THE BOOKS OF THE GODS
PART ONE

The Face of Apollo

Ariadne's Web

The Arms of Hercules

FRED SABERHAGEN

FANTASY

Published by arrangement with
Tor Books
Tom Doherty Associates, LLC
175 Fifth Avenue
New York, New York 10010

Tor® is a registered trademark of Tom Doherty Associates, LLC.

First SFBC Fantasy printing: December 2000

Visit the SFBC online at *www.sfbc.com*
Visit Tor Books online at *www.tor.com*

ISBN 0-7394-1487-9

Contents

The
Face
of
Apollo

I know more than Apollo,
For oft when he lies sleeping,
I see the stars at bloody wars
In the wounded welkin weeping . . .

—*Tom O'Bedlam's Song,* Anonymous

Prologue

TO THE PEOPLE who could not escape the Cave, it seemed that the bones of the earth were shaking. The sun and stars, sources of light and courage, were out of sight and very far away.

On and on the murderous struggle raged, filling the underground darkness with reverberating thunder, lancing it through with flares of unnatural light. Two titans fought against each other, each commanding the personal powers of a god and each supported by a squad of merely human allies. Two gods, dueling to the death in the echoing chambers of a vast cavern, came together with profound hatred and full abandon, each committing every scrap of resource, holding nothing in reserve. Here was all-out bitter violence, carried extravagantly beyond the merely human.

When their most powerful weapons had been exhausted, they came at last to grappling hand to hand. The thunder of their battle, the bellowing of their two voices raised in rage and pain, deafened and dazed the few humans—less than two dozen altogether—unlucky enough to have been trapped with the pair inside the Cave of Prophecy. The searing lightning of divine wrath, the flaring blasts of godlike power, came near to blinding human eyes that had earlier grown accustomed to the Cave's deep darkness. Clouds of dust from newly shattered rock, along with the fumes of slagged and burning earth, choked human lungs.

Well before the struggle entered its climactic stage, the two factions of human warriors had ceased trying to accomplish anything beyond their own survival. It was obvious to all of them that nothing they were capable of doing would affect the outcome, and those who were still capable of movement now bent all their efforts on crawling, scrambling, for their lives, concerned only to get out of the way of the pair of monsters wielding superhuman force.

From one second to the next it seemed that the level of fury already reached could not possibly be sustained. And yet that level not only endured but was surpassed, turning the cave into an inferno, shaking the walls of solid rock.

———

One of the mere humans who was still alive, a lithe young woman with darkish blond hair, had crawled aside, seeking shelter behind a hump of limestone on the Cave's floor. Her clothing was torn, her skin bleeding from half a dozen minor injuries.

Meanwhile the giants' struggle stormed on, its outcome impossible for anyone to know. Now one of the fighters was down and now the other.

Just when it seemed to the cowering human witnesses that there could be no end, that the fight must swallow the whole world and drag on through eternity, there came at last an unexpected lull in violence, a little breathing space in which it was possible for men and women in the Cave to regain the ability to see and hear. Some of them, recovering with amazing speed, tried to raise a chant, the words of which were promptly lost again in the renewed fury of the fight. The lips of the young woman moved, mouthing the words no one could hear:

Apollo, Apollo, Apollo must win.

And across the Cave, in another half-protected niche, another human chanted: *Hades, Hades, King of Darkness!*

In the next instant the tumult rose up again, reaching its climax in a last burst of violence more cataclysmic than any that had gone before. Once more the bones of earth were set quivering, and high in the rocky wall of one of the Cave's great chambers a rent was torn—letting in a single shaft of sunlight.

The beam of light was sharply outlined in its passage through the dusty air within the Cave.

When the echoes of that splitting rock had died away, there followed an interval of relative near-silence, broken only by shudderings, quivering of the stony walls, receding roarings, and gurglings, where veins of water had been turned to steam in the abused and ravaged earth. Here and there the lesser sound of human sobbing fell on deafened ears, evidence that breath still remained in yet another human body.

Only seven human followers of great Apollo had survived inside the Cave until this moment, close enough to see the fight and yet man-

aging to live through it. The ranking officer among them, a man accustomed to the leadership of a hundred warriors, now counted only six
behind him. Their monstrous chief opponent had withdrawn, to do so
needing the help of the remnant of his own human army. Apollo's seven
were left in possession of the field.

But the retreat of their enemies meant almost nothing when balanced
against their loss.

All seven were stunned by the fearful knowledge that their god was
dead.

Moved by a common impulse, they crawled and staggered, dragging
their wounded, deafened, half-blinded bodies out of their separate hiding
places and back into the great Cave room where the climax of the fight
had taken place. There the disaster was confirmed.

In their several ways the human survivors vocalized and acted out
their grief. One or two of them wondered aloud, and seriously, if the
sun was going to come up ever again.

They derived a certain measure of relief, these folk who had served
Apollo, simply from seeing that light shine in, however faintly, through
the great Cave's newly riven walls. The light of the universe had not
been extinguished with Apollo's death. That fact alone was enough to
give them strength to carry on.

The filtered light was faint, but it was enough to let their eyes
confirm what their ears had already told them, that their master's monstrous opponent, Hades the Pitiless, most hated of all divinities, had
withdrawn.

A haggard, bloodstained woman among the seven, her black hair
scorched, raised empty hands in a vague gesture. "Damned Hades must
be injured, too."

"He's gone to where he may recover—down, far down below." The
surviving officer was looking at one of the doorways to the Cave room,
a void of black that swallowed the faint wash of sunlight, giving nothing
back. Gray clouds of dust still hung thick in the air.

Another man choked out: "May he burn and melt in his own hell!"

"But he will not. He will be back, to eat us all." The tones of the
last speaker, another woman, were dull and hopeless. "*Our* god is dead."
In their battle-deafness the seven were almost shouting at each other,
though none realized the fact.

"We must not give up hope," said the man who had once commanded a hundred. "Not yet! Apollo is dead. Long live Apollo." He
looked round, coughing in clouds of choking dust. "We must have light
in here. Someone get me more light. There is Something I must find."

A hush fell over the other six. Presently one of them, guided in near-darkness by the sight of sparks in smoldering wood, located a fragment of what had once been a tool or weapon. The piece had caught part of a bolt of electric force, hurled by one or the other of the chief combatants. Now human lungs blew into sure life the faint seeds of a mundane material fire. Human skill nurtured a small flame into steadiness, giving human eyes light enough to distinguish objects in the deep shadows where the thin shaft of sunlight could not penetrate.

Crude torchlight flaring orange enabled the human survivors to look at one another—only three of them had picked up their weapons again; all of them were smeared with dust and most with blood. None were as old as thirty years, and all of their eyes were desperate.

Around them on the rock floor of the Cave of Prophecy were scattered a score and more of other human bodies, friend and foe commingled, and some of each still breathed. But that could wait. All that could wait.

More light as usual gave courage. First they were compelled to make absolutely sure of the tragedy—their god had perished. They could see all that was left of him—which was not much.

Apollo was dead, but hope was not. Not yet.

The officer was down on his knees, sifting through the rubble with his fingers. "You know what we must find. Help me to look for it."

"Here's something," another remarked after a few moments' search. "That way did Hades go." Now in the crude torchlight the visual evidence was plain. There were marks where someone—or something—had been dragged away, gone dragging and sliding down, into impenetrable darkness.

"Helped by humans. The Bad One was hit so hard that he needed human help, even to crawl away."

"Gravely wounded, then! Is that not blood?"

They all stared at the dark stains on the rocks. It was blood, but whose? No one could tell if it had spilled from divine veins.

"Not dead, though. Hades is not dead, l-l-like, l-l-like—" The words came stuttering and stumbling, in a voice on the point of breaking into wrenching sobs.

Another found a crumb of hope. "It might be that our Enemy will die of his wounds, down there."

"No. Down in the depths he will recover." Several people drew back a step. It was all too easy to imagine the Lord of Darkness returning at any moment and with a single gesture sweeping them all out of existence.

"I fear that the Pitiless One still lives." A voice broke in agony. *"But Apollo is dead!"*

"Enough of that!" the officer shouted hoarsely. "Long live Apollo!"

And with that he rose to his feet, having found what he had been groping for in the dust, a small object and inconspicuous. With the sound of a sob in his throat, he hastened to wrap his right hand in a fragment of cloth, torn from his own tattered uniform. Only then did he touch his discovery, holding it up in the torchlight for all to see. It was no bigger than the palm of his hand, a thin and ragged-looking object of translucent gray, with a hint of restless movement inside.

"The Face!" another cried.

"We must save it."

Hoarse murmurs echoed that thought. "Until, in time, our god may be reborn."

"Save it, and carry it, to . . . who knows the names of worthy folk?"

The people in the Cave exchanged looks expressing ignorance. Finally the leader said, "I can think of only two. Certainly none of us."

There followed a violent shaking of heads. Unanimously the seven counted themselves unworthy even to touch the remnant of Apollo's Face.

"But how can we carry it to safety?" asked the young woman with the dark blond hair. "It's damned unlikely that any of us are ever going to leave the Cave alive."

No one in the small group had much doubt that the human allies of Hades were in command of all the known exits—but the struggle of titans had created some new openings in the rock.

The weight of decision rested on the officer, and he assumed it firmly: "I think our chances are better than that. But we must split up and go in seven different ways. We will draw lots to see which of us carries . . . this."

Moments later, the seven had cast lots and the eyes of the other six were all turned upon the young woman with dark blond hair.

———

In the days that followed, the spreading reports and rumors telling of the fight were in general agreement on the fact that the god Apollo, known also as Lord of Light, Far-Worker, Phoebus, Lord of the Silver Bow, and by an almost uncountable number of other names, was truly dead. But the accounts were by no means unanimous regarding the fate of Hades, the Sun God's dreadful dark opponent. Some said that the two superbeings had annihilated each other. Others insisted that the Dark One, attended by the monster Cerberus, had now dared to emerge into the world and was stalking victoriously about. A third group held that the Lord of the Underworld, the final destroyer of Apollo, had been himself gravely injured in the duel and had retreated deep into the bowels of the earth to nurse his wounds.

And there were many humans now—none of whom had been close to the Mountain and the Cave of the Oracle during the fight—who insisted that all the gods were dead and had been dead for decades or even centuries, if indeed they had ever been more than superstitions.

The full truth turned out to be stranger than any of the stories that were told.

1

WEEKS LATER, AND more than a hundred miles from the Cave of
Prophecy, dusk had ended the day's work for the inhabitants of a quiet
riverside village. In a small house on the edge of the village, three
people sat at a table: a gray-haired man and woman and a red-haired
boy who had just turned fifteen. By the dim and flaring light of a smoky
fish-oil lamp the three were concluding an uneventful day with a supper
of oatmeal, raisins, and fresh-caught fish.

This was, in fact, a very minor birthday party. Aunt Lynn had sung
Jeremy a song—and poured him a second glass of wine.

Tonight gray-bearded Uncle Humbert had emptied somewhat more
of the wine jug into his own cup than usual and had started telling
stories. On most nights, and most days, Jeremy's uncle had little enough
to say about anything. But tonight the birthday occasion had been
melded with the prospect of a good harvest, now in late summer already
under way. For the latter reason Humbert was in a good mood now,
refilling his clay cup yet again from the cheap jug on the table.

Tonight was going to be one of the rare times when Uncle drank
enough wine to alter his behavior. Not that Jeremy had ever seen his
uncle take enough to bring on any drastic change. The only noticeable
effect was that he would start chuckling and hiccuping and then reel off
a string of stories concerning the legendary gods, gradually focusing
more and more on their romantic encounters.

Months ago Jeremy had given up expecting ever to be thanked for
his hard work. He had to admit that the old people worked hard, too,
most of the time. It was just the way things were when you lived on
the land.

As a rule, the boy consumed only one cup of wine at a meal. His uncle was stingy about that, as about much else. But tonight Jeremy dared to pour himself a second cup, and his uncle looked at him for a moment but then let it pass.

The boy was not particularly restricted in his consumption of wine but so far had not been tempted to overdo it—he wasn't sure he liked the sensations brought on by swallowing more than a little of the red stuff straight.

Earlier Aunt Lynn, contemplating the fact of his turning fifteen, had asked him, "S'pose you might be marrying soon?"

That was a surprise; he wondered if the old woman really hadn't noticed that he was barely on speaking terms with any of the other villagers, male or female, young or old. The folk here tended to view any outsiders with suspicion. "Don't know who I'd marry."

Aunt Lynn sat thinking that over. Or more likely her mind was already on something else—the gods knew what. Now Jeremy sat drawing little circles with his finger in the spots of spilled wine on the table. Often it seemed to the boy that there must be more than one generation between himself and the two gray people now sitting at his right and left. Such were the differences. Now Uncle Humbert, tongue well loosened, was well into his third tale concerned with the old days, a time when the world was young and the gods, too, were young and vital beings, fully capable of bearing the responsibility for keeping the universe more or less in order. Jeremy supposed the old folk must have heard the stories thousands of times, but they never seemed tired of telling or hearing them yet again.

Many people viewed the past, when supposedly the gods had been dependable and frequently beneficent, as a Golden Age, irretrievably lost in this late and degenerate period of the world. But Uncle Humbert's view, as his nephew had become acquainted with it over the past several months, was somewhat different. A deity might do a human being a favor now and then, on a whim, but by and large the gods were not beneficent. Instead they viewed the world as their own playground and humanity as merely an amusing set of toys.

Humbert derived a kind of satisfaction from this view of life—it was not his fault that the world, as he saw it, had cheated him in many ways. Certain of the gods seemed to spend a good deal of their time thinking up nasty tricks to play on Uncle Humbert. Jeremy supposed that seeing himself as a victim of the gods allowed Humbert to have a feeling of importance.

The other half of Humbert's audience on most nights for the past five months had been his weary, overworked nephew. Tonight was no exception, and the boy sat, head spinning over his second cup, falling asleep with his head propped up in one hand, both his elbows on the table. Nothing was forcing him to stay at the table—he could have got up at any moment and climbed the ladder to his bed. But, in fact, he wanted to hear the stories. Any distraction from the mundane world in which he spent the monotony of his days was welcome.

Now Jeremy's eyelids opened a little wider. Uncle Humbert was varying his performance somewhat tonight. He was actually telling a tale that the boy hadn't heard before, in the five months that he'd been living here.

The legend that Jeremy had never heard before related how two male gods, Dionysus and one other, Mercury according to Uncle, who happened to be traveling together in disguise, made a wager between themselves as to what kind of reception they would be granted at the next peasants' hut if they appeared incognito.

"So, they wrapped 'emselves up in their cloaks, and—*hiccup*—walked on."

Aunt Lynn, who tonight had hoisted an extra cup or two herself, was already shrieking with laughter at almost every line of every story and pounding her husband on the arm. Silently Jeremy marveled at her. No doubt she had heard this one a hundred times before, or a thousand, in a quarter-century or so of marriage and already knew the point of the joke, but that didn't dampen her enjoyment. Jeremy hadn't heard it yet and didn't much care whether he heard it now.

Uncle Humbert's raspy voice resumed. "So great Hermes—some call'm Mercury—'n' Lord Di'nysus went on and stopped at the next peasants' hut. It was a grim old man who came to th' door, but the gods could see he had a young and lively wife. . . . She was jus' standing there behind the old man, kind of smiling at the visitors . . . an' when she saw they were two han'some, young-lookin' men, dressed like they were rich, she winked at 'em. . . ."

Aunt Lynn had largely got over her latest laughing fit and now sat smiling, giggling a little, listening patiently. She might be thinking that she could have been burdened with a husband a lot worse than Humbert, who hardly ever beat her. And Jeremy was already so well grown that Uncle, not exactly huge and powerful himself, would doubtless have thought twice or thrice before whaling into him—but then, such speculation was probably unfair. In the boy's experience Uncle Humbert had never demonstrated a wish to beat on anyone—his faults were of a different kind.

The story came quickly to its inevitable end, with the grim, greedy old peasant cuckolded, the lecherous gods triumphant, the young wife, for the moment, satisfied. Judging by Uncle Humbert's laughter, the old man still enjoyed the joke as much as the first time he'd heard it, doubt-less when he was a young and lecherous lad himself. The thought crossed Jeremy's mind that his father would never have told stories like this—not in the family circle, anyway—and his mother would never have laughed at them.

━━━━━━━━

That was the last joke of the night, probably because it was the last that Uncle could dredge up out of his memory just now. When all three people stood up from the table, the boy, still too young to have a beard at all, was exactly the same height as the aging graybeard who was not yet fifty.

While the woman puttered about, carrying out a minimum of table clearing and kitchen work, young Jeremy turned away from his elders with a muttered, "Good night," and began to drag his tired body up to the loft where he routinely slept. That second cup of wine was buzzing in his head, and once his callused foot sole almost slipped free from a smooth-worn rung on the built-in wooden ladder.

Now in the early night the tiny unlighted loft was still hot with the day-long roasting of summer sun. Without pausing, the boy crawled straight through the narrow, cramped, ovenlike space and slid right on out of it again, through the crude opening that served as its single window. He emerged into moonlit night on the flat roof of an adjoining shed.

Here he immediately paused to pull off his homespun shirt. The open air was cooler now than it had been all day, and a slight breeze had come up at sunset, promising to minimize the number of active mosquitoes. To Jeremy's right and left the branches of a shade tree rustled faintly, brushing the shed roof. Even in daylight this flat space, obscured by leaves and branches, was all but invisible from any of the other village houses. In a moment Jeremy had shed his trousers, too.

He drained his bladder over the edge of the roof, saving himself a walk to the backyard privy. Then he stretched out naked on the sun-warmed shingles of the flat, slightly sloping surface; his shirt rolled up for a pillow beneath his head.

There, almost straight above him, was the moon. Jeremy could man-age to locate a bright moon in a clear sky, though for him its image had never been more than a blur and talk of lunar phases was practically meaningless. Stars were far beyond his capability—never in his life had his nearsighted vision let him discover even the brightest, except that once or twice, on frozen winter nights, he'd seen, or thought he'd seen, a blurry version of the Dog Star's twinkling point. Now and then, when Venus was especially bright, he had been able to make out her wandering image near dawn or sunset, a smaller, whiter version of the moon blur. But tonight, though his eyelids were sagging with wine and weariness, he marveled at how moonlight—and what must be the communal glow of the multitude of bright points he had been told were there—had transformed the world into a silvery mystery.

Earlier in the day, Aunt Lynn had said she'd heard a boatman from downriver talking about some kind of strange battle, supposed to have recently taken place at the Cave of Prophecy. Whole human armies had been engaged, and two or more gods had fought to the death.

Uncle had only sighed on hearing the story. "The gods all died a long time ago," was his comment finally. " 'Fore I was born." Then he went on to speak of several deities as if they had been personal acquaintances. "Dionysus, now—there was a god for you. One who led an *interesting* life." Uncle Humbert, whose voice was gravelly but not unpleasant, supplied the emphasis with a wink and a nod and a laugh.

Jeremy wanted to ask his uncle just how well he had known Dionysus—who had died before Humbert was born—just to see what the old man would say. But the boy felt too tired to bother. Besides, he had the feeling that his uncle would simply ignore the question.

Now, despite fatigue, an inner restlessness compelled Jeremy to hold his eyelids open a little longer. Not everyone agreed with Uncle Humbert that all the gods had been dead for a human lifetime or longer. Somewhere up there in the distant heavens, or so the stories had it, the gods still lived, or some of them at least, though they were no more to be seen by any human eyes than Jeremy could see the stars. Unless the stories about a recent battle might be true. . . .

Others of that divine company, according to other stories, preferred to spend their time in inaccessible mountain fastnesses on earth—high places, from which they sometimes came down to bother people or befriend them. . . . At least in the old days, hundreds of years ago, they had done that.

He wondered if the gods, whatever gods there might be in reality, behaved anything at all like their representations in Uncle's stories. People who were inclined to philosophy argued about such matters, and even Jeremy's parents had not been sure. But Jeremy preferred to believe that there were *some* gods in the world. Because magic really happened, sometimes. Not that he had actually experienced any himself. But there were so many stories that he thought there must be something . . .

. . . his mind was drifting now. Let Dionysus and Hermes come to the door of this house tonight, and they'd find a crabbed old man, but no young wife to make the visit worth their while. Neither gods nor men could work up much craving for Aunt Lynn.

From down in the dark house the rhythmic snores of Jeremy's aunt and uncle were already drifting up. Wine and hard work had stupefied them; and in the real world, what else could anyone look forward to but sleep?

Weariness and wine quickly pushed Jeremy over into the borderland of sleep. And now the invisible boundary had been passed. Bright dreams came, beginning with the young peasant wife of Uncle Humbert's tale, as she lay on her back in her small bedroom, making an eager offering of herself to the gods. Her husband had been got cleverly out of the way, and now she wantonly displayed her naked body. Between her raised knees stood the towering figure of jolly, bearded Dionysus, his muscles and his phallus alike demonstrating his superiority to mere mankind.

And now, in the sudden manner of dreams, the body of the farmwife on her bed was replaced by that of a certain village girl about Jeremy's age. Her name was Myra, and more than once this summer the boy had seen her cooling herself in the river. Each time, Myra and her younger girl companions had looked their suspicion and dislike at the red-haired, odd-looking newcomer. They'd turned their backs on the intruder in their village, who spoke with a strange accent. Whichever way Myra stood in the water, however she moved, her long dark hair tantalizingly obscured her bare breasts and the curved flesh of her body jiggled.

The boy on the shed roof was drifting now, between sleep and waking. Something delightful was about to happen.

Well, and what did he care if some ignorant village girl might choose not to let him near her? Let her act any way she liked Here, behind the closed lids of his eyes, he was the king, the god, the ruler, and he would decide what happened and what did not.

And even in the dream, the question could arise: What would Dionysus, if there really were a Dionysus, do with a girl like Myra? How great, how marvelous, to be a god!

But in another moment the dream was deepening again. The fascinating images were as real as life itself. And it was Jeremy, not Dionysus, who stood between the raised knees of the female on the bed. Even as Myra smiled up at him and reached out her arms, even as their bodies melted into one . . .

Groaning, he came partially awake at the last moment, enough to know that he was lying alone and had spent himself on wooden shingles.

Real life was messy, however marvelous the dreams it sometimes brought.

Less than a minute later, Jeremy had turned on his back again, once more asleep. This time his dreams were of the unseen stars.

2

ON THE AFTERNOON of the following day, Jeremy was fighting a heavy wheelbarrow down a steep path, moving in the general direction of the village on one of his many trips from the vineyard on the upper hillside, a lean and shabby figure, almost staggering down the well-worn path on unshod feet, his face shaded by a mass of red hair, stringy arms strained taut supporting the wheelbarrow's handles. Several times on the descent the weight of the load caused him to stumble slightly, on the verge of losing control, as he guided the mass of the crude conveyance piled with freshly picked grapes, bunches with here and there a few leaves. Purple skins with green highlights, clustered thickly on their stems, ripe and bursting with the weight of their own juice, bound for the vats in which the juice would be crushed out of them, they made a staggering load. Jeremy's skin and clothing alike were stained with the royal purple of their juice.

These were truly exotic grapes that people grew in the Raisinmakers' village. Only a comparative few, mostly those on Humbert's vines, were pressed for wine, because the real strong point of the local crop was that they made superb raisins. Jeremy had liked the homemade raisins, for the first four months or so, but for the past two months had been heartily sick of them.

Soon the village wine vats would be full and future barrow loads of grapes would have to go to the other side of the village, where they would be spread out on boards and dried into more raisins. Then Jeremy would be kept busy for weeks to come, continuously turning the grapes in the sun and guarding them vigilantly against insects. At least he might be granted a break from the wheelbarrow.

An alternative possibility was that when he had finished the job of hauling grapes he would be assigned to the job of bringing down to the river's edge some tons of rocks, of a convenient size to be used as the foundation for a new dock.

Long hours of toil since sunrise had already wiped away all thought of last night's dreams and needs. He was muttering and grumbling to himself in smoldering anger—an eternity of nothing but more work seemed to stretch out before the weary youth—when he heard a voice calling, from the direction of the patch of woods at his right side:

"Help me."

The whisper was so soft, almost inaudible, that for the space of several heartbeats Jeremy was unsure that he had heard anything at all. But the strangeness of the call had brought him to a halt. Memories of dreams very briefly flickered through his mind.

Then the faint call was repeated. The words were as real as heat and work and aching muscles, and they had nothing at all to do with dreams.

In the course of a day, other workers came and went along the path at intervals, but at the moment Jeremy had it all to himself. From where he stood right now, no other human being was visible, except for two or three in the far distance. No one was in the field that lay to his left, richly green with late summer crops, or nearby on his right, where the land was too uneven for practical tilling and had been allowed to remain in woods. Ahead, the fringe of the village, visible among shade trees, was also for the moment empty of people.

The boy pushed back his mass of red hair—he had decided to let it grow as long as possible, since it seemed to put off and offend the natives of this village—and looked a little deeper into the woods. His gaze was drawn to the spot where a growing bush and the pile of vine cuttings beside it made a kind of hiding place. In the next moment Jeremy let out a soft breath of wonder at the sight of the dark eyes of a young woman. She was lying motionless on her side on the ground, head slightly raised, gazing back at him.

The two upright supports of the wheeled barrow hit the barren earth of the pathway with a thud. Letting his load sit where it was, Jeremy stepped three paces off the path and went down on one knee in the tall weeds beside the woman—or girl. Despite her weakened, worn appearance, he thought she was only a little older than he.

She was curled up on the ground, motionless as a frightened rabbit, lying on her right side, her right arm mostly concealed beneath her body, her knees drawn up. The attitude in which she lay told him that she must be injured. Dark eyes moved, in a begrimed and anguished face. His first look told him little about the woman's clothing save that it was dark and concealed most of her body. Dark boots and trousers and a loose blouse or jacket mottled gray and brown. At some time, perhaps many days ago, some kind of camouflage paint had been smeared on the exposed portions of her skin, so it was hard to tell its natural color.

Casting a quick look around, he made sure that they were still unobserved. Then he ducked around a bush and crouched down right beside the stranger.

The stranger's dark eyes glistened at him, with an intensity that tried to probe his very soul. Her next words came almost as softly as before, with pauses for breath between them. "Don't . . . betray . . . me."

"I won't." He gave his soft-voiced answer immediately, in great sincerity, and without thought of what the consequences might be. Even before he had any idea of how he might betray her if he wanted to. Some part of him had been ready to respond to the appeal, as if he had somehow known all along that it was coming.

"I see you . . . passing . . . up and down the path."

"That's my work. I work here, for my uncle."

In the same weak voice she said: "They are hunting me. They are going to kill me." After a longer pause, while Jeremy could feel the hair on the back of his neck trying to stand up, the woman added, as if to herself in afterthought: "They've killed me already."

"Who is . . . ? But you're hurt." Jeremy had suddenly taken notice of the bloodstains, dried dark on dark clothing.

She shook her head; all explanations could wait. The dry-lipped whisper went on: "Water. Bring me some water. Please."

He grabbed up the gourd bottle, hanging on one side of the barrow, and handed it over.

At first she was unable even to sit up, and he had to hoist the stranger's slender torso with an arm around her shoulders, which were bony and solid, though not big. Even with his help, she made the move only with some difficulty. Her face was begrimed and stained with dried blood, on top of everything else.

When the gourd had been completely drained in a few rapid swallows, he handed her a rich cluster of grapes; she hadn't asked for food, but her appearance suggested that she could use some. She looked to be in need of nourishment as well as water. She attacked the grapes ravenously, swallowing seeds and all, the juice staining her lips purple, and reached for more when Jeremy held them out.

Her hair was a darkish blond, once cut short, now raggedly regrown long enough to tangle.

The boy's heart turned over in him at the appeal. It was hard to be sure with her face painted and in her wounded condition, but he guessed that the woman hiding at the edge of the brush pile had perhaps four or five more years than his fifteen.

"That's good," she murmured, eyes closed, savoring the aftertaste of the water. "Very good."

"What can I do?"

The water and grapes had not strengthened her voice any. Still she could utter no more than a few words with a single breath. "Help me get . . . down the river . . . before . . . they find me."

"Oh." He looked around, feeling his mind a blank whirl. But he felt no doubt of what he ought to do. "First I better move you farther from the path. Someone'll see you here."

She nodded but winced and came near crying out when he tugged at her awkwardly, accidentally putting his hand on a place where she had been hurt. Blood had soaked through her garments and dried, on her back and on the seat of her pants. But he did succeed in shifting her, for the few necessary yards, to a spot surrounded by taller bushes, where she would be completely out of sight as long as she lay still.

"Lay me down again. Oh gods, what pain! Put me down."

Hastily he did. As gently as he could.

"Did anyone . . . hear me?"

Jeremy looked around cautiously, back toward the path, up the path and down. "No. There's no one."

Suddenly he was feeling more fully alive than he had for months and months, ever since moving into Uncle Humbert's house. He wiped sweat from his face with the sleeve of his homespun shirt. No one else from the village had seen the mysterious stranger yet, or there would already be a noisy uproar. And he accepted without thinking about it that it was important that no one in the village must learn of her presence.

It never occurred to Jeremy to wonder who the people hunting her might be. The only thing in the world that mattered was the bond that had already sprung into existence between himself and this other human who had come here from some enormous distance. He could not yet have defined the nature of this tie, but it was very strong and sharply separated the pair of them from everyone else he had encountered since moving to this village.

The boy crouched over her reclining form, staring, wondering. He had not yet grasped any of the details of what had happened, but already he understood that his whole life had just been drastically changed.

The young woman's eyes were almost closed again. "Thank you for saving my life."

Jeremy could find no response. He hadn't done anything, yet, to earn those words. *But he would.* He only grunted, feeling like the village idiot, his face turning red beneath its thousand freckles.

The woman, her mind obviously absorbed in bigger problems, took no notice of his embarrassment. With a faint crackle of dried twigs, she slightly raised her head, squinting and sniffing. "I smell woodsmoke in the wind, sometimes. And something rotten."

"That's the clam meats. Some of the people fish for clams. To get the shells."

She shook her head. "I hear people. I see . . . Actually, I can't see much of anything from here." She squinted again, turning her head a little to the right.

"Yes. How long have you been here, lying in the woods?"

"I don't know. Hours. Maybe days. It was starting to get daylight. And I couldn't walk anymore. I was afraid . . . to try to crawl to the water. Afraid someone would see me. Is this a Honeymakers' village?"

"No. Nothing like that." He wasn't sure that he had understood the question or heard it right. "We keep no bees."

"Gods help me, then." She paused. "Is there a shrine in your village? What god?"

"Not really mine. But yes, there's a small shrine." Every village Jeremy had ever seen had some kind of shrine, though most of them had been long neglected. "Dionysus and Priapus, both. One god for wine and one for vineyards."

"I see. Not much good. Apollo help me. Bees might do some good. Do you have cattle?"

"Cattle? No." Bees? What good could they do? And cattle? With a chill it came to him that this person, with whom he was suddenly so intimately connected, might be delirious.

"Where am I, then?"

He told her the formal name of the village, archaic words meaning the town of raisinmakers, giving it the pronunciation he had learned from his aunt and uncle. But he could see in the stranger's face that the words meant nothing to her.

"But the river," she persisted stubbornly. "We're right beside a river here. You said freshwater clams."

"That's right."

"Is it the Aeron? I couldn't see it. I had to come across country."

"Yes, the Aeron."

At last the young woman had heard an answer from which she could derive a little comfort. Jeremy thought her body relaxed slightly.

"There are boats here, then," she said. "People beside a river have boats."

"Yes, ma'am. Some of them do a lot of fishing. There must be a dozen boats."

"Then there must be some way . . . I could get a boat."

"I can get one for you," the boy promised instantly. Stealing a boat of course would be the only way to obtain one, and an hour ago it would not have occurred to Jeremy to steal anything. His parents had taught him that thievery was simply wrong, not something that honorable people did.

But when he learned that, he had been living in a different world.

The young woman turned uneasily. Her movement, the expression on her face, showed that something was really hurting her. "Water. Please, I need more water." She had quickly finished off the few mouthfuls Jeremy had left in the bottle. "Is there any other food?"

He gave her some more grapes from his barrow and tore off a chunk of bread from his lunchtime supply and handed it over.

And then he almost ran, delivering his barrow load, going by way of the well to get more water, that he might get back to the stranger more quickly. He had promised her fervently that he would soon be back.

———

During the remainder of the day, Jeremy went on about his usual work, shoving the empty barrow rattling uphill, wrestling it down again with a full load, and feeling that everyone was watching him. Despite this, he managed to bring more water to the fugitive and this time some real food, a piece of corn bread and scraps of fried fish. In fact, everyone in the village was intent on their own affairs and paid him no attention at all. Ordinary river water was the easiest to get, and most of the people in the village drank it all the time.

In the evening, the first time Jeremy had seen his aunt and uncle since early morning, Aunt Lynn commented that he was moody. But then, he was considered to be moody most of the time anyway, and neither of the old people said any more about it.

———

Not until next morning, when he was making his first visit of the day to the stranger in her hiding place, did she ask him, between bites of fish and corn bread: "What's your name?"

"Jeremy. Jeremy Redthorn."

The ghost of a smile came and went on her pallid lips. "Redthorn suits you."

Meaning his hair, of course. He nodded.

After he had brought her food the first time, she told him, "If you must call me something, call me Sal."

"Sal. I like that name."

And she smiled in a way that made him certain that the name she had told him was not her own.

"When can I get you a boat?"

"I better wait. Until I get a little stronger—just a little. And I can move. Can you spare a minute just to stay and talk?"

He nodded. If Uncle Humbert thought that Jeremy was slacking on the job he would yell at him but was unlikely to try to impose any penalty. Generally Jeremy worked hard for most of his waking hours— because working was about the only way to keep from thinking about other things, topics that continually plagued him. Such as dead parents, live girls who sometimes could be seen with no clothes on, and a life that had no future, only an endless path down which he walked, pushing a loaded barrow.

Sal in her soft voice asked: "You live with your parents, Jeremy? Brothers? Sisters?"

Jeremy tossed his mass of red hair in a quick negative motion. "Nothing like that." His voice was harsh, and suddenly it broke deep. "My father and mother are dead. I live with my aunt and uncle."

Looking up at him, she thought that his face was not attractive in any conventional way, running to odd angles and high bones prominent in cheeks too young to sprout a beard. Greenish eyes peered through a tight-curled mass of reddish hair. Face and wiry neck and exposed arms were largely a mass of freckles. Jeremy's arms and legs tended to be long and would one day be powerful. His hands and feet had already got most of their growing done; his shoulders were sloping and still narrow. Today his right knee was starting to show through a hole in trousers that, though Aunt Lynn had made them only a couple of months ago, were already beginning to be too short.

⸺

Sometimes when Jeremy saw the woman again she seemed a little stronger, her speech a little easier. And then again he would come back and find her weaker than ever before.

What if she should die? What in all the hells was he ever going to do then?

Once she reached up her small, hard hand and clutched at one of his. "Jeremy. I don't want to make any trouble for you. But there's something I must do. Something more important than anything else—than anything. More than what happens to you. Or to me either. So you must help me to get downstream. You must."

He listened carefully, trying to learn what the important thing was—whatever it was, he was going to do it. "I can try. Yes, I can help you. Anything! How far down do you want to go?"

"All the way. Hundreds of miles from here. All the way to the sea."

Yes. And in that moment he understood suddenly, with a sense of vast relief, that he would get her a boat and, when she left, he was going with her.

———

"You haven't told anyone else? About me?"

"No! Never fear; I won't." Jeremy feared to trust anyone else in the village with the knowledge of his discovery. Certainly he knew better than to trust his aunt or uncle in any matter like this.

"Who is your mayor—or do you have a mayor?"

He shook his head. "This place is too small for that."

"How many houses?"

"About a dozen." Then he added an earnest caution: "The people here hate strangers. They'd keep no secret for you. This place is not like my old home—my real home."

"What was that like?"

Jeremy shook his head. He could find no words to begin to describe the differences between his home village, the place where he'd spent his first fourteen years, and this. There everyone had known him and his parents had been alive.

Marvelously, Sal seemed to get the idea anyway. "Yes. There's a great world out there, isn't there?"

He nodded. At least he could hope there was. He was inarticulately grateful for her understanding.

For the past half a year he'd been an orphan, feeling much alienated. Uncle Humbert was not basically unkind, but such daring as he possessed, and Aunt Lynn's as well, had been stretched to the limits by taking in a refugee. Both of them sometimes looked at Jeremy in a way that seemed to indicate that they regretted their decision. Apparently it just wasn't done, in the Raisinmakers' village.

The truth was that Uncle Humbert, with no children of his own, had been unable to refuse the prospect of cheap labor that the boy provided.

He could do a man's work now, at only a fraction of the expense of a hired man.

No, Jeremy had no illusions about what would happen to Sal—or to himself, but never mind that—if he appealed to his uncle and his aunt for help. He and Sal would both be in deep trouble, he'd bet on that, though he could not make out what the exact shape of the trouble would be. Nor could the boy think of a single soul in the village who might be sympathetic enough to take the slightest risk on behalf of an injured stranger.

Vaguely the image of Myra crossed Jeremy's mind. This time her image appeared fully clothed, and there was nothing vivid about it. In fact, her form was insubstantial. Because Jeremy had no time, no inclination, to think of Myra now. The village girl meant no more than anyone else who lived here, and suddenly none of them meant anything at all.

3

AGAIN, AS JEREMY hurried about his work, he had the sensation of being watched. But he saw and heard nothing to support the feeling. Everyone in the village was busy as usual, preoccupied with work, the busy harvesttime of midsummer—Uncle Humbert had explained how the variously mutated varieties of grapes came to maturity in sequence and disasters might befall them unless they were tended and harvested in exactly the right way.

The ruts in the village's only street still held puddles from last week's rain. Half a dozen small houses lined each side. Half the menfolk went fishing in the river Aeron, sometimes hauling in freshwater clams. The shells were sold by the ton to carters, who carried them off to the cities, to be cut up by craft workers and polished for use as decorations, bought by folk who could not afford more precious metals, jewels, or ivory. Now and then a pearl appeared, but these of the freshwater kind were only of minor value.

The next time Jeremy returned to the little patch of woods where Sal lay nested he traveled most of the way along the riverside path. This brought him right past the local riparian shrine to Priapus, a squat figure carved in black stone, who seemed to be brooding over his own massive male organs, and to Dionysus, whose tall, youthful form was carved in pale marble, handsomely entwined with ivy and other vines. Beside the taller god crouched a marble panther, and he held in his left hand his thyrsus staff, a rod with a pinecone at the end. His right hand was raised as if to confer a blessing upon passersby. A fountain, an adjunct to the main well of the village, tinkled into a small pond at the stone gods' feet.

Starting some twenty yards from the shrine, piles of clamshells, separated by irregular distances, lay along the bank, waiting to be hauled away by boat or by wagon. The meats, mottled black and white like soft marble, in warm weather quickly beginning to rot, were hauled up the hill by barrow to fertilize the vines and hops and vegetables. Pushing a barrow filled with clam meats, as Jeremy had learned early in the summer, was a stinking job, beset by many flies, much worse than hauling grapes.

When days and weeks of the growing season went by without adequate rain, which had happened more than once since the beginning of summer, Jeremy and others filled kegs and barrels with river water and pushed and dragged them up the hill. Uncle Humbert's vineyard was comparatively high on the slope.

Today those villagers not toiling in the vineyards were out in their boats fishing. Some kind of seasonal run of fish was on, and the general scarcity of people in the vicinity of the village during the day made it easier for a fugitive to hide nearby without being noticed.

———

Suddenly, as a result of his responding to a whispered cry for help, a great weight of responsibility had descended on Jeremy's shoulders. Now, for the first time in his life, someone else was totally dependent on him. But what might have been a great problem was, in effect, no burden at all. Because suddenly life had a purpose. The only problem was that he might fail.

Sal said to him: "This puts a great burden on you, Jeremy."

He blinked at her. "What does?"

"Me. I depend on you for everything."

"No!" He shook his head, trying to make her understand. "I mean, that's not a problem."

———

The boy had just scrounged up some food, which his client attacked with savage hunger. Her mouth was still full when she said: "My name is something you need not know." His hurt must have shown in his face, for immediately she added: "It's for your own good. And others'. What you don't know you can never tell."

"I'll never tell!"

"Of course not!" She put out her hand to gently stroke his. Somehow the touch seemed the most marvelous that he had ever known. He was touched by the fact that her hand was smaller than his. He could feel the roughness of her fingers, as callused as his own.

"I see you can be trusted." And she had turned her head again to favor him with that look, on which it now seemed that his life depended.

Before he could find any words to answer that, there came a noise nearby, a scurrying among dead leaves, making them both start, but when the sound came again they could tell that it was only some small animal.

Jeremy settled down again beside her, still holding her hand. As long as he sat here, he would be able to hold her hand. "Who hurt you this way?" he whispered fiercely. "Who is it that's hunting you?"

"Who? The servants of hell. Lord Kalakh's men. If I tell you who *isn't* hunting me, the list will be shorter." She bestowed on Jeremy a faint, wan smile and sighed. "Yet I've done nothing wrong."

"I wouldn't care if you had!" he burst out impulsively. That wasn't what worried him. What did concern him was a new fear that she might be growing feverish, delirious. He dared to feel her forehead, an act that brought only a vague smile as reaction from the patient. Yes, she was too warm. If only there were *someone* he could call upon for help. . . . About all that he could do was bring more water and a scrap of cloth to wet and try to cool her forehead with it.

When Jeremy saw the young woman again, Sal in her feverish weakness increased her pleas and demands to be taken or sent downriver. She was determined to go soon, if she died in the attempt. Jeremy tried to soothe her and keep her lying still. Well, he was going to take her where she wanted to go; that was all there was to it.

The very worst part of the situation now was that Sal's mind seemed to be wandering. Jeremy feared that if she really went off her head, she might get up and wander off and do herself some harm. And there was a second problem, related to the first: he couldn't tell if she was getting stronger or weaker. She had refused his offer to try to find a healer for her, turned it down so fiercely that he wasn't going to bring it up again. He had to admit that if she was determined to keep her secrets, she was probably right.

Several times, in her periods of intermittent fever and delirium, Sal murmured about the seven. As far as Jeremy could make out, this was the number of people who were involved with her in some business of life-and-death importance. Then she fell into an intense pleading with one of the seven to do something. Or, perhaps, not to do the opposite.

Almost half of what Sal babbled in her fever was in another language, like nothing that Jeremy had ever heard before. He could not understand a word.

When she paused, he asked: "Who are the seven?"

Sal's eyes looked a little clearer now, and her voice was almost tragic. "Who told you about that?"

"You did. Just now. I'm sorry if I—"

"Oh god. Oh, Lord of the Sun. What am I going to do?"

"Trust me." He dared to put his hand on her forehead and almost jerked it away again, the fever was so high.

She shook her head, as if his vehemence had pained her. "I have a right to carry what I'm carrying. But I can't use it. If only I were worthy."

To Jeremy it sounded almost as if she thought he was accusing her of stealing something—as if he'd care, one way or the other. Sal was his, and he was hers; she trusted him. "What is this thing you're carrying that's so important? I could keep it for you. I could hide it."

Sal drew a deep breath, despite the pain that breathing seemed to cause. "What I bear with me . . . is a terrible burden. Mustn't put that burden on you. Not yet."

The suggestion that she might *not* trust him as utterly and auto-matically as he trusted her struck him with a sharp pang of anguish.

His hurt feelings must have been plain in his face. "No, dear. My good Jeremy. All the good gods bless and help you. Wouldn't be safe for you to know . . ."

He couldn't tell if she meant not safe for him or for the secret. Her fever was getting worse again. She had started to wander, more than a little, in her speech.

Still there were intervals when Jeremy's new comrade's mind was clear. In one of those intervals she fiercely forbade him to summon anyone else to her aid.

He nodded. "That's all right. I can't think of anyone around here that I'd trust. Except maybe the midwife; but you're not pregnant. . . ." He could feel his face turning warm again. "I mean, I don't suppose . . ."

Sal smiled wanly at that. "No, I'm not. Thank the good gods for small favors at least."

When she paused, he asked: "Who are the good gods?"

Sal ignored the question, which had been seriously meant. "Don't tell the midwife anything. She can't do anything for me that you can't do."

Presently Jeremy left Sal, whispering a promise that he would be back as soon as possible, with more food.

For several hours he continued working at his routine tasks, with a private fear growing in him, and a tender excitement as well. He tried to keep his new emotions from showing in his face, and as far as he could tell he was succeeding.

And then there were hours, hours terrible indeed for the lonely caretaker, when her mind seemed almost entirely gone.

At first he could not get Sal to tell him just where her goal downriver was. But soon, under stress, she admitted that she had to get a certain message to someone at the Academy.

Coming to herself again, and as if realizing that she was in danger of death, Sal suddenly blurted out a name. "Professor Alexander."

"What?"

"He's the man, the one you must take it to if I am dead."

"Your secret treasure? Yes, all right. Professor Alexander. But you won't be dead." Jeremy was not quite sure whether Professor might be a given name or some kind of title, like Mayor or Doctor. But he would find out. He would find out everything he had to know.

"He's at the Academy. Do you know what that is?"

"I can find out. A sort of school, I think. If you want to give me—"

"And if he . . . Professor Alexander—"

"Yes?"

"If he should be dead, or . . . or missing—"

"Yes?"

"Then you must give it to . . . to Margaret Chalandon. She is also . . . very worthy."

"Margaret Chalandon." Carefully he repeated the name. "I will."

"What I carry is . . ."

"Is what? You can tell me."

". . . is so important that . . . but if only I were worthy. . . ."

Still Sal maddeningly refused to tell her savior exactly what the thing was or where it might be. It couldn't be very big, Jeremy thought. He'd seen almost every part of her body in recent hours, while trying to do the duties of a nurse. Certainly there was no unseen place or pocket in her clothing with room enough for anything much bigger than a piece of paper. Jeremy thought, *Maybe it's a map of some kind, maybe a list of names.* He kept his guesses to himself.

"Jeremy."

"Yes, Sal."

"If you should get there, and I don't . . . then you must give him what I will give to you."

"Yes."

"And tell him . . ."

"Yes."

"Seven of us were still alive . . . at the end. We did all we could. Split up, and went in different ways. Make it hard for them to follow."

"You want me to tell him, Professor Alexander, that you went in seven different ways and you did all that you could."

"That's enough. It will let him know . . . Jerry? Do your friends call you Jerry?"

"When I had friends, they did."

And either Sal really wanted to hear her rescuer's life story or Jeremy wanted so badly to tell it to her that he convinced himself she wanted to hear it.

But with her breathing the way she was and looking at him like she did, he soon broke off the unhappy tale and came back to their present problems. "Sal, I'll carry the thing for you now, whatever it is. I'll take it to one of the people you say are worthy. I remember their names. Or I can hide it, somewhere near here—until you feel better. No one will ever find it."

"I know you would . . . Jerry. But I can't. Can't put it all on you. I'm still alive. I'm going to get better yet. Tomorrow or the next day we can travel." She hesitated and seemed to be pondering some very difficult question. "But if I die, then you must take it."

Helplessly he clenched his fists. It seemed that they were going round and round in a great circle of delirium. It was impossible to be cruel to her, search her ruthlessly, impossible to take from her by force whatever it might be. "But what *is* it?"

Still something, some pledge, some fear, kept her from telling him. *Unworthy.*

"Can't you even show it to me?"

She had to agonize over the decision for some time. At last she shook her head. "Not yet."

"Sal. Then how can I—?" But he broke off, thinking that she was delirious again.

━━━━━━━━

Late that night, Jeremy lay in the damp warmth of his cramped loft, listening to a steady rainbeat on the roof above and trying to sleep on the folded quilt that generally served him as both bed and mattress. Whatever position he assumed in the narrow space, at least one slow trickling leak got through the decaying shingles and managed to make wet contact with some part of his body. He had thrown off his clothes—being wet was less bother that way—and was fretfully awake. Tomorrow the going with his wheelbarrow would be slow and difficult, both uphill and down, the steep paths treacherous with mud.

Tonight he was doubly tired, with urgent mental strain as well as physical work. It wasn't girl pictures in his mind or even the cold dripping that was keeping him awake. Rather it was the thought of Sal just lying out there, wounded, in the rain. If there were only something, anything, like a waterproof sheet or blanket, that he could borrow or steal to make even a small rainproof shelter for her . . . but he could think of nothing rainproof in the whole village. Some of the houses had good solid roofs—but he couldn't borrow one of those. Ordinary clothes and blankets would be useless, soaking up the water and then letting it run through.

Briefly Jeremy considered sliding out the window to lie on the shed roof. Exposing himself fully to the rain, he could at least share fully in Sal's distress. But he quickly thrust the idea aside. Adding to his own discomfort would do her no good at all. In fact, he had better do the very opposite. He had to get whatever sleep he could, because he needed to think clearly. Tremendous problems needed to be solved, and Sal was in such bad shape that by tomorrow she might not be able to think at all.

And she was depending on him. Absolutely. For her very life—and she was going to depend on him for something else that seemed to mean even more than life to her. *He must not, must not, fail her.* Fiercely he vowed to himself that he would not.

Well, the air was still warm, she wouldn't freeze, and at least she would not go thirsty. Also, the rain would tend to blot out whatever trail she might have left, foil whatever efforts might be in progress, even now, to track her down.

And maybe the drenching would cool her fever. At least that was some kind of a hope he could hang onto. Enough to let him get a little sleep at last.

━━━━━

The next day, when he at last felt secure enough from observation to get back to his client, he was vastly relieved to see that Sal had survived the rain. Though her mind was clear now, she was still feverish, and he cursed himself for not being able to provide her shelter or find her some means of healing.

But she would not listen to his self-abuse. "Forget all that. It's not important. Maybe—listen to me, Jeremy—maybe you'll have to do something more important. More than you can imagine."

Jeremy had been trying for days now to devise plans for getting control of a boat without letting the owner know within a few hours that it had been stolen. But he could think of nothing; the only way was just to take one and go. Getting Sal to the river unobserved would be somewhat chancier. He decided that shortly after sunset would be the best time. Leave early in the night, and neither he nor the boat would be missed till after dawn; and travelers on the river left no trail.

Sal's most troublesome wound was on her upper thigh, almost in her crotch. To Jeremy, who had grown up in one small village after another, places where everyone generally bathed in the river, the plain facts of female anatomy were no mystery. In some ways his care of Sal became almost routine. The sight of her nakedness under these conditions did not arouse him physically—rather, he was intensely aware of a new surge of the fierce pride he had begun to feel in being Sal's trusted friend and confederate.

She looked, if anything, more feeble now than she had been two days ago; when Jeremy pulled her behind some bushes and helped her stand, she still could not walk for more than about two steps. He knew he wasn't strong enough to carry her for any meaningful distance, at least not when her injuries prohibited rough handling. He had dug a series of small holes for her to use as a latrine when he was gone.

So far the village dogs had been tolerant of the alien presence they must have scented or heard from time to time, but Jeremy feared they would create a fuss if he tried to help Sal move around at night. The boy considered bringing the dogs over, one at a time, to introduce them to her where she lay hidden, but he feared also that someone would notice what he was doing. He and Sal would just have to avoid the village as they made their way to the riverbank.

When he was helping her with the bandage again he dared to ask, "What . . . what did this to you?"

"A fury—did you ever hear of them?"

He was appalled. "A flying thing like a giant bat? A monster like in the stories?"

"Not as big as in some of the stories. But just as bad." She had to pause there.

"Why?" he whispered in dreadful fascination.

"Why bad? Because it's very real."

He stared at the very real wounds, the raw spots wherever two lash marks intersected, and tried to imagine what they must feel like. "I've never seen one."

"Pray that you never do. Oh, if I were only worthy!" The way she said the word endowed it with some mysterious power.

"Worthy of what?"

She heard that but wasn't going to answer. Turning her head, trying uselessly to get a good look at her own wounds, Sal observed calmly: "These aren't healing. I suppose some of them would be better off with stitches . . . but we're not going to try that."

Jeremy swallowed manfully. "I'll steal a needle and thread and try it if you want. I've never done it before."

"No." She was not too ill to mark the awkward turmoil in his face when he looked at her. "I don't want you to try to sew me up. Just tie the bandage back. It will be fine . . . when I get downriver. Poor lad. Do you have a girlfriend of your own?"

He shook his head, carefully pulling a knot snug. "No. Is that better now, with the bandage?"

"Yes, much better." She managed to make the words almost convincing. "You will make an excellent physician, someday. Or surgeon. If that's what you want to be. And an excellent husband, I think, for some lucky girl."

He made an inarticulate sound. And cursed himself, silently, for not having the words to even begin to tell Sal what he felt. *How could she say something like that to him? Some lucky girl. Why couldn't she see how desperately he loved* her?

But of course for him to talk about, think about, loving her was craziness. A woman as beautiful and capable as Sal undoubtedly had a husband or, at least, a serious lover. Hell, she'd have her pick of grown-up, accomplished, handsome men. Successful warriors, great men in the world. They would naturally be standing in line, each hoping to be the one she chose.

Presently—putting out a hand to touch him on the arm—she asked Jeremy, "What *do* you want to be?" And it seemed that the question was important to her, taking her for a few moments out of her own pain and thoughts of failure.

Again Jeremy discovered that he had an answer ready, one that needed no thought at all. "I want to be someone who works at whatever kind of thing it is that you're doing. And help you do it. Spying, or whatever it is. That's what I'm going to do."

"You *are* doing that, Jeremy. Doing it already. Serving my cause better than you realize. Better than some tall bearded men I know, who . . ." Once more she let her words trail away, not wanting to say too much.

Suddenly Sal, as if feeling a renewed urgency, again sharpened her demands that he help her out of her hiding place in the thicket and into a boat of some kind. And then she must be taken—or sent on her own, though she feared she would never be able to lift a paddle on her own— downriver.

"Sure I can get us a boat. Whenever you say the word. Rowboat or canoe, either one." One or two people had canoes, for fast trips to nearby relatives or markets. "I'll take you. Downriver where?"

"Have you heard of a place called the Academy, Jerry?"

"I've heard the name. You already told me that the people we want are there. The worthy ones."

"Do you know what it is? Think of it as a kind of school. A school for people who are . . . well, about your age or older. Some of them much older. It's near a city called Pangur Ban, if you know where that is. Where the great river joins the sea."

Jeremy nodded. "I've heard that much. Back when I lived in my own village. People said it was like a school for grown-up people."

"Yes. That describes it about as well as . . . Jeremy. Jeremy, my love, pay close attention. I thought . . . if I stayed here and rested . . . but I'm not getting any stronger. Mind's clear right now, but actually weaker. Got to face that. Don't know if I'm going to make it down the river. It might be you'll be the only one alive when . . . No, hush now; listen. . . . So I have to tell you things. And ask you to do a certain thing, if it should happen . . . if things should work out so that I can't do it myself."

"Yes." *Jeremy, my love.* She'd really, truly, said those very words. To him. With his head spinning, he had to make a great effort to be able to hear anything else she said after that word.

She kept on trying to warn him. Between her breathless voice and her wandering mind she was not succeeding very well. She continued: "What I want you to do . . . is dangerous."

As if that could make any difference! At the moment he felt only a bursting contempt for danger. "I'll do it. Tell me what it is."

Sal looked at him for what seemed a long time. He could almost see how the fever was addling her brains. To his despair, at the last moment she seemed to change her mind again. "No. I'd better not try to explain it all just yet. Maybe tomorrow."

It made him sick to realize the fact that Sal's mind was once more drifting, that she was getting worse.

For the first time he had to confront head-on the sickening possibility that she might die, before he could take her where she wished to go. The thought made him angry at her'hat could he possibly do, how could he go on with his own life now, if Sal were dead?

That night, supper in the shabby little house was fish and oatmeal once again. For some reason there were no raisins—he could begin to hope that Aunt Lynn had grown sick of them herself. Jeremy took an extra piece of fish and when no one was looking hid it in his shirt, to take to Sal tomorrow.

Sitting at the table across from the two aging, gap-toothed strangers who happened to be his childless aunt and uncle, the boy found himself looking at them as if this were his first night at this table. Again he wondered how he had ever come to be there in their village, in their house, eating their oatmeal. The arrangement could only have come about as the result of some vast mistake. A cosmic blunder on the part of the gods, or whoever was in charge of arranging human lives.

On impulse, while the three of them were still sitting at supper, Jeremy brought up the subject of the Academy, saying that some passing boatman had talked about it.

Aunt Lynn and Uncle Humbert heard their nephew's words clearly enough. But in response they only looked at him in silence, displaying mild interest, as if he'd belched or farted in some peculiar way. Then they turned away again and sipped their water and their wine. Evidently neither of them felt any curiosity on the subject at all.

Presently Uncle Humbert began to talk of other things, on subjects he doubtless considered truly practical. Among the other jobs Jeremy would be expected to do in the fall, or in the spring, was somehow conveying water uphill to irrigate the vines on their sunny slopes.

"Mutant vines, you got to remember, Jer, and they need special treatment."

"I'll remember."

Jeremy found himself wishing that he could steal his uncle's boat, since it seemed that he would have to take someone's. But as a vine-dresser, only occasionally a winemaker, not really a fisherman, Humbert had no boat.

It was next day at sundown when Jeremy's life, his whole world, changed even more suddenly and violently than on the day of his parents' death.

He was walking with studied casualness toward the place of rendezvous, bringing Sal a few more scraps of smuggled food, when his first sight of a fury, throbbing batlike through the air, coming at treetop height in his general direction, threatened for a moment to paralyze him. *Sal's enemies have come, to kill her and to steal her treasure.*

In the distance, just beyond the last house of the village, he saw and heard a strange man, mounted on a cameloid, shouting orders, telling creatures and people to find "her."

Suddenly the darkening sky seemed full of furies, as black and numerous as crows.

4

BOUNDING FORWARD, HE reached Sal's side only to crouch beside her helplessly, not knowing if they should try to hide or take to the river and escape. Her soft voice seemed unsurprised at the sound and movement beginning to fill the air around them. "Remember. The first name is Alexander, the second Chalandon." Then suddenly her expression altered. "Listen—!"

There was a rustling and a gliding in the sunset air, and from directly above them drifted down a series of soft, strange, wild cries.

Jeremy leaped to his feet, in time to see the second wave of the attack swept in, in the form of sword-wielding men on pacing cameloids, less than a minute behind the flying creatures. Jeremy recognized the blue and white uniforms of Lord Kalakh's army—the people who half a year ago had overrun Jeremy's home village.

Tumult had broken out among the Raisinmakers, with people pouring out of houses, running to and fro. Jeremy grabbed Sal by one arm and dragged her up and out of hiding. She was now in full sight of several villagers, but none of them paid any attention.

Jeremy was ready to try once more to carry her, but Sal, driven to panic, tried desperately to stand and run to the river. She hobbled beside him for a moment, but then her wounded leg gave way. She was crawling to get away when a swooping fury fell upon her slashing. Sal rolled over, screaming in agony.

Jeremy grabbed up a stone and flung it at the flying terror, which squawked and twisted in midair to avoid the missile. When another of the monsters swooped low over Sal, he hurled himself at it, trying to beat it off with his bare hands. It seemed to him that he even caught a momentary grip on one of its whips, but the organ slithered like a snake out of his hand, impossible to hold.

Men, women, and children were shouting in the background. Another fury had just alighted in the top of one of the village shade trees, slender branches swaying under the startling weight. Another came down on the ground and a third right on the peaked shingled roof of Uncle's house. A host of similar creatures were swirling, gray blurs in the background, coming out of the east with the approaching dusk.

Finally Jeremy got a good look at one, holding still in the last sunset light. The creature's face looked monstrously human, a caricature of a woman's face, drawn by some artist whose hatred of all women was clear in every line. Actually, male organs were visible at the bottom of its hairy body.

The creature's great bat wings, for the moment at rest, hung down like draperies. When once more they stirred in motion, they rippled like gray flags in the wind. Its coloring was almost entirely gray, of all shades from white to black, and mottled together in a way that reminded him of the sight of rotting clam meats. And the smell that came from it, though not as strong as that corruption, was even worse in Jeremy's nostrils.

Even from the place where Jeremy was now crouching over Sal, trying to get her back on her feet again, the village shrine was visible. Pale marble Dionysus and squat, dark Priapus were not about to move from their carved positions but stood facing each other as always, oblivious to what was going on around them. Now their raised wine cups seemed to suggest some horrible treachery, as if in mutual congratulations on the success of the attack, the destruction of the villagers who had so long neglected them.

Jeremy had heard that in addition to his more famous attributes, Priapus was a protector of vineyards and orchards. But his statue here was dead and powerless as the stone markers in the village burial ground.

Villagers were running, screaming, pointing up at gliding or perching furies. Jeremy caught a glimpse of Myra, wearing a short skirt like other village girls, standing frozen. On her plain face, framed by her long brown hair, was an expression of perfect shock.

And here came another of the flying horrors toward Sal—

From the fury's taloned birdlike feet and from the fringed wingtips hung the half-dozen tendrils that served as scourging whips. They snapped in a restless reflex motion, making a brief ripple of sound. One struck at a small bird and sent it into convulsions.

The fellows of the first attacker, gliding above on wings the size of carpets, screamed down to it, making sounds that might almost have been words, and it launched itself into the air again, first rising a few yards, then diving like a hawk to the attack. The screams that rose up in response were all from human throats.

Someone in the village had found a bow and was firing inaccurate arrows at the furies as they darted by overhead. Someone else hurled rocks.

Another villager shouted: "Don't do that! A god has sent them."

The man with the bow had time to shout out what he thought should be done with the gods before a human warrior on a swift-pacing cameloid, decked in blue and white, lurched past and knocked the archer down with a single blow of a long-handled war hatchet.

Another blow, from some unseen hand, struck Jeremy down. Senses reeling, he had the vague impression that Myra had come hurrying in his direction, that she was briefly looking down at him with concern.

The stranger who had called herself Sal, the woman Jeremy had begun to worship but had never known, had time to gasp out a few sentences before she sprawled out crudely, awkwardly, facedown, let out a groan, and died.

Swiftly Jeremy bent over her, grabbed her body and twisted it halfway round, so he could see her face, her blind eyes looking up at him. When he saw that she was indeed dead, he twisted his body, screaming out his grief and rage against the world.

The puddle beneath Sal's head was so red with sunset light reflected from the sky that it seemed half of blood, and in the puddle an object that must have fallen from Sal's hand as she died now lay half-sunken, half-floating. Jeremy instinctively grabbed it up and found he was holding a small sealed pouch. Again he thought that it must have dropped from her dying hand, just as she had been on the point of handing it over to him.

Shocked and numbed by Sal's death, only distantly aware of the fire and blood and screaming all around him, Jeremy stuffed into his shirt the pouch all wet with water and with her blood. Vaguely he could feel that it contained some irregularly shaped lump of stuff that clung against his skin with a surprisingly even temperature and softness and, even through the fabric of the pouch, seemed almost to be molding itself to fit against his ribs.

There was something that he had to do, an urgent need that must be met. But what was it? Jeremy's brain felt paralyzed. In his shock it seemed that the world had slowed down and there was no hurry about anything. In her other hand Sal had been holding the small knife whose scabbard hung at her belt. The blade, though shorter than Jeremy's hand, was straight and strong and practical, and very sharp. The handle was made of some black wood the boy could not have named. Certainly Sal would want him to have the knife, and after looking to her dead eyes for encouragement he decided to take belt and all. His waist, he noted dully, was only a little thicker than hers. Kneeling beside the dead woman, he took the whole belt from her and strapped it on himself.

The flying creatures were stupid by human standards, yet obviously experienced in this kind of work, good at starting huts and houses ablaze, driving the inhabitants out where they could get a look at them. They found an open fire somewhere and plucked out brands, using their lash-tentacles almost as skillfully as fingers, and used the bits of burning wood as torches.

From the moment when he left the house, a minute before the attack began, Jeremy saw no more of his two relatives—he had no idea whether they had survived or not.

Shaking himself out of his near-paralysis, he concentrated his full energy on an effort to get himself away.

He cast one more look around him, then rose up running. Before him lay the river, one highway that never closed, and the escape plan he had at least begun already to prepare.

The usual complement of villagers' boats were available, tied up loosely at their tiny respective docks, as well as a few, awaiting minor repairs, hauled bottom-up on shore. A few more were drifting loose, freed of their moorings in a backwater current, their owners likely murdered or driven mad in the latest attack. Jeremy saw one human body thrashing in the water, another bobbing lifeless.

And now the voices of people screaming, under attack, came drifting down from the high vineyards on the hill above the village.

And the voices of the human attackers, raised like those of hunters who rode to hounds in the pursuit of wild game. The thud and plash of saddled lamoids' padded, two-toed feet.

A human warrior on foot was now blocking the approach to the long, narrow dock to which the boats were tied. But the man was looking past Jeremy and seemed to be paying him no attention.

Jeremy hit the water headfirst, in his clothes, and struck out hard for the outer end of the crude pier, where boats were clustered. He'd caught a glimpse of a canoe there, somehow left bobbing and waiting, instead of being pulled out of the water.

Something struck the nearby water with a violent splash, and he assumed it was a missile aimed at him, but it had no influence on his flight.

Even underwater Jeremy could feel the thing, the mysterious treasure she had given him, stowed snug inside his shirt, strangely warm against his skin, as warm as Sal's own living hand had been.

Pulling to the surface for a gasp of air, hoping to find the canoe almost within reach, he screamed in pain and fright, feeling the slash of one of the furies' whips across the back of his right shoulder.

5

GASPING OUT ALMOST forgotten prayers, Jeremy improvised a few new ones while he dived again, driving himself to the verge of drowning in his desperate effort to escape.

Lunging about blindly underwater, he almost swam right past the boat he wanted but managed to correct his error in time. Again his head broke the surface of the river, and at last his grasping fingers closed on the canoe's gunwale. His heart leaped when he saw that a paddle had been left aboard, stowed under the center seat. Feverishly he groped for and found the bit of cord holding the canoe loosely to the dock, and after some clumsy fumbling he undid the knot.

Bracing his feet against the dock, he got the vessel under way with a shove, then got himself aboard with a floundering leap that landed him in a sodden heap and almost capsized the vessel. A moment later he was sitting up and had the paddle working.

For a moment it seemed that the path to freedom might now be clear—then a fury materialized out of the evening sky to strike at him twice more. Two more fashing blows, which felt as if they were delivered with red-hot wire, fell on the backs of his legs, first right, then left. Involuntarily the boy screamed and started to spring to his feet, only to trip and fall face downward back into the water. The plunge carried him out of the fury's reach, and he stayed under, holding his breath, as long as possible. When he surfaced again he was behind the boat and started pushing it downstream, paddling furiously with his feet.

He braced his nerves against another slashing attack, but it never came. The monster had flapped away while he was underwater.

Jeremy was several hundred yards downstream before he pulled himself back into the boat and found, to his dismay, that the paddle had somehow vanished.

Then his spirits surged. There was the paddle, floating at no great distance, visible in the dark water as a darker blot, against the reflection of the sunset. In a moment he had hand-propelled the canoe close enough and had it in his grip.

With every movement, the slash wounds skewered him with almost blinding pain, pain that diminished only slightly if he held still. His sensations, his imagination, warned him that he could be bleeding to death. But no, Sal had been beaten worse than this and hadn't bled to death.

Terror kept him moving, despite the pain.

Deepening dusk was overtaking him, but with terrifying slowness. Whatever concealment full night might offer was still long minutes in the future. Desperately he tried to recall if there were any prayers to Night personified. The name of that god should be Nox, he thought, or was it Nyx? He seemed to remember both names from children's stories, heard in a different world, the early years of childhood. But neither name inspired any hope or confidence.

Avoiding the local islands and sandbars, whose positions had been fixed in his mind during the months he'd lived nearby, was easy enough. But once Jeremy's flight carried him around the big bend, half a mile downstream from the Raisinmaker's village, he found himself in totally unfamiliar territory.

He kept on working the paddle steadily, fear allowing him to ignore the pain in legs and shoulder. Fortunately, he'd spent enough of his childhood in canoes to know how to handle this one. It was his good luck, too, that the river was now high with upstream rains and moving fairly swiftly.

In the dark he found it well nigh impossible to judge distances with any accuracy. Moonlight, which ought to have helped, had he been blessed with normal vision, only seemed to add to an extra layer of enchantment and deception.

In one way fortune had smiled on him; he'd been able to get away with a a canoe, instead of being forced to settle for one of the heavy clam-fishing craft. He could drive such a light vessel farther and faster with a single paddle than he'd ever have been able to move a rowboat, even if he'd been lucky enough to get one with a good pair of oars.

———

Frequently during that long night, when a dim perception of something in the river or in the sky brought back terror Jeremy felt himself in the greatest peril. Drifting or paddling as best he could while making a minimum of noise, he muttered heartfelt prayers to every other god and goddess whose name he could remember—though none of them, as far as he knew, had ever even been aware of his existence. He had no way to tell if the prayers did any good, but at least he was surviving.

The tree-lined shores to right and left were hazy black masses, totally bereft of lights. Hours into his journey, when the last of the sun glow was completely gone, there was still a dim blurred glow, faint and familiar, high in the night sky. His poor sight could distinguish this from the more localized blur of the moon. People had told him that it came from a cloud of stars called the Milky Way. The sight of the bright smear was somehow reassuring.

Meanwhile the light of the burning village remained visible for a long time, at least an hour, in the eastern sky. But Jeremy and his boat were not molested again. Finally he gave up on trying to be quiet and used his paddle steadily.

Vividly Jeremy could recall how, when he was small, his father and mother had begun to teach him the old stories about the planets and constellations, how various celestial objects were intimately connected with different gods and goddesses.

The presence of the all-but-unseen stars above him brought back memories of his parents. One night in particular, long ago, when he'd gone fishing with his father. But Jeremy was not going to allow himself to think of them just now.

He even considered including, for the first time he could remember, prayers to Dionysus and Priapus—but in the end he declined to do that. The memory of their statues, saluting each other with wine cups in the midst of horror, convinced him that neither of them was likely to take any interest in his welfare.

Meanwhile, the wound that cut across the back of his right shoulder continued to burn like fire, and so did those on the backs of his legs. First one and then another of the three slashes hurt badly enough that he could almost forget about the other two. Only fear that the enemy might be close behind him, and the memory of his pledge to Sal, enabled him to press on, whimpering aloud.

Fear tended to make every half-seen minor promontory a ghastly crouching fury, ready to spring out and strike. Even floating logs were terrible. Several times during the night, trying to steer among the ghostly shapes and shadows of unfamiliar shores and islands, paddling or huddling in the bottom of the boat, Jeremy heard more soft commotion in the air above him, taking it to be the detestable sounds made by the furies' and the furies' wings.

And there was a certain unusual light in the night sky.

Let it burn, was all that he could think, looking back at the last embers of red light decorating the northeastern sky, reflecting off the vineyard slopes on the hill above the village and into a patch of low clouds. He could feel only vaguely sorry for the people. Already his aunt and uncle were only dim and half-remembered figures, their faces and manners as hard to call up as those of folk he had not seen for many years; it was the same with everyone he had known, everything he had experienced in the last months, since his parents and his home had been destroyed.

Everyone but Sal.

Jeremy supposed that the total time he'd spent actually in the company of Sal, adding up the fragments of his hasty visits over a period of three days, amounted to less than an hour. But in those three days Sal had become vastly more important to him,even more real, than Uncle Humbert or Aunt Lynn had ever been. No matter that he'd known his aunt and uncle since his infancy and had been eating and sleeping in their house for months.

Every once in a while his memory reminded him with a little jar that Sal had probably not been her real name. Never mind. That didn't matter. He would find out her real name, eventually—when he told the story of her last days to Professor Alexander or Margaret Chalandon.

It seemed, now, to the traveler alone on the river in darkness, that he could remember every word that Sal—that name would always be holy to him, because she'd chosen it—had ever spoken to him in their brief meetings. Every gesture of her hands, look on her face, turn of her head. She was coming with him as a living memory—and yes, his mother and father were with him as well. It was as if some part of him that had died with his parents had somehow been brought back to life by Sal.

Paddling on as steadily as he could, peering nearsightedly into the darkness ahead, Jeremy thought that, leaving aside the memory of Sal, he was bringing with him out of his last half-year of life very little that would ever be of any use, or worth a coin.

For one thing, a new understanding of what death meant—he'd certainly learned that. A good set of worker's calluses on his hands. Some creditably strong muscles—for his age. On the useless side, a few semi-indelible grape juice stains, on hands and arms and feet, marks that would doubtless stick to his skin at least as long as the ragged clothing Aunt Lynn had provided still hung on his back.

And that, Jeremy thought, just about summed it up.

Except, of course, for the three painful wounds he had so recently collected. But they would heal in time. They had to. He kept hoping that if he refused to think about the injuries, they might not hurt so much. So far that strategy did not seem to be working.

Jeremy wished neither aunt nor uncle any harm—any more than he did any other pair of strangers. But he found himself hoping that Uncle Humbert's barrow, the heavy one the boy had so often trundled up and down the hillside path, was burning, too.

With every movement of his right shoulder, propelling himself downstream, the pain of the fury's lash wound brought tears to Jeremy's eyes. But still it wasn't the pain, sharp as that was, that brought the tears. They were welling up because his injuries were the same as Sal's and tied the two of them more closely together.

———

Gradually, as the hours of darkness passed, and the heavenly blurs of the newly risen moon and fading Milky Way slowly shifted their positions toward the west, his distance from the village grew into miles. The red glow faded and at length was gone completely. When the first morning grayness tinged the eastern sky, Jeremy paddled in to shore and grounded his canoe under the dim, spiky silhouette of a willow thicket.

Stumbling ashore in exhaustion, then dragging his boat up higher until it was firmly beached, he lay down on his left side, sparing his right shoulder, and, despite his injuries and the fact that his stomach was empty, fell quickly into a dreamless stupor.

———

. . . he frowned with the breaking of the last filaments of some dream. Something important had been conveyed to him while he slept—he had the feeling it was a vital message of some kind—but he could not remember what it was.

He was waking up now, and it was daylight. Even before opening his eyes Jeremy felt for the pouch inside his shirt. Sal's treasure was still there, but strangely, the mysterious contents seemed to have softened and even slightly changed shape, so that when Jeremy had rolled over in his sleep the corners and hard edges he'd earlier detected had somehow modified their contours to keep from stabbing him.

His three wounds and their demanding pain seemed to awaken only an instant after he did. He felt slightly but ominously unwell, in mind and body, and he dreaded fever and delirium. Only too well he remembered Sal's illness, caught from the furies' slashes on her flesh, a sickness that had been close to killing her even before the second attack swept in.

With eyes open and Sal's treasure in hand he lay quietly for a while, trying to think, but only gloomy imaginings were the result. By the time he roused himself and looked around, morning was far advanced. Mist was rising from the river, his shirt and trousers were still almost dripping wet from last night's soaking, and the air was almost chill. Every time he started to move, the fury's lash marks stabbed his back and legs with renewed sensation. Pain settled in to a steady throbbing.

He hadn't yet even tried to investigate the wounds. Only now did his probing fingers discover that the cloth of shirt and trousers had actually been cut by the blows, just as Sal's clothing had been.

It was common knowledge that some hundreds of miles downstream the greater river to which the Aeron was a tributary emptied into the sea, which Jeremy could not remember ever seeing—though from his first dim understanding of what an ocean must be like he had yearned to see it.

And he had known, even before encountering Sal, that at that river's mouth there was a harbor, where huge ships from the far corners of the world sailed in and out, and that the city beside the harbor, Pangur Ban, was overlooked by the castle of a great lord, Victor, whose power largely sponsored the Academy. Before meeting Sal, Jeremy had never spent any time at all thinking about the Academy, but often he had yearned to see the ocean.

Gradually the mist began to dissipate, as if the sun, supposedly Apollo's property, were truly burning it away. Jeremy raised his eyes to behold above him a great tangle of the feathery leaves of willow branches. Beyond the topmost branches arched a partly cloudy sky. . . .

Slowly he got to his feet, forcing himself to move despite the pain, and began to walk about, rubbing his eyes. Scratching his head, he thought, *All that part of my life is over now. Sal is dead.* But he had the strange feeling that, thanks to her, he, Jeremy Redthorn, had somehow come back to life. He had a job to do now. And he was going to do it, if it killed him.

Peering about him, he tried in his nearsighted fashion to see something of what lay across the broad surface of the river. He could see a line of hazy green that must mean trees, but not much beyond that. Patiently listening for what his ears could tell him, he eventually decided that there were no towns or villages nearby—he would have heard some sound of human activity, carrying across the water, and there had been nothing of the kind. Sniffing the breeze, he caught only river smells, no traces of a settlement's inevitable smoke.

After walking along the shore for a few yards upstream and down, he concluded that he had come aground on a fairly sizable island. The river was much wider here than it had been at Uncle's village, at least one large tributary evidently having come in.

At the moment the sky was empty of any threat.

———

Jeremy's stomach, unfed for many hours, continued to insist that food should be the first order of business. He could only remember with regret the food he'd been carrying to Sal—after all his swimming and struggling, only a few wet crumbs remained. Searching his stolen canoe without much hope, he discovered under the forward thwart a small closed compartment, containing half a stale corn cake, from which someone must have been breaking off pieces to use as fishbait. The bait served as breakfast, washed down with river water. Now, in late summer, he might well be able to gather some berries in whatever woods he came across. With any luck he could find mushrooms, too. And the wild cherries were now ripe enough to eat without too much fear of bellyache.

Wading in the shallows right beside the shore, he tried without success to snatch fish out of the water with his hands. He'd seen that trick done successfully once or twice. It gave him something to occupy his mind and hands, though probably success would have done him no good anyway, for he lacked the means to make a fire, and he wasn't yet starved enough to try raw fish. He'd heard of people eating turtles, which ought to be easier to catch, and also that turtle eggs could be good food. But he had no idea where to look for them.

———

Jeremy's best guess was that he might have made twenty miles or more down the winding stream during the night—maybe, if he was lucky, half that distance as a fury might fly. Having reached what appeared to be a snug hideaway, he decided to stay where he was until night fell again. He had no idea how well furies could see at night or whether they, and their two-legged masters, might still be looking for him—but they hadn't found him last night, when he'd been moving on the open water.

If he made a practice of lying low every day and traveling only at night, he would escape observation by fisherfolk in other boats and by people on shore, as well as by at least some of his enemies aloft. He could not shake the idea that some of the beasts and people who'd attacked Uncle Humbert's village might still be following him downstream.

Now, it seemed he'd done about all the planning he could do at the moment. The urge to do something else had been growing in the back of his mind, and now he could think of no reason to put it off any longer—he meant to take a good took at Sal's parting gift.

For some reason she'd been reluctant even to tell him what it was. Not that it mattered; whether it turned out to be priceless diamonds or worthless trash, he was going to take it on to Professor Alexander—or Margaret Chalandon—or die in the attempt. But it seemed to the boy that he at least had a right to know what he was carrying.

He felt inside his shirt to make sure that the strange thing was still where he had put it.

It was time to take it out and give it a look. He didn't see how he could be any worse off for knowing what it was.

One more thing bothered Jeremy. Why had Sal, when her treasure was mentioned, kept saying that she was not worthy? Not worthy to do what?

6

MAKING A CONSCIOUS effort to distract himself from ongoing hunger and pain, Jeremy sat down on the grass, holding the pouch, meaning to examine its contents carefully. His vision had always been keen at close range, and now he was working in full daylight.

He tore open the crude stitches that, as he now discovered, had been holding the pouch closed. Taking out the single object it contained, he held it up against the light. It was a fragment of a carved or molded face, apparently broken or cut from a mask or statue.

For one eerie moment he had an idea that the thing might be alive, for certainly something inside it was engaged in rapid movement, reminding him of the dance of sunlight on rippling water. Inside the semi-transparent object, which was no thicker than his finger, he beheld a ceaseless rapid internal flow, of . . . of *something* . . . that might have been ice-clear water, or even light itself, *if* there could be light that illuminated nothing. Jeremy found it practically impossible to determine the direction or the speed of flow. The apparent internal waves kept reflecting from the edges, and they went on and on without weakening.

And, stranger still, why should Jeremy have thought that the pupil of the crystal eye in the broken mask had darkened momentarily, had turned to look in his direction and even twinkled at him? For just a moment he had the fleeting impression that the eye was part of the face of someone he had known . . . but then again it seemed no more than a piece of strangely colored glass. Not really glass, though. This was not hard or brittle enough for glass.

Whatever it might cost him, he would carry this object to Professor Alexander at the Academy. Or to Margaret Chalandon. Silently he renewed his last pledge to Sal.

Brushing his hair out of his eyes, he turned the object over and over in his hands.

Its thickness varied from about a quarter of an inch to half an inch. It was approximately four inches from top to bottom and six or seven along the curve from right to left. The ceaseless flow of . . . something or other inside it went on as tirelessly as before.

Somehow Jeremy had never doubted, from his first look at this fragment of a modeled face, that it was intended to be masculine. There was no sign of beard or mustache, and it would have been hard for him to explain how he could be so sure. The most prominent feature of the fragment was the single eye that it contained—the left—which had been carved or molded from the same piece of strange warm, flexible, transparent stuff as all the rest. The eyeball showed an appropriately subtle bulge of pupil, and the details of the open lid were clear. No attempt had been made to represent eyelashes. An inch above the upper lid, another smooth small bulge suggested the eyebrow. A larger one below outlined the cheekbone. No telling what the nose looked like, because the fragment broke off cleanly just past the inner corner of the eye. On the other side it extended well back along the side of the head, far enough to include the temple and most of the left ear. Along the top of the fragment, in the region of the temple, was a modeled suggestion of hair curled close against the skull.

Around the whole irregular perimeter of the translucent shard the edges were somewhat jagged, though Jeremy remembered that they had not scratched his skin. Now when he pushed at the small projections with a finger, he found that they bent easily, springing back into their original shape as soon as the pressure was released. Everything about the piece he was holding suggested strongly that it was only a remnant, torn or broken from a larger image, that of a whole face or even an entire body.

What he was looking at was most likely meant to be the image of a god. Jeremy reached that conclusion simply because, in his experience, people made representations of deities much more often than of mere humans. Which god this might be Jeremy had no idea, though somehow he felt sure that it was neither Dionysus nor Priapus. What the whole face of the statue or carving might have looked like—assuming it had once been complete—was impossible to say, but Jeremy thought that it had not been, would not be, ugly.

Well, few gods were hard to look at. Or at least very few of their portrayals were. He realized suddenly that few of the artists who made them could ever have seen the gods themselves.

Brushing his own stubborn hair out of the way again, he held the fragment of a face close to his nearsighted eyes for a long time, tilting it this way and that, turning it around, and trying to think of why it could be so enormously valuable. Sal had been willing to give her life to see that it got to where it was meant to go.

The expression on the god's face, the boy at last decided, conveyed a kind of arrogance. Definitely there seemed to *be* an expression, despite the fact that he was looking at only about a sixth or a seventh of a whole countenance.

When Jeremy stroked the fragment with his callused fingers, it produced a pleasant sensation in his hands. Something more, he decided, than simply pleasant. But faint, and almost indescribable. An eerie tingling. There had to be magic in a thing like this. Real magic, such as some folk had told him wistfully was gone from the world for good.

The sensation in his hands bothered him, and even frightened him a little. Telling himself he couldn't spend all his time just looking at the mask, Jeremy stuffed it back inside the pouch and put the pouch again into his shirt, where it lay once more against his ribs, seemingly as inert as a piece of leather.

Time to think of something else. He kept wondering, now that the sun was up again, if the flying devils with their poisoned whips were combing the river's shores and all its islands, if they would be back at any moment, looking for him.

Well, if they were, there wasn't much he could do about it, besides traveling at night—but maybe he could do a little more. There was no use continuing to let his hair grow long when he had left behind him the village full of people the growth was meant to challenge. With some idea of altering his distinctive appearance, to make any searchers' task a little harder, he unsheathed Sal's knife and slashed off most of his hair, down to within a couple of finger widths of his scalp. Actually using the knife made him admire it more. He thought that a man would be able to shave with a blade like this—his own face still lacked any whiskers to practice on.

Despite its hard-edged keenness, the blade was nicked in places and the point slightly blunted, as if it had seen hard use. There were traces of what Jeremy decided had to be dried blood. Probably she'd used it as a weapon, against some beast or human—she'd never talked to him about the struggle she must have been through before they met.

Struck by a new idea, Jeremy now squatted on the riverbank and scooped up handfuls of thick black mud, with which he heavily smeared the top of his head, down to the hairline all around. Most of the stuff dripped and slid off, but enough remained to cover pretty thoroughly what remained of his hair. He could hope that flyers, or men in boats, who came searching for a redheaded youth would be deceived if they saw him only from a distance. A worm came wriggling out out of his mudpack to inch across Jeremy's face, and abstractedly he brushed it away.

———

He'd been hoping that the wounds inflicted by the fury would bother him less as the day advanced, but the opposite turned out to be true. He took some comfort from the fact that so far he seemed to have no fever. The stinging wounds had fallen where he couldn't see them, but he once more explored them with his fingers.

Both legs of his trousers were slit in back, horizontally, where the second and third whip blows had landed. All three of his wounds were almost impossible for him to see, but his fingers could feel welts, raised and sensitive, as well as thin crusts of dried blood, scabbing over beneath the holes slashed in the homespun fabric of shirt and trousers. Well, he'd had a good look at Sal's wounds and thought these were not as bad. He didn't have anything to use for bandages, unless he tore pieces from his shirt or trousers—but then bandages really hadn't done Sal any good.

The boy dozed for a while, then woke again in the heat of the day, with the sun not far from straight overhead. Jeremy helped himself to a drink, straight from the river, and then decided to go into the water, hoping to soothe his lash marks. He'd have to emerge from under the sheltering willows to reach water deep enough to submerge himself up to his neck, but he thought it unlikely that anyone would notice his presence, as long as he allowed only his head to show above the surface.

As he started to pull off his shirt, the pouch holding the mask fragment fell out on the grass. The pouch, no longer sewn tightly shut, came open, and the irregular glassy oval popped briskly out of it, like something with a will of its own, announcing that it declined to be hidden.

Delaying his cooling bath, Jeremy sat down naked on the grassy bank, dangling his feet in the water, and once more picked up Sal's peculiar legacy. He wondered if some kind of magical compulsion had come with it. He'd be forced to keep on studying the thing, until . . .

Until what? Jeremy didn't know.

There seemed no reason to think the piece was anything but what it looked like—a fragment that had been torn or broken from a mask or from a statue, maybe in some village shrine. But who'd ever seen a statue made of material like this?

A mask, then? Maybe. The jagged edges argued that the object had once been larger, and certainly this one piece wasn't big enough to serve as even a partial mask—no one could hope to hide his identity by covering one eye and one ear. Anyway, there was no strap, no string, no way to fasten it on a wearer's face.

Besides, what would be the point of wearing a transparent mask? The import must be purely magical. The visible interior flow, as of water, wasn't enough to obscure his fingers on the other side. Well, he'd never seen or heard of a transparent statue either.

The more he handled the thing, the more of a pleasant tingling it sent into his fingers.

On a sudden impulse Jeremy carried the shard down to the back of his right leg, where he stroked it tentatively, very gently, along the slash mark of the fury's lash. Even when he pressed a little harder, the contact didn't hurt but soothed.

Presently Jeremy lay back on the grassy bank with his eyes closed. Raising one leg at a time, he stroked some more, first giving the injury on the back of the right leg a thorough treatment, then moving to the left leg. The medicine, the magic, whatever it was, was really doing the wounds some good. After a minute or so he thought the swollen welts were actually getting smaller, and certainly the pain was relieved. Presently he shifted his attention to the sore place on his shoulder and enjoyed a similar result.

Magic, no doubt about it. . . . Jeremy's nerves knew hints, suggestions of great pleasures, subtle and refined, that the thing of magic sent wandering through his body. . . . There was one more place he wanted to try. . . .

But even as he indulged himself his mind kept wandering, jumping from thought to thought. Sal's lash marks had been worse than his, and she'd been carrying this very thing of magic with her, all during the very worst of her suffering. So why hadn't she used it to heal her injuries, or save her life, or even to ease her pain? *That* was something to puzzle over. She must have known more about it than he did, which was almost nothing at all. . . .

Now, even in the midst of growing pleasure, the troubling notion came to Jeremy that the exotic joys evoked by the shard were not meant to be experienced by the likes of him—or at least it was somehow wrong for them to be obtained so cheaply. Because Sal was involved.

Certainly she hadn't given him her treasure to use it for this purpose. What would she think if she could see what he was doing now?

Shivering as with cold, feeling vaguely guilty of some indefinable offense, Jeremy pulled the object away from his body and held it at arm's length.

No. This—this *thing*—which was Sal's great gift to him, had to be dealt with properly. With respect.

The magic had helped his back and his injured legs. Whatever helped him to heal now would help him achieve his sworn goal. What other worthy purpose might he find for powerful magic?

Well, he couldn't eat the thing if he tried—his fingers could tell that it was far too tough to chew. But now when he tried holding it against his belly, his hunger pangs were soothed just as the pain of his wounds had been.

Suddenly the glassy eye reminded him of the spectacles he'd once or twice seen old folk wearing. Once more, as on almost every day of his life, Jeremy had the thought that doing what he had to do would be a hell of a lot easier if he could only *see*. Anything that might help him in that regard was worth a try.

Carefully, eagerly, Jeremy lifted the translucent oval toward his face again, holding it at first at a level slightly higher than his eyes. Yes, his earlier impression had been right. The world really *did* have a different look about it when seen through the mask's single glassy eye.

Suddenly hopeful, convinced that at least he was going to do himself no harm, Jeremy brought the fragment close against his nose and cheek, pressing it tight against the skin of his face, trying to seat it there more snugly. At first the results were disappointing. His left eye now peered into a field of vision even more wildly blurred than usual. It was like looking through some kind of peephole. It would be marvelous not to have to be nearsighted any longer. If he could just get the distance between his own eye and the crystal pupil exactly right, he might be able to—

A moment later, the boy let out a half-voiced scream and jumped to his feet, heedless of the fact that his involuntary leap had carried him splashing knee-deep into the river.

Because the object, Sal's treasure, was no longer in his hands. It had attacked him, like a striking snake. He hadn't seen what happened, because it had been too close and too quick to see. But he'd felt it. Sal's thing of magic had melted in his fingers, dissolved into liquid as quickly as ice thrown into a fire—and then it had disappeared.

The damned thing was gone, dissolved away—but it had not run down his arms and body toward the ground. No, instead of streaming along his skin to the earth, it had run right into his head. He'd *felt* it go there, penetrating his left eye and his left ear, flowing into his head like water into dry sand. The first shock had been an ice-cold trickle, followed quickly by a sensation of burning heat, fading slowly to a heavy warmth. . . .

The warmth was still there. Clutching at his head with both hands, Jeremy went stumbling about in the shallows, groaning and whimpering. There was a long moment when his vision and his bearing blurred and he knew with dreadful terror that he was dead.

But maybe, after all, some god was looking out for him. Because here he was, still breathing, and his body showed no signs of having sustained any damage. At the moment he couldn't see at all, but he soon realized that was only because he had his eyes covered with his hands. His feet and legs just went on splashing, until he stumbled to a halt, still in water up to his knees.

Slowly Jeremy spread his trembling fingers and peeked out. Yes, he could still see. Whatever the damned thing had done, it hadn't killed him. No, not yet. Maybe it wasn't going to.

His three savage lash marks once more throbbed with pain, because of all his jumping around—still they did not hurt nearly as much as they had before Sal's magic touched them. His head still felt—well, peculiar.

For what seemed to Jeremy a very long time, he just stood there, right below the grassy bank, almost without moving, knee-deep in mud and water. Gradually he brought his empty hands down from his head and looked at them and felt another slight increment of reassurance.

Something alien had entered his body by speed and stealth, trickling right into his damned *head,* and it was still there. But these were his familiar hands. He could still do with them whatever he wanted.

He tried to tell himself it had all been some kind of trick or an illusion. What he'd thought was happening hadn't really taken place at all. Slowly, slowly, now. *Stop and think the problem out.* He could almost hear his father, trying to counsel him.

All right. The piece of . . . whatever it was, wasn't in his hands now. It wasn't anywhere where he could see it.

One moment he'd been pressing it firmly against his face. In the next moment, it was gone.

So, it had sure as all the hells gone *somewhere.* Magical treasures, of great value, didn't just cease to exist.

Raising empty hands again, the boy squeezed fists against his temples. Again he reassured himself that there was no pain in his head, and by now even the sensation of liquid warmth had faded. Whatever had happened hadn't hurt him. *Something* of a funny feeling persisted, yes, very subtle, deep in behind his eyes, where he'd thought he'd felt the *thing* establishing itself. But . . .

But other than that, everything seemed practically back to normal. Yes, he could hope that he had been mistaken, after all.

Abruptly Jeremy crouched down in the water, moving on hands and knees. Now he was getting the cool bath he'd started out to take, but he didn't care what it felt like, because he wasn't doing it for amusement or relief from the day's heat or even to soothe his injuries. All those things had been forgotten. All the boy's attention was concentrated on searching the muddy bottom with feet and hands, working his way in a semicircle through the opaque brown water beside his private beach, groping for the missing object.

Of course the mask fragment—if that was what it was—being light in weight, might easily have been carried some distance downstream by a normal current. But the current at this point, right on the flank of the island, was only a gentle eddy, actually turning and swirling upstream insofar as it moved at all.

And Jeremy's memory kept prodding him with the fact that there had been no splash, not even a small one, when the damned thing ran out of his hands and disappeared. Even a tiny pebble made some kind of splash. No, the thing he was concerned about could not have fallen into the water at all.

Panting with new fear and exertion, he paused in his muddy, desperate search, then after the space of only a few heartbeats plunged back into it, splashing and gasping. But he knew now that he was doing it only as a duty, so he could tell himself later that he had done everything possible *to make sure.*

At last he came to a halt, eyes closed again, panting for breath, standing waist-deep in the river, leaning his body against the stern of his canoe, most of whose length was firmly grounded.

He knew quite well where Sal's treasure had gone, where her precious, priceless bit of magic was right now. Because he had *felt* it going there. It was just that he didn't want to let himself believe the fact or have to put it into words.

Not even in his own mind.

The answer was in his own head.

He had no choice but to believe it, because when he opened his eyes again, new evidence was at hand.

7

A TREMENDOUS CHANGE indeed had come upon him. The simple fact was that now he could *see,* which meant that his left eye, having been treated to a dose of Sal's magical melting ice, was now functioning, showing him things in a way that he had to believe was the way human eyes were meant to work.

Turning his head to right and left, looking upstream and down, Jeremy confirmed the miracle. No more mere smears of brown and green. Now he could not only count the trees on the far bank but easily distinguish individual leaves on many of their branches. And miles beyond that, so far that it took his breath away, he could make out the precise shapes of distant clouds.

Again Jeremy had to fight to regain control over himself. He was still standing in waist-deep water at the curved stern of the canoe, gripping the wood of the gunwale in an effort to keep from shaking. In this position he kept closing his eyes and opening them again. In spite of his improved vision, fear still kept him hoping and praying, to every god that he could think of, for the thing that had invaded his body to go away. But there was not the least sign that his hopes and prayers were going to be fulfilled.

Even at the peak of his terror, the glorious revelation of perfect sight shone like a beacon. At last there came a moment when he could forget to be terrified.

Drawing a deep breath, Jeremy insisted that his body cease its shaking. The effort was not totally successful, but it helped.

Now. He wasn't going to go on playing around here in the shallows, like a child making mud pies. It was pointless to go on looking for something that was not there.

Finally he admitted to himself that the fragment of some unknown divinity's face was somewhere inside his head. He'd *felt* the thing invade his skull, and the reality of that staggering experience was being steadily confirmed by the transformation in his vision.

Concentrating on that change, he began to realize that it went beyond enabling him to see distant things. Now in his left eye the whole world, near objects as well as far, was taking on a distinctly different aspect from the familiar scene as still reported by his other eye in its half of his visual field.

And belatedly Jeremy began to realize that his left ear was no longer functioning in quite the same way. His hearing had always been normal, so the change wrought in it was not as dramatic as that in his vision— but an alteration had definitely taken place. Some sounds as he perceived them on his left side were now underlain by a faint ringing, a hollow tone, like that resulting from water in the ear—but again, it wasn't *exactly* that.

Gently he pounded the heel of his hand against the sides of his head, first right, then left, but to no effect.

He wasn't quite sure whether his hearing on the left was actually improved—but possibly it was. The situation wasn't as clearcut as with sight.

Time passed while the boy's pulse and breathing gradually returned to normal. He was still standing waist-deep in water, clinging to the boat, but the invasion of his body appeared to be producing no additional symptoms. Eventually Jeremy stopped shaking, and eventually he was able to force himself to let go of the canoe—only when his fingers came loose did he realize how cramped they had become maintaining their savage grip.

Rubbing his hands together to get some life back into them, he waded slowly ashore, where he stood on the riverbank dripping, naked—anyone watching would be certain *he* wasn't carrying any mysterious magical object—and waiting for whatever might be going to happen to him next.

What came next was a renewed surge of fear and worry. Despairingly Jeremy thought: *I had it, Sal's treasure, right here in my hands, and now I've lost control of it. Like a fool I pushed it right up against my face, and right into . . .*

Never mind all that. All right, he knew quite well where the damned marvelous thing had settled. But just stewing about it wasn't going to do him any good.

The reassuring belief remained that Sal—well, Sal had at least *liked* him. She wouldn't have played him any dirty tricks. No. Sal had—well, she'd called him *love* that one time. At least once. He really couldn't stand to think of the most that might have meant—but yes, at least she'd liked him, quite a lot.

And the precious object she'd lost her life trying to save had now become a part of him, Jeremy Redthorn. Of course that wasn't what was supposed to happen.

Possibly what he'd just done—what had just happened—meant he had already failed in the mission for which she'd given up her life. But no, he wouldn't stand for that. He'd still fulfill his promise to her—if he could.

Even if he still had not the faintest idea of what the treasure really was, what it really meant.

Slowly Jeremy pulled on his wretched clothes again. As usual, the coarse fabric of his shirt scraped at the lash mark on his back. But that injury, like those on his legs, was notably less painful than it had been an hour ago. And it was really not possible for him to go without clothes all the time. At least during the day, he had to protect the parts of his hide not already deeply tanned and freckled. Already weakened by his lash marks and by hunger, the last thing he needed was a case of sunburn.

Once more the boy became absorbed in testing the miracle of his new vision, closing one eye at a time. Each trial had the same result. The world as seen through his left eye, especially in the distance, now looked enormously clearer, sharper in detail. Certain objects, some trees, bushes, a darting bird, displayed other changes, too, subtle alterations in shape and color that he would have been hard put to describe in words.

When he grew tied of these experiments, the sun was still high above the shading willows. He had decided to stick to his plan of waiting for nightfall before he pushed off in the boat again. Meanwhile, he really needed more sleep. All emotions, even fear, had to give way sometime to exhaustion.

Jeremy lay back on the grassy bank and closed his eyes. This made him more fully aware of the change in his left ear, which kept on reporting new little differences in the everyday events of the world around him. Whenever wavelets lapped the shore nearby or a fish jumped in the middle distance, there came hints of new information to be derived from the sound. His left ear and his right presented slightly different versions of the event. Not that he could sort it all out just yet. In time, he thought, a fellow might learn to listen to them all and pick out meaning.

It crossed Jeremy's mind that this might be the way a baby learned about the world, when sight and hearing were altogether new.

He had to try to think things through . . . but before he could think any more about anything, he fell asleep.

His slumber was soon troubled by a dream, whose opening sequence might have placed it in the category of nightmare, except that while it lasted he remained curiously without fear. In fact all the action in the dream took place with a minimum of emotion. He dreamed he was beset by a whole cloud of airborne furies, even larger than life-size, as big as the harpies that his waking eyes had never seen. Huge bat-shaped forms came swirling round him like so many gigantic screaming mosquitoes. But somehow the situation brought no terror. Instead he knew the exquisite pleasure of reaching out, catching the neck of one of the flying monsters in the grip of his two hands, fully confident of being able to summon up, in his hands and wrists, a sufficiency of strength to wring its neck. In fact, the action was almost effortless on his part. The physical sensation suggested the familiar one of chicken bones crunching and crumbling.

Then abruptly the scene changed. No more nightmare monsters. Now Jeremy was presented with an image of his lovely Sal and was overjoyed to realize that she was not dead after all. What had seemed to be her death was all a horrible mistake! She wasn't even wounded, not so much as scratched, her face not even dirty.

Jeremy's heart leaped up at the sight of her wading toward him, thigh-deep in the river, dressed in her familiar clothes—the only garments he'd ever seen her wear, but now new and clean instead of torn and dirty.

She was smiling directly at him—at her friend, her lover, Jeremy. And Sal was beckoning to him. She wanted him to come to her so the two of them could make love. *Love.* Her lips were forming the word, but silently, because the Enemy, the unknown and faceless Enemy, must not hear.

Jeremy—or was he really Jeremy any longer?—seemed to be drifting, disembodied, outside himself. He was observing from a little distance the male youth who stood waiting onshore while the young woman approached. He who had taken Jeremy's place deserved to be called a young man rather than a boy, though his smooth cheeks were still innocent of beard. He, the other, was casually beckoning Sal forward, with his outstretched right arm, while under his left arm he was carrying a stringed musical instrument of some kind.

He, the newcomer, stood a full head taller than Jeremy, and the boy knew, with the certainty of dream knowledge, that this other was incomparably wiser and stronger than himself. The nameless stranger was dark-haired, his nude body muscular and very beautiful. Plainly he was in total command of the situation. His beckoning fingers suggested that he was masterfully controlling every detail of Sal's behavior.

And something utterly horrible was about to happen. . . .

. . . and Jeremy was jarred awake, his mind and body wrung by nightmare terror, a fear even beyond anything that the actual presence of the furies had induced in him.

He sprang to his feet and stood there for almost a full minute, trying to establish his grip on waking reality. When at last he had managed to do so, he collapsed and lay on the ground in the shade of the willows, feeling drained, his whole body limp and sweating in the hot day. Gradually his breathing returned to normal.

Overwhelmed by fantastic memories, he struggled to sort them out, to decide what had really happened and what he had only dreamed. No girl, no Sal or anyone else, had really come wading out of the river to him. And no dark youth stood on the bank now. He, Jeremy, was completely alone . . . or was he?

Suddenly confusion gripped him, and he thought in panic: What had happened to the treasure Sal had entrusted to him? Something of transcendent importance, having to do with some god . . . it had come loose from inside his shirt. . . . Only after some seconds of frantic groping and fumbling did he remember where it was now.

He sat on the grass with his head in his hands. How could he have forgotten *that,* even for a moment? But it was almost as if that strange invasion of his body had happened to someone else.

And Sal had kept saying she was unworthy. If so, what about Jeremy Redthorn? Yes. Of course. But that had been *before.* Now, things were different. Whatever sacrilege had been involved was now an accomplished fact. The worthiness of Jeremy Redthorn was no longer of any concern—because Jeremy Redthorn was no longer the same person.

———

Taking stock of himself, Jeremy noted additional changes. The lash marks were notably less painful than when he'd fallen asleep—how long ago? Surely less than an hour. There were still raised lumps, sore to the touch—but no worse than that. Otherwise he felt healthy, and there was no longer any trace of fever.

And there was yet another thing. . . . Somehow the experience of the last hour had left him with the impression that he was not alone.

But not even his improved vision or hearing could discover anyone else with him on the island.

He had the feeling that there was a Watcher, one who kept just out of sight while looking continually over Jeremy's shoulder. But who the Watcher was or why he or she was observing him so steadily the boy had no clue.

Also, the feeling was gradually growing on him that he had been used by some power outside himself. But he did not know exactly how or for what purpose.

Presently he stirred and got up and stripped and went into the water again, with a sudden awareness of being dirty and wanting to be clean. Meanwhile he noticed that his body had become a nest of various unpleasant smells. Probably it had been that way for a long time—and what in all the hells had made him think putting mud in his hair would be of any use in deceiving his pursuers? He did his best to soak it out. He couldn't remember exactly when he'd last had a real bath, but he badly needed one now and found himself wishing for hot water and soap. And maybe a good scrub brush. But he would have to make do with the cool river. He brought his garments into the water and did what he could to wash them, too.

Swimming a few lazy strokes upstream, then floating on his back and drifting down, he gradually regained a sense of reality. Here he was in his own body, where he belonged, as much in control of all its parts as he had ever been. His sight had been changed by Sal's thing of magic—changed for the *better*—and his hearing was a little different, too. And that, as far as he could tell, was all. Sal hadn't been killed or hurt by carrying the thing around with her. Other things, not this, had destroyed her.

And the dream he'd just experienced was only a dream. He'd had others not too different from it. Except for the part about strangling furies, of course. And then the utter terror at the end. . . .

Well . . . all right. This last dream had been like nothing else he'd ever experienced.

Around the boy floating in the water the drowsy afternoon was still and peaceful, the sun lowering, sunset not far away.

Looking through his left eye at the sun, he beheld a new and subtle fringe of glory. At first he squinted tentatively, but then it seemed to him that his new eye could bear the full burden of the world's light without being dazzled, without dulling a bit of its new keenness when he looked away. Not his right eye, though; that was no better than before.

Despite the exquisite terror with which the dream had ended, he didn't want to forget it and wasn't going to. The bit about killing furies had been good, but not the best. No, the best part—even though it, too, frightened him a little—had been when Sal was beckoning to him from the water and for one glorious moment he had known that everything was going to be all right, because she was not dead after all.

8

THE NIGHT THAT followed was one that Jeremy would remember for the rest of his life. Because on that night he first saw the stars.

All day he had been keenly aware of his improved eyesight. In fact, long minutes passed when he could hardly think of anything else, and so he later told himself that he ought to have anticipated the commonplace miracle. But he was still distracted by grief and heavily occupied most of the time with the problems of immediate survival. So it was that the first pure point of celestial light, appearing just as the sun was going down, took him completely by surprise. Until that moment, the contents of the sky had been the furthest thing from his thoughts.

And then, marvelously, the stars were there.

Somehow the boy was surprised by the fact that the revelation was so gradual. Very soon after that first startling, soul-piercing point at sunset, there came another twinkle, in a different part of the sky. And presently another. In a little while there were dozens, eventually hundreds. The onset of the multitudes, the thousands, which required hours to reach its full development, cost him time on his journey, holding him openmouthed and marveling for a long time when he might have been paddling.

On each succeeding night Jeremy hoped for a clear sky and looked forward with keen anticipation to the celestial show. More often than not he had his wish. Also, the events of one night began to blur into those of another, and so it went with the sleepy days as well, as a kind of routine established itself in his journey downstream. Sal's bequest had markedly improved his left eye's ability to distinguish shapes in darkness, which helped him avoid snags, sandbars, and islands. But now he often lost time by forgetting to paddle, in his sheer wonderment at the stars.

Each day at sunrise he beached his canoe in the most sheltered spot that he could find. He had begun his journey fully intending to count the days of its duration. But when three had passed, he began to wonder whether the true number might be four. From that time on, his uncertainty grew. But when he considered the situation carefully, he supposed it didn't matter much.

His daytime slumbers continued to be enlivened by dreams of the strange, newly vivid kind, sometimes erotic and sometimes not. In them the nameless, bearless, dark-haired youth frequently appeared, usually unclothed, but sometimes wrapped in a white robe secured by a golden clasp. Always he played a commanding role. Sometimes he casually strangled furies, beckoning to them, willing them to fly near him, so that they were compelled to come, like moths around a flame. Then, smiling, he would snatch them out of the air, one at a time, and wring their necks like so many helpless pigeons, while Jeremy, the silent witness, silently cheered the slaughter on.

Sometimes, in other dreams, the Nameless One effortlessly seduced young maidens. And not only girls but older women, too, females in all colors and sizes, some of races Jeremy had never seen before. Many of their bodies were lovelier than he had ever imagined the human form could be, and the shapeliest of them behaved in wanton and provocative ways, making the boy groan in his sleep.

And there were dreams in which the Dark Youth remained apart from human contact, his fingers plucking at his seven-stringed instrument—a device whose counterpart in waking life the dreamer's eyes had never seen—producing fast rhythms to which the women danced. These were followed by haunting melodies to which no one could dance that seemed to have nothing to do with the body at all but stayed with Jeremy long after he had awakened. In these episodes it seemed that the musician sang, but Jeremy could never hear his voice.

And in one memorable dream the Nameless One had put away the instrument of seven strings, along with all thoughts of music and of soft amusement. Now he looked a head taller than before, his beardless face hard as stone, his white cloak rippling with what might have been a savage wind. He was standing on a field of battle, wearing on his back a quiver filled with arrows, clutching in his powerful left hand an archer's bow that seemed to be made from—of all things—silver. As Jeremy watched, awestruck, his dream companion raised his bare right fist and swung it against a towering stone wall, while hundreds of human soldiers who had been sheltering behind the barrier took to their heels in panic. Some of the soldiers were too slow to run away, and their little human bodies were crushed by falling stones. The thunder of the toppling wall awoke the dreamer to a summer storm of lightning.

———

During Jeremy's waking nighttime hours, while he kept paddling steadily downriver under the entrancing stars (he had identified two constellations, enough to make him confident of which way was north), his thoughts continued to revolve around the question of how he was to carry out the sacred mission entrusted to him by Sal *(by Sal who had called him by the name of love!).* How was he ever to accomplish that now, when the magic thing that he was supposed to deliver had vanished into his own head?

One unwelcome possibility did cross his mind. Suppose that when he located one of the people for whom the magic thing was meant, that person would have to kill the unhappy messenger in order to retrieve the treasure?

Well, so be it, then. Jeremy's current mood was appropriately heroic and abandoned. He would do anything for Sal, who had set him free and given him the stars.

Contemplation brought him to one truth at least, which was that everyone he'd ever really cared about was dead. He had to fight against bleak intervals of despair. In an effort to distract himself from endless mourning, he set himself certain mental tasks. One challenge was to recall every word that he had ever heard about the city of Pangur Ban and the Academy, which lay somewhere nearby. It seemed hard to believe that he was really traveling to such places, and yet he had no choice. And trying to remember what he had heard about them was futile, because he had never heard more than a dozen words or so. He would just have to learn what he needed to know when he got there.

In his entire life the boy had heard people speak of the Academy not more than two or three times, and always as part of a catalog of the accomplishments of Lord Victor Lugard, who ruled at Pangur Ban. But those few sentences, spoken in awe and wonder, about matters that the speaker did not pretend to understand, had created in the boy's imagination a place where might be gathered all the wise folk of the world, and where an explanation for the mysteries of the world could be available.

———

Early one morning, two days after Sal's mysterious prize had vanished into his head, Jeremy was much mystified when he caught sight for the first time of a mysterious towering shape on the horizon. It was certainly miles away; how many miles he could not try to guess.

And somehow he knew just what it was. The answer came rising unbidden out of some newly acquired depth of memory.

Everyone had heard of the Mountain of the Cave. Halfway up its slopes, at a point perhaps a mile above sea level, the Cave of the Oracle opened a supposed entry to the Underworld and offered a shrine where rich and poor alike might hope to have their futures revealed to them, might truly be told which road to take to find success. The first time Jeremy's vision showed him that strange shape was near dawn, when he was just about to head in to shore for the day. The first sight of the strange high ridge, with its top shrouded in even stranger clouds, shook him, brought him up short paddling.

What in all the worlds? And yet he had no need to ask the question. The boy stared, letting the canoe drift. He squinted—this was fast becoming a habit with him—and tried closing first one eye, then the other.

The distant Mountain stood well off to the north and west, so that the river in its gentle windings, tending generally west and south, never carried him directly toward it. In fact, there were times when he was being borne in the exactly opposite direction.

When he experimentally closed his left eye, the Mountain's distant image disappeared entirely, swallowed up in sunglare and horizon haze and, of course, the chronic blur of his nearsightedness.

———

During the afternoons late summer storms sometimes produced hard rain. On these occasions, if the opportunity offered, Jeremy dragged his canoe entirely up onshore and overturned it, creating a shelter beneath which he contrived to get some sleep. Anyway, getting wet was no real problem as long as the weather remained warm.

Sometimes now, at night when he thought he was making good headway toward his invisible goal (though getting somewhat farther from the Mountain), keeping wide awake beneath the stars, Jeremy had a renewed impression that he was no longer traveling alone. His Watcher companion was with him now.

Sal had warned him that the Academy was hundreds of miles distant and that the journey downriver would take many days. She had started to coach him on the exact location of her goal, but they hadn't got far enough with that to do him any good now. He soon gave up trying to estimate how far he had come since leaving his uncle's village—and by now he had definitely lost count of the number of days in his downstream journey. He regretted not having started a tally of scratches on a gunwale with Sal's knife.

At about this time he noted that his canoe had begun to leak, though so far only slightly; so far he could manage, with a little bailing by hand two or three times a night. Being run aground every morning, sometimes on rough shores, wasn't doing the wooden bottom any good. He could of course try to steal another boat along the way, but the theft would leave a mark of his passage, and he had little doubt that those who had hounded Sal to her death were now after him.

———

Back at the Raisinmakers' village, in sight of the twin shrines of Dionysus and Priapus, extensive interrogation was in progress. Magicians in the employ of Lord Kalakh were active—and had already set up an image of their master, stern and ageless looking, with bulging eyes, by which they meant to keep themselves in tune with his will. This despite the fact that neither Lord Kalakh nor his chief lieutenants had much faith in magicians.

Gods, now, were a different matter altogether.

His Lordship had impressed upon this crew of raiders, before dispatching them, the fact that in recent months the goodwill of at least one faction of the gods had been shown to be essential to any human being who took the quest for power seriously. And since Hades had already shown himself victorious, it was with Hades that Lord Kalakh meant to ally himself.

Questioning, most of it rather stressful, had been proceeding steadily. The surviving inhabitants of Uncle Humbert's village had been counted, along with their dead, and the survivors questioned as to who had been in the village but could not now be accounted for.

The body of the woman who had been carrying the Face was readily identified—but of the treasure itself there was no sign.

As it happened, both of Jeremy's relatives had survived and made no difficulty about telling the questioners whatever they could about their unhappy nephew. It was a shame if the lad had managed to get himself in some deep trouble, so that powerful folk had to put themselves to the trouble of coming looking for him, but it was a hard world, and there was nothing to be done about it.

Another of the villagers thought that the lad named Jeremy had been one of those carried off by the harpies.

"There were no harpies here," the officer corrected sternly. "Nothing that flew here was big enough to carry anyone."

The villager had to admit the likelihood of error.

There was also the possibility that the boy Jeremy Redthorn had been drowned while trying to get away; there was no evidence one way or another on that. At least two boats were missing, but in the confusion accompanying the attack some might have simply drifted away.

The body bore old, half-healed fury whip marks as well as fresh ones. The villagers all stared in wonder at the dead servant of a defeated god, and none of them would admit to ever seeing her alive.

The body had already been stripped and all the clothing and possessions that might have been the woman's subjected to the closest scrutiny. The officer assigned to conduct the last stage of the search had no scruples about opening her head with knife and hatchet and probing gorily about inside the skull. In the normal course of events a Face would eject itself when its wearer died—but no possibility must be overlooked.

"And of course if she had been wearing the Face we want, instead of carrying it . . ." The speaker, a junior officer in Kalakh's Special Forces, let his comment die away.

His colleague was ready to complete it for him. "Unlikely she'd be lying there now. Or that anyone as small as we are would be opening her skull," he finished dryly.

From the last stage of the search the man who'd undertaken it looked up a moment later, his hands stained with fresh gore but empty. "No, sir, nothing."

"Damn all in Hades' name!" The junior officer looked around him, at ruin and ashes, soldiers and moping villagers, a planted field and a patch of forest. "Possibly this missing Redthorn does have it with him— or she may have hidden it somewhere nearby. We must search the entire area—kill no more of these people. It will be necessary to interrogate them all over again." He paused. "If this missing youth does have it— well, which way would you flee, Carlo, if you were trying to get away from here in a hurry? Downstream, of course."

Now the river was carrying Jeremy past larger villages, here and there a sizable town, amid an increasing traffic of sailboats and barges. Now, even with superb eyesight, he began to have trouble locating places to lay over during the day, spots along the shore where he might hope to pass the daylight hours entirely unobserved. Perhaps, he thought, at this distance from Uncle Humbert's village it no longer mattered if people noticed him. But the fury's lash marks were still sore—though a little less each day—and he still felt hunted.

It was hard to keep himself from looking again and again under the thwarts of the canoe, in hopes of finding another chunk of stale corn bread, on the possibility that another might have miraculously appeared. Now and then, drifting near dawn or sunset, while his stomach growled with hunger, the fugitive yearned to catch some fish, but he lacked the means of doing so. The little cache did contain flint and steel to make a fire, but in this season he had no need of extra warmth.

He had heard of some folk who claimed magic, the power to compel fish to come within reach of their grasping hands and submit like pet animals to being flipped out of the water. Others, who could do the trick as well, said that no magic was involved. Jeremy in his hunger tried to make the thing work for himself, gave it a try without really believing it would work—and sure enough, whether it was magic he still lacked or only skill and patience, it didn't.

One night, two hours before dawn, driven by hunger to take serious chances, he decided to raid the henhouse of an isolated farm whose buildings, atop a wooded bluff a little inland from the river, showed up plainly enough in silhouette against the stars.

Roots and berries were only maintaining him on the brink of starvation. If he ever hoped to dine on chicken, on fresh meat of any kind, he would probably never see a better opportunity than this.

Tying his boat up loosely, in readiness for a quick getaway, he stepped ashore and padded his barefoot way inland as quietly as possible. The complication he had feared most, an alert watchdog, soon came to pass; the animal gave a few preliminary growls when Jeremy was still some thirty yards away, even though the boy had taken the precaution of approaching from downwind.

Under his breath Jeremy muttered oaths and blasphemies against a variety of gods. At least the dog had not yet barked. Grim determination had grown in him; he was too hungry to give up. Anyway, he had known for a long time that the worst thing you could do when faced by a dangerous animal was turn around and run.

Drawing Sal's businesslike little knife and holding it ready for a desperate defense, Jeremy stuttered out some low-voiced nonsense, meant to be soothing. To his joy and surprise, the attempt was an immediate success. The mammoth dark shape of a long-haired dog came jostling right up to him, but with a reassuring tail wag and not growling, only whining as if to entreat a favor. A wet nose nuzzled his hand. Having sheathed his knife again, Jeremy spent a minute standing in a cold sweat of relief, scratching the grateful, panting beast behind its ears. Then he resumed his progress toward the henhouse. His new friend was content to follow a step or two behind. Obviously the dog was taking a benign interest in his affairs, with the air of a guide standing by to do a favor if requested.

Every few steps the starving two-legged marauder paused to glance toward the small darkened farmhouse. But everything there remained as quiet as before.

In the stable a dromedary snorted, a long groaning snuffle, and shuffled its feet inside its stall. But that was all.

Moving cautiously in deep shadow, with the dog still companionably at his side, Jeremy approached the henhouse, only to find it surrounded by a tall fence, obviously meant to keep intruders out as well as hold chickens in. The barrier consisted of thin vertical stakes bound together with a network of tough withes and cordvines, the spaces between the stakes too narrow to admit even the body of a chicken. There was a gate leading into the enclosure, but unhappily for the boy's purposes it was fastened at the top with a kind of lock, and on top of that was an oddly shaped device that appeared to be a kind of metal box.

And now Jeremy started nervously and almost began to run. With his left ear (but not with his right, he thoughtfully observed) he could hear the box making a ghostly clamor, which grew louder when he stood on tiptoe and stretched out a hand toward it.

Looking over his shoulder, the apprentice chicken thief beheld the house still dark and silent. The dog beside him was quite unperturbed. Gradually the boy allowed himself to believe that the noise existed nowhere but in his own left ear.

And with that belief came understanding: he had just received, through his mysterious silent partner, a timely warning—the contraption was precariously balanced, and he supposed it was designed to make a racket if it was disturbed. When he began to unwind the cord, it produced a loud rattling sound.

Reluctantly he gave up on the gate and moved away, but his hunger would not let him abandon all hopes of chicken dinner. Sliding along the fence, peering in through the thin palings from one new angle after another, the boy half-absently resumed the whispering that had already served him so well this night.

"C'mon, hens—one of you anyway—how 'bout a nice fat one? Or you could just send me out some eggs, if you don't . . ." His voice trailed away, as his jaw dropped.

A sleepy bird, white-feathered and as young and plump as any thief could wish, had hopped down off its roost somewhere in the dark interior and now came stalking out of the henhouse, directly toward him. In another moment the chicken was right beside the fence and fluttering high enough for Jeremy, who had forced a lean arm between the stakes, to grab it by the neck, turning fowl into food before it could utter a single squawk.

Even as he performed the act, he recalled in a vivid flash of memory a dream in which with this same right hand (yet not entirely the same) he had exerted about the same amount of effort and strangled a fury.

He could ponder dreams some other time, after hunger had been stayed. Right now he lifted the dead chicken, wings and feet still beating, near the top of the fence, to a position where he could reach over the top with his other hand and grab it.

On leaving the farmyard, with his dinner-to-be in hand, he found it necessary to quietly discourage the watchdog, who was whining and wanting to come with him. When Jeremy was a hundred yards away, he could hear the animal howling its regret at his departure.

At the moment he was too engrossed in his hunger to try to reason out what had just happened. Still, he took the time to move his boat downstream another quarter-mile or so, just in case the farmer, wondering what the hell was wrong with his dog, grew suspicious and came looking around.

Established at last in a modest riverside encampment, protected from onshore observation by the riparian thicket where he'd tied his boat, Jeremy busily plucked feathers and beheaded and gutted and cleaned the bird with Sal's sharp knife. By now the eastern sky had grown sufficiently light to let him see what he was doing.

Starvation had not yet reached the point where he would try to eat a chicken raw. But, in order to roast the fowl, he was going to have to make a fire.

And damn it all, this was naturally the time for his bad luck to take another turn. Try as he might, the flint and steel refused to work. Somehow everything must have got wet again. To make matters worse, all the tinder he could find was damp from a recent rain. Even on the bottom of such logs and fallen branches as he could find. It seemed he'd have to wait, his stomach growling, until some hours of sunlight had dried things out.

Fumbling and cursing, Jeremy at last gave up the futile attempt to strike a spark. Then he squinted as the first direct rays of sunlight came striking in over the water to hit him in the face.

Fire? You want fire? Plenty of it, right there in the sky ... if only it might be possible to borrow just a little of *that* ... if only he had a burning glass.

A moment later, when he looked down at the wood and tinder in front of him, he was startled. Suddenly his left eye had begun to show him a small, bright spot, like a sharp reflection of the sun, right on a piece of kindling. At last the boy cautiously reached out a hand and touched the spot. He could feel nothing there but the dull, unreflective wood ... except that the wood felt warm!

This called for investigation.

Jeremy soon discovered that when he sat with his face in direct sunlight and squinted down at an angle, focusing the gaze of his left eye on the tinder he had arranged, a spark of white light flared at the spot he'd picked. When he maintained the direction of his gaze for half a minute, the white light began to generate a small orange glow that he could see with both eyes. A wisp of whitish smoke arose.

And presently, having added some more of the dampish twigs and grass and wood, he had a real fire, one hot enough to dry more stuff for it to burn and big enough to roast his chicken, after he'd impaled it on a green stick. Carefully he kept turning the fowl around, and soon delicious smells arose. In his hunger, he began tearing off and eating pieces of meat before the whole bird was cooked.

───────

When he had satisfied his belly for the time being, Jeremy tried again to raise fire from the sun, just for the hell of it and got the same result. Nothing to it. Now the feat was even easier than before—maybe, he supposed, because the sun was getting higher in the sky and hotter.

Having thrown chicken bones, feathers, and offal into the river, he sat picking his teeth with a splinter and thinking about it while he watched the fire that he had made in wood die down. By all the gods! It just beat anything that he had ever seen. He had been given magic in his eye, all right.

For the first time in what seemed years, Jeremy began to consider new possibilities of fun.

Eventually he lay back and drifted into musing over what powers the mask piece might have given him that he hadn't even discovered yet.

Of course there were nagging questions, too. Why would a chicken and a dog be compelled to listen to him, to do what he wanted, when a fish in the river was not? But the questions were not enough to keep him from dozing off into a delicious sleep.

———

His journey went on, day by day. And still, by day and night, though not so frequently now as at the beginning of his flight, Jeremy anxiously looked upstream for pursuing boats and scanned the sky for furies. Eventually the idea at least crossed Jeremy's mind of someday trying to burn a fury out of the sky by concentrating sun glare fatally upon it. Only in dreams could he—or the Dark Youth—summon up strength enough to wring their necks, but it would give him great satisfaction, in waking life, to at least mark some of those great gray wings with smoking spots of pain, send them in screaming flight over the horizon. But as a practical matter he had to admit that the damned things would never hold still long enough for him to do that. Such fire raising as he could do now with his eye was a slow process.

On a couple of occasions he'd seen a burning-glass in operation, and this was much the same thing. But . . . his *eye*?

Of course, the eye endowed with such power didn't seem to be entirely *his,* Jeremy Redthorn's, any longer.

———

In succeeding days, the traveler managed to feed himself reasonably well. Partly he succeeded by helping himself to more fruit, both wild and cultivated. Strawberries were easy to find. Apples, peaches, and cherries came from orchards along the shore, melons from a vine-strewn field. Jeremy's left eye outlined for him, in subtle light, certain pathways, certain objects, indicating where the harvest would be profitable. Several times he dared prowl close enough to houses to dig up carrots and potatoes out of kitchen gardens. Coming upon some wild grapes, Jeremy tried them, too, and enjoyed them, though he'd thought he'd lost his taste for grapes of any kind long months ago. These had a sharply different flavor from the special doomed-to-be-raisins variety that Uncle grew and of which the boy had hauled so many loads.

But his special vision was of no help at all in gathering that which grew independent of cultivation. Something there to think about—but he didn't know what to think.

And in the nights that followed he repeated his feat of chicken stealing, several times, with growing confidence and consistent success. Minor variation brought him a goose on one night, a turkey on another. Soon starvation ceased to be a real fear, and so did watchdogs—he might have had a whole pack of them, eager to join him on his journey, had he wanted to encumber himself with such an escort.

Whenever he had sunlight or even when clouds were no worse than a light overcast, he could make a fire. He tried bright moonlight once and thought he might have succeeded had he had the patience to persist long enough.

━━━━━━

During late afternoons, while he lay ashore waiting for darkness to bring what he hoped would be safe travel time, Jeremy amused himself by borrowing the sun's last energies with his left eye, to burn his initials into the wooden side of his beached canoe. He hadn't really thought about the matter before, but of course there were several different ways to make each letter of the alphabet—there, for example—*JAY—TEE*— in cursive. And there were other styles of making letters . . . other languages, of course. . . .

How many of each category could he call to mind? Too many, he realized, feeling a faint chill at heart. Far more than Jeremy Redthorn, in half a dozen years of simple village schooling, had ever learned. There were some people, his new memory recalled, living about five hundred miles over *that* way, who made their letters in *this* style. Meanwhile a certain tribe dwelling a long, long way over in the opposite direction wrote down their words in entirely different characters. And meanwhile, way over *there,* at a truly enormous distance, on the far side of the great round world—

He sat back on the ground beside his boat and sighed.

Yes, of course the world was round. And amazingly large. He didn't know when or how he'd gained the knowledge, but so it was. Now he could see it in his new mind's eye as the planet Earth. Dimly he could evoke the shape of continents and oceans. Names of distant places, cities, countries, oceans, lakes, and rivers. Might his parents have told him such things, years ago, shown him a globe? He couldn't remember them doing anything like that.

But they might have, yes, of course. They might have taught him some of all this, but not all.

How much of all this had he really learned in the school in his home village?

He couldn't remember any teacher, or his parents, actually telling him any of these things.

On the other hand, he now had a firm awareness that globe models of the world definitely existed. Along with many, many elaborate maps. Even if there hadn't been anything like that in his old village school. The Academy had them, and so did a thousand other seats of knowledge, places of learning, scattered around the world.

Now, every time Jeremy turned his thoughts in a new direction, he discovered his memory freshly stocked with dozens, hundreds, perhaps thousands of facts, likely and unlikely. One discovery in this enormous warehouse tended to lead to another, until it seemed that a whole cascade, an avalanche, of facts and words and images was about to come pouring down on his head, burying him from sight. It sometimes frightened him to think of all the things he might now find, in his own mind, if he really tried. Things that had been newly stuffed into his head, without his knowing—

Stop it, he sternly warned himself.

And yet it was impossible to entirely stop the wondering, the inward search. The freshly loaded cargo of information was in place, as impossible to ignore as were the powers of sex, now that his body had grown into them. His mind was compelled to keep teasing and worrying at the edges of the vast, the unbelievable, oversupply of memories and knowledge.

Of course, all this had come to him as a result of Sal's great gift.

But what good was it all going to be to him?

How, for example, could Jeremy Redthorn, who'd spent the entirety of his short life in a couple of tiny and obscure villages, possibly have any idea of the teaching tools with which the Academy was equipped? Yet so it was. And if Jeremy tried, he could call up a rather hazy image of the place, many white stone buildings with red tile roofs. He could even see, as if in old and hazy memory, some of the people there and how they went about their business.

Jumping to his feet, he paced back and forth on the small strip of sheltered island beach he'd chosen for his current resting place. Around him, the world was bigger than he'd ever imagined it might be—and he could sure as hell see more of it.

Maybe he should think about girls for a while and pass the time that way. It was damn sure time to think about *something* besides the thing, the god mask or whatever it was, that had poured itself like liquid into his head.

He was afraid that his new memory could tell him exactly who that Face belonged to and what its presence was going to do to its human host—but he feared the answers too much to dare to frame the questions.

9

AT LAST JEREMY'S chronic fear of pursuit assumed objective form. Once during the early morning and once again during the following night, the fleeing boy in his small boat was overtaken by flotillas of war canoes loaded with armed men.

Even in darkness, his left eye could see them clearly enough for him to distinguish what they were and whose insignia they bore—one force carried the blue flower on a white ground of Lord Kalakh, whose troops had taken part in several massacres. The second was less fearsome, the Republic of Morelles, displaying burgundy and yellow. In each case their multiple wakes gently rocked his small craft as they passed.

Jeremy's left eye saw the warboats and their occupants differently than his right. The colors of boats and people varied slightly, in subtle ways that the boy supposed must have some significance, though he was unable to interpret the variations. The craft belonging to Kalakh, though painted white and blue, glowed in small spots with a bright but phantasmal red that he took as a serious warning.

Jeremy understood, without really thinking about it, that what he was seeing was only part of the ongoing maneuvering for power among rival warlords. Basically it was part of the same struggle that had killed his parents half a year ago. Aided by his marvelous new eyesight, he was able to steer well clear of these bodies of marine infantry. They in turn paid him no attention as they hurried on their way. Each time this happened he stopped paddling and frankly stared—what else would a lone figure in a boat be likely to do?—and each time he was ignored.

On a third occasion he was overtaken after dawn, still looking for his day's resting place. He panicked in the belief that the squadron of boats coming downstream at great speed, either Lord Kalakh's or those of some unknown power, were, in fact, pursuing him. For several minutes he paddled frantically in a mad effort to stay ahead—but when he despaired of outspeeding all those husky rowers and set his course for shore, they simply ignored him and continued straight down the river. Watching them speed by, while his heart and lungs gradually resumed their normal action, he allowed himself to believe for the first time that there might be no one actively pursuing him, tracking him downstream from Uncle Humbert's village.

If it was true that no one was actively hunting him, then maybe he had overestimated the importance of Sal's mysterious gift—and of himself as its custodian and her messenger. Was it possible that the raid he had just survived had been launched for some purpose unconnected with Sal and her treasure? Or for no purpose at all except as an exercise in savagery? But Jeremy had trouble believing that. The men riding into the village had been intent and purposeful, though the creatures they commanded had blundered; and Sal, though terrified to see them, had not been really surprised.

So far Sal's treasure had escaped the hands of those marauders. Not that Jeremy felt he could take any credit. Only sheer good luck, it seemed to him, had thrown them off his track. No one could rely on good luck, but it seemed that he had nothing better.

Over the next couple of days he also saw cavalry patrols, lancers mounted on long-necked cameloids, one-hump mutated droms, their insignia obscured with camouflage, plodding their way along the shore. But the men were looking for something or someone else. Jeremy took care to keep out near midriver, but the man onshore showed no interest in him or his boat.

Except for these occasional glimpses of bodies of armed men, Jeremy encountered very little traffic on the river. He supposed that with war flaring in the region, people who had any choice about the matter had fled to safer places or were staying home. It was also possible that many boats had been commandeered by one faction or another.

As Jeremy steadily paddled south and west, the country visible along the riverbanks changed, becoming different in striking ways from anything he could remember ever seeing before. Vegetation was somewhat thicker, and the air seemed wetter, intensifying the late summer's heat. The river was broader and deeper, having merged with others— whether the stream he now traveled should still be called the Aeron was more than Jeremy could say. Wild birds he could not recognize flew crying overhead.

The information Sal had failed to give him was now available in his new memory. Still, Jeremy did not know just where he was in relation to Pangur Ban and could only guess how far he might still have to go to reach the city or the Academy. Regarding the Academy his new memory gave him relatively little help.

Once or twice when passing one of the rare fishing boats he thought of hailing them and asking how far the sea might be. But he didn't do so, not wanting the local people to remember a young stranger on a long journey.

Every night, a little after sunset, Jeremy pushed off from his day's place of concealment and resumed his cruise downstream.

And eventually there came a night when he beheld a strange sight, low in the sky ahead of him. All night long there arose in the distance, reflected against clouds, a faint, odd, attractive glow that was visible only through his left eye. On the next night it was back again, a little brighter and a few miles nearer. The source, whatever it might be, was vastly closer and lower than the Mountain.

The river was changing around him, first day by day, then hour by hour. Gradually, at first, then suddenly in an explosion of channels and multiplication of islands. The stream spread out to an indeterminate width and began to lose itself, dividing into a hundred lesser flows.

Long days ago he'd lost the count of days and nights, but the feeling was growing in him that the goal of his journey must be near. Wanting to keep a sharp lookout for the Academy or anything that might give him a clue to its location, Jeremy decided now to travel by daylight.

On the first afternoon of progress under this new regime he noted that the mysterious glow was now bright enough to be seen by day. Pallidly visible only through his left eye, it appeared low in the northwest sky, ahead of him and to his right.

By midafternoon he had drawn much closer. The source itself was still out of sight behind several ranks of island trees. This mild light, now rippling in a way that seemed to beckon, was the very opposite of the red warning signals with which his left eye had tagged the Kalakh canoes.

Jeremy paddled toward it. Now listening carefully, he could barely detect, with both ears, the distant sound of a woman's voice. It was far too faint to let him make out words, but she seemed to be shouting, ranting about something.

Accepting the glow as guidance provided by some friendly god, Jeremy was soon paddling down a smaller channel. Presently this led

him into a backwater bayou, a serpentine of water almost motionless—
and this again, at its farther end, into a more active channel. All the
land above water was thickly overgrown with trees and dense underbrush.

He thought the source of the strange illumination was now little
more than a hundred yards ahead. The brightness was slowly fading as
he drew near, as if its only reason for existence had been to capture his
attention.

When he had put a dozen or so of the taller intervening trees behind
him, there came into his view the upper portion of a strange half-ruined
building, towering above the screen of jungle that still intervened.

Jeremy had not gone much farther in its direction when he heard
the woman's voice again, carrying strongly across an expanse of open
water. It was shrill but strong, raised in fierce argument—but no, he
presently decided, not really argument, because no one ever answered.
Rather, she was engaged in a strident, prolonged, abusive harangue. He
could not make out all the words, but he got the impression that several
people were objects of her wrath. It would be an unlucky individual
indeed who caught it all.

In the boy's left ear her voice sounded with a mellow ring, distinguishing it from the fishwife screeching he'd sometimes heard from
villages or other boats as he passed them. He took this to mean that
there was something good about it—good for him at least.

Now he was no more than about fifty yards away from the bellicose
woman. Paddling slowly and cautiously, keeping a sharp eye on the
scene before him as it was gradually revealed by the curving channel,
the boy deftly pulled his canoe behind a screen of reeds close to the
marshy shoreline and looked out through them to get a good view of
the huge, looming structure, whatever it might be. Docked immediately
in front of it was a kind of boat or raft that Jeremy Redthorn's eyes had
never seen before—and yet it was disturbingly familiar. The glow that
had guided him thus far was emanating from this vessel—and now that
he had come in direct sight of it, that strange illumination faded, evidently having served its purpose.

At the edge of the channel rose half-ruined stone walls perhaps forty
feet high and of formidable thickness, the remains of a building whose
size and shape were totally unlike those of any structure familiar to
Jeremy Redthorn. Even in its fallen state the massive structure was by
far the largest that he had ever seen. It rose out of the swamp in the
form of an irregularly truncated pyramid, built of blocks of stone, most
of them much bigger than a man might lift. Here and there vegetation
was growing out of the structure, where time had eaten cracks and holes

into its fabric—some of the plants were only moss and vines, but in several spots sizable trees put forth their twisted branches. Windows in the shape of pointed arches framed various degrees of interior darkness, and here and there a doorway was visible, reached by the remnants of an exterior stair.

Looking at the ruin, Jeremy felt an inward jar, an unexpected sense of familiarity. Somewhere in the seemingly bottomless pool of his new memories he thought there lurked knowledge of the purpose of this building and even a good approximation of what it must have looked like when it was new. But those memories conveyed no sense of urgency, and calling them up could wait.

A good part of what had once been an extensive stone dock in front of the odd building seemed to have crumbled away. The unfamiliar boat tied up at the narrow portion that remained was much larger and rode much higher in the water than Jeremy's tiny craft. The single mast rising from the deck between its joined twin hulls bore a flag, marked with the stylized symbol of a burning torch. Jeremy recognized it at once as the Academy logo.

He had only a moment in which to wonder *how* he had been able to make the identification—conceivably Sal had mentioned it to him. But he had to admit to himself that the memory was more likely a part of the frighteningly great trove that had come into his head along with her mysterious treasure.

As soon as Jeremy focused his attention on the boat before him, his new memory served up the type's proper name—he was looking at a catamaran. This example consisted of twin narrow hulls of shallow draft, some thirty feet in length, surmounted by a flat platform, somewhat narrow in relation to the length of the boat. On the platform, just a little aft of amidships, stood a square-built house or shelter. Just aft of this deckhouse, an awning covered a kind of galley, which would no doubt be centered on a box of sand in which to keep a fire. Each of the twin hulls was enclosed, providing considerable sheltered space belowdecks.

The name, painted on the near side of the nearest hull (and he presumed it would be also on the far side of the other), was *Argos*. The word conveyed rich meanings—or Jeremy could tell that it would have done, had he allowed himself to probe for them in his new memory.

In a vessel of this type, the crew, none of whom were now in evidence, probably slept on deck, under another awning, which was now half-fallen, adding to the general picture of disarray. The craft could be propelled by oars or by a fore-and-aft spritsail—Jeremy could now vaguely recognize the type, and a moment's thought brought up more terminology, as well as understanding. Neither sail nor oars were ready to be used just now, being both in disarray.

When the boy directed his penetrating left-eye gaze at the vessel, he was also able to recognize certain kinds of lamps and various nautical tools and pieces of equipment, things that Jeremy Redthorn had never laid eyes on before.

But he had little time to spare just now for such details. His gaze was immediately drawn to the slender figure of a woman, white-haired but lithe and energetic, who was pacing back and forth with desperate energy on the nearby dock. Behind her, the walls of irregular stonework went up, sloped back, then again straight up, and angling back again, toward a broken pinnacle of structure more than four stories above the greasy-looking surface of the sluggish channel that curved around the building so as to front it on two sides.

Above the woman, partly over the boat and partly over the platform where she was standing, hung the single sail, half-furled, awkward and useless. Happily for sail and boat, there was practically no wind at the moment. She was waving her arms and calling at random, in distress, though more in anger than in panic. Her manner was that of a woman who fully expected someone to hear her and pay attention but was unsure of just who her audience might be or where they were.

From a distance the white hair hanging almost to her shoulders seemed to be tightly curled. Her face had a pinkish cast, suggesting sunburn. Her feet wore sandals; her slender body was clad in neat trousers and tunic, suggesting a kind of uniform, in which the color white predominated.

In one hand the woman occasionally brandished a short sword, which she waved about as if trying to threaten someone with it. But the object of her wrath was nowhere to be seen, and she seemed to have no clear idea as to the direction in which it, or he, or they might be found. At intervals she again replaced the weapon in a sheath that hung from a broad leather belt and put both hands to other use.

Supine beside her, on the stone quay along the broken, magic-glowing temple (and the oddness of the building kept demanding Jeremy's attention: who would have constructed such a thing in the middle of a vast swamp?) decorated with the headless statues of peculiar monsters, lay the figure of a dark-haired, dark-skinned man, nude except for a skimpy loincloth and so motionless that Jeremy at first believed him dead. Then he saw the man's head turn slowly from side to side; life had not fled. Experience that was not Jeremy Redthorn's, though now it had come to dwell in him, interpreted the quivering of the fellow's arms and legs as the final tremors of some kind of fit, not dangerous to life. He lay surrounded by an incomplete layout of magical stuff, debris suggesting that the fellow had been struck down in the very midst of his calculations or incantations, while trying to prepare himself for the visitation of a god.

Suddenly Jeremy took note of the fact that the *Argos* was not tied up properly at the quay. The nearest stone bollard to which it might have been secured was crumbling as part of the pyramid's general decay. Only the feebleness of the current just there kept the vessel from drifting slowly away.

A slight breeze was now stirring the leaves of the swampy forest whose nearest branches actually overhung the catamaran, and the half-furled sail flapped ineffectively. The watching boy wondered if the *Argos* was supposed to be driven or guided by some sort of magic. If so, the magic did not appear to be working. There were always stories about magic that did work or that had worked in Grandfather's youth, but Jeremy Redthorn in his own short life had never seen any—at least not until the past few days.

Ever since Sal's treasure had gone flowing like some enchanted liquor into Jeremy's head, he had been struggling more or less continuously with a kind of mental vertigo, a condition having nothing to do with physical dizziness or balance—or with traditional ideas of magic. It was as if his mind now stood upon a narrow and slippery beam, teetering over an absolute ocean of new memory, a sea of experience and knowledge to which he had no right. Fear whispered to him that if he ever fell, plunged wholly into those depths, he might very well be drowned, his very self dissolved to nothingness in an alien sea.

Trying hard now to distract himself from such horrors, he concentrated his attention on the *Argos*, which had been built with a marvelous precision. All visible surfaces were painted or varnished. The lines and the white sail looked new, not stained or rotted. The whole equipage was very well cared for, or had been at least until very recently—but now Jeremy thought that an air of futility had descended on the whole enterprise, magical and mundane.

It was not only the sail that seemed to have been suddenly abandoned. Several oars were also lying around on deck, as if the crew had simply let them fall before abandoning ship. At least one oar had gone overboard and was slowly drifting away. There were a few spare weapons also, a short spear in one place, a bow and quiver of arrows in another.

Jeremy was getting the impression that it was the absent crew who were the targets of the lady's wrath. She was carrying on as if they might be hiding somewhere nearby, in range of her voice, though actually that seemed unlikely. One of the angry woman's problems, and probably not the smallest one, was that the whole damned boat now seemed to be drifting helplessly.

Well, that problem, at least, might be one that Jeremy could do something about.

Somewhere in Jeremy's head, but by some intelligence not part of the mind with which he had been born, an estimate was being made: To judge by the fittings of the catamaran, and the number of spare oars currently available, there probably ought to be six or eight people in her normal crew. The present situation could be explained by assuming that they had all jumped ship and run off. Maybe they had been frightened by the illness of the dark-skinned man—or perhaps the explanation lay elsewhere.

Again the woman's thin, high voice was raised in imprecations, which seemed to be directed at no one she could actually see. At this distance her words carried clearly across the water, to be easily heard by Jeremy's ears, both right and left. Her language was the common one of Jeremy Redthorn's homeland, her accents quite understandable to someone from the villages. He listened with awe and a kind of admiration. She had thought up some truly venomous and special curses to bestow upon the people—Jeremy was now virtually certain that she meant the deserting crew—who had left her in this predicament. Now and then she paused for breath, gazing into the distance as if she hoped to catch sight of the objects of her wrath, who had to be somewhere out there.

These two people were obviously individuals of some importance, and their flag said they were connected with the Academy. Helping them ought to give Jeremy the very opening he needed toward the fulfillment of his vow to Sal.

The boy in his canoe, continuing to observe the couple from behind his screen of reeds, raised a hand to scratch his itchy scalp and was glad that he had decided long days ago to wash off the dried mud.

Springing into action, he paddled his canoe briskly to the woman's assistance, adroitly detouring a few yards to pick up the drifting oar before the listless current got around to bearing it away. Then, after securing his own small vessel to the catamaran, he climbed aboard and seized the line with which the woman was already struggling.

The woman quickly became aware of his approach but did not appear surprised by it; she stood nodding in Jeremy's direction, with her small fists planted on her hips, as if she wondered what had taken him so long. *It's about time*, her attitude seemed to say. About time the world woke up to its duty and came to her assistance. Her clothing, while of practical design for an active person in hot weather, proclaimed her as wealthy, and a fine gold collar around her neck confirmed this.

Quickly she sized up Jeremy—he realized that he must present an odd-looking figure—but she made no comment. She spoke to him imperiously.

"Thank all the gods." She made a brisk summoning gesture. "Come aboard quick; give me a hand here."

"Yes'm."

As he drew close, he saw that at a distance her whitish hair had deceived even his new keen eyesight. At close range he could see that the face beneath it, despite its stern expression, was very young. She was probably no older than Jeremy himself. Eyes even greener than his own and sharp elfin features. Several of the girl's small fingers bore valuable rings.

She had now ceased, for the moment, her scolding and cursing of the absent boatmen. Obviously her chief concern, as she ran about with the incongruous sheathed sword banging against her slender legs, was the man's welfare.

And again, as soon as the drifting had been checked: "Never mind that! Help me here, with him!"

Jeremy wondered if the girl could be a priestess of some god or assortment of gods. His new memory could not confirm this but neither did it find evidence that the idea was impossible.

After some difficulty the two of them got the craft turned in solidly against the stone dock. Then Jeremy, springing ashore, secured it firmly, with another line, to some stonework that seemed likely to endure for a while.

Now that she had an active helper, the young woman announced her determination to cast off as soon as the unconscious man and a few essentials had been carried aboard. She was ready to abandon certain other items; when Jeremy volunteered to go back for them, she refused his offer.

On the inner side of the dock, one or two dark doorways led directly into the broken pyramid. It was too dim in there for Jeremy to even guess at what the building might contain.

As they were making their slow progress away from the ruined dock, she looked back now and then, in the manner of someone who feared pursuit. Jeremy was quite used to that manner now, having observed it in himself for many days.

But there was one item, a small box of ivory and ebony, that she made very sure to have on board. Jeremy caught only a brief glimpse of it and did not see where the young woman put it away.

When he got the chance to take a close look at the unconscious man, Jeremy could detect no obvious injuries. Dark-mustached, thin-faced, naturally well muscled but somehow ascetic-looking, about thirty years of age. His nearly naked body was marked in several places with painted symbols, so extensively that the natural color of his skin was hard to make out. The designs showed, among other things, his Academic standing. Jeremy could read them now.

His hands were soft, those of an aristocrat.

"What happened to him, ma'am?" the boy inquired cautiously. No blood, bruises, or swellings were visible on the unconscious body, which was breathing regularly.

"Never mind. He has been taken ill. But it will pass. Be careful with him! Don't worry; it's not catching."

But after Jeremy and the girl between them had somehow got the immediate emergency under control, she tersely informed the boy that the man had been rapt in some kind of meditation when the fit came over him.

"Did you say 'the fit,' ma'am?"

She wasn't going to waste a lot of time explaining things to a river rat. "Help me move him. We've got to get him down out of the sun. Into the cabin."

"Yes, ma'am." And once more Jeremy sprang to obey.

It was a difficult job. The man was a deadweight, his lean body muscular and heavier than it looked, and his unscarred, well-nourished frame was difficult to maneuver. The belt of his scanty loincloth offered about the only handhold.

The lady—if she deserved that status—unbuckled her sword belt and with a muttered curse threw it aside to clatter on the deck.

Soon the man's inert frame had somehow been shifted to a safer, more secure position, in one of the two narrow built-in bunks inside the cabin. One bunk was on each side, and both were made up with neat pillows, and smooth, clean sheets the like of which Jeremy had rarely seen before. There was even mosquito netting.

Taking a brief look around inside the small cabin, the boy caught a glimpse of men's and women's clothing and other items to be expected in a place where people lived. Most startling was the sight of what seemed to him a hundred books—more scrolls and volumes than Jeremy Redthorn had seen in total, before today. The majority of these were stacked on a worktable, broad as the whole deckhouse, whose remaining surface was littered with more papers and parchments, weighted down by the instruments of natural philosophy. Dried bones in a round cup, used for casting lots. A kind of magnifying glass. Tools for dissecting biological specimens? With at one side a dead lizard cut open and fastened down on a board by pins. It looked like some nasty child's experiments in torture, but new memory—when Jeremy dared risk a quick look into its depths—offered reassurance. *No, this is a matter of what those who are highly placed at the Academy call odylic philosophy. You look at their entrails and seek omens therein. It is largely a waste of time.*

And he was being given little time or opportunity to gawk. They were outside again, where the young woman directed Jeremy to their next task. Working together, pushing with poles against the shallow bottom, they were eventually able to get the craft moving downstream, like an animal that had to be prodded into recognizing its master's purpose.

A shadow, not easily distinguishable from that of a large tree's limb, moved on deck. Looking up, Jeremy saw that a giant snake, scales faintly iridescent in the sun, clinging to an overhanging branch was beginning to take an interest in the boat and its contents. While Jeremy poled, the woman stood by with drawn sword, fiercely ready to try to hack the thing's head off. Its open mouth looked a foot wide, lined with lovely red and equipped with a full armory of backward-slanting teeth.

A moment later, the heavy body thudded down on deck, and she struck it and eventually drove it writhing into the water, meanwhile screaming orders at Jeremy to keep on poling. If he didn't, the mast was going to catch on more branches and they'd be hopelessly enmeshed. He understood the situation quite well; her screaming didn't help any, but he put up with it in silence.

Snake blood spattered as the huge body, thick as Jeremy's waist, contorted and the lashing tail sent small objects flying, philosophers' tools and sailors' also. But head and neck remained stubbornly connected.

When he'd got the boat safely out away from the trees he came to help. At last a combined effort sent the monster overboard with a great splash. But Jeremy's flesh crawled when he saw how other low branches, ones they'd narrowly avoided, were bowed with the weight of more gigantic snakes.

———

While Jeremy dug the lower end of a pole into the bottom of the channel and strained his wiry weight against the upper end, doing his best to steer, keeping the catamaran from running afoul again on reeds and stumps, the girl went back into the deckhouse to check on the condition of the man. Jeremy could hear her voice, low, asking something, and then a man's voice, sounding dull and sleepy, answering.

Jeremy's feet had been slipping in snaky blood, and he grabbed up a bucket and used a minute to dip water from the river and sluice down the deck.

In a minute the girl was out again, leaning on the rail. She had now unbelted her sword, as if wanting to be rid of the weight as soon as there were no more snakes. She did not look at Jeremy, and she spoke abstractedly, as if to the world in general: "He began to talk—he kept crying out, 'The god is coming near, the god—' And then he went off, like this. . . ." She turned her head toward Jeremy, looking straight through him, letting her voice trail off.

"Has he had fits like this before?" Jeremy as a child—and this, he felt confident, was certainly his own memory—had had a playmate subject to falling and convulsing fits. Jeremy didn't know why the question was important now, but he knew a curiosity that wanted to be satisfied. Perhaps it was not entirely his own.

Now the young woman's gaze did at last focus on the boy, as if she had not really seen him until this moment. She seemed to be preparing a sharp retort, only to reconsider it. "Not as bad as this one," she answered at last.

———

And, in fact, the man did not truly regain consciousness, and a little later Jeremy entered the deckhouse and put his hand on the man's forehead. The victim sighed, making a sound like one relieved of worry. But he remained unconscious.

Earlier the girl had stuffed a small roll of cloth into the man's mouth, to keep him from biting his tongue. Now she tentatively eased out the barrier, checking to make sure the fit was over.

———

A breeze had come up, feeling welcome on Jeremy's sweaty skin. It would have been even more welcome if they had known what to do with the sail, but new memory gave him no help on that. Out on deck, pieces of the torn-up parchment were blowing about. Jeremy snatched one up. The writing on it was in a language never seen before by Jeremy Redthorn, but now he could read it readily enough—at least with his left eye—the gods alone knew how. A mere glance, evoking ancient memories, told him that it was part of a set of instructions for conducting a ritual, intended to call up demons. The symbolic destruction of that ritual was part of a greater one for—not summoning—inviting, or beseeching, the attendance of a god.

And Jeremy also knew, with a certainty that came welling up from his new sea of memory, that neither form of conjuration, as they were written here, had any chance of being effective. The how and why of such matters would take deep plunging in the sea to learn.

The young woman, gathering up stray scrolls and the other things her man had been using, was putting them away, stuffing them into some kind of chest.

Also, she had evidently hidden her special little ebony and ivory box somewhere. The box had disappeared when Jeremy looked inside the deckhouse—she must have shoved it under one of the bunks, he thought, or maybe back in one of the far corners. There would be no shortage of hiding places amid the clutter.

Then it seemed that she gave up, as if admitting to herself that these other things were not worth the effort.

With a kind of automatic movement, she snatched from Jeremy's hands the scroll he had been looking at. Taking full notice of him for the second time, she pronounced judgment: "You are a bizarre-looking child indeed. Where do you come from?"

It had been years since anyone had called Jeremy a child, and he didn't know what to think of the description now, particularly when it came from someone not much older than himself. He gestured vaguely with his free hand. "Upstream, ma'am."

For the moment that was enough to satisfy her curiosity. She gazed at him a second longer, then nodded and went on with what she had been doing.

The channel they had entered was turning shallow again, and more hard work ensued. This round lasted for several minutes, with girl and boy both leaning hard on poles one minute, paddling furiously the next. Jeremy soon found himself giving orders—he had some childhood experience with boats, which had been considerably sharpened and deepened during the past few days. This made him a more logical candidate for captain, or at least for temporary pilot, than the girl. Fortunately, she accepted his assumption of command without comment and without apparent resentment. Soon they were running free and clear again, back in one of the river's more vigorously flowing channels. Still the open way was narrow, with overhanging branches.

Every minute or so the young woman turned her head, looking back along the way that they had come, as if in fear that someone or something could be following them. Her behavior added to Jeremy's own chronic nervousness.

"We must get out of this misbegotten swamp," she said aloud. "We must find an open channel and move downstream." She added another phrase that the Intruder easily interpreted as an exotic obscenity, couched in a language native to many who lived halfway around the world.

It had sounded like she was speaking to herself, but Jeremy decided to answer anyway. "Yes, ma'am. River's flowin' freer now. Not so many islands 'n' snags 'n' things. There'll be a way."

10

WHEN THE TWO young people, working together, had got the big boat moving more or less steadily downstream (though only at drifting speed and slowly spinning as it moved), the pale-haired young woman took her longest look yet at Jeremy. Then she demanded of him: "What is your name?"

"Jonathan, ma'am." He grunted as he spoke, meanwhile using his pole again to fend off a waiting snag. He'd had the new name ready, having been expecting the question for some time now. The stubborn conviction would not leave him that Sal's killers were still in pursuit of the treasure she'd been carrying and would cheerfully rip it out of his head first chance they got. If they'd lost his trail, they might well be questioning their way methodically downstream, going from one farm, village, or town to the next.

Briskly the girl nodded her head of white curls. Her thin eyebrows were almost the same color. At that moment the boy belatedly noticed that her earlobes had both been neatly punctured and on each side of her head a small metal ring, as golden as her collar, hung from one of the tiny long-healed holes. Obviously the mutilation had been deliberate and the ornaments were meant to call attention to it. Jeremy had never seen the like before, and it struck him with a shock: *Why would anyone . . . ?*

His encyclopedic new internal source of information could not precisely explain why, but it assured him that out in the great world such practices in the name of fashion were far from unknown.

"Jonathan, then." The girl nodded again with satisfaction; evidently one name was plenty for him. "You may call me the Lady Carlotta. The gentleman I serve"—she gestured toward the deckhouse with an ele-

gantly wiry wrist—"is Scholar Arnobius. You will address him as
'Scholar' or 'Doctor.' Due to a chain of unlikely, unforeseeable circumstances, the Scholar and I find ourselves here in the middle of this dismal
swamp, which one might think would be forsaken by all the gods. . . .
Some might say that he was mad, to imagine that the god *he* was trying
to talk to would show up. . . ."

Some idea had brought her to a stop, and once more she glanced
back upstream. Then her pale brows again contracted, her small fists
clenched. Her voice almost died away, then rose to a girlish crescendo:
*"And we have been abandoned by those scoundrel-bastards of row-
ers. . . ."* A pause for breath, giving the rage that had flared up again a
chance to die down.

The young woman's voice when she resumed was well controlled,
almost calm again. "We came here, the two of us, to this remote and
abandoned swampland on a noble quest. My . . . my master sought
knowledge of one particular deity, and I . . . was doing what I could to
help him. We . . ." Considering her audience, she fell silent for a moment. Then she began to speak again, slowly and distinctly. "We come
from a place—how shall I put it?—an organization . . . called the Academy. There—"

"Yes'm, I know that."

Lady Carlotta had already begun the next step in her simplified
explanation, but now she paused in midword, derailed by surprise. "You
have heard of the Academy."

"Yes'm."

Taking another long look at his mud-smeared figure, ragged and
barefoot, she evidently found that claim astounding. "But Jonathan—
how did you know . . . ? You mean to say you had actual knowledge of
the fact that we, the Scholar and I . . . ?"

"No ma'am." The boy nodded toward the mast. "But I saw your
Academy logo. On the flag."

"Oh. But . . ." Still at a loss, she frowned again. "And how did you
happen to recognize that? It's fairly new, and no one else we've encountered on this river has had the least idea about . . ." She made a
gesture of futility.

"I've seen it before," Jeremy answered vaguely. Even as he said the
words, he knew that they were not strictly true—the eyes of Jeremy
Redthorn had never rested on the Academy's flag before this hour. And
at the same moment he felt the little chill that over the past few days
had grown terribly familiar.

Soon it was necessary again to pole the boat free of a grasping patch of bottom and then to avoid another overhanging snake, dangerously low. With the boat clear for the time being of snags and mud banks, and making some encouraging progress downstream, the man in the bunk in the deckhouse began to come around. But it took many minutes for his mind to clear entirely; and even when it did, his body remained weak for some time longer.

Jeremy's new memory offered no quick and easy answers concerning the art and difficulties of sailing a boat—and he was not going to plunge in looking for them. Still he made shift to get the sail more or less tied up snugly to its proper supports. Carlotta assisted him, by pulling on lines at his polite request. Now there was less cause for concern that a sudden wind might do them damage.

By the time he had accomplished that, night was coming on, and the only reasonable course seemed to be to choose a suitable small island and tie up—taking care not to be under any overhanging branches.

Carlotta, evidently made nervous by the approaching night, had buckled on her sword again and was peering warily into the dusk. Somehow she had found time and opportunity to change her clothes. "Do you suppose it's safe to light a candle, Jonathan?"

Sticking his head out into the night, he looked and listened and was reassured that his left eye showed him nothing special. He heard no other boats, no splash of oar or paddle. The only flying shape he could make out against the darkening sky was that of a normal owl. Again he thought how wonderful it was to be able to really *see*, at last!

"I don't think snakes or anything is going to be drawn to the light, ma'am."

The girl hesitated. There was a moment in which Jeremy thought that she looked about twelve years old. "What about . . . people?"

"I still think we're all right having a light here, ma'am. Just to be safe, we can keep it indoors and the windows shaded."

"We can do that."

He'd already discovered food supplies aboard and behind the cabin a sandbox serving as a kind of hearth. There seemed no reason not to have a fire and do some cooking. Jeremy was sent to get an ember from the earth-filled fireplace. They were a fine pair of aromatic candles that the girl lit, giving steady, mellow light.

When light bloomed in the little cabin, the man suddenly raised himself on one elbow and looked around. He seemed to be trying to peer, with tremulous hope, out through the little window of the deckhouse, on which his companion had just closed the little curtain shade.

"Where is he?" he whispered.

"Who, my lord?" the Lady Carlotta asked.

"He was here," the dry lips murmured weakly. "Before it got dark. I saw him. . . ." Weakly the speaker let himself slump back.

"What did he look like?" the girl asked, as if the question might have some relevance. "Just standing on the ground, or was he—?" She concluded with a gesture vaguely suggesting flight.

"Standing still. Right in front of me."

"Maybe what you saw, my lord, was nothing but too much sun." The girl was tenderly bathing his forehead.

"But I tell you I did see him. . . . It was only for a moment. . . ."

"I warned you about getting too much sun." For the moment she sounded motherly; then she paused and sighed. "Yes, my lord, tell me about it." Her tone suggested that she knew that she would have to hear the story, sooner or later, but did not look forward to the experience.

The man on the bed was marshaling his thoughts, so his answer was a few moments in coming.

At last he came out with it: "Apollo." As the Scholar spoke, his eyes turned toward Jeremy. But as if the boy might be invisible, the man's eyes only gazed right on through him, with no change of expression, before looking away again. "The Lord of Light himself," Arnobius said in a flat voice.

The girl slowly nodded. Turning her face to Jeremy, she silently mouthed the words: *Too much sun!* Then back to the man again. "How could you be sure, sir? That it was the Far-Worker?"

Scholar Arnobius pulled himself up a little farther toward a sitting position and moved one hand and wrist in a vague gesture. "Glorious," he murmured. "A glorious . . ." His voice died away, and the two listeners waited in silence to hear more.

"I don't think, my lord," the girl said, "that any gods have really shown themselves at all. Not to any of us, not today."

No reaction.

She persisted: "I might suggest, my lord, that not everyone at the Academy is going to accept your subjective feelings as evidence of a manifestation of the Lord Apollo."

"Why not?" Rather than resenting a servant's impertinence (Jeremy had already abandoned his tentative acceptance of Carlotta's claim to be a lady), Arnobius sounded lost, a child being denied a treat.

"Because." The girl's elfin shoulders shrugged expressively. "Because, my lord, you have no proof that anything really happened. You say you saw Apollo, but . . . just standing in front of you? I mean, the god *did* nothing, gave you nothing—am I right? . . . He told you nothing? No prophecy or anything of the kind?"

A slow shake of the man's head.

"Well, you don't even have much of a story to tell. I'd say the old ruin back there has been long abandoned by gods and humans alike."

Slowly the man in the bunk nodded. Then he shook his head. It was hard to tell what he was thinking.

"Oh, my sweet lord!" Carlotta put out a small hand to stroke the man's forehead, and the head shaking stopped. He had closed his eyes now and looked as if he had a headache. For the moment he had nothing more to say.

Oh, she really loves him, Jeremy thought. One look at the girl's face now left no doubt of that. But she was worried that he was crazy or going to make an utter fool of himself.

A moment later she had turned back to Jeremy. After she sized him up again, her voice became brisk, demanding. "Jonathan, have *we* seen any gods?"

"No, ma'am."

The Scholar's eyes came open again. Squinting now like a man who'd taken too much wine, he needed a little while to focus properly on the newcomer. This time his voice came out a little harsher. "Who's this? Not one of our regular crew."

Carlotta, caught up in her dubious role somewhere between lady and servant, sidled closer to him on the bunk and took his hand. "I was trying to tell you earlier, my lord, they're all gone. They deserted their posts like rats when . . . when you were overcome back there."

"The crew deserted? Why?"

"Well, I suppose they were frightened, the miserable sons of bitches! You were unconscious, and . . . and things in general began to get a little strange."

"A little strange? How so?"

"Oh, I suppose it was not so much that anything really *happened,* my lord, as that those gutless fools were afraid it might. With your lordship lying there senseless."

"Oh." The Scholar seemed to be trying to think about it. "The last thing I remember clearly is—it seems to me that I was about halfway through the ritual. This fellow—Jonathan—hadn't arrived yet. The crew were busy, or I assumed they were, with routine affairs . . . whatever they were supposed to be doing. And you"—he looked sharply at Carlotta—"you'd gone into the temple, as I remember?"

"That's right, my lord. I didn't go in very far, wasn't in very long. Then I heard the crew—well, some of their voices were raised. I was puzzled and came out, just in time to see our little boat go round the bend, with the whole worthless bunch of them in it."

She nodded at Jeremy. "This young lad happened along most providentially, my lord, and pitched right in. Otherwise we'd still be stuck in the swamp. I'd say Jonathan has twice the courage of that whole bunch of worthless renegades who were supposed to be our crew."

Jeremy bowed. A newly ingrafted instinct for socially correct behavior, surfacing right on cue, rather to his own surprise, assured him that that was the proper thing to do.

———

The Scholar Arnobius, on fully recovering consciousness, showed little interest in practical affairs but was content to leave those to his young assistant. Judging from the occasional word Arnobius muttered, as he started to concern himself with the litter on his worktable, he was bitterly disappointed that the god he had been looking for had not, after all, appeared.

Carlotta, on the other hand, had enjoyed some kind of partial success. Jeremy's augmented memory assured him that anyone who so played the servant to a mere Academic was very unlikely to deserve the title of "Lady."

Jeremy tried to listen in without appearing to do so. From what he could overhear, it was evident that the Scholar and his helper or mistress—whatever roles she might play—had come into the swamp with the specific purpose of investigating stories of a ruined temple in these parts.

As soon as Carlotta began to talk about the purpose of their mission here, she switched languages. Jeremy was so intent on the substance of what she was saying that he didn't notice for some time that she had switched—the new tongue was as easy as the old for him to understand.

Eventually the Scholar, whose mind only gradually cleared itself of the cobwebs of drugs and his strenuous attempts at magic, remembered to express gratitude to Jeremy for his timely help and was more than willing to sign him on as a crew member to paddle, run a trapline, or catch fish or serve as a local guide. The fit, trance, or whatever it was had left Arnobius in a weakened condition, and there was no sign that any of the original crew was ever coming back.

And Jeremy's nimble little canoe proved useful to the common cause. It allowed him to go exploring ahead down twisting channels, seeing which ones grew too narrow or too shallow, scouting out the best way to get around islands. Carlotta renewed her curses of the decamping crew members, who had taken with them the expedition's own small craft.

━━━━━━━

When Jeremy's canoe was hauled on deck, Arnobius and his servant both expressed curiosity at the number of times their new deckhand had burnt his initials into the sides of his canoe—it seemed to them it must have been a slow, painstaking process. They also frowned at some of the letters from other alphabets, the ones Jerry'd been trying to make for the first time. But their shapes were sloppy, and Jeremy was relieved when the scholars decided they were only random scribblings and not writing at all. After all, the scholarly couple had many other things to worry about.

At last the Scholar, frowning, asked him: "You have a burning-glass, then?"

"Had one, sir. I lost it overboard."

"You've been hurt, Jonathan." The lady was staring at the back of his shoulder, where the rent in his shirt revealed a half-healed fury slash. He'd taken his shirt off while working in the heat. Carlotta's face did not reveal whether or not she recognized the wound as having been left by a fury's whip.

"They're getting better now. They're almost healed."

"But what on earth happened to you?" To Jeremy's relief, she wasn't seriously looking for an answer. "Go find yourself some new clothing if you can. Yes, I'm sure you can. There is a crew locker, I believe, behind the deckhouse." Her nose wrinkled. "And I strongly suggest you take a bath in the river before you put the new things on."

"Yes'm."

Jeremy discovered a chest in the small shed, from which the awning that had sheltered the crew protruded, did indeed contain a selection of spare workers' clothing in different sizes, all now available for him to pick from. His vineyard worker's garments or what was left of them, slashed by a fury's whips and still grape-stained, went quickly into the cook fire that Jeremy discovered still smoldering, on its foundation of boxed sand, under the awning. Not into the water—he could visualize the hunters, who must be still fanatically on his trail, fishing the rags out and gaining some magical advantage from them.

Remembering Carlotta's orders, he located a bar of soap and took it with him into the river, where he scrubbed to the best of his ability before he climbed aboard and clothed himself anew.

11

THEY WERE UNDER way again shortly after sunrise. Arnobius was still taking it easy, letting Carlotta make decisions, when Jeremy was officially signed on as a member of the crew. From somewhere the lady dug out a kind of logbook that Jeremy was required to sign. This he did willingly enough, putting down his adopted name in large, legible letters. To form his signature he needed no help from his new stores of memory; his early years in school had not been wasted. Neither of his new employers was surprised that a youth who could identify their flag could also read and write.

With Jeremy heating water at the galley fire and carrying buckets into the deckhouse and Carlotta scrubbing her master's back for him, Arnobius removed all traces of the magician's paint and put on clothes of simple elegance. He continued to spend most of his time in the deckhouse, hunched over his workbench, endeavoring to figure out what had gone wrong in his attempt to make contact with the god Apollo. Once Arnobius stuck his head out and called for more small animals to be used in his dissections—but the chance of obtaining any specimens just now was small.

Later in the day, Jeremy, steering pole in hand, heard the Scholar talking to the girl about his work. "It is not, of course, a matter of summoning, as one would try to call a demon—if one were interested in calling demons. Even one of the lesser gods could not be treated so high-handedly, of course, and that approach would be unimaginable in the case of the Far-Worker, in whose presence even other deities tread carefully—or most of them do," he added, apparently scrupulous about getting all the details right. "The recent rumors of his death must be discounted."

After a moment he added: "In the case of the Lord of Light, one can only offer a humble invitation." Then he sat staring, rather hopelessly, at the materials on the table before him.

Carlotta listened, warily, her attitude that of a worshiper in awe, now and then offering a sympathetic word or two of comment. Jeremy wasn't sure how she felt about Apollo, but she was close to worshiping the man before her.

Suddenly Jeremy felt himself moved, by some inner prodding, to ask a question. First he cleared his throat. "Sir? Scholar Arnobius?"

The Scholar looked up at him absently. "Yes?"

"Well, I just wondered—what was it you wanted to say to Lord Apollo?"

Carlotta only continued to look thoughtful. Arnobius allowed himself to be distantly amused. He got up, stretched, patted Jeremy on the right shoulder—clearly having forgotten about the wound there, he missed it by only an inch—and with a kindly word sent him back to work.

The catamaran was as unwieldy in narrow, shallow waters as any craft of its size and shape must be. Fortunately, the crew had not looted the food supplies before deserting. The only explanation Jeremy could think of was the vaguely ominous one that they'd been too terrified—by something—to think of needing food.

One of Jeremy's first, successful efforts on behalf of the expedition, on the first evening after his enlistment, was catching, cleaning, and cooking a string of fish, all of a particularly good-tasting species—the Scholar carried one whole specimen into the deckhouse as a subject for odylic dissection. Whatever fishing success the boy had was only a matter of natural experience and of luck. When he was sure of being unobserved, he tried whispering commands to whatever uncaught fish might be lurking in the nearby river, the same words that had worked so beautifully with chickens and watchdogs—but the effort failed completely.

Watching the women of his family in their kitchens, he'd learned the basics of cooking and cleaning skills; here was another category in which his new memory proved useless.

Each night they found somewhere to tie up. Stretching out under the awning on a selection of the crew's abandoned bedding, which Jeremy was relieved to find contained no lice, he could hear a murmur of voices from behind the closed door of the cabin. The tone certainly suggested disagreement.

If he turned his left ear in that direction, he found that he could distinguish words. He had eavesdropped on a good chunk of conversation before he realized that it was being conducted in a language vastly different from the only one he'd heard and spoken all his life. Yet the boy now had no trouble at all understanding it. After the marvels he'd already experienced, he could accept a new one calmly.

Jeremy wondered if the Scholar had decided to turn to asceticism in an effort to increase his magical powers—a common practice, if ineffective—and was therefore rejecting the advances of his mistress. Or possibly he was just annoyed with her over something.

Jeremy's Intruder, his inward partner, could smile at that idea. If Arnobius wanted to converse with gods, he needed more help than mere celibacy was going to provide.

And again, from time to time, the man and girl shifted to another language in their conversation with each other, to make sure that Jeremy if he happened to overhear them could not possibly understand.

Now they were speaking of Carlotta's work, which in the past had sometimes resulted in genuine discoveries. But this time she claimed to have found nothing useful. Jeremy got the impression that Arnobius was not entirely satisfied with her recent work—but then his own results had been so dismal that in fairness he could hardly complain.

To Jeremy's disappointment, the names of Professor Alexander and Margaret Chalandon were never mentioned.

———

Jeremy and Carlotta had a lot of time effectively alone together, during the hours the Scholar spent in the deckhouse, lost in a brown study over his failed attempts at magic. That was where he spent most of his time when his strength wasn't needed to control the boat, and Carlotta several times reminded the deckhand that it wouldn't be wise to disturb him at his work.

"What is his work?" Jeremy wanted to hear how she'd describe it.

"He seeks to reach the gods. To talk to them, establish a relationship. He's spent all his life in that endeavor."

Pressed for a further explanation, the girl said her master was contemplating what he called "the odylic force," which, he explained, meant "a force that pervades all nature."

"So he's an odylic philosopher?" New memory provided the term, and Jeremy was curious.

"One of the most advanced," said Carlotta, and blinked at her questioner. "What do you know of such matters?"

"Nothing. Not much. I've heard people talking."

The girl's attitude toward Jeremy was ambivalent—as if with the main, conscious part of her mind she was stubbornly refusing to allow herself to take him any more seriously than her master did. While on a deeper level—

And gradually Jeremy was revising his opinion about her. Maybe she wasn't so much in love with Arnobius as she had seemed at first—or she had been, but something had recently happened to cure her of that problem.

The weather continued warm, the mosquitoes, despite the surrounding swamp, not too bad, and Jeremy chose to sleep on deck. He had taken off his new shirt and, as was his old habit, was using the garment as a pillow.

On the third night after Jeremy had come aboard, he awakened, near midnight, from one of his Apollonian dreams, in which the Dark Youth had been summoning one of his concubines to attend him.

Jeremy found himself already sitting up on deck when his eyes came open. The door of the little shelter had slid open almost silently in the moonlight, and a moment later she was there.

It was if he had known for some time that something like this was going to happen.

Somewhere in the darkness beyond the open door of the deckhouse, Arnobius was snoring faintly.

The girl's legs and feet were bare beneath the silken hem. Standing almost over Jeremy, she loosened the old shirt she had been wearing as night garment and let it slide to the deck, displaying her body nude in the moonlight. Even the golden rings that had hung on either side of her head were gone.

It crossed the boy's mind to note that she was so proud of her golden collar that she had chosen to leave it on. He had a blurred impression that the Intruder's memory might have suggested a different reason for the collar's continued presence, but right now Jeremy was not concerned with explanations.

As he rose to his feet, he could hear how fast Carlotta's breathing had become. Her voice was a terse whisper: "Just don't say anything."

His body was moving mindlessly, automatically, efficiently discarding his remaining clothing as he rose. It seemed to him that the girl standing before him was somehow shorter than she had been in daylight and with her clothes on. His arms reached out to her, with perfect confidence, as if some mind and spirit infinitely more experienced than Jeremy Redthorn's were in control. And indeed that was the case. His bones and muscles, lips, face, breathing, every part of his body, had been taken over—and in the circumstances, Jeremy was perfectly willing that it should be so.

Sensation was, if anything, only enhanced by the change. The young woman's mouth presented itself hungrily to his, even as his left arm expertly enfolded her and his right hand sought her breasts. Her frame was naturally thinner, slighter than his own. One of her hands went sliding down his belly, and when it reached its goal performed a ritual of experienced caresses. Together they sank down to the deck.

And all the while, with little Carlotta's sweet rapid breathing hissing in his ear, along with the moans she was trying to stifle, Jeremy Redthorn kept thinking to himself: *So, this is what it is like, with a real woman.* Over and over he could only keep thinking the same thing— *so this is what it is like*—until matters had gone too far to permit him to think of anything at all.

———

A few hours later, just after sunrise on a tranquil morning, the girl emerged once more from the shelter she shared with her master. This time she was fully, neatly clothed, earrings and all, and her first move was to favor the new deckhand with an enigmatic look. Jeremy had been up for some minutes—though he had the feeling that the Intruder was sleeping late today—and the boy had made sure that the decks were clear of snakes and now had the fire in the cookbox going briskly, heating water for tea. The flat slab of metal that served as grill was greased and spitting hot, ready to do griddle cakes.

Carlotta said nothing at first but only looked at her new employee and shipmate as if challenging him to suggest in any way that a certain strange adventure, moments of wild abandon during the hours of darkness, had been anything but a dream or that the dream was not by now forgotten.

That was quite all right with Jeremy—and with the Intruder, too. "Good morning, ma'am." His tone was properly, even a little excessively, respectful. His recently acquired stores of memory provided, if not wisdom in such matters, at least a sense of familiarity that allowed him to feel quite at ease. All this had happened many times before.

"Good morning," responded the young woman, slowly, visibly relaxing. Her insecurity in this situation, her uncertainty, showed to the experienced eye. Her look said to Jeremy: *There are matters we must discuss, but later.*

Then she evidently decided that the general idea should be made clear at once. "You will do something for me, won't you, Jonathan? If I should ask?"

Jeremy nodded, more in response to the look than to the words, and went on making griddle cakes. The lady—he could try to think of her as a lady, if that made her happy—gazed at him thoughtfully for a long moment, then went to the rail and stood looking out over it. Her look was hopeful, as if she was expecting to make some new discovery.

"Sleep well, Jonathan?" the Scholar asked, absently, when he emerged in his turn, a little later.

"Yes, sir. Couple of dreams." Jeremy's voice was steady and casual; he didn't look at the lady as he spoke.

"Ah." Arnobius nodded slowly, gazing over the rail at something that only he could see. "We all have those."

What had happened on deck that first night did not happen again during the remainder of the voyage. All was proper and businesslike between the lady of ambiguous status and the new servant. In any case their conduct was constrained by the fact that Arnobius had snapped out of his withdrawal and at night Jeremy heard faint sounds from the deckhouse indicating that only one of the two beds was in use.

Jeremy had other matters to concern him. He thought the time was ripe to ask the Scholar whether he knew either of the people to whom Jerry was supposed to convey the message.

"Yes, though I don't know Margaret all that well—she's a visiting scholar, from Morelles I think—and Professor Alexander, of course, a sound man." Arnobius ceased his contemplation of whatever it was that he was thinking about and turned to look at the boy with interest. "How did you happen to hear of my colleagues?"

Jeremy was ready with what he hoped would be an acceptable answer. "Someone in our village . . . told me that she had worked for him once."

"Ah," said the Scholar vaguely, turning away again. If there was anything wildly improbable in the claim, he did not appear to notice it. And Jeremy had chosen a moment when Carlotta was not around.

Emboldened, he pushed his luck. "I thought if I might talk to the professor, then he might offer me a job. When I've finished with the job you've given me, of course."

Arnobius once more looked at him with his usual air of benign remoteness. "Well, who knows?" Then a new thought occurred. "I might possibly be able to retain you in my employ when we get home. Reliable people are hard to find, and you've shown yourself reliable—though of course if you wish to speak to Alexander it won't hurt for you to try." A pause. "Where is your family?"

"They're all dead, Scholar."

"I see. That is sad." Arnobius nodded, blinking. It seemed that in his remote, abstracted way he actually felt some sympathy. "Did they all die at the same time? Fever, perhaps? Or maybe you'd rather not talk about it—?"

"I don't mind. Yes, sir, they all died at about the same time." As he spoke the words they seemed quite true. "There was an attack on my home village. I don't know why."

"War," said the Scholar, nodding wisely again. "War is always . . ." He made a gesture of futility and let it go at that.

───────

It was still difficult for three people to propel and steer the catamaran, especially in narrow channels, but after all, their goal was downstream, and mere drifting would get them there sooner or later—if their enemies did not show up to interfere.

Jeremy still looked back, from time to time, over his shoulder, for the boats full of armed men, or the furies, who could be pursuing him from upstream. They were still comfortingly absent.

And from time to time he noticed that Carlotta also kept looking back, along the way they had come, while Arnobius rarely glanced up from his table of what he preferred to call not magic but odylic computations.

On the walls of the cabin there were posted maps, or charts, including one ancient-looking one.

Arnobius was about convinced now that there wasn't any real reason to go back there, and so he treated that map as unimportant.

But Carlotta studied the map so intently that Jeremy got the idea she might be trying to memorize it.

12

ON A MORNING when everything for once seemed to be going smoothly, with the catamaran drifting more or less steadily downstream, Carlotta briskly discussed with the new employee the matter of wages. In return for a certain increase in the sum already contracted, payable on reaching port, he would be expected to double as sailor and personal servant for the duration of the trip.

It appeared that the Scholar was going to have little to say on this or any other practical matter and, though now fully recovered from his fainting fit, was perfectly willing to leave all such affairs to his young companion. When circumstances required the efforts of all three people to move the boat, he followed her orders, or even Jeremy's, willingly enough and with his usual abstracted air.

Jeremy had no way of knowing whether the pay he was offered was generous or stingy, but for his purposes it hardly mattered—he would be provided with food and shelter and, above all, would be living within the walls of the Academy. There, presumably, he would be able to move around with some degree of freedom, enough to enable him to keep his pledge to Sal.

Jeremy still tended to grant Carlotta the title of Lady in his thoughts, however false her claim to it must be. As she laid down the conditions of his employment—she couldn't seem to think of many—Jeremy stood nodding his head, scarcely listening, agreeing to it all. Once he was inside the gates of the Academy, locating the man he had to find ought not to be too hard.

As the days passed, the girl's overt behavior gave little indication that she remembered the midnight encounter she had enjoyed with her new servant. And indeed, that event now seemed almost unreal to Jeremy as well.

The only clue that the girl had not entirely forgotten the interlude came when she actually blushed once or twice when Jeremy looked at her directly, as if she were reading more into his glances than he was aware of putting into them. Jeremy felt faintly amused to see her blush, but his main emotion was a remote but profound surprise at his own ability to maintain a cool and casual attitude in the presence of this young woman, who by all the rules ought to have been much more sophisticated than he was. The face and ears of young Jeremy Redthorn ought to have been turning red; his voice should have been stammering.

The explanation arrived at by the boy himself was that the young woman's midnight lover had not been Jeremy Redthorn—or not entirely. That made an enormous difference, and there were moments when the realization that he was no longer exactly himself might have thrown him into a wild panic—but whenever that began to happen, fear, like embarrassment, was gently damped away, managed before it could get a good foothold.

It had gradually become obvious to him that the Intruder was really taking over parts of his behavior. The proof lay in the fact that he could calmly accept the fact that he wasn't totally, entirely, Jeremy Redthorn any longer. One hot afternoon, on a riverbank, the boy who had grown up with that name had disappeared, never to return.

To the new Jeremy, the transformation didn't seem nearly as terrifying as it might have been. And he thought he knew why: Because the Intruder kept pushing suggestions in through the back of his mind. Kept telling him—wordlessly but very effectively—*Relax. It's all right. Take it easy.*

What had happened to him was beginning to seem like something natural. In recent days, no doubt prodded along by his new partner, he had come to realize that no one, child or adult, was ever the same person from one week to the next. The self that anyone remembered was a self no longer in existence.

———

Taking the *Argos* downstream continued to be an awkward job for three inexperienced people. But, as Carlotta explained to her two shipmates, they really had no choice—Jeremy could see that she was right, and

Arnobius, as usual, took her word on whatever she wanted to tell him regarding practical matters. Abandoning the boat and trying to walk home was really not a viable alternative. Trying to travel any distance overland, starting in this swamp and with no clear idea of the best way out of it, would have guaranteed disaster.

All three of them could have fit easily enough into Jeremy's canoe, which had been brought aboard—all six of the deserting crew had apparently crammed themselves into a boat not much bigger. But on a journey of many days that would have meant going ashore to sleep, among the giant snakes and other dangerous creatures whose presence filled the swamp; and leaving the catamaran behind would also have meant abandoning not only the bulk of their food supplies, but also almost all of the Scholar's books and magical paraphernalia, a sacrifice that was not open to discussion.

Besides, the canoe's chronic leak had been growing worse when it was taken out of the water. None of the three (or four, counting the Intruder) knew of any quick, effective method of repair. And Jeremy on thinking it over decided it would be just as well if the canoe should disappear before one of the Academy's real language experts had the chance to observe its decorations.

———

When Arnobius was sufficiently recovered to take part, he put a man's strength into the job of steering, which with the widening of the river's channel became eminently doable. The Scholar had little experience in boating of any kind and Jeremy none at all in sailing, but Carlotta claimed some, which she soon managed to convey to her companions.

———

The catamaran had made two or three days' slow progress toward the mouth of the river when a well-manned small flotilla came in view ahead, gliding swiftly upstream to meet it. The philosophic expedition was overdue, and evidently people were getting worried.

Jeremy froze and stared, but his left eye saw no warning dots of red. The Scholar, shading his eyes with his hand, squinted into the sun dazzle. "Here comes my father," he said at last, without surprise. "My brother also."

The boats coming upstream were each driven by the arms of a score of powerful rowers.

These troops wore different uniforms and displayed a different flag than any Jeremy had seen before, showing green waves on a blue background.

———

Lord Victor Lugard, a solid middle-aged figure standing in the prow of an approaching boat, was now close enough for Jeremy to study him closely. His lordship was not dressed much differently than his soldiers who were rowing.

His Lordship was obviously pleased to find his elder son alive and physically well, but Jeremy got the impression that he would not have been utterly devastated had matters turned out differently. Lord Victor smiled benignly and briefly at Carlotta and at first did not appear to notice Jeremy at all.

As soon as the fast boat that was carrying him, long and narrow and raised at prow and stern, came bumping alongside the catamaran, Victor jumped briskly aboard. Lord Victor's coloring was lighter than that of his older son, and he didn't, at first glance, look quite old enough to be the father of grave Arnobius.

Weeks had passed since the last message received from the Scholar, and his father as well as the authorities at the Academy had been growing alarmed.

The younger man who followed Lord Victor aboard the catamaran was Arnobius's brother, three or four years his junior. Actually, Lord John's lined and weathered face made him look at least as old. A modest degree of scarring on his face and body, as well as his general bearing, indicated that John was already well experienced in combat, but the short sword at his belt looked showy as well as serviceable. John obviously preferred a more flamboyant appearance than his brother—he was the second person Jeremy Redthorn had ever seen wearing earrings.

John also favored Carlotta with an admiring look, to which she returned a distant smile. And then he stared at Jeremy with mild surprise.

Explanations were begun, in which the boy received full credit for his help in salvaging the expedition. Arnobius tried to put as good a face as possible on his results, reporting at least partial success. Though the effort to find a god had come to naught, they were bringing back with them at least some of the specimens and information that Arnobius had started out to seek.

Neither Victor nor John was particularly interested. The leader asked: "You brought away nothing of value at all, hey?"

"By your standards, sir, no, nothing."

This reminded Jeremy that since leaving the temple in the swamp he had seen no sign of the small ebony and ivory box Carlotta had been at such pains to conceal within a few minutes of his arrival. He looked at her, but she was obviously not intending any surprise announcements.

The Scholar's father and brother obviously did not care much whether his expedition had advanced the cause of odylic science or not. The present audience were vastly more interested in any crumbs of valuable military information that night have been picked up. John personally questioned all members of the party.

Jeremy was quite willing to answer some questions about the attack on the Raisinmakers' village, thus briefly drawing upon himself the full attention of father and younger son. The boy said nothing about Sal but described the furies he'd encountered and the troops he'd seen. Though he hadn't caught more than a glimpse of the human attackers, he could name them as Lord Kalakh's—new memory whispered that Kalakh and the Harbor Lord were anything but the best of friends. Jeremy gave an essentially accurate account of his long, lonely downstream flight—except that he made no mention at all of Sal's treasure or of his private goal.

None of his hearers seemed curious as to why the village had been attacked—perhaps because that was the normal fate of villages and they all had some acquaintance with Lord Kalakh.

The Harbor Lord and his people did not impress Jeremy as especially villainous, and he mulled over the advisability of now Telling All, as regards Sal and her treasure. Arnobius did seem to be on good terms with Professor Alexander.

Still, after a brief hesitation, the boy decided to retain his secrets for the time being. He had no particular reason to distrust these people—but no reason to trust them, either, once momentous matters came to be at stake. It did not seem utterly impossible that they'd start carving his head open, once they learned what treasure was inside it. Under the circumstances, the decision was easy to make: he would say nothing to anyone as yet about Sal or the special mission he'd undertaken for her—certainly nothing about the weird result. That would have to wait until he'd managed to locate one of the people Sal had named.

It seemed that Lord Victor and all the rest were now inclined to trust Jeremy—to the extent that they thought of him at all. The Harbor Lord tossed him a gold coin by way of reward for helping his son out of a tight spot.

And the girl was now behaving as if she and Jeremy were practically strangers. He felt half-disappointed and half-relieved. Had they wanted to carry on the affair, it would have been impossible now to find a way to be alone together.

Five or six skilled crewmen in green and blue had boarded the catamaran and taken over the job of handling her. The wind being generally favorable, the sail was put to work. The *Argos* seemed to come alive, and the miles began to fly by. The oar-powered escort boats had trouble keeping up. Jeremy, relieved of any need to demonstrate his clumsiness as a sailor, had little to do but sit on the roof of the deckhouse and observe.

When Jeremy had the chance, he watched Arnobius and listened to his efforts to perform magic. The man was not totally unskilled, but his present attempts were doomed to failure—for the simple reason that at the moment no gods were paying him any attention. None except the Intruder, who currently was not interested in being of any help.

———

After another day's swift travel, the last and largest river brought the small flotilla to a saltwater bay, several miles in extent and ringed by low hills. One morning there were gulls and the smell of the sea, exotic to an inlander like Jeremy. For some reason, no doubt having to do with the local geography or the prevailing winds, the Academy had been built not quite in sight of the ocean.

The whole scene closely matched certain old, vague memories that Jeremy had acquired from the Intruder. On the farther side of the bay sprawled the walled city of Pangur Ban, rising from the quays at bayside in tier upon tier of white and gray, crowned by a hilltop castle with its distant blue-green pennant. The city was far bigger than any settlement Jeremy Redthorn could remember seeing. Its walls, light-colored and formidable, rose bright in the sun, and in the ocean breeze the atmosphere above Pangur Ban looked almost free of smoke. Near at hand the buildings of the Academy were set amid green hills on a peninsula.

This close to the sea, the river was tidal in its ebb and flow. Jeremy had never before seen a river that changed directions, but this one did, every six hours or so—and his new memory, when consulted, was able to provide the explanation.

Crossing the harbor from the river's mouth with a skilled crew on board, the expedition's catamaran put in smoothly to a well-made dock, a mile outside the city walls, where a few other vessels of various types were moored. One or two were large seagoing ships, the first that Jeremy Redthorn had ever laid eyes on.

And then the *Argos* was at the dock, with a small horde of deckhands and dockworkers working to make her fast.

13

AN HOUR OR so after disembarking from the *Argos*, Jeremy, his existence for the moment almost forgotten by nobility and commoners alike, was standing on a hill overlooking the low buildings of the Academy, which stretched for a couple of hundred yards along the harbor side of a long, narrow, curving peninsula. He was alone, except for his permanent, silent companion.

Here Jeremy got his first look at the full ocean, the domain (so it was claimed by the Scholar and his colleagues and others who took gods seriously) of Poseidon. Jeremy saw a gray and limitless expanse, ending at an indeterminate horizon. Here his left-eye view was not much different than his right. Only an occasional strange brilliant sparkle showed upon a wave. Nor did his left ear find anything worth emphasizing in the rush and sigh of surf.

The dark shapes of seals and sea lions, awkward on the land, decorated the rocks and beaches, their smooth bodies now and again lunging into the water or up out of it. Some were heavily mutated, their species showing great individual variety. Another amazing sight for the country boy, and another in which his left eye drew him no special pictures. And more gulls, in varieties of shape and color suggesting hundreds of mutated subspecies, crying and clamoring above.

Though the Intruder did not seem particularly interested in the limitless expanse of sea and sky, Jeremy Redthorn was. When the boy on the hilltop managed to tear his eyes away from the distant blue horizon, the Academy struck him as a marvel, too, more striking as he got closer to it. The sprawling white buildings, few of them taller than two stories, roofed with red tile and set amid gardens, connected by paths of ground seashells, created an awe-inspiring impression in the mind of the country boy.

How old were most of these red-roofed, white stone buildings? Some only a few years, as Jeremy was soon to discover; the Academy had undergone a notable expansion in recent times, as a direct result of the new stirrings in the world of magic, the profession of odylic science. But a few of the structures at the core of the establishment were very old, and of these one or two were of a vastly different style.

Here, new memories assured Jeremy Redthorn, were many men and women who considered themselves learned in the business of the gods. At first it seemed to him impossible that here his special condition, the presence of the Intruder, would not be quickly discovered.

But the Intruder did not seem particularly concerned.

Within a few hours of his arrival on the grounds of the Academy, Jeremy began to learn something about how and when the institution had been founded. The only trouble was that his new memory strongly suggested that the story as he now heard it was wrong in several details—he wasn't going to dig to find out.

When Jeremy at last found himself mingling, as a servant, with Arnobius's Academic colleagues, none of them paid him much attention to the fact that Scholar Arnobius happened to have a new servant. They took only momentary notice when he was pointed out to them by Arnobius, or by Carlotta, as a sharp-eyed lad. The boy became an object of desultory interest, but only in a distinctly minor way.

Very soon after his arrival, Jeremy was taken in charge by a female housekeeper, an overseer of the staff who tended the many Academic lodgings on campus. To this woman Arnobius, his mind as usual engaged somewhere in the lofty realms of philosophy, gave a few careless words of instruction regarding his new personal attendant.

Plainly horrified by the appearance of her new charge, still wearing an ill-fitting rower's uniform and by her standards far from sufficiently clean, the housekeeper snorted and turned away, gesturing imperiously for him to follow her. She led Jeremy down seemingly endless flights of stairs in a narrow passage between gray walls. On a lower level they emerged into a kind of barracks, evidently for male civilian workers.

Here she commanded him to bathe—the barracks boasted showers with hot running water, the first that Jeremy Redthorn had ever seen.

Gratefully he took advantage of the opportunity and afterward in clean clothes was sent to have his hair cut even shorter than his own rude trim had left it, evidently the accepted style for servants in these parts.

At the barbershop he appeared wearing new sandals and the white trousers and jacket of the low-ranked support staff. Undergarments had been provided also, and care was actually taken to see that the clothes fit him. His jacket was marked with colored threads that, he was given to understand, marked him as an Academician's personal servant. Catching a glimpse of himself in a mirror, he could see that his appearance had been considerably transformed.

"Will you need a razor, Jonathan?" The chief housekeeper frowned, inspecting Jeremy's smooth cheeks. "No, not yet." With a final look around she left him in the barbershop.

It was a well-lit, serviceable room that, as Jeremy later discovered, occasionally served as a surgery for students and permanent members of the lower class.

There was only one barber. Seated in the central chair and arguing with the civilian barber about the relative length of sideburns was a compactly built young soldier in Lugard green and blue.

"I can't grow hair where there ain't none, Corporal," the barber was remonstrating. "You want me to trim for sideburns, you got to produce 'em first. Then I can trim 'em down."

"Private, not Corporal! See any stripes on my sleeve? Private Andy Ferrante. And damn it, man, I *got* hair! I can feel it hangin' down the sides of my bloody head!"

"That's all sprouting from above your ears, son. Take a good look at yourself in a mirror sometime." Not that any such device was currently in evidence; probably, thought Jeremy, the customers here were generally not paying for their own haircuts and what they thought of them meant little to the barber.

Private Andy Ferrante appealed to the next customer in line, who happened to be Jeremy. "Ain't I got sideburns he could trim? Tell the truth!"

Jeremy moved closer, to give the matter careful study. "Truth is, you've got no more than I do. Which is just about zero."

"Yeah? That's really it, huh?" Ferrante's face, keyed up for fighting, or at least for argument, fell.

From then on the haircut went peacefully enough. Ferrante kept on chatting. When he stood up from the chair, he was shorter than Jeremy, though two years older, at seventeen. His look was intense, open, and guileless, his face not particularly handsome. When he saw Jeremy looking at his left hand, from which the smallest finger and its nearest mate were missing, he remarked that he had lost them in a fight. Gradually Jeremy's interested questions brought out that several months ago Ferrante had distinguished himself in a skirmish against Lord Kalakh's troops, in particular by carrying a wounded officer to safety, and had lost part of a hand in the process.

"Did they give you a medal?" By now Jeremy was in the barber chair and scissors and comb were busy around his ears.

"Yeah. Not worth much. Good thing wasn't on my sword hand. Ever done any fighting?"

"Couple of times I would have, but I had nothing to fight with."

"Join the army; you'll get your chance."

Jeremy only shook his head. Ferrante was not in the least put off by this lack of martial enthusiasm. "You're right; don't join the goddamned army. Crazy to join if you've got a good job on the outside, which it looks like you do." He eyed the thread marks on Jeremy's new tunic.

Ferrante, as it turned out, was here on campus as part of the permanent bodyguard of about a dozen men now assigned the Scholar. The current military and political situation being what it was, prudence dictated precautions against assassination and kidnapping plots.

Jeremy got the impression that Andy didn't get on all that well with the other members of the small military unit. Likely this was because the other men were all some years older, while his combat veteran's status and his cool attitude kept them from treating him like a kid.

Several human factions were involved in the sporadic warfare, in a tangle of alliances and enmities. Everyone wanted to take advantage somehow of whatever change impended in the status of the gods.

The barber was finally moved to comment on the fact that the roots of his newest customer's hair were growing in very dark.

"Damn, kid, never seen anything like it."

"Like what?"

"This hair of yours."

No mirror was available. Questioning brought out the fact that some of the roots were dark, scattered in random patches across his scalp, producing a mixture of curly red and curly black. The more the longer, older red hair was cut away, the more noticeable was the effect.

Again the work with comb and scissors paused. "The dye job on your hair could use a touch-up, kid. Course I'd have to charge extra. Or does your new boss want you to let it grow in natural?"

Jeremy, whose mind had been far off, trying to imagine army life, looked up blankly. "Dye job?"

"Of course with your coloring, the red almost looks more natural than the black. You can see where the darker stuff is growing in at the roots."

"The black?"

The barber began speaking slowly, as to one of inferior intelligence. "You want a touch-up, I got some nice red. If your boss likes it that way."

"No. No dye." Belated understanding came, with a slow chill down Jeremy's spine. The Dark Youth. "Just cut it."

"You still look weird, fellow." This was Ferrante again, assertive, with an easy assumption of familiarity. Evidently he had no urgent business to call him elsewhere. But somehow the words did not seem intended to give offense.

The boy in the barber's chair grinned wryly, thinking: *If you only knew.* He said: "I don't know what I can do about it, though."

The barber was still bemused by the remarkable case before him. He turned aside and after an obvious internal struggle dug a small mirror out of a drawer and held it up for Jeremy to see himself.

In the glass the boy's left eye showed him quite a different self-image than his right. He was still far from closely resembling the Dark Youth, not yet anyway—but Jeremy thought that he could now see a definite family likeness.

A few minutes later, he and the young soldier left the barbershop together.

"Not many uniforms here on campus," the civilian remarked.

"Nah. Only about a dozen of us."

Jeremy looked around with interest at the scattering of passersby. "And I guess it's easy to tell who's a servant—they're dressed like me. Most of the rest of these people must be students?"

"Yeah. Students, men and women both, mostly have long hair. A lot of 'em, especially the ones from wealthy families, dress like they just fell off a manure cart.

"And there are the slaves, of course. Only a few. They all have metal collars."

"Slaves?" A hasty internal check with the Intruder's memory: yes, all true enough. With a mental jolt the boy suddenly grasped the significance of the golden collar that Carlotta wore. Her neckband was thinly wrought and of fine workmanship; its golden thickness might be easily cut or broken. Still, in this part of the world no one but a slave would wear such a thing.

Ferrante, pressed for more information on the subject of slaves, provided what he could. As far as he knew, with one or two exceptions, the only examples on the grounds of the Academy belonged to visiting academics, who had brought them from their respective homelands as personal servants. Jeremy's memory when called upon confirmed the fact: the peculiar institution was rare indeed here in the Harbor Lord's domain. But, perhaps for the very reason that it was so uncommon, it had never been strictly outlawed.

Ancient law and custom of Pangur Ban, indistinguishably blended and extended to the grounds of the Academy, required slaves to wear distinguishing metal collars welded on.

In Carlotta's case the collar was definitely a symbolic rather than a real bond; Jeremy wondered if it was even welded into place. But it did mean, must mean, that the Scholar literally owned her.

Her story, which Jeremy later heard confirmed by several sources, was that the girl had been a gift to Lord Victor's from some other potentate, known to Ferrante only as the sultan. It wouldn't have been politic to reject her or, once the gift had been accepted, to simply set her free.

Ferrante, being off duty for the remainder of the day but currently penniless and unable to afford the amusements of the nearby town, volunteered to show his new acquaintance around the grounds.

Ferrante said to Jeremy, "Suppose your master should send you to the stables with a message—you'd best know where they are. Anyway, it's a place I like t'hang around."

Out on the grounds of the Academy, back toward the stables, Jeremy's footsteps slowed when he realized he was soon going to encounter a large number of domestic animals. Only now did he begin to fully comprehend the extreme strangeness of the ways in which domesticated beasts reacted to him. Herd animals seemed particularly keen on displaying their devotion—if that was the proper word for it. Here were a dozen cameloids or dromedaries, property of the Academy or its masters, peacefully grazing in a field fenced off from the grassy common where teachers and students, distinguished by their own varieties of white uniforms, strolled or gathered in fine weather to dispute in groups.

As soon as Jeremy came within sight of the pasture, these animals tended to congregate along the fence and look at him, sniffing and cocking their ears, as if they were greatly intrigued by his mere presence and could not wait to discover what he might do next. Fortunately, he noticed the silent scrutiny before anyone else did—even more fortunately, as soon as he silently willed the beasts to turn away and go about their regular affairs, they did so.

It was lucky, too, that Jeremy's companion's thoughts were elsewhere at the moment.

The same thing happened with the nearest members of a herd of beef and milk cattle, who slowly followed him along their side of a fence, gazing at him in what might have been some bovine equivalent of adoration. The swine in a large pen behaved in the same way. He saw a flock of chickens farther on but detoured to stay away from them.

At times he found his chief objective in coming to the Academy drifting toward the back of his mind. Jeremy had to struggle to keep from impulsively trying to question his new employers and acquaintances as to whether they had known Sal—but he could think of no good way to frame the questions, especially as he had got the distinct impression that that was not her real name. He kept his resolution to refrain from making any direct inquiries about Sal until he could be reasonably sure that he had reached the man for whom Sal had intended the message. Jeremy could only hope that there would be some way short of killing him to rid himself of the thing of power and pass it on to where it belonged.

Nor could Jeremy keep from wondering if Sal had ever lived in one of these white buildings and, if so, for how long and what kind of a life she'd had. Maybe she'd been here as a student. She would have had a family of some kind, of course. Probably a lover—or a score of lovers— but that imagined picture hurt to look at.

Somehow it was difficult for Jeremy to picture Sal, as he had known her, staying here in any capacity. Whatever controlled his enhanced powers of sight and thought had no clues to offer him regarding the question.

———

Apollo's eye provided Jeremy with fitful flashes of insight, occurring here and there across the Academic scene, coming into being unexpectedly and flickering away again. And it gradually showed him more details, when he looked at what he considered special things, things he very much wanted to ask about—but he continued to be cautious in his questions about anything he saw in the special way, not wanting to reveal the powers he possessed. Not until he could accomplish the mission that he believed Sal had entrusted to him.

It had already occurred to Jeremy that the fact that one of his eyes was still restricted to purely human perception was probably an advantage. The difference let him distinguish between mere natural oddities and the special things that only a god could see.

———

The Academy grounds and buildings held many sights that Jeremy had never seen before—as well as things that he had never come close to imagining—but in most cases the left Eye of Apollo provided at least a partial explanation. And Jeremy had begun to develop skill at interpreting the hitherto unknown sounds occasionally brought to him by his left ear.

One series of these special sounds reminded him of something he'd heard in some of his recent, special dreams—the music of the string-plucked lyre.

14

THE LIVING QUARTERS assigned to Jeremy were tiny, a mere curtained alcove off the hallway connecting bedroom and living room in the Scholar's apartment. Carlotta had her own modest apartment on the next floor up, and on the floor above that were quartered the dozen men of Arnobius's military bodyguard, one of whom was almost always on duty at the door to the Scholar's apartment, with another standing guard in the shrubbery beneath its windows.

So far, Jeremy's duties were not demanding; they consisted of general housekeeping for the Scholar, running errands, and reminding him of appointments, which Arnobius tended to forget.

Carlotta spent at least as much time in her master's apartment as in her own, so she and Jeremy were frequently in each other's company.

On the third day of Jeremy's stay at the Academy, the Scholar sent him to the library with a note addressed to one of the archivists asking if a particular old manuscript, dealing with the origins of odylic science, was available.

On entering the vast main room—really a series of rooms, connected by high, broad archways—the boy's feet slowed and his mouth fell open. It was a revelation. The hundred or so books that the Scholar had had with him on the boat and that had seemed to Jeremy (who at the time did not consult his new memory on the subject) an unbelievable number were as nothing compared to the thousands arrayed here. A faint intriguing smell of dust and ink, parchment and paper, testified to the presence of ancient texts. Marble busts of gods and humans looked down from atop some of the high bookcases. Tall windows, admitting great swathes of light, looked out on green lawns and treetops nearby, green hills more distant. Somewhere in the background a droning ar-

gument was in progress: two voices, each patient and scholarly and
certain of being in the right.

When Jeremy delivered the note, he was told to wait while a search
was made. He got the impression that the effort might well consume an
hour or more.

While waiting, Jeremy encountered Carlotta, who had been sent
here on a similar task. She volunteered to give him a tour of the library
and the Hall of Statues.

He was fascinated, and for the moment his real reason for being
here was forgotten.

The Academy complex was centered on an exhibition hall, which
had been built in a different style of architecture and had been a temple
to some specific god or gods. At least the building had been constructed
to look like a temple, in which stood two rows of statues, facing one
another under elaborate stone arches and across an expanse of yards of
tiled floor, representing many of the known gods. One of the main
structures of the Academy had been built on the ruins of some elder
temple and incorporating a portion of its framework.

The library and hall of sculpture opened directly into each other—
another way of looking at it was that they were both parts of the same
vast room. The tall shelves created plenty of recesses, where a number
of people could be unobserved.

Carvings on the many pedestals and on the walls between them held
a partial listing of gods. Hundreds of names, far more than were represented in the Hall of Statues.

Jeremy's new memory informed him that the list contained mistakes, some of which his inner informant found amusing. Certain things
that the signs and labels told him were simply *wrong*, though he certainly had no intention of trying to argue the fact.

Carlotta, who in her two years of working with Arnobius had become something of a scholar in her own right, remarked that only a
minority were from the Greek or Roman pantheons. Then she began to
explain what that meant. Jeremy nodded, looking wide-eyed, though
he'd had no trouble understanding the original comment, which had
been made in an ancient language.

One pedestal, unoccupied and set a little apart from the others, was
marked: FOR THE UNKNOWN GOD. The boy looked at it thoughtfully.

Most of the statues in the great hall had been carved, or cast in
metal, larger than human life, and many were only fragmentary. Obviously they were the work of many different sculptors, of varied degrees
of talent. They had been executed at different times and were not meant

to be all on the same scale. Some had obviously undergone extensive restoration.

Fragments of learned conversation drifted in from the adjoining rooms, where scholarly debates seemed to be going endlessly and comfortably on.

"It is, I think, inarguable that the true gods come and go in our world, absenting themselves from human affairs for a long time, only to return unexpectedly."

"Whatever the truth of the matter earlier, before the unbinding of the odylic force many centuries ago, since then the gods' presence on earth has been cyclical.

"Some scholars, our learned colleague Arnobius among them, argue passionately that the old gods have now once more returned and are now in the process of reestablishing their rule. Others refuse to credit the notion of divinity at all; nothing happens in human affairs that cannot be explained in terms of human psychology."

"Here, for example, is a statue of the Trickster. Like many other gods, he is known by several different names. He has more names than I can count—some of the better-known are Loki and Coyote."

The display devoted to Coyote/Trickster caught Jeremy's eye, even among the diversity of the others in their long rows, because of its bewildering variety of images. Here was represented the god who possessed above all others the power of changing his shape.

Jeremy thought Carlotta showed some signs of being emotionally perturbed when they came to this particular god. Right now he wasn't going to try to guess a reason.

Here on a modest pedestal stood Aphrodite, in bronze and gloriously naked. The lettering on the pedestal cataloged her with a list of half a dozen alternate names, including Venus, some in different alphabets.

Mars/Ares, arrayed with spear, shield, and helmet, had a place of honor—he was known to be a favorite of Lord Victor and several other wealthy patrons.

Here stood Hephaestus/Vulcan, clad in his leather apron and little else, one leg crippled, a scowling expression on his face, and his great smith's hammer in his hand. *How often I have seen him just so*—but that thought had to be hastily reburied in new memory, lest it bring on terror too great to be endured.

Other names for the Fire-Worker resounded in Jeremy's new memory, evoking tales of wonder that he dared not pause to scan . . . Agni, the Vedic god of fire. Mulciber, a name from ancient poetry.

In the beginning, so the legends said, Zeus, Poseidon, and Hades had been of equal strength and had divided up the universe among them. So it was according to the authorities of the Academy.

"Is there a statue of Zeus somewhere?"

"The people in charge have never been able to agree on what it should look like."

And here Poseidon, the Earthshaker, who bore a trident among his other symbols.

Other deities, from different pantheons, scattered through human history, had their own sections, rows of columns. The total appeared to be more than one hundred, and even Jeremy's augmented memory did not recognize them all.

Another point that struck him was that there was no statue of Thanatos, the acknowledged ruler of the realm of Death. Maybe, Jeremy thought, no one had ever wanted, or ever made, a statue of him. Memory had heard it often said that the Pitiless God himself wanted no such representation.

Other statues of gods and goddesses presented interesting appearances also. Carlotta could tell some stories of them that even the Intruder had not heard before.

Ancient books were stored here by the thousands, along with a great many volumes of lesser age. Some were on scrolls of vellum, some even on wax or carven tablets of wood or ivory or horn—of the few that were on display or left unrolled on a desk, accessible to his casual glance, there were none that Jeremy could not read.

"What do you think you're doing there? Hey?" But it was a rather good-humored accusation, from a middle-aged scholar who sat surrounded by books.

"I was reading, sir. Sorry if I—"

"Reading that, were you? I'd gladly give a gold coin if you could tell me the meaning of that page."

The boy looked down again at the worn scroll. Even the Intruder did not recognize all the words, some of which were likely only copyists' mistakes, but overall the text was concerned with arrangements for a funeral.

"Sorry, sir. I've no idea."

"Never mind. Get on about your business."

It sometimes seemed to Jeremy, in the first days of his new life in the alien world of the Academy, that Arnobius and his colleagues must be blind, so determined did they seem to ignore what must be the glaring peculiarities of the Scholar's new servant lad. It was a fact that cattle and cameloids turned to look at Jeremy whenever he came near them and that he did indeed possess special powers of understanding languages. But all the supposed experts were intent on managing their own careers in their own way and had no interest in anything that might disrupt them.

Jeremy was sure that more surprises, brought by the Intruder, still awaited his discovery; but he was in no hurry to confront them. He had his mission to accomplish.

He was sure that Professor Alexander and Margaret Chalandon ought to be here, somewhere; quite likely he had already seen them. But neither Jeremy nor his inner guide had any idea what either individual looked like, and there were thousands of people on the Academy grounds. It was hard to know where or how to begin a search.

Without Jeremy's recently augmented memory, the world around him would have been alien indeed, and he would have spent his first days in a state of bewildered helplessness. As matters stood, he was still frequently surprised, but never totally at a loss as to what he should do next.

On the rare occasions when faculty members took any notice of him at all, they credited him simply with natural talent or good luck. Arnobius, like his colleagues, tended to assume that non-Academics were out of the running when it came to finding answers to the deep questions affecting all human lives.

Not, someone commented, that the Academics themselves were doing very well at the task.

———

Jeremy was on another routine errand for Arnobius when a man of about thirty-five, in Academic dress, grabbed him by the arm and demanded of him sharply: "Where did you get that knife and belt?"

At first Jeremy thought his questioner was merely commenting on the impropriety of a servant going about the campus wearing a hunting knife—Arnobius himself hadn't seemed to notice, and so far no one else had commented. Knives were tools, after all, and workers carrying tools were a common enough sight.

Jeremy, as he turned to confront his questioner, was aware of a sudden inward mobilization. The stirring of the Intruder behind his forehead was almost a physical sensation. What might be going to happen next he could not guess.

Yet he felt no indication that anyone but himself, Jeremy Redthorn, was controlling his mind or body as he answered: "I had them from a friend of mine."

The man was a little taller than average and appeared to be in excellent physical condition for a scholar. "What friend was this? Come, let's have the truth."

"A friend who is now dead."

"Man or woman?"

"It was a woman."

"Young or old?"

"Young."

"Her name?"

Jeremy drew a deep breath and took the plunge. "The name she gave to me was Sal."

Jeremy's questioner's manner changed again, and after taking a hasty look around he drew the boy aside to where they might hope to hold a private conversation.

"And where was this?" he demanded in a low voice.

"First, sir, you will tell me your name."

When Jeremy's questioner stared at this insolence, the boy stared right back.

After a few seconds the man's shoulders slumped slightly. He said: "Evidently you are more than you appear to be."

Jeremy said nothing.

"I am Professor Alexander."

"Sir, I'm . . . I'm very glad indeed to have located you at last. Sal told me that I must find you and give you something."

"What else did she give you, this young woman who called herself Sal? You say that she is dead?"

"Yes. I'm sorry."

His listener's shoulders slumped further.

Jeremy pressed on. "The important thing she gave me is meant for you, but I can't hand it over right now."

The relief in the professor's face was no less vast for being well concealed. "You have it safe, though?"

Jeremy nodded.

Then an interruption came, in the form of a loud group of students, just as Alexander was starting to explain matters to Jeremy. At least the man was promising Jeremy that he would be given an explanation in due course. But at the moment any further conversation was obviously impossible.

There was only time for the Academic to demand: "Meet me in the stacks of the library, third alcove on the east wall, this evening at the eighth hour. Can you get away then?"

Jeremy thought. "I can."

"Bring it with you, without fail."

When the appointed time came round, Jeremy, his evening his own as he had expected it would be, went to keep the rendezvous. His feet dragged, as he wondered if giving up the Face as he was bound to do was going to cost him his life. Also, he found himself now intensely reluctant to give it up . . . and never see the stars again. But at least he had been able to see them for a few nights, and for that he could thank Sal.

Professor Alexander was at the appointed meeting place, a lonely and unfrequented alcove among the vast stacks of shelves. He sat at the small writing table, an oil lamp at his elbow—and his head slumped forward on his curved left arm. His right arm hung down at his side, and on the tiled floor below his hand lay the reed pen with which he had been about to write—something—on the blank paper that lay before him.

Jeremy put a hand on the man's shoulder—but there was no need to touch the body to be certain that it was dead. A quick, close look at Alexander's body revealed no visible signs of violence.

Thanatos had paid a visit. And Jeremy, looking out of the alcove with frightened eyes, froze in absolute horror. Framed in a doorway some twenty yards away stood a lone figure. It was a man's shape, yet his left eye recognized in it at once the essence of Thanatos, God of Death. There was the unkempt dark beard, the fierce countenance, the hint of red and ghostly wings sprouting from his shoulders. And at the same time the figure was as thoroughly human as Jeremy himself, a beardless man dressed in a way that indicated he must be a member of the faculty.

The God of Death. Jeremy Redthorn shrank back into the shadows. And the image of terror raised a hand in a casual gesture, a kind of wry salute to Apollo, before he backed through a doorway and disappeared.

The thing, the man, the god, was gone. The boy slumped with the intensity of his relief and broke out in a cold sweat. There was to be no direct confrontation—not now, at least.

Shivering as he made his way back toward the Scholar's quarters, Jeremy knew beyond a doubt that Alexander had been murdered and could only wonder why he himself had been spared.

In his terror it was all he could do to keep from breaking into a dead run, heading for the gates, fleeing the Academy in a panic. But then he thought that now, as when confronted in the wild by a dangerous predator, that might be exactly the wrong thing to do.

Now his only hope of keeping his promise to Sal lay in finding Margaret Chalandon. But he still knew nothing of her besides her name and the fact that she was a visiting scholar.

A few hours later, when Alexander's dead body had been discovered by someone who reported it, great excitement spread through the Academy. Officially the death was blamed on natural causes, unexpected heart failure or something of the kind—a detailed examination had disclosed no signs of foul play, no marks of injury of any kind.

———

Arnobius, like the great majority of his fellow Academics, was much upset when he heard of Alexander's death. He was also vaguely aware that his new servant was acting as if he were in some kind of difficulty or at least seemed to have taken on some new burden of worry.

Carlotta was for the time being keeping in the background as far as Jeremy's affairs were concerned.

———

Carlotta, as well as the head housekeeper, had given Jeremy some desultory instructions as to the skills and conduct expected from a personal servant. Oddly, as it seemed to him, his new memory was already furnished with a vastly greater store of information on the subject. To his teacher it appeared that Jeremy learned the job with amazing speed, as if he were able to get things right instinctively.

The task was made easier by the fact that Jeremy's new master (who thought he was rewarding him handsomely by giving him a job of lowly status) rarely seemed to notice whether he was being served well or poorly—the Scholar's mind as usual remained on larger things.

———

Repeated visits to the library, and also to the refectory, where ranking scholars took many of their meals, revealed more about the comfortably sheltered life of the ranking members of the Academy. Arnobius for the most part scorned, or rather ignored, such luxury and lived in rather ascetic style. Often his behavior surprised people who knew little about him except that he was the son of Lord Victor Lugard.

In a way this seeker of contact with the gods was the black sheep of the family, among several other more warlike sons and cousins.

━━━━━━━

Alcoholism and addiction to other drugs were definitely on the rise among those who professed skill in wizardry. So far, Arnobius showed no sign of any such tendency. All agreed that beginning several centuries ago, there had been a general decline in the world's magic. Gods had ceased to play a part in the affairs of humanity—or at least humanity had become less inclined to believe in such divine activity. But now, abruptly, within the last few weeks and months, signs and portents indicated that a general increase in magical energy was in progress.

The inconsistent rumors concerning the supposed recent battle in the Cave of Prophecy between two gods were hotly debated, at every level of sophistication, here inside the Academy's walls and outside as well.

From time to time Jeremy discussed the matter with his new friend, Ferrante, the young soldier. Neither of them were Academics—Andy could barely read—but both were curious about the world.

Ferrante admitted that he would like to learn to read well enough to try a book someday and to write more than his own name. Jeremy said he would try to find time to help him.

━━━━━━━

Among the questions continually debated by the faculty was: Is magic a branch of philosophy? Many of the learned argued that it was the other way around. A third opinion held both to be branches of odylic science, by which the ancients had managed to transform the world.

Some people continued to claim that real magic had ceased to exist, equating the time of its demise with that of the last withdrawal of the gods, which they put at various periods of between fifty and two hundred years in the past—the more extreme argued that there never had been. The latter group included an influential minority of political and military leaders, but their non-Academic ideas were not considered respectable here at the Academy.

And Jeremy, walking alone through the gallery, cutting between the long rows of divinities at a location remote from where his tour had broken off, came to an abrupt stop. He had suddenly recognized, portrayed in art, a certain figure that had appeared to him in dreams. In dreams, he had taken the figure for an alternate version of himself.

Probably he hadn't seen this one before because it occupied its own large niche, standing in what amounted to a shrine, a place of honor at least equal to that which had been allotted the God of War.

Jeremy's feet shuffled, drawing him around in front of the statue, to where he could read the name. The carven symbols reached his eyes with almost dull inevitability. It was of course the name he had been expecting to discover. What he felt was not surprise but rather the recognition of something he had known for a long time—almost, since the day of his union with the Intruder—but had been steadfastly refusing to think about.

He stood there for so long that some clerk in passing asked him what was wrong.

15

IN JEREMY'S LEFT eye, the rounded white marble arms and shoulders of Apollo's statue glowed with a subtle patina. Its colors were subtle and rich, and there were a great many of them.

Persistent rumors still had it that the Lord of Light had recently been slain. The latest in the way of secret whispers was that his followers expected him to be reborn, that among the gods rebirth followed death almost inevitably.

The legend carved at the base of Apollo's statue described a god of "distance, death, terror, and awe," "divine distance," "crops and herds," "Alexikakos," Averter of Evil.

Another name for this strange deity was Phoibos, meaning "the Shining One." And yet another was Far-Worker. A very powerful deity and very strange, even in the varied company in which the statue stood.

Jeremy found himself fascinated by the face on this statue. It had much in common with a great number of other representations of Apollo, secondary portraits and carvings in other rooms of the gallery and library.

The best of these portrayals was very like, though not precisely identical with, a certain face that had of late become extremely familiar to Jeremy in dreams. It was almost like an unexpected encounter with a friend: a beardless youth, his otherwise nude body draped in a white cloak, of powerful build and godlike beauty, wearing a bow and a quiver of arrows slung on his back and carrying a small stringed musical instrument in his right hand. The expression on the face, resonating with something inside Jeremy's own head, was one of distant, urbane amusement.

The boy felt an eerie chill. *It is you indeed,* he thought—as if it might now, at last, be really possible for him to converse with the Intruder in his own head.

There came no direct answer, which was a relief.

———

Carlotta said to Jeremy: "The gods know you're not really cut out to be a servant; you're much too bright. When I first saw you in your canoe, plastered with mud, your clothes unspeakable . . . I naturally assumed you'd no formal education at all."

"Formal?"

His questioner considered that, then shook his head. "Sometimes, Jonathan, I think that you're pretending to be stupid. The question is, have you ever been to school? With such skill as you display at reading, in music . . ."

Jeremy admitted vaguely to having had some education, letting his hearers assume it had gone well beyond the reality of half a dozen years in a village school. So, he thought, it would seem natural for him to know a little more about the world.

He had to take continual care not to display too much skill or knowledge in any subject.

What Jeremy saw of the students' lives here, particularly the younger ones in the dormitories, where he would inevitably be sent to live if he became a student, did not make the prospect of his own attendance seem that attractive.

Nor were the benefits supposedly available at the end of the Academic years of schooling particularly attractive.

And what glimpses he had, from outside, of classroom activity aroused no enthusiasm in him either.

No one at the Academy thought it particularly odd that the servants' quarters should be better than the students'. Jeremy just assumed from what he saw and heard that the students were a lower social class. He was surprised that anyone who had his welfare at heart should urge him to become a student.

———

And the lyre was intriguing, too. Jeremy had seen several different versions amid a clutter of diverse musical instruments lying around at various places in the Academy.

He was sure that servants ought not to be playing around with these things. But for the moment, he was unobserved.

Unable to resist the temptation, Jeremy picked one up and attempted to play it. His left arm cradled it automatically, in what seemed the natural and obvious position, while the fingers of his right hand strummed.

Carlotta owned a similar instrument and sometimes played it to amuse her master.

Jeremy Redthorn had never had musical training of any kind. He enjoyed listening to most kinds of music but was at a loss when it came to making any. But now his right hand immediately and instinctively began to pluck out a haunting melody.

The people who happened to hear him play, the first time he picked up a lyre, were not tremendously impressed. Neither were any of them musical. They merely assumed that the odd-looking boy had somewhere learned to play, after a fashion. Well, he clearly had a certain talent for it and would be able to entertain his master of an evening.

Andy Ferrante, visiting Jeremy in his alcove when he had an hour to spare, heard some more strumming and commented that his friend played well, then added: "But then I may be wrong—my mom told me I'm tone-deaf."

That evening in the Scholar's rooms Carlotta, while waiting for her master to come back from a faculty dinner, heard Jeremy play for the first time. Jeremy had picked up the lyre again with some vague idea of practicing, but it was soon evident that he needed no practice. Probably, he thought, he never would. She was so impressed that he thought it would be a good time to raise a subject that had been bothering him.

He put the instrument aside. "Carlotta?"

"Yes?"

"When I first met you, I didn't know what your collar meant. I thought it was only a decoration. What I'm trying to say is that I'm sorry that you . . ."

Her green eyes were quietly fierce. "And now you think that you know what my collar means?" When he started to say something, she interrupted, bending forward to seize him by the arm. "Have you ever been a slave, Jonathan?"

"No. And my real name's not Jonathan."

Her look said that at this stage she didn't give a damn what his name was. "If you have never been a slave, then you still know nothing about my collar and what it means."

"He'd set you free if you asked."

"Ha! Not likely. Not at the risk of offending the sultan."

"If you just . . . ran away, I don't think he'd—"

"You know as little about Scholar Lugard as you do about me. And let me tell you this: if and when I run, I will never be retaken."

"Is that what you plan to do?"

"If it were, do you suppose I'd tell you?"

He looked at her for a moment in silence, then asked: "Why did you once tell me to call you 'Lady'?"

Her voice changed, becoming almost small and meek. "I'm surprised that you remember that."

"I don't remember if I ever actually called you that. But I thought you deserved it."

"Well, I wanted to hear how it sounded. And I . . . wanted to impress you, and I thought I might someday need your help."

"What kind of help?"

Her only answer to that was another question of her own. "Who are you? You've already told me your name isn't really Jonathan."

"It's Jeremy." *Since Thanatos had already seen him and must know who he was, what risk was there in telling a girl that much of the truth?*

"All right. Who are you, Jeremy? Something more than a simple fisherboy from up the river."

"Whoever I am, I still want to be your friend." And he fought down a strong urge to question Carlotta about the ebony and ivory box she'd smuggled away from the ruined temple. Right now the last thing he wanted or needed was involvement with another secret treasure. "I've told you my real name—Jeremy Redthorn. I really did come down the river, to the place where you met me. All my close relatives were poor, were peasants and vinedressers, and all of them are really dead."

"I'm sorry about them. But there's got to be more to you than that. I would dearly like to know your secrets, Jeremy Redthorn. And I still think you have another name than that."

"I don't understand."

"Don't you? Also, I believe you are of higher birth than you pretend. Or, perhaps, even higher than you know."

"I promise you again, my birth was as humble as you can imagine. But . . . lately I've been thinking about such matters. Where you're born makes less difference than most people think."

"You might as well say that wealth and titles make no difference."

His curiosity flared up. "What about your birth?"

"My parents were poor, but they were not slaves." Carlotta seemed to think that summed up all there was to say about them.

It was on the next evening that the lives of everyone in the household were suddenly and drastically changed.

It began with a vague impertinence on the slave girl's part, the kind of thing that Jeremy had known the Scholar to ignore a hundred times before. But not this time. Arnobius put down his pen and swung round in his chair to face Carlotta. "My dear, you and I do not get on as well as we once did. In fact, in recent days it seems to me that we are not getting on at all."

She tried feebly to give him some witty answer.

The Scholar shook his head, not really bothered by the words—he could be, often was, indifferent to those. But Carlotta had come to be objectionable on some deeper level.

He said, unsmiling: "I'm giving you to John. He tells me he's been interested in you for some time. And you and I no longer get on very well."

Carlotta had put out a hand to steady herself on the table but otherwise was standing very still. "My lord. You don't mean it."

"Consider it a fact." He turned back to his desk. "I'll make out the paperwork tomorrow."

"Is there paperwork for me to do, my lord?" She didn't seem to have really grasped it yet.

"No, not in this case. This is one paper I must handle myself." He went on writing.

The silence lasted for several seconds before Carlotta said: "My lord, it isn't funny."

"Not meant to be funny, girl. I said I'm giving you to Lord John. I've put up with this attitude of yours long enough. You can leave your things here until he has a place ready for you to move into. Oh, of course you may keep . . . whatever trinkets I may have given you." His right hand made a dismissive gesture.

The girl stood as if she were paralyzed. John meanwhile sat regarding her happily, hopefully, as if someone had just given him a fine riding camel or hunting dog.

After a single glance at him, Carlotta turned away and ran out of the room.

"She's not going to do anything silly, is she?" John asked the world.

No one replied.

Carlotta did not return for several hours, and when Jeremy saw her again she was looking shaken and thoughtful.

Jeremy now nursed a secret hope that Carlotta might now decide to resume her affair with him, as an act of rebellion against being given away, passed from one man to another like a hunting dog.

Jeremy thought that the Dark Youth hidden in his head was now intent on matters he considered more momentous than seduction. But the Intruder was certainly not averse to attractive women.

When Ferrante heard what had happened to Carlotta, he reacted more strongly than Jeremy might have expected him to, his sympathies with the girl.

Several weeks went by. Jeremy learned to play the role of servant that was expected of him, well enough to get by. It helped a great deal that Arnobius was anything but a demanding master; in fact, he tended sometimes to forget the existence of his servants, and of other people as well.

One way or another, Jeremy had plenty of free time in which to tread the green lawns and the halls of echoing marble.

Free time also in which he might easily have become involved with other girls and women about the place—or with a certain male professor. All of these found themselves fascinated by the odd-looking lad. Had it not been for the threat of Thanatos hanging over his head, Jeremy Redthorn would have enmeshed himself in affairs with the females; but as matters stood, the threat of doom hung heavily enough to crush desire. He could not shake the image of Thanatos, waiting for him, biding his time, playing for some unknown reason a game of cat and mouse.

Other people than Jeremy were beginning now to be seriously worried about Scholar Margaret Chalandon, who had left on an expedition to the Mountain of the Oracle before he arrived at the Academy. Word from her small party was long overdue.

Simmering warfare in the region had of course put a stop to much ordinary activity. But the struggle for power involving the Harbor Lord and other potentates intruded only indirectly on the grounds of the Academy.

Forests visible in the distance, on the high slopes miles inland from the bay and harbor, made patches of changing colors. Autumn in this subtropical latitude was gently making its presence known.

———————

For a servant to spend as much time as Jeremy did in hanging around the Academic centers of the place was rare indeed. Of course, he as a personal assistant had status somewhat above that of the household help and maintenance workers. But he totally lacked Academic rank—several times he had to explain that he was not even a research assistant. Odd looks were directed his way, and his behavior would certainly have been frowned on by the authorities—unless, of course, he should be there legitimately on business for his master. His master was a man whom few cared to annoy. And much of the time the servant's business was indeed genuine; there was always at least one book or scroll that needed borrowing or returning. But Jeremy knew an urge, perhaps unreasonable, to keep on visiting the library. The place fascinated him; there were endless new things to be seen and heard, and with the grafted Eye and Ear and Memory of Apollo to help hire he thought he could understand many of the new things and come tantalizingly close to grasping others. It was hard to resist coming back to search among the books at every opportunity. It was as if the knowledge he gained in this way was truly his, and he had the irrational idea that it might somehow cushion his fall if the dreaded tumble into Apollonian depths ever came.

He could easily imagine Arnobius at some point growing angry or indifferent and discharging him. But as a freeman he couldn't simply be given away. Certainly Jeremy had no wish to spend the rest of his life serving meals and picking up clothes, but it was a notably easier existence than laboring for Uncle Humbert or robbing henhouses up and down the river. It would do quite nicely until he'd figured out how to meet his sworn obligation Sal had trusted him with before she died. What was going to happen to him if and when he managed to do that was something he didn't want to think about.

There had been no lessening of his thirst for vengeance on Sal's killers'—and those who had earlier dealt with his parents in the same way. But Jeremy knew almost nothing about the individuals responsible, except that they were Lord Kalakh's soldiers and servants. And a man couldn't sustain himself on a craving for revenge and nothing else. At least, Jeremy felt sure that he could not.

Guiltily he realized that the details of Sal's appearance were starting to grow blurred in his memory. It was becoming hard to call to mind the exact sound of her voice. But he told himself that the essentials of what she had been would never fade in his remembrance.

He also felt a strong sympathy for Carlotta, but there seemed to be nothing he could do to help.

———

Over the course of weeks Jeremy encountered a number of young students. Though he seldom or never had serious talk with them, he overheard many of their conversations.

Now and then Ferrante came into Jeremy's curtained niche and sat down and talked about his background and his wish that he could be something other than a soldier. Jeremy liked the young man and came near telling him too much. More often, they met and talked somewhere outside the apartment.

Jeremy's acquaintance with Ferrante was growing into friendship. He learned that the young soldier, like the great majority of the population, had been brought up on a farm. Jeremy could readily understand that the other had run away from home at fifteen and enlisted in the Harbor Lord's army to seek adventure.

The military bodyguard was quartered in a small set of rooms one floor up from the Scholar's suite. The sergeant in charge had a room to himself.

———

Jeremy's manners, his knowledge of etiquette, practically nonexistent by Academic standards, would have needed a lot of polishing to make him an acceptable servant—except that the magic of Apollo now and then put appropriate words into his mouth and seemed to make his head bow or boldly lift, his hands move in gestures of suitable humility and occasional eloquence that Jeremy himself did not begin to understand. Grace and authority were there. And his natively keen inborn intelligence soon caught on to the idea that he ought to trust these impulses when they came, not fight them.

Meanwhile Arnobius paid little heed to how any servants behaved, as long as they provided him with certain essentials, at minimal inconvenience on his own part.

———

Now and then Jeremy caught a glimpse, at some distance, of the man he now recognized as the avatar of Thanatos. The man's colleagues were now addressing him as Professor Tamarack. It was indeed the same man who, on leaving the area just after Alexander was killed, had saluted Apollo, in what Jeremy had interpreted as a gesture of scorn, contempt, and threat.

Once, as they gazed at each other across the width of the library, Tamarack, smiling, repeated the gesture in minimal form. In return, Jeremy could only stare. Then he walked slowly away, with the feeling that he was doomed.

16

THERE ARRIVED AN otherwise undistinguished afternoon in which some person or force unknown invaded the Scholar's rooms during the hour or two he was away attending a faculty meeting. Nothing was stolen, but the place was effectively turned inside out. Two of Ferrante's low-ranking comrades in arms who were standing guard duty at the time, one at the door and one below the windows, swore they had neither seen nor heard anything out of the ordinary, nor had any visitors come to call.

During the intrusion the whole apartment, walls, floor, and ceiling, was repainted in strange colors, laid on in irregular stripes and splashes by some unknown and amazingly broad brush. But that was not what drew awed attention. Incredibly, a *window* had actually been moved from one wall to another. The place where the aperture had been was solid wall now, blending seamlessly with the old wall around it.

Arnobius, on coming home, ran his hands unbelievingly over the fabric of the stonework.

The Scholar's face as he contemplated the turmoil was a study in mixed feelings. On the one hand, his routine of study and experiment had been seriously, irreparably, disrupted, his precious papers and artifacts of magic tossed about promiscuously. On the other, the very nature of the disruption argued powerfully for the reality of divine intervention in human affairs.

Intervening to save the unhappy guards from military punishment, he questioned the pair closely and was delighted to establish that powers beyond the merely human had been at work. Not that any other explanation seemed possible. "The very *window*, Jonathan! Look at it! Obviously no merely human . . ." He let the statement fade away in bemused mumbling.

Jeremy looked into the several rooms, not knowing quite what to think. Certainly this was not the work of Death—some other god must have come upon the scene. The nature of the prank strongly suggested the Trickster.

Arnobius's colleagues, gathering at the scene as the word spread, reacted in predictable ways. The antigod faction found ingenious arguments to explain how merely human pranksters could have accomplished the feat after all.

Jeremy's private opinion, fortified by what indications he could gain from the Intruder, was that if the vandalism had any meaning, it must be intended as a warning to the Scholar. But a warning from whom, regarding what?

Meanwhile, Carlotta was once more nowhere to be found.

"I suppose it's possible she's run away." Arnobius sighed—another of life's complications, designed to bedevil him.

―――――

Probing gingerly into his augmented memory, Jeremy could find no instance where any god had ever operated independently of a human host. Therefore, the Trickster must now be associated with some man or woman, even as Apollo had come to dwell with Jeremy. The person who now shared the Trickster's nature could be one of the faculty or a student at the Academy. It might just as likely be one of the lowliest laborers.

The fact that Carlotta had coincidentally disappeared raised Jeremy's suspicions as to who the Trickster's latest avatar might be.

In recent days Jeremy had begun to wonder whether the Intruder, after melting down to get into his head, had then reassumed some solid shape. Sometimes he had the feeling that the invader in the form of a shapeless blob lay hidden only just barely beneath his skin, in the shape of a giant snail or slug, peering out through his left eye, listening through his ear; then again it seemed to him that the thing must have taken up residence right in the center of his brain.

Wherever he imagined it, he shivered.

―――――

The military situation, across that portion of the continent surrounding Lord Victor's domain, which had seemed likely to flare into open war at several widely scattered points, had in recent weeks apparently calmed down a little.

The various potentates who were Lord Victor's chief potential enemies, along with the infamous and already hostile Kalakh, were keeping each other fully occupied, and Lugard wanted to seize the opportunity to make his own bold move. Some of the Academics tried to keep a close watch on the military and political situations as they changed, but others, including Arnobius, did not.

———

Some three weeks after Jeremy's arrival at the Academy, he was told by Arnobius that a final decision had been made on the new expedition. They were going, with others from the Academy faculty, to explore the Mountain of the Oracle. Margaret Chalandon was long overdue from her solo attempt to accomplish the same thing. Arnobius had now been given an additional reason for wanting to go to the Mountain—to help locate Margaret Chalandon.

Arnobius had long been hoping to launch an expedition for that purpose and some time ago, due to the unsettled political situation, had requested that a military escort be provided by the Lord Victor.

Arnobius's father had now at last agreed, and the Scholar found this moderately surprising.

The real reason for this acquiescence came out in a conversation between the two brothers that Jeremy happened to overhear. It was the Lord Victor's wish to carry out a reconnaissance of the Mountain and, if at all possible, boldly seize control of the Oracle and of the heights above. The uneasy balance of forces that had heretofore kept the Oracle open to most people was now spoiled.

Now at last His Lordship had assembled what he considered an adequate military force.

———

A quiet search for Carlotta was under way, though she had not been officially posted as a runaway slave. For one thing, the sultan wouldn't have liked to hear that news. And Arnobius kept muttering that he didn't want to be harsh.

Lord John, the girl's new owner—though so far in name only—muttered once that he looked forward to getting his hands on her. Soon enough his father was going to require him to marry and settle down, and when a wife came on the scene the possession of a handsome and intriguing slave girl would no longer be the simple and uncomplicated joy that it now was—or ought to be. The same would be true of the elder brother. "Maybe that's why you were so willing to give her away."

"I gave her away because she and I had ceased to get on at all well together." Arnobius smiled faintly. "And because I had the idea that you liked her."

"I'm beginning to wonder if I'm ever going to see the gal at all."

Arnobius was looking at a map, spread out on his worktable, when he noticed Jeremy standing nearby. With quiet excitement the Scholar pointed out to his young attendant exactly where the new expedition would be heading and with a finger traced the route.

The Mountain dominated the region for almost a hundred miles in every direction, psychologically if not necessarily in any other way. On the map it loomed over a nexus of roads. Possession of the heights would not guarantee military control, but control would be extremely difficult to sustain without it.

The Scholar, thinking aloud as he often did, mentioned to Jeremy in a casual afterthought that he'd need a replacement for Carlotta as a technical helper. "Do you have any idea who we might . . . but no, how could you possibly?"

Jeremy was glad to see that Andy Ferrante, as a member of the Scholar's permanently assigned bodyguard, would be accompanying the Expedition, too.

In command of the whole military escort was Lord John, who gave some signs of not being entirely happy with his military life. He was out of favor with his father because of lack of imagination in a recent battle.

"If we go up there in the guise of an expedition of philosophers and naturalists, maybe no one will notice that we're also carrying out a reconnaissance in force of the whole Mountain. Or at least as far up as the Cave of the Oracle."

The more the Scholar got into the planning and preparation for the Expedition, the more quietly excited he became. He now thought that there was reason to believe that truth was likely to be found on the peak of the Mountain, high above the Cave of the Oracle.

In what was commonly considered the Oracle, the utterances delivered by some drugged priestess inside the entrance to the Cave, Arnobius had no faith—"though I would very much like to have." He confessed that he had lately been visited by certain dreams that he interpreted as prophecy. Suddenly he had found reason to hope that atop the Mountain, if not at the Oracle itself, he could and would provide him with some credible answers to his eternal questions. "If it can possibly be true that the Mountain was once truly the home of the gods, then perhaps they are really to be found there once more."

Jeremy said, "Possibly only the bad gods, sir." Hades had won the deadly battle there, had seized the ground, and was not likely to have given up his prize.

"I do not fear them."

Then you are even a bigger idiot than I take you for. Jeremy fought down the impulse to say the words aloud.

When the military escort for the Expedition showed up at the Academy, it turned out to be considerably larger, with more offensive capability, than the Academic nominally in command of the Expedition had expected.

The center of the campus had temporarily become a military parade ground, and people goggled and murmured at the display. One of the Academics marveled: "One hundred men ought to be more than enough to defend us against any conceivable gang of bandits. Four hundred seems a ridiculous number."

Ferrante muttered to his friend that half that number of lancers would be a lot more than were needed.

And the Scholar: "Of course, it's absurd. And how are five hundred people going to feed themselves and their cameloids? Forage off the countryside? That'll win us a lot of friends in the area."

He was assured that there wouldn't be five hundred, unless he was determined to bring half the faculty with him. And whatever the number, ample supplies would be provided; there was a sizable pack train.

Arnobius suspected that more was going on here than he had been told about. His father and brother thought he gave so little thought to anything outside of his philosophical speculations that even five hundred men, under his brother's command, would not set him to wondering what was going on.

It was soon obvious even to Private Ferrante, who explained the business to Jeremy in one of their private conversations, that the ostensible armed guard for this expedition had as its real purpose a preemptive military strike, with the purpose of bringing the Mountain and Cave under control of the Lugards. More likely just a scouting effort, as above—but ready to seize the key strategic points if that should appear feasible. Lord Victor and his military sons wanted to seize control of the Oracle, with the idea of at least preventing other warlords from getting its presumed powers under their control.

Meanwhile, a rumor was going about to the effect that Arnobius had secretly had his unhappy slave girl killed.

"Do we make an open announcement, then? We haven't much precedent for setting in motion a search for a runaway slave. And I'm still reluctant to do that."

"Damn it, I never thought of her in those terms."

"Maybe she didn't *want* to be forced to move out, to be told that she now belonged to someone else."

"Maybe I won't *want* to get married, someday, when it comes to that. Matter of duty. Each of us has a role to play, according to his or her position."

In any case, someone had to be chosen to take Carlotta's place as the Scholar's lab assistant and fellow natural philosopher.

When Jeremy thought about it, he soon realized that Carlotta had been deluding herself that someday she might really be granted a lady's rank and even would be considered suitable as a bride for Arnobius. She'd managed to convince herself of that while she and the Scholar were carrying on a long-term affair, casually accepted by his father and the rest of society.

The Intruder's memory, coupled with snatches of conversation overheard, made it possible for Jeremy to see with some clarity the social and political implications. It wasn't really that the Scholar stood to inherit his father's rank and power directly. Something in the way of lands and other wealth, no doubt. Pretty much the same thing applied to his brother, John. Lord Victor's position as ruler of the Harbor Lands was theoretically nonhereditary, but in practice one of his sons was very likely to succeed him, given the approval of the Council in Pangur Ban.

Meanwhile, Lord Victor, while trying to keep his full plans secret, even from his older son (whose lack of interest in them could be assumed), was mobilizing and keeping ready a still larger force, this one a real army, eight or ten thousand strong. These reserves were prepared to march on short notice in the same direction as the supposed scientific expedition.

Lord Victor intended to forestall the seizure of the Mountain, and the psychologically and magically important Oracle that lay inside it, by any of his rival warlords.

17

THREE OTHER ACADEMICS, two men and a woman at the level of advanced students, were chosen to accompany Arnobius and serve as philosophical assistants. Several servants accompanied them. All were practically strangers to Jeremy.

The total number of people in the train was now something more than four hundred. Such a group with all its baggage was going to move relatively slowly, no matter how well mounted they might be and how well led. The journey from the Academy to the Cove of the Oracle, whose entrance lay halfway up the flank of the distant Mountain, might take as much as a month. Some cold-weather clothing was in order, as the end of the journey would take them a mile or more above sea level. Still, it was decided not to use baggage carts; everything necessary would be carried on animals' backs.

The question Arnobius had asked, as to how they were to feed themselves on the march, turned out to have a rational answer and had been routinely managed by Lord Victor's military planners. There were some allies along the way, and the chosen route afforded good grazing for the animals.

Consideration had also been given to the roads, which were known to be fairly good. Someone showed Jeremy His Lordship's file of maps on the region, which was impressive.

———

Preparations for the first leg of the journey were at their height when Ferrante asked Jeremy, "Have you ridden before? Or will you need lessons?"

They were standing in the yard in front of the Academy's extensive stables, where people were engaged in picking out mounts for the Academic delegation.

As Jeremy approached, the nearest cameloid turned its head on its long hairy neck and regarded him gravely from its wide-set eyes. The boy in turn put out a hand and stroked the animal's coarse, thick grayish fur, the hairs in most places a couple of inches long. Dimly he could remember taking a few turns, years ago, aboard his parents' mule, but outside of that he had no experience in riding any animal. Still, he felt an immediate rapport with this one.

What happened to Jeremy now was very similar to what had occurred on his first day at the Academy, when he had approached a pasture. And recalled his earlier clandestine adventures in numerous farmyards.

He had foreseen some such difficulty and was as ready for it as he could be.

Looking round at the other animals in the stableyard, fifteen or twenty of them in all, he saw with an eerie feeling that every one of them had turned its head and was looking steadily at him. The sight was unnerving, all the more so because of the side-to-side jaw motion with which most of the beasts were chewing their cud.

No. Look away from me! The urgent mental command was evidently received, for at once the animals' heads all swung in different directions.

Carefully surveying the nearest of his fellow humans, Jeremy decided that none of them had noticed anything out of the ordinary.

The common procedure for getting aboard the cameloid called for the rider, with a minimum of effort, to climb onto the back of a conveniently kneeling animal. But Jeremy had noted that some of the more youthful and agile folk had a trick of approaching a standing animal at a run, planting the left foot in the appropriate stirrup, and vaulting up into the saddle in one continuous motion.

The saddles were light in weight, made of padded lengths of bamboo, glued and lashed together. Each was in the shape of a shallow cone, with an opening at the apex into which the cameloid's single hump projected. Those of the best quality were custom-made for each animal, while lesser grades came in a series of sizes. The rider's seat, of molded leather, was actually forward of the hump, with the space behind it available for light cargo or for a second passenger, in emergency

Taking two quick steps forward, as he had seen the others do, Jeremy planted his sandaled left foot solidly in a stirrup and then without pausing vaulted right up into the saddle. Once having attained that position, he grabbed and hung onto the reins with both hands, not knowing what to expect next, while the animal's body tilted first sharply forward, then toward the rear, adjusting to the load.

Other people, surprised at his unexpected acrobatic display, were staring at him.

The position felt awkward to the boy at first, and he wasn't sure just how he was supposed to hold the reins, but the powerful animal beneath him was standing very quietly, only quivering slightly as if in anticipation of his commands. Some of the other riders, experienced or not, were having considerably more difficulty.

Mentally he urged his mount forward, requesting a slow pace, and was instantly obeyed. Taking a turn around the stableyard, Jeremy soon discovered that he had only to think of which way he wanted to go and at what speed and the animal instantly obeyed. He couldn't tell whether his wishes were being transmuted by subtle movements of his hands and body or by some means more purely magical.

It was not that his body had automatically acquired a rider's skill— far from it, for he continually felt himself on the verge of toppling out of the saddle. Nor was his mind suddenly filled with expert knowledge. But his mount obeyed his every wish so promptly—leaned the right way to help him keep his seat, stood still as a stone when that was required—that no one watching would doubt that he was experienced.

When the signal was given, Jeremy's cameloid moved out quietly with him in the saddle and seemed to know intuitively which way its master wanted to go and at what speed.

———

When they had dismounted again, at Ferrante's invitation Jeremy picked up and examined one of the lances, a slender, strong, well-balanced shaft about ten feet long. The sharp fire-hardened point and resilient shaft were all one piece of springwood. A curved shield, to protect the user's hand and forearm, surrounded the body of the lance near the butt.

"Looks like it might take some skill to use," he commented, to say something.

"It does. But not as much as the bow."

The lancers were also mounted archers. Other weapons carried by your average lancer included a large knife. Some had shields fashioned from the hides of mutant hornbeasts.

———

The military cameloids used by Lord Victor's cavalry were big, sturdy animals, their humped backs standing taller than a man's head, and powerful enough to carry even a big man at high speed without straining. They could run, pacing, much faster than a man and under an ordinary load maintain a speed of eight to ten miles an hour for hours on end.

Some of the dromedaries wore their own armor, cut from sheets of the inner bark of a special tree, a material that hardened and toughened as it dried.

A mounted party determined to make speed at all costs could cover eighty miles a day on a good road, at least for two or three days, until their mounts became exhausted. Under ordinary conditions they could do forty miles a day.

In one corner of the stables were housed a pair of animals of a species that Jeremy Redthorn's eyes had never seen before—but his grafted memory immediately provided a wealth of information. Horses were rare in this part of the world, as they were generally considered sickly and unreliable. Leaders who wanted to appear especially dashing sometimes rode them, but in general, mules were more widely used.

Some of the more observant onlookers, including a sergeant who had been assigned to keep an eye on how the civilians were doing, marveled to see the odd way in which the young servant held the reins, and before he could contrive to imitate those who were doing it properly, some of them had begun to imitate him. The same with putting the saddle on and taking it off.

Experiments carried out very cautiously confirmed that Jeremy could, if he wished, control with purely mental commands the mounts of others as well as his own.

<hr>

Each night a site was chosen by Lord John and camp was swiftly set up. Jeremy worked with other servants at putting up the few tents shared by the Academics, building the one small fire shared by the civilians and cooking their food. The latter job was made easier for him by the Scholar's usual indifference to what he found on his plate.

The military escort routinely posted sentries and sent out scouts. John was taking no chances, though everyone believed that the force was too strong to be in any real danger of attack.

Then the commander frequently dropped in on his brother and stayed for food and conversation.

On the first night out, the two brothers discussed their respective intentions, alone beside a small campfire, except for Jeremy, who tended the fire and stood by to run errands as required.

The advanced students who had taken over Carlotta's professional duties carried on somehow, as did Arnobius himself.

The last section of the chosen route to the Mountain led over a series of swaying suspension bridges, crossing rivers that roared green and white a dizzying distance below. Each time scouts and skirmishers rode ahead, to make sure that no ambush was being planned in this ideal spot.

And now the same Mountain that Jeremy had marked on his long journey downriver, whose distant mystic glow his left eye had sometimes marked against the clouds, was back in view. Often it hung on the horizon directly ahead of the Expedition; sometimes it swung to right or left with the turning of the trail. Always it glowed in Jeremy's left eye like some exotic jewel.

The cameloids' tough feet were well adapted for maintaining a good grip on rock.

When the Mountain was no more than a few miles away, they reached the last suspension bridge that they were required to cross, spanning a steep-sided gorge nearly a thousand feet deep. The structure of the bridge was slender, not meant for massive loads, and no more than about ten riders could safely occupy it at a time.

Arnobius, who habitually rode in the van, and his immediate escort were first to cross. Besides Jeremy, this party included two junior academics and half a dozen mounted troopers, one of them Ferrante, under command of a sergeant. As soon as they had put the bridge behind them, a trap that had remained concealed until that moment was somehow sprung.

Another handful of riders were on the bridge when the two cordvine cables supporting it abruptly broke at its forward end or were severed as if by some act of magic. Hoarse screams drifted up as men and animals went plunging into the abyss.

The Scholar and his immediate entourage were neatly cut off from the bulk of the escorting force. At a distance of more than a hundred feet, Lord John, surrounded by a mass of lancers, could be seen and heard waving at his brother and shouting something unintelligible.

For a few more moments it was still possible to believe that the failure of the cables had been accidental. Then some instinct drew Jeremy's attention away from the gorge, to the road ahead.

The sergeant asked sharply: "What's that up ahead there? I thought I saw movement."

"One man riding . . . who in hell's that?" Ferrante shaded his eyes and stared some more.

The road heading away from the bridge led into a small wooded canyon, and now there was a stirring in the brush on both sides of the road.

Now a single rider, dressed in what appeared to be an officer's uniform from Lord Victor's army, now appeared upon that road, waving with his arm as if to beckon them forward into the canyon.

The sergeant looked to Arnobius for orders, but the Scholar, still pale from the shock of the bridge's collapse, was paying him no attention.

Meanwhile the unknown rider, when no one immediately complied with his gesture, urged his mount swiftly nearer, then reined it out of its swaying, pacing run, so that the cameloid stopped in place with a manlike groan and a thud of padded feet. The unknown man in officer's garb leaned from his high saddle. "The Lord Victor himself is nearby. He wants you Academic people to come with me—no need for a large escort, Sergeant. Your squad will do."

Arnobius squinted at him. "My father's here? How could he possibly—? What's this all about?"

The unrecognized officer shook his head. "I've just told you all I know. Better hurry." And he turned his cameloid and spurred back the way he'd come.

The Scholar murmured his acknowledgment of the message. And grumbled about his father's interference.

———

Arnobius and his small escort had followed the messenger for no more than forty yards or so before reaching a place well out of sight and sound of John and the bulk of his force. Now they were in a narrowly constricted passage among trees and bush—then the supposed messenger suddenly spurred ahead and disappeared as if by magic among the vegetation.

"I don't like this," said Arnobius unnecessarily. Reining in his restive mount, he appeared for once to have abandoned woolgathering and to be taking a keen interest in his surroundings. As if to himself he muttered, "We should have armed ourselves—"

The bushy treetops that almost overhung the road stirred suddenly and powerfully. From places in them and behind them, concealed hands hurled out a cord-vine net, which fell as swiftly as the rocks that weighted it, engulfing the Scholar's head and arms. The snare also engulfed Ferrante, who happened to be the closest soldier to the man they had been ordered to protect.

In the next moment the ambush was fully sprung. Men in a motley assortment of civilian clothes, bandits by the look of them, some mounted and others on foot, came bursting out of concealment.

Jeremy had a moment in which to note that the face of one of them—he who was shouting orders at all the others—was completely covered by a mask.

The two junior Academics who had been with the Scholar in the vanguard tried to flee and were cut down by flying weapons.

One or two of the small military escort were trying to fight, while the others ran. Jeremy, terrified at the thought of being caught in another slaughter, kicked both heels into his cameloid's sides and added a mental command, urging the animal to full speed. Once more he was fleeing for his life. But this time there was no deep, welcoming river to hide him and carry him away.

18

JEREMY'S MOUNT WENT down with a crash, killed instantly by the simultaneous impact of two missiles striking its head and neck. Sheer good luck kept the rider from breaking any bones as he was flung out of the saddle.

All around him, noise and confusion reigned.

Dominating the ragged front rank of the enemy was a masked male figure, sword in hand, the very one who'd just killed Jeremy's cameloid. Now he was dancing in a frenzy of excitement, agonizing in the manner of an excited leader over whether the operation was going properly.

The irregular weapons and clothing of the enemy declared them bandits rather than soldiers. The sturdy figure in the commanding position at their center definitely looked masculine, despite the fact that its face was the only one concealed by a mask.

Jeremy caught a brief glimpse of Arnobius, the net still entangling his head and arms, struggling madly in the grasp of two brawny bandits, who were pulling him from his saddle while a third held his cameloid's reins. Beside him struggled Ferrante, bellowing curses, sword half-drawn, also hopelessly entangled in the net.

Noise and confusion raged on every side as Jeremy rolled over, looking without success for a place to hide as the dust puffs of more missiles spouted around him. Luckily for him, he'd been able to roll free from the animal's body when it went down.

Whirling around on all fours, he spent two seconds taking in the scene around him. Obviously the attackers had already gained a winning advantage.

Of the half-dozen members of the Scholar's bodyguard who had crossed the gorge with him, all but one had now run away, urging their mounts to dangerous speed along the rim of the gorge. The exception was Ferrante, and the net had made his decision for him.

Luckily uninjured by his fall, Jeremy leaped to his feet and ran for his life. From one moment to the next he kept hoping and expecting that the Intruder might do something to save him, at least give him guidance. But so far he felt himself completely on his own.

Instinctively he headed downhill, first close to the rim of the great gorge, then angling away from it, for the simple reason that running in that direction would be faster. He heard another slung rock whiz past his shoulder, quick as an arrow. Trying to climb down into the gorge, with enemies on the brink above, would be utter madness.

After about fifty yards, he turned his head and without breaking stride snapped a look back over his shoulder. It showed him exactly what he had hoped not to see: the masked man, a stocky but extremely energetic fellow, had leaped into the saddle and was urging his mount after Jeremy in hot pursuit. Jeremy with a quick mental command brought the cameloid to a stop, so suddenly that the animal went down, rolling over. Unfortunately, the rider leaped catlike from the saddle and landed unhurt. In another moment the masked man had regained his feet and resumed the chase with his sword drawn.

The idea crossed Jeremy's mind of getting his enemy's cameloid to run his enemy down. He flashed a command broadcast, and the animal seemed to be trying to obey, but it had been injured in its fall and could not even regain its feet.

All the cameloids in sight on the near side of the gorge, including those belonging to the bandits, were thrown into a mad panic. The usually dependable animals bolted to freedom or crippled themselves in falls, with one or two actually plunging over the brink and into the depths of the gorge. Jeremy was certainly not going to try to call the survivors back.

Having used up his animal resources and noting that the effect upon the enemy had not been nearly what he hoped for, Jeremy turned his back on the ambushers and ran.

"Stop! Stop, I command it!" The shouted order rang out imperiously, but Jeremy's feet did not even slow.

When the man spoke, Jeremy had an impression that his voice was familiar.

The masked pursuer, in his frantic energy, gave the impression of being possessed by some god or by a demon.

After half a minute of desperate flight, Jeremy found himself on one side of a tree, engaged in a dodging contest with his pursuer, who was on the other.

For a few moments the pair played death tag with a tree trunk in between. *Slash* and the other's wicked scimitar buried half its blade width in the trunk, while Jeremy danced back untouched. Trouble was, he had no weapon to slash back with, so as his next best choice he turned and ran again. Presently he was brought to bay, standing on a rock, at his back a higher rock, impossible to climb.

The bandit, standing just below him, was gasping, too, but found the breath to speak in connected words. "Who am I talking to?" His voice was rich with what seemed a mockery of courtesy.

"Guess." The boy had all he could do to get out the single word between gasping breaths.

"If you won't say, we'll find out. . . ." A pause for heaving lungs. "So . . . she gave you something to carry to Alexander? Too bad you didn't deliver. But I suppose you were holding out for a better price. Let's have a look at it, my friend."

"I don't know . . . what you're talking about."

"Don't you? Maybe that's possible . . . but no. I suppose you haven't got it on you now?" The masked man shifted his weight abruptly to his right foot, then quickly back to his left.

"No." Even as Jeremy reacted to each feint, he could feel a kind of relief of at last finding someone who seemed to understand his situation—even if the understanding one was going to kill him.

"You lie!" Death snarled at him.

And somehow as he spoke the marauder had moved a half-step closer, so that it seemed that the chase was truly over. The fierce-looking blade came up menacing. Its sharp point jabbed at Jeremy's ribs, hard enough that he felt a trickle of blood inside his shirt. "Maybe I'll have to peel a chunk out of your skull to take a look. But no, you can't be wearing it, so . . . so save yourself a lot of pain and tell me where it is."

But I am wearing it . . . yes, inside my skull. Even in the midst of fear and anger it was possible to see the masked man's difficulty. If he did open Jeremy's skull and failed to find there what he was looking for, there would be no hope of extracting any further information from the victim. No doubt it was his contemplation of this problem that made the swordsman dance a step or two in sheer frustration.

Taking advantage of a moment's inattention on the part of his foe and feeling himself urged on by his silent partner, Jeremy broke desperately out of the position in which he had been apparently cornered. He jumped squarely at his enemy, striking him in the chest with both booted feet and knocking him down. The impact jolted from the swordsman what sounded surprisingly like a cry of terror, but when the masked one bounced up again a moment later he still had a firm grip on his sword, and Jeremy, who had gone sprawling in the other direction, could do nothing but take to his heels again.

Not only did Jeremy lack any skill or experience in fighting, but he had never carried weapons and had none with him now, except for Sal's practical knife. He'd carefully sharpened it and scoured away the rust, then put it on again when starting on the Expedition.

So far, Jeremy had made no attempt to draw his small knife. Even in an expert's hand, Sal's little blade would have been no match for the masked one's sword.

In the days of his childhood Jeremy had been considered fleet of foot. Already he had put considerable distance between himself and the site of the ambush, but shaking off the man who wore the mask was proving quite impossible. The landscape offered little in the way of hiding places, consisting as it did of scattered patches of trees and undergrowth, growing amid a jumble of small hills and ravines. With the feeling that he himself was now moving at superhuman speed, the boy darted in and out among the trees and took great risks bounding down a slope of rocks and gravel. But his pursuer stuck to him with more than human tenacity.

Once the boy fell, tearing one leg of his trousers and scraping his left knee and hip bloody. But scarcely was he down when he had bounded up again, in his terror hardly aware of pain or damage.

Every time Jeremy risked a glance back over his shoulder, the grinning mask, pounding feet, and waving blade all loomed closer by a stride or two. The gasping cries the bandit uttered were all the more terrifying for being incoherent.

Behind the pair engaged in the desperate partnership of the chase, the sounds of murder and mayhem coming from the scene of the ambush faded with increasing distance. But in both of Jeremy's ears the heavy thud of his pursuer's bounding feet grew ominously ever louder and louder.

The boy strained legs and lungs to increase his speed, but it did no good. Then, just as the bandit was about to catch up, he, too, stumbled and fell. Judging by the savagery of the oaths he ripped out, he must have skinned himself, too. But judging from the speed with which he bounded up again, he could not have been seriously hurt. Grimacing horribly and still cursing hoarsely, thereby demonstrating a disheartening surplus of lung capacity, he came on again.

His quarry sprang away, avoiding another murderous sword slash by half a step.

"Curse you! You couldn't possibly keep up such speed if you weren't wearing it after all." Something in that conclusion seemed to give the man pause. But after another breath he again sprang forward, almost foaming at the mouth. "I'll have to peel your head!" And he let out a cry half fear, half wordless longing.

Ever since the moment when the bandits had come charging, leaping, vaulting, dropping out of ambush, Jeremy had wordlessly and almost continuously pleaded for help from the alien mystery that had come to dwell in his own head. But Jeremy's communication with the Intruder had never been open and direct, and he could achieve nothing of the kind now. At the moment, his alien partner seemed incongruously asleep. Only too clearly the boy remembered that Sal had never been helped by this burden either—at least not enough to keep the furies from killing her.

Breath sawing in his lungs, he pounded on. Directly ahead of him, a steep and almost barren hillside loomed, with no obvious way to get around it. He must decide whether to turn right or left—

And now, just as Jeremy had abandoned any hope of aid from the Intruder, there came evidence that his silent partner was not entirely inactive after all. Maybe his onboard god fragment had been busy making plans or just staying out of Jeremy's way until the proper opportunity arose. Because now the boy's left eye, which ever since the ambush had been refusing to provide him with guidance of any kind, suddenly displayed a tiny spot of crystalline brightness, almost dazzling, lodged in a gravel bank just ahead. The spark of brightness was high up toward the top of the bank, where the hillside steepened into a cliff, just below the place where it grew into an overhang impossible to climb.

So, he had to reach that spot at all costs, before a sword thrust came to kill or cripple him from behind.

And still the pursuer himself had breath enough to yell. "Give me your Face—I mean the magic thing the woman gave you, you bloody idiot—and I will let you live!"

Oh no. What you told me before was true—you'll have to peel my head. Jeremy wasted no breath in trying to reply but only launched himself at the bank and scrambled up.

In desperation, exhausting his last reserves of wind and energy, seeking something, *anything,* to use in self-defense, like a rock small enough to throw and big enough to kill, Jeremy sped up the hill as fast as he could go, a final lunge carrying him to within an arm's length of the dazzling spot.

Grabbing swiftly with his right hand, he scooped up the radiant little nugget, along with a small handful of surrounding gravel. Spinning awkwardly on the steep slope, he spent his last strength in a great swing of his arm, hurling his fistful of pebbles at his enemy, who was now but little more than an arm's length away.

The impact was amazing, as successful a stroke as he'd hoped for but had scarcely dared to expect. It was as if Jeremy had clubbed the masked man with a heavy weapon, stopping him in his tracks. His sword clattered to the ground, and in the next moment he clapped both hands to his masked face, uttered a choked cry, and toppled backward. The impact of his heavy body and its hardware on the steep hillside provoked a substantial avalanche. Bouncing and sliding down amid a hundred-weight or two of gravel, Jeremy's fallen foe came to a stop at the very bottom. There he lay without moving, both brawny arms outflung. The cheap mask had come partly loose from his upturned face, enough to show a spiderweb of welling blood. Meanwhile the bandit's helmet and sword had come rolling and sliding down the slope to join their owner.

Standing ten yards or so above his fallen foe, with the gravelly slope slowly giving way under his weight, Jeremy swayed on trembling legs, blood roaring in his ears, on the verge of fainting from the exertion and terror of the pursuit. But it was over now. That fall had been too genuine to allow for any suspicion of trickery.

Death's claim on him having been denied for the moment, Jeremy's quivering legs allowed themselves to collapse under him. His sitting automatically launched his own minor landslide. He was borne toward the bottom only a little more slowly than his enemy had gone.

Gradually he ceased to gasp, to hear the thudding of his pulse, as it slowed down to normal. Looking keenly about him amid settling dust, he made sure that he and his assailant still had the immediate vicinity to themselves. Now Jeremy saw with dull surprise that the face beneath the mask was . . . No, it was really no surprise at all. But he'd have to get closer to be sure.

Near the bottom Jeremy's private avalanche slowed to a trickle, and the boy regained his feet to walk the last few yards, to stand over the body of the first man he'd ever killed—who'd come within an inch of killing him.

Bending for a closer look, Jerry saw that he man had been hit in the right eye with some sharp-pointed object, for bright blood was trickling out in thin streams over the dead face.

Jeremy reached out to pull the cheap mask away to reveal the features of Scholar Tamarack. His left eye limned them in a peculiar, sickly glow.

And then he recoiled, not understanding. The human countenance revealed was undergoing a rapid succession of changes.

For a moment or two that face was no more than a grinning skull.

But it, too, was recognizable; he'd seen the same countenance, or something very like it, on a certain statue. And it had grinned at him, beneath a jaunty salute, when he had raised his eyes from the body of the murdered Professor Alexander.

Thanatos. Jeremy stood staring stupidly. His astonishment was not that Thanatos/Tamarack should be here, but that Death should be dead. It seemed that, with a pebble hurled in desperation, he'd somehow accomplished a miraculous victory. For a moment a mad suggestion flared: Did that mean that no one could ever die again? . . . but that was ridiculous, the craziest idea that'd ever crossed his mind.

And now, before Jeremy's half-believing eyes, the fallen body also was contorting, even changing its size and shape to some degree. When it settled into final death, it lay shrunken inside clothing that had become somewhat too large. It was only the corpse of some middle-aged Academic, almost anonymously ordinary. The face was still Tamarack's, or very nearly, but Jeremy could not remember ever laying eyes on this man before.

Slowly the boy straightened. He glanced briefly at the cheap, mundane mask he was still holding—it was quite an ordinary thing, and he tossed it aside.

The meaning, the implications, of what had just happened were beyond his ability to calculate.

In his left eye's gaze, the fatal missile was still marked by the luminous halo that had originally drawn Jerry's attention when its source lay embedded in the gravel bank. The boy's right eye told him meanwhile that he was looking at nothing but a dull black, oddly pointed pebble.

Objectively, the weapon he had wielded with such fatal skill and force was less than two inches long, a dark flake of razor-thin obsidian—an ancient arrowhead, Jeremy realized. It had struck point-first—more than luck had to be involved in that—and with all the force of Jeremy's lean body behind it.

The bandit—whether he should be truly called Thanatos or Scholar Tamarack—was quite dead, no longer even twitching. His head lay at an odd angle, and Jeremy supposed his neck might well be broken, after a fall like that. During the past half-year he'd seen enough dead folk to have no doubts about this one.

And now came shattering revelation, though as soon as Jeremy saw it he realized it ought not to have been a surprise at all. With a faint hissing and crackling sound, a Face fragment, superficially much like Jeremy's in appearance, was coming out of the bandit's head.

The boy watched with a sick fascination as the small translucent shape came first oozing and then popping out. Jeremy watched intently, holding his breath. What he had momentarily thought was the dead man's own proper skull, inexplicably starting to show through, now revealed itself as a portion of a Face fragment. The countenance of which this fragment was a part was very different from Apollo's Face—in fact, it was the bone bare countenance of Death. A mere translucent cheekbone filled with rippling light, a lipless grin, a pair of holes where nostrils might have fitted.

It seemed that it was Apollo who reached out a hand, a powerful right hand that had once been only Jeremy's, and for the second time peeled a masklike thing away from the dead face. Holding it up, Jeremy saw how like his own morsel of divinity it was—one-eyed, one-eared, the same slightly jagged edges, its translucent thickness marked by a mysterious inner current.

The touch of it brought no pleasure to the fingers. *I will not put on the Mask of Death.* The Lord of Light and Jeremy Redthorn both rebelled against the very thought—and if any final assurance were needed, the Intruder's memory supplied it. No human could ever be avatar of more than one god.

Over the past year Jeremy had become only too familiar with the sight of death—but this was the first time he had killed anyone. So far the realization carried little emotional impact. The thought now crossed his mind, bringing little emotional content with it, that this would probably not be the last fellow human he ever killed.

If the being whose life he had just snuffed out was really a fellow human at all. But then he realized it must be so—only another human, wearing a fragment of another Face.

There was a calculating quality in the way he noted that bit of information, distinctly alien to Jeremy's usual modes of thought. He took it as evidence that he was now seeing some things from the viewpoint of the alien dweller inside his skull.

We killed him with an arrowhead. But that—he thought—was only Jeremy Redthorn's voice.

He also thought that, if he tried, he could imagine pretty well what the Intruder might be, ought to be, saying to him now:

Ah, if only I/we had had the Silver Bow and proper Arrows! Then there would have been none of this pusillanimous running away, only to turn and strike out desperately when cornered.

An ordinary bow and arrow, or even an arrow alone, would have made an enormous difference to an avatar of the Far-Slayer, thought Jeremy with sudden insight. *Had there been time, I might have pulled a useful shaft from the body of one of the fallen soldiers back at the ambush site. . . .*

Meanwhile, Jeremy didn't know what to do with the object he had almost unwillingly picked up, the thing that had somehow turned a middle-aged Academic into the God of Death. If the feelings that rose up in him were any clue, Apollo regarded it with repugnance. Jeremy considered trying to destroy it on the spot, by hacking at it with his newly captured sword, but Apollo gently and voicelessly let him know that he would be wasting his efforts.

"All right, all right! What then? What do we do with it?"

Even as he tried to relax and wait for guidance, his right arm drew back and hurled the thing away. It went into a handy stream, the almost transparent object vanishing as soon as it fell below the surface. The flow of water was going to wash it away, somewhere, until . . . Suddenly the boy was reluctant to dig into memory for the knowledge of what would most likely happen next.

Jeremy, still surprised by what his own right arm had done, throwing the Face of Death into a stream, had to assume that the Intruder knew what he was doing. Dipping hastily into acquired memory, the boy uncovered certain facts concerning running water. The fact that the stream where he had hurled the Face of Death, or the larger stream it emptied into, soon vanished underground made it all the better a hiding place. Now the fragment would be hard for even a god to find.

Only when his hand went unconsciously to the empty belt sheath did the boy fully realize that he had lost Sal's knife. Now clearly he remembered the feel of the impact when it had been knocked out of his hand, and he felt the deprivation keenly, on an emotional as well as a practical level.

With some vague idea of compensating himself for the loss, Jeremy picked up the fallen bandit's sword, before turning his back on him. The weapon was finely made, but it sat in his hand much more awkwardly than had the stone arrowhead. The thought that he should take belt and scabbard to accompany the blade and make it easier to carry never crossed the boy's mind. He had no idea of how to use a sword, beyond the obvious basic one of cutting or thrusting at the enemy. The previous owner, in his one-eyed contemplation of the sky, offered him no guidance. Nor did the silent partner lodged in Jeremy's own head have anything to say on the matter; still, being able to swing a dangerous blade at the end of his right arm made the boy feel minimally more secure.

For a long moment he stood listening, sweeping the trees and hillocks before him with his own gaze and the Intruder's. The sword he had just taken up felt strange and clumsy in his hand. He could hear no sounds of combat. He supposed he might have run half a mile trying to get away from the masked man.

It seemed he had indeed escaped this latest batch of enemies; no other pursuers were in sight. Deciding there was no point in standing around waiting for them, he chose a direction, again heading generally downhill, and started moving. The idea of trying to find the place where he had lost Sal's knife and then recover it crossed his mind, but he pushed it aside as impractical.

The thing to do now, Jeremy assured himself, was get back as fast as he could walk, or run, to Lord John and his four hundred men and then guide them in hunting down the damned bandits and see if they had taken Arnobius and the others hostage instead of killing them.

Lord John and the main body of lancers must have seen what had happened, and riders must be speeding even now back to Lord Victor with word of the disaster. As soon as John could get his four hundred men on the right side of the river gorge, they would all be on the trail of the ambushers.

━━━━━━

And now, as Jeremy was trying to decide what to do next, a sickeningly familiar ring of bandits came pouring out from behind trees and underbrush, with their weapons in hand, to surround him.

And now again, just when Jeremy thought he most desperately needed whatever strength and cunning the Intruder might contribute, he was being given no help at all.

19

WHEN HADES LEARNED *of the death of his henchman Thanatos, at the hands of Apollo reborn, the first concern of the Lord of the Underworld was for the Face fragment that the right hand of Jeremy Redthorn had thrown into a stream.*

The God of the Underworld had a fair idea of where a Face fragment thrown into that stream was likely to reappear, and his helpers were soon dispatched to search for it. The Face of Death was only of secondary power, and Hades felt no need to concern himself as to which of them might put it on.

Meanwhile, Hades pondered who this new avatar of his great enemy might be—not one of the so-called worthy ones of the Sun God's cult of worshipers; they were all being kept under observation.

No, the answer appeared to be that this was a mere lad, chosen accidentally by Fate—

Or possibly the choice of Apollo himself?

Now the bandits, as they marched Jeremy back to the site of the ambush, were grumbling and swearing because their leader and employer seemed to have deserted them. They were upset, but at the same time their behavior conveyed a strong undercurrent of relief.

"If I'm going to take orders from someone, I want him to be strong. But not crazy." It seemed that Tamarack had never revealed to these followers, or had never succeeded in convincing them, that he was indeed the God of Death.

This time, when a dozen or so bandits came at Jeremy in a group, casually surrounding him, calling him sharply to throw down his weapon—laughing at the way he was holding his borrowed sword—it was plain to him that trying to fight was useless.

One of them grabbed up the weapon as soon as he had cast it down. "Where'd ye get this?"

Even before Jeremy's answer left his mouth, he could feel, upwelling in him, the sense that something was about to happen, an event after which his world would never be quite the same. And then he surprised himself by what he said, the words coming out in a flat, cold tone of challenge: "I met a man back there who paid a good price for me to take it off his hands."

He saw eyebrows rising on the faces in front of him, expressions changing. What was going to happen now had a whole lot to do with Jeremy's silent partner, though at the moment the Intruder was sending no gem sparkles to brighten Jeremy's left eye's field of vision. And at the same time sharp in Jeremy's memory was the image of Sal lying dead. She'd been killed with terrifying ease, by enemies no more formidable than these folk were, and the Face shard of Apollo had given her no help. Of course Sal hadn't been carrying it inside her head.

But in a moment the bandits' laughter burst. It was plain that whatever had happened to Professor Tamarack wasn't going to lose them any sleep.

The moment of tension among the bandits had passed. This time the Intruder's challenge was going to be ignored, rather than accepted.

The men (there were no women among them) who now surrounded Jeremy and tied his hands behind him treated him almost tenderly; the arguments he had started to practice, to the effect that he was someone worth ransoming, proved to be unnecessary. With his hands bound, they brought him back to a place near the site of the original ambush, where the main band of bandits were now gathered with their other prisoners.

"A servant of the Lugard family! Likely they'll pay something to get *him* back."

As soon as they reassured Jeremy that he was in no immediate danger, the interior upwelling of—what was it? power?—whatever it had been receded, so the boy once again knew himself to be no more than a tired and frightened stripling. He knew that if they were to continue their questioning, the next answer he gave them was going to be a very meek and timid one.

The boy felt a greater relief than he would have expected to see that Andy Ferrante had survived the ambush without serious injury, as had Arnobius. Ferrante was plainly steaming; had his hands been free, he would probably have done something to get himself killed. His face had some new bruises, and he had a crazy look about him. Evidently everyone else in the party was dead or had escaped.

Both of Jeremy's fellow prisoners were glad to see him alive, sorry that he had not got away. Soon they were all three seated together, all with their wrists tied behind them.

Arnobius informed the latest arrival that the bandits had evidently known all along that he was Lord Victor's son. "I think we're safe for the moment, Jonathan. They know who I am, and they plan on holding us all for ransom. My father will pay—since he really has no choice." Arnobius was taking care to sound confident on that point, on the theory that at least one of the bandits must be listening. "He'll negotiate some reasonable amount. What I wonder is *how* did they know me so quickly? Were they expecting me here?"

Maybe it wasn't you they were really looking for, Scholar. But it was unlikely to occur to Arnobius that anyone in the human world could consider him unimportant.

Jeremy, having recognized Professor Tamarack in the pursuer he'd just left dead at the foot of the gravel bank, now had a good idea of how the ambush had been arranged. But just now he was reluctant to discuss it in public with Arnobius.

Intruder, I badly need your help. But he uttered the silent plea with no real hope that it would be answered.

The man who was gradually assuming authority among the bandits, taking over for the absent Death, made no answer to the Scholar's remark. He and his people continued to treat Arnobius and his companions reasonably well, assuming that all of them would be worth a fairly good price in the hostage market.

"With perfect hindsight one can see that it was foolish for us to come this far from home without a *sizable escort*," said the Scholar to Jeremy, putting a slight emphasis on the last words. His eyes glared at his servant, trying to convey a message. Jeremy had no trouble in grasping the point: it was still possible to hope that the bandits didn't know how strong their full escort had been, that four hundred of Lord Victor's cavalry were quite likely only a mile or two away—possible, if not exactly a good bet. But Jeremy was surprised. Arnobius, of all people, was suddenly thinking in practical, worldly terms!

"Yes, my lord," said Jeremy, nodding to assure the other that he had grasped the point. The scrapes he'd got from falling during the chase were hurting.

He wanted also to convey the fact that he'd recognized the deceased bandit leader. Though it might be just as well not to try to tell Arnobius that his fellow Academic had also been Thanatos the god, the personification of Death. Knowing the Scholar, that would probably do no good at all. Anyway, Jeremy decided that would have to wait until he and Arnobius could talk without the bandits overhearing them.

The bandits were growing impatient, waiting for the man who'd hired them and given them a plan to follow. "Where's the Mad One?"

Jeremy thought that a likely name for them to give an Academician—though not one they would have been likely to call Thanatos to his face.

A tall man wearing one earring gestured toward Jeremy. "Last I saw of him, he was running after this one."

"Why should we care what he's doing?"

"Because he's paid us and he's going to pay us more."

"Hey, wasn't that the Mad One's sword the kid was waving?"

"Yes, idiot, that's what we've been talking about." The eyes of the last speaker came around and fixed on Jeremy; they did not seem unkind. "You'll lead us to where you last saw the gentleman, won't you, lad?"

All boldness had retreated, somewhere deep inside. Jeremy nodded, swallowed. "Sure."

The bandits eventually located the body of their missing leader. His death dashed whatever hopes they entertained of eventually collecting all the pay the man had promised them when his objective had been achieved.

On finding the fallen man's dead body, the band seemed neither much surprised nor particularly grieved. One or two of them declared they couldn't recognize it—refused to believe this worn- and sedentary-looking corpse was the terrible figure who, their attitude implied, had held them all in awe. According to them, even its physical size was notably diminished.

The body did appear to be wearing their leader's clothes, which gave them cause to wonder.

"He changed clothes with this one? Makes no sense. There's got to be magic in it somewhere."

"If this ain't the Mad One, then the Mad One's likely coming back." The speaker concluded with a nervous glance over his shoulder.

"Well, and if it's him, how did he come to this? Whatever killed him hit him in the eye."

Someone finally suggested that Jeremy might be responsible.

He tried a simplified version of the truth. "I threw a rock at him. He was going to . . ."

"Yes, a rock indeed." The arrowhead was still available. There was of course no sign of any shaft to go with it. "Well, one lucky throw."

Presently they gave up, though one or two continued from time to time to throw wary, wondering glances at Jeremy. The consensus of opinion among the band was coming around to the view that they should get on with their business in their own way, and if they were lucky maybe the one they feared and worried about wouldn't come back at all.

Now that they had the son of the Harbor Lord, they seemed a little vague as to what they were going to do with him. The scheme to collect ransom, Jeremy gathered, was still in effect, but the details were hazy and perhaps growing hazier.

———

At dusk, the bandits built a small fire, cooked and ate some food, belatedly and grudgingly fed their prisoners, and tied them up for the night.

Privately Jeremy tried to understand how the expedition had been ambushed and why his own strange new powers had failed to prevent it or at least give warning. The Intruder either had been willing for it to happen or hadn't been able to do anything about it.

The Scholar was even more angrily eager for some explanation.

Obviously Tamarack, the renegade Academic, had known where to intercept the party and had help, whether magical or merely technical, in setting up the ambush. But when the trap was sprung, he'd not concentrated his attention on Arnobius, who was presumably its object. No, the one he'd never taken his eyes off, had chased like a madman, was

Jeremy. Here, far from the Academy and its crowds of onlookers, Death had had a very different objective. . . .

Whenever the group stopped for a rest or to make camp for the night, Jeremy had a chance to discuss their situation with the Scholar and Ferrante. The bandits let them talk together, assuming that each would be thinking up the strongest possible arguments as to why he should be ransomed at any cost.

Actually, not much of the prisoners' time was spent on that. In fretful whispers they all kept worrying at the same question. Someone at least suggested that magic must have been involved in their betrayal to Lord Victor's enemies.

Now there was nothing for the three survivors to do but submit to captivity and allow themselves to be dragged forward under the drastically changed circumstances.

Arnobius went through the hours grim-faced and for once seemed fully aware of his immediate surroundings.

Now the gang, new leadership having taken over and modified its goals, carried its prisoners off in the opposite direction from the Mountain.

The prisoners exchanged glances but said nothing. They were now heading in the opposite direction from where they believed John and his lancers to be.

The band stayed on small trails, avoiding the larger roads, which in this region all converged upon the Oracle. On those highways parties traveling with armed escorts were fairly common. Instead the bandits preferred to look for an isolated farmhouse to attack. Next best would be a small, poorly defended village. Jeremy failed to see how this harmonized with their primary goal of obtaining ransom for Lord Victor's son. But then he had already seen and heard enough of the gang's behavior to realize that consistency was not to be expected.

Even with his left ear it was difficult to hear the leaders' words as they argued among themselves, but what he did pick up suggested they were experiencing some difficulty in reaching a consensus.

Pressing on along the road, being dragged as a bound prisoner, Jerry had the Mountain now and then in sight, when the road curved, even though they were heading away from it. It even began to dominate the skyline, but its top was still obscured, even from the piercing gaze of his left eye, by natural clouds or subtler magical effects.

The earlier loss of all their cameloids seemed to make little difference to the bandits' plans. Everyone was walking, in keeping with their pose as pilgrims. They coughed and blinked in clouds of dust until a shower came along to settle it.

Anyway, Jeremy had the hopeful feeling that the intrusive power inside his head was slowly, fitfully mobilizing itself in some new way. At least he could hope that something of the kind was going on. He wondered if mortal danger had wrought a permanent change in the nature of his relationship with the Intruder. Since showing him the sparkling arrowhead, it had at least been fully awake and aware that the body it inhabited faced grave peril. But he kept coming back to the fact that it had not saved Sal's life for her.

The longer the partnership went on, the more trouble Jeremy had thinking of the Intruder as really another *person* in his head. Maybe because the Intruder never talked to him in plain words. And the idea that he, the child of poor villagers, was now sharing his humble skull space with a god—least of all any of the truly great divinities, like Apollo—was very hard to swallow. The chilling thought came that his partner, or invader, acted more like the demons of legend were supposed to act, half-blind and fitful. . . . That thought was not endurable, and Jeremy put it from him.

It was no demon that had killed the most recent avatar of Thanatos. Or at least had killed the man who had been the servant of the real god, as he, Jeremy, had become the servant of . . .

Divinity or not, familiarity was beginning to breed contempt. If only he could *talk* to the damned thing, person, or god—or he, or it, could say something, in plain words, to Jeremy—whether the Intruder could not converse or would not, evidently that was not to be.

Sometimes, especially just before drifting off to sleep or when waking up, Jeremy seemed to catch a glimpse, out of the corner of his left eye, of the Dark Youth of his dreams standing or sitting near him. When he tried to look directly at the figure, it invariably disappeared.

———

For a while, being herded forward with his fellow prisoners, walking at a brisk pace in open sunlight, Jeremy tried to devise a plan of escape that would take advantage of his ability to sunburn himself free of ropes. But that would take some time, and someone would be sure to notice what he was doing.

He decided he had better wait for guidance. Experience suggested that the Intruder would provide what help was absolutely necessary. But only when he was good and ready.

20

HAVING TURNED RESOLUTELY in the opposite direction from where their captives had hoped to go, the bandits brought their little knot of prisoners to a halt at a place where the Mountain, looming at a distance of ten miles or so, presented them with a fine view when they turned back to look at it.

Only a quarter of a mile away, reported the scouts sent out by the new bandit leader, lay what one of their scouts reported as the Honey-makers' village.

From the recesses of Jeremy's natural memory drifted a vague recollection that Sal had once mentioned a village of that name, wondering if she had reached it. But Apollo's fund of information assured him that there were many such, scattered around the world.

What exactly had Sal's words been, on that occasion? *Bees would be a help; cattle would be a help.* Yes, she had said that, or something very like it. But then of course she'd been delirious much of the time.

Observing the village at hand from a little distance above it on a wooded hillside, where he had been herded together with his fellow prisoners, Jeremy saw that it was two or three times the size of the settlement where Uncle Humbert and Aunt Lynn had grown their grapes—and no doubt still did, if they yet lived. Here the houses seemed more sturdily built and were in a different style.

Jeremy could see a few of the villagers, moving about, and his augmented vision strongly hinted to him that there was something special about these people. There was a moment when he thought he could almost see the ghostly figure of the Dark Youth, walking among them in the swirling white cape that he wore for business. Almost, but not quite.

The majority of the bandits now pulled out pilgrim costumes, pale cloaks and habits, which they slid on over their ordinary clothes and their sheathed weapons.

The three prisoners were left, closely guarded by a couple of their nastier-looking captors, outside the town until the attack had succeeded. They were warned to make no outcry. "Unless you want to go back to Lord Victor's service with a few parts missing."

Yet another village to be overrun, to die under the impact of a surprise attack by the forces of evil. The boy began to feel ill in anticipation of what was going to happen to these innocent people. Judging from what he could see of them, small figures moving in the distance, they were common-enough folk, a natural mixture of young and old. He could hear someone in the village calling in a loud voice, speaking a dialect quite similar to that with which Jeremy had grown up.

And now, once more, Jeremy's left-eye vision, which he had begun to fear had deserted him, was definitely becoming active. When he looked at these villagers from a distance, it seemed to him that each of them sprouted a thick growth of almost invisible quills, like some kind of magical porcupines. He understood that this was only symbolic, but what did it mean? He could only assume it to be some kind of warning. Maybe these people could not be attacked with impunity. Well, that was fine with him. He wasn't going to try to pass the warning on.

And his god eye also reported that something in the center of town, other than its people, was definitely glowing, with a diffuse but steady radiance. The source of this light, whatever it might be, was still out of Jeremy's sight, hidden from his view behind a leafy mass of shade trees, but its presence was undeniable.

And the more Jeremy looked at these simple folk, the stronger grew the feeling that they were, or ought to be, familiar old friends or helpers . . . who had played a role in his life, somewhere, a long time back, though he couldn't recall exactly how or when or where. Damn it, he *knew* them somehow. . . .

Before he had time to consider the matter at any length, the attack was under way. The watchers on the hill could hear the screams of sudden terror, and they saw how a couple of villagers were cut down in cold blood.

About half the population, crying their alarm, fled the little settlement, with a bandit or two shooting a few desultory arrows after them; and the other half were not so lucky. Half a dozen girls and young women among them were rounded up; if the rest were content to sit or stand by and watch the despoiling of their daughters and their property, it seemed they would not be molested much.

A few minutes later, being prodded and herded with his fellow captives down from the hill and into the little village square, Jeremy was able to get a direct look at the source of the strange glow. It centered on the statue at the center of the crude shrine, the figure of a nude man holding what might have been a lyre under its left arm. With a sense of grim inevitability Jeremy recognized the unskillful carving as intended to represent Apollo.

━━━━━━━━━━

Now the program of serious terror got under way.

The marauders swaggered in, cowed anyone who looked at them, kicked open the few doors that were slammed at their approach, and began disarming men—though none of these village men were bearing real weapons. Still several were knocked down, cowed, disabled.

One or two brave boys and angry women met similar fates. Dogs that barked and challenged were ruthlessly cut down.

The bandits seemed unconcerned about the villagers who had managed to hide or run away—it was probably a safe assumption they had really nowhere to run for effective help.

An old man, evidently some kind of a local leader, stepped forward, trembling. Jeremy gathered, from the few words that he could overhear, that one of the young women already being molested was the old man's daughter or granddaughter.

Although his relatives were now trying to hold him back, he protested in a quavering voice, "It is a very foolish thing that you are doing—"

The old man, now being surrounded by a little circle of bandits, screamed out his plea for Apollo's help against the darkness, the barbarians.

"Other gods rule now, you old fool," one told him in a pitying, almost kindly voice.

"In fact," said another, adopting a thoughtful attitude, "we ourselves are the only gods you need. What's the matter? Don't you recognize us?"

A roar of laughter burst out around the little circle. "Anyway, we're the only ones taking any interest in you today! Let's hear some prayers."

The words that came out of the old man's mouth were not a prayer, and a bandit's fist soon shut it for him.

Jeremy meanwhile was experiencing an increasing sense of remoteness. He realized now that he'd been mistaken about the Intruder—the alien power inside his skull had not fallen idle. Something was going on, but he could not tell exactly what. Whatever it was produced a feeling of disorientation, unsteadiness, apart from what could be blamed on the horror he had to watch. And now there was a kind of humming sound—was it inside his head or out?—that he could not identify. It was a distant very faint but slowly growing noise, a wavery, polyphonic drone, that seemed to have no beginning and no end.

Jeremy closed his eyes—not so much in an effort to blot out horror as to seek something else; he knew not what. There passed before his view a parade of all the images of the gods that he had ever seen, most particularly a collection of the statues and paintings he had walked among while at the Academy.

He knew that Apollo (the being whose image at the Academy bore that label) was considered God of "Distance, Death, Terror, and Awe," "Divine Distance," "Crops and Herds," "Alexikakos," Averter of Evil.

Now and again Jeremy grew afraid that the alien thing inside his head cared not at all what might happen to any portion of his own proper mind or body.

The voices of the terrified villagers, men, women, and children, muttering, sobbing, in repeated and hopeless prayer, had blended into that other droning sound, so Jeremy could no longer separate the components of what he heard.

The repeated invocation of Apollo, the sight of the crude smiling statue, riveted Jeremy's attention. There again was the one presence he could not escape; the Intruder inside his head, however ungodlike certain aspects of his behavior, had to be in some way identified or at least connected with Apollo—with the entity to which humans gave that name.

And he, Jeremy Redthorn, now carried some portion of that god's substance—whatever that might mean—within his skull.

———

After the carnage of the early minutes of the invasion, when the feeble attempts at resistance were bloodily put down, but before the leisurely rape and looting really got under way, the bandits had the idea of putting the hostages they wanted to save in a safe place and detailing one of their number to look out for them.

"We don't want you getting hurt by accident." A wicked chuckle and a hard poke in the gut. "Wouldn't be good for business. On the other hand, we don't want you to forget where you belong and just go wandering off when we're not looking."

The safe place turned out to be the front room of the mayor's white-washed house, only the width of a narrow street from the central plaza. Neither it nor any of the adjoining houses had yet been set on fire.

Of course, the bandit assigned to look after the potential hostages might soon desert his post.

———

One of the more clever and observant bandits, as he sat with his fellows rummaging through some of the loot they were so easily collecting in the village, was made uneasy by the degree to which the Honeymaker villagers appear perfectly helpless and undefended. Jeremy heard him say to a colleague, "I don't get it."

"What's that?"

"Don't understand this place. Why hasn't someone eaten these folk up long ago? Surely there must be some bold fellows like ourselves living in this part of the world?"

The other shrugged. He reached out and broke something, just to be breaking it. "Maybe they have a protector. Or had one."

"Who? There's no flag."

"Maybe there's some superstition."

———

And now, inside one of the little houses, some anonymous voice was raised, formally calling upon the power of Apollo to protect the village.

"Sorry, old god; you're not up with the times." Someone was befouling Apollo's shrine, absently hurling a piece of garbage at it.

The bandit who had already begun to worry was worried more by the profanation.

Jeremy suddenly understood that the old man, once leader in the village, had also at one time been a priest of Apollo and maybe still thought that was his calling. Yes, the same old man the bandits had clubbed down once already. Amazingly he had dragged himself back to his feet, and now he was wiping at his blood-streaked face, meanwhile tottering toward the tiny shrine, in the middle of the little village square, beside the well.

The boy now found his attention drawn more closely to the shrine, the image of whose central statue was beginning to burn a dazzling white in his left eye. It had been a poor piece of work to begin with, when it was new, though doubtless the best that some local artisan could manage. Poor to begin with and now long-neglected. The scale of the sculpture was somewhat smaller than human life-size. Several green vines that needed water were trying to twine up the wood and stone. The central carven figure, as compared with the Academic representations of the god, was crude, thick-waisted, and with awkward legs, although Jeremy still got the sense that long years ago some would-be artist had done his or her best to make it handsome.

"Alexikakos," Averter of Evil.

Jeremy could read the names and prayers in the old scrawlings, misspelled in several languages, and the laborious carvings on the shrine, which must have been old when the grandparents of today's elders first laid eyes on it—half of the words were in no language that Jeremy Redthorn had ever seen before. But he could read all of them now—at least the ones that were not too much obscured by vines.

The new bandit leader was very confident. "I don't take much stock in gods."

. . . and all the time the droning in the background, building slowly. Very slowly. Maybe, after all, it existed only in Jeremy's head, a sign that the god who lived in there was angry. . . .

. . . and Jeremy's thoughts kept coming back to the shrine, which was probably older than the village itself and certainly had been here before any of the current houses had been built. He wasn't sure how he knew that, but it just looked old. . . .

And gradually, inwardly, a certainty, a kind of peace, was stealing over him. Jerry could feel more strongly than ever his union with Apollo. The divine Intruder's presence was now as real to him as his own.

Alexikakos, defend us now.

As seen through Jeremy's left eye, the crude old statue was gradually taking on quite a different aspect.

He turned his head a little, squinting into sunlight. On the surface of his consciousness, he was dizzy with horror and with the ache of the blood in his hands and feet being cut off by cords. Deeper down, the roaring and humming in his head had grown into something steady and reliable. Was Apollo himself going to come stalking down the little street, his Silver Bow in hand, dealing vengeance right and left against the desecrators? In the boy's current mental state, some such demonstration seemed a real possibility.

Once again the bandits were laughing at the old man, and now they watched him crawl and slowly regain his feet and stagger for a while before they clubbed him down again. Even now he was still breathing, but he no longer tried to raise his head.

Jeremy, on the verge of trance, could no longer hear either the laughter or the breathing.

Blood splashed upon the shrine, making a new noise that did get through. Jeremy's left ear could hear the liquid spattering, though there were only a few fine drops, striking as gently as soft rain. The tiny sound they made, much softer than the endless litany of prayers, so faint it ought not to have been audible in all the uproar, did not end when the blood had ceased to fly. Rather, it seemed to go on vibrating, vibrating, endlessly and ominously into the distance.

It blurred into the old droning noise, which even now was only faintly audible. No one else was paying attention to it as yet, but it was now growing ringingly distinct in Jeremy's left ear.

Looking up, the boy saw that a strange cloud had come into being in the western sky. It was almost too thin to see, and yet it was thick enough to drag a shadow across the sun.

21

THREE OR FOUR of the girls and young women of the village had been seized by the bandits and dragged into the comparatively large central house the raiders were making into a kind of headquarters. Jeremy and the other hostages who had been stuffed in here for safekeeping could hear the sounds of mumbled threats, hysteria, and tearing cloth.

One of the girls had been somehow selected to be first. Four men were beginning to abuse her, one kissing her, others' hands being thrust inside her clothing.

One of the young men of the village, who seemed to have a special interest in her, stood looking in a window and called out in mental anguish: "Fran!"

And the local youth essayed at least a symbolic struggle, as if he would interfere with what was being done to Fran—but when one of the bandits glared at him menacingly and raised a weapon, the young man fell silent. He turned away and hid his face, and in another moment he had left the window and vanished into the street outside.

The girl he was worried about screamed as the bandit leader and two of his cohorts held her down and forced her legs apart. Again there was the sound of ripping cloth. When the girl continued to struggle fiercely, one of the men struck her several blows.

Another one of the attackers had brought a jug of honey from the kitchen in the rear of the house and was pouring it over the victim's exposed body, while others held her arms and legs. The act amused his comrades greatly, and their laughter roared out.

Arnobius, who had been jammed down beside Jeremy on a kind of couch, with Ferrante on his other side, was leaning forward in a way that put a strain on his bound arms. He kept cursing the bandits, in a low, savage voice, an effort to which the men were taking no attention at all. Now the brigands began to take their turns between the young girl's legs.

And all the while, the strange new noise continued its slow growth. Jeremy was intensely conscious of it, more so than of the atrocities being performed almost literally under his nose. In another minute or two, despite the continued laughter and the screams, the unidentified sound had grown loud enough to force itself on people's attention. One after another noticed the droning and looked round, puzzled. It was not really loud—not yet—but the volume was steadily swelling. And there was a penetrating quality about it that was soon strong enough to distract even a rapist.

Jeremy was only vaguely aware of the atrocities being performed right in front of him. Or of the nagging pain of his scraped knee and hip, souvenirs of his attempt to run away from Death. Or of the bonds that painfully constrained his hands and feet. He sat in the place where he had been made to sit, among his fellow prisoners and sharing their enforced passivity. His bound hands hung in front of him; his eyes were half-closed. Here under a roof, shaded from the sun, all he would have to work with if he wanted to try fire making was the indirect sunlight from the windows. Jeremy thought it would probably have taken him a long time to burn his ropes away. But, in fact, he wasn't even trying to do that.

The Intruder had given him definite orders, though they had not come in words. Wordlessly but effectively Jeremy had been made to understand that the ropes that bound him were of no consequence—not right now. Because now his mind had been caught up, enlisted, in a far greater effort, in work that seemed likely to stretch certain of its abilities to the utmost.

In this striving Jeremy willingly allowed himself to be swept along. More than that, he was not content to accept a purely passive role, whether or not he would have been allowed to do so. His mind was fiercely willing to do the work that he was now being given—because he saw, however dimly, what the end result was going to be.

Had it not been for the days and weeks in which Jeremy had already begun to accustom himself to the Intruder, the overwhelming presence that he now felt might have proved too much for him. The sense of being invaded, possessed, co-opted, could easily have overwhelmed his sanity. As matters stood, the natural stability of his mind endured and was even strengthened by this sensation of divided sovereignty.

And perhaps—the boy was beginning to believe—the Intruder experienced natural limitations in the assumption of control.

Only gradually did the boy come to understand just what tasks he had been assigned and how his mind was to go about carrying them out. He had to put up with a complete lack of any verbal explanations, but over all was the reassuring certainty that a tremendous effort was being made against his enemies—his and those of the god who dwelt inside his head. He, Jeremy Redthorn, had been enlisted as an essential partner. His mind, most particularly certain parts of it whose existence he had barely suspected until now, was being borrowed, stretched into a new shape—and *used.*

And in the process, the boundaries of what he had considered *himself* were becoming indistinct.

Jeremy Redthorn and the Intruder—the Intruder and Jeremy Redthorn.

Inside the human skull they shared, the boundaries between the two had blurred, but the boy had no sense that they were struggling against each other for control. From the beginning of their union, deity and human had never fought each other openly. And now they were fighting side by side, in the same brain and body, making an effort of a very different kind.

Slowly, with considerable confusion at the start, Jeremy Redthorn came to a better understanding of what must be done. At first he was aware of only the necessary actions and not the effects they would achieve.

So intensely was Jeremy's concentration focused on his assigned job that he was almost able to ignore the horrors that still went on and on directly in front of the couch on which his body sat. He did not turn his head away from the endlessly screaming girl and her tormentors, did not even avert his eyes from what the grunting men were so intent on doing. The animal sounds that the girl and her attackers made seemed to reach him only from a distance. He was hardly aware at all of anything else that might be happening in the house or in the dusty sunlit village square in front of it.

Jeremy was not even aware that down the street one of the houses had been set on fire and bandits were laughing at the owner's hopeless attempt to put out the blaze with water from the village well. Two of them offered to help, but then with howls of merriment they emptied their buckets on the man instead of his burning house.

At the moment Jeremy's mind was actively serving as a source of energy, of raw psychic force, fueling the will and purpose of the Intruder. And neither was immediately concerned with what was happening in the village. Both were busy at a considerable distance from the house where their shared body sat, both engaged in an urgent business of finding and calling, of combing the grasses and fields of flowers for something that was urgently required. To find it they were sweeping the air above all the fields and woods within a mile of the village. Their task was a gathering of necessary forces, an accumulation and a summoning of vital power.

But before that job could be completed, another important task arose. The major part of Jeremy Redthorn's awareness was sent drifting back into the village again, into the house where his bound body still slumped on a couch, unharmed in the midst of horror.

Out in the street before the house, some people of the village were running uselessly to and fro, and as each one came within Jeremy's field of view he looked steadily at the passing man, woman, or child. He knew that the directed gaze of his left eye could mark them, and he was marking each of them with the Eye of Apollo, tagging them for salvation. Nor did he forget to turn his head and tag each of his fellow hostages as well. Also, he saved the girl in front of him—he was most careful to save her. Not that he could do anything about the ordeal she was enduring now. But he had the power to redeem her from sufferings considerably worse.

No human eye was able to see the markings—save only one of Jeremy's, which made them. These were signs not meant to be perceived by human sight—but when the need for them arose, they would be unmistakable to those very different organs of vision for which they were intended.

Turning his head, Jeremy impulsively marked another girl, the one named Katy, who lay on the floor of the house tied up and crying while she waited her turn at being raped. In a calm voice he said to her: "It's all right; I've saved you." Amazingly, she heard him, and turned up a face of tearstained wonder.

One of the men who stood awaiting his chance to get between the legs of the first girl also heard and didn't seem to know whether to laugh or be outraged. He turned toward Jeremy a dark and heavy mustache that jittered with the twitching of his red face. "You think you save the little bitch there, hey?"

"Not from you," said Jeremy remotely.

"What then?"

"You won't have time to hurt her."

"What?"

"From what is coming for you. Though probably she'd be safe from that anyway." The boy was speaking absently, with the larger portion of his mind still engaged out in the open air, half a mile away.

The mustached mouth was hanging open, forehead furrowed in a total lack of comprehension.

Jeremy, with his attention jarred back to the immediate vicinity of his own body, abruptly realized that he was slacking off on his other assigned job; not all of the villagers were going to come within his field of vision as long as he stayed inside the house.

A moment later he had jumped to his feet. Ferrante was now thrashing around, trying to get loose. The bandit detailed to guard prisoners was busy at the moment restraining Arnobius, who in his frustrated fury seemed actually on the point of getting his hands loose, and Jeremy's move took their warden by surprise.

In another moment the boy was hopping and stumbling, almost falling on his bound legs, out of the house and into the adjacent village square, where he took a stand and tried to focus the direct gaze of his left eye at least momentarily upon each and every villager. Now he might really be able to get them all—gods, let him not miss even one! With each such focused glance, a tiny flash of energy went forth and made a mark. A mark invisible to human eyes, but still—

Jeremy had only a vague general understanding of just what he was accomplishing by doing this, yet he never doubted that it must be done. The Dark Youth, the Intruder, had commanded it, though not in words.

On the other side of the little shrine, the old man let out one more yell: *"Alexikakos,* protect us now!"

Jeremy had only a few seconds, standing unsteadily upright in the village square, trying to mark every inhabitant with his gaze, before his bandit guardian, having settled with Ferrante and the Scholar for the moment, came screaming out to seize him by the collar and began to drag him back into the house by main force.

But before Jeremy's captor had got him back to the door, the man abruptly let him go, so that the boy on his bound legs fell flat in the dusty village street.

And all this time the droning sound had been increasing steadily. No doubt about it now—it was very real, as physical, as a blow, and it was still rising.

The bandit who had been struggling with Jeremy heard it plainly now, in the same moment as did his fellows deployed elsewhere around the village. In that moment all of them abruptly realized that they might have worse things to worry about than some rebellious hostages.

The peculiar noise had now acquired such volume, such a murmurous insistence, that Jeremy could be absolutely sure it had objective reality outside his own head. All around him other faces, those of attackers and victims alike, were turning from side to side with puzzled expressions. No one was able to ignore it any longer.

If you have keen ears, you can sometimes hear the swarm-cloud coming half a mile away. Somehow he might have remembered that— though in Jeremy Redthorn's past there was nothing remotely like it.

And now truly the cloud of insects was dense enough for its shadow to darken the sun, casting a vague pool of shadow in advance of its swift approach.

Jeremy Redthorn's eyes had never seen the like before, and he sensed that a long, long time had passed since even the Intruder had seen the like. In flight the great bees of certain swarms made a peculiar, distinctive buzz-fluttering sound, and a whole swarm in the air generates a heavy roar.

For anyone who had much experience with the bees, it was easy to tell by the sound whether the swarm was angry or just on the move somewhere.

One insect landed close in front of Jeremy's eyes, on the central pedestal of the village shrine. In his left eye the small live body glowed with a vital fire.

Some of the bees producing special honey for these villagers had bodies half as long as a man's hand. Odylic bees, some product of what the legendary technofolk had done to life a thousand years ago or more. Others of the six-legged honeymakers were only half as long—but that would be quite large enough. Large, multifaceted eyes. All workers, these, and with ferocious stingers. Their wings snarled at the air, mere blurs, too fast for Jeremy's right eye to follow, although his left, moving in the same track, could catch detailed pictures. It seemed that nothing in nature ought to move as fast as those thin wings.

When Jeremy saw the first, isolated bee scout, it was easy to mistake its right-eye image for that of a hummingbird. But when he saw it through his left eye, there could be no mistake.

A moment later it had come down on a bandit's neck. And a moment after that, with a twitching of its posterior against his skin, it had done one of the things that a bee does best.

A large swarm of them, descending in their mindless anger, could rout any human army, inflicting heavy loss of life on any who tried to stand and fight. Protective clothing was of course possible, but ordinary military armor had so many chinks and gaps that it was practically useless.

And now the bees descended in their thousands, on all who were not marked with the Eye of Apollo. Jeremy, looking around him, thought not a single citizen of the village was being stung.

Suddenly the brigand nearest Jeremy bellowed and began making frantic thrashing motions with his arms.

The three rapists who had been coupling with the girl released her—they suddenly needed all their hands for something else—and she collapsed on the floor and crawled away, trying to pull the remnants of her clothing around her. But there were no bees on her body, not a single one, and she was no longer in need of the fragile protection clothes could give.

The three who had been her chief attackers displayed much greater energy, and the sounds that they were making grew even louder than before, even less human. One man, with the lower half of his clothing off, replaced with a breechclout of buzzing brown and blue, went out of the house through a window, two others through the door. Their limbs were all in frantic motion, legs springing in a useless and spasmodic dance, arms swatting in a frenzy, hands working without hope at the task of scraping, beating away, the droning, writhing layer of gauzy, speed-blurred wings and furry bodies, poison needles, and piercing sound that had now engulfed them. The men whose legs still functioned might have tried to run, except that now they could no longer see. Jeremy observed clearly the complete disappearance of one of the bandits' heads inside a clump, a knot, of angry bees. When the pink-white surface that had once been the man's face appeared again, his head was swollen beyond all recognition as a human part, the mouth all filled with foam.

The droning had now risen to what seemed a deafening volume. It was almost enough to drown the screams of men.

Few of the other bandits were any better off. Swords and battle hatchets and short spears were waving in a few hands, but to no avail. Jeremy observed more than one demonstration of the fact that an active man or woman could catch one of the insects in one hand and crush it or knock it out of the air with a brisk arm swing. Of course the human would almost certainly survive the painful sting of a single bee. But meanwhile three more bees, or a dozen, or a hundred would be stinging him. And Apollo's memory informed Jeremy, quite dispassionately, that ten or a dozen stings from the stock of these apiaries were very commonly enough to kill an adult human.

So far Jeremy had not been stung, and he knew, with perfect confidence, that he was not going to be. So he raised his bound hands before his face and began steadily worrying with his teeth at the cord fastening his wrists. Really he was very tired, much energy had been drained from him, and as soon as this was over (it ought not to take long now) he was going to have to rest.

The droning had reached a kind of plateau; it was no longer getting louder.

Now and then Jeremy glanced up toward the elevated statue in the shrine while around him the screaming voices grew even louder. It seemed to the boy for a moment that the faint smile had broadened on the stone lips of the shrine's awkward, almost ugly Apollo. One bee landed on the lichened head, then abruptly propelled itself away again. As if, Jeremy mused, it might have paused there briefly to deliver a message—or simply to acknowledge the image of its god.

22

ALL THE LITTLE houses up and down the street that had been forced to swallow bandits were now vomiting them out like poison, and Jeremy could see and hear the invaders dying horribly, all up and down the little street. They broke and screamed and ran, each pursued by his own angry little cloud, and two of them somehow had found cameloids somewhere and appeared to be getting away.

Now the girl whom Jeremy had heard called Katy came unmolested out into the square and started helping Jeremy get free of his bonds. He welcomed her assistance, though others seemed to need it more than he did. The area of the shrine and the little square surrounding it was almost entirely free of bees, and with Katy's fingers, small but strong, digging at the knots, the loosening of his ropes proceeded steadily.

"Don't be afraid," Katy was urging him. "If you're calm, they won't sting you." She had achieved a remarkable steadiness in her own voice, considering all that had recently happened, and she was standing very close to Jeremy, as if to shield him with her body. Now and then her soft breasts pushed at his side and chest.

She was almost as tall as Jeremy himself, her body generously curved, in a way quite different from Carlotta's. Honey-colored hair hung now in disarray, and gray eyes looked startling in a tanned face. If she was going to have hysterics, following her rescue, they weren't going to hit her for a while yet.

"What did you mean, in there, when you told me you'd saved me?"

"I was trying to help you. Make you feel better."

Another village girl now came around carrying a basin of water, and Katy produced a clean-looking rag from somewhere and pulled aside the flap of Jeremy's torn trousers and started dabbling at the dried blood on the old but still untended scrape he'd got by falling in the gravel back when Professor Tamarack, also known as Death, had been pursuing him. In his memory that seemed a year ago.

"I'm not afraid," he murmured in reply to Katy's first remark. And he wasn't. But in fact he wasn't calm either, not with her standing as close as she was. In truth he was beginning to feel a mighty arousal—how much this was due to Apollo's involvement in his sex life he couldn't tell, but the Sun God had a legendary reputation along that line, while on the other hand Jeremy Redthorn considered such a reaction mighty inappropriate just now, what with all the screaming barely quieted and death and grief still everywhere around them. He supposed the right thing for him to do would be to tell Katy politely that he could manage perfectly by himself and she should go and help one of the villagers who were still screaming. But if he said that, he feared she might actually move away from him. Jeremy stood with closed eyes and let her go on with what she was doing.

Meanwhile, other villagers had shown and were still showing a variety of reactions to their winged rescuers' arrival. Some cowered down, pulling clothes and blankets over their heads in a desperate though unnecessary attempt to obtain shelter. Many others realized very quickly that they were now safe. But only very slowly, gradually, did some of those who had been most terrified come to understand that *they* were not in danger. Not anymore.

"I think you meant more than just trying to make me feel better," Katy said abstractedly. "I think you were doing something that really helped. Or at least you thought you were."

And here at last came Arnobius, red-faced and disheveled, having finally got free of all the entanglements inside the house. No longer bothered by bandit guardians, he now came following Jeremy out into the street, hopping on his bound legs, to stand there beside his young attendant. The Scholar gaped silently around him, getting a firsthand look at a major god's idea of retribution. Jeremy wondered if the man had any idea of what was really going on.

Jeremy, his own hands now free, got busy trying to help the man who had been—who still believed himself to be—his master. Meanwhile Katy had moved away, gone to try to comfort some screaming friend.

But Arnobius just now did not seem to have anything at all on his mind, beyond grossly practical matters. He was shouting in rage for the people who were trying to loose his hands to hurry up. Couldn't they see that now was the time to strike back, while the enemy was distracted?

Here, thought Jeremy, was one practical matter in which the newly worldly Scholar was mistaken. There was no longer any need for human hands to strike back and, indeed, not much chance of their doing so. The enemies of the village were far worse than distracted.

Arnobius had not been stung, nor had anyone marked by Jeremy with Apollo's protection. None of the villagers—inevitably, he'd missed a few—seemed to have suffered more than a sting or two. But he could see how each person of them winced now and then when each felt, briefly, the hairy, feathery extension of some insect's body on their backs and necks and legs, the small wind of their saviors' blurring wings . . . and now, thank Apollo for his influence, the girl who had untied Jeremy was once more hugging him in triumph and delight. Their embrace crushed the bodies of a bee or two, but against the two young bodies their stingers still remained harmlessly encased. The deaths of such units were trivial incidents in swarm life, nothing to alarm the mass of insects that still seemed to fill the air.

Once Ferrante had got free, he went mumbling and ranting and swearing up and down the street, in his hand a sword taken from a dead bandit, looking for a live one to cut to pieces.

Arnobius, sounding for all the world like his brother, John, was barking orders.

Ferrante, after only a momentary hesitation, leaped to obey—even if Lord John's brother was only a mere civilian. The two snatched up weapons from the sting-bloated, unrecognizable bodies of dead bandits. Now the Scholar, ignoring Jeremy for the moment, was snapping what sounded like orders at some of the young village men, and a few of them were nodding enthusiastically. In moments they were aboard the remaining cameloids and the animals were run-pacing out of town, at a speed that raised a cloud of dust.

When there were no more live bandits to be seen but only dead ones, the girl Katy led Jeremy by the hand back behind the houses.

"Come with me. I want to see if my family's all right."

Also, she wanted to assure them that she was all right, aside from some torn clothes. When they had reached a small house in the next small street, several family members, including small children, came running out of hiding to embrace her.

Katy's full name turned out to be Katherine Mirandola. She introduced Jeremy to her family as a man who'd tried to help her, and their enthusiastic gratitude knew almost no bounds.

Katy, not one to let questions drop when she found them interesting, still wanted to know what Jeremy had meant when he had told her that she was saved: how had he known what was going to happen?

"I have good eyes and ears." Then he saw that wasn't going to work as an explanation. "I'll give you all the details someday. But why does your village have a shrine to Apollo?"

━━━━━━━━

Katy eventually explained to Jeremy some things about the history of the village. In the old days, at least, any local band of hardy, vicious warriors would have been glad to turn back politely when confronted by a soft and innocent-looking young Honeymaker lass who was annoyed with them. Under ordinary conditions, individuals of the Honeymaker tribe or culture were introduced to at least one of the swarms, or to the Swarm, as babies—from then bees recognized these individuals as friends or, at least, folk to be tolerated.

And all the while, the stone lips of Apollo atop his shrine kept on smiling faintly. Jeremy Redthorn remembered clearly some of the things he'd learned at the Academy. Among the Far-Worker's many other attributes, he was patron of all domestic animals, including bees. . . .

━━━━━━━━

Almost all of the buzzing insects had now dispersed, sorting themselves out somehow into their proper swarms, and then those in turn gradually dissolving as individuals returned to the interrupted tasks of peace. One of the larger bees, only one, landed on Jeremy's head, just as another— perhaps the same one—had landed on the stone god, then quickly whirred away. The boy flinched involuntarily at the unexpected contact but then sat still. In a strange way the touch of power had been comforting, as if someone or something of great authority had patted him benignly on the head.

Meanwhile, the swarms of bees had efficiently dispersed and gone back to their regular peaceful activities, as industrious in retreat as they had been in attack. One villager was regretting out loud that it would probably be days before honey production got back to normal. Most people weren't worried about that yet. For one thing, they had the swollen, blackened bodies of the human victims to consider. A few, driven mad by pain, had torn their own clothing to shreds.

About a quarter of an hour after the first sting, the slaughter was over, the swarms once more dispersed, become mere vague receding shadows in the sky, and those of the former hostages whose release had been overlooked till now were soon set at liberty; none of them and none of the villagers had suffered any stings.

Some villagers formed a bucket brigade to put out the blaze in the house that had been torched. Everyone in line worked hard, though the building was already beyond saving.

Jeremy's sense of the Intruder's intimate presence now faded rapidly.

As soon as Jeremy had a few moments to himself, he walked back to the shrine, which for the moment was once more unattended, and stood there, his hand on one foot of the statue as it stood elevated on its pedestal.

Around him all the tumult of triumph and grief and anger was gradually fading into a tired silence. He thought of praying to Apollo but told himself that that was foolish. Why? Because the words he had been taught to use in childhood all sounded idiotic now. A deeper reason was that he was afraid that some clear god voice would respond, maybe with laughter, right inside his head. Somehow the thought of a plain communication from the Intruder was terrifying.

But he needn't have worried. No clear voice sounded, and no derisive laughter either.

He looked around for the Scholar, then remembered where Arnobius had gone.

There came a new outburst of shouting voices, blurred with the promise of violence. Jeremy looked around, to see that the villagers had discovered one surviving bandit, upon whom they now fell with screams of rage. Evidently the wretch had shut himself up in a closet, where the bees could not get at him, and then had been too frightened to come out.

Gleefully the more able-bodied of the man's former victims and their friends dragged him out into the sunlight and then energetically disposed of him. No one raised any objection as the villagers, with smiling, cheerful faces, maimed him horribly and seemed to be voting on whether to let him go in that condition. But before the vote could be formally concluded, several people lost patience and beat out the bandit's life, with an assortment of wooden garden tools.

Lying like ballast in the Intruder's cool memory were sights infinitely worse—Jeremy did not call them up, because he was afraid. But there they lay, and somehow their weighty presence helped.

Still none of the villagers attributed the success of their defense to Jeremy. But he knew, in a way that he could not have explained, what he had done.

Fervently he craved someone to discuss his problems with. The Intruder himself was of course no use in this regard, and Jeremy was not surprised that he seemed to have gone to earth again; the boy felt as alone inside his head as he'd ever been.

When he tried to talk to Katy about his problems, she of course could not begin to understand. But she listened earnestly and nodded sympathetically, and that helped more than he'd thought it would.

The old man who'd been almost killed in the village square was still alive. Jeremy on impulse let his hand rest for a moment on the heavily bandaged head, and a moment later the old man's eyes came open, looking first at Jeremy, then past his shoulder.

And the old man's reedy voice murmured, with great certainty: "It was Apollo, then, who saved us. Saved everyone."

Everyone hadn't been saved, but no one was going to quibble. "Of course. The Lord Apollo. I will make rich sacrifices—or I would, were it not well-known that he is one god who has little taste for such extravagances."

"What *does* he have a taste for, then?"

The old man had suddenly sat up, as if he might be going to recover after all. "Ha. Who can say? Devout prayers from his followers, I suppose. Beautiful women, certainly, any number of them—and I've heard it said that he is not averse to now and then taking a handsome boy or two to bed, just for variety."

Jeremy shuddered inwardly at the thought of coupling with even a girlish-looking lad. The Intruder was going to have to fight him for control if he had any such diversions planned.

A few Honeymakers, at least a few legendary ones in the past, had enjoyed the power of summoning a swarm by magic from a distance.

"But I have never seen it like this," the old man said. Looking up and down the street again, he shook his head. "Never anything like this. All thanks to great Apollo."

"Thanks to great Apollo," Jeremy murmured automatically, joining his voice to a dozen others.

▬▬▬

Problems sometimes arose, as Katy explained, with people who wanted to steal or lure away the queen and start their own hive somewhere else.

Jeremy tried to imagine what might happen if a swarm were summoned to try to fight off a fury or a whole flight of furies. Memory failed to come up with any examples immediately, and he let the idea drop. Bees are restricted to altitudes near the ground. If there was flesh and blood inside a fury accoutrement, the long stingers would find it out.

Heavy smoke and hailstorms offered a temporary defense against a swarm, as did sufficiently cold weather or heavy rain.

▬▬▬

"Some of the old folk claim that our bees fly for many miles, as far as halfway up the Mountain of the Oracle—there's some rare good things grow there, if you get up high enough."

"You've been there?"

The girl nodded. "Sometimes I carry bees from our hives to meadows where the flowers are good and thick. Release them there, and they know how to find their way home and tell their hive mates. Then a thousand workers, or ten thousand, will go to where the blossoms are prime."

"That's good for the honey, I suppose."

Katherine nodded, large-eyed and solemn. *Gods, but she was beautiful!*

"Do you go by yourself? Isn't it dangerous?"

"Folk around here know that we in this village are best left alone. These . . . these men must have come from far away."

▬▬▬

Due to the timely intervention of its patron god, the village as a whole had suffered comparatively little damage, though a few individuals were devastated. One house had burned almost to the ground, but none of the others had suffered more than minor vandalism.

As the day faded, and the sense of terror turned gradually to rejoicing, Jeremy was introduced to a drink made by the fermentation of honey and water and called *madhu*. Memory assured him that it was of course a form of mead.

Jeremy Redthorn had gained a minimal knowledge of winemaking, hearsay picked up while laboring at his uncle's elbow, but the Intruder had vastly more. Jeremy could step in and make mead—pretty successfully, with the magical help of his augmented vision and other magical enhancements having to do with the preservation of crops. Or at least he might discuss the process with local experts.

But the experience of Jeremy's blood and brain in the consumption of alcoholic drinks was decidedly minimal, and Uncle Humbert's wine had nothing like the entrancing impact of *madhu.*

Meanwhile, the dance of victory went on, giving signs of blending into a kind of harvest celebration. The villagers were celebrating the fact of their survival, the first real attack on their village in a long time, and the practical annihilation of their enemies.

Again he heard it said of the attackers: "They must have come from far away. Bandits around here would know better."

Fears were expressed for the young men who'd ridden out with the Scholar and Ferrante. Jeremy was asked for reassurance: "He's a crafty war leader, no doubt? Knows what he's doing? Our young men have little skill or knowledge when it comes to fighting."

Jeremy did his best to convey reassurance, without actually saying much.

Katy, he was pleased to note, was now drinking *madhu,* too. Her fingers stroked his face, with a touch that seemed less affection than frank curiosity.

"You were trying to help me, I know, and I thank you. But I didn't really need . . ."

———

After having been chased by Death, knocked down gravel slides, and robbed and wrestled about by bandits, Jeremy was long overdue for a new issue of clothes for himself. He might have taken some from a well-dressed bandit—had any such creature existed among their corpses. Nor could he find his riding boots that one of them had stolen. Katy's brother, who'd moved out last year, had left some that might fit.

"He was tall and strong, like you."

"Like me?" It was very odd to hear himself described as tall and strong. Just a little over middle height, maybe, but . . . there was hope. He thought he was still growing.

He also got some ointment applied to the old scrape on his hip and thigh—actually, it was healing quite well. And while injuries were on his mind, he took note of the fact that not a trace now remained of his three lash wounds.

Then he took the trouble to seek out another mirror. The mayor's house had a big one of real glass, no more depending upon the water in a perhaps-enchanted well. Had he really grown taller in the two weeks or so since leaving the Academy? Apart from the way they'd been damaged in his most recent adventures, he realized that the clothes he'd put on new shortly before leaving the Academy no longer fit him very well. Even if they hadn't been torn and dirty, they were beginning to seem too small, too short in arms and legs, too tight across the shoulders.

The *madhu*—he was now on his second small glass—made him giggle.

Katherine was trying to look after him. It seemed to be the other young women of the village against whom she was most interested in protecting him.

He put down his drinking cup, picked up a lyre someone had left lying about, and twanged the strings. People fell silent and turned their heads toward him. This wasn't what he wanted, being the center of attention, and he soon put the instrument down again.

Wandering the village in the aftermath of victory, Jeremy looked, in the last bright rays of the lowering sun, down into the reflecting surface of the well beside Apollo's shrine. What the shimmering surface down there showed him surprised and worried him.

Was it the reflection of the stone god that seemed to be holding out a pointing arm? Right over his shoulder.

And then the figure holding out a pointing arm collapsed. No, it hadn't been the statue after all.

People were wont to see strange things when they drank too much *madhu,* especially when the honey it was made from contained the vital chemicals of certain plants, and no one took much notice of one more vision.

———

The music went swirling out raggedly across the town square, and villagers and visitors alike took part in a wild dance, mourning and celebration both confabulated into one outpouring of emotion.

And Jeremy, with the world spinning round him in a kind of out-of-body experience, needed a little time to realize that the crashed and intoxicated figure was his own. Somehow he seemed to have achieved a viewpoint outside his body—memory assured him that *madhu* could do that sometimes.

The sprawled-out form sure as hell didn't look much like the Dark Youth. Much too skinny and red-haired and angular for that. And the face—! On the other hand, Jeremy supposed it was the Intruder after all, because the two of them were sharing the same body. Jeremy hoped it was a good-enough body for a god. Not what the Dark Youth was used to—but so far he hadn't complained.

And now Jeremy had come to be back inside it, too. He giggled. Never in his life had he imagined a god having to pee, or shit, or get dirty and hurt and sometimes smell really bad. None of those human things seemed at all right and proper. Definitely inappropriate. But there they were.

The music blared, and someone passed him a jug again. He accepted gratefully, first swigging from the jug like everyone else, then refilling his cup; *madhu* was delicious stuff. Someday he would have to thank his fellow deity, Dionysus, for inventing it.

And he belched, emitting what seemed to him a fragrant cloud.

One of the village girls whose name he didn't know danced by, flowers in her hair and smiling at him, and Jeremy reached out and squeezed her thigh in passing, giving the young skin and the muscles moving beneath it a good feel. The way she smiled at him, she didn't mind at all. But he wasn't going to try to do anything more to this girl or with her. Right now, just sitting here and drinking *madhu* provided Jeremy Redthorn with all the good feelings that he needed.

Come to think of it, though, where had Katy gone? He looked around—no sign of her at the moment.

And he, Jeremy Redthorn, no longer had the least doubt about the correct name of his own personal god—the god Intruder. The boy could even dare to come right out and speak that name, now that he was drunk enough.

Hi there, Apollo. My closest companion, my old pal, the Far-Worker. My buddy the Lord of Light. To Jeremy it seemed that he had said the words aloud, and he giggled with the reaction of relief and *madhu*.

He looked around with tipsy caution, turning his head to left and right: If he *had* spoken aloud, it seemed that no one had heard him amid all the noise. No one outside his own head.

Maybe no one *inside* it was paying attention, either. There were moments, like now, when there didn't seem to be anyone present but himself.

Time passed. The celebration inside the mayor's house went roaring on around Jeremy, while he sat with his eyes closed, head spinning.

He felt greatly relieved when enough time had passed to let him feel confident that there would be no answer.

23

FOR THE FIRST time in his life, Jeremy was waking up with a bad hangover. Whether or not Apollo was also a victim he couldn't tell. But he could hope so.

The first problem of the morning was a sunbeam of what seemed unbearable, unnatural brightness, stabbing at his eyelids. The left eye dealt with this assault no more successfully than did the right. When Jeremy turned his head away from the sun, he discovered that his head ached and his mouth felt furry. Also that he was lying on his back in an unfamiliar room, with a stiff neck, at the edge of a mound of pillows and upended furniture. Unfamiliar snoring drifted over from the other side of the mound.

Gradually he remembered where he was and how he'd got there. He'd begun yesterday as a helpless prisoner and had ended it as a victorious god—or at least as the partner of one. And the day had ended in a party—oh gods, yes, the party.

Feeling not in the least like a victorious god, he tried to get to his feet. Sinking back with a groan, he decided to put off his next attempt indefinitely.

The girls. The singing and the dancing.

Katy.

Now he had raised himself sufficiently to let him look around. Yes, this was the room where most of the party, the dancing anyway, had taken place. Four or five other people, defeated in their bout with Dionysus but still breathing, had fallen asleep in the same large room—not quite all in the same pile. The casualties included some of the village girls—but not *her*. Seen in a frame of nausea and suffering, all of the strewn bodies, men and women alike, were repulsive creatures.

As he must be himself.

And oh, oh gods, the *madhu*.

Slowly Jeremy levered his way onto all fours and from there to a standing position—more or less. He swayed on his feet. There was a smell of vomit. Well, at least it wasn't his.

Fighting down the desire to throw up, groping his way through stabbing daylight with eyes more shut than open, Jeremy stumbled out-of-doors. It seemed to him tremendously unfair that gods should be immune to these aftereffects. Or, if he himself was now indeed a god, that he should still be subject to them. Never mind; he'd think about it later.

He made it to the privy out back, stepping over a couple of snoring male villagers on the way. On emerging from the wooden outhouse he slowly found his way back to the town square, intending to slake his horrendous thirst at the fountain. When he reached the square he discovered that some saintly women had tea brewing.

When he tried to remember everything that had happened at the party, Jeremy had trouble shaking the feeling that Carlotta had been there, too, joining in last night's celebration. But that of course was nonsense. Carlotta, whatever she might be up to, had to be many miles away. Maybe there'd been someone from the village who'd looked like her, sounded like her—yes, that was quite possible, though Jeremy couldn't remember now who it had really been.

Ferrante, who soon came to souse his head in the water of the public fountain, looked about as unhealthy as Jeremy felt but demonstrated a perverse soldierly pride in his condition. Also, the young lancer was a prolific source of good, or at least confident, advice on how to deal with a hangover.

"When did you get back?" Jeremy demanded. "Is the Scholar here?"

"Some scholar. He'd make a mean sergeant, I can tell you."

Ferrante reported tersely on the punitive pursuit, which had evidently been bloodily successful. About an hour before dawn, the Scholar and the members of his impromptu posse had ridden back into the Honeymakers' village. And described how one of the local youths had been holding up, proudly displaying, the scalps and the ears of the bandits who had not been able to escape after all.

———

When Jeremy finally saw Arnobius, he wondered whether the Scholar's campus colleagues would have recognized him. The Scholar now looked tired but formidable, with a war hatchet stuck in his belt, his beard growing, and wearing different clothing, grumbling that one still seemed to have got away. The villagers who had ridden with him, a handful of young, adventurous men, regarded him with great respect.

The change was so substantial that it crossed Jeremy's mind to wonder if Arnobius had recently come into possession of a fragment of the Face of Mars. But Jeremy's left eye denied that any such transformation had taken place, and so far the Scholar had displayed no traces of truly superhuman powers. It was just that he had never been exactly the person that everyone took him for.

Arnobius said to him: "Would have brought you along, Jonathan, if I'd thought of it. As matters turned out, we were enough."

———

One of the first tasks of the morning was not wisely undertaken on a queasy stomach. More than a dozen dead bandits, sting swollen to the point where their mothers would not have known them (the lone specimen mangled by human hands and weapons looked by far the most human), had already been collected and decently covered, but this morning they had to be hauled in dung carts to a place well out past the edge of town. At a site where mounds of earth of all ages identified the municipal dump, their bodies were stripped of any remaining valuables and then swiftly disposed of in a common unmarked grave.

Meanwhile, elaborate and very sober funeral preparations were under way for those villagers who had been killed. By no means everyone in the village had been involved in last night's party.

The half-dozen seriously injured people had already been put in the care of healers and midwives.

On every hand Jeremy heard expressions of gratitude to Apollo, whose domain of domesticated flocks and herds obviously stretched to include apiaries. But as the morning wore on he realized that no one in the village seemed to have any idea of the important role that he, Jeremy Redthorn, had played by closely cooperating with the god. His only reaction to the discovery was relief.

Order had been quickly restored within the village, though half the population were still wailing in their pain and grief and rage. Others to vent their feelings had begun to play loud music and to dance. Almost every one of the villagers who had run away at the start of the raid came trickling back over the next few hours, to listen in amazement to the tales of the violence, horror, and retribution that they'd missed.

By midmorning a feast of celebration was being prepared, according to local custom.

Two or three of the villagers had gone out before dawn to the hives, which were all located well outside town, to soothe the excited domestic swarms and try to reestablish peaceful production. Having the swarms so disturbed was sure to be bad for business, and the village depended largely on trading its honey for its livelihood.

This morning Katherine Mirandola, who seemed to have spent the end of the night properly at home with her parents, looked red-eyed, her face swollen. She had been weeping bitterly, out of sympathy with several of her friends who'd suffered far worse than she. Jeremy on greeting her held out his arms to offer comfort, and she wept briefly on his shoulder.

He asked what had happened to the youth who'd tried ineffectually to help her. Turned out that he had fled the village now and no one knew where he was.

Katy explained that the young man who'd been courting the girl, Fran, who'd been repeatedly raped was now treating her coolly and evidently found her much less desirable.

"That's a damned shame."

"Yes. But now there's nothing to be done about it."

Jeremy also braced himself for more searching questions from the newly forceful leader regarding his own behavior in the crisis—but when everyone was under extreme stress, one would have to behave strangely indeed to attract notice, and he hadn't done that. Physically, he hadn't done much of anything at all.

Anyway, the Scholar had no questions for him. It struck him as odd that Arnobius should not be interested in the godly intervention by which the village had been saved. But so it was.

Arnobius, having effortlessly assumed command, did not seem inclined to relinquish it. After offering the villagers some gratuitous advice on how to defend themselves and their homes in the future, he announced that it was necessary to provide some defense for his party of Academics. Of course they were going on to the Oracle of the Cave, and they would now adopt the guise of pilgrims headed in that direction.

"That way, we're less likely to attract undesirable attention. Having now been deprived of our escort—with one notable exception—we must escort ourselves. Assuming the Harbor lancers are still in the area, if we fail to rejoin them it will be no one's fault but our own."

Ferrante, as the only member of the original military bodyguard still present for duty, was now promoted to second in command for military matters. Arnobius briskly gave him the rank of Sergeant.

It was easy to see that Ferrante had mixed feelings about this advancement—naturally he was pleased, but on the other hand, he couldn't help wondering what right this civilian had to assign him any rank at all. And when things sorted themselves out, what was his rightful commanding officer going to say?

The Scholar was frowning at Jeremy, as if he had finally taken notice of him. "Jonathan, what about you?"

"If it's up to me, sir, I prefer to remain a civilian."

"Very well. But you are hereby enrolled in the ready reserve, subject to being called to active duty at a moment's notice." The Scholar spoke quietly but was obviously in dead earnest. His servant had sidestepped one episode of military duty but could expect to carry his full share of the load next time.

"Yes sir." Jeremy decided that trying to salute would not be a good idea.

████████

Arnobius soon let the two surviving members of the Expedition know what was coming next. Moving closer to the Mountain and its Oracle, their original goal, would offer them the best chance to reunite with the troops under his brother's command, whose primary mission would take them in the same direction.

Besides, the Scholar still was drawn to learn the secrets of the Oracle.

Meanwhile the villagers were offering to provide their honored guests with a guide who would, so the elders assured them, show them the shortcut trail by which they could shave hours or even days off the time necessary to reach the Mountain!

Katherine volunteered for the job.

"Won't your family be . . . well, worried about you?"

"I think not. Why?"

"Well. Going off for days, with three men . . ."

"I've done it before, and I know the route better'n anybody else. Besides, Dad says I'll be under the special protection of Apollo."

"Oh."

████████

Arnobius and his two aides spent one more night in the village, as honored guests. That tonight's celebration was somewhat tamer. A general exhaustion had set in, and the stocks of *madhu* were depleted as well.

During the night, Jeremy dreamed that Apollo had drawn Katy Mirandola to him, just as unfamiliar maidens had come in other dreams, on other nights. But Jeremy, his mind filled with fresh and ugly memories of women being forced, awakened the sleepwalking girl and sent her back to her own house.

In the morning he was disturbingly unable to determine whether or not it had only been a dream.

Not even when he saw Kate again could he be entirely sure. He said, "I dreamed last night that you were walking in your sleep."

She sat there fingering her braids, a practical treatment for her long honey-colored hair. "But . . . I never do that."

Jeremy, uncertain of what might actually have happened, decided not to press the matter further.

On the morning of the next day, after another substantial meal consisting largely of bread and honey, and several speeches, the surviving Honeymakers, after observing the rituals of formal mourning for their murdered friends and relatives, gave the surviving pilgrims (as they conceived Jeremy and his companions to be) a joyous send-off.

With their parting wishes, the Honeymaker elders urged their visitors to watch out for more bandits. Or for soldiers of the army that was opposed to their overlord.

An elaborate ceremony in honor of Apollo was held in the little village square. Various animals were sacrificed—something in Jeremy winced inwardly each time the blood of an offering was spilled—and a pot of honey poured into the earth. There was a little *madhu* also, though not much of the precious stuff could be found after two nights in a row of celebration. The long-neglected statue was in the process of being cleaned and freshly decorated, and Jeremy learned a little more about the god with whom he had become so closely associated. Still no one else seemed to realize how intimately Jeremy had been involved in the rout of the bandits.

Before leaving the Honeymakers' village, Arnobius insisted that everyone in his little band be well armed; the weapons taken from the dead bandits amounted to quite a little arsenal, and the unwarlike village elders were content to let the visitors help themselves.

The Scholar gestured at the pile of blades, clubs, and other death-dealing devices before them. "What sort of weapon takes your fancy, lad?" Arnobius himself had belted on a short sword, suitable for a commander, and a serviceable knife, much like the one that Jeremy had had from Sal, then lost. Ferrante had put on a couple of extra belts, and he now bristled with blades, like a storybook pirate. Everyone had reclaimed a backpack or acquired a new one from the newly available stockpile, and the village was still in a generous mood when it came to filling the packs with spare clothing and food supplies.

Jeremy's hands moved uncertainly above the array of lethal tools. The fingers of both of his hands began to twitch, and something in the display glowed brightly in the sight of his left eye.

What his right hand lifted from the disorganized pile was quite an ordinary bow—actually, the Intruder silently judged it a little better than ordinary, though the man who'd been carrying it hadn't been giving it the best of care. And nearby there lay a quiver containing half a dozen arrows. With two fingers Jeremy thrummed the string, which according to his left eye looked a trifle frayed. But there was a spare bowstring, wrapped around the quiver.

Standing, he planted both feet solidly, a modest stride apart, and then angled the bow between his braced legs, with one end on the ground. Now able to use two hands on the free end, he could, without exerting any unusual strength, flex the wood sufficiently to get the old string off and the sound one on.

Ferrante commented, in mild surprise: "You look like you know how to handle that, Jonathan."

Jeremy nodded and murmured something. The truth was that he had never in his life so much as touched a bow before picking up this one. But it seemed that his body's onboard mentor had already taught his nerves and muscles all they needed to know on the subject—and considerably more.

His left eye noted meaningful differences among the arrows. With careful fingers he selected one of the better-looking shafts from the quiver and inspected it closely. Something in him sighed at its inadequacy. But for the time being, it would do. It would have to do.

The villagers' hospitality did not extend to loaning or giving away anything as valuable as the few cameloids they possessed. And Arnobius on thinking it over decided that he and his companions would do better on foot anyway, making more convincing pilgrims. All were in good physical shape, quite ready for a lengthy hike.

After getting clear of the Honeymakers' village, the party of four, Jeremy, Arnobius, Ferrante, and Katy, retraced on foot the path by which the bandits had herded and driven their hostages away from the Mountain.

Arnobius spoke no more of the Oracle except as a goal, a place where they could most likely rejoin the force commanded by his brother, while avoiding the enemy.

There was no particular reason to doubt that most of John's force of four hundred lancers was still intact, but there was equally no reason to suppose them anywhere near the Honeymaker's village.

Arnobius said: "If it was odylic force, or magical deception, that tore down the bridge and separated us in the first place, then I suppose they could be prevented by the same means from following our trail."

Apollo seemed to have no opinion.

———

For people traveling on foot, as the most serious pilgrims did whenever possible, the Oracle was several days away, even with the benefit of the shortcut trail.

People walking, if they took any care at all to avoid leaving a conspicuous trail, were bound to be harder to track than the same number mounted on cameloids. Of course the footsloggers were also condemned to a much slower pace.

Jeremy was not the only one who noticed that Arnobius no longer had much to say about discovering truth. The Scholar seemed to have been shocked out of such concerns and was absorbed now with the need to straighten out the practical business in front of him. Obviously he enjoyed the role, now that it had been thrust upon him.

"At the moment, philosophic truth is whatever happens to promote our survival."

———

Ferrante, like most of his fellow lancers, considered himself something of an archer. And now with some satisfaction he had regained his own bow and arrows.

It was only natural that, on seeing Jeremy arm himself with a bow as well, Andy would challenge him to an impromptu contest. And that their new guide should pause to watch.

"How 'bout it, Katy? Winner gets a kiss?"

The girl blushed. But she said: "All right."

Jeremy just for practice shot one arrow—at a soft target, hoping not to damage one of his usable weapons. That the shaft should skewer the mark dead center seemed only natural and right.

And the kiss, when he claimed his prize, was more than sweet. Something far more serious than any voluptuous dream had begun to happen between him and this girl.

Ferrante, whose arrow had come quite creditably close to the bull's-eye, kept looking at him strangely, more with puzzlement than jealousy.

───────

The trail along which Katy led them carried them mostly uphill, and sure enough, there was the Mountain in the distance, not yet getting perceptibly closer. After Katy had guided them through a day of careful progress on back trails, the party crossed a larger road. At this point they might fall in with and join a larger pack of pilgrims who were bound for the Cave Shrine.

Arnobius would have been pleased to join forces with a bigger group and offered Katherine's services as guide, but the distrustful pilgrims declined the union, being too suspicious to be led away from the main road.

───────

Jeremy remained as determined as ever to complete the mission that Sal had bequeathed to him, almost with her dying breath. Or so he told himself. The trouble was that sometimes he forgot what he was doing here, for hours at a time. But if he couldn't find Margaret Chalandon at the Cave of the Oracle, he didn't know what he would do next.

He tried cautiously questioning Arnobius for any additional information about this woman, Scholar Chalandon, who had been missing in the vicinity of the Mountain ever since her own expedition had miscarried. But the Scholar was evidently unable to tell him much.

Well, damn it, he, Jeremy, was doing the best he could. With this—this *god thing* in his head, he was lucky if he could remember who he was himself.

It bothered Jeremy that the image of Sal was fading somewhat in his memory—the details of how her face had looked and what her voice had sounded like. But he was still committed to fighting the entities that had destroyed her.

In the middle of the night he woke up with a cold chill, suspecting that maybe Apollo didn't *want* him to remember her.

―――――――

It was natural that, as they walked, Jeremy spent a fair amount of time talking to Katy. She listened so sympathetically that he soon found himself stumbling through an attempt to explain his situation to her.

He realized that he was becoming increasingly attracted to the girl, who was in many ways quite different from the other girls and women he had known, since they had begun to be of interest to him.

It was obvious that Ferrante was getting to like her, too, if only because she was the only young and attractive woman around.

―――――――

Jeremy told Katherine that he had made a solemn promise to someone, and naturally she wanted to know more about that.

"Then you and this girl are engaged?"

"Engaged? No. No, nothing like that." He was only fifteen; did she think he was about to get married? A pause. "The truth is that she's dead."

Katy said how sorry she was. It sounded like she really meant it.

24

THE FOUR WHO traveled together continued to make good time along the little-used trail, which after much going up- and downhill rejoined the main road comparatively near the Mountain.

Katherine continued to lead the way, giving every indication of knowing what she was about. The route she had chosen, she told her clients, went through some tough hills by an unlikely-seeming path. Apollo's memory was empty of information on this passage through the hills and woods.

After the first day, when they had come to a section of the trail with which she was less familiar, she spent a good portion of the time scouting ahead alone.

This morning Jeremy walked with Katy when she moved ahead. They exchanged comments on strange wildflowers—of whose names she seemed to know at least as many as Apollo did. Jeremy admired her backpack, which bore, in what she said was her mother's embroidery, a design showing the same flowers being ravished by industrious bees.

Katy and Jeremy spoke of many other things—including the strange diversity of life-forms, which was said to increase dramatically on the Mountain's upper slopes.

"Some say it's all the Trickster's domain, up there," Katy offered, tilting back her head in a vain effort to see the summit, which was lost behind setbacks and clouds.

He didn't want to think about Carlotta. "I've heard it is Olympus." So Apollo's memory suggested—it was no more than a suggestion, for the Sun God had no recollection of ever being that high on the Mountain. "What god do you like best, Kate?"

She gave him a look. All right, it was a strange question to be asking anyone.

Katy seemed more attractive the more he looked at her. Jeremy was impressed by her—to the Intruder she could hardly be anything but one more conquest, but to the boy she had assumed deeper importance, and Jeremy found himself sometimes tongue-tied in her presence. When he would have commanded the supposed eloquence of Apollo, it was nowhere to be found.

———

One night when they were well in among the foothills, as Jeremy was taking his regular turn on watch, while his companions slept, he turned round suddenly, feeling himself no longer alone.

Carlotta, dressed as when he had last seen her, on the day when Arnobius had given her away, stood there smiling at him.

Her neat, unruffled presence sent a chill down his spine. There was no natural means by which Carlotta could be here on the Mountain now.

Her eyes were unreadable, but she put out a hand in the manner of a friendly greeting. "You look surprised to see me, Johnny—but no, that's not really your right name, is it?"

"You know it isn't. I am surprised . . . by how much you've changed." His left eye showed him a multicolored aura surrounding her figure, as bright as that worn by Thanatos, but less suggestive of danger. On her feet were strange red sandals, more heavily marked.

"Let's talk about you first. You've grown in the days since I've seen you, Jer."

"Have I? Maybe I have." His clothes were starting to feel tight again.

Carlotta put out a hand and familiarly stroked his cheek. "Still no whiskers, though."

"Truth is, I doubt I'll ever grow any."

"Oh well. Whiskers aren't that important. Having no beard is just a way of saying that you'll possess eternal youth."

"I don't know about that."

"I do. I can now understand you much better, Jeremy—if I may still call you that? Because I have a goddess in my own head now, and I can see you through her eyes."

"And I can see you through Apollo's. . . . You have the Trickster, don't you?" The glow in Carlotta's eyes and mouth was like that of a house at dusk, where you could tell that candles were glimmering inside even though windows and door were shut. "I always pictured the Trickster as a man. That's how I always heard it in the children's stories."

"Well, she's a woman, now that she lives with me. I'm not sure what she was before."

Memory, quickly and shallowly probed, could find no hard reason why the Trickster—or, for that matter, Apollo or any other god—should absolutely be required to be male.

Jeremy looked around. He and Carlotta effectively had this spot in the deep woods all to themselves. Arnobius and Kate and Ferrante were still sound asleep.

She seemed to read his thoughts. "I put them to sleep. Apollo of course can wake them if he wishes."

He shook his head slightly. "So, the Trickster and you . . . Want to tell me the story? I mean how . . . how it happened?"

"That's one reason I came to see you. I've been aching to tell someone. Here, sit down beside me." With a gesture she smoothed the surface of a fallen log, brushing away sharp branch stubs and rough bark like so much sawdust, changing the very form of the wood, leaving a smooth benchlike surface.

Jeremy sat, close to the goddess who sat beside him, but not quite touching her. He said, "You moved the window, in the Scholar's rooms."

Carlotta's laughter burst out sharply. "It was nothing, for the Trickster. I bet he was impressed!"

"Totally confused."

"As usual!"

For a moment they looked at each other, sharing memories in silence. Then Jeremy spoke. "You were going to tell me how you . . ." He finished with a vague gesture.

His companion ran a hand through her white ringlets. "The Lord Apollo can say it, if he likes. I expect he can say just about anything he wants. As for me, it all began on the day we met—you and I."

He cast his mind back. "I *thought* maybe . . . I saw you hide a little black and white box. Never mind; go on."

Carlotta jumped up restlessly from the log and strolled about, her fair brow creased as if in meditation. Jeremy found himself distracted by the display the red sandals made in his left eye.

Presently she said, "It started only an hour or so before you showed up. I expect it was your arrival that threw Arnobius into a fit, though of course he never made the connection. I didn't know he was knocked out, because I happened to be in the temple when it happened."

"Yes, his seizure. . . . Go on."

That day on the stone wharf beside the ruined temple, Carlotta had thought her master safely occupied with his usual rituals and incantations, adequately served and guarded by half a dozen men.

"I told him that I was going into the building to take a look around, but I wasn't sure he'd even heard me. That was all right. I certainly didn't mind having a chance to do some exploring on my own."

She'd gone into the temple, not searching systematically, only wandering. Arnobius wasn't going to begin his own official exploration until he was sure he'd done all the proper incantations as correctly as possible.

"He was very big on incantations, and on trying to divine what the gods wanted—I don't know if he still is."

"He's changed," said Jeremy. "Changed a lot in the last few days."

"Has he indeed?" But the idea aroused no interest. "I didn't realize how big that temple was until I started wandering around inside. I might actually have been worried about getting lost in there, except that I could see daylight coming in at so many places. The windows and holes were all above eye level, but I could easily tell where the river was, because the trees I saw looking out on that side were far away, while on the other sides they were growing right into the ruins. . . .

"I went into room after room. Some of them were of crazy shapes, and a few were huge. On the walls there were paintings, as old as the building itself, and many of the paintings were very strange. And some statues. . . . I didn't want to look at those closely, because they frightened me. I can admit that now. Maybe some of them still would, even though I'm now who I am.

"There were . . . things . . . that I suppose had once been pieces of furniture, but by the time I saw them they'd rotted away until only scraps of wood were left.

"Everything in there was half-engulfed in lichens and mold and mildew. . . . Anyway, to cut the story short, I came at last to a place— it was a kind of strongroom, but the door was standing ajar. Inside there was a shrine to a certain god. And below the shrine a kind of cabinet, made of both wood and stone, intricately carved.

"I thought the handle of the door seemed to reach out for my hand, beckoning. And when I pulled it open, I found something inside—something very important. And at that moment everything was changed for me, forever." The transformed version of Carlotta paused, staring into the distance.

"The Trickster's Face," Jeremy supplied.

Her eyes came back to him. She blinked. "Oh no."

"No?"

"No. Finding the Face, becoming a goddess, came later. You see, that shrine in the temple in the swamp belonged to Hermes." She paused, looking at him curiously. "But hasn't . . . your own god . . . told you all this already?"

"I've been afraid to ask him much of anything. And he tells me very little. Never comes out and just says anything in clear words. I suppose he's taking it easy on me. Because I can't get over my fear of . . . of being swallowed up in his memory. Consumed by him."

Carlotta nodded. "I know what you mean. Trickster's frightening, too, though she's not . . . Apollo." The last word came out in a reverent hush.

Jeremy was shaking his head. "Carlotta, by all the gods, but I'm glad you—glad I now have someone I can talk to, about all this!" Impulsively he seized her hand. "But you were telling me what you found in the ruined temple, that day we met."

"Yes. Let me try to keep the story in some kind of order." She sighed and took a moment to gather her thoughts. "What I discovered in the cabinet, on that first day, was, of course, the Sandals." Jumping to her feet and pirouetting slowly before him, she reminded him how gloriously her feet were shod. "Jeremy, did you never guess what truly frightened our crew of boatmen into running off?"

"I never thought much about it. I've had a lot of other problems to keep me busy."

"Well, it was the sight of me that did it! Of course as soon as I found Sandals looking like these I had to try them on, and as soon as I tried them on I discovered what they were good for.

"When our worthless crew saw me fly out of the temple—dipping and darting in the air like a bird—they pointed at me and screamed and ran around for a minute like beheaded chickens. Then they chose to pile into the little boat and paddle like hell off into the swamp. Even though they had some idea of what kind of things lived in the swamp, they chose that rather than stay . . . in the presence of what I had become."

At the time, the sight of the fleeing men, whom she certainly hadn't liked, had provoked in her a giddy laughter, but the men's desertion had proven to be no joke, and soon her anger had flared. If it hadn't been for Jeremy happening along, she would have been forced to use the Sandals to get help—and there would have been no keeping them secret after that.

Now Carlotta gave a fuller demonstration of the Sandals' darting power, moving to the distance of a hundred normal paces and back again, all in the blink of an eye.

"Beautiful," said Jeremy, and confirmed with a glance that his three companions were still asleep. Perhaps if it were not for Apollo, he would have been as terrified as the boatmen.

She said: "I think that even you, even with Apollo in your body, will not be able to move as swiftly and smoothly as this."

Apollo's memory, when pressed, confirmed the fact—and pumped up more information, before he could turn off the flow. "Hephaestus made them," Jeremy blurted out, pointing at her feet.

"That's right."

"And what did Arnobius say, when you came flying out? But that's right; he didn't see you, because he was already out cold by then. So you hid the Sandals, carrying them in that little box, and kept the secret of their existence from him."

"Right again."

"I thought you loved him, then."

The figure of the goddess spread her arms in a very human gesture. "Johnny, I did, and I meant to tell him. At least that's what I told myself. But then you came along, complicating matters further, because I didn't entirely trust you.

"You remember how *he* wasn't fully himself again for several days. By the time he had recovered, I'd had time to think. And the more I thought, the more I worried."

"Why?"

"By then, I began to fear that I'd waited too long. He'd wonder why I'd kept the discovery quiet. . . . I think the truth was that I feared losing him."

"How would having the Sandals—?"

"For one thing, because it was I—his slave, his inferior helper—who'd actually made the great discovery. *The Sandals of Hermes, wrought for him by Hephaestus!* And *I'd* found them, not the great Scholar. He'd found the temple in the swamp, but then he'd failed. Suddenly things became too real for him to handle. Instead of simply exploring the way I did, finding what was there to be found, he stupefied himself with drugs and wasted his time with almost useless diagrams and spells, games he could have played at home.

"If he denied me credit for the great discovery, claimed it for himself—well, he and I would always have known the truth. And if he nobly gave his slave assistant proper credit, he would have made himself look inferior. Or so I feared. Either way it would have upset things between us—or so I thought. Turned out there was nothing much between us anyway."

Jeremy nodded slowly.

Carlotta's eyes had once again gone distant. "When I look back, I can see he'd already started the process of dumping me. There was no more talk of keeping me with him always. I had some idea that if I waited until just the exactly right moment to present him with this great gift of the Sandals—but somehow the exactly right moment never came."

Later, on the night when the Scholar had told Carlotta he was giving her away, she'd got the Sandals out of hiding and begun to use them secretly. At first she'd only gone skimming and dancing out over the sea at night, simply for the sense of power and freedom they provided, with no further conscious goal in mind. But she'd soon found herself returning to the hidden temple in the swamp, searching for more secrets of power and wealth. Any slave knew that wealth was power—gold made its own magic, at least as strong as any other kind.

Now the trip from the Academy to the distant temple, through midnight skies, took her less than half an hour.

At first she didn't know why she had chosen that place as her goal or exactly what she was looking for. Except that she now wanted, needed, a weapon, some new means of power. It was as if the Sandals heard her whispering to herself and carried her to what she needed.

Finding herself again inside that broken structure, now and then having to dance aside from killer snakes, she discovered that her instinct had been correct. She located what she was looking for, and she knew it was what she had been seeking the moment she laid her eyes on it.

She'd known since her first visit that some great treasure must be hidden in that spot but had decided it would be safer where it was. As long as she had the Sandals, she could always go back for it.

"One thing I soon discovered is that these little red shoes give their wearer more than speed. More than the ability to fly, great as that is. Even if you don't know precisely where the thing is that you're looking for, they'll take you to it."

"That's a tremendous power."

"You should know—*Apollo!*"

"Maybe I should. If I'm a god, I should know a lot of things that I don't."

"Because you are afraid to look for them."

Jeremy was still sitting on the log, and he sighed and closed his eyes. "Yes, probably. Go on; you were telling me about when you went back to the temple."

———————

There had been a time, Carlotta said, when she wanted to make herself great only for the sake of the man she loved—if she came to him as a goddess, or something like one, then he'd be forced to take her seriously.

"But I should have known better. You." She pointed at Jeremy. "You were already a god when you encountered us. Sometime before that you'd somehow found Apollo's Face and put it on."

"I didn't know what I was doing."

"Didn't you? But you did it. You were Apollo himself, the first time you stood in front of Arnobius, and he saw nothing but a grubby human. No more did I, for that matter."

Slowly Jeremy nodded. "That's true. Drugged or awake, he never knew either of us. He never understood Jeremy Redthorn any more than he did Apollo."

"And what does Apollo now have to say to me? Or to the Trickster who now lives in me?"

Jeremy waited for some inner prompting—but there was only passivity. Slowly he raised both hands, palms up. "Nothing, it seems. What does Loki have to say to me?"

The girl's eyes wandered over him. "I don't know. But Carlotta wishes you no harm.

"That night when I first came to you, out on the deck, that was of course before I knew you were a god. Still, by that time I'd noticed something about you that I found very hard to resist. A strength and value, so that I wanted you on my side.

"I was trying to recruit you as my helper, even before I went back to the temple and found the Face and the other treasure. Of course I had the Sandals then, but I needed a partner that I could trust."

Carlotta told Jeremy she'd half-suspected he was a runaway slave, who'd somehow managed to get free of his metal collar.

The plan she'd formulated then had been daring but not impossible. Jeremy could have got clear of the Academy with her help, not to mention Apollo's. They could have returned to the temple in a small boat and loaded a cargo of gold and jewels.

"Before I had the Trickster's power and skills to call upon, there was a definite limit to how much I could carry, flying with the Sandals."

Then, with Jeremy doing the heavy work under Carlotta's guidance, they would have been off across the swamps to freedom—there were other lords, other cities in which they might manage to convert some of the jewels to wealth.

He said: "It wouldn't have worked. Apollo would never have let me go running off like that. He's determined to go to the Oracle, where there are things he wants to do. He has other uses for my mind and body."

She only stared at him for a while, not saying anything.

He asked Carlotta: "What are you going to do now?"

"Do you know, I'm not sure? I want to have a talk with Arnobius—of course." She nodded in the direction of the sleeping figures by the fire. "And do something with him, or about him. Not at the moment, but in a little while. But I wanted to see you first. Is Apollo going to mind if I do something to Arnobius?"

Jeremy looked inward, for some signal that did not come. He said, "As far as I can tell, he's not."

Carlotta brightened. And in the twinkling of an eye, the Sandals carried her away.

Apollo, still earthbound, resumed his watch over his sleeping human companions.

The four pilgrims on resuming their hike soon found themselves on a trail that went angling across the Mountain's lower slopes. Viewed from their current position, the upper Mountain regained the same shape it had had when seen from many miles away—it appeared now an extended range, with a long crest of uneven height, no longer giving the illusion of being a cone with a sharp peak. Here they could be within a few minutes of John and his troops and never know it. It was perfectly possible that other expeditions, armies even, could be going up simultaneously to right and left. And that none of the rival groups might be aware of the others until they all converged near the treeless top.

At least on the side now visible, forests and meadows clothed the Mountain up to about three-fourths of the way to the top—the uppermost fourth was barren rock. The higher ranks of trees were already showing patches of autumn coloring.

For an hour or so, which on this steep path translated into a mile or two of horizontal distance, the explorers climbed with the Mountain on their right. Then came a switchback, which moved the rock wall around to their left. Meanwhile, on the lower side, their increasing altitude gradually spread before them a vista of valley, forest, and field, marked with winding rivers and an occasional road. Somewhere in the distance, more miles away than Jeremy wanted to guess, the hazy sea was faintly visible. Down in the lowlands the colors of late summer were shading into those of early autumn. Sheer height, now totaling thousands of feet, tended to give unaccustomed lowlanders, including Jeremy, a queasy feeling in their stomachs.

Katy was the only human member of the group who had previously been up the Mountain this far, and indeed all the way to the Oracle, to which she knew the trail. When the men wondered aloud what questions she might have asked there, she only shook her head in silence.

Apollo certainly had been to the Cave before, though the experience of this laborious climb on foot did not seem to be stored in his memory. With a minimal effort Jeremy could call up a clear memory of what lay just ahead at any point on this portion of the trail. But as usual, there was much in which his inner god did not seem interested.

The entrance to the Cave lay approximately a mile above the level of the sea. From that point the Mountain went up at least as far again; just how far was impossible to say. People had different ideas on the subject.

Ferrante had never been on the Mountain before, but he wasn't held back by ignorance. He said flatly: "The gods are up there."

It was Kate who asked him: "You believe in the gods?"

"Whenever I get up the Mountain far enough I do. Anyway, I've heard too many stories, from too many people, about what happened in the Cave a couple months ago."

In shade the air was definitely cooler here, though the direct sun could scorch worse than ever. At almost a mile above the sea, autumn had already begun, and the nights were sharply cold, under an unbelievable profusion of stars. In the hours after midnight, tiny icicles began to form wherever water dripped.

Wooded ravines and small, fertile valleys opened on the uphill side of the path, which was now on the right side, now on the left, according to the way the switchback had last turned. Here and there small anonymous peasants' huts were tucked away, their windows peering out of small patches of woods whose rear limits were not discernible.

Jeremy wondered if woodcutters could live on these slopes. No doubt they could, if they could get their product to market. Certainly large trees were plentiful enough. The woods, like the Mountain itself, sometimes gave the impression of being magically extended. Hermits and would-be wizards occasionally. But you'd need villages and towns in which to sell your wood. And the villages up here, if there were any at all, were uniformly tiny.

Jeremy liked to spend a fair amount of time away from his companions. He had much to think about, and thinking was generally easier when he was alone. If he was indeed invested with Apollo's powers, he ought to be doing more than he was doing. But he couldn't dart about the world as Carlotta did and wouldn't have known what to do with such speed if he possessed it.

So he spent a good part of the time climbing by himself, volunteering to forage for wood or food.

Time was passing, the sun lowering. Jeremy was beginning to be bothered by the fact that Katy was no longer in sight. As guide, she of course, more than any of the others, was likely to be scouting ahead. But now several minutes had passed since Jeremy had started looking to find her waiting beside the trail.

Soon he mentioned his concern to Arnobius and Andy.

He told himself that he wasn't really worried about her—not yet.

Would Carlotta, out of some twisted anger, possibly jealousy, have done anything to her? . . . But no, he told himself firmly, that was a foolish thought.

His thoughts returned to Carlotta, who, now that she was also the Trickster, should possess, according to all the information Jeremy could summon up, the ability to look exactly like anyone she chose.

Still he could barely force himself to probe Apollo's memory, and then only under the pressure of immediate need. He was unable to plunge down to the depths where he might find information concerning his colleagues in the pantheon and the subject of godhood in general. If he could have convinced himself that some specific, urgent need had to be met, then maybe—but Jeremy wasn't sure that he'd be able to plunge in even then.

Well, he thought, so be it then. So far the Lord Intruder seemed to be working on the plan of bringing important matters to Jeremy's attention only when the moment had arrived to do something about them. Well, he had to assume that one of the greatest gods in the world knew what he was doing.

And Katy was still missing. Jeremy moved on, all his senses in a heightened state of alertness. He was trying to call up powers that he knew must be his, if he could only find the way to use them.

━━━━━━━━━━

Goats grazing in their high, sloped pastures, some of which seemed tilted more than halfway to the vertical, looked down over their white beards at the intrusive climbers. The beasts' eyes seemed to have the penetrating gaze of wizards, and one reminded Jeremy irresistibly of a certain archivist he'd encountered in the distant library.

Except for a goatherd or two, the climbers encountered no other traffic as they ascended, but certainly the path was not overgrown. It was as if some subtle magic kept it clear. Around it, strange-looking ferns and wildflowers grew in profusion. A swarm of ordinary bees droned somewhere in the middle distance. The common noise had acquired a newly ominous significance, sounding a minor echo of Apollo's vengeance.

Already it was becoming obvious that the Mountain had a great deal of the magical about it. The summit, more crested ridge than single peak, always seemed to be only a little farther on, though perpetually out of sight behind the bulge of the nearer slopes. And yet here, even more than on any ordinary mountain, you could climb for hour after hour, maybe day after day, without reaching the top. Jeremy, now clinging to the flank of the first mountain he had ever climbed—in fact, it was the first the eyes of Jeremy Redthorn had ever seen—found it impossible to rid himself of the eerie feeling that he could go on climbing for years, forever, and still never reach a point where there were no more rocks above him.

━━━━━━━━━━

Over the last days and weeks, the phenomenon he'd first noticed in the Academy barbershop was becoming more pronounced. According to the wondering description provided by Kate, single strands and patches of Jeremy's hair were growing in a lustrous almost-black, matching the traditional look of Apollo. The dark hair was slightly curly, as were his naturally red locks, a detail that somehow made the coloring look all the more artificial.

And Jeremy's face had been ugly, or at least plain, by conventional standards—or at least he had come to think of himself that way. But it was easy to accept Katy's wondering assessment that now, over the past few days, he was growing handsome. Of course his cheeks and chin and upper lip were still as smooth and hairless as they'd ever been.

Fervently he wished for a really good mirror, then decided that if he had one, he'd be afraid to look into it.

Ferrante had a bad few moments when he realized that Jonathan, who'd been only an inch or two the taller on the day they met, now overtopped him by almost a full head. Of course it was only natural for boys of fifteen to grow.

"But this's bloody ridiculous!"

He remembered how Katherine yesterday had noticed and commented on these changes, even before Jeremy himself was fully aware of them. Katherine didn't begin to understand, but she knew there was something strange about this boy, and she liked him and tried to be reassuring.

When Jeremy came upon, in one of the small mountain streams, a pool still enough to offer a coherent reflection, he stared into it, as he had stared at his reflection in the Honeymakers' well, and knew a sinking feeling.

Because he was changing. It didn't seem that he was going to come out looking exactly like the Dark Youth, either—*more* like him, yes, but his bodily proportions were not going to be so perfect, any more than his hair was going to turn entirely black.

It wasn't only a matter of hair or of the changes that came to any boy growing into manhood. What frightened him was that his whole face—no, his whole head; no! his whole body!—seemed to be growing now according to a different pattern, trying to take on the shape of an entirely different person.

Other changes in his body were not as immediately apparent but more substantial. His muscles were no longer merely stringy but rounding into strength. His masculinity was more heavily developed—though for the time being, at least, erotic images rarely intruded upon his thoughts, either waking or sleeping. He supposed that might be because the Intruder of late had been concentrating upon other matters. He had his own business to set his mind on. Yes, all roads, all thoughts, led back to the Intruder. Apparently Jeremy Redthorn was not going to spend much time thinking about subjects in which the Lord Apollo was not interested.

Or worrying about them, either. Thank all the gods—well, thank

Apollo, anyway—that Jeremy's body was developing with a great deal more classic symmetry than his face.

It was hard to remember now, but not that long ago, back around midsummer, he'd had trouble persuading even a moderately ugly village girl—what had her name been? Myra, that was it—not to lie with him but just to tolerate his presence! Even that had seemed a mystical, practically unattainable goal.

And then the Intruder had moved into his head. And the girl called Carlotta, carrying her Sandals hidden somewhere in the boat, had done what she had done, that memorable night on the deck of the catamaran. And now women and girls in general seemed to hunger for him. Even though his body hadn't changed *that* much—the body that had once belonged entirely to Jeremy Redthorn.

And now, according to some ancient, weathered signposts, wood slabs fixed to trees and carved or painted in half a dozen languages, the famed Cave of the Oracle was no more than a mile ahead. Maybe there was also a stone marker or two.

I'm getting really worried about Katy. I thought perhaps we'd find her waiting here.

The shrine ahead of them was also known as the Cave of the Python. Believers said that in it, deep down under the surface of the earth, there dwelt a Monster of Darkness. Evidently Apollo in his previous avatar had tried and failed to conquer this creature—another hero was needed to accept the task and succeed in it.

———

The entrance of the Python's Cave—more precisely, certain features that marked the location of the entrance—were visible from a considerable distance downslope. The Cave itself, according to Jeremy's grafted memory, lay hidden by a large fold of rock until you were almost upon it. But the broad and well-worn paths and the cluster of small buildings nearby left no doubt of where the entrance was.

Having caught this tantalizing glimpse of the entrance from a distance on the path, you found that it disappeared again until you were almost on it.

The party advanced.

———

Arnobius, too, was perturbed by the fact that their Honeymaker guide had disappeared, but in his role of methodical leader he wasn't about to do anything rash because of that.

He gave his orders to his remaining people. Oh, if only he had forty of John's lancers with him! Or even twenty young and angry villagers! He'd seize the mouth of the Cave and hold it until John and the rest of his force arrived.

———————

But Jeremy was becoming more and more grimly concerned with Katy's fate. He was determined to disregard the Scholar's orders and go on to the Cave himself, alone.

And the Intruder, for his own reasons, concurred with this course of action.

Jeremy knew, with certainty and yet with frightening ignorance as to the ultimate source of his knowledge, that this hard whitish rock that stood a mile above the sea had one day been down at the bottom. In the past, the distant past . . . no, the word *distant* was inadequate. That ocean rolled on the far side of a time gulf so immense that he was afraid of what might happen to his mind if he was ever able to see it clearly.

The whitish rock on which his hand was resting contained innumerable small objects that looked like seashells. Here were remnants of what must have been tiny clamlike ocean-dwelling creatures, now encased within the limestone. His new memory confirmed the identification.

There were half a dozen people, a mixture of priests and soldiers, some showing Kalakh's blue and white, standing near the mouth of the Cave. But Jeremy could be sure, before he got any closer, that Katy was not among them. And he knew she wouldn't have gone willingly along the trail past this spot.

———————

Even as he approached the Cave, Jeremy remembered something else that had happened during the Intruder's earlier visit, or visits, to this spot. At certain hours of the day and seasons of the year, looking down into the Cave from outside, if the sunlight fell at the right angle, you could still make out the caveman paintings of some animal being hunted and speared. And another scene in the same style, depicting what could hardly be anything but human sacrifice. A small human figure was in the process of being devoured, and the thing that was doing the devouring looked for all the world like an enormous snake.

25

APOLLO'S MEMORY OF the Cave entrance showed it as one detail of a whole landscape, seen as it had been a few months ago, engulfed in war. But since the Sun God's last and fatal visit here, human activity in the vicinity of the Cave of Darkness had taken on a different character. Open warfare in the area had ended. Human powers allied to Hades were in charge but making no effort to keep others out. Lord Kalakh's priests and soldiers were endeavoring, with some success, to encourage pilgrimages.

Appearances from as close as a hundred yards were still deceptive. At that distance, neither of Jeremy's eyes could see more of the Cave's entrance than a kind of high, shallow grotto, framed by a fringe of tall, thin trees. What Apollo perceived as a grotto was a rough concavity, not deep in comparison with its height and width, that had been formed by natural forces in a towering steep wall. That wall formed one flank of the upper Mountain, which beyond it went on up for an immense distance. From where Jeremy stood now, the summit was still completely out of sight behind intermediate elevations.

The true mouth of the Cave did not become visible until you got much closer, and as Jeremy drew near he saw an enormous hole, ten yards wide, going down into the earth at the base of the grotto. The opening went down almost vertically, so that you could fall into it if you were careless or jump down into it if you tried.

These details seemed new to the Intruder's memory; his previous entrance to the Cave must have been accomplished by a different route.

The pilgrims' road ended here, at the Cave of the Oracle. But as Jeremy approached, he could see that a much smaller path continued climbing past the Cave's mouth and its surrounding clutter of small buildings, people, and animals. For as far as his vision, or Apollo's, could follow that extended way, it appeared to be unobstructed.

Arnobius had commanded the members of his small group to maintain their disguise as pilgrims but not to closely approach the Cave and to avoid as much as possible any contact with Kalakh's people, or the Gatekeeper's. The Scholar was mildly concerned about the fate of Katherine, but then one had to expect some casualties in war—and he had little doubt that a state of war existed, or would soon exist, between Kalakh and the Harbor Lord.

———

But neither Jeremy nor Apollo was minded to wait for Arnobius's permission to look for Katy. Her welfare had now become Jeremy's overriding concern. He didn't see how that could possibly be the Intruder's goal as well—but whatever Lord Apollo's plan might be, it, like Jeremy's, evidently called for a prompt approach to the entrance of the Cave. Jeremy kept expecting that he would have to fight some internal duel, at least a skirmish, with the Intruder over control of the body they both inhabited. He more than half-expected something of the kind to develop now. But Apollo did not dispute him in the matter.

———

Here, of course, was the site of the world's most famous oracle. That was one point on which the vast memory of the Intruder and the very skimpy one of Jeremy Redthorn were in agreement.

And here, of course, in one of the Cave's deep rooms, was where the recent but already legendary battle between Hades and Apollo had taken place. Memory assured Jeremy that it had been much more than a legend.

Traditionally the Cave stood open to anyone who wanted to try his or her luck at gaining power or advantage out of it or obtaining a free prophecy. And Apollo's vision showed Jeremy something that made him want to make the attempt.

What kind of questions did most visitors ask the Oracle? Apollo's memory could readily provide an answer based on hearsay. As a rule, rich and poor alike wanted to know basically the same things: whether they were fated to enjoy success in love and in money matters. Generally the poor were able, for a small fee, to take part in a kind of mass prophecy.

Arnobius had chosen a campsite about a hundred yards from the Cave entrance, and here the Scholar planned to wait for some indication that Lord John and his lancers were in the vicinity.

Winter tended to come early at this altitude, but so far the weather remained mild, and an abandoned hut provided sufficient shelter, though one wall had fallen in. There were a number of similar structures standing about, put up and used and abandoned by successive parties of pilgrims.

Ferrante was beginning to share Jeremy's worries about Katherine. But to the soldier she was not important enough to disobey a direct order. To Jeremy she had become just that. Soon his need to go and look for her became too strong to resist. Without a word to anyone, and with no clear plan in mind, he set out alone for the Cave entrance.

Neither Arnobius nor Ferrante was immediately aware of Jeremy's departure, and none of the people near the entrance to the Cave paid much attention to the boy as he came walking calmly down the path.

While the little knot of attendants were chatting among themselves, Jeremy came to a casual merchant's table, suitable for some small bazaar, on which a miscellany of items had been set out for sale.

Almost at once Jeremy came to a halt, his gaze fixed on one item among this merchandise: he was looking at Katherine's homemade backpack, the one with the bee and the flower embroidered on it.

He grabbed up the pack, which was empty now, and held it up to the sunlight and could see his fingers trembling. She'd told him that her father had made the thing from leather and tough canvas and her mother, required to use a special needle for the heavy fabric, had sewn on the design.

One of the men who dealt in buying and selling came sliding close to him, bringing a scent of cheap perfume. "A pretty and useful object, sir. The price is very reasonable."

"It may be higher than you think." Out of the boy's throat came a remote voice that seemed to have little to do with Jeremy Redthorn.

The man drew back a step.

Some items of women's clothing were on display also, on the same table. Jeremy, knowing himself to be outwardly calm except that his hands were still shaking, opened the empty pack and began to restore to it what he assumed were its proper contents, including some items of spare clothing that he thought he recognized. Then he strapped it shut and hooked it over his shoulder, next to his own pack.

"Here, sir, payment is due on that!"

Jeremy turned and looked at the man. "Do you insist on payment?" the voice of Apollo asked, not loudly, and there were no more protests.

The boy turned away, with the feeling of one moving in a dream, again facing the Cave entrance, not knowing exactly what would come next but confident that whatever it was would be the necessary thing.

There came a sound of a single pair of feet behind him, hurrying, and suddenly Ferrante was at his elbow, dressed as a pilgrim and not a soldier, looking agitated but trying to conceal it. In a low voice he said to Jeremy: "Scholar's looking for you. I got my orders to bring you back."

Jeremy was still walking toward the Cave. "I've got my orders, too, Andy. I'm going on."

Ferrante didn't get it. "Orders? From—?"

"This pack I just picked up is Katy's. I think the worst thing that could have happened to her has happened. I'm going to find out."

Ferrante looked upset, but he wasn't going to create a disturbance by taking physical measures to stop Jeremy—not here, in the public eye, with a dozen or more armed enemies in sight.

———

Half-consciously Jeremy was still bracing himself for conflict with the Lord Apollo over what their next joint move was going to be. But the precaution proved quite unnecessary. His left eye began to supply him with symbolic guidance, and the direction chosen seemed appropriate for aggressive action.

The two who walked in one body were going on, into the Cave. To locate Katy if they could, to bring her out if she was still alive. On all these points the Intruder was with him all the way.

The question of what Apollo might want of him, later, in return, came up in Jeremy's mind, but he brushed it aside for now, as of no importance. Steadily he walked forward, with Ferrante, not knowing what to do, following uncertainly a couple of steps behind.

Almost immediately Jeremy was challenged again, this time with serious intent. The sentry was well armed, equipped with helm and shield, a figure of burly confidence, almost twice Jeremy's bulk.

"No passage, this way, you!"

Now there was no need for patience any longer—anyway, he and Apollo had both had enough of patience. But neither, the Intruder assured him wordlessly, was there any need to waste an arrow here.

How, then?

Easily. Like this.

Jeremy watched as his own right arm swung to the left across his body, then lashed backhanded at the sentry. It was a casual blow but effective. In one direction soared the soldier's shield, painted with the black and red device of Hades, while his spear, now in two pieces, flew another way. The man himself went dancing straight back, feet scarcely touching the ground, until he hit the wall eight feet behind his post. Sliding down that barrier, he lay unmoving on the ground.

Seeing the way ahead now unimpeded, Jeremy walked on, forward and down. His mind was glowing with pleasant surprise, but the sensations in his right arm were less agreeable. It had gone numb, from fingertips to shoulder, and now life was slowly returning in the form of a painful stinging.

A few people standing in the middle distance had turned their heads at the sound of the sentry's demolition, but no one had actually seen anything happen. The body lying at the foot of the wall was hard to see, and there was nothing alarming in Jeremy's measured pace.

As the boy moved ahead, he thought: *Damn it all, Intruder! Remember, this body we share is only human flesh and bone. A few more shots like that one, and it won't be any use to you!* Then briefly he felt aghast at his own impudence—but, damn it, as long as he was allowed his own thoughts he was going to have them. He had never taken a reverential approach toward the god who shared his flesh and blood, and he was in no mood to start now.

Evidently his impudence was not resented; perhaps it meant no more to his resident divinity than a dog's bark or cameloid's groan.

Still Jeremy's hands were empty, the bow and quiver on his back, not yet needed. *Maybe I should have picked up the sentry's knife, or the sharp end of his broken spear, to use in the next fight.* But no, he could feel that Apollo's approval for that course of action was lacking. He had his chosen bow and arrows. If Jeremy at any point needed to gather additional equipment or detour for any other reason, the god would doubtless let him know.

He'd actually forgotten Ferrante for the moment. Now a small sound made him turn, to see the young soldier petrified with astonishment. Jeremy's finger pointed. Out of his throat came Apollo's voice, not loud but commanding: "Go back to the Scholar, and tell him that the Lord Apollo has gone into the Cave."

"The Lord . . ." Ferrante's face had suddenly gone gray, his eyes as they regarded Jeremy turned into those of a frightened stranger.

"Yes. Tell him." Turning, Jeremy strode on.

Obviously the Intruder had been in this part of the Python's Cave before and was familiar with many of its details. Now it was possible to get a better idea of the location of the room, buried in the earth somewhere ahead, where about two months ago the last previous avatar of Apollo had been slain by some overwhelming enemy.

Many additional nuggets of information were suddenly available, a bewildering variety of clues leading up to that event, and much emotion attached to it, but Jeremy firmly refused to dig into any of that now.

A minute ago, he'd been fearful that his Apollo component might come bursting out of hiding and take complete control of his behavior—that Jeremy would become a prisoner in his own head and eventually perhaps be ground up and compressed to nothing there. But now he had no sense that anything of the kind was happening. It was Jeremy Redthorn who was putting one foot ahead of the other, determined to head down into the Cave, whatever anyone else, human or god, might want from him. Certainly he was no puppet. . . . People stared at him, salesmen and priests and would-be guardians, as he strode past them and went on down. They must have wondered who he was, but none of them had noticed what had happened to the sentry.

Looking down from very near the sharply defined brink of the entrance, Jeremy beheld a winding path, almost too narrow for two people to edge past each other, but smooth and well-worn into rock, clinging to the side of the Cave, which was almost vertical here at the start. An easy place to defend, if your enemies were trying to fight their way up out of the ground. The path in its first descent went halfway round the great hole. Then it started to switchback lower, fading and losing itself in the devouring darkness after a distance of perhaps a hundred paces. His left eye could follow it only a little farther than his right. How far beyond that the Cave might descend into the earth he had no means of guessing. Nor did the stories offer much real information, except that it was very large and some of them claimed that it connected with the Underworld.

Jeremy tried a gingerly search of Apollo's memory for details of the Cave's configuration at this point but came up blank. To reach the Cave beyond this point, the Intruder, in the course of his previous visit, must have traveled by some different route.

Lord John and the almost four hundred troops under his command had found their way down the western side of the gorge, forded the tumultuous stream at the bottom, and located a trail to bring them up the eastern side, all the while trying with belated caution to guard against another ambush. The kidnappers' trail had been more than a day old by the time they reached it. More long and painful hours had passed before the searchers were able to pick up the right path and follow it to the Honeymakers' village.

——

Now the boy Jeremy was standing in the cavern's first great room, a roof of rock some thirty feet above his head. But he was still so close to the surface that the sky was barely out of sight. There was still plenty of daylight with which to examine the details of his surroundings.

Stalking from one to another of the prisoner cages that stood near the entrance to the Cave, inspecting the contents, the visitor made sure that Katy wasn't in any of them. Once that was accomplished, Jeremy now felt certain of where she had gone—down and in. The only remaining uncertainty, and it seemed a slight one, was whether she was already dead, somewhere under the earth.

Here the Gatekeeper's people, who were also the merchants of sacrifice, were definitely open for business. Half a dozen intended victims, their number divided equally between girls and boys, were even now awaiting their turns, in the same number of wooden enclosures. All were young; all had probably looked healthy when they were caught, not many days ago—unblemished specimens were generally preferred. Now they had the appearance of being drugged, their naked bodies slumped in awkward positions or crouched, like animals, over their own droppings. They turned to Jeremy eyes that were very human but utterly lost.

He held his breath until he had made sure that Katy was not among them.

In similar cages nearby there also waited an assortment of animals. Posted prices indicated that one or two of the beasts, rare and almost perfect specimens, cost more than some of the humans. Doubtless they were more difficult to obtain.

The cages were rough cubes about five feet on a side, and some of them at least were set on wooden platforms, to raise the contents somewhat above the ground. This no doubt made easier such cleaning and feeding as was undertaken.

Several of the cages were new, which Jeremy took as evidence that business was good. Generally the heavy cages were left here and only the helpless occupants, their bodies painted with magical designs, were dragged or carried down into the earth, to Hades's kingdom.

Jeremy, who despite his recent adventures still looked reasonably prosperous, was given additional information by one of the attendants, who wanted to sell him an animal or a human.

Lord Apollo was eager to proceed, his spirits were high, and his attitude imbued their joint progress with a certain style. Jeremy Redthorn might have advanced at an anxious run, but that would not do for the senior partner. Regally he stifled the impulse to trot and infused the boy's walk and carriage with a kingly grace as he approached the next set of attendants, who now gave him their full attention as he drew near.

One man in particular came out bowing and fawning, smirking as if he thought he was approaching an incognito prince. His object was, of course, to sell the prince one or more humans. The other attendants smiled and bowed. There was nothing like youthful specimens of humanity, perfect in every limb, if you wanted to please the Dark God with a really classy sacrifice.

Did the Cave Monster, Jeremy Redthorn wondered, have any real interest in devouring helpless humans? Yes, the Intruder's memory assured him. One point was surprising—the hunger of the thing below seemed to be more for beauty and rationality than for meat. The monster, then, was some perverted god, surviving from the last cycle of deity creation. It may have played that role, as well as many others. In past cycles, if not placated by sacrifice, it had come out to ravage the countryside.

Exactly which member of the partnership, Jeremy Redthorn or Apollo, made the final decision to smash the cages in this Cave anteroom before going farther down Jeremy was never afterward quite sure. It seemed to be one of those things that they agreed on, though their motives were quite different.

One of the attributes of Apollo, as cataloged at the Academy, was that he was not readily impressed by sacrifices. Rather, what he looked for in his worshipers was a seeking for purification, a willingness to atone for guilt.

Nor, one would think, would Apollo have any particular interest in the welfare of a humble village girl named Katherine, any more than he would in any of the other intended sacrifices. After Jeremy had looked internally for an answer, he decided that the Far-Worker's reason for smashing the cages was that he, Apollo, meant to claim the Cave as territory from Hades, his mortal enemy. Eventually, perhaps, he would relocate the true oracle where it belonged, up on the peak of the Mountain, in open sunlight.

———————

Jeremy's right arm, which he had bruised against the sentry's bony mass and armor, still pained him—not a disabling injury, but certainly a warning of this body's vulnerability. The boy thought that, for once, he could almost follow the Intruder's thoughts: *First, before I enter serious combat, I must attend to this body, this tool, which is my best and only essential weapon; limbs so feeble and tender must first be strengthened.*

And Jeremy's hands and wrists came up before his face, in such a way that he could not be sure if he himself had willed their rising up or not. A moment later *something,* as if pumped by his heart and in his blood, came flowing through his back and shoulders, spreading, trickling, down into both arms. He could follow the interior flow by the feeling that it generated of a buzzing, liquid warmth. He was intensely reminded of the never-to-be-forgotten sensation of the mask fragment melting and flowing into his head through the apertures of eye and ear.

The feeling of warmth and flow abated, leaving him slightly dizzy and with a pounding heart. His arms looked no more formidable than before as he raised them and gripped the cage—and yet he knew that the power of the Dark Youth had entered into them. He pulled with the right hand, pushed with the left, in almost the same motion he would have used to draw a bow. Moderate effort yielded spectacular results. Under the pressure of those arms, green logs four inches thick went splintering in white fragments, and the tough withes that had bound the cage together exploded from it. Briefly there was the sound of timber breaking, a forest falling in a gale. The noise put an end to any hope that his further progress would remain unnoticed by those in the room with him.

There was shouting and confused activity among the humans milling around.

Noncombatants, women and a scattering of children, as well as a few aged men, were screaming and shouting in panic, getting themselves out of the way as rapidly as possible.

There came a well-remembered flapping, whistling, sighing in the air around him. Apollo was suddenly happy, an emotion so vital that Jeremy caught it almost at once from his senior partner. How marvelous that there should be furies here! They must be kept like watchdogs by some greater power, for a whole swarm of them now came soaring and snarling out of the depths of the Cave.

It crossed Jeremy's mind to wonder if these might even be counted as domestic animals and thus be readily subject to his control. He wasn't going to find out, and, in fact, he immediately forgot the question, for the sight and sound and smell of them had triggered a killing rage in both of the entities inhabiting Jeremy Redthorn's frame. His—or the Dark Youth's—left arm lashed out like a striking snake and clutched a handful of mousy skin, stopping the creature in midflight. It screamed while its whips flailed at him, with no more effect than on a marble statue.

A moment later, the Lord of Light had seized a wing root in each hand and was ripping the beast apart, with no greater effort than Jeremy Redthorn would have used tearing paper. A maimed body fell to the Cave floor, and black blood splashed and flew. Only later did Jeremy realize how his face and clothing had been splattered.

Then he seized one of the dealers in human souls and bodies by his neck, took one long-clawed fury foot in his other hand, and used the talons to obliterate the slaver's face.

———

Again Jeremy stalked forward. Now he was approaching the first internal barrier he'd encountered since entering the Cave, a gate of wood or metal that was already standing open. The smoke of pungent incense rose from a wide, shallow bowl supported atop a tall three-legged stool of black wood.

The debauched priestess who mouthed the prophecies swayed on her three-legged stool, staring with drugged eyes at the newcomers. An aging woman, her sagging breasts exposed, a tawdry crown poised crooked on her head.

She reacted violently to the presence of Apollo/Jeremy. "Lord of Light, I know you! You come to die again!"

Jeremy/Apollo ignored the nonsense she gibbered at him and stalked on, leaving behind him a growing pandemonium. The captives that he'd freed would have to see to themselves now—his own real task lay ahead.

On he stalked, and down.

Once more a single figure, this time a man, confronted him. And out of memory new material suddenly emerged: At the inner entrance to the Cave there ruled, partly by cunning, partly by tradition, the Gate-keeper—a human remembered only vaguely by Apollo and of whose actual age even Apollo could not be sure. But it was hard for even Apollo to remember a time when there had been no Gatekeeper at the Cave.

Could it possibly have been the same individual, all that time?

. . . quite old in his appearance, and of a lean and vicious aspect, who a few months ago, at the time of the great duel, had commanded the debased remnant of the traditional attendants of the shrine.

In Jeremy's left eye he looked even worse.

And now he himself hardly ever emerged from the Cave but rather shunned the sunlight.

He had wisps of graying hair, once red, curling around a massive skull. Once he had been impressively muscled, and still his body possessed wiry strength, fueled by meanness. Large portions of his tawny skin, wherever it was visible, were covered with tattoos. Once there had been rings in his ears and nose, but now only the hard-lipped scars remained.

He was cynical and evil—but in his heart he was still waiting for the true god to reappear.

For almost as long as Apollo could remember, the world had accepted the Gatekeeper (really a succession of Gatekeepers, the god supposed) as chief overseer of all sacrifices at the shrine. The only ones in which he took keen interest were those in which a human was set before the God of the Underworld—the immolation of youth or maiden, their nude bodies painted, then carried, drugged and helpless, down into the darkness, where they were bound to their log frames and left to whatever might come for them.

Later, so the whispers said, he sometimes went down again, alone, to revisit the victims. If Hades or one of his creatures had not yet accepted the sacrifice, the Gatekeeper sometimes tortured or raped them. Once or twice, acting on an impulse he could not explain, he had killed a victim mercifully with a swift knife thrust.

———

"I see," called Apollo to the waiting figure, as Apollo/Jeremy strode near, "that your master, Hades, has not yet decided to devour you."

"It may be that he will, someday, Sun God." The voice that came from the ravaged face was surprisingly deep and firm and unafraid. "But the knowledge has little terror for me."

"Have you forgotten what terror feels like, torturer? It is very dangerous for any human to entirely forget that."

"Only one thing, my Lord Apollo," said the deep voice from the ruined face, "any longer is capable of filling me with true dread—and so long as I am not confronted by that one thing, I seem to have forgotten what it is."

━━━━━━━

The Gatekeeper had been the first of Hades's human allies to reach the scene after the most recent killing of Apollo. Prophecies were handed out under his auspices. He controlled, most of the time, the demented woman who generally uttered them. More often than not she was just putting on an act and saying what the Gatekeeper told her to say. Sometimes she was passing along what came down, in some jumbled way, from the summit.

━━━━━━━

The Gatekeeper was not trying to block the path, and Apollo/Jeremy strode on past him. Once more the man spoke briefly to Apollo, then dodged and fled when Apollo merely raised a hand to his bow, as if to grasp and draw it.

The Gatekeeper fled down into the depths, to bring his dark master word of the new incursion.

━━━━━━━

Jeremy now was in the third great chamber of the Cave, out of sight of the entrance by some hundreds of feet. But there was still plenty of indirect daylight to let him find the path.

His attention was focused on the way ahead. There he could see with his left eye the reflections of a distant reddish glow and hear with his left ear the echoes created by the shuffling approach of the monster Hades.

He knew that these were signs of the approach of Hades, who must now be coming up, with strength renewed for renewed battle, from however far down in the earth his last retreat had carried him.

Jeremy strained his senses listening, wondering if Cerberus might be coming up also. Apollo's memory was not reassuring on the subject of Cerberus, picturing a multiheaded, doglike shape of monstrous size—and neither human nor divine. Apollo seemed reluctant to push the image of that shape forward, where Jeremy might have a good look at it.

And what of Thanatos? What Hades had said might well be true:

If that mask fragment had been retrieved from the stream carrying it under the earth, then the God of Death might already have been reborn in the body of another human avatar. There would be no shortage of people ready to enter the great game in that role. Still, Apollo seemed to believe that the odds were against Thanatos having been already revived.

So an active Thanatos was a real possibility, and so was a reconstructed Cerberus. If all three of those dark allies should come against him at the same time . . . but he could not think yet of turning back.

The Enemy's chief avatar, when he finally appeared, was, like Jeremy himself, no more than man-size, physically. But his true dimensions were hard to see at first, such was the dominant impression of overwhelming strength.

Even Apollo had difficulty in determining practical details from a distance. Minor changes in form had occurred since the two gods' last encounter. The only clear impressions coming through to Jeremy were of malevolence and enormous destructive power.

The one who approached seemed to move in the form of rippling shadows, which the light of the torches spaced around the walls could do nothing to disperse.

This was a presence monumentally powerful. Beside the Lord of the Underworld, even Death, which Apollo, if not Jeremy, had already experienced, faded toward insignificance.

Hades, on coming at last into conversational range, put on a show of mockery and feigned obeisance. "I go to prepare a place of entertainment for you." His voice was not loud, but it boomed and echoed, as if it were coming from some great distance.

Jeremy had not long to wait to hear, from his own lips, Apollo's reply. "Indeed I am ready to be entertained. Prepare whatever objects and ceremonies you choose. But remember that whatever is in this Cave, inside this Mountain, will soon be mine. I intend to take the Oracle from you and make it speak the truth."

"Truth, great Far-Worker? The simple truth is that you will be dead."

"Here I am," said Apollo simply, spreading out Jeremy's boyish-looking arms.

The dark shape nodded, shifted. "Perhaps, Sun God, you count the death of Death a few days ago as a great victory. You sent his mask into the earth, but I can bring it out again. A new avatar of Thanatos will step forward, and you should be warned that it will make little difference to you; you and your friends will still be subject to death."

The Lord of Light was unperturbed. "So will everyone else."

"Not I. I am surprised that you value your own life so lightly. The body you have chosen to wear this time looks a poor one, and inadequate."

"Not so feeble that you can knock it down with words. Here I am, standing in it. What do you intend?"

There came a grating sound that might have been a laugh. Even the Lord of the Silver Bow had better beware of this opponent. Others might have been fearful, but not Hades. Yes, even the Far-Worker, and even had he still been possessed of his full strength. The Lord of Light was not all that he had once been, as the history of his last visit to this Cave showed, and certain vague but terrible memories warned . . .

And Jeremy's vague opponent bowed in mockery. "Here all the ways lie open before you. Let us see what your new avatar is able to accomplish."

Apollo had nothing to say to that, and Jeremy knew that at last the time had come to unsling his captured bow.

He noted without surprise that his hands, however human and puny they might be, handled the weapon with easy familiarity. And he noted once more, with cool regret, how mediocre, not to say poor, were its materials and workmanship. No Silver Bow, this, but it would have to do. Unhurriedly he reached back into the quiver and drew and nocked against the bowstring one of the dead bandit's knobby arrows—the first three fingers of young Jeremy Redthorn's right hand, curling themselves around the string, seemed to know precisely what had to be done next, even if his conscious mind did not.

26

HADES HAD RETREATED, for the moment, without Jeremy or the Intruder even getting a good look at him. But the Intruder already knew their enemy well, and Jeremy needed no advice from his partner to know that their problems were not over.

The thought now dominant in Jeremy Redthorn's consciousness might have been entirely his own: *We are going to be tested.*

There sounded a clatter of rocks under clumsy feet. Here, scrambling and stumbling about in nervous eagerness, came a dozen human skirmishers, those calling themselves Guardians of the Oracle. They claimed to serve the Gatekeeper and to protect all pilgrims, but Apollo knew with certainty that they were the people who had taken Katy—and they were in the service of Hades.

The first guardians to react to Apollo/Jeremy's intrusion were all male and lacking any common insignia or uniform. They appeared to be a mixed bag indeed. Two or three of them, in the Intruder's judgment, looked the part of competent warriors, professionally equipped and moving with the air of men who knew their business. But all the rest were poorly armed, wielding mere sticks and knives, and not dressed for the part at all. Their movements were uncertain. Obviously they had been hastily summoned from other duties and pressed into service. Mixed groups of such men were assembling, more slowly than their leaders would have liked, out in front of the Cave, with their vanguard close inside its mouth. Some had been pressed into service from the attendants outside, while others came moving up out of the earth in advance of their dread master.

Jeremy had the feeling that the Intruder was not impressed by the quality of the opposition so far; his forward progress neither slowed nor hastened.

Someone running by in haste toppled the tripod of the pythoness; she had already disappeared. Torch flames swayed in the flow of air generated by human movement. The noncombatants who fled turned back to watch as soon as they had reached what they judged was a safe distance. *Quite possibly they are wrong about that,* Apollo's memory assured his human partner.

The half-dozen prisoners intended for sacrifice who had suddenly found themselves no longer on sale had evidently been shocked out of their drugged lassitude by the experience, for they had all disappeared when Jeremy looked back; he supposed they were climbing toward the surface and some of them could get clean away.

Instead of rounding up the prisoners again, their guards had turned their backs on the wrecked and splintered cages and now formed the nucleus of Apollo's opposition. Someone in charge of Underworld operations here on the surface had been suitably impressed by the progress so far of the lean youth with the particolored hair.

With Apollo's concurrence, Jeremy took a moment to adjust the position of the two packs and the quiver on his back, where in his anger they seemed weightless.

Now, with his borrowed bow of mediocre quality clutched firmly in his left hand, he stepped across the unmarked threshold of the entrance and warily set his booted feet on the descending path.

Rage still burned in him, too huge and active a force to leave room for much in the way of fear.

And almost immediately, rage found its next object.

On the trail ahead, and also flanking the trail on both sides, Jeremy's left eye made out bright-rimmed shadows, advancing furtively through the thick gloom. Human figures, much like those he had just seen mobilized on the surface. Human, or something close to human, armed, many bearing shields, wearing helms and partial armor, and intent on his destruction.

Among them were several specimens of a type of enemy only just recognizable, not familiar, even to Apollo. These were apelike creatures, hairy and shambling. Naked zombies, dropping their dung when they walked, like animals. Jeremy's god-companion was surprised to see such creatures this near the surface of the earth.

When the most aggressive of them slung a stone at him, Apollo's right hand came up—before its original owner had begun to react at all—and caught the missile in midair, with a meaty but quite painless impact. In the next moment a flick of the wrist returned the projectile to its sender, faster than his sling had sent it. Jeremy saw the small rock glance off a dodging figure and knock it down.

Five seconds later, he loosed his first arrow, again almost without having made any conscious decision. Drawing and releasing were accomplished in a single fluid motion, delayed until the precise moment when two of the advancing foe were lined up, one behind the other. The first arrow, broad-bladed and meant for hunting, darted away at invisible speed, taking its first target precisely where the bowman's left eye had focused, in the small space between his heavy leather belt and armored vest. At a range of no more than a dozen yards, the shaft penetrated completely, pushing the broad hunting point through layers of clothing, skin and muscle and guts, and out again through the man's back. The primary target let out an unearthly cry and fell, his fingers clutching uselessly at the place where the feathered end of the arrow had disappeared into his paunch.

Scarcely deflected by some contact with hard bone, the dart sped on, to bury half its length in the neck of another trooper who had been climbing close behind the first. Another of Apollo's enemies who moved in human shape was down.

But Jeremy's quiver now held only five arrows more. The fingers of his and Apollo's right hand, reaching back behind his head, counted them, making sure, before he drew another out.

He killed repeatedly; he dodged more missiles. He caught and hurled back another stone, swiftly nocked another arrow, and killed again. Sliding silently away when his two-legged foemen managed to work their way too near him—he was willing to let them live, if they would let him pass—with unerring skill dropping one after another of those who remained in his way, Jeremy successfully fought his way through the monster's advance guard of humans.

Eventually a slung stone caught him in the left shoulder, when he was unable to dodge two in the same instant. But on his magically strengthened flesh the impact, which would ordinarily have broken bone, was no worse than a punch from a small boy's fist. Moments later an arrow hit him in the back, and then another, but both bounced off, after delivering no more than gentle taps.

Reaching back a hand, Jeremy could feel that only two of his own arrows were now left in the quiver. But he had no quarrel with Apollo's evident intention of going on.

Farther down would be the room in which today's sacrifice had been exposed, to await the pleasure of the Lord of the Underworld, or such creatures as he might allow to accept it in his name.

The room Jeremy was in now, like many of the others, was cluttered with stalactites and stalagmites. Rock formations offered good cover, especially in the near-darkness.

Though Jeremy sought cover in shadows as well as behind rocks, he knew deep darkness was his enemy and sunlight his friend—such little sunlight as came this far into the Cave, filtered and reflected.

A few of Hades's fallen warriors had been carrying bow and arrows also—most fighters would choose a different weapon for close work in bad lighting—and Jeremy/Apollo, stalking from one body to another, stooping and taking when no live enemy threatened, was able to replenish his armament. He obtained three usable shafts from the quiver of one of his victims, five from another. Already he had noticed that it seemed to matter little how true the arrows were, how sharp or broad their heads. They carried death with them, unerringly, when the Far-Shooter willed that they do so.

Soon those of the Enemy's human allies who were still on their feet had withdrawn into the depths, leaving half a dozen of their number, who would fight no more, on the Cave floor. There was some light down there, because their human eyes needed some to see.

Methodically, Jeremy stalked on, going to the next chamber farther down.

Somewhat worried by Jonathan's prolonged absence, the Scholar had moved forward to a position no more than about fifty yards from the Cave's main entrance. There Arnobius had climbed a tree, establishing himself in a good position to overlook whatever might be happening at the portal. He had settled himself on a limb of comfortable thickness, some fifteen feet above the ground. At this height he had an easy view downhill, overlooking lower growth.

From that vantage point the Scholar considered the situation. During various cycles of enthusiasm, some lasting for centuries, parties of pilgrims from places far and near had come to visit this consecrated spot and had worn a network of paths among the nearby trees. Those who sought help from the Oracle had been coming here for centuries. The business of pilgrimages had recently started to boom again, after a long decline.

So, this was it, the world's most famous site of prophecy. As one who had been much interested in the gods and their history, the Scholar might well have been here before, under conditions far more peaceful. As far back as Arnobius could remember, the thought of coming to the Oracle had tempted him. But always it had seemed that he was unready, unworthy, his preparations incomplete.

Over the last few months the Oracle had rapidly acquired, in the popular mind, a close association with Apollo, for it was widely said to be the place where the god had died.

Arnobius wasn't entirely sure what to make of the human hangers-on and parasites at the mouth of the Cave, who were evidently pretending to be in charge of the Oracle.

After observing for a little while what went on at the entrance, he thought to himself: *Even though the real power lies far below, in the Underworld, and well they know it, they try to exact a toll from all who approach. If a strong party refuses to pay, the attendants do not press the point.*

He wondered whether they had any control over what prophecies were made. How much did Hades, their master, interest himself in such matters? Maybe, the Scholar thought, they were as legitimate as any set of humans in this place could be. Only trying to make a living—of course they would prefer to make a damned good living, if that were possible. But all prophecies now were fraudulent, without exception.

Once, a long time ago, he supposed that things had been much different here. Now, all was in the hands of opportunists. He'd heard they kept on hand a half-demented woman with the ability to go into convincing trances on demand, a performance that satisfied the usual pilgrims.

Arnobius considered that his father was certainly not the only powerful warlord who would dearly love to be able to secretly control the prophecies given to his enemies. In fact, Lord Victor would probably care less than most about having such control. But Lord Victor was one of many chieftains who would all give a great deal to be in charge here—but at the same time many of these powers were reluctant to become too closely entangled in the affairs of the Oracle.

But as far as the Scholar knew, no useful prophecies had issued from this oracle for a long time. Probably whatever power had used to make them had been for a long time dead or disabled.

And of course the presence of Cerberus and other horrors inside the Cave was a powerful deterrent to at least some of the adventurers who would otherwise have swarmed in eagerly, seeking power and treasure.

Arnobius was beginning to be convinced that all human attempts to understand the gods were doomed to failure. People, now, were a different matter. Much more comprehensible. And amenable to being controlled.

He was disturbed about what Jonathan might stir up in his mad intrusion of the Cave. Even the newly cynical Arnobius, as he watched, began to be impressed by the approach to this particular Oracle.

He wondered if the place below had really been the site of a deadly battle between two gods. Paradoxically, now that he was actually here, the whole business of gods and magic seemed distant, hard to believe in at all.

Conversely, practical political and military matters seemed to stand out in his mental vision as solidly as the Mountain itself. He wondered why it had taken so long for him to discover his own considerable natural talent in those fields.

Ferrante had come with him, and the Scholar soon sent the young soldier off to scout.

"I'm concerned that Jonathan will get into some kind of trouble, do something foolish. If you find him, tell him to get back here at once."

"What about the girl, sir?"

"Well—tell her also if you see her." He raised a hand to hold the sergeant in place for one more order. "On second thought, tell her she can go home now if she wants to. Perhaps that would be best for her."

When Sergeant Ferrante had saluted and moved away, Arnobius resumed his contemplation of the scene below. He began to wonder whether one of the people near the Cave entrance might spot him in his tree, and this led him to reflect upon the kind of clothing he was now wearing. Glancing down at himself, his clothing, the Scholar took note of the fact that over the last few days, since being ambushed by bandits, he'd more or less fallen into a style of dress very far from the academic.

It hadn't been a matter of trying to imitate the military or, indeed, of any conscious decision. But given the kind of business in which he was now engaged, there were certainly practical reasons for strapping on weapons, wearing a broad-brimmed, chin-strapped hat, a plain coat with many pockets, and sturdy footgear.

Another newly discovered need nagged at the Scholar: as soon as he had the chance, he intended to learn the fine points of using weapons; the next opponent he met in that way was liable to be much more formidable than a demoralized bandit already poisoned by bee stings. The further use of sword and spear was not something he looked forward to; it was just something that had to be done, and he had learned that one could not always count on having skilled subordinates around to handle it.

All in all, the Scholar had been forced into a new way of looking at the world. Somewhat to his own surprise, he found himself quite well suited to it, possessed of a latent ability to inspire others to follow him. It seemed he had that, though until very recently he'd never needed or wanted to put it to use. The young men had been quite willing for him to lead them into combat. Except for a few like Jonathan—

Was that Jonathan, striding toward the entrance? Certainly the lone figure seemed taller than Arnobius's servant, and it did not move with a menial's walk. But there was that red-black hair. And here now, disposing of all doubts, came Sergeant Ferrante, perfectly recognizable, in awkward and tentative pursuit.

Turmoil below, around the Cave mouth, interrupted the watcher's train of thought. Arnobius didn't know what to make of it, at least at first. Some of the words being shouted below carried to his ears, but at first they made no sense.

One word that he heard shouted was: "Apollo!" And another, in the language of Kalakh, was: "Mobilize!"

Suddenly it crossed the Scholar's mind to wonder whether the people down there might actually be convinced that his servant Jonathan was, in fact, an avatar of the god Apollo.

Arnobius was pondering the ramifications of this when his thoughts were interrupted by a sudden feeling, apparently causeless but far too strong to be ignored, that he was no longer alone. Turning his head without any special haste, Arnobius first glanced down at the foot of the tree—no one was there. Then he turned to look behind him.

Sitting on an adjacent branch, only little more than an arm's length distant, was a slender figure wearing what looked like a comic actor's stage mask and a simple sexless costume, loose blouse and trousers of conservative cut and drab color, set off by a pair of bright red Sandals. At first glance it was plain to the Scholar that his visitor had to be a god or goddess, because no mere human could possibly have come to occupy that place in undetected silence.

A long moment passed while mortal and deity contemplated each other in silence. The shaded eyes behind the jester's mask appeared to be studying Arnobius intently. The apparition had assumed its place so simply and naturally that so far the Scholar felt himself remarkably calm; it was as if he had known all his life that sooner or later he would have some clear and unambiguous confrontation with divinity.

At last, having taken in the details of the other's appearance, he cleared his throat and said with certainty: "You are the Trickster."

The figure did not reply.

When another half-minute had passed and the god figure still maintained its silence, the Scholar tried again: "If you are a god . . . ," and let his words die away.

The other leaned toward him. The tones of the voice that now suddenly erupted from behind the mask were feminine and staggeringly familiar.

" 'If'? What else should I be, sitting up here? A monkey like yourself? You've always lacked the wit to recognize divinity, even when it stood right in front of you, trying to get your attention."

"I—"

"Shut up!" The command was so forceful that he obeyed. "You are a remarkably stupid man, even for an Academic and a scholar." And she crossed her ankles, calling attention to the remarkable red Sandals.

Then she raised a small hand and pulled aside her mask and hurled it away, revealing the perfectly recognizable face of the woman who had once been the Scholar's companion, concubine, and slave.

"Carlotta!" He hadn't really believed in the familiar voice, but here at last was surprise enough to knock him over. He had to grab at a branch to keep from falling out of the tree.

The familiar greenish eyes stared hatred at him. "So, you remember my name. Is that all you have to say to me—*master?*" The last word had the tone of an obscenity.

Cautiously—his seat was still none too secure—the Scholar lifted both hands in an open gesture. His mind seemed to be whirling free in space, beyond astonishment. "What should I say?"

She smiled at him, simpering in mockery. "Why, nothing at all. I can do the talking for a change. I can give the instruction, and the orders."

Arnobius was scarcely listening. Slowly he shook his head in wonderment. "So . . . you bring me evidence that I can see with my own eyes. A Trickster does indeed exist. Female, evidently. And she has chosen you as avatar."

"Oh, has she, indeed? Maybe *I* have chosen to be the Trickster—did that possibility ever cross the mudhole that passes for your mind, that I might be able to make choices of my own?"

"Carlotta!" He was still clinging with both hands to branches and shaking his head. Still couldn't get over the transformation.

"Oh, now I am to hear your famous imitation of a parrot! I suppose that is the best way to advance one's career at the Academy—but then you never need worry about your career. Not as long as your father is who he is."

"You are Carlotta—and now an avatar of the Trickster. For some reason he has chosen you to wear his Face—then the theory of masks is true." He sighed, and his thoughts turned inward. "There was a time when a discovery of such magnitude would have crowned my life's work—or so I thought." He continued to stare at her for the space of several breaths before he added: "I've experienced a profound change, too, over the last few days. I no longer take much satisfaction in philosophy."

"Oh?" The Trickster pantomimed an overwhelming astonishment, ending with her head tilted sideways. Her voice was low and vicious. "Just what in all the hells makes you imagine that your likes and dislikes are of any interest to the world?"

At last the true intensity of her anger was starting to get through to him. Blinking, he said: "You speak as if you hate me."

"Do I indeed? Is there, do you suppose, some faint possibility of a reason why I should do so?"

Arnobius tried to gesture but had to grab again at a branch to keep from falling. He began what seemed to him a sensible argument. "Carlotta, it was not my doing that you were a slave when you came to me. I would have given you your freedom, but as you know, there were reasons—of policy—why that wasn't possible. It seems to me that I always treated you with kindness."

"Kindness. Arnobius . . . you gave me away as if I were a hunting dog! *'Reasons of policy'!"*

"Only because you were, technically, a slave. What else could I have done? I meant you no harm. And now . . . now it seems the question of your status is academic, because you have been chosen." Despite his recent lack of interest in matters theological, he found himself becoming mightily curious. "I wish you well. How did it happen, this apotheosis of yours? Do you mind telling me?"

"Considerate, aren't we? My social standing has gone up remarkably."

"But how? Carlotta!" he added, shaking his head, still marveling that *she* had been chosen.

"How did that sad little bitch, the poor piece of property named Carlotta, how did she become a god? Right under your nose, you stupid bastard!"

"Here, there's really no call to—"

"The truth about my being chosen, as you put it, is that I discovered a great treasure. Oh, and by the way, let me tell you that legally the treasure must be yours, for my discovery was made while I myself was legally your property." She leaned forward on her branch. "But let me tell you also that you are never going to see a single ounce of it. It seems to me that gods are safely above the law."

"Treasure," he said numbly. Revelations were coming too fast for his thoughts to keep up.

"Yes, a whole stockpile of treasure. Gold, gold, gold. Besides, everything else. Ah, that got your attention, didn't it?"

Actually, it hadn't. Money in itself had never mattered to the Scholar much—he'd always had a plentiful supply. "So, then, you found some treasure in the temple. . . . Yes, it always seemed to me that there ought to have been at least one or two items of importance in there. I regretted that we couldn't stay to search . . . but go on."

Her eyes were fixed on him. "I came into possession of more than one object of fabulous value. The first one I found, these Sandals, was the most important—because it made the others possible. And would you believe that when I held the Sandals in my hands, my only thought at that moment was how I might use the discovery to help you? Can you imagine such insanity?"

"I don't know what to say. Carlotta! I'm sorry—"

"Oh, what an idiot I was! Sorry, are you? It's a little late for that, O great Scholar who has never managed to learn anything. You didn't recognize Apollo himself, when he was standing right before you."

"Nonsense!" His first response was automatic. Then: "When? What do you mean by that?"

"Never mind. Maybe I should force you to address me as Lady Carlotta. I remember very well what it was like to be your slave, Scholar. Now I want to see how it feels to be your goddess."

"My goddess?" The Scholar still didn't know where to start in grappling with all this. The depth of Carlotta's hatred came as a great surprise, and as her former master, he felt that her attitude was unjust. He'd always treated her well, shown real generosity, and now she was downright ungrateful. He noted that her golden collar was gone and wondered in passing what had happened to it.

But he could still refuse to believe her, thinking the statement her own idea of Trickery.

The Goddess of Trickery, clothed in the body of a vengeful slave, leaned toward him on her branch. Alarmed, he cried out, "What are you going to do?"

"I have not yet decided what to do with you."

"Do with me?"

"Gods, but you sound stupid! Even worse than before. I might, of course, give you away—but who would want you?"

"Give me away? What are you talking about?"

"But I have a better idea. It will do for the time being—*for reasons of policy.* You seem to think that a good excuse for anything."

Carlotta leaped suddenly from her branch. Arnobius cried out in alarm, then groaned in a different tone when he saw her not falling, but hovering in midair like a giant hummingbird, her Sandals shimmering like a dancer's shoes. Then with a single dramatic gesture she caused the tree in which Arnobius was still sitting to grow to a fantastic height. The ground dropped away below him with the magical elongation of the trunk, as if he were riding a sling beside some tall ship's mast and twenty hearty sailors were heaving energetically on the rope.

The tree below him now sprouted branches so thickly that it looked impossible to climb down. If he fell, he was going to bounce many times before he hit the ground—but he could remember in his gut how far below it was.

The hovering toe-dancing goddess called up to him from far below: "I'm going, now. I think I'd better take a look into the Cave. But I'll be back, my noble Scholar. Perhaps I should convey you back to that temple in the swamp. A lot of treasure still waits there, my Scholar, and it could, all of it, belong to you. When you starved to death there, or when the great snakes came in and ate you, you would die a wealthy man."

Turning back as an afterthought, Trickster conjured from somewhere and gave him a mirror. It was circular, the center of the smoothest, brightest glass that he had ever seen, surrounded by a broad frame of ivory.

"What's this?"

"So you can see what a fool looks like."

When the figure changed into the likeness of a giant, shimmering butterfly and then darted away in a miraculous dancing flight, he wondered for a moment if he'd been dreaming. But no, the tree was still stretched out like no other tree that he had ever seen, and here he was, at an elevation that looked and felt like a hundred feet above the ground.

He had a confused memory that at some point his visitor had just told him that he'd failed to recognize Apollo. Now what had that meant?

If his visitor hadn't really been Carlotta, he didn't have to believe all those confessions and accusations.

Meanwhile, he clung to his tree. The trunk, and the branches near the trunk, felt far too slippery for him to attempt any climbing down. All he could think of was to wait for Sergeant Ferrante to return from his errand, and shout down to him for help.

Yes, it must really have been the Trickster who had confronted him.

But that, as he suddenly realized, didn't prove that the woman he had known as Carlotta, his former companion, colleague, mistress, slave girl, was now or had ever been the Trickster. Every serious student of odylic philosophy knew that Coyote was the premier shape changer and it could have been anyone under that outward appearance of Carlotta. Oh, his recent visitor had been a god, all right, the Trickster—but not Carlotta.

What a bizarre thing for a god to do, to take the shape of a slave girl—but then one had to expect that that particular god, if he existed at all, would have a predilection for the bizarre.

Poor Carlotta! He wondered what had really happened to her.

He promised himself that he'd do something nice for the girl if he ever ran into her again.

Coming back from his nerve-racking encounter in the Cave, Sergeant Ferrante at first had trouble relocating his new commander. He'd come back with a disturbing message—it sounded like young Jonathan had gone completely mad—but when Ferrante had looked into those eyes, and listened to that voice, he'd been ready to believe.

This was the very spot where he'd left Arnobius. Except that now here was this damned great unnatural tree—when Andy heard the Scholar calling him and looked up and located him at last, he decided that the world had gone mad, too.

Even the Eye of Apollo had trouble descrying the truth about people— or about any people, for that matter, as complex as humans were. And this Cave did not yet belong to Apollo and probably never had. Though certain things within it might be clearly enough marked as Apollo's property.

When Jeremy thought back over the chain of events that had brought him here, beginning when Sal's unknown voice had first called to him for help, he could discern only a few links in the chain that he would prefer to have been wrought differently.

He was gradually gaining more knowledge regarding the nature of the fantastic powers vested in him by Sal's gift. A simple arrowhead in his hands took on great and deadly capabilities. And domestic animals, including the bees and the cameloid, could be placed firmly under his control. And the energy of the sun itself was his to command, at least in some limited degree.

Apollo had never told him what his own fate was to be; Apollo had not told him anything, strictly speaking.

Jeremy heard the priests of Chaos, trying to nerve their followers for their next battle with Apollo, proclaim in their triumphant ritual chant that this was the place where great Apollo had been slain.

Still, it was reassuring that they had felt it wise to summon reinforcements before tackling the pitiful remnant of the god and that it was necessary to whip up the enthusiasm of those recruited to do the fighting.

Jeremy knew that he was going on, down into the deep Cave. There was a long moment in which Jeremy as he trudged on felt himself to be utterly alone.

But I'm not a god, really. I'm only me, Jeremy Redthorn, pretending. Not pretending that the god is here—he's real enough. Pretending I'm his partner. What's really happening is that I'm being used, like a glove that will soon wear through.

His feet in their light boots, made for riding, crunched lightly on the path. His feet—and Apollo's. Behind him—behind them—daylight was growing dim. And ahead of them, neither Jeremy's right eye nor his left could see anything but darkness.

27

JEREMY HAD NOW entered a room in which deep silence held sway, broken only by a distant echoing drip of water.

After pausing to listen for the space of a few heartbeats, he moved on. Apparently Apollo's enemies had been scattered for the moment, the survivors of the clash sent scrambling in retreat. But godlike wisdom was not required to realize that the seeming withdrawal might be a ruse intended to lure the Sun God's avatar deeper underground.

Even so, the risk must be accepted. The parallel purposes of the god and of Jeremy Redthorn both required their shared body to make a descent farther into the Cave. And for the moment the way was open.

He could feel his anger against the creatures of the Underworld grow stronger than ever, now that it had been tempered, like a blade, by action.

At the moment he felt that his will and Apollo's were the same, indistinguishable.

Steadily he made his way forward and down, into the heavier shadows of the true Cave, while the entrance with its blessed sunshine fell farther and farther behind him. Some time ago the upper world of air and light, of trees and sky, had passed out of sight behind a curve of dark Cave wall.

After another brief pause to make sure his puny borrowed bow was still in workable condition, he set his foot upon the switchback path and advanced at an unhurried pace.

There would be no racing recklessly down into the depths. No, not just yet; not until he was good and ready. His advance so far had been in the nature of a probe, testing his Enemy's strength—which had turned out to be formidable indeed.

The Far-Worker was ready and determined to face his enemies, even if that must be done on ground of their choosing and not his.

———

After tribulations and confusion that would grow in the retelling to legendary proportions, Lord John Lugard and his force of four hundred lancers had at last found the proper trail, leading them first to the Honeymakers' village and then away from it again. The lancers were now arriving at the foot of the hundred-foot tree. This would have been an excellent moment for an enemy force to take them unawares—almost all of the four hundred were goggling at the spectacle of ten stories above their heads. But the Harbor Lord's enemies were no better organized than his own troops, and the opportunity was wasted.

A few men, working at Lord John's orders, had begun an effort to help Arnobius down from where he was marooned. A pair of volunteers who claimed some skill in tree climbing had started working their way up from the bottom, cutting handholds and steps in the slippery trunk and thinning the dense branches as they climbed. In a few minutes enough brushwood to thatch a large hut lay piled below. Meanwhile hundreds of riders continued to gawk at the monstrous tree and in dubious but respectful silence pondered the Scholar's shouted attempts to explain his strange situation.

Lord John on discovering the giant tree had at first stared at it in amazement and then reacted even more strongly when he realized who was in the topmost branches. After a phase of laughing that lasted several minutes, he went back to marveling again.

Now he called up: "Certainly *something* outside the course of nature has happened to you, Brother!"

The answer that came down was couched in terms of odylic philosophy and left the questioner no wiser; he felt he had been listening to a foreign language.

A few minutes later, Arnobius was back on the ground, but still looking at the world from a different viewpoint from the one he'd held before he climbed the tree. Soon he was thrashing over the evidence with his brother, while Sergeant Ferrante was called as a witness.

"Was it really Carlotta whom I saw?" the Scholar pondered aloud. "I can't be sure. But Jonathan's—or Jeremy's—case is more important. More to the point, is the being called Apollo, whoever or whatever that may be, actually present when these remarkable things happen? Was Apollo actually in possession of Jonathan, or Jeremy, or whatever his true name is? I don't know. Whatever the theory of the business is, the *fact* is that the lad's now doing things that no mere human could accomplish."

John, despite the presence of the altered tree, took something of a skeptical attitude. "Yes, it must have been some god. But I doubt that it was really Carlotta."

There came a whirring and whirling in the air behind him and above him as he sat his saddle. Before he could even turn his head, hands stronger than any he'd felt in many years took him by both shoulders and snatched him from the back of his cameloid, straight up into the air.

John gave a wordless, helpless cry. A tumult broke out among his troops, but they were as helpless as so many ants in the face of this attack.

In only a few moments their commander had been whisked away through the air and had vanished, with his kidnapper, from their sight.

Arnobius, his feet once more on solid ground, found himself in command, more or less by default, of four hundred lancers. The officer who had been second in command after Lord John hesitated only briefly before yielding the point to Lord Victor's son.

Arnobius, like those around him, gaped after the figures of John and his kidnapper, dwindling rapidly with the speed of their flight into the west. But in only a few moments he turned back with a look of determination. "Major, are your men ready to ride on?"

"Sir? . . . Yes, sir. Ready."

"Since we don't know where my brother is being taken, it would be pointless to attempt any pursuit." He faced the Mountain's cloud-wreathed summit and extended an arm in that direction. "We are going up there."

"Yes sir." The major reacted automatically to the voice of confident command.

Sergeant Ferrante was soon relieved to discover that his promotion in the field was apparently going to stick.

Meanwhile, down in the Cave, Jeremy was interrogating the latest victim of Apollo's archery.

Before the arrow-pierced soldier-priest of Hades had breathed his last, he had confirmed Jeremy's worst fears regarding Katy. She had been grabbed by the Gatekeeper's crew, who were always on the look-out for salable young people. Not understanding what was going on, she had been simple enough to approach them and pay them to have some purification ceremony performed.

Still Jeremy dared to hope that she might be still alive. Because if she was not, the world would have become more than he could handle.

Inside his whirling head, plans of stunning grandeur, regarding the seizure of the Oracle from Hades, contended with the fears and hopes of a frightened child—and which of the two was himself? He could no longer feel sure of that.

When you got deep enough into the Cave, far enough away from the wind and the warm sun, the air moved only very gently, and it became dry and cool, independent of what conditions on the surface might be. The Intruder's memory supplied the information that day and night, summer and winter, would all be much the same in here.

After walking steadily for another ten minutes or so, Jerry/Apollo paused to listen, at a spot well down inside the Cave. Here the visual and auditory evidence was unmistakable—once more some ghastly entity was approaching, dragging itself up from the frightening depths below. The presence that had been detected by Apollo's senses when he stood near the entrance was now a great deal closer. The glow was definitely brighter in Jeremy's left eye, and he could distinguish details in the sound of the approaching footsteps.

At one point the audible steps changed into sounds suggesting the dragging of a giant serpent's coils. Apollo's memory confirmed that Hades, as well as Coyote, could really change his shape, as well as render himself invisible. It was a power possessed to some degree by many gods—whether or not Apollo was included was not something Jeremy wanted to examine at the moment.

Still, Apollo surely recognized the other as it drew nearer. Even invisibility was not certain protection. This time Pluto himself was now gasping, fumbling, and mumbling near, coming up from somewhere deep down in the earth. Hades, "the one who never pities or yields."

The thing from far down in the earth approached erratically, but it approached.

Once more a dim shape, vaguely human, but of uncertain size, came rising out of the depths into partial view. What Jeremy could see of it, hardly more than suggestions of a massive shaggy head and shoulders, killed any curiosity that might have prompted him to try to see more.

The voice of Hades now sounded deeper and stronger than on his previous appearance—all dark tones filled with echoes. Jeremy was reminded of cold water running, a shifting of red lava, and cold granite, far under the earth. "So you are determined to try my strength again."

Jeremy waited to hear what words might issue from his own throat; he himself couldn't think of any at the moment, and it appeared that Apollo also had nothing to say.

Hades waited a polite interval before he added: "Lord of Light, I tell you this—the sun is great, but the darkness is greater still."

And Jeremy, with the feeling that this time the words, if not the voice, were all his own, said suddenly: "My sun is great indeed. Compared to it, your Cave is pitifully small."

The shape of darkness accepted the answer as coming from the god. "I need no pity, Sun God, even as I grant none. This Cave is but a little room, but for this world it is big enough." A gesture, movement black on black, a shifting of the blurs of deeper darkness that must be the figure's arms. "My whole domain is infinitely more. What is your sun? It may dazzle one who gets too close, but it is lost in the Great Dark. Look at the night sky if you do not believe me."

"I have seen the night sky," Apollo said. And Jeremy, suddenly remembering, broke in, in his own voice: "And I have also seen the stars!"

The Lord of the Underworld seemed to ignore both answers. A dark blob of a hand played with the dark chain that he seemed to be wearing round his neck as a decoration. "You will not abandon war? Then abandon hope, Far-Worker. O herder of flocks and fertilizer of orchards! 'Abandon *all* hope, ye who enter here!' " There followed a wild peal of maniacal laughter, shocking after the solemnity that had gone before.

Jeremy's borrowed memory understood and recognized the quotation.

The impression came across that this avatar of Hades/Pluto had forgotten what it was like to be human—really believed, now, that he had never been anything but a god, tragically mistaken.

Apollo remembered differently. He knew exactly how human this avatar of Hades was, or had been before his humanity had gradually eroded away. The details of the man's name and face lay buried in the depths of memory where Jeremy was still afraid to tread, but he considered that they were probably not important anyway.

The two beings moved closer together, began to stalk each other, Jeremy with an arrow nocked and his bow drawn. He had to summon up all his courage to keep from opposing Apollo's will to advance and fight.

Darkness enveloped them, and silence, save for a distant drip of water. Out of unbreathing silence and darkness, a hurled rock bigger than Jeremy's head came at him relatively slowly, affording the youthful target body plenty of time to dodge. The missile crashed away behind him, wreaking destruction among the stalagmites. Not a truly hard blow, probably intended not so much to kill him as to render him over-confident.

When he had worked a little closer, it became possible for Jeremy/Apollo to get a somewhat better look at his archenemy. The boy had expected a gigantic figure, but what he saw was small, no taller than the body he was sharing, and the surprise was somehow disturbing. Then he understood that the visible shape before him, the body in which his Enemy lived, had once been purely human, too.

Again an arrow darted from the bow in Apollo's hands, as true to its target as the previous shots had been—but Jeremy could not see that this one had any effect. Blackness in a blurred shape simply swallowed the darting shaft. To this Enemy, an ordinary arrow from an ordinary bow might well be no more than a toothpick.

The Lord of the Underworld unleashed a horrible bellowing, threat and warning no less frightful for being wordless.

Apollo had heard it all before and was not particularly impressed. Urgently he tried to recall what additional weapons Hades might have at his disposal.

A lurching of the rocks, great house-size slabs coming together to trap and crush the Lord of Light between them. Again Apollo danced to safety in the quick young body he had borrowed. Certain sounds and smells suggested to him that somewhere, deep down, an effort was under way to bring up molten rock.

Hades was given no time to bring that effort to fruition. Apollo, with first a blow of his fist and then a kick, shattered a rock wall and sent a lance of reflected sunlight deep into the Cave. And of course shot more arrows at his enemy.

It was impossible to know whether any of his clumsy wooden shafts or the faster, straighter beams of light he now employed had inflicted serious damage. The Lord of the Underworld was keeping his own heart shielded behind heavy rock. The arrows and the sun fire of Apollo pained and wounded but did not kill.

Bellowing Hades fought back, somehow causing darkness to well up like a thick liquid out of the Cave's floor, to slow Jeremy's feet and drag against his spirit. He had the sensation of a giant suction working on his entire body, and had he been no more than human he must have yielded to it and been drawn into the earth.

Yet something told Jeremy that Hades, like Apollo, was now weaker than on the occasion of their previous fight. The Lord of the Underworld was also working in close league with some human mind and body, and that human, like Jeremy, would be drained and eventually used up in heavy conflict.

Apollo could not remember who the human was who had last put on the Face of Hades—or Jeremy could not dig deeply enough into the available memory to find out. But it seemed certain that he or she was gradually being destroyed by the partnership.

From the mad certainty of Hades's utterances it seemed that the man who had become the Dark God now labored under the delusion that he had never been anything less than a god and that he was truly immortal—the Lord of the Underworld rejected bitterly, as some enchantment of his enemies, any memory he might still have of existing in a state of mere humanity.

A corollary of this delusion seemed to be that Hades genuinely believed that Apollo, too, was purely a deity, as perhaps were all the others who had put on Faces.

Hades, limping away in retreat, had once more broken off combat rather than risk an all-out direct attack. But he turned his head and shouted threats as he withdrew, promising to send a destroyer after Apollo.

"I have patience, Far-Worker, great patience. You will come to me again, and I will kill you. Next time with finality."

Jeremy stood panting, getting his breath back, listening. His clothing was ripped and torn. His body, even though it had been strengthened and toughened magically, ached in every muscle, and his heart was pounding at a fantastic rate.

The echoes took a long time to die away.

28

IT WAS NOW obvious to Jeremy why his other self had made sure of having a bow in hand, and arrows, before entering the Cave. Such weapons would doubtless be hard to obtain by any means once inside—the advantage of any bow was that it killed at a distance; it would not be the armament chosen by most warriors doing duty in the cramped spaces of a cave.

Now Jeremy's strides were carrying him and his onboard partner ever farther away from the sun and into confinement in a cramped space, bounded by walls of massive rock. This was the home territory of the Far-Worker's chief Enemy, his very opponent.

When Jeremy came to another branching of the subterranean path, Apollo's memory, when called upon, readily provided him with a partial plan of the underground network, a whole intricate system of interconnections. The Lord of the Underworld had just retreated on the wider trail, headed down; the narrower branch took another turning and kept going more or less on the same level.

Jeremy had more than half expected the Intruder to force him, willy-nilly, into a continued descent, but such was not the case. Vast experience within his memory assured him that the downward passage would lead to a trap, down at some depth where no sunlight could be brought in.

It seemed that the god dwelling in Jeremy's head had reluctantly conceded that their shared body must gain strength before he could finally defeat his chief enemy.

And only now did Jeremy notice that he had suffered a slight wound in the most recent passage of arms. Some missile he had not even seen—memory supplied the image of one possibility, a special kind of dart—had torn the flesh on the back of his left arm, a little above the elbow. The pain was growing in intensity, despite the fact that Apollo must be diminishing its force.

Apollo's memory immediately raised the disturbing possibility of poison—

—and almost simultaneously assured the human partner that the injury would not be fatal in itself, to a body wherein Apollo dwelt. But it certainly was going to complicate matters.

The wound was bleeding freely, and Jeremy let it bleed, hoping that poison, if there was any, would be washed out. Any real treatment would have to wait. But the fact of the wound presented another argument, and a telling one, against an immediate advance. For the time being, it would be the summit of the Mountain and not the depths beneath it that lay ahead of him.

————

Once more Jeremy's thoughts became focused on his search for Katy, and he resented the time that had been spent in arguing and skirmishing with his and Apollo's common enemy. The boy found himself angry with her for being so incautious as to let herself be caught. But he could picture, in unnerving detail, any number of plausible scenarios in which she had been caught.

Driven by a need whose intensity surprised even himself, he began to shout Katy's name as he descended. Through one after another of a series of chambers, his cries evoked great echoes, reminding him of Hades's voice. On he stalked, holding an arrow ready at the bow, three fingers curved to hold a gentle tautness in the string.

Jeremy had counted five large chambers down into the earth and estimated that he was more than a hundred feet below the level of the main entrance before he came upon what he had hoped and dreaded that he would find.

The glow he had detected from a distance was not intruding sun but faint torchlight. As he advanced, the illumination became somewhat brighter. But he would be unable to focus and magnify torchlight as he could sunlight.

————

This room was more artificially modified than those that had come before, a rounded, almost perfectly circular chamber, the most elaborately decorated though by no means the largest he had encountered so far. Some ten paces in diameter, and a domed ceiling four or five yards high. There were four entrances, spaced at irregular intervals around the curving wall.

And there, raised on a platform of rock that had long ago been laboriously flattened, one more cage was waiting—the door of this one stood open, but it was not empty.

Suddenly aware of his heart beating wildly, the boy called out something incoherent and went stumbling hastily forward—it was left to the senior partner to look keenly to see if any traps had been set for would-be rescuers.

A motionless figure, its unclothed skin painted for purposes of magic in multicolored patches, was sprawled facedown on the floor inside the cage. She was able to raise her head and call back, but only feebly.

"Katy." Jeremy spoke her name, once and quietly, as he came within arm's length of the open cage.

And in a moment he could be sure that this was Kate indeed, though she had been changed. The colors black and red, the insignia of Hades, were dominant in the painting of her body. Something had been done to her hair as well, adding to the difficulty of recognition.

The round room was not in deep darkness but dim in the light of only three guttering torches, fixed in sconces spaced evenly around the walls.

There came a whisper of wings above, and Jeremy realized that there were three furies in attendance. They were not going to touch the sacrifice, who was reserved for a mightier power. They had been drawn by the scent of death to scavenge the bodies of those recently slain by Apollo's not-so-painless arrows.

A triumphant joy surged up in him, blending with his anger—renewed anger when he saw what had been done to her.

One of the winged creatures came, with the compulsive stupidity of its race, to attack the Intruder, and meanwhile the others escaped to spread the word of Apollo's intrusion into the Cave.

The door of this cage had been left standing open, evidently on the assumption that the prisoner would be too drugged, too weak, to try to get away. For a few more seconds, with all the paint, he could not be absolutely sure that he had found Katherine, but when her eyes at last looked straight at him, he knew.

Apollo, looking into those eyes, knew that the victim had been drugged, as well as ritually abused. At first she didn't recognize her rescuer when he appeared. For a moment Jeremy had wondered if he himself could possibly have been so changed in the brief time since she'd seen him last.

But with the first touch of Apollo's hand, she began to emerge from her state of stupefaction.

"Jerry? Are you—am I imagining you, too?" The last words were dragged out in an utterly despairing voice.

"I'm here. I'm real." He wanted to say something important, tremendous—but there were no words. "Thank Apollo, and . . . thank the gods you're still alive."

With the borrowed strength of Apollo in his fingers Jeremy snapped whatever bonds were constraining her wrists and ankles. Then for a long moment he held her, fiercely, tightly.

Then one of their inhuman enemies, a fury flapping into the chamber near its roof, tried to douse the remaining torch, knocking it from its high sconce—but it still burned fitfully as it lay on the Cave floor.

And then in a soft rush through the thickened darkness there came the sudden charge of a squad of fanatical humans. There were half a dozen of them. Once they were seen they abandoned secrecy and came on howling, swinging, and thrusting with a variety of weapons.

They came on so boldly that they might have been expecting to encounter an Apollo already drastically weakened and worn down by a poisoned wound—or they might have been drugged themselves or hypnotized into a fanatical certainty of victory. In any case, they were fatally mistaken.

A vicious struggle surged in near-darkness around the broken cage while the girl, still weak and helpless, cowered. One or two of Hades's folk went howling in retreat. The last man standing was too slow, and Apollo seized him by the neck and wiped away his screaming, bubbling face against a rough outcropping of rock.

Then with his two strong hands the Lord of Light undertook a further splintering of the wrecked cage, the object this time being to gain another weapon, for use when the arrows should all be gone. The action also served as a symbolic wrecking, a weakening of Hades's magic, all his powers in this chamber. Darkness or not, Apollo meant to have this Cave and all its prophecies all to himself one day. And then, with flint and steel taken from one of the dead soldiers, he set fire to the wreckage, so that for a little while an artificial light flared up.

The cord vines came loose when the logs that they had been holding together were broken. This small cage was more strongly made, much more elaborately carved and decorated, than those up on the surface.

Apollo poured extra strength into the human fingers and lingered lovingly over the job. He knew with an inner certainty that it was important to ruin the ritual property of Hades.

When the latest skirmish was concluded, Katy, crawling, stumbling, out of the wreckage of the cage, collapsed in Jeremy's arms. Some of the paint that covered her naked body came off on his hands and clothing.

He could see well enough, even with the last torch almost gone, to know that the two of them were alone. But at any moment Hades's troops or even the Lord of the Underworld himself could reappear.

She was shivering in the dry coolness of the Cave.

He had restored some of Katy's own garments to her backpack when he picked it up from the sale table, and she was soon lightly clothed again but still chilled. Jeremy pulled off his own tunic and put it on her as a coat. In his undershirt he bustled about, ransacking the packs of fallen enemies for extra clothing. One of their bodies also yielded a pair of boots small enough to be a reasonable fit for Kate. Meanwhile the Intruder seemed to watch but gave no clue to his reaction.

Maybe, thought Jeremy, it was important in terms of magic, of the commerce of the gods among themselves, that the sacrifice intended for the God of Darkness be denied him, reclaimed for light and life.

What to do now?

Jeremy realized that it would be foolish for him and Katy to simply turn their backs on their nearest enemies and make their way back to the main entrance. For one thing, the enemies were almost certainly still there and now in greater numbers than before. The Lord Apollo, wounded arm or not, could probably fight his way through them. But neither he nor Jeremy would be able to protect Katherine in the process.

Besides, the Sun God had some further vital business of his own yet to be accomplished in the Cave. Jeremy was sure the god had not launched this raid simply to turn back before encountering his chief opponent.

When he had Katherine clothed as warmly and practically as he could, Jeremy cradled her gently in his arms. "Listen to me, Katy."

"Jonathan? Jeremy?" Her voice was small and wondering.

"Yes, it's me—call me by whichever name you like. Listen. We can't get out the way we came in. We're going to have to go on. There's a branch of the Cave that goes up from here, up inside the Mountain . . ."

He paused, consulting his engrafted memory. "All the way to the top, I think." Then he winced as the wound in his arm delivered what seemed a gratuitous jolt of pain.

"Just get me out of here somehow. Just don't leave me."

"Leave you? *Leave* you?" He shook his head in wonderment that she could imagine such a thing.

If Apollo wanted to leave her, he and Jeremy were going to have the showdown that had been so long postponed. But at the moment, the Lord of Light was nowhere to be found.

But their advance toward freedom was delayed again, after they had climbed only a little way. Now Apollo's ear could hear the servants of Hades coming after them again. A moment later, Katherine could hear them, too.

Before the fighting had started, Jeremy had regretted his own youth and inexperience, the fact that he was completely awkward and untaught in any of the normal techniques of combat.

But he had come into the Cave armed with a consuming anger and a grim resolve. And by now he had learned, in the most exhilarating way, that Jeremy Redthorn's original limitations mattered very little.

He was handling the mediocre bow at a level of skill vastly beyond what any human archer—let alone an untaught boy—could have accomplished, but yet his eye and his strength and his magic were far below those of a whole Apollo.

And his left eye and ear continued to show him helpful things. He had to be ready to trust these strange new senses and interpret properly what they were telling him.

It was not surprising that furies turned out to be nesting in the Cave, hanging upside-down like bats from the rocky ceiling. Air stirred by their great wings gave warning of their approach. Jeremy/Apollo could strangle them with ease, when the god let power flow into the human's arms and hands.

It seemed to Jeremy that by lingering here, committing himself to the defense of a mere human girl, Apollo was trying to draw the Lord of the Underworld up out of the deep earth into another confrontation.

But at the same time the Sun God was too wary to go deep underground to try to root him out.

———

Jeremy and Katy were now getting ever farther from the Cave's main entrance, although they were actually ascending. Following this branch of the underground trail, they traversed rooms where even Apollo had not trod before. Still, when the Sun God passed the dismembered and thoroughly devitalized carcasses of would-be wizards, explorers, and adventurers who'd fallen in the attempt to establish their authority in this place, he knew them for what they were.

Jeremy refastened his tunic around her when it started to come loose, drawing the belt tight.

"Who are you?" She asked the question in an exhausted whisper, her body shivering in the chill.

"Jeremy. You know me, Kate. For a while I called myself Jonathan. I told you, use either name you like."

"No." She shook her head. "I don't mean that. And I don't know you."

The fear in her eyes told him that he would have to come up with a proper answer. But he could feel that Apollo wasn't going to help, and at the moment that seemed too much to ask. "We can talk about that later. We'll have to talk about it."

"They said . . ." He could barely hear her voice.

"Who said what?"

"Things down below, in the dark. Told me that I . . . I belong to Hades now."

Jeremy took her by the hand. "You don't. No longer. Not that you ever really did." He paused, thinking the matter over, trying to hear his god-partner's wordless inner voice. "I don't care what rituals they performed over you, or what magic they think they did. Apollo—you hear me, *Apollo*—says otherwise. From now on, nothing in this whole damn Cave is going to belong to hell." And that, Jeremy realized, was why he had been so willing to take time to smash the cages near the entrance. The Sun God would have nothing to do with human sacrifices.

Katherine's legs and arms moved only stiffly, and she was still somewhat dazed, though fortunately she had suffered little actual physical harm. And soon life and strength began to come back to her arms and legs.

Dimly Jeremy's left eye could discern a wash of faint, diluted sunlight coming into the Cave from somewhere far above. A little more came oozing up from below, where he'd already broken open a wall to the outdoors.

Aided by the powerfully enhanced vision in his left eye, and also by a torch improvised from the fire of the burning cage, the boy-god made his way forward, still guiding the newly rescued Kate who was newly clothed in his own tunic.

Presently Katherine was able to move along fairly briskly without his support.

But there would be no safety for her, and none for him, until Hades had been defeated.

The couple passed through almost perfect darkness, past the place of sacrifice, to the spot where the last avatar of great Apollo had fallen.

In Jeremy's head a kind of dialogue took place, in which the answers to his questions came floating from Apollo's memory.

Where are we going? Jeremy wanted to know.

Then he had to concentrate to be certain that he caught the answer: *Stronger weapons are absolutely necessary.*

All right. How do we get them?

As yet there was no good answer to that one.

29

FOR SOME TIME now both Jeremy and Katherine had been aware of the sound of roaring water. Echoes in the Cave made it hard to determine location, but the flow could not be far away.

The couple had climbed only a few score paces from their latest resting place when a new, faint light became visible ahead, coming from a small crevice, high enough to be far out of reach, which let in a trace of sun. Jeremy's left eye could follow, all the way up through the darkness, the growing strength of its distant radiance.

When they reached a position under the source of light, they stopped and stared at what lay just ahead of them.

A column of clear water approximately a foot in diameter rose from unknown depths, just forcefully enough to maintain the level of an irregularly shaped pool the size of a swimming bath. This pool emptied itself spectacularly at its other end, where the water for no visible cause again began to rise, moving smoothly into an ascending column, which as it climbed gained speed as if it were falling in the opposite direction under the influence of normal gravity.

"I don't understand," whispered Katy after a moment.

"It's called a waterrise," her companion informed her. Even Apollo had rarely seen the like of it before, but he knew the name. "An ancient trick of the Trickster. Harmless. The ones in the Cave should be safe to drink from."

Cascading up through a network of small cracks and fissures in the irregular ceiling of the cave, the stream went up to fill another pool on a higher level, which Jeremy and Katy saw after another minute's climb through the twisting passage.

Before they left the area that was still comparatively well lit with filtered sunlight, the thought came, whether from Apollo or not, that it would be wise to stop and rest. Jeremy got bread and cheese and sausage out of his pack. Katy stared at the food as if she did not know what it was, then grabbed up a small loaf and began to eat. She sat down on a rock ledge shivering, the fingers of her free hand absently rubbing at her upper arms and her legs where they emerged from the borrowed tunic, worrying at the paint that still disfigured most of her body.

Jeremy, chewing with his mouth full, knelt before her, tightening the straps of the sandals he had given her, trying to make them fit her feet. It seemed years ago that she had volunteered to guide him and his companions to the Oracle.

To Jeremy she said: "I saw what you did back there. To the cage. And to the fury."

He changed his position to sit beside her on the ledge. "You were right, Katy, about what you told me before we ever reached the Cave—Apollo has possessed me." He paused. "No. That's not really the right word for what's happened. He's made me his partner."

She said in a tiny voice: "I don't understand."

"I don't either." He made a helpless gesture. His left arm was stiffening; the gash on the outside of his elbow had stopped bleeding, but it had swollen and hurt more than before. "Why a god would do a thing like that. But I'm not the only one it's happening to. I finally got a chance to talk with . . . another person who's in the same boat. It seemed to be working out about the same way for her."

Frightened and bewildered, the girl looked a question at him.

He tried to make a gesture with both arms, then settled for using his right while he let the throbbing left arm hang. "Now I can see some things that ordinary people can't see—when I'm not afraid to look for them. One of them is this: the only Apollo that lives anywhere . . . is in this body, the one you're looking at right now."

"Apollo? *You?*" It was the merest whisper, expressing not doubt but astonishment. He could find no words to answer her, but it seemed he needed none. Looking into his eyes, his face, she had seen what she needed to see.

The watching girl could only shake her head, wide-eyed. He could feel her shivering beside him and put an arm around her to give warmth. She started a movement, as if she meant to kneel at his feet, but his good arm held her on the shelf beside him.

Jeremy sighed. "I'm stronger than any human, Katy. But now it turns out that I'm still not strong enough for what Apollo wants to do." He raised the fingertips of his free hand to his temple. "He's in here, but I can't even *talk* to him. Not really. Now and then ideas pop up in my mind that I know must be his and not my own."

"Oh," she said. The sound of someone giving up on someone else.

He tried again, with renewed energy. "I know it sounds crazy, but you've seen what he can do. What *I* can do, when he helps me."

In the dim light Katy's eyes were enormous, staring at Jeremy. Then she nodded, her eyes wide, still not saying anything. Jeremy wondered if she was still dazed from drugs or mad with fear. If she were now afraid of *him.*

Turning away from her for a moment, he scanned the Cave. Apollo's senses assured him that they still had time before the next Enemy onslaught. Holding Katy's hand, Jeremy persisted in trying to explain. The story of his life, since the day when he'd met Sal, came pouring out. It was a bursting relief to be able to speak plainly about the business, at last, to someone. But in a way it had been easier to talk to Carlotta—not to someone as important to him as Katy was becoming.

When he had brought the girl up-to-date on his situation, all that she asked was: "What are we going to do now?"

"I have to get you to a place—" He had to pause there, such was the pang that came from his small wound. *How about taking care of our body, you who are supposed to be the God of Medicine? We're going to need it in good working order.* "—to a place where you can rest. And myself, too. We both need it. After that . . . there'll be a lot I have to do."

"We must get out of this Cave."

"Right." He patted her hand. "Doesn't seem likely we'll get any rest in here."

She stood up suddenly, craning her neck to try to see the source of light ahead of them. "Gods, take me back to where I can see sunlight!"

Thoughtfully Jeremy examined their current choice of several passages. "I will. We must go up again. Getting nearer the light, even if it's dark for a while." Looking ahead, he wondered if even Apollo would be forced to grope his way.

After resting a little longer, they used the opportunity to refill Jeremy's canteen and then slowly resumed their climb.

Presently in the distance Apollo's ear could detect the Enemy, once more mobilized and moving in force. Scores of human-sounding feet were warily but relentlessly following them, with those who walked upon those feet so far taking care to keep out of the Sun God's sight.

And the pain in his poisoned wound was getting worse instead of better.

Meanwhile, in the back of Jeremy's mind his inward partner kept up a wordless prodding, holding before him the imperative to seek out weapons, means of increasing strength. In particular the shimmering image of the Silver Bow (a heavy longbow, strung with a silver string) was being thrust imperiously into his consciousness. Vivid images showed him the weapon not as it had been depicted in some of the statues at the Academy, but in a more realistic and powerful form.

While he walked with Katy, Jeremy tried to explain to her, in whispers, that without the Bow and Arrows, or some comparably powerful addition to their armament, Apollo was not sanguine about their chances of even surviving the next round of battle—let alone winning it. And the next round might very well be the last chance against Hades they ever had.

Despite the bad news, Katy was reassured by his ungodlike behavior. She asked: "But if you must have this Bow . . . where will you look for it?"

"Apollo is perfectly sure that the best place—the only place—to look is in the workshop of Hephaestus. If my old Bow can't be found, that's where I'll have to go to have a new one made."

On hearing that, Katy only began to look dazed again. Well, Jeremy could see that it might be hard to think of a sensible reply, especially for someone unaccustomed to sharing skull space with a god. Meanwhile Apollo's memory, when called upon, brought forth the image of a sinewy lame giant, wearing a leather apron and wreathed by the smoke of a glowing forge. That was Vulcan, whom some preferred to call Hephaestus.

Suddenly it occurred to Jeremy that it might prove necessary for him to talk to the Lame God in person. For the Lord of Light to commission from his colleague a new Bow and Arrows, the old silver model having been somehow lost or destroyed. He reeled under the burden of trying to imagine Jeremy Redthorn playing a role in such a confrontation.

And where was the forge?

Yes. Memory was ready to show him not where it was precisely, but what the place looked like—a small, rugged island in a violent sea—and how to get there. Trouble was, the journey would be immensely long, with the greater part of it over the ocean. And there might be no way to gain entrance once he'd reached it.

Finally Katherine, some of her old practical manner coming back, asked him, "Do you know where this place is, where you must go?"

"The workshop? Not clearly. But I know which way to start toward it, and once I get started, Apollo will show me the route to take." *And, he hoped, some means of crossing more than a thousand miles of sea.*

"It's far from here, though."

"I think so. Yes, very far."

"Then how will you get there?"

Posing the question inwardly brought forth only a vague mental turmoil. "I don't have an answer for that yet. Even if I am . . . connected with a god, I can't just . . . fly." He looked down at his feet.

Meanwhile, Jeremy faced even more immediate problems. There were tremors in his wounded arm. He thought his body was beginning to grow weaker, and his poisoned wound was festering, lancing him with pain.

Still he felt confident, with the wordless inward assurance that had become so commonplace, that the powers of Apollo were fighting against the onslaught. The poison in itself was not going to kill him. But it could easily leave him too weak to survive another attack by Hades or some other superhuman power.

"Jerry, what's wrong?" Katy could see clearly enough that something must be. Meanwhile she herself grew somewhat stronger, as she began to recover from her imprisonment. Food and drink had done her a lot of good, and so had the fact of freedom. Part of her improvement came through sheer will, because she saw that she was going to have to be the strong and active one.

The couple stumbled on, leaning on each other for support, as Jeremy's body weakened. With Sal's fate never far from his thoughts, he feared that he was beginning to grow delirious.

"He keeps telling me that we can't win—at least he doesn't think we can—unless we have the Silver Bow."

"Then you'd better listen to him. Find out how to get it."

"I am. I will. The trouble is, he doesn't know how to get it either."

Not Hades, this time.

This was the Python, the monster come to fulfill the threatening promise made by Hades at their last meeting. A looming snake-shape whose body thickness equaled the height of a man—how long it was Apollo could not see, for fifty feet behind the smooth-scaled head the rearmost portion of the body vanished in a curve of the descending passageway.

And it had an escort of human auxiliaries. Katy had to take shelter against their arrows.

The first and second of Apollo/Jeremy's ordinary arrows only bounced off the thickness of its armored scales. The third sank in too shallowly to accomplish any vital harm. At last he scored an effective hit, when he thought to aim for the corner of one small eye in the moving head. The enormous body convulsed, the vast coils scraping the sides of the Cave, dislodging loose rocks. Apollo's next shot hit the other eye.

Meanwhile, Jeremy could hear and feel that Katy was close behind him, screaming even as she hurled rocks at the enemy. It was the sight and sound of her more than the rocks that helped to drive the human foes away.

The monstrous serpent, now probably blind and perhaps mortally wounded, broke off the fight and turned and scuffed and scraped its scales away. Even wounded, it still moved with impressive speed. They could hear it shuffling, dragging, stumbling.

In the aftermath of their latest skirmish, Katherine and Jeremy found it possible to gather more supplies, including arrows, from their fallen human enemies. This they did in the failing light of sunset, which oozed into the Cave through yet a few more high crevices. Soon even these portions of the upper Cave, more than a mile above sea level, would be immersed in utter night. Meanwhile they conversed in whispers. The air was damp around them, and their voices echoed whenever they were raised.

Jeremy, stimulated by the urgency of the fight, felt temporarily a little stronger. Now he prowled cautiously into a vast, poorly lighted chamber that the Intruder instantly recognized.

Through part of the night, the couple took turns sleeping and standing watch.

Splits and cracks, only some of them natural, in the mountain's walls were letting in the light of early morning, at least indirectly. In one place a glorious sliver of blue sky was visible. Even the faintest wisp of daylight was better than the brightest torchlight for Apollo's eye. Each time darkness fell outside the Cave, he was going to be at a disadvantage.

———

There had been a hell of a fight in this room, at some time in the not-too-distant past. Jeremy's nose, one organ that was still functioning without divine help, informed him that the smell of burning, of rock and cloth and flesh, had lingered for many days in this confined space and would linger on a whole lot longer.

A couple of hours' sleep had helped a little, but he could no longer deny the fact that he and Apollo seemed to be losing ground in their battle with the poisoned wound. The body they shared was getting weaker. He picked up a small log, really no more than a stick. When he tested his strength, trying to break it, his left arm was almost useless, his right quivered in futility, and a wave of faintness passed over him.

He could no more break the log than he could lift the Mountain. Soon he once more had to sit down and rest.

"What are we going to do, Jerry? How do we get out of here?"

"I'm not sure. Let me think."

He—at least the Apollo component of his memory—had been one of the combatants in that historic fight. And Apollo's opponent then had been Hades, the same entity that he had fought against today. *The same, yet not the same.* Today's version was somehow diminished from the image in memory.

Jeremy stood leaning against the Cave wall, his head slowly spinning. Katy was speaking to him, in a worried voice, but he couldn't quite decipher what she was saying.

Here and there on the rocky floor of the Cave were scattered the metal components of weapons and of armor that had survived. Soldiers from at least two competing forces had died here. He wondered if Sal had been here—Sal. She was why he had come here in the first place.

He was fueled by a feverish curiosity to see what the remnants of the fallen god—of his earlier self—looked like. Whatever was left of him now was inconspicuous, unimpressive.

Yet there remained a certainty that Apollo in all his majesty could be somehow revived and reconstituted, as a bulwark against the darker gods who had survived.

This, then, must truly be the lace where the seven had held their famous meeting.

"This is it. There is where it happened—where I died."

"Jerry!"

Advancing slowly, a step at a time, the boy discovered the fragmented remnants of a human skeleton, of normal adult size, somewhere near the fallen Bow, and assumed these bones were those of some other intermediate owner of the Bow or some mere human ally of Apollo, like Sal—but really they had belonged to the last human being to serve the god as avatar.

Jeremy could only wonder what the person had been like; he couldn't even tell now whether it had been man or woman. The god's memory seemed useless in this, holding no record of anyone who'd ever filled the role.

No doubt mere humans weren't considered sufficiently important.

Jeremy couldn't tell which fragmentary skeleton was that of Apollo's previous avatar. It gave him an odd feeling, as if he were trying to identify the remains of the brother he'd never had.

The bodies themselves (perhaps no human from outside had dared to remove them or even to visit this room) had been reduced to skeletons by Cave scavengers, during the months since the fight had taken place.

The Apollo fragment in Jeremy's head provided an agonizing memory here. Remembered defeat blended with the current pain and sickness caused by his wound.

Then for a moment or two he stood motionless, with his eyes closed. Sal played a role in this particular memory, though under a different name—not that he cared any longer what other name she might have used. It was as Sal that she'd belonged to him. And he could see her face.

The images dissolved in an onset of delirium. His arm throbbed and had swollen frightfully. He was poisoned and tottering. Katherine now had to lead him forward for a time.

———

Katy was calling him, shaking him, dragging him up out of a nightmarish sleep. Jeremy came awake to the echoes of a distant uproar, what sounded like some kind of skirmish in a far part of the Cave.

"We'd better move on."

Jeremy had been dreaming of Vulcan's workshop. Apollo's memory supplied some accurate details.

That site was of course a place that every combatant wanted to control—but it was guarded by some kind of odylic fire. Traps, dangerous even to other gods, lay in wait there for the unwary.

"Someone's coming. But—" Sounds as of speeding footsteps, light and rapid, came echoing up from below. The approach was being made at an impossible speed.

A last broken arrow shaft clutched in his right hand, Jeremy braced himself to make a desperate resistance—then he relaxed. As the couple tried to take shelter in a niche, a slender form he quickly recognized as that of Carlotta came staggering, dancing on the red Sandals, up from the lower Cave, to stop right in front of them.

Jeremy slumped in relief, but Katy recoiled in fright when the figure came near. Her companion did his best to reassure her.

Carlotta, looking weary but apparently unhurt, reported that she had just concluded some kind of skirmish with the bad gods, down in the depths. Then, as her breathing slowed down to normal, she told them: "It was too easy for me to find you just now. If I could do it so quickly, so can Hades."

"Where is he now?"

She gestured back in the direction from which she'd come. "Way down there. Still resting, as you should be, gaining strength. He's also trying to recruit more help. I'd say you have a few more hours before he's ready to try again. He believes that time is on his side now, and he wants to be sure to be strong enough to finish you the next time he finds you—I see that you are wounded."

"It's not much."

"It's too much!" the Trickster corrected him sharply. "Any weakness on your part would be too much—and who is this?"

Katy had started to get over her fright when she saw Jeremy calmly talking to the apparition. Now, with Jeremy's hand on her arm, she summoned up the courage to open her eyes and watch.

Carlotta looked thoughtfully at them both, the way they were clinging to each other. Then the Trickster sat down on the Cave floor and began to untie her Sandals.

"What are you doing?"

"I'm giving you these." She slid them off and held them out.

"Why?" But Jeremy automatically put out a hand to take the gift when it was thrust at him.

"Because I want Apollo to survive. You don't look well enough to get through a round of heavy breathing, let alone one of fighting Hades. I'd hate like hell to see him and his take over the worlds." Carlotta sighed. "I only regret that the evil twins, I mean the Lugard brothers, aren't on the other side. I think they'd fit right in."

"Where is Arnobius? Where are Lord Victor's troops?"

"A little while ago the Dunce was up a tree. I don't speak metaphorically." Carlotta smiled faintly. "His brother got him down, but now his brother is engaged in some heavy exercise, I think. I tell you, I can't really decide what ought to be done with either one of them."

"Up a tree?" Neither Jeremy nor Apollo understood.

"Yes. And their father's army was milling around, looking for both of them, and making a great effort to get itself organized—but none of that is your immediate concern, my dear colleague.

"Apollo needs to get away, to rest and heal. And you are going to have to acquire some superior armament before you face Hades again. It would be suicidal otherwise."

"I know that. But you're going to need the Sandals yourself."

"Pah, have you forgotten I am a god? It's not easy to kill a god. I'm not going out of my way to pick a fight with Hades, and he has enough on his mind without going out of his way to make another enemy. I'll be safe enough." Carlotta looked at Katy, then back to Jeremy: "Do either of you have any place in mind where you might be able to rest and heal for a few days in safety?"

"I do," said Jeremy. "Apollo does." Another ocean-flavored memory was trying to bob up, now that a need for it had arisen, and now it came popping into place. Another island—this one very different from the first, surrounded by warm seas, with warm mists and sandy beaches.

"Then put on what I have given you and go there immediately. Don't tell me where it is; one never knows. . . . Take whatever time you need to recover and rearm yourself. Then hurry back here, to the Mountain, as soon as you are ready."

"What will you do in the meantime?"

"I have some plans . . . but never mind. On your way now, both of you."

"Thank you," said Katy. "Thank you very much."

"You're welcome, child. How old are you? Fifteen? A couple of years ago I was fifteen, and now I am about a thousand. . . . Never mind. Listen, dear. Katy, is it? A fine strong god you have there for your lover. Let me reassure you that no human body inhabited by Apollo is likely to die of poison, even a dose administered by Hades—but you must see that he gets some rest."

Kate nodded, overwhelmed, and Jeremy added his own thanks. Then, despite his weakness, he insisted on trying the Sandals before he would let Katy have them.

"After all, I am Apollo."

Kate didn't know what to say. Carlotta grumbled but let him have his way. It was as if she did not dare to try to be forceful.

Now at last he took a close look at Carlotta's gift. It was easy to see that this footgear was of no ordinary material or construction. The thongs and trim were of silver, around the red. They didn't feel at all metallic—unless their straps were almost like thin strips of chain mail. A smaller, finer version of the chain mail worn by some of Hades's fallen warriors. And by some of the lancers, too.

Apollo had no hesitation about putting them on. Doubtless he'd had these before, or another pair just like them—or even better.

In another moment Jeremy was strapping the red Sandals on. At first he feared they would be too small, since they had exactly fit Carlotta, but they conformed magically, perfectly, to the size of his feet.

When he stood up, it was almost with the feeling of floating in water. Looking down, Jeremy saw with alarm that his feet did not quite touch the Cave floor—but in a moment they had settled into a solid contact.

A quick experiment proved that he could still walk normally—but now that was only one, and the least useful, from a menu of choices.

The instant he decided to move more quickly, a single stride carried him floating, gliding, clear across the great room. Stopping, or changing direction, in a single footstep was as effortless as starting had been.

But weakness and dizziness quickly overcame him.

Jeremy had to admit that he was now too weak with the poisons of his wound to use the Sandals effectively himself. He saw that they were given to Katy, who gave him his own sandals back in return.

They bade Carlotta a hasty farewell.

———

Apollo's memory was reliable. Eventually it turned out to be possible to leave the Cave by the same exit used by one of the waterrise streams.

Building up speed, the couple raced through the Cave and out through some aperture known to Apollo, so fast that anyone who might be on guard to keep them in, a picket line formed by the army of Hades's human allies, had not even time to raise their weapons before Katy was past them, Sandals barely touching the earth, and gone from their view.

They had emerged from the Cave along with the stream of a wa-terrise, in a rainbow shower of frosty spray.

They were coming out into daylight substantially farther up the mountainside than the main entrance and out of sight of the people gathered there, where, according to drifting sounds, a skirmish had now broken out.

30

WHATEVER REMNANTS OF his childhood Jeremy might have taken into the Cave had been purged away there long before he emerged. There had been moments underground when the business of killing men seemed of no more consequence than swatting flies.

That was a godlike attitude that he didn't want to have. But until the war was over, he would wear it like a piece of armor.

His empty quiver and his mediocre bow (a useless weapon for a man with only one effective arm, but it never crossed his mind to give it up) were still slung across his back when Katherine carried him out of the Cave. The first three fingers of his right hand were sore from the repeated pressure of the hard bowstring.

Katy was still weak from her captivity, but even fragile feet could fly like eagles once the Sandals were strapped on. But Vulcan's footwear healed no injuries, counteracted no poisons.

Once they were clear of the Mountain, Katy, who fortunately had no terror of heights, soon mastered the simple procedures for controlling course and speed—and her own fear of the powers that had come to her from Carlotta. Jeremy told her in a faint voice which way, and how far, she had to go to reach the sanctuary. Only vaguely did Apollo remember the way—only vaguely, for the god could not recall, in all of his own indeterminately long life, any time when he had needed sanctuary.

Looking down from his position on Katy's back, her honey-colored hair blowing in his face as he clung weakly to her shoulders, Jeremy could see her feet in the red Sandals, striding as though she ran on earth, treading air at a vast distance above a surface of gray cloud, gliding like a skater's on a frozen river—almost as if time itself could be frozen in place. In his present condition, the rhythmic running movement of her hips between his clasping legs was no more erotic than the measured drifting of the clouds below. Through holes in the distant floor of gray cloud he could catch glimpses of the ocean, its waves almost too tiny for even Apollo's eye to pick them out. Then Jeremy drifted into unconsciousness, even as he was borne off through the howling air.

When he regained his senses his muscles felt weak as a child's, his god-tenanted body trembling and sore. And he shivered, with the persistent wetness of the fountaining stream.

Both he and Katy had been wet coming out of the Cave, and the outer air, screaming past them with the speed of their running flight, was so cold that Jeremy thought he would not long survive. Katherine might have found something in which to bundle him.

With Katy dancing on magic Sandals and with Jeremy rousing himself at intervals long enough to sight landmarks, providing guidance as the information came flowing from Apollo's memory, they swiftly accomplished the long journey.

The air was warm about them, the breezes gentle, as they descended, as if on invisible stairs, toward what seemed a spot of garden rimmed by surf and coral.

Jeremy said: "This island was Circe's, once."

Her head turned slightly back. "A goddess. The one who turned men into beasts, in the stories. This was hers?"

"Some of the stories have her a goddess, but she's not. I'd call her a witch, or enchantress."

"You know her, then?"

"Apollo does."

Kate was silent briefly, almost drifting down. "If this island was hers once, whose is it now?"

They were now going down so slowly that the air was almost still around them. He tried to sort vague, hazy memories. "A long story, I think, a complicated business. I don't want to dig for it." He made a gesture at the side of his own head. "But it seems to me we can depend on friendly spirits."

Now Katy was only walking in the air, instead of running. As her steps slowed, so did their darting passage. They were coming down to the inner edge of a broad beach of white sand, rimming a peaceful half-wooded island in a warm sea. Birds flew up squawking, but as far as Jeremy or Apollo could see at the moment, the place was deserted of intelligent life. The god's memory presented the fact that certain immaterial powers that served as guardians and keepers here were no doubt hovering close by.

Jeremy passed on this bit of information to his companion. Then he added: "Circe's house was built of cut stones, and it stands in the middle of that patch of woods." He pointed weakly toward the center of the island, luxuriant with greenery, a quarter of a mile from where they were about to land.

"You've been there? I mean . . ."

"I know what you mean. . . . The clearest image I can get from Apollo is of a young woman, sitting in that house. She's dark . . . and beautiful . . . and she is singing as she works at her loom."

"Weaving? Weaving what?"

"Nothing ordinary. I can't describe it very well. A thin . . . web of some kind." In memory the material looked incredibly soft and delicate. And it was shot through with spectacular colors. "People said that no one but a goddess could have made it."

Kate made no comment on that. The invisible stair created by her Sandals had run out softly beneath them, and they were on the ground. Jeremy's weight hadn't posed her a crushing burden as long as they were Sandal-borne, but now she was glad to be relieved of it.

Stiffly Jeremy extended his legs and found them capable of supporting him, though with not much capacity to spare.

"The place looks deserted," Kate said quietly, gazing around them.

"Almost." No sooner had Jeremy said that than the visitors were treated to a peal of tinkling laughter, nearby but proceeding from some invisible source that not even Apollo could at once identify. Kate was startled, but Jeremy, still reassured by borrowed memory, made a sign to her that she ought not to be concerned.

"Which way is east?"

He didn't even need to look up at the sun. "There."

Another body of land, whether island or continent, was visible at a modest distance across the water, in the direction of his pointing hand.

Fortunately, much of this island was blessed with a southern exposure that bathed it in life-sustaining sunlight. Here the surface rocks and beaches of white sand were pleasantly warmed.

With Jeremy now and then leaning on his companion for support, the couple followed an irregular path of shell fragments and white sand to the small house in the center of the island. Another, fainter burst of fairy laughter accompanied the opening of the front door, which un-latched itself with a loud click and swung itself in just as they reached it. A brief tour of the sunny rooms inside discovered no visible occupants; the place was snugly furnished and obviously well cared for, and the couple settled in for a rest. Both fell asleep in comfortable chairs in the front room and awoke an hour later to find that invisible servitors had placed food and drink on tables beside them.

Katy, having seen her patient settled in the most comfortable bed, spoke of her desire to visit her home village and see her family again but feared the enemy might seek them there.

"It seems safe here."

"It is. I'm going to sleep again."

The poison dart of Hades had been fearfully potent. Even Apollo could not keep his body and Jeremy's from sliding into recurrent bouts of fever and delirium. Sometimes he thought he saw Death, in the form of a great fury, smiling at him, closing in with talons like those of a raptor.

No matter how warm it was, Jeremy was chilled with fever. He opened his eyes to see that Kate was standing by his bed and that she had taken off her clothes. She said, "If you are still shivering, then I must warm you properly." And she slid in under the blankets with him.

In time the fever went away, and Kate still comforted him with her love. When he slept again, the chills and shivering came back and with them a dream of the three-headed dog, catching up with Jeremy at some temple halfway around the world, where he had gone by means of the Sandals, looking for the Bow—and he also felt an urgent need to find the unnamed treasure that Carlotta had hinted was hidden there.

Katy's embraces soothed him, and he woke feeling better and spoke reassuringly to his companion: "On this island one tends to have prophetic dreams."

He shouldn't have said that, for within the hour he slept again and his next dream was a nightmare, from which Jeremy woke screaming, in which it had seemed that a hangman's noose awaited him.

"Don't . . ." He gasped. "I don't want to have any more dreams like that. Not ever again."

Katy held him and petted him and soothed him.

After a long silence, she said: "If she—Circe—is only a mere human, like me, how can she defend her island, herself, against Hades?"

"She is . . . what she is. She doesn't intrude into his domain, and he doesn't see her as a threat. I don't doubt he'd like to have her as an ally."

———

By the next morning Jeremy was feeling much better and was up and moving weakly about. The swelling on his arm was much reduced.

Covered dishes appeared, as if from nowhere, holding delicious food. Here and there, inside the house and out, were traces, carved initials, showing that other humans before Jeremy and Katy had visited and lived upon this island, over a period of many years. "Some of them were shipwrecked sailors."

"Was Circe as kind to them as she was to you? To Apollo, I mean?"

"Circe is not always kind. . . ." Memory suddenly produced an unwanted offering of ghastly pictures, of men turned into animals. "But she is Apollo's friend. . . . Also, other gods have been here, coming and going over a long, long time."

———

In the evening, just as sunset light was fading, a fire came into being on the small hearth, radiating all the gentle warmth that even a sick man might need.

The two backpacks Jeremy had made a point of bringing contained a number of useful things, including a couple of blankets, and some spare clothes for warmth. It seemed that the effort to carry them had been wasted—except that the couple could expect to need the packs again when it came time to depart. In fact, the sanctuary turned out to be furnished with almost anything that a couple of exhausted humans might need.

Sometimes music of a heavenly sweetness played, coming from an invisible source, but never for more than a short interval.

⸻

After two days in sanctuary, both visitors were beginning to feel rested, and a start had been made toward healing Jeremy's wound.

Now he was able to stroll about the island, talking with Katy about exactly what they ought to do when it came time to leave.

That would be when the poisoned wound upon his arm was healed enough to serve him well in combat again. Already the arm felt much better and the swelling was almost gone, but it would be wise to wait a few more days and make sure.

⸻

Briefly blissful in their new status as lovers, the couple lay on the white beaches and swam in the warm, clean sea. Jeremy warned his companion to stay inside the barrier reef, for beyond it was the realm of Poseidon, one of the very mightiest of gods, of whose friendship Apollo could not be sure.

Katy worried about sunburn, but Apollo only laughed. "I will mark you with my left eye—and the sun will never burn your pretty skin again."

"Oh?" She splashed a little water at him, not knowing whether to take him seriously or not.

"The more I think about it, Kate . . ."

"Yes?" She paused, prettily shaking the water from her hair and treading water.

"The more that I could wish that I was not a god." The lure of immortality meant little—not after he'd seen one god die at his feet.

"For a moment there, you almost *looked* like Apollo!"

Almost he laughed aloud. "And what does Apollo look like?"

⸻

When he was better, but still weak, Katy left him alone for hours at a time. She put on the Sandals fairly often, having learned to enjoy the heady feel of using them. She also felt a need to return briefly to her home, at least long enough to reassure her family. Tentatively she brought up the idea of going there and back on a solo flight.

"Jerry, I want to see my family. I have a father and a mother, a brother and a sister."

"I don't know that you could find your way."

"Never fear; I've a good sense of direction. Now that I've been here I'll not forget the way. And she—Carlotta—said the Sandals help whoever is wearing them to find things."

He shook his head solemnly. "Don't count on being able to find your way back here, Sandals or not. Not to this island."

Subject to vague feelings of unease, and with the sense that Circe was never far away, Kate postponed her visit home, restricting her flights to the vicinity of the island.

Once, as soon as she had gone on one of these, Jeremy stretched out on the warm sand for a nap but soon awoke to find a beautiful darkhaired woman sitting beside him, clad in a cloud of fine fabric woven of all colors and of none.

The enchantress, when she saw that he was awake, managed a graceful kind of seated bow. "The Lord of Light is welcome to my home, as always."

"My gratitude for your hospitality," said a voice from Jeremy Redthorn's throat, in tones that had grown familiar though they were not his own. A nod of his head returned his visitor's bow.

"Any favor I may do my Lord Apollo will be reciprocated, I am sure." Her eyes appraised his unclad form. "The lord has this time put on a younger body even than I am accustomed to see him wear. All to the good—it will facilitate healing."

"I shall do what I can for you, in turn," Apollo said, and paused. After a moment he added: "I have wondered sometimes why you never seek divinity for yourself."

"I am content with what I have." Circe's smile was serene and private. "As I am sure the Lord of Light must know, the fire of divinity is a consuming one when it catches in a merely human mind and body."

Apollo was not much interested, it seemed, in pursuing the subject further—and Jeremy Redthorn was afraid to do so.

"Two words of warning, my lord," the dark-haired woman said, after the silence between them had stretched on for a little while.

"Yes?"

"First, not many days ago, my lord held in his hands the Face of Death and cast it in a certain stream."

"True enough. What of it?"

"It has been picked from the water and will be worn again."

"I feared as much. And what is your second warning?"

"It is for Jeremy Redthorn and not the Lord Apollo, and it is only this: that the human body when serving as the avatar of any god will, as a rule, fairly quickly wear through and collapse; there is a limit to how long the power even of Apollo can sustain it. He should expect that the Sun God will seek a fresh human to use when the one called Jeremy Redthorn has been used up. The immortality of the gods is only a cruel hoax where human beings are concerned."

Whether the voice that answered was Apollo's or truly his own Jeremy could not be sure. "And that I suppose is one reason why Circe herself has turned down more than one chance at divinity."

The enchantress ignored his response. She went on: "And there is a third item—take it as a warning if you will—that I pass on for what it may be worth: I am told there is a place atop the Mountain of the Oracle where the Faces of the gods can actually be destroyed."

Apollo was immediately skeptical. "How is that possible?"

"Some instrument of Vulcan's devising—how else? It was told to me that the destruction must be accomplished while the target Face is being worn inside a living human head."

"Ah."

"You know that it is your Face, Lord of Light, that Hades in particular wishes to destroy."

"Rather than have one of his henchmen put on the powers of Apollo and try to use them?"

"He would much prefer, Lord, to see your Face and your powers wiped out of existence."

Jeremy nodded slowly. "A question for you, friend Circe. Since it seems you are in the mood today to provide information."

The enchantress slightly inclined her lovely head.

"There was a woman, known to . . . to Jeremy Redthorn only by the name of Sal. She carried the Face of Apollo with her, through great dangers and suffering, and made no attempt to put it on. Though she must have known as well as anyone that wearing the Face of Apollo would intimately connect her to the god. Why was she ready to die rather than to achieve that connection?"

"Fortunately, my lord has chosen to question me on a subject whereof I have some knowledge. The woman you knew as Sal chose as she did only because she was deeply convinced of her own unworthiness to share Apollo's life. The fact that she was female and the god embodied in the Face was male was another reason. But that in itself would not have decided her. When humans are confronted by death, a great many preferences, such as those involving sex, are easily forgotten."

And the sex difference, Jeremy mused, *hadn't mattered in the case of Carlotta and the Trickster.*

"Is it possible?" Apollo mused aloud. "Yes, I suppose it is." By the standards of the Cult of the Sun God, to which Sal had belonged, she had been unworthy. "As I recall, only two members of the cult were considered qualified to become my avatar—and one of them is now dead. What the other is like I really have no idea. Foolish mortals!"

"Have you never met the other?" The idea seemed to amuse Circe.

"No."

If only Sal were still alive, to tell him, Jeremy Redthorn, what to do now!

But Sal was dead. And anyway, Jeremy now had a far better grasp of the relationship between gods and humans than that young woman ever had. She had been a member of a cult, a worshiper, and the god, the image of Apollo, she'd prayed to had been mainly a creature of her own hopes and fears.

The real god was something else. Just what Jeremy was only beginning to find out.

"Mortals have no monopoly on foolishness, my lord."

"I suppose not."

"Consider Thanatos, in his most recent avatar, whose life was so swiftly and violently terminated at my lord's hands—consider the misplaced courage that led Death to challenge Apollo face-to-face."

That statement was at first so shocking that Jerry was more or less compelled to consider it. Doing so, he realized that he had almost entirely lost or outgrown his fear of his own—Apollo's—memory. And when he looked boldly into those vaults, he realized that what Circe had just implied was true. He saw how deeply the Monster of Darkness, the antithesis of sunlight, must fear the mighty Apollo—even though Hades boasted and tried energetically enough to kill him when it had the chance. And Thanatos, being so much less powerful, must have been even more afraid. . . . Professor Tamarack had nerved himself somehow to take a reckless gamble and had paid the price. When Jeremy had discovered Alexander's body, Tamarack had retreated—because terror lay in Apollo's power to inflict.

"Then it is true that Hades fears me."

"He is absolutely terrified. Which does not mean, of course, that he will not attack you; quite the contrary."

Circe had one more caution to pass on: "Hades has a helmet, made long ago by Vulcan of course, that grants him invisibility. Other people ought to be able to use the same helmet if they could get their hands on it."

Now they were coming into view, truths that Jeremy might have found for himself, weeks ago, in Apollo's memory, had he dared to dig for them. The truth was that almost every god and goddess feared and tried to steer clear of the mighty Apollo, even at times when there was no particular enmity between them. Thanatos, and Cerberus, and even powerful Hades, despite all his bluster, had to nerve themselves just to hold their ground when they came within sight of him.

Circe had gracefully risen, in what seemed to be an indication that she meant to take her leave. She assured the Lord Apollo that he was welcome to remain on the island as long as he wanted.

"And your companion, too, of course. The girl who is so enthusiastic about her Sandals."

"Thank you."

One of the thin, dark eyebrows rose. "A most human expression of gratitude. One final bit of advice."

"Yes?"

"I strongly recommend that on leaving the Isle of Dawn the Lord Apollo should pay a return visit to the temple of Hermes, in the great swamp, before going anywhere else."

"And why is that?"

With her eyes closed, Circe added: "What my lord finds there will make a profound difference in what happens to him over the next few days."

"A difference for good or ill?"

Circe avoided answering that directly. She bowed deeply—and disappeared.

A few minutes later, when Katy returned, flushed and cheered, from her practice flight, Jerry was sitting alone on the portico of the small house, waiting for her. Feeling not at all godlike at the moment, he had spent the time in struggling with the decision of whether to tell her of the other woman's visit.

The struggle had been brief and not very hard. "I had a visitor while you were gone—Circe herself."

Katy had a hundred questions, including: "Was she as beautiful as you remembered?"

"Good-looking enough, I suppose; I hardly noticed. Not my type." Apollonian wisdom had guided that reply, but whether it was truly wise enough . . .

Long before the two lovers emerged from their sanctuary, Katherine had heard Jeremy's whole story regarding the process by which there had come to be something very much out of the ordinary about him. She'd heard it the first time when her own mind was still unbalanced with terror and maltreatment and wanted to be told again. And so she was.

If he'd saved Katherine's life down in the Cave, she'd certainly saved his by carrying him here. He felt now that he really owed her the best explanation he could manage regarding what he thought was going to happen next. Besides, he now *wanted* to tell her everything that was of importance to him.

"You deserve to know all that I can tell you. The trouble is, there's so much I don't understand myself. Despite all the languages I can now understand, all the powers that seem to keep coming and going in me."

"You don't have to tell me."

He considered that. "No, I think that's just what I have to do. I just don't know how to go about it."

Being Katy, she didn't insist on knowing everything. But he wanted to tell her anyway. As much as possible.

"Well—what happened was not that Apollo exactly picked me out. And I certainly didn't choose him. I had no idea . . ."

The girl found this talk puzzling. "What, then?"

"And a fantastic story it is." She stroked his particolored hair—at the moment he was lying with his head in her lap. "If I hadn't seen what I have seen . . ."

"You'd think me mad. Of course. But it's true. I am a god."

"I'm convinced. But will others believe you when you tell them?"

"If it's important that they believe—why, I can do things that will make them listen." His voice was dull. He raised his hands and looked at them. "I think that all of the other gods must be like me. None of them are grander beings than I am."

───────

The silent help and comfort of the efficient powers of sanctuary enabled the couple to hide out successfully for several days—days in which Katy fed Jeremy, until he regained the strength to feed himself. Days and frigid nights in which they became true lovers and she warmed him, not least with her own body.

Katy here told him what questions she'd once hoped to get the Oracle to answer. What the girls in the village had talked about. How she hoped her family was in good health—she worried about her aging father.

"I'll see what I can do for him, when I take you home."

Jeremy no longer had any doubts about the seriousness of his feelings for Kate. Therefore, he'd have to take her into his confidence. Which would mean, among other things, telling her the important things about Sal and his own attachment to her.

Kate if she loved Jeremy would feel jealous in some sense of Sal. And she suspected she had reason to be jealous of Carlotta, too.

Jeremy tried to be reassuring. "But you don't need to be jealous. You never need worry about that. I know Sal's dead now. And at that time I was someone else."

———

Katherine had spent more time—a full day, by ordinary measure, but a subjective eternity—than Jeremy down in the Cave, and now in a sense she possessed a better understanding than he did on what the behavior of the Enemy was and also how great was the danger that the gods of the Underworld were about to launch another excursion from below.

And, maybe, she could better estimate how badly Hades and Cerberus had actually been hurt.

Even while the couple were secure in their temporary sanctuary, she dreaded more than anything else being caught again and once more dragged under the earth.

She feared that even these golden sands could part, and instead of some inroad of the sea below there would be dark Hades, reaching up. . . .

At Jeremy's urging she told him of important things she had experienced, seen and heard, down there while awaiting rescue.

She'd gained a working knowledge of the strengths and weaknesses of hell itself.

"The darkness was almost the worst part. There were . . . things . . . down there, talking to each other. . . ."

And he had to hold her. Stroked by the healing hand of Apollo she fell asleep. And into that guarded sleep he thought that no foul dreams would dare intrude.

Despite the weakness brought on by his wound, he had gained an inner assurance. He'd now acquired confidence in the powers he was being loaned and even some skill in the weapon's use—mainly it was a matter of getting his own thoughts, fears, and instincts out of the way once he'd picked out a target. He'd had to learn how and when to abandon his own nerves and muscles, the fine control over what had once been exclusively his own body, to the Intruder.

After an interval of several days, when Jeremy'd regained his strength he went looking around their bedroom to see where the Sandals had got to. It was a measure of how secure they had come to feel here that they made no effort to guard their treasure.

"Kate, I must go looking for the Bow. My Bow and Arrows. I'm well enough now, and this is my fight more than anyone else's. I am the one who has a god inside my head."

After some discussion, Katherine agreed to his plan, because it had to be his task to carry on the fight. It was up to Jeremy to carry on the fight because he was the one who carried the god inside his head. Sandals or not, she lacked the powers of godhood and would have been helpless against Thanatos, Cerberus, or Hades. "You might succeed in running away from them, but now just running away is not enough."

Superficially it seemed that the safest place for Katherine was right here on the island of sanctuary, even if she were alone.

Jeremy thought hard about it, holding an inner consultation. "No, not a good idea. Not if Apollo is not here with you." He thought it completely impossible for Hades to come here, but he didn't trust Circe, dead or alive.

He had to assume that Hades also could find his way to Vulcan's workshop. But according to Apollo's memory, the Lord of the Underworld couldn't go there himself, because the journey could not be completed underground. It was doubtful whether the prohibition was absolute, but certainly Hades would avoid any prolonged exposure to sunlight and open air, at almost any cost. Other memories, remote in time, assured Jeremy that his chief Enemy would find the varied composition of starlight even more painful.

And the Lord of the Underworld would also hesitate to trust any emissary not to seize for himself the powers that were bound to be available in Vulcan's laboratory—assuming Hades himself knew the secret of getting in.

But Hades would not scruple to send some of his allies and auxiliaries to deny access to Apollo or any of *his* followers.

Would Vulcan himself be in the workshop? Apollo didn't know, but he could remember that the Artisan invariably locked up the door, whenever he left the place unoccupied.

Apollo did not know the secret of getting into the workshop either. But he was willing and eager to make an effort to find out whether even Hephaestus could really hide something from the Lord of Light.

Gradually Jeremy was daring to probe deeper and deeper into the vast stores of memory available, to discover practically everything that Apollo himself knew about the god's own recent history. . . . It worried him that even in the Far-Worker's memory gaps existed. Here was no perfection or omnipotence.

———

Gradually everyone was being compelled to the belief that the great fight between Apollo and Hades, said to have happened a month or two ago, had actually taken place. The commonly accepted version was that Hades had struck down the previous avatar of Apollo. That version of the Lord of Light had fallen on the spot, and the mere human who then wore the gods's Face had died instantly. But the servants of the Oracle didn't understand this?

One thing Jeremy felt sure of: neither the servants of the Oracle, nor anyone else he'd yet spoken to—certainly not the Academics— knew what the hell was going on in general with regard to gods and people and the part each species played in the universe. Folk like Arnobius, and his colleagues at the Academy, who'd spent their lives wrestling with the theories about gods, seemed really no wiser on the subject than anyone else.

31

BY DAWN ON his fourth morning in sanctuary, Jeremy had the feeling that the benign environment of the Isle of Dawn had done its work; his arm was as ready as it was going to be, and Apollo was once more ready to take over the controls of the shared body. It was time to go hunting. He knew this when he awoke from a dream in which he had seen his familiar dream companion standing tall, pointing toward the horizon.

Inwardly the most important thing to Jeremy was that from now on he had Katy at his side.

It was now unavoidable that Kate and Jeremy separate for a time while he went to seek the required Bow and Arrows.

"I have to go back to the Mountain. Hades will be behind, but not too far behind, the humans who are fighting for him."

Jeremy had no doubt that with the Sandals on and strength regained he could have carried his lover on his back or in his arms for almost any distance—but when he entered combat, her presence would probably be disastrous for them both. Then his overriding concern would be for her safety. He knew, without any divine guidance, that that was not the way to win a fight against an opponent of Hades's stature.

Now he could race safely down the Mountainside or up a nearly vertical cliff. It was almost as if the Sandals had their own voice: *Where do you want to go? I will take you there.*

It proved possible also to race like a gliding spider across the surface of a body of water, tripping over the waves or dodging them. The water had a different feeling to it than the earth when it passed beneath his flying feet.

Jeremy's plan on leaving the sanctuary had been to transport his love back to her village. He could think of no safer place for Kate to pass the time until Apollo had settled his business with the Underworld.

He was still nagged by an inward fear, not supported by any evidence, that Apollo disapproved of Katy and Jeremy's powerful attachment to her—that the god at some point would ruthlessly move to get her out of the way.

Jeremy worried, but so far nothing of the kind had taken place.

Now it was her turn to ride on his back while he carried bow and arrows in his hands. "Hold on tight—as tightly as I held to you."

———

A human could do marvels wearing the Sandals. But with a god's feet in them, the effect was transcendental. The air rushed past his face at a speed that made it difficult to breathe. Katy's arms held tight, and her face was buried in his shoulder.

"We are making a small detour."

"Why?"

"There's something I have remembered." He didn't want to tell Katy that he was following Circe's advice, in going first to visit the temple of Hermes in the swamp.

Katy wanted to arm herself, before they risked reentering the great world, and asked his advice on how to do so, even though she had no training or experience in using weapons of any kind. He looked at her fondly. "Then carry whatever makes you feel comfortable. Anyway, there don't seem to be any arms here, except for what we brought with us."

Jeremy hoped this would be only a brief stop before he took Katy home and then went Bow hunting.

———

Carlotta had hinted at a vast treasure remaining in the temple in the swamp, and Jeremy assumed that her urging him to visit the place might have something to do with the treasure.

But as matters worked out, all thoughts of gold were promptly driven from his mind.

When Jeremy and Katy arrived at the swamp temple, he landed on the crumbling quay just outside the shadowed main entrance to the temple. Apollo's ear soon detected a faint sound from inside—they were not alone.

Cautious investigation promptly discovered Carlotta/Trickster inside one of the rooms not far from the entrance.

She was dying, and even the healing power of Apollo, or as much of it as Jeremy was able to apply, was not enough to pull her back. As the Trickster she knew this and was not afraid. But the girl Carlotta was afraid of death. She said that she had taken refuge in the temple in an effort to hide from the bad gods.

Katy went to get the dying girl a drink. Apollo continued to exert his curative powers, but at this stage they were not going to be enough. Perhaps if he had found her earlier. Jeremy said, trying not to make it a reproach, "You told me you would be safe."

"I misjudged Hades' nastiness."

Jeremy was no longer much concerned about Arnobius—but Carlotta, evidently unable to stop thinking of him, brought up the man's name and mentioned his brother, too.

What with one thing and another, she'd never got around to punishing either of them further.

Her last words were: "What bothers me now is . . . I have to die, and the Trickster doesn't."

Jeremy Redthorn could appreciate the point.

———

Carlotta in death looked worn and small, her body insignificant.

Moments after her last breath, the god Face she had been wearing ejected itself from inside her head. There came a visible bubbling out of eye and ear. A flow of something clear and active that within a couple of seconds had solidified to make a small familiar shape, one-eyed and one-eared. It was sharper-featured than the Face of Apollo or Thanatos but showed the same transparency alive with mysterious movement.

Gently Jeremy lifted the strange-looking object free of the dead face and handed it to the living girl who was standing petrified beside him. The thought had crossed his mind that he ought to warn Katy to put on gloves or, if that was impractical, to wrap her hands in something before she touched the Face—but then Apollo decided that such a warning would be pointless, given what was certain to come next.

The girl stood looking down at the Face in her hands as if it was a cup of poison—as if she understood already what must be. Jeremy knew that there was no blood on it, no material trace of any of the human bodies it had inhabited down through the centuries.

When Jeremy spoke he thought that his voice was purely his own. "Katy? We have to decide what to do with this."

Her startling gray eyes looked up. " 'We'? How can I have any idea of what's best to do?"

"Because you're involved. It's not possible to destroy the thing; at least, Apollo doesn't know any way of doing it. I'm wearing one god Face now, as we all know, and this seems to mean that I can't put on another." Though even as he spoke he was trying recklessly to do that very thing, pressing the Trickster mask against his eyes, to no avail.

Kate watched, still not understanding—or not ready to admit that she understood.

Jeremy said to her: "*You* must wear it. In the long run that will be safest for you, and everybody else."

Long seconds passed before Kate could speak. "I? Become a goddess?"

When Jeremy was silent, she shook her head and put her hands behind her back and took a small step backward, away from him.

He said: "Apollo is telling me that that's what you should do."

"Well. How can either of us argue with the Lord Apollo?"

Suddenly Jeremy was as weary as if he had been wounded again. "I don't know if I want to argue with him, Kate. Anyway, I can't. Not in this. We can't destroy a Face; we can't hide it where it can't be found. The point is that if you don't wear the Trickster now . . . someone else will eventually get his hands on it and use it. Quite likely it will be one of those men who held you prisoner in the Cave. Because they'll be looking for this Face now, looking like crazy, and no one else will be."

"Jeremy. What are *you* telling me I should do?"

"I—all I know is that the god in my head ought to know what he's talking about." He raised both hands to his head as if he weren't sure whether to crush his skull between them or tear it open and let the Intruder out. "Damn it, Kate, what I want most is to protect you, but I don't know how!"

Kate's voice was quieter now. "What will it mean to us, Jerry, if I do wear it? What'll it mean to you and me?"

Slowly Jeremy Redthorn shook his head. "It's not going to change how I feel about you. You're never going to have to worry about that."

With a gesture like one downing a fatal cup, she raised the thing of magic in both hands and pressed it hard against her face.

In the next instant she moved staggering back a couple of steps, as if her balance had become uncertain. Jeremy was at her side in an instant, offering support. "Kate? Are you all right?"

The face she raised to him showed no sign of change—except that her expression was suddenly transformed, full of life and almost gay. "*Of course* I'm all right, darling! My, you didn't tell me it was going to feel as good as this." She stretched her arms and turned, this way and that. He was glad, of course, that the transformation seemed to have been easy for her—all the same, he found the very easiness of it somehow unsettling.

"You don't have to carry me any longer, Jeremy."

"How will you travel? Get anywhere?"

"Carlotta managed to get here, from the Mountain, remember? The chariot she used is still available. It's waiting out behind the temple, and I can use it now."

"Do you still want to go home?"

"Eventually I will."

"I still want you to be safe."

"The safest place for a country girl may not be the safest for a goddess. Besides, I don't know that I can sit still for very long."

Jeremy, not knowing what else to do, soon agreed that it would be a good idea for Katy/Trickster to try to get word to Lord John Lugard, or to Arnobius, that the Cave was open for occupation—and maybe even a better idea to seize control of the Castle on the heights.

Solemnly Apollo warned Katy, as she tentatively tested her new powers, to steer clear of the deep Cave and the monstrous things that now ruled there. They were not to be provoked until Apollo at last descended in his full power to root them out, kill them, or drive them deeper still.

Naturally both Jeremy and Katy wondered what had happened to Ferrante and to Arnobius.

Katy, getting used to wearing the Trickster's Face, giggled, finally, a surprising and uncharacteristic sound. Her eyes flashed at Jeremy with unwonted brightness. She had changed—of course she had, he told himself irritably. No one could put on a god's Face and remain the same. But nothing really important had been altered. She was still Kate—

Just as he was still Jeremy Redthorn.

Bidding a cheerful Katy an uncertain good-bye, Jeremy, retaining the Sandals for himself, now went looking for Ferrante.

"Will you go home soon?" he asked once more.

"Of course. After I've . . . looked around a little, got used to . . . to being what I am."

———

Locating Ferrante took some searching, among the skirmishing that simmered around the Mountain's flanks. Hundreds or thousands of men belonging to the army of Lord Kalakh, their colors blue and white, had now come on the scene.

Apollo, putting to work the special powers of the Sandals, concentrated on finding the man he wanted. Within a quarter of an hour he had located him.

———

The Sandals brought the Sun God swooping down on Ferrante in the bottom of a wooded canyon on the Mountain's flank, where the sergeant had to be pulled out of a hot fight. The task was easy enough in this case for Apollo, the sight of whom was sufficient to dissolve a fierce skirmish and send half a dozen of Lord Kalakh's men scrambling in terrified flight.

Andy was aghast, relieved, and shocked all over again when he realized who had saved his life and was confronting him. The young soldier's left hand, already lacking two fingers, was dripping blood again. "Jerry? My gods, it's true! What you told me before you went into the Cave."

"True enough. I need help, a fighting man I can rely on. Are you ready for a ride?"

Andy wiped his blooded sword on the leaves of a nearby bush and slapped it firmly back into its scabbard. "Ready as I'll ever be—if that's what we need to do."

Jeremy said: "That hand looks bad. Give it here a moment."

Gingerly the other held out the mangled part. At first it was as if they were simply shaking hands, left-handed. Then Ferrante, shooting him an uncertain look, said: "We stand here holding hands like two schoolgirls."

"Don't worry; the next person I take to bed will be a schoolgirl and not you."

Ferrante looked at him sharply, then suddenly asked: "Kate?"

Jeremy only nodded. Later, he thought, would be time enough to explain what had become of Kate.

Apollo's powers could compress ten days or more of healing into as many seconds; at the end of that brief time the bleeding had stopped and some function had come back.

Jeremy bent over and gestured toward his own back, and Andy hopped aboard.

There followed another long airborne jaunt, over water, some of it during the hours of darkness. Dawn at altitude was spectacular. For Jeremy this was becoming almost routine, but for his passenger it was a different matter. Ferrante clung to him as tightly as a one-armed tackler in a game of runball, and his bearer, glancing back once, saw that the young soldier's eyes were closed.

Keeping his voice as calm and matter-of-fact as possible, Jeremy explained to his passenger en route that they were looking for the workshop of Hephaestus and that Apollo knew where it was—or where it used to be. The age of the memory inspired awe even as it undermined confidence; and even then, the Sun God had only glimpsed the place from outside.

Even as Jeremy talked, a new suggestion, born in Apollo's memory, came drifting up into his awareness: that if they could enter Vulcan's workshop, they might well find there yet another god Face—or even more than one. Now it became clear why he had felt he must bring Ferrante with him—if indeed another Face became available, it should be given to a trusted friend to wear, as soon as possible.

When Jeremy looked down and saw their destination take form out of the mist, below his jogging feet, what he beheld was nothing like the Isle of Dawn.

"We'll be down in a minute."

Ferrante growled something unintelligible.

"Are you ready to move?" Jeremy asked his passenger when they had landed and were both standing on a shelf of dark, slippery rock, only a few feet above the level of the sea. Atop the rock a large building fit the image of their goal as carried in the god's memory. "I know, we both need food and rest; but I think this cannot wait."

Ferrante at first shook his head, too much overcome to speak. At last he got out: "Give me ten minutes." He stretched and limbered his arms and legs, drew his short sword, and practiced a few cuts and thrusts.

Then Andy paused, staring at what two hours ago had been the freshly wounded remnant of a hand. The new cuts were quite solidly healed, and even the long-healed stumps of missing digits on the same hand were itching and stretching. Each remnant of a finger was longer, by half an inch, than it had been.

"In a few days you should have them back," Jeremy assured him.

━━━━━━━

The two men advanced on foot, Apollo in his Sandals leading the way, and circled partway round the tall building as they climbed toward it. Seabirds rose up screaming, but so far their approach had provoked no other response.

Ferrante asked, "You expect fighting?"

"I don't know what to expect, except that I'm probably going to need some kind of help." It was a shading of the truth.

"Well, I'm here; I'm ready." And spit and once more loosened his blade in its scabbard. "Seen what you can do. Less'n the sons of bitches come at us in a whole army, we oughta be able to whip their ass." He shook his head, held up his left fist, and flexed it, still marveling at the healing and restoration of his hand. "Itches like hell."

"Sorry about that."

"Have to get used to having five fingers again—but I ain't about to complain."

This glacier-bound island, in the middle of a fog-bound northern ocean, gave no sign of ever having been inhabited by humans at all. That, thought Jeremy, was probably one reason why Vulcan had chosen the site, at some distant time in the past.

The place seemed to have been sited and designed with the idea of making it approachable only by a god. Someone who could fly. When Jeremy thought about it, he knew that few of Apollo's colleagues possessed any innate powers of flight—a pair of Vulcan's Sandals, or the functional equivalent, were required. If conditions were stable for a long time, most deities would manage to get themselves so equipped.

As they were clambering around the outside, looking for some way to obtain entrance, their efforts apparently disturbed only gulls and other seabirds.

"Tell me—damn it all! Do I still call you Jerry?"

"I hope so. I'm trying to hang on to being human."

Ferrante needed a moment to think about that. "All right then, Jerry. Tell me—look into that extra memory you say you got and tell me this—did Vulcan or Hephaestus or whatever name you give him build his own workshop? If not, who built this place?"

"I've been trying to come up with that, and I don't know. Apollo doesn't know."

Now they had almost completed a full circuit of the huge building and had come back on a higher level to a position directly in front of what appeared to be its main entrance. Flock after flock of wild birds flew up screaming. Waves pounded savagely against sheer cliffs of ice, which offered the seafarer little choice of landing places. Cliffs half rock and half ice, the latter portion thunderously fragmenting into glaciers. A thin plume of natural smoke promised that the Artisan (Apollo recalled an ugly face, bad temper, heavily muscled arms and shoulders, and gnarled legs that did not quite match in size) would be well provided with handy volcanic heat to draw on as a source of power.

At places the climb was so steep and smooth that Jeremy had to give his human helper a boost up. Now they were approaching the place whose appearance from a distance had suggested it might be the front door.

And when he came to consider the walls of the workshop itself, even the Far-Worker wondered what power could have wrought metal and stone into such configurations.

Down far below, under the sea and earth alike, the senses of Apollo perceived fire—life of such intensity, and energy, as to keep dark Hades from any underground approach against this spot.

Still there was no apparent means of getting in.

There were visible doors, or what from a little distance had appeared to be doors, but with surfaces absolutely smooth and no way to get a grip to try to open them. Beating on them, even with all the strength the Lord of Light could muster, blows that would have demolished ordinary masonry, made no visible impression. At the most they only bent slightly inward and then sprang back elastically.

One wall seemed to be composed entirely of doors, so that there was no way to tell which of them might be real and which were only decorations on a solid surface.

When Apollo let out a god-voiced bellowing for Hephaestus to come out or to let them in, Ferrante grimaced and plugged his ears with his fingers. But the noise drew no response from inside.

Anxiously Jeremy/Apollo looked around for some tool or weapon to employ, but there was nothing but chunks of rock and ice.

An alternate possible entrance was suggested by a visible door, or transparent sealed window, of ice, fitted neatly into a thick wall of the same material. When the door was forcibly attacked (Apollo battering it with the hardest rock pieces he could find, then focusing upon it the full heat of the magnified sun) the body of it went melting and crumbling and sliding away, revealing what had been behind it—another door of ice, this one just a little smaller than the first. Each of the series was a few inches smaller than the one before it and, long before the progression had reached its end, too small to squeeze through. Each door frame seemed to be of adamant, impossible to enlarge.

"Dammit, there's got to be a way! Nobody builds a place like this without there's some way in!"

Hours passed, and darkness fell. It was fortunate that they had brought some food with them, carried in a pack on Ferrante's back as he himself had been borne on Apollo's. Apollo could wring fire out of driftwood and drifted seaweed and pile rocks for a makeshift shelter so that his merely human companion was able to pass a night of no more than ordinary discomfort, by a soldier's standards.

When dawn arrived with no improvement in their position, Jeremy decided to leave it up to the Sandals to find a way in for them—they, too, were a product of Vulcan's art.

Finally they gave up on the doors and sought some other means of entrance. Their attention was then caught by a raw hole, in a part of the rock that served as the building's foundation, which Apollo's strength was finally able to sufficiently enlarge, to allow them to squeeze in.

But when at last they burst inside, momentary triumph turned quickly to dismay. The sweating intruders stood reeling in a shock of bitter disappointment. All the rooms of the workshop inside lay in ruins. Several overturned workbenches and a floor littered with fragments of tools and materials—but nothing, nothing at all of any value left.

It was obvious that the place had been thoroughly plundered, long ago, so long that the seabirds were coming in to build their nests. The only practical way to gain entrance was to enlarge one of the cracks that had admitted birds. The place smelled of the sea and of ice and rust and of desertion.

The doors of cabinets and lockers stood open, and raw spots on the walls and ceilings showed where some kind of connections had been ripped free.

"Cleaned out. Everything's gone."

For Jeremy it was a sickening blow—and he could see the same reaction in Ferrante's face and feel how deeply his invisible companion shared it, too. "This means that someone else may have come here and made off with a hundred Faces. Or two hundred. But who?"

For the moment, neither Jeremy nor his companion could come up with a useful idea. They were about to leave, in near-despair, when . . .

"Wait a minute."

Some idea, some clue, led Jeremy/Apollo back. "Those doors, where we were first trying to get in, weren't really doors."

"True enough. So?"

"Then maybe . . ." He couldn't express his hunch clearly in words. But it led him back into the ravaged interior.

"What the hell we looking for?"

"We won't know till we find it. A hidden door. An opening. A . . . something."

A thorough search ensued, probing examination of all seemingly blank, unhelpful surfaces.

At last it was Apollo, aided by some subtle secret sense or the trace of an ancient memory, who found it out. At the back of the smallest, dirtiest cabinet in one of the ruined rooms, a panel remained unopened. But at the Sun God's touch it silently swung aside.

Andy, crouching beside him, swore. Apollo muttered something in an ancient language.

Before them, when they had passed through the small aperture, stretched a whole suite of undamaged rooms, larger than the decoy rooms. Here was the true workshop of Hephaestus, packed with strangeness and loaded with wonders. Inside, the air was warm and clean. Soft globes of bioluminescence filled the sealed rooms with pleasant light.

The central chamber of the suite was circular, and in its center stood a massive forge, now all unfueled and empty. When they laid hands upon its edge, it felt as cold as a rock on the bottom of the arctic sea. Going down from its center, deep into the earth, was a round black hole in which a single spider of surpassing boldness had spun a web and taken residence.

32

THE TWO COMRADES stood under miraculously clear lighting, produced by white tongues of inexplicable magic fire that danced across the room close under the high ceiling, heating the space below to a comfortable level as well as illuminating it.

But neither Jeremy nor Andy was watching the flames. Their whole attention was drawn to an object that lay, as if carelessly cast down, in the middle of a cleared space on the scarred upper surface of what seemed to be the main workbench.

"What's this?" Andy demanded, pointing.

Jeremy had come to a halt on the other side of the bench, which had been wrought of massive timbers. "Just what you think it is. A Face."

"So that's what they look like. But whose? Which god?" Ferrante obviously didn't want to touch the thing.

Even Apollo couldn't be sure, without touching it, of the identity of the god whose powers had been thus encapsulated. But the moment Jeremy picked up the Face, he knew absolutely, though he could not have explained his certainty. What he held in his hands was a model of the rugged countenance of Vulcan himself, showing a furrowed brow and a hint of ugliness, the whole combining to suggest great power. Jeremy noted, without understanding, that this Face, like the three others he had seen, had only one eye and one ear.

Neither of its discoverers could think of a reason why the Face of Hephaestus should have been carelessly left lying here.

Carefully Jeremy put the object back exactly where he had picked it up and then with Andy began a careful search of the whole inner, secret workshop.

At the beginning of this search Apollo's avatar had substantial hopes of discovering some version of the Silver Bow, or some of its Arrows, left by some previous incarnation of Vulcan. But nothing of the kind was to be found, nor did the searchers turn up anything at all that seemed likely to be of practical value. The most interesting discovery was in a room next to that containing the workbench, where one wall held a row of simple wooden racks, of a size and shape that suggested they might have been designed to hold a score or more of Faces. But all the racks were empty. There might be a space marked for the Face of War, suggesting it had been kept there—and in this case the empty space struck Jeremy as ominous.

God or not, he was feeling tired, and he sat down for a few minutes' rest, his face in his hands. The situation reminded Jeremy of one of the logic puzzles with which his father in bygone years had sometimes tried to entertain him: *If there exists an island where one god makes masks or Faces for all the gods who do not make their own ...*

Up on his feet again, he went prowling restlessly about. Here stood a row of statues, busts, of godlike heads, in bronze and marble, reminding Jeremy of the display at the Academy. Why would Hephaestus have wanted to provide himself with such a show?

Other shapes of wood suggested molds or templates for body armor in a variety of sizes. But again there was nothing that looked useful waiting to be taken, only a bewildering variety of tools, materials, and objects less readily definable, about which Apollo seemed to know no more than Jeremy Redthorn.

Putting down an oddly shaped bowl—or it might have been a helmet, for someone with a truly strange head—Jeremy looked around and noted without any particular surprise that Ferrante had returned to the central bench. There the young soldier stood, his head over the bench, leaning on his spread arms, both hands gripping its edges. He was staring in utter fascination at the Face of Vulcan. In a near-whisper he asked the world: "What do we do with this?"

"You put it on," said Jeremy softly. The decision had been building in him over the last few minutes—not that there had ever been much doubt about it.

Eyes startled—but not totally surprised, not totally reluctant—looked up at him. "I *what?*"

"Andy, I don't think we have any choice. Much better you than some others I've run into. *I* absolutely can't do it."

Everything Apollo could remember, all that Jeremy could learn from others, including the new memories now available to Ferrante, confirmed the idea that no human could wear the Face of more than one god or goddess at a time.

"Sort of like the idea that an egg can be fertilized only once."

"We could destroy it?" Ferrante's tone made it a question.

Jeremy spread his hands. "I don't know how. Even Apollo doesn't know a way. I've heard a rumor that on top of the Mountain of the Oracle there's a place where Faces can be wiped out of existence—"

The young soldier's face showed how much credence he put in rumors.

Jeremy continued: "Maybe Hephaestus knows how to destroy a Face—but he won't even exist until someone puts this on." He concluded his thought silently: *And then maybe he won't want to reveal his secrets—and then you won't want to either.*

Ferrante with a sudden grab picked up the Face. But then he stood for several seconds hesitating, juggling the thing like a hot potato, struck by whatever sensation it produced in his fingers. "I'd be a god," he murmured.

At the last moment Jeremy felt compelled to give a warning. "It will mean, in a way, giving up your life."

Troubled eyes looked up again. "You glad you put yours on?"

Jeremy thought for a long moment. "Yes."

"Then here I go. . . . How?"

"Just press it against your own face, as if you just wanted to look through the eye. That's how it worked for me. And for Carlotta." *And for Kate.* He didn't want to worry Andy with that news just yet.

When the Face of Hephaestus had disappeared into his head Andy Ferrante stood for a long moment with his eyes closed, looking as if he were in pain.

"It'll be all right, Andy."

There was a slight sound behind Apollo/Jeremy, and he/they spun around, both startled. The doors of a closet-size cabinet, previously locked, had opened, and from inside two life-size golden maidens had emerged, walking in the manner of obedient servants.

From the first look it was obvious that the pair were not real women, let alone goddesses, for there was no glow of life about them. Rather, they were marvelous machines. Their beautifully shaped bodies were nude, but no more erotic than metal candlesticks. Jeremy was sure they would be hard as hammers to the touch.

They spoke, when questioned, in golden voices, assuring the Lord Hephaestus and the Lord Apollo that there was no Silver Bow here in the workshop now, nor were there any Arrows. New weapons would have to be manufactured.

Ferrante's eyes were open now, and he regarded the maidens with a thoughtful, proprietary air. Jeremy's left eye could already read the subtle beginnings of a tremendous transformation in the young soldier's face and body. Of course it would take him weeks, months, perhaps even years to grow into the part as Jeremy had grown into his.

Then Ferrante suddenly clutched his right leg. "Ouch! What the hell—?"

"What is it?" asked Jeremy—although Apollo already knew.

"Like a goddam stabbing pain—" Within a minute the pain had abated, but Ferrante was left limping.

Jeremy spent the next few minutes reassuring his friend about the various strangeness of the transformation. Each individual who underwent the transformation was affected differently; Katy hadn't needed nearly so much help, and he himself had muddled through unaided.

"Everything looks different," Ferrante murmured.

"Sure it does. I just hope you can see how to make the things we need."

"Let me think a minute. Let me look around." The new avatar of Hephaestus hardly had time to catch his breath before he was required to get busy making weapons—in particular the Silver Bow and its complement of arrows.

When Ferrante hesitated and fretted, Jeremy told him, "Don't ask *me* how to do things; look into your memory. You'll find more things in your mind, more plans, more schemes, than you know what to do with."

The young man turned away, staring numbly at the pair of golden women, who looked back solemnly with yellow eyes. Slowly Andy nodded. The expression on his face was now that of an old man.

————————

Even as the new Hephaestus began preparing to produce a Bow, Apollo wanted some questions answered about the business of making Faces. Whether or not some previous avatar of the Artisan had manufactured the current supply, Ferrante said he could find no clue in memory as to how the feat had been accomplished. Making more god Faces wasn't going to be immediately possible.

He paused in his labor, looking at Jeremy out of an altered face, speaking in an altered rumble of a voice. "Anyway, I don't see how I—how Vulcan—could have made the original batch. That would mean he somehow manufactured his own memory. In effect, that he created himself. No, I don't think so.

"Some great mystery's involved here. I can't remember the beginning of Vulcan's life—if it ever had a beginning—no more than Andy Ferrante can remember Andy Ferrante being born."

Jeremy/Apollo couldn't argue with that. "That's about how things stand with me."

Ferrante raised his hands (did they already look bigger, with gnarled fingers? in Apollo's eye, they had acquired that kind of ghostly image) to his head. "Jer, I'm not gonna dig into memory anymore. Not now. It could show me some terrible things . . . if I let it. But just like you say it is with you, there are holes in my new memory. Huge gaps."

"All right. We can't take the time now to go looking for ultimate answers. We'll have to do the best we can. What I need are my Bow and Arrows."

Now the new Artisan had begun to putter about, in a way that seemed purposeful though not comprehensible to his companion. As Ferrante worked, limping from bench to cabinet and back again, evidently taking an inventory of tools and materials, he tried to keep up a conversation. "Maybe I'll grow taller? Like you?"

"I think you will."

Andy nodded. "That's one part of the business I'll enjoy."

Jeremy hadn't mentioned other probable changes that had popped into his mind. He was thinking that the other would doubtless grow uglier as well, which he would not find so enjoyable. Strength and magical skill would flow into his hands—and into his eyes and brain, for measuring and planning. As well as a knowledge of all the marvelous tools with which his workshop was equipped.

Already he had begun to issue orders to the two handmaidens who were the color of gold. They murmured obediently and started doing something in the rear of the workshop.

Then, for a moment, Andy was only a young man again, terribly out of his depth.

Jeremy/Apollo said to him: "It's your workshop now."

Ferrante looked round nervously, then whispered as if he didn't want the two golden women to hear him. "Until the goddam god comes back."

"He has."

Ferrante started and turned quickly, first to one door and then another, as if he expected another Presence to come striding in. Only when he turned back to meet Jeremy's level gaze did the truth finally sink in: ". . . oh."

Apollo was nodding at him. "Yes. Take it from me; you are now Hephaestus. There is no other."

Hesitantly Ferrante called orders back to the two golden maidens, who had been watching him impassively: "What we've got to do now is make a Silver Bow—and the Arrows to go with it. Bring out whatever the job's going to need."

As Ferrante's body began its slow, inevitable alteration, Vulcan's image flickered in Apollo's eye, like a tongue of flame—which reminded Apollo that on the rare occasions when the Artisan was driven to use weapons, fire was generally his choice. Apollo could remember how the Smith had once driven off Ares himself, with a mass of red-hot metal.

And now Vulcan's new voice, not much like that of a soldier named Ferrante, was raised, chanting words, ancient names, beyond the understanding even of Apollo: "Agni . . . Mulciber . . ."

. . . and with a pop and a *whoosh* the forge fire had been lighted, a column of flame springing up from concealed depths below, radiating a glow in which red and blue were intermingled.

The workshop was certainly equipped with marvelous tools, and to Jeremy and Apollo both it appeared they might enable the construction of anything that could be imagined. Here and there some project looked half-finished—Apollo had no idea what these were, and Vulcan's new avatar already had more to do than he could readily handle.

The new avatar of Vulcan, looking around him, already becoming thoroughly enmeshed in his new memories, became less communicative as he gained in understanding. The looks he shot at Jeremy/Apollo were still friendly, but more reserved.

Also, thought Jeremy, you would have to know how to use the tools. Some of the implements scattered around on benches or visible in open cabinets looked almost ordinary, while others were very strange indeed. If you didn't know what you were doing, messing around with them could be dangerous—and even Apollo did not know. They worked by magic—or by technology so advanced as to be indistinguishable from magic.

And then Apollo—even Apollo—was brusquely commanded to step out of the room during some phases of construction.

"Go out now. Soon I will bring you, or send you, what you need."

"Sure." Jeremy hesitated. He wanted to ask again about the possibility of destroying Faces but did not want to distract the new Smith from his task of Bow and Arrow making. Abruptly Jeremy turned and left, crawling out again through the little cabinet. Over his shoulder he called back: "If I don't see you for a while, good-bye. And good luck!"

Before exiting the building through the broken place in the foundation, he peered out cautiously through the riven rock where he and Ferrante had come in. Jeremy was not much surprised to note that snow had started to fall, nor did it really astonish him that the Enemy had arrived.

Before deciding what to do next, Jeremy took a careful inventory of the opposition. There was Cerberus, and there a human he was able to recognize as the Gatekeeper, accompanied by about a dozen human and zombie auxiliaries, who had taken up positions behind various outcroppings of rock, from which they could observe that side of the workshop that looked the most like a front door. That seemed to be all.

In another moment Jeremy had spied out his enemies' means of transportation, now almost concealed behind rocks—a kind of airborne chariot, pulled by winged horses that were no more like natural animals than the golden maidens were like women. As soon as he posed the question seriously to himself, Apollo's memory informed him that few gods were for long without some means of swift, long-range travel.

From behind him in the inner chambers Apollo's keen ear picked out what sounded like a whoosh of bellows—of course, plenty of heat would be needed for working silver. Though how either Bow or Arrows could be fashioned of that metal was more than the Sun God could say.

Turning his back on the enemy, he crawled deep enough into the interior again to encounter one of the maidens and informed her: "Visitors have arrived."

By the time Apollo got back to his observation post, Cerberus had moved to a position allowing the god inside the building to get a better look at him. So had the Gatekeeper, who was now sitting, wrapped in furs, a little apart from his companions. Cerberus was obviously not human, not even a human wearing some god's Face, but an artifact of the mysterious odylic process. The mechanical beast looked like nothing in the world so much as a three-headed dog, shaggy and elephant-size, though built closer to the ground than any elephant. Apollo had no important information to offer on the subject of Cerberus; Jeremy concluded that the Dog, too, had been built by some earlier avatar of Vulcan.

Thinking it over, the Sun God decided that Hades's minions must have been here to the workshop before, scouting. Perhaps they had come here many times over a period of decades or centuries. They'd evidently had some agency watching the place and so were informed when Apollo arrived.

It was quite possible that on some earlier reconnaissance the villains had penetrated far enough to observe the interior ruin. That would account for their attitude of nonchalant waiting, which indicated that they didn't expect either Jeremy/Apollo, or his merely human companion, to have acquired any new armament when they came out.

In confirmation of these suspicions, the Gatekeeper now raised his voice, with surprising confidence for a mere mortal, and called out: "Are you finding a new Bow in there, apprentice god? I don't think so! We can discuss the matter further when you come out. My good pet here wants to meet you."

Jeremy/Apollo turned, in response to a small sound behind him. Approaching from the direction of the inner workshop, crawling out through the inconspicuous cabinet, came one of the maidens, carrying his required weapons, the great Bow still unstrung. While the cabinet door was open, Jeremy could hear from inside the workshop Hephaestus/Andy hammering on his forge.

"One Bow, three Arrows, sire," the golden woman, really no more human than Cerberus, murmured in her resonant and mellow voice.

Apollo accepted the gift with a few words of appreciation. His favorite weapon, when Jeremy Redthorn's eye at last got a good look at it, was as tall as he was when he set one tip on the stone floor. It appeared to be laminated with horn from some magical beast and some special metal still hot from the processes of manufacture. The string appeared to be metallic silver—just like those of the perfect lyre that lay also in his memory.

The enemies were behaving restlessly outside. Someone, or something, out there hurled a rock with terrific force, so that the missile striking the workshop's outer wall shattered and splintered into tiny fragments. Following the booming impact, Jeremy/Apollo could hear the little fragments raining, dusting down.

Jeremy tried to calculate whether a mere three Arrows might be sufficient to dispose of the array of foes that now confronted him. Certainly one should be enough, and more than enough, for the merely human Gatekeeper—but then Jeremy remembered the powers of the merely human Circe and no longer felt quite certain.

The Arrows he held in his hands were just as Apollo remembered that they ought to be: very long, perfectly straight, and distinctively feathered. The feathers, if that was truly what they were, must have come from no bird that Jeremy Redthorn's eyes had ever seen—he thought no draftsman could have drawn such linear regularity in all the fine details. These all bore the broad-bladed, barbed heads of hunting arrows—Apollo could remember some Arrows in the past that carried quite different points from these, but he felt satisfied that these were what he needed now.

He turned to see that the maiden had retreated. Andy/Hephaestus had stuck his head out of the inner workshop and was regarding him.

Jeremy held up one Arrow. "Will one of these kill him? Hades himself?"

The answer seemed to come more from Vulcan than from Andy Ferrante: "Wouldn't bet on it. But he won't like the way it feels."

Jeremy nodded and turned back to business. It was time to string the Bow.

The more he looked at it, the more he was impressed. Jeremy Redthorn's eyes had never before even seen a bow anything like this one, and he would not ordinarily have imagined that he had the strength to draw it. He could feel something in his arms and shoulders change when he picked it up; his restored strength drew it smoothly

The Bow felt heavier than any normal wooden weapon, even heavier than a bar of silver ought to be. Jeremy estimated that normal human strength would not suffice to bend it—scarcely to lift it. But Apollo's arms, of course, were more than adequate.

. . . *as the Bow bent, it seemed to him that tremors afflicted the deep earth beneath the workshop, and from somewhere came a ripping sound reminding him of the noise a great tree made, moments before it went down in the wind.* . . .

And (his memory assured him) distance would offer his enemies no protection. Even if Apollo could not see a target, let him imagine it clearly, Far-Worker's weapon could put an arrow through it. He could even attempt to slay Hades from halfway around the world—but no, he had better deal with the immediate peril first.

The Gatekeeper and the great Dog must have been at least half-expecting him to sortie from the workshop, but the Bow and Arrows were evidently a considerable surprise. The immense doglike three-headed machine was scarcely higher than a large normal dog but at least thrice bulkier than a cameloid. Each head was supported by an extra set of legs, and each set of jaws was filled with long, sharp teeth. Cerberus was ready to attack, whatever the odds might be, and came roaring and scrambling forward, over rocks and snow.

Apollo's first Arrow killed one head of the Dog, striking it squarely between the wide-set yellow eyes.

As the beast recoiled, an idea occurred to Jeremy/Apollo. Ignoring a thin rain of missiles from the auxiliaries, he turned his aim in another direction. The second Arrow well placed into the middle of the chariot split it in half, bright wood splintering, as clean as freshly broken bone. Now Hades's creatures would be stranded here unless they could find some other means of transport.

If any of them survived this fight.

One of the Dog's still-functional heads now seemed to be trying to speak, but Jeremy could understand nothing that it said, because its fellow growled and roared, drowning out the words. Meanwhile the slain head hung down limply, while the extra legs beneath it were starting to lose function, threatening to bring the whole beast down.

Now, thought Apollo, it was time to dispose of the auxiliaries, lest they cause some mischief after he had departed. Now Jeremy wished he had the support of Ferrante, the simple soldier, in this fight, but he could manage without it.

Thanatos had not been with the war party when it arrived, but death had come among them, all the same. Even ordinary arrows leaped from this Bow straight to the target, striking with terrible, unnatural force, within an inch of the place the archer willed them to go. There was no need now to aim for chinks, for the missiles were driven right through armor, even a succession of armored bodies, even if the targets were not arrayed in a straight line. The flight path of the missile curved to take in a goodly number.

The blood of the human/zombie auxiliaries was a startling red against the fresh snow. The few survivors among them scattered with, Jeremy thought, little hope of survival amid rocks and surf. Drowning or starvation ought to be the fate of any who escaped immediate slaughter.

Jeremy's ordinary shafts had been used up now, and his single remaining Arrow was now required to finish off the monster three-headed Dog.

The Gatekeeper had vaulted onto the creature's back, in an effort either to make his escape or to control the creature and direct its fury against Apollo. When the third Arrow leaped from the Bow to strike the Dog, it also mortally wounded the man who was trying to ride it.

Cerberus was finished now, and beside the huge and grotesque body the man in furs lay sprawled on his back, motionless in a pool of his own blood.

The Gatekeeper's face looked cynical and infinitely weary. He blinked and squinted, as if trying to bring into focus the Face of Apollo bending over him.

What had been a commanding voice came out in a thin whisper. "Once I wanted to be you."

Apollo did not understand that, but often the dying babbled nonsense. The god was paying attention to this death, listening carefully, withholding the healing force that might have saved. His Bow was still in his hand, though no more Arrows—or even arrows—were left in the quiver.

The god's voice came out through Jeremy Redthorn's lips.

"You are an evil man."

The Gatekeeper breathed twice, shallowly, before he answered: "And you are still a child. . . . Never mind. It doesn't matter." He was showing his age now, as he lay Arrow-pierced and dying, and in truth, as the watching god remembered, this man was extremely old.

There was one last thing the Gatekeeper had to say to Jeremy/Apollo: "Still a child . . . I made you."

Whatever Jeremy, or Apollo either, had expected to hear, it had not been that. "What are you talking about?"

Three more slow and shallow breaths. "A little while ago I thought . . . that if I could only deliver . . . your Face, the Face of Apollo . . . to Hades, then no one else would be able to oppose him any longer. And he, he would give to me at last . . ."

"Give to you *what?*"

". . . but the gods . . . the gods make many promises, to many humans, which they never intend to keep."

The listener waited to hear more, but the ancient man was dead. No Face came trickling and bubbling out of the Gatekeeper's head when breath was gone. There might have been the passage of a soul, but not even Apollo could see that.

33

WHEN THE FIGHT was over and Jeremy slung the Bow on his shoulder, he could feel how its size diminished just enough to fit him comfortably. The workshop was silent, though now a thin column of smoke ascending from a hidden chimney near its center gave evidence that it was no longer unoccupied.

Wanting to bring its new occupant news of his victory, Jeremy started back inside. He also wanted to let Andy know that Apollo was now returning to the Mountain.

That was where the decisive fighting was going to be, and he had to go there—if necessary, without waiting to get more Arrows.

———

A golden maiden met Jeremy in the ruined, deserted-looking anteroom, holding out in her right hand three more Arrows. Handing them over with a light curtsy, she informed the Lord Apollo in her golden voice that many hours must pass before more shafts could be made. The reason given had to do with a shortage of vital materials.

"I must talk to Andy," said Jeremy. "I need more Arrows." And Apollo pushed past the machine that made no attempt to stop him.

———

"I have demolished Cerberus and killed the Gatekeeper."

"That's fine." The Toolmaker, eyes on his task, reached for a heavy hammer. Andy's altered face of the Toolmaker was ruddy in his forge fire's light, his newly muscular torso bare and sweating.

"What are you working on?"

"Necessary things." Andy/Vulcan appeared irritated at being distracted from his work. "Look, Jer, I'm going to be busy here for some time. I can't just make Arrows. I've got to strengthen the defenses of this place and fix myself up with some fast transportation—I don't have any Sandals."

"I need more Arrows."

"Hell yes, I'll do your Arrows, too."

"Hades is . . ."

"Then go fight him," Hephaestus growled. "I tell you I can't leave the shop just now." And he turned back to his forge. On the anvil lay a small object whose vital glow was so dazzling that even the Sun God's vision could not quite make out its true shape, but it did not appear to be another Arrow.

———

Apollo took himself away, vaguely unsatisfied but afraid to provoke an argument with his strongest ally. The uncertainty worried him, but he dared not wait around to discuss the subject. He was disturbed by the fact that he'd been given no congratulations on winning the skirmish, no expression of enthusiasm; it wasn't like Andy. The situation brought home the unpleasant fact that the Andy he'd come to know no longer existed.

But Jeremy's greater worry was for Katy—partly on account of sheer physical danger and partly because he feared the changes that must inevitably have taken place in her when she put on the Face of a goddess. If only he could have followed his original plan and carried her back to her home village, instead of—but there was no use fretting about the unchangeable past.

The bleak thought came that, in a sense, he'd killed the woman he loved. The Katy Mirandola who had grown up in the Honeymakers' village no longer existed, any more than did the boy named Jeremy Redthorn, who'd once had only dreams to tell him what the stars were like.

———

He adjusted the straps of his Sandals and sprang into the air, headed for the Mountain again.

———

His plan was not to immediately search for Kate. He calculated he'd have a much greater chance of defeating the Lord of the Underworld if he could somehow rejoin Lord Victor's four hundred lancers and persuade the troops in green and blue to accept his leadership. He supposed that would not be hard for Apollo to accomplish.

He thought it impossible that any human being could stand against him in single combat, but *leadership* was a different matter—not his strong suit. Nor, when he came to think about it, was it Apollo's either.

Arnobius, having been left by default in command of the 400 lancers when his brother was snatched away, ordered an advance on the entrance to the Cave. There the remnants of the Gatekeeper's force, outnumbered about thirty to one, either fled into the surrounding woods or surrendered immediately.

The Scholar decided to leave about a hundred men to hold the entrance. Meanwhile he meant to advance, with the remaining three hundred, toward the summit.

"Up there ... up there at the top. That's where things will be decided."

His harried second in command stared at him. "Sir?"

"Up there, Major!"

As Trickster, Katherine's first important decision was that Lord John ought to be rescued from the punishment to which her predecessor had consigned him and restored to his proper position of command. For one thing, his presence as a skilled and familiar leader ought to be good for his army. For another, she didn't want a son of the Harbor Lord to fall into Hades's or Kalakh's hands and be used as a hostage to hinder the war effort.

Not that she approached the task of rescue with any enthusiasm. Through the Trickster's memory Katy could recall perfectly that Lord John had been ready to take Carlotta and use her as a slave.

Fortunately, the place where she had taken him, a stone quarry that used up a lot of slaves, was relatively nearby, not ten miles from the Mountain.

Her borrowed chariot, behind its galloping horses whose hooves magically found purchase in the air, swooped low to scoop John up, out of a cloud of rock dust and hammering noise, under the eyes of a gaping overseer who was so astonished that he dropped his whip.

Looking at the totally bewildered man she'd just dumped beside her in the zooming chariot, Katy/Trickster told him: "Don't suppose that I have suddenly become your friend. Maybe before the day is over you'll wish that you were back there, breaking rocks."

He appeared to be in bad shape, half-naked now and his remaining clothes in shreds. His costly earrings of course were gone, one having been ripped right out by some impatient robber, turning the lobe into a raw and ugly fringe.

Slowly he righted himself and got to his feet, fixing his gaze on her with an expression of haggard hope, mixed with desperation. "Who're you? You're not . . ."

"Not Carlotta, no. Lucky for you," Katy told him, increasing their airborne speed with a flick of the reins on the white horses' backs. "But I am the Trickster, and I remember her and what happened to her. I suppose you are not a good man—but maybe not *that* bad. In practical terms, you should be very useful."

Clinging to the low rail in front of him, the man beside her started to stammer through some kind of explanation, but Katherine wasn't really listening. She felt troubled by new inner doubts about her relationship with Jeremy. "The Bride of Apollo," she muttered to herself, wondering if anyone would ever call her that, and tried to laugh at the idea. There were moments when it seemed to her ridiculous that the two of them could have any kind of a future together.

She still *felt* human—and then again she didn't. This new state of existence was something more. If neither of them was going to be human any longer, would marriage between them even be possible? The Trickster's memory gave reassurance on that point, as did the old stories, in which divinities frequently wedded one another and brought forth offspring.

Driving over the spot where she had left Arnobius and the lancers, Katy observed that they had moved on to the Cave entrance, less than a hundred yards away. Bringing her chariot to earth there, she reined its magnificent horses to a standstill. "Where is Arnobius?" she demanded of the junior officer who appeared to be now in command.

"Gone up the hill, my-my lady," the man stammered, his eyes as wide as those of the lowliest common soldier.

Katy/Trickster reached out a hand to assist John out of the chariot.

"The military situation here will be your job," she informed him. "I have other business to attend to. Don't make me sorry that I brought you back." She flicked the reins, and a moment later the chariot had leaped into the air again.

———————

John ached in every bone and in a good many other places. But he was not too hurt, or too exhausted, to know what had to be done and settle down to do it.

He was also burning to be avenged upon those who had whipped and starved him for the last four days or so. But that would have to wait.

Meanwhile his older brother's thought and energy were being entirely consumed by the increasing nearness of the Oracle—the true Oracle, if any in the whole universe was true. With Olympus itself now practically within his reach, he would at last be granted a clear look at the nature of the gods.

The Scholar looked around and found himself alone in the woods. The last of his troopers had somehow wandered away—but no, they were probably good soldiers, and vaguely he remembered sending them off.

But doing what was really important here would not require soldiers.

———————

When Jeremy/Apollo arrived at the main entrance to the Cave, there were no ordinary pilgrims to be seen, which was hardly surprising, given the fighting in the area. Instead of pilgrims he found lancers, with Lord John newly restored to command. But he had no more than about fifty men in the immediate vicinity. The elder brother's inept orders had scattered the bulk of the force up and down the mountainside, generally out of sight and out of touch with each other, where they were engaged in ineffective skirmishing with Lord Kalakh's troops in white and blue.

When Apollo appeared, John turned pale, evidently with fear lest this new god had come to snatch him away again.

Once reassured on that point, he tried to explain what had happened to him. "It was the Trickster, my Lord Apollo, who brought me back here, about an hour ago. The same goddess who snatched me away— but not the same woman, if you take my meaning."

Jeremy's heart leaped up. At least Katy was still alive. "I do. Where is this woman now?"

John had not the faintest idea. She'd hurried away in her chariot again, airborne as before. But he passed on the information that Arnobius was pressing on toward the summit, determined to find Olympus.

Jeremy moved in the same direction. Now, with the Silver Bow in hand, an advantage that Apollo's previous avatar had lacked, it was time for him to lure Hades out into a decisive combat.

Might it really be true that at the summit of the Mountain there existed a means of destroying god Faces? Apollo had no direct memory of any such device or even of the possibility of one, but that, Jeremy decided, didn't rule it out. The Sun God's memory was shot through with lacunae, some of them in places where vital matters ought to have been available.

And Jeremy Redthorn was willing to risk much to destroy the Face of Hades. At least the power of destroying Faces must not be allowed to remain in Hades's grasp.

Jeremy considered praying for help—but to whom should a god pray? Father Zeus? That name called up from memory only a shadowy, forbidding image, oddly similar to a gnarled tree. He could only hope that after dropping off Lord John Katy had managed to get herself back to the Honeymakers' village or to some other place of safety. Carlotta's fate had proved that the Trickster's powers were no match for those of Hades in a direct contest.

Katy. The idea that he, Jeremy Redthorn, might have destroyed her was now continually preying upon his mind. It was too terrible to be thought about, and yet it refused to go away.

——————

With the power of the Sandals to aid him, Jeremy could readily enough dash off to visit Lord Victor in Pangur Ban or somewhere in the field, if he had good reason to do so. He pondered whether he should do so and decided against it. Surely His Lordship had learned by now of the great perils his sons were in and had taken the field with his full army.

His mind once more focused on finding Katy, Jeremy let the Sandals carry him where they would. After whirling him above the treetops for two minutes in a curving ascent, they brought him to the Scholar, who through carelessness had become separated from the last of his troops, and was climbing alone, on foot, toward the summit.

Arnobius looked almost exhausted but content. At the sight of Apollo his face lit up, and his whole body seemed to slump in the relaxation of one who had finally achieved an almost impossible goal. He had now at last established the contact with Apollo that he had once so desperately craved.

He gave no sign of recognizing, in the figure before him, anything of the peasant lad he had once enlisted as his servant. Inclining his head in an awkward kind of bow, he said, "I am the Scholar Arnobius. What is your wish, my Lord Apollo?"

Apollo on Sandals, armed with the Silver Bow and with a fold of his white cape over his arm, was an impressive sight and a formidable antagonist. Jeremy now conjured up the white cape whenever he wanted it.

"I recognize you, Scholar. My wish is to defeat Hades. But first, to find out what has happened to the Trickster." When he saw how the Scholar's expression changed, he added: "She is no longer Carlotta—Carlotta is dead."

"Ah." Obviously the man did not know what to make of that.

Jeremy was not going to try to explain—not now. "Where is your cameloid?"

"I had to leave the animal behind, my lord, when I decided to climb some rocks. I was hoping for a short cut to the summit." Arnobius squinted up into the clouds. "But it seems to keep . . . receding from me."

———

Because the Sandals had brought Jeremy to Arnobius, he thought it would be wise to retain the man in his company for a time. With Apollo's three precious new Arrows in the quiver on his back and his new Bow slung over his other shoulder—and with Arnobius now thrilled to be tagging along as his companion—Jeremy allowed the Sandals to carry him on toward the top of the Mountain, as he tried to concentrate upon his wish to rejoin Katy/Trickster.

Together god and scholar advanced along the aboveground trail, at a pace no faster than a well-conditioned human might sustain. Jeremy wondered why the Sandals were guiding him this way, rather than at the speed of the wind and through the air. Perhaps there was no hurry or approaching on foot would allow him to see something he would have missed in hurried flight.

The winds gusted more savagely and hour after hour became more fierce; soon after sunset, a fist of icy cold clamped down. People who had come up here in summer clothing suffered from the cold.

Other difficulties were less easily explained by events in the realm of nature. From time to time Jeremy and others observed monstrous suffering animals and birds—most of them dead creatures that had not lived long, some of the more tasteless jokes perpetrated by one or another of the Trickster's avatars.

At this altitude the climbers encountered no one, and the trail Jeremy followed seemed never to have been much traveled, for it was narrower and less deeply worn than on the lower slopes.

Looking out over the ocean and land from up here was quite a dizzying prospect. At night you could see the occasional little fire sparks of villages and isolated houses.

Again Jeremy wished that Andy Ferrante could be at his side, ready to fight his enemies or give him counsel. One simple human friend would be of more comfort than a dozen divine promises . . . but he saw now with cold clarity that he had killed Andy Ferrante, just as he had destroyed Kate.

━━━━━

The closer Arnobius got to the crest, the more he hungered for the certain knowledge that would be available there. No more mysticism—the Mountaintop was real and solid, and whatever was there would be as real and solid as itself.

━━━━━

Jeremy was unable to shake his dread that he had gone through all his various sufferings and struggles only to lose his love again, and for good.

━━━━━

The trail on this side of the Mountain wandered back and forth across the middle slopes, not always for obvious reasons, sometimes traveling miles to get up the hill a few hundred yards. In places it was quite difficult, but a couple of trials soon demonstrated that trying to shorten the hike by climbing off the path was going to be considerably worse.

Now and then the Scholar had to stop for breath on this leg of his climb, and each time he expressed his wish that they were at last near the top. But, in fact, they could always see that there was *something,* in fact a good many things, still above them. And as often as not, they had stopped in a place from which it seemed impossible to climb any farther. Yet every time there was some means discoverable of going on.

Signaling his companion with a wave indicating that he wanted to stop, Jeremy let himself sink down upon a handy rock. It was time to do some planning. He felt confident that rest had restored him, that when the need arose again he would once more have mighty powers to call upon.

––––––

Deciduous trees, the leaves of birch and aspen already burning orange and yellow with the steady autumnal shortening of the days, had gradually given way to evergreens as the ascent continued. And once a certain height was reached, trees of any kind were fewer and stunted and growing bent and twisted by the winds that almost never ceased. Jeremy's imagination transformed their images into those of elderly enchanted wizards, their deformed arms frozen in gestures of power that would never be completed.

The rocks seemed to grow ever sharper and the paths and trails steeper.

Distant mountains, some of them weirdly shaped or colored, were visible from up here, some more than a hundred miles away.

"Lord Apollo, we approach Olympus." The man's voice was hushed, exalted.

"I suppose we do. I have never been there before." Then Jeremy asked his companion, "How high are we above the level of the sea?"

"Something like two miles." Here it grew very cold at night, and fires and/or tent shelters at least were necessary for human survival.

Here, too, Apollo was at least a little closer to the sun and had brighter and less filtered light to work with, when he set out to burn or to illuminate. And so were his enemies closer, to their disadvantage.

––––––

And now again, as on the island of Vulcan's workshop, there was snow on the ground, only gradually being eaten away by direct sunlight and persisting in the shade.

And then at last, Jeremy/Apollo and the Scholar, after tramping across a broad meadow covered with masses of wildflowers, peered over a ridge of rock and saw clearly ahead of them, no more than a hundred yards above, what they had been expecting, with a mixture of hope and fear, to find. Here the Mountain and their climb were coming to an end at last.

The House of the Trickster. That was one name, supplied by

Apollo's memory, for the sprawling structure that clung along the crest, its walls surrounding the actual summit. The grander title of Olympus seemed to apply at a different time in history—but again, as often before, memory was confused.

From somewhere far down in memory there floated up another name: *The House of Mirth.*

Echoes of maniacal laughter, perhaps launched by an earlier Trickster's avatar, seemed to haunt the high rocks, coming and going with the wind.

The structure's low crenellated walls and squat towers were visible from certain places a long way below.

The closer Apollo came to the building, the stranger it looked. Very strange indeed, as if different deities had at different times been in charge of its construction—which, Jeremy supposed, was actually the case. *The House of the Magician.*

Whatever other attributes the strange, half-ruined structure might possess, it provided a kind of fortification, on the highest ground available, and a comparatively small force ought to be able to hold it against a larger army.

At first glance it seemed unlikely that this sunlit scene, the broad, high meadow and the flowers, could ever form any part of Hades's territory—though the idea became less startling when you knew about the steaming vent that led down secretly to the Underworld again. Steam came rising visibly into the chill air.

Jets of boiling water and scalding mud imperiled the underground explorer.

The Trickster had left her/his mark everywhere around the summit, in the form of balanced rocks and twisted paths and natural-looking stairs of rock leading to blank walls or, without warning, over precipices.

Apollo's hearing could detect the murmured clash of widespread fighting, drifting in and up from miles away. There were signs that a major battle between human armies was shaping up.

And right now some zombies, their bodies the hue of mushrooms, were coming out to fight, coming right up out of a hole in the ground.

34

THE NAKED BODIES of the zombies gave no sign of being affected by the cold of the high summit—but they recoiled swiftly from direct sunlight. They had emerged from hiding, welling up from various of the Cave's upper entrances, only a little below the very summit, when the sun was temporarily hidden by thick cloud. But they swiftly retreated under the rocks again when the rays of Apollo's heavenly personification once more pierced the clouds.

Arnobius had not seen such creatures before, and their presence disturbed and frightened him. "What does it mean?"

Apollo, on the other hand, was quietly elated. "It means that the one I'm looking for can't be very far away. It means that there still exists a dark tunnel allowing such creatures to come all the way up here to the crest."

Now the very summit was only about fifty yards above where the two men were standing. Even now, in broad daylight, the air hurled by the howling winds along the crest was grayish, filled with a strange unnatural mist, when it was not opaque with snow. All this before the last greens of summer had faded from the sea-level lowlands visible below. Here and there Jeremy could barely distinguish some building, maybe a barn, that happened to be bigger than the ordinary.

Looking down from up here at the world from which he had ascended, the young man sometimes thought it was the normal land down there that looked enchanted—and this strange place the stronghold of grim reality.

Rising winds sometimes blasted gusts of snow straight toward the driving clouds above, ascending in twisting columns that threatened to coalesce in the shape of howling faces, reaching arms.

———

The Scholar, his gaze turned upward, let out a little moan, and the expression on his face suggested that he had now entered into an exotic, exalted mental state.

Jeremy looked at the man sharply and saw that he was going into one of his recurrent fits. A moment later Arnobius had toppled softly into a bank of flowers, where he lay with eyes closed and arms outstretched, hands making feeble groping movements.

His companion pondered whether to let him lie where he had fallen or carry him on to the very summit. But at the moment the Sandals were giving Apollo no impulse to move on, and so he decided to wait where he was till his companion snapped out of it.

———

Jeremy had never forgotten his sworn promise to Sal. His Sandals had brought him here and were not yet ready to carry him all the way to the summit. But she was not here. Once more he expressed a thought that he had already repeated so often that it had become automatic: "Find me Margaret Chalandon."

This time, it seemed, he was granted an almost immediate response.

He had thought himself alone except for the unconscious, entranced Arnobius. In the background, the song of larks was audible between fierce gusts of wind. On every side, but where the summit of the Mountain lay, there stretched a view that seemed to encompass all the countries of the earth.

But Apollo/Jeremy was no longer alone. A woman of regal bearing, her dark hair lightly streaked with gray, came walking toward him through a flowery meadow—and Apollo remembered now this was the Meadow of the Sun—dressed in the practical garments, including boots and trousers, that an intelligent scholar would have worn on a field expedition. She carried no tools, no weapons, no canteen or pack of any kind.

It was the woman's clothing, as well as the timing of her appearance, that instantly suggested a name for her. "Scholar Chalandon?"

She stopped, ten paces away. "Yes?" Her attitude was calm, her voice mild. If she found the youth standing before her particularly impressive in any way, her face did not reveal it.

Jeremy came right to the point. "I swore an oath that may now be impossible to keep."

"Regarding what?"

"I carry with me a great treasure that was entrusted to me by a young woman, a little while before she died . . ."

Apollo's voice trailed away. He had never seen Circe wearing clothing anything like that of the woman before him, and also this woman was apparently years older than the sorceress. Therefore, it, had taken the god a space of two or three breaths to recognize her. Now he continued: ". . . but I recall having told you something of the matter before. Tell me, were you also one of the seven?"

"No, my lord. But you may count me as a worshiper of Apollo— your humble servant." The voice of the enchantress was soft, but her eyes and bearing were anything but humble.

"I want no worship, but I need help. I am still Jeremy Redthorn— and I am afraid."

"So is Apollo, sometimes, I am sure. So are we all. I include Hades, too, of course—and even the great enchantress Circe." The last words carried a tone of something like self-mockery. She paused, as if to collect her thoughts, and as she did so the appearance of age fell away and her clothing changed, all in an instant, to the kind of filmy stuff that Circe was wont to wear. Now she strolled the meadow on bare feet that seemed to require no boots, or Sandals either, to carry her around in perfect comfort on the flank of a mountain. The intermittent fierce blasts of wind had little effect on her, barely stirring her hair and garments.

Jeremy waited.

Presently Circe ceased her pacing and said to him: "In the old stories the gods are forever disguising themselves as humans, ordinary mortals, and prowling around the earth in search of adventure. The Lord Apollo must realize, as soon as he allows himself to think about the matter, that such disguise is, in fact, no disguise at all."

The larks had fallen silent, but in the pines beyond the sunlit meadow wild birds were screaming frantically at one another, caught up in some conflict that had naught to do with either gods or humans.

Revelation, when it came, was something Apollo had doubtless known all along but Jeremy Redthorn had been afraid to look at. "You mean that only when the gods put on human bodies—like mine—can they ever have any real life."

Circe smiled at him.

"I spoke with the Gatekeeper," Jeremy told her. "Before he died."
Her dark eyes expressed a gentle curiosity.

"Certain things he said to me," Jeremy went on, "fit very well with
other things I see in some of my . . . in some of Apollo's deepest memories.

"The Faces that turn people into gods were never made by Vulcan.
What really happened was that the Face of Vulcan and all the others
were created, long, long ago, by clever humans. They were made to
embody certain . . . certain powers . . . that even then had been with humanity from time immemorial. And the Gatekeeper, in that time before
he became . . . what he became, was one of the clever ones who fashioned Faces."

Circe was nodding gently.

Jeremy/Apollo went on. "Now and again, down through the centuries, people have tried to destroy the Faces, but that can't be done.
Sometimes people have hidden them away. They may lie in concealment
for many years, but someone always finds them out again.

"The Scholar, if he could ever grow wise enough to understand,
would call the Faces triumphs of engineering with the odylic force. The
Gatekeeper in his early life would have called them *biocomputers*." It
was a word from a language too old for even Circe to recognize it;
Apollo could see in her face that it was strange to her.

"My lord gains wisdom," said she who had been known as Margaret
Chalandon, and now bowed to him lightly. Then she added: "So far I
have been conversing with my Lord Apollo; let me speak now to Jeremy
Redthorn."

"Go ahead."

"It is not out of kindness that the mighty god who shares your body
refrains from seizing total control of the flesh and bone. Kindness has
nothing to do with it. The real reason you retain your freedom is that
Apollo, who is granted life and being by your body, cannot *exist* without
a human partner. As long as he lives in you, he can do nothing that
Jeremy Redthorn does not want to do."

Nerving himself at last to probe the depths of borrowed memory,
Jeremy saw, and his new understanding deepened. "Then neither is Hades a true, pure god, as he believes himself to be?"

A nod of confirmation. "The power called Hades can commit no
greater wickedness than the human who wears that Face. Who but an
evil man or woman would seek to wield the power of death?"

Jeremy/Apollo took a step toward the woman. "Then answer me
this. Where did the *powers that are captured in the Faces* come from,
in the first place? Who created them?"

"As well ask where we humans came from." Then Circe added: "Fare you well in the battle you must soon fight; I cannot help you there." And the image that had been Circe became only a pattern of wildflowers, seen against the meadow, and then the pattern was gone from Jeremy's perception and there were only the flowers in themselves.

From ground level at his side there came a faint mumbling and a crackle of broken flower stems. Arnobius was sitting up and rubbing his eyes. Looking at Jeremy, he said: "I dreamed . . ."

"Yes, I think I know what you dreamed. Never mind. Get up, if you are coming with me. I want to stand in Olympus, on the very top."

"You wish me to come with you, Lord?"

"Yes. Why not?" It was on the tip of Apollo's tongue to say that if he were to discover yet another Face, he would want to have some halfway decent human being on hand to give it to. Arnobius for all his faults would be less objectionable as a god than any of Hades's henchmen.

Turning his back on the Meadow of the Sun, Jeremy found the trail again and went on up. Behind him he heard the Scholar's booted feet crunching on gravel, trying to catch up.

Meanwhile Lord John, having borrowed a few garments from various of his officers, was once more dressed in something like a fitting uniform and chewing on field rations as he rode—he'd lost some weight in his brief tour of duty as a quarry slave.

After reducing the guard at the Cave entrance to about fifty men, he was making his way uphill with all the others he could muster, trying to regroup his people into something like a coherent fighting force, after his brother's absentminded amateur commands had scattered them almost hopelessly about.

The ascent of John and his small force, unlike his brother's or Apollo's, was not unopposed, and the results of combat so far were unhappy.

Jeremy and the Scholar climbed on over the last few yards, against a sudden howling wind that stirred the piles of old bones, human bones, that lay about. It seemed that today's was not the first battle to be fought upon these heights. Now and then the wind picked up a skull and hurled it, dead teeth grinning in a great silent shout that might have been of fear or exaltation.

They now observed, at the foot of the stone walls that were almost within reach, another waterrise, an enchanted stream flowing in a closed loop, part of its course uphill. White ice from splashes covered all the nearby rocks. Its water might have frozen in this bitter cold, had it not gained warmth continually from some underground source. Only a few yards away, another pool lay bubbling and steaming and stinking of sulphur, from time to time emitting dangerous jets of steam. And yet a little farther on, two such streams were linked together, so that their waters, while never mingling, crossed and recrossed each other in an endless system of circles. Fish, mutated aquatic animals, were shooting up the waterrises, leaping with broad silvery bodies bending left and right, tails thrashing the air, like salmon headed upstream to spawn. In each dark, small pool the stream itself seemed to rest for a moment, gathering its strength for the abruptness of the next leap up.

There had been fighting here only hours ago, and dead men lay scattered about, along with a couple of dead cameloids. Some of the lancers, following the age-old tactical doctrine of seeking the high ground, had preceded their commanders to this spot; evidently some of Lord Kalakh's troops had had the same idea. Jeremy was able, as in his earlier combat, to replenish his supply of ordinary arrows by scavenging from the fallen.

Time and again in recent days Jeremy had heard rumors of the real Oracle's being up here. And now Arnobius was certain of the fact, with a true believer's faith.

The mad world of the upper heights was littered with strange objects. One who had not seen the vicinity of the workshop might have thought that the world could hold no other display like this.

During the years of the interregnum of divine activity, an incredible number of magicians, would-be magicians, adventurers, would-be saints, and fortune seekers seemed to have come this way, each striving desperately for his or her own goal. Here the seekers of knowledge, of wealth and power and glory, had left their bones, both broken and whole, and their weapons in the same variety of conditions. Here were rags of clothing, much of it once fine, purses and boots and headgear, now and then an armband of gold, a broken dagger beside a jeweled necklace, lying here forgotten and abandoned. Furs and blankets were more valuable booty, for folk who had to spend the nights outdoors at this altitude.

Possibly, Jeremy/Apollo thought, some of this junk had simply been abandoned by mundane human workers, who had been brought up here by one divinity or another, to contribute human effort to the construction of Valhalla. Building with only one set of hands, no matter how strong and how much assisted by things of magic, had probably turned out to be practically impossible.

No doubt there had been some tearing down to be accomplished also. Obviously the plans for the structure had been changed, repeatedly, while it was under construction.

There were broken flutes of wood and bone and an abandoned drum. The shape of other fragments suggested that they had once been parts of a lyre.

Passing through one of the many gaps in the outer wall, they found grass growing through the holes in what had been a fine tile floor. So far there was no sign of the tremendous Oracle of whose existence on these heights Jeremy had received hints.

Fighting flared and sputtered at no great distance below, but so far all was quiet right on the summit—except for the wind. If the old stories had any serious amount of truth in them at all, this barren place had been, perhaps still was, Olympus. To Jeremy and Apollo both it seemed within the realm of possibility that Father Zeus might come stalking out from behind the next half-ruined wall, coming up or down one of the ruined stairs.

Apollo was ready to challenge this possibility and boldly raised his voice: "Where is it, this deadly machine that can destroy Faces? Where is great Father Zeus? Apollo has a question or two he'd like to put to him—and so does Jeremy Redthorn."

His only answer was a gust of wind more violent than before, hurling a whole shower of grinning skulls and swirling a powdering of snow in the rough shape of a pointing arm. The indication was to the place where the piled stones reached their peak.

━━━━━━━

Brother John had reassembled a hundred or more lancers into a coherent fighting force and was commanding them with some skill. Every time he had a moment free for thought, he thought about the gods—and every time he did that he looked up at the sky, afraid that woman in her chariot might be coming back. And then, Apollo! He and his brother, the Scholar, had both failed for a long time to detect any trace of divinity in the skinny red-haired peasant fisherboy one of them had picked up in a swamp.

━━━━━━━

Up on the very summit, magic was thickly present in the strangeness of the way the world behaved. Under a gray sky, amid gray stones, you tried to catch your breath while flecks and streaks of improbably colored birds were driven past like missiles in a breathless hurricane of wind. Some of their eggs came flying, too. Yes, winged eggs, sprouting wings in midair at the last second, veering away from a smashing collision. Arnobius was struck by the mad thought that these might be the winged eggs of flightless birds—and then he saw a pair of great gray eagles riding the whirlwind, broad pinions almost motionless, apparently in full control.

Now Jeremy and Arnobius, climbing the very highest rocks, which seemed the remnant of a demolished tower, were able to look down at the portion of Olympus that had until now been hidden from them behind the very peak. They saw a sprawling, clinging structure, clinging low to the Mountain's rock, but still one of the biggest buildings that Jeremy Redthorn's eyes had ever seen. Apollo had seen bigger but could not recall any that looked more odd. From this angle, Olympus appeared to have been built as an ancient crude rock fortress. It would only be fitting that great horrors, great marvels, or both should lie behind such walls.

Fierce fighting raged not far below the crest, between the Lugard lancers and the forward units of Kalakh's army; the sound of men's voices, bellowing, came up on the wind, but for the moment Arnobius and his companion had the summit to themselves.

"The Oracle of the Gods," Arnobius breathed, and went scrambling up, scaling the very pinnacle of tumbled rocks.

Apollo's keenest interest lay elsewhere, and he went down a little on the eastern slope, where the bulk of the vast enigmatic structure lay. Scouting inside, Jeremy came to a place where the howling of the wind faded a little, shielded now behind thick stone walls. He had entered a huge central room. Enough seats and benches to hold hundreds of people were arranged in concentric rows, all empty now, but the heavy wooden frame on the small stone dais at the center looked more like a gibbet than a throne. Directly above it, the domed ceiling was open, at its center, to the sky.

A slight sound caused Jeremy/Apollo to turn round. Back in the dimmest shadows at the rear of the auditorium, a pool of deeper blackness was suggestive. Apollo walked in that direction and stood at the edge of the pool, peering downward into the depths. He had discovered the uppermost entrance of the Cave.

35

JEREMY CAME OUT of the sprawling half-ruined building again. His thoughts, as he looked about him at what was supposed to be Olympus, kept coming back to the revelation of his last talk with Circe, in the Meadow of the Sun: His union with Apollo had brought him marvelous tools, powers, including memory, worthy of a god. And with Apollo's memories, including those of his death struggle against Hades, had come a kind of inherited purpose. But whatever wisdom or foolishness Jeremy demonstrated, whatever courage or fear, did not come from the Sun God. Whatever Jeremy Redthorn now possessed of such qualities could only have come from within himself.

He stood for a moment looking about him at the ruin, part of which was older than Apollo's memory. If *this* was Olympus, then there ought not to be any gods.

The wind brought noisy news; the fighting between Kalakh's troops and Victor's was now sweeping up the mountain again, to rage once more upon the highest rocks.

Jeremy/Apollo took his Bow in hand and once more gathered ordinary arrows from the fallen, as he needed them. Wreaking havoc among the troops in Kalakh's blue and white, he meant to provoke a showdown with Hades, at all costs.

The Sun God yearned for help from Hephaestus. But Andy did not appear, and Jeremy supposed the truth was that the enemy was likely to get more help from Hephaestus than Apollo did, in the form of jealously guarded tools and weapons, crafted in olden times, by previous avatars. Jeremy had not mentioned anything of the kind—but then he could not have had time to fully explore his memory before Jeremy departed.

Jeremy kept in mind Circe's warning that human bodies pressed into service as the avatars of gods tended to wear out and collapse rather quickly; there was a limit to how long even the generally beneficent power of Apollo could sustain a framework of flesh and blood through extraordinary stresses. He should expect that the Sun God would seek a fresh human to use when the one called Jeremy Redthorn had been used up.

But there was nothing that Jeremy could do about that now.

Meanwhile, Lord John was bravely rallying the remnant of his original four hundred lancers, as many of them as he could gather under his control. He had dispatched messengers to his father's army and now could only wait for some reply—and, above all, for reinforcements, before it was too late.

Once more the most ordinary of arrows, springing from Apollo's Bow, wrought fearful havoc among the enemy. He wished he dared to use his stock of special shafts, that they would magically replenish themselves in his quiver as fast as he shot them away—or that Andy would come whirling in an airborne chariot to bring him more. But that was not the way things were working out today.

How long his human flesh could stand the strain and stress of combat he did not know. But for the moment he endured, and no human could stand against him in single combat—unless it were another like himself, strengthened from within by the help of some god.

This battle could not be won until he had challenged and conquered Hades. He went back into the auditorium, nocked one of his three special Arrows to his Bow, and prepared to go underground.

Pausing at the very entrance to the Cave, Jeremy found himself looking into the eyes of an old man, standing no more than an arm's length away. A moment passed before he realized that the image was his own, reflected from the visual depths of a glassy wall. The left eye was dark and keen, the right as greenish and nearsighted as Jeremy Redthorn's had ever been.

He started down, into the darkness.

Somewhat to his surprise, not Hades but Thanatos, in a new avatar, stood there confronting him.

Apollo was not impressed. "Nothing to say to me, Death God? The last time we met, you were full of words."

"This time I am a soldier, not a scholar," replied a sharp new voice. "You may find it a little harder to kill me, this time."

Jeremy raised his Bow just as his opponent dodged back out of sight.

Arnobius, wind-battered but still clinging to the stones that seemed to him the top of the world, could feel his mind wavering, on the brink of being plunged into another fit. Grimly he fought to retain his consciousness; he was only dimly aware of the fighting going on a short distance below.

But here came a startling sight indeed; he saw a chariot swooping down out of the sky and the Trickster in it, about to enter the fighting. But that was not to be, for grim Thanatos rose from behind one of the high rocks and put the curse of death upon the magic horses, so that the running animals collapsed in midstride and the chariot crashed to earth.

The Scholar blacked out for a moment, and when he could get his eyes to focus again, he saw the goddess, who was no longer Carlotta, on the ground now and in the grip of Death himself. She was being dragged under the earth through one of the little openings by which the zombies had earlier come out in their abortive sortie.

In the midst of his near-swoon, trying to get his body to work again, Arnobius thought he understood why the gods had ceased for many days to fascinate him: that had happened as soon as they became uncomfortably real. Just as he had turned away from Carlotta when she became a real person in his life. But here and now, on the Mountain, reality had become so overwhelming that he had no choice but to yield to it.

This was Olympus, the abode of Zeus, the place where answers ought to be available, if the truth could be found anywhere in the universe. Here, if anywhere, it could be possible to read or hear the inner secrets of the gods.

The Scholar gritted out: "Once the gods cease fighting among themselves, they may slay me for intruding. But first I will demand, of whatever Power rules here, some *answers!*"

At the very peak, three massive stones, one supported by two, formed a kind of niche or grotto, and half-sheltered in this recess there grew, or crouched, what looked like a squat and ancient tree, almost entirely denuded of leaves, trunk and branches fiendishly twisted by centuries of wind.

On the side of the tree toward Arnobius, an image was forming, even as he watched. A knob of the thick trunk fashioned itself into a head, twice as large as human life. On it was a countenance, gnarled and grim and powerful, that might have belonged to Zeus.

Two great eyes stared at the human visitor. "Ask," said a voice, seemingly wrung out of the wood, branches, and whole sections of the gnarled trunk, squeaking and grating against each other in the wind. Then it repeated the same word, four or five times, in as many different languages.

The Scholar could understand all of the languages but one. "Apollo, Apollo!" he screamed at it, surprising himself with his own choice of a first question. "I want you to tell me about Apollo!"

He had been expecting the voice to convey whatever response the Oracle might deign to make, but instead his answer came in an even more amazing form. The right eye of Zeus quickly expanded into a rough circle, a hand length in diameter, and its surface became glassy, translucent. There was an appearance of a ceaseless motion, flow, of *something* very active inside the eye, and presently small dark lines spelled out letters and words. The Scholar, clinging close to the trunk, had no difficulty in deciphering the ancient language:

> I KNOW MORE THAN APOLLO,
> FOR OFT WHEN HE LIES SLEEPING,
> I SEE THE STARS AT BLOODY WARS
> IN THE WOUNDED WELKIN WEEPING

If Zeus was really a talking tree stump, then the world was indeed completely and utterly mad, and the Scholar burned with the daring of despair. "Who are you?" he shouted. "What is this gibberish? Is there or isn't there a god somewhere, hiding in these ruins, who can explain it all to me?"

The wind howled, tearing at the rage of his clothing. New words formed inside the eye:

> THERE IS NO GOD—(WISDOM 12:13)

More nasty tricks. He might have known. He stood up straight and howled at the universe. "Who are you? Father Zeus?"

Doing so, he almost missed the next line:

—OTHER THAN YOU, WHO CARES FOR EVERY
THING

Arnobius gripped the rough bark with all the fingers of both his
hands, clutching at the cheeks of Zeus. "Tell me; I demand to know . . .
whether the gods made human beings or humans somehow created
gods?"

YET GOD DID MAKE MAN IMPERISHABLE
HE MADE HIM IN THE IMAGE OF HIS OWN NATURE
(2:23)

"Who are you?"

I AM HE WHO FOILS THE OMENS OF WIZARDS,
AND MAKES FOOLS OF DIVINERS (ISAIAH 44:24)

"All trickery, all sham! What kind of knowledge is this? This is no
god. I could give better prophecies than these myself."

KNOW THYSELF

Arnobius jumped to his feet again. And in the next moment, as if
responding to a signal, flying furies came buffeting him with whip-
fringed wings, tearing at him with their claws.

Moments later the furies were driven off by a pair of eagles—birds
known to Arnobius as the symbol, sometimes the incarnation, of Father
Zeus.

The Scholar fell down gasping. The pangs of a new seizure clawed
at him, and this time he had no choice but to give way.

━━━━━━━━

Jeremy, having advanced a few more yards into deepening gloom, made
out in front of him, to his utter horror, the form of Katy. She was
struggling in the grasp of Death, and he lunged forward to save her. A
moment later, his Arrow had plunged unerringly into Thanatos's head,
even though the Death God was trying to shield himself behind his
hostage.

A moment later, Jeremy/Apollo had scooped up Katy in his arms
and had turned with her, striding back toward the daylit dome of the
big amphitheater.

The way to sunlight and the upper air stood wide open for them. No opposition here. Only the faintest imaginable blot of shadow, moving along the wall of the Cave passage—

"Look out!"

Katy's warning came just too late. Hades, wearing his Helm of Invisibility, came seemingly from nowhere to strike down Jeremy/Apollo with a rock. Apollo's powers shielded him from the deadliest effects, yet he fell down senseless before he even realized that his great Enemy was near.

———

On regaining consciousness, Jeremy/Apollo discovered that he was lying on the stone floor of the great auditorium, bound hand and foot, his Sandals gone; he remembered slaying Death—for the second time—but knew that his own death was near.

Straining against his bonds, the Sun God discovered that this body's muscles had again been worn and exhausted into weakness. He had no chance of breaking even a single cord.

The fight, the whole battle, had been lost. Among the common soldiers in green and blue, those who were unable to get away downhill, the Enemy took no prisoners.

But worse than that, worse than anything, was the fact that Katy lay bound beside him, as helpless as he was.

The first thing he heard on regaining consciousness was: "Don't kill either of them yet. We must not spill Faces where they might flow away and be lost."

Kate still lay beside him, and her eyes were closed, but the rise and fall of her breast showed that she still lived. He thought of calling, trying to wake her—but then thought that perhaps he had better not.

Instead he turned his head and looked around. His mind, now confronted by inescapable doom, was refusing to settle down on anything. Somehow the atmosphere here under the great stone dome was utterly businesslike. If this was still the Trickster's house, in this room even the Trickster seemed to have abandoned whimsy; even she, it seemed, must be compelled to take seriously this ultimate assertion of power.

Jeremy realized now that it was not an audience chamber so much as a place where executions would be carried out, and witnessed by an orderly crowd.

The fine workmanship of this room, at least, if no other part of the fortress in its present form, showed that it must have been built by Hephaestus—who else?

Apollo thought that in some of the stonework he detected faint clues to some fairly recent remodeling, but he could not tell by whom it had been done or for what purpose. . . .

But that mattered little. Of course, this was the place, the room, the device, in which Faces could be destroyed.

Occasional crevices in the thick walls and the central opening of the dome let in the howling of the wind. Looking up, he could see blue, and moving clouds, but the sun and its power had now gone low in the western sky. There would be no direct beam of its light to lend Apollo new strength.

Yes, the chamber must have been designed to accommodate rituals with hundreds in attendance and possibly to double as a throne room for the intended ruler. Certainly that had not been Hades, who would never dare to risk the brightness of daylight or even the piercing pin lights of the stars, under the centerless dome of stone. As many as twenty concentric rows of seats ascended toward the dome's circular base at the rear. And now, an hour after the end of the battle, it appeared that almost all of the seats would be occupied, by the officers of Kalakh and the ministers and hangers-on of Hades. Lord Kalakh, stern and ageless-looking, with his bulging eyes, an enemy of Lord Victor and therefore an ally of Hades, had a place of honor in the front row.

Jeremy's mind was clearing now. He could wish that it was not so, but so it was.

And even in the midst of fear and overwhelming loss, Jeremy could not help being struck by how *serious* this chamber was, in its surfaces and its proportions! After all, it could hardly have been built to the Trickster's specifications. Darker forces must have commanded here.

Now executioners came, to lift him up while others lifted Kate. They were being hoisted now onto the central dais of the great room, where other men were busy, bending over, testing something. At the last moment the two prisoners were held aside, but not so far that Jeremy could not see what was being tested. In the center of the stark wooden scaffolding, a circular stone trap, big enough to accommodate two bodies side by side, fell open smoothly.

When the round slab hung open, it revealed what looked like a bottomless well beneath. The details of whatever was down there remained invisible. It reminded Jeremy of Vulcan's forge before the flames came shooting up.

"That is where the two of you are going," said a male voice at

Jeremy's side. He looked around, to discover an unfamiliar male countenance, yet another avatar of Death—there seemed no shortage of humans willing and ready to put on that Face.

The man said: "Our master Hades bids me explain the matter to
you: You will discover no quick end to life below. Instead, slow horrors
await you in the pit. There will be prolonged agony for you both. The
Faces now inside your heads will rot there. Your gods will decay, eroded
by your pain, until there is nothing left of them. Days from now—to
you it will seem like many, many years—when your two bodies at last
cease to breathe, both Apollo and the Trickster will have been long
dead."

Whatever reaction the newest Thanatos had hoped for was perhaps
there to be seen in Jeremy's face—perhaps not. Jeremy was past caring
what his enemies saw or thought.

When Death had turned back to report to his master, Jeremy wondered a little that Hades should prefer to destroy the Trickster's powers
rather than take them over for his own ends, but then on second thought
he did not wonder. Any trick, even the nastiest, contained an element
of joy, of unpredictability, that would be unacceptable to the gloomy
ruler of the Underworld.

Kate, oh, Kate! Her eyes were open now and wandering. As for
himself, he'd done what he could and there was nothing more to try,
and they would kill him now. Let his fate, and Apollo's, be in the hands
of Father Zeus . . . if there was any Father Zeus, apart from the odd
presence upon the summit, which he had never had the time to see for
himself.

But Kate! Oh, Kate.

On second thought he diverted his prayer, directing it to the Unknown God, whose empty pedestal waited in the hall of deities back at
the Academy.

Hades had removed his helmet of invisibility—perhaps it was a
strain to wear or interfered with the wearer's own vision—and could be
seen by those brave enough to look directly at him. The Lord of the
Underworld was standing heavily shadowed in the rear. About as far as
he dared to get away from the opening of the tunnel. Now and then
someone in one of the forward seats turned his head, glancing back
toward that brooding presence—but soon turned back again. He didn't
like people in front turning around to try to see him clearly. He had a
bodyguard of shadow-loving zombies around him.

And it hurt Jeremy far more than his bruises and his bonds, more than defeat and death, to see Kate, his helpless love, now tied in place beside him.

Looking at Kate once more, he thought, for just a moment, that deep in her eyes lay a hint of some wild hope. He wanted to speak to her, but he could find no words.

———

. . . his eyes had sagged closed, despite his effort to keep them open. But now they opened again. Because someone, either Katy or some invisible presence, had put lips close to his ear and whispered, *"Remember whose house we are in."*

Willing hands were busy making the final arrangements, freeing the doomed couple from all their bonds except those that held them to the central stake above the trap and would slide free from that support when it opened.

Toward the rear of the auditorium, Hades, as if hoping to observe more closely, was leaning forward a little more toward the light.

Someone, perhaps it was Lord Kalakh himself, was concluding a triumphant speech, of which not one word reached Jeremy/Apollo's mind.

"But where does the great jest lie?" he asked himself. And whether the question had been spoken aloud or not no longer mattered, for even now the lever was being pulled.

The villains' laughter rose in a triumphant roar—

Kate's startling gray eyes were open, looking steadily at him, and meaning and courage poured out of them. As if that could be enough, even now, to sustain them both.

As the executioner leaned his weight upon the lever, the small circle of doom beneath the couple's feet shuddered once and only slightly—and the round lid of stone over the pit remained right where it was, solid as the living bedrock. But in perfect synchrony with that small shudder, a heavy jolt ran through the whole enormous edifice. Bright cracks sprang out zigzag, with the suddenness of lightning, down the curve of the dark stone dome, at half a dozen places round its encircling curve.

In the brief and breathless interval that followed, the Trickster's laughter suddenly burst up, a clear fountain of sharp sound from Katy's lips. That sound and all others were drowned out an instant later by a great avalanche of noise. On every side of Jeremy and Kate, leaving them standing together, bound safely in place on what was now a pinnacle, the entire massive amphitheater crumbled and fell away, its fabric dissolving, in the time-space of a long-drawn breath, entirely into thunder and dust. In the background, audible even above the thunder of collapse, rose the terrible bellowing of Hades, engulfed in rage and pain, stabbed by a flaming lance of afternoon sunlight, sent crawling and scurrying in a desperate retreat.

The sun in all its vast and soothing energy shone full on Jeremy as well. In a moment he was able to turn his head and focus light and burn Katy's rope bonds through, first in one place and then another. In another moment her hands were reaching to support him and then to set him free. And presently, at whose command he was never afterward quite sure, two great eagles, of a size and strength that was more than natural, came to carry them both to safety, letting them down easily from the now-isolated pinnacle that had been the trapdoor into the descending shaft. The dungeon of horror below was filled with rubble now—and with the bodies of the audience.

Fresh wind was whirling a great cloud of dust away. Jeremy could now get a fresh view of what, only a minute ago, had been the inside of the auditorium and was now an expanse of rubble covering an open slope. With the pulling of the executioner's trigger, the whole of the packed chamber had collapsed, dome, sides, and sloping floor alike gone sliding thunderously away, careening and crashing in all directions down the steep slope of natural bedrock that moments earlier had been its support.

Gone in the crash, and doubtless now buried in its debris, were Lord Kalakh and all of his key aides and officers who had been present with him.

It was hardly possible to hope that Hades had been killed. He would be sun-scorched and beaten now but no worse than half-dead, and he would have found underground passage home through the Mountain-piercing tunnel.

No sooner had the eagles set Jeremy and Kate down upon a fresh mound of rubble than Vulcan was suddenly present and a golden maiden to hand Jeremy his recovered Bow and the one Arrow he had never used. Armed again, though still almost staggering with pain and weakness, he looked around for his foes—but those few who were still alive were already out of sight as they went scrambling in retreat.

———

Minutes had passed, and still it seemed that the last echoes of the prolonged crash refused to die. The fact was that it had provoked landslides, whose sound rose in a great but now diminishing roar, down the Mountain's distant flanks. More clouds of bitter dust came welling up, mixed with a little smoke.

And the Trickster, gripping Jeremy by the arms, then hugging him, once more laughed her glorious laugh: *"Couldn't you remember whose house this is?"*

———————

"It wouldn't have destroyed either of your Faces anyway," Andy was assuring him, a little later, leaning out of the new chariot in which he'd just landed on the Mountain's top. Now it was possible to observe how much the new Hephaestus looked like Andy—and sounded like him, too. "At least I don't see how it could have. That was nothin' but a latrine rumor from the start. Oh, the dungeon was real enough. Don't know who built it, but I had to fix it up a little."

"Small comfort." Apollo/Jeremy was sitting on a rock in the full light of sunset, trying to regain some strength and sanity. His right arm was around Kate, who was sitting close beside him.

Jeremy Redthorn's brush with death had freed him of the fear of being used up, worn out, a human body too frail a vessel to bear all the forces that a god pours into it. It seemed to him now that that view was based on an essential fallacy. Humans were stronger than they looked or felt, and the gods with their Faces, however powerful, were only human creations. Eventually the human body that he still shared with Apollo would die—but Apollo would not be anxious to discard him when he tired and aged. Apollo, as long as he remained Jeremy Redthorn's partner, could want nothing that Jeremy Redthorn did not want.

Hephaestus produced what actually looked like a guilty blush. "Damn it, Jer, we didn't *want* it to work out like this—we hoped you could get a couple Arrows into Hades, kill him dead. But you never know what'll happen in a fight, so Katy and I thought we better work on the house here, and we got this little business ready, with the trapdoor and the walls and so on. Just in case."

"Might've told me."

"*Meant* to tell you, damn it! But by the time I got in touch with Kate and we settled what kind of plan would have the best chance, you'd already gone rushin' off to fight. Damn, boy! For someone who didn't want to join the army . . ."

"I *did* manage to whisper in your ear," said Katy, almost whispering again. Suddenly her lips were once more very close.

Arnobius could not be found anywhere. Not even his body. But after those climactic landslides, a lot of other people were missing, too.

Some of the Lugard reinforcements had eventually arrived. Lord John had come through the battle alive and despite his injuries and weariness was now directing the search for his brother's body.

It appeared that the Lugards would now have at least nominal control over the new ruin atop the Mountain and of the supposedly important Oracle as well.

But, Jeremy thought, everyone who came to the Cave, whatever happened to its Oracle, would have to realize that both Cave and Mountain had now come under Apollo's control.

This might be an excellent time, Apollo's thought suggested, for a Council of Gods to be convened, to debate the future of the world—excluding, of course, those deities who wanted to destroy it or preserve it as their private plaything. Other Faces, other gods, must now be abroad in the world again, and there must be some way of making contact with them. But that could wait a little while.

"If Zeus himself shows up to dispute the matter with me, to put in some kind of a claim about Olympus—well, we'll see. But I'm not going to argue with a tree stump. Anyway, the point is that an end is now decreed to human sacrifice upon these premises—anywhere on the Mountain. Apollo will not have that."

"What manner of worship would my lord prefer?" This was Katy, putting on a face of what looked almost like innocent humility.

Jeremy smiled, but very faintly. "I want no one to worship me." (And he wondered privately just what the Gatekeeper had meant when he told the Lord Apollo: "I made you.")

"A god who wants no servants! Well! But I expect many a spotless animal will be sacrificed in your name, here in the Cave and elsewhere. Folk want to worship someone—or something."

"If killing animals makes them feel better, let them. At least they'll have some meat—Kate?"

"Yes?"

"What I really wish is that you and I could go and live on our own farm somewhere—even growing grapes. Or be Honeymakers, maybe."

Katy nodded her head, very slowly. Obviously humoring him. And with a sigh he had to admit that she was right.

The possibilities arising from such intimate union with a god range far beyond anything conceivable by ordinary human imagination. All the doors to the great universe would be open to you, if you dared to use them. You would be no longer merely human.

"Merely?"

Once incorporate a fragment of divinity within yourself, and there may be no way to ever get rid of it, again.

"But maybe there's a fragment already there, in all of us. And anyway, who would want to get rid of it?"

Ariadne's
Web

1

ALL THROUGH THE hours of darkness there had been a howling of the wind, and perhaps of livelier things than wind, in the chimneys and around the parapets of the sprawling palace in the elder city of Kandak. A scud of low clouds kept driving in from the empty reaches of the Great Sea, across the island kingdom of Corycus. Outside the stone walls of the palace, winter's offensive from the northland seemed at last about to conquer the territory that had been occupied for several pleasant months by autumn. Inside the palace walls, a frightened king, driven to desperate steps in his efforts to cling to his throne, had spent the night attending to the efforts of his chief magician, a wrinkled and shriveled man named Creon.

For long hours a young soldier called Alex the Half-Nameless had watched them both, the king and Creon, as they went through the recitation of spells, and the bloody sacrifice of animals, all seemingly without producing the least result. The mess of the sacrifice had been cleared away, and king and magician, conferring together in low voices, had seemed on the point of abandoning the effort, when suddenly the god they had been trying to summon stood towering over them, bleary-eyed and swaying like a drunk.

With the first light of morning, Alex the Half-Nameless was shivering, mostly with excitement, though with the fires ignored and untended a damp cold had begun to dominate the great hall of the palace.

Except for the business going on in front of him, it had been a night of routine guard duty, interrupted only by a couple of short latrine breaks. With his short spear in hand, Alex had spent the hours of the night standing more or less at attention with three of his comrades in arms. All four, like soldiers everywhere, were waiting to be told what to do next. A fair amount of effort had gone into trying not to think. For tonight's duty all had been ordered to wear full battle dress, including light helmet and breastplate. Greaves armored their shins above their sandaled feet, while chain mail reinforced the kilts of their uniforms. They were accustomed to the weight of their formal arms and armor, but it had been a long night, and the hardware was becoming burdensome.

Much earlier in the night, when the king's magician had begun his efforts to evoke the god, a fire had been roaring in each of the huge hearths, one at each end of the hall, flames surging and bending as the wind drove down the chimneys. But by now the light and heat had dimmed to mere ghosts of their full selves. The only visible flame was in the north hearth, small and wispy, in the heart of a section sawn from a great log. Meanwhile, half of the torches burning in sconces on the high walls had guttered and gone out.

Gripping his short spear, tensing and relaxing youthful muscles in an effort to generate some bodily heat, Alex, like most of the handful of other people present, was looking at King Minos on his throne at the moment when the god arrived. Two other men were standing near the throne, and naturally none of the three, not even the seated king, was more than merely human mortal. There came a moment of silence in which Alex happened to blink. At that same instant, a fierce gust of autumn wind rattled the closed shutters defending all the windows, and jostled the doors of the hall's two entrances against the latches that held them shut. And in the next moment, in the time consumed by a mere flicker of a young man's eyelids, there were four figures in his field of vision. So it seemed to the young soldier that the new arrival must have ridden the very wind to appear where he was.

The fourth figure was no mere human being. A god was standing in front of Alex the Half-Nameless now, and a single glance was enough to tell him that this god was Dionysus.

Like the great majority of humans anywhere in the world, Alex had never seen a god. But unlike many of his fellow mortals, he had never doubted the existence of such beings. Tonight he and the handful of others gathered in the great hall had been waiting through the hours of darkness for this amazing thing to happen—and now at last the wonder had occurred, a real deity had manifested himself.

A swirl of mist, and a stale odor as of wet, dark, dead leaves had entered with the visitor. There sounded also, in the four corners of the hall, a murmuring of soft voices, snatches of song from invisible throats, accompanied by the music of invisible flutes. Alex could recognize details from many of the stories. By all these signs it was obvious that the being who stood before them was an avatar of Dionysus, the Twice-Born.

But a silence had fallen over the humans gathered in the great hall. This was not quite the appearance which Alex, at least, had been expecting. The realization forced itself upon them all that the visitor was no greater in stature than humanity—there was of course no reason why he should be—and at the moment he appeared less impressive than many merely mortal men.

The shocking and ugly fact was that Dionysus was fat. Not only fat, bloated, his once-fair skin blotched red and gray. At a closer look, Alex could see that there was gray in the god's hair and beard, and patches of both had fallen out. There were still remnants of a once-considerable beauty in that face, a comeliness now all but erased by the all-too-human ravages of age and dissipation. The cloak of the Twice-Born, which he kept tightly wrapped around his massive body, was stained and frayed.

Judging by the strange newcomer's appearance alone, Alex might have dared to suspect that he was an impostor. But no impostor, unless he were a god himself, could have contrived such an entrance.

As a child and youth, Alex the Half-Nameless had been fascinated by stories of the gods, and had eagerly gathered every scrap of knowledge that he could regarding them. Now it crossed his mind to wonder that the Twice-Born had not arrived in a chariot drawn by panthers, bedecked with vine branches and ivy.

But what had actually occurred so far was quite marvelous enough to keep the young soldier staring, open-mouthed.

Now and then, mingled with the continued wind, there was a rapid, light clopping sound, suggesting to Alex's active imagination the hooves of invisible satyrs on the paved floor.

Greener leaves, conveying no hint of wet or darkness, were garlanded around the brow of the newcomer, entangled with the flow of his brown hair, and his right hand clutched a golden wine cup. His laughter boomed. But the longer Alex watched, the more he was convinced that there was something wrong with this divine visitor. Besides the look of bloated shabbiness, there seemed an attitude of desperation.

King Minos was an unimpressive monarch, well into middle age.

He still sat staring silently at the new arrival, and the expression on the king's face was one that Alex had seen there before, that of a man accustomed to dealing with disappointment. Tonight Minos wore a gloriously brocaded robe, of scarlet interwoven with the blue of the sea, and a light gold circlet of a crown. He carried no arms, nor did anyone in the great hall, except for the small detail of soldiers.

"Welcome, my Lord Dionysus." It was Creon, the cadaverous magician-priest, who broke the silence at last. In his sepulchral voice there was more wonder than heartiness, as he extended his hand in a ritual movement toward the god. "In the king's name, welcome."

Dionysus did not move forward the two or three steps that would have allowed him to touch the magician's outstretched hand. The Twice-Born gave no sign that he was impressed by his welcome, or by the king's magician who claimed to be his priest, or, for that matter, by the king himself. Silently the visitor directed his world-weary gaze, in turn, at each of the humans who had been anticipating his arrival. To judge by his reaction, what he saw was no better or worse than he had expected. When the god's gray-eyed gaze fell on Alex, the main impression the young soldier received was one of exhaustion.

"What do you know of the gods?" The voice of Dionysus was a kind of parody of a conspiratorial whisper, but still it had a resonance, and was so far the most impressive thing about his person. Again the god glanced from one human to another, as if he hoped for answers to his question not only from the king and his magician, but from their soldiers too, and even from their menial servants.

But it was only the king who answered. After exchanging looks with his priest-adviser, Minos evidently decided that this was a time when protocol and ceremony should be minimized.

In a tone and manner that seemed to claim his equality with the one he addressed, Minos said, "I know what it is necessary to know, Twice-Born Lord. That all of you who are now gods began your lives as mortal men and women."

Perhaps the royal manner and tone sounded simply impertinent to Dionysus. The pudgy chin lifted. "Oh?"

"Yes." Minos persisted bravely. "That each god or goddess whom we see on earth has attained divinity by somehow coming into possession of a Face. Yours is of course the Face of Dionysus—or do you prefer to be called Twice-Born, or by the name of Bacchus?"

"It does not matter."

The king nodded. Now his hands, bejeweled and soft with years of luxury, sketched a flat, small object in the air. "Each Face is a thing as clear as fine glass, they say, but with a suggestion of flow, of movement, visible inside it—is that not correct?"

But the visitor seemed tired of the subject. He made an impatient gesture. "Why me, Minos? Of all the deities you might have tried to summon, why did you choose me?"

The king paused, as if to consider. Then he said: "We have long worshipped you, great Dionysus. From one end of my kingdom to the other, my people have long sought your favor, with prayer, and sacrifice, and—"

"Yes, yes. And the real reason?"

There was a pause, in which Minos exchanged looks with his magician before answering. "The truth is, Lord Dionysus, that we chose to summon you because, of all the mighty powers who could be helpful, we thought you most likely to respond."

"Because you thought that I was weakened, I suppose."

There was a rustling sound, sharp but not loud, almost at the king's elbow, running up along the massive column that stood there supporting stone arches that curved above. The young soldier Alex, gaping like everyone else, began to notice a process that was already well under way, the greening of the great hall, the writhing of vines up through the stone-and-timber floor, wrapping the columns that held up the roof.

Alex thought he heard a faint birdsong, and felt a welcome ghost of summerlike warmth. And now there was more evidence that the god had not come unattended, for some of those who had accompanied him were now taking on half-visible form, in the far corners of the great chamber, where the light was faintest. The little that Alex could see and hear of them suggested they were less human than the one who'd brought them. The soldier glimpsed what had to be a kind of satyr darting by, the upper body small, like that of a naked child, but that appearance belied by the beard that curled around the chin, and by the hairy nether parts. The creature, whatever it was, moved with great nimbleness upon two shaggy goat-legs. Now the faint voices from invisible throats, some of them sounding too high-pitched to be human, were crooning a drinking song, to the accompanying music of unseen flutes. Any suspicion that the visitor could be an impostor had long since vanished into the realm of fairy tales.

For a moment Alex had been distracted from what Dionysus was saying. But he caught the end of it: "—right enough. Right enough, so far, as far as you go."

And then without warning the god fell into a paroxysm of coughing that almost bent him double, a racking noise that sounded as if it might be damaging his lungs.

The king politely ignored his guest's spasm. But, magical vines and satyrs notwithstanding, Minos gave the impression of being less and less impressed by his visitor as the interview went on. The king's own voice was gradually reverting more and more to its accustomed royal tone.

"One day," said the king, now almost lecturing, "when you were still only a mortal man, you somehow found, or were given—or perhaps seized by force—the Face of Dionysus. That might have happened a year ago, perhaps a hundred years—"

"Sometimes it feels a thousand," the other wheezed, when he had done with coughing.

The monarch pressed bravely on. "—and at that time you were brave enough, or perhaps frightened enough, to put it on. The Face melted into your head, as Faces always do when people wear them. And there yours still rests at this moment, somewhere behind your eyes, as invisible as your soul. And like your soul, your spirit, it will remain with you until you . . . for the rest of your life. And as long as it is with you, you enjoy all the powers of a god."

The Twice-Born did not seem to have been bothered by the casual suggestion that he might once have been frightened. Indeed, it did not seem impossible that he could even now be well acquainted with fear. He only nodded his head gently.

" 'Enjoy.' Oh, I enjoy them, yes." *Cough* again, and *cough*. "You have said nothing," he observed hoarsely, "about all the pain."

Then the visitor gestured negligently toward Creon. "Tell me, King Minos—did this adviser of yours, this self-anointed priest of mine who stands beside you—did any of your wise informants, your magicians, or perhaps they call themselves odylic experts—did even one of them tell you anything about the pain?"

The gaunt magician frowned, but held his peace. The king said, "I am sorry if you are currently experiencing any kind of discomfort, Lord Dionysus, but I suppose it will get better. All authorities agree that gods are very hard to kill."

"And so we are." In the left hand of Dionysus there suddenly appeared, clean out of nowhere, a sturdy wooden staff, perhaps seven feet long and thick as a man's wrist. *That is the* thyrsus, Alex told himself, in silent awe, recognizing an element from the stories. The shaft was ivy-covered, and tipped with a pine cone, just as in the legends and the tales.

Dionysus was now leaning part of his considerable weight upon his staff, as if he really needed its support.

"You should remember that," the god continued. Once more he

turned his head to look around the hall. "So, this is the welcome you've arranged. Lucky for you that I place little value upon ceremony. But you're right, for now my wants are simple, I desire only a few months of peace. I must rest until the spring. As you say, things'll be better then."

"Would you care to sit down, Lord Dionysus?" The monarch gestured courteously toward one of the empty chairs, of which there were a few nearby.

"I'll sit when I'm ready."

Now Alex was having a hard time taking his eyes off the *thyrsus*, as if with some part of his mind he could sense that power was centered there. All the mortals in the room, except for the king and his chief magician, had been impressed by the sudden appearance of the ornate staff. Alex thought there was something written on it, thin lines of small, graven characters going up and down the wooden shaft. The writing was too small for him to read, even supposing that it had all been in the only language that he knew. Certainly no more than one of the sets of characters was in that tongue.

Minos was speaking again. "There is nothing in this world that I want more than to provide my Lord Dionysus with a secure place to rest during the tiresome winter that is only now beginning. All the comforts, magical and, um, otherwise." The king paused for a deep breath. He seemed to have finally found the tone, the manner, that he wanted to use; one that might have been appropriate speaking to an important ambassador, a human from one of the kingdoms ringing the shore of the Great Sea.

"But," the king continued, "there is a certain problem that must first be solved, before any of us will be able to rest in safety."

"Ah, hum. Yes, I supposed there would be. Everyone has problems. What is yours?"

"My brother," said Minos simply. "He wishes to take the throne away from me."

"Oh he does, hey?" Dionysus drew himself up a little taller, straightening his shoulders. "Seems a damned unbrotherly thing to do."

In the privacy of his own mind, where as a private soldier he entertained nearly all of his important thoughts, Alex was coming to the conclusion that what his early quest for knowledge had taught him about the nature of the gods, and what the king's brief speech had just confirmed, was very probably the truth. The one who stood before them, staff in hand, gave the impression of possessing a dual nature. The man, who was one component of that nature, was terrified, feeling that death was near, even if the god was not.

Alex stared, with a mixture of fear and fascination, at what a great god had become—at the evidence that those who were called immortal were not, after all, immune to damage and to failure. Only the Faces were immortal, indestructible, while their wearers came and went. He remembered all the stories that were told, of all the marvels wrought by the one some called the God of Many Names. Dionysus, Bacchus, Twice-Born . . . there were indeed a host of other titles, most of which the young soldier could not now recall.

Three or four of the ordinary household servants of the palace had also spent the night in the great hall, standing by to serve the king and his magician, though so far the servants had had little to do. Now, somewhere in the background, at least two of these people were being drawn into interaction with some of the entourage of inhuman attendants who had come with the great visitor. Alex could hear a man and a woman in low-voiced talk, but he did not want to spare a moment to see what they were up to.

———

Almost since the moment of his entry, Dionysus had been standing in one place, swaying a little on his feet. But now he suddenly lurched forward, so that the king on his throne involuntarily recoiled. But the tottering god had suddenly decided that he did, after all, need a place to sit down. He threw himself not into the chair Minos had indicated, but another, taller, not quite a throne, that had once been occupied by the queen on state occasions, and had now been practically unused for almost two decades. There seemed no special significance in this choice of a resting place. Rather it was as if the distinguished visitor had simply made the handiest selection, to keep himself from falling.

As soon as the god's substantial bottom was firmly supported by the chair, he rapped the floor sharply with his ornate staff. His resonant voice boomed out, more loudly than before: "Let's settle your little problem now. Where is this treasonous brother? Let him be brought here, so I can warn him—do you think, Minos, that a warning will be sufficient?"

"Regrettably," said King Minos, clasping his soft hands together, "I have grave doubts about that. And at this moment I am not even sure exactly where my brother is."

Suddenly he looked sharply at the soldier standing nearest to Alex, who happened to be the corporal in command of the small contingent. "And the commander of the guard still has not appeared. Where is he?"

The corporal saluted awkwardly. "I don't know where either of them are, majesty."

At that point, everyone was distracted by Dionysus sliding out of the seat he had just taken, a movement quite obviously involuntary, that left his divine form sprawled on the rush-strewn floor, his *thyrsus* clattering down beside him. In the next moment he was grabbing at the breasts of a kitchen wench, a poor and simple girl, but not unattractive, who for the last minute had been approaching him slowly from across the room, as if drawn by some invisible thread of fascination. Only a moment ago this girl had been engaged in murmured conversation with the sprites and satyrs halfway across the room, and now she was lying with their god on the floor. Dionysus pawed at her bosom without even turning his head to look at her. It seemed a purely reflex action, as joyless and even hopeless as his booming laughter.

And over in a far corner of the great room, one of the household's male servants, who had also somehow become involved with the inhuman Dionysian entourage, had evidently just taken something to drink that did not agree with him. The servant was suddenly vomiting, abandoned to helpless, hopeless retching.

And now the god himself, forcing himself to sit up straight on the floor, appeared to be struggling to regain some shreds of dignity. Absently he let go of the girl, and tried to straighten the garland of vines that now perched crookedly on his head.

It was growing more and more obvious to the onlookers that this specimen of divinity was hopelessly drunk.

But again his impressive voice filled the hall. "Must reassure the rightful heir—who's that, by the way? Your son, I s'pose? Is it any one of these wretches here?" And Dionysus squinted at the handful of people present, again taking them one at a time, as if he suspected them of trying to hide their true identities.

Minos, who had been rubbing his forehead wearily, raised his head. "I have no son, Lord Dionysus. In fact there is no undisputed heir; a matter that I have not yet had the time to rectify."

You have had almost eighteen years, thought Alex, in silent accusation. Everyone knew it was that long since the true, respected queen had died; since then there had been only royal concubines, and no offspring worth mentioning. *You have delayed shamefully, oh king, and in doing so you were unfair to your two marvelous and deserving daughters.* His grip tightened on his spear. *And some would even say that it is not true that you have no son.*

To judge from the expression on the king's face, it seemed that the royal thoughts might possibly be running along similar lines. Minos did not seem drunk, despite the formidable amount of wine he had consumed during the night, a little at a time. But he did seem very bitter.

"My late wife . . ." the king began to say, then let his words rest there, as if he could see no point in going on with them. He looked around him, at the small gathering of his fellow humans in the great hall, and their disgraceful visitor, and it was as if he were asking himself, *how have I come to this*?

———

Abruptly the god rolled over on his side, turning his back on all three of the people who had so far been most affected by his presence—the lamenting monarch, the feebly vomiting varlet in the far corner, and the dazed serving wench. As Dionysus rolled, the folds of his cloak came open. Scanty and wretched undergarments hung loose, revealing gross nakedness, including a flabby paunch that the deity swung around only with some difficulty.

The move had brought the Twice-Born into a position directly facing Alex. Now, thrusting with one elbow on the floor to raise himself a little, squinting at the lithe form of the young soldier, who was standing only about ten feet away, Dionysus addressed him in a low voice: "Once I . . . I was . . . like you."

Being spoken to directly by a god, any god, was something of a shock for Alex—though not quite the shock it would have been an hour ago. Still, he was flustered and did not know what to think, let alone what he ought to say if he should be required to answer. The note of envy in the god's voice was staggering.

Alex had never had cause to consider himself particularly handsome. He was of average size, generally healthy, and perhaps physically a little stronger than most young men, at least when his anger was aroused. His brown beard was at last starting to grow in with a reasonable thickness. But no one had ever found any godlike qualities in either his mind or body. Vaguely he could foresee humorous taunting in the barracks when it became known there what the god had said.

To Alex's relief, he was not required to respond. Already Dionysus had turned his back on him, and was groping for a wineskin, obviously looking for a drink. When he found what he sought and held it up, the skin hung flat and empty on his hand. Whatever magical sources of wine he might possess, they seemed to be running dry.

Alex could only stare at the divine visitor sitting helplessly on the floor. In the young man's mind, fear, disillusion verging on embarrassment, and a great curiosity were struggling for dominance.

———

The king had fallen silent after his own small outburst, and was evidently making an effort to collect himself. As an awkward silence grew in the great hall, Alex noticed that the general transformation which had been wrought by the entrance of Dionysus was already fading, as if the power that had brought it into being was waning fast. The vines that had begun to climb the pillars in the hall were dying, the luxuriant growth of leaves turned dry and dead and falling. The drafty air was distributing them in little swirls around the floor. The thicker stems were turning to stone, so that they now seemed to have been carved as part of the pillars by some master artisan. The lesser sprites and powers, all but invisible presences that had accompanied the entrance of the god, were dying too, or perhaps only silently taking their departure, one by one. Fading with the flute music into nothingness.

Minos started to speak again, then stopped. He cocked his head, turning it slightly as if trying to listen to some faint, unwelcome noise.

Now Alex could hear it too. There were at least two men, it seemed, making no particular effort to be quiet, for he could hear their voices just outside the closed door of the main entrance to the hall.

2

"YOU SENT FOR me, my brother?" The last two words were spoken in a tone of mockery, by the man who was standing just outside the door when it swung open. It was a harsh voice, one that Alex immediately recognized, though he had seldom heard it before.

In through the open door strode a tall man garbed in a robe of royal splendor, wearing a sword and a bronze breastplate. His head was bare. He advanced with a confidence that did not seem at all shaken when his gaze fell upon the immortal visitor. It was as if Prince Perses, the king's younger brother, had expected nothing less.

A step behind the prince came a military officer, General Scamander, commander of the Palace Guard, fully armed and armored, younger than the prince, and much more massively built. The commander swung the large door shut behind him, and in a few clipped words ordered Alex and his three comrades to see that it remained that way. There were only two exits from the great hall, the second being a small door commonly used only by servants. The soldiers of the guard were to prevent anyone from going in or out by either way.

"I did not send for you, no," said Minos, who appeared suddenly diminished upon his throne.

"I see you have summoned another." Perses nodded, unsurprised. "Well, so be it. I, too, have decided that my affairs might prosper better with an ally."

"And you are not to interfere," Scamander added, speaking in a low voice, but certainly not a whisper, to his men.

"Yes sir," responded Alex, in ragged chorus with his comrades. And like them, he wondered silently: *Interfere in what?*

General Scamander, informally known among his troops and behind his back as the Butcher, for some feat of pacification accomplished on the mainland many years ago, turned and stood with his hands behind his back, smiling benevolently in the general direction of Minos on his throne.

The corporal was now hastily giving orders, and Alex and the other two privates instantly obeyed. Two men were now stationed at each door, Alex being assigned to the main entrance, and all of them were now slightly farther from the throne than they had been.

Alex understood the confidence of the new arrivals, their casual attitude about the presence of Dionysus, when he observed the next figure to appear in the great hall.

All ordinary portals were closed, but this newcomer minded that no more than Dionysus had. It was a truly impressive form which now materialized just behind the prince; and at his first glimpse of it, Alex understood that after a lifetime without ever seeing a single god, he had encountered two in the space of a few minutes.

This second divinity was physically somewhat smaller than the Twice-Born. Not a bulky shape, hardly more than half the size of the commander of the guard; but beside it, even the Butcher seemed to have shrunk to insignificance. A male body, thin to the point of emaciation, wearing almost nothing but a necklace of small round objects. When Alex looked more closely, he could see that they were human skulls, somehow shrunken or miniaturized to the size of oranges. The skin was grayish overall, mottled here and there with shades of blue. Matted locks of almost colorless hair fell in coils on either side of the thin, beardless face, and at first the young soldier thought there was something wrong with the high brow. But then Alex realized that what he was looking at was not exactly a defect. There was a third eye, browless, no trick of decoration but a real organ, centered in the forehead, perhaps an inch above the usual two.

Not everyone at first recognized the newcomer. The soldier standing beside Alex asked him a question, in a whisper so low that it was barely audible an arm's length away: "Who?—What—?"

And Alex, with the hair standing up on the back of his neck, mouthed one soft word in reply: "Shiva."

Shiva the Destroyer.

A movement at the far end of the hall caught Alex's eye. Looking in that direction he saw the figure of a bull, a little larger than life size. In the faint light of dying fires the hide of the animal (that was of course not really an animal at all) looked the gray of dead wood ashes. Nandi, the bull, was wingless, but capable of the swiftest flight . . . a creature as inseparable from Shiva as the leopards and chariot were from Dionysus.

Alex, who from childhood had been fascinated with the stories of the gods, saw the bluish neck—legend said that Shiva was thus marked as a result of holding in his throat the poison thrown up at the churning of the cosmic ocean, near the time of the creation of the world, and thus saving humanity from its effects.

The Third Eye of Shiva now winked briefly, partially open, just long enough to afford an anxious onlooker a hint of destructive fire somehow impounded.

If the king had been right in his earlier claim, about the Faces of the Gods—and Alex knew nothing to suggest that Minos had been wrong—then even this dark god, like all the other gods, was only a transformed human.

But somehow that thought made the presence of the Destroyer no easier to bear.

At his first sight of Shiva, Dionysus had frozen momentarily, as if turned to stone. A moment later the Twice-Born one let out a hoarse yell, half of terror, half of challenge, then grabbed up his *thyrsus* staff and struggled to his feet.

Ignoring both gods for the moment, Prince Perses strode straight forward toward his brother, drawing his sword as he advanced. Minos, still looking weary as well as frightened, stood up unarmed from the throne and barked an order to the commander of his guard—

Alex did not hear the words of the command clearly. But whatever they were, they were ignored. And by that the king knew his fate.

Minos spoke a few words to his brother, in so low a tone that Alex could not hear them. Prince Perses, grinning mirthlessly, said nothing, but only continued his advance without pause, and when he came within reach of the throne used his sword, once, twice, in a thorough and workmanlike way.

Minos met his death with stoic dignity.

The slain man fell, his blood leaked out. Royalty had been reduced in a moment to a mere object. Alex had seen killing before—such matters were all in a day's work for a soldier—but never had he seen a human life ended quite as cold-bloodedly as this.

Any of the handful of other humans in the hall who might have been inclined to fight for Minos were held motionless by a combination of fear and habitual obedience. The soldiers all stood frozen under the Butcher's glare.

"Hold your posts," the general advised them, in a hard but yet not unfatherly tone. "That's it. Good men."

And Dionysus, after that one blustering moment in which he had seemed to challenge the intruders, was suddenly no more to be seen. The Third Eye of Shiva had opened fully for a flicker of time, emitting a dazzling narrow lance of light, and the dropped and abandoned staff fell clattering on the floor. At a touch of the ray from Shiva's forehead, the stout wood smoked and flared and disappeared.

When the surviving people, Alex and his fellow soldiers among them, had the chance to look around again through eyes that were no longer dazzled by reflections of the Third Eye's beam, no trace of the terrified Dionysus was to be seen. His entourage of satyrs and invisible, discordant singers had vanished with him, leaving only a residue of vomit, and grape leaves, and crumbling, dying vines. The servants who had taken part in his last celebration went crawling and slinking away, as well as they were able. The man who had been retching was silent now, perhaps terrified into a semblance of self-control.

The smell of wet leaves had been covered, smothered, by the sharper smell of blood.

"I am now Minos," said the old king's brother, speaking clearly into the sudden silence. He who had been Prince Perses was standing now with the empty throne just behind him, as if very nearly ready to sit down on it. His sword was back in its scabbard on his belt. Alex could not remember seeing him wipe the blade on anything.

"You are Minos, majesty," acknowledged the Butcher, and offered a sharp military salute. Then the general shot a quick glare at his soldiers, to make sure that they were following his lead. Alex's right arm shot up obediently. Behind the general, Shiva was standing like a statue, and said nothing.

The new Minos stood looking down with satisfaction at the dead body of his brother, lying almost at his feet. Behind him, the priest-magician Creon had been standing with folded arms during the violence, obviously not much perturbed and perhaps not surprised.

"You are now Minos," Creon echoed quickly. Then he added, "I do not know the fate of Dionysus, majesty."

The usurper, now bending over the body of his brother, shook his head, as if to say that he did not know either, nor much care, where the defeated god had gone.

General Scamander stepped forward suddenly, picked up from the stone floor the slender golden circlet that was the traditional crown of Corycus, and with a humble gesture offered it toward the throne. With steady fingers Perses accepted the emblem of authority, and casually put it on his own head.

The commander of the guard, who had drawn his own sword only to salute with it, now slammed it back into its scabbard. Turning around again, he began in his harsh voice to tell the simple soldiers what they had just seen.

Alex's own eyes and ears had told him a wildly different story, but now was certainly not the time to suggest that there might be some discrepancy, or even think about it. Alex found that his eyes kept returning to the dead body of the old king on the floor.

Having concluded his narration, the general immediately began to go over it again, repeating his explanation in short simple words, as if to children. Anyone who had been too shocked or stupid to understand the business the first time had better get it now. The main point to be grasped was how Dionysus, the treacherous god who had just fled the hall, had slain the old king before departing.

"You saw that, did you not?" His glare swung from one soldier to another, making sure to get the reaction that he wanted from each one before moving to the next. Now it was Alex's turn. "You?" the officer demanded.

"Yes. Yes, sir." And at the same time Alex remained perfectly aware that that was not at all what he had seen. But that knowledge must be suppressed. And anyway, with true gods and great magic involved in these events, could a simple man trust his own senses, his own thoughts, in anything?

"Good lad," said the Butcher, heartily, and turned away to begin the same process with the servants.

"Enough," said Shiva, speaking for the first time. Every head in the great hall—excepting only that of the dead king—turned to look at him. All who had not heard Shiva's light, smooth voice before were surprised at how it sounded.

"Enough," the god concluded. "It matters not, what any of them saw."

———

And, with no more fuss than that, the bloody business had been finished.

General Scamander, who was still commander of the guard, assured the new king that troops who could be depended on to support him were now holding the palace.

He who had been Prince Perses, who now formally repeated his announcement that he was taking the name of Minos, exchanged a few words with his two close human supporters, while Shiva stood in the background, his arms folded. Whether the god was presiding over the scene or simply attending would have been hard to judge by looking at him.

Then the new king raised his voice, speaking to all the humans within earshot. "Rouse the household, there is news that everyone must hear. And a terrible sight that all must see."

———

Within a few minutes, a small, excited group of newcomers had gathered, and was growing by the minute. Alex heard someone remarking, in a low, cautious voice, on the fact that the old king had left no legitimate son—there were two daughters, and in the normal course of events the elder, Phaedra, might have expected to assume the throne upon her father's death.

"And no son," someone else observed, whispering. As if that might have any bearing on the legitimacy of succession, which according to the traditional rules it did not.

"His only son is—Asterion," murmured another. And there was muttered laughter, accompanied by looking over shoulders. It was the way common folk behaved when one of their number dared to tell a sexual joke about someone far above them.

———

And only moments after that, the younger of the old king's two daughters, Princess Ariadne, came bursting into the hall before anyone there had begun to expect her. Alex and his partner at the main entrance each took a hesitant step in her direction, but then hung back. Not even the Butcher would expect anyone to hold back the princesses from their father's body. This was the woman Alex had come to worship, helplessly, beginning on the first day he had seen her, long months ago, on his first day in the palace.

Ariadne fell on her knees beside the corpse, and for a long moment only crouched there, stunned, her white hands spread like a dancer's on outflung arms. From the moment she entered the great hall, Alex was unable to tear his gaze away from her, and his grip tightened on the shaft of his spear.

Oh Princess, I swear to you that I could do nothing. Had you been here, I would have gladly died for you. Not even a god would have touched you, not while I was alive. Alex with a pang could imagine the

princess demanding of him: "Then why did you not die for my father?"
To which his only answer must have been: *Then I would have been
unable to ever serve you again in any way.*

Ariadne was nineteen, light brown hair hanging loose in long ringlets about her shoulders, her slender body wrapped in a white robe that
she would ordinarily have worn only in her chamber. Her feet were bare
on the stone floor, as were those of her personal servant, a slave girl
who had swept in beside her, almost unnoticed. The slave girl's name,
as Alex remembered, was Clara.

Ariadne's first loud cry of grief was still hanging in the air, when
Princess Phaedra, some two years older than her sister, came bursting
in, completely unattended.

Phaedra was the shorter of the two sisters, her hair dark, her body
compact and womanly. Her cries of grief were not as loud as Ariadne's,
but Alex had no doubt that they were every bit as sincere.

"Father! They have killed you!" The scream seemed torn from the
bottom of Ariadne's heart.

And in that moment Alex, though he still did not stir an inch from
the post where he had been commanded to stand guard, knew in his
own heart that he was ready to cheerfully give up his own life, if by
doing so he might spare the woman he worshipped even one minute of
such horror and sorrow. *If he were now to dart quickly across the room,
and thrust with his spear for the usurper's throat . . .*

But it was almost certain that the other soldiers would be quick
enough to stop him before he could kill Perses. Also, Alex thought that
Shiva was watching him, from the far side of the room, and the Third
Eye could dart death as quickly as thought.

And even if, by some miracle of skill and endurance, he succeeded
in cutting down the usurper, what then? Ariadne would be spared nothing in the bloody turmoil that would be sure to follow.

All good reasons for holding back. But perhaps not the real reason.
The truth was that in this matter he was not the master of his own will.
He had been ordered not to interfere.

When the first spasms of grief had subsided, the princesses confronted
their uncle, who affected an air of great sympathy, told them the tale of
murderous Dionysus, and strongly suggested that now it was time for
them to return to their respective rooms.

Phaedra, on regaining control of herself, dared to raise her eyes and confront Perses. In a low voice she asserted, "Many will say that on my father's death I should be queen."

The new king was gentle and tolerant. "My dear niece, your grief has naturally unsettled you. Your dear father with his dying breath insisted that I take the throne. All these witnesses will confirm the fact. Is it not so?"

And so it was.

Gradually the sorrowing princesses allowed themselves to be led away by their own attendants, and what was left of the assembly broke up. Alex was soon free to confirm the official version of events among his wondering barrack-mates, who had already heard a formal announcement from an officer.

Soon the body of old Minos was removed, at the orders of his brother the new king, to another room, where it would lie in state. The new Minos was announcing plans, so well organized that they might almost have been prepared ahead of time, for a public display of Dionysus's victim, in the plaza before the palace.

Then the new king said to the last of his remaining attendants, "Leave us alone. The Lord Shiva and I have certain matters to discuss between us."

He had to tell the Butcher twice; then the big man saluted briskly and withdrew.

At last there were only two figures left in the great hall.

"Certain matters . . ." the former Prince Perses began, and had to stop and clear his throat, and make a new beginning. "There are certain matters, Lord Shiva, that ought to be spelled out clearly between us. So there will be no chance of later misunderstanding."

The light was brighter in the great hall now. Before the last servants retired, more torches had been brought, and fires rekindled. The figure that had assumed the throne was grayish-blue, in a way that suggested the residue of fire. Facial features sharp and thin, almost to the point of caricature. The rest of the body seemed hardly more robust, essentially little more than a skeleton. The Third Eye, lid closed as if in sleep, made no more than a modest bulge in the middle of the forehead. In the changed light the necklace of skulls took on a deceptively artificial look. But for all that, it was a body, a solid human body, not any mere apparition.

The god's two normal eyes were fully open. In his light and somehow metallic voice he replied, "Let there be understanding between us.

You will kneel when you address me." And he extended an arm, to point with a skeletal forefinger to the floor.

For a long moment Perses observed a frozen silence. Then: "I am the king!"

Shiva was unmoved. "Only because I have made you so. I can unmake you just as easily. I am a god, and you will kneel. Or you will learn what it means to incur the anger of a god." A pause. "Don't be concerned, our agreement stands. Later, I will let you have your throne back. I do not plan to spend much time with toys."

Muttering under his breath, he who was determined to be Minos looked around to make sure that they were still alone in the great hall. Then he rose from the throne and moved two hesitant steps forward. Then he lowered his heavy body to one knee.

Few of the scores of people making up the household had ever seen a god before. Now as they all came trickling into the great hall, murmuring and whispering their astonishment, they found themselves also confronting the awesome presence of Shiva, not enthroned but standing behind the throne.

A first search for the divine fugitive had already been made, through the palace and its immediate grounds. But of the god Dionysus there was not a trace to be seen. There was no thought of looking for a secret passage. Gods, even failing gods, could be expected to have the power to vanish when they willed.

And already the dark god was demanding sacrifice, and of no ordinary kind.

The man who had now assumed the name of Minos turned to his soldiers and exhorted them, "We are going to discover those responsible for my brother's death, and punish them."

And the wind howled mournfully, around the parapets and down the chimneys. The first clear sunlight on that morning seemed woefully slow in coming.

3

"ASTERION?"

I did not answer the call at once, but stood in silence, looking out through leaves. Spring sunshine striking through the fresh leaves of the tangled vines made patches of bright translucent green, leaving caves of shadow within the roofed-over sections of the endless, intertwining passageways that comprised the great bulk of the Labyrinth. Somewhere just out of sight, perhaps in the next open courtyard, or maybe in the one after that, water was trickling musically from one of the Maze's many fountains into an adjoining pool. In the years of my youth, the sound of running water, far or near, was almost never absent. The curving walls and tunnels, most of their surfaces hard stone, sometimes played games with sound.

"Asterion, where are you?"

The young, clear voice was of course that of Ariadne, the younger of my two sisters, both older than myself. (Phaedra, the eldest of our sibling trio, was by the test of flesh and blood only my half-sister—more on that subject later.)

Even at Ariadne's second call I did not answer. First I wanted to make quite sure she was alone.

To find me today she had come more than half a mile out of the palace, which stood right at one edge of the great Maze. Most people would have been utterly lost before they walked five minutes in the Labyrinth, but I had no fear that that would ever happen to Ariadne, who had been coming to visit me since both of us were only children. I had not seen her for more than a week, an unusually long time between her visits.

But I was not at all surprised that she had come today. On the previous night I had dreamt of encountering her in this small courtyard, and in such matters my dreams are seldom wrong.

When Ariadne called my name a third time, and still I could perceive no sign that anyone else was with her, or had followed her in stealth, I advanced out of deep blue shadow, and came pacing on my two very human legs across the small sunlit plaza. On its far side my sister stood, looking up at me in trusting welcome. I am seven feet tall, almost exactly. A little more if the horns are counted, curving up as they do, one on each side of my inhuman skull, in rather graceful symmetry, to a level about an inch higher than the top of my head. (My ears sometimes rise higher too, but they are so mobile that I don't count them.)

Ariadne was two years older than my seventeen, and by most human standards she was beautiful. Her light brown hair fell in long curling coils on both sides of her heart-shaped face. On that day she was wearing, as typical day-to-day costume, gold-painted sandals, and a linen shift. It was not her custom to wear much jewelry, and today she had on none at all, save for a medallion Daedalus had given her. (He had given Minos and Phaedra their own, equivalent gifts at the same time—and I had mine a month later, after the Artisan had become acquainted with me.) Ariadne's bright disk of gold and silver was tucked inside her dress and out of sight, but I could see the silvery chain that held it round her neck. On the island of Corycus, women of the upper class exposed their breasts only on formal, dress-up occasions.

Her face lit up at the sight of my advancing form, clad in a kilt and large, plebeian sandals. (My feet, like my legs, are very human, comparatively hairless, and no bigger than those of many normal men.)

"There you are!" she cried, and burst out at once with an announcement that could not wait. "Oh, I have so much to tell!" My sister was in a fever that seemed half anxiety, half joy.

"Some of it at least must be good news," I observed, accepting a joyful hug. For most of my life I have been aware that my voice does not sound quite like those of other men. There is no way that it possibly could, given the inhuman shape of my throat and head. But to my sister the tones of my speech were quite familiar, and she had no difficulty understanding.

It was almost the first time in half a year that I had seen Ariadne smiling, that I had been able to catch sight in her of any happiness at all.

"You are right," she told me, nodding her head for emphasis. "But some of it is not." And her smile faded rapidly, as she considered some problem that I was certainly going to hear about within the next few minutes.

My stomach like my limbs is very nearly human. Extending an arm to a mutant tree nearby, I plucked an early fruit that hung within reach, and ate it while we talked. Still a trifle green, but that was only to be expected so early in the season. Each day I grew wearier of the dried stuff that had largely seen me through the winter. It was something like an apple, and a little like a peach, but not that much like either, and a thing for which I had no name. Names sometimes bewilder me. Each spring the fruit of this tree, like that of many others growing in my home, was something different. The ashes in the little hearth nearby were long dead. The nearby vines that had looked dead a week before were springing forth with fresh new green.

Much vegetation grows wild inside my home, and in several places there are even groves of trees. In very many places grass has started up in the cracks between paving stones, especially in the hundreds of miles of passages where almost no one ever walks. But some strong protection, odylic magic perhaps, or only a dearth of moisture, has so far kept the place from being entirely overgrown.

I had been rather expecting Ariadne to bring me some news on this day, probably details of the long-expected arrival of the Tribute people, whose black-sailed ship had entered the harbor of Kandak at least a week ago. And she began to do just that, but in fact I was listening with only half an ear, because I had an announcement of my own that I wished to make.

The idea had been growing for some time in my monstrous head that I was long overdue to venture once more out of the Labyrinth. I wanted to see for myself what the world out there was truly like, not just how it looked when reflected in my dreams and those of other folk; I had been so young when I was immured in the great Maze that I could remember very little else. For some months now, ever since midwinter when the days began to lengthen, dreams had been urging me to go on an excursion.

My sister paused, and out of habit glanced back briefly, first over one shoulder and then the other, before she went on speaking, even though in the remote fastnesses of the Labyrinth we had no real worry about being overheard. Now, I thought, she had come to her real news.

She said, "Our uncle's god grows stronger day by day—stronger and more demanding. Now they are killing slaves, almost daily, in one of the courtyards of the palace. At least it isn't under my window. Slaves and prisoners, for no good reason but to feed Shiva's joy in killing." She paused. "Have you dreamt about him yet?"

"About Shiva?" I shook my horned head, no. "But of late I have seen our father more than once in dreams, and heard his voice."

"Our father?"

"I mean Minos," I said, and Ariadne relaxed slightly. I went on, "It is as if he calls me from a great distance. I can't tell what he's saying."

"From the realm of Hades?" Now my sister shivered.

"I—don't know." I didn't think the communication came from the Underworld, but it had always been difficult for me to try to explain to her my adventures in the realm of Oneiros, god of dreams.

I did not and do not remember, of course, how I came to be born in the shape I have. There were occasional dreams—and I was certain that these particular visions were no more than ordinary dreams—in which the monstrous transformation had happened to me only after birth. In these dreams, my mother might still have died in childbirth, but it would not have been because of the horns I bore on my inhuman head.

Why had anyone suffered such a monstrous child to live? My old nurse, the first of a short succession of folk who had cared for me in childhood, and whom I only dimly remembered now, had sometimes whispered fiercely to me that I was, must be, the offspring of Father Zeus himself. "They say that the Thunderer will sometimes take the form of a bull—and it is in that form that he came to your mother!"

My memories of what had happened to me in dreams became confabulated with what I could recall of reality, and I was by no means always certain which were really the most real. Once, so long ago that I could not remember details, I, Asterion, had looked into a mirror, a real mirror of fine smooth glass. And more than once I had lain on my belly on the pavement, somewhere in the endless cool recesses of the Labyrinth, gazing into one or another of the many quiet pools. In those reflecting surfaces I always saw something very different than what I beheld when I looked at the faces of other people. The most unpleasant of my dreams were those that had to do with mirrors.

One part of my spotty education had to do with the gods—how those strange and awesome beings had played a vital role in human affairs some generations ago, but then had faded from sight, so effectively that many people had begun to doubt their very existence.

Not that I, Asterion, could remember ever seeing a god myself. Not with my waking eyes.

━━━━━━

On that spring day in the Labyrinth, Ariadne brought as one item of news certain details that had only recently reached the island of Corycus, from a certain place on the mainland hundreds of miles away. The details elaborated on a story that was already somewhat old, telling how the great gods Apollo and Hades, and the comparatively trivial human forces that supported each of them, had within the past year fought a tremendous battle. And how Apollo had established his Oracle upon the site, and how on that mountain, on whose summit some said Olympus lay, the great Sun-God had forbidden human sacrifice.

"Much of that is old news," I remarked.

"Of course." My sister jutted her fine chin at me. "But wouldn't it be a good thing if the people of Corycus served Apollo too?"

"Probably—but they no longer have much chance to do so. I doubt that there is any longer even one active shrine or temple of Apollo, anywhere on the island. Our noble uncle remains devoted to a very different god."

"I have just been talking with some of the people of the Tribute." That was not changing the subject, at least not the way Ariadne thought.

"Nine youths and nine maidens, just as Uncle demanded of his tributaries?"

My sister nodded.

"And now that these people of the Tribute are here, what is Uncle really going to do with them? I understood that they were not to become slaves."

"No, several of them are even of noble blood. The official word that Uncle has announced to the people is that . . ."

Ariadne hesitated at that point and had to start over. "There are several things that I am anxious to tell you, my brother, and one of them is painful."

"So you said. Well, let me hear the painful message first." But though I asked so boldly, I was afraid of what my sister might be going to tell me. Afraid of hearing in real life a frightening message which had already been given to me in some dream, and which I had then mercifully forgotten. But there would be no forgetting it this time.

Ariadne said, "Our noble uncle, and all the priests of Shiva that are now coming to our island, like flies gathering on a dead body . . ."

"Yes?"

". . . they are telling everyone that the nine youths and nine maidens are going to be sacrificed to the Minotaur. To you."

I knew that people called me by that name sometimes, gave me the appellation of a monster, as if to remind themselves never to think of me as human. But there was nothing to be done about it. " 'Sacrificed,' "

I said. "You mean killed. Like the slaves and prisoners you mentioned earlier."

"Yes."

Some time passed in which I endeavored to make sense of this latest announcement. "And sacrificed to me? To *me*?"

"I know that the idea must sound foolish—"

Suddenly angry, I turned away and went stalking about the little plaza, clenching and unclenching my fists. " 'Foolish'? That doesn't begin to describe it! Do they think me some kind of demon, demanding human sacrifice? What am I supposed to do with youths and maidens? Eat them? I don't even eat meat. Drink their blood? Or maybe love them to death, go rutting on them like—but you know I don't even . . ."

"I know! I know, dear Asterion." Gently my sister tried to soothe me. Grabbed one finger of one of my enormous though manlike hands, and tugged me to a halt, when my pacing would have carried me away from her. "Zeus has made you different. And I love you, and understand you as you are. But the world does not know you as I do. People are always ready to hear tales of a monster, and I fear the official story is going to be believed."

"And of course the people of the Tribute *are* really going to be slain in sacrifice."

"Shiva is demanding it. Or so his priests are whispering. We seldom see the god himself. The whispers are that he spends much of his time worrying about assassination plots."

———

I thought that human sacrifice had not been the original intention of the usurper, when he claimed the Tribute. He had wanted the young folk as hostages, perhaps. As a way of encouraging our enemies to discover ways that they could live with us. Part of the justification given when the Tribute was first announced was that the new Minos, emboldened by the god-power of Shiva at his back, was more than ever determined to assert his authority over those poor fools and weaklings in their dis-united kingdoms on the mainland. Send tribute, or my matchless navy will attack your ports, destroy your shipping!

In a little while I had talked the sharpest edge of my anger away. "But something else has happened to you, sister. Something good, it must have been, for despite our uncle's wickedness you are beginning to be happy."

Immediately she brightened. "Oh, yes! I don't doubt that you can see in me the effects of what has happened."

"Describe this happy miracle to me."

She jumped up lightly and walked about, unable to sit still. "His name is Theseus."

"Ah."

"I am in love, desperately in love!"

"Somehow I suspected as much."

"His name is Theseus!" This time Ariadne almost sang the word.

I was happy for my sister, but also already beginning to be jealous, in a way. "Yes, I understood that the first time. So, who is Theseus, where does he come from? What is he like?"

"He is one of the youths of the Tribute. What is he like? How can I tell you? Like a god, strong and handsome beyond my powers of description. He is really a prince, who was taken prisoner in one of those foolish mainland wars, and then . . ."

"Stop. Wait." Finally I managed to break in upon the rhapsody. "Back up a moment. You seem to be telling me he's one of the eighteen—? Ariadne, you can't be serious!"

"Asterion, I've never been so serious in all my life."

I stared at her. "Perhaps you haven't. This is the first time you have ever told me that you were in love."

"Yes, it is . . . Of course I am going to arrange it somehow that his life will be spared." To Ariadne, an effective sentence of death hanging over her newly beloved was only an awkward detail that had to be managed somehow, on the order of a conflict of dates when a party was being organized. My sister, being who she was, had no doubt at all that she would be able to accomplish that. Confidently she added, "I know that I can count on you to do whatever may be necessary to help."

"Of course, my sister." I took her small hand in both of mine, and patted it. "Tell me more."

"Have you seen Prince Theseus in your dreams, Asterion? Tell me what you have seen!"

Thinking the matter over, I realized that I very well might have seen this supposed paragon, some night when my eyes were closed and my senses absent from my body, without knowing his name. Lately I had dreamt of bad things happening to several people I could not identify. From my sister's description I began to understand just who that stalwart youth might be, what role he had played in those dreams.

What I had seen would only alarm my sister to no purpose, and so I lied to her. "I have seen a great many things as usual, a great many people. And in my dreams people do not always look like themselves in real life. It will take time for me to sort them out."

She accepted the lie happily.

"But look here, Ariadne, surely all these people of the Tribute — nine youths and nine maidens—are being held as prisoners?"

"They are."

"Then how is it you are able to talk with this Theseus at all?"

Before answering, my sister once more cast worried glances over both shoulders. "Their confinement is quite mild. Actually they are not in the cells under the palace, but are only being held aside, apart, in a section of the Labyrinth close by." She supplied a few details of the local topography, from which I was able to visualize the area.

"But surely they are guarded."

"Yes. But I have many friends in the palace, and I even still have a few among the soldiers. So it wasn't too difficult for him to get a message out to me." She paused, sobering. "The message said that he was the son of a sea lord, from somewhere in the Outflung Islands, and he had information of great importance, that he wanted to give to me in person. It concerned our father's death."

I thought that over for a while. "If your Theseus is telling the truth about his parentage, then his father must be in some way a rival of our respected and noble uncle."

"Yes, I suppose that's true."

"But he didn't actually give his father's name."

"No."

Several names suggested themselves to me, of powerful men active in current affairs around the world, but I saw no reason to prefer any of them to the others. Later I would try to narrow down the field. "So, you naturally thought it necessary to meet with a prisoner who sent you such a message. And when you met, did he actually have anything new to say, about what happened to our Father Minos?"

Ariadne frowned slightly. "No, not really. Slightly different versions of the rumors we have already heard. But more and more I am coming to believe that Uncle must have had something to do with killing him."

"Very likely," I agreed in a quiet voice. Lately there had been revelatory dreams.

———

When I had listened to all that Ariadne had to tell me, I cut short her glowing descriptions of her lover, in which she was beginning to repeat herself, to make an announcement of my own. "Sister, I am determined to go out into the city. I want to see and hear for myself something of what is going on."

She looked concerned, perhaps because my project might delay one of hers. "Is this because of something I have just told you?"

"No, it's nothing to do with you or Theseus. I've been thinking about it for a while."

"But is it wise?"

"Are you the one to counsel me on wisdom? But no, lately I have very often dreamed about such an outing. So much, that I take it as something I must do."

Immediately Ariadne had something new to worry about. But as usual my sister was (and I had counted on the fact) more than half ready for a prank, for almost any adventure. There was a new eagerness in her voice as she said, "If you're determined to go out, maybe I can help. When do you want to go? Tonight?"

"That was my thought."

Briefly she was serious again. "Of course Uncle will be very angry—if he finds out."

"Let him be angry if he wants."

"You're not afraid he'll kill you, as he did our Father Minos?"

I shook my head.

My sister nodded slowly. "Of course if he got rid of you, he could hardly claim that you were demanding sacrifices."

"But why not? I suppose I would live on in legend. No, I doubt very much that dear Uncle will try to inflict any serious punishment on me. Not for such a minor offense. Not for one so obviously a child of Zeus—unless he thinks that sending eighteen hostages to live with me in the Labyrinth will be my punishment—I can see how that might work."

I paused. "Of course your situation and Phaedra's is quite different, living in the palace as you do. How is Phaedra, by the way?"

"I see little of her, as usual." Then Ariadne tossed her head defiantly. "As for punishment, I'll take my chances. Even if Uncle learns you've gone on an excursion out of the Labyrinth, he needn't know that I had anything to do with it. And the less Phaedra knows about it the better. Not that she would ever betray us willingly, but . . ."

"Yes," I said. Our elder sister generally tended to keep to the rules, until they became totally unendurable. And she had never been able to conceal her thoughts and feelings with any degree of success. "Have you told her about Theseus?"

"No. Asterion, you *will* help me, won't you? His life must be saved, whatever else happens."

"Whatever else?"

"I mean it."

"Then I promise. I'll do whatever may be necessary. But I don't know anything about him. The next time I go to sleep, I will try to find out what I can, about him and about what Uncle may be planning. Then we can devise some stratagem of our own."

"You will find out nothing bad about Theseus." Tossing her head again, Ariadne turned and started away. "Excuse me, but there are many things that I must do."

"Wait. Just how do you mean to help me, in the matter of my visiting the city?" Knowing my sister as I did, I was certain she would not forget the matter, and I thought it prudent to know as soon as possible what scheme she was concocting. Ariadne meant well, but any recipient of her aid could count himself lucky not to be involved in new perils.

"You'll see!" Already at the nearest branching of the passageway, she waved goodbye vivaciously. "Meet me in the courtyard of the three statues, one hour before sunset!"

4

TO PASS THE time before the appointed hour of my next meeting with my sister, I decided to go and talk to Daedalus, who I considered by far the wisest counselor among the few I had available.

Impractical as I was in many matters, it seemed to me that saving the life of Theseus was likely to be a far more difficult problem than Ariadne was willing to admit. But my personal search for a solution would have to wait until I could sleep and dream again. In the meantime, possibly Daedalus could help.

Headed toward the place where I expected to find him, I gave little conscious attention to the course my feet were taking, yet I made good time.

I suppose that you who have never walked those convoluted pathways cannot really conceive what they are like. Passages within the Labyrinth transform themselves from wide to narrow to wide again, according to no pattern that the sole permanent inhabitant, myself, has ever been able to ascertain. Stairways appear, seemingly at random, never any more than eight or ten steps in any one flight. When a passage is elevated it is quite likely that another one, or two or three, will cross beneath the high place, out of sight.

But most of the Maze, as you may know, is roofless, and walls in those uncovered portions are generally about fifteen feet high. They also display a notable lack of useful projections, so climbing them is very hard work at best. One person standing on another's shoulders gains no real advantage. And the top of each wall, more often than not, is an almost blade-sharp edge, impossible to walk on, difficult even to grasp. In keeping with this theme, the roofs of the covered sections of passageway tend to be steeply sloping, and precarious. There are also some low-level roofs, easily climbable but useless for getting out, or even seeing over the adjoining walls. What flat and solid covering there is, is thin, and at the time of which I write it was badly rotted in places, so people tended to fall through when they tried to walk on it.

At frequent intervals a passageway will widen a little, doubling or tripling its breadth to create a space that could be called a room, if it happens to be covered, as it sometimes is. Occasionally such a room contains a fireplace or open hearth, and the vines that in summer grow so long make good fuel when they are dead and dry in winter. Not that Corycus ever experiences a real winter, by the standards of the northern mainland, with persistent snow and ice. Instead we have shorter days, gray skies, dull rain.

There are a few spots within the Labyrinth from which it is actually possible, when one stands up high enough, to see, at a distance of ten or twelve miles, the sometimes snowy peaks of the low ridge that the inhabitants of Corycus call a range of mountains. But the points from which such an observation is possible are hard to find.

The center of the Maze was less than a mile, as a bird might fly, from the place where I had spoken with my sister. But to get from one point to the other through the passages required a minimum walk of almost three times that distance; and one who did not know the Labyrinth might easily have walked a hundred times as far to arrive at the same destination. Assuming (and it is a large assumption) that he or she would be able to find the way at all. Many are incredulous when they first hear that a square of the earth's surface, only two miles by two, might, without the use of magic or any special cleverness, contain a thousand miles of passageways, each broad enough for human traffic. But so it is.

Here and there I managed to subtract miles from my journey, by climbing over a wall, or walking briefly atop one of the roofed segments of a passage, the narrow supports bending under my weight.

Still, to reach a portion of the Maze where I might reasonably begin to look for Daedalus took me the better part of an hour. I knew that I had almost reached my goal when I entered the central region, which was more ancient and stranger than any of the rest. Here the possibility of confusion was even greater, and the walls and floors were made of panels and blocks formed from a different material, some product of the era when the gods were born, not readily identifiable as either stone or wood or metal.

———

The central part of the Labyrinth, an area about a quarter of a mile square, had the look and feel of being older than any of the rest. The style in which it was built, and the materials, did not match those of the surrounding work. Where there had obviously once been buildings, now there were only rooms, many of them roofless and half-overgrown with the same kinds of vegetation that sprouted in the endless miles of the surrounding passageways. Patches that once were garden had now gone wild, but continued to produce some edible stuff. There were conflicting stories, legends, regarding this construction, which must have taken place back in the ancient epoch, at the time when the gods were born— or created. This portion of the Labyrinth included endless rooms, some roofed, some open, filled with complex, incomprehensible apparatus. All of this, or almost all, had fallen into ruin decades or even centuries before I was born. Following that notable event, another seventeen years passed before Daedalus arrived, and was assigned by our noble uncle the task of trying to unravel the truth of ancient mysteries.

Gradually, over the centuries since this center portion was constructed, the whole stone-walled Maze had been built up around it, for reasons that now seemed not only mystical but often totally obscure. For generations the rulers of the city and the island seemed to have taken up the erection of more walls and tunnels as a holy task. The reasons underlying this tradition remained obscure.

———

I found the Artisan about where I had expected he would be, not far from the center of the relatively small area in which he had chosen to confine his labors.

"Greetings, Daedalus."

"Asterion." He had been sitting cross-legged in a shaded corner, perched on a kind of bench or table that was made of some ancient, incomprehensible material, seemingly neither wood nor rock nor metal, dark and smooth and hard. Once he had told me that such tables were antique workbenches.

As I approached, Daedalus was studying intently a small fragment of twisted, ancient metal, holding it up in both hands close before his eyes. When he heard my voice he looked up at me, startled and yet not really surprised to see me, the vagueness in his eyes showing that most of his thought was still elsewhere, engaged I suppose upon some baffling problem. Yet he was not displeased to be interrupted.

Nothing that I had ever seen in the Artisan suggested to me that he was a violent man; but the story that had come with him, on which I had never sought his own comment, was that he had fled to Corycus after killing his nephew and chief assistant, Perdix, in some quarrel on the mainland.

The master artisan, said to be a widower, was a lean man of about forty, of no more than average height, with a large nose, his brownish, gray-streaked hair tied behind him with utilitarian string. Nothing ornamental about Daedalus. Today, as usual when he was on the job, his only garment was a kind of combination belt and apron of patched leather, equipped with pockets and loops to hold small tools. His arms were all lean, practical strength. All of his fingers were ringless as a slave's, both hands callused and scarred from the use of every kind of tool, and marked by accidents. Even now one knuckle was bleeding slightly, from a fresh scrape.

I had heard that while laboring for his previous patrons on the mainland, Daedalus had usually worked with many assistants. But since Minos had set him the task of making sense of the ancient apparatus of odylic force, he was almost always alone.

When we had exchanged a few commonplace remarks, I asked him, "What do you know of a youth, a man, called Theseus?"

"Who?" It was plain from his blank look that Daedalus knew nothing. "Who is he?" Now he was giving me his full attention, his technical problems for the moment set aside. Even the fact of the Tribute was news to this dedicated worker, who seemed to know even less than I of events outside the Maze.

I shook my head to show it did not matter. "Never mind, I will ask elsewhere. Is your work successful?"

"Successful?" Daedalus's brows knotted. He searched the sky with his fierce gaze, and blasphemed several gods. Savagely he hurled aside the bit of twisted metal he had been examining, so that it bounced on stone pavement and vanished somewhere. "The truth is, I have been here on Corycus for almost four months now and I still don't know what I'm doing. I curse the day I became entangled with these mysteries they call odylic. That's why I currently have no assistant. My ignorance would be hard to conceal from any intelligent person who might spend an entire day with me."

"I don't suppose you've confessed to the new king that you still don't know what you're doing?"

Daedalus snorted.

"Do you wish that you were elsewhere?"

He looked at me sharply. "To you, Asterion, I will admit that I curse the day I ever came to Corycus. But what I wish on that subject does not much matter. King Perses is not going to let me go."

"You have asked him?"

"I don't need to, I know it would be useless."

I tried to let my concern show in my voice; my face does not much lend itself to the expression of emotion. "Well, I'll help you if possible. Is there anything I can do?"

"I doubt it. But I suppose it's conceivable that you might be of help sometime, and I certainly thank you for the offer." The Artisan drew a deep breath and let it out. "You've spent more time in this damned Maze than anyone else, myself certainly included. My question is quite fundamental: What in the Underworld *is* all this stuff?" And Daedalus gestured with one scarred hand toward all the heaped-up business, unidentifiable, strange enough to be unearthly, almost indescribable, upon the nearest bench.

"I don't know," I admitted simply. "You've been here four months; I've been here most of my life, and I have no idea." It did not seem the kind of question that could be answered by pursuing it in dreams.

"Look at it! Table after table of it, room after room. Long glass tubes to make connections in the mass. They stretch from one chamber to another here on ground level, they go down at least two levels lower. But they convey nothing at all that I can see, or imagine."

Here the Artisan paused, and fixed me with a gaze of burning intensity. "Asterion, do you know anything of the art of handling molten glass? No, how could you. But let me tell you, just to duplicate one of those tubes would be a serious challenge to the finest glassblower. And that's only the beginning. Strands of copper, intricately woven, binding other objects. Glass, metal, other materials I can't even tell if they're mineral or vegetable—or maybe some kind of horn, or bone. No two rooms are quite identical, nor are the contents of any two tables, but to a casual inspection most of them are very much alike. If these are tools, then it can be no ordinary matter on which they are designed to operate, no ordinary task that they were meant to do.

"I am not entirely sure that I have even found all of the rooms in this section of the Labyrinth, let alone examined them minutely, or even determined their exact number—though I suppose I will do that. That would at least give me something quite definite to report, which might at least sound like progress." He glanced over his shoulder at the shaded doorway of the modest roofed room in which he and his small son had taken up their residence; at the moment there was no sign of anyone.

Then Daedalus added, as if in afterthought, "And there is supposed to be a god's Face discoverable somewhere in all this."

"What?"

The Artisan nodded. "The king, the new king, is convinced of it, for some reason, and so it must be there." Daedalus took a deep swig from an opaque water bottle that stood by him and set it back on the bench with a thud, like a workman putting down a tool. It occurred to me to wonder if there might be something besides water in the bottle; but I had never seen him appear to be the worse for wine.

"Really?" I asked. "The Face of what god?"

"Actually I didn't ask, because I didn't think it mattered. Because, whoever it might be, I have no idea of how to go about such a task. Asterion? Have you ever seen a god's Face? I suppose the great majority of people never do."

"Not I." As usual, I found Daedalus's calm acceptance of me as a person, despite my grotesque shape, very heartening. "Except in dreams, where I am liable to see almost anything. How should I see a god? Shiva has never summoned me, or visited the Maze—which suits me fine. Have you ever seen one?"

The Artisan nodded slowly. "Once, long ago, I may have done; not a detached Face, but a being who looked almost like a man, though I believe it was one of the gods."

"You said: 'a detached Face'?"

Daedalus patiently explained what everyone more or less knew about the Faces, and how the king was interested in a particular one, unspecified.

"He came to visit me a while back, and without much preamble demanded, 'Where is the Face of Dionysus?' I said to him, 'My lord king, though I am Daedalus, I am only a mortal man, and there are things I do not know, and that is one of them. The missing Faces of the gods may be here, somewhere within reach, or they may all be at the far end of the earth. I can only go on searching.' "

"And what did our new Minos have to say to that?"

"He grumbled, and told me to go on looking, and that was about all. But I tell you, Asterion." Here the Artisan paused to look around, and dropped his voice. "I regret the day I came here, and I devoutly wish my son and I were somewhere else."

"I suppose it is not impossible that a man of your talent should find a way to leave. If you do, I wish you would tell me, and soon. I know others who have the same wish."

"Ah," said the Artisan, sounding slightly and hopefully surprised. He gave me a long, guarded look, then nodded slowly. "These others you mention . . . have they taken any steps toward a practical solution of the problem?"

"I think not. No, I'm sure they haven't. Would it be impertinent to ask if you have done so?"

"Impertinence should be the least of anyone's concerns when such matters are discussed. No, I have taken no pragmatic action. But now perhaps it is time I did so."

———

And with that he went back to talking of other things. What Daedalus had said to me on the subject of Faces tallied with much that I had heard before. It was a story so common that I supposed it had to be fundamentally correct: how ordinary mortals could, when given the opportunity, put those Faces on, clothing themselves in divine power.

Then he added, "Now that the subject of gods has come up between us, Asterion, there is a personal question I would like to ask you, if you do not mind."

"I don't mind it from you, Daedalus. I suppose I can even guess what the question is."

"There are folk who say great Zeus himself was your father."

I nodded. "There seems reason to believe that is the case. But I know no more about that than you do."

At that moment Icarus came running up to us, a wiry boy of seven or eight, clad only in a small copy of his father's leather apron. Daedalus had never mentioned the boy's mother, who she might be, or where she was, and I had never asked. Evidently the child had seen that Daedalus was not, at the moment, concentrating upon his work, and thus could be safely interrupted. Icarus had been frightened of me, months ago when we first met, but had soon adopted his father's cosmopolitan attitude.

The Artisan's son was willing enough to help with his father's work, when his parent told him to do so, but I thought Icarus showed no great native skill or interest in such matters.

Absently Daedalus stroked his small son's uncombed head. "If this were some ordinary job, I'd have the boy assisting me. But this . . ." The artisan shook his head. "I must come up with some kind of an answer here. Or the king will be seriously displeased."

Studying Icarus critically, I said to him, "You have grown taller since I saw you last. I think you are old enough to swim, and I could teach you. We wouldn't have to leave the Labyrinth. I know where there is a pool quite long and deep enough, not many miles from here. No one else ever comes to that place, only the birds, from year to year, and sometimes a big fish."

For some reason, what I had just said had caught the father's interest. Slowly he came back from his dreams of work to look at me. "How big? The fish, I mean."

I raised my hands, almost two feet apart.

"What species?"

"A sort of salmon, I think, judging by its resemblance to a fish I have seen people eating."

"I would like to see this pool," said Daedalus, and at the same moment his son said, "I already know how to swim," in a tone that expressed his scorn of anyone who might not.

"Then I won't need to teach you," I agreed. "And I will show you both the pool," I said to Daedalus. "But it will have to wait until another day." Looking up at the sun, I estimated how many hours must pass before it set. I turned away to go, and then turned back. "Remember what I said, about how others share your wish."

"I will remember."

At an hour before sunset, Ariadne was waiting for me at the agreed meeting place. This was a little plaza, wider by a stride than most such in my domain, that my sister and I in our private talks had come to call the Courtyard of the Three Statues. Because indeed there were three marble carvings, of a man, a woman, and a satyr, each on its own pedestal, carved by some unremembered artist in some lost century before our own.

But on that afternoon I paid little attention to the statues as I approached; I was surprised to see that my sister was not alone. The small figure of a single companion stood beside her, anonymous and sexually ambiguous in an elaborate mask and costume.

Ariadne was carrying a mass of fabric in her arms; it might have been another costume, or a small tent. As soon as I appeared, she told me that she had brought something for me to wear when I went exploring in the town. The chosen outfit included loose trousers, and a large, baggy shirt or blouse that I thought rather strange-looking, to say the least. Both garments were of coarse cloth and gaudy colors. On a bench nearby rested a lacquered box that I thought I recognized as her own modest makeup kit.

"And who's this?" I demanded, pointing. Ariadne giggled and

pulled the mask from the face of the short figure by her side. I was not really surprised to see the face of her regular attendant and frequent companion, Clara, a pert slave girl with dark, straight hair.

Clara had accompanied Ariadne on many of my sister's earlier visits to the Maze, but I had not expected her or anyone else today. It had seemed to me that the fewer people who knew about my planned foray into the outside world, the better.

Ariadne was smiling, as if daring me to guess what these preparations were all about. I took the gaudy shirt from her hands and shook it out. It was enormous, too big even for me. "Where in the world did you get a garment like this?"

"We found it in a storeroom. It was made for the last Festival, and then it didn't quite fit the straw dummy that was going to be burned, and they had to make another. I happened to remember that this one was just left over."

I waved the mass of fabric like a flag. "And wearing this is supposed to make me inconspicuous?"

"Actually, yes. You'll see."

"And Clara. Why is she costumed?" The slave girl smiled at me uncertainly.

"She's going with you," Ariadne informed me, observing my continued puzzlement.

"Oh." My first impulse was to protest, but on second thought I could see advantages. Clara's outfit was a showy one, I suppose on the theory that it would also serve to distract attention from me.

Now I turned my attention to the box of cosmetics. "Do you imagine that with a little paint you can make my head look human?"

My sister shook her head at my obtuseness. "No, silly! But what I *can* do is make your head look like a mask. One of those great, hollow masks that people often wear at Festival."

"I don't know . . ."

"I do. Come over here, where the sun still shines." She patted the stone bench beside her. "Sit down. Sit still."

Over the next few minutes the two women busied themselves making up my horned head with rouge, lipstick, and paint, so that in the end they assured me that it did indeed look like a giant mask. And they helped me, as if I were a child who needed help, to pull on the huge blouse as a costume, and the oversized, awkward gloves. Now I began to appreciate the plan. Had I gone out without a costume, I would necessarily have spent my time lurking and scurrying through shadows, trying to avoid being seen by anyone.

When I had been thus thoroughly disguised, my sister assured me that I could pass, for a while, and at night, as an ordinary human, though indeed a man of impressive size. Clara had brought with her in her kit a small mirror, and I was now encouraged to try to see the alteration for myself. Fortunately or not, the small mirror was of but little help.

Studying the total effect, Ariadne planted her fists on her hips and sighed. "There's no way, short of magic, to disguise your height; and I don't know any magician I'd want to ask to do that job." But the huge blouse covered just those upper parts, those portions of my body that looked least human.

———

At last the artists were satisfied. "When are you going?" my sister inquired.

"Now. It'll be dark by the time I get out. It will take us half an hour to walk from here to the nearest exit, on the city side."

"Longer than that, surely."

"Not by the route I'll take." I had good reason to be confident that no one else knew the Labyrinth as well as I.

Ariadne sighed, and rubbed my gloved hand in a proprietary way. "Then go, and the gods of fortune with you. I am half tempted to go with you myself—I want a full report tomorrow on your adventures."

"You shall have it." I paused, wanting to change the subject before my sister could convince herself that she should come along. "Have you had any further word of your Theseus?" I had no fear in speaking that name in front of Clara, taking it for granted that the slave girl shared all her mistress's fears and schemes.

Ariadne shook her light brown curls. "Not since I spoke to you a few hours ago. Why?"

"I have had a talk with Daedalus during the interval. I think that you, and he, and this Theseus now all have something very important in common—a wish to be away from Corycus."

Both young women were listening with keen interest. "Then I think I should meet with Daedalus," Ariadne said.

I bowed lightly. "Allow me to arrange it—tomorrow."

5

I NEEDED NO one's help in accomplishing my actual emergence into the world. I had managed that feat several times before in my young life, quite without assistance or companionship. There were a number of doorways, spaced around the eight-mile perimeter, and to the best of my knowledge four of them always stood open between the outermost layer of the Labyrinth and the rest of the world. There was nothing physically difficult about getting out, once you could find one of those doors. And of course the doors were infinitely easier to discover from the outside, so it was not at all hard for outsiders to get in. People had done so, of course, at irregular intervals over the years. Every now and then, some fanatic or adventurer, drawn by the urge to explore a mystery, bemused by some foolish rumor of hidden treasure, or simply acting on a dare, would venture into what I considered my domain. Certain evidence obtained in dreams had convinced me that most of these explorers were newcomers to the city and the island.

These occasional wanderers caused me no trouble, and I seldom gave them any thought. Only twice, while roaming the Maze during my childhood, I had stumbled upon human bones that must have belonged to members of this ill-fated fraternity, dead of panic and despair, or possibly of starvation—vast regions of my domain offer little or nothing in the way of food. In each case the remains were lying miles from the nearest entrance to the Labyrinth—which, of course, might not have been the portal by which the unfortunate one had entered. In each case, again, a rusted weapon lay near the skeleton; doubtless the intruders had come armed to protect themselves against the monstrous Minotaur. Or possibly they planned to collect my great horned head and lug it home as a trophy.

How many similar fallen ones might still lie undiscovered, even by me, in the remoter byways, was hard to estimate. I felt most comfortable with the belief that the majority of such experiments ended with the adventurer making it safely out of the Maze after an hour or two's adventure. No doubt some of them carried balls of string to unwind as they explored, in an attempt to keep from getting lost. But I had no fear of ever being overrun by trespassers. As I had once told Ariadne, I was confident that none would carry a thousand miles of string.

My own previous excursions beyond the walls of the Labyrinth had all been brief, and unaccompanied, impulsive midnight dartings into a world that I had never really known outside of dreams. My last such sortie had been years ago, and my memories of the world that I had seen outside were old and hazy, like troubled dreams.

This time, as on those earlier occasions, I naturally waited until after dark. And as before, I carried no ball of string to help me find my way back through the mysterious city to my home. I planned to go much farther this time than I had ever gone before, but this time I had a guide to help me, and in any case I was willing to rely on my own sense of direction.

Meanwhile, my sister, having bidden her brother and her slave farewell, turned away to make her way home to the palace alone. I had no more fear of Ariadne's ever getting lost in the Maze than I did of losing my own way. From our real father she had her own special inheritance, which fortunately for her was far less conspicuous and troublesome than mine.

Now, walking beside Clara, I made an effort to observe more details of her true appearance, but the effort was thwarted by her mask and the clothes she had put on.

My escort's costume was of colors considerably brighter than my own—but that she should draw attention away from me was, of course, a key part of Ariadne's plan. Clara's mask was of papier-mâché or something of the kind, and it altered the shape of her whole head, though it gave her feline rather than bovine form—of course there was no need for her to match me in that way.

From the sound of my companion's occasional laughter behind her mask, from the feel of her hand when I took it to guide her through certain turns of the passages, I thought that she was still a little afraid of me. She had seen me often enough in the company of her mistress, but this was the first time the two of us had ever been alone.

Now that darkness had fallen, had already become impenetrably thick in some of the roofed areas, the Maze was more confusing than ever. Once, as I led her down a byway that must have looked particularly unpromising, I am sure that my companion started to ask me if I knew where I was going. But then she bit her tongue and did not fairly launch the question.

As we walked, I described to the girl a certain winter night that I remembered very clearly. One night, several winters ago, when snow fell briefly, out of a cold and moonless, starless sky, swirling and drifting in the roofless stretches of the endless passageways. That had been the first and only snow that my waking eyes had ever seen, excepting the occasional white stain along the crest of the distant mountain ridge. Several times, on that long-past night, even I had begun to be confused about directions.

My girl-companion evidently did not know what to say in response to my little story. Eventually she murmured something. I took her small hand in my great gloved one as we walked, and being a slave she made no effort to pull her hand away. She asked, brightly enough, "Where are we going? I mean once we are out in the city?"

"I'm not sure. Perhaps I'll leave the final decision on that up to you. I want a place where I can see many people, face to face. And where it is likely that they will all accept me as a man in costume."

Clara was ready with a suggestion. "I know a place where many of the soldiers, the enlisted men, go when they're off duty. At night during the Festival, there will be many fantastic costumes there."

"What Festival is this?"

"Quite a new one, I think. It's been proclaimed, in connection with the Tribute."

I asked her, "And have you been to this place of celebration with the soldiers? Is one of them perhaps your lover?"

"I am a slave, Lord Asterion." Clara raised a hand to finger her silver collar, beneath the concealing fabric of her costume.

"I know that, but does that mean that you can have no lover?"

"My Lord Asterion's questions are too profound for me to understand. I would be overwhelmed, if my lord was suggesting that he and I—"

"No, nothing like that. I have no lovers, in the way that we are talking about. I want and need none. I thought my sister would have told you that much about me."

"No, Lord Asterion. My lady has told me very little. Only that the stories that you are some kind of a cruel monster are all utter nonsense— not that I would have believed them in any case, when I saw how she regards you."

"That's good." For a moment I thought of asking Clara to tell me exactly what some of those stories said; but quickly I decided I did not really want to know. "Lead on."

———

The doorway, or gateway, through which we left the Labyrinth that night was one of those that I knew were generally unlocked and unguarded, and so indeed we found it. Somewhat to my surprise, I noticed now that this high-arched portal was no longer furnished with any real door at all. Holes in the masonry showed where bolts must once have secured strong hinges. The only hindrance to intruders was what I took to be a warning, graven over the arched opening, on the outside of the high wall. The message was written in what appeared to be three languages, all so old that I was unable to read any of them. In passing I reminded myself to come back here sometime in a dream; then, more likely than not, I would be able to decipher all the words.

When my companion and I had emerged from the Maze and were standing in an open street, it was dark and at the moment almost unoccupied except for ourselves. Turning to my left, I could see the palace, less than a mile away. The huge, daunting House of the Hammer (as it was sometimes called, for what reason I know not), level after level of it rising up, lights burning on certain corners of the roof, and in many of its windows. Having visited that building in many dreams, I felt I knew it very well. Indeed, I supposed it very probable that I had been born inside it, but that of course I could not remember.

No one has ever told me the detailed story of my birth, nor had I ever sought to learn it. When in dream-life I found my steps tending in that direction, I always shied away.

Looking in the opposite direction from the palace, Clara and I could see out over the harbor, where there were berths for many mighty ships of war, as well as the bottoms of a busy trade. Most of those berths were empty now, but there was moonlight enough for me to see a scattering of ships, skeletal masts and spars, furled sails. Including some moored biremes. Here and there the orange flame of some warning beacon burned. If the whole world did not fear Minos, as they had once feared his predecessors, at least most of the people who knew him did. Of course, as always, a great part of his formidable navy was at sea.

As soon as we were fairly out of the Maze, Clara seemed to lose all her remaining timidity regarding the Minotaur who walked beside her. Now she was eager for a party, and held my hand quite willingly.

———

"I wonder—" I said aloud.

"Lord Asterion?"

"I was only wondering how many thousand people live here in Kandak. I've heard that it is one of the great cities of the world, but that saying may be only local pride."

"Lord, I have no idea how many there may be."

I still thought it strange that I had lived in the capital of my native land, or more precisely beside it, my whole life, and still had no idea what the number was.

We moved on. Tentatively exploring the darkened streets, steering a course neither directly toward the palace nor away from it, Clara and I were drawn to a scene of music and laughter.

Parties of laughing folk went by us in the street, and on impulse I tugged my partner into following one such group.

There were cameloids in the streets of the city, pacing on their great soft feet, some being ridden swiftly, and others swaying slowly under heavy cargo. Draft cameloids, one-humped droms even taller and heavier than the others, pulled the heavier carriages and carts. I knew that these were common animals, but in waking life my eyes had never seen the like before.

From behind the high gates and fences guarding private homes, dogs barked at me as we passed. I hesitated, but Clara murmured reassuringly, "They would bark at anyone."

———

The group of people on foot we had begun to follow soon turned in through the gateway of a private house—no place for me there, certainly. But my companion knew where she wanted to go, to another building in another street, and in a few more minutes we had reached the place. There was the sound of laughter, and the rich smells of roasting meat and fresh-baked pastry, to me unappetizing. Torchlight came spilling out through all the doors and windows that pierced a certain white adobe wall, while most of the neighborhood around remained in darkness.

A door in the middle of the wall stood wide open. Ducking my head and turning, to get my horns in through the doorway, I entered the hall. I thought that something in the overall shape of the building suggested an earlier history as a temple, but the walls were scarred where symbols must have been chiseled away, and I could not tell which god it had sought to honor. Later, I thought, when we were outside again, I would ask Clara.

Inside the crowded room, the music of drums and strings throbbed loudly, and unclothed bodies whirled in a wild dance. Not professional entertainers, but free folk, mostly of the working classes, dancing for their own amusement. There sounded the lyre, Apollo's instrument. Torches and braziers flared, somehow cleverly made to burn with flames of different colors. Laughter went up in many voices. I was almost entranced. Never, except in dreams, had I even seen so many people in the same place at the same time. I supposed there might have been a hundred in one room. This was not a haunt of the wealthy. I thought a number of the men were soldiers, as Clara had foretold, young enlisted men out of uniform for their night's revelry.

Along the walls of the room and in its corners there were tables, with people sitting at them, some consuming wine and food. Moving close to the broad table where drinks were being poured and handed out, I heard disturbing comments, and saw startling sights, including a number of people costumed even more spectacularly than I was myself.

Looking closely, I observed that one or two of them were actually versions of the Minotaur, larger and fiercer-looking than I had ever been, with long horns carved of wood or bone. The mouth of one of their great masks sprouted predatory fangs.

And again, something about the shape of the scarred walls nagged at my attention. "I still wonder," I murmured to the girl beside me, "what god they once served here, whose house we are in? Not Apollo. And not Bacchus, surely." I was sure that Bacchus, one of whose other names is Dionysus, was proscribed in every quarter of the island, and had been for the last six months.

Clara said in a low voice, "They might once have served the Twice-Born. I have heard that when the new king came to power, he sent his soldiers here and they tore the place apart; they wouldn't say what they were looking for."

"There are many gods whose interests lie in the same general direction as those of Dionysus. Priapus would do, or any of half a dozen others."

On entering the hall, I had rather foolishly hoped no one would notice me. But even in this gathering, my appearance was more conspicuous, and drew more attention, than I would have wished. This was so even if the other Minotaurs were more monstrous than I.

Fortunately, Ariadne had remembered to give the slave-girl coins, trusting her more than me to understand the details of using money. Presently something to drink, carried in a strange flagon, appeared on the broad table before me. I should mention that I was not entirely unused to wine; Ariadne had brought me some from time to time, and in the old days it had sometimes come, in small glasses, suitable for my youth, with the official meals that were then sent out to me from the palace. That an intoxicating drink would be served in this establishment suggested Bacchus once again. Beside me a loudmouthed man had now ceased haranguing the world long enough to empty a flagon of foaming beer. I had heard that the new god of Corycus frowned on most kinds of merriment; well, people were not going to give up wine, let Shiva threaten as much as he liked.

The noise, the press of the crowd around me, more solid than in any dream, tended to be confusing. I had emptied my first flagon of wine and started on another before it occurred to me that if I drank or ate anything, I risked revealing that my mouth was mobile flesh, not part of a lifeless mask.

But the hesitation was only momentary. To the Underworld with it! I was going to enjoy the wine.

The unaccustomed drink produced a swaying of the room, a roaring in my ears. I had to wait for a long moment, until everything began to settle down again. Then I banged the empty flagon on the table, and made a bull-sound deep in my throat. I wanted to drink still more, and yet I was afraid.

Only now, with the drink beginning to act upon my senses, did I begin to pay attention to a large mirror, hanging on the wall behind the long table where the drinks were poured. The broad, smooth glass was as long as the table itself, and from that position it reflected all the dim lights of the large, low room.

Looking at my image in the mirror, I beheld a figure seven feet tall, weighing, as I knew, a little over three hundred pounds. Two sharp horns on the head, large brown eyes set wide apart, on a long bull-like face, now painted in stripes and dots that struggled to give a look of artificiality. Muffled in the great shirt were massive shoulders and arms, the latter terminating in hands that were trying to hide their almost inhuman size in grotesque and fancy gloves. The face and most of the body (now concealed by my costume) was covered with short cattle-hair.

The removal of a glove, the better to deal with a drinking glass, revealed long fingers, heavy nails.

But my gaze kept coming back to the reflected image of my face. Here it was, at last exposed for everyone to see, and had been ever since I entered the hall. But no one had really seen it yet.

Standing in the middle of such a crowd, it was hard to know what to think, what to do next. In all my life, my waking eyes had never seen more than six or eight people at one time at close range, and fewer still had ever seen me. Men and women were almost as unfamiliar in a mass as cameloids. Now to be surrounded, almost imprisoned by swarming humans, was more unsettling than I had expected it would be.

One of the young women, whose costume, or rather lack of one, suggested that she was a hired entertainer, put a hand upon my arm, only to withdrew it suddenly, a moment later. She must have felt skin that had the touch of fur, of something very much like cattle-hide.

Suddenly brutal voices rose up nearby, and I feared that my disguise had been somehow penetrated—but no, it was only being ridiculed, by drunken celebrants.

"What is it, man or monster?"

"Not very convincing, if it's supposed to be the Minotaur."

I turned toward the voices, but could find no words. Looking back at the situation now, I can see that my lack of ready speech must have only encouraged those who were looking for an opportunity to torment a victim.

"Hey, cow-face!" The speaker was large, though not, of course, as large as I. He was in costume too, some kind of parody of a military officer—not, of course, of the Minoan Palace Guard.

I was being picked on, first from one side, then another. Emboldened by drink, I shouted back at them. My voice, tolerably human when I am calm, sometimes escapes control when I am greatly excited, making a braying noise. What words I might have used have escaped my memory now. Certainly I meant them as insults, but I lacked all skill in such matters, and perhaps I only sounded stupid.

"Your mask is uglier than mine," was perhaps my best attempt, addressed as it was to a lounger who, like myself, wore none.

With that, the space around me grew ominously quiet. Clara had taken me by the arm, and was trying, first gently and then fiercely, to tug me away. But even when she pulled with all her strength, it was hardly possible for her to move me. And some accidental surging of the crowd in our immediate area had made the press so thick that quick movement was hardly possible.

The tugging and shoving grew more violent. My tormentors and I were thrust together. It would have been hard to pinpoint a moment when the fight began. Someone swung into my midriff with a clumsy fist; I scarcely felt the blow.

This was not why I had come here. Neither reality nor my world of dreams had prepared me for anything of the kind.

I had, and have, no particular skill in personal combat. I could send bad dreams upon someone I hated—if I hated anyone—but that is all.

But the sending of dreams required me first to go to sleep, and at the moment that was not feasible.

Some of the men who joined the brawl were soldiers, off duty and here to spend their pay, and some were not. Several were armed, though weapons were not drawn at first. One struck me with his fist, a much harder blow than the first attempt, and I struck back, and he went down, flat on his back.

My own more serious armament, such as it is, is always ready. When the brawl started, one of my opponents grabbed the bull by the horns, no doubt with the intention of tearing off my mask. What kind of shock he experienced when he discovered that the horns were of one piece with my skull, I do not know. Perhaps he was too far gone in wine to notice. I am no skilled fighter, but I am very strong, and my temper is not always mild. With an awkward heave of my bull's neck and shoulders I cast him loose, so that his body flew across the room, sweeping a table clean, reducing a chair beyond to kindling.

Someone else came at me with a weapon, and I saw the gleam of steel, but a young man whom I took to be a soldier, though now out of uniform, intervened on my side of the fight, helping to protect my companion. Clara, her mask dislodged in the scuffling, was huddling on the floor, trying to protect her head with folded arms. I hurled a chair at the man with the drawn knife, and he was seen no more.

"Call the Watch! Call the Watch!" First one voice, then three or four, were bawling.

The brawl had not become a general riot yet, but neither was it over. I realized that I had no choice but to flee, back to the Labyrinth. Quite possibly some of those in the room realized my true identity, but there was no general awareness, or alarm that the monster had actually come out. Those who screamed that they had seen the Minotaur were laughed to silence by others convinced that the witnesses had mistaken one of the cruder costumes for the real thing.

If this was the real world, I thought, I wanted no more of it. In my innocence I then imagined that I had really begun to understand what the real world was like.

After the figure in the monstrous costume had been driven out into the outer darkness, the young soldier Alex, who was in the room but taking no part in the fighting, recognized the slave-girl who served the princess that he worshipped from afar.

She had run out into the street, following the costumed Minotaur, and Alex ran out after her.

"Clara?"

The sound of her name stopped her in her tracks. She stood looking over her shoulder, waiting fearfully. In the distance sounded the whistles and rattles of the Watch. Alex knew he had a little time in which to act before they could arrive.

"You serve the Princess Ariadne, don't you? I've seen you with her more than once."

"Yes." Now Clara turned fully around.

"How lucky you are!"

"Why do you say that?"

"Why? Because—because you can be near her, every day."

The girl paused for what seemed a long time, as if she were unsure just what to make of that. At last she said: "Your name is Alex, is it not? A soldier of the Palace Guard."

"Yes." Then, as if involuntarily, the secret that had been poisoning him for half a year burst out. Still, his voice was so low that no one but the girl standing directly in front of him could hear. "Tell your mistress I must see her."

"Why?"

"There is something of great importance that she needs to know."

"What?"

"Something about her father, and the way he died."

"You must see her. Very well, I'll tell her that."

"And, slave-girl—repeat to no one else what I am telling you!"

Clara nodded, wide-eyed. The young soldier got the impression that what he had just said had frightened her, perhaps more than the fight itself.

———

Clara had already screamed, and run away in the direction of the palace. She had seen that I was loose, and knew I could certainly run fast enough to overtake her.

Some man with a loud voice was bellowing, "The Watch is coming. Look out for the Watch!"

I ran, my very manlike feet in sandals pounding the pavement in the direction where I had seen the young girl who was my escort disappear. I can move very quickly, and I had no fear that they would catch me, unless they came on cameloids.

How ironic it would be, I thought, if I became bewildered, lost my way in the city, and had to ask directions back to the Labyrinth. But once I was out in the street, I looked up to see the familiar stars and moon. They had followed me out of the Labyrinth as if they intended to stay with me, and now they were on hand to guide me home.

6

ON RETURNING TO the palace, the slave-girl Clara found, as she had expected, that her mistress was waiting up in their shared bedroom for her report on Asterion's adventure.

As Clara closed the door behind her, the Princess Ariadne pushed aside the small harp on which she had been practicing, and jumped to her feet. "What happened? Come in and tell me everything!" She blew out the single candle, leaving the room to the moonlight that entered by the high window.

With the doors closed, the two young women were as safe from being overheard as it was ever possible to be inside the palace. While discarding her costume and mask, Clara hastened to pass along what the young soldier had said to her in town.

Ariadne was immediately fascinated, but wary. "It couldn't be some kind of trap, could it?"

"I really don't see how, my lady. That would mean someone knew I was going to be there, and arranged for Alex to tell me what he did. But neither the Lord Asterion nor I were sure where we were going, until we were well on our way."

"Did anyone recognize him?"

"I really don't know, my lady. I couldn't tell. Many people looked at him strangely, of course . . ."

"Of course."

Quickly the princess decided to take the risk of arranging a secret meeting between herself and Alex, at a time when the young soldier would be off duty again, and might be expected to be in town enjoying himself.

"First we must find out when he will be off duty again."

"I expect I can easily do that," said Clara. "I know a certain corporal, who keeps track of the rosters."

———

A day later, Alex received a summons to a meeting, whispered to him by one of the greasy kitchen scullions, who managed to catch the soldier alone as he was leaving the small mess hall. For the next twenty-four hours his head was awhirl with the news that the princess wanted to see him. At the end of his next shift of guard, on being relieved from duty, instead of walking into town or back to the barracks, he made an excuse of weariness that separated him from his fellows.

Then, still in his workaday uniform though without armor and unarmed—only guards on duty were allowed to carry weapons inside the palace—he walked around the huge building, entering the grounds through a side entrance at a good distance from the barracks.

In the gardenlike expanse just inside the gated wall, he was met by Clara, dressed inconspicuously in ordinary servant's garb, who seemed to be waiting for him.

"Good day," Alex offered timidly.

"Good day to you, corporal."

"I'm only a private." His lack of any insignia of rank was plain enough.

Clara smiled faintly, and Alex supposed she had only been trying to flatter him a little. She said, "The princess is waiting for you. Come this way."

As he followed the slave girl, it occurred to Alex, not for the first time, that there must be many members of the royal household, even as he knew there were in the barracks, who loved the princess, though some of them had not cared for her father all that much. Certainly most of them cared even less for her ambitious uncle and his terrifying god. One thing Alex was sure of was that there could be none who loved the Princess Ariadne more than he.

Somewhat to his surprise, his guide led him not into one of the side doors of the palace itself, but in almost the opposite direction, along a small gravel path that curved across a corner of the parklike grounds. Now he could see that they were headed straight toward one edge of the mysterious Labyrinth, which here immediately adjoined the palace grounds. The Maze's outer wall of stone, tall and slightly curving, loomed up ominously ahead of them. Soldiers were warned frequently against ever entering that realm on their own.

"We are going there?"

His escort tried to be reassuring. "The princess goes into the Labyrinth almost every day. She's done so for a long time, and no one takes notice."

"Why does she go in every day?"

He expected to be told that what her royal highness did was none of his business. But Clara responded readily enough. "Mostly to see her brother."

Alex, like the great majority of the Corycan people, and of visitors to the island, had never set foot inside the Maze. What little he knew about it came almost entirely from the legends and the stories. It was a vast construction, sprawling over some four square miles. It was also the home of the legendary Minotaur, and the almost equally legendary Artisan, Daedalus—and rumor had it that for the last six months the god Shiva had also made the Labyrinth his chief place of residence.

At any given time there were sure to be two or three different rumors, stories, jokes, circulating in the barracks about the horrible monster who dwelt inside the Labyrinth—and two nights ago, in town, he had seen for himself someone, or something, who . . .

But it was going to take more than a Minotaur to frighten him when he had a chance to be of service to the princess.

Now the arched entrance to the great Maze was looming close ahead of them. "They say," said Alex to the slave girl, "that there are monsters here."

"People say many things that are sheer nonsense," Clara told him briskly. Without slowing her pace, she turned her head to give him a penetrating glance. "There is no monster in the Maze—unless perhaps you mean a certain god. The only mortal creature who lives there is the brother of the princess. You saw him the other night, when he was in costume."

"Yes. All right." Alex nodded. If the being he had encountered in town two nights ago was not to be considered monstrous, whether it was costumed or not . . . well, so be it.

He paused briefly, on the very threshold of the arched doorway. Ahead were blank walls, and a quick choice to be made of sudden turnings. "Is this the same part of the Maze where the people of the Tribute are being held?"

"No, they're over there." With a slight movement of her head the girl seemed to be indicating some other section of the Maze.

And even as she made that gesture, she went in. Alex followed, keeping close behind his guide, who led him first beneath a grating that striped the sky with iron bars. They turned right at the first branching of the passageway, then left at the second. In these early stages the passage between tall walls of smooth stone was so narrow that Alex walked with his elbows almost brushing on each side. Then abruptly the overhead grating was gone, but the way was wider, so wide that a man could not hope to climb by bracing himself between two walls.

Three more turns inside the Labyrinth, three choices of branching roofless corridors, brought Alex and his guide to a place where the walls opened out a little more, making a kind of narrow courtyard. The soldier felt his heart leap up inside his chest. The Princess Ariadne, today almost as plainly dressed as her servant, was seated there on a stone bench, waiting for him, while the afternoon sun awakened glories in her light brown hair.

Alex dropped to one knee on the pavement. This was the woman he had come to worship, helplessly, beginning on the first day he saw her. His escort had somehow vanished, and it came upon him with overwhelming force that now he and the Princess Ariadne were utterly alone, surrounded by the grotesque, curving pattern of the tall stone walls, as if this were only some fantastic daydream. Alex assumed that Clara had remained nearby somewhere, probably keeping watch to see that they were undisturbed.

"Your name is Alex?" Her voice was achingly familiar; of course he had heard her speak in public now and then.

"Yes, my princess!" For a moment he was afraid that the words were going to stick in his throat.

Of course she was not going to offer her hand to a mere private soldier. Her marvelous eyes were well-disposed toward him, but they were not patient. "Yes, I think I can remember seeing you on duty now and again, as a member of the Guard." She paused to draw a breath. "Last night you told my servant that you knew something about my father's death."

So, he had made some impression on her memory! The revelation was immensely heartening.

"Yes ma'am." In his own ears, every word he said sounded utterly stupid.

The eyes of the princess were not only kindly, but enormous. They were pools in which a man might lose his way forever. Under their gaze, Alex made two false beginnings to his story, tried a third time and was not doing well. Eventually she had to prompt him. "So you were there, in the great hall, on the night of my father's murder?"

"Princess, I was there. One of the men guarding the main door, when you came in."

"I remember only that there were some soldiers. Never mind, tell what you have to tell."

And Alex, with much sincere worship, finally told his story. It was not, of course, the version of events the general had forced upon all witnesses, but the version his own eyes had seen.

It needed a couple of minutes to stammer through. When Alex was done, and the eyes of the young woman before him were clenched in tears, he added, "Gracious lady, I am so sorry to reopen the wound . . ."

"The wound has never closed." She wiped her tears away, and in a few moments it was almost as if they had never been. She said to the young man before her, "I thank you with all my heart, for telling me the truth, when no one else has dared to do so. You may stand up. Yes, now I seem to remember seeing you in the great hall that night. I would like to give you a present to show my gratitude."

"All I want is the chance to serve you, Princess!"

"The gods know that I may call on you for help. But you should have something finer and more immediate than that." And, rising to her feet, she impulsively pulled a small medallion up on the golden chain by which it hung around her neck. It looked like a thin disk of gold, between two and three inches in diameter, one flat side welded somehow to a disk of silver of the exact same size. Both gold and silver circles bore in low relief an image of the sun, surrounded by intricate fine metalwork suggesting leaves and vines.

"Come closer," she commanded.

And when Alex had nervously edged closer, so close that he hardly dared to breathe, the princess reached out and with her own hands put the chain around his neck. On each side, her fingers touched his skin. "You will probably be safer if you wear it inside your shirt, where no one will notice."

Obviously she was not familiar with living conditions in the barracks; but Alex could not possibly have raised any objection at this point. "Yes, my lady."

Somewhere in the distance, probably in some remote portion of the palace grounds, one of the officers of the guard was shouting something at his men. The voice was a familiar sound, but at the moment it had nothing to do with Alex.

And now, having sealed his loyalty even more tightly than before, the princess insisted on his going over once more the events of that terrible night. This time she craved more details, in particular the identities of the other soldiers and servants who had been there at her father's death, and who had never come forward with the truth.

"You can give me their names, can you not?"

"I could, lady, and of course I will if you command it. But . . ." Alex slowly shook his head.

"Would any of them be willing now to tell me the truth, as you have done?"

"Great princess, I think that's very doubtful. I don't know about the servants, but I think that after what the general said to us, the other soldiers almost certainly will be too much afraid."

Suddenly Ariadne seemed to be really looking at him for the first time. "But you are not. You are willing to disobey orders, coming here and talking to me like this."

"Majesty, lady, for you—I would do anything. I . . ."

"I thank you again for your loyalty," said the princess, her attention sliding away from him again. Then her gaze shifted, sliding over Alex's shoulder to a point not far behind him.

He turned to see the Minotaur regarding him, standing on two human legs not ten feet away.

No trace remained of the facial paint the monster had worn two nights ago, so his head and face were even more inhuman than Alex remembered them. The loose garments of carnival costume were gone, the huge body clad in little more than a kilt, leaving the massive chest and shoulders exposed in their coating of short cattle-hair, in black and white. Here was the beast of legend, in the full light of day.

Ever since that night six months ago, when he had witnessed the arrival in the kingdom of two gods, Alex had been ready to accept, to believe in marvels when he saw them. Now his blood seemed to freeze in his veins. He couldn't interpret the expression on the Minotaur's face, if that inhuman countenance could be said to have an expression at all. Alex's first impulse was to reach for the sword he wasn't wearing, following an instinct to defend the princess.

If either the princess or the monster noticed the aborted movement of his arm, they paid it no attention. Instead they exchanged with each other a few words of almost casual conversation.

Then the terrible, frightening figure turned to Alex, and said in its strange voice, towering over him, "I am the Lord Asterion. We recently saw each other in town."

"Yes. Yes, lord."

"You have spoken to others about my presence there?"

"No . . . sir."

"If you would serve the Princess Ariadne, you will say nothing. About last night, or about this meeting here today."

"I will say nothing, Lord Asterion."

"Then you may go."

As soon as the soldier had been escorted away by Clara, Daedalus emerged from the place of concealment from which he had been watching, and bowed deeply before the princess. The slave-girl had kept him waiting until the coast was clear. Icarus had been left in the care of the woman who usually looked after him whenever his father was busy.

Ariadne wasted no time in getting to the point. "Theseus wants to meet you, Artisan—you know who Theseus is?"

Daedalus made a perfunctory bow. "Your brother has told me, my lady. Let me say that I advise against it, unless there is some reason stronger than mere curiosity. The fewer meetings we have, the less chance that anyone will suspect our plot. My suggestion is, let the Lord Asterion go back and forth, and act as go-between."

"That sounds wise," said Ariadne cautiously, and looked to her brother.

The horned head nodded in agreement. Then Asterion asked, "Daedalus, have you devised a means of escape we might all use?"

The Artisan cleared his throat, and spoke with modest satisfaction. "It was your mention of the deep-sea fish, my Lord Asterion, that gave me the essential clue."

"How is that?"

"They are a kind of fish who spend most of their lives in Poseidon's domain of deep salt water, but once or twice in their lives ascend fresh-water streams to spawn. Somehow those fish in what you call the Deep Pool must have got there by following an underground conduit, open only at intervals to light and air, all the way from the coast of the island to a place well within the Maze."

Having deduced this much by logic, Daedalus, bringing his son with him, had spent almost a full day following the hidden stream, down to within sight of the sea, and within the sound of its waves.

"It was not a very long walk—say three miles down to the sea, and three back—but over most of the distance it was not possible to move quickly."

Then Daedalus had warned his child fiercely to say nothing to anyone about having recently seen the sea.

"Why did you take the boy with you?" Ariadne asked curiously.

"Because, gracious princess, I thought it quite possible that I would not come back."

"I am not sure that I understand."

"I mean, my lady, that had I been able to pass one final obstacle on that day—and had my son and I been able to find a boat at the water's edge—and had we been willing to brave the sea alone—then I must admit to you, princess, that the two of us might have left this island forever behind."

"I see."

"But to obtain a suitable boat, or passage on a ship, we are almost certainly going to need help."

"That will not be impossible to arrange. But tell me, Daedalus, what is this 'final obstacle' you speak of?"

"My princess, with your permission, it will be easier if I show it to you when we reach it—if it is agreed that we are going." They both looked at Asterion, who nodded silently. "And rest assured that this time I will be prepared to overcome it."

"I see. Yes, I think that we are now agreed to go . . . I will speak for Theseus, since he cannot be here to speak for himself. Then the only remaining question seems to be, how are we to obtain a boat? No, I suppose there is one more: when we put out to sea, can we escape the patrols of my uncle's navy?"

She stood looking at the two men, and they at her. At last Ariadne added, "I must speak to Theseus about this."

7

IN THE EARLY evening of that same day, Ariadne and Theseus met secretly once more. Like all their other meetings, this one took place in a corner of a walled-off passageway of the Labyrinth, very close to the palace.

When communication by smuggled notes and surreptitious glances had advanced their relationship to the point where a place of rendezvous was certainly required, the princess had closed her eyes and taken thought, in the special way that had come to her as a legacy of her divine father. A familiar scene, recognizable to her as a portion of the Maze, had appeared as if it were a product only of her imagination. And in the scene there appeared two glistening parallel lines; the princess had been following those lines almost all her life, through one kind of imaged background or another, and they had never yet led her astray. As always, they reminded her of imaginary spiderwebs; and on this occasion the lines had run straight from just below her own eyes to the next corner of the Maze, where they took a sharp turn to the left. Ariadne had relaxed. From lifelong experience she knew that she had only to follow the two lines and they would almost infallibly lead her to the thing that she most wanted or needed at the moment—in this case, a place where she might meet in secrecy with her new lover.

It had needed no more than a trifling bribe to a sympathetic guard to enable Theseus to slip from one pocket of the Maze into another, out of sight of guards and of his fellow prisoners as well. So easily was it possible for him to leave behind the section in which the eighteen young people of the renewed Tribute were still confined, waiting to meet their doom in a few days.

On the following day the couple had met in the secret place again.

Since then, hardly a day had passed without a rendezvous. Today, as soon as Theseus saw her, he caught her in his arms, with princely boldness, and kissed her feverishly. So far, faced with the constant possibility of being observed, he had not attempted any further demonstration of his love.

How beautiful he was! Taller than any other man that Ariadne knew, her brother of course excepted. Her new lover's body, clad now in the special kilt and cape that all the young men of the Tribute had been given to put on, was fit to be that of a young god. A thick curl of golden beard adorned his square jaw.

In an urgent whisper, she told him, "It's been decided. You are going to escape, and I am coming with you, and so are several others."

He heaved a sigh, as if a large weight had just dropped from his shoulders. Then he asked, in his usual quiet voice, "Others of the Tribute?"

"No! It won't be possible to get them all away. You must say nothing to them."

Immediately Theseus was suspicious. "Who is coming with us, then?"

"One is Daedalus—you've heard of him?"

"I think that everyone in the world has heard of Daedalus. And most people know that he has come to Corycus to work for the new king."

"Yes. And now he has his own reasons for wanting to escape my uncle, and this island. Also, he has discovered a way by which we can reach the seacoast."

Still her lover's suspicions were not entirely allayed. "How?"

"Daedalus doesn't want to say, until the day comes. Probably that's wise, and I believe him."

"Then when are we going? How will it be arranged?"

Ariadne lowered her voice to an even softer whisper. "We are going to depart, from somewhere near the very middle of the Labyrinth, on the very morning, the very hour, when the sacrifice is scheduled to take place."

Obviously Theseus did not understand. "In broad daylight? Why then?"

"Because Asterion—he's my brother, and he's coming with us too, at least I think he is—has learned in a dream that that will be the best time."

Theseus was obviously not impressed by such a revelation. "Are we to be controlled by our dreams, then? Shall I tell you what mine was last night?"

But the princess lifted her chin and defended it. "My brother's dreams are as different from those of most men as his body is from theirs. As I believe Daedalus when he says the thing is possible, so I believe Asterion."

When her lover saw how serious she was, he did not press the argument. But he had more questions. "And how am I to get free? Somehow I must reach the starting point of this secret route that Daedalus has discovered."

Ariadne grabbed up one of his big hands and kissed it. "All these details will be worked out. We will meet in a certain place, inside the Maze. Those who do not already know the way will be guided when the time comes."

"Fine. Reasonable, I suppose. And then—?"

"Daedalus has not revealed the details of his route yet. When the day has come, and we are all together, he will show it to us."

The prince still brooded, not quite satisfied. He took a pace or two, all that the confined space would allow, and then came back to her. "And this is all you can tell me now?"

"It's all I know, my love. Many details must still be worked out, of course. If you don't want to trust Daedalus, can you come up with a better idea? He seems to be a good man, and he wants to escape almost as much as we do."

Theseus had no concrete suggestions of better ways to offer. He kissed her, and said, "I am a stranger on this island. If it were up to me to plan an escape, I'd be at a dead loss. If you trust Daedalus, I will too."

"Good." Then a shade of new concern grew in Ariadne's face. "How is it with you, among the other prisoners? Are the others . . . ?"

"Are they what? Trying to escape? No. Terrified? They really don't seem to be." Theseus shook his head. In a different tone he said, "The truth is that I don't understand them. Even if I had not found you—"

"Don't say that, dear."

"Oh, my darling! . . . But my point is that no matter what, I would still be trying to get away. Making some kind of effort. What I can't understand is that none of my fellow inmates seem to care a fig for their own lives. It's beyond me—having been told that they are doomed, they accept the judgment without a murmur. They've given up and said good-bye to the world. Well, I haven't."

"I should hope not." Ariadne snuggled into the curve of her prince's arm, which seemed to soften to accommodate her. "I suppose they think it hopeless to struggle against a god—or even against my uncle. Still, I worry that your absence will be noticed, when you come here to meet me."

"I really don't think we need worry much about that. It's not as if all eighteen of us were being kept in a single room. No one is taking roll call every hour. One of Shiva's priests does that, usually only once a day."

Theseus went on to describe the interior layout of the quarters he shared with the seventeen others of the Tribute. Ariadne had not seen that portion of the Labyrinth since it was partitioned off from the rest. The young people of the Tribute were rarely all in sight of one another at the same time—in fact no one room of their quarters was big enough to hold them all. The section in which they were confined was in itself a maze of narrow passages and small compartments. Here and there draperies had been hung, affording some measure of privacy.

The captives were being well fed, provided with wine and certain pleasant drugs, allowed and even encouraged to spend their time amusing themselves with each other's bodies, or with the entertainers who were brought in from time to time.

The princess was relieved that her lover was not being cruelly treated. But at the same time she was vaguely perturbed. "What luxury! Of course I hope you have no interest in the others' bodies."

"Of course I do not! Believe me, dear one, from the moment I laid eyes on you . . ."

When another prolonged kiss had been concluded, Ariadne said: "I am relieved. Somehow, though I should have known better, I was picturing a kind of dimly lighted dungeon. Rats, and dirt . . ."

"Not at all. It seems that nothing is too good for those who are to be blessed by Shiva."

The princess winced, and her voice dropped. "Have you caught a glimpse of my uncle's god yet? I have seen him only a couple of times."

"No, the Lord Shiva has not honored us poor folk of the Tribute with his presence," Theseus observed dryly. He paused, then added, "Nor have I yet been able to speak to your uncle the king."

That made the princess blink. "Why should you expect to be able to do that?"

Theseus drew a deep breath, like a man coming to a decision. "I didn't say anything to you about it, not wanting to cause you extra worry, but—many days ago, I sent a message to King Perses—addressing him as King Minos of course—saying I was willing to act as go-between in arranging an alliance between him and my father. On the condition, naturally, that my life should be spared, and I released."

Ariadne's eyes widened in surprise, and she held her breath. "And what did Uncle say?"

"Nothing at all; at least I have received no answer. I suppose the new Minos—no, I really shouldn't call him that—I suppose your uncle doesn't trust me. I'd be a fool to rely on any promise he might make. Not that he's likely to make any."

Ariadne said impulsively, "I will go to him, and plead for your life."

Theseus was shaking his head slowly. His face was grim. "I don't think so, princess. I believe we ought to rely on some other means, more dependable than your uncle's word—even assuming that you could persuade him to give his word. No, I'd much rather trust the plans of the clever Daedalus. Your pleading should be kept as a last desperate resort."

After that the couple tried to work out some of the details of the effort they were soon to make.

The princess said, "Daedalus swears that he can somehow lead us all the way to the seashore, with little danger of discovery. But after that of course we'll need a ship."

Her lover was listening intently, squinting with an effort at concentration. "To what point on the shore is he going to lead us? There are hundreds, maybe thousands, of miles of coastline on this island, taking into account all the inlets and promontories."

"I don't know where, but I'll find out."

Ariadne told Theseus she was going to smuggle a message out to certain sailors, men who had remained loyal to the memory of her father. The new king was feared and obeyed, but he was not enormously popular among the people.

But Theseus assured her that it would be much easier for him than for her to summon ships and sailors to their aid, provided her secret allies could get a message out for him. He felt confident of being able to communicate with seamen who would be loyal to him. Vaguely he spoke of elements of his father's navy.

"In fact," he added, "I had better give you the message now. Take this." And he slipped from one of his big fingers a distinctive ring. It was of bronze, thought Ariadne, of little intrinsic worth, but curiously wrought. "So my friend will believe it truly comes from me." He gave her also the name of a man in the city ("he is one of my father's agents") who would pass it on.

The name of the ultimate recipient meant nothing to Ariadne, and she commented on the fact.

Theseus shrugged. "There's no reason why it should. It's only a kind of code word. He is really an officer in my father's navy."

The princess was daring, but seldom careless, and she wanted to make sure that the whole escape effort was as solidly organized as possible. "How many will we be, then, besides you and myself?"

"Is Princess Phaedra coming too?" her lover asked.

"No." Ariadne answered calmly, but without hesitation. "I know my sister, and she will not leave the island. She would see running away as deserting her suffering people. Besides, Phaedra is one of those people who become transparent whenever they try to keep a secret—everyone who looks at her can see at once that something is amiss. No, she mustn't even suspect what we are doing."

"All right. I leave your sister to you. Not that I have any choice about it."

"Fine. Let me see, where were we? You and I, and Asterion, if he will come with us, makes three."

Ariadne's lover raised a golden eyebrow in a perfect curve. "Will your brother be willing to leave the Labyrinth?"

"I don't know, but of course I have offered him the chance, and he hasn't yet said no. And Daedalus, who will be our necessary guide, makes four—and little Icarus, five. I'm sure the father has no intention of leaving the son behind."

Theseus nodded thoughtfully. Then he suggested, "What about this soldier—you say his name is Alex?—the one who confirmed the manner of your father's death. How deeply involved is he in the plan?"

"Quite deeply, now."

"Then I think he should join our party too. Or at least it would be wiser for us not to leave him behind, alive. Now that he knows so much of our plans."

Ariadne tossed back her hair with a decisive motion. "That makes sense. Say half a dozen, then. And we should also add my personal attendant, for the same reason. Clara will make seven. That is a lucky number, is it not?"

"A large number, to keep anything a secret. But it seems we don't have much choice."

———

The couple's talk moved on, to the things that would have to be managed at the last moment. Ariadne had learned, and now warned her lover, that the maidens and youths were to be given a slow-acting poison, in a ritual cup, just before they were led deeper into the Maze, and to their deaths. "A few hours later they will all be dead. They will disappear from the world forever, and their fate will of course be blamed upon the Monster."

Just at sunrise on the chosen day, the eighteen were to be guided, by priests of Shiva and a detachment of the Palace Guard, to a spot near the center of the Labyrinth. "It's only a short distance from where Daedalus is working, and he says that a crew of maintenance workers from the palace are building a kind of holding pen. Some of the walls of the Labyrinth have been knocked down to make an open space."

"What method is to be used to take our lives?"

The princess had heard rumors about that, but it was not the kind of thing she wanted to mention to her lover. "It's not going to happen to you. It's not!"

"Of course not." And Theseus patted her arm. "Now, while we have the chance, let us try to consider some of the details. Where things might possibly go wrong."

"Of course."

"But before we get into that—I've wondered, how does your uncle plan to explain to the world what he is doing with the people sent to him as tribute?"

"From what I hear, the world had already given them up for lost. As for my uncle, he sees no reason why a king has to explain anything. Dear, what will you do when they hand you a poisoned cup and order you to drink?"

Theseus shrugged impatiently. "I can manage that somehow. I might just pretend to drink the stuff. Hold it in my mouth and spit it out, it can't be instant death, if they mean to march us a mile after we drink. Or, if you can find out what the poison is, it might be possible to get an antidote—but that's even chancier. I hope we can get away before that moment comes."

He went on to relate to Ariadne a rumor that had been allowed to spread among the victims themselves: Minos secretly hoped to create from these fine specimens of mainland youth the nucleus of a legion of powerful and fiercely loyal warriors, with the girls of course destined to be the mothers of warriors. With such a legion he hoped to be able to conquer the world.

Ariadne's eyes were wide. "Do you believe that?"

Theseus shook his head. "Frankly, no. There are few of the other intended victims that I would choose as fighters."

Another tale that had gained some currency was that the youths and maidens were simply to serve for a year as attendants in a temple, containing the altar of some god whose help Minos considered vital, perhaps Mars, or Hermes; and after that the eighteen would be returned safely to their homes.

"Maybe some of the seventeen others have swallowed that one," Theseus speculated. "That might account for their complacency."

Ariadne was shaking her head slowly. Her voice was more frightened than he had heard it yet. "The truth is, of course, that Shiva wants you, and the others."

"To be his servants?" The question was asked in mockery.

She answered solemnly. "He wants you to walk the road that so many slaves and prisoners have already traveled in the last few months—in the form of sacrifice."

The prospect did not seem to disturb the youth unduly. "But why? I don't doubt what you say, everything points to it—but still it puzzles me."

"Why does any god want sacrifice? And yet almost all of them seem to find it pleasing."

My horns rather limit the number and kind of positions in which it is possible for me to sleep. When I, the Minotaur, awakened, I was exactly where I had lain down, in a certain small plaza of the Labyrinth where I liked to sleep in the warm weather. My big body was suspended in a hammock I had tied up between two trees, within a ring of murmuring fountains. I lay in a curved position, clasped hands under one cheek, supporting my head.

I, Asterion, slept and dreamt deeply, for several nights before the morning on which the great sacrifice was scheduled to take place—I experienced vivid dreams, in which my spirit wandered far abroad, over sea as well as land.

When asleep, I can sometimes gain ready access to the minds of others, through the medium of dreams, my own and theirs. I can sometimes exert considerable influence upon my fellow dreamers, often without the subject suspecting the presence of an intruder. In a lifetime of such nocturnal wandering, out of my misshapen body, I have had many strange encounters, some of them with figures that I gradually began to recognize as gods.

As the day of sacrifice and escape approached, I was not certain yet whether I would be one of the fugitives. But in any case my sister and her party were certainly going to require a ship.

Ships were virtually always in the control of men. Sending my dreaming spirit drifting out from the Labyrinth, out from the island, over the waves, through the breezes of a spring night, I posed the question to the universe, or perhaps it was only to myself: *Where is the man I have to find?*

Tonight the beauty of the sea had no attraction; my thought was too much concentrated upon our needs. But I knew it was on the sea that I must search. At last my search was rewarded, a good contact established with the dreaming captain of a small merchant ship.

The detachment of the Palace Guard who were detailed to watch the youths and maidens of the Tribute took head counts only casually and sporadically, generally leaving that business to the priests of Shiva, who took them about once a day. The portion of the Maze in which the youths and maidens were confined was only casually sealed off from the rest—none of the victims seemed inclined to try to escape. And, after all, where would they possibly go, with the wide ocean between them and their homes? The two doors which had been cut into the old walls to connect their quarters with the outside world were steadily if not very intensely guarded.

From time to time the young soldier called Alex the Half-Nameless, like many of the other men in his barracks, pulled a shift of guard duty at one of those portals.

There Alex was able to observe, to his relief, that most of the guards were deployed on the wrong side of the people they were trying to guard. The escape plan, as it had been stealthily conveyed to Alex, in bits and pieces by the slave-girl Clara, did not require Theseus to break out into the palace grounds. Rather he was to accompany the others of the Tribute on their forced march deeper into the Labyrinth. Ariadne's lover was a superb athlete, and, as he assured her, confident that he could get right over the wall, at a certain point she had described to him in detail, where the barrier was no more than about ten feet high. All he would need was a moment or two to prepare himself, and a little space in which to run and jump. Alex himself, along with the princess Ariadne and Clara, would be waiting on the other side, ready to lead Theseus away to join the others who were taking part in the escape.

Before the time arrived, the plan had been worked out in some detail. The planners, chiefly Daedalus and the princess, were proud of their achievement. If all went well, it seemed entirely likely that seven people were going to vanish as if the earth had swallowed them up.

━━━━━━━

In the course of their secret meetings, Theseus several times expressed to Ariadne his admiration for the famous Daedalus, and said he looked forward to meeting the Artisan. Theseus was also intrigued by the participation of the Minotaur, whom he had not yet seen, and he questioned Ariadne about her brother.

"So, he eats no meat at all? Then it's a pretty good joke to think that all these people are supposed to be somehow devoured by him. He eats no meat, can't handle wine, and goes to bed with no one. And we are all supposed to be terrified of this—cow."

Ariadne's face suddenly looked swollen around the eyes, and her voice quavered. "Asterion is my brother. He is placing his own life at risk to help you get away."

Theseus looked at her, and something altered in his face. "I am sorry." The words had a sound of beautiful sincerity.

When they had kissed again, Ariadne observed, "I don't suppose the Lord Shiva is really going to eat seventeen people either. Is he?"

"Not exactly." At the moment, Theseus wasn't much interested in Shiva. "But tell me more about Asterion. I'm sorry I spoke rudely about him, I didn't understand. Is he really a child of Zeus? And does he really have prophetic dreams? And what is his contribution to the escape plan going to be? Apart from dreams, I mean."

Her response was sharp. "He is as much a child of Zeus as I am. Asterion is my brother, and to me he seems . . . almost ordinary, despite his strange appearance. And don't laugh at his dreams. Over the years he has told me many wonderful things, gathered in his own dreams and those of other people."

The young man smiled faintly. "I think it is your dreams that interest me more than his."

"I would like to hear about what you do in the land of Oneiros, when you sleep," Ariadne breathed.

"And I of your adventures there."

"And I will tell you of them."

Theseus said intensely, "What I would really love, is to lie beside you as you dream."

Fiercely Ariadne squeezed his hand. "I, too, desire that very much, my love," she whispered. "And it will come about, I promise."

"I believe you."

Moving back half a step, she drew a deep breath. "As to how my brother will help you, on the day of the escape, that depends. If I should be delayed for any reason, he will appear when you need a guide. You can trust him with your life."

"I am trusting him with your life, too. And to me that is infinitely more valuable than my own."

"Oh, love!"

8

SEVERAL DAYS BEFORE the sacrifice of the Tribute was scheduled to take place, the priest Creon had approached the Princess Ariadne quietly and discreetly, conveying to her official notice of just where and when the ceremony was to be conducted. The ceremony would definitely not be open to the public. It would take place in the presence of a select few witnesses, in the assured privacy of a certain restricted domain within the Labyrinth, and not far from its center. At Shiva's orders a new ritual site had already been created there, by flattening and removing some of the old walls across a circle about a hundred feet in diameter. A semicircular viewing stand had been erected in about half of the cleared space, and an elaborate stage upon the other half.

Creon, obviously enamored of his subject, seemed about to go into greater detail, when the Princess Ariadne interrupted to make it plain that whatever the arrangements were, she had no intention of attending.

The priest had obviously expected that response. "Your uncle and I assumed that that would be your attitude, your royal highness." And he seemed content to let the matter go at that.

But now that the subject of Tribute and human sacrifice had been raised, Ariadne was not going to let it pass without further comment. She said, "You are going to murder people, to please your damned new god, and it is a foul and vicious business."

At that the high priest managed to look pained and shocked. "If I may say so, highness, that is not a very constructive attitude to take. It is even rather dangerous. Our lord Shiva has graciously consented to accept the offering of our most royal king, your uncle."

"Since you use the form of asking my permission, no, you may not say so. What kind of god is it who demands an offering of human lives? What kind of king, who struggles to provide it?"

Creon's countenance seemed to have become a mask. He bowed slightly, and silently took himself away.

━━━━━━━━

The morning on which the sacrifice of the Tribute was scheduled to take place dawned clear across the island of Corycus, on a day that promised to be very warm for spring.

Ariadne had given everyone to understand that on this morning she would be visiting her brother, as she often did, in some remote portion of the Maze.

She and Clara were just about to depart when the princess Phaedra was announced. Phaedra had come unattended, paying an unusual visit to her younger sister's room. "Have you heard what kind of sacrifice is to be performed?"

Ariadne was eager to get rid of the unexpected visitor, without arousing her suspicions. "Of course. I have even been officially invited to attend it—haven't you?"

"I have." Phaedra shivered. "But of course I am not going."

"Nor am I."

━━━━━━━━

Meanwhile the slave-girl Clara was standing by, trying to conceal her nervousness, watching and listening to the conversation, but taking little part. None of the Princess Phaedra's personal attendants were granted anything like the freedom of speech and action that Clara generally enjoyed in the company of her own mistress.

Now Ariadne was saying, "Today's will not be the first human sacrifice Shiva has claimed here in our homeland."

"I know that. There have been prisoners, slaves—"

"Do you know who the first one was?" the younger sister interrupted. She paused briefly for effect, before adding, "Our father, Minos."

Phaedra was aghast. She had to admit that the suspicion had crossed her mind, but until now she had been inclined to give their uncle the benefit of the doubt.

When she stammered some remark along this line, the younger woman quickly cut her down. "Nonsense. Perses killed his brother." Ariadne spoke with firm conviction.

"Why do you say that?"

"Because I know it to be true."

"But *how* do you know—? No, don't tell me!" Phaedra paced nervously among the feminine furnishings of the room. She glanced several times at her sister, who continued to regard her silently.

At last the elder sister stopped her pacing. "I must think deeply about this."

"I wish you would."

"We must not—not take any hasty action. I must consider all these things, very carefully."

"Yes, I agree. Oh, if you are concerned about Clara here, you need not be. I trust her with my life."

The older princess knew that well enough, and was not worried about Clara. She was thinking again of the ceremony of sacrifice, due to get under way in less than an hour. She said, "I will not attend any such horrible event. What is our uncle thinking of?"

"What he's usually thinking of—his own power. I suppose he will not be satisfied until he rules the world, may the gods forbid that ever happening." Ariadne paused, then added deliberately, "That is why he killed his brother."

Phaedra turned pale, and this time involuntarily glanced toward Clara. Again she said, "We must talk of this later."

"You keep telling me that, Phaedra. Yes, I agree, we must."

For a moment Phaedra seemed on the brink of breaking down, under the weight of confirmed suspicions. "Ariadne, what can we do?"

"At the moment, nothing."

"But who is going into the Labyrinth today, to watch this horror? Ariadne, I have sent our uncle word that I am indisposed and will not be there. Will you stay with me this morning?"

"Today there are reasons why I must be elsewhere," the younger told her tenderly.

"Reasons? What reasons?"

"I have promised Asterion."

"Oh." Phaedra never spoke of her half-brother in the Labyrinth, much less went to see him. And the sisters embraced and kissed each other, a rare occurrence with them.

One of the regular household servants now appeared on schedule, ready to serve the usual morning tea.

But Phaedra protested that she was too upset to think of tea, or any other food or drink. Moments later she had taken herself away.

"Thank all the gods," Ariadne murmured when her sister was gone, and the innocent servant too. "She dawdled until I feared that she would make us late. Clara, see that you have good sturdy sandals on. Beyond that, we dare not make any preparations."

"I have, my lady."

Clara and her mistress had already put on their ordinary clothes.

As the princess looked down from her window, only the leaves of nearby treetops prevented her seeing into the section of the Labyrinth where the young people of the Tribute were being held.

What might have been the entire crew of odylic priests and wizards who attended the new king and his strange god, perhaps a dozen men in all, were busy arranging and decorating a table in one of the larger plazas of the Labyrinth, an open space that served the captive youths and maidens as a kind of common room. Two or three sections of wall had been taken down, enlarging the plaza by converting sections of several passageways into a single open space.

Ariadne could not exactly see just what the servants of Destruction might be doing down there, chanting as they did so. But it was an easy guess that they were drugging the wine which was to be ritually served to the victims just before the young people were led off to their doom, in another recently created plaza perhaps a mile away.

Ariadne looked sharply at Clara, who was now visibly trembling. "Do calm down. You're as nervous as my sister."

"Yes, my lady."

Then she asked Clara, "Did you hear anything in the room last night? See anything?" For about a month now the princess had addressed those same questions to her servant almost every morning—and on the few mornings when she failed to do so, Clara had asked them of her. The ritual of questioning had been going on ever since one memorable night when the suite of rooms shared by the two young women had been plagued with a mysterious flurry of strange midnight whisperings. The unintelligible voices, coming from no visible sources, had been mixed with other sounds, hard to identify but suggestive of small objects being moved about.

On the following night, similar phenomena had taken place. Each occasion, both occupants of the room had arisen, Ariadne from her huge canopied bed, Clara from her cot nearby, and had consulted in whispers as to whether they should call the guard. But neither young woman put much trust in the guard, since their uncle had taken over. Neither mistress nor servant had been molested in any way, and a careful inspection of the contents of the rooms by daylight showed nothing was missing.

On the second night of the strange visitation, which had turned out to be the last, Ariadne had dreamt, or thought she dreamt, of a shadowy figure bending over her in her bed. But in the morning her jewelry—

quite a modest collection for a Corycan princess—lay in its strongbox undisturbed, and the gold and silver medallion, the gift of Daedalus, still hung on its fine chain round her neck, lying just above and between her breasts.

"I heard nothing last night, my lady," Clara said now. "I saw nothing." For almost a month, inhuman intruders had been as totally absent as any of the human kind.

"Do you suppose anything of the kind has been happening to my sister?"

"I doubt it, my lady. Today would have been the Princess Phaedra's chance to tell you all about it. And . . ."

"And she probably would have done so, had there been anything to tell. But she said nothing."

The princess and her slave-girl had both felt confident from the start that at least the trespasser, if there really had been one, had not been Shiva. The thought of an unknown power was somewhat disturbing; but whatever it might be, they feared it less than they did the one which now had the kingdom in its grip.

Now, on the morning of the Tribute, Ariadne put the matter of strange intrusions completely out of her mind, and looked out of the window again. She breathed a prayer to her favorite goddess, Artemis— and then to be on the safe side, she added silent pleas to Athena and Aphrodite.

He was down there; and she was going to save him.

On that morning of mixed omens, good and bad, I, Asterion, awoke somewhat earlier than usual, my sleep having been tortured by strenuous and disturbing dreams. These were only partially concerned with the escape plan, in which my personal part was simple. Because of my own uncertainty as to whether I was really going to escape or not, I had been assigned no duties in the way of helping others.

I opened my eyes about half an hour before dawn, when certain stars, and a single planet, that I could interpret as favorable omens, were still visible. The Morning Star, that humans have sometimes identified in a mystic way with the Goddess of Love, was plain in the slowly brightening sky. But Venus had nothing to say to me.

Much, much closer to where I lay, but still at a considerable distance, I could hear loud chanting from the priests of Shiva, and I muttered useless curses under my breath.

My slumber had been fairly long, and my body should have been rested, though my mind had labored even while I slept, but in fact even my flesh and bones felt tired. Near the middle of the night, in a determined search for allies, helpers, wherever I could find them, I had once more visited the dreams of a certain seafaring man named Petros, the captain of a small trading ship, and had reinforced the message I had conveyed to him on the previous night, and also on the night before that.

Now I knew, in the effortless way one knows such things in dreams, that Petros, still at sea and many miles distant, was the one I needed to accomplish the second stage of the escape. With what seemed to me the willing assistance of Oneiros—though I was aware of no direct contact with the God of Dreams—I had planted in the trader captain's mind the vision of a particular swampy cove, at only a few miles' distance down the coast from the main Corycan harbor.

Then, in the hour before waking, when come some of the clearest visions, I had dreamt, involuntarily and quite naturally as it seemed, about the coming into my world of the eighteen young folk from the mainland. It was an ambiguous perception, which I took to indicate that the impact of the business of the Tribute on my life was going to be so violent that there could be no certainty about my future for a long time afterward.

Uncertainty was rising about me like a sea. I was not to be left simply to manage my own affairs. Once I had pledged to Ariadne that I would do all I could to make sure that Theseus escaped, she had taken me at my word and begun to assign me tasks. When the ceremony began, I was to be in a place from which I could watch the sacrifice itself—just in case the inconceivable should have happened, and at that point Theseus was still penned in with the other prisoners. Then it would be up to me to somehow contrive to set him free.

And in the back of my mind I was somehow satisfied that I would be able to witness the horror, or part of it at least. Not, of course, that I expected to derive any kind of pleasure from the sight; rather, Shiva's worshipers had contrived so egregious an evil that I dared not turn my back on it, and feared to let it out of my sight.

On the morning of the sacrifice, shortly after the sun came up, the youths and maidens of the Tribute were thrust into the great Maze and began to tread the path marked through its windings, I, Asterion, was actually somewhat more than a mile away, the distance measured as a bird might fly, or the sound of a scream might carry. They could be singing at the top of their lungs as they marched, and banging drums, and I would never hear them. There might well be a thousand miles of twisted passageways between us.

I wondered what the young folk might be saying to one another, as they talked among themselves on this last morning of their lives. Probably nothing that made sense, after the massive doses of drugs they had ingested. With Theseus, I marveled at their passivity. And what fears they did have were all of harmless shadows, and would be as useless as their songs. As they walked, or danced, or were dragged unthinkingly to their doom, some of them at least would be looking over their shoulders to see if I was about to pounce on them from behind.

I might easily enough have probed their dreams during the night just past, and discovered their secret thoughts during the last sleep of their lives. But that was something I preferred not to know.

And now it was time for me to close off my mind from the realm of dreams. Today's issues were going to be decided in the less manageable world that men and women call reality. Before setting out I breakfasted, forcing my stomach to accept more than it really wanted, not knowing when my next meal might be. I picked up and weighed in one hand a small pack I had prepared. At that moment, I was still uncertain whether I might today be leaving forever the Labyrinth, my lifelong home. After a few moments' indecision I left the pack behind, telling myself I would have time to come back for it later.

As I had expected, I found Daedalus and Icarus waiting in the spot designated for our rendezvous, close by what the Artisan called the Deep Pool.

As soon as I appeared, the small boy jumped to his feet. His father, almost literally pouncing on me, demanded, "Have you seen the princess this morning? She has not changed her mind?"

"I assume you mean Ariadne. I have not seen her, but she will not change her mind in this. Today is the day when Theseus must either escape or die, and I think my sister will die rather than be separated from her lover."

"And you are coming with us, Asterion? I don't see the pack you spoke of bringing."

"There will be time for me to get it."

Having, as I thought, a little time to spare, I briefly joined father and son in their silent vigil. We all three sat waiting for the princess and her servant and her lover, and for the young soldier who was also supposed to attach himself to our party. Icarus fidgeted, so that peri-

odically his father scowled and muttered at him. Daedalus had packed
a very few things, which he carried in a small pouch or wallet secured
to his belt.

The place where we were waiting was half a mile from the center
of the Maze, and a somewhat greater distance from the small area where
the youths and maidens were confined.

Daedalus was unarmed as usual, except for the plain knife, more
tool than weapon, that he habitually carried at his belt. He explained to
me that he had been up through much of the night preparing a balloon,
and getting the feathers ready.

I doubted that I had heard his speech correctly. "Did you say 'a
balloon'? What are we to do with a balloon, and feathers?"

"Nothing. Oh, I didn't tell you about that, did I?"

"No."

"It is a matter of misdirection." He went on to describe, in the gray
predawn light, how the balloon, stitched together from some kind of
treated fabric, would be released by a timing device of his invention,
just as the escape was getting under way. How the flying machine once
launched, sustaining itself in the air, would automatically drop the false
clues of feathers, and so on, even as the wind carried it out to sea. "With
any luck, they will think we have escaped in a balloon. That I have
fashioned wings."

"Well . . ."

"They will, depend upon it." Now it was the Artisan's turn to look
me over. "You are unarmed, Asterion?"

"Not really." And I moved my head slightly, so that the sharp tips
of the two horns drew circles in the air.

The father nodded grimly. His whole bearing was tense, and the
look around his eyes indicated that he had slept but little. The son, who
today was also wearing a small knife on his small belt, was fretting at
not being allowed to roam as usual. But Icarus was old enough to understand that today they were going to leave Crete.

"Where are we going, Father?"

The answer was a growl. "Haven't I told you not to talk about it,
before we start? We'll see where we're going when we get there. It'll
be another island, or maybe the mainland."

I, Asterion, had but little time to visit them this morning.

You must also understand a thing that seemed impossible for anyone else on the island to realize: that although I had spent something
like fifteen years inside the Labyrinth, almost my entire life, there were
still many passageways—by my best estimate, hundreds of miles of
them—within that marvelous creation that I had never seen, at least

with waking eyes. I had heard that some foolish folk now ascribed its construction entirely to Daedalus.

I mentioned that idea to him, on the morning when we waited to escape. The Artisan himself smiled at the thought, even in the midst of his fretting about today's desperate adventure. No more than a tiny portion of the Maze could possibly have been his doing, and in fact he had not built any of it at all.

"The work of Hephaestus, then?"

"I think not; I have seen some of the divine Smith's constructions, and they are marvelous. Looking at them, one understands what it means, or ought to mean, to be a god." Daedalus shook his head, and his voice dropped. "But the Labyrinth is not particularly marvelous, except by reason of sheer size."

"Really? There, Artisan, I might disagree with you for once. Consider the strangeness which lies at its center."

"If you include that, yes, of course. I am already dizzy from months of considering it."

I was talking to Daedalus, as we waited for a little time to pass, while Icarus lingered nearby, playing some private game that involved hopping on one foot—I noticed that he, like his father, was now wearing sandals—alternately fretting and trying to come to grips with the sudden changes in his childish world. It seemed we were all of us as ready as we could be to set our rescue/escape plan in motion.

Eventually I had to admit that it was time for me to perform that certain thing I had promised my sister I would do. Ariadne had not been able to rid herself of the idea that Theseus might need help to get away. I was more inclined to credit her forebodings, because dreams had warned me that a great chance of difficulty lay there. On this morning I felt some concern also for the young soldier who was to join in the escape, for in the normal course of events he would have less freedom of movement than any of the rest of us, except perhaps for the prisoner Theseus.

But it was not, of course, the soldier's fate that concerned Ariadne. She had asked me to go to the very scene of the ceremony, because nothing must prevent Theseus from escaping.

9

DAYS AGO, ALEX the Half-Nameless had told Clara what the duty roster showed his assignment would be on the morning of the escape—interior guard. That meant a comfortable station inside the palace. This considerably simplified the secret arrangements being made for the escape.

The next time Clara saw Alex she informed him of the details of the plan as they concerned him: When, on the fateful morning, the princess Ariadne left her rooms on her way to the rendezvous, with Clara at her side, they would keep an eye out for Alex as they passed the various guard stations. When the princess saw him, she would simply and openly beckon him to come along.

Alex nodded. "Yes, I see. That should work." There was nothing very unusual about a soldier being summoned by a member of the royal family or some high official, to perform some chore, undertake an errand, sometimes to administer punishment to an erring slave or servant. It seemed highly unlikely that anyone who saw Alex walk away in obedience to Ariadne's summons would pay much attention. With the exception of a few key locations in the palace, there was no very rigid requirement that men on interior guard remain precisely at their posts at all times.

And at last that dawn arrived, in the light of which all their fates were to be decided.

Alex had not slept much during the night. He awakened in his bunk a little before dawn, as he did on almost every morning of his life—the sergeant saw to that. Around him his comrades were likewise launched on their regular morning routine, groaning and farting and complaining of tiredness, grabbing for their garments and weapons. Despite efforts at disciplined cleanliness, a vague stink hung in the air, the result of too many men in too little space. Amid the predawn grouching, grumbling and scratching in the dim and crowded barracks, the only men excused from duty today were those few who had manned guard posts through the night.

As usual he had taken off his clothes before rolling into his bunk, but this morning, as on other recent mornings, no one appeared to notice the gold and silver medallion that for the past few days he had been wearing around his neck. Alex had hoped and expected that that might be the case, because at least half the men wore some kind of charm or amulet, and many were of metal that resembled gold or silver.

Around him now, some of the men were muttering prayers to various gods, Mars—whose other name was Ares—and Priapus being the most popular. Several soldiers were conducting a variety of small rituals, some rubbing their amulets or breathing on them. Traffic to and from the latrine was busy as usual.

"You look a little worn this morning, Al." This was Sarpedon, who slept in the next bunk, a tall young soldier with curly dark hair and a world-weary look that belied his village background.

"I'm not a short-termer like you, Sarp." Sarpedon had only six months to go on his enlistment.

The other nodded. "Can't wait to get out."

"What'll you do when you get home?" Everyone in the barracks knew that Sarpedon was looking forward to returning to his home on the northern coast of Corycus.

Rummaging in his duffel bag for a clean shirt, Sarpedon mumbled something.

Though every move Alex made on this morning was routine, for him today everything looked and sounded different. Every commonplace detail stood out with eerie clarity, as things did sometimes when he had a fever. Consumed with worry, more for the princess than for himself, he had been unable to sleep much.

All day yesterday, from dawn until he rolled into his bunk at the usual time, he had forced himself, by concentrating with all his will, to do nothing that would cause any of his fellow soldiers to notice that he was under any unusual stress, or about to undertake anything out of the ordinary. Fortunately the great majority of them were anything but keen observers, being wrapped up in their own plans and problems.

And then Sarpedon, coming back from the latrine, sent a chill through Alex by asking him if anything was wrong.

"No." There was a rote response to that kind of question, and he repeated it now without enthusiasm. "Another day, another copper coin. Two coins for the corporal."

Then, looking over his friend's shoulder, his eye was caught by a group of men standing near the front door of the barracks, clustered around the place where the duty roster was posted on the wall. The voice of someone up there was raised abruptly, uttering crude words describing various bodily functions. Alex felt a sudden premonitory shifting, as if a heavy weight had abruptly intruded somewhere near the pit of his stomach. Shouldering forward, jostled by other men moving in the same direction, he reached a position where he could read the listings. The paper was crisp and new, not the thumb-printed sheet that had been up there yesterday.

Assignments had been changed. There was his name, but no longer in the list of those who were to draw spears from the armory and pull interior guard. Instead, he and a number of others from his barracks were to arm themselves with short swords and join the detail assigned to convey the people of the Tribute to the place where they would honor Shiva.

There was no way out. It would be unheard of, of course, for a mere private soldier to protest any assignment. Unless he reported himself sick; but the only sure result of that would be to draw unwelcome attention to himself.

Fiercely Alex tried to resist showing any of the sudden turmoil welling up in him. What was he going to do now—now that he was going to be right on the scene when Prince Theseus made his break for freedom? In the back of his mind, apparently, he had been unconsciously preparing for some such eventuality as this. Because he knew without thinking about it that he was not going to stand inertly by. For the princess's sake, he, Alex, would do whatever was required at the time to make sure the prince got away. And then he would simply have to do the best he could for himself.

The best tactic might well be to allow Theseus to break away, then give chase, but in such a manner that the quarry was in no real danger of being caught.

That might work, though of course he could hardly expect to be the only one chasing the fugitive.

But almost as soon as Alex began to try to make a plan, he gave it up. It was impossible, without knowing the specific situation he'd be facing. There was only one thing Alex could be sure of now: For the princess Ariadne he would do anything.

Back at his bunk again, cleaning up the area in case there happened to be a barracks inspection, he was aware that Sarpedon was once more looking at him strangely. Sarpedon was now going to be on the same detail. They exchanged a few routine grumbles. "Not a job I wanted. Well . . ."

So far this morning nothing was really out of the ordinary—roster changes, including some that seemed wildly arbitrary, were not that uncommon—and yet nothing was the same at all. Even if Alex somehow managed to join in the great escape as planned, he was about to set out on the longest and most dangerous journey he had ever undertaken. There had been no question of his packing anything, or even stuffing anything into his belt pouch, to take with him on the journey. When he fell out of the barracks this morning, with his squad, to stand in formation for roll call, he would be carrying with him his short sword and his usual clothing, practically nothing else.

Of course, if the escape plan should fail . . . but he wasn't going to let himself think about that possibility.

It had already occurred to Alex that as soon as his defection was discovered, as he had to assume it would be within a couple of hours at the most, everyone in his barracks would be called in, methodically, for questioning, and those among his fellow soldiers whom he considered his best friends—Sarpedon, for example—were going to be in for a hard time, whether the escape succeeded or not. But there was nothing in the world that Alex could do about it.

The sergeant was now calling names of the detail set to guarding the Tribute youths and maidens. Alex and Sarpedon stepped forward in their turns.

━━━━━━━━

Minutes later, they had joined a squad from another barracks. The whole detail, some twenty men in all, were marching in loose formation under the sergeant's command, crossing the parade ground behind the barracks to the place where the youths and maidens of the Tribute were being held.

Muttered exchanges as they trudged along soon established that none of the men of the detail had been told exactly how the sacrifice was to be accomplished.

Looking around him in formation, taking note of who was present and who was not, Alex decided that men of proven reliability had been wanted for this job. Probably this was one reason why he had been chosen, since he had happened to be on duty in the great hall on the night of the usurpation, and there—to his own lasting shame—he had acquitted himself well, in the Butcher's estimation.

Standing at ease in one of the little plazas just inside the Labyrinth, waiting for the people of the Tribute to be brought out of their quarters, the soldiers of the detail continued muttering and speculating among themselves. When the actual ritual got started, were they going to see another skull or two stripped of flesh and dried for Shiva's necklace? Or maybe more were needed, to be mounted in his new temple, which was outside the Labyrinth but in easy walking distance of the palace.

One rumor whispered among the soldiers now said that the priest-experts were intent on creating a god-face for Shiva's consort, Kali, by in essence boiling down parts of human victims. The hearts of ten brave men, and so forth. Each rumor sounded worse than the one before it, and Alex was sure some of the men were making them up on the spot, trying to outdo each other in gallows humor.

The nine girls, according to a murmured rumor passed along from the other side, were scheduled to be used up in an effort to summon the goddess Kali, traditionally Shiva's consort. Another claimed that the real purpose of the whole sacrifice was directed toward finding the Face of Zeus, supposed to be buried somewhere within the Labyrinth.

Alex had been too long in the army to give credence to any rumor that lacked supporting evidence.

Now it was time to supervise the administration of the ritual drinks to those whose lives were now forfeit to Shiva.

When Shiva's priests brought the victims out of their confinement, Alex had no trouble recognizing Theseus, and had to admit to himself that Ariadne's secret lover looked as if he might almost be worthy of the part. But Alex was curious: Of what kingdom was this man a prince? He had never heard anyone name the place; and he wasn't about to suggest his own interest by asking.

Watching the priests begin to serve their victims what was widely supposed to be drugged wine and water, he saw how Theseus took the cup into his hands as readily as any of the others. But no one besides Alex seemed to be watching the actual consumption of the wine all that closely. If the tall prince let some of it run down his chin in the act of drinking, and more dribble from his mouth after he'd handed the cup back, no one else was going to know about it.

Presently all eighteen had been served the ritual draught, and the soldiers began the business of escorting the people of the Tribute to the place where they were to die.

As the march got under way, following the marked route through the Labyrinth, Alex wondered if Shiva would be waiting for them up ahead. It seemed likely.

He wondered also if Theseus would recognize him, and decided that was highly unlikely.

Even if the princess had mentioned Alex to her lover, at one of their secret meetings, there would have been no point in her describing the soldier who was to accompany them on their getaway.

Alex wondered again what had caused the princess and Daedalus to choose this exact time, the very hour of the sacrifice, for the escape. Not that it was up to a mere private soldier to question anything such folk decided; but he had once tentatively raised the question with Clara.

It might have been troubling her too, for she'd had a kind of answer ready. "The Lord Asterion says that the time that seems the worst may sometimes be the best. We go when the Lord Shiva will not interfere."

That was too much for Alex to understand. Why would Shiva not interfere, when everyone knew he would be present at the ritual? He could only hope that the dreaming bull-man knew what he was doing.

And at the moment when the squad of soldiers, and the eighteen victims they were escorting, reached the cleared site where the sacrifice was to take place, Shiva was very much present, reclining nude in a throne-like chair of silk and leather, on the very stage of the sacrifice.

The scene of the planned sacrifice was the recently constructed small amphitheater, with concentric semicircles of seats, enough to hold forty or fifty people, far more than it seemed were going to be needed today. Facing them, a kind of elaborate altar, built upon a stage.

The very complexity of the arrangement suggested ominously that today's sacrificial harvest would not be gathered by means of a swift roasting with the Third Eye. Alex supposed that might be too quick and bloodless to produce the desired effect on victims and onlookers, and even in the celebrant himself. There were human beings, he knew, who took great pleasure in inflicting pain; and he supposed that the same was true of certain gods.

Shining cages of a peculiar construction had been set up. Also, at the base of the scaffolding, a kind of holding pen, crudely constructed, in which the prisoners were evidently meant to wait until their turns came to mount the stage.

The sun had been barely at the horizon when the younger princess, attended only by her usual companion, Clara, walked out of the princess's suite of rooms in the palace.

In the freshening morning light, the two young women traversed one corridor of the huge palace, went down some stairs, and then followed another long, broad hall. Here and there, as usual, were soldiers of the Palace Guard, on duty. But none of them was the man Clara was watching for. To cover all the guard posts, it was necessary to make a circuit of the ground floor, and this they did. And now they had almost reached the exit.

They had entered the last corridor on the ground floor before she touched the princess on the arm, something she ordinarily did only in private. "Where is Alex?" Clara dared to whisper.

"I don't know," came the soft-voiced answer. "I haven't seen him anywhere. I'm not going to stop and look for him, we haven't time."

"But my lady . . ."

"No. Either he'll find a way to catch up with us, or he won't. There can be no more delays."

"If *he* dies today," the princess added, obviously no longer speaking about Alex the Half-Nameless, "I will die too."

"Don't say that, my lady!" Clara seemed near tears with fear and worry, and her mistress grimly ordered her to smile. With an effort the slave-girl got herself under control.

Past another pair of soldiers at the door—neither of them the man they hoped to see—and the young women were out of the palace altogether, walking in new morning light, over well-tended grass now glistening with dew. And now the familiar entrance to the Labyrinth loomed close ahead, open and unguarded. And then they were in among its windings, out of sight of the rest of the world.

━━━━━━━

It occurred to Alex, as he quivered in suspense, trying to look calm while waiting for Theseus to make his break, that no one among the group of plotters had really considered the possibility of doing anything to help the other seventeen scheduled victims. It would have been inconceivable to get them all away, even had they not been more than half-stupefied with drugged wine.

Of course, if a man could somehow set them all loose, running in a panic, that might well create a distraction to help a chosen few to get away . . .

Without much hope, Alex tried to come up with good possibilities. Setting them loose, even for a little while, would entail opening certain doors in the Labyrinth which the priests of Shiva wanted to keep closed; leading or driving the sacrificial victims down alternate paths, so that confusion reigned, and time and effort would be required to get them back.

———

Having left the palace and its grounds behind them, Ariadne and Clara were now traversing the Labyrinth by means of the marked path, about a mile and a half in its frequently curving length. Perses in his crown and formal robes would soon be coming along this way—it was how he was wont to travel to and fro between his palace and the center of the Maze. And then the intended victims, under guard. There were of course many intersections, and sometimes the chosen route went under or over crossing passageways.

Daedalus no doubt had traversed the intricacies of this way several times, when he came to the island and was set to work, and when Perses called him out to give a progress report.

This way was marked through the Maze by painted spikes driven into the pavement.

The princess and her attendant followed this first portion of the route each time they went to visit the Prince Asterion. And today, as on most other days, on reaching a certain point, Ariadne calmly turned aside, as if she were going to one of her regular meetings with her brother.

From this point on, she walked part of the time with her eyes closed, relying on the web-strands of her inner vision. And during the intervals when her lids were shut, her small feet in their sturdy sandals moved as surely as before.

Presently, after a look back to make sure that she and Clara were unobserved, she turned aside again, leaving the route that usually brought them to Asterion. The two women were now on a way that, if all went well, would take them to Theseus.

———

The king and Creon were also traveling the marked path. They had the two women briefly in sight ahead of them, and naturally assumed that they were going to see Asterion.

King Perses, dressed in rich ceremonial garments, had given few signs as to whether he expected to enjoy the forthcoming spectacle or not. Not that Perses had any real choice; Shiva would certainly insist upon his being there in any case.

"I suppose, lord, that neither of your nieces are going to attend today's ceremony?"

"So they have both informed me."

"I don't know what the Lord Shiva will think."

Perses frowned, but considered this was not the proper time for a real test of wills. "Really, Creon, I don't know why their presence should make any difference to him."

———

When the king arrived on the scene, well after dawn (no one really expected any elaborately planned event to start sharply at the scheduled time), he found Shiva waiting, surrounded by his priests. The emaciated body of the God of Destruction was perched on an improvised throne that was higher if not more glorious than the one in the great hall of the palace.

Only the cages were higher than the throne, in fact almost directly above it, so that if Shiva, his scrawny frame lounging naked in a silk and leather chair below, wished to luxuriate in the rain of blood from them he had only to move his body slightly.

The god shifted his position, as if he were growing impatient.

The mortal king, who was now arriving with Creon at his side, would have to be content with a place of secondary importance.

The Butcher and perhaps a dozen lesser officers were in eager attendance, occupying portions of two rows of seats. Alex and the rest of the cohort of the Palace Guard had been deployed casually around the space.

———

I, Asterion, having taken leave of Daedalus and his son, trotted quickly back through the Labyrinth, to a vantage point I had been careful to select beforehand, which would provide me with a good view of the actual site of the sacrifice. I suppose that if I had applied to Perses for permission to attend, it would have been easily and even eagerly granted. But of course I had not thought of doing so, any more than the usurper had thought of volunteering an invitation.

One of the refinements of the Maze, known to comparatively few, is the existence of movable panels, which on casual inspection are indistinguishable from sections of a certain type of solid wall. With strength only a little beyond that of an ordinary man, it is not hard to move the panels, and the judicious shifting of a few of them can, if the shifter knows what he is doing, redesign whole regions of the Labyrinth.

In the current situation my object was not so ambitious. I was using a loose panel, carved into a kind of lattice-shape, to block off a short section of passage. Peering through this latticework, and the screen of greenery which came attached to it, I expected to be able to look on at the ceremony without being seen.

I would not have been surprised to observe, on the newly-constructed stage, blood drained by stone knives in the hands of priests. I feared that if my monstrous shape were suddenly to appear before the doomed ones, even drugged as they were, total panic would be inevitable. Of course, just such an effect could have been calculated as part of our escape plan. My form would not only be monstrous in their eyes, but the very shape of all the nightmares that the Maze engendered. But when it was desirable to create confusion, then total panic was just what we wanted.

I had known in a general way what was going to happen. Still, I was utterly horrified when the details actually began to take place right before my waking eyes.

The first of the eighteen, still glassy-eyed with drugs, was separated from the group, stripped of his ceremonial garments and led up the steps to the stage, from which another skeletal stair to the small, twin cages above. A young woman soon followed.

Now both of the iron-ribbed torture chambers were occupied, almost above Shiva's throne. From every side of the interior of each cage, sharp dagger-blades projected toward the naked victim there confined, the clearance between skin and dagger-point being never more than a few inches. None of the blades were long enough to inflict a single, fatal wound.

Now one of the priests approached on a catwalk outside the cages, carrying a bar of iron whose free end was heated red. The object soon became plain—recoiling involuntarily from the hot iron, the victim's body would inevitably be punctured repeatedly by the sharp blade-points that drained their blood, one small wound at a time. Life would run out slowly, with the trickling blood that ran to bathe the God of Destruction who was taking his ease below.

The eyes of almost everyone were on the hot iron in the torturer's hand. The eyes of Alex were still on Theseus, who had pasted a foolish smile upon his face, and stumbled about restlessly among the other intended victims, singing as they sang.

Then, choosing his moment with superb skill, Theseus abandoned his pretense of being drugged.

The sergeant spoke to him sharply. "Get back in line. Where d'you think you're—?"

Despite Alex's determination to be ready, still Theseus moved so fast that the young soldier was very nearly taken by surprise.

———————

An armed sergeant moved quickly to block Theseus, who did not shy from contact as the soldier must have expected. Instead, the prince, already running at full speed, lowered his shoulder into the sergeant's midriff, knocking him down, and with almost the same fluid motion grabbed up the short sword that had fallen from his hand.

Then Theseus went bounding and climbing over a wall, under his own power. He threw the weapon he had just captured up and over the wall ahead of him. Then, with one more explosion of strength, he was up and over after it.

And Alex was running at full speed after him.

———————

Watching from behind my screen, I saw that the alarm caught Shiva in something of an awkward position in his silk-and-leather chair, just beginning to enjoy the bath of young blood that trickled on him from above. The God of Destruction was immediately convinced that his life was in great danger. I saw him leap into action, calling the bull Nandi seemingly out of nowhere and jumping on the creature's back. It seemed that with decisive action he might have recaptured Theseus in short order; but my dream-omens were proven accurate. Shiva's purpose was only to break away and take flight, and in a moment he and his mount were dwindling together in the distant sky.

Meanwhile, Theseus had escaped, as far as I could tell, without the need for any last-minute heroics on my part. But before I could turn away, I beheld something else that froze me in my tracks. A young woman whose name I did not know, one of the eighteen, inadequately drugged and running desperately, seemed to be appealing to me for help.

No dream, and of course no conscious effort to foresee possibilities had ever warned me that such a thing might happen, and for just a moment I cursed mentally the chain of decisions and impulses that had caused me to become so entangled in the real world.

When seen from its other end, the short spur of passageway at whose end I waited was, to all appearances, a dead blind alley, and so no guard had been posted at its entrance. But the girl by running into it did put herself momentarily out of sight of the watchers in the tiers of seats (who of course were themselves just out of my field of vision). She came running toward me as if she believed, or trusted, that a way to salvation must exist somewhere, as if unaware or unwilling to believe what her eyes reported, that only a few feet ahead a solid barrier walled her in.

In such circumstances, I suppose it was impossible for me to do anything but what I did.

Behind the one who had awakened to reality, the other drugged ones were groaning and moaning now, turning and trying to stumble away as a vague consciousness of what was happening began to get through to them. Others had been made so happy by the drugged wine that they kept on singing.

Many of the guards had run after Theseus (I had noted that Alex was first among them), and everyone had witnessed the shocking fact of Shiva's taking flight. Only a few soldiers were left at the scene of sacrifice, and the rest of the scheduled victims were largely forgotten in the uproar. Not that any of them actually got away, but some were not retaken for many hours.

Bursting from my place of hiding, I charged at full speed, brushing past the petrified girl in the narrow passage. A moment later I had smashed my horned head into the torso of the unready priest, so that the stone knife fell from the man's hand and his gored body, much less massive than my own, went flying.

The priest of Shiva I had so brutally struck down lay flat on his back, blood already puddling under him. Whether he would survive to accuse me I did not know, nor at the moment did I much care. In the open space beyond the stub of passageway, men and women were running to and fro, none of them yet paying me any attention. The noise of mass panic suggested that I still might have a few moments in which to act. It was quite possible that no one but the priest and girl had noticed my rash interference.

The girl I had just saved had slumped to the pavement. Bending swiftly, I scooped the drugged and helpless figure up into my arms, and carried her away.

Having quickly regained my original hiding place, I stopped and turned to restore the screen-barricade that made the stub of passageway look like it was blocked. Then, gently carrying the girl, I turned away and raced on.

Behind me, the sounds of panic and of rage lingered in the morning air, fading only slowly.

———

Theseus, having vaulted over the wall, came down catlike on his sandaled feet, steadying into a fighting crouch, ready to spring. But he was utterly alone. He found himself now in another passage, practically indistinguishable from the one from which he had just departed so precipitously. There was the sword he had just captured, lying on the pavement where his toss had landed it, and he hastened to grab the weapon up.

A hasty glance to right and left, and away he ran. There was no one here to guide him, but he had not been relying on that anyway. It was ingrained in him never to trust that people were going to do anything they promised.

Ariadne had given a list of directions to memorize and follow— turn right, right again, then left at the next corner, and left again, after a longer run than either of the two preceding.

The whispered words were carved into his memory. *Then you will see a kind of alcove on your right. Turn into it, though it looks like a dead end, and behind the column in the rear you will discover a small door. Come through that door, and someone will be waiting for you.*

If anyone had noticed him going over the wall, then almost certainly some pursuit would follow. But they would have to spend a little time in scrambling to get over, especially if they carried weapons.

The tumult behind him was increasing in volume, but so far no one was right on his tail. He could hear voices shouting in confusion, and screams that spoke all too eloquently of blood and death.

Theseus sprinted on.

10

THESEUS, RUNNING AS fast as he could through the memorized list of turns, rounded a corner in the Labyrinth to find Ariadne and Clara hastening toward him. Smothering a cry of joy, the princess threw herself into her lover's arms. Moments later, she was leading him and Clara on a sinuous path toward the place where they were to meet Daedalus. Ariadne's eyes were closed at least half the time, as she strode sure-footedly ahead.

The prince had not yet noticed this fact. "How can you find anything in this place?" he demanded, after the third or fourth additional branching of the ways. "My head is spinning already."

"I can always find what I need, my love." The princess smiled at him proudly. "Especially in here."

As far back as she could remember, the Princess Ariadne had always been willing to put aside the comforts and privileges of her high birth, for the sake of an adventure—she had endured considerable discomfort for the sake of much less exciting outings than this one promised to be. And this, of course, was vastly more than a mere escapade. For Theseus, she would have sacrificed everything she had, her very life.

In a few minutes, when they had reached the Deep Pool, Daedalus greeted them with relief. Asterion and the young soldier, Alex, were still nowhere to be seen, and the newcomers reported that Alex had not been in the palace. The princess and her lover huddled democratically with Clara and the child of the Artisan. They were all about to put their lives into the hands of Daedalus, relying utterly on his word that he would be able to provide them with an effective means of escape.

Icarus was a study in wide-eyed, silent fear, caught from the tension among the adults around him. He clung close to his father as much as possible.

All of them but Theseus were now sitting, while he paced nervously on the edge of what Asterion called the Deep Pool. The artificially constructed basin, some ten paces long by five wide, looked fresh and was evidently filled and drained by unseen subterranean flows. It was a surprisingly large body of water compared to the few other ponds Ariadne had seen in the Labyrinth—though after years of roaming in that immense complexity, often by herself, nothing she discovered there really surprised her anymore.

Right now, her instinct urged her to trust to Daedalus; but when she gazed into the unplumbed depth of water before her, she knew that she could find her own way to the sea if that ever became necessary. Closing her eyes, willing her thoughts into the proper channel, she could see the beginnings of the thin, ghostly filaments that would lead her to the correct path. Though it wasn't possible just yet to see which way they led . . .

The agreed-upon time to begin the next stage of their journey had now arrived, the sun was several handsbreadths above the eastern wall of the little courtyard. But still, two of the group's original seven had not appeared at the meeting place.

Theseus told the others he had no idea whether Alex might have been among the detail of soldiers from whom he had just escaped.

"I thought that one of them kept watching me, and then the same one took a cut at me when I ran. But the fates were with me, and he missed."

"About middle-sized, with a straggly brown beard?" Daedalus inquired.

The prince stared thoughtfully at the older man. "He might have been. I wasn't paying much attention to the details of anyone's appearance."

Ariadne and Clara were worried about what might have happened to Asterion. But the princess comforted herself with the thought that her brother had never seemed firmly committed to joining in the escape, and had probably simply decided at the last minute not to go. Knowing him as she did, she would not have been much surprised if it were so.

Clara, despite her mistress's earlier command to do no packing, had managed to tuck under her dress a small belt pack with what she considered a few essentials. There were now some dried dates in a kind of purse that ordinarily held for the princess a mirror, a hairbrush, and a few cosmetics, all trinkets that had been left behind.

Theseus suddenly halted in his pacing, and announced commandingly, "We can't wait any longer. Whoever is not here by now is probably not coming."

The princess quickly agreed. "You're right, we mustn't wait."

If Ariadne was not determined to wait for her brother, no one else was either. And certainly no one was going to suggest a delay in hopes that the young soldier, Alex, might, after all, be able to catch up with them. Nor was there any real discussion of his possible fate. He might have lost his way, might have been killed or captured, or perhaps had simply lost his nerve at the last moment. As Theseus observed, "Anyway, he didn't know the place of rendezvous, or the escape route. He won't be able to tell them much."

For Ariadne, the fact of overwhelming importance was that her lover Theseus had managed to get this far, and for the moment he was out of danger. It seemed to the princess that her whole life was now invested in her concern for his welfare. As long as *he* was safe, nothing and no one else, herself included, counted for very much.

———

It would have been almost impossible for anyone to accidentally stumble on Daedalus's secret way, even had there been daily visitors to the site of rendezvous, which there certainly were not. People might have camped here for years and caught no inkling that it existed. Now, speaking quickly, in a low voice, the Artisan explained how he, trying to determine for himself how large saltwater fish could have come this far inland, had spent some time investigating. Once he had located the underground stream, he had fashioned a secret entrance, at the edge, just below the waterline in the deep pool that Asterion had once described as being long and deep enough for swimming.

Immediately agreeing that they should wait no longer, Daedalus quickly explained to the others what they were about to do. Then he, with his son clinging to him, drew a deep breath and slid down into the dark waters of the pool and disappeared, with scarcely a ripple, under the water-lily pads that covered a portion of its calm surface.

Without hesitation Theseus, still clothed in the cloak and kilt of sacrificial garments, and with his captured sword in hand, drew a deep breath and went after the man and boy. One after another, the other members of the party followed, each keeping the one ahead in sight. Each ducked underwater, groped along the side of the pool beneath an overhang, slid through a hole, and popped up again on the other side of the wall, where the pavement was higher than that immediately surrounding the Deep Pool. There they all found breathing space, though there was no room to stand up properly. They were in a dark and clammy cavern, where the noise of running water was somewhat louder than it had been on the surface, while the occasional shouts of soldiers in the distance had faded almost to inaudibility. Only enough of the brilliant morning sunlight filtered in through chinks and crannies in the upper rounds of masonry to turn the cavern into a half-lit grotto.

When it came Ariadne's turn to immerse herself in the pool, a stray thought momentarily crossed her mind: what a thorough way to ruin one's fine clothes. There was a curious satisfaction in the image.

When all five had crowded into the dank little cavern, Daedalus murmured a few words of encouragement and led the way again, his son still clinging tightly to his back. This time the Artisan plunged boldly into the descending course of the underground stream, managing to keep his head above water. Theseus, as if jealous of the leadership position, kept close behind him. Here the current was swifter. Water gurgled and rushed around them, sometimes as high as the adults' armpits.

Now and then, in muttered comments, the Artisan tried to explain how water from mountain springs flowed in diverse channels through the Maze, across its almost-level tableland, while other streams had been diverted to the streets of the city. Various aqueducts and channels had been added over the centuries.

From time to time Theseus raised a hand, calling a halt so he could listen carefully for sounds of pursuit. His cloak, now water-soaked, was weighty but he did not discard it. Each time, after only a slight pause, he shook his head and motioned them on again. There was no sign that anyone was coming after them.

Now and then the slave-girl, Clara, took a turn at helping the child through some of the more difficult places, and Daedalus looked at her gratefully. Ariadne noted the fact in passing; in these circumstances, she herself certainly did not need the constant attendance of her slave.

After perhaps an hour underground, sometimes wading, sometimes crawling over wet rock, the party had reached a half-lit cavern a little bigger than most of the similar rooms they had passed through. Here, as they paused for a rest on a dry ledge, the Artisan told the others about the hot-air balloon he had put together, the fire that kept it inflated, and the timing mechanism, involving a slow-burning rope, he had devised for its launching. If all had gone well, the balloon should have risen in morning sunlight from near the middle of the Maze, and should even now be riding the prevailing winds out to sea. The idea was to deceive the army of searchers, who by now were sure to be hunting the escapees, into believing they had made an aerial escape.

"Look!" It was an urgent whisper from Icarus, who stood peering up through a crevice in the masonry, at the world outside. "Look!"

Looking up through other gaps, where tree roots met the pavement overhead, Ariadne and one or two others were able to catch a glimpse of the Artisan's balloon. The princess saw a crude sphere bound in some kind of ropes, with a basket hanging beneath it, soaring overhead. There were dots, that at such a distance could be mistaken for human heads, showing just above the basket's rim.

The slave-girl, having seen the balloon, turned openmouthed to stare at its creator. She obviously found Daedalus interesting.

Theseus, a new respect in his tone, said to him, "It seems that going through the air might be a better, faster way than this."

Now they were getting under way again. The Artisan replied, "Watch out for the bottom here, all slippery mud. No, my balloon was not even large enough, you understand, to carry one man, let alone a party of five or more. And it will come down, as soon as the air inside cools off. A balloon, or any flying device, big enough to bear us all away would be a vast project—though a truly interesting one." For a moment Daedalus could not keep himself from being distracted by the challenge of such a task.

━━━━━━

Once more the party moved on. Ariadne kept close behind Theseus, and close behind her came the slave-girl, tugging the child along by the hand.

There were places where the stream, in its long rush seaward, went through ancient culverts, one of which it almost filled. Fortunately a sufficient breathing space remained open along the top.

━━━━━━

Now and then their guide muttered and mused that parts of this escape route seemed to have been designed, by some ancient engineer, to serve the function of a tunnel, and other parts were only the natural course of the stream bed.

Who knew, thought Ariadne, how many hundreds of years the little creek might have been flowing here—or any stream anywhere, for that matter? This one had been at it long enough, certainly, to carve its way deeply into the ground, forming a channel that enabled a few big fish to swim all the way up into a portion of the Maze. Any fish ascending as far as the Deep Pool were evidently required to leap up one or more waterfalls in the process.

When they had stopped once more to catch their breath, Daedalus explained that in the course of his earlier reconnaissance down this stream, only a few days ago, he had briefly toyed with, then quickly discarded, the idea of improvising some kind of boat. For most of its length the channel was simply too shallow and narrow for that to be practical. A true underground stream of more than minimal length would have made breathing apparatus necessary, but fortunately that was not the case.

After about a mile of progress, carried out in a generally southwesterly direction, Ariadne was sure that they had left the Labyrinth behind them. Looking up through the occasional aperture, past natural rocks, exposed roots, and spiderwebs, it was no longer possible to catch a glimpse of its distinctive walls or pavement. Neither were they beneath the grounds of the palace, or the city, both of which lay in a different direction. The route now seemed to lie beneath a rocky wasteland, and the spaces that let in light and air were mere crevices between outcroppings, or piled boulders. Here and there, at the bottom of an otherwise almost impenetrable ravine, the little stream came fully out into the open for a few yards, before it once more plunged under the earth.

Ariadne, more familiar than anyone else in the party with the island's overall geography, announced that she knew approximately where they must be. "Little or nothing grows here. The land above us is good only for grazing goats."

By dint of walking, crawling, clambering, occasionally swimming, once or twice going underwater again, the fugitives continued their descent, almost all the way to the small stream's inevitable junction with the sea. Eventually it would become a creek, which must find its way down to the marshy wetlands, and then the sea.

Daedalus gave his estimate that the whole journey would be about three miles long. At the best rate of progress the little band of fugitives could manage in the circumstances it took them more than two hours.

Once the slave-girl asked her mistress timidly, "What do we do when we reach the sea?"

Ariadne was silent for a time, hoping someone else might come up with a better answer than she had ready. But no one did, and at last the princess said, "If there's no useful ship or boat immediately available—and of course we can't count on there being one—we must find a hiding place, and wait."

For a moment Clara seemed on the point of asking: *Wait for what?* but then she let it go in silence.

Two days before the morning of the escape, Theseus, with some help from Ariadne's sympathizers, had dispatched by secret means a message, to a man he said was an officer in his father's navy. It would of course take time for that message to reach his pirate cohorts, and more time for them to respond. But Theseus hoped that they would come looking for him on a series of nights, beginning only a few days from now, on a certain practically uninhabited stretch of the island's rugged coast, long familiar to pirates and smugglers.

The trouble was that that stretch of coast was halfway around the island from the area in which Daedalus's discovered tunnel seemed to be about to bring them out. But Ariadne had been given some encouragement by her brother as well; her lover had not been the only one trying to arrange transportation.

Theseus was aware of the difficulties, but remained grimly optimistic. "We'll get to a place where we can be picked up. Or we'll find a way to take a boat from someone."

After struggling down the narrow waterway for several hours, more often than not wading in its bed, picking their way with difficulty down slippery rocks beside the falls where the salmonlike fish came leaping up, the fugitives reached what was undeniably the end of the tunnel, blocked by a coarse grillwork of thick, rusty metal bars. Just beyond that the stream emerged into full sunlight, then went wandering on, beyond a fringe of small trees, to lose itself in a marsh, under an open sky. A gull cried in the distance, and they could hear the encouraging sound of surf on hard rocks. Theseus, gripping the bars of the terminal barrier, announced hopefully that if he craned his neck he could just see a blue sliver of watery horizon beyond the reeds and bushes of the marsh.

From inside the tunnel it was possible to see occasional furry movement in the middle distance. Daedalus called attention to the fact that there were mutant beavers living and working in the waters that drained the Labyrinth. The stream the fugitives had been following emptied here into a kind of wetlands. From the nature of more distant vegetation, it appeared likely that the area soon became a salt marsh, and would be a good place for pirates or other surreptitious folk to land.

Evidently some authority had once at least suspected that the stream offered a pathway directly into the heart of the Labyrinth, and had attempted to seal it off. Rusted iron bars as thick as a man's arm, some underwater and some above, ran both horizontally and vertically across the opening where the small stream debouched at last into the open air. There was plenty of space between the bars for fish to go in and out, but not nearly enough for people.

The others all looked at Daedalus. "This is the 'final barrier' you mentioned?" asked Theseus.

"It is." The Artisan proceeded calmly. He had carefully studied the details of this problem on his earlier scouting trip, and it was soon obvious that he had been thinking the matter over ever since.

"We need a tool," he said. "And on my first visit I marked one that I believe we can use."

Taking from a pouch attached to his belt a small coil of thin, strong-looking cord, he handed it to Icarus. Now, moving at his father's orders, the boy squeezed his small body through the largest of the irregular openings in the grill, and went splashing off downstream toward the fringe of trees. When he got there he followed directions called to him by Daedalus. Soon he had knotted one end of the cord to a green log or pole, as thick as a man's arm, that lay where it was visible from the end of the tunnel. Ariadne, watching, supposed it was probably a small trunk chewed down by beavers.

Icarus had to draw his little knife, and work industriously at the log for several minutes, trimming off twigs that got in the way of his knot-tying. Meanwhile his father, watching from behind the iron bars, continued to call out instructions and encouragement, while the others managed to keep quiet.

As soon as the boy had a firm knot in the right place, he ran splashing back to the end of the tunnel, swimming through a couple of deep spots in the stream, carrying with him the free coil of the cord, unwinding it as he came.

Moments later the Artisan had the loose end in his hands. Drawing it taut, he raised it to one of the higher openings in the coarse grill, then engaged in some skillful and energetic tugging. In response, the distant pole leaped up, and began to progress in fits and starts toward the grating.

Icarus, who had run back again to stand beside the pole, now kept pace with it as it moved, and when necessary cleared its pathway of minor obstacles. Now and then he helped with a tug or push on the weight that would have been too great for him to lift or drag unaided.

Ariadne, not fully understanding the plan as yet, still let out a whispered cheer as the slim log came loose from the last entanglement of brush. A minute later it came sliding right up to the bars. Working together, with hands extended through the grating, Theseus and Daedalus turned the log endwise and pulled it through, a process delayed by the necessity of hacking off one more branch.

Once the two men had the long lever in their hands, inside the tunnel, they needed only moments to force one end of it into the gap between one side of rock and the nearest bar, only a few inches distant. Then, using a conveniently located bulge on the side of the tunnel for their fulcrum, they leaned their weight against the free end of the lever formed by the log.

The green wood of the fresh timber bent, but stubbornly refused to break. The metal barrier was very old, and the rock around it had started crumbling years ago. Presently there came a rasping sound of tortured metal. Now the men were able to force their lever farther into the aperture. They heaved again. First Clara, then Ariadne, came to try to help, but space near the end of the lever was limited, and the women soon stood back out of the way again.

Once more the two men strained their muscles. This time they made some progress. Ancient bolts and rivets formed of bronze, much thinner than the bars, were giving way, one at a time, in small, sharp explosions.

Daedalus stood back, wiping sweat from his brow with a bare forearm. "Prince Theseus, if you would help me, please. There are some hard rocks here of a handy size to make good hammers." There was no use, at this point, in trying to be quiet.

Theseus picked up from the stream bed a stone the size of his two fists, and with it delivered powerful, clanging blows to a bolt that now stood with almost its whole length bendably exposed. Then he dropped the hammerstone and went back to stand beside the Artisan, once more laying hold of the lever.

"It's tougher than I thought," Daedalus grunted.

"We'll get it, old man. This is a brilliant idea of yours. Now heave!"

After a few more minutes of grunting, straining effort, the massive, rusted iron tore loose from rock with an explosive noise. One whole side of the grating sagged.

An exit two feet wide stood open to the world.

11

WHEN THESEUS WENT over the wall and vanished from sight, Alex was already running in hot pursuit. There was no need for him to hold back or deliberately stumble. Compared to most men Alex was fast and agile; matched against Theseus, he was clumsy and slow, and on his best day he would not have been able to overtake the prince.

Nor would he ever be able to match the leap that enabled Princess Ariadne's lover to catch the top of the wall, or the strength of arm that pulled him over and out of sight in just the blinking of an eye. But Alex remained grimly determined not to let the fugitive permanently out of sight. Whatever route Theseus might be following to reach the point of rendezvous with the princess and the others, it would presumably work for Alex also.

All this ran swiftly through the young soldier's mind as he darted round the first corner in pursuit. There was no trace of Theseus to be seen, and with a shock Alex observed that the passageway he had now entered seemed to curve in the wrong direction, and was going to carry him farther from the spot where Theseus must have come down.

But at this point Alex had no choice. Hoping that the next turn would bring his quarry in sight once more, he dashed on, committing himself entirely to chance.

Behind him, the uproar attendant on the shattered ceremony faded quickly, the noise baffled in the endless turnings of the Labyrinth. Before his racing feet there appeared always another branching of the way, and then another. The occasional stair going up or plunging down beneath ground level. Each time he had to choose, Alex followed his instincts; but his instincts were evidently wrong, for there was never a sign of the fleeing prince, or indeed of any living being.

In this way Alex ran until he was exhausted. When at last he stopped, chest heaving for breath, he turned and looked about. There were the twisting walls on every side, and the sky above. The realization came to him, with a blending of horror and relief, that he was now hopelessly lost.

Resting, he thought he heard someone approaching, the steps of a single pair of feet, coming along the way that he himself had come.

He could see no place to hide. On he went, desperately crawling through one odd low passage that was really only a small tunnel, breaking his fingernails on the rough stones that paved its floor. Now it seemed to him that he could hear the sounds, padding feet and clinking metal, of armed men running in pursuit, behind him and around him. On his hands and knees, peering round a corner, Alex's worst fears were confirmed when he caught a glimpse of one such figure. These were men who until minutes ago had been his comrades, but who now might well have been ordered to cut him down on sight.

For the moment he was still safe, but he might be discovered at any instant. If he simply waited where he was, they were certain to find him sooner or later. But if he ran on, turning corners at random as before, he might very well run right into the men who were looking for him.

Near despair, he almost called aloud to the Lord Asterion, and to Prince Theseus, for help; but with an effort he kept himself from doing that. Even when the enemies of the princess caught and tortured him, as now it seemed almost certain that they would do, he must do his best to keep from naming names.

Fighting to shake off the grip of panic, Alex told himself firmly that it was possible, even likely, that he was not yet being hunted, or even under suspicion. Of course people must have seen him running after Theseus, but that could be easily explained as his attempt to catch the fugitive. Other soldiers must have gone pounding in pursuit as well. He might, he probably could, rejoin his comrades now, assuming he and they could find their way out of the toils of the Labyrinth, and perhaps remain free of suspicion.

But meanwhile, every passing minute and hour would see the princess getting farther and farther away, by means of whatever cleverness Daedalus had chosen to employ. And he, Alex, would be able to do nothing at all for her, never see her again or have a chance to serve her. Never again would she look at him with approval; nor would her fingers ever touch his skin, as they had when she gave him the medallion—

though she was unlikely ever to touch him again in any case. Ah, if only he could be sure that she was safe!

Restlessly he moved on, and soon began to run again, driven by a sense of urgency to find the princess. But in a little while he stopped, aware that he had not the least idea where she was, or where he was headed. Flattening himself against the wall, he thought his own gasping breath was so loud that the sound of it must betray his presence to any searchers who came near. If only he could keep from breathing! But he was likely to reach that state of perfect silence soon enough.

Now it seemed to Alex that not only soldiers, but also the priests of Shiva, carrying their instruments of torture, must already be searching for him, and that the men who sought his life must hear the pulses pounding in his head. At any moment they were bound to come upon him; and a few minutes after that, if he was lucky, he would be dead.

His mouth was dry, with normal thirst as well as with fear. Too bad that a canteen had been no part of this morning's prescribed uniform.

He moved on, still nursing a fading hope to join the princess and her party. But gradually it was borne in on him that it probably made no difference whether he tried to desert or rejoin his squad; he was now hopelessly lost. Maybe if he climbed one of these walls, he could at least see where he was, in relation to the palace and the city . . . but when he looked up he saw that here the high walls, difficult enough in themselves, had been topped with a stiff growth of some mutant thorn. It would be impossible to walk on that.

The sun as it progressed across the sky could give him some clue as to the points of the compass. But since he did not know in which direction he wanted to move, knowing them would be no help.

Once, encountering a cheerful fountain, Alex paused gratefully, long enough to plunge his head into the pool at its base, and drink deeply. There was no telling when he might have another chance.

After resting a few minutes, he felt unable to sit still, and moved on at a steady walk. Now he had to fight against a helpless feeling much akin to that of drowning. For a long time now, he had not had the slightest idea whether or not the path he was following was bringing him any closer to the princess and her party. For all he knew, his every move was carrying him farther and farther away from her.

Turn right.

Alex stopped in his tracks, body swaying with the impetus of suddenly arrested motion. The voice that had uttered those two words had been so plain, though soft, that he did not doubt for a moment that he had really heard it. But it had issued from no visible body; his eyes assured him that he was still utterly alone.

Only once before had Alex ever heard a similar voice. Half a year ago, on a certain never-to-be-forgotten night, a night of wintry wind and bloody horror; and the voices he had heard then had been those of the auxiliaries of Dionysus.

Now, even as he stood waiting, listening, beginning to fear that imagination was after all playing tricks, the breathless little voice came back again, as clearly as before: *Turn right, then up the little stair, and right again.*

In his disoriented state of mind, the next thought Alex had was that the beings who spoke to him had somehow joined in his persecution, and he cried out, "Why are you doing this to me?"

But at the moment he could get no answer to that question. The only sounds that came, very faintly, were those of music and merriment.

Then at last, a few words: *Not to you, for you. We want to help.*

And then, as if his interlocutors grew impatient, Alex saw a mysterious, insubstantial figure, beckoning to him from around a corner. At once he recalled a glimpse of a similar presence, on that night of death and horror in the great hall, six months ago.

Above the loins, the body was that of a naked human male, while all the lower parts, including the two hoofed legs, were thickly covered by the rough fur of a beast. Whatever it might be, it at least was not a soldier, or a priest of Shiva, and Alex instinctively obeyed the wordless summons.

And now, off in the distance somewhere, he could hear soldiers shouting excitedly, fired with the excitement of the hunt.

And in the same instant, the rapid voice in his own ear: *They chase after phantoms.*

The inhuman presence was frightening, and he tried to run. Gasping, sobbing for breath, he plunged back into the windings of the Labyrinth.

Once more the sounds of pursuit, or of a search at least, grew less and faded away. Still, in spite of everything, he had not been caught. Luck seemed with him, and luck might count for as much as an army.

Then, there it was again, in front of him, the ghostly figure waving a beckoning arm. Again, having no hope of any better chance, Alex followed.

Apotheosis will be a good treatment for any wound—therefore see the apothecary. A voice that certainly sounded like a woman's giggled those words into his ear. Alex only wished that he could have known what the two big words in the statement meant.

Rest here.

And gratefully he sank down.

If only he'd been able to find Asterion, who would have told him where to go and what to do . . . but Asterion was probably long gone now, with his sister, and Daedalus, and the others. If only the Lady Ariadne had managed to escape! That, after all, was far more important than what might happen to a half-nameless soldier.

At last Alex heard the horn, the usual signal for a recall of the troops. Now the officers would be reorganizing, planning a methodical search, and in a little while they would be back in earnest. The Maze might shelter him from that. But by the same token, he was still lost in the Maze, utterly and hopelessly lost . . .

Sitting against a wall, Alex dozed, to snap awake again with a nervous start. The sun was gone now, light fading from what he could see of the sky, darkness beginning to enfold the Labyrinth. He had been on the move since dawn, and had accomplished nothing, except to keep himself alive. Which he might have managed just as easily by sitting still. Would there be searchers through the night, groping about in the Maze with torches? He couldn't guess.

Trying to burrow his way into the deepest, darkest hole he could, in which to hide, he tumbled into the closest thing to a hideaway that he could find. Not underground, but the cramped dead end of a coiled passage that just wound in on itself, going nowhere.

He lay there breathing deeply, feeling utterly worn out. Now he was bottled up for sure. Never in his life had he felt so weary and alone. If only he could find some reason to hope that what he had done today had been in some slight way a service to the princess . . .

Totally exhausted, Alex knew despair. He had missed his appointed meeting with the princess and the others, he had no idea where they were going or how, and he would certainly be unable to follow them. The only bright side of his situation seemed to be that if he were captured he would be unable to betray them. Even the Butcher, even Shiva himself, would not be able to extract information a man did not have.

But if only the princess could get away! He kept coming back to that, which was the all-important thing. But the truth was that he would probably go to his own death without ever knowing what had happened to her—or to her lover.   •

Alex had to admit that he would have been unlikely to find a better hiding place than the one to which he had been led. If the powers that had brought him here were as friendly as they claimed to be, then it might offer real refuge for a time. Alex had slept very little on his last night in the barracks; and his weariness soon overcame him now.

He was not even aware that he was close to falling asleep again, until a jolt of nervous tension jarred him abruptly awake. For a moment he lay there afraid to breathe. Then there came a rustling in the darkness, and a faint glow, and once more the helpful powers were on hand.

Someone—or something; he barely felt a touch upon his hand—handed him a smooth stone cup, brimming with cool liquid. A taste informed him that it was wine, fine wine, and water mixed. Not only did the draught quench his thirst, but it sent him right back to sleep.

He was awakened again, with another jarring start, this time from dreamless oblivion, and with the conviction that someone, or something, had just said to him in a clear voice, *Now it is time.*

Had he been dreaming after all? No, because he suddenly realized that he was not alone in his small stone refuge. For a moment he could remember that the vast Labyrinth enfolded him, and wonder whether he was waking in a prison, or a tomb.

"Time for what?" he whispered back. "Who are you?"

In answer there came a giggle, then a whisper of what sounded like nonsense words. With a deep inner chill, Alex suddenly remembered that madness was the real signature of Dionysus. But the being confronting him now was only some satyr, sprite, or other minor power.

Gradually he became aware that there were two or three of them—he could not be certain of the number—with him in the confined space. They glowed in the dark, with a gentle light to which only the corners of his human eyes seemed sensitive. Each of them interchangeably took on and put off again the appearance of man and woman, child and goat, sitting or standing or lying at full length. Somehow his new companions seemed to occupy little or no room, but it was hard to be certain of anything about them. Whenever Alex tried to look closely at one of the figures, it dissolved into grayish back-of-the-eyeball blurs, exotic shifting shapes that made no sense and had no permanence.

"Tell me who you are." He breathed the words as much in weariness as fear. If something horrible was going to happen, then let it happen and be done.

Only a faint whisper came back, and at first Alex couldn't be sure that he was hearing anything but the wind. Still he could see them moving, and he knew that they were with him.

Once the Lord Dionysus was like you.

"Ah," said Alex. On any ordinary day, the fact that any nonhuman being had chosen to speak directly to him would have stricken him with awe. Today, however, he seemed to have no capacity left for such emotions.

After a pause he continued, "Yes. Yes, I remember he told me that himself." Alex paused again, waiting for an answer.

Faint, very faint and far away, the music of a single flute. Of course they were the creatures of Dionysus; what else could they be? But even the mad must sometimes tell the truth.

Alex swallowed, then got out a whisper through a tight throat. "Lord Dionysus? Where are you?"

Our god is dead.

"Oh." He swallowed. "Then what do you want of me?"

Come. A little patch of blurred fog. The ghost of a pale hand, beckoning.

Shakily Alex rose to his feet. He wondered if he was weakening, though at the moment he felt no particular hunger. Led by the sprite, for no great distance, but by a convoluted path, to a cranny, a buried recess, that he would not have found unaided in a hundred years of searching, Alex came upon the body of the previous avatar of Dionysus. At first, all he could recognize was the cape.

A swirling of half-visible forms was followed by what sounded like a whispered consultation, and then one who had been delegated to do so came back to the young man again, an image becoming minimally plainer, the mere outline of an old man, bearded like a goat. *When no one wears the Face of Dionysus, we grow weaker and weaker. If our god stays dead much longer, most of us will fade and die.*

Alex looked about him on the dusty pavement, starting at the spot beneath the mummified head of the late god. Nothing. "Where is the Face? Does one of you have it?"

The vague form gestured, with what might have been its hands. *None of us can ever wear it, for we are not human. We are allowed to touch it only briefly.*

A spotted panther, looking like a creature from somewhere deep in the mainland jungles, south of the Great Sea, came into view, silent as a ghost, regarding him gravely. It was a very strange sight indeed, though not the strangest that Alex had seen today. And now there were two panthers, enough like each other to be twins. And, just behind the great cats, an image as of a small chariot, hardly more than toy-sized. In a moment the animals withdrew, or disappeared. The great cats had looked neither more nor less unreal than all the other visitants; and as soon as they moved away, the chariot too was gone, if it had ever been there.

For a moment Alex recoiled in fear. But then he moved forward again to look. At last he knelt down, cautiously, beside the inert figure.

As a soldier he was no stranger to death in all its phases. Obviously the god had been dead for a long time. Judging from everything he knew about the case, Alex concluded that six months would be about the right interval. Dionysus—this avatar of Dionysus—had probably hidden here half a year ago, on the night when he fled from Shiva.

"Who are you?"

This time he was asking about the individual who spoke to him, not the whole collection of them, and so his question was understood. *My name is Silenus. But that does not matter. What matters is that spring has come again, and yet our god is dead.*

A second voice now joined in the ghostly whispering. *Our god is dead, yet spring has come to the world regardless. Is that not strange and unbelievable?* It was a weird, affecting lamentation, all the more intense because it was so inhuman.

This was one turning of the year when the previous avatar was not going to revive. The body was little more than a skeleton by this time, but the rich cape that Alex remembered was here, now only a weathered rag. The golden winecup Dionysus had drunk from in the great hall now lay near the skeletal right hand. Dionysus, at least in this most recent avatar, had not bothered to bear weapons, at least none of any ordinary sort. If a divinity became so weak that he needed a commonplace sword or spear, they weren't likely to do him any good.

The fleeing god had left his *thyrsus*-staff in the great hall, where it had been incinerated by Shiva. Alex wondered whether the staff might have reconstituted itself somehow, as sometimes the tools of the gods did in legend. If so, it was not here.

And there was no sign of the Face.

Overcoming first his awe, then a growing distaste at this disturbance of the dead, Alex began to search, first carefully, then more vigorously. But what he was looking for was not to be found.

The countenance of the corpse, eyeless and noseless now, was still utterly and routinely human. No more and no less horrible than that of any man long dead, a kind of placid and routine horror. Nothing that ought to frighten an experienced soldier, or raise his hopes. Yet a wild hope, that had in it a strong component of new fear, had been born in Alex now. He repeated his question, this time as a demand. "Where is the Face?"

We took it away. We wanted to make sure that it remained out of our enemies' reach.

"You mean someone else has put it on?"

It would be a mistake to bring about our god's rebirth just now here on Corycus. When the Twice-Born lives again, he must be given

*time to grow, develop, become familiar with his powers before he needs
to use them. Here and now, Shiva would allow him no such time.*

"Then where is the Face?" Alex persisted. "You've hidden it somewhere?"

*When you have arrived at a certain temple of Apollo, we will tell
you more. In that place you may discover our god's Face, and put it
on.*

There was a silence that seemed long. Those last three words kept
echoing in the young soldier's mind, while their meaning seemed to
stay just out of reach.

"I?" Alex cried at last. Abruptly he was very conscious of the
strangeness of the Labyrinth around him. The passageway in which he
crouched seemed to be constricting around him. "*I* am to put it on?"

*On the night when our god last breathed, he spoke favorably of
you.*

Suddenly Alex could remember again the fallen avatar in the great
hall, looking directly at him and saying, with something like envy, *Once
I was like you.* It seemed to the young man now that he could hear in
the echo of that booming voice all the false heartiness and bravado that
had concealed a great fear.

Aloud he asked, "And this—my discovering the Face—is to happen
in some temple of Apollo? Not one of Dionysus?"

No response.

His mind was whirling. Sudden dreams of unbelievable glory alternated with sharp pangs of terror. "Anyway, I think there are no longer
any temples of Apollo on this island. Shiva has ordered them all destroyed, or converted to base use."

The only answer was faint music, and fainter laughter. The man
could hear nothing of joy, but only a kind of madness in it.

"All right, so I must reach a certain temple of Apollo. Where does
it stand, if not here on Corycus? And how am I to get there?"

*We are weak. Without our god to give us strength, the long trip
over the water may be too much for us.*

The voices babbled all together suddenly, sounding confused, not
to say mad. But what else to expect from the entourage of Dionysus,
God of Frenzy? Alex resisted the urge to repeat his search of the immediate area, to make sure that despite their babble, the Face was not
simply lying here unclaimed.

Struck by a sudden thought, Alex raised his head and whispered
into the air, "Does Shiva know that your god is dead?"

The God of Destruction does not care. He has not taken the trouble to search for Dionysus. Shiva is very much afraid of certain other deities. But not of our lord. Not yet.

There came an eerie sound, a kind of high-pitched rumbling, rolling down one of the twisting corridors—Alex could not at first be sure which one. Soon the chariot, pulled by the two ghostly panthers, pulled up in front of him and stood there, waiting, its car unoccupied. The whole equipage seemed much bigger now, too wide to have negotiated the narrow pathways of the Maze—yet here it was.

Get in.

Drawing a deep breath, Alex put a hand on the low side rail of the vehicle, just in front of one of the two tall wheels. The sensation of solidity beneath his palm and fingers wavered once, then firmed. It had the feel of ivory, or horn.

Drawing another deep breath, and holding it this time, he vaulted up onto the wheeled platform. Before he could locate the reins, or even confirm that any existed, he heard a warbling of flutes and a clash of ghostly cymbals, the panthers sprang forward, and the chariot shot up, lurching into the air.

At that moment the rattle of wheels on pavement ceased abruptly. Gripping the railing with all his strength, Alex groaned and involuntarily closed his eyes. The last thing he saw was the moonlit vast complexity of the Labyrinth falling away beneath him, many of its thousand miles of twisted passageways now visible all at once.

When he opened his eyes again, moments later, most of the island of Corycus was spread out below, with faint points of light outlining the sprawling city, and marking the other settled places. Here and there a lone spark from lamp or hearth marked, he supposed, an isolated dwelling.

Everything was quiet, except for the rush of air. The soft feet of the leopards, running over a soft carpet of mere air and cloud, made no sound that human ears could hear.

At last his ears were able to pick out a fainter murmur in the air around him. He understood that the tattered remnants of the minor powers were accompanying him upon this journey. Somehow the little chariot was able to contain them all, or drag them with it through the sky.

12

THE LAST THING that Edith, the girl from Dia, could remember was
. . . a monstrous, animal-like figure looming in front of her . . . her own
voice, shouting in terror, pleading with Apollo, *Alexikakos*, averter of
evil, to save her from the bloody horror that threatened.

Standing in line with the others of the Tribute, she had been shocked
by an outcry, and had looked up in utter amazement to see Prince Theseus escape. She had watched, as with startling fury he struck down a
guard, with what speed and strength he hauled himself over a wall and
out of sight.

Such feats were not possible for her. But suddenly it was no longer
possible to simply, meekly, wait for pain and death. In a moment, she
too was running as fast as she could . . .

Now, regaining consciousness with the sense that hours of drugged
sleep must have passed, she remembered few details of the peril from
which she had been rescued. Her head ached, and thirst was parching
her mouth and throat.

Then, with a shock, something like full memory returned, and she
sat up.

Even on the last morning of their lives, many of the eighteen had
not believed that they were doomed to die. The upcoming ceremony
meant only that they would be initiated somehow into Shiva's cult.

For days she and her doomed companions, an assortment of young
folk who seemed to come from every quarter of the Great Sea, had been
aware that this was the morning when they were to meet the god. Shiva,
the Compassionate, as his priests described him, who took an interest
in their welfare . . . then the first victims were marched up to the cages,
and shut in. There followed the glowing iron and sharp, cruel knives,

the dripping blood. What Edith now remembered most clearly of all was her own body's reaction, the burst of panic breaking through the fog of drugged wine, to send her running madly for her life . . .

Now everything around her was silence, tranquility giving at least the appearance of safety. Bright sunlight, coming at an angle not far from that of midday, touched part of one high wall above her. *Apollo, lord of light, you have not yet entirely forsaken me.*

━━━━━━

She had awakened lying on a kind of curved stone bench, built into one wall of the Maze at a place where several passages came together, forming a clear space roughly circular, about three yards in diameter. The miniature courtyard thus created had five entrances or exits, five doorless apertures, each leading to a different corridor. Three of the connecting ways were roofless, and all of them curved out of sight after only a few yards. She was still dressed in the clothing of the ritual. There was more cloth beneath her body, a kind of blanket that she had never seen before, padding her away from the sun-warmed stone, and a folded robe to serve as pillow under her head.

There was no need to ask herself: where am I? For the tall, laterally curving stone walls that shut her in told her with certainty where she was—still inside the Labyrinth. Some of those walls seemed waves of stone, frozen in time, about to topple in and crush her. For all she knew, she could still be near the very place where the sacrifice was to have been carried out. But she sat up with a sudden movement, provoking a wave of dizziness. And now she began to wonder what could have happened.

Her belt had been loosened, and a cup of water and some fruit placed at her side. Indeed, she was very thirsty, and drank the water in a few quick swallows. She had had nothing to eat or drink since that early morning draught of delightful wine and water, administered by Shiva's helpers. They had poured hers carelessly, filling the goblet less than halfway. Something in *that* cup must have been potent enough to begin to dissolve even the fear of death.

Now she had drained the last drops from the simple cup of water before it occurred to her to wonder whether it too might be drugged. But the taste of this drink was clean and cold, not like that poisoned wine at all.

Every part of her body ached as she forced herself to get to her feet. Repeated waves of dizziness made her sway as she stood listening. Somewhere in the distance she could hear what sounded like soldiers' voices, shouting back and forth, though it was impossible to make out what they were saying, and even hard to tell how far away they were.

Had she been retaken, then? Carried to this spot by soldiers, who might reappear at any moment, to carry her back to the place where Shiva's victims bled and died?

But no soldiers appeared. Instead, there came a slight sound behind her, and she turned quickly. She of course recognized the shape before her as the Monster of the Maze, dreaded by everyone. It was the last sight she had seen at the place of horror and blood. Whimpering, she shrank back against the wall. She might have run, but was engulfed by another wave of dizziness, motes swimming before her eyes.

The monstrous figure paused, spreading huge manlike hands as if to show they were empty of any threat. In an unlikely, low-pitched voice it said, "You needn't be afraid. I'll keep my distance, if that will ease your mind."

Desperately Edith pressed her body back into the curved corner, feeling rough stone against her back. "What do you want?"

The beast, the monster, answered as calmly as before. "My name is Asterion; at moments of formality, the Lord, or Prince, Asterion, though we needn't be bothered about titles. And you are—?"

The possibility that the creature might have a name, might be *someone*, had somehow never occurred to her before. Automatically she told him her own name.

"Edith. Yes, I like that. I am the one who brought you here, you know, after snatching you away from the killing." Here he paused, as if to give her time for some response. But Edith could only shake her head, and Asterion went on. "Or perhaps you don't remember. But I am not one of those you must fear." There was a longer pause. The creature sat down on the opposite bench, and as it ceased to tower over her it became a touch less threatening. "As for what I want—well, to start with, you might oblige me by answering a question or two."

"Yes?" She managed to get out the one word clearly.

"To begin with: Just what is it that you're afraid I'm going to do to you? Eat you? I don't even eat lamb chops."

It took her almost half a minute of confused effort to come up with a kind of answer. "I remember the blood . . ."

"None of it was of my spilling. Well, only a little bit, perhaps."

———

Still the young woman had very little to say, but I could see that her fear of me grew less as I sat at ease and conversed with her.

It was all very well to congratulate myself for having rescued one of the eighteen, and I had no second thoughts about having done so. But now, I was growing more perturbed as she grew calmer. Minute by minute, a certain question was becoming more urgent: what was I going to do with her?

I had no means of inducing the girl to fall asleep again; all I could do was listen to her hopeless weeping until it ceased. Later on, when she slept again, I ought to be able to prolong her slumber by a little bit, and also to see to it that her dreams were pleasant, and reassuring. Maybe, if we were very lucky, I could do more than that.

But such plans failed to come to grips with the basic question: what *was* I going to do with her? Certainly by now it was too late for me, let alone my new companion, to join my sister and her desperate band of escapees. Daedalus and the others would not still be waiting for me, and I could only hope that they had all gotten away. In dreams lay my best hope of getting an accurate report on what had happened to them; but that would have to wait. Dreaming required sleep, and it was pretty plain that I was not going to sleep again for many hours.

———————

Within an hour or so I began to realize that Edith might have to live with me in the Labyrinth indefinitely. While she was still unconscious, I had carried her to a remote area, where it seemed practically impossible that the inevitable searchers would ever find their way. Here, a human presence of any kind was exceedingly rare; the grass grew thick in many places between the paving stones. Probably none of Shiva's priests, or the Butcher's soldiers, had yet come closer than a mile— which meant that they were effectively hundreds of miles distant, by any route that they were at all likely to discover.

And now, as the young girl lost her immediate fears, the larger difficulties of her situation became plainer in her eyes. "I want to go home!" she moaned, again and again.

I did my best to remain calm and soothing. "No doubt you do. But I don't know when that will be possible." I thought, but did not add: *probably never.* I could understand, being so attached to my own terrific home that I was ready to die rather than leave it.

"Where is home, Edith?" I asked, after a little silence. I was thinking that gentle talk was probably the best thing for her just now.

"The island of Dia."

"Is that so? I've heard of it, of course, but never been there. Tell me about it."

And soon she was able to take food, and enjoy an almost-peaceful sleep. But soon I felt I had to awaken her from that. Time was passing, and there were things I had to do. I explained to my guest and new companion that I had to leave her for a little while. "There has been much excitement, as you can imagine—as we have both heard." Indeed, certain phases of the great search had been quite noisy, some of the military trumpet calls audible a mile away. "I expect there may be messages waiting for me, and I had better see them."

The shade of alarm that crossed her face was flattering. "Asterion, you won't—?"

"Abandon you? Certainly not." But I emphasized, and repeated, that she should stay where she was. "I can almost guarantee that no one will find you here." That guarantee would be void if Shiva ever nerved himself to take an active part in the proceedings; but I saw no reason to mention that. "And where would you go? Believe me, you won't be able to find your way out of the Maze. On top of that, you wouldn't *want* to find your way out, because everywhere outside are the soldiers of King Perses, and the priests of Shiva, and I have no doubt that they are all still looking for you.

"Besides, if you go wandering about inside the Labyrinth, you may lose yourself so thoroughly that even I won't be able to locate you when I return. There is fruit growing here in this courtyard"—I pointed to a patch of exposed soil, where two trees grew, as well as the mutant vine—"and running water. And I promise you, I will return, as soon as I can. With some more food for you, and with good news, I hope. Though naturally I do not promise that."

By the morning after the escape, Uncle Perses had become exceedingly eager to interrogate me. During the previous afternoon, the usurper king had taken time out from his other efforts to send messengers into the Maze, who claimed to know where I could usually be found. One of these messengers, actually an old woman who had once been my nurse, had succeeded in leaving a written message for the Minotaur.

Dutifully I checked in certain odd locations, nooks and crannies of the Labyrinth which my sister and I had used, in our early years, as places to exchange communications. Today there was no such good luck as a note from Ariadne. But I did find a brief note, as sort of memorandum, from the usurper.

To judge by the contents of the note, Perses had already questioned Princess Phaedra extensively, and I silently congratulated myself on our wisdom in keeping all knowledge of the plot from her. Nor had Phaedra any idea of where I might usually be found inside the Labyrinth; Ariadne had almost never discussed such things with her. My elder sister had met me only a few times, generally in dreams. I could not remember whether we had ever laid eyes on each other in waking life; if that had happened, it must have been when I was very small. I knew that Phaedra wished me well, but couldn't help being profoundly upset by the mere sight of her half-brother.

But the main point of the king's written message was a proposal, almost a supplication, for a meeting with me. It did not mention Ariadne, and the wording of it raised my hopes that the attempted flight had succeeded.

———

The usurper and I had had very little contact with each other at any time, and none at all in the six months since Perses came to power.

Somehow it did not concern me greatly that I had irrevocably missed my chance of escaping with the others. It seemed to me almost as if someone else had made the decision for me, knowing I would approve. Maybe I had known somehow, even when I so impulsively rescued the girl, that her presence would prevent my flight.

Nor did I greatly dread my coming interview with the usurper. Even if Perses was aware that his monstrous nephew had aided the princess and others to get away, he was not going to kill a son of Zeus. And now, looking back, I see that there was another possible reason for my remaining where I was: I might simply have been too much afraid to leave the only home that I had ever known.

———

Our meeting took place in a portion of the Labyrinth that lay quite near the place where most of the youths and maidens of the Tribute had been done to death, and from which Theseus must have made his escape.

My uncle was wearing full battle dress, as if he thought an invasion was impending, and was attended by a bodyguard of half a dozen soldiers, all picked men from the Palace Guard. Also present was a priest of Shiva, who with his necklace of small imitation skulls was obviously trying to cultivate a similarity of appearance with his dread master.

The monarch's rage grew as the evidence mounted that Daedalus and his son were among the missing. That made six people in all who were unaccounted for.

"Vanished as if the earth had swallowed them." The priest decked out in imitation skulls seemed to think he had just invented a particularly apt comparison.

"All the inducements I showered upon the man," Perses grumbled again. "I made him wealthy."

The Artisan's simple quarters near the center of the Maze had of course been found deserted. A small room containing two small beds, and nothing special in the way of furnishings. A few of their scant belongings were lying about, but there was nothing to indicate whether the man and boy might be coming back. I saw that a satchel containing a set of fine, small tools had been opened and its contents scattered.

"Surely he would have wanted to take his special tools with him?" I suggested helpfully.

"Maybe they were too heavy for the balloon," muttered one of the searching officers nearby. I gave no sign that I had heard.

The woman who sometimes cared for the child, a duty she had shared with other members of the regular Cretan palace household staff, had been going about her routine business of cleaning and preparing food. No, she could tell nothing about where the Artisan and his son might have gone. Both man and boy tended to be irregular in their habits.

And, though he remained reluctant to admit the fact to me, Perses was forced to acknowledge that his niece Ariadne was also among those who had disappeared. No one had a clue as to where they might be now.

My heart leaped up in joy. For me it is always easy to keep my emotions from showing in my face.

The concern in the usurper's voice was very real when he informed me, "Princess Phaedra is greatly worried about her sister's welfare."

For once I could easily believe that the murderer spoke the truth. "Naturally," I responded. "As I am."

———

In the course of this conversation I refused to show any sign of respect to the priest, whose name was Creon. Looking him up and down, I observed, "Somehow I was expecting to see the god himself."

"Be glad that you do not," snarled the priest.

"Why?" the king demanded of me. "What do you want with the Lord Shiva? Some favor to ask?"

I returned the usurper's gaze curiously. "I want nothing from him. Certainly no favor."

The new Minos was obviously trying to repress his loathing when he looked at me; and yet, I could tell that he was impressed, almost intimidated, despite himself.

"Asterion, you are my nephew, and I wish you well."

"Half-nephew, at least, half-uncle."

He was not going to try to respond to that. "They tell me you have all the understanding of a normal man. Despite the shape of your head."

I was already angry at this man. Very angry, because of the killing of our father, the pain he had caused Ariadne, and for the lies he spread and encouraged about the Minotaur. "They tell me the same thing about you," I returned sweetly.

At that the king's anger flamed, so that his bodyguard looked at him expectantly, and tightened their grips upon their spears, as if they anticipated an order to attack the warped creature before them, and put it out of its misery. But, as I had expected, Perses gave no such command. He had business to transact with me. Obviously there was some kind of help he wanted from the impertinent monster, and he managed to control his temper.

Motioning Creon the priest to withdraw to a little distance, the usurper said to me, placatingly, "Your father and I were never bosom friends. But neither were we enemies."

"Does your majesty mean my father King Minos, or my Father Zeus, the ruler of the universe?" That last was perhaps an exaggeration; though not, as I thought, by much.

"I am speaking of my brother."

On rare occasions in my childhood and youth I had tried to explore in dreams the question of what my foster father, or adoptive father, Minos, had really thought of me. But in truth I was afraid to learn the whole truth on that subject. Minos had not slain me in my monstrous infancy, even though my horns, already present at my birth, had cost him the life of his unfaithful queen. Of course, for a wife, especially a royal wife, to betray her husband with a mere man is one thing, and for her to bear the children of the Great Lecher Zeus is quite another. Also I found it not always easy, and sometimes quite impossible, to cause the visions of the night to develop in the exact way I wanted them to go.

I said, "I never considered King Minos my enemy, and indeed I hardly knew him. When I heard that he was dead, the news at first had little impact. But having had half a year to think about it, I find I'm truly sorry." I paused for a moment. "Of course my sisters are still grieving deeply."

"So are we all, my boy. So are we all." A stranger would have believed his sorrow, his willingness to be reconciled, perfectly genuine. "Now, speaking of your sisters: tell me, where is Ariadne?"

"I do not know," I said quite honestly. Once more I could be glad of my inhuman face and voice, which make it vastly easier to conceal my emotions.

"If you did know, Asterion, would you tell me?"

I tried to give the impression that I was thinking the question over very seriously. "Any answer I might give you now, majesty, would be only speculation."

The usurper, his face totally expressionless, stared at me in silence for a full ten seconds. Then he tried once more. "Also among the missing is a certain slave-girl, Clara, who is the regular attendant of the missing princess. You know the girl I mean?"

"I may know the girl you mean, Uncle. But I don't know where she is now. Probably with Ariadne."

I thought our noble uncle winced slightly at the familiar form of address. But he remained outwardly calm.

"Another is a young Dian woman named Edith, one of those who were to have been honored by the Lord Shiva."

"I have no information to give you about her either. So, am I to understand that only one of the eighteen is missing? What exactly happened? How many are still alive?"

"Actually two of the Tribute are among the six people unaccounted for. The second is a youth named Theseus. We have learned from a servant that he held a private meeting with your younger sister, several days ago."

"A private meeting?"

"Yes."

I shook my head, expressing ignorance.

With an effort at patience, Perses went on with his list of questions. "Have you seen anything at all, since the day of the ceremony, of Daedalus, or of his child? Or of a lost soldier, who may be wandering in the Maze?"

So, I thought, *Alex also may have got away.* My horned head continued to shake slowly from side to side. "Don't tell me they are missing too? But if I do encounter any of these people, my uncle, I will inform them of your concern."

"Make sure you do." Our noble uncle paused to draw a deep breath. "But I see you are still here."

I inclined my head in a slight bow; let him make of that answer what he would.

"Where were you, Asterion, when the sun came up yesterday morning?"

I considered pretending to have difficulty remembering. But that would have been childish. "Uncle, I was busy trying to explore the world."

The usurper leaned forward, frowning. "Trying to explore—what do you mean?"

"In the only way possible for one whose movements are so restricted. I explore the world by means of dreams."

It seemed to me that our uncle did not have much belief in his nephew's dreams—but likely he could easily be convinced.

Now he said, "You and I, Prince Asterion, have not always gotten on very well together." He said it with the air of a man who had recently made a discovery that gently pained him.

"I fear that is true, Uncle."

"Will you believe me when I say that I would like to be your friend?"

"How could I doubt my true king?"

Impulsively, or so it seemed, he reached out to grasp my hand in friendship. At that moment I might have seized the opportunity to jerk him toward me and wring his neck. But moments after doing that, I too would lie dead, and Edith would be left completely unprotected. And the death of Perses would have achieved nothing, really, to my sisters' benefit. There would still be Shiva, ready to put some other human puppet on the throne.

And still I wondered why Shiva was not present at this meeting. It seemed to me that the king, and even the chief priest Creon, might be uneasy over the same question.

Naturally Shiva had been enraged at the disruption of the sacrifice, and the loss of some of the youths and maidens whose painful deaths would have fed his cravings. But the question kept looming larger and larger—where had the God of Destruction gone when he departed so suddenly? And, where was he now?

Even gods—some of them might say, *especially* gods—had enemies. Envy and jealousy raged among them as violently as in any merely human group.

"I see that bravery is not the Destroyer's most conspicuous quality." The people around me blanched when they heard me say those words.

The usurper said he did not find it surprising that Shiva was not available just now for consultation, or to inspire his followers and allies. The hunt for the escapees would have to be conducted without divine assistance. The God of Destruction, before vanishing, had told Minos that he had more important things to worry about. "You must see to these details yourself. Other powers of some kind are near, I tell you!"

But Uncle Perses and the Butcher had wasted no time before organizing a mass search of the Labyrinth for the escapees. The king also dispatched riders on cameloids, commanding that all the coasts should be watched. But it was a long, long, winding coastline, that with its many bays and promontories extended for hundreds of miles. The king's word would need at least a day to reach the farthest points of the island; and how comprehensively it would be honored was a question. Any fugitive who once got clear of the palace and the city was in a fair way for getting away entirely.

And the king suspected that, if Daedalus was seriously involved in their escape plot, the fugitives might well enjoy some extraordinary means of transportation. "If you know the man's reputation as I do, you will worry."

The Butcher agreed.

And Shiva agreed, but had little thought to spare for Daedalus, or any of the other humans involved. Rather he was consumed by his suspicion that the escape was only a diversion, planned by certain other gods who were jealously trying to destroy him.

———

The attempted search of the Labyrinth, by a hundred men of the Palace Guard, had achieved little but to get half a dozen of the Butcher's soldiers fairly seriously lost. In spite of some measure of planning, military discipline, and stern precautions, several of those men became separated from their comrades, and did not find their way back for several hours. By sunset on the day following the escape, almost all had been recovered, but the new Minos was left with the uncomfortable feeling that if he ever chose to deploy his soldiers in those endless passageways, an entire army could easily be swallowed up, like water flowing into sand.

At last only one man remained unaccounted for, a certain private soldier known as Alex the Half-Nameless, last seen running after the escaping Prince Theseus. None of other members of his squad seemed to have any idea where Private Alex might have got to. Of course it was possible that he had caught up with some of the plotters, they had killed him, and his body lay undiscovered in some winding of the Maze.

Before our conversation was quite over, an urgent report was brought to the king, concerning the finding of some parts of a balloon, and feathers, in an outlying portion of the Maze.

"A scattering of feathers?" Creon's voice went up in an unseemly squawk.

Several people had reported seeing a kind of balloon-shape, heading out to sea. The thing was visible only at a distance, and it was impossible to gauge its size.

To those who knew Daedalus by reputation, it was entirely possible that he had contrived a miraculous escape.

13

ON EMERGING FROM the mouth of the secret tunnel, the princess and her companions immediately scanned their surroundings, looking for the best hiding place nearby. The land nearby was mostly waste, with a small marsh where the stream they had been following trickled into the sea. There were no houses in sight, and no sign of human presence, apart from a couple of narrow paths, so the danger of accidental discovery appeared to be no worse than moderate.

A cluster of small caves offered the most convenient hiding place, and virtually the only one in the immediate vicinity. The caves were clustered forty or fifty feet above the marsh, near the top of a sandstone cliff, the highest point of land within half a mile. Within a minute or two the fugitives had scrambled up to the high ground and were established in the caves. The stream was still near enough to provide a source of water. Obviously the lack of food would soon become a problem, if they were forced to stay here for any length of time.

Looking inland from the top of the cliff, it was easily possible to see the towers and walls of Kandak, less than four miles away. In the circumstances this was not a reassuring sight.

The openings of the high caves also afforded a good view of the sea. Theseus, sounding confident, assured the others that it would be easy for him to spot the sail, or the hull, of the ship he was expecting to come looking for them.

Of course the five people spent most of their time doing their best to stay out of sight, keeping their heads down in one cave or another. At any moment a patrol of soldiers might come along to take them alive and drag them back to Shiva and King Perses, or perhaps to kill some of them on the spot. Or some vessel of the Corycan navy might sail by, and spot them on the shore. Or the God of Destruction himself might finally decide to come looking for them, mounted airborne on his bull. Everyone suffered with the heat and the confinement, but the threat of a much worse fate, if they should be overtaken by Shiva or his followers, stifled protest.

All day, at intervals of half an hour or less, Daedalus or Theseus, or sometimes both together, would emerge restlessly from a cave and crawl to the top of the small cliff. There, crouching or lying flat to avoid presenting a conspicuous silhouette against the sky, an observer had a view of the sea that was both broad and deep. Now the men searched the horizon anxiously. Once or twice during the day a distant sail came into view, but none headed for the island.

Meanwhile the slave-girl Clara moved about restlessly, going back and forth between the two most habitable caves, until her mistress ordered her sharply to settle down somewhere and be still. At that, Clara seemed to pull herself together and concentrated on inventing quiet games to play with the child.

Theseus spent most of his time, between visits to the cliff top, waiting in a cave, looking moodily out to sea, or tossing pebbles, one at a time, at sparrows that came near. He never managed to hit any of them. Ariadne spent most of her time looking soulfully at the man she loved, and trying to think of ways to cheer him up.

Icarus whined, sometimes, when Clara's games grew boring, until his father threatened to cuff him. Daedalus fretted, and drew in the sand before the entrance of the largest cave odd diagrams that none of the others could understand.

When darkness fell, and it was no longer possible to keep a useful watch on the sea, Theseus took the princess by the hand and pulled her into the smaller of the two most easily habitable caves. At the moment the two of them had its modest space entirely to themselves. Willingly enough she allowed herself to be drawn to him, and there they lay together through the night, while no one else came near them.

Shortly after the two lovers came together, the slave-girl Clara appeared at the entrance of the largest cave, only a few yards away, into which there now began to drift soft, eager moaning sounds made by the princess.

"If you do not object to my presence, sir," Clara said to Daedalus.

"I do not mind at all." The Artisan spoke in a low voice; he glanced toward his son, who, worn out by the day's adventures, was already asleep, huddled on a patch of sand where the warmth of the day's sun still lingered. Daedalus had partially covered the small boy's body with the warm sand. "I suppose your mistress is not likely to need you for anything?"

"Not tonight, sir." The girl answered quickly and with certainty. She tilted her head, listening to the soft sounds from the other cave, and wrapped herself more tightly in what had been a fine linen dress twenty-four hours ago. The garment had sustained serious damage in the travail of the escape, and patches of Clara's smooth skin showed through holes. "She and Prince Theseus are busy keeping warm together."

"I understand. And do you have a plan for keeping yourself warm tonight?"

"Not really, sir." Her long eyelashes flickered. "But I am open to suggestions."

———

In the other cave, there came an interval of sleepy rest, and relaxed murmuring. "I am glad, Prince Theseus," whispered the Princess Ariadne, "that your plans for the future include me."

"Absolutely—certainly they do." His voice sounded vague and tired, as well it might, after all he had been through.

"Isn't it strange?" the young woman mused. "A year ago—six months ago—I had no idea that anything like this was going to happen."

"How could you have had?"

"Did you?"

"Did I expect to meet the woman who would become dearer to me than my own life? No."

The princess moved a little, snuggling herself more comfortably against her lover. "Where were you a year ago? I suppose you were safe at home, in your father's palace."

That brought a chuckle from Theseus. "My father doesn't have a palace."

"You said he was a king."

"Well, yes, but . . ." The prince seemed to be groping for words. "He has a nice big house. Even if he had a palace, neither he nor I would spend much time in it. We are both men with many affairs—affairs of state, I mean—to keep us busy."

Ariadne raised herself on one elbow. "I want to know all about your family. So far you've told me practically nothing. What is your mother's name? What's she like?"

"She's been dead for many years."

"Ah. Like my own mother. I'm so sorry for you. How about your brothers, sisters? Tell me everything. I can't believe I don't even know the name of your country, or how far away it is."

"All that can wait. Right now isn't it enough that we are both alive? And that we have each other?"

————

Theseus and the princess who loved him lay together in the soft, clean sand of the cave floor, keeping warm through the night. Ariadne kept exchanging whispers with her lover in periods of sleepy talk, between the bouts of feverish activity.

"If you don't want to talk about your family, then we can at least plan what kind of wedding we are going to have. I mean when we have finally reached your mysterious homeland."

"All in good time. You know what I would much prefer to think about right now."

"Tell me."

"This."

"Ahh."

————

And still later, the princess returned yet again to the subject of her lover's family and home. But the more Ariadne tried to press him for the relevant details that she so craved to hear, the more he put her off.

When she pressed harder, Theseus curtly broke off the discussion. "I don't want to talk about all that just now."

"Really? Then when?"

"When I feel we are truly safe, my princess. Then I'll be able to relax."

————

The best way to break off the discussion was to change the subject. Fervently Theseus protested his love for Ariadne, doing all he could to insure that she remained devoted to him. He never ceased to marvel at her beauty—for a few seconds at a time.

Privately he also marveled at the fact that she seemed really to have been a virgin—until this night. But then he supposed that was not really surprising in a princess.

Theseus slept fitfully, between bouts of passion and sleepy intervals of talk. Whenever his attention was not totally engaged with the body of the princess, he nursed his dreams and plans, which in general had little to do with her. Meanwhile he never entirely gave up watching and listening for the patrol of Minoan soldiers, who wouldn't be making much noise when they came, but would be carrying plenty of power of their own, in the form of weapons. It was important not to sleep too soundly.

———

Under a brilliant moon and piercing stars, Theseus stood confronting Asterion, deep inside the Maze. A night breeze whispered, and there was as always the faint sound of running water.

But he wasn't even thinking about Asterion at first. Instead his thoughts were confused, as if he were on the point of falling asleep. Theseus's next plan, now that his own survival seemed assured for the time being, was to get Ariadne away somewhere. It would have been great if he could have brought her sister away too. Then he might even have held both of the girls for ransom—though in his heart he would have been better satisfied if it had been Phaedra who had fallen in love with him at first sight, and who lay with him tonight. He thought she would have been more interesting, perhaps only because Phaedra had never paid him any attention. But he had done all in his power to seduce Ariadne, because she *was* clearly interested. And after all, he had no intention of ending his life as a mere sacrifice, one of a row of sacrificial dummies.

On second thought, he rather doubted that their Uncle Minos would really want either of his nieces back on Corycus, as a potential rallying point for the disaffected, once someone had been so obliging as to kidnap them. Trying to collect ransom would have been useless.

And, besides saving his own skin for the moment, Theseus wanted to find out whatever this girl knew—if she knew anything at all—about the god-Face supposedly hidden in the Labyrinth. That rumor had been passed around even among the youths and maidens of the Tribute.

Already he had tentatively questioned Clara on that subject. She had heard the same rumors as everyone else, but had been able to tell Prince Theseus nothing concrete that he did not already know.

———

Prince Asterion (as far as Theseus could determine, that seemed to be a genuine title, his real name) was half a head taller even than Theseus. His massive, hairy upper body was exposed above the beltline of his kilt, making Theseus, for all his muscular development, seem no larger than an ordinary man. The strange voice from the bull-throat said: "I am sorry to see that you have come carrying a sword on your visit to me, Prince Theseus."

"As a prince and a warrior, it is my business to carry a sword. Whether strange creatures approve of the practice or not."

"I only said that I am sorry. *Are* you a prince indeed? I know you've told my sister that you are."

Theseus made a little jerky motion with the bright blade, stirring sparks of starlight. "I am whatever I say I am. Whatever *this* says. Are *you* a prince indeed? Are you even a human being?"

"I am the brother of the woman you say you love. Does that mean nothing to you? If not, consider this: I am determined that she will take no harm through you."

Theseus made no answer to that. He was pondering whether he ought to kill the monster right away. The act would doubtless boost his reputation mightily in some quarters—but of course he would be damaged irreparably in the eyes of Ariadne, and right now that was much more important. Also, it would be much better if he were somehow able to put Asterion's powers to work for his own benefit.

Taking the bull-man hostage, holding him for ransom, seemed yet another possibility. But the objections that applied to kidnapping the sisters were valid here as well. No one, except possibly Ariadne herself, was going to pay ransom to get a monster back.

In a bright glow that impressed the dreaming eyes of Theseus as intense and silvery moonlight, the two of them still faced each other, somewhere deep inside the Maze.

The odd voice from the bull's head said to him, "What you and my sister need now, prince, if you are in fact a prince, is not a sword but a ship. I am doing my best to provide one, and if all goes well it should soon be there."

But Theseus refused to be distracted. "I don't fear your powers, monster."

"Why should you? Powers? What powers?" The creature spread his vast and leathery hands, as if to show their emptiness. "The only powers that I have exist only in dreams."

Theseus was not at all sure that he ought to believe that, of the supposed son of Zeus. The prince cast a hasty, nervous glance over his right shoulder, then very quickly another over his left. He was reluctant to take his eyes off the monster before him, even for a fraction of a second, but he could not escape the uneasy feeling that the Maze was closing in ominously around him.

"Set me free," he demanded, brandishing the blade again, "or I will kill you!"

The monstrous hands were still spread out and empty. "I do not hold you prisoner. If you would depart from me, all you need do is turn and walk away."

This time Theseus turned fully around, but saw only the endless Labyrinth, hedging him in. The walled space in which he was standing seemed to have a million doorways, but he knew, with the certainty of dream-knowledge, that they all led nowhere. With a great cry, he spun around again to face the Minotaur, leaped forward and thrust with his sword, aiming for the middle of the barrel chest, where he supposed the heart must be. The sword plunged home; the monster went down quite easily, and lay in a great heap, leaking blood.

For a long moment the prince stood frozen, in the position in which he had finished his thrust, staring at the weapon with which he'd struck the Minotaur down. Dark blood was on the blade, running down toward the hilt when he tilted up the point. How and where had he obtained so fine a tool? He could not remember. Somewhere, somehow, he'd laid his hands on a sword of fine steel—although in the moonlight he was suddenly reminded of a weapon of his father's he'd once envied, the blade of magically hardened and toughened bronze.

Certainly what he held now was not the common sword that he had taken from a common soldier, in the midst of his desperate scramble to escape the Labyrinth. Dark blood, almost black in the moonlight, oozed onto his hand, and he shifted his grip on the sword and tried to wipe his fingers clean against his thigh, realizing as he did that he was naked. How had he come here without clothing?

The monster was dead, a mound of fallen meat, but the monster's Maze still held him prisoner.

Above him now, what had been a clear night sky was darkening, immense thunderheads rolling into position, emitting a cosmic grumbling. Beneath such power, the Labyrinth itself seemed meaningless, shorn of terror. Theseus cowered down, suddenly terrified of the wrath of Zeus—what had possessed him to actually kill a son of the Thunderer? Then he wondered, with a more immediate pang, how he was going to justify to Ariadne what he had done.

He was going to have to give her some kind of explanation, because she was already watching him—how could she be here—?

—But in fact she was, and her face came looming over him, faintly visible in starlight, as were her bare breasts. Anxiously watching her lover Theseus, calling him repeatedly by name, even as he at last broke some chain of sleep, and woke up in their hiding place in the little sandstone cave.

The night was far advanced. His hands were empty, and the only available weapon was the cheap sword that he had taken from the soldier, and even it was lying now on the other side of the narrow cave. He, Theseus, had killed nothing and no one tonight. Only in a dream, under the spell of divine Oneiros, had he been anywhere near Asterion or his Labyrinth during the past few hours.

Groggily, Theseus said, "I thought I was . . ."

"What is it, darling?"

"Dreaming," he got out. Rolled over, wiped sweat from his face, looked at her intently. But her eyes were innocent, as usual. Her body as naked and innocent as a baby's. She knew nothing of what her brother, the invader and changer of dreams, was trying to do to him.

The sky outside the cave was starting to brighten. Soon it would be time to go up on the clifftop again and look for ships.

Early on the next morning, beginning the second day of their escape, great excitement spread among the fugitives when a small ship, moving under a single sail, came to stand by just offshore.

Theseus and Daedalus crouched together atop the little cliff, squinting into the morning sunlight, holding consultation.

The Artisan said at last, "It's only a trader. Not Corycan, as far as I can tell, so I can't see that they're likely to pose us any danger."

Theseus nodded. "Come, let's go down. Make sure they see the women and the child, they'll be less suspicious of us then."

The men called to the women to bring the child and follow them. Theseus put on the cloak that he had shed during the night, Daedalus slipped on his workman's belt and apron, and both men went down to the shore to make contact with this alien captain and his crew.

Theseus, striding forward across the little strip of beach, greeted them boldly and heartily. "Good day to you, captain—and to all of you. We are five, altogether, and we require passage across the sea."

The sailors soon relaxed—these five seemed a harmless enough bunch. The captain, who introduced himself as Petros, was a short, bearded, pot-bellied man wearing a single earring, his hair and beard of curls so dark as to resist the slightest bleaching by the sun. He had a red cloth tied around his head, and was wearing a pair of shorts and a worn vest of some leather that had once been fine. He stood with arms folded, watching the approach of the three refugees with no particular surprise. Meanwhile the half-dozen men of the trader's crew stood by their captain. They were a motley group, varying in age from a white-bearded elder to a beardless boy. About half of them were armed, like their leader, with long knives or short swords.

Captain Petros looked over his prospective passengers, while the crew of the small trader regarded them with what seemed wary speculation. Then almost at once, to the fugitives' surprise, Petros promptly agreed to take them to any reasonable destination within range of his craft. And the faces of the crew showed no objection to this decision, only a kind of watchful waiting.

Theseus accepted the offer as if he had expected nothing less. But the Artisan was more circumspect. "Captain, are you accustomed to taking on odd lots of passengers?"

Under cautious questioning by Daedalus, Captain Petros offered an explanation: for the past two nights in a row, he had been promised by a strange figure in a vivid dream that his fortune would be made if he put in at this particular beach, and accepted an offer that would be made to him when he had done so. No one, especially a seafaring man, could ignore such a message.

Now Theseus was interested again. "This strange figure in the dream—did it seem entirely human?"

"Now that you mention it, no. There were great horns on its head. Why?"

"That's fine, I was just curious."

Petros explained that he had discussed the series of dreams with his crew, and by a unanimous vote they had decided to stake their fortunes that the promise he had received was true—the business of carrying cargo had not been prosperous of late.

Captain and crew were still worried, however, about the patrols of the Minoan navy, whose prowess was almost legendary. So far they had been lucky in that regard.

So it was best not to waste any time. Yes, he was willing to take them where they wished to go. "Where will that be?"

"Away from this coast, to begin with," said Theseus. "As soon as Corycus is out of sight I will consult your compass-pyx."

Nor did Petros press his new passengers as to when he might expect to receive his reward, and exactly what it was to be. All his life the captain had believed earnestly in dreams, and he expected much from this one, which had promised him great things.

14

AS THE CHARIOT drawn by two swiftly pacing leopards bore Alex westward into the sky, even the practical fear of falling could not distract him from his steady anxiety about the princess.

Vertiginously he clung to the thought that the creatures of the god would not have whirled him to this giddy height simply so that they could watch him plunge to his death. Alternately, his thoughts soared with dreams of glory, in which he triumphed over some nameless, faceless enemy of the Princess Ariadne. Gradually his opponent took on the form of the king, her uncle—but in almost a year of pulling guard duty in and around the palace, Alex had seen too much of royalty to be overawed by the mere thought. Even if he had to fight against the Butcher himself, Alex could still face him.

Now he had a god as an ally, even if it was a dead god. A deity known for, among other things, his many names: among others, Dionysus, Bacchus, the Twice-Born, for which last name there was a legendary explanation. A god renowned also for the yearly cycle of growth and decline to which he and his powers seemed to be subject—and also for a tendency to fits of madness, sometimes bloody, in which his followers were constrained to join him.

Hastily Alex tried to think of something else. That last attribute was not one he wanted to contemplate in an ally.

The leopards paced on, their paws spurning the air, running as firmly as if they were on solid ground.

Gradually Alex came to understand that his terrifying distance from the earth was easier to bear when he did not look down. Therefore he spent much time studying the sky. He could tell by the moon and stars that the chariot was still carrying him to the west.

Several minutes passed, while his terror and confusion slowly diminished. When at last he changed position, his hand fell by accident upon something that felt like fine leather. He had discovered the reins, which had been tied around one of the carved spindles which served as support for the rail that encircled the car at about the level of the occupant's waist. But the knot of leather strips would not yield easily when Alex tugged at it, and after a minute he let the reins stay as they were, and went back to gripping the rail.

Even had he been able to establish control over his exotic team, he would have been afraid to use it. His experience at driving any kind of animals was minimal, and it seemed that the powers who had launched him on this flight were much better equipped than he was to see it to a safe conclusion.

His hand went more than once to the medallion the princess had given him.

He had been able to bring his soldier's short sword with him, and it was still vaguely comforting to be armed, though at the moment keen edges and hard metal were of no help at all.

Hours passed as he stood clinging to the rail, swaying on his feet with the motion of the speeding chariot. At last, exhausted by the tension in his muscles, he let himself slump into a sitting position, with the wooden spindles of the railing at his back. Maintaining a grip on one spindle with his hand, he let his eyes close, though he could not sleep. As long as he had no control over the direction of his flight, there was no use in even trying to see where he was going.

The time, as indicated by the rotation of the stars, had been a little past midnight when the inhuman auxiliaries of Dionysus had scooped him up into the air, and the flight lasted long enough to afford Alex the privilege of seeing the dawn in all its glory, the world and the morning coming to life over the flat immensity of the sea, the boundless domain of Lord Poseidon. By the time that daybreak was starting to wipe the stars away, he was shivering violently in the endless rush of air. The fugitive thought, but could not be sure, that some of the sprites managed to warm him a little as he flew, or at least to break the force of the wind with some invisible shielding.

There were certain minutes when he slept, in spite of his precarious position. Each time he awakened with a start of terror, sure that Shiva had somehow overtaken him.

Shortly after one of the awakenings, his invisible escort furnished him, somehow, with a fragile crystal goblet almost filled with wine. The drink went straight to Alex's head, with in its way a sharper impact than any cheap, throat-burning soldiers' booze he'd ever swallowed. Yet this was totally different from the last drink these Dionysians had given him, which had put him utterly to sleep. He was not sleepy now, but energized, keyed up to the brink of some extraordinary effort. When he had drained the goblet he set it down on the chariot's wooden floor. When he looked for it again a moment later, it had disappeared.

On departing from Corycus, Alex had had the idea that the whole diminished host of Dionysian powers, or at least all those strong enough to make the journey, were accompanying the chariot. By daybreak he had a definite impression that their numbers were diminished, though he still had no clear idea of what the count should be. Perhaps, he thought, the wind of the chariot's passage could not support them all, and those who had been left out had trouble keeping up. Even as that idea occurred to Alex it seemed to him that one of the unseen beings cried out faintly, as if it were swiftly dropping behind.

———

Only a few moments later he became aware of an odd-looking flight of birds, visible in the growing morning light, bearing in from the dim, gray north as if to head the chariot off.

Perhaps five minutes after first sighting the flying things, Alex realized that they were not birds at all, at least in any ordinary sense. His blood chilled as he realized that they seemed little more than large, inhuman heads with great wings attached. Of course the true scale of size was difficult to determine, but surely such shapes lay outside the ordinary forms of nature.

The creatures were closing upon the chariot with remarkable speed, and before Alex had time to be fully alarmed, there came a midair clash between his own half-visible escort and a dozen of the winged heads, all streaming long, tangled hair. Flying near, the attackers opened beaked mouths that shrieked and honked with laughter, then swerved away as the leopards unsheathed their claws and snarled, causing the chariot to rock wildly in its flight. A moment later, the pair of great cats had somehow increased their pace.

Alex, on his feet again, drew whatever weapon he had, and tried to shout defiance, but the wind of flight whipped his words away so that he himself could scarcely hear them. Some of the heads and faces were more birdlike, and others more batlike, than human in design, and he thought they were built on a scale somewhat larger than humanity. Still it was hard to be sure of size, with nothing near them to judge by.

He could feel his own hair trying to rise upon his scalp, when his eyes told him that the visitors' scalps were each thickly overgrown with a crop of hissing, writhing snakes.

Moments later the largest of the things, wings laboring frantically, drew close enough for him to see its bloodshot eyes, squawked words at him. The language was one that Alex had never heard before, but the content of menace, the intention to inspire terror, were unmistakable. And now from the chariot's other side, another creature suddenly swooped close, near enough to strike at him, it seemed, although he could not see what weapon it might have.

Suddenly it displayed a thin, bonelike arm, wielding a kind of twisted javelin. Evidently the damned thing had six limbs in all, counting its wings. And Alex could also see the claws in which its thin legs terminated. Another of the beings gripped in one hand what appeared to be a living snake, thick as a man's arm, and raised it like a weapon, ready to strike with the reptile's fanged and gaping mouth. Two long snake-fangs came thudding down with a hard impact, to remain embedded in the wood.

A moment later he saw, almost too late, that the flying horror, whatever it might be, also used its beak for a weapon. A savage thrust of head and neck just missed Alex as the chariot swerved, and tore splinters from the wooden railing.

There was no way to retreat, and no place to run. Instinctively Alex thrust back with his blade, feeling the steel go into solid flesh. Then he dealt a hacking blow, decapitating the snake, whose head stayed where it was, while the thick body writhed and fell away.

One of the flying creatures he had struck dropped like a stone. Another, wounded, screamed and fell away, laboring to stay airborne with a damaged wing.

Meanwhile the chariot was rocking and bouncing in midair, as if it had encountered some kind of obstacle, so Alex was terrified of being thrown out; then once more the motion of the vehicle straightened out, and it bored ahead at increased speed.

The leopards were bounding straight for a cloud. Moments later they plunged into the insubstantial barrier and through it at high speed, so that it passed in a mere flickering of disorienting whiteness.

A second cloud was skewered in the same way, and then, after some broad intervening spans of empty sky, a third and then a fourth. Gradually the monstrous enemy was left behind.

Now the passenger noticed that two thin streams of smoke emerged from the wood around the two embedded fangs of the snake's detached head, to be quickly blown into nothingness by the wind of passage. Using the tip of his weapon he pried the thing loose and let the wind of passage whirl it away.

Alex kept looking back. After the last band of clouds had been passed, he thought that the flying heads retreated, falling back farther and farther as the Eye of Apollo rose fully clear of the horizon, launching itself on its long daily passage across the sky. At last, with a reaction of relief that left him feeling weak, he allowed himself to be convinced that they had abandoned the chase and turned away. Soon they had shrunk to mere elongated dots against the far clouds on the horizon, and not long after that disappeared altogether.

A few minutes later Alex, looking ahead and to the right, past the spotted backs of the rhythmically coursing leopards, thought that he could see some kind of island, though at the distance he could not be sure that it was any more than a low-lying cloud. Details were impossible to make out.

Abruptly the chariot altered course, so that now the cloud, or island, lay straight ahead.

"Is that our goal?" the passenger demanded loudly of the rushing air. "The island where I am to find the Face?"

Nothing and no one answered him.

"What's wrong now? What's going on? Why don't you speak?"

He had to shout his questions again and again before at last there came a few words in response: *We grow weak.*

"But is that the island we want?" He was sure that they were now gradually descending.

We must land somewhere soon, or the chariot will fall and you will perish.

The island—now he could see that it was certainly more than a cloud— may have been farther away than Alex had first estimated, or else the great panthers' pace had slowed considerably.

Another hour of the day wore on, and then another. With nothing below him but the trackless sea, it was hard for the weary passenger to even guess at his altitude, but he felt sure that they were considerably lower. And now at last he could see clearly some of the details of their goal. It was a mass of land with the shape of a thick, rough horseshoe, curving a strip of beach around a narrow-mouthed harbor, which at the moment held no ships.

At this range he could still distinguish nothing that might be a Temple of Apollo. Indeed he began to get the impression that there were no buildings at all.

Without warning, the chariot wavered again, not only in its course but, as the passenger thought, in its substantiality, the very reality of its existence. There was a long, horrible moment when Alex thought that he could see right through the rims of the spinning wheels, and even the floor beneath his feet. Then solidity came back, but the vehicle was rapidly losing both speed and altitude. Now abruptly the leopards and their burden plunged down at a sickening angle, the water coming closer with frightening speed. Alex gritted his teeth, then screamed unashamedly in fright.

Keeping his eyes open, he waited until what he judged was the last possible second, then leapt clear of the plunging chariot.

Inevitably he had misjudged the height, and endured a longer free fall and a harder splash into the sea than he had expected. Warm salt water closed over his head, and he struck out blindly. Heavy metal was dragging him down unmercifully, and he unfastened belt and harness, let go all his weapons. A moment later he had slid out of what remained of his clothing, realizing he was going to need all the buoyancy that he could get.

Holding his mouth closed, he framed a silent prayer to Poseidon, a promise of rich sacrifice if his life should be spared. After a frighteningly long struggle he popped out on the surface, gasping. When the motion of the sea lifted him to the top of a gentle swell, he could see the island clearly, with its shoreline still a quarter of a mile away.

Alex had never been better than an average swimmer, but fortunately the sea was calm, the surface water warm. By now the sun was well along in its climb toward the zenith. It remained high in the sky, but it seemed that a long time had passed, before Alex finally waded and crawled ashore, to lie shivering on a sand beach, his naked flesh shriveled with immersion, feeling more like a drowned rat than any kind of conquering hero, or even a useful servant on which the princess might be able to depend. When the last small wave slapped at him from behind, he felt immensely grateful for the last little push of Poseidon's helping hand, though he doubted that any conscious effort by the sea god was involved.

All he could be reasonably certain of was that at least one powerful god, Shiva, would probably be very angry to see Dionysus returning.

The one thing Alex had not even considered abandoning to the sea was the medallion given him by the princess, and the thin double disk of gold and silver still hung on its chain around his neck. He now raised it to his lips and kissed it fervently.

As soon as the castaway felt a little stronger, and had distributed a few heartfelt prayers of thanksgiving among various deities, he got to his feet. Shading his eyes, he turned to scan the sea from which he had emerged. The chariot seemed to have sunk immediately, or perhaps simply disappeared on contact with the water. The two panthers had also vanished without a trace, along with the rest of his inhuman escort. He could only hope that they were not all entirely dead.

Facing inland, he studied the thin scrubby woods beyond the beach. There were a few palm trees, and the ubiquitous laurel on the modest heights inland. There seemed to be no coconuts. Along the first edge of solid land, a few feet above the pale sand of the beach, there straggled a row of dying olive trees.

As soon as he had recovered his breath a little, he started to explore inland.

Alex felt a little better as the sun began to toast his back and shoulders, already heavily tanned, and his activity warmed him too. More than a day had passed since he had eaten his last meal, a poorly digested breakfast in the mess hall, in a place and among people that, if he was lucky, he would never see again.

Here and there he found a few berries he couldn't recognize, but which looked and tasted edible. He wondered if the island held any permanent inhabitants.

Over the next few hours, while the sun slowly declined toward the west, his wandering investigation confirmed the impressions he had gained on his approach. The island was roughly horseshoe-shaped, its outer shoreline perhaps a mile in diameter. The neat natural harbor that Alex had observed while still airborne was indeed currently unoccupied by any ships. He also discovered, to his relief, a small stream flowing right into the harbor, and he immediately bent to drink. The water was brackish close to the beach, but when he had followed it upstream for a quarter of a mile, to near the springs where it had its source, it became good and fresh.

For the first hour or so he found himself looking frequently over his shoulder. But gradually he became convinced that he had the entire island to himself.

He soon came to the conclusion that there were indeed no buildings anywhere, but in several places he found traces of recent human occupation, an occasional footprint and discarded bits of trash. Any place with fresh water conveniently available was likely to be visited frequently by ships.

Thirst was evidently not going to be a problem while he was marooned here, but hunger could certainly become one. There were no cultivated plants, and what grew wild was not reassuring. Scarcity might be due, of course, to the land having been picked over by frequent visitors. There were a few mushrooms that he could recognize as edible, and some berries growing in the patch of woods that covered the island's central elevation. On the next hill he could see what looked like wild grapes, and he walked that way to investigate.

If only he could know that the princess was somehow safe—but he could not know that. He was no closer now to being able to help her than he had been when he was lost in the Labyrinth. Assuming she had been able to escape at all, she was probably getting farther and farther away from him all the time.

On reaching the hilltop, he discovered that the fruit of the wild vines growing there was still much too green to eat. But rummaging around among them soon led to an intriguing discovery. Almost completely hidden by the vines and the surrounding bushes of tall laurel, a few whitish bones of marble came poking out. Digging into the mass of vegetation, the castaway discovered the shattered and age-worn remnants of a building.

There was not much of the structure left, only the skeleton of a single room, a paved floor covering a somewhat larger area, enough for two or three more rooms perhaps, and a low rim of surviving stone wall. If only this could be the temple of Apollo that the sprites had spoken of—but that possibility seemed remote in the extreme. On this island the best that Alex thought he could hope for was survival.

At sunset, some hours after Alex's arrival on the island, one sprite came back to talk to him, much to his relief.

He greeted his almost invisible companion joyfully. "Thank all the gods! I feared that all of you were dead."

Not all the gods are worthy of your thanks.

"Well then, I confine my thanks to those who are. Tell me, tell me, what of the Princess Ariadne? Did she get away from Corycus? And what of the others who were with her?"

There was only a whispering, as of a faint wind, before the contact broke, the visitor vanished. Alex got the impression that the auxiliaries of Dionysus were grown too weak even to talk to him at all. He could only hope that now they might somehow be able to rest and regain some strength.

"Tell me, tell me I beg you, is the princess safe?"

But that question received no answer.

15

CAPTAIN PETROS AND his crew were eager to put out to sea again as rapidly as possible, and energetically assisted the five fugitives as they scrambled aboard. There wasn't much room on the small vessel, and comfortable spots to sit or even crouch were at a premium, but no one was complaining. Petros and his crew kept casting worried looks about, and their comments indicated that they were chronically worried about running into some ship of the Corycan navy, who were likely to demand tribute. But so far their luck was holding.

Ariadne repeated her earlier question. "Where are we going?"

"I have an idea or two about that," her lover said, frowning into the distance. "But Petros is right, the first thing is to get away from this coast as fast as possible."

At first the wind was unfavorable, and a great deal of maneuvering with the sail was necessary. Theseus was not shy about giving the captain advice on the details of how to do this, while Daedalus grumbled that the whole design of the ship was inefficient. Petros mainly ignored the arguments of both.

It would also be possible to man about ten oars, now that the fugitives were available to pull. Theseus and Daedalus as potential crew members added two strong men, and Ariadne volunteered herself and her slave-girl to row if necessary.

The offer was received in bewildered silence. When the princess proudly announced that she had often rowed for sport at home, the crew looked at her without comprehension.

In any event, the men took care of the oars, while the women contributed by keeping out of the way as much as possible. An hour of rowing was necessary before the wind came around to the right direction, and gained enough strength to be useful. The shoreline receded only slowly.

At last the peaks of the island's small mountains disappeared under the horizon.

The breeze kept on after sunset, and the stars provided guidance. The Princess Ariadne, clinging to her lover's arm, was in a mood to contemplate romantic tales, and she began to relate some of them, that Theseus said he had never heard. There were legends told about some of the constellations, and the role that Father Zeus was supposed to have had in creating them. One was called the Bull, and another, small and comparatively obscure, the Princess. Theseus listened, saying little, now and then nodding indulgently with approval.

One of the crew, perhaps inspired by listening to the stories, began to twang an untuned lyre. In a surprisingly true voice he began to intone an ancient song, in which the singer bragged that he knew more than Apollo—

"—for oft when he lies sleeping,
I see the stars at bloody wars
In the wounded welkin weeping—"

Ariadne had never heard that song before. "What is the 'welkin'?" she asked, perpetually curious, hoping that at least one of her shipmates could provide the information.

But no one knew; or at least no one was interested enough to want to answer.

"What had you planned as your next stop, captain?" Theseus's tone conveyed the idea that the question was not entirely an idle one.

Petros sounded relieved, now that Corycus was out of sight. "Refuge Island. Not too far, and it's a good place to take on water."

It was really necessary to replenish the store of water on board before undertaking a voyage of the length required to satisfy the hopes of either Theseus or Daedalus. For the time being the Artisan pronounced himself content to be leaving Corycus behind.

Refuge Island, as the captain had said, lay at no great distance and offered a dependable supply. Theseus nodded, and said that he had some acquaintance with the place. Ariadne grudged the delay, but when she looked at the depleted water casks she had to admit that it was probably necessary.

The first night the fugitives passed on board the trader was almost un-eventful. Ariadne had to fight off seasickness, and got little sleep. Icarus, who had slept longer ashore, now kept people awake reveling in the adventure of it all, and several times came near falling overboard. Petros from time to time questioned his passengers, trying to get a clue as to what his reward was going to be, but they could tell him nothing helpful.

The princess was determined to be gracious. "I repeat, captain, that we are grateful for your help."

"Thank you, ma'am, thank you."

Captain Petros continued to be accommodating. He explained that all his life he had depended heavily on dreams, and had picked up the fugitives after being promised, in a remarkable dream, that his fortune would be made if he did.

When Ariadne questioned him, she was comforted to hear that in his dreams he had spoken with a figure that looked like the Minotaur.

But he hadn't wanted to delay on the shore of Corycus long enough to get water—not a moment longer on that coastline than was absolutely necessary, not even long enough to fill some jugs. Besides, the water there at the marsh had a bad reputation among seafaring folk, it just didn't look or taste right.

Use of the compass-pyx was well-nigh universal. Navigation across the open sea, out of sight of land, was difficult enough even with the help of such devices, and would have been all but impossible without it. The basic device was proven, but Petros, like many sailors and fish-erfolk, relied upon some special private magical addition to the instru-ment that he was keen on keeping secret.

What Petros's secret addition might be was hard to say. The compass-pyx that Ariadne was inspecting now looked much like the instruments that she had been required to practice with in the course of a royal education.

The pointer, or cusp of the device, balanced on a needle-sharp pivot, consisted of a narrow crescent of horn and ivory. A sliver of each of the disparate materials, identically curved and not quite as long as a man's hand, were bound together in a particular way. Some swore that silk was the only proper material to use for the binding, but Ariadne saw now that Petros, like a number of others, preferred the web-stuff of certain mutant spiders.

That gave her pause. She closed her eyes, but no vision came im-mediately.

Once a pilot or steersman had attuned his mind to the device, it indicated with great accuracy the bearing that the ship should take to bring him to his goal. Few people placed any reliance on the compass-pyx on land; its effectiveness on the Great Sea was credited to Poseidon's having long ago given the device his blessing.

There were of course refinements in the construction and operation of the compass-pyx. Some extremely simple versions were good only for indicating true north; others, if the cap/cover was shifted to the first end, pointed to the nearest dry land.

Many swore that the compass-pyx worked best, indeed that it was only reliable at all, if hooked up with a strip of pure copper that ran deep into the central timbers of the ship.

Daedalus looked at the device mounted in a binnacle near the steering oar of Petros's craft, and pronounced it of tolerably good workmanship. Coming from him, this was a high compliment.

Early the next morning, despite patchy fog, the merchant raised the small island he was seeking, and maneuvered in through the narrow mouth of the harbor.

Petros's crew dropped a small anchor in the still harbor, and then, wading ashore from the shallow-draft vessel, broke out water jugs and wooden kegs from below the single deck, and began to carry them inland. About half a mile upstream, the captain informed his passengers, they could fill them from where a spring flowed pure, into a little rivulet that soon became the brackish stream.

Hardly had they begun this operation, when a larger craft of ominous appearance materialized out of a drift of fog at the mouth of the harbor, and soon dropped anchor there, blocking the narrow entrance.

Everyone froze and stared at it. Giant eyes, suitable for some legendary sea monster, had been painted in bold colors on the bow, and glared threateningly at the pirate's potential victims.

The newcomer appeared to be manned by an energetic crew of twenty, who, even at a distance, gave the impression of being all too eager to drop their oars and pick up weapons. Blades of steel or bronze glinted in the distance.

About half of the merchant crew, loaded with every empty container aboard, had been just about to hike inland and get some fresh water. But the stranger's appearance stopped them in their tracks. The merchant crew knew at a glance that they had no chance to get away from the newcomer, bottled up in the harbor as they were, nor any hope of outfighting her if matters came to that.

Ariadne, bewildered for a few moments, took her cue from the trader captain, who quickly identified the newcomer.

She cried, *"Theseus, they're pirates!"*

Everyone but Theseus seemed perturbed to hear this rather obvious discovery so flatly stated, although no one but Ariadne herself appeared surprised.

Her lover only raised one perfect eyebrow, then nodded, smiling ruefully. "I'm afraid they are," he acknowledged.

"What are we going to do?"

"Well, I wouldn't worry about it if I were you." And then, instead of leading Ariadne inland as she expected, running into hiding on the heels of Petros and his crew, he strolled casually in the opposite direction, out across the sand, waving across the narrowing gap of water at the new arrivals.

A minute later the pirate put a small boat overside, and two men got into it, one of whom rowed energetically for the beach, while the other sat with massive bare arms folded. Theseus walked down toward the water line, to stand, fists on hips, with the wavelets washing over his sandals.

When the little rowboat was close enough for handy communication, he waved an arm, and called in a loud voice, "Hello, Samson. I see you got my message. It took you long enough to get here."

The other acknowledged the greeting with a friendly word of surprised recognition. "Theseus." It was a familiar mode of address, and for a moment Ariadne wondered if this fierce-looking man could be her prince's brother, or some other close relation. "What message? I've had no message from you, or anyone."

What she saw of the passenger as he drew closer was not reassuring. He was an evil-looking man dressed in a loincloth and a vest, his whole body massively muscled. The hilts of blade weapons protruded from three separate sheaths at his belt. Hair grew on his scarred and tattooed shoulders as thickly as on his chest. He wore two rings in each ear, and what appeared to be a small, straight piece of bone in his nose.

"Was expecting to meet you, mate, but not here."

"Don't worry about it. Matters worked out all right."

Looking around her in bewilderment, the princess observed that the trader captain and his crew had now entirely vanished from her sight, having disappeared in the general direction of the center of the island. Only a couple of empty water containers, dropped in haste, and the stirring of some bushes about a hundred yards inland, indicated which way they had gone.

Ariadne moved a step closer to Theseus, and rested one hand on his arm. Her love, and her lover, provided all the protection she would ever need.

The two men who had rowed the little boat ashore were appraising the beached merchantman. One of them climbed aboard, took a quick look into the tiny space belowdecks, and reappeared nodding his head.

"Small, Cap'n Sam, but sound. We can find a use for her. Or get a price."

"Cargo?"

"Not much."

Captain Samson squinted inland. "Too bad the crew's run off. I'll be short-handed for two ships. Think any of your people might be ready to take shares in our enterprise?"

"They won't have gone entirely out of sight just yet," Theseus put in. "Let me see what I can do." Giving Ariadne's hand a reassuring squeeze, he dropped it and strode inland. After a moment's hesitation, the princess followed.

Her lover walked steadily toward a screen of bushes about a hundred paces from the beach, where the princess herself had already noticed movement.

Stopping before he got close enough to alarm anyone who might be there, he called out in a clear, calm voice, "How about it, lads? Samson here's ready to take you on as shipmates. I can vouch for him, he's not a bad sort as a captain. What say you to a different kind of cruise, that has a little profit at the end of it? Otherwise you'll be left here. Not the worst place in the world to be marooned, but . . ."

Slowly, cautiously, part of a head appeared from behind a bush. The trader's captain and at least some of his crew were in there listening.

━━━━━━━

Daedalus and Icarus, who had already started upstream along the brook when the pirate ship appeared, continued to hurry inland, determined to hide out. Clara had been walking near them, and with a look of mingled fear and determination, had attached herself to them, and the Artisan with a brisk movement of his head unhesitatingly signaled her to come along.

Theseus, who seemed to be blithely assuming that he had full power to represent the pirate captain in negotiations, was now heavily engaged in bargaining with the people who remained hidden in the bushes. At issue now were some details, regarding matters such as the food available on the buccaneers' craft, and the plan according to which future booty would be divided. Meanwhile Samson kept aloof, with folded arms, waiting for the result.

When several questions had been answered, Theseus stood back and folded his arms too, awaiting the decision of Petros and his people. He seemed perfectly at ease, though his manner was absent when he returned Ariadne's anxious smile. There were dozens of questions she wanted to have answered, declarations she wanted to make, but this did not seem the right moment to bring any of them up.

Presently there was a rustling in the bushes. After less than a minute of discussion, the trader captain and his small crew, having evidently discussed and voted on the matter among themselves, emerged as a unit, announcing that they had vowed to stick together.

When Theseus had shepherded them all back to the beach, the pirate captain took his time looking his new recruits over, with the attitude of a man considering the purchase of slaves. At last Samson nodded as if reasonably satisfied.

While these negotiations were being concluded, Ariadne, giving her hair its familiar toss, stood waiting proudly beside her prince, trusting in the calm assurance he had already given her that everything was going to be all right.

Belatedly remembering Clara, she looked around and observed that the girl was missing, as were Daedalus and his child. Briefly the princess was annoyed by her slave's defection. But when she thought about it, she could hardly blame the girl for running off, given the way that any female of low rank was likely to be treated by pirates.

Theseus was back at her side, smiling at her. Only now was it really sinking in. She repeated, "These men are *pirates*!"

He frowned slightly. "There are nicer terms, my love, like 'gentleman adventurer,' or 'soldier of fortune.' I'm one of them, you know. Let me be plain about that, just in case you were still harboring any doubts."

"But your father! The kingdom . . ."

He was quite ready to debate the point. "Well, everything I told you is quite true—in a sense. My father is a pirate too, only much wealthier than I. But of course he's been at the business much longer. He lives in a big house when he's ashore."

"You told me he was a king!"

"And so he is. King of the Pirates—a lot of people call him that. Ariadne, I suppose I should warn you that often Dad and I don't get along. That has a lot to do with how I found myself shanghaied into being one of the Tribute people sent to your damned uncle." Theseus sighed, with the sound of a man finishing a disagreeable chore. Then he brightened. "Anyway, since we are home now, I thought it was time I filled you in on the family situation."

"Home?" The princess looked around her blankly.

Her lover's gesture took in the sea before them, and the two ships, on the smaller of which Captain Samson was now affixing a striped banner that was evidently his own flag, from the pride he took in fastening it to the mast.

"Home." Theseus pronounced the word with an air of finality, and a certain pride. "I don't have a big house, let alone a palace, anywhere. Not yet."

Ariadne took a step away from him. "Then you lied to me," she got out at last. Her voice was low, almost choking.

"Maybe I did stretch things a little." Theseus paused and grinned at her. "Can't really blame me, can you? After all, I didn't want to take any chances. Not with what Shiva was planning to do to me."

16

SUCH CARGO AS the pirates had been able to discover in the small hold of the trading vessel—water casks, oil jars, dried fish, and extra coils of rope—was nothing to cause wild jubilation in their ranks. But, as Theseus explained to the princess, such modest hauls added up, and formed a large part of the business of pillaging. What they could not use, they could probably sell in some congenial port, and make a small profit thereby. The ship itself, of course, would fetch a nice price—if it were not quickly used up, consumed in the general wear and tear of pirating, which tended to be stressful on men and equipment alike.

Samson manned the captured ship with a prize crew composed mainly of his own people, and including only two or three of the trader's original crew, the captain not among them. Petros accepted the decision philosophically. Despite the fact that the best deal Samson felt able to offer him was service as a simple seaman on the original pirate vessel. "But once a man decides to trust his dreams, he might as well go all the way. I've been a soldier of fortune before. No reason I can't be again."

Petros expressed his philosophy forcefully. But still he continued to appear just a little worried.

Theseus assured him heartily that he had nothing to worry about. Then he turned, and, looking thoughtfully inland, said he was considering whether it might be worthwhile to try to find Daedalus and bring him along. "There are a lot of places where a man like that would bring a very good price."

The princess at first could not believe that she had heard him properly. "You mean—you'd sell him? *Daedalus?* After he helped you to escape?"

Theseus looked at her blankly for a moment, then shrugged. "I thought the idea had some merit; I won't insist on it."

In turn, Ariadne was staring at her lover as if she had never seen him before. She thought that the prince—she had still been thinking of him as a prince though it seemed he really had no legitimate claim to that title—was demonstrating a poor attitude.

"If it weren't for Daedalus," she said to him, "you wouldn't be here now. You'd probably be dead."

Theseus shrugged. "He helped us, we helped him. If he had power over me, and I stood in the way of his solving some problem, how long do you think I'd last?"

Samson overheard some of the talk about trying to chase down Daedalus, but decided quickly that it would involve a lot of effort for a doubtful return. The same went for the slave-girl—it was annoying to have a valuable and entertaining girl get away, but there were plenty of others in the world, and in general they were not too hard to find.

Presently both ships put out to sea.

Ariadne had not been aboard ship long before she became aware that the crew were eyeing her with several varieties and degrees of speculation. Much of this attention was not at all of the kind a princess had been brought up to expect.

"They stare at me," Ariadne said to Theseus, the next time he stood beside her.

"I'll bet they do, you're well worth gaping at. But none of them are going to forget that you are mine—I'll see to that."

"How long are we going to be on this ship?"

"Depends on where we go. As I said before, I've got a couple of ideas about that. I haven't quite decided. It's just great to have a ship again." And he filled his lungs contentedly with ocean air, and let his gaze roam the horizon.

Ariadne continued to be troubled. "You say you 'have a ship.'"

"Mm-hmm."

"But this one is not yours, is it? It's still going to be Samson who decides which way we sail? That's the impression I got from listening to him."

As if regretfully, Theseus ceased his enjoyment of the view. Looking at the princess again, he smiled thinly. "That reminds me. I suppose Samson himself probably still clings to that opinion. I'd better go have a talk with him." And Theseus gave her a wink and presently moved aft, to engage the captain in serious conversation.

Which soon began to grow heated. Ariadne could not hear much of what Theseus and Samson, at the other end of the ship, were saying to each other. But it was plain enough from their faces, and certain gestures that they made, that they had begun to disagree.

The dispute had nothing directly to do with her; she felt reasonably confident of that. From the few words drifting her way, she gathered that it was about what the next object of their pillaging should be. Most of the men were listening too; enough of a breeze had come up to make the oars temporarily unnecessary.

The princess still couldn't hear much of what was said, but the key point of contention was not hard to discover. Theseus was claiming authority, simply as his father's son, and Samson had no intention of turning over his ships and crews to an upstart, on that basis or any other.

Now Samson at last raised his voice. "Once and for all, *Prince*, I understand that's what you like to be called, you'd better get it through your head that both of these vessels are mine now. Both their crews follow my orders, no one else's. I plan to build up a fleet the way your father did."

"My understanding is not the same as yours, Samson."

"Well, I s'pose your father will understand, if I have to feed you to the fishes."

The two men were now standing tall, staring each other levelly in the eye. There was still no murmuring among the crew, but rather a watchful stillness. Ariadne had the impression that some of the men, at least, knew Theseus, though they hadn't seen him for some years. Earlier she had heard one remark that when the prince was last seen he had been only about two-thirds his present size. It seemed obvious to Ariadne that few or none would be ready to side with him in a mutiny. A number of the crew, like the newcomer Petros, obviously didn't know what to think, except that any threat of serious trouble aboard ship made them nervous.

What the usual code of ethics among pirates might be, Ariadne had no idea, but to her it seemed a bad idea for her lover, or anyone, to try to steal another man's ship right out from under his feet. The princess had already edged away from the developing conflict, as far as it was possible to go on a small ship, which was only a few feet—and in her own mind was trying to construct excuses for her lover's unacceptable behavior. Now that they had fallen among pirates, he must of course try to look and sound as much as possible like one of them.

Suddenly turning her back on the argument, she scanned the seas ahead, then closed her eyes. Useless. Now was one of those times when it seemed almost impossible to generate any kind of inner vision—

Ariadne was aroused from fruitless inward contemplation by a shout behind her, and then the sound of some kind of impact, like that of one chunk of solid flesh and bone against another.

If there had been a blow, it seemed to have left no physical mark.

Samson, blaspheming the names of several deities in the process, was telling the young upstart that it made no difference on *his* ship whose son anyone else might be.

Theseus's face was turning red with anger, but his voice stayed steady. "And if I have a remark or two to make on your own parentage?"

The crew had long since given up any pretense of going on with any of their shipboard duties.

The newly acquired ship, Petros's former trader, had been sailing close enough for those aboard to see and hear something of what was going on, and now she was maneuvering closer alongside. This was a matter in which all members of both crews were deeply interested.

There was evidently a protocol for how these things were done. A formal challenge had evidently been issued, Ariadne was not sure exactly how, and a space for the fight was swiftly being cleared on deck. The sun was going down in a welter of bloodred light, and a couple of men were lighting torches against the coming dark.

One of the older crew members had taken charge of managing the formalities.

Ariadne could hear him spelling out the rules, reciting mechanically and grimly what sounded like a well-known formula. A loser who was forced into the sea, or jumped in to escape, would not be picked up again. If both contestants went into the water, neither would be helped out, until the fight had been concluded.

One point remaining to be decided was the choice of weapons. Theseus seemed gloriously indifferent. "Knives if you like. Or hands and feet are good enough for me."

Samson smiled at that. He had respect for the youth's quickness and ruthlessness with a blade, but retained as usual supreme confidence in his own strength and rough-and-tumble skills. "Hands and feet it is." And he shot a meaningful glance in the direction of the princess, which she had no trouble interpreting.

Each man was allowed to wear only a loincloth, doubled and knotted in such a way as to provide some protection against disabling blows to the crotch.

Empty-handed, the two men faced each other. A signal was given and the fight began. The men struck at each other with clenched fists, in boxers' blows, and tried to use their knees and elbows to good effect.

Gripping a railing, Ariadne watched. Just looking at them, she was sure that Samson must have an edge in brute strength and ruthlessness. The only advantage she could see for Theseus was that he looked quicker, and more agile.

If Theseus loses, she thought to herself coldly, *I will throw myself into the sea*.

Again the combatants exchanged blows—Samson missed twice in rapid succession—and then they grappled, wrestling. It was hard for either to obtain a grip. The princess could hear the animal sounds of their lungs working. And now, somehow, Samson's nose was bleeding heavily.

The crew, silent at first, soon erupted in cheers and grunts of sympathy. Ariadne could not tell who they were for, or if they really cared who won, as long as they had the spectacle of the fight to entertain them.

Then somehow Theseus was taken by surprise, tripped, shoved or knocked off his feet. However it had happened, he was down. Ariadne's heart leaped up like a wounded bird inside her, and she uttered a small cry as Samson leaped on his fallen victim. But the leaner body of the man below twisted and writhed away. Several men jumped to their feet, but none attempted to interfere, as the grappling bodies on the deck rolled back and forth.

First Ariadne could not see what was happening, and then she dared not look. Her eyes were turned away when she heard first a horrible choked cry, surely that of a dying man, and then a great mindless roar from the men who had been watching.

Slowly she turned her head back, compelled to know her fate. Theseus was standing erect, his golden curls visible above the ring of watchers' heads surrounding him. Now he seemed to be pushing hard, with one foot, at something on the deck, something that Ariadne could not see for all the men's legs in between. And now that something had gone into the water with a weighty splash, provoking another cheer from the assembled crew.

Scarcely had the waves closed over Samson's body, when Theseus proclaimed himself the new commander.

Looking around him at the crowd of men, he asked, "Anyone else in need of a workout?"

No one else was minded to challenge the victor, who took a plunge in the sea to rinse off the blood and grime of combat, and then was showered with congratulations. Ariadne thought a number of the men were genuinely pleased to be rid of Samson, who had been blustering and unpredictable. Unexpectedly she was reminded of the situation at home, when Minos was overthrown, and Perses hailed and acclaimed.

Theseus was looking back toward the spot where the body of Samson had vanished tracelessly among light waves. "One owner, two ships," he mused. "Yes, I like that idea." He smiled at Ariadne. "We're making progress."

Unable to think of anything to say, she smiled back.

Now in command of two vessels, he had a new look about him, that of a man who felt much more at home in the world than the harried prisoner Ariadne had helped to escape. Now Theseus began to plan what work of piracy he wanted to accomplish next. Ariadne heard only bits and pieces of these plans, as he commented on the jewels and furs she would soon be able to enjoy.

"I had jewels and furs at home," she remarked.

"Why, I suppose you did." Her lover's glance turned speculative, as an idea occurred to him. "Didn't smuggle any gems along with you, by any chance? No? Too bad."

Her reply broke off in the middle of a sentence, for it was obvious that Theseus was no longer listening to her at all. His gaze was fixed somewhere high over her left shoulder, and the look on his face made the princess spin around quickly, eyes searching the sky.

There was a figure there, approaching swiftly, traversing the air like a bird, without any visible means of support, though its shape was all wrong for any bird that she had ever seen, in dreams or waking life.

Shiva had flown within a hundred yards of the ship before the princess recognized him. Ariadne had seen the God of Destruction only once before, and had paid him little enough attention on that howling autumn night, as he stood in the background while she crouched over her father's corpse.

Now the whole crew, eyes wide and jaws dropped in consternation, were watching the god approach.

Some of them still did not understand. "What in the Underworld is that?"

"There's only one thing it can be."

The crew were absolutely in awe, and Ariadne shrank back in terror of this being who had played a role in her father's murder.

When Nandi made his first pass over the ship, most of the crew went down on their faces, prostrate on the deck. One or two got no farther than kneeling. One actually hurled himself overboard, convinced that he personally was the target of divine vengeance. But Shiva ignored the man, and a couple of his shipmates fished him out.

Shiva had never taken a close look at any of the youths and maidens of the Tribute—except for the two or three who had actually been used up. But now, making a rapid survey of the assembly on the deck, he had no doubt from the first moment which of the men was Theseus. Only one still stood erect, and had actually drawn a short sword.

And there beside her lover stood the Princess Ariadne. True to her heritage of royal blood, the princess was standing as straight as she could on the pitching deck.

Shiva flew low, hovering for a moment only a few yards from the ship, studying the man he had come to see.

The young man holding the drawn sword called out in a clear, loud voice, "Dark God, if you mean to claim me as your sacrifice after all, I don't suppose I can stop you. But I mean to try."

There was a long moment of silence. The bull-figure, posing in the air, was steadier than the wooden ship riding the light waves below. Then the god said in his harsh voice, "I have chosen you for greater things than that, son of Aegeus. Perhaps I want for you exactly what you want for yourself. You have not been easy to locate, but as you see, I have taken the time and trouble to do so." And Shiva on his wonderful steed swooped low, and, disregarding the drawn sword, seized the prince of pirates by one arm, and snatched him up into the sky full of low-scudding clouds.

Ariadne and the others watched them go, and she expected her lover to vanish at any moment from her sight—and as soon as that happened, she would hurl herself into the sea.

But that was not to be. Shiva was circling the ship at no very great distance, holding before him on the bull's back the larger body of the mortal man, as he might have held a child. Theseus seemed to have sheathed his sword again.

Several minutes passed before the wingless bull, hooves gracefully and powerfully treading the air, swooped low again, slowly passing directly above the ship, and Theseus was deposited casually on deck, so smoothly that he needed only one brief running step to keep his feet. Then the bull with its divine rider once more shot high into the air, and this time soon disappeared into the distance, in the direction of Corycus.

Theseus waved after it, the gesture of a man speeding some departing friend on his way. But the rider did not look back.

"What happened?" Ariadne breathlessly demanded of her companion. "What did he say to you? What did he want?" Around the couple, most of the crewmen were daring to raise their eyes.

Theseus was standing with his fists on his hips, still gazing after their departed visitor. He had a look on his face the like of which the princess had never seen there before, and had never imagined he would wear. As if he had been stunned, then treated to a vision of glory before he had quite regained his senses.

Time passed, but still her question hung in the air unanswered.

17

SHIVA, HAVING CONCLUDED his meeting with Theseus, was coming back to Corycus, wind howling in his ears as he traversed the sky astride the galloping bull-creature, Nandi.

He had delayed his return and prolonged his journey in order to search out alliances and information in certain other portions of the world. Unfortunately for himself, the Destroyer had not succeeded very well in either effort. It seemed to Shiva that other gods had secretly arrayed themselves against him, and he was stubbornly determined to discover who they were who so stubbornly plotted his destruction. That such a conspiracy existed, he did not doubt for a moment.

He had some very good candidates in mind, but he wanted to be absolutely sure.

The more he brooded on the matter, the broader and deeper grew his mental image of the plot against him. It was becoming more and more obvious to Shiva that his divine enemies had engineered the whole course of events over the last few months. The escape of the youths and maidens of the Tribute, the defection of the Princess Ariadne—all these events and others took on sinister meaning as part of an elaborate scheme to attack him.

He brought his mount down on the flat roof of the king's palace, an acre of stone and timber and hardened plaster, presenting to the sky a variation in levels in accordance with the layout of the various rooms below. Welcomed home by Creon the high priest, Shiva informed his human servants that he wanted to determine the full roster of his active enemies.

Creon looked groggy, and was shivering with cold. Rain had wet him while he was waiting for the god's return, though he was accompanied by a pair of acolytes who were trying to hold a silken cover over him.

The Destroyer's Bull of course needed no stabling, in the sense that any ordinary animal would require it. In obedience to his master's will, Nandi had already disappeared.

Shiva looked forward to the time when he would be able to identify his foes with certainty. Then he would rapidly proceed to build an alliance against them—and then, no matter how great they might be, how high in the hierarchy of divinity, he meant to pull them down. And he thought he saw the means of forming a coalition that could accomplish that.

Descending from the roof of the palace, with Creon walking beside him, and the two acolytes following at a respectful distance, Shiva said, "One very important thing that must be remembered about the Faces of the Gods is that they cannot be destroyed. Nor, as history and legends testify, can they ever be buried deeply enough or hidden well enough to keep them out of human hands indefinitely."

"Very true, lord," Creon said. He had no idea why Shiva was suddenly talking about the Faces of the Gods, but he presumed that the reason would be made clear in time.

The god went on, "Since it is very likely that some human will again wear the Face of Dionysus in the near future, I would much prefer it to be a human of my own choosing—so I intend, if I can, to put that Face into the chosen human's hands before some unreliable person, or even one of my enemies, can pick it up."

Creon asked deferentially, "Is it permitted to ask whom you have chosen to be the Twice-Born, great lord?"

It was only natural, Shiva thought, that at least one of his own worshipers would like to claim that privilege for himself. But the god considered that that man would be too ambitious, as a divinity.

He looked sideways at the wet and worried man walking beside him. "My dear Creon, you make a much better high priest than you would a god."

The other's face fell. Bitter disappointment, obviously. But such was the fate of human dreams in general.

Shiva continued thoughtfully, "But you wanted to know my choice. A fair question. Easy enough to say, that it should be someone easily led. Who would continue to take my orders, even when he felt the divine power flowing in his own veins. But strange things happen to mortal men, aye and to women too, when they undergo that transformation."

Creon had regained an appearance of calm. He said, "Your Lordship's own power is certainly greater than any that some mere mortal might gain by putting on the Face of Dionysus."

"Yes, of course. Greater where it counts most, or so I should like to think. More direct, at least. The abilities of the God of Many Names are . . . subtler than my own. Nevertheless, they are considerable. Whoever gains those talents, those attributes, will want careful watching.

"Therefore, my chosen candidate is—Theseus, Prince of Pirates. And I have just come from telling him so."

"Theseus?" Creon was shocked and uncomprehending. The infant skulls of his necklace displayed their almost toothless grins, as if mocking the dismay of the one who wore them.

Maybe, thought the God of Destruction, this man was not even worthy of his present office. But who was better qualified?

Shiva said to him, "I know the objection you are about to make— he is far too ambitious, and as a god he could become a mighty rival. However, I think you are mistaken. The prince of pirates is aggressive and unpredictable as a mortal, true. But with his talent for self-defense, I think Theseus will last a long time in a position of divinity—as did his predecessor. Why bother to give a Face to a weakling? Likely he would soon manage to lose his life, and the business would have to be done over again."

Creon bowed low. He had managed to recover fully, and was once more projecting his usual appearance of happy subservience. "Your will be done, lord. The ways of your wisdom are unfathomable to mere humans like myself."

"And, unlike yourself, the pirate prince displays an almost unlimited capacity for wine, women, and song. When he finds all the opportunities of godhood lying open to him in those directions, I think he will have little energy left over for serious matters."

Having now reached an interior courtyard of the palace, Shiva dismissed his high priest and the other attendants who had begun to follow him. Now he entered a covered passage through which he could pass privately to a certain nearby temple, which had now become his own. On the way the walking god encountered only a few humans, all of them bowing deeply, or crouching in attitudes of terror, faces averted. All this was as it should be.

As soon as Shiva had passed inside his private citadel, a place where he felt relatively safe, a divine weariness came over him. With a gesture he banished the temple prostitutes who had been waiting; all his energies must be conserved, channeled into the purposes for which they were needed most. Dismissing also the few remaining servants, he entered a hidden room where he lay down to sleep. In this inner sanctuary, a private retreat within a fortress, he knew he would be fiercely guarded by the humans and the things of magic that he commanded. Still it was not without misgivings that he barred the room's only door and went to his couch.

━━━━━━

Even a god, it seemed, was not exempt from the requirement of having to sleep sometime. And even here, in his stronghold, strange dreams continued to annoy him.

Slumber claimed him quickly, and Shiva was plunged promptly into a bewildering dream. There was a bull, with baleful eyes, whom he could not recognize. It was certainly not Nandi.

This vision included, among its other strange events, a troubling vision of Apollo. Turning restlessly on what should have been a comfortable couch, the God of Destruction saw the beardless youth, wrapped in his white robe, gripping his Silver Bow, and engaged in what seemed a friendly conversation with the Minotaur.

Even while he remained asleep, the man who was an avatar of Shiva suspected that it was Asterion who was sending him this vision. Someday he intended to meet the bull-man, face to face in waking life. But dreaming or waking, Shiva was in no hurry. He had many enemies, and one could never be too careful.

Next in his dream he saw the seared and wasted ghosts of those he had destroyed. The nearer ones, the more recently slain, were plainest in his sight. These included the caged and naked youths and maidens of the Tribute. But Shiva was able to see many of the others clearly too. There was a long, long line of them, and the previous Minos stood among them. Their shades would still be active in the Underworld, and it would be reckless to assume that even from there none of them could ever act against him in revenge.

Memory, accumulated by a long series of previous avatars, held substantial evidence that Shiva had sometimes played a constructive role in the world—but he who wore the Face at present was not interested in such matters.

Rolling over on his couch he muttered, half-asleep, "Perhaps my predecessors did not understand what power is for."

He could gladly endure some troubling dreams, if only they would provide him with the information that he needed.

———

In a few hours he awakened fully. Though he felt far from rested, there were things he must do. Unbarring the door of the small secret room, he quickly called in his attendants to report to him on all that had happened while he slept.

Shiva listened to a series of reports, all rather useless, from his Corycan priests.

Left alone again, Shiva returned obsessively to his chief concern, determining exactly the identity of certain other divinities who were conspiring to destroy him, and what their next move against him was going to be.

Of the names of one or two he could feel absolutely certain. He had no doubt that Apollo must be his enemy, and gods and men alike might well tremble to have such a foe.

The latest avatar of Hephaestus, said to be new in his position and recently allied with Apollo, had given no signs of friendship for Shiva either.

On the other side of the ledger, Shiva's most reliable supporter would probably be Hades, Lord of the Underworld, and it would be hard to find a mightier ally than that.

Some help could be expected from a host of less eminent denizens of the Underworld. Thanatos came especially to mind. Not that any of them were particularly trustworthy; but most, and Hades in particular, could be counted on to try to help any enemy of Apollo.

———

Later in the day, Creon was back, once more talking matters over with his god. The chief priest toyed with his necklace of imitation skulls, perhaps with the stuffed cobra he also wore, and said, "And . . . the Thunderer?"

The skulls in Shiva's own necklace were all genuine bones, and of course all human. As adult human crania would have been awkwardly large, the god found it more convenient to use only those of infants and small children. Sometimes he wondered how his predecessors had managed. The available memories on the subject were fragmentary; the current avatar took this as a sign that the question had not much interested the god, whatever his mortal predecessors in the character had thought.

To his priest he said, "I think that for a long time, no one has had certain knowledge of the whereabouts of mighty Zeus." A lowering of the voice. "It might even be that his Face lies unclaimed, somewhere."

"My lord, I believe King Perses has had this idea for some time. I assumed that he had communicated it to you."

Shiva nodded calmly, trying to remember whether Perses had ever said anything of the kind to him. Sometimes his memory was not all that he could wish it to be.

"Somewhere in the Labyrinth," added the god at last, making it half a question.

"That is the indication, lord."

Creon always swore that his sources were reliable, even though for magical reasons he was forbidden to reveal them. Of course it was impossible to check on them directly now.

"The most priceless object in the universe could be here, waiting to be picked up!"

Once the idea had begun to grow in Shiva's mind, it was impossible to forget it, or to keep from speculating on the subject. But neither god nor man could be sure. A hush followed that declaration.

———

Shiva considered ordering his priest-magician to try to arrange a face-to-face meeting with Hades. But, in truth, even he, the God of Destruction, was somewhat afraid of that dark power. In the accepted scheme of classical theology, Zeus, Poseidon, and Hades divided the rule of the whole universe among them, being respectively the lords of sky, sea, and the Underworld. But in this late age of the world it seemed that gods seldom or never did anything except through the medium of their Faces, and then only when those were worn by humans. However the system might have been established, great confusion and uncertainty resulted.

Pondering all these matters intensely, the God of Destruction decided that he would first try to call Asterion to account. "I am going into the Labyrinth. We must talk to this great beast and see what we can learn."

But even Shiva, like everyone else, would think twice before doing grievous harm to any child of Zeus.

It occurred to him to wonder whether Asterion might know where the Face of Zeus was hidden. And what might happen if the Minotaur himself tried to put it on and become a god?

Looking for Asterion, determined to try to settle the matter of the dreams, he once more called up Nandi, and on his wingless, galloping mount went flying back and forth over the four square miles of the Labyrinth, looking down into the thousand miles and more of tedious windings.

Whether he skimmed low or soared to an eagle's height apparently made little difference. There were literally thousands of places where man or monster could be hiding, in the scattered clumps of vegetation or in any of the many roofed segments of passageway. The God of Destruction could not escape the uneasy feeling that Asterion, mortal or not, was not likely to be found, even by a divine power, unless he wanted to be found.

But at last he spotted the Bull-man, standing still on his two human legs and looking up.

Shiva commanded his mount to land.

Even before dismounting, he said, "This time, monster, we are both of us fully awake. That should put you at something of a disadvantage."

I, Asterion, had been looking over the mysterious central portion of the Labyrinth when the God of Destruction came upon me. Most of these windings I had visited a hundred or a thousand times before in waking life, and so I was not sure what I expected or hoped to find. If Daedalus had not been able to fathom the secrets of this ruin, how could I expect to do so?

For some time I had observed the God of Destruction in his cruising search over my domain, and when he descended I was as ready for him as I could be. Meanwhile the girl, Edith, who had begun to grow accustomed to my Minotaurish presence, still cowered down when Shiva appeared. At the last moment, his close approach proved too much for her. Reminded inescapably of the horror of the day of sacrifice, she panicked, screamed that the devil had come for her again, and ran away.

I did not even attempt to call her back, but hoped that she might safely lose herself for the time being in the endless convolutions of the Labyrinth.

The god, perhaps annoyed at having to cruise for so long above the Maze before he could locate me, dismounted promptly. While Nandi stood snorting and pawing the pavement in the background (perhaps wondering who this being might be with a head so like his own) his master exchanged chilly greetings with me. Then Shiva demanded, "Where is the Face of Dionysus?"

The question startled me at first. "Still buried in the head of the human who was wearing it last fall, for all I know." But as soon as I began to think about the question, I was no longer surprised. The avatar of the Twice-Born who had visited the palace in the autumn had certainly seemed unhealthy.

The lid of my visitor's Third Eye cracked open just a trifle, offering me a hairline glimpse into a pit of molten silver. "You will show me some respect, Bull-man. Or suffer for your impudence."

At last I was beginning to be frightened, but I reminded myself that it is always a great mistake to show fear when confronted by a dangerous wild beast. I folded my huge human arms and looked straight back at the Third Eye. "The world holds greater gods than you, Destroyer. I give respect where it is due."

And then I winced and moved involuntarily when a lance of fire darted from the Third Eye, passed close over my right shoulder, and with a sizzling sound incinerated a small section of one of the Maze's walls behind me, stone and wood vanishing together, as I saw when I slowly turned my head to assess the damage. Of course my movement would have been much too slow to save me, had the beam been directed at me.

Wisps of smoke had been left hanging in the air. But so far Shiva had been careful not to harm a hair on the heads of the children of Zeus.

Now Shiva's hoarse, strained voice dripped words on me like liquid acid. "You persistently intrude upon my dreams, Minotaur."

Still I stood with folded arms, not retreating an inch, though I could feel a fine trembling in my limbs. I hoped that I could conceal the effort that it was costing me to be brave; my antagonist seemed excited beyond the point where he could pay any attention to subtleties. "I might say the same about you, slayer of infants." My voice remained reassuringly steady. "Understand that I do not particularly enjoy your company, either waking or asleep."

"Listen, monster! You ought not rely too much for protection upon legends concerning your illustrious parentage."

I could think of no quick answer to that, and I could see in the three-eyed face that Shiva believed he had made an impression upon me. After a moment he added, to press the point, "There are the princesses, your sisters, to be considered."

"Harming either one of them will not endear you to the people of Corycus."

Shiva's expression showed what he thought of the great mass of ordinary humans.

"Or to the Thunderer, either," I added.

"I have warned you not to rely on that. No one wants to claim you as a son—certainly Minos never did. It seems to me he spent almost twenty years plotting ways to be rid of his monstrous burden—you are a rather ghastly creature, after all."

The idea was hardly a new one to me, and I was able to confront it calmly enough. I shook my horned head. "Whatever Minos may have thought of me, he never contemplated my destruction. It would have been perfectly easy for him, as for any king, to quietly dispose of any infant born in his household and under his control."

"Still," said Shiva, "he did choose to hide you from the world."

"Did he?"

"Of course." My enemy's gaze moved about, taking in the Maze. "What do you mean?"

"What do I mean? Just think about it." And I gestured at the surrounding walls. "What a flawed and futile way to try to conceal someone's existence! To house him in the center of one of the world's most famous mysteries, making it impossible for people ever to see him—or forget him. Creating a legend, demanding international tribute in his name.

"No, it seems to me much more likely that my royal father—or stepfather if you will—had some goal in mind for his wife's offspring, Zeus's bastard. And my uncle is planning something now, you may be sure."

Shiva's lip curled, a sign of contempt for any plans that Perses might be making. "What other gods have approached you lately, monster?"

Again he had surprised me. "Other gods? None. What do you mean?"

But a silent sneer was all the answer I received. My visitor called Nandi to him, and in a moment had sprung into the air again.

———

When Shiva was gone, I looked around for Edith. At first I assumed that she had not gone far, but soon I became worried and began to search for her. At last I called her name repeatedly, aloud.

All in vain.

For days now I had been trying to think of some way to arrange
for Edith to get home—as well as to get the Princess Phaedra out of
house arrest—but even if that could be managed, I feared it was even
possible that Edith's father, when he saw her return home, would assume she had escaped unlawfully, and, fearful of the wrath of Minos,
send her back to Corycus.

But, as I discovered later, only minutes after Edith fled in panic
from Shiva's presence, she had fallen into the hands of some of the
Butcher's soldiers, who were using the marked pathway to maintain a
presence near the center of the Labyrinth. She was soon put aboard
Aegeus's ship and dispatched toward Dia.

The next time I fell asleep, I had a dream of darkness, in which I heard
the voice of someone (I could not see who) observing, "What do you
suppose would happen if—but no, that's too grotesque."

"What?" responded another invisible being.

"*Suppose the Minotaur tried to put on a god's face?*" The unknown
speaker sounded shocked.

There was a murmuring, as of an audience. It seemed that no one
felt confident of what might happen in that case. But several were frightened by the thought.

Including me. I stirred in my sleep, and must have groaned aloud.
Suppose I were to come upon the Face, the power, of Dionysus—or of
Zeus himself? What would I do with it? Would I be too frightened to
put it on, or too frightened not to do so?

Shiva was holding audience, for a group of flying heads, creatures similar to Furies, the product of ancient odylic engineering. They came
before him, groveling extravagantly, nightmare things, some of them
with snakes for hair, others with the heads of dogs. They entered his
chamber hovering in a swarm; those that entirely lacked legs or bodies
were more or less compelled to remain airborne at all times.

In some jockeying among them for position, one of these last had
been forced down to the ground, and now for the time being it could
only lie there, like a winged egg, the ugly face tilted far to one side.

These creatures reported, to Shiva or his priest, that one morning,
very recently, they had seen the usual entourage of Bacchus in full

retreat, leopard-drawn chariot and all, westward bound from Corycus, high above the sea. The Dionysian powers had been carrying a mere mortal with them in their retreat, and they were obviously weakening.

Shiva demanded, "They were carrying only one?"

That was confirmed, in a chorus of ugly voices and jerky gestures.

"This is very important. Can you be sure that the figure in the chariot was a mere mortal?"

The heads—some mutant version of Harpies, it would seem—pirouetted on their wings in midair, and tried to find the breath to laugh. They could be absolutely sure.

Speaking of the Dionysian powers they said, "They know where the Face of their dead master lies; and they are carrying someone there to put it on."

"Do they indeed?" the God of Destruction questioned. "If they were originally headed for Dia, perhaps so. But my candidate ought to get there first." That too was very likely. But the leopard chariot had changed course abruptly when the heads attacked, and made for a scrap of land known as the Isle of Refuge, a place where human sailors of all kinds often took refuge in storms and other emergencies, and stopped to replenish their stores of fresh water.

Doubtless the satyrs' and sprites' original destination had been some other island, more directly to the west, and more distant from Corycus. Dia was a good possibility. Or maybe they had even been heading for the mainland in that direction, beyond the rim of the Great Sea.

"No doubt the Face of your enemy can be discovered there, Lord Shiva."

"Very likely. Who was the man the leopards were transporting?"

The heads, the Furies, did not know. They had never seen him before.

18

ALEX, AFTER SPENDING a few hours in exploration of the small island, mastered his impatience as best he could, and settled down to wait. For his vigil he chose a spot on one of the higher hills, very near the ruined temple, from which he could conveniently keep an eye on the harbor. Everything he had observed about the island so far suggested that ships put in here fairly frequently, to get fresh water, or to take refuge from bad weather. But it would be important to be able to look each visiting vessel over, from a safe distance, before applying to be taken aboard.

Since coming ashore he had been mentally rehearsing a short speech, in which he intended to present himself to the populace as a shipwrecked mariner, and appeal for their help. But within a couple of hours of his arrival, he had been forced to the conclusion that there was no permanent population at all. He was going to have to make his speech to another crew of sailors.

The ruined temple—on second look he thought it had probably been no more than a shrine—occupied a position where, except for the overgrowth of greenery, it would have been fairly conspicuous, on one of the highest points of the island. Its location was further disguised by the fact that most of the walls and roof had fallen in. What was left of the building was almost completely overgrown by wild grapes and laurel, the latter in the form of evergreen shrubs and small trees.

He had never tried the taste of laurel berries before; he sampled one now, making a face at the bitterness and spitting out the single seed. One was enough to convince him, despite his hunger, that they must be poisonous.

The building, temple, shrine, or whatever it was, could never have been large, even when it was intact; that much was shown by the limited size of the foundation, and the relative thinness of the remaining walls. The higher portion of one of those walls bore inscriptions, carved with an air of permanence, doubtless as old as the building itself. They appeared to be in several different languages, none of which Alex could begin to read. The only section of roof remaining, a kind of miniature dome, was small and covered a chamber that must once have been a kind of anteroom. Now birds had adopted what was left of the dome, as a good site for nest-building. Well, it would offer some shelter from the rain that was sure to come.

Alex spent what seemed an interminable series of hours impatiently watching for a ship, meanwhile trying to stave off hunger by nibbling such fruit and mushrooms as he could find, and were not too bitter to be eaten. Once, when the tide seemed at its low, he went down to the beach, to search for shellfish in the shallows. The effort proved futile, shellfish being absent while other small creatures darted away over the sandbanks before he could try to grab them; had he been able to retain his knife, he would have tried to whittle a fishing spear.

In this manner he passed the remainder of the day. Most of his hours were spent in the shade, out of the broiling sun, brooding on the possible meanings of the various things the Dionysian spirits had said to him, and on the problem of what he was to do if he should never hear from them again.

The moon was getting on toward full, appearing vague and blue in the eastern sky before sunset; and when, after sunset, Alex watched it from his high place, it made a vast shimmering on the sea, like silver burning. When he slept, choosing for his bed the anteroom of the shrine or temple, he tried to keep watch in his dreams for the Lord Asterion. But such visions as came held nothing that he could recognize as helpful, and when he awoke even their trivial content had slipped from his memory like water from a clenched fist.

———

As Alex had expected, he did not have very long to wait for the next ship. On the second morning after his own arrival, two of them appeared in rapid succession. First a small trader, rather nondescript, entered the harbor. Then within the hour a larger vessel, of perhaps twenty oars, hove into sight, blocking the entrance.

Watching as closely as he could from his vantage point in a tree well up on temple hill, perhaps two hundred yards above the harbor, Alex didn't like the look of the bigger vessel, with the ominous painting on its bow. He had no personal experience of pirates, but like everyone else had heard some hair-raising stories.

Anxiously he shifted from one observation post to another, working his way closer to the beach, trying to get a better look at what was happening. A few people were milling about down there, but he couldn't see any of them very well. He had about decided that he must work his way closer still, when he observed three people, energetically making their way inland together. In the lead came a nearly naked man whose brown hair was turning gray, closely a young woman and a child, neither of them much better clothed. Already the three had put a substantial screen of vegetation between themselves and the people on the beach. They were all looking back frequently over their shoulders as if in fear of pursuit—there was none—and were coming toward Alex at a good pace, though they had not seen him yet.

Quickly he decided that he must question these folk, and dropped down from his tree.

The trio had not come much closer before he realized that there was something familiar in the woman's appearance.

Alex had never actually seen the Artisan, who had spent almost all his time on Corycus in the middle of the Maze; but this man certainly fit the descriptions he had heard of Daedalus.

The man and boy stopped in their tracks, staring at the naked man who seemed to have popped out of nowhere, perhaps thinking they had come upon some savage native of the island. But the slave-girl hardly paused, having recognized Alex at once.

And Alex was now close enough to be certain that she was Clara. Eagerly he looked downhill past the girl, nursing a faint hope that the princess might be following her slave in flight. But it was not to be.

As soon as Clara had finished the necessary introductions, she said to Alex, "We had given you up for lost. What happened to your clothes?"

"They're gone. I couldn't help losing them, I had a long swim getting here. I very nearly drowned—and I didn't know whether any of the group managed to get away or not. Tell me, where is the princess?" It came out as an urgent plea.

"Down on the beach." The slave, sounding not terribly concerned about the fate of her mistress, turned her head slightly in that direction.

"Really? Is she—is she—?"

"She was quite all right a few minutes ago, hanging on her lover's arm. But I had no such protector there."

Meanwhile, Daedalus was squinting at the gold and silver medallion, which still hung on Alex's naked chest. "I made that ornament for the princess, soldier. May I ask how you come to have it?"

Alex straightened his shoulders. "The Princess Ariadne gave it to me, sir. It's the one thing I was determined not to lose, even if I drowned."

"She simply made you a present of my handiwork?" Daedalus seemed to find this difficult to understand.

"It was a reward, sir. I was able to tell her something she considered very important."

"But how did you get here?" the Artisan demanded of him. "Don't tell me you swam all the way from Corycus."

"No sir, hardly that far. But you may find the true story not much easier to believe. I was helped by the powers of Dionysus, though the god himself is dead. How about yourself?"

The three new arrivals on the island took turns in relating the essentials of their own journey. Among them the newcomers had nothing in the way of a spare garment to lend Alex, being themselves down to the minimum in that regard. The fine linen shift in which Clara had begun her journey out of the Labyrinth had been shredded in a number of places, and was in danger of disintegrating entirely. The man and boy were still wearing the leather aprons in which they had begun their flight, and Icarus had lost his sandals somewhere. Nor had they any food to offer the other castaway, and hope dimmed in their faces when he related the difficulties of foraging.

While Alex led them on to higher ground, the three offered more details of their escape. There was some discussion of the recent arrival of a pirate ship, and the different reactions of Theseus and the Princess Ariadne.

On being reminded of the princess, Alex once more scrambled up a tree, and strained his eyes studying the people on the beach in the sun-bathed harbor. He was a little farther from them now, much too far away for ready identification, but all the people he could see down there now looked like men.

Daedalus, grunting, clambered up beside him, squinted into the sun, shook his head, and said, "The ship we arrived on is lost, I fear. The pirates have surely taken her over. And I believe the crew of our ship has joined them."

"But what will happen to the princess?"

The older man remained calm. "That the fates must decide. The last I saw of her, she was still clinging quite willingly to her handsome prince, who is quite nonchalant about his real profession as a pirate. She may well be regretting her attachment by now."

"Why do you say that?"

"Well . . ."

Both men dropped down from the tree. Alex was mightily upset, having to face the fact that the princess would be taken aboard a pirate ship, by her lover Theseus, who had turned out to be no better than a buccaneer himself. Alex feared for Ariadne's safety—nor did it ease his concerns to hear that in spite of everything she still clung closely to her lover's arm.

In his helplessness he reacted by becoming unreasonably angry with Clara. "Could you not have stayed with her?"

The girl gestured awkwardly. "I don't know, sir, what good that would have done."

"No. No, you are right, of course." Alex raised both hands and tugged at his hair. "Oh, gods! If only I could *do* something!"

It crossed his mind that he might, of course, run down to the beach even now; if the pirates did not kill him at once, and if they were willing to take him aboard their ship, he might at least be near the princess for a while. But how could he be of any possible use to her under those conditions?

It seemed that, short of being able to summon some kind of human army or navy, only the powers of a god had a chance of helping Ariadne now. Therefore, before he, Alex the Half-Nameless, could be of any use, he must gain the strength that the helpers of Dionysus had promised him—but to do that he must somehow reach the proper island, and the proper temple!

Another look in the direction of the beach, and the two ships, confirmed that all the people there seemed to be getting along peacefully, at least for the moment. Daedalus, counting heads at a distance, confirmed that the entire crew of the merchant had decided to join the more irregular enterprise.

"Which is not really surprising," the Artisan observed. "The distinction between trade and piracy is often somewhat unclear, and many seafaring men change back and forth several times during their professional lives."

"I suppose so. But . . ." Alex was not comforted.

In a little while, everyone on the beach had gone peacefully aboard one or another of the two vessels. Soon both hoisted sails, and tacked their way out of the harbor, carrying with them Alex's last chance to attend the princess as a mere human. It now seemed to him that on the deck of the larger ship, he could make out a bright speck that might well have been sunlight on Ariadne's light brown hair.

After watching the two ships out of sight, the refugees agreed that there was little they could do now but wait for yet another ship to put in. When one that looked like a decent trader arrived, one that was not Corycan, they would emerge from hiding and ask to be taken aboard.

"If only we don't all die of hunger first," Icarus complained.

Alex led his three new companions back to the heights, near the place where he had been waiting alone, where they established a kind of camp.

Restless Icarus soon returned from a mushroom-hunting foray into the brush, with the announcement that he had discovered someone's broken house—it was of course the same building that Alex had already started to examine.

Daedalus, perpetually and professionally curious, went to see, pulling some vines away from the crumbling masonry that he might have a better look.

"Practically useless as a shelter," he observed.

The building was mostly ruined, but the Artisan thought that the paintings on the wall-remnants depicted some worship of a sun-god. No one else could tell what the dim and doubtful figures were supposed to be doing.

Daedalus soon produced flint and steel from a waterproof oilskin wallet that he carried attached to his apron's belt, and quickly had a small fire going in a slight hollow of sandy ground. There was a notable lack of things to cook, but at least a symbol of civilization had been established.

The Artisan told Alex that his ultimate goal was to reach a certain mainland kingdom, Megara, whose ruler had once offered the Artisan a place of honor at his court. There he could hope to bring up his son in reasonable safety and stability.

The slave-girl asked, "And will there be room in that household for me, as well, my lord?"

Alex was somewhat surprised to see how familiarly the Artisan reached out a callused hand to stroke her hair. It was the gesture of a man who knows a woman well.

"There had better be," Daedalus said. "I grow fond of you indeed." When his fingers touched her slave's collar he added musingly, "We must soon find a way to get this off."

In his continued desperation regarding the Princess Ariadne and her fate, Alex soon found himself confiding in the others more details of his search for the Face of Dionysus.

After their evening meal of roots and berries, augmented by some eggs Icarus had pillaged from a nest in a tall tree, Alex asked Daedalus, whom he considered a wise and trustworthy older man, for his advice.

The question now having been raised, of what a man ought to do if offered the chance to put on a Face, Daedalus said without hesitation that he would definitely refuse.

"Would you really?"

The Artisan nodded slowly. "I find that merely being a man presents me with quite enough problems; I have no wish to assume those that must come with being a god." With a finely splintered twig he picked out a bit of eggshell from between his teeth.

Alex found this attitude hard to understand. "But think of the powers one would gain!"

"And what have the gods ever done with all the powers they have accumulated? Do they experience great happiness? Contentment? Such glimpses as we catch of their lives do not encourage that idea." Daedalus picked up a handful of sand, letting it sift through his fingers. "There are other ways for a man to increase his capabilities. To find a plan for dealing with the universe."

The slave-girl, on the other hand, proved to have a head full of glorious daydreams that she yearned to put into effect, if she were ever given the chance.

"If I could only be Artemis—" At that point Clara broke off, evidently deciding that some of her dreams were still best kept private. To cover the sudden pause, she turned to the youngest member of the group. "What god would you like to be, Master Icarus, if you had the choice?"

The boy looked up with shining eyes. "I want to be Ares!"

"Bad choice," his father growled. "Who've you been listening to? Ares means war, and war destruction. Any fool can kill, and break, and burn."

Icarus was subdued, but did not appear entirely convinced that his selection was a bad one.

Clara had returned to her own dreams, and was fingering her simple metal collar. "But what would a goddess do, if she found herself wearing one of these?"

"I have no doubt that it would be gone, in the next instant." The Artisan nodded briskly. "Yes, I must find a way to get that collar off your neck."

Alex offered no comment. In most lands ruled by law, or by the authority of a monarch, the removal of the badge of slavery, by any mere mortal human, would of course be seriously illegal; but on this island, he supposed, the only lawmakers were the pirates and the gods. Certainly the Princess Ariadne would not begrudge her favorite companion a chance at happiness.

Daedalus was looking at him shrewdly. "What of your future, soldier? We would all of us like to help the Princess Ariadne, who has done her best to help us. But we don't even know where she's going now, or where we may be tomorrow. It's quite likely that none of us will ever see her again. Under the circumstances, you may find it hard to continue your devotion."

Alex explained that the sprites and other Dionysian powers had revealed to him that the Face of Dionysus was hidden in some Temple of Apollo, on some island. "But I don't know which temple, or where to look for it. They were gone again, off into thin air, before I could find that out."

"That is unfortunate," the Artisan observed. "There are a thousand islands in the Great Sea, as a conservative estimate, and shrines to the Sun-god can probably be found on most of them. Not to mention the countless numbers on the mainland."

Alex nodded wearily, and glanced at the broken wall nearby. "I doubt this ruined structure was the temple they had in mind. Or that this island was their original goal, because when I was riding in the chariot we had to alter course to get here; and here I am, and I see no Face. And I very much doubt that the temple the powers were talking about is on Corycus, or they wouldn't have carried me so far away. Besides, I don't think the island where the usurper rules contains any temples to Apollo."

Daedalus shook his head. "Not any longer. Shiva, may all three of his eyes go blind, has seen to that."

———————

When night fell, the fire was allowed to die down; the air remained reasonably warm, and the Artisan felt confident of being able to kindle another when required.

Alex soon found himself alone, Daedalus having indicated in certain polite but definite ways that he and his woman would appreciate a bit of privacy, to make sure of which they retreated out of sight, a little distance down the hill. Well, that was natural enough. Clara was well-shaped and young, and her torn dress was definitely provocative. Had Alex not been obsessed with thoughts of his princess, he would very likely have been trying to persuade the slave-girl to spend some time alone with him.

Sleep would not come at once, and the young soldier soon found himself sitting upright in what had once been the main entrance of the ruined temple—or perhaps shrine—staring out at a sea exotically silvered by moonlight. He was hoping without much hope for some return of the Dionysian sprites, when a slight noise nearby made him turn his head, to see small Icarus emerging from the bushes.

"Hello," said Alex.

"Hello." The boy was naked as an egg, having evidently shed his leather apron in preparation for sleep. "They are keeping each other warm over there, and they wanted me to go somewhere else."

"I see. Well, you are welcome to stay here, if you like. It seems I am to have no other visitors."

Icarus sat down close beside Alex, and immediately reached out to finger the medallion hanging on the man's chest. "My father made this," he said. "I watched him do it."

"Yes, I know. We were talking about that, but I suppose you weren't listening. He gave it to the Princess Ariadne, and she gave it to me."

"Why?" the child demanded.

"To reward me. As I explained to your father, I was able to tell the princess something that she . . . considered to be very important."

"What do you keep in it?" the boy asked curiously.

"Keep in it?"

"Yes. Don't you know? It opens up. Like this." Shifting position, the son of the Artisan worked on the medallion momentarily with two small, nimble hands, and suddenly it sprang open, the thin disk of silver that formed its back separating from the equally attenuated circle of gold that made the front. Only a single hinge of ingenious construction, practically invisible, still joined the two halves together.

And something, a certain object that had been folded with eerie skill, compressed with supernatural cleverness, into the thin secret compartment between the gold and silver—that something now fell out, to land on Alex's right thigh.

It was a transparent thing, roughly the breadth and thickness of a man's hand, and it felt warm and tingled when it touched his skin. Alex made an odd sound in his throat, and a moment later he had jumped to his feet, clutching in both hands what he knew must be the Face of some god—doubtless Dionysus.

Never before had he seen or touched anything of the kind, and yet he had not the least doubt of what it was. It was shaped like a mask, or rather a fragment of a mask, large enough to cover about half a human face. From near the middle of the fragment, a single transparent eye stared back at the man who clutched it in his hands.

Again Alex uttered a strange noise, born of joy, astonishment, and fear. Young Icarus, alarmed by Alex's behavior, jumped to his feet also, and backed away.

———

For a short and yet unmeasurable time the young man stood there, holding the object that he could not doubt contained the powers of a god. For the moment it seemed impossible to breathe.

The moonlight seemed to show that some substance, or some kind of energy, inside the Face of Dionysus was engaged in rapid movement—a ceaseless, rapid flow of something that might have been ice-clear water, or even light itself.

Inside the semi-transparent object, the waves of—of something— kept reflecting from the edges, top to bottom, side to side, and they went on and on, crossing and recrossing one another in the middle without any sign of weakening.

The most prominent feature of the Face was the single eye—the left—carved or molded from the same piece of strange, warm, flexible stuff . . . around the whole irregular perimeter of translucent shard, edges were somewhat jagged . . . small projections bent easily, springing back to original shape as soon as pressure released.

Alex became aware that the mere touch of the fragment was producing a pleasant sensation, an eerie tingling, in his hands, and the spot on his leg where it had landed still felt warm.

———

And, just as he knew the identity of the object that he was holding, he was aware, without the least doubt, of what he was required to do next.

The decision to put on the Face was really no decision at all, because it was obviously what the princess must have wanted him to do— otherwise she would not have given it to him.

But Alex had some idea of what to expect from a Face. So at the last moment, even as he raised the tingling thing toward his own eyes and nose and forehead, and despite the joy and determination with which he did so, he had an intimation of something of what a suicide must feel.

But that pang endured only for a moment. He ignored the Artisan's son, who in his childish voice was babbling something that might have been intended as a warning. Alex breathed a certain name, and pressed the transparent thing against his countenance, so that his own left eye looked out through the corresponding transparent lens of the Face of Dionysus.

And instantly something began to happen to him. He was undergoing a transformation that was simultaneously tremendous, marvelous, and horrible.

19

FOR THE REMAINDER of the day I, Asterion, continued my search for Edith. But she was gone, beyond my power to locate in a few hours, and as the time passed I had to admit to myself that she had very likely been recaptured.

Of course it was still possible that the girl had only fled deeper into the Labyrinth, beyond the range of my comparatively brief search. I hoped that when I had the chance to sleep again, a dream would reveal her fate. But for the moment I was helpless to do anything.

Her loss affected me strongly. Despite the short time that we had been together, I had a strong impression that she had been learning to trust me, perhaps even to feel some regard for me—

Looking at what I have just written, I see a hopelessly inadequate attempt to express profound complications. But if I were to write that Edith had begun to develop an attachment to me, beyond simple gratitude, how idiotic that would sound.

Let me stick to the facts. She had begun to tell me something of her ordinary life, before the dreadful conscription of the Tribute had taken her away from home, and I got the impression that as a girl she had been happy. She'd been destined from childhood to serve some god or goddess, and eventually had somehow become attached to the service of Apollo.

At one point in our talk I asked her, "Have you ever seen him, girl?"

"Who?" It took her a moment to understand. "The *god*? Apollo himself?" Just the thought was enough to make her wide-eyed. "Never. Have *you* . . . ?"

"No. Not I."

The bull with its divine rider had disappeared into the sky above the distant sea-horizon, in the direction of Corycus. Around Ariadne and Theseus, on the deck of the pirate ship, most of the crew were daring to raise their eyes again.

"What happened?" Ariadne breathlessly demanded of her companion. "What did he say to you? What did he want?"

For the time of several breaths after Ariadne had asked her question there was no sound but the whine of wind and the whisper of water past the hull.

The princess was not in a mood to cultivate patience. "What happened?" she demanded again. "What did Shiva have to say to you?" From the edges of her vision she could see that all the faces of the crew were turned toward her.

Theseus, still wearing only the loincloth in which he had won the fight, was standing braced on the deck, his bare feet planted wide apart. For a long moment he said nothing, only shaking his head slightly, staring after the departing form. Then, turning aside, he barked orders at his crew, commanding them to man the oars, establish a change of course. "We are going to Dia!"

As the helmsman bent over the compass-pyx, Theseus turned his face back to Ariadne, looking at her with a strange, unreadable expression. But still he had not replied to her questions.

The princess was not accustomed to such rudeness. "Are you going to tell me or not? It seemed a long time that he held you in the air. What in the Underworld did he want?"

When her companion's answer came at last, his voice was so low that she could barely hear it. "He told me that I am to become a god."

Again a silence fell aboard the ship.

Almost within arm's reach—it seemed to Ariadne that everything on the small ship was almost within arm's reach—some of the crew were pulling at their oars, aiming the ship into what little wind there was. Meanwhile others tugged at lines to get the lowered sail properly out of the way. They had gone back to work at the captain's orders, and were obeying his instructions, being too much afraid of him to do anything else. Meanwhile there was no doubt that they were also listening avidly to the conversation, knowing that their own lives and fortunes were surely at stake in any dealings that their master had with gods.

"Are you joking?" was the next question that burst from Ariadne's lips. She was painfully aware that sun and salt were cracking her lips and spoiling her skin. Her fine linen dress was gone, dissolved into threads and rags, her present clothing a haphazard collection of rags extorted by her companion from several members of the crew. At the moment she was fully conscious of how little she resembled the beautiful princess who had awakened in her palace bedroom only a few mornings ago. If she were to appear at the gate of the palace in her present condition, no one would recognize her.

"Not at all," said Theseus. Now she could see just how elated he was, and how grimly serious in his delight. For the first time the princess realized that, though her lover could smile and laugh as readily as any man, she could not remember him ever making a joke.

She was still angry at him, and felt a growing disgust with her whole situation. "And how and when is this great transformation supposed to take place?"

"As to how, simply enough. I have been told where the Face of a god can almost certainly be found, and Shiva wants me to go there and get it and put it on. As to when this will take place, within the next few days."

"Which god are you to be?" was Ariadne's next question. It came out in a small voice.

"Does it *matter*?" Now his triumph was beginning to show more plainly. She had to face the fact that the look he gave her was actually scornful. "Actually it's Dionysus. Gods and demons, but you're starting to look strange with your nose peeling like that."

"So, Shiva himself promised you this?"

"Shiva himself." And Theseus, shaking his noble head, drew what sounded like a deep breath of pride.

"So Shiva told you this." Somehow she couldn't believe it.

"Are you deaf? That's what I said."

The more Ariadne thought about the strange claims her companion was making, the less she liked them. "Of course it matters! You're not going to be—you can't be—allied with something like Shiva! Not with the demon who killed my father!"

"Shiva didn't kill him." This man had a way of saying things that made them supremely convincing. Sometimes, she had observed, he applied this talent to things she knew were false.

Ariadne was not going to be meekly convinced, and her attitude showed in her look. "I suppose the Destroyer himself told you that as well."

This irritated Theseus. "We had other things to talk about."

"Such as what?"

The Prince of Pirates ignored the question. "As for your father, were you there that night in the palace?" he demanded. "Did you see what happened?"

"I saw my father's body!" As Ariadne spoke, the ship fell smoothly away from under her feet, starting down a swell, her hungry stomach lurched, and for a moment of distant horror she wondered if she was going to be seasick. "My sister and I both saw that."

Theseus, still clinging with one hand to one of the lines that thinly webbed the single mast, seemed oblivious to the plunging of the ship, as he was to so much else. "But you didn't see how he died."

"That was plain enough. He died of . . . horrible injuries." Her outrage had grown so great that she could hardly speak. "Injuries that looked like sword wounds."

"There you are. Shiva strikes down his enemies with a beam of fire. He never carries a sword."

"Not only his enemies does he strike, but a lot of innocent bystanders as well. He would have cheerfully devoured you, had we not escaped."

Theseus was not moved by her arguments, but he had paused. Now she could perceive in his face a shade of something uglier than sheer indifference. He said, "He didn't devour me, as you put it, just now when he had the chance. Instead, he has chosen me as his ally. And what makes you so sure that Shiva is really *your* enemy? He hasn't hurt your sister, has he?"

"Phaedra may be dead by now, for all I know. Burned to a crisp, or tortured in a cage. He's allied with my uncle, isn't he?"

"So's the whole army back there, and you still have friends among them. I don't say that your uncle is totally innocent, maybe he's not, but why do you accuse Shiva? You admit you didn't see what happened to your father. They say your father also called up a god on that night."

"No, I didn't see him killed with my own eyes. But I had a . . . reliable report."

That made him frown. "A report from who?"

Ariadne didn't care to answer that.

"So, you won't tell me?" But Theseus, hanging with one hand on a rope that ran up to the mast, his eyes probing the horizon, spoke only out of habit, trying to force everyone else to do his will. He really was not interested sufficiently to try to force an answer. Now Ariadne could see that his thoughts had already turned sharply away from her and all her questions. Doubtless he was imagining the glorious adventures that would come within his grasp when he became a god.

But she wasn't going to let him get away that easily. "So, you think you are going to be Dionysus. Why would Shiva grant you such a favor?"

"That's easy enough. No Face can lie around indefinitely unworn, everyone knows that. Some divine power, some kind of law, keeps them all from getting really lost. Sooner or later someone's bound to find it and put it on. And the Lord Shiva would rather see the Face of Dionysus worn by someone he can depend on as a useful ally."

After a pause, Theseus advised her offhandedly, "If the report that worries you came from your brother, I wouldn't put too much reliance on it. He wasn't there either. He dreams things, and then imagines they are real."

Ariadne said coldly, "Sometimes they are. Very real indeed." But despite her anger, a seed of uncertainty had been planted. Theseus's point about the army was well taken—officers and men who called themselves her friends were still willing to serve the usurper and his new god. And she really knew almost nothing about the young soldier— Alex something—who had claimed to have seen what had happened.

Her quest for love and adventure had landed her in a sea of uncertainty. But it came to her with a rush of emotion that there was one man she must never doubt. Her lover, the only man she had ever allowed to know her body. Theseus was so handsome, and at this very moment he was looking at her, so intently that her knees felt weak.

The Island of Dia had a much smoother coastline than the Island of Refuge, besides being enormously larger, with perhaps a hundred times the area, and several thousand permanent inhabitants. There was nothing that could really be called a city. The last time there had been a strong central government was so long ago that memories were vague. The most prominent topographical feature was a range of tall, rugged hills, locally called mountains, never rising more than about three thousand feet above sea level. These ran down the center of the island from north to south. This range was rugged and barren along its crest, but there was plenty of moisture in the smooth slopes of the lower elevations.

Dia was roughly rectangular, about sixteen miles by ten. Vaguely Ariadne could remember from her history lessons the name of a certain tyrant, Lygdamis, who had ruled here several centuries in the past. The present government was a loose and ineffectual confederation of townships. Exports included beautiful white marble, white wine, and some fruits. The capital and chief port lay on the west coast, the opposite side of the island from that where Theseus's two ships were approaching.

Naturally the mountains were the first landmark to become visible to an approaching ship.

As the pair of raiders drew near, their crews could see a few small sailboats near the coast, craft that seemed to be taking care to steer clear of the attacking force; and they grumbled that now the natives had probably spotted them as well. The locals, given warning, might be able to arrange some kind of a defense, or at least to hide their women and their valuables. "Of course they don't know where we're going to land."

The Dians were among the peoples who had been forced to send tribute to Minos; in recent years they had not been well organized among themselves.

Theseus took note of the fact that there was as yet no sign of his father's ship. "Shiva said he might be here, and that I could expect some other help as well. I expect the old bastard will show up, but who knows when."

Ariadne asked Theseus, "Are you and your father still on speaking terms? I thought it was somehow because of him that you were shanghaied into being one of the youths of the Tribute."

Theseus looked into the distance, smiling faintly. "We have our disagreements, Dad and I. So far, neither of us has tried to conceal any of them from the other."

What kind of greeting he intended to give the old bastard when he came was hard to tell from his manner.

Back on the island of Corycus, Shiva had ordered Perses to see to it that such forces as were available and could be spared, were dispatched to aid the cause of Theseus.

Fortunately several suitable ships were in the harbor or nearby, among them that of Aegeus, also known as King of the Pirates. Theseus had agreed with Shiva, in the course of their brief airborne discussion, that his father would be a good man to have along when matters came to fighting. Provided, of course, that it did not take months to locate him. But as fate would have it, Aegeus had already put in at Corycus; months ago, King Perses had let it be known that certain gentlemen of fortune would be welcomed at his court, and that profitable alliances could be arranged. Before putting out to sea again, Aegeus had taken aboard his ship the girl Edith, who had been recaptured in the Labyrinth. It was thought she quite likely would be useful on her native isle of Dia, both as a guide and as a hostage.

Now the God of Destruction was engaged in directing the furnishing of his new temple. King Perses had come to the temple, to make sure, as he said, that the work of furnishing and decoration was going to the god's liking. Laborers and craftsmen, ordered to keep the work going despite the immediate presence of divinity and royalty, were pounding and sawing on the upper levels of a high interior wall, now and then ripping out oaths and dropping fragments of wood or stone, so that the god and king who stood below had taken shelter beneath a platform of scaffolding. A faint cloud of dust, pierced here and there by sunbeams entering at windows, filled most of the large interior of the structure.

Perses, paying careful attention, listened to the news that Theseus was very likely to soon put on the Face of Dionysus. The king knew very little about the amazingly fortunate young man, except of course that he had just escaped being part of the recent Tribute, and had by some amazing feat established a romantic connection with Ariadne.

Now it suddenly occurred to Perses, with a sharp inward chill, that Shiva might be planning to depose him as king, and invite Phaedra to take the throne instead.

He said nothing of his suspicion to Shiva, but asked cautiously, "This Theseus bears me no ill will?"

As usual, most of the god's attention seemed to be elsewhere. He was squinting upward past the scaffolding, trying to make important decisions. Should the rows of human skulls on the interior wall run vertically or horizontally? It was a high wall, and broad, and its surface held room for many rows of skulls. Maybe a random scattering would be more effective. "No more than he feels for humankind in general, I suppose."

The king said that if he could be assured of that, then he had no objection. Not that it would have made any difference, he supposed, if he did object.

"How do we know, oh great lord, that the Face of Dionysus is likely to be found on the island of Dia?"

"Because that is what your man Creon assures me, on what he claims is very good magical authority."

"May I ask, lord, what this good reason is?"

Shiva made a gesture of impatience. "Something he has heard from one of his familiars." Actually Shiva had been unable to follow Creon's involved explanation, but he had no intention of confessing any such failure to a mortal. "Of course he may be wrong, but we cannot afford to let the opportunity pass by."

Perses meanwhile was thinking that some of Creon's other predictions, notably those about the Face of Zeus, had not been fulfilled. But the king, dreading his god's reaction, did not want to voice that comment aloud. Investigations, both physical and magical, were continuing. But legend and experience alike assured him that in the Labyrinth, answers of any kind, to any question, tended to be difficult.

The god had fallen silent. Perhaps, thought Perses, Shiva's thoughts were running along the same lines.

Presently they were joined by Creon himself, who brought word that Hades was ready for a meeting.

Shiva drew himself up to his full height. "That is satisfactory," he allowed.

"Will the Lord Shiva be going to Dia personally?" the high priest asked. Then he looked up apprehensively, as another fragment of something fell from the ongoing work above.

"Not now." Shiva's original plan had been to allow Theseus time to get to Dia with his ship, and then to appear to take a personal hand in the proceedings. But the meeting with Hades must come first. By his very nature, the Ruler of the Underworld was vastly more powerful and important than Dionysus was ever likely to become.

He did not wish to try again to explain to this mere mortal how he, Shiva, could be so certain that his many enemies were trying to entrap him. Besides, there were other matters, like trying to arrange his alliance with Hades, that were really of overriding importance. Seeing to it that the right human got to wear the Face of Dionysus was certainly a task worth doing, but Shiva did not think that his own fate depended utterly on the result.

To Perses he said, "The Lord Hades has expressed a wish of forming an alliance with me."

"Great are the ways of the gods," the king murmured placatingly. Now the man was being so ostentatiously awe-stricken that Shiva found his attitude irritating. "How soon does my lord plan to conclude this alliance?" No doubt the humble tone of the question was intended to make it sound less impertinent, but the effort did not succeed.

"Very soon," Shiva responded shortly. Later there would be time to deal properly with impertinence.

The current human avatars of Hades and Shiva had never met, and, as far as Shiva could remember, none of the contacts between their respective earlier embodiments had been more than brief and incidental; so Shiva knew he must approach their impending conference warily.

In a little while the humans who were working as liaison between himself and Hades came to Shiva and told him where Hades wanted to meet him, and when. The rendezvous was scheduled to take place on a new volcanic island, many miles from Corycus, and still almost glowing with heat. Shiva had already scouted the place, airborne, from a distance; he supposed that Hades and his creatures of the Underworld could stand on it unscathed, but Shiva and everyone else would find it excruciatingly hot. Shiva expected that he could stand there and shield himself from damage, by an exertion of will, but he could not be comfortable.

The attitude of these human servants of Hades toward him was not at all like Creon's. Shiva burned with inward rage at being treated with arrogance by these mere mortals; yet he dared not strike them down, or even rebuke them strongly. And they were so confident in their impudence that they did not even flinch when he allowed the lid of his Third Eye to open slightly. Perhaps they did become just a shade more respectful.

These humans were relatively new to their job; their predecessors had been discharged—if that was the right word to describe their fate—in a general shakeup of Hades's staff following last year's encounter with Apollo.

———

The meeting got under way at last.

Lightning flared, rain fell toward rocks still not cooled very far below their melting point. The falling water, caught up in the rising heat, was turned to steam before it even touched the rocks, and so sprang up again at once, hissing and boiling away in white clouds that spread across the cooler ground, knee deep on mortals and deities alike.

There were no formal introductions made, and most of those present seemed to be taking steps to cloak their identities. For a moment Shiva wondered whether all these who were gathered here were part of the great conspiracy against him. Well, even if they were, it was too late now to simply turn around and leave.

Hades had to remove his Cap of Invisibility before he could be seen, even by his fellow gods. But even before the cap came off, Shiva was certain that he could *feel* that mighty presence near.

And then he saw it, standing where the shadows of the thunder-

clouds above seemed to be deepest. Not so much a shape, as a gathering
of darkness, only vaguely human. It was difficult to be sure of Hades's
size, though he received a definite impression of a shaggy head and
massive, rounded shoulders, with a dark chain of some kind hung
around the neck.

The voice when he heard it was dark and deep, and sounded full
of echoes, as if it were issuing from some deep cave.

As was true of all the gods, Shiva's human body had once walked
the earth with no name or identity beyond those of mere humanity. But
the Destroyer, unlike many other deities, had long labored to force himself to forget that epoch of his existence. He would have given a great
deal to possess that Cap. He was impressed despite himself by the power
and majesty of Hades, but also vaguely sickened in a way. *An utter
blackness, an infernal gloom, that defied the Sun itself to brighten it. It
would have swallowed up the lancing beam from the Third Eye, as the
ocean swallowed sparks.*

Exchanging whispers with those around him, Shiva began to comprehend the situation. Some of the gods that the Lord of the Underworld
had hoped to recruit had declined to join him, while his aides had been
unable to locate certain others. Some might be absent because no one
was wearing their Faces at the moment. Others simply disliked Hades,
or feared him too much to consider entering a partnership.

An alternate explanation could well be that they were mightily
afraid of Apollo. Even those who had never been the Far-Worker's
enemies, who considered themselves ready to be his friends, tended to
be uneasy in his presence. Of course, very much depended on the nature
and behavior of the particular avatars involved. In general, it seemed
that the worldwide community of gods—if such a loose assortment of
beings could be called a community—was not taking sides in this conflict. Most of the members, as far as could be determined, were simply
waiting to see what happened next.

One god commented, "Too bad that Thanatos is missing. I have not
seen his Face on anyone for some time."

"Have never seen him, that I can remember—and won't be too sad
if I never do." That got a chuckle.

And another observed, "Yet I have noticed no difficulty in terminating mortal lives, even in the absence of Death himself."

Hades had his own ideas concerning any god-Faces that might be available, and who should put them on. He wanted to make sure that this

new upstart avatar of Dionysus was slain without delay, though he was not at all sure which human should receive the prize. Ideally, the Lord of the Underworld would have preferred to carry that Face down to such a subterranean depth that none of his potential enemies would ever be able to get at it.

Shiva protested that he had in mind a certain human who, he thought, was very well qualified to wear the Face of Dionysus.

Well, said Hades, who as yet had no particular human in mind, maybe the candidate of Shiva would be acceptable—this Theseus. "But I must meet him first."

While the gods conversed, they observed a new version of Cerberus in operation. Cerberus was not a god, of course, and certainly had never been a human. But a formidable weapon and tool in the arsenal of Hades, the creature had just broken open the new gateway to the Underworld.

First a quivering of the ground, then a savage eruption, flying rocks and mud. Powerful limbs moving in a blur of speed, claws harder and sharper than any bone, any tooth or claw, rending the earth, pulverizing even rock.

And now Cerberus, unbothered by the infernal heat, was working to pave the smooth, round wall of a tunnel, circular in cross-section.

"I seem to remember a different creature of that name. Much more doglike."

"That was the old version—Apollo killed it, more than a year ago."

The introduction of Apollo's name cast something of a chill on the proceedings.

Looking at the thing, Shiva decided that it was not, and had never been, alive, even though it certainly had hair—even red hair, calling to mind something he had heard of Apollo's new avatar—and its surface showed some of the complex irregularity of life. Even its eyes looked dead, and there was no sign that it was breathing.

Some kind of artifact, no doubt, of the mysterious odylic process of the ancients.

"Where does Hades get them?" an anonymous voice wondered.

"No one knows."

The thunderheads of the ongoing storm were massing ever more tightly above the island. The suggestion was inescapable that Zeus might be taking an interest in their meeting.

Hades professed indifference, but many of the others who gathered here would have preferred to meet at night, out of sight of the great Eye of Apollo.

The subject of the Sun-God having arisen, Hades assured his prospective colleague that he was quite ready to go another round with Apollo.

"That Bloodless One will not escape me, next time."

Shiva had been impressed by the presence of Hades when the meeting began. As it went on, the Destroyer moved from being wary to being frightened. The dark presence before him was one, with Poseidon and Zeus himself, of the triumvirate who ruled the universe. It had become a habit with Shiva to toy with the lid of his Third Eye, no matter whose company he was in, deriving pleasure from the nervous reactions of whoever he was with. But now the Third Eye stayed tightly closed.

And he remained frightened of Hades even after the conference was over. Even if Hades had promised that his, Shiva's, rule on Corycus would be confirmed and strengthened.

———

The high priest Creon, making his own calculations, had decided that the unknown power that had advised him about treasure was probably very reliable.

The thought that it might be untrustworthy was very frightening indeed, and he quickly put it from him.

20

IN THE MOMENT before Alex slipped the Face of Dionysus on over his own, he had only a vague and general idea of what shape his impending transformation was going to take—but that his metamorphosis would be awesome in some way he had not the slightest doubt. The young man clapped the strange thing over his left eye and ear, and cheek and forehead, in the full expectation of being seized and shaken by all the powers of Dionysus, mentally as well as physically, like a rat in the jaws of a dog.

What actually happened seemed less violent than he had expected, but every bit as thorough.

Through his left eye he now saw the world quite differently than he ever had before. Potentialities of life, perceptible as shimmering, transparent reds and greens, were visible in almost everything he looked at. Not quite everything; the empty sky was least affected, along with certain dark rocks, whose shapes and colors told him they had been unchanged for almost as long as there had been an earth. The vision of his other, un-Faced eye, like the hearing in his right ear, remained unaffected. The dual perception thus created in his senses was disorienting at first, but he soon began to get used to it.

In his left ear there now came sounds that were not quite sounds, only hints of whispers that might have been or were yet to be. And, if he listened for them, the throb of pulse and sigh of breath of every human who was near him.

Outside of the sudden alteration in his senses, the young man was at first aware of very little physical change in his own body. Unthinkingly he had somehow expected to be ten feet tall, but of course that was not to be. It seemed to him that there had been a broadening of his chest, a slight rounding of his limbs. When he wished silently for a mirror, one of the newly revitalized sprites brought it to him, materializing what felt like solid silver and glass out of the air.

Presently Alex realized that he was now able to see the sprites, and the other creatures of his entourage, clearly, whenever he wanted to see them, in somewhat the same way as a human could always monitor his own breathing when he cared to think about it. He could have named them now, or most of them, individually, had he wanted to take the trouble. At the moment about a dozen sprites, also called maenads or bacchantes, were visible, about half their number naked, the remainder wreathed in wispy veils. All were beautiful in both of the young soldier's eyes. Most of them appeared to be no more than half-grown girls, in a great variety of sizes and shapes. Their smooth, bare skins bore all the ordinary colors of humanity, along with several hues that neither Alex nor Dionysus had ever seen on mortal flesh.

Then there were the hairy-legged satyrs, all emphatically male, ranging in apparent age from elderly to hardly more than children. Their leader, as Alex could now remember, was a paunchy and debauched elder specimen named Silenus. As soon as Alex willed their forms into clarity, there they were, satyrs and maenads alike, making obeisance to him as soon as they observed that he was taking notice. The moment he wished them away, they promptly disappeared.

Let them stay vanished for the moment. He needed at least the illusion of privacy, to try to come to grips with a new world, his new self.

Now memory, vastly augmented over what that of mere mortal Alex had ever been, assured him that only the chariot and the two panthers were still missing from his usual entourage. The stored experience of a god's lifetime, a depository of marvels bewilderingly enormous, warned him that the restoration of those items might still take many days.

But it was not only the potentialities of life outside his own which were now open to his observation. New memory also assured him of the possibilities of frenzy, that he would experience and that he would bring to others, embodied so clearly in his inhuman escort. And there were depths now visible within himself, from which he recoiled after his first look.

The moment Alex wondered about the *thyrsus* staff, it suddenly appeared. It had come from nowhere, and now it was in his hand. He knew that his marvelous new memory, if he consulted it, would tell him what miraculous feats might be accomplished with the staff, and how to go about doing them. He would be able to work marvels, he was sure. But first. . . .

———

The first really disturbing change to manifest itself was a raging thirst for wine, easily enough satisfied. He had only to extend a hand, and a filled goblet appeared in it. Then came a vivid daydream of naked women, sinuous bodies twisting in a lustful dance. But in the very first moments of the experience Alex realized that it was not a dream at all. The sprites were back, as he must have wanted them to be, at least a dozen of them now, as convincingly real and alive as any people he had ever seen.

Satyrs in their several varieties came trooping and cavorting with the females, bearing torches whose flames spurted up wildly in different colors. Romping lustfully, stamping and prancing to the beat of the music, the goat-men, led as usual by Silenus, grappled the girls and women to them in a wild dance that had hardly got under way before it was transformed into an orgy.

———

His human mind and body had a limited capacity to sustain such passion. Soon there came an ebbing of the tide that had drawn and whirled his blood into such frenzy. The storm ebbed, and was soon followed by an exhausted calm.

How many minutes had passed, Alex could not have said. He came to himself, gasping and with the blood pounding in his head, keenly aware that he had just finished satisfying his own lust on the body of Clara. Now she moved again beneath him, but this time the movement was only a simple, awkward, sexless shifting of her weight, as if trying to ease some painful pressure. With a kind of groan the new god—still Alex, but no longer only Alex—raised his body, enough to let her get up and withdraw to a little distance. Then he collapsed on his side and lay there panting.

His mind was filled, overwhelmed, with the memory of naked bodies surrounding him, the rhythms of joining and rejoining. When he closed his eyes they were still there. But gradually the excitement and its visions faded.

Evidently Clara had been caught up in the madness of Dionysus almost as fully as he had himself. Nor had Daedalus been immune—but there was another matter that Alex now found puzzling. When the tide of mania ebbed, he retained a confused memory of having been observed, even while the frenzy was at its peak, by the figure of a woman. A beautiful, dark-haired woman, clad in a cloud of fine fabric that shimmered with the ghosts of many colors, she had watched with evident amusement while declining to take part.

Who was this woman, who could resist so successfully not only the grappling efforts of the satyrs, but all the charisma of Dionysus? His vast new vaults of memory held the answer, readily available—Circe, no goddess but a mortal woman, though still in appearance as young and beautiful as she had been two hundred years ago. Beyond that distance in the past, even the memory of the Twice-Born started to grow cloudy, on this subject at least. Dionysus thought it would have been good to speak with Circe, but now she was gone again.

Alex found a kind of ease in the exhaustion of his own, still very human, body. Not sleep, not yet. Sleep would come, as it came to gods and men alike, but it would have to wait.

The *thyrsus* was lying on the ground, and he bent and picked it up. He looked around, but there was still no sign of chariot and leopards.

Thinking about all that had happened to him during the last few hours, pulling up memories of a vast number of similar events in the god's past, Alex gradually came to understand that a great part of what he had experienced during the orgy—but not all of it, by any means—had taken place only in his own mind.

Well, he had never anticipated that the Face of Dionysus, the arrogant intruder he had so eagerly invited into his brain, was going to bring him peace. Tranquility of any kind, physical or mental, was exactly the wrong thing to expect from the god whose nature Alex had come to share. But the change had been more overwhelming than he had expected it to be. The presence of the deity was racking him with madness.

He had just experienced a prolonged wave of divine craziness, that like an enormous ocean surge had drawn him under, and held him beneath the waves until he knew that he was quite thoroughly drowned. The god was used to such experience, surely, and would survive. But Alex was far from certain that his human nature could stand it.

For a few moments he dozed, sprawled on the broken floor of the ruined temple in divine exhaustion. From that slumber Alex awoke with a shock of guilt, for having entirely forgotten the princess for what must have been many hours. On waking he was himself again—as much, he supposed, as he in his new life was ever going to be entirely himself. The god seemed to have partially withdrawn from him, leaving only the confused human, with enhanced senses and capabilities.

In the aftermath of madness he felt, for the time being, thoroughly human, and very weak.

Again his human heart experienced a sudden lash of guilt at the thought of how, at the very moment, the Princess Ariadne might be in desperate need of the help that he had now been empowered to provide. And he, instead of spending the precious minutes and hours trying to reach her, he had been . . . but the god had possessed him, he reminded himself hastily. He had been given no real choice.

That was a good excuse, but he wasn't sure he could believe it.

Through his own, old, human memory, a vision of his sodden, drunken predecessor, sprawled on the floor of the great hall of the Corycan king, came to Alex like a nightmare. It spurred him to move, to get back on his feet.

———

"Hello." The voice was quietly thrilling, unmistakable. The mortal enchantress Circe, arrayed in fine garments of her own weaving, was once more standing near, this time certainly no vision, but a solid presence. The coloring of her hair, her skin, seemed as inconstant as that of her clothing.

"So, you are the new Dionysus. I see you are enjoying your new body, great lord." He thought the enchantress pronounced the title with just a hint of mockery. "Let me offer my congratulations on your escape from the Destroyer."

"Thank you, my dear." Dionysus spoke as a prince might, to a favorite artisan or entertainer. To Alex the Half-Nameless, the words seemed to come automatically, in the same language that his visitor had used. It was a tongue that he had never heard before—but of course Dionysus had not the least trouble understanding it. "Perhaps next time—?"

"I am invited to join you?" Circe gently mimed surprise. She was standing at her ease, small hands clasped, graceful head tilted to one side. "All things are possible—but I think not. You never seem to lack for willing partners in your madness."

Alex nodded silently. Then the god with whom he shared his body bowed lightly to the visitor, a gesture containing a hint of mockery.

Then Dionysus saluted her with his staff. "But none as experienced as you, Circe—and very few as lovely."

"Oh Twice-Born Lord, I very much appreciate the compliment. But in truth, your romps are far too energetic for a poor mortal woman of my years." To Alex's right eye, still purely human, the female figure before him appeared no more than twenty years of age. Even his augmented left eye could discover no trace of the decay that time must leave on mortal flesh, though to vision of divine acuity, subtle hints were visible in plenty. But that, the human realized, was not the sort of detail that Dionysus ever wished to see.

"Where is Apollo?" the god asked.

"I think you need not bother to search for him. The Far-Worker will be seeking you, and he will find you soon enough." Circe paused. "I do believe you two will get along splendidly in your present avatars, different as you are."

"I rejoice to hear it. Where is the Face of Zeus?"

"Ah, Lord Dee, if I knew that . . . would I be standing here, consuming time in idle chat?"

"I see. No doubt you have other affairs of pressing importance."

"You mock a poor woman, lord; but in fact I do. Besides, it is not good for mere mortals like myself to spend much time in such exalted company."

"Do you mock me, woman?" Alex alone would have been hopelessly enthralled by the shimmering beauty before him, not only of form but of voice and gesture; but Dionysus was beginning to be annoyed.

Silver laughter trilled, and before the god could decide whether to pursue his protest, the woman who had been standing before him was gone. No deity could have vanished more smoothly and magically.

Shortly after awakening from the restful sleep that followed, Alex became aware that he was no longer naked, but that his body was draped in a rich purple cloak. He became intimately and vitally aware of everything that grew and lived on the island, and even the nightbirds flying over it.

At dawn, the growing light revealed trampled bushes and discarded garments, discarded sprite-wear—those glorious shreds spontaneously disappeared even while Alex looked at them. This litter was mingled with the stubs of burnt-out torches, whose persistent reality indicated that most of the light must have come from some kind of real fire.

Ready to attend to business once again, Alex found plenty of practical matters awaiting his attention. He knew, even without any warning from Circe, that Shiva, a damned efficient killer, would be hunting him with murderous intent, and that, despite his own new godhood, he was in mortal peril.

So was the entire world, perhaps. If the Face of Zeus was really lying about somewhere, waiting for someone to pick it up . . . Alex alone could never have fully appreciated what that might mean. But Dionysus could, and Alex could feel the god's fear.

His determination to help the princess had not been in the least diminished by his apotheosis. He felt immensely reassured by the knowledge that he was still fully human, still as much the individual Alex as he had ever been, despite the unarguable fact that he was now also someone else—and something rather more than human. Before putting on the Face, he had been afraid at some deep level that his own identity would vanish when he became Dionysus; but now the very memory of the god himself, recording the fate of more of his avatars than Alex cared to think about, assured him that was not going to happen.

Not unless he was driven mad by repeated bouts of ecstasy and frenzy. Memories that were new to Alex, but ancient in the god now bound to him, assured him that too was distinctly possible. More than one avatar had led only a short life after putting on the Face of Dionysus.

The worn stones paving the floor of the grass-grown shrine were stained following the orgy—but not with blood. The only redness was of wine. There were worse gods by far, and bloodier, than Dionysus. Alex was afraid to probe his new memory for information about them, but he knew that soon it would be necessary to do so.

The great majority of the participants in last night's revelry, never having been burdened with real human flesh, had vanished into the air, or perhaps into the earth—neither Alex nor Dionysus knew. Only four solid, living bodies, including his own, remained in sight. One of the solid bodies was that of the child Icarus, who had slept peacefully through the night, and now, still deep in the absolute sleep of childhood, lay curled in the lingering warmth of the ashes of last night's fire. And none of the four, as far as Alex could tell, had been seriously harmed, though both the Artisan and Clara looked a little worn this morning.

Clara's metal collar was gone, and whether it had been removed by the power of the god, or through the cleverness of Daedalus, Alex did not try to remember. A pale ring around the girl's neck showed where the vanished band of metal had shielded a narrow circle of her skin from the sun. She had reclaimed the torn remnants of her once-fine linen gown, discarded early on in the bout of shared madness, and was clutching them around her, as if in shame. Clara's movements were tentative and slow, suggesting that many parts of her body were sore this morning.

She gave Alex a slave's unreadable glance, but said nothing, and quickly looked away again, as if she were afraid. Memory assured him that as a god he could expect many people, mere mortal humans, to look at him like that.

The Artisan, who had evidently come fully awake even before Alex, had put his apron on again. His face looked pained, and there was a tremor in his fingers as he endeavored by purely natural means to rebuild the ordinary fire. Meanwhile young Icarus was still asleep.

Alex got up and moved a little apart from his three fellow humans, realizing that they would feel easier if he did so. Moodily he began tracing with one finger the ancient inscriptions on the walls of the ruined temple, while he waited for his companions to recover fully. Suddenly he realized that he had gained the ability to read in a great number of languages. In the litter on the ruined floor he located a sharp-pointed fragment of rock, and on a blank section of remaining wall he proved to himself that he could write many of them also, tracing his own name and that of the Princess Ariadne. His new memory assured him that a great many gods shared such linguistic abilities.

Soon he became aware that the Artisan was approaching him, slowly and tentatively.

"What is it, Daedalus? Don't be afraid." Vaguely Alex realized how different his transformed self must now appear to the other humans, even though the changes in him were comparatively subtle on the surface.

Daedalus, as usual, was making an effort to understand the world around him as well as possible. "Lord, was there—was there someone else here, a few minutes ago? Another woman?"

"There was. Circe. But no cause for you to worry." Feeling a sudden, restless urge to explore more of his grafted memories, Alex reached out with the tip of his staff and pointed to one series of weathered markings. "Daedalus, what is this language called?"

The Artisan rubbed his head, as if it were still throbbing with last night's wine, exertions and emotions. Squinting at the words, he could name the tongue in which they were written, and read a little of it. He could also identify a second kind of writing, but was unable to read it at all. And the third script was something he could not remember ever having seen before.

Alex/Dionysus could not only name all three, but could read them with perfect ease; and he could, if he thought about it, tell in what parts of the world each was in use. All conveyed pretty much the same ideas, being litanies of praise directed to the Sun-God.

Now the new avatar of Dionysus could not only see, and read, but feel, with a mysterious new inward sense, that the temple in which he'd found the Face had indeed been dedicated to Apollo.

"Then it truly happened as my powers foretold," he murmured to himself. "Silenus? Where are you?"

Under questioning by Dionysus, the paunchy one readily admitted that of course the sprites and satyrs had known that the Face was hidden in the locket—they had put it there, trying to hide it from Shiva and the new King Perses. "I doubt we could have done better, lord," the satyr concluded.

"Perhaps not," admitted the Twice-Born, and spread his hands— Alex's hands, of course—and looked at them, as if trying to assess the quality of this new body in which he found himself.

Meanwhile Icarus had begun to stir and yawn. When the child sat up, rubbing his eyes, Daedalus, excusing himself from the god's presence with a few murmured words, went to his son and led him away. The faint sound of their footsteps descending the pathless hill went on for a long time, and Alex realized that the Artisan was taking his boy to some other part of the island.

When Clara looked inquiringly at Alex, he nodded slightly, granting permission, and without saying anything she turned and followed the father and son.

Alex sighed, in sudden loneliness. As a result of sharing an orgy, the three of them now seemed more remote from one another than before. But Dionysian memory assured him that some separation now was for the best. The Twice-Born knew that other humans would generally be more comfortable away from him.

But the god also realized that the three mortals would soon be seeking out his company again. Because the divine keenness of his hearing could pick out a new sound in the distance, that of the ocean's surface being crisply parted by the sharp bow of a ship. The sound was steadily approaching; the harbor would soon entertain another visitor.

By the time the sun had risen a good hand's breadth above the sea, Alex and the god were watching it alone, sharing the same pair of eyes. Right now he was content to be alone, but he knew that it would not always be so.

And now the ship that Dionysus had detected at a distance was at hand, coming right into the harbor.

Several hours passed before Alex saw his fellow refugees again. As he had expected, the arrival of the ship had brought the man and woman and child all back to him, seeking protection against the unknown.

But Alex did not yet realize, and the god did not care, what the effect of his new self on them would be. When the three mortals drew near, Icarus and Clara fell down before him, hiding their faces, and even Daedalus assumed a position indicating a certain humility. Alex spoke to them absently, giving reassurance; but his main thought was already far away, considering what he must do next.

The new arrival proved to be another trader, to all appearances reasonably honest, or at least showing none of the outward signs of piracy, putting in to the harbor to take on water.

Unhurriedly Alex walked down to the beach, where he was presently joined by Daedalus and Clara and Icarus. Calmly he hailed the sailors as they came ashore.

Slowly the timidity of the newcomers was relieved. The captain, who gave his name as Ottho, bowed deeply when he stood before Alex. He was astonished to find himself in the presence of a god, but not paralyzed.

This captain knew the Artisan by reputation, and was impressed to meet him. Also his eyes, and those of his crew, lit up at mention of the reward that the God of Joy now promised them for taking on these passengers, and conveying them to where they wished to go.

The crew of this new ship were, like their captain, ready to acknowledge the young man, whose dazzling presence stood before them, as an avatar of Dionysus. At first they took him for some lord, or prince, who had been marooned here by chance; then, one by one, they began to realize the truth.

"Lord Dionysus!" one said clearly. And a murmuring of prayer and incantation began among them.

"Stand at ease, men!" Alex held out his hands as if in blessing. "If you would please me, take my friends here on a voyage to where they want to go." And he gestured with his staff.

Crew and captain eagerly agreed. And they were pleased and enchanted by the presentation that the god now gave them, large bunches of purple grapes, fully ripe and almost bursting with their juice. "If you will save the seeds and plant them, I think you will be pleased with the results."

"We thank you, lord! We thank you heartily!" Once more the demonstration of gratitude was impressive.

The ship's new destination would be a seaport of Megara, the kingdom where Daedalus hoped to find that the ruler's generous job offer was still open to him.

"And you . . . my lord?" Ever since Alex had put on the Face, the proud Artisan gave the impression every now and then that he was about to fall to his knees—and Clara had already done so.

Alex put out a hand to tug at the arm of Daedalus, holding him upright. "Call me your friend rather than your lord. But let me be alone for now. You should take ship away from here, with your woman and your child, while you have the chance. I want to go where Ariadne is— can you tell me where?"

"Not I, my lord."

"And so I must stay here, and gather my strength, until I can find the right place and time to use it."

"My lord, I—"

"No. Leave me now." Alex—though it really came more from his new, internal partner—made a dismissive wave, a regal gesture. "I will miss your company, all three of you. But the battle I must now fight is one that you had better avoid. In any case, none of you are the kind of people who can spend a great deal of time in the presence of Dionysus and escape unharmed."

Daedalus straightened to his full height. Alex thought he was probably curious about what kind of people that might be, who were able to live on easy terms with the God of Frenzy. But the Artisan's question was: "What will you do now—my friend?"

"My full powers will be restored to me—soon, I think." The god's memory of many previous transitions gave him that hope. "And when they are, I must rely on them to tell me that. But they are not yet . . . fully gathered. For now I can only wait."

In quick succession he shook the callused hand of Daedalus, playfully ruffled the child's short hair, and briefly and tenderly stroked Clara's tender cheek. Then he sent his three mortal companions on their way.

———

In another hour the ship had sailed free out of the harbor, Alex himself was once more the only human being on the island. But this time he was not alone. It aroused in him mixed feelings to reflect that he, whose name had been Half-Nameless, would never be unknown or alone again.

"Princess Ariadne, be calm, be brave, wherever you are. As soon as I can locate you, I am coming to your aid."

Not that he really expected she could hear him. His only answer was the almost mindless singing of his sprites, and a bass chuckle, very distant, from Silenus.

21

FOR SOME HOURS after his transformation, Alex never doubted that the Princess Ariadne had meant to bestow on him the powers of a god. Miraculous as it seemed, this daughter of the royal house of Corycus had chosen *him*, out of all the men who must have been—who *had to* have been—eager to devote their lives to her service. He, Alex the Half-Nameless, the humble private soldier, was the one Ariadne wanted to be her champion, her defender. In effect she had surrendered her fate into his hands. The princess must have had, after all, some idea of the depth of his devotion, because she had picked him to be the one who, when the time was ripe, would descend with divine power to intervene in her affairs, and save her from . . .

From what, exactly? From the man she had chosen as her lover, who now, if Daedalus and Clara were telling the truth about him, had turned out to be a pirate? No, Alex couldn't believe that it was Theseus from whom the princess wanted to be rescued. Although, to judge from the evidence Alex had heard from his fellow fugitives, she'd be much better off without him. The man Ariadne feared most was of course her uncle.

And above all, and with the best of reasons, she must be terrified of Shiva.

Vividly Alex could remember that dark autumnal night in the great hall of the palace, and how his own predecessor in the role of Dionysus had fled in abject terror from the God of Destruction. By all the gods, even had he lived out his human life as nothing more than human, he would never have forgotten that.

Already, he had enough experience of his own new powers to know that they were tremendous. But the memory he had from Dionysus assured him that they were also terribly disorganized just now; a certain period of confusion in the life of any god was only to be expected when one avatar died and another one took over. On top of that, Alex still had no idea just where the pirates' ship might have carried his princess by this time, or how to go about locating her.

From time to time Alex's new memory presented him with an item of disquieting information. For example: the sprites and satyrs could be expected to become distinctly unreliable, every now and then. Not that they had ever engaged in serious, deliberate treachery, or anything like it. But when those auxiliaries became involved in anything more important than an orgy, it would be a foolish avatar indeed who neglected to keep an eye on them. One or two of the members of his entourage in particular required watching.

Distracting the new god somewhat from such concerns was another question, now beginning to nag at both components of the dual mind of Alex/Dionysus. Why had the princess never told him about the treasure hidden in the medallion?

The first explanation to suggest itself was that Ariadne hadn't wanted to worry a callow young soldier prematurely. It would have frightened him, to know what treasure he was carrying, and ultimately the knowledge must have made his mission harder to accomplish. Of course, the princess must have intended at some point to reveal the truth to her chosen champion. She also ought to have let him know just what she expected from him when he became a god. But Fate had intervened to separate her from her servant before she'd had the chance to break these matters to him gently.

It took a little longer for Alex to become aware of a less flattering possibility. Princess Ariadne had trusted him to carry the Face, but only as she might have relied upon a faithful dog or a cameloid, to bear a burden without any idea of what it meant. At some point she would have asked for her medallion back, and her dazzled worshiper would hand it over. Never had the princess intended that such tremendous treasure should be buried inside the skull of Alex the Nameless, for the rest of that young man's life.

He had to face the fact that the glorious Ariadne must have intended that the Face of Dionysus should be worn by someone else.

It must be that she had intended it for Prince—if he really was a prince of any kind, which was looking very doubtful—Theseus.

Alex the Half-Nameless might well have been overawed by Prince Theseus, but Lord Dionysus certainly was not. And as far as Alex could tell, the Twice-Born seemed to have no innate preference for having his existence inside the brain of one avatar rather than another.

If Theseus had indeed been Ariadne's choice, she might well be displeased when she saw how Alex had taken personal advantage of the priceless object she had given into his care. Well, there was nothing he could do about it now—nothing but prove to the princess that he was worthy. Once a human had put on a Face, only death could separate it from him.

———

Alex's efforts to deduce the princess's motives inevitably led him to consider a second question, which he thought might well have a bearing on the first: how had Ariadne herself come into possession of the Face? Most likely, Alex thought, some of the invisible, comparatively minor powers who formed the Dionysian entourage had brought it to her, at some time during the interval of six months or so when the Twice-Born lay dead, his Face unworn by anyone.

Of course, once the princess had the Face of Dionysus in her hands, there would have been nothing to prevent her putting it on herself. The legends and stories all agreed, and the god's own memory confirmed, that humans of either sex could wear the Faces of either male or female deities. So it would seem that the only thing standing in the way of Ariadne's apotheosis must have been some innate reluctance on her part to undergo such an irrevocable transformation.

Dionysus now seemed to have nothing to say about that attitude. But Alex thought that his own mortal mind needed no divine help to understand it. Any princess, and particularly this one, was very like a goddess already; why should anyone as beautiful, as perfect, as Ariadne, ever want to change her identity, even to become a deity?

———

After sunset, a full twenty-four hours after Alex had put on the Face, he thought he had made a good start, but no more than that, on getting accustomed to the fact of his apotheosis. That word now lay handily within his vocabulary, part of the seemingly inexhaustible memory of his new partner. Some of the treasures waiting to be discovered within that memory were ideas which had never occurred to Alex before, even in the form of questions.

The experimental possibilities now open to him were endlessly fascinating. By a mere act of will, which he demonstrated to himself again and again, he could cause vines to grow, bursting from barren ground into the air. And, by the same token, induce even dead or dying plants to burst into bloom, or sag suddenly with fruit that developed and grew at a fantastic pace, and provided welcome food for the human component of the one who had brought it into being. The olive trees in the hills of the small island, and even those that had been dying along the shore, now burst out with a great new crop, the cycle of growth and ripening requiring only minutes instead of months. The god's power of promoting fertility and growth did not seem to fade or grow tired with repeated use, and in a day the whole island was notably greener than it had been. No doubt when autumn came, his new powers would at least decline somewhat—if only he could stay alive till then!

It worried Alex that he was still temporarily without his chariot—but the god's memory, extending back through a seemingly endless chain of avatars, assured the new possessor of the Face that the vehicle and its team of leopards would be restored to him in time. The process might take no more than a few days but it could require as long as months. Therefore he would have to find some other means to cross the sea, and that meant waiting for a ship.

Had he known that his wait to regain the chariot was going to be this long, he would have boarded the merchant ship with Daedalus and Clara, and started his journey to Dia by that means. But there was no use fretting about it now. Calling up Silenus, Alex asked if anything could be done to hurry the thing along. Silenus was not hopeful, but swore he would try.

And again and again, Alex's new memory brought him back to that scene in the great hall of the palace of King Minos, on what must have been the last night of the previous avatar's life. Now, through the god's vivid memory, Alex could see himself, his earlier, purely human self, as a clearly seen but generally inconspicuous figure in the background of that brief drama. Indeed, he had been, even then, a better-looking young man than he had imagined himself to be. And even, perhaps, a little taller.

Once I was like you.

———

Sleep and dreams were evidently going to be at least as large a part of his new life as they had been of the years when he was merely human. On the first night following his possession by the god he had not slept, in any sense of the word implying repose, but tonight he was alone and needed rest.

Even the tiredness of a god was somehow of a different quality than the same feeling in a mere mortal human. But Alex soon discovered that he could now see more sharply than ever before the faces and objects in his dreams, and also remember them more clearly when he awakened. This clarity of vision came from Dionysus, he was sure, but he thought much of the content of the dreams was sent him by Asterion.

———

In this one, his first real dream since his apotheosis, he remained throughout strangely but comfortably aware that he was dreaming. He was wandering a rocky shoreline, not that of the Island of Refuge, nor any place that either he or Dionysus could remember ever having been before. The waves as they broke before his feet were the color of dark wine, and each time the withdrawing water left a fizzing, a whispering, of small bubbles on the rock. Like the sparkling white wine that once— how many centuries ago?—he and his colleagues in divinity had drunk in the crystal halls of a vast palace that he now thought might have been Olympus. But that scene lay beyond such a gulf of time that even the memory of divinity began to be uncertain.

"It *is* you," the odd voice of Asterion said, sounding behind him in his present dream. Dionysus identified the speaker even before he turned. The bull-man gave the appearance of wandering comfortably through this world created by the new man-god's sleeping imagination. He stood relaxed, wearing his usual kilt and sandals, looking around him at the odd scenery, as if he had come to visit an old acquaintance in a strange new house. In one of his very human hands Asterion was gathering what looked like spiderwebs, and somehow Alex knew that this was material used by Ariadne in some private and very mysterious weaving.

In his other hand the bull-man held a long, pointed stick, and with its tip had been sketching in the sand a diagram that Alex knew at once must be the map of the Labyrinth itself. Though each corridor in the map was only an inch or two wide, the whole plan was enormous, stretching over sandhill after sandhill, so that its far end was lost in darkness and distance.

Asterion threw the stick down, as if the diagram was now complete. Then he proceeded to ignore what he had sketched. His gaze remained fixed on Alex. "And yet," he continued, "it is not you any longer."

"Wrong. It is me, but it is someone else as well."

"Of course. You are a god now, and I think that is good." The Minotaur appeared to be pleased, but far from overwhelmed, by the discovery.

"Circe seems to think so too."

"So you know the enchantress now? I've never met her. I am enormously surprised, of course, at what has happened to you. Tell me as many details as you can."

Looking into his own mind as best he could, Alex could discover no Dionysian objections, and he related an outline of his recent adventures. In turn, Asterion told him of Shiva's plan to make Theseus a god.

The Twice-Born asked, "I suppose you have gained this knowledge in a dream?"

"It is the world in which I am most at home. And now in another dream I pass it on to you." Asterion's next question was: "Are you strong enough to oppose Shiva?"

Looking into his new memory for clues, Alex could find little to give him confidence on that point. "I don't know. I will do what I can, when the time comes. Where has the princess gone?"

The horned head turned slowly sideways, back and forth. "The dreams of both my sisters are always hard for me to find, difficult to enter. But I know, I feel, that Ariadne is beginning to consider herself lost. And once she understands that she is lost, she will probably be able to find her own way home."

"*I* don't understand." And now it seemed to Alex that the god inside him was speaking with him, sharing his concern. "If you can't tell me where Ariadne is, how am I to locate her?"

It seemed that the Minotaur could find no answer. From that point on, the dream gave promise of dissolving into the visions of the mad, with parts of the landscape that should not have been alive behaving as if they were. This was not the green and healthy growth normally inspired by the Twice-Born, but something cancerous and gray and ugly. Alex/Dionysus with an effort of will pulled himself free of it, awakening to the second morning of his new life.

He had not been awake for very long on that bright morning before there blew into sight, far out to sea, yet another ship with bellying sail, that appeared to be steering a course directly for the mouth of the harbor. Before it had come within a mile, Dionysus had descended from the hill to sit on the inner shoreline as before. He watched its approach from a seat so close to the water that the waves now and then lapped his sandaled feet, in the luxuriant shade of newly blooming olives.

He was not in the least dismayed to observe that, even at first glance, there was no possibility that this could be anything other than a pirate ship. It was a slightly larger vessel than the peaceful trader on which the princess and her new, crude entourage had departed only a few days ago. Two days ago, the sight of the dark flag, the swarm of armed men, would have sent Alex jumping to his feet and sprinting away for cover. But it would never have occurred to Dionysus to do anything of the kind, and Alex, bonded to his new partner inside the skull they now shared, felt quite secure enough to wait without fear.

It appeared there were a great many pirates in the sea. Well, the waters around the Isle of Refuge were probably one of their favorite hunting grounds. This vessel of freebooters, like its predecessor, anchored in the mouth of the harbor, blocking it while avoiding the possibility of being itself blocked in. Next the visitor, like its sister ship before it, launched a little boat; the difference was that instead of only two armed men, this dinghy contained five, one standing, in an attitude of command, while four others rowed.

Alex felt no apprehension, and little excitement, except that the way was now opening for him to go to Ariadne. With a sense of being intimately connected with the reassuring presence of Dionysus, he sat waiting, watching the men approach. He had no plan regarding them—except that they had brought him a ship.

When the small boat had come halfway across the harbor's inlet, he was suddenly struck by the pirate captain's strong resemblance to Theseus. The closer the man came, the greater the likeness seemed, and Alex was soon firmly convinced that this was Theseus's father, the Pirate King.

Splashing ashore through the shallows, and tugging their boat up after them, the pirates behaved cautiously, lodging only the very prow of their rowboat on shore, as if they feared an ambush, and wanted to be ready to put out again at a second's notice. But very soon they began to relax. The nearest cover that might possibly hide ambushers was more than a hundred paces from where Alex waited.

Alex studied the pirate captain, whose face was burned and wrinkled by the sun, his body richly scarred and tattooed in the course of an obviously eventful life, and hung with the sheaths of what seemed an inordinate number of weapons. With this model in view, it was easy to imagine what the son would look like in twenty or thirty years.

"Captain Aegeus?"

"Aye?"

"I have seen your son, Theseus," Alex told him.

If he had thought to surprise the buccaneer, he was mistaken. "Have you, now?" Aegeus did not seem startled by the news, or much impressed.

On impulse Alex asked the pirate chief, "Wouldn't you like your son to be a god?"

The King of Pirates did not seem startled by the question, or even much impressed; maybe he simply did not take the announcement seriously. "I don't know that it would make much difference. My lifelong tendency has been to ignore the gods, and so far they've done the same for me. Anyway, my son has considered himself to be endowed with divine powers, as far back as I can remember."

"You don't seem surprised to learn that Theseus is still alive; I understand you arranged to have him sent to Minos as part of the new Tribute."

"Did I? Must have slipped my mind." He gave vent to a burst of laughter. "That's one thing that I'll never be surprised to hear of my son. That he's still alive."

The captain and his four men surrounded him, their carefree voices booming now. "Someone's marooned you, hey, matey? How unkind!" And all five demonstrated that they thought it extremely funny.

Alex said no more. To argue with these men now, to try to persuade or threaten, would only delay his getting aboard the ship, if it had any effect at all. When they were at sea again, the Lord Dionysus would make his wishes known.

The most talkative of the sailors had some more to say. "Bad luck for you, good for us. Your family will pay a mighty ransom to have you back—I'll bet your life they will! Haw, haw, haw!"

Now two of the buccaneers menaced him with their weapons, while two others seized him. Dionysus tolerated their roughness, indeed scarcely felt it, nor did Alex—but only because his thoughts were elsewhere, on matters of great moment.

They hauled him to his feet and started to drag him away. In less than a minute they had taken the utterly unrecognized Dionysus into their rowboat, where they pushed him down in the bottom of the boat, so that the glorious youth in his purple robe seemed to be practically cowering at the pirate captain's feet. But the god's mind, melded with the mind of Alex, was focused far ahead, on plans for dealing with serious enemies, and finding the princess. Scarcely did either of them notice the indignity. Now the quest for Ariadne would soon be under way in earnest, and their thoughts were concentrated on that.

The small boat had been pushed off and was halfway across the harbor, the four oarsmen pulling with a good will, when the captain called out something to one Acetes, who was evidently the helmsman among the crew still waiting on the pirate ship.

Roughly the captain cried out that they would be hoisting anchor immediately. A stroke of good fortune had changed his plans, and they would not delay even for the short time necessary to take on water.

Acetes, a lean fellow with a red cloth tied around his head, and a curved sword at his belt, shouted back some acknowledgement of the order. Then he added, with a shade of concern in his voice, "Who've ye got there, mates?"

One man pounded in triumph on the captive's shoulder. "A prince's ransom, that's who! A bag of gold in a purple cape!"

22

MINUTES LATER, THE little boat was right under the ship's bow, with its painted, staring, devil-face. There was a story in that painting for Alex's new right eye to read, but he would not allow himself to be distracted by it now. Rough hands were pulling and pushing him aboard the ship. Again the minor mistreatment was easy to ignore, with other things to think about. Flies droned, trying to extract nourishment from old bloodstains on the deck. Garbage lay about. Whatever the captain's serious interests might be, they did not include cleanliness.

A faint moan, issuing from some cabin or locker, reached his ears. There were tones in it of great interest to the god. Suddenly concentrating once more on his immediate environment, Dionysus thought in a certain way about the sailors, who were still endeavoring to terrorize him. And the brush of his thought against their minds caused them to forget about him for the moment. As soon as they went slack-jawed and stood back, he reached out a hand to touch the latch that secured the door of the locker or cabin, and the fastening fell open.

Alex tugged open the door and looked inside, wrinkling his nose against the smell of heat and human confinement. A young woman lay slumped in one corner of the small space, barely conscious and obviously in great distress.

Edith had changed in the few days since Alex had briefly seen her in the Labyrinth, so that he did not recognize her at first glance. Even the ceremonial garments she was still wearing were stained and torn and faded out of recognition. Alex, in those distant-seeming days when he had been no more than a young soldier, had seen all of the youths and maidens of the Tribute more than once; and presently he understood

that this young woman had been one of them. Somehow she had survived the murderous terror of Shiva, to become a harassed prisoner.

And now, as if dimly aware that the door was open, she stirred at
last, muttering what sounded like some desperate prayer to Apollo.

Moving forward into the dim space, Alex bent down and put out a
hand to raise her up. He was gratefully aware that the Twice-Born must
be helping, for he could lift her as easily as a doll.

He said, "Your name is Edith—isn't it? Of course. You were on
Corycus when I was there. How did you come here? Did any of the
others in the Tribute manage to survive?"

Gradually, in halting phrases, a story came out. Captivity, as one of
the Tribute people. Then freedom for a short time, in the Labyrinth.
And finally, a worse captivity by far, a hell of repeated rape and other
torments.

"Why have they done such things to you? Because they are bad
men, and you are pretty, and young, and helpless, yes—but was there
some other, special reason? Take your time in answering. Soon you will
sleep, and there will be no more pain."

"I was a servant of Apollo, once," she whispered back. Her lips
were cracked and dry.

The right hand of the god accepted a crystal goblet from the air.
Carefully he gave the girl a drink. "And will be again, if that is what
you want. Is that the reason why these men have so abused and tortured
you?"

"They wanted me to tell them the secrets." Her voice was a little
stronger now. "They said there must be secrets in Apollo's temples, and
I must tell them what they were."

"Secrets? What could they be?" Dionysus wondered aloud. "Of all
the gods I know, the Far-Worker seems least inclined to have mysteries."

"They wanted to know about places in the temples in which something could be hidden. I told them all I knew," said the girl in her small,
hurt tones. "Which was little enough. I knew of nothing hidden."

"Of course you told them." Alex patted her hand. "Don't worry
about that. But why have they carried you here, all the way from Corycus?"

Again, Edith needed a little time to gather the strength to speak.
"Lord, they kept saying to me that they would bring me back to my
home on Dia, and there I would serve them as a hostage. They also
think that I will serve them as a guide, to some particular temple there
in my native land."

With human concern Alex examined the young woman. The traces of the terror and abuse she had been through were very plain. Was there nothing he could do to heal her? The skills and attributes of Dionysus offered very little. It would be easy enough to cause her to forget her troubles utterly, for a long time if not forever; and possibly in a little while Alex would use the powers of the Twice-Born to accomplish that. But right now more urgent matters must claim almost all of his attention.

Anger was mounting swiftly in him. But Dionysus was no Shiva, to deal out death in the winking of an eye; and Alex was no Butcher, either.

Slowly Dionysus shook his head. A purpose was growing in him, though he had not yet formed it in clear words, even in the mind he shared with Alex. Backing their shared body out of the cabin, he allowed the crew once more to remember the fact of his presence. Now they stood squinting at the young man they had carried aboard, evidently trying to make up their minds what to do with him next. Alex wanted to demand of the pirates: *What have you done here*? With the memory and experience of Dionysus to draw on, he had already realized that he was unlikely to get anywhere trying to work with and through these men.

Still, he could feel enough human sympathy for them to make the attempt. Also it would be useful to have a full crew, or something like one, to man his ship.

He stood up straight and raised his voice. "Will you not listen to me?"

Sadly, it seemed that they would not. They had given themselves to some darker power, and accepted a kind of blindness. Except for one member of the crew, the man named Acetes, who seemed on the verge of saying something sympathetic—but then the steersman fell silent, when he realized what strange things had begun to happen before his eyes.

———

Alex had left open the door of the little cabin, or locker, and now Dionysus reached in, with their shared right hand, to stroke the head of the captive girl. Soon he would bring her out into the open air, but not just yet. He feared that she might be frightened by certain things that were soon going to happen on the deck. Her freedom was now assured, and could wait just a little longer.

"All will be well," Alex tried to comfort her. "But tell me again what has happened to bring you here. I'm not sure that I understand. Somehow, you got away from Shiva?"

Slowly her gaze focused on him. Whatever she saw evidently gave her strength to talk, to speak clearly. "I was with Asterion, and he protected me."

"In the Labyrinth?"

"Yes. But then—Shiva came again."

"I see. All right, it doesn't matter now. No doubt you would like to go home, to Dia? In freedom, I mean, of course."

"Lord, if only I could go home!"

Dionysus nodded. "As soon as we can hail another ship," said Alex, "I'll send you home by that one, or by this, whichever is the slower. The faster one I must keep, and use. I would be inclined to escort you to your home myself, but there are other things that I must do. Matters so urgent that they must not wait."

Now a handful of crewmen, suddenly struck by the fact that their lordly prisoner still remained unbound, approached Alex, and were actually making an attempt to bind the youth whom they still imagined to be their prisoner.

As soon as the ropes had been knotted round the god's wrists and ankles, Dionysus, irritated and distracted from the plans he was trying to make, caused them to loosen and slide off.

When he did this, the men who had tied the ropes on simply tried to tie them on again—the madness that had now taken possession of the crew was none of his doing, but rather sprang from their own cruelty and greed. They were too far gone in their own quiet, hopeless insanity to comprehend the meaning of what they were trying to do.

But Edith, looking out through the open door of the cabin where she still lay huddled, had the beginning of understanding. And so did the helmsman, Acetes, whose eyes widened when he saw what was happening, and who began to plead with his shipmates to stop. But they could not or would not hear him—it was as if some kind of curse had seized them.

From scraps of conversation Alex overheard, he soon understood that, in a kind of circular chain of circumstance, the pirate king intended to sell him to King Perses, having heard that the Tribute levied this year was going to be repeated, next year, or even sooner.

In the god's memory Alex could find the image of what he himself ought to look like now. His hair should be fuller and darker than it was, and it doubtless would take on that aspect soon—provided Shiva let him live long enough. Even now, with his purple cloak covering his broad shoulders, he looked enough like the popular image of royalty to account for the sailors' optimism in the matter of being able to collect a great ransom.

Now some of them had picked up scraps of rope and cord with which to fetter him, but to their amazement their efforts along that line met with no success. The ropes would not hold together; the fibers separated, the knots came undone as soon as they touched Alex's hands or feet. And he sat looking at them with a smile in his dark eyes.

"Stop!" This was the helmsman crying out.

"What's wrong with you?" Aegeus demanded, what little patience he possessed now badly frayed.

Acetes said, "You are trying to abuse a god." But his voice had suddenly fallen so low that the others in their impatience, and with their own ongoing clamor, failed to hear him.

"What's that? Speak up?"

Once more the steersman screamed in anguish at his shipmates.

The captain shouted abuse and mockery at him, and with a volley of oaths ordered the crew to get the sail up.

The wind at once filled the sheet of cotton canvas, and the mast creaked and strained, but the ship did not move.

"Are we aground? We can't be!"

"What's going on?"

If they had thought about that question instead of merely shouting it, they might still have saved their lives. The power of a god was taking their ship away from them. Men were splashing in wine up to their ankles, wading in sparkling red that poured from nowhere to run across the deck and into the sea. But for once they found no joy in wine. The lines on which they tugged and heaved turned into green vines in their hands.

Jarred at last into his senses, the captain gave up trying to begin a voyage, and ordered the helmsman to put in to land.

He was too late. Ghostly images of two leopards appeared, and at that sight some of the men began leaping overboard.

Dionysus said to them, "If you will behave like wild beasts, then you ought not to wear the shapes of men." And in midair the bodies of those who jumped took on the smooth and limbless shape of dolphins.

Turning to face the one he had tried to kidnap, Aegeus drew one of his weapons from his belt, brandished it for a moment, and then saw it fall clattering to the deck when his own hands and arms betrayed him, flailing the air in madness.

Now Aegeus was no longer able to grip a weapon, or anything else. The King of Pirates, the father of Theseus, could see and feel his own arms contracting, the bones in them changing, his hands losing their fingers, warping into the digitless shape of fins.

Driven into a frenzy by their fear, the remainder of the sailors, all but the captain himself, leapt for the rail and over it, and even as they jumped, their arcing bodies were transformed in midair, grimaces of fear transformed to mindless dolphin smiles, taking on in midleap sleek streamlined shapes.

All of them losing, among the million other things they lost, any chance of ever becoming gods.

One cried out, just before his mouth took on the mindless dolphin smile, "Lord, mercy!"

The Twice-Born was calm, regretful. "Another god might have done much worse to you than I have done. Be glad that it was not the Far-Worker whom you brought on board. Now leave my ship!"

Now, of all those the god had condemned, only Aegeus himself remained standing on the deck. The pirate captain's hands had disappeared, his feet were now barely large enough to let him stand on them. His clothes were gone, his skin no longer that of a man, but his head and the sound of his voice were human still. It was as if he still maintained them in that form, by a supreme effort of his own will.

"A prophecy once said that I would never hang—by all the gods, it was right!"

Dionysus had nothing to say at the moment. Neither did Alex.

But the King of the Pirates was not quite finished. On the edge of doom he bragged and blustered to the new avatar of Dionysus that his son, Theseus, was going to be a god—he had the word of Shiva for that.

"And you have faith in the Destroyer's word, do you?"

The pirate's voice was failing now, but he could still form words. "My son is going to be a god. Seek out Theseus. Will you do that for me? Seek out my son!"

"Why should I do that?"

"So he may kill you."

"Has he the Princess Ariadne with him?"

Triumph flamed in the pirate's ruined face. "He has her with him. My lad has her, and he'll keep her, too. Go search for them on the island of Dia. You'll find your princess there, and Theseus and Shiva too. Shiva will burn you to a cinder, puny god! And my son will have your Face!"

"That may be. But you will not be there to see it happen. Go!"

And at last the King of the Pirates screamed in despair, a scream that mutated into a croaking and inhuman noise. The change had overcome his head and face before he went overboard.

Now, in helpless obedience, they were all gone.

Dionysus turned away from the suddenly unpopulated deck, and went to stand beside Acetes, who had not moved from his post, though he had let go of the steering oar. Alex put out a hand and laid it on the trembling helmsman's arm, restraining him, when he too would have tried to escape by plunging into the sea, and at the same time giving him the courage that he needed to stand fast.

Now the young man spoke in a different tone, perfectly human and friendly. "Take back the steering oar, Acetes, and don't be afraid."

Obediently the man clamped both hands upon the worn and weathered wood. But both his eyes were tight shut, as if he was afraid to open them. "My lord. Lord Dionysus, God of the Many Names, have mercy on me!"

Gently the god squeezed his arm. "Be at peace, steersman, I say. Open your eyes; now there is nothing terrible to see. The wind will change, and I will need a good sailor to advise me. We are going on to Dia."

Edith had fallen into a faint, and lay where the men had pushed her. Abstractedly, with half a thought, Alex/Dionysus sent a sprite to comfort the young woman softly, and ease her slumber, so that she might rest and heal. The door of the cabin was standing open, and when the girl felt ready to come out on deck she could.

He hastened to tell her the good news: she would see her home even sooner than she had expected, and in far better circumstances.

Then he faced around. "Acetes, I suppose you know the right course for the Island of Dia?"

"I believe I do, great lord. But the wind is wrong."

"I do not have the ordering of winds, so you must do the best you can. I can raise or lower the sail, if you will let me know which way you want it."

An act of will, and the ship was free to move again, once more subject to the mundane forces of wind and wave.

Alex/Dionysus soon discovered that he needed no crew to sail this or any other ship, or at least none beyond his sprites and satyrs. He soon discovered that, with a little help from them, he could drive the vessel anywhere by the sheer power of his will, even against the normal wind. But to have the mundane forces on his side was a great help. He caused the compass-pyx to glow so that the helmsman could read it when the sun had dipped below the sea.

Alex was beginning to find the handholds that he needed, not on ropes and oars, but on the very fabric of reality. There were limits on what Dionysus might accomplish, but they were very far beyond the limits that constrained a mortal.

What was going to happen when he faced Shiva, Alex did not know; his new Dionysian memory seemed to hold no clue, no plan, that would help him survive the Third Eye's dazzling, incinerating lance of light. But now, apart from his lack of any tactical plan, he thought he was as ready for the contest as he was ever going to be.

When they were driving swiftly through the sea, more or less in the right direction, he glanced toward Edith again, and saw that her eyes were open and fixed on him. Reluctant to leave the helmsman's side just now, Alex beckoned her to him, and she crept out of the open cabin, trembling, and came across the deck so Dionysus could hold her in the curve of his arm and gently comfort her.

Then Alex raised his head, and called into the wind, "Princess, be of good cheer. I'm coming to you."

23

THE GREAT ESCAPE had indeed turned out to be a tremendous adventure, just as the Princess Ariadne had expected from the beginning. But for her it was also a great deal more. For many days her only real goal in life had been to help Theseus, first to save him from destruction, eventually to claim him as her true lover. Someday, somehow, they would be betrothed, and then, by some means and ceremony, she would become his beloved wife. Eventually she would sit somewhere on a throne beside him—but that was vague in a distant future, and at the moment not at all important. She still refused to doubt that her lover was, or could be, in some sense a real prince—she was all the more determined to believe it, now that she could no longer deny that he was a pirate.

Once more blessed by favorable winds, the ship under direct command of the pirate prince bore on through the sea at a rapid pace, her compass-pyx tuned to the mind of Theseus. The captured trader, once the property of Captain Petros, was sailing more or less with it, sometimes within bowshot, sometimes forced by the vagaries of wind and wave a mile or more away. Near Dia they were going to join forces with whatever additional ships Shiva and Perses might have managed to dispatch, and which could reach the point of rendezvous in time.

As the days passed, Ariadne was increasingly beset by seasickness and fear, but was grimly determined not to meekly let such feelings master her.

"And what are we going to do when we get there?" she demanded.

No one had seriously discussed the matter with her yet. Her companion might not be minded to answer questions, but now on the small ship he couldn't very well avoid her.

"*You're* not going to do much of anything. Certainly not going on shore with the raiding party." Theseus made no pretense of asking, or trying to persuade her. He was simply telling her how things were going to be. "You'll stay aboard ship, locked up, so I'll know where to find you when I get back."

"Locked up!" The idea left her speechless for a moment, so protest would have to wait. But she had no doubt he meant it.

"As for what I'm going to do—the first thing will be to meet with the other captains, the leaders on these other ships, and work out a coordinated plan. Make sure they all realize that I am in command."

"Uncle Perses may have appointed his own commander, if he's sending a squadron."

"I hope he is, we can use the ships and men. But what a mere king says won't matter. Shiva has appointed *me*."

Ariadne's anger at the man who had deceived her had grown great, but even worse than the anger was the hollow feeling that lay beneath it. Sometime, somehow, the anger must recede, and when it did, how much of their love would still be left?

Once or twice she had looked into the ship's single tiny cabin, really only a storage space, and once, shortly after they came aboard, Theseus had taken her there, as the only place on board where the two of them might be together out of sight of the crew. No one would spend any more time than necessary in that uncomfortable space; it was only a little smaller than the second clothes closet in her bedroom back in the palace on Corycus, but crowded with stores and intolerably hot and close, under the baking sun, so that it seemed much smaller still. Even when she had lain there in her lover's arms, she could hardly wait to get out again, into the fresh air. To be shut up in that smelly hole alone—

Finally Ariadne found her voice for protest. "And suppose I don't choose to stay in that oven?"

"You'll stay." His calm assumption of control was totally infuriating. "When we go ashore, I'm leaving a skeleton crew on board each ship. Pegleg, for one." That was the nickname of a sailor who had lost part of a lower limb, and hobbled on a foot carved out of ivory. "Along with our graybeards, anyone who can't move fast on land. But I don't want 'em distracted—and you can be very distracting, in several ways, when you're running around loose."

"I won't be shut up in that miserable hole." The refusal came in a royal tone, one that in the experience of a princess had always produced results.

But the only response it provoked from Theseus was a faint smile. "You'll stay," he repeated. "There's a good strong latch on the outside of the door."

Since she had been a child, no one, not her father or Phaedra, not even her oppressive uncle, had ever told her so flatly what she must do, and she found the treatment intolerable.

She turned her back on him, taking her turn at staring out to sea. He must not see any hint that tears of rage and humiliation were threatening to break out.

Several days passed. The wind held, and the compass-pyx seemed to be working well—though the only sure proof of that was arrival at one's destination. Theseus spoke to her less often than before, and made no attempt to take her into the cabin out of the crew's sight. Theseus had not approached her as a lover since that single hurried and uncomfortable encounter shortly after they came aboard. She slept alone, when she slept at all, in a small space on deck half-sheltered against the outer wall of the cabin in which she would be locked away. Ariadne thought that he seemed to have forgotten first her needs, and then her very existence.

No, he had not quite put her entirely out of his thoughts. Once Theseus demanded to know whether she had visited the Island of Dia before. Ariadne still yearned to be of help, but had to plead ignorance. He was trying to learn all he could about the island and its people, from those of his men who had been there. He wanted the most recent information possible.

About the time that the Island of Dia came into sight, so did a couple of other ships, soon identifiable as two of those dispatched from Corycus by Uncle Perses.

"Is that all the help I'm going to get?" Theseus complained, squinting into sunlight. But it was hard to tell from his tone whether the fact pleased him or alarmed him.

Before sunset, the four small vessels came together behind a tiny islet, little more than a sandbar, that screened them from the Dian shore, and a hasty conference was called.

Any additional ships dispatched by Perses or Shiva would need several days to get to Dia from Corycus. Shiva had not promised any direct, personal help, no doubt having what he considered more important business elsewhere.

It would have been too much to hope that Perses, the new Minos, would somehow have been able to assemble and dispatch a large invasion force on such short notice. A regular fleet or squadron might be on its way, next week or next month, if he used his regular navy; but the two captains who had just arrived had no knowledge that any such effort was being planned.

As matters stood, there were still only four ships. And, as Theseus soon discovered, one of the newcomers was seriously undermanned. Counting noses on crews, he arrived at a total of sixty-four men. As it would be necessary to leave minimal crews aboard each vessel, he would be able to lead only about forty ashore, as an effective raiding party.

Perses had told his sailors that Theseus was to be in undisputed command, so that theoretically there should be no doubt as to who was going to put on the Face of Dionysus when it was found.

Yet Theseus couldn't imagine that even the weakest man among his crew, if that wretch should have the tremendous good fortune of being able to put on a god's Face, would worry much about whether Theseus or any other mortal might be angry at him. Even the wrath of a merely human king, like Perses, could be safely disregarded. The anger of Shiva, now—*that* would be worthy of some consideration.

━━━━━━━

Theseus remained too impatient to wait for any more ships to show up—whether there would eventually be more or not was an open question. And he was ready, in fact eager, to trust to luck, and his own strength and skill.

The subject of prayers and sacrifices came up in the captain's meeting, and it was decided to let each crew satisfy themselves in that regard.

Theseus said to the other men, "Let Samson be my blood sacrifice, if I am required to make one. It seems to me he leaked enough to please any god who is interested in that kind of thing." He paused and thought before adding, "And at the moment there is no one else who can readily be spared."

Theseus had no personal experience of previous forays against Dia, but most of what he had heard about that island from others in his profession, including his father, tended to raise his confidence. He was ready to assure his shipmates that on the Island of Dia a foray to collect a treasure might, if everything went smoothly, amount to little more than simply sailing in, taking a little stroll on shore, filling one's pockets and sailing out again.

One of the other leaders of the raid, Mochlos, the captain of one of the two ships that had been waiting at the rendezvous, was not convinced. "If everything goes smoothly. Yes. If one knows exactly where the treasure is, and is lucky enough to lay his hands on it at once."

Mochlos was almost as tall as Theseus, of angular build and indeterminate age, dark hair hanging in two braids beside jutting cheekbones.

Theseus gave him a steady stare. "Others have raided Dia before, with little difficulty. My own father many times."

Mochlos returned the stare. Suddenly Theseus wondered if the other might be taking that side of the argument in a deliberate effort to provoke an accusation of cowardice. What kind of madman would do that?

Mildly enough Mochlos went on, in a cultured voice that belied his general appearance, "True, the Dians have never had an army, nor do they continually patrol their coasts—unless they have just recently begun such an objectionable practice. But there are, after all, about a thousand men dwelling on the island, and like everyone else they are doubtless rather touchy about certain things. Such as uninvited visitors coming ashore and carrying off their wives and children, or their cattle, or their works of art. Or their food, or their casks of white wine—I hear they press some fairly decent grapes, in certain valleys inland. They're probably also sensitive about their temples being desecrated. Most people are."

The Prince of Pirates was contemptuous. "A thousand scattered farmers, vinedressers, goatherds and quarry workers."

The other could be stubborn too. "That means two thousand arms with muscles in them, two thousand hands clutching weapons—even if it's only reaping hooks and pitchforks. And you say the object of our visit is to hoist something out of a temple of Apollo . . ."

"It's not only my whim that we do that. Shiva says the same thing."

"Of course. But doesn't the thought of arrows worry you a little bit?" When the others looked at Mochlos, he amplified, "Silver arrows,

I mean?" He shook his head, dark braids swinging. "If I had to select a deity of whom to make a mortal enemy, the Sun-God wouldn't be my first choice."

"Any gentleman of fortune who feels much concern about making enemies—well, that gentleman is probably in the wrong business." Theseus drew a dagger and began to play with it, thunking it solidly into the wood and pulling it out again. "And if *I* were inclined to fret about what any of the gods are thinking—mind you, I'm not, but if I were— my absolute last choice as an enemy would definitely be Shiva." *Thunk.*

The others looked at Theseus soberly as he sheathed his dagger and went on. "I have seen and talked to Shiva, very recently, at his invitation. I have looked into that Third Eye when it was partly open. And I'm due to talk to him again, ere very many days are past.

"As for Apollo, I have never seen him, I don't know where he is— and I doubt he's ever paid me much attention either."

The others looked at Theseus with respect. One of them laughed appreciatively.

One suddenly, rapping out a string of oaths, came around to his side. "Spoken like a true prince of pirates! That's the talk for me."

"All right, then," said Mochlos, and paused. "From all that your description tells me, the temple we want may very well be the one that's miles inland. For the kind of raid you contemplate, we had better take several ships."

One of the sailors, who had spent time on Dia and knew the lay of the land fairly well, had sketched with charcoal on the deck an outline of the place that they were going to attack. They talked about the island's dimensions, in miles, and the location of towns and villages, hills and streams and harbors.

"There's only one fort, one real strong point, that I know of. It's on the far side, the north side, and we don't need to go anywhere near it."

Theseus could tell from the attitude of the men who had just joined him, the look on their faces and the questions they asked, that they had not yet been told the real object of the raid. Not even the captains knew.

The second of the newly arrived captains, who had had little to say so far, now asked, "Is this a treasure that will need a crew of many men to carry?"

"Not at all," said Theseus. "One man will carry it easily. Myself."

But he realized that now they were all going to have to know what they were looking for. "There is a god-Face there, that I am to have. Shiva wants me to have it."

That was so impressive a statement that it produced silence instead of murmuring. At last the man who had first mentioned the treasure spoke again. "Oh. Which god?"

"Not that it makes any difference, for our purposes, but the god is Dionysus."

"Ah, well. Wouldn't mind putting that one on my own head." And soon the tension had relaxed sufficiently to allow a round of bawdy laughter.

Mochlos inquired, "I suppose there'll be no objection if the rest of us make some profit from this trip too?"

"No objection—as long as we see to it that the main objective is accomplished first."

The temple of Apollo, in which Theseus first intended to seek the treasure, was right on the coast, so the raiders would not have to fight their way inland. Maybe this temple had been chosen as their first target because of its location.

The leaders in their conference went over their reasons for thinking the Face of Dionysus was to be found in one of these two temples. There were various theories according to which it might be so. But the only real reason to believe it was that Shiva had told him so.

He distinctly remembered Shiva mentioning, as if in passing, that there was a possibility that the information about the Face was wrong. But Theseus wasn't going to tell the captains that.

Ariadne was soon aware that Theseus had explained his mission to the men, for she could overhear some of them arguing about it among themselves.

"How does Shiva know where the Face of some other god is to be found?"

"How does a god know anything? What's the point of mortals wondering about that?"

"If the Destroyer's so interested, why didn't he carry it himself to the man he wants to have it?"

"Maybe he was too busy. How in the Underworld should I know?"

"If the local people know that the Face is there, why has no one put it on?"

"Probably because they're not aware. I'd bet that no one on Dia now realizes that it's there."

The whole business made little sense to Ariadne. But she was beginning to realize that that might often be the case when gods were involved.

She had never seen Dionysus in any avatar; but when she tried to picture Theseus in that role, she did not at all like what her imagination showed her.

The raiders were encouraged, and considered their prospects for success much enhanced, when none of their number who had local knowledge could recall there being any large settlement very near their goal. The nearest village, of about a hundred people, was two miles away. If things went smoothly, they could be in and out, and at sea again before most of the people on the island even knew they had arrived.

The captains were gathered on the deck again. "Now as I recall, there's one sizable house, a kind of country estate I think, on the coast within a quarter of a mile of the creek where we're going to put in." The stick used as pointer made a dot on the sketched map.

"Still, that looks like the best place. Anywhere we go ashore, there's bound to be someone near."

The planner stared at the crudely sketched map. "If we don't find what we seek there—well, getting to the next temple will be tougher. That's miles inland."

"The next one will be impossible, if we give the whole island time to mobilize."

"Time for them to run into the hills and hide, more likely."

"It wouldn't be wise to count on that."

"I thought we had this settled. No one ever took any treasure by being timid."

"It's settled that we're going for it, but no one's even mentioned tactics yet. High time we did."

One of the buccaneers had some fairly recent news to pass along about their potential opposition: the leaders of the Dianite villages, tired of being despoiled, had banded together and sought the help of a man to organize, unite, and command all of their defense forces.

"Hired a professional, did they? Too bad. What's he look like? Maybe I've met him somewhere."

"Wiry fellow called Nestor, maybe about thirty years old. Sandy hair, his nose looks like it was once broken. Not a native Dianite, but a real professional."

"Did this Nestor bring any people with him to the island?"

"Could be one or two. Maybe a small handful. I think no more than that."

During the hours of daylight, one or another member of each ship's crew was always scanning the sea, hoping to sight the sail of the ship captained by Aegeus, Theseus's father. The bow of that ship, Theseus said, was adorned with a distinctive painting, showing a pair of monster eyes.

"I hope he arrives soon," said Ariadne. "I want to meet him."

"I hope he brings some fighting men."

But when morning came again, no other ships had yet arrived. Now and then Theseus sent a small and agile man up the mast, which was little more than a stick of slippery wood, in an effort to see farther.

When the first light of morning showed no helpful sails in sight, he said, "We're not going to wait. We've enough men now. More than we need, in fact." He sounded as if he believed that, but the men only looked at one another.

"So we go in now, as soon as we can get ready."

Before the morning sun had fully cleared the horizon, all four of the pirate ships made their final approach to the island, with crews under strict orders to minimize the noise of oars.

They lowered anchors cautiously in a small sheltered bay, at the mouth of a muddy creek, all prows pointing back toward the open sea, and the raiding parties quickly prepared to go ashore. This was one time when no one wanted to run a ship aground; it might be necessary to put out quickly, and with only a skeleton crew to pull the oars or hoist sail, if the wind happened to be right to make that profitable.

"Time to put you in the coop, my little chick."

When Theseus beckoned imperiously, Ariadne meekly bowed her head and went into the cabin—her fists were clenched so that her fingernails, raggedly uncared-for since the adventure started, bit into her palms, but every instinct assured her that this was not the time to resist. When she did fight for her rights, she would do so with all her strength; but in these circumstances all the strength that she could muster would have done her no good at all.

In the doorway she hesitated. "Water. At least give me some water to take in there with me."

One of the crewmen put a jug into her hands. It felt half-empty, but she took it and went in, making no further protest. The wooden overhead of the cabin was not quite high enough to allow her to stand upright. The place was just as hot and foul, and crowded with miscellaneous seafaring baggage, as she remembered it to be. A folded sail, coiled ropes and cords, dried fish piled on the deck like dark slats of wood. She heard the small splash of an anchor going overboard on the end of a line, and then the voice of Theseus, urgent and energetic.

She sat down on a spare folded sail, and folded her arms. If she had to find some way to get out of here without help, absolutely had to, she was confident that she could.

As long as most of the men still remained on the ship, Ariadne could hear them talking in excited voices, but as soon as Theseus gave the order to go ashore, a sudden near-silence fell, broken only by the sounds of splashing and an occasional oath.

Through the chinks in the walls of the low deckhouse, Ariadne watched them climb away.

The men were all professionals who knew what they were doing, and soon the bulk of them were gone ashore, except for the skeleton crew. For a few moments she could hear Pegleg's oak foot thumping on the deck. Then that noise stopped. In the distance, a gull screamed, and then another.

Time passed. Ariadne sipped at the warm water in her jug. The morning sun warmed rapidly, its heat beat down upon the decks and walls, and the cabin became even less endurable. Of course there would be some way out, and if she absolutely had to have it she would close her eyes and find it. There would be a loose plank somewhere. Or—

She sat imagining her web. When the thing was difficult to get started, as it was today, it helped to visualize a giant spider, weaving a web-pattern with concentric circles of fine strands. And then the imaginary creature growing, moving away, leaving one glistening filament to mark the path of its departure—

The eyes of the princess suddenly came open at the sound of an alarm, if not a panic, among the skeleton crew. Their voices were not raised, but the princess could hear a rapid muttering that was all the more alarming because it was trying to be quiet.

All the cabin walls had chinks in them, as did the overhead, and these defects had the accidental benefit of allowing a certain amount of air to circulate. Presently Ariadne, peering out through the small gaps between boards in the shoreward wall, caught her breath. A gang of men she had never seen before were approaching at a run, carrying among them a random, amateurish assortment of weapons. Each man had a white scarf tied around his upper arm, evidently as a kind of emblem or insignia; otherwise they were casually dressed as field-

workers or artisans. One loosed an arrow toward the ship. She heard
the impact smart against the planking.

Looking out through a chink in the cabin wall, Ariadne could catch
a glimpse of the man they were calling for, standing with folded arms
on the very edge of the shore, and looking about him alertly. He was
perhaps thirty years old, sandy-haired and wiry, simply clad, with nothing amateurish or showy about the sheathed sword at his side.

A couple of the men on shore were waving torches, their flames
only marginally visible in the bright sunshine. Suddenly terrified by the
thought of fire, Ariadne screamed to let whoever was out there know
that she was in the cabin, and pounded on the thick door with ineffective
hands.

Pegleg and the other limpers and graybeards of the skeleton crew
had begun, too late, a futile effort to put out to sea. Oars clattered and
clashed and fell; as far as Ariadne could tell, there was no attempt to
hoist sail. Cowering unarmed in the cabin, she heard the struggle, the
swearing and the screams.

─────

Every minute or so some excited Dian man or boy, running at full speed,
would come pounding up on shore, calling for someone named Nestor
and then shouting to the leader some kind of a report as to where the
main body of the raiders now were, what they were doing, and how
many they were. Each report, it seemed to Ariadne, was more likely
than not to be contradictory of the one just preceding it. The consensus
on the number of pirates who had come ashore seemed to be around
two hundred.

Applying a rule of thumb learned from experience, Nestor decided
in the privacy of his own mind that if he cut that number in half he
would probably be somewhere near the truth.

"They're headed for the Temple of Apollo?" The leader was keeping deliberately calm, but he sounded mystified. "What do they expect
to find there in the way of loot?"

Ariadne could not hear the response clearly.

"Well, maybe more are landing elsewhere, and they're using the
temple as a rendezvous point. Or else they're just confused—that happens a lot. Or possibly they know something that we don't." He raised
his voice in the tone of one giving a decisive order. "Let's see how well
she burns!"

─────

The scream seemed to come bursting out of her throat without any conscious intention on her part, and it threatened to tear the top of her head off.

She had really been locked in the cabin—a firm try on the door proved that—but moments after the scuffling was over Nestor opened the door, in response to her screams. She could see blood spattered on the deck when she came out.

The ship was already actually on fire; at least the sail was burning spectacularly.

She shrank back momentarily when the grinning man confronted her, not at all certain what treatment she was going to be given. But then she gritted her teeth and burst out of the cabin, regardless of whether missiles might still be flying. Ariadne had determined that if she was to die, it would not be in that miserable hole.

The lean man called Nestor caught her effortlessly with his left hand, as she would have gone running past him, and at the same time lowered the sword that he was holding in his right. Briefly he looked past her, satisfying himself that no one else was in the cabin.

He was not nearly as big as Theseus, she thought, but possessed of all the wiry strength he seemed to need, and moved and spoke with the same air of confidence.

When the man who had caught her spoke to her it was in the common language that everyone who traveled much on the Great Sea, or dealt with travelers, learned to use. "You're free now, lass. Where're you from?"

He thinks I was a prisoner, Ariadne suddenly realized. And in the next moment she realized that he was right.

One of Nestor's men barked at her to answer.

But Nestor only shook his head. "That's all right. After all she's been through, it's only natural that she's mightily upset."

Then he faced back to Ariadne. "Who's the leader here, girl? Of the people who locked you up?"

"A man called Theseus." The name came simply and automatically, and called up no emotion.

Nor did it seem to mean anything to her questioner. "Don't know him. The two ships that got away looked Corycan."

She nodded.

"And what do they think they're after here?"

Some remnant of loyalty, or maybe it was only innate stubbornness, kept her from blurting out the truth, or giving any reasonable answer. She could hear herself repeating, idiotically, "I don't know, I don't know."

Nestor did not press her but turned away again, conferring with his men. Presently he once more turned back. "You don't talk like a slave or servant. What's your name, girl?" His voice softened. "Don't be afraid, no one will hurt you now."

"Ariadne," said the princess softly, without thinking. And a moment later she felt a faint pang of fear for having revealed her identity, because it was more than possible that these folk would be unfriendly to the lords of Corycus. But Nestor heard the name without blinking, and it was borne in on her again how far she was from looking the part of a princess now.

For many days, until now, Ariadne had continued to assume, without really thinking about it, that if she remained loyally with the romantic prince she had come to love so terribly (not that she could really imagine herself doing anything else), then her life, barring a few exciting and odd adventures, would continue to be that of a princess.

But the time had now come when she could no longer make excuses for her lover, not even to herself—there was no getting around the fact that Theseus had been downright cruel to her.

Not that Theseus had ever physically mistreated her—unless you counted his locking her in the cabin. But she could almost wish he had been moved to slap her—that would at least have shown strong personal interest.

"I see now," she murmured to herself, "that to be a princess is really nothing in the great world. To be loved is perhaps everything—but now I doubt that Theseus loves me. If only I were a goddess—but I am not. There is no Face of Ariadne that anyone can put on—the only one who can wear the Face of Ariadne is myself."

———

She, Ariadne, had her pride. She was the daughter of King Minos of Corycus—the real king, who had been unlawfully deposed and murdered—and of his true queen, Pasiphae. And she was the younger sister of Princess Phaedra; and the older sister of Prince Asterion, known to the vulgar as the Minotaur.

In her imagination she could hear her own voice now, trying to explain all this to the man called Nestor. Meanwhile she knew quite well that it was really herself to whom she was trying to explain, how in the name of all the gods she, a princess of Corycus, had come to be here in this situation. And in any case, Nestor seemed to have given up listening to her, once he decided that she was babbling.

24

IMMEDIATELY ON COMING ashore, Theseus had picked out half a dozen of his men, choosing the youngest and most agile, and sent them straight for the seaside villa that practically overlooked their landing from its nearby cliff. It seemed to him that the first thing he had better do was to prevent any local people who might have seen the landing from getting away and spreading the alarm.

The small band of fast-moving pirates went scrambling up the rocks in the gray light of dawn, soon broke into the stable behind the large house, where, shouting their reports downhill, they said they had found no one at home, but were able to report the capture of two cameloids. Shouting up the hill, Theseus quickly ordered a couple of his agile six to mount these animals in swift scouting probes. He thought it an ominous sign that the house was unoccupied. Whether any of the inhabitants might already be busy spreading the alarm he couldn't tell.

He had come ashore with forty men, and now the thirty-odd who made up the main body of the raiding party were quickly moving inland. Theseus was already able to make out, in the distance, the classical white rectangular shape that had to be of one of the temples they were looking for.

The band kept advancing rapidly on foot, following the course of a ravine. The bottom of this natural ditch was mostly dry, with only a puddle or two here and there along its twisted length, and the head-high cliffs of crumbling earth on either side would offer them concealment part of the way to the seaside temple. Halfway there, the ravine went twisting off inland, climbing gradually into higher country, and the attackers had to climb out of it and go running across an open pasture.

"Let's go, lads!"

Moving at a quick trot, some with weapons drawn, they began to cover the uneven space of land between them and their goal.

One of the men who had gone on an impromptu scouting mission on a cameloid came back in a few minutes, driving his mount in a quick pacing run, with a report for Theseus.

"No signs of opposition, cap'n. Saw only three, four people, all running the other way."

"Good. Which way did Hector go?"

"Couldn't say, chief."

"All right. Get off that damned animal and come with us." If he'd had twenty or thirty mounted men, that would have given him a considerable advantage, but one just drew attention to the raiders' presence.

Theseus was not making any plans beyond the moment when he was going to find himself inside the temple. Somehow he had been visualizing the treasure as lying out in the open, on an altar or table of some sort, waiting for him to come along and pick it up. He had to keep reminding himself that there was no reason to believe that getting his hands on a Face would really be that easy.

Scanning the landscape for signs of potential opposition, he could see three or four buildings, all on hilltops, that had the look of temples of one kind or another. All were more than a mile away, and Theseus gave them no thought except to suppose they were dedicated to other gods, deities who might be expected to be neutral in this present conflict.

━━━━━━━

Now the raiders, moving on foot, were rapidly drawing near the temple on the shore. Nearby, just a few yards inland from the formal erection of marble walls and columns, there clustered some shabby wooden outbuildings, not nearly as fine to look at. Even the most austere temple, dedicated to the most exalted god, needed a latrine nearby, if humans were going to spend much time there. Suddenly it occurred to Theseus to wonder, for the first time in his life, whether men when they became gods still required such a facility. Soon he ought to know.

With Theseus still in the vanguard, and men bunched closely at his heels, the raiding force covered the last few yards. They went bounding across a grassy terrace, up the broad steps of Apollo's temple, and in between the massive columns. There were no doors here to be locked or broken down.

The walls and columns, the decorated entablatures and cornices, were all of the fine local marble. The structure was only partially enclosed, standing broadly open to the sun and air, oriented less with regard to the cardinal directions than to the shape of its natural rocky base.

On the very verge of crossing the threshold, some of the raiders hesitated before intruding upon the shaded solemnity before them. Trying to squelch this reluctance before it could get a foothold, their leader strode right in, and bellowed, "Are there any gods in here? If there are, damn you, come out and fight!"

When Theseus shouted that, his companions looked at him, and the terror and awe they felt were briefly visible in their faces. But he roared his laughter at them, and they got on about their work.

The handful of people already in the temple froze in place after a single look at the grinning men who were advancing toward them so rapidly with drawn swords. A moment later most of the worshipers of Apollo were running away at top speed.

By chance the raiders had interrupted a ceremony in progress. A short procession, consisting of five or six men and boys, all but the chief priest ritually naked, had been approaching the altar. A bearded man who was evidently the priest in charge was bearing in both hands a slab of wood, and piled on the slab like food on a platter were the offal and bones of some newly slaughtered animal, the portion traditionally due the gods. Two boys in the procession were carrying strips of the edible meat, already cut up and wound onto wooden spits, ready to be cooked.

Two of the worshipers, one of the boys and the bearded chief priest, did not get out of the way fast enough and were cut down. Terror sent the others flying out onto the seaside rocks behind the temple, past the place where the animal had just been slaughtered, and from which the smoke of the cooking fire went up. It was not the best choice of directions in which to flee, because from there their only escape from pursuers would be to hurl themselves into the sea. But today was a lucky day for those who scrambled to the rocks; this pack of raiders was not interested in hunting them down.

Whether the tubby, bearded priest was foolhardy enough to try to stop the raiders, or whether he was simply slow, was a question that remained unanswered. When the priest lay on his back on the stone floor, with a dead acolyte beside him, Theseus tried to interrogate him on the subject of hidden treasure in the temple, but his mouth was bubbling blood, and there would be no useful answers.

━━━━━━

Theseus took a deep breath, stood back, and looked around.

Temples of Apollo were common enough everywhere, but Theseus had rarely been inside one before. This one was big enough to hold perhaps a hundred worshipers, if they didn't object to a little crowding. Or weren't bothered by getting wet when it rained—most of the roof seemed to have been deliberately left off. The structure had been positioned on a rocky promontory, so three sides of it were only a few yards from sunlit water. From inside it was quite possible to hear the waves, of only ordinary size, eternally patient at their work, casually smashing at gray rock, not many yards below the portico.

Most of the interior of the temple was one open, central space, and at one end of this, behind a wide-spaced row of marble columns, were arrayed the hearths and altars used in offering sacrifice. There were no old bloodstains here, nothing that crude in this austere environment. The actual killing of sacrificial animals would take place somewhere outside. Within the temple, everything was clean, well kept.

The intruders stood looking around them, wasting precious moments, stalled by the lack of any evidence of treasure.

"Where is it, chief?"

"We'll find out."

Other men were rummaging through a kind of cabinet on the other side of the broad interior open space, pulling out rich cloths, ritual vestments, knives for slaughtering animals, tossing them on the marble floor. One called over his shoulder, "Not here either."

On the floor, the lungs of the dying man kept bubbling, like a kettle on a fire. Theseus's men were beginning to stand around, as if they had run out of interesting things to do. "Keep looking!" he shouted at them.

Meanwhile the statue of Apollo, his bow in one hand, lyre in the other, looked down on the scene from a pillar behind the altar. The marble Apollo in this case was a little more than life-sized, and executed with some skill, showing a beardless but well-muscled youth gazing into the distance. It had been crowned with a circle of real laurel, the stiff oval leaves clinging close to the marble head.

At one side of the temple, behind the first row of towering white pillars, were a few wooden storage chests, all quickly upended and their contents turned inside out. One was empty, the others filled with common-looking cloth and various instruments of ritual. Nothing of mundane value but a few delicate tools of silver, and not enough of that for any of the men to argue when Theseus commanded them to let it be.

The structure of bare stone, scoured by the sea wind, standing open to light and air, did not appear to offer much in the way of possible hiding places.

He strode back into the open center of the temple, looked about him, and then pointed with his sword. "Maybe it's under the altar. Heave on this chunk of rock, you bastards, tip it over."

So heavy was the stone, so low its center of gravity, that they wanted to drive a lever under it to make any progress; but unfortunately there was no suitable tool on hand.

At last, with six strong men tugging and pushing, the tall stone went over with a breaking crash. And there was nothing under it, not so much as a spider or an ant, nothing at all but the blank solid stone of the floor, not even the suggestion of a hiding place, let alone treasure.

Men swore, and blasphemed the gods. But none of their curses mentioned Shiva by name. Or Apollo, or Dionysus. It was as if an unspoken agreement existed among the men, that to speak such names just now would be pushing one's luck just a bit too far.

"It must be in the other temple, then," Theseus muttered to himself. "The one inland." Or the possibility that Shiva had hinted at was real, and the Face was not here on the Island of Dia at all.

And he turned, trying to catch a glimpse of that distant structure through the spaces between the nearby columns, to see just how far away it might be, as if he did not already know.

He was starting to have serious doubts. *It appeared that Shiva might have been wrong. Or deliberately lied to him? But why should a god do that? Simply as a joke?* No, Shiva might be many things, but not a joker. When Theseus thought about it, he was aware of no reason why a god could not be misinformed, or simply wrong, just like any human.

Maybe someone, or something, had lied to Shiva, trying to provoke a wild goose chase. If so, they had succeeded.

At that moment came the unmistakable sound of an arrow, launched at some distance but passing nearby at deadly speed. The veterans around Theseus did not even look round for the bowman. They came close to ignoring the missile's faint whir, as they might have a droning hornet. Something of the kind had to be expected when you went around tearing up people's houses and temples, and one arrow though certainly unwelcome, was not in itself cause for genuine alarm. Still, it had to be taken as a definite portent, like the first snowflake of a northern winter.

———

The raiders, after withdrawing in good order from the first temple, advanced to the second temple, dedicated to Dionysus, some three miles from where they'd left their ships. This time there were no worshipers on hand—evidently word of the raiders' coming had spread ahead of them.

Time was passing.

Having actually got into the temple of Dionysus, Theseus thought maybe the Face he wanted might be hidden in the larger-than-life-size mask, mounted on a sturdy column, which to the devotees represented their god if it did not actually embody him. That would at least be a good place to start looking, as long as they were here. He strode to the column and seized the effigy.

The lower half of the mask's face was covered by a heavy black beard, probably formed of cameloid hair, from some of the dromedaries of the northern mainland, or from the rarer shaggy pelt of horses.

Not quite the Face I wanted. Right now it was only a puzzle, an obstacle. And only lightly fastened in place. Theseus ripped it from its mounting and shattered it on the floor. Fragments flew, and cameloid hair and marble dust went drifting in a beam of sunlight. But the smashing revealed no secrets that he could see.

"Nothing here."

Occasional arrows and slung stones began to come at them out of nowhere, whizzing into the temple between stone columns. One or two of the stones, hurled at invisible speed, chipping the solid marble when they struck.

It was in that sacred space that the first of the raiders fell, struck down by stone and arrow, both hitting him at the same time.

"Lucky man," one of the others standing near Theseus remarked, when the body was turned over. "Never knew what hit him."

One of the pirates yelled at the marksmen outside, "Hey! Quit shooting that stuff in here! Don't you know this is holy ground?" For a minute there were no more missiles; then the slow shower resumed, tentatively at first.

"Let's go, men. Back to the ships."

———

But when another quarter of an hour had gone by, it was ominously apparent that resistance was developing from somewhere among the people of the island. Arrows and slung stones were now beginning to come in occasional flurries, and the possibility of a real storm had to be recognized. Along the flanks of the raiders' small, irregular column, armed locals could occasionally be seen, running in groups of two or three, from one spot of shelter to the next.

So far the raiding party had lost only one man. But Theseus was now virtually certain that enviable record would not last until they got back to their ships.

As he moved, he kept hoping to catch sight of the second scout, one of the two men who had ridden out on stolen animals to reconnoiter. One had come back, but one had vanished. That was not a good sign.

Meanwhile the main body of the raiders kept moving of necessity on foot. The locals on the other hand had the benefit of mounted speed, at least for a few important messengers. Within an hour or two of the landing, a formidable number of defenders could be mobilized.

Gradually it became easier and easier to believe that the defenders had received some warning of the impending raid, an hour or two at least, and had started to rally their forces and make a plan.

"Gave 'em time to hide their treasure, too."

Very quickly a second raider fell. The stone that had knocked him down had struck him in the back, high up near his neck; but the man was not hit squarely, or killed instantly. A couple of his comrades got him up, wobbly on his feet. Theseus yelled at them to keep moving; if they wanted to slow themselves down trying to help him keep up, he was not going to make an issue of it.

Maybe, thought Theseus, the Dians had learned somehow that he was coming for the thing he wanted, and had hidden it away; but on the other hand, maybe Shiva had been misinformed, and it had never been here at all. Surely if any of these Dians knew where a Face was to be found, one of them would have picked it up and put it on; and in that case Dionysus would be here to defend his house in person. And that would be that—unless, after all, Shiva came to help his men.

But Shiva had never promised to do anything of the kind. No, Theseus kept coming back to the idea that the Face he wanted had never been here at all.

Fiercely he put down his suspicions. It was not that gods were above lying, most of them at least, far from it. But why would Shiva lie to him, about a thing like this? What would be the point? Theseus could not conceive that the god would have had any motive, any possible reason to do so.

———————

Now Theseus, talking with Mochlos, observing certain maneuvers in the distant landscape, began to wonder whether the enemy was less intent on driving them away, than on cutting them off from their ships and destroying them.

A third man went down, felled by a slung stone to the head. One look was enough to know that there would be no helping this one to his feet again.

There was no point in trying to count up losses. But it was becoming obvious that a great many Dianite men had not reacted to the raid by heading for the hills in panic.

"Guess maybe you were right about this fellow Nestor. I wonder if he's really any good?"

As if in answer, a stone came buzzing by within inches of Theseus's nose.

———

Theseus was an intelligent commander, as well as a bold one, and his troops were experienced men. But now he was becoming convinced that the thing he was trying to find was really somewhere else, probably right back on Corycus.

Theseus could see no reason to believe that the Face of Dionysus, or that of any other god, had ever been in any of these temples. If it had ever been in the temple they had already ransacked, certainly he couldn't find it.

It was a bitter disappointment, but life was full of disappointments, and the only way to deal with them was to plow ahead.

———

So far they had ransacked two temples, killed about a dozen people, and suffered almost that many casualties themselves. They had found no sign of the marvel they'd come looking for. Theseus supposed there could possibly be a third temple of the kind Shiva had been trying to describe, somewhere on the island. But if such an establishment existed, he obviously wasn't going to get to it today.

His men grumbled when Theseus began to lead them in a forced retreat. Some were laboring to carry a couple of wounded comrades with them, and these were ready to withdraw, while others argued that they should turn in the direction of the nearest village, and try there to take something that would compensate them for their time and trouble.

Overruling this latter group, Theseus kept his people together, pressing on toward the landing site.

Suddenly his eye was caught by a faint column of smoke in the air, rising from very near the place where the raiders had left their ships. His anger flared, and he felt something like the beginning of real apprehension. It was, as usual, a sharply enjoyable sensation.

As soon as he could see that his ship, or one that he now counted as his, was being burned, he cursed at the loss.

Neither Theseus nor his lieutenants had really expected such an effective counterattack, but still had planned for the contingency. The men who had been left aboard the ships were to put out to sea, and keep watch over a long stretch of shore, waiting for their comrades to reappear.

"There they are, I see 'em. Two ships."

Suddenly he remembered Ariadne. Now he was going to have to make a quick choice on what to do about her—assuming she had survived the burning of the ship. It was an irritating decision to be forced to make, but certainly not a hard one.

For a few minutes, at least, he had totally forgotten about his woman. Well, he had certainly enjoyed her, but her real usefulness had ended as soon as they were away from Corycus. Anyway, she did not match his idea of a pleasant companion for a long cruise.

Someone aboard one of the ships had the idea of lowering a single small boat into the water, but that wasn't going to do the thirty or so survivors of the landing party a whole lot of good.

Theseus and a few others plunged immediately into the surf and swam out to the waiting ship. As soon as a few more men had got aboard the ship, they managed to work the vessel a little nearer shore. Moments after the leaders took the plunge, the whole band was in the water, some abandoning their weapons and helmets.

Strong swimmers did their best to drag the wounded along. One man had found a handy log to push into the water to provide additional support. A few missiles, launched from far away, came pattering ineffectually down.

Theseus, ever mindful of his personal reputation as a leader, and himself a very strong swimmer, went back to the beach, this time in a small boat, into which he loaded a man who wasn't going to survive even an assisted swim. Determined to make sure that all his men who were still breathing had gotten offshore, he contemptuously ignored the missiles that sailed from inland to patter around him in the water and on the sand.

In moments when he had nothing else to think about, Theseus found himself wondering briefly what might have happened to Ariadne. The pair of ships that had got away did not include the one on which he'd locked her up. Then he caught a glimpse of her on shore, a distant figure readily identifiable by her hair, and her odd grab-bag selection of clothing. She was waving both arms, doubtless trying to attract his attention, for her face seemed to be turned directly toward him.

It appeared that no one else was near her. The spot on shore where she was standing would be difficult, but not impossible, to reach with a small boat. It would only take a couple of minutes to row over there and pick her up, and the risk of doing so not much different from the risk he was already taking.

"There's the lady, cap'n. Do we get 'er?"

"No. Pull on for the ship." The answer was given without hesitation. The memory of the body now hidden beneath her ragbag clothes caused him to sigh faintly with regret. Very nice, yes—but on the whole, his best move right now was simply to leave her here. Her presence aboard ship was always threatening to cause problems among the men, and sooner or later those problems would erupt. Everything in his earlier plans had given way to the chance of becoming a god, and Ariadne was only going to get in the way of that.

His life that he was risking was no longer merely a human life. The prospect of immortality, or something very like it, made a difference. No woman compared in importance with the possibility of obtaining godhood.

Besides, there was a good chance that she would do all right where she was; any good-looking woman could usually talk some man into being her protector.

Theseus wished the Princess Ariadne well.

25

THE MOMENT AFTER the young woman came popping out of the ovenlike little box of a cabin, Nestor had started impatiently barking questions at her. She was a strange-looking wench, too young-looking and healthy to have long been a pirates' girl, though she was dressed like one. To his great disappointment, she had nothing meaningful to say to her rescuer, only mumbled a few words and looked at him dully, as if she was in shock, while around them Nestor's men were doing the best they could to encourage the fires they had set aboard the vessel.

His urgent need for knowledge kept him trying for a while. "Who are they, girl? How many ships are coming in? Did any of them talk about that?" The raiding force as reported so far seemed ridiculously small, and Nestor kept wondering if this might be only a diversionary attack. If so, where was the main body going to strike? Somewhere near the fort? He had done all he could to put his people on that side of the island on alert.

Naturally he was also wondering about the identity of this bedraggled prisoner, and where she might have come from. But her personal story could be put off until later. Anyway it seemed not to matter which line of questioning he followed, because the answers she kept giving him were practically incoherent anyway.

Well, there was nothing strange about a pirates' prisoner being shocked and terrorized into a state approaching idiocy. Or possibly she'd been an idiot to begin with. Still Nestor kept hoping from minute to minute that if he allowed the girl just a little more time to pull herself together, she might be able to tell him something useful.

So far only four raiders' ships had been spotted, and two of them had managed to escape his counterattack by putting out to sea. A third vessel, drifting away and abandoned by her crew, was now satisfactorily on fire, sending up a good column of smoke that was sure to alert the raiders who had gone ashore. The fourth, on whose deck Nestor and the strange girl were standing now, was soon going to be ablaze, if only his half-trained home guard troops could show a little competence.

It seemed to Nestor, shading his eyes with one hand and squinting out over the sun-shimmer on the water, that neither of the two escaped ships were able to put more than four oars in the water—not enough men aboard. Therefore it should be possible to overtake them, if any Dian ships, most of which were ordinarily harbored on the other side of the island, could be gotten around here in time.

Long hours would have to pass before that happened, though of course he had sent messengers riding inland. Anyway, Nestor had more immediate things to worry about. His men, local militia lads who'd come aboard the pirate with him, kept giving the impression of intense activity, but they weren't the most skilled arsonists he'd ever seen. Even now one energetic youth came running up to Nestor, breathlessly complaining that they hadn't any fire with them at the moment.

"What happened to your torches?" Nestor inquired, reasonably enough as he thought. In an effort to calm down his amateur troops, he was now sitting on one of the rowers' seats, affecting a pose of tranquility he didn't feel. His hands were clasped in front of him, and he was thinking of twiddling his thumbs.

"We threw them in the sea when the other ship caught fire. We forgot we'd need 'em for this one."

Nestor nodded thoughtfully, and looked about, silently calling upon various spiritual powers for assistance. He forcibly reminded himself that people weren't always as stupid as they sounded at their worst. There were times when it paid to lose your temper, but he didn't think this was one of them.

The youth had dashed off again, without waiting for an answer. Nothing like tight discipline—there was nothing like it around here, anyway. Where to obtain fire in a hurry? There was, of course, a whole burning ship in sight, but that source of ignition had now drifted well out of reach.

One of the local men, a sturdy farmer and council member who had turned out to be a brave fighter, and was willing to go to great lengths to protect his property, protested, "These are solid vessels. We should be saving them for our own use, not burning them!"

The professional commander raised an eyebrow. "Want to grab one for yourself?"

"That's not the point!"

Nestor shook his head. "I've no crew of sailors to put aboard, and if I did I wouldn't want to tie up that many of our people. Our fight ashore's just getting started. Most of the crews from four ships must be in the landing party, I'd guess between fifty and a hundred men, and they're not just going to drops their blades and say the joke's on them. Besides, it would just fit the pattern of pirate raids if there were twenty more pirate ships coming right after these."

"Twenty ships!" The young farmer had dark skin to begin with, and was deeply tanned, but still he seemed to pale. Nervously he scanned the horizon once again. "That could be—what? A thousand men?"

"I don't say it'll happen, but it's possible. If they see one or two of their comrades' ships on fire, they may be discouraged enough to stay offshore. No flint and steel?" This last was addressed to the eager youth who had earlier reported difficulty with torches. Now the lad was back again, panting, seemingly waiting for orders.

"I don't know, Nestor—I mean captain. I'll ask the others." In a flash the boy was gone again. At least one volunteer was hugely enjoying his first experience of war.

Nestor blasphemed the names of several obscure deities, and shouted after him, "If you can't get a fire going, chop a hole in her bottom."

Now he did start twiddling his thumbs. Ariadne, watching from only a few feet away, thought that if this man was only trying to give an impression of being perfectly at ease, he was doing a good job.

She had cast herself down on another rower's bench, where she sat huddled and silent, not really frightened at the moment, vaguely aware of the strangeness of her own mental state. Now that she was freed of the immediate terror of being burned alive, she felt only a remote curiosity about what was going on around her, as if it were some kind of staged show, not particularly interesting. She had no doubt that this fellow called Nestor and his men were going to kill Theseus if they could, and she could scarcely blame them for that. Right now she felt profoundly numb, and anyone or everyone in sight could have been killed without exciting her very much.

Now a sound strongly suggesting the solid blows of an ax falling on heavy wood began to come from somewhere behind the low cabin. Now it sounded like two axes working.

Meanwhile, a couple of members of the Dianite ruling council, pudgy men in merchants' gowns, had come aboard to confer with Nestor. These were his employers, and he sat up straight and began to explore options with them. With the situation as it now stood, he thought it would be best to lure the raiders farther inland, and destroy them, rather than merely drive them away.

Nestor was strongly in favor of this plan. But the ranking civilian, president of the ruling council, let it be known that he would actually be better satisfied with a less drastic result.

The other man from the council was wringing his fat, white, merchant's hands. "Captain Nestor, if the attackers are now *trying* to withdraw, then does it make sense for us to be standing in their way?"

"Seems to me the whole idea is to keep these bastards from doing whatever they want."

"What *we* want to do is get rid of them!"

"Of course, chief. But you don't want them coming back next month, do you?" Nestor paused, staring at his two visitors. Then he added, "By all the gods, I think you're scared you're going to make them angry."

The civilian drew himself up. "I'm afraid of what may happen to our people."

"Right now, I'd say your people are winning. Sure, war is a scary business. But as the proverb says, there are four or five things in the world even worse than war, and most of them happen to you when you're defeated."

Nestor was telling the truth; he viewed the current situation as a considerable victory in the making. There was a good chance that most of the enemy who had come ashore could be trapped and slaughtered.

In fact the council president, listening to the list of his own dead and wounded, was beginning to view the situation as a disaster. Someone had just brought him a paper bearing what appeared to be a list of names, and he shook the paper almost in Nestor's face. "Have you seen this? Have you heard the reports of the slain? Fifteen massacred in the Temple of Apollo. Is this what you call victory?"

Conflicting reports kept coming in from scouts who had been ranging inland, as was usual when a protracted fight was on, even a small one like this. Nestor was sure that many of the details of slaughter and destruction would prove unfounded, while others would be unhappily confirmed.

One of the merchants suggested that it might be a good idea to deliberately allow a few of the marauders to escape. "Let them spread the word among their pirate brotherhood, all across the Great Sea, that Dia is now well armed and capable of resistance."

"That's not a bad idea," Nestor admitted. "But you see, two of their ships did pull out before we could board them. Looks to me that some of these mother-humpers are likely to get away whether we want 'em to or not."

Presently the excitable young man reappeared again, panting, to report that there was now a hole in the planking of the hull, and some water coming in.

"That's what I kind of expected, once you made a hole." Nestor got to his feet, dusting off his hands as if the thumb-twiddling might have dirtied them. "Let's go ashore." After a last glance around at the still-smoldering fires, Nestor took the rescued prisoner gently by the arm. "We're going ashore, lady."

Ariadne came with him meekly, saying nothing.

———————

While guiding her splashing through the water toward the shore, he tried the young woman again with more questions, thinking maybe a moderate dunk in the sea would prove refreshing enough to wake her up. But she came out of the water as glassy-eyed as she went in. She still couldn't or wouldn't give him any helpful answers. Vaguely he wondered if whatever the pirates had done to her might have driven her completely mad. That would be too bad, but meanwhile other folk were dying, including men under his leadership, and he didn't have time to worry much about one girl.

Nestor made sure that Ariadne got safely ashore, a process which required swimming a few strokes, as well as some heavy wading. The brackish water near the creek mouth felt good, cool and clean after her confinement in the cabin. But she let out a gasp of relief at the feel of solid ground under her feet once more.

Nestor urged her along a path that ran inland.

"Take her back to headquarters," he told a small group of armed youth, who were standing around with the air of being temporarily unemployed. "Go easy, she's had a rough time."

"She's a prisoner, Nestor?"

"Not our prisoner, by Hades. Not anyone's anymore. Just take care of her."

———————

The princess hadn't gone far with her new escort, when he was summoned away to attend to some other emergency. Before leaving, he assigned a gray old man to carry on as Ariadne's guide. In the background men were cheering. Now it appeared to her that the ship she'd just left, the one with the hole chopped in her bottom, might be going to catch fire after all.

The way along which she was now being conducted led past the intermingled bodies of slaughtered attackers and defenders. Ariadne had rarely seen such gruesome sights before, and never on such a comparatively large scale. It crossed her mind that one or more of these inanimate things might have been her living shipmates for the past several days, but she could recognize no one. And in any case she would have felt no sense of loss had Theseus's entire crew been wiped out.

What she could see of the landscape stretching inland from the rocky coast looked peaceful and pastoral. In one place she could see the red, tiled roof of a distant farm. Most of the grass in the rolling fields seemed to have been cropped short, though at the moment she could see no grazing animals. She wondered if these efficient defenders had somehow rounded up their herds and driven them to safety.

The silent old man who now had Ariadne in charge, ushering her along courteously if not very helpfully, was following a path that ran along the bank of a small creek or stream.

Part of the time they were walking knee-deep in the stream, so the banks on either side reached over their heads, and kept Ariadne from seeing much of what might be happening in the nearby countryside. Here she wished earnestly for shoes or sandals; the stones in the stream bed and along the path were too much for her tender feet. When she limped and stumbled, her elderly escort showed not the least concern, and it appeared fantastically unlikely that he was going to offer to carry her. Had he done so, she would have been afraid to accept.

When the path brought them up out of the creek again she was able to see, beyond two or three miles of rolling countryside, a building of white marble on a rocky promontory, bathed in brilliant sunlight. Without thinking about it, she knew that building must be the temple of Apollo where the raiders had launched, or were going to launch, their main attack.

To distinguish individual people at such a distance would be impossible. Some figures were visible at a range of two or three hundred yards, but Ariadne could not tell if they were soldiers or shepherds, or even if they were men or women. Certainly they were not in uniform, but then none of today's combatants were regular troops.

So far, since she'd come ashore, everyone had been treating Ariadne kindly, as a rescued prisoner. But the terrible numbness that had settled over her mind and spirit still had her in its grip. Now and then someone asked her a question. All the princess could think of in the way of answer was to keep murmuring that she did not know. Since they were assuming she had been a prisoner on the ship, they seemed to find this acceptable—until another man in his excitement began to question her all over again. But no one pressed her very hard.

Exactly where Nestor's senior auxiliary was taking her, she did not know, but as things turned out, it didn't matter what goal they had in mind. Before she and her escort could reach their destination, some other men wearing white armbands appeared in the middle distance, shouting something to the old man. Ariadne couldn't catch the words, but they must have indicated some military emergency, for her escort immediately turned his back on her and scrambled away at surprising speed to join the others. Whether they were trying to get into the fight or away from it she couldn't tell, and didn't care.

Ariadne ran away.

Their weapons were urgently needed somewhere, and they all ran away from her. Barefoot, she could not have kept up with them had she tried—and she felt no wish to try.

Now she was left to her own devices.

Glancing back to the ships she had just left, she saw how a second one was burning now, smoke black with the tar and pitch of caulked seams, the resin of pine and fir, going up and up into the clear sky.

Looking inland, she saw the pirates, twenty or thirty men in a band, running along a distant trail. They appeared to be hell-bent on getting back to their ships, at the moment dreaming no dreams of pillaging or conquest. Ariadne's heart was briefly in her mouth. But they were out of sight again before she could distinguish Theseus among them, and for one more moment that was her chief concern.

For the space of a couple of breaths she came to a full stop on the path. Then she left the path and moved off at a fast walk, sore feet notwithstanding, instinctively heading away from the sounds of fighting. Somehow the worst fate she could imagine for herself at the moment was being retaken by Theseus and his corps of raiders.

The princess slowed her pace as soon as she felt herself out of immediate danger. But she kept moving, away from the screams and the sound of clashing metal, away from the column of smoke that still went up from the burning ship. Still her feet refused to take her far inland.

To a Corycan princess the sea was much less strange, after all, than the rocks and vegetation of this alien island.

Eventually the last sounds died away. When she thought she must have come at least half a mile, she paused to catch her breath and rest.

Wondering if the man called Nestor had already forgotten about her, or if he had set some of his men to searching, she sat down wearily and closed her eyes, only a pebble's toss from the shoreline. Now she had got clear away from all the men of both factions, and all their fighting. Here on this desolate portion of the coast, all she could hear was the sound of seabirds, and unhurried waves as they came in splashing and gurgling between huge rocks. Here it might almost be possible to believe that she had the entire island to herself.

But now the numbness that had gripped her all through the fight, ever since Theseus had ordered her shut up in the cabin, was failing, like a broken dam. She could no longer avoid coming to grips with the truth: the man who had played the role of her lover had locked her away as a kind of afterthought, a toy he might someday want to play with again. And then he had abandoned her. Maybe he was dead by now. But the truth was, she no longer cared whether he was or not.

A storm of rage and weeping swept the princess now, followed by helplessness and hopelessness.

Ariadne fell asleep, in a total exhaustion of mind and body, nestled in the sand between a pair of wave-worn boulders.

She woke again after only a short doze, feeling hungry and thirsty and cold, just in time to see, at a distance of less than a hundred yards, her lover and one of his men in a small rowboat. The face of Theseus was turned in her direction, and Ariadne was sure he saw her, but he made no response to her calls and waves.

She stood up, waving with both hands, and he would have to be stone blind not to see her now. A strong arm might have thrown a stone across the gap of open water in between.

"Theseus!" One last time Ariadne stretched out her arms to him.

He saw her clearly, there could be no doubt. He must have heard her calling. But when he spoke to the man with him, the man only rowed the boat away, intent on making sure there were no more pirates in need of rescue.

26

MUCH LATER THE bards would sing it, and most of those who heard them would believe: how the hero Theseus abandoned the Princess Ariadne, shortly after he had carried her to the Island of Dia. In the songs the reasons for his behavior were left obscure. There was no reason to doubt that the princess was still a very young and attractive woman when he left her there—but heroes were generally considered to have their pick of attractive women, and those who listened to the bards were generally more interested in hearing about heroic deeds.

Above all, the Prince of Pirates intended soon to become a god, and to a god, no woman ought to be worth the effort to woo and keep her. It was a law of nature that to a prince, let alone a god, all women should be readily available.

She watched Theseus climb aboard the ship, the size and beauty of his body conspicuous amid a tangle of other men. Soon he had them getting up sail, and when everyone who could make it to the ship seemed to have been gathered aboard, the vessel headed out to sea. It remained in sight for what seemed a very long time, and Ariadne had sat down on the rock again long before it disappeared.

Once she had possessed a home, and family, and friends, and it seemed an evil dream that all of that could have been swept away so rapidly. Half a year ago her vicious uncle and his cruel god had deprived her of her father, and now, over the past few unhappy days, fate had robbed her of all the rest. Everything had been sacrificed for Theseus, who had pledged her his eternal love—and now he, too, was gone, and his promises had meant no more than the whisper of a stableboy to a kitchen maid.

In a profound sense he, the man she loved, had never existed. Now she supposed the best fate she could reasonably hope for was to be taken captive by the Dianites and held for ransom. Not that Uncle Perses, who if he thought about her at all must consider her a threat to his power, was likely to reward anyone for bringing her back—more likely her uncle would judge himself well rid of her. Quite possibly he would even pay someone to make sure she never did come home.

The only ray of hope the princess could discern, and that not very bright, lay in the fact that her brother Asterion would almost certainly be doing all he could, working in the world of dreams, to try to help her—but in her current situation, she needed much more than dreams. Not even visions as powerful as those her brother could invoke were likely to bring her any benefit.

But she couldn't even be certain that her brother was still alive. He had stayed behind on Corycus, perhaps by his own choice, and Shiva and Perses might well have taken their anger out on him. That thought in itself was enough to bring on tears.

The questions kept forcing themselves upon her tortured mind. *Why* had Theseus abandoned her? How was it possible for the man she had loved so desperately to do a thing like that? Maybe there was some other woman in his life. Maybe . . . but a storm of weeping came, wiping away all thought in pure emotion.

He wouldn't have had to fight his way to me, or anything like that. Only a short row across an open stretch of water. *He saw me, but he turned away.*

He might have come to get me, as he went back to the beach to pick up his pirates.

Ariadne roused from an exhausted sleep in her lonely hiding place. For a moment she was utterly confused, then she remembered she was on Dia. She had just awakened from a strange and twisted dream in which her supposed lover, Theseus, had returned and come ashore to watch her sleeping, and then had faithlessly stolen away again. In the dream he had come and gone without even leaving her any message, and the only explanation she could think of was that he had never learned to read or write. Somehow that seemed unlikely.

Her body ached, as if she had been through some great physical exertion. Slowly, cautiously, she moved to a slightly higher spot where she could see more of the sea. All the ships of the raiding party were completely out of sight by now, the hulk of the one that had been burned evidently sunk beneath the waves, and she could just see in the distance, along the shore, the mast of the one that had been sunk, protruding above the water.

A wave crashed on the rocks, almost at her feet, wetting her borrowed pirates' clothes with spray. The tide had changed, she realized, and now was coming in.

───────────

Now, once more left to her own resources, Ariadne remained in hiding. Theseus had sailed away, but she imagined there must still be pirates on the land. And the defense forces, the irregulars captained by the man called Nestor, might be searching for her. She preferred that they not find her either, though perhaps that attitude did not make sense, because sooner or later she would have to come out, if only to beg someone for food in this alien and probably unfriendly land.

Hunger was fast becoming a problem, and the princess could foresee that it was quickly going to get worse. In her last day on the ship she had eaten only some hard biscuit, and a couple of raw carrots, gone rubbery with dehydration. It seemed to her that she had not had a hearty, solid meal since the evening before the great escape effort had begun. If she now had one of those boardlike dried fish from the cabin floor in hand, she would have tried to chew on it.

As the tide came in and the wind shifted, the spray from incoming waves kept wetting her, so she moved. Then she moved again, cowering first behind one rock and then behind another, but reluctant to go anywhere out of sight of the sea—it was as if with part of her mind she still expected her lover to come splashing up boldly out of the waves and rescue her. But that was not going to happen. The truth was that she had no lover, no such being existed. Men had paid court to her from time to time, and one of them, to save his own skin, had managed to seduce her. (There were names for men who behaved like that, though a Corycan princess was not supposed to speak such names.) But there was no man who loved her, and probably there had never been.

And another truth was that she was hiding now because she hated and despised them all, all the men with swords in their hands, like the one who had killed her father.

Now she must find her own way; and since her earliest childhood, she had never been entirely helpless. Settling herself in the driest corner she could find between tall rocks, in a position that minimized her various discomforts as much as possible, she closed her eyes and tried to visualize a web.

When the familiar, gossamer strands began to glisten in her inner vision, they formed a pattern that Ariadne had never seen before. They came together to form a great, complex network, with herself at the center, nexus, of many radiating filaments.

In the circumstances the vision was frightening, and she quickly opened her eyes again. Never had she seen the threads do that before. They seemed to be telling her to stay right where she was—advice that did not seem to make any sense at all. Unless it meant that her condition was now utterly hopeless.

For most of her life, she had relied upon her own almost unerring ability to find, to locate, whatever she was looking for. But today, after what had happened, she no longer quite knew what that was. Certainly she was not making an effort to locate Theseus.

"Father Zeus, why have you deserted me?" It was the first time in Ariadne's life that she had ever uttered such a prayer aloud. There was no answer. Of course she had not really expected one.

Homeless and friendless and lost, the princess considered hurling herself into the sea and dying. Maybe Poseidon would welcome her, grant her the peace that had escaped her on the earth.

She needed no extraordinary perception to be aware that something very strange, but something very real, that was not an inner vision, was approaching the island from well out at sea.

The president of the ruling council saw the strange-looking ship approaching before Nestor did, and called his attention to it.

"Another pirate?" the merchant demanded anxiously.

Nestor looked for a long time, shading his eyes with one hand. At last he said, "I don't think so. If it is, it's the weirdest-looking pirate I ever laid eyes on."

On second thought, when he had looked a little longer, he decided it might well be the weirdest-looking ship of any kind he'd ever seen. The vessel's mast and lines were festooned with greenery, its sides growing grass and vines that trailed in the sea as if they could be nourished by salt water.

As the princess watched the same ship from a different distance and angle, the thought momentarily crossed her mind that the craft might belong to Theseus, that he was engaged in some trick or magic, coming back to get her after all. But she could not convince herself of that, and did not try.

Now Ariadne could be sure that the strange vessel was coming in to land. But of course it was not going to land within a quarter of a mile of her, where the coast was all jagged and forbidding rocks.

———

Dionysus, immediately on landing, escorted Edith ashore, and tenderly sent her on her way homeward.

A smooth plank, magically supported, ran ashore and steadily supported those who walked on it.

Alex had done what he could, but had not been able to work any miracles of healing on the girl. But freedom and the prospect of being reunited with her family, along with a couple of days of proper nourishment, had had a strong beneficial effect. Edith now seemed quite capable of making her own way home through a friendly countryside.

Alex also dispatched a couple of sprites to dance attendance on the girl, to see that she came safely to her destination.

She was wearing soft, clean garments now, there were flowers in her hair, and she had passed a full day without weeping. "Thank you, thank you, my lord!"

"You are welcome. I envy you the joy of your homecoming. And I envy your family when they see you. There will be much rejoicing when you arrive."

Before walking away from the vessel that had brought him to Dia, Alex gave her to her faithful steersman, who was still with him. "This ship is yours now, good Acetes. Make what profit from her you can."

"Thank you, great lord!"

———

Ariadne's presence on Dia had been strongly suggested by Aegeus, before he was turned into a dolphin.

Some of Alex's sprites and powers, sent ahead to look around the island, now brought him a report.

But at first Alex could not believe what he was hearing. "Theseus has done *what*?"

The whisperer told him. Alternate waves of outrage and joy engulfed the latest avatar of Dionysus. She had been badly treated, mortally offended—but she was physically unhurt, and she was here.

Despite his recent access of divinity, Alex still felt very shy at imagining
himself in the presence of the princess—he thought that with the Twice-
Born to support him, he could face another god now, calmly enough, if
required. But somehow this was different.

"She is only a mortal woman, why am I so nervous?"

His entourage had no answer to that question, but to chide him. *It
does not behoove a god to take the presence or absence of mortal flesh
so seriously.* These were the words of the disreputable Silenus.

His reply was stiff. "Thank you for your advice. But I am the god,
not you." And it occurred to Alex to wonder, not for the first time, how
and why Silenus, who had no real body, should show in his image all
the ravages of dissipation.

*You see me as I am, lord; your true servant, incapable of guile or
deception.*

Even Dionysus seemed to be taken aback by such a fabulous claim,
and unable to find words for an immediate reply. Eventually Alex got
out, "Oh, compelled to be absolutely truthful, are you?"

*My devotion to the truth, Your Divinity, requires me to qualify that
description. In pursuit of the highest truth it is sometimes necessary to
deviate from strict accuracy in less important matters. In such a case—
for example, in my service to yourself—the greater good to be accomplished must work to purify the means that are necessary to achieve it.*

"I see. Of course. This is your roundabout way of admitting that
you are an incorrigible liar. I ought to have remembered that fact before
now."

I am most honored that Your Divinity remembers me at all.

Wondering how best to approach the woman he so desperately loved,
Alex could this time find nothing very helpful in the long memory of
Dionysus. Probably the god's usual approach to such matters was simply
too different from his own. Left on his own, and feeling strangely awkward, the young man pondered how to introduce himself. To say "I am
a god" would be no more than the simple truth, but an unaccountable
shyness held him back from that approach. He was a god, but like the

avatars of other deities, he was also something less—or something more. To say "I am Alex the Half-Nameless" would also be the truth, or at least a half-truth, but now seriously misleading.

In the end, Alex decided that he would neither announce his name to the princess at once, nor make any effort at disguise. Let Ariadne recognize him if she could—though, as he reminded himself, she had never been very familiar with the face of the young soldier whose only name was Alex. Nor had she ever seen him dressed in any other garments than the uniform of the Palace Guard.

He was still wearing around his neck the medallion of silver and gold that she had given him long days ago, but all of it except the chain was hidden under his purple cloak, where that garment was clasped around his neck.

When Alex saw her crouching in among the rocks, and the image of her as it appeared in the eye of Dionysus assured him that she had taken no great harm, his relief was so great that for a moment he could not speak.

When Ariadne suddenly became aware of the figure of a lone man standing there, wrapped in a rich cloak and gazing directly into her hiding place, she caught her breath in fear. Then she summoned up her courage and, with no trace of recognition in her eyes, demanded, "Are you a soldier?"

"No, my lady." And the young man opened his hands, showing them empty of weapons. Indeed he wore no belt or armor, and his tone was so humble that it set fear at rest.

But the wearer of such a fine cloak, standing idle in such a commanding attitude, could hardly be a slave or menial. "A landowner, then?" Ariadne demanded. "Or the priest of some local god? If you have no weapons, and no soldiers at your bidding, you'd better take shelter while you can."

"Why?"

"Why? You fool, pirates are ravaging the land! One shipload of them have run away like cowards, but others may still be here. More ships may be landing. If you don't care for your own safety, at least try not to give my hiding place away."

"That's the very last thing I'd want to do." Appearing concerned, he moved forward with alacrity, and slipped in among the rocks to stand beside her. There wasn't much room in her hiding place, and he had to stand very close to Ariadne.

Ariadne, her nerves already drawn to breaking point, had to fight to stifle a scream; but a second look assured her that the man was only standing there, calmly, being a perfect gentleman. Despite his fine clothes, there was still something humble about his attitude, and with an effort she controlled herself. "I don't suppose you know where I could get my hands on a boat?"

"No, my lady. Do you think you would be safer in a boat?"

Why had the fates sent this idiot to pester her? "I don't know, but I've got to do something. I can't just hide among these rocks until I rot!"

"Certainly not. Would it please you to have some food? Something to eat and drink?"

"Yes! Please. I'm very thirsty. And hungry too."

Her mysterious visitor made a little bow, the best he could do in the constricted space, and took his leave. "I'll be back shortly." He started away, then turned to call over his shoulder. "And I'll see what I can arrange in the way of transportation."

———————

And when he had gone apart from her by thirty or forty yards, getting himself just out of her sight, Dionysus began getting his chariot mobilized, calling up out of its usual state of invisibility his whole exotic entourage.

"Should I send a sprite to her with wine and water?" Alex asked himself, muttering aloud. "No, those things I will bring to her with my own hands—in a minute. And—what an idiot I am!—food, too, of course. She said that she was hungry."

Critically he studied the display that was now being presented for his approval. Six or eight varieties of fruit, of course; that was good. He tasted a morsel of the presented cake. Not the very best he, Dionysus, had ever enjoyed, but—definitely satisfactory. There was no time just now to strive for absolute perfection.

Then he addressed his permanent escort. "And now, show me, how are you going to display yourselves?"

The entourage exploded suddenly into visibility, making an impressive array. Even the satyrs, commanded to appear more or less fully clothed, in suitable raiment, could achieve a kind of nobility. Alex would have been dazzled, but now, equipped with the mind of Dionysus, able to recall many occasions when the team had done much better, he was forced to judge it an inadequate, shambling sort of show.

"No, that is not good enough," he demanded of his inhuman servitors. "It's plain you haven't practiced this kind of thing for a long time. I have seen and heard better than that at a merely human court. Improve your costumes, and your manners, quickly. As for music, let us have first a fanfare, suitable for a great lady, and then a kind of serenade. But softly! Let her not hear until I have given my approval."

And now there seemed to be a greater variety of instruments tuning up to play. Strings and horns, flutes and timpani. And stuff for the eyes to feast upon: a whole panoply of lights and colors, gold and silver, scarlet and purple, was borne in the seeming substances of gems and fabrics. The whole scene was lighted by flames that burned coldly in the air, or with no heat greater than that of human bodies fired with passion.

"No, it must not turn into an orgy this time. *No*, it certainly shall not." Alex paused, trying to find the exactly proper words and thoughts with which to instruct his helpers, to produce exactly the effect he wanted. "Let the style of madness with which we approach the princess be of quite a different sort."

After the third or fourth revision of the whole display, all accomplished in accordance with the god's instructions, even the Dionysian memory at last found it acceptable. Besides, the princess must be growing impatient, and it would hardly do to let her faint from hunger.

And, besides that, Alex was reluctant to prolong their separation for even another minute. "That's more like it. Forward!"

27

THE SLENDER, HUDDLED figure stirred. Ariadne began to say, "Sir, I feared you were not coming back. If I could have only a cup of fresh water . . ."

Then, at the sudden crash of timpani and horns, she lifted her head, so all the colors of the flames of the procession were reflected in her heart-shaped face, between her hanging strings of grimy hair.

A moment later the princess had sprung to her feet in utter wonder at the leaping, marching music, at once sweeter and stronger than anything most mortal ears had ever heard. As the procession came fully into her view, swaggering and dancing past the entrance to her rude shelter, she remained motionless, getting a good look at every part of the parade. Spreading her hands in a gesture of unconscious grace, she stood there marveling.

Alex/Dionysus had made no effort to disguise himself, or to conceal his new nature. Still there was no sign as yet that the princess had recognized either the god who now stood before her, or the young soldier who had once pledged his undying loyalty.

But when the parade had passed, and turned, and was coming back again, her wondering eyes became fixed on Alex. As he approached she could see that he was carrying in his right hand a crystal flagon of what appeared to be clear, sparkling water, and in his left, a delicate dark bottle of what must be wine. Beside him and a little to the rear, a silver tray of choice dishes floated waist-high in the air, pastries and cheese and fruit borne by invisible hands. Mechanically she took the water from his hand and drank.

Never in her young life had the Princess Ariadne looked upon any god but the cruel Shiva; but now she understood at last that she stood in the presence of some very different deity.

The proud neck of the princess, that in the course of her young life must seldom have been bent to anyone, bowed low, but only for a moment. Then she raised her head again.

"You are—you must be—the Lord Dionysus." Somewhere in the back of her mind passed the thought that this was the form Theseus had been planning to put on. But evidently that effort had miscarried—the young man now standing before her was certainly not Theseus.

"Whatever I am, my lady, I owe to you," the noble-looking youth said now. And to Ariadne's amazement, she now beheld what seemed the enormity of a god going down on one knee, offering obeisance to a mere mortal woman.

But her wonder at the gesture was overwhelmed in a new mystification. At last her attention was fully concentrated on the one who stood beside her.

She said, "But . . . it seems to me that I have known you. Your face is almost the same as that of a young soldier I remember, the one named Alex. How can that be?"

In sober fact it was hardly strange that the princess should remember him—only a few days had passed since they were engaged in planning desperate deeds together—but still Alex felt a rush of joy at the acknowledgment.

"My name was Alex then," he said. "And it still is."

"I don't understand," she breathed.

"Don't you? Princess, I think you must be well aware of how I came into possession of this Face."

Her cracked lips made a perfect O. "I? How should I know?"

"Don't you?"

"Great Dionysus! I have no idea what my lord is talking about. You are the second god that I have ever seen. The first was more a devil. Never in my life have I laid eyes on the unworn Face of any god."

Wondering, Alex raised a hand to touch the medallion that still hung around his neck. "You gave this to me, when I was no more than a young soldier."

"Yes. Yes, so I did." A sharp sound made the princess turn her head. Around them, the surfaces of barren seaside rocks were cracking, green shoots peeping forth, the tendrils of vines beginning to make progress.

Again she faced the man before her. "You?"

He wondered if the troubles she had endured had left her mind confused. "Yes, my lady. My name is Alex," he repeated. "I am the new avatar of Dionysus. Here, sit down." On a rock behind the princess, soft green moss had already grown thick enough to make a cushion.

"Yes," said Ariadne, nodding her head slowly. "Thank you." She sat down. But her face indicated that what she had just heard explained nothing for her. "Yes, I did give my medallion to—to the young soldier. But what of it?"

"The Face of Dionysus was concealed inside it." And Alex snapped the two halves of silver and gold apart, displaying the empty compartment. Then he sighed; obviously the princess was as surprised as he had been at the revelation.

Dionysian memory suggested . . . if not an explanation, then a likely place in which to seek one. Whenever the god's affairs took a turn that he himself found particularly mystifying, the solution was usually found to have some connection with his inhuman associates.

With one of them in particular.

As the result of a silent summons, Silenus once more appeared as their spokesman.

Dionysus posed the question in a godly voice. "Can you explain this business of the medallion, Silenus?"

Everything has worked out in a most satisfactory way, Lord Dionysus. Again Your Divinity is united with a congenial mind, in a suitable host body.

"I begin to understand," said Alex after a pause. "It was you who put the treasure where I found it."

Evidently the satyr took that comment as approval. *My lord is perspicacious as always. I ask no special reward. But would it not be a good thing, lord, to begin a celebration at once? The lady appears to be in a receptive, congenial mood.*

"It would *not* be a good thing," Alex rebuked his servant sharply. "Not what I suppose you mean when you say 'celebration.' Certainly not with this lady. Do not suggest it again."

Of course not, lord! Silenus seemed aghast at the possibility.

"Do not suggest what?" the princess queried, obviously mystified, and Alex understood that her mortal ears had heard nothing of what Silenus said to him.

"Never mind," the god continued sternly. "We can speak of all that later." The last remark was addressed to his entourage; he had more questions that he meant to ask of them, especially of Silenus.

But for the moment he focused on Ariadne once more. "I would be pleased if you would allow my servants to minister to you."

There were suddenly in the air clouds of fragrant steam, and gauzy curtains, enveloping the princess. Now her wide eyes, along with the rest of her, disappeared from the view of the man-god who watched.

A sprite, taking the form of a nearly invisible blur in the air beside his head, whispered a suggestion to him.

"Oh yes, her clothes," Alex responded, in a whisper too faint for the lady herself to hear. "Of course. What to do? Yes, good idea. See to it, I command you!"

Foreseeing that there would now be a time of waiting, Alex sat down on a handy rock. "Here, I have brought you food and drink," he called into the clouds of steam, and clapped his hands.

There came trickling sounds, as invisible hands poured wine and water into crystal cups. A chorus of singing, dancing satyrs and maenads, beginning on schedule the next phase of their performance, as their master had commanded, took form out of nowhere to surround their master, and the princess, who was still lost from view inside her improvised bathchamber of steam and gauze.

Meanwhile, the revamping of the princess's dress proceeded quickly. Coarse dirty cloth, only briefly visible as it emerged from the chamber of the bath, appeared to be consumed in a white flame, fire that burned or heated nothing but the stuff that it destroyed. Replacing the discarded rags came gauzy fabrics, silk from somewhere past the edge of the known world, gold thread and fine embroidery. In the traditional high fashion of the queenly women of Corycus, the style left her breasts bare.

As always, the entourage of Dionysus managed to convey, even in their dullest routine actions, a hint of frenzy. For a moment Alex could feel the turmoil strongly and he cringed inwardly. But this time the onslaught was not overwhelming. Something—something that even the god found strange and unfamiliar—tempered the impulse toward madness, turned it away from the mania that sought blood, and even from lustful coupling, toward a less fleshy and more inward ecstasy.

Now, with his beloved for the time being out of earshot, Alex took the opportunity to call Silenus to a full accounting.

As soon as the goatish figure stood before him, he demanded of it, "Explain the matter of the Face."

Which Face does my lord mean?

"Which Face do I—? How many Faces are we talking about? You know what I mean." Alex tapped his own forehead. "How it came to be in the medallion."

While we were still on Corycus, lord, one of us who now make up your loyal entourage—one of us observed the work of clever Daedalus, a man who in my opinion, lord, is himself most worthy of apotheosis.

Indeed, we might have left your Face where he would find it, had I not been fearful that instead of putting it on, he would have wasted much time in a useless attempt to cut it open, looking for its secrets.

" 'One of us' meaning yourself, I suppose. Stop these damned circumlocutions and get on with it. Why didn't you simply tell me, the first time you dragged me into the chariot, that the treasure I sought was hanging around my own neck . . . ?" Alex's voice died before he had finished the question. Now, with the experience of a god to draw upon, he could find a reasonable answer for himself, even before the ready voice of the satyr furnished one.

Great lord, had you been reborn while still on Corycus, your new avatar would inevitably have been exposed to great peril. There could have been no time of accommodation, of the necessary development of your new avatar, before you had to face your enemies again.

"That might make sense," the Twice-Born admitted. "Especially if Shiva were taking an interest in what happened on the island. It *might*, I say. Any other reason?"

The satyr briefly hung his head. *Also it is possible—remotely possible, I must admit—that your poor servant Silenus was experiencing the joys of wine when he hid the Face.*

"Yes? Go on."

And when . . .

"Yes?"

When sober again, had forgotten where he put it.

There was a silence.

"Ah, Silenus," Dionysus whispered at last. For once it seemed the god had been shocked into solemnity.

Evidently mortified by that stunned whisper, the satyr remained silent, eyes lowered, shuffling the goat-hooves that he used for feet.

Presently Dionysus sighed. "I see. We must let that pass, for now. Now wait, don't go darting away. I have another question for you."

Yes, lord?

"A moment ago, you seemed genuinely uncertain as to which Face I was talking about."

Alex was vaguely surprised as Dionysus moved forward two long strides on Alex's legs, reached out an arm, Alex's right arm, and with the power of a god closed the fingers of his right hand upon Silenus's throat, now held by the same power in a tangible and bruisable form. The voice of the Lord of Frenzy roared, with sudden power, *"Tell me, ancient villain, what do you know of the Face of Zeus? And be sure that this time you speak the truth."*

Ariadne's eyes were filled with wonder, some minutes later, when the clouds of steam and walls of gauze were dissipated, and she emerged from her bath already wearing her new clothing.

Her eyes were wide with wonder as she brushed her fingers, newly clean, over the fabric. "But—but this is—I have never had a dress as fine as this. Nor have I even seen one, I believe." And with a distinctive motion of her head, she tossed back her coil of light brown hair, almost the color of fine Corycan honey, that had never been so lustrous.

When the princess had slaked her thirst from crystal goblets, and nibbled at some food, she again looked closely at her rescuer.

"So, you were—are—Alex the Half-Nameless, who once served me. And now you have become a god, and I, a werely mortal—merely wortal—woman—must serve you. Even if I am a princess. That is the way of the world," she pronounced wisely, and finished with a light hiccup.

"One cup of strong wine has been too much for your empty stomach," Dionysus mused. "And my very presence brings on in many folk a touch of lunacy. There are important things I must discuss with you, an important discovery I have just made. But I see that for the moment they must wait. Ariadne," he added softly. "Now I have the right to call you Ariadne."

"Indeed you—*hic*—indeed you may. And I may call you . . ."

"Call me Alex. Please."

It was soon obvious that what the princess needed most of all just now, more than additional finery, reassurance, celebration, or even a declaration of undying love, was rest. And for a time the God of Joy considered causing his beloved to fall into a deep sleep that should last for many hours. There appeared a couch, as finely appointed and as temporary as her bath had been. Surrounding the princess where she slept, his powers could construct a wall, an encirclement, of protective greenery. He might hope by such means to keep her safe, until he had concluded his business back on Corycus, and could return here for her.

But as Alex thought it over, he doubted they had many hours to spare for the luxury of rest. And neither he nor Dionysus was convinced that it would be safer to leave his beloved here than to carry her along—there was not time to construct a stronghold of safety. Nor, indeed, had

Alex any reason to believe that anything Dionysus could build would protect her against Shiva.

———

Events precluded any chance of the princess being allowed a long time in which to recruit her strength. Ariadne had been napping for only a few minutes when one of the sprites alerted Alex to the fact that a couple of men were watching him, from behind some rocks about a hundred feet away.

He turned and studied them with the augmented power of his divine vision. The taller, younger observer, standing with folded arms, looked military, capable, and stoic, not as nervous as most people would be, confronting divinity at close range; the older man looked fretful and nervous and so out of shape that he had to be civilian, though he had brought along a spear that now stood leaning against a nearby rock.

"Pirates?" Alex softly inquired of his entourage.

Not so, lord, whispered the nearest sprite in her soft voice. *Quite the opposite.*

Gently Alex reached out a hand and touched the dozing princess on the arm. He had to touch her twice before she stirred on her silken couch and opened her eyes.

"We are being watched," her guardian informed her. "Do you know either of those men?"

Ariadne stretched luxuriously, frowned, and then turned on the two watching men a gaze still mellowed by that single cup of Dionysian wine.

She said, "I believe—yes, I'm sure—the one wearing the sword is the same man who got me off the ship when it was burning. Nestor, the others called him."

"And did he treat you well?"

"He did. Actually he did. You see, he and his men were fighting against, against Thes—*hic*—Theseus. And I was sick of it all, sicker than you would believe, my lord—my Alex—sick of all the things men do—and all I wanted was to get away. Do you know, my head is still a little light?"

28

NESTOR AND HIS former employer continued to observe, in awe, and from some distance, the meeting between Dionysus and Ariadne.

"He's seen us," the civilian was whispering, shivering in a kind of agony of anxiety. "Let's get out of here."

"Of course he's seen us, that's why we're standing here. Withdraw if you like," said Nestor, making no attempt to keep his voice down.

The older man twisted his body, the tense writhing of one struggling to control his bowels. "But—but *he* may be angry if I turn my back on him and walk away!"

"Walk backwards, then." Nestor was irritated. "I don't know, chief. You've said that you're displeased with my methods, that you'll need my services no more. So naturally I must try to find another client."

The civilian did not seem to be listening. "What does it mean?" he pleaded, in a near-frenzy of doubt and worry. "What is a god doing on our island? No one living can remember the last time that happened."

"So now it's come to pass. I assume there's some connection with the raid we just fought off. Or it might be simple coincidence—though I don't believe that. I'd surely like to find out."

"Oh gods! *The god is beckoning to us to approach.*" Nestor's companion moaned the words, and was practically paralyzed at the prospect. "What shall we do? I can't walk. I can't move!"

Nestor shook his head. "Then why don't you just stay here, chief? Sit where you are. I suspect I'm the one he's interested in." He lowered his voice to a mere whisper. "Won't be the first immortal I've ever talked to face to face; and this one doesn't look as scary as some I've seen."

Once more the male figure standing in the rocky recess raised one hand in a gentle beckoning motion, and Nestor moved forward slowly, the chief still groaning at his back.

He came to a stop, and bowed, two or three yards from the couple in their stony niche. "Lord Dionysus? My name is Nestor." It was easy to feel confident of this deity's identity, with fronds of greenery bursting out of the rocks on every side of him, and strains of wild music half-heard in the background.

"So I have been told," the figure in the purple cloak responded. "This is the Princess Ariadne, of Corycus. How she comes to be here is a long story."

"I have already met the princess," said the soldier, bowing again. "Though I was not aware of her exalted rank."

Ariadne responded with a distant, mellow smile. The god beside her nodded. "She tells me that you treated her well, and brought her to safety from a burning ship. For which we are both grateful."

"It seemed the least I could do, lord."

"How do you come to be here, Nestor? Surely you are not a native, your speech has not the Dian sound."

"That's quickly explained, my lord. Some months ago, certain members of the Dian ruling council got together and decided they were tired of being harassed by pirates. They sent a delegation to the mainland to hire some help, and after interviewing several candidates, made me a good offer to come here and take charge of the island's defense."

"And now they are dissatisfied with your work?"

"So it would seem." Nestor glanced back in the direction of the chief. The chubby man was lying so still, curled up against the base of a rock, that he might have fainted. "Would you like to talk to a council representative?"

"Not necessarily. But I would like to talk to *you*. My powers tell me that you have discouraged the raiders pretty effectively."

———

A few hours later Alex, walking now with a somewhat revived Ariadne on his arm, and accompanied also by Nestor who said he had urgent military matters to discuss with him, strolled in sight of the recently defiled temple on the Dian shore. The only images of Apollo that he could find recorded in the Dionysian memory were fragmentary, and they were also of an extreme age. So frighteningly old that Alex made no attempt to compute the gap in years. The avatars who had then worn the Face of the Far-Worker, and that of Dionysus, must have ceased to walk the earth long ages hence.

Suddenly the sharp senses of the Twice-Born were recording something—odd. Faint, and odd, and interesting. Dionysus said, "Let us walk a little closer to Apollo's temple."

"As my lord wishes," said the princess demurely.

Alex had in mind the need to discover some kind of sanctuary where the woman he loved might stay safely for a few hours or days. In the present situation, he was afraid to leave her alone and unprotected, even for a few minutes. Not that he was at all confident of his ability to protect her from an angry Shiva.

Now they were steadily approaching the defiled temple. There was a strange glow in the tall, marble structure, subtle lights that did not seem to come from any natural flame, and corresponding shadows. And Dionysus, if not the mortals with him, could, if he chose to harken in a certain way, detect a series of tones, unearthly music. Very different from the tunes of sprites and satyrs, but strains of ineffable rightness, sounding more in the mind than in the ears.

There is someone in the temple now, lord, said a low, disembodied voice, in which a note of stress was evident.

"Yes, no doubt about it."

Nestor's footsteps had been gradually slowing, and now they stopped. When Alex turned to look at him, the mercenary said, "Lord Dionysus, in my life I have encountered several gods."

"Yes?" Alex prodded.

"I have even achieved a certain—I might even call it friendship—with one or two divinities. As I would like to do with you." Nestor paused and swallowed. With a nod he indicated the temple ahead of them. "I'm not sure why this case is different. But . . ."

Alex was nodding. "But Apollo is something else again. Lord of Terror, Death, and Distance, among his other attributes. I understand. It's all right, most of the gods themselves are uneasy in his presence. Without necessarily knowing why." Alex was trying to avoid being too sharply aware of the usual attitude of Dionysus in that regard. By comparison with the one who waited just ahead, he himself felt more completely human than he had for several days. He said, "So wait here, Nestor, if you like." He turned. "Ariadne?"

The woman beside him laid her hand upon his arm. "I will come with you." Her voice was warm and confident.

Slowly the couple moved forward. This time it was Dionysus, even more than Alex, who was reluctant to advance. Alex's own feet felt leaden, though he could not have said precisely what he was afraid of. He knew that the being he was about to encounter was no friend of the Destroyer. And it was necessary to go forward.

He had advanced only a couple of additional steps when he realized that his usual escort of inhuman hangers-on had suddenly left him. Even Silenus for once was silent, offering no jests or jabbering. The sprites and satyrs had withdrawn in awe, or were hanging back, desperately reluctant to draw any closer to the Far-Worker. Their absence produced an unaccustomed sense of emptiness in the space around him, and that further fed his own uneasiness.

Somehow Alex, the mere mortal, continued to be less affected than the god whose nature he now shared. And on entering the temple, there was nothing intrinsically frightening to be seen, though in his left eye, the figure before him shimmered mightily.

Alex with his right and merely human eye, and Ariadne, beheld only the figure of a beardless youth, perhaps not quite fully grown, his athletic body partially wrapped in a belted robe of snowy white. A lyre hung at his belt, and a great bow, improbably silver in its color, was slung over one shoulder. The youth was standing straight, cradling weightlessly in his arms a burden of pale flesh that had once been a boy. At his feet lay the butchered corpse of a priest, still laurel-crowned like the god himself.

When the Far-Worker saw the couple approach, he gently set down the body he was holding, and stood up straight again, several inches taller than Alex.

"I am Apollo." The voice was mild, nothing like Shiva's commanding tones; still, it had a resonance. Seen at close range, the figure in the white robe was of striking appearance, rendered odd by the fact that his hair of glossy black contained a strong admixture of red curls. Had it not been for a certain dignity in the face, a shadow of divinity tinged with sadness, Alex would have assumed the other to be a year or two younger than himself.

Even though Ariadne stood with her hand resting on the arm of one deity, in a touch that claimed the beginning of familiarity, that name was enough to silence her. But Alex, aware of the powers of a god in his own blood, managed to answer steadily enough.

"We join our lamentations to yours, Lord Apollo, on the death of your worshipers here. I am now Dionysus—as I have no doubt you can see. My human name was—is—Alex," he added on an impulse. Then with a touch of defiance he supplemented, "No family name. And this lady with me is Ariadne, princess of Corycus."

The youth before them nodded his odd shock of hair. "Not exactly of a famous ancestry myself. I grew up in a village. I'm Jeremy Redthorn." He extended a hand, and Alex immediately took it. It felt completely human. Apollo was looking at him searchingly. "Alex, then, if I may."

"Of course."

"And I am pleased to meet you, princess."

Exactly what protocol demanded of a princess, on being introduced to one of the mightiest of gods, was a question that Ariadne's early lessons in deportment had never covered. But she took Apollo's hand, and did the best she could under the circumstances.

Having greeted her casually, Apollo turned back to her companion. "If you don't mind my asking—I have good reason—have you been very long involved in this god-business?"

Dionysus remained awed and wary. But Alex was conscious of the beginning of a feeling of considerable relief, at having encountered another deity who was willing to make a simple confession of humanity. "Not very." Then Alex impulsively decided to trust the other. "Actually only a few days."

The tall youth nodded sympathetically. "I thought so. It took me much longer than that before the thing began to feel at all natural. I've had more than a year now to get used to it."

Alex let out a sigh. "Lord Apollo—"

"Jeremy, if you prefer."

"Jeremy, then. There are about a hundred questions I would like to ask you. But I expect most of them can wait."

"I expect you are right," Apollo said. "But I have a few that had best be answered quickly. Tell me where you are from. And how you got your Face."

The Sun-God listened attentively, and when the story was finished, he advised the neophyte deity to take the Princess Ariadne back to Corycus with him.

"It could be more dangerous for her there than here," Alex suggested.

"Possibly. But in my opinion, even riskier to leave her here, unprotected. Understand that whatever you do, I can offer no help as bodyguard; I'm going to be very busy."

"I understand."

"Besides, there is another reason why she ought to go on with you to Corycus. From what you tell me, it might be possible to see this lady here—or more likely her sister, Phaedra—installed on that island as the true queen."

Alex shook his head. "Realistically, I can't believe that I am strong enough to overthrow the usurper. Not if he has the help of Shiva."

"I wanted to be sure you understood that point."

"I do. And to make matters worse, I fear Shiva may have assistance from the Underworld."

"No one would expect you to overcome such an alliance—without substantial help."

The two had many things to discuss.

Especially Alex wanted to pass on to Apollo the information he'd recently had from Silenus, that the satyr had in fact been spreading the rumor that the Face of Zeus was really hidden in the Labyrinth.

"There is no truth to that rumor, then?"

"Ah, there, Jeremy, we run into complications. Truth and lies and guesses are so entangled in what passes for the satyr's mind that I doubt he could give us a straight accounting if he tried. Ages of debauchery, of celebration without thought, have warped his—"

"I see. I believe I understand. We can't afford to deny the possibility that the Face of Zeus is really there."

"I think that's it." And Alex heaved a sigh of relief.

When the recent developments involving Corycus had been explained to him, Apollo reiterated, "I think the people of that island might rise to overthrow this usurper Perses, and support a decent human ruler, if you could find a way to offer them such a choice."

"Many people would find it hard to believe that whatever happens in the lives of a few mere mortals, on one small island, could matter much to Apollo."

"It could matter to Jeremy Redthorn."

"I'm glad to hear that."

"And Apollo, at least in my avatar, is very reluctant to see Hades increase his power."

When the chariot and the leopards arrived, Alex and Ariadne left the Far-Worker in his temple and went out to meet Silenus, who lingered in the vicinity long enough to turn the reins over to Alex.

And with her first ride in the chariot of Dionysus, Ariadne lost the last trace of any longing for the Prince of Pirates. Beside her now was not only a god, but, and this was foremost in her thoughts, the man whom she had once thought to embrace in the person of Theseus. She took his strong arm in both her hands, and he turned his head to smile at her.

"Princess Ariadne." It was his human nature rather than divinity that gave him the strength to say the next few words. "I love you."

For a long moment she did not respond. Then she said, "Once— how long ago it seems!—once I dared to ask my . . ." She paused, and started over. "I prayed and sacrificed to great Zeus, to send me the man who above all men I could love, and who would love me, and marry me."

"And what happened?" Alex prompted when she fell silent.

"I thought I had found that man in Theseus, but I was wrong. Terribly wrong."

"Do you want to tell me more about it?"

"No. Except that there was a moment—only a few hours ago, how strange!—when I came near throwing myself into the sea."

"My dear—!"

"But I could not see drowning as an improvement, and that impulse did not last long."

"Let it never come near you again."

Whether he himself or the princess was the first to raise the subject of marriage, Alex could not afterward remember. Spontaneously the princess admitted (or perhaps it was more of a complaint) that she and Theseus had never gone through any kind of ceremony.

"Princess Ariadne. Will you be my wife?" Alex drew a deep breath. Somehow the moment he had thought might require all of his strength was past before he had time to dread it.

"I will," said the princess at once. Then her eyes grew wide. "Oh, I will, I will!" After a moment she added in a small voice, "At this point, were I at home, and had I just become engaged to some prince from a neighboring kingdom, there would be required official testimony on the subject of my virginity."

"When the world knows that the Lord Dionysus has proposed marriage, I believe it will also know that the time is long past for any such tests or testimony."

Her eyes were miracles of joy, of promise. "I will gladly do whatever my Lord Dionysus asks of me. But I am only a mortal woman."

"My Ariadne. Mortal or not, you are the only one that I have ever asked to marry me." And the immortal memory of Dionysus assured Alex that it was so.

And Alex took Ariadne in his arms and kissed her tenderly.

It was obvious, even without discussion, that any more formal ceremony was going to have to be postponed indefinitely, until certain great obstacles to true happiness should have been removed. But it would not be forgotten, and they could only hope that the delay would not be great. "One must make an effort to do these things properly," said the god who had fallen in love. But Alex could feel that Dionysus could never make more than a half-hearted effort at propriety.

The god's memory held numerous examples of marriage between gods and mortals. The rate of success, both in terms of happiness and progeny, had been as varied as it was in unmixed human unions. Children born to such mixed unions were not gods—no Faces issued from their heads when they died. Nor did their identities survive death, in any form that could be passed on—but as humans they tended to be extraordinary in ways that were unpredictable, Asterion being a rather extreme example. Alex supposed it would be surprising if they were not.

———

Ariadne protested the presence of the sprites and satyrs, who had quickly returned to close attendance on their lord, as soon as the Far-Worker's overpowering presence had been removed. "They make me feel faint."

"Sometimes they have a similar effect on me," sighed Alex. "I will see to it that they stay farther away." And with a gesture Dionysus banished his escort to a greater distance. In his left ear he could still hear them, but by now he knew from experience that not even he could banish them entirely.

One thing this avatar of Dionysus knew that he would never do with Ariadne—and that was to subject her to, or induce her to take part in, one of the rawer episodes of madness that now and then afflicted him, and especially afflicted his followers.

With vague distaste Alex recalled his orgy of sex on the Isle of Refuge, and the later one of blood and death aboard the pirate ship.

"Some call you the god of madness. Frenzy. Ecstasy." The young woman sounded frightened and fascinated at the same time.

"Many do. And I call you my lady—my princess. Ariadne, I think that as long as you are with me, my madness will be only of the most welcome and creative kind."

"My love and my lord!"

29

THE YOUNG SOLDIER Sarpedon was asleep in his bunk, dreaming that he had to perform some incomprehensible military exercise under the Butcher's eye. General Scamander was glaring at him, shouting orders in some language that Sarpedon had never heard before, and in another moment the general's temper was going to snap, and he was going to order some horrible punishment, worse than flogging.

In the dream the executioner had Sarpedon in his grasp, but at the last moment whipped off his hood, revealing a great bull's head on a tall man's broad-shouldered body. And suddenly all the military trappings of the dream were gone, as was the dread scaffold of punishment.

"My name is Asterion," said the bull's mouth in an odd voice. "Seek in the Labyrinth if you would find a friend."

A moment after that, Sarpedon woke up gasping, relieved beyond measure to find himself amid the sights and smells and sounds of the familiar barracks, much as he had come to dislike the place in waking life. And as for the Minotaur . . . he had never dreamt or imagined a monster yet as terrible as the Butcher could be in his wrath.

He had had the same dream, or one very like it, for several nights in a row. He could no longer try to convince himself that it was only an accident.

After another morning of waking life, having worked his way through routine duties, including a weekly inspection that required polishing of weapons and uniform metal, Sarpedon was off duty for the next half-day. He changed into a civilian tunic and made ready to set out as if for an ordinary foray into town.

Lurid rumors continued to circulate in the barracks, concerning the aborted ceremony of the Tribute, and what had really happened in the Labyrinth on that occasion. Sarpedon, as one of those who had actually been there when Theseus got away and their comrade Alex disappeared, told the truth as he had seen it. But soldiers, like people everywhere, tended to believe what they wanted to believe.

As he left the palace complex behind, he felt the ground quiver faintly beneath his feet. Sometimes strange minor tremors passed underfoot, and the breeze brought a sulphuric smell. Now and then in the air there hung a sound so deep it might have been the whole earth groaning. Other parts of the island were said to be shuddering with a volcanic oozing, in which Cerberus, dread three-headed guardian of the nether regions, was said to be crafting a new opening to the Underworld, somewhere in the mountains. No one on the island had ever seen Cerberus, but almost everyone claimed to know someone who had done so recently.

Sarpedon looked back over his shoulder. A wisp of cloud was indeed hanging over the high country, wisps of ashes in the air that city-dwellers breathed.

There was griping in the barracks, but then there was always griping. Sarpedon wondered how many of the others were nursing ideas as rebellious as his own. So far as he knew, none of those thoughts had yet broken out into barracks conversation, even among close friends. Units had recently been reorganized, people shifted around. There were strangers everywhere, and probably informers were among them.

One thing the men of the guard did talk about was the increasing presence on the island of mercenary troops.

"Who're they going to fight? Not a hell of a lot of doubt about that. The plan has to be to use them against us. The king must think we're unreliable."

"If the king's bringing in people like that, he already *knows* he doesn't want to trust us."

The official announcement from the palace had said that new mercenary troops were being imported, as a precaution against a threatened invasion, and against terrorism by unspecified foreign troublemakers.

The mercenary units were some which had a bad reputation, even among their kind.

On the day of the aborted ceremony, when Alex had run after Theseus, Sarpedon had followed Alex for a short distance into the Maze. But as soon as Sarpedon had lost sight of the man he was chasing, he stopped and turned back in fear of getting lost.

For a few hours, he had nursed hopes that some kind of coup was in progress, that a glorious conclusion of the day would see the usurper deposed, and, ideally, one of the princesses on the throne. Maybe their father hadn't been the greatest king who'd ever ruled anywhere. But he'd been a hell of a lot better than his replacement.

But then Sarpedon, along with many others, had been plunged into gloom when it very quickly became obvious that nothing remotely resembling a coup was taking place. And when you thought about it, it was hard to see any way that could have happened. A Palace Guard might manage to depose a king, especially an unpopular one, but how could any combination of mere humans overthrow a god? At the last minute, old Minos had tried to enlist some divine help to save his throne, but the best he'd been able to come up with was Dionysus, in an avatar who looked almost dead when he arrived—such were the facts, as Sarpedon had heard them, from one of the few people who'd actually been present in the great hall on that momentous night. You could hardly do better than recruiting Dionysus if your objective was to have a party, but winning a civil war against the God of Destruction was quite a different proposition.

When a quick roll call was taken, shortly after the debacle of the Tribute, and Alex still didn't show up, Sarpedon had been eighty percent convinced that his friend was dead.

But now he wasn't at all sure. Day after day had passed, with no announcement made of the discovery of any of the escapees, living or dead. Shiva made an appearance now and then, in the palace or flying over the city, often enough to squelch any germinating hope that he was gone for good. As for the Princess Ariadne, the official story put out soon after the event was that she had been kidnapped—again "troublemakers" and foreign agents were to blame.

———

When questioned by officers on the very afternoon of the great escape, and in several sessions after that, Sarpedon had stoutly denied having caught sight of Alex doing anything out of the ordinary on that day, or anything disloyal at any time. Nor had Sarpedon heard or seen anything else that might help in the search for the fugitives now.

He could tell his questioners truthfully, and with impressive conviction in his voice, that he had been as much surprised by that day's events as anyone else.

So far he had managed to divert suspicion from himself.

"I don't know what happened to Alex. Maybe he was kidnapped, like the princess, and Daedalus."

But the officers and Shivan priests who did the questioning were not so easily put off. They had fastened on the fact that Sarpedon and Alex were known to be friends. "I understand you went to town together fairly often?"

"Once in a while, sir."

"Did his girlfriend live in town?"

"I don't know that he had any particular girl, sir. When he had some money he went to the houses, just like most of us."

"Which house did he prefer? The one where men lie with each other, or with boys?"

"No sir, not that I ever noticed. Just the regular ones."

"The one for those who enjoy being beaten with whips?"

Sarpedon hadn't heard of any such establishment in Kandak, and had serious doubts that one existed. But he wasn't going to debate the point. "No sir."

They would stick with one line of questioning for a while, then switch abruptly to another, as if they expected to shatter his whole structure of lies by confusing him. Or maybe they were just doing it for practice.

"Maybe his girlfriend worked in the palace?"

"Sir, I don't know that he had any particular—"

"Tell me what you know about a slave-girl named Clara, personal attendant of the Princess Ariadne."

No official announcement had ever listed all the missing. But by now, everyone knew the names, and Clara's was on the list. "I've seen her around the palace. Everyone's seen her. Before the day when—"

"Ever speak to her?"

"No sir, not that I can remember—no sir."

"Take her to bed?"

"I—no sir."

"What about your good friend Alex the Half-Nameless? How close was he with Clara?"

"As far as I know, sir, no closer than I am. Was. Knew her by sight, and that was all. Never said anything to me about her. I can't remember ever seeing them together."

"Who else was a particular friend of Clara's?"

"Sir, I can't remember anyone. As I say, I hardly knew—"
"One of the men in your barracks, maybe?"

———

The interrogation sessions tended to run in a pattern. Eventually, after going over and over the same territory until Sarpedon thought he would go mad, they had told him to return to duty.

"Keep thinking about it, soldier. Maybe something will come to you. Wait, don't be in such a hurry to leave. Before you do, let's go over again what happened on the day of the insurrection, and the kidnapping."

———

And of course there still hadn't really been anything like insurrection on Corycus. The way things were going, though, it might not take much to start one. You could smell it in the air.

Sarpedon thought there would be no use trying to get aboard a ship and leave the island altogether—everyone knew the harbor was being closely watched. Maybe if you had a friend with a ship, or even a small boat, departing from somewhere else along the coast could be managed readily enough. But Sarpedon was out of luck in that regard.

Having made up his mind as to what he was going to do, he had gone into town, alone, taking care not to deviate from what he commonly did on his day off—except that today he was wondering if some agent of the Butcher's was following him. Once, only once, he looked back, casually, and could see no one.

———

For several blocks after leaving the palace complex he stayed on the route he regularly took on the way to his usual taverns and houses. But on reaching a certain point he suddenly turned aside, careful to maintain the same steady walking pace. He was now headed straight for one of the entrances to the Labyrinth, that as he remembered always stood open.

The few passersby seemed to be paying him no attention, and he ignored them as well. The opening ahead, drawing nearer with every stride, looked in fact quite ordinary, like an archway in the outer wall of the dwelling of any solid citizen. And it was still unblocked and unguarded. Evidently Shiva and his pet king had decided that if disaffected elements of the population wanted to lose themselves in the Labyrinth, they were welcome to it. There was nothing easier than to plunge inside . . . legend had it that once you got deep into the Labyrinth, there were fountains everywhere. You might be hunted down and eaten by the Minotaur, but you weren't going to die of thirst.

My name is Asterion. Seek in the Labyrinth if you would find a friend.

———

Shiva, getting a report from some creature of the Underworld, now knew with certainty that his informant had been wrong about the location of the Face of Dionysus. There could no longer be any doubt that a man who was not Shiva's preferred candidate had picked up the essence of the Twice-Born somewhere and put it on.

Shiva looked forward to imposing a punishment on Creon, for allowing himself to fall victim to this deception. More than likely it was all a part of the great plot against Shiva. He could not decide whether to have Creon arrested at once, and interrogate him under torture, or wait a little longer, until the details of the plot became clearer, and he could be certain of everyone involved.

Another chronic, major concern was the Face of Zeus. Was it really possible that the most valuable and powerful object in the universe was lying about somewhere, waiting for any human who stumbled on it to pick it up? Creon had suggested that too; more false information, very likely.

If it was indeed hidden in the Maze, who had put it there, and when? Certainly it hadn't been Zeus himself—even the most powerful deity in the universe could not remove his own Face from his head, and set it aside somewhere. Unless he did so in the accidental way that the previous avatar of Dionysus had accomplished exactly that feat: by crawling into a hole somewhere and dying.

Suppose some other god had come into possession of the Thunderer's Face—in that case, of course, the finder would be unable to put it on himself, and might well seek a hiding place. Or find a human ally to give it to. But, to what human being would this hypothetical deity be willing to entrust a power so much greater than his own?

———

There are certain regions within the Labyrinth that I, Asterion, consider unlikely ever to be penetrated by even the best-organized searchers from outside. I had taken myself to one of these zones in search of rest, but even there, I no longer felt entirely secure. When Shiva came looking for me, he would come by air, and at an altitude from which whole sections of the Maze would be simultaneously exposed to his penetrating gaze; and probably he would be able to muster additional powers that I had not yet even imagined. Dreams had shown me all too clearly that if the Destroyer made a determined effort to locate me, he would succeed.

Still, I needed sleep. It afforded me a kind of rest, even though I could not afford to be idle in my dreams. There was now a task before me that I feared and disliked, but yet I felt compelled to undertake it. It was now required that I try to spy on Hades himself.

Oddly enough I thought it helped my approach to Hades when I deliberately thought of myself as the Minotaur. That slavering monster was daring enough to try to interfere with the dreams even of a god like Hades.

Before I began to play that game, I viewed the feat as comparable to that of trying to find and enter the dreams of Zeus himself—which was one exploit the Minotaur had never quite managed to nerve himself to attempt.

Ever since I had been old enough to think at all, I had known an inner conviction, doubtless based on little more than a few hints and clues received in earliest childhood, that made me certain that Zeus was, or had been, my true father.

All the evidence indicated that Minos, my stepfather, had been a moral and reasonable man—as kings go. In contrast, my true father, the most powerful being in the universe, was generally acknowledged to be quite a lecherous monster, and traditionally his offspring over the centuries were legion.

There was every reason to believe that Ariadne shared the same parentage, and was indeed my full, true sister.

Though one might observe that there is not much family resemblance between my sister and myself.

The affair of Zeus with the mortal queen of Corycus had ended only with her death in childbirth.

Sometimes, as I grew older, I wondered whether the Thunderer had ever been able to feel grief. There were days when I wanted to meet him, face to Face, and demand from him an answer to that question. But lately I had grown uncertain of his very existence. Somewhere, of course, his Face must still exist; but quite possibly no one was wearing it.

But my latest dreams (besides allowing me to give Sarpedon directions to find me) had led me to an intriguing discovery, that I thought might be connected with Zeus. Actually finding him was not my immediate goal. My objective was much more modest and practical. What I needed was a messenger, to convey a certain item of urgent news unambiguously, and in waking life.

───────

And at last I succeeded in intruding upon one of the visions that marked the slumber of the Dark God, Hades.

But very quickly my psychic surroundings grew so terrible that I was forced to withdraw, unable to endure that overwhelming presence even for a few minutes. The dream that engulfed me, defying all my efforts to control it, was almost sightless, filled with heat and the smell of sulphur, as well as with fear and discontent. And almost the only sounds in it were what seemed to be the sobs and screams of human torment.

───────

When I awoke, I saw a human figure standing at a little distance, and I feared for a moment that my nightmare had somehow trapped me.

But when I sat up, and my mind cleared, I discovered to my relief that the truth was much simpler: I once more had a human companion. He stood before me a weaponless, weary, bedraggled youth, still wearing the uniform of the Palace Guard.

His voice was tired, and not so much afraid as filled with resignation. "Lord Asterion? My name is Sarpedon."

Slowly I got to my feet. "Yes, I see. I recognize you now."

"I am glad to hear that . . . sir." The young man took a deep breath and drew himself up. "Yesterday I deserted from the barracks. Last night I slept in the Labyrinth. I've had strange dreams, last night and before . . ."

I nodded. "And I have visited you in some of them. Otherwise you could not have found your way in here to me."

Gradually my visitor allowed himself to relax, and told me his story in some detail.

I in turn was grateful for any friendly human presence, and after we had talked for a while, I tried to relieve myself of my own most recent dream by telling it aloud. "I dreamt I stood on the brink of a black and empty nothingness. And what made it unendurable, was the fact that it was dark and empty by its own deliberate will."

The dreams of Hades, if one could call those sickly nightmares dreams, were profitless for an intruder, and I suspected they could be deadly.

"But enough about nightmares," I told my new ally. "I have good news for you as well."

The last time I had tried to penetrate the dreams of Dionysus, a surprise awaited me. I found myself in close contact with the mind of the young man I had known only as Alex; and what the mind of that youth had now become astonished me.

I was vastly cheered to discover that Alex, who was certainly no ally of Shiva, had now put on the Face of Dionysus. The fledgling immortal now stood in mortal danger, but at least Alex seemed to be aware of the fact.

And I came upon hints, obscure indications, that there was, after all, something of overwhelming importance in the Maze—in or near the center, where Daedalus had spent his fruitless months in search of something he could understand well enough to be able to investigate.

"I can try to communicate this discovery to Alex/Dionysus at a distance, in a dream. But we cannot wait to see if this attempt at communication succeeds. I badly need a messenger."

30

IT WAS JUST sunset when the magic chariot of Dionysus, drawn by twin panthers through the high wind above the sea, arrived on Corycus. Nestor was in the chariot with the god, and so was Ariadne, who throughout most of the long flight had been clinging to her lover. The mercenary captain had stood most of the time with his eyes closed, keeping a white-knuckled grip on the chariot rail; meanwhile Ariadne seemed less affected by the experience of the ride. As long as Alex's arm was around her, and her eyes fixed on his, speed and altitude appeared not to bother her at all.

Alex had timed the flight from Dia so as much of it as possible took place in daylight, the vast memory of Dionysus containing evidence that the considerable dangers would thus be minimized. The influence of Hades was diminished when the sun itself, the Eye of Apollo, dominated the sky.

With the island only a thousand feet or so beneath them, Alex directed the leopards to land in some place where he was not likely to be forced into an immediate confrontation with his chief enemy. He left it up to Silenus, who as usual was on hand with the rest of the inhuman entourage, to make the final choice: a rocky glen, through which a small stream trickled, high up in the rugged hills that were locally called mountains. No human habitations were in sight, save for the roofs of a small village a quarter of a mile down the slope.

The chariot of Dionysus came down to earth as silently as a falling leaf. Still, a pair of owls, sacred to Athena, flew up in alarm as the chariot came down. It had left a very faintly luminous streak behind it in the dimming sky, which Alex supposed must have been noticed by numbers of people on the ground. He tried to brace himself for a sudden attack by Shiva, but so far the evening remained peaceful.

Nestor hopped out even before the vehicle had quite come to a stop, and stood with hand on his sword-hilt, slowly regaining his composure, and trying to look as if a long flight was only part of the day's work. The two leopards licked their paws and took their ease. Now, on the ground, they might almost have been mistaken for ordinary animals.

Dionysus looked out, frowning. "It seems we were expected," he told his companions in a low voice, and nodded toward a lone figure that had emerged from among some trees to greet them.

Alex gazed, frowning in surprise. "Sarp?"

"Alex?" called Sarpedon, tentatively. There was a pause, while the two old friends looked each other over.

"You look like nothing very bad has happened to you," Alex said after a moment.

"I've been lucky." Sarpedon swallowed. He refrained from saying anything about how Alex looked. "I bring a message to Dionysus from the Lord Asterion. He saw in a dream that your chariot was coming, where and when you were going to land."

Ariadne said, "What my brother sees in his dreams is generally true."

Alex performed introductions. Sarpedon bowed low to the princess, whom he had seen many times before, but never spoken to. He said, "The burden of my urgent message is that Master Daedalus must be brought to the Labyrinth as quickly as possible."

"Daedalus? Why?" the princess wondered.

"I don't know why, my lady. If your brother knows, he thought it wise not to risk the knowledge in my care."

"Perhaps I can find out," Ariadne murmured. "My lord Dionysus, Alex, you must excuse me for a few minutes." Stepping gracefully over the railing of the chariot, she moved a few yards away. There she stood with eyes closed, hands folded before her, as if deep in meditation.

Alex looked at her, then at the leopards and the chariot, then back at her again, undecided. "If that's what Asterion wants, we must try to do it. But I don't want to leave you here while I fetch Daedalus."

"Now that I have come home," said Ariadne, eyes still closed, "I must stay."

"Very well. Sarpedon, old friend."

"Yes?"

"Will you recognize Daedalus, if you see him? Yes, of course you will. Therefore I want to lend you my chariot. You must catch up with the Artisan—he must be still aboard ship en route to Megara—and bring him back here."

"But if he's at sea—can I find him?"

"My helpers will locate him for you. All you need do is speak to him."

Sarpedon, after hearing some further explanation, accepted the task willingly. "I'll rout him out of his snug mainland cottage, if I have to."

"Ask him courteously, at least at first. But convince him that he must come back to Corycus."

"And if he still declines that honor?"

Alex heaved a sigh. "Tell him that at last there is a promise that the secret of the Labyrinth may be solved. Tell him anything you think may help, but bring him here. If all goes well, it shouldn't take you more than a few hours."

The soldier started toward the chariot, then stopped, gesturing helplessly. "Lord Dionysus—Alex—how do I control the leopards?"

Alex thought. "You don't—you won't be able to. They'll locate the Artisan on their own, once I have given them their orders, and bring him back when he's aboard. But they can't talk to him. That's your job."

And in another moment Sarpedon had climbed aboard the chariot and was on his way.

————

Nestor's sufferings during the long flight had been considerably greater than he had allowed to show. Not that either of his fellow passengers had paid him much attention en route; indeed he thought he might have fallen out of the chariot and not been missed.

To occupy his mind, he had speculated privately as to how many human bodies the chariot might be able to accommodate. It seemed that a pair of human passengers, in addition to Alex/Dionysus himself, posed no problem. Nestor thought that the space inside the chariot's enclosing rail had expanded modestly, just enough to give them all comfortable elbow room. And as far as a mere mortal could tell, the leopards betrayed no signs of weariness or strain from coping with the unaccustomed load.

Nestor had also been distracted from his fears by the rowdy chorus of maenads and satyrs, almost always invisible, that kept near-perpetual attendance on the Twice-Born God. Occasionally during the flight Alex had encouraged his sprites and satyrs to manifest themselves quite openly. Traveling airborne as easily as smoke, they went rushing and capering along in a lively torrent beside the chariot, doing their best to entertain the passengers with song and dance. Nestor was grateful for their efforts, though he was unable to enjoy them to the full.

━━━━━━━

Ariadne had already assured Nestor he would be welcome in her homeland, where the faction loyal to the princesses would soon be organizing in an effort to overthrow the usurper. And she also promised him that he would be well paid, when she or her sister, or some ruler sympathetic to their cause, should be restored to power.

And Dionysus had also pledged a substantial reward. "Provided of course that we both survive until this matter has been settled."

"I could ask no more than that, lord. What do you want me to do?"

━━━━━━━

As the sun went down, and night began to well up out of the valleys and creep over the lower foothills, the lights of the city of Kandak were plainly visible from the hills, a thin scattering of orange sparks of hearth fires and wall sconces. Larger fires marked the two great lighthouse fires bracketing the entrance to the harbor from the sea. Also conspicuous, by contrast, was the adjoining patch of absolute, unbroken darkness where the Labyrinth sprawled over its square miles.

The princess, having for the time being learned all she could from her visionary web, emerged again from meditation, looked around at her homeland and asked, "And are we really now in Corycus again? Or is this all another vision?"

"We are here, my love." Alex took a long look around as well. "All that you see is grimly real and solid. I'm afraid I've brought you to a place of greater danger."

"I'm not worried. I have a god to protect me."

"A very new and inexperienced god. And not much of a warrior, as gods go."

The princess murmured something loving, expressing great confidence in his abilities.

"My love," Alex murmured in return, kissing her again.

"My sweet love," she murmured back. "*You* are the one I have been looking for."

Nestor recalled them to their current situation. "Look. People with torches, coming up the hill."

"Someone must have got a good look at us, when we were landing, and spread the word about what they saw."

The torches in the hands of people climbing burned brighter as twilight thickened.

Soon the god and his entourage of divers beings were surrounded, at a little distance, by a small murmuring crowd. The mood seemed to be one of eagerness, only slightly tinged by apprehension. Gradually the curved line, marking the farthest advance of the less timid, was edging closer, and again a little closer still.

Obviously some of the people of Corycus had observed the chariot's landing, and had correctly interpreted it as a welcome sign of divine interference. Some of the braver folk, or those who were more desperate, had started climbing toward the place to see what was happening, but maybe it took them an hour or more to reach the remote spot.

Some had already recognized the princess, for her name was being spoken in hushed tones.

Close on the heels of the first climbers came a steady trickle of others. Humble people, peasants and workers of the island, who saw the princess shortly after her arrival, recognized her at once, and greeted her joyfully.

The torchlit circle of welcomers grew, and thickened, and the happy murmuring grew louder. Alex thought that the village below, or several villages, must have emptied out completely.

As it became obvious how fervently she was being welcomed, and by a great number of people, Ariadne responded to the demonstration with tears of joy, and impulsive gestures.

"Oh Alex! I never realized how much I missed my good Corycan people until now, when I see them around me again. I feel as if I've been away for a year."

"Let's show them we appreciate their attitude," said Alex.

"How shall we do that?"

"Probably a little refreshment is in order." With a minimum of thought and effort the god, making himself relatively inconspicuous, created samples of magic fruit, grapes of a dazzling perfection and incredible taste. These he handed to his betrothed who passed them out to the people who were bold enough to come to get them. Emboldened, the crowd soon lost almost all of its timidity, and was pressing closer.

One of the young Corycans cried, "We thank all the gods, princess, that you have come back! We will burn rich grain and fat meat upon the altars of Dionysus and Apollo!"

"The temples of all the good gods have been destroyed," another onlooker mourned aloud.

A third chimed in. "But the stones of altar and hearth were taken away and hidden, and I know where."

And Alex had a little speech to make. "My friends, my people, you had better go home now, before our gathering here becomes so big and noisy that it draws unwelcome attention."

"According to what the people here are saying, the island is swarming with mercenaries. More have landed even in the few days since we left."

Alex and the princess wanted Nestor to go into the city and scout. Other mercenaries by the hundreds, hired by Perses and his ruthless god, had begun arriving on the island shortly before the great escape. More were still coming in now. So anyone Nestor encountered in the city or in the countryside would almost certainly assume that he was there at the invitation of the new rulers, the supporters of Shiva.

"Find out all you can about the mercenaries," Alex instructed him. "If you can, get some of them to change sides."

Nestor nodded thoughtfully. "I'll see what I can do. I may very well see one or two colleagues who know me fairly well, and I them. Of course it's bad for a soldier's professional standing to get a reputation for changing sides. But that doesn't mean it's never done."

"It would be a big help if you could persuade some of them to do it this time."

Speeding over the sea, in silent obedience to the orders of their divine master, the twin leopards soon located the ship that was carrying Daedalus, and brought Sarpedon in the chariot alongside in the moonlight, wheels spinning gently as it hovered in the air, the chariot's rail just a little higher than the deck.

The crew goggled and yelled in terror, and Daedalus emerged from somewhere below to stare in frank amazement.

On hearing in whose name he was summoned, and for what purpose, the Artisan grumbled, but finally grabbed up his bag with a few small tools, reached up boldly enough to grab the chariot's rail, and swung himself aboard with Sarpedon.

Clara and Icarus remained on deck, wailing their sorrow that he was leaving them.

"Goodbye, husband! I fear I will never see you again!"

"If I'm not back before you reach Megara, tell the king there you are my true wife—Captain Ottho can testify he's married us." Daedalus quickly explained to Sarpedon that he had planned to arrive at his new home in the character of a married man with a family. He wanted his time free to concentrate upon whatever work his new patron might assign him.

Leaning over the chariot rail, cupping his hands to yell, the Artisan had a few last instructions for Clara. "And tell our new master the king that I will be back as soon as possible. Promise him . . ."

"Promise him," suggested Sarpedon, "that he may name his own compensation for your absence—within reason, of course—from Dionysus himself."

The chariot rose higher over the moonlit waves, turned in the air, and gained speed rapidly. Daedalus seemed already to have forgotten wife and child, in the sheer fascination of having a god's odylic chariot at hand for close inspection. He stood upright, gripping the railing, obviously enthralled. "How does it work?"

———

When Daedalus arrived back on Corycus, the time was almost midnight. Some of the local people had gone home, but many were still in attendance on the god and princess. The sight of the returning leopards had a powerful restraining impulse on their tendency to crowd forward.

Alex/Dionysus greeted the Artisan warmly, and said to him, "Since divine Hephaestus is currently not available, you are our next choice for this task, of all the gods and humans we know." A little flattery wouldn't hurt.

Daedalus accepted the flattery absently; his main concern was the job for which he had been summoned. "Princess, it seems to me wonderful that you moved about inside the Labyrinth for years, and yet only now have your powers revealed to you that the Face of Zeus may lie hidden there."

"Not so wonderful. I think, Prince of Artisans, that you may have forgotten how vast the great Maze is. Also, I have never till now thought of trying to find my father's Face."

Now there was a murmur from the remaining crowd as a little girl came forward with a gift of wildflowers. The leopards only yawned benevolently as she passed close in front of them. Dionysus accepted the bouquet gravely, and passed it on to Ariadne.

———

There had been many moments during the past few hours when Alex could hardly resist the impulse to insist on having some time as absolutely alone with his bride-to-be as it was possible to be. But too much was at stake, including Ariadne's safety, for them to be able to shut themselves off from the world.

Alex said to Ariadne, "Our wedding is going to have to wait." Then he added, only half in jest, "I fear that if we were to hold a ceremony now, Shiva and your uncle might insist on being invited."

She emerged from the laborious interpretation of her web-images long enough to kiss him lovingly, perhaps to eat and sleep a little, and hold brief conversation—then she had to plunge back into the effort that haunted and consumed her.

———

Alex considered offering the gathering a hint or two that any effort to overthrow Perses could expect to be blessed with strong support from Apollo himself. But on second thought he decided to save that cheering news for some time when it was really needed. Also he had to assume that whatever was said or done in public now would be known to his enemies in a day or two.

Some in the crowd impulsively pledged themselves to fight for the princess and her sister. They had come armed with pitchforks, sickles, and scythes, to be ready for attack or defense as seemed to be required, and now waved their weapons in the air.

When Ariadne assured them that neither she nor her husband had any personal interest in crowns or thrones, the denial was quite credible: Why should any god be interested in ruling a merely mortal realm? Support for Ariadne's sister grew more vociferous and open. In the estimation of most of the people of Corycus, Princess Phaedra had become the rightful ruler of the island on the death of her father, Minos.

———

Judging by what the welcoming committee had to say, everyone on the island seemed ready to believe that the two younger children born to Pasiphae had been fathered on her by the god Zeus in one of his mysterious manifestations; Pasiphae's affair with Zeus had endured for years, ending only when the birth of their youngest child, Asterion, had resulted in the queen's death.

One of the villagers cried, "Better even the bull-man for a king than what we have now!"

Many of the people would be more comfortable if their human ruler was entirely human.

Nestor said, "In my experience, most folk are of two minds as to whether they want their ruler to be entirely human or not."

Tonight the joyous welcome extended, with growing enthusiasm, to Ariadne's high companion, who was standing back a little so as not to interfere with her reunion with her people. Apparently everyone on the island had long since learned that the earlier Minos, the father (at least by adoption) of Ariadne, had shortly before his death concluded an alliance with the God of Revelry.

The newly returned princess, when it was obvious that everyone wanted her to make a longer speech, said something gracious in return. Once more she explained that she had no personal ambitions for the throne.

"My new husband probably would not want me to assume such a burden." There was a murmur of applause, and faces turned toward Alex, who smiled and did not contradict her.

Then, when it seemed to him that some direct comment was called for, he said, "My dear, you would make a lovely queen. But the memory of Dionysus assures me that gods do not make good kings, as a rule; and he has no wish to try."

Ariadne assured everyone that she fully supported the claim of her older sister, Phaedra, who was really deserving of the crown.

Now certain people, who had close relatives in the military, assured the returned princess that there was still a faction in the army and the navy who would be ready to support her, and even more readily her sister, in a power struggle with her uncle—especially if they believed there would be a good chance of winning. None of the current senior officers, all chosen or vetted by the Butcher, had such an attitude.

Alex and his divine partner both kept hoping that Apollo would show up soon. The Sun-God had pledged his help in the coming battle, but had warned Dionysus not to expect to see him on Corycus immediately.

Ariadne suggested to her bridegroom that one of their first moves should be to find Phaedra, and offer her half-sister protection against the forces of darkness. It would also be necessary to sound her out on her willingness to lead a rebellion against their usurping uncle.

"I don't want to alarm you, dear one. But first we must make sure that she's still alive. She has not the protection of being thought a child of Zeus."

"She will be. Shiva still hopes to be able to use her as a figurehead, if Perses proves unsatisfactory. And Perses would not dare go against the wishes of his god."

"I don't know your sister at all. When I was a soldier, everyone in the barracks wished her well, but we never saw much of her. How do you think she'll respond?"

"We have never been truly close, as some sisters are. Phaedra's usually the quiet one, but I think not easily frightened. I know she loved her father, and that she loves the people of the island. I anticipate that she will be ready to be a queen."

Now there was a bustle among the local people. A messenger coming up from the village had just brought word that Perses the usurper had placed the Princess Phaedra under house arrest. There were rumors that he had ordered her to be killed.

"Then show me to the place where they are holding her."

Ariadne was clinging to his arm. The sprites had given her new garments again, including the simple tunic of a warrior woman that covered her body almost completely. At her belt hung a short sword of mainly symbolic value; Silenus had obtained it somewhere and presented it as a gift.

Now the princess was saying to Dionysus, "I fear no danger when you are with me."

"If only I could tell you truthfully that you need fear none!"

But the princess was already busy with her web.

Alex thought to himself that Theseus might well be on his way back to Corycus also.

"Shiva might very well go to fetch him, if he wants him here to receive the Face as soon as it's removed from my own shattered head."

Also Alex could not keep from wondering what would happen when Ariadne saw that man again. So far, the subject of her previous lover had never come up between them.

31

WHEN DIONYSUS TOOK the leopards' reins again, Ariadne, Daedalus, Sarpedon, and Nestor were aboard the chariot with him. Alex held the vehicle at or near ground level on their swift foray into the city, only going airborne when fences, walls, or the occasional building presented obstacles in the most direct route.

Ariadne repeated her web-spinning search at intervals as they drew closer and closer to the city of Kandak, and the adjoining Maze and palace. Her findings steadily confirmed what Asterion had told Sarpedon—the place they sought lay somewhere near the center of the Labyrinth.

The Artisan's ride in the chariot, and the prospect of being able to come to grips with a supremely challenging problem, freed him from the last traces of shyness in the presence of the god. Daedalus grumbled briefly about the stresses of the flight that he had just endured. But actually he did not seem displeased by his near-kidnapping. He told the princess that in a way he had been sorry when they had left Corycus several days ago, feeling that he was abandoning puzzles unsolved, secrets undiscovered, somewhere in the monstrous Maze.

━━━━━

Princess Ariadne was reluctant to try to use her powers to probe into the affairs of Zeus. Perhaps, she thought, she was afraid to be brought closer to the man who had been wearing that Face when she and Asterion were conceived.

But she dared not ignore the possibility that the overwhelming power of the Thunderer was almost within reach, ready to be taken.

With gods and a king against her, help of that magnitude was desperately needed, to save her own life, and her sister's, and above all the life of the god she had so suddenly come to love.

When Ariadne in secret silence, in the privacy behind her closed eyelids, asked the oracle of her webs to show her the best way to keep the love of Dionysus, she received no answer at all.

This upset her so much that she could not keep from blurting it out to Alex. "What does Dionysus have to say about that?" she concluded.

He took her in his arms and answered immediately. "That only means that there is no way you can lose my love. As long as my spirit lives, it will be yours."

The chariot had covered a mile or more before either of them was ready to speak again. Then Alex whispered in her ear, so close that the other passengers could not hear. "There is something we should decide now, my love. If we do discover the Face of Zeus, who is going to put it on?"

And she whispered back, "There is at least one man with us who I think can be trusted."

Daedalus, when he was offered the chance, declined—Alex was not surprised, having already heard the Artisan express his reluctance ever to be a god.

Ariadne knew the moment might come when she herself would have to put on the Thunderer's Face, if that should prove to be the only way to deprive the enemy of its powers. She feared such a transformation would cost her the love of Alex/Dionysus—but she would make that sacrifice, if necessary to save his life. Again she and Dionysus conversed in low whispers.

The princess said, "Perhaps, if and when Daedalus is confronted with the reality, he will change his mind."

"Perhaps. In any case, we must find the Face before any of us can put it on."

Meanwhile, Alex continued to wonder what had become of Shiva. He kept turning his head, searching the night sky with Dionysian vision. What was distracting the Destroyer, keeping him occupied with other matters? Could he possibly be waiting simply until he had all of his chief enemies in one place, subject to one blast of destruction?

———————

A journey that would have taken many hours of steady travel by wagon or cameloid, from the high hills to near the center of the Labyrinth, was accomplished in less than half an hour. The time could have been much less had Alex not stopped several times to observe conditions, and once to drop off Nestor in a deserted alley near the waterfront, where he assumed that when daylight came he would find it easy to mingle with imported mercenaries.

The observations en route revealed evidence of military repression in several portions of the island. It seemed that numbers of people had been arrested. Alex saw bodies hanging at a crossroads; the dead wore placards accusing them of treason to the great god Shiva. If anything like a rebellion had actually been attempted, so far it was evidently going badly for the rebels.

When at last the chariot began to skim low over the Maze's twisting walls and narrow passages, Ariadne kept a sharp eye open for her brother. But she saw nothing of Asterion before they began to descend, guided by her private visions, to land near the center of the Labyrinth.

They found a squad of soldiers present, men of the Palace Guard gathered nervously in torchlight, who, after a moment's shocked retreat, came forward again to unanimously welcome the princess and pledge her their loyalty. The presence of Sarpedon, whom they all knew, helped put the men at ease. Some of them recognized Alex, despite his apotheosis, and he propped one foot up on the chariot rail and made them a little speech.

"When I joined the Guard, my friends, I remember the recruiter told me I had a great future ahead of me. Well . . ." With a gesture he indicated the chariot, and the princess at his side. After a moment's silence, the men burst into a roar of laughter.

Disembarking from the chariot, leaving it waiting in the space that had been cleared for Shiva's sacrifice, Alex and Daedalus advanced on foot under the guidance of the princess, with most of the squad of soldiers following.

The time was now a little after midnight, and Dionysus called upon his invisible entourage to provide some light. Bright flames that gave no heat were soon dancing erratically across the pavement and along the enclosing walls.

Ariadne's web-spinning vision brought her party closer and closer to the spot she sought.

It was on a lower level, almost below the central space where Shiva's stage of sacrifice had been erected, certainly one of the most-traveled sections of the Labyrinth. And at first glance there seemed nothing to distinguish this spot from any other, though the eye of Dionysus, when he looked at it steadily, noted certain subtle peculiarities.

The soldiers were set to digging, moving earth. Busy hands were excavating a cavity that had been filled with rubble, deeply saucer-shaped and perhaps twelve feet across.

As the underlying basin of solid rock was cleared, gradually a strange configuration was revealed.

Getting his first good look at the mystery, Daedalus said nothing for what seemed, to his nervous companions, a long time indeed.

Curtly he dispatched one of the squad of loyal soldiers to his old quarters to look for a certain bag of small tools, telling the man where he thought it could be found. Everything he'd left behind had been ransacked and scattered by the new king's agents, in a fruitless search for clues to where he might have fled, but his small tools would have been meaningless to those angry searchers, and though they had been scattered most of them were still there.

Then, gesturing at the problem before them, the Artisan invited comment by his associates. "How would you describe this?"

The center of the revealed pit was a round concavity about two yards in diameter, a series of concentric rings, like the design on an archer's target, with the innermost circle the lowest. At the very center was what seemed obviously a door, a circular panel no more than about two feet wide, set in the lowest spot of the floor. A single massive hinge was visible, as was a handle of bronze with which to lift it open.

"The door must swing up, not down," said Alex, stating the obvious.

"Of course," the princess agreed. "Look at the hinge."

"But the lock keeps it from opening," the god observed.

Daedalus gave him a look that was far from worshipful. "To prevent a door from opening is generally what the designer has in mind when he creates a lock."

The solid rock near the hinge had been carved with the lightning-symbol that was sometimes used to represent Zeus.

Looking over the door and its intricate lock, Alex's left eye, armed with the vision of Dionysus, showed him some meaningless color variations, but nothing special that he could interpret in any useful way.

But Ariadne could see more. Now, standing near the locked door, she reported a vision of a thread of her imaginary web-stuff, weaving its way through the intricacies of the lock.

She frowned, squeezing her eyes more tightly shut. "It is as if the thread were attached to some invisible, impalpable needle. And as soon as it has been pulled all the way through, the trapdoor swings up and open . . . I can see no more beyond that."

And of course the door in the real world remained solidly closed and locked.

Somewhere under the earth, quite nearby, a murmur of unseen water could be heard. To the Artisan it was obvious that the nearby streams must be channeled past this spot in conduits, or even wholly contained in round copper pipes, as if here, over a kind of fissure in the earth, they might otherwise be in danger of plunging all the way to the Underworld, never to be seen again by mortal eyes.

Daedalus muttered to himself, "And of course there may well be—there probably is—more to the trick than appears on the surface."

To Alex, what appeared on the surface certainly seemed challenging enough.

The lightning-symbol of Zeus was not the only carving in the rock. Around the circular rim of the broad depression ran a lengthy inscription. The seven lines of symbols, each seemingly in a different tongue, reminded Alex of the words carved in the wall of the ruined temple on the Isle of Refuge.

When he looked at these letters through the eye of Dionysus, he could read what amounted to the same verse seven times. Alex recited:

" 'Who would hold in his hand what lies below
Must subtly plan and gently go.
The key required is a supple strand
One might think only a thread of sand—'

"—and there it breaks off."

The Artisan nodded slowly. "Then the inscription confirms the princess's vision. To solve this puzzle we must thread a string, or length of fine yarn, or some equivalent, all the way through the shell. That is the only kind of key that is meant to fit this lock."

"And I doubt that even you can make a thread out of loose sand, or a key either."

"So it would seem. But let me think about it for a bit."

━━━━━━━━━

Dionysus was the first to admit that cleverness in problem-solving was not his own strong point. It might be within his power to transform the vault and all that it contained into a mass of living growth—but he feared that would blur and probably destroy whatever secrets it might now contain.

His residence within the Labyrinth had allowed him to begin to appreciate its strangeness. Therefore he was not surprised that a marvel like this locked door had lain almost under his feet for several months, without his ever suspecting its existence.

"We can try digging down here beside the door," Sarpedon suggested tentatively.

Bigger tools were soon brought from the Artisan's old workshop. But digging in the hard and solid rock was going to be difficult at best. And the very first attempt along that line ended in frightening failure.

Daedalus himself tried first, hitting the shell-like structure with a sharp steel chisel, driven by a hammer of moderate weight. The chisel slipped away, and sudden tremors went coursing through all the surrounding earth.

Someone let out an involuntary cry, and clutched the rough stones of a shortened wall for support. But the wall was swaying noticeably too.

"Hold up, no more of that!"

The lock itself was not even scratched; the unknown material from which it had been made was extremely hard and tough.

By now one of the loyal soldiers had brought the Artisan his bag of small tools, or such of them as could be found, and he tried one of them against the mechanism, and then another. But this preliminary poking and probing accomplished nothing either.

"The entry passage, where our key of sand must enter, is no thicker than a baby's finger, and intricately curved."

Daedalus found it simply too hard to see clearly, to get a good look at the problem. "I must have some air to breathe in here, and room to turn around. And give me some light!"

The Artisan ordered the low overhead to be broken away, opening the tunnel-like passage to the plaza above it. The soldiers set to energetically, fracturing ancient stonework and tossing away the fragments. *If anyone takes notice of our noise,* thought Alex, *well, let them.* Dionysus feared no opponent except Shiva or some other malignant god— and he expected, fatalistically, that the ones he truly feared would come when they were ready, noise or not.

A couple of the upper walls in the immediate vicinity were also knocked down, and the ivy and laurel growing on them cleared away. The loyal guardsmen, eager to serve the princesses, broke and slashed and heaved with a good will. The moon, almost full, shone down on the secret door from the western sky, an hour or so after midnight.

Now, with steadier, better light available, the mysterious encircling inscriptions became a more insistent presence.

Now the Artisan gave the impression of settling in comfortably, to do a job.

"We must hurry!" the princess burst out impulsively.

Such urgings made no impression on him. "Did you ever see a lock like that? I've never seen one in my life before." Coming from Daedalus, that was an impressive statement indeed.

Now it could be clearly seen that the key part of the puzzle was shaped like a shell of the many-chambered nautilus, or some very similar seashell. It might have been a real shell of some obviously mutant creature, heavily bioengineered in ages past.

No one could forget that a single hammer-blow, directly on the lock, had provoked a serious shaking of the earth beneath them.

"Open it by gentle means, I pray you, Daedalus!"

"It seems I must use subtle means, or none at all." And Daedalus growled at his would-be helpers to stop standing in his light, keep quiet, and let him work.

Transparent forms came whispering in the air, and then Silenus took solid shape, as real as a cameloid and almost as odorous as a goat. Sometimes Alex thought it would be an excellent idea to rid himself of Silenus permanently, but such Dionysan memories as were readily available offered no encouragement for such a hope. The satyr murmured a warning that the Princess Phaedra had just been placed under house arrest, confined to her apartment in the palace.

Leaving Daedalus to begin his task, with Sarpedon and the squad of loyal soldiers as protection, Alex set out with Ariadne to rescue her sister.

At first he hesitated. "You might be safer if I left you here—"

"But nowhere will be safe until we win. Come, and I will find my sister." And once more the princess assumed the role of guide, deviating from the marked route to take an even shorter pathway to the right side of the palace.

Alex was also quite familiar with the interior of the palace, having pulled interior guard duty many times within that rambling structure. Certainly he could find his way without difficulty to the private quarters of the princesses, though he had never actually been inside those rooms.

Now when he approached and entered those corridors and rooms, exerting his power to clear a path, they underwent a transformation similar to that which had happened aboard the pirate ship, when the powers of Dionysus had it in their grip. Around the advancing god, stone columns sprouted branches and green leaves. What had been an iron grillwork, recently installed, had become a screen of gentle branches, easily brushed aside.

Some of the soldiers and servants here greeted Dionysus as their savior, while others fled in terror. Alex could hear one of the mercenaries cry out, "No one's paying me enough to battle a god. Let them fight it out among themselves."

32

PHAEDRA STARTED UP in wonder when Dionysus suddenly appeared at the door of her apartment. Joyfully she recognized Ariadne at the god's side. "Sister, is it you? Thank all the gods!"

"Not all of them are against us, Phaedra. You are free, for the time being at least." The two young women fell into each other's arms.

"Praise be to the good gods!" Phaedra cried.

"I promise I will offer a worthy sacrifice," her sister said. "To one of them, at least." She looked over her shoulder toward Alex, who had withdrawn a few paces and was keeping watch.

The older sister said, "My life was about to be sacrificed for nothing, and I thank you for returning it to me."

"You are entirely welcome. Now we must be on our way."

"Where?"

"Back into the Labyrinth. I have much to tell you as we walk, and much I want to hear from you as well."

Dionysus had transported Nestor into the city in the chariot, and dropped him off in an alley near the waterfront, where it seemed likely he would soon be able to make contact with some of the mercenaries imported by King Perses.

Nestor found this chariot ride mercifully much shorter than the previous one. It also helped that the trip was conducted over land, practically at ground level. Observing the countryside as well as he could by night, Nestor saw that the state of roads and fences showed that it was, or recently had been, a prosperous land—even if the prosperity had been founded, over generations, on tribute and taxes extracted from other kingdoms on the shores of the Great Sea, mostly by the powerful Corycan navy. What he could see of the land had the lush, innocent look of a country that had forgotten, if it had ever known, what it was to be invaded and despoiled.

Well, if civil war erupted here, as now seemed practically inevitable, there were plenty of lessons in horror soon to be taught.

───────

Nestor's biggest personal worry at the moment was that among the villagers welcoming the returning princess might have been one or more secret supporters of Shiva and Perses. That would mean his own arrival on the island would soon be reported, and much increased the odds that as soon as he showed his face in the city he was going to be arrested.

The locals had warned him that a curfew had been declared in Kandak, and though he arrived a little after midnight, he was forced to lie low until sunup. At least this enabled him to get a few hours' sleep.

───────

Once the sky brightened with morning, and the streets began to be busy again, Nestor emerged from hiding and bought some fresh melon and fried cakes from a vendor. The man seemed surprised that this hard-looking foreigner paid without dispute. He was willing enough to vent his displeasure with foreign mercenaries in general—present company of course excepted—but he could provide little in the way of specific information.

Munching a fried cake, Nestor strolled around, getting his bearings. It would be an interesting city to return to someday, as a man of peace.

He walked with a touch of arrogance, nothing furtive in his manner. And he saw, here and there on the streets and in the markets, other men with the air of self-confident strangers. Some of these were simply merchants and sailors, as might be expected in any busy seaport; but some had a definitely military look.

Nestor sat for a while on the quay, chewing a wad of the leaf favored by many seafaring men, and at intervals thoughtfully spitting the yellow juice, observing the traffic in the harbor. Only those people attempting to board ships were being stopped and questioned. Among the many vessels visible, he was able to spot a familiar ship or two, belonging to colleagues, with some of whom he was on good terms.

An hour or two after sunrise, on one of the streets adjacent to the waterfront, Nestor recognized one or two of the men he saw on shore as colleagues with whom he'd had dealings in the past.

He had parted with one of these on particularly good terms, and he chose this one to approach now.

"Hello, Rafe."

The man turned and looked at him in mild surprise. "Nestor. I see Perses is really working at this business of beefing up his army."

What more natural than that they'd turn almost automatically into a tavern to share a drink and exchange ideas about their new jobs. It was a little early in the day for serious drinking, but Rafe said he'd discovered yesterday that the beer in this establishment was not too bad.

"Glad you came to Corycus?" Nestor inquired cheerfully.

The other shrugged. "It's a job. What about you?"

Nestor naturally had to remain closemouthed about his own supposed job here on Corycus.

His companion was not surprised. "Can't talk much about it, hey? That's all right."

"What about you? I've not seen anything of this King Perses yet, have you?" Rather leaving the implication that the god Shiva might have hired him.

"Not much, one quick meeting in the palace. But so far he's paid on schedule, and I'm content."

But Rafe was pessimistic about the prospects for success. "When a king must hire foreign troops to keep down his own people, my thought is he's not long for this world."

"Who else is here?"

━━━━━━

On leaving the tavern, half an hour later, the two men went their separate ways.

Nestor thought that if his mission in Kandak went sour, he might want to seek out the Labyrinth as a place of refuge. In there he might have a powerful friend in the person of the Minotaur.

Alex had cautioned him, "Don't be, ah, put off by his appearance."

Thinking about that, Nestor could not repress a slight inward shudder. But he'd certainly run to embrace a monster rather than face Shiva or interrogation in a dungeon.

━━━━━━

Alex/Dionysus had been introduced to Phaedra, and he and the princesses were threading their way back into the Labyrinth, when the sprites, who seemed to live almost always on the verge of one kind of frenzy or another, brought Alex word that Shiva was approaching.

Lord, thy enemy approaches with the speed of the whirlwind, and in terrible wrath. He cries that he will burn to a cinder this body you now wear, and recover thy immortal Face!

"We must see to it that he does nothing of the kind," said Dionysus.

Alex's chief concern now, when a deadly battle with Shiva seemed only minutes away at most, was to arrange some kind of protection for Princess Ariadne, and for her sister. The best expedient currently available seemed to be to send Phaedra and Ariadne into the Maze, to rejoin Daedalus. The Artisan might profit from the younger sister's help once more, and whatever powers were guarding him would protect the princesses as well.

And, even as Ariadne and Phaedra entered the Labyrinth once more, they felt the earth quiver and lurch beneath their feet.

Ariadne, frightened as she was, was still very confident of her own ability to locate some safe hiding place for herself and her sister within the Maze. Finding her way in the predawn darkness was no problem, not with the strands of her web always ready, behind her eyelids, to offer guidance.

Not many days ago, she had guided Theseus through these windings. Then she had imagined that she was escaping to freedom and adventure. The idea that the Face of Zeus might be nearby had never entered her mind—nor had many other things of great importance. Like a child, like a fool, she had believed with all her heart in her great true love, that brave and handsome Theseus was devoted to her, that in his arms she might find everything that she would ever need. . . .

What an idiot she had been! And she was really frightened now.

But it would not do to show that fright. Grabbing her older sister by the hand, she tugged her ever onward, deeper and deeper into the engulfing Labyrinth.

Phaedra had lived near the Maze almost all her life, and yet had seldom set foot in any part of it. Now she found its high, curving walls and constricted spaces frightening and unfamiliar. She hesitated briefly, protesting, "May we not become hopelessly lost?"

"That, at least, will not happen." The younger sister was calmly certain.

"Why not? We've made so many turns already, that for all I can tell, we might round the next corner and find ourselves right back in the grounds of the palace, with Shiva waiting, and Uncle Perses grinning at us."

Ariadne paused in her flight, giving both of them a chance to catch their breath. She decided that it was time at last that she explained a few things to her half-sister. "We haven't talked about this for a long time. But you must remember that I have a talent for finding things—and, which may not be so obvious, for hiding them. So we can be reasonably confident of being on the right track."

"What are we looking for, besides a place of safety? You strongly implied that there was something else."

"Something I never thought to look for, in all the years I traveled through these passageways."

"And that is?"

"It might be dangerous for you to know."

At this point Phaedra was not going to insist. "You were always good at finding, Ariadne. I remember having one or two long talks with you about that. But that you were good at concealment as well—that is something I never noticed."

"Perhaps because I concealed the fact." It was a sober answer, and the half-smile died from Phaedra's face. "Now watch, and I will do my best to conceal us both." Closing her eyes, the younger sister took the older by the hand and led her forward.

"You are walking with your eyes closed," the elder whispered.

Ariadne nodded silently, not breaking the rhythm of her stride.

———

I, Asterion, had been asleep most of the night; in my case, of course, sleeping does not mean I was inactive. I hoped that Sarpedon had accomplished the mission I had entrusted to him; but my dreams had brought me no reassurance on that point, and therefore I could not be sure.

To say that I had devoted that night's precious dream-time to a continued search for Edith would be exaggerating. But while roaming the visionary corridors of night I kept my eyes open for any sign of her, and I nursed hopes. It was perfectly possible that she might still be somewhere nearby. There were certainly convolutions within the Maze that I had never seen. There were whole sections, acres in extent, where for years, for centuries perhaps, no human feet, not even mine, had ever trod. As a child I had often thought that some day, if I could live long enough, I would have memorized every room and space and passage-way. I suppose I might possibly have achieved that end had I made it my life's work. But the world of dreams was an even vaster puzzle, and also more intriguing, and most of my hopes and plans were invested there.

———

Waiting for his enemy to attack, trying to concentrate on matters of life and death, Alex/Dionysus could not banish from his thoughts hopeful visions of the time when he would at last possess his bride. At that moment, he was thinking now, all the sprites and satyrs were going to be shut out, kept at a distance. He did not want them intruding upon that holy time, any more than he would have wanted other humans present.

He doubted it would ever be possible to rid himself of his entourage completely, but at least he could banish them to the middle distance, where he could still hear them singing.

Earlier, when he had tried to discuss these matters with Ariadne, in one of the brief periods when they seemed to be quite alone, she had felt sure enough of her divine companion to gently tease him about it. "Some would think it strange to meet an avatar of Dionysus who is opposed to orgies, or at least chooses to avoid them. How will the world change next?"

"Orgies . . . have their place. Or so says Dionysus, who ought to know all there is to know about the subject. But I am also Alex, who was once half-nameless, and I say that I no longer want anything to do with such events. Certainly not when I am with my love."

And somewhere in the background he had heard a murmur from invisible Silenus: *We will see if the Twice-Born can be content with such a monogamous relationship.*

———

Loyal soldiers patrolling near the center of the Maze raised a sudden alarm: a new version of the monster Cerberus had burst up out of the earth, at some unknown location on the island, and was approaching swiftly.

Alex, mounting into the air in the chariot of Dionysus, soon caught sight of the thing. He could not tell where it had come from, but it seemed to be following the path the sisters had taken into the Maze, tracking one or both of them like a hound on the scent. Driving in pursuit now, urging the leopards to greater speed, he closed in rapidly on Cerberus: big as an elephant and with three fanged heads, stalking and striding on long legs through the Maze, stepping right over walls at places where they were no more than ten feet high.

Cerberus was not a human, nor a god, nor yet a normal beast of any kind. In part, at least, it was no more than a machine; and yet his Dionysian memory assured Alex that earlier versions of the monster had possessed enough of life to render them subject to madness and to frenzy.

Had there been an open volcano nearby, he might have tried to plunge it in. Still, Dionysus had doubts about the beast's susceptibility to that kind of damage, coming from the Underworld as it did. Prolonged sunlight might wear it down, but that was not a helpful hint now in the middle of the night.

Anyway, there was no volcano handy at the moment.

Alex shouted, "After it, you sprites and satyrs! Goad it, tempt it, turn it from its course!"

And his crew of invisible, inhuman helpers soon afflicted the machine with madness. It turned away from the center of the Maze, bursting through walls at random, stopping and retracing its steps, wandering off course.

Meanwhile, Alex had driven his chariot closer and closer to Cerberus. The influence of Dionysus was strong enough to cause its lifeless surface to break out in plant growth. Gradually, whatever power it was that steered and energized the machine was disrupted, weakened, confused into chaos and helplessness.

The thing staggered on its long legs, and at last crashed down in a heap. The stalks and tendrils of new life, springing from its flanks, finding themselves now with motionless ground to grow in, turned to grope toward the sun.

Nestor, as he made his way across the troubled city of Kandak, could feel some of the earthquakes that Hades had now begun to induce, sending minor temblors rumbling clear across the island. Such disturbances were usually interpreted as evidence of the displeasure of some god. The God of the Underworld could bring houses and shops and palaces tumbling down, if that was what he chose to do.

Nestor, having learned from Rafe that his old acquaintance Captain Yilmaz was quartered in this section with his troops, had come looking for him. Yilmaz would not be Nestor's choice for a bosom companion, but his reputation for venality and untrustworthiness was great enough to raise Nestor's hopes of getting him to defect.

Among the beautiful older buildings in the city of Kandak, there stood one in particular that had once served as a gathering place for worshipers of Apollo. It had been repeatedly desecrated, profaned, by the new Minos and the fanatical devotees of Shiva. Maybe some of Hades's earthquakes had begun to crumble it.

While in the process of tracking the captain down, Nestor happened to look in through an open doorway of the former temple of Apollo. High windows filled the interior with cheerful morning sunlight, showing him a band of four or five priests of Shiva, identifiable by their skull-necklaces, who had stripped a young girl of her garments and were stretching her out between them on the floor; the victim seemed to have given up struggling, but she was obviously still alive. A couple of irons were heating in a small fire in a brazier nearby.

Adopting his best sergeant-of-the-watch voice, Nestor called in through the open door, "Anyone know where Captain Yilmaz is? And what do you think you're doing there?"

To these men the sergeant of the watch was apparently not an impressive figure. "Yilmaz is not here, outlander, nor any of his company. I am Creon, high priest of Shiva."

"Whatever you think you're doing, looks to me like you'd better stop." Nestor wasn't sure, when he said the words, if he was only bluffing or not.

Maybe they were just the wrong words to have used to a high priest of Shiva—or maybe there were no words that could have made a difference.

It turned out that Nestor wasn't bluffing, and a savage swordfight quickly ensued. None of the skull-wearers had looked to Nestor like men who really felt at home with weapons in their hands, but he knew better than to trust to first impressions in such matters.

If he had underestimated his opposition to begin with, they had made the same mistake. In the space of a few heartbeats, Nestor had killed one of his opponents, going after the most aggressive first.

Then he cut down a second.

There must have been one more opponent than he had mentally accounted for, because the blow that struck him down came from behind, and was totally unexpected. It allowed him only an instant to feel regret, or anything else, before the world went glimmering away.

Regaining his senses, slowly and painfully, Nestor at first was uncertain whether he was truly dying or only felt that way. His head ached fiercely, and pain in his upper chest told him that he had been stabbed there also—his shirt was wet with blood. His enemies had not bothered either to tie him or to finish him off—that would have been good news, if he could move. As matters actually stood, it didn't seem to be good news at all.

In the middle distance he had a good view of the one who had called himself Creon, and two or three others, gathered within reach of a small fire in the middle of the temple, preparing to get on with the business at which Nestor had interrupted them. The young girl was stretched out on the paved floor while four men each held one of her limbs. It seemed that only a minute or two had passed, and Nestor could not have been unconscious long. Not long enough.

But the proceedings were not going to proceed, not just yet anyway. A tall young man had just appeared in one of the doorways leading to the street, and stood there surveying the scene inside. The newcomer wore a white robe or cape, and nothing else, suggesting that he too was one of Apollo's acolytes. Now he stepped inside, advancing with steady strides.

"Who in all the hells are you?" The priest of Shiva who had just picked up a hot iron from the brazier, causing the girl to scream and faint, now waved it in the newcomer's direction. "You want a taste of this too?"

The tall youth came right up to him, and spoke in a tone of gentle remonstrance. "This is not your house, after all." And he put out his hand and gently caught the wrist of the arm that held the iron, guiding it even closer to his own calm face; and then with a gentle puff of breath, like a man extinguishing a small candle, he cleansed the metal of its fiery heat. The one breath drenched and quenched the orange glow and its radiance, in an icy cold that might have come from the dark side of the moon; even Nestor at the distance where he was lying could feel a faint chill spreading through the air.

"Rather this house is mine," the newcomer added quietly.

For a long moment, the girl's tormentors gazed unbelievingly at what had happened to the iron. Then, with Creon in the lead, they jumped to their feet and fled in screaming panic, the necklaces of toy skulls rattling madly. Terror himself came under their new enemy's dominion.

Apollo only watched them go, allowing them to leave his presence unharmed. But as the last pair of running legs vanished through the doorway he shouted after them, in a voice that might have been heard half a mile away, *"Let me never see you again under the sun!"*

A moment later he was bending over the unconscious girl, touching her so that she roused from her faint. Nestor heard him murmur, "More than enough blood has already been shed inside my house."

Then the Lord of Light came to Nestor, and with another touch sent renewed life flowing into him, body and mind. Nestor thought that he could feel, could almost see, the black wave of death receding.

"You will tell me your story later," said the voice of Apollo, which seemed to reach him from a great distance; and that was the last thing he was aware of for a time.

Nestor slept briefly, lying as he was on the floor, and when he awoke he felt almost entirely restored. The back of his head was still sore when his fingers pressed it, but that was all. Of the stab wound he thought he had discovered earlier, there was now no trace, though his shirt was caked with dried blood.

The sunlight in the temple was even brighter now, a clear and steady illumination that seemed not to depend entirely on the windows for its source. The thought crossed his mind that Shiva and Hades might someday succeed in tearing down Apollo's temple, but they were never going to put out the sun.

The girl was gone. And now Nestor saw, with no capacity for surprise left, that his recent acquaintance Dionysus had come to join Apollo. At the moment, Alex was indicating with a gesture the bones and offal that had been burnt for Apollo on the nearby altar. "Some of them mean well," he observed.

Jeremy Redthorn nodded. "People most often do mean well, while they are praying to Apollo; they would rather turn toward the sun than to the darkness. But why even well-meaning folk should think I crave burnt guts and bones . . . ?" He shook his head. "So it has been for ages."

Alex agreed. "I don't care for sacrifices either." He paused, looking inward and considering. "I speak for Dionysus as well as for—me."

"If it makes people happy to slaughter a few animals in my name—well, let them. They could be doing worse; and wisely they keep the good meat to eat themselves, while putting the gristle and guts and bones in the fire as my share. Fortunately I need not depend on them for nourishment."

"I understand." Alex drew a deep breath. "What are we going to do now?"

"I am going to seek out Hades, as soon as the sun comes up," Apollo said quietly. "There's no use waiting longer. I see no reason to think that I'll be stronger tomorrow, or the next day, or that he will be weaker."

"Are you strong enough to stand against him?"

"In daylight I think I will be. But there is no certainty about the outcome. He has hurt me badly in the past. You must do all you can to see to it that he gets no help from his allies."

"I will do all I can. I am—I was—a soldier. But Dionysus isn't . . ."

"I understand."

"Can we count on help from anyone else?"

"Hephaestus is my friend, and would stand with us if he were here. I know of no other Olympians willing to risk their necks." Apollo paused, then added, "I think that we can win, but I will need all the help that you can give."

"You can count on that."

"Let me tell you, my colleague," said Apollo, "that I have sworn a great oath to foil Hades wherever and whenever I can, in this great game that we and others play."

"I see it as no game, but war."

"It can be both. A war whose first battles were fought so long ago, that the gods themselves can scarce remember. A game, with the whole world at stake."

33

AT DAWN ON the morning following the arrival of Dionysus, Shiva returned to Corycus, with Theseus riding behind him on his flying bull.

Nestor had climbed to the roof of the temple of Apollo, intending to get a view over the city as the sun came up. He observed what appeared to be a mob of angry citizens, more or less spontaneously marching on the palace.

Nestor was about to report this to his two divine allies, when his eye was caught by a startling image in the sky. Looking up, he saw in the distance Nandi, with two man-shaped figures on his back, air-trotting downward as if intending to land. Nearly as Nestor could tell, the creature was coming down close to the edge of the Labyrinth opposite the palace.

The mob dispersed in panic, and the mercenary captain ran to tell the gods who had now become his companions.

Grumbling and discontent had been gradually becoming more and more open among the officers and men of the Palace Guard, and most of them were now ready to join the revolt. Unfortunately much of the Guard's strength had been dispersed to distant regions of the island, as Perses became doubtful of its loyalty.

Wild rumors had been flying regarding Shiva's whereabouts. There had been speculation that the God of Destruction was really a coward, and had fled the island altogether at the first hint of serious opposition.

Others feared that Shiva was only standing back a little, to encourage all his enemies, mortal and divine, to raise their heads, that they might be more readily and thoroughly cut down.

And still others feared, with good reason, that an even stronger and more terrible god than Shiva might now appear on Shiva's side.

When Nestor had reported Shiva's arrival to Apollo and Dionysus, Apollo took leave of his two allies, saying he had to try to find out what Hades was up to. He hoped he would be able to rejoin them soon.

Dionysus and Nestor rode the chariot back into the Labyrinth, there to join Sarpedon and the other loyal soldiers in defending Daedalus.

On the way, they wondered who the second rider might have been, on Nandi's back.

Alex observed, "Well, I don't like him or her, whoever it was. Shiva is very powerful indeed. But Shiva can only be in one place at a time."

Also Shiva tended to treat people with an arrogance that quickly made enemies, if only secret ones, out of the majority of those he met.

The bull Nandi had come down to land inside the Maze, only a few hundred yards from its very center. "The Face of Dionysus will yet be yours," said the God of Destruction to his human client, nudging him unceremoniously to the ground, so unexpectedly that Theseus failed to get his feet under him in time, and sat down hard. "Stay right here, so I can find you quickly when I need you. I will kill this God of Many Names, this Great Party-Goer, again, and as soon as he is dead you shall have the Face he wears."

As soon as Theseus regained his feet, he forced himself to make a deep obeisance. It had been a long time, but with a little effort he remembered how.

He might have saved himself the trouble and humiliation, for Shiva totally ignored him. Nandi bounded into the air again, and a moment later the god was gone.

Theseus, right hand on his sword hilt, stood staring after the divine figure, which had already vanished over the surrounding Labyrinthine walls. The man was thinking dark thoughts, and wondering to himself. "Do I really want to be a god of wine, madness, and lechery?" All amusing things in which to dabble—but are such matters really the important part of a man's life, after all?

Besides which, he was already tired of being carried along like a child, or a mere woman, on a god's magic steed.

His sword had been ready at his side, and now it was ready in his hand. He decided that what he really wanted to do now was to slay the Minotaur. Shiva would be angry—but when he, Theseus, started worrying about who might or might not be angry at him, it would be time to retire. Or to die.

He said to himself now, "It never does a man any good to be furious with a god. You can of course defy him." In the legends, that course was likely to lead to some eternal and truly heroic punishment.

He moved on.

Somewhere in the Labyrinth ahead of him he could hear the shouting of men's voices. He could not make out any of the words clearly, yet somehow he felt sure that they were soldiers. He set out to investigate.

───

The true rebellion had broken out first in the city of Kandak, only hours after the first rumors of the return of Dionysus. From Kandak it spread rapidly across the island. People in the hinterland had always resented Perses's usurpation, and away from the capital there was little support for Shiva and his puppet.

Even in the big city their support, apart from the mercenary troops, was very thin. Nestor in his reconnaissance of the city had seen that in the narrow streets of the old quarter, citizens were constructing barricades, tearing up cobblestones, as if they planned to stop a cavalry charge. On observing this activity Nestor judged it a total waste of time, as no good cavalry officer would launch a charge down a narrow, winding street like this. But he supposed it gave the people a feeling that they were doing something useful.

In the wealthier quarter of the town, some houses and other buildings owned by people suspected of being especially close to Perses and his imported, bloodthirsty god were set on fire.

Strong factions of the army and navy were ready to join in the revolt. The Butcher remained loyal to Perses, but the Palace Guard he commanded had largely been already transferred out from under his supervision. He really had no choice but to stay with Perses; the Princess Phaedra would have nothing to do with the man who had connived at her father's murder.

As was usually the case at any given time, more of the navy's ships and sailors were out to sea than were in home port; but the royal sisters and their allies were confident that most sailors would approve of the revolt when the news reached them. But by then, of course, the matter would have been pretty well settled, one way or the other.

People loyal to "our true queen, Phaedra" were determined to put her on the throne, and to depose the usurper and his gang.

I, Asterion, with the help of Sarpedon and a squad of guardsmen, continued to do my best to stand guard over Daedalus, as the Artisan concentrated on his investigation of the locked door.

As dawn approached, I had withdrawn from the area where Daedalus was working. Feeling a weight of weariness, I withdrew to one of the remoter fastnesses of my domain. There I lay down on a couch of stone, well-padded with moss, and was soon asleep. Almost immediately I plunged into a kind of nightmare, in which Theseus had captured Edith again and was trying to wring secrets out of her.

Other people and gods well known to me were taking part in the dream as well, but I was encountering only their images, not their minds. Some of them, I knew, were dead. There were Shiva and Dionysus, the old King Minos and the new—

There was Theseus, again, shouting a challenge and waving from some elevated place quite near the Labyrinth—

The dream changed abruptly, and I was alone with Daedalus. The Artisan was talking earnestly, trying to reveal some great secret; but with all the noise and shouting, I could not make out a word of what he said.

Presently I dreamt of my sisters too—and realized suddenly that what was happening was something more than a dream.

Out of sleep I fell, cold and disoriented, into the world of wakefulness, where as always I was immediately bothered by the lack of control. Even before my eyes were open, I was aware that Ariadne and Phaedra were nearby, calling my name, beseeching me to come and help them. There was shouting in the distance, and the sounds of fighting.

I rose to my feet, stumbling clumsily for once, as dreams became entangled with reality, and lumbered away.

I dashed around a corner and there they were. Ariadne immediately ran forward and threw herself into my arms.

When my gaze fell directly on Phaedra, she shrank back involuntarily. It had been many years since she had laid eyes on her brother.

All she could get out in her confusion was, "You were much, much smaller when I saw you last."

Then slowly, while Ariadne and I embraced in greeting, our older sister moved forward, obviously in awe of the gigantic, bullheaded and beardless figure dressed in kilt and sandals. But she took the hand that I stretched out to her.

I made sure that the pressure of my fingers was very gentle. She did not seem startled by my odd voice when I said, "My sister. Now you shall be my queen."

"My brother."

"I suppose," said Ariadne, "that you two have never actually seen each other before."

"Not strictly true," her sister said.

"Not true?" Ariadne was amazed.

"No." The elder sister's gaze remained fixed on my face. "In fact you are one of my earliest memories. I remember feeling so—so terribly *sorry* for you."

She told the story to us then. Phaedra had been about four years old when I was born, and had only the haziest and most fragmentary memories of that time. She had not, of course, actually witnessed her mother's death.

Ariadne would have been only two, unable to remember anything at all.

Phaedra as a small girl had had at least one long look at the horned and monstrous infant. In the realm of fact and logic, that horror was of course intimately entwined with the fact of her mother's death. But in the memory of the four-year-old, the two events had nothing directly to do with each other.

Princess Phaedra would not have chosen to bring up that subject now, but there seemed no way to avoid it. And maybe a direct confrontation was really for the best.

"After that we were kept apart," she said to the bull-man.

His huge head nodded slowly. "Yes. Sometimes I wonder that our father on earth, King Minos, did not kill me on the spot, when mother died. But I suppose he had received some omen, some warning against that."

"Minos was not a ruthless man. And I believe he loved his queen. Even as she loved all her children."

Ariadne, as she grew older, had not been prevented from seeking out her brother and spending time with him.

The visits had started early, with the connivance of a nurse, who had been the early wet-nurse of the monstrous infant, who thought that siblings ought to know each other.

Naturally both girls had been forbidden to wander in the Labyrinth, as children in general would be, by their parents. But Ariadne's special talent had enabled her to find ways around the prohibition, while her older sister, naturally more inclined to follow rules, had stayed in the palace grounds like a good girl.

When King Minos eventually learned that Ariadne had made several visits to her brother, he had been shocked at first. But then he had not forbidden the meetings.

I doubt that my foster father Minos ever laid eyes on me. Whether he did or not, he could never bring himself to acknowledge that such a creature might be one of his family, or bring it into the palace.

Ariadne had to leave us, to go on with the all-important business of her visions and her web. But Phaedra stayed with me for a time, and for the first time in our lives we could begin to know each other.

34

ALEX WAS INTIMATELY aware of Dionysus's chronic reluctance to engage in battle. The God of Many Forms had been a hunter, in the past, and might someday hunt again—but being a warrior was something else again. When, as now, the god faced unavoidable armed conflict, his overwhelming reaction was not so much fear as a sense of his own total incompetence. His instinctive preference was to enter combat, if he must, moving at high speed aboard his chariot. On the other hand, Alex the simple soldier, considering the situation as unemotionally as possible, quickly decided that such a conspicuous presence in the sky would only make him a better target for Shiva's lancing rays of death. Staying close to the ground, where he could at least try to shroud himself with greenery, might make the enemy's task a little harder.

In this question it seemed that Dionysus readily yielded to the superior experience of his human component.

As to what direct action the God of Joy—the Great Party-Goer, as some irreverently called him—might be able to take against Shiva, or any other divine opponent, his Dionysian memory was anything but reassuring. He was no better at fighting than he was at puzzle-solving. Alex's divine partner could command no armament to match the Third Eye. His chances of being able to turn the God of Destruction into a dolphin, or working any similar transformation on him, were practically zero. On the other hand, driving Shiva into a frenzy might be all too easy to accomplish, and might require no effort at all. But Alex was not at all sure that that was the result he should be trying to achieve.

Now the young man could better understand the behavior of his predecessor on that cold night, half a year ago. As soon as Shiva had shown his face in the great hall, the previous avatar of Dionysus had simply turned and fled for his life. It hadn't done him a bit of good, of course—save that it had prevented the Face of Dionysus from immediately falling into Shiva's hands.

The only effective weapon he could use against Shiva must be his wits; but the sharpest wits in the world could be quite helpless unless provided with something material in the way of tools.

The twin leopards could be deadly fighters against any ordinary opponent. Unfortunately Alex could find no memories to suggest that the magical beasts would be able to stand long against Shiva, let alone kill him.

Reluctantly he summoned his inhuman auxiliaries, intending to give them instructions on what to do if he, the present avatar of Dionysus, should fall in battle. His predecessor seemed to have decreed certain behavior along that line, if only indirectly.

If Fate granted him the chance to pick his own successor, whom should he choose?

It would not be Ariadne, even though Faces seemed almost indifferent to the gender of those who wore them. Alex could not give her to satyrs and maenads, who were always beckoning their lord to dances and orgies. His soul recoiled from the image of Ariadne in that role. Nor could he hand over to her the Face of Zeus, if that should fall into his hands. To enter into such intimate union with the Ruler of the Universe, to become the Thunderer, must change her, or any human being, beyond all recognition; somehow, even her death would be more bearable than that.

When Silenus appeared, in his usual role as spokesman for the entourage, Alex issued his own orders. "If I am killed, I command you to pick up the Face I now wear, and carry it to the soldier, Sarpedon. If that proves impossible, bring it to Daedalus. If you cannot do that either—to one of the princesses." He added those last words with great reluctance. Still he could not bring himself to consent to Ariadne's melding herself, body and mind, with anyone, human or divine, besides himself. As for Phaedra, Alex still thought the elder sister should be queen of Corycus, not a goddess.

But who else was there worthy of being trusted with such power? Asterion came to mind. But Dionysus found it hard to believe that Asterion's bull head would ever be able to wear a Face. Asterion was too much the son of Zeus to partake of the nature of any other deity.

We will not desert you in the battle, Lord! Silenus managed to infuse his wheezing protest with tones of deep sincerity. He even sounded vaguely offended, as if Alex had suggested that the satyr might value his own personal safety higher than his god's.

Dionysian anger flared. "Whether you might desert me is not the question. Why do you persist in misunderstanding? What I am talking about is the need to prevent Shiva or Hades from gaining control of *this*." And Alex raised a hand to touch his forehead. Then he added, "If you do run away, don't go too far."

The ancient satyr looked sadder than ever. *If any of us survive the battle, master, we will do then what we must do.*

Neither Alex nor Dionysus found that very reassuring, but it seemed to be the best that either human nature or divinity could hope for.

Memory assured Alex that it was undoubtedly a very long time since any sprite or satyr had been killed by violence, but they were certainly not immune to such an attack. Not when it came on the scale employed by Shiva.

Trying to make war against Shiva might be hopeless, but against merely human opponents the Twice-Born had every reason to expect success. In the memory of Dionysus Alex discovered that one effective method consisted in the god's driving opposing soldiers mad, causing them to kill each other.

This scanning of the past evoked certain related memories, including scenes of cannibalism, which so revolted the young man that he turned his thoughts quickly away from them.

———

His main task continued to be the defense of the princesses, and of Daedalus, who must be protected from interruption as he worked.

Anxious to know what success Daedalus was having, Alex went to look, and found him still hard at work upon the puzzle-lock. At the moment the investigator had his ear pressed against the shell-like surface, face scowling in concentration, while his fingers tapped and probed at various places on the mechanism. Watching the Artisan now, Alex got the impression of a man who was making progress on a job, though Alex would not have been able to say exactly what made him think so.

If the enemy did not yet know that Daedalus was present, and in what kind of task he was engaged, then it was worth some considerable effort to keep Hades and Shiva and their creatures from finding out.

On the plus side, Alex again had the chariot and leopards available for his own tactical use. But he wanted to keep them hidden as long as possible.

———

Alex had not yet called forth the chariot when he found himself facing a company of mercenaries, the really bad ones from the company of Captain Yilmaz, men who, as Sarpedon informed him, had been used by Perses to interrogate people suspected of disloyalty. They were following the marked pathway leading to the center of the Maze, and in the process getting uncomfortably close to the site where Daedalus still labored. Of course it was still possible that they would never reach it, but it was dangerously exposed to discovery.

Nestor, who knew these men professionally, saw them approaching, and came running up, out of breath, to deliver a warning about them.

Drawing on his own experience as a soldier, his familiarity with the men in the ranks, Alex understood that most of the men in any fighting unit would be terrified at the prospect of face-to-face combat with any god. The only ones not terrified would be the berserk, some of whom were likely to show up in any fight.

Taking a cue from Apollo, he did not pursue the soldiers who ran away from him. But he could not ignore those who were brave enough, well-disciplined enough, or simply vicious enough, to try to stand and fight. Also any orderly retreat would be difficult in the Maze, and the troops might well feel that they were cornered.

He knew he must do all he could to weaken the usurper's human army, before he had to meet Shiva, an encounter that would more than likely result in his own death.

Reacting with professional instinct, the mercenaries sent a concentrated hail of projectiles at him, arrows and slung stones, and it was not beyond the bounds of possibility that one such missile might do his human body injury. Sprites and satyrs, virtually immune to such gross physical attacks, formed a defensive screen before their god, and his own powers, almost without conscious effort on his part, could deflect stones, turning them into ripe fruit even as they flew.

Turning his human opponents permanently into animals would take more time and effort than he could spare just now, with much greater demands upon his powers looming in the near future. Recalling commands from some of the Twice-Born's earlier memories, Alex inflicted on some of his opponents a temporary transformation. Hogs grunted and squealed and ran. Even when those men returned to human form, they would remain out of action, in shock, for some time.

But he must not become too absorbed in this business to watch for Shiva. Turning away, Alex left his company of sprites and satyrs to conclude the skirmish. Capering phantoms immune to sword and spear and arrow, they first distracted the remaining enemy troops, then maddened them into frenzy.

The satyrs especially took on martial forms, brandishing illusory weapons.

As Alex turned away, Silenus began blustering in a position of assumed leadership—waving a broken wine bottle, as if it were a sword. Alex knew that he would be perfectly willing enough to relinquish what he thought of as his command, as soon as it began to appear genuinely dangerous—but that was hardly likely to happen until Shiva or Hades came on the scene.

Soldiers infected with new frenzy began trying to catch and rape and kill the phantom females, or come to grips with taunting, leaping, chanting goat-men. Instead the mortals only crashed into each other, and in the growing madness of their rage, took out their frustrations upon each other's solid flesh.

What had been a squad of working professionals quickly fragmented into a swarm of individuals—but instead of separating, those individuals quickly came together again, in an orgy of mutual destruction.

Alex took note especially of one pair, locked in a desperate death-grapple.

The voices of the struggling mob rose in a cacophony of screams, threats, howls and insane laughter.

Alex/Dionysus stalked away. His mind was quivering, thoughts jumping, with the burden of his own divine madness. Resolutely he refused to think about the horror he was leaving behind him. He had to struggle hard to free his own mind of the craziness he had invoked, and part of him remained revolted at his own nature.

Alex closed his eyes and leaned against a wall. The God of Madness must not be undone, defeated, by his own nature. *I am more than a God of Madness. I was a human being before I became a god, and a human being I still remain. And I always will.*

When Alex opened his eyes, the world was reasonably steady once again.

His invisible escort swirled around him again. They were highly excited with the results of the just-concluded skirmish, exulting in the bloody deeds they had provoked. To these inhuman servants the only thing that seemed to matter in the war was the degree of frenzy to which the participants could be driven.

Alex, and for a moment even Dionysus, was repelled by this attitude.

Dionysus, like any other god, could not long hold any emotion, any wish, unless it was shared by his human avatar.

Alex hurried to catch up with Ariadne. He called her name, but received no answer. She was nowhere in sight, and sprites and satyrs reported anxiously that they had lost contact with the princess.

He also wanted to make sure that Daedalus was still on the job, and see if he was any closer to success.

There came a distant shouting, as of the enemy in triumph. Shiva had paused to visit destruction upon some rebel formation.

Alex could only hope that Ariadne and Phaedra, and Daedalus as well, might find some place of safety with Asterion.

Because now at last Shiva was in sight, airborne astride the great bull Nandi, gripping in both hands indeterminate shapes that must be weapons. The mouth of his death's-head face was open in a howl of rage. The necklace of skulls was swirling with the speed of the Destroyer's motion through the air.

Alex turned at bay to face his deadly enemy. At all costs he must avoid leading the killer to the woman he loved.

His soldier's instinct urged him to pick up a spear that had been dropped by one of the squad of scattered and slaughtered mercenaries. Alex the soldier felt a shade less terrified, with hilted metal in his hand. But he might as well have saved himself the trouble. The world seemed to dissolve in a burst of white light, eating into his eyes and brain like acid.

The first lance-thrust of light from the Third Eye hit the chariot directly and knocked it out of the air, spilling its divine occupant rudely on the ground.

Alex lay stunned, god-powers at an ebb, waiting for the next blast to sear away his life.

35

ALEX LAY SPRAWLED on the ground, shrinking in expectation of the death blow that must fall on him at any moment. But heartbeat after heartbeat passed, and he was spared. In the background, he thought he could hear one of the princesses screaming.

Granted another moment of life, he tried to move his body, to go to her aid. But all of Alex's half-formed plans for survival in combat had been shattered instantly by Shiva. There was no use deceiving himself; Dionysus was helpless before the Destroyer's deadly power.

And in the back of his mind, as he waited for the searing bolt of death to strike, Alex realized that the entourage of Dionysus had suddenly and finally deserted him. Only an hour ago, he would have sworn that when this moment came, his sprites and satyrs would stand by their master to the death. But now they had all fled in panic . . . not that either Alex or Dionysus could blame them, with Shiva already triumphant and Hades no doubt looming near. Only once before, in recent memory, had his creatures ever forsaken him. That had happened when . . .

. . . when they found themselves suddenly in the presence of . . . but no, that hadn't been Shiva. Someone else.

Groggily Alex, his flesh still cringing in anticipation of a fatal stroke, turned over and tried to focus on the sky. His vision cleared.

Nandi was prancing strangely in the air; Shiva had reined his great mount around, as if preparing to make a charge. Or maybe in an attempt to flee. It was hard to determine which, and suddenly it did not matter. The bull's body had just been transfixed front to back by a Silver Arrow, a shaft so long that a portion protruded on each side. Nandi let out a long bellow, a sound seemingly pure animal and almost deafeningly loud, and at the same time lost the power of flight, fell like a stone, all four limbs frozen in position.

Before Nandi's lifeless shape could hit the ground, Shiva had vaulted nimbly from the dead beast's back, coming down catlike on his feet in the space cleared days ago for the Tribute, not far from the silken chair where he had once reclined at ease, intending to enjoy a sacrifice of blood. Now the God of Destruction, brought to bay, crouched facing his new foe.

Apollo, embodied in the straight-lined, youthful body of Jeremy Redthorn, Silver Bow in hand, was standing atop one of the high walls of the surrounding Labyrinth. The Far-Worker had drawn a second Arrow from the quiver on his back, and was nocking it to his Bow.

Alex/Dionysus, looking over his shoulder as he tried to crawl to safety across the broken pavement of the Labyrinth, had the scene in clear view before him.

First Alex could only crawl, and then he found that he could get one foot under him, though he could not yet stand. But still his thoughts were chiefly for the princess. *If I am dying*, he thought, *let it be for Ariadne. All good gods, protect her!*

In the next instant, Alex winced in sympathy, squinting his eyes shut, as the silver lance of Shiva struck home on its mighty target. His eyes were open again in time to see how Apollo almost lost his footing atop the wall, as he staggered in the act of fitting his next Arrow to his Bow.

When the beam from the Third Eye struck the body of the Far-Worker, obviously it inflicted pain, as Dionysus supposed it must have done even on Zeus himself. But even the Third Eye could not kill a god of Apollo's stature. He whom the legends credited with mastery of the Sun itself, seemed immune to mortal damage by any lesser fire. Few opponents indeed could ever claim victory over the being who held authority over Terror, Death, and Distance.

Apollo's weapons had remained firmly in his hands, and now the Bow was drawn again. In the split second before it was released, Alex had the impression that the whole world was tilting sideways around that arc-segment of metallic silver. Echoes of a deep sound, so low-pitched as to be almost beyond the range of human ears, like movement in the world's foundation, went chasing themselves around the sky.

This time Alex attempted to follow the Arrow in flight, but there was no hope of that, not even for an eye of godly power. Missile and target seemed to have come together even before the Bow had thrummed.

Shiva was down on the ground now, gut-pierced and spouting blood though not yet dead. Some immense reserve of vitality kept the God of Destruction moving. Howling like a demon, laboring and scrambling in a crawling progress on all fours, he was trying to reach one of the newly created chasms in the earth. But just as he gained the brink of one of them, another of Apollo's shafts struck like a lightning bolt before him, blasting up chunks of stone and soil, hurling fragments of wall foundation, sending the Destroyer reeling and rolling backward, still mortally exposed.

At the last moment Shiva, with the Arrow still protruding on each side of his body, got his feet under him and stood erect again, bravely turning his face and his own terrible weapon back toward Apollo.

Only an eyeblink later, Alex saw the head of the Destroyer's avatar explode in a great blur of blood and fragments. He had a clear, momentary look at the glassy Face of Shiva leaping free undamaged, with Apollo's final Arrow perfectly centered in the eye that marked the center of its forehead.

The Face, still transfixed by the Arrow, was only briefly visible before it slid into the new hole in the ground.

One of the soldiers who had been crouched down nearby, seeking shelter, went scrambling in an effort to catch the Face before it disappeared. But the young man was too late, and had to scramble back to keep from falling into the hole himself.

The only visible remnant of the God of Destruction was a headless human corpse, scrawny and nearly naked. The pitiful remnant of the avatar's human body seemed suddenly only a symbol of itself, no more than one of the tawdry emblems of death with which it was still adorned.

In another moment, Apollo was kneeling beside Alex, helping him to regain his feet. Dionysus must have exerted some protective power over the body that they shared, for Alex felt jarred and bruised by his fall, but no part of him had been burned or broken.

Ignoring Alex's outpouring of thanks, Apollo was already talking about the evidence of the locked door, which he had just seen for the first time, and speculating on what might lie beneath it.

When Alex mentioned the Face of Zeus, even Apollo seemed taken momentarily aback. He looked at Daedalus, and the delicate investigation the Artisan had now resumed, and declined to interfere.

Alex asked, "Do you think the story is true?"

"When Zeus is involved—" began Jeremy Redthorn, then stopped, shaking his head. Then he added, "There was an hour, not too long ago, when I was standing atop a mountain that might once have been Olympus—then I thought I might be about to encounter Zeus. But he turned out to be a tree stump."

"What?" Alex and Dionysus were about equally astonished.

"It's a long story, and not very helpful for our present purposes. I'll tell it to you someday."

While the fight had been taking place almost over his head, Daedalus, like all the other humans in sight, had crouched down trembling. Now he was already back at work. It seemed he was in a dangerous position now, for the solid rock surrounding the puzzle-door had been rayed with fine cracks by the impact of Apollo's Arrow on the earth.

Jeremy Redthorn was saying to him, "Find the answer for us, Artisan. No one will attack you while you work." Daedalus looked up, nodding abstractedly, perhaps hardly aware of who had just saved his life and was speaking to him now.

Apollo discussed with Alex the next move that he was contemplating: a raid on what he thought was probably enemy headquarters—the huge temple newly dedicated to Shiva, adjoining the royal palace, a couple of miles straight from the center of the Labyrinth.

Apollo told Dionysus that he preferred to do most of his aerial travel with a pair of winged Sandals; the story of how they had come into his possession would have to wait until another day.

Dionysus offered his colleague the use of his chariot. "The leopards seem to tolerate your presence if my other servitors do not."

But the Lord of Light declined. On his Sandals, he thought he could probably move as fast as any other being in the universe.

Another round of combat seemed inevitable. Everyone knew that a little more than a year ago, Hades and the Sun-God had fought a bitter and inconclusive duel, from which both had retreated with serious injuries.

"It's very fortunate that you were able to kill Shiva as quickly as you did."

Testing the string of his great Bow, Apollo confided to Dionysus that he wasn't entirely sure that he wanted to kill Hades. "Assuming that it's even possible."

"But why shouldn't you, if you can?"

"If he dies, it is inevitable that another human will find that Face and put it on. Thus a new Hades will be created, who will be perhaps even more of a curse to the world than this one."

"Possible, but unlikely. We would at least have something of a breathing space, while the new avatar began to feel at home with the Underworld and its powers."

"That may be the best outcome that we can hope for."

"No, the best would be to have a decent human assume the rule of the Underworld. And if we are gentle with Hades, what about Shiva? Was it a mistake to slay him too?"

Apollo had come to understand that no god is truly good, or bad, except by the will of the person who wears the divine Face at the moment.

"Not even Shiva?"

"Not Shiva, or even Hades. Destruction and death have their place in the universe."

Apollo confessed that he knew nothing of what might be under the secret door. "It's true that, as far as I know, years have passed since the Thunderer was last seen by either gods or mortals. I have certainly not laid eyes on him for many years; and it may be that his last contact with anyone was shortly before the death of Pasiphae, and the birth of Asterion."

"What did he look like?"

For a moment Apollo only stared at his questioner. Then he gave a short burst of laughter that seemed to have nothing to do with Jeremy Redthorn. "What does the lightning look like? Or the thunder?" Then the Far-Worker condescended to explain. "At one time or another, my eyes have seen Zeus as an eagle, as a bull, as a shower of gold, among other manifestations. The possibilities are unlimited."

"But underneath it all, behind it all, there must always be a man. A man like you or me."

Jeremy's personality seemed in full control again. "I suppose. Or, for all I know, a woman."

Apollo shrugged. "I see no reason why not."

"But could a woman have fathered two children on Queen Pasiphae? That's what some Jovian avatar did, almost twenty years ago."

"A woman who wore the Face of Zeus, or Jupiter—in some lands they call him by that name—might be capable of that, or almost anything. The powers inherent in Zeus are as far above those of an ordinary god, as your abilities and mine are above the merely human."

"Would we, gods and humans in general, somehow be aware, would anyone necessarily know, if Zeus was dead? Would the universe be any different than it is? We see the lightning flash as it always has, we hear the thunder sound, as it must have sounded a thousand years ago."

"The world seems to be able to keep itself going without the immediate supervision of gods and goddesses."

"How many avatars have worn the Face of Zeus, since the beginning of the world?"

It would be a wise deity indeed who knew the answer to that one.

36

ALEX/DIONYSUS, SEIZING the opportunity to make sure that Ariadne was still safe, paused to take a close look at the woman he loved. Some of the things he had learned about her during the last few days were surprising. He thought her beauty had not been damaged by rough treatment, and exposure to the sun and wind, but only made more real. Her wit, and energy, and the fierce devotion she had now begun to show to him, seemed greater marvels even than the mysterious and special powers she had inherited from her father. Even though he himself had attained godhood, he still stood somewhat in awe of the Princess Ariadne.

When Ariadne stood in front of the locked door in the floor of rock, she reported seeing in her vision a thread of her imaginary web-stuff weaving its way through the intricacies of the lock, as if the thread were attached to some invisible, impalpable needle. And as soon as the thread had completed its progress, the trapdoor in her vision swung up and open.

But the vision refused to show her what might lie beyond the seal.

Visions were all very well, and poetic ideas of a thread of sand, but a real strand of some tough fiber seemed to be needed to solve the puzzle and open the lock.

Alex, now watching the Artisan closely, got the impression that Daedalus, incredible as it seemed, was far from being ready to give up. Instead, his look of quiet satisfaction suggested that he might be on the point of succeeding in his seemingly impossible task. Alex thought that the Artisan possessed formidable qualities that in a soldier would have swept the enemy from the battlefield.

Some of the watchers kept silent, but others could not. Phaedra at last cried, "Hurry, hurry!"

The Artisan, with magisterial calm, ignored all efforts to hurry him. When people had specific advice to give, he listened, but so far had quickly dismissed every suggestion as to what he should do next.

At the moment he was lying sprawled on his belly, head lower than his feet, contemplating the mystery that lay a little below his nose. His position looked painfully awkward, but somehow he was managing to ignore the resulting discomfort, as he did the sweat dripping from the tip of his nose. He appeared to be ignoring, also, the ominous rumblings and tremblings of the earth.

———————

Alex, returning to the scene after a short absence, heard a little murmur, as of wonder and appreciation, go up from the small group surrounding the Artisan.

Approaching more closely, Alex noted with surprise that Daedalus was now sitting back, hands clasped, watching the lock with an expression of satisfaction. Alex in astonishment beheld a moving thread of gossamer fineness being gradually pulled into the windings of the shell. This filament was so like one of the gossamer threads of Ariadne's web, as she described them, that for a moment Alex wondered whether her powers might have objectified it into solid reality. But that was not the case.

He could not at first imagine what agency was doing the pulling. With a shock he saw that the thread was moving, progressing into the miniature maze in little fits and starts, a quarter of an inch now, half an inch more a moment later. About two feet of the thread remained outside the lock, and its visible end had been tied, or glued, to a slightly larger and stronger filament.

"But—what magic is this?"

"No magic," said Daedalus. "Watch." And pointed with one gnarled finger to the tiny hole that formed the exit of the passage through the lock.

A tiny creature emerged from the hole, and the mystery was solved. The Artisan had somehow glued his slender filament to the back of an ant, which he had then somehow induced to go crawling through the many-chambered nautilus, dragging the thread through after it.

With a gesture Daedalus indicated the other side of the concavity, where dozens of similar insects, large, red, and active, were darting about over the rock. Dirt had spilled through a crack in the rock there, and doubtless their nest had been disrupted, when the earth moved in its most recent tremor.

"In the past," said the Artisan, "I have found them to be excellent helpers, for certain very special jobs."

And now he leaned forward, taking in his strong fingers the end of the fine thread that had already been pulled through the windings of the lock. Delicately pulling, Daedalus gently tugged the heavier strand, to which it was connected, into place after it.

There came a sharp click, to Alex unmistakable as the sound of a fine mechanism peacefully yielding. A moment later the Artisan reached for the handle of the door, and started to lift it open. The door began to open, for whatever bolts had been holding it in place had smoothly and suddenly been withdrawn.

———

But the motion of the opening door was interrupted. As swiftly as a sprung trap, the fine cracks in the surrounding rock split open and yawned wide. A crash, like a great explosion, sounded from underground. In the next instant the round door and the whole of the broad depression surrounding it disappeared as if by magic, vanishing down into the earth.

Thunderous noise accompanied the disappearance, a roar that went trailing away below, muffling itself at last in distance and interior gloom. Belatedly a light cloud of dust rode up out of the hole on a faint air current. When someone looked over the brink, his line of sight went down and down, disappearing at last into a vertiginous darkness, relieved near the bottom only by a sullen red glow as of heated rock.

The collapse was so sudden that the Artisan and several soldiers came very near to falling in. Daedalus was only saved by the prompt action of Dionysus, who sprang forward to grasp him by the collar. In the next moment Alex had hurled the Artisan backward, away from the new hole, saving him from being badly burned by the hot gases that came belching up from below, a sulphurous exhalation of the Underworld.

As he recovered from being thrown yards away, Daedalus was a little dazed, though basically uninjured. He muttered, "The door—the door was just starting to swing open. I almost had it in my grasp."

"But what was under the door?"

The Artisan gasped and coughed, exhaling dust. "All I can say is that there was certainly—something there. I mean a structure, a vault, a room. Stone walls and a floor. But whatever was inside it fell clean away, in a cloud of dust, before I could get a decent look."

"*But what was in the vault?*"

He shook his head disconsolately. "I tell you I couldn't see."

"Then if the Face of Zeus was in there, it's now tumbled into the Underworld."

"Or simply into a crevice in the earth." Dionysus, though he had never entered the domain of Hades, understood that it did not extend everywhere beneath the surface of the ground. He tried to explain this to his comrades.

"Hades may be setting a trap for Apollo, trying to lure him underground."

The huge cavity shocked the eye.

A funnel-shaped volume of soil and rock, some five or six yards in diameter at the top, had gone sliding and collapsing down into the bowels of the earth. The whole apparatus of nested rings had completely disappeared, along with whatever might have been immediately beneath it.

The great, gaping hole, as seen by some observer who found himself hanging precariously over it when the pavement broke, indeed looked as if it might open a passage into the very Underworld.

"In fact—" Apollo began to say. But he stopped abruptly, and after standing frozen for a moment, peering down into the pit, quickly jumped back.

Dionysus stood close enough to see a little of what was going on. Darkness was moving down there, as if a negation of sunlight, of all light, had taken on a solid, objective form. And it was hurtling toward the surface, at the speed of a slung stone.

Hades came erupting out of the earth, a boiling cloud of shadow. The Cap of Invisibility concealed his precise form, even from the other gods nearby, but everyone could feel his presence.

One Silver Arrow, and then another, went flying into the heart of the darkness; and in return, there came back a shaking and rending of the earth beneath the Sun-God's feet, a hurling of chunks of solid rock.

And then another Silver Arrow, this time drawing blood. Darkness flecked with red burst open, like pus from a boil, and seemed about to engulf the entire Labyrinth. Alex felt the need to brace his feet, straining against what seemed a combination of wind and gravity, that threatened to suck him down into the earth.

Gradually, irresistibly, the sunlight seemed to be eating away the billowing darkness.

The awesome weapons of Hades and Apollo shook the rock beneath the feet of all the humans unlucky enough to be caught nearby. Those who were able went scrambling to find some kind of shelter.

The earth was trembling again.

Now Alex/Dionysus saw, with a chill of horror, another figure emerging from the newly enlarged pit.

Dionysus recognized the new shape, superficially quite human. It was that of the God of Death. The lower half of his ugly face was covered by a ragged growth of dark beard, and the eye of Dionysus could make out the red and ghostly wings sprouting from his shoulders.

Thanatos struck at him, a staggering blow whose force was borne by no visible weapon or movement of the arm; and in another moment, a four-way fight was in progress.

The weapon of Thanatos was a subtle extraction of life; but it was hard to extract life entirely from anyone when Dionysus was defending.

Neither Alex nor Dionysus had thought ahead of time how the God of Joy might be able to fight the embodiment of Death. Laughter to shake him to pieces? That would not work. But if Dionysus could not strike back at Death directly, he could maintain his own life against the onslaught, and spread it as far as possible into the world around him.

How long their silent struggle lasted, neither Alex nor Dionysus could have said. But a time came at last when he realized, with a kind of desperate relief, that Thanatos was in full retreat.

Death fled close on the heels of Hades, who had been wounded, perhaps mortally, by a barrage of Silver Arrows, and had gone tumbling down through the opening from which he had emerged.

For hours, Theseus had been prowling the Labyrinth, sometimes with sword in hand. When he heard human voices somewhere ahead, he followed the sound as best he could, until the voices faded away, to be followed by the crashing noises of divine combat. In a few minutes, that too had faded.

Still he kept going, trusting to the luck that almost never failed him; and after several hours he emerged in the central open space, the very spot from which he had escaped, some days ago, by bounding over a wall. He looked around him warily, but the plaza with its central tiers of seats, and torture-cages, was now deserted. But for the seats and cages, he might not have recognized the place, so drastically had it been transformed, with some of the surrounding walls torn down and a great ragged cavity hollowed in the earth.

But still there was no sign of the Minotaur.

In frustrated anger he turned round, glaring at the walls, and shouted, "Come out and fight, damn you, Cow-head. Where have you got to now?"

Only silence answered.

And suddenly, for the first time since returning to the Maze, Theseus knew fear—fear that he was dreaming again, and that he would not be allowed to recognize the fact that he was dreaming—not until something truly horrible had happened to him.

But Theseus would rather die than allow his life to be ruled by fear. Moving on, a moment later he almost stumbled over the blasted, headless, shriveled-looking body of Shiva's most recent avatar. The necklace of skulls made it impossible to mistake—though for just a moment he had almost taken it for some fallen priest of Shiva's service.

Theseus raised his head, and looked around him, and listened carefully. For a moment, a moment only, he thought of Ariadne. "Time to go home," he said aloud at last. He was speaking to no one but himself.

No, it was not a dream this time. He was not going to allow it to be a dream.

━━━━━━━━

That evening, an irregular string of mercenaries' ships were putting out to sea from the harbor of Kandak, oars working the water in a steady rhythm. Captain Yilmaz, like many of his colleagues, had not waited to hoist sail; Theseus, leaning on the rail beside his friend, remarked that it was easy enough to tell when a fight had been lost, when there was no longer any prospect of getting paid.

━━━━━━━━

Dionysus understood that the killing of Hades would have more far-reaching implications than the deaths of Shiva or the God of Death. But was the Lord of the Underworld truly dead as a coffin-nail, his Face lost somewhere down a fissure in the earth? Neither gods nor humans could be sure.

No one really depended on the Destroyer for anything, but the Underworld had widespread and far-reaching business—some said that the soul or shade of everyone wound up sooner or later in that dark domain.

Apollo, though once more victorious over the Lord of the Underworld, had been weakened by the conflict, and had withdrawn to rest and try to restore himself; and not even Dionysus knew where his great ally had gone. He had promised to return in time for the wedding.

Gazing down into the pit, as well as he could while keeping at a safe distance, Daedalus said, "Not easy to see how any object that falls down there will ever be brought back within reach of a human hand. Yet I must believe that it will."

But the satyr Silenus, who had launched, or at least helped to spread, the rumor concerning the Face of Zeus, had already confessed the fact to his master Dionysus.

Princess Phaedra asked, "Then whether or not there was any truth in the story of the face of Zeus being there . . ."

"Is something that we simply do not know," said the Twice-Born.

The current avatar of Dionysus, he who had once been Alex the Half-Nameless, could only hesitate as to whether to punish his servant, who was now prostrate before him and putting on a show of great repentance. The god said sternly, "Whatever effect you intended, the result was to sow great confusion among our enemies—and among ourselves as well."

It was easy to bewilder the foolish Creon. He had already befuddled himself, with much seeking after exotic wisdom. Next time we will be more careful, lord. Oh great lord, is it time yet for another celebration?

It would be time, and very soon, for a great wedding feast. But the Twice-Born was not ready to allow his erratic servant the joy of making such a plan—not just yet. Instead, Dionysus told him, "We will be lucky, you ancient fool, if any of us live long enough to see another celebration. Hades will always be waiting somewhere."

The
Arms
of
Hercules

1

A Blind Man Witnesses

I DO NOT sing this story, for I have neither the patience nor the voice to hold an audience. Rather I will write it down, so I will have the time to choose my words and amend them as I go along. Those who wish to read may do so. Those who do not will be under no compulsion to appear polite.

I have, among other things, this in common with all other members of the human race: that the seed of my life was planted, the roots began to grow, before I could be there to witness any part of the process. Therefore I can tell the first chapter of my story only in the form in which others who were there have told it to me.

Years ago, in the kingdom of Cadmia, there came a certain summer night on which the prophet Tiresias, in vivid dreams, beheld the descent of the mightiest of living gods. A few hours later, when Tiresias awakened to the first birdsongs of the bright spring morning, he climbed from his bed and called unhurriedly for his servants and his guards, sending his young companion to seek them out. The blind seer was an old man then, and he had been an old man for a long time, but the joints of his limbs still moved freely enough, all the vital parts of his body functioned, and he still craved young girls. As a member of the king's household, in a high position, he had the power to indulge his craving. His companion on that morning was a girl, and very young.

The prophet enjoyed the sound of young girls' voices, and the touch of their smooth skins, but whether or not they were beautiful in the world's eyes was a matter of total indifference to him.

When he could be bothered to explain his preferences to anyone, he put it this way: "In the first place, the dear little creatures are more grateful for the attention; and in the second place, very few of them deserve to be called ugly. You are handicapped in your vision by having eyes, and I can see the girls much better than you can."

The prophet himself, on the other hand, was ugly by almost any standard. He had been eyeless since birth. His face had eyebrows, but under them there were no lids to break the smooth expanse of skin, and the skull had no accommodating sockets.

Preparing for their master for that unexpected morning foray out into the world took the servants a little time. For this purpose they arrayed him in his own and his servants' idea of barbaric splendor, garments of bright colors and fine cloth, golden rings around his arms and in his earlobes. Tiresias bore all these procedures patiently, for he wanted to be sure not to arrive too soon at his destination. It was two hours after sunrise when he left his apartment in one wing of the king's palace, and set out on the road.

When he left the palace on that morning of birdsongs and sunlight, he went singing, in a cracked voice, some ancient song that no one else who was still alive in the kingdom of Cadmia had ever heard before. He mounted for his ride with his arm around the bored-looking young girl who had shared his bed. As far as anyone knew, there was no tie of blood between them, though the girl was certainly ugly enough to be his descendant. She might possibly have been a daughter or great-granddaughter, carried to almost any number of iterations that you care to name.

When the ill-matched couple had climbed aboard the mastodrom, it started walking, and the bodies of both passengers lurched with the motion of the howdah that rode just forward of the great beast's single hump. The huge, phlegmatic mastodrom had been brought at great expense from somewhere south of the Great Sea. A wizened little driver, a male of indeterminate age, sat straddling the animal's neck, guiding its motion with slight pressures of his callused feet, just behind its huge fanlike ears.

"Where are we going?" the girl asked, doubtless hoping that the day would bring some break in her routine.

"There is a house that has been visited by a god," the old man said to her. "And the man of the house does not know about it yet. I want to be the first to tell him."

"And the woman of the house?" the girl asked, when the mastodrom had carried them on a few more rocking paces.

The blind man laughed. "Ah, she knows already that she has had a visitor. She knows *that* in much more detail than I do. But who the visitor was—that will be a big surprise, I think!" And his laughter boomed out, as loudly as if he were still young and healthy.

Accompanying Tiresias, besides his youthful concubine, was an escort permanently assigned to him by King Eurystheus, a squad of half a dozen armed men on their own smaller and more agile mounts. The seer did not really want them, or believe he needed their protection, but the old king insisted that they always go with him; and this morning Tiresias had made sure they were alerted for his foray.

The morning's journey was only a few miles. Less than an hour after it began, the chief of the armed escort reined in his own much smaller mount, an ordinary cameloid, and turned closer to the mastodrom to tell its passengers that they had reached their destination. The estate on which I was conceived and born was a large and important one. The manor house was only a few miles outside the seven-gated city wall of Cadmia, whose massive stones were just visible in the distance from our own front gate.

The blind old man seemed somehow to know exactly where he was as well as anyone. Even before the soldier began to speak, the prophet turned from the public road to face the great ornamental gates of the estate, lifted his chin, and called out loudly: "Open, Alcmene, lady of the manor! I bring you marvelous news!" Eyewitnesses of the event confirm that the seer did not call for Amphitryon: thus even at that time he knew that the lord of the manor was not at home.

Amphitryon, who for many years was called my father, was a nephew of the late king Electryon of Megara, and he had been banished to Cadmia as a result of one of the intrigues afflicting that royal family, like so many others. (According to family tradition, Zeus was his great-great-grandfather; and a similar tradition in my mother's family gave her the same god as male ancestor eight generations even further back; in truth almost every family aspiring to high social status claimed divine blood.)

There was a pause while the gatekeeper inside sent some junior servant running for instructions, up the long hill to where the big house stood amid its ornamental plantings.

Meanwhile, out on the road in the sunlight of the summer morning, Tiresias waited patiently, singing. There were moments, even epochs, in which Tiresias seemed but little aware of what was going on in the world around him. The special seats with which his howdah was equipped were shaded by a canopy, which insured that the waiting would be comfortable. His armed escorts, taking their cue from him, were patient also. But what they thought of the quality of his song could be seen from the expressions on their faces.

Tiresias was by far the most famous prophet in Cadmia, or for many and many a mile around. Some said he was a child of Zeus, one of the Thunderer's uncountable bastards who were scattered all around the world, and that this explained both his deformity and his occult powers. Whatever the truth of that theory, I do not remember that Tiresias ever denied it.

The seer did not seem to object to being kept waiting in this way. Every minute or so the mastodrom swayed restlessly, treating its passengers to a soporific rocking. Meanwhile the tuskless creature groped about with its trunk, which was shorter than an elephant's but bifurcated for half its length, and therefore almost as handy. When the time came, the mastodrom would use its flexible trunk to help its passengers dismount.

———

On that summer morning, Alcmene, she who was to be my mother, awoke stretching on rare and expensive silken sheets, her body luxuriously sated by a night of tempestuous lovemaking, the like of which she could not recall. Somewhat to her surprise and disappointment, she found her bed partner gone when she turned in the direction of the empty pillow beside her own.

Her dreams, when at last her husband's importunities had allowed her to fall asleep, had been vaguely disturbing.

At the time of which I write, my mother was still considered a remarkable beauty, though the first years of her youth were past.

Pulling on a robe, a thin wrap designed to display her superb figure, she went out into the hall. The first servant she encountered was actually on his way to tell her of the unexpected caller at the gate, but she brushed aside this news and demanded: "Where is the master this morning?"

The question earned her a blank look. "Where should he be, mistress? Still a great many miles from home, I fear."

My mother's protests died on her lips even as she heard the news of the distinguished visitor; already a fearful suspicion had been aroused in her heart. There might be something seriously wrong. But what could it be? She knew, unquestioningly, that her husband had come home quite unexpectedly about midnight and had been with her through the remainder of the night, joined to her very closely most of the time. But now his familiar presence had vanished, completely and unaccountably.

Alcmene looked into room after room, but there was no sign of Amphitryon anywhere, nor of his weapons, nor of the clothing and the armor that he must have been wearing when he came home from the wars, must have discarded before coming in to her. She could clearly remember hearing his weapons and his breastplate clang together when they were thrown down on the floor.

Another servant, hurriedly dispatched to reconnoiter, came swiftly back to report that the cameloid Amphitryon always rode was not in the stable.

Now the lady Alcmene had to put her uneasiness momentarily aside to greet her illustrious caller, as Tiresias, the king's adviser, was being conducted to the house and offered refreshment.

When she entered the room where he was waiting, the eyeless man turned his pale face toward her. If he was aware of what effect his appearance could have, at close range, to one who was not accustomed to it, he made no allowance for it.

He said: "I wish to speak to your husband, my dear, as soon as he comes home. That should be soon."

Despite the servants' evidence, Alcmene was on the point of correcting her visitor, telling him that her husband had been home for many hours. But she remained silent, remembering how the servants had already started to react to that claim, absolutely refusing (though silently and subserviently, of course) to believe her.

She never even considered the possibility that the events of the night just past might have been a dream. Whatever else might have happened to her, it was not that. Dreams did not leave the dreamer's body pleasurably sore, and bedsheets stained.

While servants spread through the household in a futile, half-hearted search for a master they knew could not possibly be there, old Tiresias began to explain to my mother the reason for his visit.

"Young lady, last night I saw the great god, all-powerful Zeus himself, descending on this house. I saw the Thunderer enter your bedchamber, and what transpired there, between the two of you."

"Merciful gods!" the lady murmured, low-voiced. Her first thought was that the man who stood before her now was mad.

His voice, though, was horrifyingly reasonable. "But even from me"—he thumped his chest—"from me, Tiresias, the *why* of the matter is still concealed."

The lady drew a deep breath. Her second thoughts were even more frightening than her first.

"If," she began, "*if*, as I say, my lord Tiresias, anything of the kind had happened . . ."

But the lady was spared any effort at deception. The seer had turned his blind head and was listening to sounds from another direction.

A moment later, the unexpected return of Alcmene's husband was announced, by a servant who at least pretended to be joyful as he proclaimed the news.

The fact was, of course, that until the night when my true father first visited my mother, Alcmene had enjoyed a justly deserved reputation for chastity. The great god Zeus knew this, of course, and so for the duration of his visit, which lasted only a few hours, he had assumed the likeness of her husband. If you know anything of the history of Zeus, in legend and in fact, you will not be surprised.

The legends will tell you also that to make sure Alcmene was thoroughly deceived, Zeus gave her a gift of a golden cup, which Amphitryon could have captured from his chief opponent in the war, and also told her of many things that had happened on the battlefield. Later, when Amphitryon tried to tell her of his adventures, she amazed him by filling in some details he had forgotten. But on the truth of these particular stories I make no judgment.

———

Usually Alcmene was genuinely glad to welcome her husband home. But this time it was with a heavy, sinking feeling that she first saw Amphitryon, as he came riding in with two or three companions, all of them dismounting from their cameloids with weary groans. She felt nothing at all of the lightening of spirit with which she usually witnessed his arrival.

The general was really of no more than ordinary size, but so strongly built, with powerful hands and arms, that he seemed larger. He was about forty then, somewhat older than his wife. Much of his long hair had already turned gray, which secretly annoyed him, though it gave him more credibility as a leader. His eyes were gray, too, and they could turn very cold and hard.

"Hello, wife. We've ridden all night." Amphitryon had arrived wearing helmet and breastplate, just as his surrogate had on the preceding night, and his round shield hung from the horn of his wardrom's saddle. The returning general was in good health but looked somewhat dirty, tired and worn, after a journey of several days.

He came to his wife and kissed her hungrily, locking her in an embrace. If the general had not been entirely without women for the past several months (and he certainly had not), he had endured that time without the one woman he preferred above all others.

Iphicles, my half-brother-to-be, then a mere beardless fourteen years of age (not very large but strongly built; a younger edition of his father), awakened by the stirring in the house around him, came running to welcome his father home, demanding at once to hear tales of glorious battles.

Answering Iphicles, Amphitryon said: "Well enough, I suppose. I suppose we win more than we lose, if we count up all the scores. Well, this is not the first year that this war has taken up our time, and I don't suppose it'll be the last. But enough about battles. I've come home for a rest."

When the tired general finally took notice of Tiresias and his squad of escorting soldiers, he was surprised.

"To what do we owe this honor, soothsayer? Has the king sent you?" Amphitryon tried to keep out of his voice the disgust he felt in looking at the eyeless face.

"I am here by reason of a greater power than King Eurystheus." Tiresias smiled faintly, as if he could still hear the general's loathing in his guarded speech. "Amphitryon, I bring you news of your extraordinary misfortune."

The general's shoulders slumped, and for a long moment he stared in silence at the prophet. Then he looked around him, making sure that the members of his immediate family were all well. But Amphitryon, who did not know yet that he was to be my foster father, was too well acquainted with the seer, or at least with his reputation, not to take him seriously. "If you bring bad news, let me hear it in private."

Giving the prophet his arm, he guided him to an inner room and shut the door.

When the two men were alone, and Tiresias settled in a comfortable chair, he raised his blind face toward the warmth of the cloud-filtered sunlight coming in a window. Then, at the sudden passing of the cloud from in front of the sun, he tilted his head away from the light, as if its new brightness hurt him in some way.

The general half-sat on the edge of a table, folding his arms and swinging one leg. "Well, sir?"

"Last night your house was visited by a god," the prophet told Amphitryon bluntly.

"Indeed." It took the general a little while to come to grips with this announcement. Like the great majority of people anywhere, even those of high rank, he had never in his life seen any god. Had anyone else told him the same thing, he would have laughed. But this was Tiresias.

"Which god?" Amphitryon demanded at last. "And for what purpose?"

"It was the Thunderer himself. As for his immediate purpose, it was the same that generally brings Zeus to the bed of a lovely mortal." The blind man raised a cautionary hand. "You ought not to blame your wife, for the god appeared in a perfect semblance of yourself. Any mortal would have been deceived."

For almost a full minute after the general heard those words, he seemed unable to speak. At last he managed to choke out a brief response: "But why?"

The question got no answer—not then. At that time the seer knew no more than the cuckolded general exactly what purpose Zeus might have had in committing this outrage, beyond relieving his chronic lust. No doubt that was purpose enough for the Thunderer, to whom legend attributed all the fine moral stature of a rutting beast.

Tiresias had to repeat his unwelcome message several times before the general began to believe what he was being told.

Amphitryon's first reaction, when at last he began to believe what he was being told, was violent anger. Jealous rage swelled in him, and he stalked about, muttering.

Then he stopped and looked at the closed door of the room. "Where is my wife now?"

"It will do no good to question her," the seer advised him.

But Amphitryon, angry, would not listen to advice. Summoning Alcmene, he brought her into the room and closed the door again, shutting the three of them off from the rest of the world, and made her listen to the prophet's story.

In a low and deadly voice he ordered: "Tell my wife what you have just told me."

"Tell her yourself." Tiresias, himself more puzzled and uncertain than he wanted to admit, was in no mood to be ordered about.

"What have you to say to that?" the general demanded of his wife.

"Oh, my lord. I don't know what to say." She who had just become my mother felt confused and injured—and at the same time, secretly, gloriously honored at the thought that the greatest god in the universe had chosen her as his lover, if only for a night.

Her first thought, on hearing the prophet's revelation, had been that Zeus had simply lusted after her; only now, as she listened to the two men talking, did it occur to Alcmene that she might be going to bear the god's offspring.

Mixed in with shame and surprise, my mother felt a wonder and a gratitude that she dared not show. She fixed pleading eyes on Amphitryon. "My lord . . . I repeat, I don't know what to say. Last night I was sure that I was with you—as I am sure of your identity at this moment."

Her husband grunted something, a stunned and almost unintelligible sound. "For now," he said at last, "better go on about the business of the household."

———

Obediently Alcmene bowed her head and moved away. When she was gone, her husband turned back to Tiresias.

"Prophet, I am sorry if I spoke rudely to you a moment ago. I apologize, and humbly I ask your advice."

The blind head nodded slowly. "Your apology is accepted, great general. My first advice is that you do nothing in haste or anger."

Amphitryon might not have heard him. He almost seemed to be mumbling to himself. Another wave of shame and anger had come over him and seemed about to overwhelm him. "The law says—tradition has always said—that a woman so grossly unfaithful can be, even should be, burned alive."

Before he could even begin to pursue that idea, there came what might have been a response that effectively prevented any serious consideration. A burst of savage thunder sounded from not far overhead. Looking out the window, the general gazed incredulously at the thick clouds which had been gathering, with amazing swiftness, since his arrival home.

Moments later, rain poured down. There would be no outdoor fires today, anywhere in this vicinity.

———

Over the next few hours and days, suspicions of some baser plot began to creep in on Amphitryon, taking possession of his imagination. For a time, even despite the warning cloudburst and its thunder, he almost managed to convince himself that Zeus was not really involved. Rather it seemed to him possible that the king or someone else had been playing him false, and Tiresias was in on the plot somehow.

———

My young half-brother, Iphicles, moped about for a day or two after his father came home, upset by the knowledge of what had happened, and worried about what might happen next. Any suggestion that his mother might be burned would have terrified him, but fortunately for his peace of mind, he never had to hear it.

———

Tiresias and his armed escorts took their leave of the estate on the afternoon of the day of their arrival. The ancient seer was accustomed to unpopularity, but he was still unshakably certain that he had seen the god descend.

Of course the seer made sure that his concubine was with him when he left. Meanwhile she had spent the time chatting with the kitchen girls, delaying them in their work; and Tiresias in the intervals of his own conversations had enjoyed listening to their voices, even at a distance.

And that is basically the story of that day as it has been told to me. There are questions which I have never been able to answer to my own satisfaction. For example: Was it Tiresias who told the general what my name was to be? If so, was it his own idea, or did it come from Zeus? And did the seer advise that the name should be well publicized, on the theory that calling the child "beloved of Hera" might forestall the wrath of the Thunderer's jealous spouse?

In any case, I can now assure you, with the benefit of firsthand experience, that the gods, the real gods, are not bound in their behavior by what the legends say they ought to do, how they ought to feel.

———

The next days—then weeks and months—were difficult for everyone on the estate. Amphitryon, like any other general, was not averse to handing out punishments when he deemed them necessary—he enforced his will firmly enough, but he took no particular joy in making people suffer.

But he was jealously possessive of Alcmene, and he took his own honor very seriously. In this case there seemed no one else to blame for his wife's infidelity, no one to punish except her. But any move along that line had been effectively forestalled.

Once Amphitryon had firmly put out of his mind his first wild impulse to burn his wife alive, he meditated taking a great vow never to touch her again, for fear of bringing down on his own head the jealousy of Zeus. And it is a fact that my mother had no more children.

In later years, when my personal history began to be severely confused with legend, until matters had reached a point where even I could scarcely be sure where one ended and the other began, some stories had it that the mother of Hercules, still "fearing Hera's jealousy," caused me to be exposed, shortly after birth, just outside the walls of Cadmia.

There the goddess Hera herself was said to have come upon me by accident and to have been tricked into nursing me, not realizing that the sturdy infant at her breast was the illegitimate spawn of her lecherous husband.

In fact, the truth about the relationship between the goddess and myself is even a little stranger than the stories. Time and the gods permitting, I will have more to say about it later.

People love wonders almost as much as food and drink, and sometimes more, and so they insist on creating legends. But mere mortals lack the storytelling skill of Fate, and legends tend to be less marvelous than truth.

Some nine months after god and prophet had made their respective visits to our house (visits which were never repeated, by the way) my mother gave birth to me; and an hour after giving birth she was tottering on her feet, sacrificing at the altar of Zeus, giving extravagant thanks that I had not come into the world with a bull's horned head, or any such overt indication of my paternity—such a consequence of the god's mating with a woman was not unknown.

Years later, Alcmene became fond of telling me that for the first few months of my life, everyone around me had the impression that I was entirely normal. Mother always shook her head in wonder when she told me that.

2

Lessons Gone Awry

IN LATER YEARS my mother always told me that I had been a gentle child. Somewhat moody now and then but, fortunately for myself and others, almost never aggressive or quarrelsome. I have the impression that my mother controlled me easily, during most of those early years, with soft words and much love. But as the wife of an important general, she had many obligations, and a large part of my upbringing was left to others. As for the general who played the role of my foster father, I saw even less of him than I did of my mother. Only very recently have I begun to develop some real sympathy for this man, Amphitryon, whose own scruples would allow him neither to adopt me wholeheartedly as his son, nor cast me out as a nameless, shameful bastard.

I suppose my childhood was happy enough, as mortal childhoods go. Yet a few unpleasant memories endure, beginning very early. (I am not talking now about the snakes, for on the day they came to kill me I was much too young to retain any memory of the event—more later on the snakes.)

The earliest scene of any kind that I can recall with any accuracy took place when I was three or four. One of my succession of nurses, irked I suppose at having been sternly forbidden to administer even the mildest paddling, locked me in a closet as punishment for some childish offense. Standing alone in the dark was not frightening so much as boring, so I put my hands on the door and gave it one determined but still easy push, which broke it neatly from its hinges and shoved it flying across the room. Standing out most clearly now in memory are the wide eyes of the woman who had locked me in, and the way that I, ready to accept the whole business as some pleasant game, laughed at her astonishment.

Being shut up in a dark place had meant no more to me than brief inconvenience, and I might have continued to assume the whole episode was only one of play, except for the frightened look on the face of the nurse when she heard the loud splintering of wood and saw how I emerged—and worse, the expression on my mother's face when she came in response to the noise, beheld the wreckage, and learned what had happened. The adult reactions, which were more of fear than of disapproval, puzzled me and brought on in me a deep, unsettling anxiety as well.

Very much the same thing happened also some years later, on the one time when Amphitryon beat me, in an effort to inflict punishment. He may have been half drunk at the time.

Up to that point in my life, you understand, I had been given no official account of my true origins. I suppose it was not until late in my childhood that I began seriously to doubt that Amphitryon could be my real father. When the suspicion arose, I found it not particularly disturbing. The man had rarely demonstrated any enthusiasm regarding me—his parental energies seemed to be concentrated almost entirely on Iphicles, for whom he arranged a promising marriage when the lad was only sixteen, and I was only two or three. Not that my half brother and I engaged in open rivalry. As long as I remained a child, there was too much difference in our ages, and afterward I was rarely home. And Iphicles was assured of inheriting the whole estate.

Nor was Amphitryon especially cruel by nature—actually I can only recall him beating me that one time, and for that he had some justification. In the process of testing the strength of a certain object that he valued highly, a fine steel dagger that was a present from the king, I had broken its blade.

As a child I was credited with being stoic, because I had no clear idea of what real pain was like; and fortunately my special powers had always protected me from real injury as well.

Their onset must have been gradual, and at first they were restricted to purely defensive service—I never bit a nipple from the breast of my mother or any of my wet nurses, never crushed an adult's finger in my instinctive baby grip. My seeming stoicism on the day when Amphitryon beat me was not the result of any grim attempt at fortitude, but rather a near indifference to what was happening. Having reached the age of ten or so, I had practically full voluntary control over all my powers. I might of course have pulled the strap out of his hands and torn it into shreds, but I was well aware that any such feat would only have worsened an emotional climate that had already become extremely unpleasant.

As the flogging went on, and on, without having any noticeable effect, the man who had never quite been my father—though I still called him that—grew frightened by my reaction, or rather by my lack of any that he could understand. Suffering and fright on my part would have reassured him, and sturdy defiance would have been understandable. But I remained sullenly unmoved, and he grew fearful. Only then, by contagion, did the experience become frightening for me in turn. Thus, by means of a complicated process, the thrashing did at last have its intended effect, causing me to mend my ways.

As proof of the impact the experience had, the images are with me still. Amphitryon's arm rising and falling, rising and falling, swinging a leather strap, while I stared impassively and wondered at the ritual in progress. I realized that any normal child would have been left bruised and screaming, but I was in no way qualified to play my expected part. Each loud impact on my exposed flesh was met precisely by an involuntary countersurge of invisible power from within my body, a nullifying force that afforded me virtually complete protection. After the beating had continued for what seemed many minutes, I began to be aware of a faintly unpleasant stinging sensation, not enough to keep me awake had I been sleepy, and later in a mirror I noted a slight reddening of the skin.

At last the man who had never been my father cast the strap away from him and left the room in silence. I suppose he must have spoken to me—uttered threats, admonitions, curses, *something*—while the punishment was in progress, but whatever it might have been, I retain not a word. And he never spoke to me of the matter again.

When I had outgrown my succession of nurses, my mortal parents provided me with a series of tutors in their stead. Mathematics, geography, an elementary grounding in certain languages (for language I had an aptitude), literature. Of these instructors the last one, Linus, taught me music. More accurately, he made an effort to do so.

I liked the pure sounds of Apollo's instrument, the lyre, or of a good singing voice—mine was not. I could be entranced by intricate melodies, calling up captivating dreams that went beyond what could be put into words. But the musical details I was actually expected to learn, all the tedious-seeming business of tones and notes and scales, remained as indigestible as bits of gravel.

Linus was middle-aged, and not a large man physically, though he could seem so when he made the effort, which he did fairly often. As far as I knew he lived alone, and whether he had wife or family he never said. He had gray curling hair, very little beard, a fondness for jewelry, and an aristocratic manner, more so than many of us who were supposedly the genuine aristocrats. He knew much about music, and cared much. But I soon learned that he cared about power more. There was in him also a sadistic strain, which he for the most part kept concealed.

I was already fifteen years old when Linus arrived to teach me. For the past few years it had struck me as odd that Amphitryon never said anything about starting me on a course of military training. The other boys with whom I was best acquainted, those of my own age and class, were all now keenly concerned with sharp blades and other military matters. I had never been encouraged to play with weapons, except that practice with the bow was tolerated, and I had acquired moderate skill in archery. Not that I was particularly eager to be a soldier, but the fact of my special treatment left me uneasy, because it emphasized the importance of my difference from everyone else. I suppose I dimly understood that my parents were afraid of what might happen if someone put a sword or spear in my hand and urged me to use it, even in a controlled practice. And now here I was, for some reason expected to do well in music.

I suppose it is hardly necessary to mention that my peers respected me for my strength, although I carefully controlled it when in their presence, using only just enough to outwrestle any one of them when called upon to do so, or lift a slightly greater weight than any other boy could manage. I think my efforts at concealment succeeded, to the extent that none of my companions, with the notable exception of my nephew Enkidu, had the faintest suspicion of the true state of affairs. I myself had reason to believe that my powers went far beyond anything they had yet been called upon to do. But I did not *know* that for a fact. I had no wish to know the true extent of the gulf dividing me from everyone else.

The immediate cause of my problem with the tutor Linus had to do with a certain servant girl attached to our household. Megan had come from somewhere among the savage tribes to the far north; she was a couple of years younger than I, and I had started an affair with her.

In a way I suppose that was almost inevitable. Young masters in manors, from time immemorial, have begun affairs with young servants, slave or free. Down through the years I have often told myself that, more often than not, the menials are rather pleased, at least at first, to be so singled out.

But in contrast with the way such affairs usually progress, I had fallen in love with Megan.

Linus came upon us when we were making love in one of the makeshift hideaways we favored. Perhaps his intrusion was sheer accident. I will not repeat now exactly what he said or what he did (some incidents are not worth telling), but it involved a kind of blackmail—as far as I knew, my mother and foster father were not aware of my serious involvement with a servant.

The girl was much in my thoughts. But she was absent when the crisis came.

There arrived a certain summer afternoon, in the courtyard shaded by trellises and grapevines where I usually had my lessons, when Linus, unwisely going beyond mind games for the moment, struck his unmusical student. It was a casual, contemptuous, almost absentminded slap, of a kind he had administered to me two or three times before. The impact of a music teacher's hand was no more painful to me than a falling feather. But this time the teacher had chosen precisely the wrong moment, had overstepped an invisible line, and the unmusical student immediately, impulsively hit him back.

He ought not to have attempted blackmail and then struck me with such casual contempt. The two together added up to a fatal mistake. He thought he had established a new hold over me that gave him the privilege of inflicting such abuse, but in fact the very opposite was true: he stood in special danger. His words and act together were like a spark in the air of a granary filled with dusty grain. My anger flared explosively.

I knew beyond a doubt that my teacher was dead before his body hit the courtyard tiles, as soon as I felt in my right arm and shoulder the small shock of the backhanded, unpremeditated blow and realized, too late, with how much angry force it had been delivered.

For the space of several breaths, which to me seemed a long, long time, the routine of the surrounding household flowed on just as before. I could hear the steady murmur of incidental sounds. No one else was aware of what had just happened, and I remember realizing that in some sense my world, the world in which I had grown up, was coming to an end. That world had only a minute more to live, and maybe less. I could hear the servants being merry about something, in the direction of the kitchens, and in another courtyard someone pouring water from an urn.

I remained utterly alone in the small, shaded courtyard, with the body of the man I had just killed. In fact I had never felt so utterly alone in all my life. My right fist with the lyre still gripped in it—I have never much cared to listen to the sound of that instrument since— had caught him awkwardly on the jaw, making a breaking noise that seemed quite loud, and my tutor had gone down on the pavement as if felled by an arrow through the heart. Now he lay with eyes open and his head twisted far over. He might have been gazing at the sky, or maybe at the intervening grapevines on their trellis, and there was such a look of complacency on his dead face that I doubted whether he had had time to feel a thing, much less to understand just what had happened to him and why.

Fortunately for me, Linus was not a member of the aristocracy, nor was he attached to the king's household. But neither was he an utter nobody, whose shattered jawbone and broken neck might never be noticed, whose death could be practically ignored and forgotten. His only relatives were . . . who were they, exactly? I could not remember at the moment, but I seemed to remember his saying that they lived somewhere far away.

My trial took place two days later, in an audience chamber of the palace, before Eurystheus the Second, the teenage king of Cadmia. Following the advice of my lawyer, who happened also to be a friend of the royal family and of Amphitryon as well, I pleaded self-defense, and on that ground I was acquitted. The whole business took less than half an hour.

Eurystheus was a cautious youth, still ill at ease being king, feeling his way into a job for which he had never been properly prepared. He was not one of the lads with whom I had grown up. He was somewhat taller than me, and it was easy to see that by the time he was twenty years old he would be fat. His father had fallen unluckily in some minor battle, and he himself was grandson of Eurystheus the First, who had been on the throne when I was born. In those early months of his reign, Eurystheus the Second, a lifelong slave of caution, went nowhere without a guard of picked soldiers in attendance. I think he had nothing to say during the entire trial without first getting advice from the legal adviser who stood just behind him.

━━━━━━━

Tiresias was in the room during the trial, along with a score or so of other onlookers, but he had nothing to say.

In the course of the arguments, my lawyer, one of the cleverer of his profession in the city, had occasion to say several helpful things, one of which was: "The truth is, Majesty, this young man is growing rapidly and he does not know his own strength." My lawyer tended to perspire heavily, and yet in fact he was quite calm and confident under almost all conditions.

The truth was, of course, that I knew my own strength better than anyone else who was still alive. But I was not going to argue the point.

The king was only a few months older than I was, and he could sympathize with that. Thinking back, I realize that he also might have had a tutor or two whose violent deaths would not have totally displeased him.

There was learned medical testimony that Linus's neck had been broken, as were certain bones in his skull and in both his upper and lower jaws. The fatal lyre, itself basically undamaged, was exhibited in evidence, and we all stared at it solemnly.

Only one more brief whisper from his adviser, and the king was ready to pronounce his verdict. That I was speedily acquitted was, I am sure, partly due to the fact that the king wanted to retain his general Amphitryon as his loyal follower. It also helped that Linus had only distant relatives alive anywhere, and no one of importance was seriously offended by his death—indeed, his abrasive manners probably caused a number of citizens to feel a certain satisfaction.

━━━━━━━

Acquitted though I was, it was universally agreed that I ought to go away for a while. As my sixteenth birthday was still almost a month in the future, I was considered still a bit young for the army. The king recommended that I be sent out to tend the herds for an indefinite period—this frequently happened to the youth of prominent families when they grew hard to control. As we were leaving the palace, my lawyer told me confidentially that in practice my stay with the herds would almost certainly be prolonged for at least a year, more likely two or three. But there was no reason why I should not pay brief visits home during my period of exile, provided I was discreet about it.

As we returned home after the trial, my mother was in tears, though she could hardly have hoped for a more favorable outcome. Amphitryon was somewhat grim, as usual, and had little to say. But he appeared reasonably well satisfied.

My lawyer, like most other male adults, was a military veteran, and he shook his head. "Besides, any young man, especially a general's son, who reacts to the first touch of discipline by breaking the neck of someone in authority—that young man would not fare well in the army."

So my official innocence was declared, and in the same breath my punishment, for it amounted to that, was settled. With the king's verdict gratefully received, and a date for my departure set, the household was caught up in a general sense of relief. I scarcely saw Megan, and I had the impression that she was deliberately trying to keep out of my sight; but I would not have known what to say to her had we had a chance to be alone. The fact that everyone, even my mother, seemed ready to ignore me during my last few days at home did not bother me at all: The less attention anyone paid to me in my current state of mind, the better.

But before I turned my back on home and went to learn to be a herdsman, I decided to make a greater effort than I ever had before to probe the uncertainty of my own origins. I waited until I could feel reasonably confident of having Alcmene to myself for a quarter of an hour, and then approached her, when she was alone and reading, or perhaps weaving or spinning.

It did not seem to me a good omen that this meeting was going to take place in the same courtyard where I had killed Linus, but I refused to put off the business any longer.

"Mother?"

She raised her lovely eyes with slow reluctance. "What is it, Hercules?"

"I want you to tell me the truth about the snakes."

There was a long silence, during which my mother refused to look at me at all, and picked at her woman's work with nervous fingernails, and, I suppose, dropped or made a stitch or two. Then at last she raised her eyes to mine again and asked: "What snakes?"

When I only waited wordlessly, standing with hands clasped behind my back, she fell silent again, and it seemed a long time before she sighed. "You've heard the stories."

Of course I had been hearing them, in several garbled and fragmentary versions, from the servants, from my playfellows, year in and year out, from the time that I was old enough to understand any stories at all. Still I said nothing.

At last she gave in, and set aside the fabric she had been holding in her lap. Folding her well-kept hands, she said: "Of course you have. Well, I suppose your father and I should have told you the truth about it all much earlier."

The many stories I had been hearing all my life were of course concerned with more than snakes. *My father?* I thought. *I have never seen the face of my true father nor heard his voice.* But I said nothing. I wanted to take things in order, and now it seemed that I might hear the truth about the snakes at last.

Another sigh from Mother, another pause. Then at last she began. "It happened in this house"—she turned her head—"in what is now my sewing room, which was then your nursery. There were two snakes that came in—into the house—somehow. One day when you were no more than ten months old."

"How did they come in, Mother?"

"We were never able to determine that. The doors had all been closed, or so the servants swore. There were the drains, of course, but everyone agreed the snakes were too big for the drainpipes. When they were dead the servants measured them, and one was fully eight feet long, the other almost ten." And she repeated: "You were ten months old."

"Some enemy sent them, to attack me? Or could it possibly have been an accident?"

"I don't know." She shook her head and sighed. "No, that's not really true. I was sure from the beginning that it was not a—not a natural event. We've never been able to determine any reason. That anyone would have had."

"Did you try?"

"For a time we did. I consulted soothsayers, but they could tell me nothing."

"Tiresias?"

"No." She shook her head. "I suggested going to the king's prophet, but your father didn't want to consult him."

"You mean it was Amphitryon who didn't want that."

"That is what I said."

"He is my father?"

My mother was silent.

After waiting awhile I asked: "Of what species were the snakes?"

"I think they were not natural snakes, but monsters. Although they might have been vipers of some kind, I suppose. I have never learned much about snakes, but I have no doubt that they were poisonous. I saw their fanged heads later." Alcmene's face was still almost calm, but she made a strange, small noise in her throat. "One of the magicians cut their heads off, so he could use them in his rituals. But he was able to find out nothing."

"Tell me exactly what happened," I pressed her.

My mother sighed loudly, as at a painful but familiar sight. "There's no doubt about it, the serpents were coming after *you*. There was a servant's child, an infant, in the room as well, but they ignored her. Their path into the room took them directly past the cradle where she lay, and they came past it, straight to you. We could see the slimy trails they'd left—not natural snakes, but monsters. And you were still too young to walk. But somehow you had caught one snake in each of your two hands. You grabbed each one just behind the head, just as if you knew that was the proper way."

My witness had tilted her head back now, and her eyes were closed. "Snakes never die quickly, and they were still thrashing about when we—when I heard the noise and came running into the room. Their thrashing had pulled you from your cradle, but you still held on. Your little fists did not seem big enough to grasp those scaly bodies properly. But when we tried to pry them away from you, we saw how deep your tiny fingers had dug in through skin and scales, how you had crushed bones."

I did not know what to say. Of course I could remember nothing.

"You were not crying, Hercules," my mother said. "You were laughing, as babies laugh. You thought it was a game."

There was silence in the courtyard for a time. Finally Alcmene said: "That was when your father and I knew how truly—how truly special you were, Hercules. Though we had begun to suspect, even earlier."

"My father?"

My mother's eyes came open, and their look was sharp. "Hercules, you know who I mean. The lord Amphitryon has been a father to you."

So, it was true. I nodded slowly. "More or less. Most of the time. Some of the time, anyway." I knew boys who had suffered much worse treatment in their homes, and from true fathers; I had seen their bruises and heard their stories.

"He has not been cruel," I had to admit. "But I think he will be glad when I am no longer living in this house. But, Mother, now that you've started to tell me about the snakes, tell me more. Please. Every little detail that you can remember."

While Alcmene talked, confirming what had seemed the wildest rumor as cold fact, I stood before her listening carefully, but most of the time I did not look at her. Instead I looked down at my own hands. They were well kept, sunburned, but not at all callused—it seems that I never develop calluses, or blisters, either, even from hard manual labor. For a youth of fifteen my hands were not particularly large or muscular, though they were no longer childish.

At the moment they were resting on the back of a heavy wrought-iron chair, the top of the chairback formed by a bar of curving black metal half an inch thick. I thought the bar must have been bent into its present shape when it was red hot, by the blows of a heavy hammer in the hand of a skilled smith. That rod of iron was cold now, and many a strong man could have held it over his knee and strained and groaned and not been able to wrench it out of its congealed shape by so much as the thickness of a fingernail. I knew I could easily—easily!—have tied it in a bow, but I did nothing of the kind. Not for many years had I performed any truly extraordinary feats in my parents' sight, or in the presence of anyone who was likely to report to them.

The story of the snakes was deeply interesting, but now that words and thoughts were flowing I had even bigger questions that I wanted answered.

When my mother fell silent again, I asked her: "How often have you seen my father? When was the last time?"

Her eyes went closed again, and her head was shaking slowly, side to side.

She said: "Hercules, enough. It will be better if you don't try to dig into such matters."

"What will be better? How can it be better?" Receiving no answer, I drew a deep breath, and persisted. "When was the last time you saw my father?"

For a moment I feared that my mother was going to faint. But at least she did not pretend not to know whom I was talking about.

She said: "I have had one meeting with Zeus in my entire lifetime, and you seem to know about that. I suppose there is no possibility that you could not. I swear to you, Hercules, that since that night I have never seen him, or heard from him again. Not ever."

"I believe you," I told her. "Yes, I believe you, Mother." My throat was dry. I had never seen him or heard from him at all.

She nodded. "Amphitryon has always been suspicious, but I have sworn to him again and again, as I swear to you now: That night was the first, and last, and only time."

"I see." After a while I added: "I thought that there could possibly have been some message. Some word for me, even passed on indirectly. Maybe after I was born—?"

"Nothing." Mother shook her head emphatically. "Never again the slightest communication from *him,* the god we are speaking of. You must understand that, Hercules. I have no reason to think that he, your true father, even knows that you exist, or would care if he knew."

My hands were tightening on the iron chairback, and I could feel it begin to give a little, like soft wood, or something no harder than the body of a snake. I knew that what I was doing would leave fingerprints. "Someday I mean to find him, Mother."

Alcmene had been upset by my questions, but now, for the first time, she was frightened. *"Hush!"*

"I mean to find him, Mother. Find him, and talk to him, and learn from him what he knows and cares about."

"Hush, I say!" And she started from her chair.

On the day after that interview with my mother, I left home to be a herdsman.

At that time, most of the locally owned cattle were grazed in a district called Nemea, miles from the city. Herds of cattle, mixed in with lesser numbers of droms and cameloids. The animals and the herders who followed them spent eight or nine months of the year wandering among treeless hills, with ribs of rock protruding here and there through a thin skin of soil and grass. If the winter promised to be mild, the stock might be kept out in these fields all year round.

Once again, on the morning of my departure, my mother expressed her great relief that the king had declared me not guilty, and that my punishment had not been more severe.

"You must be thankful, Hercules. A man who strikes a fatal blow by accident sometimes has his right hand cut off."

I was in no mood to be told how I should feel. "I don't suppose that happens very often to any son of any family as important as ours. And I doubt it could happen at all to any son of Zeus."

I remember how she stared at me then, aghast at my dangerous pride. "Perhaps we have spoiled you in bringing you up—spare the rod and spoil the child."

Alcmene had to stop there, probably remembering the day when

Amphitryon had tried to beat me. And I suppose she was also thinking of Linus, who had not believed in sparing the rod—not as long as his hand held it.

At last my mother was able to continue. "Hercules, you have a princely pride. But you must remember that you are not a—prince." She hesitated just slightly before the last word, and I thought, with an eerie sensation down my spine, that she had been on the point of warning me that I was not a god.

"I know what I am not, Mother. But what *am* I?"

She could not tell me that. But I was determined that some day my father would.

3

A Real Lion

IT SO HAPPENED that my twelve-year-old nephew Enkidu, the son of my half brother, Iphicles, was also scheduled to take a turn at herding. I had managed to avoid that sort of duty until now, but Enkidu already had a year's experience in minding cattle. Of course when the summer ended I would be required to remain in exile with the herds, while he would return to Cadmia to go to school and to begin his military training.

My nephew was tall for his age, only a few inches shorter than I, and of wiry build. His hair was curly black, and most of his skin, like mine, had been burned dark by the sun. He might have been considered handsome, were it not for the fact that his ears stuck out outrageously. The difference in our ages was small enough, and we saw each other frequently enough, that my attitude toward him was what it might have been to the younger brother I had never had.

There I was, at the age of sixteen—my birthday overtook me on the road—undertaking what was really my first unsupervised trip away from home. Propelled by the well-nigh irresistible force of a royal suggestion, armed with my mother's blessing, and with a bow and arrows presented to me at the last moment by Amphitryon, I put on sandals and a herdsman's long shirt and started out into the countryside, with Enkidu at my side.

The army had taken almost all the cameloids and droms that were of any use, and so the two of us had to walk to the grazing grounds. We made fairly good time, but still the journey took us almost two weeks, on roads that alternated between dust and mud, depending on the weather.

As familiar territory fell behind, and the road ahead opened more or less straight and clear into the unknown, the gloom that had hung over me since the death of Linus began to lift. Enkidu helped to raise my spirits, too; he was a cheerful, energetic rascal most of the time, telling jokes and propounding riddles, looking forward to a repeat of what must have been a pleasant adventure for him during the previous summer. Sometimes during that two-week hike my companion and I were fortunate enough to find a hospitable farm, and sometimes we slept under the stars. One night when it was raining, we were lucky enough to find a hollow tree big enough to let us put our heads inside.

We heard nothing about any lion until the fifth or sixth day out, when we encountered an itinerant peddler who was trekking in the opposite direction, tugging the reins of a llamoid that bore in its panniers his meager stock in trade, tightly covered to protect it from the rain. According to the story this wanderer told us, the herds that we were going out to watch were being steadily depleted by, and one herder had already been killed by, an enormously powerful and savage beast, a great cat whose hide through some unnatural magic was proof against the point or edge of any weapon.

Neither my nephew nor I had ever laid eyes on any feline bigger than the household tabby. And I suppose neither of us was overly imaginative, at least not enough to be frightened by the story the peddler told. Rather we were intrigued—a lion seemed to promise some excitement in what might otherwise have been a boring job.

Enkidu had seen enough of me in recent years, observed enough in the way of occasional secret demonstrations, to have some awareness of my awesome physical strength, a factor that no one else in the city or on the estate, not even Amphitryon, had yet fully appreciated. As I may have mentioned already, there was nothing about me at first glance to give the secret away. At the age of sixteen I was coming to terms with the fact that I was never going to be above the average height. My hands were on the small side for a man's, my wrists still relatively thin, arms and shoulders quite ordinary in appearance, revealing nothing of the invisible might that coiled within. What I had not yet begun to understand was the full extent of my own powers.

Among the few items I carried with me into temporary exile were a quiver of arrows and a heavy bow, both, as I have mentioned, parting gifts from my foster father, bestowed before either Amphitryon or I had any idea that I would soon encounter a lion on which to try them out. The bow was so heavy in the pull that only the strongest men could draw it and shoot with any accuracy. It was elegantly made and decorated, and I am sure that Amphitryon would have kept it with him except that he, who by ordinary standards was far from weak, found it impossible to aim steadily.

Despite Enkidu's having made the long journey to the herding range once before, he still managed to lose his way as we drew near our goal. But after an extra day or two of wandering, my companion and I eventually located the herds belonging to several owners, about a thousand animals in all, gathered in one place. Naturally the grass in the immediate area was rapidly depleted, and the herd had to be kept almost continually, if slowly, moving.

On our arrival, the herdsmen turned out to be a small pack of frightened boys, fewer than a dozen in all. When they saw that newcomers had arrived, they slowly gathered around us.

Their leader, a tall youth called Tarn, gave us a cool welcome and seemed to be determined that we should be properly frightened, at least of the lion if not of him. He introduced us to the others, a scrubby crew varying in age from ten years to about fourteen, of assorted shapes and coloring. Some, like Enkidu and I, were clad in herders' shirts, others wore nothing but belts to hold their slings or knives. They were armed with an assortment of poor-looking weapons, including blades, slings, and simple sticks.

We soon learned that our new colleagues, particularly after dark, spent as much time huddled fearfully together as the animals did. And they were interested in me. Word of what had happened to Linus had already reached them; news of such violent and dramatic events always got around fast. I was only surprised that the truth had not yet been greatly exaggerated.

But talk of the lion naturally dominated everything else. All the boys swore that they had seen the beast again and again, though no two of them gave exactly the same description. All agreed that it was a fearsome monster indeed, and of a gigantic size.

Fear is one of the more contagious ailments, and Enkidu and I began to feel a touch uneasy.

The cattle tattooed with Amphitryon's brand, about two hundred animals in all, were mixed in with those of other owners, several varieties of sheep and mutant cows and steers all jumbled together. Until a few days ago there had been a herd bull, a fierce animal who had challenged the lion and had been promptly eaten.

"We wanted to get the animals all in one place," one of the more talkative lads, who had been on duty for the last few months, told me. As I immediately suspected, the truth was that with the lion prowling almost every night, and sometimes during the day, the boys all wanted to stay together, for which I could hardly blame them.

The more experienced herders among them explained to me that the traditional plan for trying to fend off a large and active predator called for three watch fires to be built each night, and the herd kept inside the triangle as much as possible; of course it was often hard to scrape up enough fuel for one good watch fire, let alone three. The animals were so frightened that they stayed without much wandering. Of course it would not have taken much to launch them all in a stampede.

"Since the lion usually comes at night, I doubt your bow would be of much use," observed the leader of the herd boys, "even if it wasn't much too thick for you. Unless you can see in the dark?" Tarn was determined to hang on to his leadership, such as it was, especially as he was a couple of inches taller than me, though probably a little younger. I think it cost him a valiant effort not to be impressed by the fact that I had not only killed a man—no one else in our crew had done as much—but had somehow escaped serious punishment for the deed.

I thought of demonstrating how easily I could draw the bow, then offering to let him try. But at that tender age leadership had no more attraction for me than it does now; it is a burden I unwillingly assume when necessary and drop again as soon as I am able, because in my view it brings unpleasantness at best.

"Afraid not," was all I said.

"We hoped they would send men this time." This from the second-oldest of my new colleagues.

"All the young men older than me are busy with the war. And none of the old men want to do this kind of work. Besides, when we left home, no one there had even heard about your lion."

"But," I added after a moment, "I might be man enough to deal with it." I suppose it was only the calm tone in which I spoke that forestalled an outbreak of derisive laughter.

Tarn thought about it, then demanded: "If you're sixteen, why aren't you in the army?"

"I just turned sixteen on the way here." I wasn't going to try to explain that my parents had kept me out of the army because of their deep though unspoken fear that I would mangle someone—not an enemy, but some comrade in arms who, according to the rules, ought not to be mangled. Probably it had even occurred to them that whatever violence I might commit in this remote place would be more easily ignored or covered up.

At that age I had as little acquaintance with physical pain as I had with serious fear. No doubt my claim sounded to my new associates like idle boasting, but I meant it only as hopeful speculation. Having lived all my life with my extraordinary powers, I felt confident that they would see me through an encounter with a lion as effectively as they had through confrontations with snakes and music teachers. I wasn't *absolutely* confident, no, not quite—but what doubts I had were no more than enough to excite a certain sense of danger, and only to the level where it was still pleasurable.

One of my listeners, at least, was not convinced by my offhand optimism. "Deal with it how?" Tarn asked, going back to the subject of the lion. He was still looking dubiously at my oversized bow.

"We'll see. I'll do the best I can." And I turned away, avoiding argument. That had become my habit, more than ever, in the weeks since Linus lay in the courtyard with his eyes turned for the last time to the sky.

Unlike most of the other herders, who kept finding various honorable reasons not to undertake the job, I readily took my turn, and even volunteered for an extra one, walking between small watch fires in the dark.

On the next night after our arrival, the lion came again, terrorizing the herd, and killed again. I heard the great beast roar, but wanted to wait for better light before trying to do anything about it.

When the first light of dawn arrived, there the predator still was, great mane and tawny hide and switching tail, crouched in the middle of what was now an otherwise deserted plain. The successful hunter was still feeding leisurely on its kill, a steer with its throat torn out.

Most of the other boys were looking at me, ready to be amused as soon as I presented them with whatever good reason I might have found for not approaching the enemy just now. But I paid my audience little attention and instead began to walk steadily toward the lion. Enkidu stayed with me, only a step behind.

With the impatience of youth, and well aware that my aim was less than expert, I loosed my first shaft at what I considered long range, something more than a hundred yards. My bow was bent far enough to propel the arrow with tremendous force. But unfortunately I missed the mark by several yards, so badly that with majestic scorn the lion ignored my efforts. Not till my third shot did I manage to hit the beast, squarely on its wide flank, with a broad-blade hunting arrow. The boys behind me drew in breath with a collective gasp as the keen-pointed shaft only bounced off.

The lion turned its head, gave us a look, and unhurriedly went back to feeding.

Now we had solid evidence confirming the rumors that this was no purely natural beast. Odylic magic was involved.

In a quiet voice, Enkidu, standing beside me, said: "Then it's true, what the stories say, about sharp points and edges, how they can't dig into its hide."

I grunted something. We might indeed be facing powerful magic, but I had no intention of giving up. The other herders stayed where they were, well in the rear, watching, desperately gripping their inadequate weapons.

"If I bend the bow any farther," I muttered, "it'll break. Or the string will." And that was exactly what happened on the next shot. The tough cord snapped and lashed me, imprinting a line of what would have been fiery pain on any mortal human arm save mine.

The boys squinted at me from a distance, as if getting a more detailed look might help them understand just how I had managed to break the string on a bow that none of them could have begun to pull. Tarn, who had been anxious about maintaining his leadership, was now as silent as the rest. Eventually, on his making a reasonably courteous request, I had let him try the bow, and he had strained his thin arms to draw it without having much effect.

Now I violently blasphemed the various bodily parts of several gods and cast away the useless stick, trailing a length of broken bowstring. Clenching my fists, I looked around me in frustration.

Had I had any experience with a shepherd's sling, I suppose I would have borrowed one and tried it; as matters stood, I had no reason to think that I could hit the beast with a slung stone in more than one out of a dozen, or maybe a hundred, tries. I would be at least as likely to brain one of my companions, no matter where they stood. With a little imagination, I could picture that kind of performance rendering the great beast helpless with laughter—I supposed it was not entirely impossible that a magic lion could laugh.

Still, such missiles did not depend on sharp points or edges to do their damage, and on thinking the matter over I doubtless would have tried to borrow a sling, except that the lion had turned to look at us once more, with an attitude of speculation, and when I looked around again the other herders had all retreated to an even greater distance. Except, of course, for Enkidu, who, though far from cowardly then or later, was careful to stay close to my side.

When the lion had made its latest kill, the herd had scattered, as it usually did when one of its number was brought down. The others had dispersed quickly to a distance of a couple of hundred yards. But once the predator settled down to eat, some instinct evidently told them that they were safe again for the time being, and they stopped running and resumed their life's work of turning what grass they could find into meat and milk and dung.

After the shot that broke the bowstring struck near the lion, kicking up dust from the rocky soil, the beast coughed a little roar and regally prepared to withdraw. But there was no thought of abandoning its dinner. Once more sinking its fangs into the fresh carcass, it gave a single heave and slung the inert mass over one shoulder. Then it walked away, carrying the dead weight greater than its own with the ease of a man wearing a small traveling pack.

Shrugging off the useless quiver of arrows, in my frustration I hurled them scattering to the ground. "I'm going after the beast," I told my nephew. "You can stay here with the others, if you like, and watch the cattle."

"No need to watch the stock while the lion's gone," Enkidu protested. "I'm coming with you. I know how to track," he added hopefully, after a moment.

Obviously my nephew's confidence in my abilities was at least as great as my own, and I found that somehow reassuring.

"All right," I agreed. At the moment the lion was still in sight, and I did not need a tracker. But before going after it I wanted to arm myself with some more effective weapon.

The twelve-year-old looked back toward our timid colleagues, then suggested: "One of these others might loan you a sword."

"I've seen their swords; you borrow one if you want. And bring a waterskin. No, if an arrowhead won't pierce the damned thing's hide, I'll bet a blade won't, either."

"You could try thrusting right down its throat."

I looked at my helpful colleague. "I'm going to try a club." I might have thrown rocks at the lion, of course, but again I distrusted my aim.

"Are you sure?"

"No, I said I was going to try."

Pacing away in a direction opposite to that taken by the beast, I climbed a nearby hillside where there were scattered trees. Such fallen trunks as were available proved on close inspection to be soft and rotten, so I soon found myself engaged in the difficult business of cutting and tearing a big club out of a live tree. Picking up an edged rock as the best tool available for severing and breaking wood, I hacked and splintered the green, live trunk of a wild olive into an approximation of the shape I wanted. The task took me the better part of an hour, while Enkidu stood watching in near silence.

———

My weapon, when I had finished shaping it, tearing away with my fingers the last unwanted bark and splinters, was about five feet long and almost straight. The thick end was as big around as my leg, the small end much thinner, enabling me to grip it comfortably. The wood was springy and heavy, and when I swung it hard it sighed nicely in the air, with faint whistling overtones.

———

By the time I had finished these preparations, the lion of course was out of sight again. Silently my nephew led the way to the spot where we had seen it last. Casting around there, he soon picked up its trail.

We had to follow the beast across half a mile or so of barren ground, and around another hill or two. In this effort my nephew's tracking ability proved of considerable help.

We came around yet another hillock in the great plain, and there the lion was, not a hundred yards away. It had dropped its burden and was once more chewing contentedly. We were close enough to hear the bigger bones crunch sharply, as if a man were cracking nuts. A few scavenger birds had begun to circle overhead.

This time when the lion raised its head, displaying a bloody muzzle, I had the feeling that it recognized me as the one who had been shooting arrows; and by now it was tired of being pestered. The beast once more coughed a short roar in our direction. I suppose our antagonist viewed two young humans more in the category of dessert than as a serious challenge, but was gentleman enough to give us a warning anyway.

As we began our final approach, Enkidu's sandaled footfalls, which at first sounded only a pace or two behind me, fell more and more slowly, and farther and farther to my rear. That was fine with me; I needed no tracker at this point, and if my club swung wildly, I did not want my kinsman to be at risk. He was a brave lad, with a lot of confidence in me, but a real lion is a real lion, and I had to admit that this one seemed to grow ever larger as I approached.

I suppose that if my former mathematics tutor had been at my side, and I discussing the business with him, I might have described my state of mind at that moment as 90 percent certain of victory. If there was only a 10 percent chance that the lion would be able to rend me limb from limb and eat the pieces—well, that chance did not seem real at all. Sixteen-year-olds are almost universally convinced of their own personal immortality.

Now only a hundred feet separated me from my quarry, and I plodded steadily on. The lion looked away from me again and around the barren landscape, as if in search of witnesses who might later be called to testify to my insane behavior. Then it looked back. It raised its head and coughed once more, seemingly puzzled by this two-footed creature of less than half its size, who kept inexorably advancing.

Something in the way the animal turned its head to one side suddenly reminded me of Linus. And like Linus, it felt perfectly confident of its own authority, even when confronted with things it did not understand. Or was my own confidence all a horrible miscalculation, and was I going to be eaten? But it was now much too late to entertain such doubts.

Now there were only forty feet between us, now no more than thirty. As I continued my methodical advance, with club upraised, the lion crouched and sprang.

I swung my five-foot log with two hands, and all the power that I needed was there to draw upon, unfailing and seemingly unlimited, as I had never really doubted it would be.

But on that day, in my instinctive reaction to the onrushing threat, I must have called upon more than I really needed, far more than I had ever tried to use before—though the surplus was not so extravagantly disproportionate as it might have been. Under the impact of heavy green wild-olive wood striking its extended forelimb, head, and shoulder, the massive tawny body changed direction instantly in midleap, ricocheting almost at right angles. It was as if I had swatted a large insect out of the air. The lion hit the ground ten yards away, rolled another five, and lay there with its four legs sprawled. Its body was convulsed by violent spasms, which even as I watched declined into a sporadic twitching.

My greenwood weapon had survived intact the crushing impact, though the force of the reaction, descending through my body, had driven the heel of my right sandal, on which my weight was braced, several inches into the hard, dry ground. Neither my heel nor any other part of my anatomy was bruised, or even tender. Power had simply flowed from its mysterious, invisible source through all my joints and tendons, bones and skin, seeming to turn my modest muscles momentarily into steel, the flow protecting my own frame even as it worked destruction on another.

Warily, somewhat awed at my own success, I approached the lion, club upraised. But it was easy to see at once that no second blow was needed. The tawny hide was still amazingly intact, but my one stroke must have created chaotic internal ruin. The body on the ground looked shrunken and half-boneless. One eye had been popped out of its socket, leaving a raw hole, and dark blood was trickling past the white fangs of the open mouth to form a little pool on the bare ground.

There was a sound of running feet, and Enkidu came up, panting, to stand in awe beside me, muttering in a high childish voice the names of gods and demons.

"I saw it. But no one will believe it," he observed after a moment. I looked around and saw that the other boys were only now coming back into sight, atop a little hill two hundred yards away.

"They will if we show them the hide," I said.

We drew our knives and got to work upon the grotesque, almost boneless corpse. Or rather tried to get to work. Our blades could make no more impression on that skin than had my useless arrows.

———

Belatedly the bright idea occurred to me that it might be possible to skin the beast using its own claws or fangs as tools. We soon discovered that the claws of a great predatory cat were ugly things, filmed with rancid grease from rotting bits of raw meat. Whatever the special nature of those sharp, stained points, they worked. Skinning the cat was still a clumsy job, but no longer impossible. Gradually the other herders came to gather around, trusting the evidence of their eyes that the lion was dead.

———

Soon I decided that the job of skinning would be more easily completed back at camp. With a single heave, I lifted the beast's dead weight easily onto my shoulders and went stalking away with it.

The other herd boys soon rejoined us. After a quarter hour or so of near speechlessness, they began to be generous with praise, and with advice on how to cure the hide.

A couple of them claimed to know something about the process. "We'll just stretch it in the sun for the time being." And some began to gather poles of wood to make a frame.

———

"See?" Enkidu was poking at the dead, misshapen head. "You could make the jaws into a kind of helmet. So you'd be looking out through the open mouth."

"Sounds uncomfortable." And so it proved to be, when at last I was able to try it on. But by that time, I had other matters to worry about, of far greater moment.

Later, as months and years went by, a legend somehow spread far and wide that had me wearing the lion skin as my chief garment from that day on. In truth I tried to do so for a while, but the smell of a hide so crudely tanned was hideous, and there were other inconveniences. The poor beast's pelt survived in legend vastly longer than it did in fact. Before long I parted with it in disgust, and I have no idea whether anyone ever picked my discard up.

4

A Visitor

NATURALLY THE FLURRY of questions continued. I grunted responses, and Enkidu kept thinking up new answers. To begin with I had told the simple truth, that I hit the lion and it died. The only trouble was that no one was going to believe that. All right then, so be it. Actually I felt uncomfortable about letting the simple truth be known. I could not forever keep my terrible strength a secret, but I wanted to postpone as long as possible the day when everyone knew about it.

None of the other boys had actually seen me kill the beast, though some were puzzled by having heard, from beyond the hillock, a single sharp jolt of sound, reverberating from other nearby hills to give the impression of something like a thunderclap. It came to me that they meant the impact of my club.

"Was the lion struck by lightning?" one naked urchin demanded of me.

"No." Ready to give up attempts at cleverness, I repeated in a few terse words the plain truth of how I had killed the beast.

Still it did not really sink in. "We heard a noise," remarked another. "Like a big thump."

But Tarn only shook his head. "No, seriously, Hercules. What happened?" He seemed convinced that I must be joking; but now there was a certain deference in his tone.

"All right, then," I agreed. "Enkidu and I walked around that hill and found the animal dying. Maybe a big rock fell on it out of the sky."

"What?" Boys looked up, startled, craning their necks and hunching their shoulders as if they feared a shower of stones was on its way. "What rock?"

"All right." I shrugged my shoulders. "That couldn't have been it. Then someone or something must have poisoned it."

"What?"

By this time most of my other colleagues were gathered closely around the carcass, beginning a detailed inspection. Soon a couple of them were waving hands smeared with lion's blood and reporting that many of the big cat's bones were broken. How could that happen, one wanted to know, if the beast had died of poison?

If my fellow herders had scarcely known what to make of me before I killed the lion, they were now totally confused. But gradually the conviction became established among them that I must be somehow responsible for the monster's death, and soon no one any longer disputed that idea. As long as they ceased to pester me for explanations, I did not mind. In later years, of course, when my fame had grown, the legends never left room for any doubt about how I had slain the beast. And in this case the legends were remarkably near the truth.

It was soon plain that the boys who had boasted of their skill in curing and tanning animal skins had stretched the truth considerably, as boys are wont to do. In fact, none of us knew much of anything about the process. Gloriously magic that tawny hide might be, but it stank so that even a pack of unwashed ruffians like us could not endure it. We stretched it on a vertical frame made from thin logs, using the lion's teeth and claws as tacks or points to hold the skin in place. Then—I had some eager volunteers to help—we scraped the inner surface clean, as thoroughly as possible, and rubbed it down with sand. After that we left it exposed to the sun and rain. A day passed, and then another, but still the hide retained a prohibitively powerful stench.

———

The lion's carcass was scarcely cold, and we were still working on the skin, when the business of tending the herd, exciting a few hours ago, already began to seem to me excruciatingly dull. At first, saying nothing to anyone, I contemplated sallying out into the great wide world to seek my fortune in some form of high adventure. The animals I had been sent to look out for were no longer in any particular danger, so I thought I could hardly be accused of violating any important trust if I simply left.

About all that held me back was my uncertainty over which way to go, what to do next when I did leave. Unlike many young men, I had no wish to go to war; there had been a certain satisfaction in crushing the lion, but my memory of killing Linus had nothing pleasant about it, and I would have given much to be free of the dreams in which I relived that scene.

On the other hand, if I went home, I could expect to lead a dull and controlled life. Not only would I be subject to parental authority again, but, as in my last few days under Amphitryon's roof, everyone would be walking around me on tiptoe in fear of some fresh act of violence. Within a year or two I could expect to be pressured into an arranged marriage with some woman or girl from one of the families with whom Amphitryon wanted to cement an alliance. And I was afraid I knew just which girl the general would have in mind.

Moodily I tried to explain all this to my nephew. We were both chewing on straws, sitting in the shade of one of the few live trees that dotted the grazers' landscape.

"What will they make you do?" Enkidu asked, wrinkling his forehead in an evident effort to imagine parents compelling anyone as strong as me to do anything.

Downwind from us, the lion's skin was stretched out. It seemed to be willfully ignoring the bright sunshine that was supposed to cure and dry it, and was continuing to poison the air. Maybe the magic that kept it from being pierced was going to keep it from being tanned as well.

I said: "Get married, I expect, for one thing. To someone . . ."

"Who you don't want to marry."

"Right."

My confidant thought that over a bit. "She's not good-looking, hey?"

"If it's the one I think it is, she's a couple of years younger than you are, and already ugly as Cerberus. No reason to think she'll be any handsomer when she grows up. And then I'd have her whole family for my relatives, and that . . ." I made a helpless gesture, despairing of being able to explain. My private thoughts had turned to Megan, as you might suppose, and in a persistent daydream I imagined myself standing beside her in a formal wedding ceremony. But of course nothing of that kind would be tolerated.

Enkidu wasn't listening to me anyway, but shading his eyes with his hand, gazing into the distance. "We have a visitor," he said.

———

That happened to be the evening when a traveler, no doubt worried about lions and glad to find any honest-looking company, approached our fire and asked to be allowed to spend the night. We had no objection, being always ready for some news of the world. He was a burly, bearded man, and now and then he would suddenly look back over one shoulder or the other, as if he had just heard behind him a certain footfall that he had no wish to hear. He was wearing a short sword, in itself nothing out of the ordinary.

Naturally the first thing our visitor took notice of on his arrival was the lion's pelt—it was not an easy object to ignore, stinking as it did, and framed as it was, held up like a banner. He claimed to have heard, in a city many miles away, about the famous lion whose hide was proof against edged weapons, and he said he had come our way deliberately, detouring many miles into the remote backcountry, hoping to encounter someone who had actually seen the beast.

But now he squinted dubiously at the stretched-out hide. "This is the one that was killing so much livestock?" He sounded unconvinced.

"The very same," said Tarn, sounding as proud as if he were the slayer.

Our visitor frowned at it critically. "I expected it would be bigger."

"Maybe it's shrunk," Enkidu put in. Then he was inspired with what he thought was a better idea: "Actually there were two lions, and the really big one got away." But I was the only one listening to him, and that only with half an ear.

"Any lion can be a killer," the stranger admitted, still considering the stretched hide. "Of course not the worst monster I've heard about. Not by a long bowshot. Lucky for your little lion there it didn't try hunting in the eastern swamps. Likely it would've been eaten if it went there. Swallowed whole, even if no tooth could pierce its hide."

"Eaten?" Tarn's jaw dropped. "What could eat a lion? What do you mean, swallowed whole?"

And the stranger began to tell us.

Around the fire in the herders' camp that night, we sat with open mouths, listening to the traveler's exotic stories. When the wandering stranger found how ignorant we were on the subject, he began to entertain us with stories regarding the Lernaean Hydra, which he claimed was terrorizing folk who lived near the marshes of Lerna near Argos, which lay hundreds of miles overland from where we were. None of us had ever been there, of course, or anywhere near.

Aye, there were great things being done out in the great world! Privately I came near deciding that I would be gone with the first light of morning. I could see that Enkidu's mouth was hanging open as he listened, and I decided to invite him to come along.

Our informant swore to the truth of another item that also stuck in my memory: that a wealthy man named Augeus had recently offered a reward, of what seemed a truly fantastic sum of money, to anyone who could rid the land of the Hydra. So far, only two men had tried to claim the prize, and both of them had promptly disappeared into the swamps, not to be heard of again.

At this point all my colleagues simultaneously turned their heads, as if unconsciously, to look at me. Our visitor seemed to take note of this, but his only reaction was a frown, as if he resented the fact that momentarily he had ceased to be the center of interest.

One more quick look over his shoulder into darkness, and he who had been telling us the wondrous news was ready to expand on it.

"Compared to the Hydra in the Lernaean marshes, your upland lion is nothing," he concluded. His tone and attitude, as he glanced once more at the stretched skin, seemed to say that it couldn't even have been much of a lion if a couple of herd boys had taken off its hide.

Enkidu spoke up sharply, suggesting that our visitor try his own knife on the hide. But the traveler seemed to be paying him no attention.

"What *is* a Hydra, anyway?" asked one of the younger herd boys, too humble to worry about seeming ignorant.

The visitor was eager to reply to that one, in some detail. "The Hydra is enormous. It has twenty heads, and each head has a set of jaws filled with teeth as big as my hand. It eats lions as readily as it eats deer, or cattle—or people. What I'm telling you lads about is a monster born of monsters—they say that Typhon was its father and Echidna its mother." On the last word, he tossed one more quick look back over his shoulder into darkness.

"Typhon was a Giant," put in the tallest herd boy. Tarn was gradually beginning to feel secure in his leadership again, seeing that I had no interest in the job; but he had made no attempt to give me orders.

"Still is, as far as I know," put in someone else.

"What's Echidna?" asked the smallest urchin.

"Another monster, of course," I replied. But I think none of us really knew.

───

It was on that night that I encountered in my sleep, for the first time, one of the strangest figures I had ever met, awake or dreaming. And the oddest thing about it, as it seemed to me while I lay lost in slumber, was that the apparition bore no resemblance at all to any of the creatures of wonder we had been discussing around the fire.

In my dream I stood surrounded by high stone walls, so close on every side that I could not help feeling closed in, very nearly trapped. He who stood confronting me was very tall, looming over me as if I were a child. The figure stood on two legs, and in general it was very manlike, strongly built and wearing a kilt and sandals. The chief exception to its human appearance was the head. That was a bull's head, complete with two long, sharp, curving horns; the head of a creature that, if discovered in the herd, might have given even our lion pause. And when the man, if he was indeed a man, opened his bull's mouth to speak, the voice that came out of it was very odd. Still, every word was clear.

"Come to me, Hercules. Come to me and learn. Bring your great strength to me and I will find employment for it."

And I awoke, sweating, and afraid of I knew not what.

———

In the morning, the traveler moved on, leaving us with a few words about the marvelous country he was bound for, where he said he expected to find giant birds capable of impaling people with their beaks. He might have been hoping that one or more of us would volunteer to come with him, but no one did. And even as he cast a last nervous look back over his right shoulder, I had a sudden flash of insight. I understood, as surely as if I had suddenly been granted the gift of prophecy, that as soon as the wanderer reached the glorious land he spoke of, he would begin to tell its inhabitants about the fabulous lion whose stretched skin he had just seen, more wonderful than any creature they had ever beheld or imagined. And he would tell them also about the godlike strength of a youth called Hercules, who had felled the monster with a single blow.

———

My restlessness had not abated overnight. The traveler's stories, though I understood that they might be mostly lies, had only made it sharper. I began to tell my nephew what I was thinking. A little later on that same morning, Enkidu and I took leave of our fellow herders, whose lives had suddenly become much safer and more peaceful, and went heading out in the opposite direction from that our visitor had taken.

When I issued my invitation, Enkidu was willing and even eager to abandon his assigned job with the herd and come adventuring with me. And why not? So far, his time away from home had all been fun.

"If people come asking after you—" Tarn began, when he understood that we were really leaving.

"Tell them Hercules and Enkidu have gone out to see the world."

We had not been an hour on the road again before my nephew asked me: "Herc, what are Giants like? If one of them could father a monster like the Hydra."

"Huge, I guess. Well, of course, that's why they're Giants. But I've never seen one, any more than you have."

"But where do they come from?"

"How in the Underworld should I know?" He might as well have asked me what kind of people lived on the far side of the moon.

It bothered me that I knew so little about Giants. Sometimes I found it disturbing that the number of subjects on which I was ignorant seemed so vast.

Our minds held only the vaguest kind of map, based entirely on hearsay, of the strange lands before us, but we were satisfied with that. We told each other that we could always ask directions, and we were willing to work for our keep as we went traveling.

Enkidu asked: "Shall we go first to see that man who's offering the reward for killing the Hydra?"

I had been thinking about that. "I'm not sure we can find him. I'm not even sure that there's really any reward." I cast a glance back over my shoulder, a habit I seemed to have picked up from our recent visitor. "The messenger, or merchant, or spy, or whatever he was, just wanted to talk of marvels, and maybe half of what he said was true. *Maybe.* When you think about it, he told us nothing of any practical use."

My nephew looked disappointed. "He told us about the reward! We can try to find the man who's offering it. He said the man's name is Augeus; I remember that plain enough."

I thought some more. "The pair of us don't look much like monster slayers," I said at last. "If we tell people we're going to kill this Hydra, they'll only make fun of us."

"You *could* kill it, couldn't you? If you hit it the way you hit the lion."

I let my feet carry me on a few more strides before replying. "I don't think there's anything living in the world that I couldn't kill."

"That's what I thought, Herc. But you don't sound happy about it."

I grunted something.

Enkidu persisted. "So if anyone laughs at us, you could show them how strong you are."

"Yes. But . . ." But that was the very thing I had spent most of my life trying to conceal. Any such demonstration of superhuman strength, it seemed to me, would inevitably lead down roads I did not want to travel. "No, Enk. I say we find this Hydra monster, kill it if we can, and *then* go to the man who's put up a reward—if we can find him. Bring him the thing's head, or one of its heads, to show as evidence. Then he'll have to pay us off."

Not much of a plan, true. But it was enough to keep us going.

5

A Dirty Joke in the Stable

AS WE TRAVELED, I talked with Enkidu about what my mother, though she knew better, hopefully thought of as the secret of my parentage. Of course it was no secret at all. My nephew, like everyone else in Cadmia, seemed well aware that I was the son of Zeus, even though Amphitryon had never mentioned the subject to me, nor had Tiresias in any of our brief encounters. My mother had only admitted the fact to me reluctantly. But my paternity, if far from secret, was still not something my family wanted advertised to the world, or even discussed openly within the family. This at least was the attitude I had absorbed while I was growing up.

I had brought along my club, of course, when Enkidu and I abandoned our duties as herders to go Hydra hunting. After thinking the matter over, I had also brought along my foster father's last gift to me, though the great bow still lacked a string and I had only a few arrows. You never knew. Actually Enkidu carried the bow and arrows for me most of the time.

Our other resources were very limited, consisting of the few coins we had happened to have in our pockets when we left home. And naturally the distances on our mental map were all quite hazy, but we agreed that a journey of some hundreds of miles would be required to reach the swamp where the Hydra was said to live. That of course did not seem much of a problem to us at the time. Shortly after leaving the grazing range, we departed Cadmian territory, but fortunately the lands that we traversed were peaceful.

To earn our keep, on the days when that was necessary, we stopped at farms and in villages along the way, asking for odd jobs. Sometimes people had no work to offer but fed two wanderers out of charity; and sometimes there were days when we went hungry. Once we killed snakes for our bread, in a village that was overrun by them, but they were only ordinary snakes, and we dealt with them by means of ordinary sticks and rocks. More typical was the farm on which we worked to build a wall of rocks.

The construction work went quickly. I suppose that my speed of movement and my endurance, as distinguished from pure strength, were no better than average for an active youth of sixteen. Certainly they were nothing superhuman. But sheer strength makes most physical tasks much easier, and less tiring.

As we traveled, the country around us had been gradually changing, so that my nephew and I now walked a road that wound among wooded hills, and now and then crossed a fiercely plunging stream. And everywhere we stopped, we asked where we might find the man who had posted a reward for the Hydra; so far, everyone we spoke to had heard of the monster, but only a few had heard any rumor of a reward. Still, the number of helpful responses increased.

We came at length to a considerable estate, where the house and its chief outbuildings only became visible after we had walked a long alley of cypress and other trees.

This estate, according to the people we had most recently spoken to, belonged to the man who was putting up the Hydra reward. Augeus was his name.

"Sure, lads, he lives up there." The man who answered our latest question looked as if he wondered why in the world we might be looking for the man we had named. But then he closed his mouth and said no more.

"Is there work available?" I pressed him.

"I'd say so. Ought to be real shorthanded, right about now." And the man seemed to be absorbed in some private amusement as he watched us walk away.

The next people we talked to were workers on the estate, field hands who only stared at us when we asked questions. For a time I thought they might be slaves, but I saw no metal collars. They had a general appearance of unhappiness, and none of them looked well fed, and had we been older and wiser we might have taken warning from those facts.

One of them, speaking in a dull and lifeless voice, told us where we could find the foreman.

The foreman was a heavyset man of indeterminate age, who carried a cudgel at his belt. Seated on a tree stump, he had a stylus and a tablet in his hands and appeared to have been working his way through some problem in arithmetic. He looked us over quickly as we approached, and did not appear to be impressed.

Some instinct was trying to warn me to turn around and walk away. But, having come this far, I stubbornly pushed ahead. "Sir, they tell us you need workers. We're just passing through, and—"

"You'd like some work? Sure, lads, we'll give you a good day's pay for a good day's effort."

The food we were given was poor, and the beds likewise, but in our brief time on the road we had already encountered worse. After a hard day's work of digging and planting, I fell quickly into a deep sleep. And in that sleep there came a dream of birds, like those of which the traveler had told us: iron talons and feathers sharp as arrows. It seemed that Enkidu was clashing an enormous pair of bronze castanets to frighten the birds out of the thickets, and when they flew out I was doing my best to shoot them with arrows. But I was not having much success . . . the flying things were the size of cranes, and closely resembled the ibises which I had seen only in illustrated books. Except that the beaks of my dream birds were straight, not hooked, and the voice of someone I could not see warned me that they could pierce a bronze breastplate.

The bull-headed figure who had appeared in my dreams before was back again. This time on awakening I was able to remember some of what he had said.

"I would bring you dreams more practical than this one, Hercules. This one is not of my devising, but I have entered it, because it is important that we talk."

"And who are you, dream bringer?"

The answer was unclear, but perhaps that was only because I did not want it to be plain.

The speaker's imaged appearance was perfectly distinct, and in my dream I knew that I ought to be able to name him, but that the name I had for him, that was hovering just beneath my conscious knowledge, was wrong. I awoke feeling as close to fear as I had in a long time.

———

On our second day of work for Augeus, the foreman assigned Enkidu and me to a new task. The foreman had a certain surface joviality about him, but we both liked him less the more we saw of him.

"Come with me," he commanded, and led us out of the farmyard and down a hill.

When we halted, we were still within easy sight of the main house. "Master's just taken over this land." The foreman seemed to take satisfaction in the claim, as if it benefited him personally. Perhaps it did.

It was plain that the previous owner had allowed things to deteriorate.

"Stables have got to be put in order," our boss observed laconically.

The stables were built in a kind of ravine, below a reservoir. Here the enterprising new landowner, Augeus, had already employed clever artisans. His engineers had obviously come to work with many men and animals at their command, and they had dammed a stream, creating a huge pond to give his livestock water, and also to hold a stock of fish. I could see that there was even a kind of waterwheel under construction, eventually to be incorporated into the dam that held back the water of the pond. Augeus was a rich man now, and he meant to be wealthier in the future.

Even at a distance, I could see that a monumental task awaited us.

The stables, a row of low, ramshackle buildings, were in considerable disrepair, but an even more immediate difficulty was that they were horrendously dirty. For some reason the simplest chores had been long neglected. I saw before me a long structure, whose stone walls had once been painted white. There were between fifty and a hundred stalls in a row, with a roof partly of thatch and partly of tile, that had fallen seriously into disrepair. None of the stalls were occupied at the moment, but there was plenty of evidence that they had been, in the recent past.

Enkidu and I were handed shovels and brooms and told to get to work. New piles of manure were to be created, in a place from whence it could be eventually hauled away for distribution on the fields.

We put in another hard day's labor, and then another after that, shoveling and carrying muck. Experience on our own estate at home assured me that no cameloids or droms could be safely housed here until the cleanup was accomplished. Not only dung, but the nests of rats and mice had to be removed. There was nothing particularly enjoyable about the task, but as farm work went, it was not the hardest or most uncomfortable. We gritted our teeth and told ourselves that it would last a few more days at most, and we would be on the road again with food in our bellies and some coins in our pockets.

As we cleaned out stalls, other hollow-eyed workers from time to time brought in animals to reoccupy them. None of these stable hands had much to say.

About halfway through the third day of our labors, I suddenly paused in my work—breaking off some irritable talk with Enkidu—and for a moment came near forgetting where I was. I had just caught a glimpse of a girl riding by, a slim young figure elegantly dressed, mounted on a fine cameloid, with silver ornaments upon the saddle and bridle—an elegant vision that seemed to belong to an utterly different world from the one in which I labored and fought off flies.

At first I was sure this glorious apparition had not noticed me at all. But then in passing she turned her head, just once, and looked at me, while I continued to gaze at her. I am sure that my pose and my expression were unconsciously more those of a general's son, or perhaps even a god's offspring, than they were those of your ordinary stable boy. It must have been my manner that caught her attention and caused her to prolong her silent gaze for the space of two or three breaths. For surely there was nothing else about me that might have done so, as I stood, pitchfork in hand, dressed as I was in a tattered herdsman's shirt, and standing up to my ankles in manure.

That evening, when Enkidu and I reported to the foreman that we had finished our day's work, he stalked over in the gathering dusk to inspect the place. The moment he saw fresh droppings in one of the newly reoccupied stalls, an anger grew in him visibly. I understood later that he seemed to be able to turn his anger on and off at will.

"Look at that! I said you make it *clean*. This here place is still shit-dirty!" And he aimed a halfhearted kick at Enkidu, who dodged nimbly away.

"We want to leave in the morning," I said on a sudden impulse. Until that moment I had been planning to stay on another day or two and earn a few more coins. But Enkidu had already begun to push for a quick departure.

Eyeing me from under his lowering brow, the foreman only grunted. "So," I asked in a clear voice. "What about our pay?"

"Pay? *Pay?* You be paid nothing until the stables are all *clean,* like I tell you in the first place. Meanwhile, what about all the food you been eating? There's a cost for that. And what about the place where you been sleeping?"

"What about it?" I was dumbfounded.

"You owe us for that, too."

"*Owe* you for it? We've been sleeping here, among the animals."

"This is not a charity! You got that, dimwits? Now I want to hear no more about pay until you've earned your keep."

Before I could close my gaping mouth and begin to think again, the man was gone.

———

When the two of us were alone again, my nephew said: "Damn it all, Herc, a stable is never going to be spotless. Not with live beasts penned up in it. And they'll be moving more back in tomorrow. The way he talks, we could spend our lives here shoveling and still owe *him* money."

I grunted and nodded. The true state of affairs had begun to dawn on me some hours ago, but I had said nothing until I could decide how best to deal with it. And for once Enkidu had been a little slow to catch on.

"Does he think we're stupid or something?" Enkidu steamed.

"I guess he does. Or at least he's sure we're scared."

On top of everything else, my valuable though not very useful bow was suddenly missing, and naturally none of the other workers whom I asked knew what had happened to it—or so they said. Most of them seemed afraid to talk to me at all. Neither did anyone seem interested in anything but their own immediate survival.

Not for the first time, I wished that I was six and a half feet tall and muscled like a god, with thick, dark stubble on my cheeks and a frowning brow. Then, I thought, no one would have touched my bow.

When we next encountered the foreman, he also suggested, in the manner of a calculated afterthought, that we should not think of running off before we got the stable cleaned out properly—there were a couple of large fierce dogs that the master employed to find those who departed without paying what they owed. With grim satisfaction at what he assumed to be our helplessness, he took his leave.

"I want my bow back," I said in a low, thoughtful voice, when he was steps away.

Almost eagerly he whirled around again. His ears were keener than I had thought, and he evidently thought that we were not worth trying to deceive. "S'pose you don't get it. What'll you do about it?"

My fists were clenching automatically, but I remained silent, backing away from a physical confrontation.

When the man was gone, my nephew looked bitterly disappointed. "Why'd you let him do that?" he demanded.

"Because. If I fight one man, I'll have to fight another, and another. And if I fight I'll break someone's bones . . . and someone else would draw a weapon . . . there'd be all kinds of trouble. It's no fun killing people."

Enkidu was silent for a time, trying to assess my mood. At last he asked me: "Hercules? What will we do?"

"Let's forget about our pay and hit the road. We'll head out about midnight, when they're mostly all asleep. We can live without the pay."

"What about the dogs?"

"I'll take care of them, if they come after us. But I don't want to start killing people and have to fight a war." Yet, having said that to my friend, still I dallied; neither did I want to leave without relieving my anger.

Shortly after dark on that evening, the girl we had seen riding reappeared. Obviously some relative of the owner's, I thought. Maybe his mistress, though she seemed too young.

This time she came deliberately to seek us out. She rode her cameloid straight up to where Enkidu and I were standing, and sat in the saddle looking down at us as if we were a problem that duty required her to solve somehow. Straight brown hair, parted in the middle, framed an entrancing face. Seen at close range, her green eyes and slender body were more fascinating than ever.

"My name is Hercules," I volunteered, to start a conversation. "And this is Enkidu, who happens to be my nephew."

The girl appeared to have no interest in our names, nor did she tell us hers. Well, I had to admit it was really none of our business.

"I just happen to be visiting here," she said at last. Her tone was almost that of one offering an apology. She sighed and seemed to come to a decision. "I heard them talking, up at the house, about you two. They were making jokes."

"Is it your father's house?" I asked.

"It belongs to Augeus, who is my uncle. I don't like him much. He's a cruel man. So are his foreman, and his slave drivers."

"I had begun to form that impression myself," I said. And Enkidu put in, indignantly: "We're not slaves."

She turned her gaze in his direction. "My advice to you is, if you don't want to *become* slaves, you'd better make some plan to get away from here."

"He owes us money!" Enkidu piped up furiously. "Three days' pay! No, now it's four!"

The girl fumbled out a small purse from somewhere and dug into it. Then she whispered a fervent oath. "This is all I have with me." She held out her hand with two substantial coins on her soft palm. "Take this and go!"

I could feel the warmth of her body in the two coins when they came into my hand. "We're planning to head out around midnight," I said.

"That would be wise."

"But there's one more thing," I said. I was intent on prolonging the conversation, though I hardly had any rational reason for doing so. "Would you happen to know, my lady, what has happened to my bow? I had it with me when I came here, a special gift from my stepfather. And now it's gone."

She took thought. "What does it look like?"

When I had described the sturdy stave as best I could, she let me know, shaking her head solemnly, that it was now in the master's collection. "I fear you'll never see it again."

I felt an urge to contradict the dear girl on that point. But she was not the one with whom my disagreement lay. Instead I only said: "Your uncle must be a strong man if he can draw that bow."

"He is indeed. And a dangerous one. Take my advice: forget your bow and leave as soon as possible." She turned her cameloid and rode away while we called our thanks to her back.

———

As soon as we judged the hour had come, the two of us quietly left our wretched sleeping quarters. When we came to where we had a choice of paths, Enkidu hesitated. "What about the bow, Herc?"

"Forget the bow, let's get away from here." I did not turn toward the house, but instead set out in the other direction. After turning this way and that several times, the path climbed to the top of the wall confining the great pond.

No one now, in the middle of the night, was fishing in the pond or working on the waterwheel. The place was deserted by all human activity, but noisy with its frogs. There was a steady murmur of falling water from the dam on the other side, over which the big pond continually drained itself.

"What're we doing?" Enkidu demanded eagerly. By now he was well aware, from my look and the sound of my voice, that I had something in mind more exciting than mere flight. But he had not yet discovered what it was.

"This," I said, and only finally made up my mind even as I spoke the word. Having now confirmed for myself the structure of the dam that made the pond, I laid hands on one of the great stones in the topmost tier. The anger that I had suppressed was suddenly running fierce and high in my blood; at such a moment had Linus died. The rock I grasped was almost big enough to have filled the stall in the stable where we had been assigned to sleep. While the smaller stones above had doubtless been dragged into place by teams of powerful droms, struggling and suffering under the whip, this one looked as if it might have been here since the creation of the world.

"You can't move *that!*" For once my nephew was seriously taken aback.

I only grinned at him. As soon as I had found a satisfactory grip, I braced my feet on lower rocks and tugged. By all the gods, but it seemed to be stuck! I gritted my teeth and pulled harder. The softer rock on which my feet were braced began to crack, and I shifted my stance a little and tried again.

Enkidu was making a little whining, whimpering sound, half protest and half amazement but then suddenly he fell silent.

There was a heavy grating noise.

Moments later, I could hear the water bubbling and laughing to itself, finding a new way out of the pond, this one right in front of me. Only a light gurgle first, but then as I moved a couple of additional rocks it deepened into a heavy rushing sound.

———

Later, legend had it that I had diverted two entire rivers through the stables to flush them out. But in this case legend, as usual, overshot the mark. There was no need for any such complicated feat of engineering. One pond, of medium size, with a lively stream behind it, was quite sufficient. All I really had to do was to break through the wall, or dike, of the reservoir, which stood in effect holding back a river. There was only one key point that needed to be attacked.

The flood, when it burst out, took me by surprise and came near to bearing me away, but I grabbed a nearby tree branch with one hand and hung on.

The water poured violently down the narrow ravine, sweeping brush and small stones and fallen trees before it. But the full fury of the flood was not unleashed until about half an hour later, when a big section of the constructed wall, undermined by rushing water, suddenly gave way. By that time a watchman had discovered the leaking dam, and Augeus himself and several of his officials had been roused from bed to deal with a disastrous flood. They were gathered in the area of the stables, making plans for a new dam, when they were swept off their feet. The master and several others were borne downstream screaming and swearing, almost drowning in a torrent heavily flavored with liquid manure. Some stone walls were undermined and went down, too, and when, hours later, the flood finally subsided, the stables were smaller than before.

But most of the stalls were practically clean.

Naturally, none of the people who were so absorbed in dealing with the disaster had any reason to connect it with a couple of itinerant laborers. Stone blocks that ought to have taken a team of droms to move had been flipped about like small mud bricks, and the explanations put forward varied from earthquakes to the sudden displeasure of some god.

For a brief time Enkidu and I watched the fun from a high place near the broken dam. Then we moved on. My blood was still up, and this time I chose the path leading to the big house without particularly caring whether anyone tried to get in my way or not; as it happened, no one did. Two big dogs came running out from somewhere, but the beasts that might under other circumstances have been fierce defenders seemed too upset by the general turmoil to care if strangers approached, and only bounded past us howling.

The two of us marched on, and moments later entered the house through a back door carelessly left open. A cook fire burned low in the hearth, giving light enough to see that there was no one else in the kitchen.

"Look at this, Herc." Enkidu's nose had led him to some almost-fresh baked bread.

There was other good food available as well, all of it much better than the stuff Augeus fed his workers on. We helped ourselves.

Curious Enkidu, half-eaten sandwich in hand, pushed open the door to an adjoining room, which proved to be almost entirely filled with sporting weapons. Evidently Augeus, or someone in his household, fancied himself as quite a hunter. There was my bow, leaning against a wall, and I thought that I was entitled to a new bowstring as part of my payment for days of hard work. I bent the bow of Amphitryon easily enough, between my two hands, while Enkidu slipped on the heavy cord.

Then I saw him stiffen, and I looked up. The girl, whose name I still had not learned, stood in the doorway. This time she was wearing a thin, fine wrap she must have grabbed up on leaving her bed, a scanty costume that made her look even younger than before.

"Why are you here in the house?" she demanded in an urgent whisper. "He might whip you to death if he finds you here, but luckily there's been some kind of flood. You should be on the road. Take this lucky chance the gods have given you."

"We are going," I said. "Right away. We're practically out the door."

"Actually," Enkidu added, "we left two minutes ago."

I hesitated briefly and then, swept by an irresistible impulse, burst out with an offer: "Do you want to come with us?"

Something lighted in the girl's eyes, and for a moment it seemed that she was actually on the point of accepting my impudent overture. But then she shook her head.

"It wouldn't work. They'd come after you and kill you for sure if I did that. Go, quickly; I'll be all right. I'll soon be going back to my own home anyway."

Yielding to a sudden impulse, I cross the space between us in two swift strides. Before she could try to avoid me, I had taken her in my arms and kissed her. She stiffened and turned her head at the last moment, so my lips fell on her cheek.

———

A minute after that, Enkidu and I were once more on the road, well fed for once and unmolested.

6

Swamp Games

THE THREATENED DOGS never materialized, nor did any other kind of pursuit; I assumed that the noble Augeus had his hands too full with more urgent problems to give any thought to two missing laborers, or to connect them with the ruin of his dam, or even the disappearance of his fine new bow.

Another couple of weeks on the road carried us well into autumn. The heat of summer faded swiftly, and the colors of the trees were changing, it seemed even as we watched.

Sometimes Enkidu and I tried to count up how many miles we had walked since leaving home. But there was no sense of urgency about the calculation, and the only time it caused me uneasiness was when the memory of Megan crossed my mind. I thought of her clear eyes, her soft voice, her warm and generous body, and I regretted the fact that I had come out into the world adventuring without having one more chance to lie with her, or to speak to her at least.

———

The more closely Enkidu and I approached the great swamp where the Hydra was supposed to have its lair, the more extravagant were the stories we heard regarding its appetite and ferocity. We were told that the monster was quite capable of devouring whole herds of sheep and cattle at a sitting, along with anyone who was rash enough to try to defend his livestock. What impressed me most was the intensity of the terror the creature had inflicted upon many who had not even seen it— some of the locals were ready to swear that even the smell of the monster could be fatal.

It was said to be the size of an elephant or greater—I nodded wisely when someone told me that, though at the time I had no idea of what an elephant might be. The smallest number of heads that anyone was willing to credit the Hydra with was nine. All agreed that the central head was perfectly immortal, though it struck me that that would be a hard claim to prove, short of cutting the head off and then seeing if it died.

Our strange visitor at the herders' camp had told us, and a number of local informants had confirmed, that the great beast we were seeking was indeed the offspring of Typhon, an awesome Giant, and Echidna, who was said to have the torso of a woman, along with a serpent's tail.

Not that we believed very much of this. We were young, but not that young. Probably, I told Enkidu, about a third of it may be true. The difficulty lay in knowing which two-thirds were false. We were still eager to press on.

———

The nights were growing cold, and since my companion and I had been so generously rewarded for our few days' work as stable hands, we sometimes paid our way into an inn or private household, and slept indoors.

During an evening at one such inn, it happened that tales regarding the Hydra and its parentage were being told in the common room when we came in. I was just in time to hear one of the locals say: "What I want to know is this—at what point on her anatomy does the woman skin stop and the serpent scales begin? Or vice versa. Must be right around her crotch somewhere, and this could be an important question, if you see what I mean. From ol' Typhon's point of view."

As always, when there seemed even a slight chance of gaining information, I asked questions. "Have you seen the monster, then? Where? How long ago?"

"Seen it? Oh, aye. I have. If *you'd* seen yon Hydra, you'd not be looking to see it again."

And that was about the best we could do in gaining any serious information.

———

We took it as a good indication that we were getting near our goal when we passed through first one village, and then another, that had been totally abandoned for no apparent cause. All of the forsaken houses stood intact, with most of their furnishings inside, undamaged. This, when I thought about it, was a grimmer warning than any tales of monstrous depredations.

After spending a comparatively comfortable night in one of these deserted dwellings, we came out on a brisk morning to meet a well-dressed, substantial citizen of the district, trundling a barrow along a road. He was accompanied by a woman who could hardly be other than his wife, and two small children. It seemed obvious that they were abandoning their home, bringing with them such remnant of their flocks as they had been able to save, one or two animals.

When the crofter saw us, he set the handles of his barrow down and wiped his face. "You're not from these parts, are you?" he demanded as we came up. His speech sounded strange in our ears, for though he spoke the common language, by now we were what we considered a long way from our homeland.

"No sir," I admitted. "We are not."

The man went on: "I must warn you, lads, you've chosen a perilous road. If you ever want to see your homes and families again, go elsewhere."

I shook my head. "If this road leads to the Hydra," I said, "it's the one we want."

The man's eyebrows went up. "And just what do you plan to do when you've located the monster?"

I paused to give the question due consideration. "I think I'll milk it," I decided at last. "I've heard that Hydra cheese fetches a great price with the city traders."

"*I've* come to kill it," put in Enkidu. He flexed his scrawny arm and frowned critically at the muscle that became barely visible in that position.

On hearing our replies, the woman only gave us a weary took and trudged on ahead, tugging her two children with her. But the man kept staring at us. He said nothing at all for several seconds, and his eyes were wide. It seemed we had come across one of those folk who take all statements seriously, no matter how incredible. Finally he got out: "Oh? And how do you propose to accomplish that?"

"We'll think of something," I assured him.

"You are mad, children. Did your parents never tell you that you are both totally mad?"

"They tell us that all the time," said my companion. "But we never listen."

———

Enkidu would have been happy to stand for a long time debating earnestly with the wide-eyed man, but I was growing impatient, and we moved on. For the next couple of days the two of us kept poking around the edges of the swamp, accomplishing little, except that the deep mud irretrievably swallowed Enkidu's sandals, which were not buskined on like mine. Fortunately his soles were virtually as hard as leather.

Eventually, by persistence and sheer luck, we stumbled across a trail that a blind man could scarcely have ignored. To my untutored eye, it looked like some body much bigger than a lion's had been dragged through the swamp by main force. Enkidu at once proclaimed that it could belong to no other creature under the sun or moon. "This is a Hydra's track!" he announced, and slapped one bare foot in the ooze for emphasis, spattering us both with mud.

"How in the Underworld do you know?" I demanded. "You've never seen one before."

"Never mind what I've never seen; I can see this plain enough. What else could it be?"

My colleague had a point there, I had to admit, as we turned to follow our discovery. Whatever beast had left this giant spoor, it was easy to tell which way it had been traveling by the direction in which the trampled growth was bent. We advanced slowly, looking over the crushed underbrush and the deep ruts, and I was holding my club ready.

———

This time no expert tracking was needed to locate our prey. In an hour or so we had come to the end of the trail, which led into the mouth of a low cave, a scooped-out cavity just at water level, big enough to accommodate a couple of Augean stable stalls. This, we were certain, could be nothing but the Hydra's lair.

As we stood on the other side of the narrow, sluggish creek that separated us from the cave, gazing into the dimness and wondering what to do next, there came a heavy scraping sound from deep within the watery recess. Then I caught a glimpse of something moving, a huge thing, far back in shadow. Whatever it was gave an impression of dull scaliness like a fish's skin. But the part I could see was definitely above water level, and the creature seemed to be moving in ways I thought no fish could ever move.

"It's in there, all right," I decided.

We both shouted into the cave, hoping to provoke its tenant in to coming out, and Enkidu threw a flat stone hard, skipping it on the water across the little channel and right into the dark cavity. But there was no response.

"It seems we must lay siege," I said.

"Then let's get to work."

The high ground nearby held a generous supply of dry wood, and with the aid of flint and steel we soon had a small fire going. And at last my great bow became useful, as I fired one burning arrow after another into the creature's lair.

"Look there, Hercules," Enkidu said.

Pausing in my labors, I turned in the direction where he was pointing. A couple of hundred yards away, a small audience was gathering to watch the struggle. Eight or ten people, all facing in our direction, stood on a kind of low bluff overlooking the marshes. Some of these onlookers, to judge by the variety and brightness of their clothing, were no mere peasants and herdsmen. A minute later I caught sight of a second group of watchers, observing us from a different angle. These last were in a fairly large boat. They were equipped with oars but at the moment neither rowing nor paddling, being evidently intent on maintaining their distance.

"Where in the Underworld did all those people come from?" my companion marveled.

"Well, we've been bragging to all the folk for miles around what we intend to do, and some of them must have believed us, enough to get their hopes up, anyway. We may not look like much, but they're probably desperate to get rid of the Hydra, and we're their only chance. And its trail sure isn't hard to find. Let's get on with the job."

My next burning arrow might have hit a sensitive spot, for it seemed to cause the occupant of the cave considerable irritation. The Hydra came out in a rush, splashing muddy water about as if it meant business, and we got our first good look at the thing we had been hunting. It filled the mouth of the cave completely in its passage. At once I could feel the hair rising on the back of my neck. *Here,* I thought, *is some magic power truly as strange as my own.*

And as the beast's monstrous body emerged into full view, any lingering idea that it might turn out to be purely natural had to be abandoned.

It made a noise like steam, hissing and bubbling out from under the lid of some boiling, giant cauldron. Its skin was scaly, mottled in shades of gray and fishbelly white. A body as big as a full-grown mastodrom's, or an elephant's for that matter, came wading and swimming on four massive legs, with clawed feet of appropriate size.

Moving straight in our direction, the Hyrda reared up its heads and towered over me. The number of necks, if not twenty, was certainly not less than half a dozen—I didn't try to count. Each neck ended in a head that would not have looked out of place on a good-sized alligator. More red eyes than I cared to total up were looking at me balefully.

Stepping forward to the very edge of the swamp, I met my foe halfway, swinging my club with a good will, and now with something of a practiced aim. My first hit smashed a head into a spray of blood, with flying bits and pieces.

I had killed one head, but three more instantly came snapping and lunging for me. Fangs ripped at me from two sides at once, but a moment later I felt justified in my confidence that they would be no more than a distraction. Their sharp points could find no purchase on my body, but caught a grip on my tunic, a substantial garment I had recently acquired to see me through the chill nights, and immediately tore it away.

Equal strangeness I was willing to concede this enemy, though I still felt confident that it would not be as strong as me. My belief in my own general superiority was somewhat shaken when, while sparring with the remaining necks, I saw the first head that I destroyed begin to grow back. At first I could not believe my eyes, but it was so. In a matter of seconds the neck stump had healed itself into a scaly, swelling lump, and in no more than a minute new eyes were glowing a sharp red, and a mouth full of new teeth was snapping.

One blow had settled the lion, but I quickly learned that now I was competing on an entirely different level. Not until the fight had lasted for several minutes did I begin to keep count of heads as I destroyed them, and when I got to eight there still seemed as many glaring eyes and slashing jaws in front of me as ever.

I raised my club and advanced a little farther, splashing kneedeep in the slimy water. Somewhere deep inside, I was beginning to grow frightened, and it was a strange and unpleasant sensation, not least because it was so unfamiliar.

Again and again the Hydra struck at me with its claws, which were larger than the lion's and just as sharp. But the power of Zeus still flowed in my nerves and veins, and the beast could not break or bruise my skin, or even knock me down. My swinging arms brushed out of the way more lunging heads and the thick necks that tried to entangle me like tentacles.

So far I had remained unhurt, but still there were moments when I feared that I might have met my match. Despite what I was doing to it, the Hydra was not at all disposed to flee. I stood my ground and kept on flailing with my club, but this creature was capable of harmlessly absorbing, on its necks and body, blows even harder than the one that had killed the lion.

The trees rang back with echoes, as if someone were pounding a giant drum. This monster seemed to shrug off the impacts, and kept on coming. Not only that, but the heads continued to grow back as fast as I mashed them. Even faster. On some of the long necks two heads were now growing where only one had been originally.

Changing tactics, I directed my attack at the body, but the springy necks, each as thick as my own body, kept coming in between, carrying their inexhaustible supply of heads to the unavailing slaughter. The great legs pawed at me, pushing me off balance.

Calling upon reserves of power, I added yet more force to my blows. (Later, Enkidu, indulging his chronic curiosity, discovered one of the beast's long fangs embedded in a tree by the energy of the stroke that had smashed its head.)

But still the damned monster was growing new parts, restoring itself by some odylic magic, as fast as I did damage.

I was becoming winded, all my clothing gone in shreds, and my swings with the club grew wild. At last I retreated, backing out of the swamp, naked except for my lashed-on sandals. Part of me wanted to turn and run, and keep on running; but I fought down the urge.

When he observed my withdrawal, my small ally was disappointed. "We're not giving up, are we?" Enkidu panted. When he was not dashing back and forth along the shoreline, shouting encouragement, he had been gathering more wood and building up our fire.

"Flames of the Underworld, no!" I got out between gasps. "But I need to take a breather. And I have to think. There's got to be some better way to go about this."

Heaps of dry, fallen timber lay nearby, on small islands of high land adjoining the marsh. Taking a break in the combat, we withdrew a few yards to one of the larger islands. There I stood guard on shore, leaning on my club and trying to catch my breath, while the Hydra, writhing and hissing, seemed to be debating among its assortment of heads whether to follow me onto firm ground or let me get away. I could have sworn that there were now more heads than when the fight started; and as far as I could tell at that point, the monster was little the worse for all the pounding it had taken, or all the blood that it had lost that was now spattered up and down the shoreline. Now I could well believe that the thing I had challenged in its lair was capable of feeding on lions as well as cattle.

Enkidu soon had an even bigger fire going, up on the high ground where there was a plentiful supply of wood. By this time it was necessary for me to fashion a new club, having worn out my original one. And this took time, prowling among the live trees and the dead, then hacking and shaving at the wood.

Now it was Enkidu who, in a sense, came to my rescue. It was he who had the key inspiration: "Let's try fire, Uncle!"

"You mean more burning arrows?"

"No. I mean, when you mash a head, if I had a good-sized torch, maybe I could get close enough to sear the neck stump. Then maybe the head wouldn't grow back."

So far no better idea had occurred to me. "All right, it's certainly worth a try. Be sure you stay clear of my swings when you come dancing in with your torch." And I practiced a few swirls of my new club.

"You don't have to tell me that." Fortunately some of the available wood was naturally oily enough to burn with some intensity, and a search produced a few good torches.

I suppose Enkidu's chances of surviving the next phase of combat would have been small indeed were it not for the fact that the beating the monster had already taken had actually slowed it down considerably. That became apparent in the next round. Wading into the marsh again, I pummeled and pounded my antagonist some more. I suppose that each of my blows falling on the monster's body, rather than the springy necks, had done some internal damage, and the Hydra's movements steadily grew weaker. The end of the fight was at last in sight, and we no longer felt any temptation to retreat. Doggedly I smashed more heads, while Enkidu, a burning brand in each hand, darted in and out, scorching and searing the raw neck stumps. As we had hoped, this proved an effective means of keeping the heads from growing back.

———

Time passed, and as the bright daylight of afternoon began to wane toward sunset, even the monstrous vitality of the Hydra was exhausted. The creature was down, sprawled all but flat in the mud and all but helpless, right on the shoreline, barely able to hold up one or two of its remaining heads, while others dragged in the ooze. The process of regrowth had entirely stopped, and most of its necks now ended in charred stumps. Feebly it tried to drag itself entirely into the water, but that we were not going to allow.

And now the eyes of all the heads, save one, were dulled with death. At last, when my great antagonist was almost motionless, I threw down my club. Then, exerting strength behind the blade of one of our poor knives, I severed the last head from the body. Enkidu with his torch was quick to scorch the stump. Then he threw back his head and let out a long, yodeling scream of triumph.

Moments later I posed with one foot on the scaly body, holding up the severed head. It had been the central one, supposed to be immortal, and indeed its eyes still held life, and its jaws still tried to snap. There came a faint cheer from the distant watchers, and then awed silence.

I found their voiceless scrutiny somehow unsettling. "What's wrong with them? The monster that they feared so horribly is dead; you'd think they'd be jumping up and down with joy. Why don't they at least come over for a close look? Don't tell me the thing's mate is still around here somewhere."

For a time Enkidu gazed in the direction of the silent watchers. At last he said: "They're not coming over here, but they're not going home, either. It's almost like they're afraid to leave. I don't think it's another Hydra they're worried about, Uncle. I think it's you."

"What do you mean, me?"

"They've been watching; they saw what you just did. They could hear the sound of the blows. Now they're almost as scared of you as they were of it."

"But I mean them no harm."

"You can be scary, Herc," my nephew said. Not knowing how to answer that, I mumbled something.

A few minutes later we buried the head, still hissing weak, lungless gulps of air, on solid ground, under an enormous rock. Later, it was said by many that arrows, when dipped in the creature's poisonous blood or gall, inflicted wounds that were invariably fatal. Possibly so, but they were never my arrows; from that day when the lion survived my shots, I have rarely used any bow.

Just as I finished working the big rock into position, Enkidu called to me again, this time in a different, quieter voice. "Look, Hercules."

It seemed that, after all, one of the onlookers was not too timid to approach. The man was standing in a second boat, and where he and his craft had come from exactly, I could not have said. One moment it seemed that he did not exist, and the next he was right there, no more than thirty yards away, much closer than the other onlookers, a tall, solitary figure poling a small, narrow boat in our direction.

I expected the stranger to land directly in front of us, but instead he stopped his small craft just offshore, where he remained standing in it. Effortlessly he kept his body erect and the boat steady, with one hand holding the pole, its lower end stuck hard in the muddy bottom of the swamp.

Ignoring Enkidu entirely, the tall man fixed his gray eyes on me. The light of the setting sun struck in under his hat's broad brim, creating there a curious appearance of small, folded wings above his forehead. But still something seemed to prevent my getting a clear look at his face.

"Greetings, Hercules, son of Zeus." Our visitor's voice had a resonant, faintly echoing quality; I had never heard anything exactly like it. For a moment I recalled the bull-man's speech that echoed in my dreams, but this voice had a very different sound.

"Greetings, sir," I replied after a moment. The man was wearing a long robe or cloak of some fine, smooth material—I remember thinking that I had never seen a garment exactly like it. It covered his broad-shouldered body almost entirely, but I had the impression he was vigorous. At first I assumed he was young, then old, then young again—and then I simply did not know.

I had seen other men as tall as the figure before me, a few even taller. And yet I was somehow certain, before our visitor had been with us a full minute, that for the first time in my life I was looking at a god. Beside me, my nephew, reaching the same conclusion at practically the same time, had lost his accustomed boldness and was suddenly trying to hide behind me. Enkidu, more upset than I had ever seen him, was whimpering words I could not understand. I put my hand on his shoulder and made him face our visitor—wasted effort, I suppose, for the god was steadfastly ignoring my young colleague anyway.

The resonant voice of the deity rang out across the swamp: "Hercules, I have a new task for you to undertake. Will you accept it?"

For several moments I did not answer. I was naturally impressed by the fact that a god had come to talk to me, but I think it is only honest to say I was not overawed. Perhaps my pride was foolish, rooted as much in ignorance as in justifiable self-confidence, but whatever its cause it was substantial.

I said: "You know my name, sir, but I do not know yours."

Our visitor did not seem offended by my boldness. "Humans call me Hermes. Or sometimes Mercury, or the Messenger. Today I have come in that capacity."

Now the pole with which Hermes had propelled his boat seemed to have turned into a long rod something like a herald's staff, except that it was entwined with two carven serpents, and I remembered that it should be called a caduceus. And the boat was closer to shore than it had been, though I had not really seen it move.

Now I was more impressed, but I persisted. "Whose messenger are you, Lord Hermes?"

Broad shoulders moved a little under the cape. "Again, I suppose you have the right to ask. Your father has sent me to you, Hercules." Suddenly most of the shadow had cleared from our visitor's face. The orange light of sunset showed me the countenance of a man who might have been thirty years old. Handsome, yes, but I had seen mortals who were at least equally so. A face perfectly human—and yet with something in it that was more.

When I said nothing, the god added quietly: "Your payment, for accepting and performing this new task, will be something more magnificent than you can imagine."

At this second mention of my father, a great anger welled up unexpectedly within me, confused with a surprising longing.

All I could think of to say was: "My imagination has never been strong."

"Will you accept the new task?" Hermes persevered, standing a little taller than before.

"You must tell me what it is." I have no doubt that at that moment, in my ignorance, I was convinced I was invincible. I had just killed the Hydra, and I was my father's son. All things considered, I refused to be cowed by the mere presence of a god—not of this one, anyway.

The Messenger was still patient. Letting go of the pole with one hand, so he could point, he said: "Hundreds of miles to the north and east of here, on the slopes of Mount Erymanthus, a monstrous boar is ravaging the land. The beast is as much a curse to the countryside around it as the Hydra has been around this swamp."

"A boar?" I think my jaw dropped open. Whatever I had been expecting to hear, it was not news of yet another monster. "A giant *pig*?"

Gravely our visitor inclined his head. "A boar like no other that has ever lived."

"And I suppose you want me to kill it."

Then Hermes surprised me again. "No!" His voice was suddenly commanding. "You are to capture the beast alive and carry it to a place that I will specify."

"Alive!" I marveled, and felt Enkidu's shoulder move under my hand as he raised his head; evidently my nephew's wonder at this dialogue was getting the better of his fear.

"Alive, Hercules," warned Hermes. "And when you have caught the Boar, you are to bring it—still alive, I emphasize, and if possible uninjured—to the port city, called Iolcus, that lies on the northern shore of the Great Sea. Do you know the place?"

"I have heard of the Great Sea but never seen it. Nor do I know any city called Iolcus. That will be totally strange to me."

"But you will undertake the task?"

"I would do much for my father," I surprised myself by saying. "I would do more than that, if he would only do a thing or two for me, in return."

Mercury seemed to sigh, as if in relief that I had agreed to what he asked. "So much to be taught and learned, so little time," he mused aloud. Then, raising his voice again, he said to me: "You should have no trouble in finding people to tell you where Iolcus is, for it is also where the Argonauts are gathering."

My mind was still engaged in trying to imagine the attributes of this monstrous Boar, and how I was to overcome it without doing it serious injury. So for the time being I ignored the puzzle of who or what in the world might be called Argonauts, why they were gathering, and what they might have to do with me. But in passing I seemed to remember that our talkative visitor at the herders' camp, he who had refused to be impressed by our dead lion, had also said something about Argonauts. That man had spoken of many things that none of his hearers understood.

But Hermes/Mercury was still talking, and now I had to pay close attention to what he was telling me.

"Before you hunt the Boar, Hercules, I strongly advise you to seek out the centaur named Pholus. He can tell you much that will be of use to you in the hunt."

"Centaurs? I know nothing about any centaurs."

"You will learn," said Mercury dryly. "I have told you there is much to learn." And he went on to give me some further details, including a geographical description of a place where centaurs were likely to be found. "Visiting the centaur first will require a detour of several days' travel, perhaps more. But it will be well worth the effort. Pholus can tell you the best way to go about capturing the beast. And he may have other information that you will find to your advantage."

Hermes seemed to have finished with what he had to say, and a silence stretched out between us. My nephew at my side stirred slightly, probably, I thought, trying to get up the nerve to leave the clutch of my protecting arm. Small waves lapped at the shore and at the sides of our visitor's boat, and in the distance the onlookers still gazed in our direction, as if they expected to witness some new marvel. I wondered if any of them were able to identify the tall man in the boat.

At last, in my pride, I demanded to know: "If it is really my father who wants me to do all this, why doesn't he come and give me these instructions face-to-face?" As I dared to speak so boldly to the god, I felt Enkidu's shoulder twitch again.

"You may ask your father about that when you see him," the Messenger responded imperturbably.

And in the next moment Hermes surprised me. I had had the impression that he was ready to leave, but now it seemed he intended to accomplish one more small task first.

He turned his head this way and that, for all the world like a man nervous about being seen (and who, or what, I wondered, might have the power to make a god so nervous?). Then, with a smooth thrust of the caduceus, which was also his boatman's pole, he brought his boat in closer to the shore, right beside the Hydra's huge corpse.

He bent toward the silent mass, and a short, bright blade suddenly appeared in his immortal hand. He braced one foot upon the body, and with a faint shock I noted that his shoes were winged, like his hat. Neatly Hermes sliced off a fragment from one of the charred neck stumps, and then another from a Hydra head that, although stone dead, was still attached to the body. These ghastly souvenirs quickly vanished, along with the knife, somewhere into the god's pocket, or his sleeve.

And in the next moment it was evident that Hermes, with divine assurance, had decided that our interview was at an end. If I was not overwhelmed by him, he did not appear all that much impressed with me. Gracefully he lifted the long pole out of the water, whose surface was blackening steadily with the approach of night. The last rays of the sun had faded now, and the god's face was all in darkness. But he was not yet quite done with me. "Remember, Hercules, what I have told you of the Boar. I will speak to you again after you have brought it to Iolcus. Do you swear that you will bring it there?"

"If that is what my father truly wants of me, I swear that I will do my best to accomplish it."

I was starting to form the words of one more question for the god, but his back was already turned to me, and I had the feeling that it would be useless.

And with that the Messenger turned in his boat and moved the pole in his two hands; and somehow the few thin trunks of trees that rose through the dark water seemed to provide concealment, for neither the god nor his boat were any longer to be seen.

At last I did call after him. "When will I be allowed to see my father?"

No answer.

I raised my voice: "Also, if I am being hired like a laborer to do a job, I have a right to know just what payment I am being offered. I know you said it is 'greater than I can imagine,' and that sounds very generous, but all the same . . ."

I allowed my voice to die away, for I was shouting into the empty swamp.

7

Saurus

THE FIRST BREATH of real winter soon overtook Enkidu and me as we pressed steadily on, up into the high country. That, we had been told, was the place to look for centaurs; but so far we had not seen so much as a hoofprint of that legendary race, let alone gained any clue as to the whereabouts of the individual named Pholus. Again and again I regretted not having pressed Hermes for more detailed information; and again and again I wondered whether I had been completely foolish in agreeing to the pledge that Hermes had demanded of me.

As for my earlier determination to confront my father and demand some answers from him, my failure was so complete that it pained me to think about it. I had not abandoned the idea, but of course had made no progress at all in carrying it out.

Several weeks had passed since I had beaten the Hydra into a mass of fish food and Mercury had carried away his samples of the creature's flesh. Enkidu and I had gratefully accepted the food and clothing bestowed on us in gratitude by some of the people who had watched the fight. On the day I wish to speak of next, we were trudging along a high mountain path, in accordance with the only clue we had that might help us locate Pholus. My chronic impatience was made somewhat the worse by the realization that we were getting farther and farther from Mount Erymanthus, where we must eventually hunt the Boar.

Our new clothing was somewhat warmer than the garments that had been lost and torn away while we were chasing down and killing the Hydra. But, coming from the warm lowlands as we did, we had failed to appreciate what real winter on a mountainside might mean, and whenever we stopped walking we began to shiver. What we needed were furs and hats and boots.

My nephew's teeth were chattering as he asked: "Herc, do centaurs speak the same language we do?"

"I wouldn't be surprised if Pholus speaks ours, along with maybe a dozen others. I've heard that some of his race are very well educated." In childhood Enkidu and I had both learned a smattering of a couple of tongues besides our own, and in our ignorance I suppose we felt beautifully equipped, linguistically, to make our way anywhere in the wide world.

As Enkidu and I strode along, now and then swinging our arms to keep warm, my mind had moved ahead to future difficulties, and I kept trying to think of what would be the best way to wrestle with the Boar. If the creature we were soon going to hunt was in any way comparable in strength and ferocity to the two terrible beasts I had already conquered, catching it alive promised to be fiendishly harder than clubbing it to death.

My companion's thoughts were running on a parallel track. "Herc, we still don't know just what this great Boar looks like."

"True, but that should be the least of our problems. I don't doubt we'll recognize the cursed thing when we see it. It must be a special beast indeed."

Actually, Hermes had given us practically no description of the Boar. But, having seen farmyard and pasture boars, of a more or less ordinary variety, I thought there would be no problem of recognition. I could picture fearsome tusks, of course, but I didn't really suppose that they would hurt me, when the Hydra's fangs had failed to inflict so much as a scratch. Maybe, I thought, I could first stun the great pig with my club, or with my fist, if I could calculate just the proper amount of force.

I felt sure that the cloaked figure who accosted me in the marsh had been a god. But for some reason, as I continued to mull over the experience, I was no longer entirely convinced that our visitor had been Hermes. Nor could I understand why Hermes—if he had been Hermes—had been so insistent that the Boar was not to be killed.

———

Enkidu and I were striding along with our minds on these and related topics, also speculating on the nature of centaurs, as I recall, and paying little attention to our surroundings, when a huge, heavily armed man surprised us totally by stepping out of concealment behind a tree and onto the road just ahead of us, where he stood blocking the way.

At his first appearance, the man's face was contorted into a scowl of menace, but as we remained passive, that soon smoothed away into a gap-toothed smile. I suppose his age might have been thirty, though it was hard to judge. He was clad in leather trousers and a leather vest with boots to match, his reddish hair hung in two pigtails beside large earrings, and his face and his enormous arms, quite bare in total indifference to the cold, had been heavily tattooed and ritually scarred. His barrel-like torso was festooned with belts and holsters, from which sharp weapons sprouted like thorns from a cactus.

I saw with faint, unreasonable disappointment that there was nothing of the centaur about him, though at first glance he was not much smaller than a horse. A robber, certainly, I thought; and I realized that we were lucky not to have encountered others of his profession in our wanderings to date. Somehow I retained presence of mind enough to take a quick look around, and I was vaguely surprised that he had no band of ruffians with him. Any lone bandit was going to have a hard time of it, I thought, if his potential victims tended to travel in groups. But perhaps this one made a specialty of lone travelers, or feeble-looking pairs—like us. I was of course carrying my latest version of a club, but I knew that it looked too big and clumsy to be an effective weapon, especially in hands no more impressive than mine.

Meanwhile the huge man had put his fists on his hips and was regarding us with satisfaction, as if we might have been two mushrooms he was about to pick and eat.

"Good morning, lads." The voice of our new acquaintance was suitably large and deep, but well controlled. And indeed, he sounded truly pleased to see us.

"Good morning, sir," I said. It seems to me now, as I look back, that half my mind must have been still on centaurs, and the Boar. I kept looking about, still more than half expecting a dozen or so of the robber's henchmen to come springing out of their own ambushes. But we three were still alone, so I turned back to him. "Do you know where we might find some centaurs?" I asked, on the off chance.

The man did not appear to hear the question. "My name is Saurus," he announced, then paused, as if expecting a reaction. When none came, he went on, frowning. "You both look cold. I think you should come along to my cave—it's nice and warm. I have some warm clothes there that would just fit you."

If these were the words of genuine hospitality, the tone certainly had a false ring to it. I exchanged glances with Enkidu, who shrugged minimally. As long as he was standing close to me, he was no more frightened than I was, and his eyes actually brightened at the prospect of adventure. I looked back at the man, who no longer seemed quite so satisfied. I suppose our reactions, neither innocent gullibility nor craven fear, were odd enough to awaken some uneasiness.

"Which way is your cave, sir?" I asked politely.

As if reluctant to be outdone in courtesy, Saurus made a motion with his head, then stepped aside to let us precede him. A small path, practically invisible from the road, led from behind his tree of ambush into the woods. I turned my back on the man and walked along the path, without really stopping to think about what other options might be open to me.

I did, of course, take the precaution of making sure that Enkidu was safely in front of me; he had scampered at once into that position, making sure to keep me between him and the big man. My stick rode in its usual place on my right shoulder. If Saurus, who was now walking behind me, should try to wrench it from my grasp, or more likely, to strike me down from behind with one of his own weapons . . . well, he'd be in for a surprise. But I still was not absolutely sure he meant us any harm. Very likely he did, I thought, but simply had no respect for any weapon so big and clumsy as my club, especially in hands as small as mine.

"Been traveling far, boys?" asked the large voice behind me, retaining its joviality. "Is home a long way off?"

I turned my head back slightly to reply. "All the way from Cadmia, sir. Thanks for your concern."

He did not reply, and I wondered if he had ever heard of Cadmia.

We had not quite gone a hundred yards along the path when the cave suddenly appeared in the form of a dark oblong window in a natural limestone wall, the opening covered by a hanging stitched together from the hides of large and furry animals. Saurus stepped up to push the hairy curtain back, and moments later we were all inside. I left my club outside, thinking there would probably not be room enough to swing it in a small cave anyway.

Enough daylight to see by came in through high crevices in the rock. It was a surprisingly warm chamber, roomy but snug, but despite the promise of comfort it was hard to relax, because of the dozen or so human skulls and other bones which the proprietor had incorporated into the luxurious decorations, and which ran like a frieze, up high around the irregular and slanted walls.

A small fire was burning, making an optimistically merry sound, in a recess in one wall of the cave. A hole in the rock above the fire made a fair chimney, and the stone floor formed a handy natural hearth. On a flat stone near the fire, a lidded pot was keeping warm, sending out a vaguely appetizing aroma. Had it not been for the charnel-house decorations, the place would have been quite cheerful. Much of the stone floor was actually covered with a carpet, incongruously fine.

Even a robber can have a home, I thought. And suddenly, I suppose because of the image of coziness and home, I thought of Megan. But she was far away, and I thanked all the gods that she would never be anywhere near this cave.

Something much larger than a mouse went scampering near my feet, and I looked down, startled, to see a couple of exotic little animals, lizards of some kind, the size of rabbits, running around inside the cave. At first their dark-scaled bodies moved too fast for me to get a really good look, but when they paused I saw that they were wearing collars, like pets. One of them was carrying a bone in its monkeylike forepaws and chewing what looked like the last fragments of meat from it. The bone looked ominously like a human ulna. Crouching on the hearth, the creatures stared at us with their large yellow eyes, and it seemed to me that they looked hungry.

"Your pets?" I asked.

"Meet Deimos and Phobos. They keep most of the vermin out. And they're better company than people."

I said nothing, but only shook my head. If a man prefers the companionship of lizards, what use is there in arguing with him?

Saurus invited us to shed our packs and sit down. But as soon as I had slid mine from my shoulders, he snatched it up, opened it without hesitation or comment, and dumped out the meager contents on the single, narrow bed that stood against one wall. Enkidu's burden followed quickly.

"Not much," the robber observed in disappointment. "Too bad, lads, that you're both so poor."

"Help yourself," I offered. "If you see anything there you like." Then I drew a deep breath, feeling for some reason that I owed the man fair warning. "But if you empty my pack, then before I leave your cave I'll likely fill it up again, maybe with things more valuable. Like some of those warm clothes you mentioned. And I suppose you have a good supply of food."

Saurus gave his imitation of a laugh. It would need more practice if he wanted it to be convincing. He was still watching me with amusement, but now with caution, too. Most likely my continued calm suggested to him that I was mad, and the mad, no matter how small or poorly armed, are always dangerous opponents.

"As for clothes," the huge man said, "you lads won't need to worry about such things anymore. I understand they're just not needed in the Underworld. In fact, you'd better take off the ones you're wearing—that'll keep 'em from being damaged and save me the trouble later."

I was glad to see that Enkidu had already done what he could to remove himself from harm's way, scrambling back as far as he could get in a blank corner of the cave. Now I would not have to worry about protecting him in the conflict that seemed likely to begin at any moment.

Still, with the image of Linus before me, I felt a need to make the whole business thoroughly explicit, so I asked our host: "Don't robbers usually have helpers? I mean, don't you like the odds to be in your favor, as a rule?"

Saurus looked at me almost pityingly. "Why, bless you, lad, I don't need any helpers. Not in dealing with anyone I might invite into my home. Maybe you've heard of me by my other name. Some call me the Lizard." Again he paused, as if expecting that the name would produce some effect. But Enkidu and I had never heard of him.

Now the robber was growing angry. "And the odds *are* in my favor, boy. If you doubt it, try me. What do they call you, by the way?"

"Hercules," I said. But that name meant no more to him than his had to me.

"And my name is Enkidu!" came from the corner, in a brave, piping voice.

"All right, Enkidu," said the Lizard equably, turning his head a little toward the corner, while he kept his narrowed eyes on me. "I'll let you live until later, so you can clean up the mess that it seems I am going to have to make. But it'll be outside. Little Hercules is going to come out there with me; I dislike staining my good carpet."

The Lizard had scorned to draw his sword for me but already had one of his big knives out. When I reached to grab his arm he was far too quick for me—not that being quick did him any good at all. Before I could get hold of him, the blade came slicing through my tunic, and I felt it slide cold and sharp along my ribs. There was a biting sensation, but, as I verified with my own eyes later, sharp bronze or steel in a man's hand was no more able to break my skin than the Hydra's fangs and claws had been. And in the next moment I had managed to catch his arm, and the fight, if you could call it that, was effectively over.

When Saurus felt his muscles crushed in the power of my grip, his bones about to break, and he saw in my eyes that he was soon to die, he said, in a changed voice: "A god has come against me, and I can do nothing."

I wondered if someone, sometime, had given him a prophecy to that effect. For he believed what he said, and he said no more, and put up almost no further struggle. Somehow the Lizard's calm acceptance only made me the angrier, so far was his behavior from what I would have said and done in his place.

He did not scream but only grunted twice, once when I broke his arm, making him drop the knife, and again when I snatched from its scabbard another of the blades that sprouted from his leather-strapped torso, and awkwardly pushed the keen point through his heart. It seemed to me fitting that death should come upon him through one of the tools of his evil trade. Deimos and Phobos screamed and ran away, and bright red stained his good carpet after all, and no one was ever going to clean it up.

In that manner died the second human being that I had ever killed. I found my second slaying less upsetting than my first—and had I been wiser, that fact would have troubled me.

But could I have been so cruel to the world as to allow such a robber and murderer to live? The skulls nailed high on the walls grinned down at me—victims having the last laugh on their killer after all, for they had told me beyond a doubt what manner of man he was.

A god has come against me. But no, I had seen Hermes, and I knew that *I* was not a god.

———

As soon as he saw Saurus crushed, Enkidu came out of the corner of the cave where he had taken shelter, and stepped carefully over the robber where he lay, no longer breathing, on his good carpet. Then the two of us unhurriedly went through the cave, looking for useful supplies and miscellaneous loot. Most of it we found in a back room, its entrance half-concealed by another curtain of animal hides. Here were the stores I had expected and hoped to find, of dried meat and fruit and fish, and warm clothes enough in different sizes, including fur-lined boots, to complete our outfitting.

After a little searching, I dug out another tunic for myself, one lacking a knife slash, and some leggings and a fur hat. While we were rifling the storeroom, my nephew picked up a fine, fur-lined hooded cloak, which I suppose might have once belonged to some elegant lady, and better footwear. But he thought all this was incidental, and kept on looking anxiously for treasure.

There was indeed a considerable store of gold and silver. This was cunningly buried under the floor, but Enkidu searched diligently until he found it. I pocketed only a handful of coins, which would be useful in buying provisions on the way.

"Look at this, Herc. And this! By all the gods, it's gold!"

"Heavy stuff to carry." I was trying on some boots, of which there was a good selection.

"But *gold!*"

I shook my head. "I've got all I need. You take what you want. But don't expect me to lug an extra load, or defend a big pile for you." Coins and jewels, gold and silver, in themselves have never seemed to me a great prize, or worth much trouble to accumulate; the world contains vast quantities of such things, after all, and enough to meet immediate needs can usually be found when they become really necessary.

For a minute he was quiet, rummaging around. Then: "Look: earrings! I wish I had my ears pierced, Herc. Are yours?" I suppose my hair hung thick and low enough to keep my ears from being a familiar sight to my companion.

"They're not," I said. "I doubt that anyone could find a tool to pierce them with. But Saurus's ears have large holes." I could remember that detail of the body in the other room.

I doubted also that the boy was paying any attention to what I said, for he did not reply. He tried on an assortment of golden armlets, rings, and necklaces, one after another, as well as belts that carried jeweled swords and daggers. But in the end, under my disapproving stare, he contented himself with a bag of coins of comparatively modest size.

Then my nephew looked around the little space and sniffed the air. "Do we want to spend the night in here? It'd be warm."

"I don't want to spend the night with him," I said, nodding toward the curtain and what lay in the room beyond.

"We'd put him outside. We could even bury him."

That was widely supposed to make the walking of a ghost less likely. "Burial might be a good idea, but I'd rather not stay in his cave at all. We're in no danger of freezing to death, especially with these new clothes. We'll find somewhere."

Enkidu shrugged. "All right. The stew in the other room smells tempting, though."

So the Lizard had turned out to be hospitable after all. Before leaving his cave, we tasted the contents of the simmering pot, decided that it was nothing worse than it first appeared to be, stewed rabbit, and dined on it heartily.

As we were leaving, I stopped just outside the entrance to the cave, tore down the furry robe that kept in warmth, and put my hands on the edge of the doorway, trying out this grip and that. Soon I found one that I thought would do the job. Pulling steadily, I dislodged a few key supporting rocks from the limestone cliff so that a portion of the steep hillside shuddered, and my nephew and I had to jump briskly to get out of the way. Nearby trees vibrated as in an earthquake, shaking dark leafless branches, and the whole front of the cave collapsed, belching a cloud of dust and dirt into the chill air. It was just too neatly situated for a robber's roost.

Meanwhile, on the death of their master the two little lizards had fled the cave, screaming in their high small voices. When we got outside we found their tracks marking the thin snow. But I doubted that Deimos and Phobos had run far, and supposed they would come back before long. The collapse of the entrance had still left room for their small bodies to pass, and the inside of the cave would stay warm at least until the fire went out. And there they would now find fresh bones to chew.

8

Centaurs

AFTER LEAVING THE robber's cave, Enkidu and I resumed our quest for centaurs, in particular the one named Pholus. We roamed about for several weeks, seeing few people, zigzagging back and forth across the region in which we had some reason to believe we might be able to locate our quarry. More than once I was on the point of giving up our intermediate objective and trying to get back on the direct road to Mount Erymanthus, where the Boar was supposed to be. I was impatient to find the damned monster, whatever it was like, deliver it as instructed, and then get on with my life—Hermes, after all, had not insisted that the centaur's help was absolutely essential.

Several times my nephew and I thought we were completely lost, and the fact that we were now warmly shod and clothed no doubt saved our lives.

Among the other treasures contained in the robber's cave had been a small arsenal of captured weapons, and we had picked up slings, almost as an afterthought, along with our other booty. My nephew, putting in long hours of practice in the following days, became skillful enough to bring down some small game to tide us over when we could not find a hospitable farm to give us food and lodging.

Our wanderings during those weeks took us well away from Erymanthus, whose snow-capped peak we could glimpse in the distance now and then. But we persisted.

At last we found ourselves among settlements where people did not look blank when we mentioned centaurs, or speak of them as fantastic marvels. In this rugged country of wooded hills and deep ravines, there were few human settlers. None of the people we encountered in this region had any doubt that centaurs were real enough. But they insisted, almost to a man, that they knew nothing about such creatures, and wanted to know nothing. It seemed that in these parts, at least, the two races were well aware of each other's day-to-day presence, but still good at keeping out of each other's way.

Eventually we met one woman, an elder and also a healer, who not only had seen centaurs but claimed to be personally acquainted with the very one we wanted. She confirmed that Pholus was much more likely than most of his tribe to seek out human contact.

Our informant not only described the appearance of Pholus in great detail but (once she was convinced that we were not out to hunt and kill him as a form of sport) advised us where we were likely to find him.

Armed with this information, Enkidu and I stubbornly pressed on. On the afternoon of the second day since leaving the house of the helpful woman, we came upon a strange trail that at last sent our hopes rising.

Every one of our informants, including Hermes, had assured us that we might track centaurs by looking for what seemed to be the prints of horses' hooves.

The marks before us had clearly been made by hard hooves that were certainly not a goat's, or a deer's, nor belonged to any animal that my nephew and I had ever seen.

"Are these horse tracks, Enk?"

The expert tracker squinted at them carefully. "Maybe. Or maybe a centaur's. What do you think?"

"Could be a demon's for all that I can tell."

Despite difficulties, at last we had some success. The ground again was covered in light snow, which made the tracks easy to follow, and even one as little skilled in the art as I was could study them in some detail.

Having proceeded on some further distance, through moderately thick woods, we began to hear a chopping sound.

I stopped in my tracks, holding up my hand. "Hear that? Sounds like a woodcutter up ahead."

"Maybe he's seen the one we're looking for."

"Maybe. Or . . . centaurs have arms, don't they? One of 'em could swing an axe."

Moving on as quietly as we could, we soon came to a stop at the edge of a small clearing and stood there, hardly daring to breathe.

My first impression was that a horse was standing at the far side of the little clearing, facing away from us, tail switching now and then, broad flanks steaming faintly in the cold. I thought it was an ordinary man, his torso naked despite the cold, who sat astride the horse. It was an awkward position for chopping, but the man's arms were vigorously wielding an axe against a thick dead branch projecting from a tree. A moment or two had passed before I noticed that the human legs of the apparent rider were nowhere to be seen. Nor were the horse's head and neck.

I snapped a twig underfoot about that time, trying to move to get a better look; but the being on the far side of the clearing did not turn around. Either he had not heard us coming, or he was indifferent to the approach of a mere pair of humans.

At last I called out in a loud voice. "Greetings!"

Now he who was standing with his back to us did take notice at last, and turned gracefully on his four hoofed legs, and answered with a nod, as if he were loath to be interrupted at his work. He had long hair and a long beard, adorning a face as fully human as the rest of his upper body. All of these made him a good match for the description given us by the woman.

Moving forward a few more steps, I called out boldly: "My name is Hercules. This is my nephew, Enkidu. And if you are Pholus, we have walked a long way indeed to find you."

The centaur pushed back long hair from his face. "I am Pholus. But why have you gone to all that trouble? And just how far is a long way?" His voice was deep and pleasant.

"All the way from Cadmia. I have gone to so much trouble because a god commanded me to do so."

Pholus frowned, as if he were thinking over very seriously what I had just said. Our new acquaintance now grabbed up and pulled on some kind of shirt or jacket, which I supposed he had earlier taken off in the heat of chopping. His arms looked brawnier than those of most entirely human men—he could easily have been a match for the late Lizard.

When he had his shirt on again, he picked up a bow and quiver of arrows from the ground and slung them over his shoulders, just as a normal man might do. The fresh carcass of a deer lay at his feet, I saw now; evidently his hunting had been successful. His mode of carrying a deer was different, of course, as he tucked it behind his human torso.

I am sure that you who read this must have seen pictures of centaurs, if not the thing itself: the head and arms and torso of a man, in the case of Pholus strongly built and in the prime of life. But where you might expect to find the hips, the body as it were began over again in its equine stage, as if the man's torso were a horse's neck. Human hair and beard were the same color as the horse's tail—there was no mane on his human neck or upright torso.

Only later, months and years after this first meeting with one of their race, did I begin to realize how hard the life of a centaur truly was.

For one thing, the huge body requires much nourishment, and it all must pass in through the small human mouth, where whatever chewing was necessary had to be done by small human teeth. Centaurs eat meat, when they can get it—to chew and swallow enough vegetables to support the massive body would be well-nigh impossible. There were of course other problems, too, including those that come of having two stomachs—but in my ignorance none of them occurred to me at that first meeting.

When we had introduced ourselves and had at least begun to discuss the Boar, Pholus invited us to his house, actually only a kind of hut. It was a mile or two away, and our host courteously slowed down his normal cantering pace to one that we could match.

The little house with its thatched roof stood by itself in a modest clearing, with no other buildings near. The front door was large enough to fit a stable, and the place smelled faintly like one, though it was as clean as any house might reasonably be expected to be—in fact cleaner than I have seen the palace of the king of Cadmia, especially on the morning after a late revel. There was little in the way of furniture inside—natural enough, I realized, when I considered that the owner and his usual visitors must rarely sit down and commonly slept while standing. A couple of tall, shelflike tables, skillfully made, offered space for reading and writing, and there were some books, stored on even higher shelves. At one side of the large room a fire of modest size, built on a stone hearth that was raised chest-high to a man, gave out comforting heat and light. There was no sign of any other occupant, and the look of the place strongly suggested that Pholus lived a hermit's life.

The interior was not as cheerfully lighted as that of the last dwelling

that my nephew and I had been urged to enter; but in this case we were
urged by a gesture of genuine hospitality. Almost involuntarily I cast a
glance around to reassure myself that here there were no skulls.

Enkidu volunteered to play the role of butcher and cook, and
dragged the deer outside. After some rummaging in a large cupboard
or closet built into one wall, Pholus brought out one ordinary chair,
which was I suppose the only one he had, and offered it to me. Enkidu,
looking quite content to be almost ignored, sat tailor-fashion on the floor
against a wall. Obviously the lad was fascinated by our host, and he
could not keep from staring at him.

There was a notable jar of wine here, our host informed us, and at
once began to tell us the story connected with it. The huge container
had been in his house—which, he assured me, was older than it
looked—for generations.

According to this ancient tale, all totally new to me, the wine was
to be kept, unopened, until a son of Zeus should come for a visit.

"Since you make that claim," said Pholus, "I will take you at your
word and open it. Another reason is that I have always been curious
about the wine."

By now Enkidu's efforts had born fruit, and the smell of roasting
venison enriched the air. When Pholus rolled the wine jar into view,
tilting and balancing it on one side of its bottom edge, I saw that it was
indeed huge, and made of clay. The top was dusty, the lid closed with
a seal of wax so dark and crusted that it might well have been as ancient
as he claimed. Pholus grappled it with powerful arms and rolled it out
of its closet to a position near the center of the room.

Next he wished to lift the barrel up, into a kind of rack that held it
in a position where it could be easily tapped. I could see that this was
a job that would ordinarily take two men to accomplish, and I offered
to give him a hand.

When I did, of course the great cask went up easily between us. He
stepped back, wiping his brow and frowning at me. "Where does your
strength come from, lad?"

"An inheritance from my father."

"I see."

When I heard how long the wine had been there, I was not optimistic about its quality, having learned that any left aging for more than
a few decades would turn to vinegar, or worse.

Returning to my chair, in which it seemed impossible for a human
to get comfortable, I asked our host: "Folk don't usually keep their tuns
of wine that long, do they?"

Rummaging in another closet, he had come up with a mallet and a wooden spigot, which he was now holding, one in each hand. "I am the wrong one, Hercules, to question on the habits of humanity. Are you then a good judge of fine wine, Hercules, son of Zeus?"

"Nothing of the kind, good Pholus. But of course we had wine in the house where I grew up, and now and then I've listened when people were talking on the subject. I might repeat some of their words, if that would amuse you."

He laughed and gave me all the details he could of the ancient prophecy, which were not many. According to the story passed down among the centaurs, bad things would happen if this cask was tapped before a son of Zeus arrived—and some catastrophe even worse might be expected should it *not* be broached when the proper time was reached.

When he had driven in the spigot with a few sharp blows and turned it properly, he handed me a flagon, filled with a liquid that looked rich and almost solid red, save for a tiny froth of bubbles on the top.

As my nephew began to serve us dinner, the centaur filled another cup for himself. Nor did he completely forget Enkidu, but tapped him a little wine as well, in a broken clay cup, the only other vessel that seemed readily available. Evidently drinking parties were not a common occurrence in this house. The boy looked sourly at this poor share, but brightened as soon as he tasted it.

For my part, I had to admit that my drink was as far from vinegar as any that I had ever tasted. Even to my uneducated palate this wine was superb, and I wanted to have one more cup at least, to wash down my bread and meat.

I began to tell Pholus of our adventure with the robber. Our host heard me out with close attention, and he was openly impressed. He said that the Lizard was locally quite infamous, and that the folk for miles around would rejoice that we had finished him.

"Congratulations, son of Zeus, on your escape."

"I'll drink to that."

We both smacked our lips with satisfaction.

Now the centaur was squinting at me intently. "Just how *did* you manage to foil the Lizard's plans for you? If you have no objection to explaining?"

"None in the least." Realizing that my previous demonstration of strength had been insufficient, I picked up an iron trivet that lay as a decoration on his table, and with my fingers twisted the thick bar that formed it into quite a different shape. Then, reminding myself that my host had not much furniture to spare, and even this trinket might have value in his eyes, I bent it back again.

Pholus said: "Ah," and leaned his human torso back, like a man settling himself more comfortably in a chair, though of course his body remained standing on its four strong, stable legs. And I thought his manner altered subtly. Not that he was suddenly afraid of me, but now I thought that he truly began to believe what I had told him about being a son of the Thunderer.

The strong wine was certainly beginning to go to my head, and I was on the point of asking Pholus rudely whether there was not a stallion or mare in his immediate ancestry. But our friendly conversation was soon interrupted by a noise outside, the thudding on hard ground of many hooves, and it was plain that either more centaurs had arrived, or else a group of men riding on horses.

Getting up from my chair, I peered out at the side of a window and saw the heads and shoulders of about a dozen men, and the dark bulks of the same number of horses. In the dim light I could not be absolutely sure that I was really looking at a gang of centaurs until one cantered closer to the house. At least half of those I saw were armed with bows and arrows, and some were carrying other weapons, too.

The one who had come near the house now called out in a raucous voice: "Pholus, we see by the trail that you have company. Two of those ugly creatures, so-called humans, that have only four limbs, totter and toddle on only two feet, and move not much faster than rocks and bushes. Ugly and clumsy monsters, they must be."

These words were hardly reassuring, and I thought the tone of the newcomers' voices boded ill for the success of my mission, though I was not personally afraid. Their mood was obviously less than jovial and seemed to resent my presence. So far they had not taken any particular notice of Enkidu, and he had shrunken so far into a corner that he seemed on the verge of utter invisibility.

Pholus looked worried and seemed uncertain of what to do; I opened the door of the house and stood out where the newcomers could see me plainly.

One centaur—later I learned his name was Nessus—conspicuously the rowdiest of the group, for some reason seemed to hate me on sight, more than any of the others did.

On getting his first clear look at me, Nessus declared: "So, this is the spawn of Zeus, of whom so much has been prophesied! What do you say, god-bastard, are all the things that the prophets say about you true?"

I remained standing in the doorway, leaning on my club, as if it were only a walking stick. Feeling the wine, and arrogantly conscious of my own strength, I called back: "It would take a wiser man than me to answer that. Especially since I have no idea what your prophets say. They may be only ranting fools. In fact, that seems quite likely."

A round of jeering answered me.

Without the further warning, one of the gathering loosed an arrow at me. It struck me before I saw it coming, and stuck in my winter jacket. I pulled it out and looked it over negligently, then broke it between my fingers.

Another individual, whom I heard the others address as Chiron, cantered out to a spot midway between me and my opponents and attempted to be a peacemaker. Pholus added his pleas in the name of common sense, but the peacemakers were only two, while all the others, ten or so, seemed bent for some reason on doing me great harm.

Chiron bravely, even foolishly, I thought, tried to keep himself between me and the angry ones.

I shouted at him that I didn't need his help and that he should look to his own safety.

Another well-aimed arrow came at me. I ignored its stinging impact and responded by hurling back a small rock that I snatched up from the bare ground at my feet. It missed the archer I was aiming at, and went on to crisply snap off a branch somewhere in the dark woods beyond.

A moment later, Chiron sidestepped at the wrong moment, while endeavoring to head off a threatened charge, and went reeling back with an arrow through his upper chest, shot at me by one of the mob behind him. I must correct the legendary error that the shaft was one of mine. I was no longer carrying a bow and had not done so for some time. I had traded the gift of Amphitryon for food, in the hungry days before we reached the cave of Saurus.

———

Rocks were fairly plentiful on the ground before me, and I let fly with a barrage that effectively dispersed the mob for the time being. As soon as the crazed centaurs had been temporarily driven off, I went to where the fallen peacemaker lay, and tried to help him.

The wound in itself ought not to have been fatal, but he warned me, between gasps of his dying agony, that the arrow must have been poisoned. And he gave me another warning, too, that at the time I failed to understand: "Hercules, do not get any of my blood on you."

Of course I could have picked him up and carried him, but the horse-sized body would have been an awkward burden and I might have hurt him in the process. Also I realized that it would do little good to carry him inside the house.

The fumes of wine seemed to have been driven from my brain, and now I regretted my shouted insult. And I still wanted to know, from anyone who was capable of telling me, why the centaurs had grown so angry. Had they somehow realized that Pholus had broached the wine? Was it simply because they wanted that good red stuff for themselves?

Neither Chiron or Pholus gave me an answer. Perhaps they were unable.

But before I could learn anything more from the dying Chiron, there came a thunder of hooves in the middle distance, and the mad ones renewed their attack.

So much for any hopes I might have had for an evening's enlightening conversation. Now I found myself engaged in another all-out fight.

———

Looking back over the years, I can now see that, yes, it is quite true that with more maturity, more sense, and a little diplomacy on my part, the worst of the trouble might have been avoided. But three cups— perhaps even a little more—of that strong wine had made me first irritable, then irascible, then launched me well on my way to drunkenness. Naturally, I was no stranger to wine, having been brought up in a well-to-do household, but at home my consumption was invariably quite modest. And the drink in that aged cask was truly something wondrous.

"What the hell are they so upset about?" I again demanded of Pholus, when another brief interval in the fighting gave me a chance to talk. Looking around, I noted that his house was being ruined in the process. A fire had started in the thatched roof, and I tore down a burning reed bundle and scattered it into dying sparks.

"Sorry about your house," I added. "But I'll be damned if I'm going to turn tail and run."

"And I am shamed," he said at last, "that this could happen while you are my guest." After a pause he added: "It is the wine, of course."

"Are they afraid I'm going to drink it all? The whole damned jar? There's enough to take a bath in. It's great stuff, but I'm only good for . . . well, maybe one more cup."

My host, I seem to remember, counseled moderation.

I was having none of it. "Moderation, is it? A bit too late for that. By the balls of Mars, I've half a mind to go out there after 'em. But they're safe enough from me. I'll never catch 'em while they all can run like racehorses. But they'd better not come within my reach."

And I seem to remember gulping yet another draught of the red wine, which seemed to be running like liquid fire in my veins. No damned horse was going to tell me what to do. Horses in general were a strange, exotic species, and horses like these, that seemed half-human . . . angrily I began to express my contempt.

With the renewal of the attack, Enkidu once more took shelter in a corner, first thoughtfully refilling his small clay cup to the brim and taking it along. If he was going to die soon, he would have some measure of enjoyment first. Unhappily I thought that the corner was not going to do him much good—the walls of this house were not as sturdy as those of the robber's cave—but I had nothing better to suggest.

Once more the attack swept in on us, and this time it was better organized. Our assailants had armed themselves with rocks, dead tree branches, and axes like the one that Pholus had earlier been wielding. They charged the house. At the sight of this determined onslaught, Pholus turned away and fearfully tried to hide himself.

Throwing rocks at me was a mistake, for it only provided me with a supply of ammunition. When a couple of logs were knocked out of the walls by the battering from outside, I used one after another as a swinging club, and then pulled another wall apart to gain more missiles. Horrible screams, half-human and half-animal, went up from the wounded creatures when my thrown logs, coming with the speed of spinning arrows, hit them squarely or scraped them and knocked them down. Had I not been somewhat drunk, I would have killed more of the attackers than I did.

Among the centaurs whom I failed to kill that night was Nessus, who here conceived a great enmity for me, so that ever afterward he remained determined to do me some lasting harm.

———

Enkidu, who somehow came through the fight unscathed, and I spent the remainder of the night with Pholus, in what remained of his house, expecting at every hour that our enemies might return, perhaps with reinforcements, and try again to wipe us out. For an hour or so after the last clash, we could hear them intermittently in the distance, bellowing like drunken men and crashing through undergrowth somewhere. Our host had sustained a couple of minor injuries, and we tried to help him with his bandaging.

All the centaurs I had yet seen were male, and I wondered if the whole race was of one sex. If so, I thought, reason enough for them to be chronically angry.

Pholus, when he could pull himself together, did what he could to explain.

Some of the males of his race, he said, on occasion mated with mares. Some undetermined number actually preferred that sort of coupling. The great convenience, of course, was that the organs of centaur and horse were well matched in physical size. As far as he knew, no issue ever resulted from such unions.

But, he explained, the majority of male centaurs, himself included, found such intercourse fundamentally unsatisfactory, as their own essentially human minds persisted in regarding women as infinitely more attractive than horses.

"That seems to me only reasonable," I said. And Enkidu nodded wisely.

At about that point, it also occurred to me to wonder how any female, even a mare, could give birth to such an odd-shaped body as my host's. But then I supposed that if droms and cameloids could manage, Mother Nature would find a way in this case, too.

Pholus went on with his explanations. Unions between male centaurs and women were sometimes fertile.

It was not a subject I cared to hear any more about. In the gray light of morning, the fumes of wine had all but completely evaporated from my brain. I was tired, and my garments were torn in several places where my enemies' weapons had struck home, but otherwise I had sustained no damage.

No, there was one exception, and excited as I was with wine and violence, I finally had to take notice. On the back of my right hand, a red spot burned, smaller than a small coin, but sharp as fire. Looking closely, I could see there was no wound, but definitely a blister. Something, somehow, had caused me injury. I rinsed the place in water, which did not help much.

My host took no notice; he had graver matters than my blister to be concerned about.

He said: "But to couple with a goddess, now . . ." And with a sigh he left the comparison unfinished. At the time, I took his behavior for a subtle kind of bragging; in my callow innocence I thought it would be difficult indeed to find any goddess willing to pair with a centaur.

9

Delivering a Boar

BEFORE ENKIDU AND I left Pholus, we helped the noble centaur start to rebuild his ruined house, at least to the extent of clearing wreckage and salvaging materials that could be used in reconstruction. After that, I labored for another hour, cutting and carrying wood, including parts of the house that had been reduced to wreckage, to make a suitable funeral pyre for Chiron. Our host informed us that few centaurs ever found their final resting place in graves—I suppose the reason is that huge holes would be necessary, and the bodies of that race, their arms so high above the ground, are ill-suited for digging in it.

The moderate chill of early winter soon gave way to bitter, freezing cold as my nephew and I made our way across the high country. We were working our way steadily toward Mount Erymanthus, aided by the fact that the peak itself was now and then visible through a frame of tall pine trees. The mountain above the timberline was covered in pure white and displayed a plume of blowing snow on windy mornings. Even at the lesser altitude where we trudged along, snow lay deep in places and looked as if it intended to remain for many months. The stories we heard from the natives as we toiled through the high country confirmed what Hermes had told us about a wild boar of exceptional size and ferocity, ravaging the land.

If I had ever been inclined to curse the Lizard, I was almost ready to bless him now for having, however unintentionally, furnished us with warm clothing. My special powers had never afforded me any protection against the common discomforts of heat and cold, though in my more optimistic moments I thought that my father's blood might prevent my actually freezing to death, or perishing of sunstroke. My only other chance to demonstrate a soldier's fortitude, and that in a very minor way, was to stoically ignore the pain of the blister on my hand, and in a few days that had faded, leaving only a small scar.

Enkidu, too, still clung to the memory of the Lizard and his store-room, but chiefly as a reason for continued grumbling. My nephew's unsatisfied craving for wealth had transformed that rustic chamber, in his memory, into something like a royal treasure vault. He still regretted that we had left behind any of the gold and gems. I failed to respond to these sullen protests, and in time, to my relief, he gave them up.

Besides, there were current problems that demanded our continuous attention. For a time we were much concerned that Nessus and some other angry centaurs might be on our trail, determined to cause more trouble. I could not rid my memory of the expression of hatred I had seen on the face of Nessus when I got my last look at him.

And still the words that Mercury had spoken to me on parting, at our last encounter, lay clear in my mind. The god had been very specific in his instructions—in passing on to me what he said were the commands of Zeus. According to those, it was very important that the beast we were now hunting should be still alive when we carried it to Iolcus. As we traveled, my nephew and I speculated endlessly on possible reasons for this requirement, but as you might expect, we got nowhere.

Another question that nagged at me from time to time was exactly where we were supposed to bring the Boar, supposing we did manage to capture the beast and carry it as far as Iolcus. Who, if anyone, would take delivery of our strange cargo when we got there? And, beyond that, what precisely was it wanted for? Hermes had left me with the impression that he intended to meet us there in person, but I had trouble imagining any god making an appearance in the middle of a busy city.

We continually worried at these and related questions, but came no closer to finding answers.

Other delays compounded those brought on by weather. We wasted, or so it seemed to me, another month or so in an effort to equip ourselves with suitable nets, some of which had to be woven. Only when these problems had been surmounted did we turn our efforts to actually tracking down the Boar.

All reports agreed that our new quarry was a very big animal. They were in accord also that it left no Hydra-sized trail across the rugged high country, and in this they were proven right. All of Enkidu's tracking skill was necessary. We were by no means always blessed with fresh snow, good for tracking.

We had now been gone from home approximately five months. Deep winter had come upon us, and the hours of daylight were short indeed.

After spending many days in a patient, methodical effort to locate the animal, our efforts were at last rewarded with the discovery of tracks that Enkidu swore could have been made by nothing but some kind of giant pig. The size of the imprints was somewhat reassuring, in that the animal producing them could not have been the size of the Hydra, or even much bigger than the lion. And when we actually caught sight of the Boar at last, I was relieved to find this reading of the trail proved correct.

By dint of much effort, we finally chased the beast out of its hiding place into deep snow—we were high on the mountain by that time— and there trapped it with nets.

Enkidu's nimbleness and courage were a great help, necessary complements to my strength. Oh, I could tell you in more detail of the various stratagems, involving much patience and many ropes and nets, by which the Boar was subdued and imprisoned, but I have no wish to turn this chronicle into a monotonous catalog of monsters. Finally I had to stun the creature with a series of sharp, comparatively light, blows to its shaggy head.

One of the local ranchers, overjoyed to see the beast removed (though it caused him much anxiety that I did not kill it while I had the chance; he said he had sworn an oath to boil it into soup), donated a large, strong cart, and another loaned us a team of droms to pull it, with his son as driver. Still others chipped in still more ropes with which to bind the beast, once it was entangled, and some stout timbers from which we cobbled together a crate, or pen, in which it might be carried. And presently we were on our way to Iolcus.

The air steadily grew warmer in the course of our long, tortuous descent toward sea level, and before we had been on the road for many days the land was free of snow again. Partly this was because we were at the same time moving steadily southward. We did our best to feed our captive and supply him with water, but any merely natural beast confined as the Boar was would probably have expired. As matters actually stood, the odylic force that had made the creature huge and formidable operated also to keep it alive, though caged and bound. Whenever I came in view, its red eyes glowered hate at me.

We asked directions as we progressed, but actually that would hardly have been necessary. All roads seemed to tend toward our goal. Hermes had been right, and we had no trouble locating the port of Iolcus, on the northern shore of what was by far the largest body of water that Enkidu and I had ever seen.

When we first came in sight of the Great Sea, we marveled that we could not see the other side of the vast watery expanse that lay before us, slate gray, under a gray sky—although of course we had known all along, from travelers' stories, that it must be so.

Even before we actually passed through the gates of Iolcus, Enkidu and I found ourselves immersed in a kind of country fair, or carnival, atmosphere.

As we drew near the city, we encountered more and more evidence that a remarkable gathering of noble heroes was in progress. Some six months had now passed since Enkidu and I had left our homes in Cadmia. Behind us the high country was still deep in winter, and snow capped the peaks of Erymanthus and its neighbors. But here, many miles to the south and at much lower altitude, the weather on the northern shore of the Great Sea was already as mild as spring. Here were green palm trees, pelicans, and other wonders for two country boys to marvel at.

━━━━━━━

The city of Iolcus was not as large as Cadmia, nor were its walls as formidable, being mainly logs and not stone; but it still held by far the largest gathering of people we had seen since leaving home.

As we drew near the chief inland gate, our progress was slowed by the numbers of people who stopped to marvel at the Boar, and at the way we were carrying it alive.

But our arrival, though it drew a considerable crowd, was not the only or even the chief cause of excitement in that town.

"Jason himself is here!" more than one of the locals excitedly informed me.

That name meant something to me, as I thought it must have done, at the time, to almost everyone in the world. Jason's fame as a warrior and adventurer had spread swiftly during the last few years. All sorts of heroic deeds were attributed to him, and probably he was even more famous than Theseus, and had not the same piratical reputation. When it became widely known that Jason was seeking forty or fifty volunteer adventurers to accompany him on a special quest, men had come from everywhere, seemingly from every corner of the earth, certainly from as far away as the news had had time to travel. I suppose there is really no need to say that very few of those who applied without a special invitation were accepted.

———

Speaking of Theseus, almost everyone we met expected that the youthful adventurer, sometimes called King of the Pirates, would sooner or later put in an appearance. But there was no sign of him yet, and no one knew where he might be. Many assumed that his name was on the list of those to whom Jason had sent personal invitations; if Theseus was not a hero, who could claim that title? True, his remarkable career consisted of little but acts of piracy. But if a consistent concern for others' property was made a qualification, Jason might have a hard time filling his roster.

Someone had posted on a wall, on one side of the town square, an impressive list of other heroes, whose presence was confirmed.

No one who observed our entrance into the town would have mistaken me for one of those summoned—at least, not until they saw what freight was carried on the cart that I was driving (our borrowed driver, unnerved by the constant red-eyed, bristly presence of the Boar, had defected before we were halfway to the port). One look at the creature in my cart was enough to assure any observer that I was probably no ordinary teamster.

The crowd that had begun to gather around us and our cargo was growing larger, minute by minute.

———

Once within the city walls, I drove on to the city square, in part simply because I wished to avoid blocking the narrow street. On the edge of the square I reined my team of droms to a halt, not exactly sure where to go or what to do next.

I was only slightly surprised when, true to his promise, Hermes materialized, seeming to come from nowhere. One moment I was unaware of his presence, and the next he was standing right beside me. The god was wearing the same winged hat and long cloak in which he had appeared to us in the swamp, and bearing in one hand his caduceus, the staff with the twined serpents.

Before I could decide for myself the proper degree of respect to offer him, Hermes announced that he was ready to take delivery of his fresh, live monster.

Traffic in the crowded square flowed by us without pause; and I soon realized that the other people must see a totally different image than Enkidu and I did when they looked at the god Mercury. Perhaps they also heard different words, if they could hear his speech at all. Not that the Messenger was totally invisible in their eyes; they walked around him instead of bumping into him, while they continued to marvel at our captive pig. But it was as if some spell prevented them from paying him much attention.

What really surprised me about Hermes/Mercury was that this time he had a mortal man as his companion. This fellow was middle-aged and of impressive bearing, though garbed in the clothing of a common workman, a mere loincloth, cheap vest, and sandals. He stood close beside the god, and the two were in earnest conversation.

I was about to ask the Messenger who his associate might be, but before I could do so, the man himself turned to me and extended a hand in greeting.

"I am called Daedalus," he announced in a brisk voice. His hand felt callused, hard as wood, against the permanent softness of my palm and fingers.

It was a name that I had heard before, while still living at home. Indeed, who in the world had never heard it? The name seemed to me to belong to some legendary character and was vaguely associated in my mind with feats of great skill and wisdom; I could not at the moment recall the details of what Daedalus was supposed to have done, but I was sure he had accomplished marvels. Was this indeed the same, the legendary Daedalus? But why should this man not be of legendary fame, if he consorted on friendly terms with Hermes?

No doubt my surprise showed in my face. "The master Artisan?" I asked.

Daedalus smiled faintly, like one who found it gratifying to be recognized. "There are those who call me that," he said. And he promptly shook hands with Enkidu as well, having evidently determined quickly that my companion was no mere servant—or, perhaps, his attitude suggested, not caring whether he was or not. And then he turned his attention to the Boar, which obviously interested him more than either of us mere humans.

The name of Daedalus, if shouted in the marketplace, would not have created nearly as much excitement as that of Jason, but was perhaps just as widely known. Trying to recall everything that I had heard about the Artisan, I finally remembered hearing that he was a widower. I saw before me a lean man of about forty and of no more than average height, with a large nose and brownish, gray-streaked hair tied behind him with utilitarian string. His fingers were ringless as a slave's, though there was no reason to believe his corded neck had ever worn a collar. Both hands were scarred, as if from the use of every kind of common tool.

As soon as Hermes and Daedalus got their first look at the Boar, they put their heads together and began what was obviously an intense discussion concerning the monstrous beast. They poked and prodded its legs and ribs, and tugged at handfuls of its hair. Meanwhile, as its flanks rose and fell in great, shuddering breaths, my living trophy glared back at them with its red eyes and seemed to yearn to get its huge tusks into their flesh.

Presently the Messenger turned back to me. He inclined his head toward me very slightly; and I understood that, from a god, this was an impressive mark of favor indeed.

When Hermes began our serious discussion, he was standing closer to me than on his previous appearances, so I was able to get a better look at his face. I understood that what I saw was not, of course, the actual Face, the indestructible object of transcendent power that conferred all the powers of a god upon the human who happened to put it on. The Face of Hermes, like that of any other god, had to be inside his head, where it must have been ever since the day this avatar slid it over his eyes and nose, and where it was certainly going to remain until the day he died.

But what I was able to see at close range helped me to fully realize what I had known in theory, that he who was now Mercury had begun life as a mere human being. Naturally it must be the same for all gods and goddesses. As usual, I found myself wondering particularly about the case of Zeus.

He said: "Congratulations, Hercules, on your success. This beast should be of considerable value to our cause."

"Thank you, Lord Hermes." I drew a deep breath and was about to inquire regarding my payment, but Mercury was already speaking again and paid no attention to what I was trying to say.

"Having accomplished this," the Messenger informed me, "you must be considered worthy to undertake another assignment for the one we both serve. This new task is of an importance that would be difficult to overestimate."

When he paused for my reply, I said: "Before we talk of new assignments, what about our reward for struggling to bring in this huge pig? The last time we met, you assured me that it would be marvelous, beyond the range of my imagination. Your exact words, as I recall, were: 'Your payment, for accepting and performing this new task, will be something more magnificent than you can imagine.' "

The god stared at me with divine hauteur—or maybe the look that I interpreted as such was no more than godly indifference. "What reward would you consider fitting?" he inquired.

"I think, Lord Messenger, that I have already made this clear. To begin with, I want to see my father, and speak to him, face-to-face."

Mercury seemed not to have been expecting any such demand. He was silent for so long that I began to wonder whether he meant to ignore my request altogether, or was perhaps trying to devise some ingenious punishment for insolence. But then at last he only said: "You do not know what you are asking."

"It seems simple enough to me."

"But it is not. Is there any alternative reward that would please you?"

"Not until my father agrees to see me and to let me have a talk with him."

"I see." The god sighed and shook his head. "Meanwhile, I am prepared to offer you a reward anyway, for what you have done already. The gift of Zeus is one that I think you will not refuse."

"Perhaps. How soon will I be allowed to see this different gift, and know whether I will refuse it or not?"

"You will see a portion of it very soon. Be patient."

Few people in the great world knew the name of Hercules as yet. But it did not hurt my local reputation any when I lifted crate and boar and all from cart to ground unaided.

Once Hermes and Daedalus had officially taken possession of the Boar, the God of Thieves magically whisked the animal away, crate and all, by some means that I could not detect. Still no one else in the square seemed aware that anything out of the ordinary was happening. In the process, the Messenger and Artisan disappeared as well, along with the cart and draft animals.

———

"I don't understand," I brooded, when my nephew and I were once more alone. "Why couldn't the mighty Hermes have laced up his winged Sandals, and flown up there onto the snowy mountain, and plucked the Boar out of its cave himself? And I wonder what plan it is that requires the presence of Daedalus as well?"

When my nephew wondered aloud who Daedalus might be, I did my best to enlighten his ignorance. By then I had begun to remember a few details of the Artisan's career.

Then I added: "Who knows why gods do what they do?"

The boy shrugged. "I don't. This one never even seems to notice that I'm around. But maybe that's just as well." Enkidu continued to puzzle over it all for a moment, then asked: "And what was all that about giving you another assignment? It sounded like he thought he was doing you a great favor."

"It sounded that way to me, too. Well, I don't doubt we'll find out before long what the great Messenger had in mind."

"And what was all that about giving us a reward? Do you think he will?"

"I suppose. He said it would come 'very soon.' All right. But maybe to a god, 'very soon' means something like a hundred years. Damn him, anyway. Why can't he just give me some straight answers?"

Enkidu looked around nervously. "Hercules, be careful. He might hear you."

"Let him hear. That's all right with me. Gods are only people wearing Faces. Anyway, you were complaining only a minute ago that he never pays you any attention."

"Yes, but . . ."

The more I thought about my situation, the more annoyed I became. "I tell you, Enk, I'm not going to stand around and wait to be given a handout, like some attendant at a stable. If Zeus is really my father, that ought to count for something. I'm fed up with this crawling and climbing through all the swamps and brambles and useless places of the earth. I've had it with endlessly digging and chasing after monsters."

Enkidu sighed. "All right, Uncle, whatever you say. But what are we going to do instead?" Then he brightened. "I know what I'd like to do, if we could choose. If only we could join the Argosy! That's what Jason calls his expedition."

The same idea had already begun to take root in the back of my own mind. One alternative of course would be to go home; but I never seriously considered returning to Cadmia, where I thought I would certainly be ordered into a marriage I did not want to make, or into the army, now that I was sixteen and old enough. Probably both.

What few scraps of news we heard from our homeland indicated that the war—I supposed it was the same one—was still on, afflicting the land like some lingering skin disease. And we learned also that everyone was getting so tired of unending struggle, endless lists of casualties, that some kind of an arranged peace might soon be possible. I was now well into my seventeenth year, and were I to go home, no one would object to putting weapons into my hands when the army faced real enemies.

But I had no wish to subject myself again to the authority of my foster father, or even of my mother. Having come this far, I meant to take whatever further steps were necessary to dig out the truth of my relationship with Zeus. Whatever that truth might be, the gods were evidently taking a special interest in my affairs. Hermes was an impressive presence, to say the least, but still I was not awed, and I wanted him to stop ordering me about, so I could get on with some kind of life of my own.

Mercury had seemed to assume that I would not be able to do this even if I tried. And in this case Mercury was proven right.

———

Entering a prosperous-looking, busy tavern, with Enkidu tagging along behind me, I put a couple of the Lizard's smaller coins down on a table. Immediately a well-dressed young man nearby, whose size, confident attitude, and youthful vigor made me assume he was probably one of the heroes, announced that he was buying this round of drinks and I should save my money. When I had saluted him with thanks, he presently came walking over, his arm carelessly around one of the giggling tavern girls, so that he dragged her with him, apparently without really noticing the fact.

When he stood beside me, he introduced himself as Meleager.

"Those who know me well call me Mel." His great hand swallowed mine.

For a moment there seemed something familiar about his greenish eyes, and I tried to remember whether I might ever have met him before.

But that seemed unlikely, as he had never been to Cadmia, or so he said, while I in my early years had rarely been anywhere else.

He went on to explain that I had been pointed out to him as the lad who had carted a gigantic, somehow magical Boar into town, and he wondered if this were really so.

When I admitted that it was, Meleager proclaimed himself an experienced boar hunter, too, and one of some renown. He had some technical questions about the feat I was supposed to have accomplished, queries about ropes and knots and so on that I tried to answer. His accent seemed to me strange, but with a little effort I could make out everything he said. I did my best to explain what I could about the Boar, but in the general din (the tavern was becoming crowded) I could not be sure that I was being heard or understood.

We had been talking for several minutes when he suddenly paused, a hand to his forehead as if it ached. "Hercules, Hercules—it seems to me I've heard that name before."

"Really? Was it in connection with a beast called the Hydra? Or maybe with a lion?"

Mel seemed to have no idea what I was talking about. "Are you coming with us on our little trip?" he demanded. "I mean the one that Jason's cooking up. Maybe your name's familiar because I saw it on one of his lists."

"I don't know if I'm coming with you or not. Tell me about the trip." But now another huge young man, Meleager's equal in heroic stature, was bellowing something at him from his other side, and he had turned away again and in the noisy tavern failed to hear me.

Meanwhile, strong drink of an unfamiliar kind had been set before me, in a foaming tankard. I was young, but looking around I could see that I was not the very youngest being served. Tasting the beverage cautiously, I reminded myself that what had happened when I drank wine among the centaurs must not be allowed to happen again here.

Two women were dancing on a kind of platform at the far end of the room, stripping off their clothes one garment at a time, while patrons shouted and whistled encouragement at them. Even I could see that they were not good dancers, nor was the music pleasing, but their bodies were young and taut and healthy, and the sight threatened to distract me from everything else. In only a few of the farmhouses where we had slept on our long walk had any female company been available.

Meleager had turned back to me again, and soon I learned that he was the son of a noble family who lived very close to Iolcus. Again he went out of his way to point out that he was something of a famous boar hunter in his own right.

That, I thought, would explain his continued curiosity, while leaving unexplained the strange sense of familiarity evoked by his green eyes. Meanwhile, he was still asking questions.

"What happened to the creature, by the way? I mean, where is it now? I spoke to several people who were there in the town square when you brought the animal in, but no two of them could agree on who took it away or where. One said you sold it to a butcher."

"I doubt you'll find it in a stew pot anytime soon." I took another long pull at my foaming tankard. My eyes kept turning back to the wiggling women.

"Then where?"

"I sold it, got a good price." Later, a time came when I realized that curious ears other than Meleager's must have heard me say those words.

"Wish I could remember where we've met before," said Mel. Then, as if in professional curiosity, he began to question me again on the technical details of hunting and capturing the Boar. Distracted by the dancers, I responded to his queries as truthfully as I could, but I could see that he was having trouble understanding. Naturally his mind was working on the assumption that no mortal man could be strong enough to handle such a beast in the way I seemed to be describing.

When Meleager, letting the matter of the Boar drop for the time being, kindly asked me how things were going in my life in general, I tried to express my dissatisfaction. "One of my parents is a god. And one of my gods is a parent. What a combination!" Well, it seemed a profound statement at the time. Meleager must have thought so, too, for he frowned and appeared to be giving it serious thought.

Though I ignored the fact at the time, others were observing both of us. Anyone, even an insignificant-looking outlander like me, who was engaged in such a serious conversation with a hero must be someone worth knowing, too.

The performance at the far end of the room was over now, the musicians devoting themselves to drink. One of the girls who had been dancing on the platform came up to me and commented on how nicely my beard was beginning to grow in. Something about it must have caught her eye from clear across the room. Her hair was yellow and thin, her face sharp-featured, and in the warm room she had not bothered to resume even a single stitch of clothing following her dance. As she stood near me the tip of one of her small breasts brushed my arm, as if by accident. And brushed again.

I rubbed my cheeks and chin, feeling the scratchy, bristly patches that had recently developed. "It's been a long time since I've seen a mirror," I admitted.

Enkidu, having been given no tankard of his own, had sipped more than was wise at mine. Now he was tugging at my tunic and telling me that his stomach felt queer, and he would wait for me outside. I nodded and brushed him away.

Meanwhile my very latest acquaintance was still speaking to me in her soft, eager voice. "Ah, but you must look in one, for you are very handsome."

"Look in one what?"

Her laughter tinkled pleasantly. "A mirror, you silly man! I can show you a room upstairs, in this very house, where there are many mirrors, all clear as air—big ones, on the walls and ceiling."

My head was whirling, dancing. I saw, as in a vision, a centaur dancing on a stage, then coupling with a mare. "So, you think I'm handsome, hey?"

"Oh yes," she said, and added: "They say you are also a strong man, and I can see that they are right." She reached out and squeezed the modest-looking muscle of my arm.

"No, you can't. See it, I mean. But I am. Even stronger than I am handsome."

The dancing girl laughed and put her hand on my arm again, more lightly this time, and the stroking touch of her fingers burned like fire.

10

Argonauts

IT WAS MIDMORNING when I emerged from the tavern, rubbing my eyes and blinking in the sunlight, with the sights and smells and sounds of a strange city all around. At once I spotted Enkidu, sitting on the steps of a market across the street, eating some toasted bread and waiting for me.

Evidently the youngster found something amusing in my appearance as I shuffled across the street, wincing at what seemed to me the inordinately loud noise of cartwheels thundering past.

"Did you sleep well, Uncle?" he demanded impertinently as I approached. "Or was that upstairs room with all the mirrors too bright for you?"

I sat down beside him with a groan. Holding out both hands in front of me, I marked how the fingers trembled slightly. My head was throbbing faintly, too, a phenomenon almost totally unknown in my young life. Something strange indeed must have affected me, more than putting down a mere half-gallon or so of wine. The drink had not had anything like the exotic, intriguing taste of the centaurs' ancient vintage.

"I slept passably well," I grumbled. "Though I could have done with another hour or two."

What had deprived me of sufficient rest, apart from the energetic activities of certain dancing girls, had been the insistent presence of strange dreams, prominently featuring the strange, bull-like figure who had now been intermittently invading my sleep for several months. Again I thought the bull-man had been trying to convey some warning to me, but my dreaming mind had been too fuddled for it to come through clearly.

I started to try to tell Enkidu about my latest experience of these puzzling visions, but he had heard me speak of similar things before and was not much interested. He said he had spent most of the night in a nearby barn, where he slept well and got over his troubled stomach. Fortunately for our fortunes, he still had most of our money safely with him. But he was not now in a mood to do much listening, once he realized that I was not going to relate in great detail my adventures in the room of mirrors.

And now, in a sudden change of mood, my nephew no longer seemed at all amused. For once he was unhappy enough to be serious, and even glum. Looking listlessly at the remnant of toast he had been chewing on, he complained: "I wish I was strong."

"You're quite strong, for your age."

"You know what I mean, Herc. Strong like you. And I wish that girls and women came flocking around me."

"We all have things we'd like to change. I wish my head would cease to ache. A philosopher would say that sooner or later all our wishes will be granted." As soon as I had made that pronouncement, it did not sound quite accurate to me. It was close, though. I was sure I could remember hearing something of the kind from the most philosophical of my former tutors. At least my version was encouraging.

My nephew told me, in a few disapproving words, what should be done with all philosophers.

Now only a few of the Lizard's coins remained to me, and those only by accident, a few that had become stuck in the lining of my tunic, where they were almost impossible to find. It seemed the wrong time to ask my nephew for money. I thought of looking about in the market for food and drink, but decided not to. Enkidu offered me a fragment of his toasted bread, but at that moment my stomach was too queasy. Getting up, I made my way carefully to a nearby fountain, where I slaked my newly raging thirst in the jet from a stone dolphin's mouth, and soused my head. That helped some, but still my head and belly were not right.

Only at that point, I think, did it occur to me to wonder whether my companions in last night's revelry might actually have put some foreign substance in my drink, with the intent of increasing its potency far beyond that of the natural power of wine.

Thinking it over, I realized that there might well have been some plan under way to drug me into a stupor and then rob me. I had talked in the tavern about selling my great pig for a good price, which meant I would be carrying money. It would have been no trick at all for one of the girls to drop something in one of the several—all right, one of the many—drinks I had consumed upstairs, or even in the one I had started on before ascending to the room with mirrors.

Well, if their plan had indeed been to knock me out and rob me, it had certainly miscarried, because here I was, and my few coins still with me. I had remained reasonably alert, and certainly functioning, for hours after going upstairs ... though when I had awakened in mid-morning and had decided to get up, everyone else in the upper room had been still totally passed out.

While I was struggling to sort out my more reasonable memories of the last twelve hours or so, and to see if any of even the clearer ones were worth retaining, Enkidu tugged at my sleeve. A familiar figure was making its way toward us across the square.

Out of courtesy I got to my feet as Daedalus came up.

One shrewd glance from the experienced Artisan allowed him to deduce my condition. "Bit of a hangover, young man?"

"I believe that's what it's called, sir. I don't have a lot of experience along this line."

With a shake of his head he expressed his sympathy. "Being young has great advantages. But of course there are drawbacks, too." He paused, then added expectedly: "I have a son at home, somewhat younger than either of you lads."

Enkidu was still gloomy. "I'm not very big. I was just telling Hercules, I wish I was six feet tall, and strong like him."

"I'll never be six feet tall," I said.

Daedalus nodded thoughtfully. "Having a wish not immediately granted is often grounds for sorrow. Unhappily, having one granted often produces the same result."

That sounded like a more accurate version of the philosopher's precept I had been trying to remember, and my nephew began to repeat his prescription for practitioners of that art. But in the midst of it he was suddenly struck by an idea, and broke off to ask a question.

"Daedalus, sir? Could Hermes make me strong, do you suppose?"

"I doubt it, lad," the Artisan responded absently. "That is, he might, but I doubt he will." Though he spoke to Enkidu, he was looking at me now, and he began to frown. "Hercules, I feel I should warn you about something."

"Sir?"

"I myself have some experience of celebrity—though not nearly as much as you seem destined to endure. It can be a dangerous drug, more dangerous than wine."

My stomach gave a queasy stirring at the thought of wine, and my head felt in no shape to cope with sage advice. "Thank you, sir—Daedalus, if I may—actually there's something else I'd like to ask you about."

"Ask away."

I began to tell him of my strange dreams. As soon as I described the horned figure, Daedalus said unhesitatingly that it was Prince Asterion of Corycus whom I had met.

"Who's that?"

The Artisan seemed mildly surprised at my lack of knowledge. "There are some—ignorant people in many countries—who do not know him, and who call him the Minotaur."

Enkidu, who was listening, let out a faint gasp—and I said: "Ahh." I said it thoughtfully, for certain things that had not quite made sense suddenly began to do so.

Daedalus was still talking. "But you are very fortunate, Hercules, if Prince Asterion takes an interest in your welfare. He is a friend of those gods who are most friendly to humanity. Had he any special message to convey to you? Perhaps a warning?"

I clenched my eyes tight shut and tried to think. "He had a message of some kind, I think. But I was too fuddled, even in my dream, to understand it."

Meanwhile Enkidu's attention had been captured, and he was still quietly marveling, repeatedly whispering that other name. *The Minotaur.* In his mind, and in mine as well, the word called up more legends: of the island kingdom of Corycus and its fabled Labyrinth; of a queen who had lusted unnaturally for a bull, and of the grotesque offspring that had resulted.

Daedalus, taking note of the boy's mutterings, suggested sternly that he had better not use that name at all. Then the Artisan looked around, as if to make sure that we were not being overheard.

"I assure you," he said, "it was no ordinary bull, but great Zeus himself, who visited Queen Pasiphae some twenty years ago and is the father of the prince. May the good queen's spirit rest peacefully in some quiet corner of the Underworld. If any such place actually exists."

"You doubt it does?" I asked.

"I have seen too much of the world to be very certain of any part of it. But one thing I know is that the monster called the Minotaur is a creature of legend, and very little more than that. The prince, on the other hand, is very real."

"The figure I have seen in my dreams, and who has spoken to me there, is certainly more than legend, Artisan. Having seen centaurs, I am more ready to believe in him."

Daedalus nodded reassuringly. "The prince Asterion, the real visitor in your dreams, indeed has the skull and horns of a bull, though the heart and hands and brain of a man. He almost never leaves the Labyrinth, but he has the power to roam the world in his dreams, and also to enter the dreams of others. If the prince has given you a warning you had better heed it."

Presently Daedalus squinted up at the sun and announced that there was business he had to be about. After saying that he would probably see us soon, the Artisan took himself away.

My nephew and I soon got up and, for want of anything better to do, strolled in the opposite direction.

"Oh, Hercules." It was a faint whisper, luxurious, weary, and admiring, all at the same time. Looking around, I saw the girl who had spoken my name in passing, and who was now retreating in the direction of the tavern where I had spent the night. She had now clothed herself for an appearance on the public street, but my brief glimpse of her face was enough for me to identify one of my bedmates of the mirrored room. One of those who might have been trying to rob me. What was it that Daedalus had said about celebrity?

Having turned our backs on the street of taverns and easy women, my nephew and I kept moving in the opposite direction. Our feet seemed to carry us automatically toward the nearby harbor. After all, water lay always downhill, and that was the easiest direction in which to carry an aching head.

There was no doubt as to which of the ships along the busy docks was the one being prepared for Jason's much-celebrated expedition. That was plain even before we came close enough to see the name of *Argo* painted on the bow. And presently, working our way through a scattering of idle onlookers, we got our first close look at the ship, resting unguarded against the quay.

Long and narrow, with places for fifty oars, her every line breathed adventure, and a great, challenging, staring eye was painted on each side of the prow, just forward of the name.

The *Argo,* the ship in which the heroes planned to accomplish their great adventure, was an impressive sight. There was a notch in the raised central deck where a mast could be mounted, though neither mast nor sail were visible right now.

I fell into conversation with some local idler—or perhaps he was a worker, for there were brushes and a paint pot at his feet, suggesting that he or someone else might have just completed the job of painting on the giant eyes. My curiosity was greatly stimulated. "And the object of this expedition is—?"

The man looked at me as if he thought I might be having fun at his expense. "To find the Golden Fleece and bring it back."

Overhead a gull was screaming, as if in derision. But I was just bewildered. "Back where? Here to Iolcus? And what is this Golden Fleece?"

My informant shrugged. "That's what everyone tells me, but I don't know what it means."

I thought that my new acquaintance Meleager would surely be able to tell me, and I supposed I would see him somewhere in town today. But I hesitated to betray my ignorance by pestering everyone else with questions.

———

Enkidu was tugging at my arm. "Look, Unc. What the man is carrying. That must be the compass-pyx for Jason's ship."

I had wondered what sort of navigational instrument the heroes would be provided with, and now I could see. It looked like something special indeed.

The man I had been talking to explained. "That's one of the heroes, the steersman Tiphys. Last night he carefully removed his compass-pyx from the ship, to make sure it wouldn't be stolen. Hah, who would dare swipe anything from that bunch?"

Tiphys, a very solid-looking fellow though not especially large, now came carrying the device onto the pier, obviously ready to reinstall it, a job that I had always heard was easily accomplished with a few simple, routine rites of magic. He acted as if the instrument belonged to him, treating it with the familiar care of a man who handles a treasure that has been passed down in his family for generations.

By now a little crowd had begun to gather onshore, just behind Enkidu and myself, as we stood there on the narrow pier. There was a murmuring from the crowd, and it gave me a strange sensation to hear people I had never met, or even seen, using my name, pointing me out to one another as someone worthy of notice. It seemed that word had finally reached the people of Iolcus regarding what had happened to the Hydra in its swamp, and how the Boar had been carried into town. And I had been observed to be in earnest conversation with a hero. Many now presumed me to be of that company.

I could hear some muttering behind my back: "Is it true that he clubbed a lion to death as well?"

Soon there came a louder murmuring among the crowd as a small group of young men, most of them taller than the average, made their way into it and through it. Now the pier swayed slightly underfoot with the weight of several heavy bodies moving briskly along it.

I turned around to face the shore just as a deep voice approaching from that direction asked: "You are the one called Hercules?"

"I am."

The speaker, perhaps ten years my senior, towered over me. He was arrayed in fine garments, and his whole head seemed a dark, luxuriant mass of hair and beard. "My name is Jason. And do you think yourself qualified to join us in our quest?"

"I don't know the answer to that, sir. I'm not sure just what qualifications you expect."

The mass of dark hair nodded judiciously. "A reasonable answer."

Jason explained that he and some of the others had begun just recently to hear of a certain youngster named Hercules, who was said to have achieved great things. They all assumed that I had come to Iolcus to join the heroes on their quest, and by the time they joined us on the crowded pier, it was obvious they had already decided among themselves that the next step must be to test my worthiness in some way.

Various murmurings around me soon informed me that the gods only knew how many other youthful would-be heroes had already been disposed of in the same way. In most cases, a bout or two of one of the milder forms of wrestling had sufficed to do the trick. I have no doubt that a majority of the qualified heroes on hand thought this would promptly eliminate me.

I felt relieved, having been worried that some bloodier test would be suggested.

"A little arm wrestling, then?" Jason was proposing jovially. "It's a warm day, whoever loses shouldn't mind a little swim." Actually, as we were all quite fully aware, the water just below the pier looked quite foul, a state of affairs only natural for a busy harbor that received much of a sizable city's waste. Today the wind and tide were doing a poor job of flushing, and it was not the place that any of us would have chosen for a refreshing dip.

———

Before the test could actually get started, more of the Argonauts appeared and introduced themselves to me. Eventually it seemed that their whole number came crowding onto the quay, forcing the retreat to shore of an even larger number of spectators. Among the newcomers I recognized Meleager, evidently no worse for his own visit to the tavern last night—of course his visit had probably not lasted nearly as long as mine.

Meleager asked me how my head felt this morning, after my adventures last night. "My own skull feels a bit thick," he added.

———

And then there happened that which I had not expected—and my life was changed forever. First I heard her voice, talking at a little distance, utterly unexpected, tantalizingly familiar . . .

. . . and then I raised my eyes and saw her, standing on the next pier over, only a few yards away, beyond a gulf of noxious water. She was looking, I realized, not at me, but directly at the man who stood just next to me. A pair of green eyes that I had seen only three times before, and then in very different circumstances, but could never have forgotten. The last time I looked into them it had been by candlelight, in a dark kitchen.

Looking at Meleager now, and at the family resemblance between them, I realized why I had thought his face familiar at first sight.

She was dressed differently now than on the last occasion when I saw her, but I did not doubt for a moment that it was in fact the same girl who had helped two young itinerant laborers who had been badly cheated.

Now she was calling to Meleager in a familiar way. He waved back casually and then turned to me to make the introduction.

"Over there you see my sister, Deianeira, informally known as Danni. Danni, this is Hercules, who says he wants to come chasing the Golden Fleece with us."

Then he paused, awareness slowly dawning in his honest face. He smote his forehead with his palm—then seemed to regret the act.

"But no, what am I saying? Of course you two have met before. *That's* where I heard the name of Hercules!" He raised his voice again. "By Hades, Danni, I ought to have remembered what you told me!"

The other heroes were meanwhile wrangling among themselves, so far good-naturedly, about which of them was to administer the test of wrestling. No one was that eager, for testing an undersized recruit was not the kind of trial that seemed to offer any chance of glory. Danni took advantage of the delay to come around and join us on the same pier. When she came near, I took her hand gently, as a man of quality does in Cadmia when introduced to a fine lady of his own rank.

She nodded a greeting to Enkidu and then turned back to me. Her straight brown hair was blowing a little in the breeze. "I see, Hercules, you and your friend have abandoned your earlier profession of farm laborer."

"The hours were long, the pay not great—though that improved toward the end, and I felt well rewarded by my stay on your uncle's estate. How is he, by the way? In bad health, I trust?"

I was rewarded with a giggle. Soon she was explaining to her brother, in more detail than before, her version of what had happened at the estate of the wicked Augeus.

Of course in Danni's version of events, which she unquestioningly believed to be the truth, the destruction of the dam, and the resulting flood, were put down as merely a coincidental stroke of good fortune that had allowed my nephew and me to get away without being noticed.

"Anyway," she concluded, "the remains of Uncle's stables are now clean. He tries to take some comfort from that fact."

Meleager stared at me for a long moment, before finally deciding that the whole story was worth a hearty laugh. Evidently he and his greedy uncle were not on the friendliest of terms.

Then he clapped me on the shoulder in good fellowship, a blow that would have staggered any ordinary man. "Lucky for you and Enkidu that there was such a flood that night!"

"Yes," I said. "That was very fortunate for us." But I was already looking at his sister again, and all I could think of was the depth of those green eyes.

"I hope you're able to come with us," Meleager said. He was sincere, but his tone made it clear he thought it wasn't likely, given the test that had been proposed.

I had looked at Danni only briefly the first time my eyes fell on her. But then I found myself looking back at her, again and again, over what must have been a period of several minutes.

When she turned her eyes to me again I said: "I think I ought to go back and arm-wrestle with your brother there."

What she said in response somehow failed to register with me. Green eyes—or were they after all some oceanic shade of gray?—quickened my pulse, seeming to convey a kind of wordless promise. I have seen something of the same seeming change of color on the sea in troubled weather.

But she was so young. Of course I was actually not yet very old myself. Perhaps she was not every man's ideal of great beauty, and perhaps she would never be . . . but I considered her a vision of loveliness, despite her youth, her age less than mine, body barely rounding into womanhood. A quotation, gleaned from some romantic tutor, drifted into my mind: ". . . upon whose neck was still the verdancy of youth. Nor was she yet familiar with the ways of Aphrodite, charmer of men."

But however great an impression Danni had made on me, I had little time to talk to her just then.

The Argonauts, after some prolonged though low-key wrangling, had finally decided on what test I was to undergo. In a general murmur of heroic voices I learned that it would be the same one that had been used on several others who had recently applied to join their company.

Jason, taking the lead in administering the test, as he did in almost everything else, stepped forward, smiling, and stuck out his big hand. He was almost a head taller than me, and his hand seemed to swallow mine. I thought there was a genuine friendliness in his attitude; he would not try to hurt me as punishment for my impertinence.

"We must make it a fair, strict trial," Mel warned me, half-apologetic.

"Of course. I understand."

And in the privacy of my own thought, I reminded myself strictly that I must be careful not to crush the hand of the brother of the girl who had been of such help to me. Nor should I do permanent damage to any of her brother's friends—of course, in truth, her green eyes would have saved *him* whether she had been my friend or enemy.

Whether I was to be invited to join the glorious quest or not was suddenly not so important to me as the chance that I might be able to impress a certain girl. But luckily the two goals were not exclusive. When the signal was given, and the match began, it was Jason who, tugged irresistibly forward, swayed and moved in a couple of helpless running steps before going off the pier and into the cool, refreshing water of the harbor. I thought the expression on his face was richly comical, and I heard my nephew's giggle plainly in the shocked silence of the watching crowd. Danni was also stricken dumb for a count of four, but then she added her own scream of delighted laughter.

Other Argonauts, suddenly alerted to the fact that something un-expected was happening and that they had better be prepared to do their best, followed their leader into competition. After four or five had copied his dive over the edge, the shallows beside the quay began to look even uglier than before, churned up as they were by the thrashing of brawny arms and legs.

When the next two contestants were disputing briefly as to who was next, pride, the heady fumes of sudden celebrity, at least as strong as those of wine (yes, Daedalus was right) once more got the better of me.

I shifted my stance and stuck out my left hand as well as my right. "Two at once?"

That was a dare such men could not refuse, and a moment later there was a double splash. In such a competition I found it hard to distinguish the strength of heroes from that of herd boys.

There were more than forty heroes present (I made no attempt at an exact count) and before my test had been completed, all of them had stepped up manfully to take their turns. There was some grumbling among my victims, and I received some formal congratulations when the farce was over, but mostly the crowd onshore and on the other piers looked on in an awed silence.

My credentials as a hero had been established beyond any shadow of a doubt, but in my foolish pride I had brought some who might have been my friends into the stage of envy, first stop on the road to being enemies.

11

A More Pleasant Swim

THAT AFTERNOON I was welcomed aboard the *Argo* by Jason personally, in effect formally granted heroic status. The leader of the Argosy seemed a trifle reluctant, and at the time I could not understand why. But following the exhibition I had put on that morning, I suppose he could hardly have done anything else.

Each qualified and accepted hero was allowed to bring aboard one companion, who was not required to pass a test, and so Enkidu came with me. No one bothered to ask whether he was present in the capacity of friend, relative, servant, catamite, or some combination of those categories, all of which were already represented among the chosen adventurers and their various associates.

That very day the expedition got under way, taking advantage of a favorable midday turning of the tide. I pulled an oar with the others, a few minutes being long enough to acquire the necessary skill. Some of my new shipmates, who had noted the soft skin of my hands, looked forward to seeing me quickly blister; but they were doomed to disappointment. Most of my body was already tanned from almost lifelong exposure, and the sun reflecting from the sea did no further damage.

Within an hour or two we had run into some choppy seas, and after half an hour of that I was unheroically seasick; my only consolation on that boatload of heroes was that I was not alone in my suffering.

Some of those who were not sick seemed to find amusement in the plight of us who were. Before my wretchedness had persisted for an hour, my anger at these mocking ones, and at myself, grew great enough to drive out seasickness from my guts and brains. Yet fortunately it was not great enough to goad me to violence.

As we rowed, the conversation around me touched on many things:

women and the sea, Giants and gods. I listened mostly, now and then contributing a word or two; but to my surprise what I had vaguely expected to be the chief subject of conversation was scarcely mentioned. That was of course the Fleece itself. Neither I nor my nephew had yet been able to discover just what kind of treasure this might be, and gradually it dawned on us that some considerable number of those who were now on their way to seek it did not know, either.

Our first night out we spent at sea, mostly dozing at our oars, while clouds covered the stars, and Jason, who apparently did not completely trust Tiphys and his elaborate compass-pyx, decided to wait for dawn to push ahead.

On our second day at sea we raised some hills around noon, and soon came ashore at a different place on the mainland for a scheduled final outfitting and to once more refill our water jugs and jars and waterskins. This was, of course, another part of the world that I had never seen before.

Before landing, we rowed up into the mouth of a good-sized stream, and one of my shipmates informed me that this was the river Chius, and the land that we had reached was Mysia.

Most of the crew might still have had some lingering taste of Iolcus harbor in their mouths, for none of us were eager to restock our water supply in this muddy stream. The party split into several groups, and most of the groups went inland, searching in several directions for a clear pond or stream.

At the time I assumed it was by sheer accident that Enkidu and I were separated, assigned to different parties; but before long I realized that it was nothing of the kind.

I was the chief subject of the following conversation but did not hear it, for it took place in a water-fetching party of which I was not a member. But it was later reported to me by a source I considered reliable.

Jason was shaking his head as he trudged along, carrying several empty jars, like all the other members of the group. "I am a strong man," he announced matter-of-factly, and others nodded. "But when he gripped my paw, I might as well have been a child." Jason raised his own right hand, large-boned, thick with muscle, callused in certain tell-tale spots that indicated a habitual use of weapons, and stared at it as if he beheld some troubling flaw. Then in a lower voice he mused: "Do you know, that wasn't the worst thing of all."

"No?" prompted one of his companions.

"No. The worst thing of all was—and it was easy to see—that Hercules wasn't even trying very hard."

"And he's not at all large," someone else put in, after a pause in which they all considered the implications.

"Wait till he gets his full growth," another voice speculated ominously.

For a while after that, no one said anything at all.

The heroes of the Argosy, every one of them having personally tested the strength of this upstart Hercules, knew that not one of them could stand against me for an instant in any direct contest. Later I learned that whenever I was not present, they tended to sulk and scowl and mutter among themselves, trying to devise some way to be rid of me. From accounts I was able to piece together later, the business went something like this:

The group of which my nephew was a member had gone ashore like the others, everyone carrying appropriate containers, in search of clean water.

When Enkidu's party had made their way inland half a mile, one member of it suddenly recalled having heard where a suitable pool might be.

When they had reached its shore, one muscular young giant approached Enkidu casually and asked him: "Are you *sure* your uncle's not some god in disguise?"

"I'm sure." The boy was calmly matter-of-fact about it. "I've known my uncle all my life, and he wears no Face. Zeus *is* his father, though."

The little squad of heroes who had casually managed to separate us muttered and discussed it among themselves. A number of the Argonauts also claimed divine ancestry, in one form or another; sometimes it seemed that half the people in the world, at least those who hoped to advance in society, did that. But among this boatload of adventurers, a great many of their claims might well be true, to judge by the various powers they could demonstrate. They were not overawed by me. But they were worried.

By now, Enkidu's group had come out of the woods to stand beside a long, broad serpentine of water, almost an acre in extent. Its grassy shores were shaded by the trees of a grove the local folk deemed sacred to some ancient god, a deity whose name had been forgotten. For the moment, the party seemed to have the place all to themselves.

Enkidu asked the others, innocently enough: "Why did we have to come all this distance for water? I heard someone else talking about a clear stream a lot closer to where we came ashore."

"Clear, yes. But not with water like this one. This is a very special pool." This was said with such a winking emphasis that my nephew's suspicions were immediately aroused, and he refrained from drinking from the pool until he saw several of his companions stretched out on the bank, slaking their thirst with no apparent concern and starting to fill their water jugs. Then Enkidu in turn bent down and drank. The water was cool and refreshing.

And very special it proved to be.

———————

When we had all been in the boat, and I had tried to pin Jason down as to exactly where the expedition was headed, his response had been a little vague. The most I could learn about our destination was that it lay somewhere in the East, and that we were going in search of a reputed Golden Fleece. For guidance in the details, he told me, they meant to rely on visions and omens.

Later, I began to wonder if Jason had withheld details because he knew I was not going to remain with the Argonauts for very long.

A sizable faction among the Argonauts, having been convinced of how strong I really was, seeing for themselves confirmation of the wildest rumors, feared that I would hog all the glory of their quest for myself if they allowed me to come along.

I was ready then to give Jason himself the benefit of the doubt, to believe that he was too noble a soul to be involved in such chicanery. In later years I became more cynical about the likely motives of all human leaders.

But whether he was personally involved or not, there is no doubt that a certain clique among the Argonauts decided among themselves to throw Enkidu into the pond of nymphs, the Pool of Pegae. They were in fact reasonably careful not to do the youth any real harm.

———————

Before Enkidu could say or do anything else, two of them had him by the wrists and ankles, their four hands locking him in a quadruple grip no ordinary mortal could possibly have broken. Another hero began a chanting, lightly mocking count: "One, and—"

"What're you doing? Let go!" the boy cried out, beginning to be frightened. The water under the overhanging trees, while much cleaner than the harbor, was somewhat darker and more mysterious than most people would choose for a casual swim.

"You *can* swim, can't you? Good! Fear not, lad, there are no monsters in the depths. Only some girls who say they want to meet you."

—*girls?!*

"—two, and—"

"You'll find it cool and refreshing, much better than that damned harbor water."

"—three!"

So it seemed to Enkidu that he was only in for a dunking; nothing so terrible about that. And what could they possibly mean, about girls who wanted to meet him? He even managed to relax a little as he went in with a splash. Even while still in midair he caught a glimpse below him of a slender, silvery body, quite dramatically female; and when he opened his eyes, under the clear water, he saw drifting before him a girlish face framed in wild wet hair and wearing an expression of devilish anticipation, as of some delightful game about to be played.

And now, close beside this first apparition he beheld another, at least as beautiful; and then another, and . . . with a strange feeling in his gut, he realized that there must be at least a dozen of the water sprites in all, and that they had him thoroughly surrounded.

He was swimming freely now, but was suddenly not so much concerned to get out of the pool as to investigate the wonders that its depths had so unexpectedly revealed. And the more he saw of those wonders, the more willing he was to be detained by them. He had never met a naiad before, though I would not be surprised to learn that he had dreamed of them without knowing what they should be called. Had my nephew known what sort of welcome awaited in the pool, it might have taken several heroes to keep him out of it.

———

Before long, I was quietly tipped off by the companion of one of the other heroes. The information came in the form of vague and disconnected hints that something might have happened to Enkidu. My informant told me he had last been seen alive on the shores of a certain pool, called the Pool of Pegae, which lay more than half a mile inland. At that point the name of the pool meant nothing to me.

Paying little attention to the suggestive fact that none of the heroes were coming with me, I dashed in that direction. I have never been able to manage anything out of the ordinary in running speed, but still I soon located the pool, which was easily approached by a couple of well-marked trails.

When I reached the shoreline, the boy was nowhere in sight, and for a moment I was totally convinced that he was drowned. Detecting some kind of disturbance below the surface, I threw off my clothes and dove into the pool to see what I could find. I was far from being the best of swimmers, but I was determined to do all I could.

Even in a pool that size, the tumult under the water was violent enough to be easily discovered. To my great relief, I soon saw and heard him sporting in good health.

Soon I had joined Enkidu in his watery sport. We both enjoyed the romp.

I quickly noted, with considerable relief, that nothing like scales and fish fins were in evidence, either on his body or those of his new playmates. The nymphs' bodies below the waist were as fair and womanly as they were above.

While we were both still below the surface, his voice reached me with the sound of a stream of bubbles.

"Uncle, Uncle! There's great magic in this pool! These girls can fix it so we can breathe underwater!"

I thought about it, then bubbled back: "That can't be good for you, in the long run."

But a moment later I was trying the technique myself, under the guidance of a fair instructress. The long run always seems very far away when you are young.

The naiads offered superb sport, I must admit, and it might have been possible for a man to spend years in that pool, coming to the surface only now and then, or not at all if that should please him, so long as the fair natives were on hand to protect him with their special magic; but I had other aims in life. Several hours had passed before I finally succeeded in disentangling my nephew from the silvery bodies of the naiads. We surfaced among a stand of lily pads, I retrieved my clothes from the border of the pool (Enkidu's had all permanently disappeared somewhere underwater) and we went looking for the Argonauts.

But by the time we had returned to the landing place, the sun was setting, and the *Argo* and its load of heroic voyagers were long gone. Only a couple of the less sophisticated natives stood and gaped at us.

For a time I stood on the muddy riverbank, now and then chucking a pebble into the stream, my mind busy with unsettling thoughts and mixed emotions.

When Enkidu told me what the men who threw him into the pool had said, I realized that the heroes' whole object in so treating him had been to delay me.

I had to face the fact that the Argonauts, or at least a strong faction among them, did not want Hercules adventuring with them. They were jealous of the glory that I would win when their serious adventures began; and resentful of the fact that they would appear weak whenever they were compared to me.

"So," I said aloud, when understanding finally forced itself upon me. Now I felt resentful, too, and yet buoyed up with a strange, sullen pride in my own peculiar nature.

"What do we do now, Unc?"

"I don't know."

He brightened slightly. "Well, we could just walk back to the—"

"No! That's one thing we're not doing, just walking back to the Pool of Pegae. We are not going to spend our whole lives there." Tiredly I looked up and down the riverbank. "I wonder if there's a real port around here somewhere?"

"We might not need one, Herc. Because here comes a boat. Maybe we can ask whoever . . ." And Enkidu's voice trailed off.

Yes, indeed there was a boat. Here it came, a small, strange, trim, single-masted craft the exact like of which neither of us had ever seen before. It came sailing silently around the nearest upstream bend of the little, nameless river to put in just where we were standing.

I had no need to look twice to recognize the tall figure that stood up in the boat and stepped ashore.

Hermes, the patron of thieves and honest merchants, as well as travelers and athletes, was still carrying his staff with its careen serpents, but was no longer using it as a boatman's pole—this craft was moving under some other, invisible, means of propulsion. He had discarded his long cloak in favor of a simple tunic, and I could see again that he wore winged Sandals, as well as the familiar winged and broad-brimmed hat.

"Hail, Hercules," Hermes greeted me in his resonant voice as he drew near. "I bring you the reward I promised—and also a message from your father."

"Hail, Lord Mercury," I responded. "When am I to see him?"

"That is difficult to say."

"I thought it might be." Suddenly the memory of the day's sport in the deep pool seemed only tiresome, a distraction best forgotten as soon as possible. "Well then, where is Daedalus?" I asked the god. "There are matters I would like to discuss with him."

"He is busy working on the Boar," Hermes answered shortly. "And both man and beast are far away from here by now."

"Working on it? Do you mean butchering the creature, for some feast or sacrifice?"

It seemed to me odd that Mercury had to consider that question before he answered it. "Neither sacrifice nor feast," he allowed at last. "But there is a kind of butchery involved."

Moments passed, in which little waves slapped at the small hull of the new boat, which had been painted a plain white.

"All right." I sighed, and felt my shoulders slump. "I cannot compel a god to answer questions."

"I am glad, son of Zeus, that you realize that fact."

"What message does my father send?" I asked.

The Messenger seemed to relax a bit. "He wishes you well and urges you to travel on as quickly as possible to the island of Corycus."

Once more Hermes had surprised me, and for a long moment I could only stare at him blankly. I of course knew something of Corycus, where grew the legend of the Minotaur, and where the real Prince Asterion, who was my counselor in dreams, must live; but I could see no connection between this new demand and any of the other efforts I had made so far.

Mercury seemed ready to take my silence for agreement. "Also, I am pleased to offer you the first part of the reward you have been promised." With a gesture he indicated the little boat. Though neither anchored nor grounded, it did not drift off in the current, but remained just where the god had stepped from it, its prow barely touching shore.

"A boat?"

"Yes."

I gazed at the small vessel without understanding, while it bobbed lightly in the water. "Whose is it?"

"Yours, if you will accept it as the promised portion of your reward."

"It is not what I have asked for. You still refuse me that."

Mercury did not reply.

I sighed. "Somehow I was expecting that great gods, like yourself and Zeus, would offer more than just a boat—something in the nature of a fabulous treasure."

"Would you prefer a fabulous treasure?"

"I have told you, Lord Hermes, what I would prefer. Well, I suppose the boat may well be useful."

"I assure you, son of Zeus, it is no ordinary craft." The Messenger's voice was solemn.

Once more I studied the vessel, but still it looked quite ordinary to my untutored eye. I saw the name, *Skyboat,* emblazoned in two languages on the prow. "Just what makes it so special?"

"For one thing, it will help you to complete your journey to Corycus very speedily."

"I see. A gift to the workman of a new tool—so he can more quickly accomplish his work. Well, what sort of monster am I to wrestle with when I get out to that island? Maybe an octopus, or a bat? Where do you want the creature delivered, and should it be alive or dead?"

"When you are on Corycus, it will be better if you can avoid wrestling, and highly advisable that you do no fighting at all. You are going there to meet a being of very unusual appearance, but he is no more a monster than you or I."

"I assume you mean the man some call the Minotaur," I said. "More properly known as Prince Asterion. Daedalus, before he rushed away the last time, did his best to enlighten me about the prince."

"I am glad to hear it," said Mercury. "For in fact Prince Asterion is your half brother."

I had already been vaguely aware of that fact, but to hear it stated plainly made me stop and think.

Now Hermes seemed ready to depart, leaving the boat behind; the wings on his Sandals and his hat were twitching, and now he rose effortlessly into the air, graceful and easy as a hummingbird.

"Who is to pilot the boat for us?" I called after him, in something like alarm.

"No pilot will be needed," Mercury responded calmly.

I looked in bewilderment at Enkidu, who was looking back at me with a similar expression on his face.

"But neither of us knows anything of the sea," I protested to the god. "We're likely to drown ourselves before we're out of sight of shore."

Hermes paused momentarily in midflight. "You do know something of the compass-pyx, and of its use?"

"I've never touched one, nor has Enkidu. We saw a little of the instrument they were putting aboard the *Argo.* All the sailors on board remarked how fine it was."

"The one in your new boat is finer still. It will serve you well no matter how great your ignorance. But to save time I will detail a certain sprite to help you."

"A sprite, Lord Hermes?"

"A creature usually attached to the Twice-Born, Lord Dionysus. You will not see it, but you will have help with the boat when you need help. Also your new servant can do duty as a messenger. If you should happen to make some great discovery, you will be able to communicate it quickly to the gods or humans who are your friends."

And Hermes pointed toward the boat.

I found nothing new to see in that direction, and when I looked back again to where he had been standing, the God of Merchants and Thieves was gone.

━━━━━━━

Enkidu could hardly have known any more about boats than I did, but he was desperately impatient to give this one a trial cruise. We climbed in and gingerly shoved off into a river that invited the experiment by being almost calm.

The boat drifted in a straight line, or so it seemed, with none of the aimless turning I had been expecting.

Enkidu was enthralled. "Uncle, this is even better than the *Argo!* This is a damned sight better!"

"Not as big, not by a long way."

"But this boat we don't even have to row!"

━━━━━━━

Mercury had been out of sight for some time before Enkidu and I got around to wondering exactly where the Argonauts might have got to by this time. They had talked of heading east, but that was about all we had been told.

"When we have finished whatever we are supposed to do on Corycus," Enkidu suggested, "we might get in our boat and look for them. If this compass-pyx is as good as it looks, it could probably find the *Argo* for us."

"No, they sure don't want us with them. Certainly they don't want me, so to the Underworld with them. Besides, I suspect that when we have finished whatever is to be done on Corycus, my father will have thought up yet another task."

My nephew nodded, and let drop the matter of the *Argo* and its crew, so jealous of their fame. Enkidu hardly seemed to care where we were going next. I think I might have ordered him to set course for the Underworld, and he would have complied, so long as the journey could be made in our beautiful new boat.

12

Visiting a Queen

BEFORE HEADING OUT across the sea, my nephew and I put in at a small settlement a quarter of a mile downstream from where the *Argo* had landed, almost at the river's mouth. It seemed about the only place approximating a real port on that sparsely inhabited coast. Here we were able to obtain some decent clothing, that we might present a proper appearance at our arrival on Corycus, and also some food for the voyage. Small lockers aboard the *Skyboat* already contained jugs of water and several days' supply of fruit, dried meat, and fish. But Hermes seemed to have ignored all other needs that a crew or passengers might have.

The townsfolk stood staring after the two of us as we carried our purchases aboard, and that night we slept in the boat. Early in the morning, with our audience reassembled and gaping at what they must have supposed to be our folly, we awkwardly (and doubtless incorrectly) hoisted our small sail. Enkidu closed his eyes and pressed his forehead to the compass-pyx. The *Skyboat* began to move, propelled directly by its own magic, and we set out boldly through the mouth of the river and into the open sea.

Our destination, the locals had warned us, lay about two hundred miles to the southeast, half the width of the Great Sea away. They marveled at what they thought was the stupidity of two landlubbers, attempting such a feat in a small and practically open boat.

In the press of other concerns, I came near forgetting what Hermes had said about detailing a sprite to help us through any difficulties we might have with navigation. But so far it seemed we might be managing on our own. When Enkidu had moved away from our compass-pyx, and I cast my untutored eye at it, it seemed to me that Hermes had been right, and it might surpass even the model they were carrying on the *Argo*, of which Tiphys had been so justly proud. Our navigational device was just as big, and the box that housed it was made of real ivory, as far as I could tell, and the carved and painted patterns on the surface of the box were more complex.

The style of construction of our craft provided a tiny cabin, just about large enough to shelter two people, if they crawled in on hands and knees and could endure each other's closeness. The sail proved to be almost entirely for show—fortunately, for neither of us knew the first thing about sailing—though later it proved perfectly capable of functioning in the ordinary way. It also filled itself out with a phantom breeze when there was no real wind in the direction chosen by the steersman. There were no oars, but a couple of paddles had also been shipped aboard, again mostly, as I thought, for show. *Skyboat* was perfectly capable of propelling itself by sheer magic.

At this time, I sorely missed the company of Daedalus. I was keenly aware of my need of a wise counselor, but the only confidant I had, had now attained the ripe age of thirteen. So far, for my nephew, our wandering had been mainly a series of glorious adventures, culminating in a chance to sport with naiads. And to top it all off, he had now been provided with a wonderful new toy in our magic vessel. Small wonder that at the moment Enkidu was perfectly convinced that the world was an endlessly wonderful place.

As the two of us put out to sea, I caught a brief glimpse of a girl with hair almost the same color as Danni's, hard at work bending her slender, nude body over a fishing net on a nearby beach. It was of course not Danni. But I found myself wishing fervently that Meleager's sister might appear onshore and wave good-bye to me; far better yet, that she should be waiting to greet me when I landed somewhere. But alas, she was naturally nowhere in sight, being miles away.

Somehow the sight of one girl, and the thought of another, evoked in my mind the thought of yet another very different one. The face and body of Megan, our unhappy household servant as I remembered her, appeared briefly in my imagination; but as I sat in our little boat, Megan seemed to me to belong to a different world, one that had little or nothing to do with the one I now inhabited, away from home adventuring. And at the moment, her very remoteness invested her with a kind of glamour that made her all the more desirable.

The weather at the start of our voyage looked a trifle ominous, and had either of us any real experience of the sea, we might well have been frightened at what we were about to attempt. But in this case our ignorance was a shield. While Enkidu, clutching the compass-pyx and gloating over the power it gave him, confidently set our course, I sat thumping my hand gently on our new boat's solid side.

So, this construction of wood, canvas, and magic was the reward I had been promised. Certainly not what I had asked for, but real and solid, and if the Messenger had told the truth, quite marvelous enough to be the gift of some benevolent god. Solid proof, if any were needed, that Hermes was no mere impostor, or creature of my imagination. The whole game had now been raised to a different level.

We had been under way only a few minutes, gradually picking up speed, before all land had dropped from sight behind us. But still our boat, under the control of the magical device given us by Hermes, ran straight and with unhesitating speed. Since my life now depended on it, I wanted to find out as much as I could about how it worked. I reminded myself to ask Daedalus when next I saw him. Possibly the compass-pyx was too magical to fall fully into his realm of expertise, but I would try him anyway.

It was installed in a containment box, or binnacle, very near the exact center of the boat, and the four side walls of the ivory compass were connected, with magical effect, to the corresponding walls of the binnacle in which it rested.

The first time I put my head near the compass-pyx, the air nearby sounded with a thin whining from some invisible source. I jerked back nervously and looked about, one hand raised to swat a giant insect. But there was no such creature to be seen.

"You hear some buzzing, Herc?" Enkidu was grinning at me. "I did, too. But it didn't do me any harm."

Sudden realization dawned on me. "Lord Hermes said that he was leaving us a sprite to help us navigate." And as I spoke, the humming sound peaked sharply, then fell abruptly away.

My nephew looked more interested than worried. "What will it do?"

"Not much of anything, I hope, unless we need its help." Actually I knew no more of such beings than Enkidu did, but I wanted to be reassuring. "Try to use the box again; the less help we need, the better."

He followed my advice and had such good success that both of us were able to forget for the time being about our invisible companion.

My main concern was with more basic and important problems, on which I doubted that the sprite could give me any help. Nor could Enkidu, surely. All the great business of my life lay between me and the gods. I kept turning over in my mind what facts I thought I had made sure of, and those I only suspected, regarding my past life and what I might expect in the future.

Whatever faint doubts I might once have had that Zeus was really my father were becoming harder and harder to sustain—from what other source could I derive my special powers? And everyone agreed that the Thunderer's children were legion, scattered around the world along with his more remote descendants, all products of his obsessive lechery down through the ages. But rarely if ever, according to legend, did he sustain any interest in any of his bastard children. So I was less than confident it was really Zeus who had sent the Messenger to give me orders and to provide a magically powered boat. Mercury, speaking with all the lordly authority of deity, had clearly said as much—but was the God of Thieves and Merchants always to be believed?

Soon I began to share my thoughts with Enkidu, who was wondering what made me so silent and thoughtful. My nephew and I speculated as to whether we might someday be treated to an interview with Helius, the Sun, or maybe Apollo himself. Or possibly Hera or Aphrodite.

Of course the gods, as usual, provided an inexhaustible subject of conversation.

"Herc? I've been wondering."

"What?"

"If your father is . . . who he is . . . then why does he need to send you all around the world, beating the shit out of these monsters? He could just . . . just smite them with a thunderbolt."

"How in the Underworld should I know? Why did he insist on our hauling the Boar around, alive, if they were going to butcher it anyway? Maybe it just amuses him to watch. He never tells me anything."

"But now you're making a great effort to do what he wants you to do."

"Well. He is my father. Though he's never spoken a word to me since I was born."

"I know, you keep telling me that."

And that put an end to conversation for a time.

"Corycus is where the Minotaur lives," Enkidu observed, after a period of thoughtful silence.

"Are we back on that again? You should have been paying attention when Daedalus was talking to me, and Hermes, too. You'd better not use the word *Minotaur* at all when we get to Corycus. He's Prince Asterion, half brother to Queen Phaedra, and like me, he's a son of Zeus. And Hermes wants me to talk to him."

"But he's really got a bull's head?"

"So it seems."

"But he talks like a human being? And all you have to do is talk with him?"

"That's the way I understand the business so far."

"I was just wondering if maybe they expected you . . ." Enkidu didn't finish.

"If they want me to pack the Minotaur in a crate and cart him off somewhere? No, listen, Enk, we'd better get this straight, once and for all." And I did my best to pass on to my nephew the information that Hermes had conveyed to me.

When I had accomplished that, or thought I had, we were silent for a while. Then at length Enkidu said: "Corycus will be really different, though, won't it, Herc? If Lord Hermes said we don't have to kill anything there. How long are we going to stay?"

"Not having to hit anything with a club will be a pleasant change, as far as I'm concerned. Not having anything trying to bite me will be even nicer. I don't know how long we'll stay."

Again long minutes passed, and then my companion offered: "I wonder where Jason and his pals are now."

I turned my head and looked out over the empty sea. "A good many miles west of here, I'd say. And getting farther away from us all the time. It'll be all right with me if they just keep going, on and on, until they fall off the edge."

"But wouldn't it be neat if they could see us in this boat? I bet we could run circles around the *Argo.*"

———

Even two passengers as ignorant as we were of seafaring could hardly fail to recognize how marvelous our *Skyboat* truly was. As we gained more experience of its capabilities, Enkidu was ecstatic, almost literally entranced, and went through spasms in which he seemed to be bubbling over with joy. "They gave it to us. They just *gave* it to us!" And he drove us swirling in circles on the surface of the great calm sea, while gulls went screaming past above us, never having seen the like before.

"Just gave it to us? No. It represents a partial payment; weren't you listening?" My gaze went sweeping around the empty place where sky rimmed water.

Finally I added: "And when we reach Corycus, Hermes will show up again and tell us there'll be more to it than talking. We'll be expected to do something else—something pretty difficult and dangerous. Now get us back on course."

"Difficult and dangerous? What'll that be?" But he obeyed my order, as if reluctantly.

"I don't know what, or why. All I do know is that the great god Zeus has never—never—paid any attention to me. Until only a few months ago. Then, good old Dad seems to have suddenly decided that the world is suffering from a plague of monsters. And that I, just one of his innumerable bastards—I suppose one of about a million that he's never even seen—I am just the one to clean it up. And to speed up the job a little he sent one of his helpers to give me a boat."

"You can be scary, Herc."

———

Despite the vaguely threatening aspect of the sky and sea when we set out, the weather actually remained fine for many hours. Evidently, if Poseidon did not belong to the cabal of gods who were supporting us, he had not become an active enemy.

After we had been for a time out of sight of land, and of all other craft, I took a second turn at crouching over the compass-pyx (I almost had to drag Enkidu away, to get a chance) and with the aid of its powers called up a vision of our destination. This time I heard the sound of no invisible companion.

Soon I discovered that it was sufficient for me to whisper the island's name while resting my forehead against the ivory box. On each trial the device showed me, behind my closed eyelids, a new view of the island, very slightly nearer than the time before but from the same angle.

With a superb instrument like this, even a landlubber who had never used a similar device before had no trouble in navigation. When our course seemed well established, in a general southeasterly direction, I urged our new craft to full speed.

I supposed we might even be able to go faster in the case of dire emergency.

Even now we were going so fast that a white bow wave sprang into existence, and the small waves could be heard slapping the bottom in a regular rhythm as they raced beneath. On the rare occasions when we came in sight of other craft, I insisted that we limit our speed to something less than the apparently miraculous. Still, the cool wind in our faces was strong enough to tear our breath away.

But now we had a vast open stretch of water all to ourselves. Dolphins appeared to challenge us, and raced along, but soon they, too, were left behind.

As I have said, our destination was no less than two hundred miles from our starting point, but we made the voyage, straight across open water, in no more than half a day. When eventually a line of squalls blew up across our course, I took the compass-pyx with me into the tiny cabin. Our boat slowed its speed considerably, and with no human hand upon the helm maneuvered itself among waves to minimize their impact and the roughness of our ride. But still I thought that we were making steady progress.

Soon we raised the mountainous, partially wooded spine of Corycus above the waves. The island was more than a hundred and fifty miles long, but very narrow. Only about an hour later we were cruising, at a much reduced speed, into the busy harbor of Kandak, the capital. It was clearly, as I had expected, much larger than any city I had ever seen before. Plainly visible in the middle distance was the sprawling palace, where less than a year ago, as everyone knew, young Queen Phaedra had ascended to the throne—I remembered how much excitement had been generated in Cadmia at the time, by news of the strange and violent events leading up to her succession.

By the time we reached the mouth of the harbor, much of Kandak had come into view. Also in sight, adjoining the palace, were the outer walls of the famous Labyrinth, sprawling over what was claimed to be four square miles of land.

Laborers and craftsmen of several kinds were at work, and folk with more leisure in their lives were strolling along the waterfront, but few took much notice of a small boat carrying a young man and a boy and looking utterly normal. Our sail put up a convincing show of being driven by nothing but the breeze.

But one man at least had evidently been expecting us, for he came walking along the pier before we had finished tying up, and bade us welcome in the queen's name.

We were hardly ashore before we learned that the gossip of current affairs on the island included considerable speculation as to whether Queen Phaedra might be going to marry. So far there seemed no certain answer to that question. People still spoke in hushed tones of the recent marriage of her sister, Ariadne, to the newest avatar of the god Dionysus.

───

The guide who had been sent to meet us happened to glance back along the dock, as we were walking away, at the place where we had tied up the gift of Hermes.

"What happened to your boat?" was his bewildered question. "It was right there, but now . . ."

I could still see it, and Enkidu told me later that he could, too, though only as a kind of transparent wraith of a small boat. At the time, we reassured our guide as best we could, and followed him on.

───

We were conducted first to the palace, where we had scarcely arrived before being told that Queen Phaedra had been informed of our arrival and was awaiting us impatiently.

As Enkidu and I walked along, we kept half-expecting to catch a glimpse of the divine Dionysus somewhere; but then we were told that neither he nor his bride, the princess Ariadne, were on the island.

The queen of Corycus received us privately. She was an attractive woman in her early twenties, with dark hair and a compact figure. The general assumption among her people was that she would not long remain unmarried, but naturally any match she made would have to be carefully considered.

Given the prominence of some of our relatives in Cadmia, neither Enkidu nor I were utter strangers to royalty, or to the procedures expected of visitors at court. So we were not as completely awed as many youths of our age might have been; and the young queen seemed to go out of her way to be friendly and gracious.

The queen concluded: "My brother feels an urgent need to see you, and I must send you on to him. But there is one other here who must speak with you first."

Now a familiar voice sounded, and a figure appeared whom we immediately recognized. And Enkidu and I saw, to our considerable surprise, that the Artisan had somehow got to Corycus ahead of us and was watching us with some amusement.

At first I blinked at Daedalus and was unable to believe my eyes. In the next moment, anger and suspicion surged up in me, and I was convinced that the apparition before me had to be some kind of a deception.

Jumping to my feet, I grasped the figure by one arm, taking care not to crush flesh and bone, but forestalling any attempt the man might make to pull away.

"Majesty," I cried, turning to the queen, "this cannot be truly Daedalus. We left him behind on the mainland, and we came here faster than any other boat could travel."

The queen and her attendants were at first greatly alarmed at my energetic action, and guards with spears leveled came bustling in. But in a few moments the cooler heads in the royal party had understood where the difficulty lay. They left it up to the Artisan himself to explain it to me.

"Swift as your little boat must be, Hercules, you should accept the fact that the transport which brought me here was even faster."

"How can that be?"

He looked around before speaking, and lowered his voice. "You should keep the matter a secret for now, but I actually came here in the chariot of Dionysus."

For a moment I thought the Artisan was joking; but then I saw that he was perfectly serious. It was evidently not the first time that Daedalus had ridden in the chariot, for he seemed to take the whole business with amazing calm.

And a little later, I was actually able to catch a glimpse of the supernatural leopards and the chariot, waiting inside the palace, at the end of a dim hall, even though the god whose property they were was somewhere else.

"Where is Dionysus?" I heard myself whispering to Daedalus, who walked beside me.

The Artisan looked at me severely. "I do not question the comings and goings of such a one. He may be very far away by now; the chariot will not be his only means of getting around."

I walked on in silence, past uniformed guards and lovely statues, all the panoply of wealth and power. Enkidu, trailing me by a step, had not uttered a word for a long time. We had come a long way from the herders' camp in Cadmia.

13

Talking to the Minotaur

WHILE I WAS waiting to hear word that Prince Asterion was ready to see me, I took the opportunity of seeking out the Artisan. Though I knew Daedalus only slightly, I had begun to trust him, and there were several matters on which I wanted his advice.

Meanwhile Enkidu, who was usually not given to worrying about anything more profound than the size of his muscles or the amount of gold he might someday manage to accumulate, had disappeared into the palace kitchen. I felt confident of being able to find him there, telling stories, eating, or chasing wenches, when I wanted him.

I had no problem locating Daedalus. He sat alone on a rooftop terrace of the palace, staring blankly at the surface of a table before him, on which he had arrayed an assortment of small objects, none of which I could recognize. I took them to be the parts of some cunning machine. They were of divers shapes and sizes, some carved of a substance that looked like bone, while others appeared to be polished wood, and yet others were clear glass.

Not wishing to break the Artisan's concentration, I remained standing quietly at a little distance until he noticed me, and then I apologized for interrupting him. But he seemed glad to see me, and bade me sit down. The elevated site provided us with a fine view of the Great Sea, beyond the palace and the harbor of Kandak.

The objects arranged on the table, Daedalus told me, were parts of an antique device with which he hoped to be able eventually to make some astronomical observations. But the problem of properly assembling the device had so far baffled him.

"Maybe some are missing," I suggested.

"I fear that's all too likely." But then he seemed to put the matter aside with a gesture of his work-hardened hand. "How do matters go with you, Hercules?"

"The *Skyboat* is a great help in getting from place to place. It does marvelous things. I hope you can examine it eventually."

"I hope so, too. If I had time . . . but there are only so many years, days, and hours in the life of any man. What else?"

"I have no real complaint about any of the tasks the gods have asked of me so far." I paused, and let time pass. In the distance, two servants were quarreling about something. The scar on the back of my right hand itched, and I scratched it absently. At last I added: "The truth is, matters do not go as well as I would like."

The man across the table nodded slowly. "I understand that you are determined to meet your father."

"I am."

As I began to make my usual complaints about my father, Daedalus listened intently, and a frown grew steadily upon his face.

"Is that how the situation seems to you?" he asked at last. "I did not realize you were so angry."

"How else should it seem?"

The Artisan sat for a time, still frowning. But now he gazed out at the distant waves, obviously deep in thought, while in front of him the collection of small parts lay totally forgotten for the moment. At last he sighed deeply and turned around to me again.

"Hercules, there are some things I dare not tell you, and other things that I simply must not. But I can tell you this: I have seen your father, and spoken to him, and—"

"You have seen Zeus?" I was impressed, and at the same time not totally convinced. For Hermes the Messenger to appear openly before mortals was one thing; for Zeus himself to do so would be quite something else. But neither could I wholly doubt. He who sat before me now was only a man—but a man who had ridden at least once in the chariot of Dionysus.

Daedalus responded calmly. "Yes. I have seen the Thunderer and spoken to him, not many days ago—"

"Where?"

"On the mainland—let me finish, Hercules—and it is my belief that not a day has passed since you were born when you have been absent from his thoughts."

"He must have a thousand bastard offspring, scattered around the world."

Daedalus nodded his grizzled head. "That may well be. But you are one of those he thinks about and particularly cares about. Do not forget that Zeus, like all gods, is first of all a human being."

Now it was my turn to sit silent, trying to digest a bit of information. I was staring at the sea but did not see it. At last, turning back to my adviser, I told him: "By all the gods, I wish I could believe that."

"You can."

"The man who currently wears the Face of Zeus is the man who sired me?"

"That is my belief."

"So, what have you heard my father say about me?"

But the Artisan was shaking his head.

"Tell me!"

"Let your anger fall upon me if it will, Hercules, but now I must say no more. Probably I have said too much already."

————————

After that, we spoke for a time of other things. Within an hour a messenger came to tell me that Prince Asterion was ready to see me. Soon the Artisan, forgetting his clockwork puzzle for the moment, was guiding me into the Labyrinth. Enkidu had emerged from the kitchen, evidently sated for the moment, and came tagging at my heels; no one objected to his presence.

Our guide led us out of the palace by one of the small side doors, then along a small gravel path that curved across a corner of the parklike grounds. Now I could see that we were headed straight toward one edge of the mysterious Labyrinth, which here immediately adjoined the palace grounds. The Maze's outer wall of stone, tall and slightly curving, loomed up ominously ahead of us.

And then we were inside, following a curving, stone-walled passage, barely wide enough for two to walk abreast, that branched, and branched, and branched again. Some sections were roofed, and here and there a stair went up, and another down. There were small courtyards, with ponds, and plants, and statuary.

It was, I learned, easy to find one's way to certain destinations within the Maze by following a series of painted spikes, which had long ago been driven into the pavement.

Not that my guide seemed to need them. I soon realized what I should have known all along, had I given the matter even a moment's thought: Here Daedalus was on familiar territory, having labored in the Labyrinth for many months on a project for Phaedra's predecessor on the throne. Many fascinating stories were connected with that effort, and some real events seemed to have already transformed into legend. I told myself that when the time seemed right I would ask the man himself to tell me the truth of all those marvelous events.

But that would have to wait, for now we were moving rapidly into the depths of the great Maze. Unlike many other famous sights in the great world, the Corycan Labyrinth, with its thousand miles or more of knotted narrow passages, most of them open to the sky, was truly as impressive as I had imagined it might be.

I had been told by several people that the prince dwelt alone in the middle of the Labyrinth, continuing by choice a style of life that had once been enforced upon him. He lived simply, with almost nothing of the panoply of rank, and was attended only occasionally by servants. He had spent almost his entire life within these walls, relying chiefly on dreams to keep him informed about the great world outside. He welcomed us even more eagerly than his sister had.

I had been told on good authority that Asterion, only a few years older than myself, was like me a child of Zeus. I had to repress a shudder when I saw for the first time with waking eyes just how the divine power had expressed itself in this, my half brother. Somehow this version of a composite creature, with the outward appearance of the head so totally inhuman, was more disturbing than the horse-bodied centaurs had been.

The prince was every bit as large as his image in my dreams had shown him, seven feet tall if an inch. Even a little more, I thought, if you were to count the horns, which went curving up one on each side of the inhuman skull, in graceful symmetry. His feet and legs as they showed below his kilt were very human, no hairier and no bigger than those of some normal men. In the course of his brief life, he had become known to most of the world only as a monster, a kind of bogeyman who feasted on human flesh. The reality of course was very different, and in fact the prince ate no meat at all. He also differed from ordinary men in having been born a eunuch.

The prince bade me be seated beside him on a simple bench, under a trellis of mutant grapevines, whose fruit looked more like miniature peaches. Enkidu, after being introduced, hung about uncertainly. Daedalus warned him sharply not to wander off.

"The Labyrinth is not the worst place in the world to go wandering, but it is one of the very easiest in which to lose yourself."

Enkidu flushed, and bowed in acknowledgement of the order.

When I had recovered somewhat from my first embarrassing but un-
controllable reaction to the sight of a man with a horned beast's head,
I questioned the prince eagerly on the subject of the father we were said
to share; but Asterion could not, or chose not to, tell me anything on
that subject that I did not already know.

I sighed and moved on to other matters. "Do you know, Lord Asterion, why Hermes sends me to you?"

"Yes. Because we have important things to talk about, and communication is much more reliable when both parties are awake. You
know I have the power to visit the dreams of others, and also to draw
others into mine. But those contacts made in sleep are too uncertain for
the proper conduct of some kinds of business."

The prince paused for a few moments and seemed to be gathering
his thoughts. Then he said: "Hercules, you have done well so far. But
all that you have done till now is as nothing to the tasks that still
remain."

He paused again, then added: "I hope that you will trust me, Hercules, when in the future I intrude to speak to you in sleep. I will never
do so without good cause."

The idea that anyone could so invade the privacy of my own
thoughts did not sit well with me. I said: "So far I have no reason not
to trust you, Prince Asterion. But then I have no proof that I should
trust you, either."

He shifted his great weight on the bench beside me, so that the
woodwork creaked. "You speak boldly, son of Zeus."

"Because there is little that I fear."

"No one here on Corycus bears you any ill will. Certainly I do not.
But I advise you to fear Zeus, if no one and nothing else."

"And what is the Thunderer himself afraid of?"

"Giants."

Had the prince answered with the one word *nothing,* I would not
have been surprised. But the word he actually used astonished me
enough to quiet my simmering resentment for a time.

"What do you know of Giants, Hercules?"

It was not the first time since my leaving home that affairs had
taken an unexpected turn. First gods, then centaurs, and now this.

"Very little, Prince."

"Have you ever seen one?"

"No."

The prince pressed on. "And have you heard of a war between the
race of Giants and the gods we know?"

"Something of such a conflict, yes. But only in nursery tales, when I was very small."

Asterion leaned his head back into the vines that grew behind our bench, as if he were trying to rest his neck from the weight of many dreams, or worries. He said in his strange voice: "I wish that the war was only a matter of nursery tales, and of dreams. But no, it is very real, and very terrible, though for most of the humans on the earth it is still invisible. That will not always be the case."

The Artisan, who was sitting in on our discussion, nodded his head in confirmation.

"The prince and I have decided," he said, "that it is time, and past time, that you know more of what your father Zeus is planning, what problems he and the other gods who stand with him must face. We can only hope that they will approve of our decision."

"Understand, first," said Prince Asterion, "that all the gods, whether they admit the fact or not, are deadly frightened of a terrible and secret weapon that the Giants use against them. Like Apollo's Arrows, it can strike at a distance of a mile or more. But it is completely invisible, even to divine eyesight. It has never been known to injure a mere mortal human, like you or me"—for a moment I thought the bull-face smiled, at including us both in such a category—"but on a god or goddess the effect is devastating."

"What sort of weapon?" I demanded, my throat suddenly dry.

"One that is hard to identify precisely, or describe." The prince raised both hands in an odd pointing gesture. "The projection from their very fingertips of some invisible beam, or force, which ravages the memory of anyone in its path who happens to be wearing a god-Face."

Each Giant, or at least a great many of them, possessed some form of this weapon, which must be somehow built or grown into their very bodies. Therefore any god who came within a mile of any Giant was at risk of losing part or all his memory, temporarily or permanently, even to the point of forgetting his own identity.

———

Then the prince and Daedalus led me into a different corner of the vast Maze, where a massive door was set into a thick stone wall. As I approached the door, the smell of the sea grew very strong, and I marveled at this, for I knew that the shore was more than a mile away. My guides indicated that I should look through a small hole in the door, and when I did I saw beyond it a room that had been converted into a stone prison cell.

The furnishings of the cell were simple. Its single inmate, a middle-aged man, was clad in a simple garment that might have been fashioned from a fishing net, and he sat on a simple bench studying his own hands, a blank expression on his face, like a man trying to remember what hands were for.

"Hercules, do you recognize that god?" asked the prince, who was standing at my side.

I had had no idea that I was looking at a god. "I do not, should I?"

"He is Palaemon, called by some Portunus, the God of Harbors. Now he is a horrible example of what the Giants' mind weapon can do. He has been so badly affected that he has forgotten what it is to be a god. I'm not sure that it still makes sense to call him a god, though the Face of Portunus is still buried in his head."

I was aghast at the sight. Now Enkidu came to the door to get a look.

"He cannot see us or hear us," the prince assured us. "Dionysian magic has sealed him off."

"Why is he imprisoned?" I asked in a low voice when we were headed down the twisting branching corridor again, back to the room where we had begun our conversation.

"For his own protection. Palaemon has been so enervated mentally that he neither knows nor cares where he is, or what might be happening to him."

"Terrible," I said.

"We are trying to find a cure, of course. But so far none of our treatments have much effect."

I was more shaken by the sight of a fallen god than I could have been by any fabulous monster or towering Giant. "But—if the Giants prevail, and all the powers of the gods should fail—how will the Universe endure?"

"It is not the fate of the Universe that worries me," said Daedalus grimly. "The Universe can take care of itself. The real problem is what is going to happen to ordinary, mortal humanity, should the Giants win."

"I don't understand. If the Giants' weapon doesn't hurt ordinary people, then what is the special danger to them?"

The Artisan spoke convincingly about the monstrous ways in which the Giants treated ordinary humanity whenever their paths crossed those of ordinary people. Fortunately such encounters had so far been fairly rare, because of the Giants' fondness for desolation. But the numbers of both races were increasing, and more contact was inevitable in the future.

"And then there is the problem of monsters. Some cases of severe deformity"—he looked around, I supposed to make sure that the prince was out of earshot—"are the result of interbreeding between gods and mortals. But others come from experimentation by the Giants. Your Hydra and your Boar are good examples."

"And the centaurs?"

Daedalus frowned. "I am not yet certain about them. They have an ancient history."

———

My pair of tutors also told me about their examination of tissues from the Hydra and the Boar; they both regretted never getting any sample from the Nemean lion.

"There are grounds for believing that the lion, too, was a monster created by the Giants. You say that no weapon could pierce its hide."

"Quite true." Enkidu and I both nodded.

"What do you know, Hercules, of the Golden Apples of the Hesperides?"

"I have never heard of them," I said, after exchanging glances with my equally puzzled nephew.

Hermes and Daedalus and their assistants were also struggling with the problems of learning exactly what the Golden Apples of the Hesperides meant to the race of the Giants, and of obtaining a sample of this mysterious fruit.

"For all we know, the Apples may have something to do with the Giants' secret weapon."

———

Our talk drifted on to other matters. The Artisan observed casually that he had analyzed some of Prince Asterion's blood and would like to be able to analyze some of mine as well. But, considering my impervious skin, he was not sure how to go about trying to draw a sample.

I was not sure whether I ought to be worried, annoyed, or only amused. "So, you'd like to see me bleed?"

"Yes indeed," he answered absently. "Of course, were you a female," he mused, "there would be your monthly cycle as a source."

"Yes, and were I an olive, you could squeeze me for my oil." The idea that my skin might actually be broken, my blood flow like that of other humans, grew more disturbing the more I thought about it. No doubt my feelings were so sensitive because nothing of the kind had ever happened to me. Not for me the scraped knees and cut fingers that normal children suffered without much thought, being inured to such damage from earliest childhood.

The thought was frightening, and I began to bluster.

"Yes, and were I a duck, I would probably lay eggs. But as I am, I think you will not get any of my blood."

The Artisan said there was nothing urgent about the matter; he was willing to wait until he could think of some good method of collection.

Asterion went on: "Sooner or later, Hercules, we are going to discover just what effect the special weapon of the Giants has on you. You are no god, but you are hardly an ordinary mortal, either. Nor am I, of course, but I am not going to leave the Labyrinth."

Asterion raised a very human palm in my direction, forestalling protest. "No, we are not asking you to volunteer for any experiments. We would all like you to avoid the test as long as possible, but in the end it will not be possible to escape."

———

We all of us rested overnight, and in the morning we held another lengthy conversation.

Meanwhile, I had still seen only a little, here and there, of the great Maze. I found it deeply fascinating. Daedalus pointed out the spot where he had labored for the young queen's predecessor, and other places where marvelous events had happened, many of them over the last two years.

I discovered that on Corycus, spring came early—more accurately, that there was hardly any winter. Now sunshine striking through the tangled vines made patches of bright translucent green, leaving caves of shadow within the roofed-over sections of the endless, intertwining passageways that comprised the great bulk of the Labyrinth. Somewhere just out of sight, perhaps in the next open courtyard, or maybe in the one after that, water was trickling musically from one of the Maze's many fountains into an adjoining pool. While we remained within those walls, the sound of running water, far or near, was almost never absent. The curving walls and tunnels, most of their surfaces hard stone, sometimes played games with sound.

———

Asterion surprised me with the claim that he had recently been able to enter the dreams of certain Giants.

"It was not an experience that I would willingly seek to repeat. I felt as if my mind, my nature, was in danger of being absorbed into the earth."

And Asterion, as was so often the case, had dreams of his own to tell. Rarely had his physical body ever left the confines of the great Maze, but in sleep his mind roamed to the ends of the known world, and sometimes beyond.

As our conversation went on, digging deeper into the topics of the previous day, Asterion and Daedalus explained a little more of the ongoing problem between the gods and the Giants, until I began to understand why even Zeus was fearful.

Speaking of the Giants, Asterion said: "Even if we could find some way to nullify their special weapon, they would still be, in many ways, as strong as the gods we know, or even stronger in some cases. They would be formidable antagonists. But as matters actually stand now, Zeus and his colleagues, the beings we have been taught to think of as the rulers of the Universe, are doomed to eventual defeat."

After hearing that, I walked on for some time, slowly and in complete silence. That Zeus, the greatest of gods, with thunderbolts at his command, could be afraid, of anything or anyone, was a new idea to me and required some digesting.

At last I said: "Then we know that our father Zeus lives, whether or not still in the avatar that sired you and me."

"He lives indeed, I can testify to that. Though in recent decades he has been exceedingly hard to find."

"It sounds better if we simply say that Zeus and Apollo and the rest are simply behaving prudently."

"I don't care how it sounds."

———

Prince Asterion also told me that he had been warned in a dream that it would be important for me to know something of the Underworld.

"Is this some foretelling of my death?"

"There is an implication of danger, certainly. And death waits for us all. No, there was some warning apart from that. But too vague to be of any real use."

"What have either of us to do with the kingdom of Hades?"

"As little as possible, I hope," said the odd voice from the bull's mouth. "Speaking of formidable gods, the Messenger also expressed a hope that you would be able to talk to Apollo while you were visiting our island. But Apollo is not on Corycus now."

"Oh," I said. At the sound of that name, so casually uttered, something inside me seemed to cringe a bit and make an effort at withdrawal, turning inward even farther. True, we had just been speaking of almighty Zeus himself, and it was also true that I had confronted and even argued with great Hermes face-to-face. And I had now been privileged to catch a glimpse of the chariot of glorious Dionysus.

But . . . Apollo.

Far-Worker, Sun God, the Lord of Death and Terror and Distance. And of many other things besides. Shiva the Destroyer was known as a god of tremendous power and was feared by many—but on Corycus, people said that Lord Apollo had shot down Shiva's most recent avatar with the authority of a man swatting a fly.

Beside me, Enkidu was now sitting still. The sound of Apollo's name seemed to have knocked him into the attitude of a chastened child, very nearly afraid to move.

At last I asked the man who was sometimes called the Minotaur. "You *know* Lord Apollo? The Far-Worker himself?"

"He calls me friend," said Prince Asterion simply. "It was his Arrow that struck down Shiva—was it only about a year ago? Sometimes I tend to lose track of waking time—not far from where we are standing now. The Face of Shiva was of course not destroyed, but it fell into a pit—I will soon show you where—with an Arrow still protruding from its Third Eye."

For a moment or two I was silent, not knowing what to say. No doubt to be a child of Zeus was a glorious distinction, even if there were more than a few of us scattered around the earth. But to claim *Apollo* as a *friend* . . .

When I remarked on this to Daedalus, he, too, claimed some familiarity with the Far-Worker, though the Artisan was generally more interested in solving problems without magic than in consorting with the gods.

———

Now Prince Asterion strongly recommended that I should leave Corycus as soon as possible and set out on a voyage to try to discover the truth about the Apples of Hesperides. Daedalus strongly concurred.

"*Hesperides* sounds to me like a chain of islands," was Enkidu's comment this time. Our tutors quickly explained to both of us that the three Hesperides were women, or perhaps nymphs, named Hespere, Aegle, and Erytheis. But in any case, the Apples might really have nothing to do with them at all.

"This task is different, Hercules, from any you have undertaken yet. This time we can give you but little in the way of specific instructions."

Enkidu was, as usual, ready for new adventure. But reaching the land where the Apples were thought to grow would involve serious traveling.

Even with *Skyboat* to speed us on our way, a journey of that length would take us many days.

But before leaving the island of Corycus, I wanted to make sure that it afforded no possible passage down into the Underworld; Asterion had suggested this as one possible meaning of the blurred dream-message. Daedalus also was strongly curious about what lay just underground; and Prince Asterion agreed that it was only reasonable that I should be the one to make the attempt.

He and the Artisan both accompanied me to the very rim of the pit, with Enkidu as usual tagging along.

We were standing in a kind of courtyard, created by a partial destruction of the Maze and larger than most of those located within it by design. In the center of this space of devastation was a crater, perhaps fifteen yards wide, and at the bottom of the crater a dim abyss of uncertain depth. The bottom, some ten or fifteen yards below us, was piled with rocks of such size that the crevices between them might very well offer passage to a much greater depth.

Glad to accept advice from Daedalus, I allowed Asterion's attendants, supervised by the Artisan, to wrap my body in layers of thick wool, then drench me in water, against the heat, before I started down.

Now I had reached the lowest depth yet attained by mortal men since the formation of the crater. From that point it was my decision to go on alone. I worked my way lower for a little distance, using natural handholds and steps in the rough rock wall of the great cavity. Descending cautiously a little farther under the Labyrinth, I felt the heat increase steadily with every step I took.

Enough daylight still came down through the opening to let me see my way. I called up to my friends that I now saw a kind of tunnel, seeming to lead farther down.

I entered this aperture but could advance for only a few yards before it narrowed so drastically that it became impassable. Where the passage narrowed, I began to widen it by breaking chunks out of the walls with blows of my fists.

Progress by this means was painfully slow because of the difficulty of concentrating the force in precisely the way I wanted. And not many minutes passed before I was brought to a halt, then driven into a retreat, by the tremendous heat of nearly molten rock not far ahead. If there had once been a passage leading farther down, it was certainly closed now. Whether the shadowy realm called Tartarus was anywhere nearby was more than I could guess.

I might have tried to force my way through, at what appeared to be considerable risk; but there was no real reason to believe that I would encounter anything but greater heat, and more rock, behind the layers that were now visible in front of me.

Whether my special powers might be equal to the challenge of protecting my body from damage by molten rock, I did not know, but I had to assume that the pain of such a contact would be terrible. Beside this, the dangers posed by lion, Boar, and Hydra were shrunken into insignificance. Here, it seemed, I was at last beginning to encounter the powers that really ruled the world.

Slowly I climbed back to the rim of the pit, where the onlookers expressed their relief at seeing me emerge alive. Enkidu especially was grateful, and the Artisan had a dozen questions about the nature of the rock below.

As to what might have happened to the Face of Shiva, I could only speculate that it could have been picked up by one of the minions of infernal Hades and carried off to some stronghold deep in Tartarus. I wondered if the Lord of the Underworld might have made a secret alliance with the Giants, and by concealing the Face intended to keep any human from regaining its powers and putting them to work on the gods' side in the great conflict. But I supposed a more likely possibility was that Hades meant to create a new Shiva by giving the Face to some mortal he thought he could trust to be his ally in the uncertain times that seemed to lie ahead for gods and men alike.

Enkidu and I now prepared to depart on our next mission. Again I wished fervently that Daedalus might come with us, but again he declined—reluctantly, I thought. He had essential tasks to perform elsewhere.

14

A Place Called Ilium

UNTIL THE LAST minute I hoped that Daedalus might change his mind and agree to accompany us on our quest for the Apples. By his own admission he was eager to get his hands on one of those strange fruits. Also I thought he would have given much to be present at my first encounter with a Giant, which seemed likely on my current mission. The true nature of those creatures, the gods' Titanic enemies, seemed to be what now interested the Artisan above all else. But Daedalus only repeated regretfully that he had very important work to do elsewhere. I did not doubt that; but I strongly suspected also that he was deeply afraid of such things as Giants, as every man has a right to be.

———

Enkidu and I found the *Skyboat* just where we had left it, at the quay in Kandak harbor. Larger vessels were now tied up on both sides, but our boat continued to occupy its small space, invisible to any eyes but my nephew's and mine, until we came to claim it.

The Artisan had taken the time to walk with us to the boat, and as we stepped aboard he gave me some final words of advice.

"Your strength is awesome, Hercules. But you are not immortal."

"I know that," I responded impatiently. But deep in my heart I thought I was immune to death, as all strong and healthy young men are wont to do.

Voyaging boldly out from the island of Corycus, with the full confidence of youth, in our small boat that seemed, happily, almost immune to the adverse effects of wind and wave, Enkidu and I set about trying to fulfill the expectations of the gods.

I was determined, at the very least, to keep the bargain that I now seemed to have made with Zeus, and with that faction of the gods who were allied with him.

Would you believe that we were so young and foolish as to entertain every expectation of success?

Had the Artisan been with us in our little boat, he could have told us much more, in the long hours of our next days of travel, about the gods and about the Giants, too. Though his usual concern was mundane matters, still he knew more about the Olympians than almost any other human being on earth, by reason of the fact that he so often had dealings with them.

On Corycus, Enkidu and I had learned some disturbing things: not only how frightened the gods were of these same Giants, but how little Zeus and the others knew, how much they seemed to have mysteriously forgotten, about their ancient enemies.

I also had at least begun to have some understanding of the special role that I was required to play. How I had been designed and bred to order, as it were; created as a handy tool to carry out the will of Zeus.

We soon discovered that the tutelary sprite assigned us by Hermes still accompanied the *Skyboat.*

Our voyage this time was much longer than our previous trip from the mainland to Corycus. We sailed even at night, trusting to the work of the gods to keep us on course under the stars. Blessed as we were with a superbly reliable compass-pyx, we felt no need to creep along the coast, keeping land in sight at all times, to avoid getting lost. Even so, the great irregularity of the northern shore of the Great Sea several times brought land into our sight on our right hand; and so it happened that our route took us close to the seaside plain and city of Troy, which some prefer to call by the name of Ilium.

At one point, several days into our journey and hundreds of miles from Corycus, where the shoreline curved out near our almost straight westerly course, my eye was caught by the sight of something there on shore, a spot of pink, of a shape appropriate for a human form. I tapped Enkidu on the shoulder and told him to steer in closer yet. The pink spot was moving, or rather wiggling about in the same place.

"Steer in closer," I ordered again, shading my eyes with one hand

and squinting into the sun-glare. Enkidu, with one hand resting on our compass-pyx, thought the appropriate thoughts, and our small boat steered itself according to his will.

When we were near enough, the spot of tawny pink began to look for all the world like a long-haired human being chained naked to a rock, halfway up a small cliff and only a little above the sea. It might be expected that any victim left in such a spot would drown if the tide came in high enough. From the top of the little seaside cliff, the barren land sloped gradually inland for half a mile or so, to a kind of crest. Along the elevation, many tents had been erected. At a distance, I could not yet tell if there were people on that ridge, but there were what looked like piles of stone, purposefully arranged. It was evident that a huge construction project was under way.

And when we had slowed our *Skyboat*'s speed and come a little closer still, we could see plainly that the chained human was in fact a young and comely female. Soon we could be sure that she was completely unclothed, and also that she was still very much alive, for she began to move her arms and legs, as much as the burden of her chains allowed, and began to cry for help, sounding a thin wail of despair that raised the hairs on the back of my neck.

"What in the Underworld is the meaning of this?" I demanded of the world in general. I had heard of human lives being offered to the gods, but never seen the business before.

"Must be some kind of sacrifice," Enkidu suggested. "Or this girl's done something that deserved one monster of a punishment. Or maybe both."

Meanwhile, our sprite seemed agitated, buzzing invisibly about my ears. This conveyed a sense of urgency, but was no help in choosing a course of action.

"Whatever it's all about, I'm putting a stop to it." I suppose a majority of men in my place would have been afraid to interfere, not wanting to risk insulting any deity by thwarting an intended sacrifice. But I felt I was beginning to grow accustomed to the gods, and Enkidu was generally brave enough for anything, provided no Olympian was actually present.

"So what are we going to do, Herc?"

"I'm not sure yet. But put us in to shore, and we'll do something."

———

We beached our small boat amid some lively surf, and I more or less tucked it under my arm and carried it up above the current level of the waves. My club I carried on a little farther, before putting it down at the base of the cliff so that I might have full use of both hands. Then I began to climb the small cliff toward the girl. Enkidu as usual was close on my heels.

The cliff was less than thirty feet high, and its face was rough enough that no great climbing skill was required. In fact as we drew near out goal, I observed just above me a fairly well-worn path, which must have been used by those who had placed the maiden in such a perilous state, to bring her down from the cliff top to the ledge where she was bound. One branch of the path swung down the cliff, and I changed course slightly to reach it, making swifter progress possible.

Walking erect again, coming around the last bend of the small trail, I found myself close enough to the victim to read the expression in her eyes, which were now locked on me in desperate entreaty.

"Who's done this to you, girl?" I demanded. "But never mind, I'll have you free in a moment." And Enkidu did his best to reassure her, too.

"Hurry, oh hurry! In a few minutes it will be too late!" And I could see where her wrists and ankles were raw and bleeding from struggling against the chains.

She seemed very near my own age. Her body was shapely, or would have been had not the metal fetters stretched and pinched her into an awkward position. But I was not too much distracted to observe that, contrary to my earlier estimate, the site where she was chained stood substantially above high tide, as was plain from the appearance of the beach. Obviously it was not the ocean itself, not Poseidon as represented by a rising tide, that was expected to receive the sacrifice.

The girl was whimpering. Now that help was at hand, she seemed ready to dissolve in helpless tears.

"Don't worry, I'll have you out of there in no time. What's your name?"

"Hesione. Oh, hurry, hurry! But my chains are welded on, and you have no tools."

I was almost within reach of the intended victim when her gaze suddenly moved past me, and she screamed out: "It's coming, I see it! Quick, help!"

———

Murmuring something meant to be reassuring, I turned to behold the sea monster, a great blackish shape breaking the gray-green sea, heading in from deep water toward the shore. It looked at least twice as big as the Hydra, but I was glad to see that this time I would have only one head to contend with.

Turning my back briefly on the horror again, I started to break the girl loose from her shackles. That job was more difficult for me than you might suppose, reluctant as I was to do even the slightest harm to her tender wrists and ankles. Also I had to shield her soft skin from flying fragments when the links gave way. But still, in less than a minute it was done.

Meanwhile, Enkidu had gone sprinting back down the path to the foot of the cliff, where he snatched up my club. In a few moments more he had lugged it up the hill again and handed it to me.

Thinking I might as well discourage further human sacrifices as much as possible, I tore out of the rock the bronze rings and spikes to which Hesione had been chained. Then I broke the links of the chains near to the wristlets and anklets that had been welded on by some skilled smith, who had somehow managed not to burn the soft skin. Very considerate of him, I thought.

"Run, get up the cliff, the beast is coming!" I commanded the girl. And at the same time I turned to face the sea, ready for whatever it might bring against me. Still there was only the one great beast, now standing in the shallows, its head on its long neck looking levelly at me where I stood halfway up the cliff.

The young woman's limbs were so stiff with being chained that she could barely stand and walk. Enkidu did not run ahead but gallantly pulled off his own tunic and draped it around Hesione's pale shivering shoulders. Then he began to help her up the path toward the cliff top.

"Everywhere we go," I growled, "it seems the world is full of monsters." Hermes had given me no instructions regarding this one, so I felt free to deal with it as I thought best. Picking up a chunk of broken rock the size of my own head, I slung it with some violence toward the serpent. Unhappily my aim was no better than usual, and the missile missed by several yards, only kicking up a small splash a quarter of a mile out to sea.

Then it would have to be the club again. As a rule, I did much better with the club. Sliding down the steep slope to the strip of beach, I took a couple of warm-up swings and waited.

I had not long to wait. When the beast came out of the water, I could see that its entire body was darker than the Hydra, and vastly larger, but similarly reptilian in its overall appearance. Again I reassured myself that indeed this creature possessed only a single head, though its jaws looked large enough to seize and crunch up our boat in a bite or two. I thought I could feel the sand beneath my feet jar slightly each time one of its feet came down.

And the huge head came swinging toward me, mouth agape, letting out a wave of foul breath almost enough to send me staggering. It seemed that at first the monster expected to be able to swallow me at a gulp, for I was evidently standing below the rock that served as its regular feeding tray, or trough. But as its head swayed near, instead of tender food it got a good knock from my club, which broke its lower jaw—all it managed to swallow on that particular attempt was a few of its own teeth.

In the end this vast sea creature proved not as hard to finish off as the Hydra had been. Its single head, large as it was, evidently lacked enough brain to try to find a strategy, or even to know when it was time to retreat. Three or four more solid whacks on that ponderous skull were enough to crack thick bone into fragments, and in no more than a minute the whole vast body was down in the surf, where it twitched a few times and then lay still.

The sprite came buzzing around my head, invisible as some benevolent mosquito. Perhaps it was offering congratulations. But I only shook my head in irritation. After a moment the humming presence moved away again.

"Well, Daedalus," I murmured, in imaginary conversation with my mentor. "I suppose you might be eager to examine samples of this beast's flesh, as you did the Boar's. You missed out on the lion, but Hermes brought you some pieces of the Hydra, didn't he? I don't know if you might want this one—but if so, you're out of luck. It will all be eaten by little fish before I ever see you again."

But a moment later a new thought occurred to me, and my actions contradicted my words. Picking up a new rock to use as a tool, and thinking that raw flesh would certainly spoil, I broke out a sample of the sea monster's bone, intending to take it when I could to the Artisan, on the chance that he might want it for his continuing investigations.

———

Later, the story would spread that I had actually leaped, fully armed, down the sea monster's throat and had spent the next three days fighting in its belly. Some folk are eager to believe anything, provided only that it be marvelous enough.

Briskly I climbed to the top of the little cliff, and asked the girl, who had already named herself Hesione, some questions. She proved to be the daughter of Laomedon, king of Troy.

"And where is the king, that he allows his daughter to undergo such treatment?"

The only answer to that question was a burst of tears.

Now, standing at the top of the cliff, I could get a better look at the enormous construction project on the crest half a mile inland. Up there, someone had made a start at erecting huge, thick walls of stone. Below the walls I could now discern a mass of color that I supposed might be a throng of people. At either end, the foundation tiers of the wall curved back over the crest and out of sight. I decided that there was probably going to be room for a great city in the space they were enclosing. Here and there I began to imagine I could discern some scaffolding of logs. How tall the walls in general were intended to be could be seen by the impressive height of a certain tower that stood already virtually completed. A little farther inland I could just make out the roofs of what seemed to be many tents and other makeshift dwellings.

It seemed to me very doubtful that the people who were building their city on the hill would not know that such a terrible sacrifice was being made right on their doorstep.

Whoever might have been watching from the high ridge would not have been able to see what happened to the monster down below the level of the cliff. But someone up there might have been able to see the reappearance of the girl atop the cliff, accompanied first by Enkidu and shortly afterward by me, and that would certainly have riveted their attention.

Soon a squad of uniformed spear-carriers, followed by another of seeming dignitaries, the latter moving more slowly, appeared on their way down the long slope from the unfinished walls. When they got closer I could hear some of them shouting loudly, but whether they were inflamed with joy or outrage I could not tell at first.

"There is my father," said Hesione, muffling a final sob and pointing to someone in the latter group, now only a couple of hundred yards away. "King Laomedon."

As soon as I faced the advancing people boldly they grew cautious in their approach—and they stopped in their tracks when they came close enough to look over the little cliff and see that I had already killed the monster. Their angry cries faded to a cautious, marveling murmur as they saw the vast body rising and falling in the crashing surf. A few people ran down to the shore, and soon a clamor of voices went up, demanding to know what had turned the creature's head into a bloody ruin.

The group led by Poseidon's priest reached us before the group surrounding the king.

The servant of Neptune was garbed chiefly in seaweed, and he seemed a hybrid of priest and warrior, carrying weapons as well as what were obviously ritual objects, dishes and stalks of wheat. I thought him on the verge of apoplexy when he saw that the girl had been freed, and his rage was directed at me when he determined that I was somehow responsible.

Not stopping to talk, or even, I fear, to think things out, he commanded one of his warriors to attack me.

"Hector! Deal with this man!"

Burly Hector's blade came down hard on my left shoulder, before I could try to argue my way out of the situation. Even as I reached to grab the swordsman's arms, I felt the now almost-familiar sharp sting, the signal that my body, had it been no more than human, would have suffered a serious wound.

I had not done much killing, by a warrior's standards, and I had no wish to do more. Grabbing my assailant around the middle, I lifted him into the air, turning his body parallel to the ground. Then I held him that way, tucked under my left arm, as I might have carried a squalling child of two or three. My left hand gripped his right wrist, and his left arm was pinned between my forearm and his body. It was a comfortable position for me, leaving me with one arm free, though I had to lean far sideways to balance the additional weight, somewhat greater than my own. By the time we reached that situation, Hector's sword had fallen from his grip, and he could do no harm to anyone, unless they happened to stray in range of his violently kicking legs. My captive writhed and strained, to little purpose, and a strangled sound, compounded of rage and fear, came from him in short gasping bursts.

"He'll do no harm to me," I assured his countrymen, "but he might be dangerous to bystanders. Is there somewhere I can put him safely down? Or must I hurl him into the sea?" With my free hand I pointed out toward the blue horizon. "I fear he'll sink like a rock, with all his armor on."

The priest of Poseidon could only gape in stunned silence at me as I stood leaning sideways, and at his helpless champion. Eventually two of Hector's comrades stepped forward, hulking men who swore that they would hold him securely; and so I was relieved of my burden.

Talking with the more peaceful citizens of Troy as they gathered around while I stood leaning on my club, I learned the reason for Hesione's being in the terrible situation from which I had rescued her. Somehow the idea had spread among the people that Poseidon was angry with the city because Zeus had compelled him to help build its walls. Therefore the Sea God had sent the monster. Somehow the king had been convinced that the monster would be appeased if it received his daughter as a sacrifice; his only reason for such a belief seemed to be that some soothsayer had told him so. I thought that any king who was so spineless would probably not be long on his throne.

I suppose I should note here what I heard later: that the Trojan princess, once she had been set free, behaved in such a shrewish way that I could begin to understand how everyone had been willing to get rid of her.

———

Once it seemed certain that the natives had given up trying to attack us, Enkidu began to mingle freely with them. People eyed him with wary respect; no doubt they were more than half convinced that he shared my godlike strength. I noticed that he said and did nothing to correct their error.

When I told the Trojans that my nephew and I had sailed out from Corycus, someone asked our purpose in making such a lengthy voyage in a vessel far too small for trade. Naturally I raised the subject of the Apples of the Hesperides.

Somewhat to my surprise, this brought on a veritable buzz of marveling and speculation, with the graybeard counselors exchanging knowing looks.

Immediately my hopes leaped up. "What is it? What can you tell me about them?"

At length, several of our new hosts brightened and told me that a sample, at least, of one of those very Apples was much nearer than I suspected.

Enkidu and I exchanged a hopeful glance. "Just what do these Apples look like, then?" I asked.

A man who had the whitest and longest beard that I had ever seen seemed to take his role of wise counselor very seriously. He made vague gestures with his hands. "They are not unlike ordinary apples, young man—you are familiar with that fruit?"

"I am."

"Not unlike the common fruit, I say, save that each one grows to about the size of a man's head."

"I suppose the tree must be gigantic?"

That seemed to be the general consensus, though a few minutes' additional questioning convinced me that none of these people had actually seen the tree, knew what it looked like, or were even certain where it grew.

"But someone started to tell me, earlier, where I might find a sample of the fruit, at least."

After holding another conference among themselves, the Trojan counselors assured me I could find a specimen of this strange fruit inside a certain cave, which also seemed to be the regular dwelling place of someone named Antaeus. When they spoke his name their voices dropped, and their faces fell, as if in dread.

Persistently I tried to dig for solid information. "This Antaeus keeps an orchard and grows the Apples? He eats them? Feeds them to his animals? Or what?"

The people gathered around me proposed a variety of answers. No one knew.

"I see," I said, nodding as if I actually understood. "And you yourselves have seen this marvelous fruit inside this cave?"

No, as it turned out, actually none of these people had ever been near the cave. And they thought it only right to warn me that no one who went into that den had ever emerged from it alive.

"Is someone watching the entrance day and night, to make sure that never happens?"

My informants did not seem to hear the question. But eventually one of them told me that a few daring souls, keeping watch from a distance, had seen Antaeus carry the Apples into his stronghold, and had recognized them for what they were.

"May I speak to one of these daring souls myself?"

"Alas, sir, they are none of them here now. They have gone voyaging again. One went with the Argonauts."

If they thought I was going to be much impressed by that, they were mistaken. When they told me the man's name, I failed to recognize it.

One point upon which my informants were eagerly agreed was that the den, or cave, of the formidable Antaeus was only about a hundred miles away, westward and northward along the irregular coastline.

After squinting uselessly toward the watery horizon in that direction, I turned back to my informants. "You interest me greatly, my friends. Now tell me, just who, or what, is this Antaeus? You speak of him as if he were something more than merely human."

The answers I was given to that question were not terribly enlightening, but they confirmed me in the opinion that anyone who lived within a hundred miles of the fellow might be anxious to get rid of him.

After an afternoon and night among the tents and lean-tos of the builders of the new walls, enjoying wary Trojan hospitality, Enkidu and I were ready for a few hours of sound sleep, during which time we took turns keeping one eye open—it was an arrangement we practiced more often than not during our travels. By an hour after sunrise we were getting back into our boat again.

15

Antaeus

THE ROSY-FINGERED dawn had come and gone before my nephew and I put out to sea again, shoving our boat off from the beach that lay half a mile below the rising walls of Troy. By the time of our departure in full daylight, no trace of the sea monster's body was any longer to be seen; I supposed the great ugly mass had been washed away by waves and tide during the night. And in the talk I heard in Troy that morning, from those who had witnessed the event and others who had not, the beast had already grown to twice its authentic size.

Enkidu and I piloted the *Skyboat* more or less steadily along the coast in the direction that our hosts had indicated, searching for the cave of the strange being, known to them by the name of Antaeus, that they had described to us. We took turns at the helm. Progress was slow at first, because the compass-pyx kept giving us contradictory indications. This, I had been told by Daedalus and others, was a sign that the pilot could form no clear mental image of his goal. We had both tried our hands at piloting, and I could believe that was our problem, but there was nothing we could do about it.

When we had crept along the coast for twenty miles or so, we put in to shore at intervals and began to look seriously for likely caves, and also for people to question on the subject, on the theory that our informants' estimate of distance might have been wildly wrong and some of their other information unreliable.

In one respect, the legends concerning the being we were looking for proved to be ludicrously inaccurate. My brief stay in that savage and little-populated land convinced me that Antaeus was really king of nothing, not even of the tribe, or guild, of bandits—assuming any such organization could exist. A bandit he was, I suppose, preying on humans whenever he could catch them, though we found no hoard of gold and jewels as in the Lizard's cave. But his predatory nature was the least remarkable thing about Antaeus.

Another falsehood concerning him, told and believed by many who had never come near his cave, was that he was the son of Poseidon and Mother Earth. Other claims, both quite untrue, were that he forced strangers to wrestle with him and that he saved the skulls of his victims to roof a temple of Poseidon. In the course of our brief visit, I had a chance to examine the interior of his cave thoroughly. There were indeed some skulls about, human and animal both, but only as part of a collection of general organic garbage that made the whole place stink. It was nothing like any temple that I ever saw—more like the lair of some wild animal, much danker and gloomier than the Lizard's cheerful parlor.

I had been solemnly assured, by the folk who were building the walls and towers of Ilium, that I could find a specimen of Golden Apple, the very kind that I was looking for, inside the cave of Antaeus. But about the time we were getting close to our goal, it occurred to me to wonder if the Trojans might have said that simply to get rid of me. No doubt I would be welcome back at Troy again, or anywhere else, whenever there was a sea monster to be slain; but I was beginning to realize that at other times I tended to make most people uncomfortable.

"Enk, do you think they might possibly have done that?" I asked, discussing the matter with my nephew after our third or fourth cave had turned out empty. "Given us a wild story about this bandit and his magic Apples just to get rid of us? You tell me I can be scary sometimes."

"Well, you can be, Herc. And yes, I guess they might have been anxious to see us on our way."

But that was one problem we need not have worried about. Antaeus and his strange fruit turned out to be as real as any of the other monsters I had faced.

━━━━━━━━

It was a forbidding stretch of coastline along which we slowly labored, patiently asking directions of each of the few people we chanced to encounter, poor fisherfolk and gatherers of birds' eggs. Eventually, from certain individuals who were not too terrified to speak of Antaeus at all, I heard confirmation that he indeed lived in a cave, where he slept on the bare ground as a means of maintaining his strength in readiness for any eventuality. And these informants even gave us a fairly precise idea of the cave's location, along with urgent warnings that we had better stay away from it.

When we identified the beach we had been told to look for, we pulled our boat a little way up on shore and simply left it there, trusting to its own mysterious powers to protect it from thieves or destruction by the waves. Then we started making our way along the rocky shore as best we could on foot. It was a strange, wild region dotted with seemingly innumerable caves, through many of which the waves went drenching and thundering at high tide.

───

Enkidu pointed out to me some signs of our quarry's presence before we saw him.

My nephew had been bending over, studying the ground, but suddenly raised his head to tell me, in a very low voice: "I realize now, Unc, what the people back there at Troy forgot to tell us."

"What's that?"

Enkidu made a show of giving it thoughtful consideration before he answered. "I suppose it was for our own good. They didn't want to discourage us, not when we were doing so well."

"Are you going to tell me *what*, by all the gods? Or am I going to have to strangle you?"

"Hush. This character Antaeus is a Giant." And my nephew stepped back and pointed with a flourish at the ground.

I was shocked into silence for a moment. Then I was on the point of angrily commanding my companion to stop clowning and get on with business. But then my eye fell on the sign that he had seen. Wet sand along the shoreline bore the clear imprint of a giant foot, human in shape if not in size, the five toes clearly marked.

"Indeed he must be," was all that I could get out, at last, in a whisper. The track was fully twice as long as one of mine, and my feet are not particularly small.

Carefully we moved on, in the same direction the marker of the footprint had been going. I half-expected to come upon some Titanic dung droppings among the rocks, but we found no such spoor. I had known humans who were much less fastidious in such matters.

We had gone only another hundred yards or so when Enkidu suddenly stopped and laid his hand upon my arm. His whisper was almost too low for me to hear. "Unc, there he is."

I looked where he was looking, and saw the shaggy brown back of a gigantic head, just visible above some rocks some thirty yards away. And I in turn whispered the names of several gods, in awe.

Cautiously and quietly we stepped sideways until we could get a full-length look at our discovery. Of course the first thing that struck us both about the man, the creature—at first glance I was not sure how to classify our discovery—was his abnormal and truly gigantic size. Imagine a human figure, or rather the crude outline of one, about twelve feet tall and sturdily built.

The second thing that struck me was that there seemed to be something vaguely wrong, out of proportion, with his overall shape.

Continuing to study our quarry from a distance of some thirty or forty yards, I wondered at first whether this might be some mutant man, imbued with earth magic, instead of one of the real, and yet legendary Titans/Giants, supposed to be the sons of Poseidon and Gaia. Considering the matter as coolly as I could, I decided that if Antaeus was a real Giant, and the legends had any truth in them at all, he was certainly one of the smaller ones.

Still, twelve feet in height is a very great deal more than six, and I stood less than that. *That cannot be a human being,* was my inevitable conclusion, after only a brief observation. I came to that evaluation even though the one before me was clothed after a fashion, wearing a rude, patchwork garment that seemed to have been stitched together from the skins of different beasts.

And the more I looked at him, the more certain I became that his body was not only larger than that of any man, but made of some different stuff. I had no doubt at all that this was one of the fearsome beings that Daedalus and Hermes had tried to describe to me.

The next most notable thing about Antaeus was his skin, which was mostly dark but with the appearance of a grainy, earthy texture. It was somehow surprising to see that it gave and stretched with his movements, as any practical skin must do. The few wrinkles that it bore were at places where in humans wrinkles are slow to form.

Rather than advance at once to confront this strange figure openly, I decided to watch him for a while. There was always the possibility that others of his kind were nearby. Working our way slowly inland so we could observe from a better angle, then peering out from between two rocks on the next hill, we watched him kill a full-sized sheep, wringing its neck as if it had been a chicken. Then he roasted the carcass whole over a fire, and then he ate it, bones and guts and all, avoiding only the woolly skin, which he peeled off and used to wipe his hands. I saw no other sheep around, and we assumed that Antaeus kept no flock of his own and that the one he killed was stolen.

Now and then, during the minutes we spent observing this rude feast, Enkidu and I exchanged whispers, but for the most part we watched in silence. Presently, watching our chances, we were able to move a little closer without being seen. This Giant looked less and less human the closer I got to him and the longer I watched. The difference, as I have mentioned, was not entirely due to the discrepancy in size. His forehead sloped back more sharply than that of any god or human I had ever seen.

His hair, on head and body, emerged from the skin in awkward tufts rather than in the more even distribution generally to be seen upon a human.

The face, which bore no trace of beard or mustache, was almost completely expressionless, and remained that way through all that followed. The massive jaws worked steadily, pausing now and then so the Giant could spit out some morsel he found less than tasty. His eyes were dark, and I thought that there was something wrong with them.

The creature, or thing—I found myself less and less able to think of it as a living person—was so eerie that it made my flesh creep.

———

Enkidu and I continued to stalk the Giant, gradually working our way closer. I wanted to see, among other things, how keen my enemy's senses were and how alert his mind. In the course of this stealthy maneuvering, I found it convenient to leave my club behind, tucked into a crevice between rocks, handle uppermost so I could grab it quickly if need be.

Eventually, inevitably, we pushed our luck too far. This Giant, the first I ever encountered (had he had his way, he would have been also the last) finally caught sight of Enkidu at a distance of some forty feet, sprang up, and ran after him, obviously with no good intention. It was as if a man who had no love for mice or beetles had spotted one of those vermin in some place where they were particularly unwelcome.

Naturally the boy took to his heels and sprinted away, and I jumped from concealment and dashed forward. The Giant, his back to me, gave chase to Enkidu, and was within a few feet of seizing him, before I could get close enough to intervene.

"Antaeus!" I bellowed at him. "This way!"

At the sound of the name, the huge figure stopped in its tracks. In the next moment it had turned, quickly enough; the huge mouth opened, showing a ragged interior whiteness that might have been a row of teeth. A rumbling bass voice came from it, uttering what sounded like words in some language I did not know. How can I describe that voice? I cannot. But I have heard it often, since that day, in nightmares.

Now our enemy came lumbering toward me, long legs devouring the intervening space.

His first ill-advised and rather clumsy attempt to squash me by stamping on me failed when I grabbed his raised foot in midair and twisted his leg until he fell with a great crash on his back. Thinking over the matter later, I realized that at that moment Antaeus must have assumed, not unreasonably, that I was a god.

Still lying on the ground, he tried to use what I had to assume was the magic weapon described by Prince Asterion—pointing all ten extended fingers of both hands at me and glaring. The gods had planned well, and the Giant's deadly instrument had no effect on me. Stepping close to the enormous body, I kicked it hard in the ribs, lifting it from the ground and spinning it over, so that a sound like a drumbeat issued from the Giant's mouth.

———

If I cannot describe the voice of my first Giant, how can I even attempt to convey the effect produced by a first close look into his face? Here the appearance of graininess was more pronounced. In that brief moment it seemed to me that his countenance might have been carved from clay, or perhaps sandstone, with two hard, dark pebbles set into it for eyes.

While still sprawled on the ground, he persisted in his gesture of unleashing magic. Somewhat unnerving, as you may imagine. But in practical terms, all his finger pointing and glaring had no discernible effect upon my memory or any other faculty.

Though I felt no ill effects, I still retreated, something I had not done while fighting any of the other monsters. Now I wanted to gain a better understanding of my enemy before I tried to utterly destroy him.

As I moved back, the Giant clambered to his feet, an awkward-looking, stiff-bodied series of movements. He swayed on his huge feet and clutched his middle awkwardly, as if my kick had broken a rib or two and now they hurt.

Meanwhile, Enkidu was hurling fist-sized stones from a point of vantage he had gained among high rocks. The boy's aim was not bad, and I saw one missile bounce high from the Giant's shaggy skull, but I do not think Antaeus even noticed it.

Now my antagonist and I were stalking each other once again.

The huge body proved able not only to move, but to change directions, with surprising speed. My club was too far away for me to reach it handily, and so I simply waited. In the next moment my opponent's hands had closed on me and grabbed me up into the air.

My earlier success in twisting him off his feet ought to have prepared him somewhat for my strength. But still, there followed a few moments in which he seemed almost paralyzed by surprise. After exerting what he must have thought would be a crushing grip, Antaeus tried to dash me down upon the rocks. But he quickly discovered that my smaller grasp, which I had fastened on one of his great arms, was quite unbreakable. Next he attempted to crush me in a hug, but the heel of my right hand under his chin forced his arms straight and his head back.

The Giant dropped me to the ground, stepped back, and uttered a few more words of peculiar speech, which I could understand no better than his earlier remarks. Then he threw himself prone on the ground, in what I first thought was a gesture of submission. But in the space of a few heartbeats he had sprung to his feet again and hurled himself upon me. To my amazement, his strength seemed even greater than before.

Never had I felt anything like his grip. His strength was truly enormous, compared to that of any human wrestler. I was still not afraid of being overpowered, but the brief struggle had left me gasping with exertion.

Meanwhile, keeping track of Enkidu as best I could from the corner of my eye, I saw that he had now scrambled from one pinnacle of rock to another even taller. He also maintained a steady barrage of rocks and kept on shrilling insults at Antaeus, who paid no attention to either. Some of the rocks came close to hitting me, but I thought I would probably not be hurt if one did land.

In the intervals between acts of attempted violence, the Giant barked words at me, phrases that somehow had the sound of questions, though they came in a language I had never heard before.

Again we broke apart, and again we closed with each other. I made no attempt to kill him quickly, because I was rapidly becoming convinced that I ought to ask him some questions, and insist on some answers, before he died.

The hands of Antaeus that would have crushed me were instead broken themselves when I pounded them on rocks. The bellow he let out when his knuckles were smashed seemed more of astonishment than pain. But I was staggered by his strangeness. His skin did not feel like skin, but more like the hard surface of bone, or even rock, with flexibility only at the very joints, where it was essential.

And for a second time during our wrestling match, the Giant flung himself down of his own accord, not waiting to be thrown. Fearing that when he sprang up again he would be even stronger than before, I seized him by the seat and collar of his shapeless garment, lifted him as high as I could into the air, and held him aloft, meaning to keep him well above the earth until he died.

Antaeus was not too strong for me to manage. But he was too big for me to keep him from the earth—my arms would not stretch far enough to let me maintain a grip on more than two of his limbs at once. Stretching and thrashing in my grip, he managed to get one foot on the ground, and when I lifted that away, one of his hands came down to grasp the earth.

Simply holding him aloft was not going to work. Shaking my head, I hit him with my fist once or twice, seeking to diminish his boisterous energy. His flesh did not seem to yield and bruise, so much as it simply crumbled. I followed with a good kick that had the same effect.

I might say that he screamed and bellowed with pain and rage—but those are not really the right words to describe the sounds he made. He seemed to fall on me as if he meant to smother me, and once more we were grappling. Of course he was so large that I had to fold him, almost like a parchment scroll, in order to hold him in a position where no part of his body dragged on the ground. When I exerted myself strongly, part of his body burst open under the stress, spilling out versions of muddy-looking blood and wormlike guts, for which my mind was unprepared.

It was so astonishing that for a long moment I could not move but only stood and stared.

When at last I had broken the great figure into complete helplessness, I stood over it, panting, while it lay impotent on the ground. What remained was not yet still, you understand, but writhed and heaved. The lower half of the face was gone by then, and the staring eyes above seemed to have turned into mere glassy pebbles.

———

By this time Enkidu, unable to restrain his curiosity any longer, had come scrambling down from his high rock. One knee was bleeding where he had scraped it in his jumping about, but he was otherwise unhurt.

Surveying the ghastly ruin that had once looked almost like a man, my nephew sounded even more shaken than I felt.

"Herc, what is all this? What does it mean?" Now that the practical danger was over, he sounded almost tearful, really frightened for the first time.

I could only shake my head in wonder.

"For one thing," I told him, "It means that the world is stranger than I ever imagined it might be."

"This is stranger even than the Hydra. Because—because it's almost like a man."

"If only Daedalus were here," I muttered.

"He's not here," said Enkidu. "But we'd better take him some of—some of this."

"Nephew, I think that is one of the better ideas that you have ever had."

———

The Giant's rude garment had come loose in the course of the fight, and when I turned the body over again, we saw that he lacked pubic hair but that his male organs were, as might be expected, of a size for a centaur. Immediately an image sprang to mind of Antaeus ravaging human women.

For what seemed a long time we stood there marveling, unable to decide just what to do next. At last I said: "It is as if a sculptor wished to copy the proper outward form of humanity—but didn't bother to get it completely right. Close enough was good enough for this designer."

"Yes, that's it." Enkidu nodded. "What this creature looks like. But what it really *is* . . ." He shook his head.

"But why a clumsy imitation?" I went on. "And who was the designer?"

I doubted that even Daedalus could give me answers to such questions. Perhaps my father could.

When I examined the ruin of Antaeus's dead mouth, looking at the teeth with which he had chewed up the sheep, I could see that they, too, were rocklike. His tongue was small and, by human standards, deformed.

"Here. I think I'm going to be sick." And indeed my nephew looked pale under his tan.

This was worse than dealing with dead centaurs. I could feel the same impulse lurching in my belly, but grimly fought it off. "No, you're not. We don't have time for that, we have too much to do."

Now that I had time to think, questions came swarming, like the flies that had already gathered. Were all the Giants in the world built on this same plan? Or was Antaeus a kind of dwarfish monster, an odd shape and strange material even for his race?

Feeling dizzy with a mixture of horror and relief, and with my own stomach on the verge of rebellion, I backed away and sat down on a rock to think.

I would now be able to make a serious report to those who had sent me to discover the truth about Giants. One part of the report ought to make them happy, I thought—I had been exposed to the weapon that somehow scrambled the brains of gods, and it seemed to have had no effect on me at all.

"Enkidu, whether you are going to be sick or not, take a close look at our friend here, so you can confirm what I say when I report back to Hermes and Daedalus."

"I saw you beat him up and kill him, Uncle. I can see what he looks like now, not much more than a pile of clods of dirt. I don't know if I'd believe it if someone else had told me. Can all Giants be like this?"

"I think it must be so."

Seeking to gather all the information that we possibly could about Antaeus, Enkidu and I searched his cave as soon as we were sure that he was dead.

"Suppose his mate is hiding in the cave?" Enkidu suddenly piped up, looking over his shoulder toward that dark mouth in the rocks.

"How could a thing like that have a mate?" I demanded. But then I thought better of my answer; the situation was already alive with what seemed impossibilities, so why not one more? And where did Giants come from, if they did not breed?

"No one said anything to us about a mate. But we'd better find her, or it, if such a creature exists." And I hefted a rock and held it ready to employ as either club or missile.

But there was no living thing inside the cave—except the Apples, which I suppose must be counted as alive. Without much trouble we found, in a kind of chest or locker at one side of his cave, a true sample of what had to be one of the Apples of the Hesperides. It was a dried fruit that when fresh must have been fully the size of a human head. The stump of a stem protruded from the amplexicaul curve at the top, as if it had been a real apple.

Also the cave held almost nothing in the way of ordinary furnishings, as if its occupant preferred the dry, bare rock of its floor to sit or lie upon.

In a dark corner we found more Apples. Antaeus had been keeping ten or a dozen of the fruits in all.

Holding up one of the bulbous, yellow, almost head-sized shapes,

Enkidu commented: "I wouldn't call this thing an apple, Herc. If it is, it's like no apple that I have ever seen before."

"I'll call it that," I said. "Until I learn some better word." And it did look more like an ordinary apple than like any other fruit or vegetable with which I was familiar.

━━━━━━━

We slept that night in the *Skyboat,* rocked and lulled by a sea that was almost calm, pulled out a little distance from the shore. I dozed off feeling that I was at last making some real progress in my great quest, and when I awoke in the morning, I found I had somehow come to an unexpected decision while I was asleep. If dreams had played a role in it, I had forgotten them.

"Little nephew, I think this would be a good time for us to return home for a visit."

Before replying, Enkidu, who had been poised for a refreshing morning dip, dove off into the water with a splash. When he surfaced, shaking wet hair from his eyes, he did not seem much surprised at my suggestion. "What about Lord Hermes, Unc? He'll be wanting a report about this Giant. And there's the bone from the sea monster that we ought to take to Master Daedalus. And these Apples, too; our clients will want to get a look at them."

"Lord Hermes has never had any trouble finding me. I think he'll catch up with us again whenever he is ready, whether we're in Cadmia or anywhere else. Besides, he'll probably send me on some new adventure, and I'd like to get in a visit home before that happens. I'd like to see my mother."

All that was quite true. What I did not fully admit to myself at the time was that in the back of my mind was the idea of another one who lived in our house, whom I also yearned to see—and you are quite right; I was not thinking of Amphitryon.

━━━━━━━

Enkidu and I had made our decision, and he was doing his best to enjoin an image of Cadmia upon the compass-pyx, when Hermes came, this time materializing out of thin air to perch on *Skyboat*'s small stern seat.

We showed him the materials we had gathered, and told him of the fight with Antaeus, and its outcome.

Hermes came ashore with us to view the body, but when I first pointed out the spot to him, I thought for a moment that I was mistaken.

The remains of the fallen Antaeus now resembled a mound of earth more than a rotting corpse.

The Messenger was much pleased and expressed to us the thanks of great Zeus himself for collecting the samples we had gathered. He also relieved us of the burden of responsibility and carried them on to Daedalus himself.

Besides the Apples, the collection we were carrying included samples of the hair of Antaeus (more human-looking than any other component of his body), and fragments of his strange skin and flesh.

I would have liked to pack the latter in salt, to preserve them during what I expected would be a long voyage, but the best I could manage was a kind of pickling in jars of sea water, which shortly reduced the specimens to the appearance and consistency of thin mud. I could only hope they would still be of some use to Daedalus and the gods.

Hermes praised us for our discovery and for the proof we had provided that Zeus's secret plan was so far successful—I was immune to the Giants' most terrible weapon.

And as he was about to depart, he added one important statement to his congratulations.

"Your true father is greatly pleased in you, Hercules."

Almost despite myself I felt a thrill of pride rising against my chronic anger.

16

Megan

HAVING BEEN RELIEVED of responsibility for our collected trophies, my companion and I rearranged our meager store of other belongings securely inside *Skyboat*'s tiny cabin, and hoisted sail. Enkidu crouched before the binnacle, laying his forehead against the ivory side of the compass-pyx, and directed it to lead us home.

The course it chose for us turned out to be quite roundabout. We first spent days traversing a thousand miles or so of open ocean, in a great curved path. This was followed by an intricate, time-consuming passage through a number of streams and lakes—some broad, some narrow—and one canal. The latter was an adventure in itself, of which I may have more to say some other time. Then we were guided out into the open sea again. But the gift of Hermes had so far served us so well that I did not hesitate to put my trust in it. For all I knew, our compass-pyx might be avoiding great storms or other dangers in its choice of routes.

Finally, it directed us up a large river, then a tributary, and then a tributary of that again, at last running the boat gently aground when we were still, by my best estimate, more than a hundred miles from homes and families.

I stepped ashore and stretched, shouldered my club and a sack containing some food and an extra pair of sandals, and looked about me. "Well. It seems we walk from here."

"All right, Herc, but my feet are tired. Let's see if we can find some way to ride."

We abandoned the boat only with reluctance, though we assumed that it would once more be invisible to any eyes but ours and would be waiting when we came back. No immortal messengers appeared, and our attendant sprite seemed to have deserted us. For the time being at least, the gods seemed content to leave me alone, and now, having just gone to the trouble of providing them with trophies from a Giant, I found this irritating.

We had to walk only a few miles before coming to a large village, where it was possible to buy cameloids. We were carrying money, gifts and rewards from those who had wished to show their gratitude, and we purchased two animals, along with a little extra gear, and so were no longer forced to walk.

From there our journey overland, occupying several more days, took us past the margin of Nemea, where lay the grazing lands where I had slain a lion—by all the gods, but that seemed a long time ago! Counting up the months, I realized that nearly a year had passed since then. The herds had evidently been moved to a different grazing ground this summer, and Tarn and his colleagues, if they still followed the herdsman's calling, must have gone with them.

The closer I got to home, the more impatient I was to encounter its familiar scenes and people. Still, by the time my nephew and I once more came in sight of the walls of Cadmia, full summer had come around again. From a distance, so little about the city appeared to have changed that it seemed we might have been gone only a day.

But we soon discovered that very much had changed. For one thing, something of my new reputation had preceded me. Everyone who had known me before looked at me now in a different way, and some were glad to see me again, and some were not.

But at first I paid little attention to such matters, for I was shocked by the unexpected news that my mother was dead.

There had been some attempt to send me word of her death, some six months earlier, but as no one at home had any idea where I was, it was little wonder that the message had never reached me. I supposed Hermes might have told me, but he had not. And I was long past expecting any communication from my father. The period of formal mourning had now expired, and there was little required of me in the way of ritual. Such real grieving as I did was very private.

Amphitryon formally welcomed me home, and I thought he was actually pleased to see me, but as usual we had little to say to each other. I no longer called him "Father," but I remained respectful, and thought he did not notice. Nor did he ever ask me what had happened to the bow, his parting gift to me when I went off to be a herdsman. Possibly he had forgotten it.

Iphicles, my elder half brother, who was now more than thirty years of age, met Enkidu and me on the day of our return and marveled at how his son had grown.

"Another year or two and the lad will be ready for some military service," the proud father proclaimed, thumping him heartily on the shoulder.

Enkidu offered no open argument against that statement, but it was plain to me that he had a different future for himself in mind.

"We've heard some interesting stories about you," my brother observed when he decided my turn had come to be evaluated.

"Some of them may even be true," I answered carelessly, and did not bother to ask what any of the stories were. And I thought that he was bothered by my indifference, which was mostly genuine.

———

I had been home now for a full day, and one of our neighbors was giving me a reasoned explanation, full of clever deductions, as to why the accounts of my miraculous victories over incredible monsters could not possibly be true. "Now, the lion, for instance . . ."

I listened in polite silence for a little while, then walked away, no doubt leaving the arguer with the conviction that he had shown me up as a fraud.

In fact my account of how I had killed the lion, though basically true, was widely disbelieved. Later, I heard that many of the gods themselves had doubted the report at first—though I doubted whether those who told me that had ever seen a god.

"You look different, too, Hercules," said another old acquaintance on seeing me again.

"I suppose I do." I was a few inches taller than when I had lived at home—certain homely benchmarks, in the form of scars on tree trunks and on doorposts, provided confirmation of that fact—and definitely more mature. And my beard was starting to grow in nicely. Critically studying my arms, I decided that I really did look stronger now than I had when I went off to herd cattle. Perhaps I actually was more powerful; offhand I could think of no way to make an accurate test.

Weighing myself on a familiar balance scale, in one of the familiar barns of the estate, showed that I had gained some ten pounds, though my body still showed very little fat. But certainly no sculptor would have chosen me as a model of the ideal.

While I was on that visit home, I took part in my first crocodile hunt, joining my stepfather and my older brother, by invitation, in an expedition they had been planning for some time. It was a dangerous kind of game that warriors played on occasion, to enliven their intervals of peace.

The three of us were in a rowboat of shallow draft, and I was leaning over, trying to see the bottom, while my two companions were busy catching fish. The fish were going to be useful in our hunt, as bait.

"The best bait for crocodile, Hercules, is something bigger," Iphicles was explaining. "Like a sheep or goat. But fish are cheaper."

"You try to lure the creature into the shallows and then surround it with men armed with sturdy spears," Amphitryon added.

I nodded my understanding, and father and son took turns adding explanations.

"We won't use the boat for the actual hunt."

"When the croc's in shallow water, we'll get five or six men and come at it from all sides at once."

"You've got to watch out for the tail, as well as for the head."

The experts had judged that we had enough fish on the string, and the servant rowing the boat had us almost back to shore, when I heard the last bit of advice, this delivered in tones of some urgency. "Don't lean over there, Hercules. Watch out!"

The sight of what I thought was a large fish, moving underwater, had captured my curiosity. I had no more than an instant's warning, in the form of a swirl beneath the surface, before the enormous gray-green shape came lunging up out of the muddy shallows, jaws spread to clamp my shoulder and neck. My startled, instinctive withdrawal was a forceful move that dragged the big croc with me; the boat overturned, and I was standing hip-deep in water.

While my companions screamed and splashed, waving their barbed spears ineffectually, I got my feet solidly planted, then brought both hands up, forcing my fingers in between the large teeth that were vainly trying to puncture the skin of my face and shoulder. There was no odylic magic about this creature, but mere nature could sometimes be quite monstrous enough.

The people in the water around me were still thrashing uselessly. Meanwhile the servant, who had already reached the shore, was running for help. Ignoring them all, I found the grip I needed and peeled the beast's jaws loose—it was no more trouble than folding back a tough fruit rind. Flipping the crocodile lightly in the air, I caught it by its thick tail, called out a warning for onlookers to stand back, and swung the great mass forcefully, sending the head end hard against a massive rock that happened to be standing conveniently near.

I made my relatives a present of the valuable hide. From then on I heard no more doubts expressed about my other feats as they had been reported. And the subject of crocodile hunting was dropped for the duration of my visit.

———

In the course of my visit I naturally kept encountering familiar faces. Yet one face in particular, the very one I had come looking for, was not to be seen anywhere.

"Where is Megan?" I finally inquired, making a conscious effort to be casual. I chose to ask the question when I was away from my close relatives.

The people who were with me at the time exchanged glances that I could not read. Someone finally told me that they thought the young woman I asked about had been seen at the palace.

"But what would she be doing there?" I wondered aloud. In response, people hesitated, coughed, and changed the subject.

It seemed it would be easier to go and see for myself than to get anyone to give me a plain answer.

———

The palace grounds were busy with a casual flow of people coming and going on all kinds of business, and no one challenged me as I wandered about. At the moment when I laid eyes on Megan, she was seated in a kind of arbor in a garden behind the servants' quarters. In her arms she was holding an infant, some two or three months of age, while it nursed at her breast. My mind began automatically counting up the months of my absence from home; and in the space of a few heartbeats, before a word had passed between us, I felt certain that her child was mine.

Megan was clad in a simple, familiar garment, of a type commonly worn by female servants, loosened from one arm and shoulder to enable her comfortably to nurse. Her wide brown eyes were fastened on me, but at first, neither of us said a word as I approached. The infant's hair was scanty, but in color much the same as mine. A diaper concealed its sex. I put out a careful hand and turned back the blanket from the tiny face, which stayed nuzzled against Megan's tender breast.

"Our child." I did not make the words a question.

"Yes." She looked at me, as I thought, reproachfully. "I have lain with no one else."

I shook my head; that had not been what I was concerned about.

Somehow it had hardly occurred to me that she might have done so. "Is the baby—?"

Now she knew what I meant to ask, before I had decided just how to put the question. "He's a fine healthy boy, Hercules. If there is anything strange about him, I haven't found it out yet."

"All the good gods be thanked for that," I said sincerely. "What is his name?"

Megan told me that the baby's name was Hyllus. She had to spell it out for me.

I thought about it. "I know of no one else called by that name," I commented at last.

"It means 'a woodsman.' And it was my father's name. If my lord Hercules wishes to change it—"

I had stuck out a finger where Hyllus could grasp it, and now he clamped his tiny hand on with surprising strength. Only later did I realize that this was not very convincing proof of our relationship, that all babies could exert a powerful grip. I said, "No, no, let his name stay as it is. His mother gave it to him, and I like the way it sounds."

I must have been with Megan for almost a full minute before my mind fully registered something that my eyes could hardly have failed to see at once—the fact that she was wearing a slave's metal collar. It was a simple ring of iron, such as the lowest of the low would wear, rather than decorative silver, or even gold.

"But what in all the hells is this?" I suddenly demanded, touching the offending object with one finger.

"Just what it looks like, lord."

" 'Lord' is not my name. Let there be no use of titles between you and me."

"As my lord wishes." And she smiled in a way that let me know that she was teasing me.

"Now, tell me who in the Underworld has put this thing around your neck. You were never a slave, and you are not going to become one."

"I had no intention of becoming one."

"Then tell me, whose hands put this on?"

Now she looked at me with something like alarm. "They were a slave's hands, Hercules, those of a simple blacksmith, and he liked the business no more than I did. I hope you don't hold him responsible."

"All right. By whose orders, then?"

"It was done, they told me, by order of His Majesty the king. Although the king himself has never had anything to say to me. So far they have only given me easy tasks to do here, sewing and taking inventory."

"But *why*?"

"No one has bothered to give me an explanation. But it seems that servants, like me, whose agreements with their masters are not perfectly in order, as mine with the lord Amphitryon perhaps was not, may sometimes be forfeit—"

"Hush! Never mind. The laws can be a greater labyrinth than Corycus has ever seen. But whatever the laws say, or the king, either, you are not going to be forfeit to anyone."

"It may have had something to do with the lord general Amphitryon's failure to pay taxes."

"Hush."

I wanted very much to kiss her, but even before doing that I reached with both hands and with gentle fingers cleanly, safely tore the iron collar from her neck. It seemed to me that the spot where, as I saw now, the royal seal had been stamped in, was likely to be the weakest, and so I chose that place to rip it right across. Somehow my hands, that had doubted their skill to do as much for Hesione on her seaside cliff, were certain in their power now. I crumpled the heavy scrap of metal into a ball and threw it on the ground, and in the same motion turned at the sound of footsteps to confront whoever was approaching. In that moment I hoped it might be the very one who claimed to have made slaves of my son and his mother.

Instead, I found myself looking into the blank face of blind Tiresias. The prophet looked more infirm than when I had seen him last, and he was walking with a cane in one hand and his other arm around the shoulders of a young girl, who I supposed served him as a guide around obstacles so small and practical that they fell below the scope of his inward vision.

"Hail, Hercules," he greeted me, coming to a stop at a few paces' distance. "I see that you are healthy."

"Hail, Lord Tiresias. I hope that you are the same."

"I am not healthy, young man, and in fact I will soon be dead. You stand in danger of death from a centaur."

That was something of a surprise, and I felt Megan grow tense beside me. "Do I indeed?"

The blind man smiled his faintly horrible smile and offered no explanation.

When I saw he did not mean to speak, I said: "I thank you for your concern, prophet. But it has been shown over and over that no point or blade can pierce my skin. I doubt that any hoof can kick me hard enough to do me harm. Besides, centaurs have had their shot at me already."

"Not everything that does harm, Hercules, is hard and sharp. Beware the soft and subtle."

"Again I thank you for the warning, Lord Tiresias. . . . Speaking of the soft and subtle, whose idea was it to make a slave of this woman who nurses my son?"

"She has already told you almost as much about that as I could tell you." The blind man paused. "What will you do now, Hercules?"

"Do you need to ask? Are there some things you can't foresee?"

"There is much."

"This is my woman," I said, putting my arm around her shoulders. "And I mean to have her for my wife." And as I said that I turned and met her eyes and kissed her.

Tiresias offered no comment. His girl was staring at me in evident fascination. Turning back to him, I asked: "Do you think the king will want to exact some kind of purchase price? If he does, tell him he may deduct it from my share of the estate of Amphitryon, of which I assume some part will come to me."

Tiresias was smiling in amusement now, silently laughing, which made his blind face truly hideous. "You may tell Eurystheus that yourself," he said. "He has sent me to tell you that he wants to see you."

An hour later, I was standing before the young king in the great hall of his palace, the very room in which my trial had taken place a year earlier. This time Eurystheus received me in the oddest way. In place of the throne I had seen in this room before, there stood an enormous vessel of bronze, approximately rectangular in shape, all of its outer surfaces decorated with gods and humans in high relief. This casket, or box, was the size of a large sarcophagus or bathtub, and was topped by a hinged lid, also of heavy bronze. The opening of the lid was in my direction, and it was propped up several inches with wooden wedges. Peering out at me through the small gap thus created were a pair of human eyes that I soon recognized as those of King Eurystheus. On each side of the box stood an attendant, holding one end of a cord whose other end was tied to one of the wooden wedges. The arrangement allowed these to be yanked away at a moment's notice, removing the last chink from the king's brazen fortress—and dropping the lid resoundingly on his head if he failed to duck in time. When, in the course of our conversation, one of the guards' spears accidentally bumped the lid of the great casket, it vibrated softly but richly, like a huge gong.

Of course the box in which the king seemed to be trying to hide was flanked by ranks of armed warriors, a dozen spear-carrying men who eyed me nervously. Those I had more or less expected.

So absorbed was I in attempting to guess whether the king had gone completely mad, or what the meaning of his strange bahavior might be, that now I can hardly remember exactly what words I addressed to the king, or he to me. But our conversation went something like this:

"Your Majesty has sent for me."

"We would like to hear the story of your adventures, Hercules, from your own lips." The young king's voice had an odd metallic echo to it, coming out of his cave of bronze. "But first, is there anything we can do for you?"

I wasted no time in raising the subject of Megan.

The result of our talk was that the king, with an air of graciousness, granted me the girl and her baby as a free gift.

Politely I expressed my gratitude. The audience did not last long after that. When it was over, and I encountered Tiresias while on my way out of the palace, I asked him if I might briefly speak to him alone.

The seer motioned with his head, and I fell into step beside him. This time his arm was draped around the shoulders of a different girl.

He said to me: "Someone, a certain prophet of great reputation, fell into a trance. And while in a trance he prophesied, in the king's hearing, that 'Bronze is protection for the most powerful.' And the young king, in his natural arrogance, assumed that the phrase 'most powerful' must refer to him."

"I see. That might begin to explain the bronze casket. Is it safe to assume that the prophet was yourself?" Tiresias did not contradict me, and I went on: "Would it do me any good to ask who the prophecy *does* refer to? Well, never mind. But tell me this, Tiresias. Why should the king think he needs protection when I'm around? Why should he think he's in any danger from me?"

"Many people fear you, Hercules. And are jealous of you."

Slowly I nodded. "At the moment I can't think of anyone who has cause to be afraid. But you are right, I do sometimes see the dread in people's faces, though they try to hide it with a smile of friendship. Still, it seems to me that the king must feel some special terror, to cause him to go to such lengths to fortify himself." I shook my head and made vague gestures.

"Hercules, your strength does not extend to your perceptions. The king only hides in his bronze box when you are present. He believes that you are determined to have revenge on him."

"Revenge? For what?"

My face must have shown my stupefaction, but I don't know whether the blind man could read my face. Probably my voice gave the same evidence; and now I think it equally likely that Tiresias was past dreading or even caring for anything that anyone might do to him.

This time he answered me directly enough. "For having cheated you out of the throne."

My feet unconsciously slowed to a stop, while I tried, without success, to sort that out. "But what have I to do with thrones?"

"Some eighteen or twenty years ago there was, or may have been, yet another prophecy, to the effect that the next descendant of Zeus born in the land would rule all Cadmia. Eurystheus believes himself to be, like you, a descendant of the Thunderer. Also the king believes his own development in his mother's womb was somehow magically accelerated, and yours possibly retarded, to move him ahead of you in the line of succession. And that you are fully aware of this course of strange events, and must resent him for it."

Again it took me a little while to digest the information. "That last, about my resenting him, is wrong, now that the business regarding Megan has been settled. Totally wrong! Is there any truth in the rest of it?"

"Very probably."

"Then some god or goddess is my enemy?"

"Rumor says Hera."

That was bad news, if true. "Is there any use in my asking why the consort of Zeus should have taken a dislike to me?"

"No use in asking me."

I shook my head. Here were more questions that I could put to Zeus, someday. Or to Hera, if I should ever meet her face-to-face. I could try Hermes when I saw him next, but I had no real hope that the Messenger would be of help.

To Tiresias I said: "But there was no reason to think I'd be a king anyway, was there? Amphitryon's not royalty, nor is there any such thing on my mother's side. I've never been in line for the throne, or anywhere near it."

The blind man shrugged. He seemed gently amused. "I only said there was a prophecy—certainly that was not one of mine. You know what prophecies in general are like—or perhaps you are still too young to have heard very many of them. The less sense they make, the more people are impressed by them. And the harder it is to tell whether they are fulfilled or not."

"But, I repeat, I don't want to be a king. I wouldn't have his throne or his crown if you gave them to me."

"I know that." A pause. "The truth is that you were destined for greater things."

"Such as what?"

"Time will tell."

Now we were walking on again. I thought that in any case the old man would tell me what he wanted to tell me, no more and no less, so I did not bother to press him.

I said: "So, let His Majesty hide himself in a bronze pot, if it makes it easier for him to talk with me. Very likely I will want to talk to him again." At the time I fully expected there to be some opposition to the marriage I planned.

And on that day I left the palace wondering whether the bronze casket did not simply represent a great joke by the blind prophet, who had chosen this means of making the king look ridiculous, and thus getting even with him for something.

Before leaving home again, I took care to make Megan legally my wife, in a full public ceremony, so both she and my son would have such social standing and protection as my name could give them.

The loss of one slave could hardly make much practical difference in the vast royal household. And the young king must have been pleased to see me taking a wife who could not, according to any rational calculation, be of the slightest help to me in any dynastic struggle.

Meanwhile Amphitryon and Iphicles, though they raised mild formal objections to the wedding, I think were secretly relieved to see me marrying so far below my station. What could have been a thorny problem for my foster father, of negotiating alliances by arranging a marriage for me, was thus taken out of his hands. But I knew that my mother, if she still could watch me from the Underworld, would be sad to see me united with one who had worn the collar of a slave. The gods alone knew what dreams of greatness, as she understood greatness, she had still been cherishing for me.

On the night after the ceremony, when my bride and I were in bed together, the one I loved, who I had thought for a time was sleeping, suddenly turned over and whispered to me.

"You are so gentle, Hercules. As you always were."

The gods knew I had tried to be gentle, with her especially. "You do not fear me, then? My strength?"

"Fear you?" she seemed astonished. "No."

And the baby in his nearby cradle cried, a tiny whimper first, swiftly building to a lusty yell. And Megan caught him up and began to nurse him at her breast, which brought quick silence; and in that peaceful bed I slowly drifted off to sleep, in what seemed the most perfect rest that I had ever known.

17

I WAS HAPPY to enjoy a week of dalliance with my new bride and to amuse myself with speculation about what happy achievements my son might someday be able to attain. But of course I was not going to remain peacefully at home in Cadmia for any considerable length of time. Even had no summons come from great Zeus himself, still I doubtless would soon have found some other quest to carry me away from the peace and security of home.

Attached to the house, which had been a wedding gift from King Eurystheus, was a small staff of servants, none of whom were slaves; no doubt some were the king's spies, but that did not worry me, as I had nothing to conceal. It was no less luxurious than the manor in which I had grown up, even if it was smaller than I would have liked. Actually I felt somewhat reassured because it was not too close to the palace. The upper strata of Cadmian society would never be really open to this former servant girl and slave, I supposed. I expected that they would be for my son, someday. But that was a matter he would have to work out for himself when he was grown.

Enkidu had dropped in for a visit, and stood frowning thoughtfully at the baby I was holding. Then he asked me: "What will he be, do you suppose? A warrior?"

"I hope not," I said, without thinking. My nephew gave me a puzzled look.

So far he had not enjoyed his stay at home nearly as much as I had. Enkidu chafed under the close attention of his father, and on the day after our arrival was already suggesting to me that it was time to be off again on some new adventure.

But then in succeeding days I heard no more suggestions from him along that line—being busy with my own new family affairs, I gave the matter little thought at the time.

———

Our visitor had only just departed when a shadow fell across a window, and I thought for a moment that he had come back. Megan, peering out of the house, was tremendously impressed when she caught a glimpse of the one who had come calling.

Her mouth and eyes were round with astonishment, and she pointed toward the outside with one finger, seemingly almost unable to speak. "Hercules! It is . . . it is . . ."

I had been trying to estimate the strength with which my son could grip my finger. But now I came to the window and caught a glimpse as well. "I know who it is, my love." Gently I put her aside. "Wait here, while I go out and talk to him."

"Hercules—?"

"It's all right." I patted my wife's arm. "No harm will come to me. The Messenger and I are required to have these little conversations every now and then."

But my jaunty attitude began to drain away when I stepped out into our small rear courtyard and beheld the somber expression on the face of Hermes.

———

"Daedalus and Vulcan," Hermes assured me when we were quite alone, "both send their thanks for the sample of Apple you provided them. And of course for the other objects also."

"That's good." I had hoped that the other objects would be more than mere jars of mud when they reached their destination. "They are quite welcome. . . . Lord Hermes, did you say *Vulcan?* Do you mean the god Hephaestus? The Smith himself?"

Hermes seemed faintly pleased that he had managed to startle and impress me. "That is who I mean. Hephaestus vouches that all the samples you have furnished them have been of inestimable help."

"I rejoice to hear it, even if I don't begin to understand just what Vulcan and Daedalus are doing. Now, Lord Messenger, will you answer another question for me?"

"Perhaps."

"Perhaps you can also guess what it is: When will my father see me?"

"Before he does, Hercules, there is one more task you must perform."

"Ah." I put my hand on the branch of a fruit tree but restrained myself from breaking it off. "Does it surprise you, Lord Hermes, that I am not astonished by your answer?"

As usual, Mercury remained imperturbable. "What Zeus asks of you now is a mission more important than any you have previously undertaken—I am quoting your father's very words. And he solemnly assured me that he is ready to see you as soon as you have completed this next assignment."

I had been perfectly prepared for any kind of an indefinite answer. This sudden acceptance of my demand, even qualified as it was, left me not knowing what to say.

Again Hermes seemed to be smiling faintly.

At last I got out: "I promise to undertake any task that my father may set, if he will promise to meet me immediately afterward."

The Messenger raised an aristocratic eyebrow. "Do you not want to hear first what the task is?"

I could feel my face reddening. "I have said what I have said."

Mercury nodded slowly. He turned his head this way and that, studying our surroundings, eyeing the open windows of the house. Then he said: "Let us find a place where we can be comfortable while we talk. It is not a matter that can be spelled out in a dozen words."

Turning out of the courtyard, we moved through a small passage, screened by arbors and grapevines, leading to the small orchard in the rear of the house. There my distinguished visitor adopted a thoughtful attitude, strolling with his hands clasped behind his back.

Hermes said: "You have of course heard of Mount Olympus, home of the gods from ancient times. It was long the favorite dwelling place of Zeus."

"Yes, of course I've heard of it. But do I understand you to say that Zeus lives there no longer?"

"Sadly that is true—but where Zeus dwells now is not our immediate concern. I mention Mount Olympus because somewhere in the vicinity of that place there lives—I should say exists—a man called Prometheus."

I shook my head: No, I had never heard of him.

Mercury went on. "This Prometheus has for a long time suffered a strange and terrible punishment, of which confinement is only the lesser part. Your father sets you the task of locating this sufferer, ending his torment, and setting him free. In the process—and this is the most important part—you must learn from Prometheus whatever he knows about the nature and whereabouts of a Giant named Atlas."

"I see," I said slowly. "And then, having done that much, I am supposed to find Atlas. And then—?"

Hermes held up a restraining hand. "Your father may want you to look for Atlas also. But that will come later. I meant what I said, Hercules. Zeus will see you, face-to-face, as soon as you have found Prometheus and gained his knowledge. Your father will want to hear from you directly what you have learned."

Briefly I considered this, while the god and I kept walking. Then I stopped in my tracks. "I have said I'll do it and I will, whatever it takes. But tell me more about this Prometheus. How is he confined, and what are the other parts of his strange punishment?"

The Messenger picked some fruit from a tree and tasted it with appreciation. For a moment or two he looked no more than human.

Then he said: "Long ago—no need to worry about exactly how long ago, or why—Prometheus was an enemy of Zeus. Of some earlier avatar of the god, I mean, long before your father's time."

"I see. And the nature of the man's punishment?"

"I believe he is chained to a rock." Mercury suddenly seemed oddly uncertain and, I thought, uncomfortable. "There is also, I think, a large and ugly bird involved. Or maybe several of them. Kill the birds if they get in your way. Now I have told you all I really know. You are going to have to deal with the details as best you can."

But then the great god suddenly recalled one detail that he wanted to convey. "Oh, and one more thing. When you set the man free, Zeus wants you to leave some small fragment of the chain attached to him. That way, a certain oath once sworn by an earlier avatar of Zeus need not be broken."

We had resumed our pacing under the fruited trees. I said: "And oaths, of course, are tremendously important."

"Of course."

"All right. I can do all that." The story of the oath and the strange punishment intrigued me, but I was not going to pursue it now. "Tell me where I can find Prometheus."

"That I cannot do."

Once more my feet stopped moving in the grass. For the space of several deep breaths the Messenger and I studied each other in silence. Then I said: "Lord Hermes, I have promised to perform this task. Now, tell me, are you playing some kind of game with me? Or giving me a test? Do you have some reason to want to make the job more difficult?"

"Not at all, Hercules. I will answer any other questions you may have, if I can."

I drew a deep breath and let it out.

"Very well, I do have several. To begin with, why send me, or anyone? Either you or my mighty father could reach this Prometheus much more swiftly than I can, even if I use the *Skyboat*. Especially if you really do know where to find this chained man, which I suppose you must. Either of you gods, I am sure, would make short work of any difficulties the man may be having with rocks and chains and birds."

Hermes was silent, staring gloomily at nothing.

"The chief reason we are sending you instead of a god," he said at last, "is that there are probably Giants in his vicinity."

"I see. And Giants really do pose that much of a danger to you, or to Zeus, that you are not going to risk your necks by going near them."

Gray eyes turned on me with such a look that at last I began to be a little frightened. Mercury said: "We would not pretend that it is so, if it were not. I thought that on Corycus they had explained these matters to you." At last the god was starting to grow angry. "Hercules, you take grave risks! Remember you are mortal. There are gods who would crush you like an insect if you spoke to them with such insolence."

"I see," I said again, and briefly bowed my head. "Very well, Lord Messenger, I dispute with you no more. I have sworn I will do this service for my father, and I will. Where is Olympus? Tell me that much at least, and I'll be on my way."

This time I really did expect a simple answer. But instead of giving me one, Hermes only seemed to grow even more uncomfortable. He hurled the fruit core from him, only a casual motion of his arm, but the soft missile went ripping like a slung stone through the leaves of another tree.

Turning back to me at last, he said, "That is another thing I cannot tell you."

"The location of Mount Olympus?" I was incredulous. "Cannot or will not?"

The Messenger now looked more ill at ease than I had ever seen him, though it seemed he had reasoned himself out of his anger, or got rid of it some other way. He said: "I can give you a rough idea of where it is, and Prometheus, too. But I cannot reveal to you his precise location, or that of Mount Olympus, either, because I no longer know. The truth is, I have forgotten both. I had forgotten the very existence of Prometheus until Zeus reminded me."

There was silence for a little while, and I could feel a cold chill creeping down my spine. Eventually I nerved myself to ask: "Lord Hermes, is one of us mad?"

"You are not mad, Hercules. As for myself, the question is not so simply answered—but yes, I *am* partially deranged, at least when it comes to memory. And so is every god I know."

I sat there for what seemed a long time, not knowing what to say. For the first time I began to realize how grim was our situation regarding the Giants.

Eventually Hermes began to speak again. It came out that all the gods, or all of them with whom he had had any recent contact, had fought skirmishes with Giants who used their secret weapon, or had been attacked by their great enemies from ambush, and all the gods, or almost all, had forgotten pretty much the same things.

I was under more than ordinary strain, and my temper got the best of me. Also I was very young and had not yet been much pounded by my world. I said: "So, your brains have all more or less gone rotten."

That got me glared at again, and for a moment I was afraid that I had indeed gone too far. In a voice that made me wince and recoil, despite myself, he barked out: "Hear me, mortal! We who appeal for your help are the wounded veterans of a great war!"

I apologized for my rudeness. But presently I had taken up the argument again, though on a considerably lower key. "You, a god, expect me, a mortal, to find Olympus for you, as well as this fellow who is somehow bound to a rock?"

Hermes tried to be reassuring. "The search may occupy you for some time, Hercules. But there is every reason to believe you will succeed."

Most of the citizens of Cadmia were really pleased to see me looking for my club and making other preparations to leave home again, though of course they expressed their regrets when I told them I was going. Young king Eurystheus was especially two-faced. As he peered out from under his bronze lid during my farewell audience, I could see in his eye a glint of self-satisfaction at how cleverly he was blocking my plans to seize his throne. Meanwhile he halfheartedly offered me an escort of warriors on the expedition I was about to undertake. I courteously declined, not wanting to be burdened with a squadron of mouths to somehow feed, of minds to argue with, and of bodies to keep out of trouble.

Before leaving, I made sure that Megan and little Hyllus were established comfortably in our new house.

After telling Megan that I was ready to push on, I informed Enkidu before telling anyone else, more or less assuming that he would choose to accompany me again.

But when my nephew heard the news, his eyes did not light up as I had expected. He briefly hesitated, and then told me: "I'm not going with you this time, Herc."

"Ah." For a moment I was astonished, but as soon as I took thought on the matter, surprise vanished. My nephew was now almost fourteen years old, and he told me he wanted to stay home and marry the girl who had grown to be attractive in his eyes. Once my mother and Amphitryon had intended that I should marry her, but there was no longer any hope of that. Also the wealth that would come with the wedding was beginning to loom up real and solid in Enkidu's eyes.

I reminded my old comrade that if he settled down and stayed home, the army, and the chronic war, were waiting for him in a year or two, as soon as his father thought him old enough to fight.

But Enkidu had already taken these matters into consideration. "I know, but it sounds like the war's about over. At last. And by the Underworld, Unc, you don't need me. You can get anyone you want to come with you now. You're really getting to be famous."

When it came time for me to depart from the happy cottage where Megan and I had enjoyed a sort of honeymoon, I took my leave with some regret, made sharper by the tears of my young wife. But in my heart I had never abandoned my quest to learn all I could about my father and finally to confront him face-to-face. And however attractive home and hearth might be, particularly after a long wandering, it was a man's business to be out and active in the world.

Getting back to the place where we had left the *Skyboat,* and where I hoped to find it waiting for me, would entail a long overland journey. But this time I was riding a good cameloid from the start. On the eve of my departure, a number of people offered various gifts, all calculated, as I thought, to speed me on my way. A few others, would-be adventurers, had volunteered to accompany me, though I had told no one where I was going or on what mission. None seemed desirable as companions, and firmly I told them that I preferred to go alone.

Up to that point my solo journey was uneventful. I was just about to step aboard the *Skyboat* when some inward sense told me that a god was near. Ready for another argument with Hermes, I turned around to confront a tall male figure. But the face I saw was not the one I had expected.

This time, in the appearance of the image before me, there was an undercurrent of something infinitely more terrible than any Messenger. This time I confronted Apollo himself.

I had never laid eyes on the Far-Worker before, but somehow I knew him instantly and unmistakably. The movements of my body seemed automatic. Letting my club slide from my shoulder, I went down on one knee before him, something I had never thought of doing before Hermes. My mouth had gone dry, and I began to know, perhaps truly for the first time, what it is to be afraid.

Not that there was anything intrinsically awe-inspiring in his shape, though he was certainly impressive. Apollo stood before me in the form of a beautiful, beardless youth, a little taller than I, his lean, muscular body draped in white tunic and cape, with Bow and Arrows slung on his back and a small lyre fastened to his belt. His face and arms would have been naturally pale, but they were tanned, and his curly hair grew strangely, in an entangled mixture of red and black.

When the great god spoke to me his look was grim at first, and his greeting came with the sound of a harsh accusation.

"You are Hercules," he growled.

"I am, lord."

He made an impatient gesture. "All right, Hercules. Who are they? Tell me their names, the gods and humans who plot against me."

I was too bewildered to attempt any reply.

My situation must have shown in my face. Apollo shook his head, and some of the stiffness went out of his pose.

His voice became lower and less threatening. "But no, there are too many logical reasons against that, and deep in my heart I feel it cannot be so. And Daedalus and the prince Asterion speak well of you, Hercules. Hermes does, too, but he . . ." He left the phrase unfinished and stood staring at me uncertainly.

At last it was up to me to break the silence. "Lord Apollo, Hermes has explained to me that his memory is damaged. Is it possible that you have suffered in a similar way?"

"He said that, did he?" The Far-Worker glared at me again for a moment, then relaxed a little further. "It is only too possible, I fear. Only too possible."

"I am sorry to hear that."

Suspicion was rapidly being replaced by uncertainty. "I must admit, Hercules," said Apollo a moment later, "that my own memory of Olympus, its nature and whereabouts, is regrettably inadequate. In fact, the more I contemplate the situation, try to estimate the number of things I must have forgotten, the more it alarms me."

"Then you, too, have fought the Giants, lord."

"Yes, fought them indeed. When I was in an earlier avatar." His right hand rose for a moment to touch his slung Bow, then fell back to his side. "Destroyed a few, but at a cost. And part of the price I paid was that for a long time, many months, the mere existence of the Giants seems to have been blotted from my memory."

Now Apollo asked me more questions, fortunately free of accusations. In response, I told him about my repeated meetings with Hermes, and what Daedalus and Prince Asterion had told me.

The Far-Worker had had his own meetings with those men, some of them comparatively recent. But he had partially forgotten them, and he found my point of view on the subject very interesting.

"And where is Hermes now?" he wanted to know.

I had no idea.

"Lord Apollo, if you have come to ask me, or command me, to do what my father has ordered, you should know that I need no special urging. Hermes has convinced me of the need. It was only that I needed another day here at home, to set my affairs in order."

"It isn't that," Apollo said. Now his manner was much milder than it had been on his arrival. "I had forgotten so much, certain things began to seem so inexplicable, that I began to think there was a conspiracy against me . . . but now memories are beginning to come back.

"Fortunately, the damage that the Giants do to gods is not always permanent." He ran distracted fingers through his hair, an action that drew my attention again to the strange mixture of red and black. But I was not going to offer any comments.

Suddenly the Far-Worker's suspicion flared again. "You," Apollo challenged me, "seem to know more about Zeus than I do. Can you explain that?"

When confronting the Messenger, I had been able to summon up a brash defiance. But in Apollo's presence that attitude had utterly evaporated, and I felt like a small boy called by some powerful authority to account for his misdeeds.

"Sorry, my lord Apollo, but I can explain very little. I know that great Zeus is my father, but nothing of any conspiracy."

For the first time he favored me with something like a smile. Gradually the Far-Worker seemed to be completely conquering his suspicions.

At last he relaxed somewhat. "Call me Jeremy, if you will. My mortal name was—is—Jeremy Redthorn. Actually I'm still rather new at this god business. I was younger than you are now when I put on Apollo's Face, and I seem to remember that my hair was all red . . . that must have been about two years ago, though keeping track of the past has become a matter of uncertainty. Maybe in another year or so it will be all black."

"Oh. Yes, your hair, of course." While Apollo had been speaking, my perception of the figure before me shifted. Before me I saw an unsettling combination of youth and majesty, uncertainty and imperial power.

In the midst of our discussion Apollo paused, as if suddenly struck by a new idea. "Have you ever been to Vulcan's workshop and laboratory?" he demanded.

"Never."

"It would be a good thing," he announced, "for you to pay that place a visit. Daedalus is working there, too, you know, and he and the Smith will want to hear everything you can tell them about this Antaeus. I saw those jars of muck you sent, and they made me wonder."

"I agree," I said. I had for a long time been curious as to what the gods were doing with the material I had provided them. "I would be delighted and honored to see the workshop where Hephaestus works his wonders. But how am I to get there?"

"How are you to get there? I can take you, easily enough. But Zeus says that learning all we can from Atlas must come first."

18

The Man on the Rock

BEGINNING TO FEEL a little more at ease with my divine companion, I tentatively suggested to him that we could both ride in the *Skyboat*. But great Apollo brushed this idea aside. He raised a hand and made a slight gesture. From out of somewhere, I could not tell where unless it was the empty air, there came a magnificent chariot, empty of passengers, that looked much like the one I had seen on the island of Corycus, belonging to Dionysus. But as it rolled to a stop beside us I could see that this one was pulled by horses instead of leopards. They were a pair of huge, white, fiery animals, obviously as much creatures of the supernatural as was Apollo himself.

The Sun God leaped in and seized the reins. "Come, Hercules," he said. "I have some vague idea of where this Prometheus may be."

"Near Olympus."

"Yes, and I also have a vague idea about that. Between the two of us, we ought to have a good chance of finding him."

I was not eager to board the chariot, but it seemed I had little choice. Taking my club in hand, I boldly climbed in, and a moment later we were airborne. Flight of any kind was a new experience for me, and moments later my eyes were closed, and my two-handed grip on the rail before me was crushing wood and metal.

Apollo urged me to relax. "Don't look down, if it bothers you. I'll try to make the ride as smooth as possible."

———

Making an effort of will, I succeeded in opening my eyes. Trying to take my mind off the fact that I was now hurtling through the air, several hundred feet above the ground, I asked the Far-Worker how we were going to find Prometheus, and Mount Olympus, if neither of us knew exactly where they were.

"I have a vague idea," Apollo repeated. "Say, within a couple of hundred square miles. But no clear memory of the exact spot." He rubbed a hand over his handsome face, the gesture of a man brushing away cobwebs. "I do seem to remember that there are Giants in the vicinity. If they allow us to complete this little trip, I'll take you on to Vulcan's laboratory."

"Hermes warned me about Giants, too." I discovered that it helped to keep my eyes raised, watching the clouds instead of the earth.

"He did, did he? I suppose the Messenger has also skirmished with them. . . . I tell you, Hercules, if I could even recall much about the enemy who has robbed me of so many memories, I might fear to face that power again. But as it is . . . in ignorance is courage." Apollo shook himself and straightened his shoulders. "Enough of that. Why exactly are we looking for Prometheus?"

I explained to my new companion that Zeus now wanted his former enemy rescued from his endless punishment.

"Because it seems," I went on, "that only this Prometheus can tell us where the Giant named Atlas is to be found—can you remember anything of Atlas?"

"Afraid not. Almost nothing."

"Oh. Well, Atlas, in turn, is important because he knows something, or can do something, that Daedalus and Hephaestus dearly want to find out, or accomplish." I was having to shout above the rush of wind. "I don't understand the details. Maybe when I meet Zeus he'll fill in some of them for me."

"Ah." Apollo shrugged his powerful shoulders. "Well, if Hermes says Atlas must be located, then that's what we'd better do. The Messenger may have retained more of his wits than I have of mine."

That was not the most reassuring thing he could have said. The chariot flew on in silence, except for the continual rush of wind. Now and then Apollo mentioned certain landmarks, towns and mountains, streams and lakes, as they passed below, while I for the most part kept my eyes fixed firmly on the horizon. To judge by the rapidity with which the earthly features hurtled by, our passage through the air was amazingly swift, much faster even than *Skyboat*. Fortunately our conveyance was also much steadier than the *Argo*, whose motion had once made me seasick.

————

No more than an hour had passed before our flight path began tending downward. We descended to lower and lower altitudes, until we were only skimming over a remote and rocky wasteland. There was no body of water in sight, not even a small stream. I had to agree that *Skyboat* would not have been of much help in reaching this land-locked region.

Now that we were at little more than rooftop height, I found I was able to watch the ground without being overcome by terror or illness. Apollo guided our team of unnatural beasts to and fro in a methodical search pattern. We spent a long time flying back and forth before we located the rock we wanted.

"There he is," my companion suddenly announced. Apollo's eyes were, unsurprisingly, much keener than mine, and it was he who made the discovery. "That looks like a man, lying on a rock." And with a touch on the reins he sent the chariot into a sharp bank.

Soon we were directly over the forlorn-looking individual on his slab of stone, and I looked down and nodded. "That must be the fellow we want. Few would choose this place for sunbathing."

———

There was no sign of any human settlement, not even a hunters' or herders' track, anywhere nearby. Prometheus had been chained down atop a small, rocky hill between two slightly larger heights. Occasionally, during the minute or two while we were making our close approach, he moved his head or limbs, and once or twice let out a hoarse cry of pain.

His situation was amazing, and horrifying. I had never seen anything remotely like it.

As we approached more closely, we saw a naked man, of muscular build and indeterminate age, chained flat on his back on a stone bed. As far as I could see, he was totally exposed to day and night, heat and cold, sun and rain. Obviously something out of the ordinary kept him from dying, in this situation where ordinarily a man might have expected to live and suffer for only a matter of hours, or a few days at the very most. What kind of nourishment was keeping him alive was more than I could guess.

His beard was not gray, but it had grown so long that it wound almost entirely around the rock.

But mere exposure was not the worst that Prometheus had to endure. A kind of hunchbacked vulture, parts of its body naked of all feathers, flapped into view even as we drew near. The great bird landed on the rock, as if on some familiar perch, and immediately began tormenting the victim, the sharp beak opening a bloody wound in the man's side.

As we approached, the creature looked up, spreading its wings to their full ten-foot span, a drop of blood falling from the tip of its beak. Apollo touched his Bow, and the bird sprang into the air and flapped away, screaming.

Moments later we were on the ground. Leaping out of the chariot even before its wheels ceased to roll, I rejoiced in the reassuring feel of solid earth beneath my feet.

At once I hurried to the side of the onetime enemy of Zeus, whose chains yielded promptly to my strength.

Prudently I remembered my father's command, passed on to me by Mercury, to leave some fragment of the chain still fastened to Prometheus so that the oath of an earlier avatar of Zeus need not be broken. I left a circlet, with a single link attached, on his left wrist.

The man on the rock had not reacted to our approach and hardly stirred even when I broke him free. Though his eyes were open, I quickly decided that he could not be fully conscious, but rather in a kind of suspended animation.

Now Apollo came and took him by the hand, and now Prometheus sat up and frowned at his rescuers in puzzlement. A touch from the hand of the God of Healing, and the ugly wound in the victim's side closed over and ceased to bleed.

But now, even as Prometheus seemed on the verge of recovery from his ancient ordeal, the predatory bird reappeared, looking ready to deal him a setback.

A moment later an Arrow from Apollo's Bow produced a sharp midair explosion, after which only a feather or two survived to come drifting to the ground.

———

After disposing of the ugly bird, Apollo stood watch, brooding with his Bow in hand and a second Arrow ready, while I pulled from the rock the anchor bolts with broken chains attached, so that no one else might ever be held captive in the same place.

Prometheus was now standing on his feet and beginning to look about him. He took no notice of Apollo, who was a step or two behind him, and he paid little attention to me, though I stood right at his side. Obviously his mind was far from clear as yet.

But at last the man did speak, gasping out: "But is this real? I am now truly free?" I could barely comprehend him, his accent had such a strange and antique sound.

"Truly free," I assured him. "By order of Zeus himself."

"Ahh!" It was a kind of groaning noise that might have expressed either pain or triumph.

"What can you tell me about Atlas?" I demanded, seeing no reason to waste any time.

Seeming to come more fully wake, Prometheus frowned at me. His voice when he finally spoke was scratchy, as if it had not been used in a long time. "Why do you want to approach Atlas? Do you know what you are asking for?"

I exchanged glances with Apollo. "Probably I don't know everything I should," I admitted. "But I am here in the service of Zeus himself, trying to locate Atlas the Giant."

Prometheus seemed surprised by my last words. He knotted his hands in his long beard and tugged at it nervously.

"A Giant?" His hoarse voice almost broke. "No. Not Atlas. Well, maybe he once was. I expect there may be Giants about. But the one you are looking for is nothing as simple and uncomplicated as a mere Giant." And from the corner of my eye I saw Apollo turn his face to us, concentrating on this remarkable response.

Meanwhile the man we had rescued was turning back and forth, studying his surroundings in every direction, as if he needed to orient himself after his long, tormented sleep. When he at last took notice of Apollo, he merely acknowledged the Olympian's presence with a slight bow, as if gods in general were truly familiar sights to him. An arrogant attitude, I thought, that might well have got him into trouble in the past.

Then Prometheus raised an arm, from which a single link of chain still dangled, and pointed off to the northeast.

"You will find the one you say you are looking for in that direction," he said. "No more than a few hours' walk. See, there, that peak on what looks like the very edge of the world?"

I stood behind our informant and peered along the length of his extended arm. He seemed to be indicating the top of a rugged, truncated cone, blue with distance, that fitted into a notch in the rocky horizon. I doubted that it was really the edge of the world, though at the time I could not feel absolutely sure.

"You will find Olympus there," Prometheus was telling us, "in the middle of a flat space ringed by hills. Seek Atlas on the top of the central cone. He'll be there still . . . though I haven't seen him for centuries."

Apollo was standing close beside us now and gazing into the dis-

tance. He seemed to have no need to shade his eyes from the lowering
sun.

"Olympus? Yes, that may be it," he murmured, in the tone of a man
who is talking chiefly to himself. "That may well be the place." Then
he rounded on Prometheus. "If you haven't seen him for centuries, what
makes you so sure that he will still be there?"

Now it was the former captive's turn to appear puzzled. "He's not
going anywhere—how can he, when he supports the heavens?"

Apollo and I looked at each other. "We thank you for your information," he told Prometheus.

Then the god made a sign to me with his head, a slight but commanding nod, and I followed him as he began to walk in the direction
indicated, leaving Prometheus behind. The chariot followed us, just
keeping pace, the rims of its wheels turning slowly a foot or so above
the uneven ground.

"If there are truly Giants about," Apollo observed, when we had
trudged along for a hundred yards or so, "it might be a good idea for
us to walk the rest of the way. A man-sized shape on the ground is a
much less conspicuous target than a flying chariot."

In the past, folk who have heard my description of that day's events
have asked what happened to Prometheus after he was freed. I can only
tell my present readers what I told them, that I do not know. The Far-
Worker and I had many other things to think about. My last glance at
the man we had rescued showed him standing with one hand on the
rock that had been his place of torture, gazing out over the land in the
opposite direction. His back was straight, his wound was no longer
bleeding, and the tormenting bird was dead.

———————

It crossed my mind as we walked that perhaps I ought to persuade
Apollo that my duty was to report to Zeus before doing anything else.
But how could I be sure that Atlas had now been located unless I saw
him for myself?

My companion set a brisk walking pace, but not one that I found
impossible to keep. As we moved along, with the chariot keeping pace
behind us, Apollo described his own mind as like a painting on a canvas,
one that had been torn full of holes, so that the scene depicted was now
barely recognizable.

He added: "I ought to remember something about Atlas, and almost
I do. But 'almost' is no help to us."

"What I can't understand, Lord Apollo—Jeremy—is how can any being, however great, support the sky?"

"I suppose that's one of the things we may find out, if we keep going."

I walked on, trying to picture what Atlas could be like, trying to picture what might happen if he simply got tired and let go. And again I thought to myself. *The edge of the world?* But no, one of my early tutors had taught me that wise folk had demonstrated in several ways that the world was round.

———

As we hiked along, Apollo told me the little he could currently remember about Atlas. As time passed since his last brush with the Giants and their exotic weapon, some details about the case were starting to come back to him.

"I am now beginning to recall a certain legend," he added. "One that says Atlas represents another case of fearful punishment inflicted by one of your father's predecessors in the endless chain of avatars of Zeus. That earlier Zeus sentenced a certain particularly rebellious Giant to bear the weight of the firmament, for all time to come."

"The firmament. I suppose that means the sky?"

"That is correct."

"Is this some poetic figure of speech?" Somehow I could not imagine that even I myself would be strong enough for that.

"My thought is that it must be." And Apollo turned and looked at me, as if the fact that I might think about poetry had surprised him.

As we trudged on, the chariot still following us at a little distance, my companion added suddenly: "If we happen to meet a Giant, and if I should fall in combat with him—"

"Zeus forbid it!"

"I doubt your father has the power to forbid such things. So, listen to me, Hercules. If I do fall, you must press on, to do the next thing that Zeus asks of you."

"If we meet a Giant," I said, "other than this Atlas, who of course must be questioned, to find out what he knows—the first thing I'll do with any other Giant is beat his brains out with my club." And I made it sing through the air.

"I wish you success in the endeavor."

"I've fought one of them already," I assured my companion. "Antaeus tried to use his memory-destroying magic on me, but it had no effect, as far as I could tell. So, it might be wise if I went first. It might save you from losing another chunk of memory."

Apollo seemed to give the matter serious thought, then came to a prompt decision and nodded his agreement. With divine assurance, he judged himself too valuable to our cause to risk his life unnecessarily; and the risk to me in fighting another Giant would probably be minimal.

We held a brief conversation, after which Apollo waited for his chariot to catch up with him and then climbed into it. He promised to keep an eye on my progress from a distance and to come to my aid at once if I appeared to be in trouble.

When I turned again to look around, neither god nor chariot were anywhere to be seen.

Pushing on alone at a steady pace, I came in two or three hours to the cone-shaped hill and began to climb. The slope looked much longer now than it had from a distance.

The day was far advanced by that time, and presently I sought a place to rest for the night. I am a creature of daylight, basically, and I also thought my ally Apollo would be at his strongest when the sun was bright.

The stars were over me when I drifted off to sleep, and my last clear thought was something to the effect of how ridiculous it was that any creature of the earth could hold them up.

I slept soundly, and in the morning resumed my climb. On top, I found a spring where I could slake my thirst. Looking about me, I gradually convinced myself that I had found what seemed to be the place that Prometheus had described.

The big hill I had just climbed had on its top a cup-shaped indentation perhaps two hundred yards across. In the middle of this, in turn, stood a small hill. And it struck me that from a vantage point atop this small interior elevation the whole sky would seem to be spread out for comfortable inspection. So I went there as soon as I had caught my breath.

After my encounter with Antaeus, I thought I had a pretty good idea of what Atlas would be like, but it soon turned out that I was wrong.

The small hill had, again, a small depression at its summit. This concavity was no more than ten yards wide, and it seemed to have been paved at some time in the remote past, for remnants of a regular layer of stones or tiles showed through the clumps of grass and deposits of dry earth that overlay it now. And at the middle of the small depression stood an object that inevitably drew my attention, first because of its position, and second because it looked something like a tree stump, at the very center of this concentric series of otherwise completely treeless hills and hollows.

With a faint chill I realized that its rounded upper surface had some vague similarity to what I imagined the grainy head of a bald Giant must be like. But the resemblance was still greater, I thought, to a tree stump.

Something like a tree stump, about four feet high, and half that in diameter. But the substance of it did not look like wood, but rather like a pillar of rock, or of compacted earth. In fact the color of it and the grainy surface made me think of Giants' skin. Around the base of this pillar, or stump, the earth was muddy, and I supposed that any hard rain must cause quite a puddle there at the bottom of the once-paved bowl.

I went to stand beside the peculiar stump, rested an arm on it familiarly, and looked around. For all I could tell, I was indeed now positioned at the very center of the earth and sky, my line of sight clear to the remote blue horizon, which seemed equally distant in all directions.

Then it occurred to me to wonder if Atlas, for all his strength and possible bulk, might be invisible, like a sprite; and that possibly the giant pillars that held the sky, if any, were invisible as well. But I could walk in every direction around the central stump without bumping into anything of the kind.

When at last I grew impatient, and called out for Atlas, no one and nothing answered, leaving me feeling a curious mixture of disappointment and relief.

On becoming even more impatient, I took hold of the strange tree stump and began to exert the force that would soon have wrenched it from the ground.

Then at last a great voice, that seemed to come from everywhere around me, boomed out, commanding me to stop.

You may believe that I stopped at once.

"I am Hercules of Cadmia," I informed the world, and the invisible owner of the voice. "I have come here in search of one called Atlas."

The top of what had looked like a dead stump clicked open suddenly, an abrupt flowerlike blooming that revealed not petals but what I took to be a huge eye, glassy and translucent, staring back at me with an intensity I took to signify intelligence.

"I am Atlas," said the same voice, at last, now diminished to a more reasonable volume.

Had I been even ordinarily susceptible to fear, I would probably have taken to my heels at that moment. As it was, I recoiled a couple of steps, then demanded of the thing bluntly, "Are you a Giant?"

The voice regained its former volume. "A CASTLE CALLED DOUBTING CASTLE," it boomed out. "THE OWNER WHEREOF WAS GIANT DESPAIR."

"I do not understand you."

"THE PEACE OF GOD, WHICH PASSETH ALL UNDER-STANDING."

It certainly passed mine. I stood silent for a while, trying to think. If this—this *thing* confronting me was all there was to see of Atlas, he certainly bore no resemblance to Antaeus.

At last I said: "You are no Giant, then. And you are certainly not a man. Nor like any god that I have ever seen or heard described."

"YE SHALL BE AS GODS, KNOWING GOOD AND EVIL."

"I do not understand you. I am trying to determine if the legends about you are true or false. They say that you hold up the pillars on which the stars are supported."

"AND WHEN THE STARS THREW DOWN THEIR SPEARS, AND WATERED HEAVEN WITH THEIR TEARS, DID HE SMILE HIS WORK TO SEE?"

"I assume that question is somehow rhetorical. Yes, yes, very well. What can you show me, or tell me, about whatever it is that holds stars in their places?"

Finally I had managed to ask a question of my own that evoked something like a real answer.

And then there occurred something so far beyond my understanding that even now I have difficultly trying to describe it. Somehow Atlas conjured into existence, atop his stump-head, a much larger visionary space, spread before me like a kind of stage.

The apparitions on this stage were clear and brilliant, and moved in a way that seemed perfectly lifelike. Yet it seemed to me that none of them had ever truly been alive.

I regretted that Apollo was missing this show, and even more that Daedalus could not see it.

A voice spoke to me, in my own language, and the marvelous pictures came and went. I have neither the space here nor the inclination to set down all that Atlas told me on that day. But among other things, it was revealed to me that every star I saw in the night sky was really another sun—and that many of those stars were actually bigger and brighter than the sun that gave us all life, and that our poets called the Eye of Apollo.

The voice from the pillar spoke to me also of inconceivable times and distances.

And gradually I came to realize that, in a symbolic sense, what the legends said about Atlas was quite true. When later I had a chance to talk to Daedalus again, I had this thought confirmed: Atlas indeed supported the celestial sphere, sustained the structure of the Universe, in the sense that he retained and preserved many basic truths about the world that would otherwise have been utterly forgotten.

When I asked Atlas where the Giants came from, he told me that they had issued from the earth.

The beginnings of new understanding grew in me. My imagination relaxed, glad to be relieved of the effort of picturing huge pillars, by which the weight of the whole sky might be transferred to one unimaginable set of shoulders, part of some Giant body sitting or standing in this spot.

———

As I continued to question Atlas about the world, another thing he showed me was a parade of human shapes, or images. And he told me also about something he called the machinery of Olympus, which still diligently made such records of certain folk, records in the form of images, which were then caused to appear in the Underworld.

But I was no longer listening carefully, because my imagination had been truly caught by that one phrase. *The machinery of Olympus.* Those words, if they meant anything, must mean that Olympus still existed somewhere.

Meanwhile, the strange being who dealt in the tree stump, or issued from it, spoke on, telling me about the spritelike creatures who had made the shadow images that I watched, in pursuit of some vast project that all human and Olympian minds had long since forgotten about.

There was more, more than I will attempt to set down now, more than I can even remember. When at last the demonstration ceased, I fell into a kind of reverie of contemplation.

———

Apollo had to call me twice to rouse me. I looked around to see him standing in his chariot, behind his pair of magnificent white horses. All the marvelous display that Atlas had stunned and enlightened me with was gone, and the day was far advanced.

I thought the Far-Worker was looking at me strangely. He said: "My curiosity got the best of me, Hercules. What's going on?"

I pointed at the peculiar central column. "Atlas, here, can probably explain things better than I can."

"This—is Atlas?" But the god did not stay for an answer to that question. Instead he immediately faced the tall stump and demanded: "Tell me, oracle—where is lost Olympus?"

The reply this time must have come in a form perceptible only to divine senses, for I saw and heard it not. But Apollo understood something, because he grabbed me by the arm and pulled me back into the chariot. A moment later, the horses went bounding away at top speed.

I thought at the time that our hasty departure was probably a mistake, and now, looking back, I am sure of it. The god and I might both have learned much more from Atlas, had it not been for Apollo's eagerness to find his way back to Olympus, and my eagerness to be at his side when he made that discovery.

How far we traveled, or even in exactly what direction, I could not have said, for our flight was extremely rapid, and the sky around us was full of clouds much of the time. When Apollo and I finally came to the place that he said had once been Olympus, we discovered it deserted now, another almost barren mountaintop.

We landed a short distance below the summit, dismounted from the chariot, and began to climb. The danger of being seen by Giants had apparently been forgotten. I felt my ears pop on the ascent.

The air was so thin and cold, and there were moments in my short stay there when I had trouble breathing.

"Was this it? Yes, I think . . . but I can't be sure." Coming to a temporary halt, Apollo pressed his fists against his temples.

Old memories, long forgotten, began to come back to him. He tried to convey them to me, sometimes stammering in a most ungodlike way, and I could tell he felt a grievous sense of loss. Once this place must have had the appearance of an earthly paradise, but now it was only dust and blowing tumbleweed.

As we advanced, the Far-Worker began to tell me, in a dreamy, abstracted voice, about another mountaintop he had visited, only a few years ago, and in his current avatar. There, for a brief time, he had thought he had rediscovered Olympus.

"It was the similarity between that place and this that half awoke old memories, made me almost think that I had really returned here."

I murmured something.

He went on: "Somehow, when I found myself facing a sudden howling wind that stirred piles of old bones—it reminded me of this. Of the last time I, Apollo, saw Olympus—that was many years before Jeremy Redthorn was born. Oh, many years indeed."

But I paid little attention to what sounded like an old man's reminiscences, coming from the lips of a beardless youth. Instead I was caught up in trying to discover more marvels somewhere on the dusty, barren, flattened hilltop where we were now. Alas, that effort was doomed to disappointment.

Evidence of one kind and another, visible to us on every hand— broken glass and tile, shreds of what might once have been fine cloth— suggested that the site once known as Olympus had been raided, perhaps occupied for a long time, one way or another ruthlessly despoiled by Giants. Apollo told me that for years all the gods and goddesses had been afraid to show their faces there. And then, what was worse, almost all of them had totally forgotten.

I shuddered faintly, inwardly. For the moment, Jeremy Redthorn seemed to have disappeared, and it was the Sun God, the Far-Worker, who walked with me around the blasted mountaintop. But he was still a mentally crippled deity. As we progressed, he sometimes thought he saw the remnants of familiar landmarks, but in no case could he be really sure.

For a time, Apollo sat on a rock with his face buried in his hands. When he looked up, it was to tell me that before the Giants' first onslaught, this had been a place of surpassing beauty.

"I gathered that much, Lord Apollo, from what you have already said."

He sighed. "Memories are coming back, a little at a time. Do you know anything of that war, Hercules?"

"Nothing, my lord—nothing, Jeremy."

My companion did not seem to be listening, or to care which name I addressed him by. He said softly: "It must be a thousand years. But if I stop now, and close my eyes, I can almost hear the music again . . ."

And to my amazement—though I really should not have been amazed—I saw tears on his young face.

19

Downed

MY RECENT ADVENTURES had wearied me, in mind more than in body, and left me profoundly confused. In the course of the last few days I had confronted the awesome deity Apollo, had almost incurred his enmity, and then had finally joined forces with him. Together Apollo and I had rescued Prometheus, and then had managed, or at least survived, an encounter with the entity called Atlas. *That* meeting in itself would have been enough to befuddle me. But when it was over I had been privileged to walk beside the Far-Worker as his comrade while he rediscovered and explored the ruins of Olympus.

The two of us left Olympus together, once more riding the chariot, cruising at low altitude behind slow-pacing horses. At first it seemed to me that we had no definite destination.

I could only hope that my experiences since leaving home had begun to teach me something about the world. Certainly they had begun to reveal to me the depth and breadth of my own ignorance. Physical strength could give a great advantage, and sometimes it could be vitally important. But I had begun to realize that it did not guarantee success in any but the crudest trials.

Very little of the knowledge I had gained so recently and with such difficulty was reassuring. In fact, the more I learned about the world, the more I felt that it was on the verge of collapsing around me, and I was not sure what to do next.

Looking back over my shoulder, I cast a last look at the rugged slopes of what had once been high Olympus.

Apollo's mood seemed to mirror my own, a readiness for rest and reflection.

As we were crossing a small stream, he turned the chariot and brought it down for a soft landing on the grassy bank. Getting out, I promptly sat down in the grass, feeling tired in body and mind.

Apollo said he would be back very soon, clucked to his magnificent white horses, and drove away.

The appearance of the surrounding land struck me as restfully neutral. It was less barren than the hills we had just left, but there were no rich crops or lush forests to be seen. The scenery was soothing rather than dramatic, with gentle hills of grazing land and a few trees here and there. Such surroundings were peaceful after the wonders I had just experienced. It seemed an undemanding spot, and I welcomed the opportunity to relax.

I dozed off, but could not have been sleeping for very long when I heard the soft rushing sound of the chariot moving through the air, and opened my eyes to discover that my companion had returned. He brought welcome food and drink, both of a quality worthy of the gods. Then we rested for a time, well out of sight of the place that had been Olympus, and well away from the immediate effects, which had been greater on my companion than they were on me, of our encounter with Atlas.

While resting, Apollo and I compared notes on what we had seen and experienced there.

We came to the conclusion that nothing Atlas had told us had any direct bearing on the outcome of the gods' struggle against the Giants—except possibly we now had evidence confirming our enemies' earthly origins.

When we had reached that point in our discussion, the Far-Worker repeated his advice that I should pay a visit to the laboratory where Daedalus and Hephaestus were working with the materials that I had gathered for them.

"I am ready to do so, Lord Apollo—Jeremy. Where is it?"

He gestured with the piece of fruit that he was eating. "On a secret island, far to the north of here. Let us rest a little, and we'll go. They will certainly want to hear everything we can tell them about Prometheus and the strange encounter we had with Atlas. I don't doubt they'll have many questions to ask. Anyway, I have an urge to see the very latest achievements of the wizards on their island."

When we had finished our repast, the Far-Worker leaped into his car and grabbed the reins. He gestured to me, and I climbed aboard.

———

Once more the earth swiftly fell away beneath us. As we flew, my escort told me that the two wizards of technology, one divine and one human, were anxious to talk to me as soon as possible.

"Daedalus will want to know whether you managed to gather any new samples while you were having your encounter with Atlas."

"I would as soon have tried to take a sample of some god's hide as to dig into that little pillar. I consider myself lucky to have come away from that meeting with my life. All I gained was—the experience."

"That can be the most valuable prize of all."

My companion told me that my mentors yearned more than ever to fathom the mysteries of the enemy's weapon that robbed gods of their memories.

"I would not be surprised if Atlas was equipped with even more marvelous weapons than that," I told him. "But I saw nothing of any of them."

———

The god and I continued our discussion as the chariot carried us along.

We were flying over land, just above a patchy layer of thin clouds, and the god who was transporting me was talking to me about something when he was cut off abruptly in midsentence.

The chariot swerved suddenly, and I had the impression that some gigantic, invisible hand had swiped at us, almost knocking us out of the sky—for a moment I did not understand that the only real impact we had suffered came from some Giant's magic weapon, which was felt in Apollo's mind, and from there transmitted through his hands and the reins to his great white horses.

I thought that Apollo was able to recognize our attacker, for he cried out a name: "Alkyoneus!"

Even as we lurched about in midair, my eye fell on a towering figure that stood on a hilltop hundreds of feet below us. It was a Giant, both arms raised, fingers extended and pointing straight at us. This was Antaeus writ large, the tufted hair, blank eyes, and grainy skin, equal to the worst my imagination might have done. I stared at a figure of the same almost-human shape as the Giant I had killed, standing among trees as if they were small bushes, kilted in what seemed a patchwork sail of animal skins, but enlarged, engorged, to what appeared in my shocked eyes as a height of perhaps a hundred feet.

In a moment the weapon struck again, an invisible club whose impact seemed to be felt only in my companion's brain. Nothing happened to affect the chariot directly, nor the wondrous animals who bore it after them, nor even me, the helpless passenger. But this time the blow to the god's memory was severe enough to make him lose all control. His hands jerked awkwardly at the reins, as if he had no idea of what he ought to do with them.

My escort was now clinging to the rail as desperately as I was. Apollo turned a strangely distorted countenance in my direction and was looking at me wildly, as if he had never seen me before. As if he did not know who I was, what we might be doing together, or where we were going.

I grabbed him by the arm and tried to shake him, but it was like gripping a marble statue.

In the next few moments it became plain that he had utterly lost control over his chariot. It seemed that he could only stare stupidly as the ground came rushing up at us.

As in my battle with Antaeus, I was not directly affected by the weapon, or curse, or whatever the right name was for the thing that struck at us. But now it seemed quite possible that I was going to die anyway.

As we spiraled lower, I was able to get one last clear look at the man-mountain who had shot us down. His great, slab-sided, rock-grained face was as blank in triumph as I supposed it would have been in defeat.

———

Now we were so close above the treetops that from time to time the chariot's wheels tore at a branch. My last glimpse of the Giant showed him walking, his huge body moving with surprising quickness, as he attempted to get in one more invisible shot. I had the impression that he was uncertain of his aim, and I could only hope that this time he would miss.

Looking at the form beside me, I saw to my horror that my god-pilot had temporarily lost consciousness. I again tried to rouse him, but failed.

The magic team that pulled the chariot still retained their full strength. But the injury to their great master had upset them, thrown them into a panic. We were flying low now, barely skimming the tree-tops, and still performing wild gyrations.

I grasped the reins and tried to exert control. I shouted commands at the backs of the great plunging beasts that pulled us through the air, but the animals ignored me. I might have pulled harder, but feared that if I did so, I was going to break their necks.

In seizing the reins, I had released my two-handed grip upon the railing. As the chariot swayed back and forth, scraping tall branches in a wild ride, a sharp turn suddenly hurled me out over the side. At the last moment I grabbed desperately for something solid, but the whole equipage was already far out of my reach.

My body was as helpless as a falling doll, but fortunately somewhat tougher. Shielding my face with my hands, I crashed violently through a screen of branches, then bounced off a trunk to hit the ground. Any normal human would almost certainly have been killed by the successive impacts, but I suffered no serious damage and a moment later was getting to my feet, feeling only a few sore spots.

———

Trees stood close to me on every side, the branches of the nearest showing new white wood, splintered by the shock of my fall. The forest had swallowed me up. Flocks of disturbed birds were racketing around over the treetops; but attacking Giant, wounded god, and speeding chariot were all out of sight and sound. As far as I could tell from where I lay, they might never have existed.

And on top of all my other problems, my club was gone. Either it had remained in the chariot, and so was possibly many miles away by now, or it had been thrown out and there was no telling where it had come down—in either case, there was little hope of finding one small log in a dense forest, and I was going to have to do without it. Partly to settle my nerves, and partly because I did not know what else to do, I began to make myself a new one.

Finding a sturdy trunk of suitable wood took some time, and so did shaping it to the right size, using only my bare hands; but when it was done I had regained a measure of control over my destiny.

Now I thought it was time to reconnoiter. On a slight rise in the forest I found a promising-looking tree and climbed it to scan the sky and the horizon for signs of Apollo and his chariot—or for the Giant, who I swore would suffer grievously for his ambush if I could catch up with him. But nothing was visible but trees and more trees. After the high-speed flight and its sudden unplanned ending, I really had no idea where in the world I was.

My first act, on finding myself in this situation, was an amateur's attempt at magic, trying to summon *Skyboat* to me. I closed my eyes and concentrated fervently on the vessel as I had seen it last, in a place that must now be many miles away.

I had no reason to believe that I was anywhere near a river, or the sea. Even if *Skyboat* responded to my call, there was no reason to believe that I would see the vessel again for many days. I was going to have to find my way on foot out of this trackless forest.

I also tried to imagine the humming presence of the invisible sprite, and call it to me that I might employ it as a messenger; but I was unpracticed in all matters of magic and could not be sure I had succeeded.

The only map of the world that I could visualize was, I feared, too woefully inaccurate to be of any use. My travels, since that distant day when I was sent out to herd cattle, had already convinced me that my early tutors had taught me practically nothing about real geography, especially with regard to those parts of the world that lay at any substantial distance from Cadmia.

It would obviously be hopeless for me to press on and try to reach Vulcan's secret laboratory, as I had not the least idea where it was. Even in my confusion, it was obvious that regaining my homeland, or even Corycus, would entail another long journey, and something of a weary one, as it seemed likely I would be compelled to do it all on foot.

After several days of almost aimless wandering, during which I saw few people, had little to eat, and gained no clear idea of where I was, I found myself crossing a small stream, which as it turned out represented a border between kingdoms. As I waded out of the stream and on the eastern side, I found myself confronted by a warning sign. The message, in several languages, was carved into a broad wooden panel, which in turn had been nailed conspicuously to a tree.

KNOW BY THESE PRESENTS
THAT ALL MEN ARE FORBIDDEN ENTRY HERE
by order of
HER ROYAL MAJESTY MOCTOD
QUEEN OF THE AMAZONS

This suggested rather forcefully that I ought to consider turning back. But over the last few days I had come to believe, though my grounds for doing so were not very strong, that the Great Sea lay in the direction I had been walking, and that my *Skyboat* might very well be cruising through it even now, drawing closer to me at every moment. If that was indeed the case, swift transportation might be awaiting me only a few miles deep in Amazon territory, along the coast, or up a river.

The sign confirmed what legend had long held, that the Amazons did not much care especially for men, except as occasional partners in sex or commerce. But still I dared to hope that a lone traveler, unarmed and hungry, might be charitably received.

Of course I could hardly be considered unarmed as long as I was carrying my huge new club. But I had invested some time and effort in its making, and I decided to wait at least until I was challenged before throwing it away.

So I boldly crossed the river, and shortly after met a lone woman, rather elderly, gathering firewood. When I asked directions, she told me I had now entered a land called Themiscyra, on the river Thermodon, and if I followed the river downstream I would come in a few days to a good-sized city. While telling me these things my informant stared at me as if she had never seen a man before. Perhaps she was intimidated by the sight of my huge weapon; in any case, she made no objection to my presence.

Taking the downstream path, on the theory that it must lead me eventually to sea, I soon encountered a shrine to Diana, standing at the next river ford. This gave me strong confirmation that I was really in the land of the Amazons.

I had long known, in a vague way, as everyone did, that the Amazons were worshipers of Artemis. (That goddess, as everyone knew, was generally identified with Diana, traditionally thought to be the twin sister of Apollo. Legend called her a virgin huntress who carried Arrows and a Spear, was of a vindictive nature, and enjoyed a close association with the Moon.) If I could get the backing of Artemis/Diana, in some convincing way, then the warrior ladies ought to be cooperative.

It was true that most humans lived their entire lives without ever encountering a god. But since beginning my wanderings, I had personally met several, and so far had had good results. So perhaps it was not strange that I began to nurse hopes of somehow confronting the goddess Diana, in this the land of her worshipers, and then making her my friend by claiming acquaintance with her twin brother.

Somehow, in this later time when I am writing, certain legends have twisted the facts around to say that my trip to the country of the Amazons was a deliberate foray, undertaken to capture the girdle of their queen.

I find it hard to understand how my obtaining this garment would have inconvenienced the Giants, mighty enemies of the gods, in any way. And now, as long as the subject has come up, it strikes me that this might be the time to review the whole business of my supposed Twelve labors. These are tasks which are often said to have been imposed on me—the gods alone know why—by King Eurystheus. The list is given differently in different sources, but the following sequence is widely accepted.

1. Slaying the Nemean lion, whose skin I was supposed to have worn ever afterward. I feel I have already discussed this at sufficient length.
2. Slaying the nine-headed Hydra of Lerna. I have said how this came about, and how, because there were credible witnesses, my fame began to grow.
3. Capturing of the Hind (in some accounts the Stag) of Arcadia. Purely fictional. In this case, legend, unadulterated by any facts at all, provided this stag with antlers of gold and hooves of brass, and sent me chasing it for a full year in a determined effort to bring it back alive.
4. The wild Boar of Mount Erymanthus. In this tale, as in the next item on the list, there was a good deal of truth.
5. Cleansing the Augean stables.
6. Shooting the monstrous man-eating birds of the Stymphalian marshes. The second purely imaginary adventure in the list. The story may have been based on a dream I once endured, though how the stuff of private dreams could be transmitted into legend is more than I can fathom, unless someone with the talents of Prince Asterion might have been responsible.
7. Capturing of a mad bull that had terrorized Corycus. A very twisted transformation of my activities in cooperation with the prince.
8. Ditto the man-eating mares of King Diomedes of the Bistones. Some authorities on my career omit this tale altogether, as well they might. I believe Enkidu in his own memoirs classifies it,

correctly, as mere legend. Certainly unnaturally carnivorous horses (possibly something to do with centaurs) were supposed to be the property of the Thracian king, Diomedes. And I, in an effort to inflict condign punishment, fed the mares Diomedes himself.

9. Seizing the girdle of Hyppolyte, queen of the Amazons. Most sources even name the wrong queen here. I am shortly going to introduce Her Majesty Moctod into my narrative; let me only add here, parenthetically, that the gods never really favored the idea of my marrying and settling down—I was too useful to them as a footloose adventurer. On the other hand, the Titans would probably have supported my adopting a sedentary lifestyle, had they been consulted.

10. Seizing the cattle of the three-bodied (alternately, three-headed) Giant named Geryon, supposed to live in the island of Erythia, somewhere in the remote west. On my way to pillage Geryon of his cows, I supposedly strangled one Cacus, a three-headed shepherd who puffed flames and lived in a cave decorated with the bones of his victims. A number of factual events seem to be confabulated in this adventure, along with some creditably artistic lies; disentangling them would take more time than I am willing to devote to the subject.

11. Bringing back (I think to King Eurytheus) the Golden Apples kept at the world's end by the three sisters called Hesperides. We have already seen something of the real Apples, and will see more. I think this needs no further comment from me, except that the king in his bronze box would not have had the faintest idea what to do with them.

12. Fetching up Cerberus from the Underworld. We will soon come to the basis of this tale.

It was said of Queen Moctod and her followers that they kept a few men around as servants; that at designated times they sought out strangers and lay with them to accomplish the reproduction of their race. Boy babies resulting from these unions would be sacrificed, or given for adoption to neighboring tribes. Each young girl suffered the amputation of one breast—generally the left, presumably in early childhood—to facilitate the use of the bow.

An alternate version was that every girl was required to kill a man before she was allowed to take a husband. My own thought was that women meeting this qualification might soon face a real shortage of prospective bridegrooms.

———

Early on in my visit to the Amazons' country, I observed some evidence that other male adventurers had recently intruded in this space presumably reserved for women only, and even that some of my own sex were still on the scene.

One distant figure, dark-bearded and almost breastless, labored in a field, guiding a plow pulled by a cameloid. Almost certainly a man, I thought, but very possibly a slave.

The only children to be seen were girls. If there were any pregnant warriors about, they seemed to be making an effort not to appear in public.

Evidence of a more recent intrusion could be seen in the occasional glimpses I had of wounded women warriors, limping, or nursing the stumps of missing arms or legs; and once I saw in the distance what appeared to be a funeral, but whether the death might have been a result of recent combat I had no way to tell.

Again, I once glimpsed on a stout limb of a distant tree three dead bodies, hanging by their necks. Whether men or women I could not distinguish at the distance, but they might have been three pirates when they walked and breathed.

It seemed to me distinctly possible that the rule against men, like many other rules in many other lands, was not strictly enforced, and as I have mentioned, some adult males, probably slaves, were in fact to be seen. Also I could imagine exceptions being made for merchants or skilled workers.

There were also the charred remnants of some ship to be seen, along a muddy riverbank, and the painted symbol still visible on certain planks suggested it had been a pirate vessel. This was of course encouraging in that it suggested I was somewhat closer to the sea than I had thought.

———

The weather was mild, and sleeping out of doors posed no problem to an experienced traveler. Water was plentifully available, but food was another matter, and before long I was ravenously hungry.

Almost the only people I saw anywhere, at least for the first several days, were women, who did (or at least officially claimed to do) all the heavy work of farming and hunting. Of course it was hardly unknown in my own land, or any other, that females should perform these tasks, but it was strange to see no men at all. An ignorant stranger, coming on the scene, might have supposed that the entire male population had been wiped out in some war. Which, when I thought about it, seemed possibly the truth.

***

Not until I had been several days in the territory of the Amazons was I challenged by an armed patrol—and I was lacking any *Skyboat* in which to flee from them.

I was facing in the other direction when I heard a shrill voice call: "Over here, girls. Looks like another of that damned gang of pirates."

Other voices responded, and there was a general trampling and crashing in the underbrush. Presently nine sturdy figures came into view to stand with weapons ready, gazing at my solitary figure.

"You're right. I thought we'd seen the last of 'em, but here's another."

All of the women confronting me were young, vigorous, and well armed. They wore a kind of uniform consisting of short skirts and sandals, and each was bound across her upper body with a kind of sash that covered the right breast, passing also across a flattened area that showed the left had been removed.

Unhappily I considered the one-breasted warriors and their spears and arrows. They all looked lithe and agile, and I doubted very much that I would be able to outrun the slowest of them. Most carried bows, and each had a short shield, shaped like a halfmoon and dabbed with gilt paint, as well as a sword. The fact that I had dropped my club voluntarily kept them from trying to cut me down at once. Meanwhile I thought I might be able to retrieve the weapon later, and that the lack would mean no more than an inconvenience.

The patrol commander barked again: "One more damned pirate. We know how to deal with your kind!"

"I hope so, ma'am," I assured her. "But I have my doubts."

When I thought about it, I could hardly blame them for their mistake. If I was not a pirate, where was the ship that had brought me across the sea? Anyway, I looked more like a pirate than a merchant. I did not attempt to disabuse them of this notion, calculating that there was no chance they might believe the truth.

As you might expect, I prepared to strongly resist any attempt to take my life. It was my evident readiness to face their several blades that gave them pause, I think.

Raising both hands in what I hoped would be interpreted as a peaceful gesture, I said: "I consent to be your prisoner."

"You do? How noble of you!"

"If I am your prisoner, then it would seem that you ought to feed me."

"We should hang him right away!" The second in command decided briskly. I gathered that was what had happened to the last straggling pirate to be discovered.

They bound my hands at first, of course, and I allowed this on the theory that it might be easier to talk to them if they believed me to be quite helpless—alas, they paid no more attention to my peaceful protestations after my hands were trussed up than before.

Then they hoisted me up to sit on the back of a phlegmatic cameloid they were using as a pack animal, tossed a rope over an overhanging limb, and soon had a noose around my neck.

But of course, when they drove the cameloid out from under me they were disappointed with the result. There I was, hanging in midair as they intended, but a slight tensing of my neck muscles enabled me to keep on breathing easily enough and even to carry on my argument as to why they should let me pass freely through their territory. Not that the women were listening. But presently they cut me down, and were recoiling the rope in preparation for starting over when a superior officer arrived on the scene.

———

While this officer was receiving the report of the patrol leader, I renewed my worries about what might have happened to Apollo. But I could not be sure that the flying chariot had crashed, or where it might have come down. Possibly a hundred miles away.

Actually my hopes of being able to summon the *Skyboat* had grown somewhat brighter. It was encouraging news that some pirate ship had evidently been able to make it within a few miles of this spot, and gave me reason to hope that my little craft could approach even closer. Once *Skyboat* was positioned as near me as the sprite could bring it, it could lie there in its mode of concealment until the sprite found me again and guided me to my means of escape. But how much time must pass before the magic vessel might be able to accomplish this approach I could not guess.

———

And only now, for the first time, did they search me thoroughly, without finding additional weapons, or anything that might qualify as stolen treasure.

The officer now in charge made a sound of disgust at the failure to discover anything incriminating. "I'd say you threw away the tools of your trade as soon as you saw you were about to be caught. But it won't do you any good."

After a short discussion among the leaders, they agreed to keep me alive until their queen had had a chance to question me.

There was some discussion of binding and dragging me, but I saw no reason to put up with that, and laid hold of a stout tree trunk, this one rooted firmly in the soil, and would not be persuaded to let it go. Blows with fists and blunt instruments failed to make me change my mind.

One had her sword poised above my wrists when the officer ordered: "Don't hack him! It'll be easier to deliver him to the queen if he's all in one piece."

The fact that my would-be captors were all women was not what kept me from more violent resistance, but rather it was my reluctance to be drawn into a full-scale battle with any nation. Surely that would have to be a losing proposition for me in the end.

After several minutes of fruitless effort, their complete inability to pry me loose began to convince some of my captors—if that was indeed their status—that I was a god.

I got the impression that male gods would not be welcome in this land, any more than mortal men.

One stood back panting. "If he is a god, why doesn't he say so?" she demanded of her comrades.

"Just bring me to your queen," I kept on patiently repeating.

"Shut up! I'll cut off your head first, and bring her that!"

"You won't cut my head off. You can't. And if you could, I'd insult your queen by refusing to answer any of her questions."

Some took me for a madman, and some for a god, and others were quite ready to make an all-out effort to kill me first and then decide into which category I might fit best.

Again the possibility of real fighting loomed. One or two women I might have overpowered harmlessly, just as I had Hector the Trojan. But someone would be sure to get hurt in a general onslaught, with weapons waving and thrusting in every direction.

Eventually their contemptuous abuse began to make me angry. I said: "I have not killed women before, but I imagine you will die as easily as men." And I loudly regretted the fact that I had thrown away my club.

When they gave up trying to tear me loose from the tree, I let go of it and stood there flexing my arms and fingers, which were somewhat cramped, waiting to see what approach their commanding officer decided to try next. Fortunately she proved willing to be reasonable.

20

Amazons

I SOON REACHED the conclusion that the lands ruled by Queen Moctod could not be very large. When we reached the capital city of the women, I thought it surprisingly small, and the royal palace little more than a middle-sized fort. Fortunately word of my capture had already reached the queen, and she was curious to see me. When at last I stood before her, several days after being taken into custody, she looked me up and down, her expression a mixture of contempt and puzzlement. My hands were still unbound, and no doubt she found this odd. Meanwhile, the women who had brought me in were telling her that I was more impressive than I looked, but still the queen, naturally enough, failed to understand.

Having evidently just come from the practice field—or, I thought, perhaps from punishing some other band of pirates—she who faced me now was fully armed with a steel sword, a shield of bronze and wood and leather, and a helmet of fine workmanship. Not as hard, I was sure, as some of the fine helms I had seen, first on Amphitryon and on a number of others since, forged of black iron; but so beautiful of workmanship that I could see how it might be the superior choice to carry into combat, for the impressive effect that it would have on one's opponent.

The queen's size, her evident strength, and above all her attitude convinced me that she would be more than a match for most of the male warriors I had ever seen.

Moctod wore no binding on her upper body, and where her left breast ought to have been there was only an old, pale scar, so faint and puckered that I could well believe it resulted from a wound made in infancy. Her right breast was full and firm.

"Why did you not tie his hands?" she at last demanded sharply. The queen's voice was strong, in keeping with her appearance.

The patrol leader cleared her throat. "He made a lot of fuss when we tried that, Majesty. Whereas if we left him unbound, he was willing to walk along with us. . . ."

"Your prisoner 'made a fuss,' you say? So you asked him politely to walk along?"

My old antagonist seemed to wilt. Almost I was able to feel sorry for her. She said: "Actually we had to fight a sort of skirmish with him, ma'am."

"Almost a dozen of you, and he made it a fight? I don't think it could have been much of a skirmish, as none of you seems to have been wounded in the process."

The junior officer raised her hands and let them fall, a helpless gesture. "Ma'am, he is . . . very strong."

The queen raised her eyebrows and let them fall, as if to say that she was accustomed to having a lot of strange problems brought before her—that was all part of the job—and she felt quite capable of dealing with this situation, as she had with all the others.

" 'Very strong,' " she repeated the words under her breath, as if trying them as an incantation. Then Moctod looked at me and made an imperious gesture with one finger. "Come stand before me, outlander," she ordered. "What is your name?"

I did as I was bidden. "I am Hercules, Your Majesty. Hercules of Cadmia."

And I saw at once that my name meant nothing to the queen; celebrity was not going to be my problem in this country.

Moctod, now focusing an intense, blue-eyed gaze on me from under her steel helm, was an inch or two taller than I. People usually view extra height as conferring some kind of an advantage. I often do not take that viewpoint seriously.

The queen said: "You seem to have impressed my soldiers as a mighty fighter. They say you were carrying a club. Did you knock their swords out of their hands with it, or what?"

One of the fighting women was now carrying my improvised bludgeon over her strong right shoulder.

I shook my head. "Majesty, I voluntarily threw my club away when I encountered your patrol. At first I was even willing for my hands to be bound. I claim no skill at all in combat. I have never practiced with the sword, or even clubbed another human being."

"But you *are* very strong."

"Oh yes, ma'am, that is true enough."

The queen nodded slowly. "One of you loan him a sword and shield. I want to see a demonstration of this strength that so impressed my fighting women." And she drew her sword. "Do you think you are strong enough, Hercules, to keep me from killing you?"

"I am not afraid of being killed, Your Majesty."

And the queen, her voice sharpening, said: "Then perhaps you should learn a little fear. Just because it has not happened to you yet, you seem to think that it cannot. Let me tell you, men as a rule die very easily. I have proved that to my own satisfaction often enough."

There was a murmuring among the elder women who served as the queen's counselors; evidently my seeming bravery had already made something of an impression upon them.

Experience had convinced me that usually the fastest way to get past the difficulty of an unwelcome fight, or proposed test, was to appear ready, and even eager, to go through with it. Leaving the offered shield where it lay on the ground, I bent and picked up the sword, running my gaze over it as I did so, just as if I knew what I ought to be looking for. The blade looked keen and true, and I suppose it might have been as well made as the queen's own weapon. Then I stepped back and nodded to the queen, signifying that I was ready.

My opponent was angry now, of course; insulted that I had scorned to take the shield. But she was too experienced a warrior to take even the most unlikely-looking opponent for granted. She approached cautiously, circling first right, then left. The sword in her hand made feinting movements that I suppose were meant to provoke certain reactions in a trained fighter, but of course they were entirely wasted on my ignorance.

I was not minded to prolong the farce. Let her defend herself, I thought. Doing my best to convince without killing (which certainly would not have made my situation any easier), I struck with an overhand swing, applying what I hoped was a nicely calculated amount of force.

The queen had no need to move her half-moon shield, and caught the stroke on it quite neatly. But the impact, of course, was far beyond anything she had been expecting, or could possibly have been ready to withstand. Her shield, of tough leather bound with bronze, was cut nearly in half, the arm that held it dislocated at the shoulder, and any counterblow was rendered totally impossible. Her balance broken in an instant, the Amazon went staggering back to hit the ground in an ignominious fall. My borrowed sword had broken, the blade staying pinched in the ruined shield, while most of the handle remained in my hand.

A cry of shock and outrage went up from the watching circle. The ring of watching warriors first drew back, then raised their weapons and would have assaulted me en masse—but the queen, still on the ground, raised her voice and stopped them.

When the Amazon elders saw the strength of my sword arm, even those who had earlier favored killing me now entirely abandoned the idea—not, I think, out of fear, or serious doubt that they would be able to accomplish the job, but because I had suddenly become greatly desirable as the father of some of the next generation of female warriors. Now I understood what all the talk of testing had been about.

A babble of discussion rose up, then quieted almost at once. They were now universally agreed that I should be invited, or if necessary compelled, to stay on as an honored guest until I had impregnated at least several dozen women—what might be done with me after that still seemed an open question.

The queen, like any other serious warrior, was angry at having been bested. A physician had to be called to pop her dislocated joint back into place. But she bore the pain stoically, suppressed her personal feelings, and went along with what her people wanted.

It was up to Moctod to put the matter to me officially: "We invite you, Hercules of Cadmia, to live with us for a year, and in that time to get as many of us as possible with child."

I muttered some kind of a response, which was probably not as gracious as it could have been. Many young men would have wholeheartedly accepted such an offer on the spot, and indeed I felt tempted; but as matters stood, I had to be about my father's business. Still, an outright refusal would only have made my task more difficult. First of all, I wanted sleep and food.

But what response I made did not much matter, for no one was really listening. It was taken for granted that I was going to consent, whether I agreed or not. My new hosts pointed out a kind of villa, a large house with stuccoed walls and a peaked roof, built against a hillside, which they said would house me for the duration of my stay. Wearily I made my way in that direction. I was vaguely surprised, and amused, to see that now I was apparently going to be left unguarded. Either they could not imagine a man wanting to escape from confinement on such terms, or they could not imagine one succeeding.

As I approached the villa set against the hill, I heard, somewhere inside
the house, a deep voice singing. I could only hope that its owner was
not one of the women I was expected to impregnate.

A short, sturdy, rather ugly servant girl came to meet me at the
door, then stood back, gaping in surprise at the sight of an unfettered
man. A shrine to Diana, only a little smaller than the one beside the
border road, occupied most of the entryway of the house.

Investigating a little further, I discovered the singer and was relieved
of my latest worry. He was wrapped in a silken robe and relaxing on a
pile of pillows, and courteously enough he stood up to say hello. He
was a handsome man, too youthful for any gray to have come into his
fair hair and beard, though sun and wind had started to carve lines in
his face. He was tall enough to tower over the servant girl and me. Had
he introduced himself as a god, many would have taken him at his word
without an argument; but in fact he said that he was Theseus, and acknowledged that he had come to the land of the Amazons as leader of
a pirate expedition that had proved a trifle too ambitious.

"I've heard your name," I offered. I did not doubt this introduction
for a moment; this, indeed, was how the famous Theseus ought to look.

"Most people have." He smiled faintly. "I trust you heard nothing
too good associated with it."

"You can feel at ease about that. Nothing in your record as it was
told to me would make me envious. Mainly tales of piracy."

Theseus laughed at that and seemed well satisfied that it should be
so. He, too, as it turned out, had been invited to stay among the Amazons, for the same reason as myself. He said he had been on the job a
month and thought he was already well along in his task of siring a new
generation of warriors. When I asked what had happened to his men,
his face darkened, and he did not reply at once. It seemed to me that it
would be unwise to pursue the subject, and I let it drop.

Theseus was obviously wondering why *I* had been recruited for the
stud farm. Nor did it take him long to put the question plainly. He
squinted at me thoughtfully, looked me up and down, and scratched his
bearded chin. "I wonder why they gave you such a special invitation,
sprout?"

I smiled faintly and stuck out my hand. "Try a turn of arm wrestling?"

He looked at me in some surprise, then shrugged. "Don't mind if I
do."

Several turns were necessary, the result of the first being put down
to some kind of unmanly magic or trickery. It was even necessary to

squeeze his hand a little to finally make my point. But once it had been made, Theseus accepted it philosophically.

———

Ten minutes later, the two of us were sitting side by side on a comfortable couch in the main room of the guest house, sipping cool drinks brought by the servant girl (yes, said my new colleague, she was one of those selected for breeding purposes; he supposed one of us would get around to her, in time) and having a peaceable discussion.

"Understand, Hercules, that in the first place, these women are not, on the average, anywhere near my ideal of feminine beauty. I've seen one or two, here and there . . . and one in particular . . . but the ones they keep sending to my bed to be plowed and planted aren't. In the second place, whatever other merits some of these girls might have, it grows monotonous when a man finds only half the usual number of breasts available for his enjoyment." Unconsciously he had begun massaging his own right hand, the one that I had squeezed.

"I understand," I said. To me also it had seemed likely that the largest and strongest Amazons, rather than the most attractive, would be selected for our attentions. Vaguely I wondered whether there would be many eager volunteers. And of course politics would play some part, as it always seemed to do.

I went on: "I, too, find the prospect of a long stay in these parts not all that alluring."

It turned out that Theseus, too, had fought a duel with the queen. He complained that it was never in actual combat that he lost out, but in the complications that arose when people were trying to make peace.

"I'll admit it to you, Hercules—I had a long struggle, trying to put her down without doing her any serious harm. Of course I managed it in the end, but I have no doubt that in a fair fight, one on one, she'd kill nine out of ten of my men; and my men are—were—hardly milksops. Maybe even nineteen out of twenty."

From the moment that Theseus had spoken his name to me, I had been ready to dislike him, knowing his ill repute for vile deeds as a pirate—there was no doubt that in his case it was justly earned. Another reason to feel aversion for him, if any were needed, was that in appearance, Theseus was everything I would have liked to be, tall and handsome with bulging muscles and graceful movements—sort of a blond, sun-bleached Jason. I could well imagine that the new warriors he sired for the queen would match the very Amazon ideal.

But at the same time, he gained my respect by refusing to either be afraid of me or fawn on me, even after he felt my strength. In this he was unlike those so-called heroes of the Argosy, or at least that faction among them who had resorted to base trickery to get me off the ship.

Another matter that Theseus and I discussed was to what extent we were really prisoners. As far as he could see, he told me, the house was completely unguarded, and no one followed him when he walked out of it and strolled about. No specific rules had been spelled out to either of us, but we were both certain that any attempt on our part to leave would have been strongly discouraged.

Our peaceable conversation was soon interrupted by another young woman, whose name, as I soon learned, was Antiope—she was the "one in particular" he had mentioned earlier. Antiope had originally been one of the pirate's assigned bed partners (and, according to my taste, much better-looking than the average of them) who, while playing her as-signed role, had fallen desperately in love with the handsome intruder. She was obviously quite willing to be abducted by him.

When he caught sight of her looking in at us, he called: "Come in, sweet one. This is Hercules, he's just arrived."

My name meant no more to Antiope than it had to Moctod. She looked from one of us to the other, and appeared pleased. "I see that you are friends," she commented.

"We're working at it, honey," said Theseus, and kissed her.

Antiope adopted a friendly attitude toward me as soon as it became apparent that I posed no threat to her beloved. And when Theseus strongly hinted that I was not to consider her as one of my own clients in our joint fertility program, I assured him that I would take no girl or woman to my bed who was unwilling to be there.

With these points settled, the three of us conversed as friends. I found myself rather liking Antiope and silently hoping that the man she now adored would not desert her, if the pair of them did succeed in getting away to the great world.

Theseus talked for a while about what might happen to any of his crew who still survived, if he escaped on his own. But it seemed prac-tically certain they were all dead.

———

I am not sure how many warriors I actually fathered for Moctod, but quite possibly there were several. However, the number cannot be vast.

———

Not many days after my arrival, the sprite whose arrival I had been hoping for came in secret to me at night, making its presence known when I was alone in bed. The creature seemed as incapable of speech as ever, but I took its cheerful buzzing to mean that the *Skyboat* was conveniently nearby—or at least as near as it was going to get by water—and that the sprite would somehow guide me to it when I was ready.

I told Theseus nothing of this visitor but, when the two of us were alone, let him understand that I had some magical reason to believe the time had come.

No doubt it was my strength that made him consider me trustworthy. He and I made our getaway from the Amazons in a cooperative effort.

He began to outline a plan that would have involved killing to get our hands on a boat, but I strongly urged that we do no harm, if we could avoid it, to any of the women—I reminded my colleague that there was no point in offending Diana unnecessarily by injuring her worshipers. I also let my companion know I had reason to believe that we would find a boat available.

With these facts in mind, my nonviolent method was adopted. Rising from our respective beds in the middle of the night, we joined Antiope, who had made her own way to the rendezvous and was waiting for us with provisions. The three of us then headed into the hills, in the direction of the nearest stream that was big enough to carry a small boat. If anyone had seen us, Antiope would have played the role of slave master, conducting two docile males to some new farmland where there were plows for them to pull.

———

To my great relief, my sprite had materialized again on cue and kept buzzing invisibly in my ear, so softly that no one else was aware of the inhuman presence. Naturally Theseus was curious as to how I could know that a boat would be waiting in a certain place. But he was ever ready to take a chance.

As we trod our way as silently as possible through the moonlit woods, I thought Antiope was quietly but almost hysterically happy at the thought of having her lover to herself, away from all those other women, for as many days and nights as the two of them might choose. I thought her a lovely creature, even if she had only one breast. And she had fallen desperately in love with Theseus and was eager to get away. Again, I hoped that he would treat her kindly.

———

I have no doubt that had Theseus still possessed even a remnant of a crew, he would have considered it essential to his honor, and to his reputation as a commander, to recapture his ship somehow. He would also have made a valiant effort, at least, to get his crew out of captivity and take them along. But as matters stood, he had only himself to look out for.

———

Gray dawn was lightening the sky when we reached the bank of a small river. "There she is," I said, and pointed.

When Theseus got his first look at the *Skyboat,* I let him think that it was the means by which I had come traveling to Amazon country. Not that the question of my mode of travel, of no immediate practical value, concerned him much.

At the first sight of the little craft, he had no high opinion of it—but when we three climbed aboard and it began to move, even before we had so much as touched a sail or oar, that was a different matter.

The way we went skipping and darting down small streams, even harmlessly through rapids, to plunge triumphantly into the sea at last, soon convinced the master pirate that there was more to this mode of transportation than at first met the eye.

For once Theseus was almost at a loss for speech. But finally he said: "I swear, Hercules. Ordinarily, I'd be sorely tempted to take a boat like this one away from its owner, whoever that might be. But I'll make an exception in your case." He showed white teeth in a smile. "Of course one reason, though not the only one, is that you'd break most of my bones if I tried anything like that." And he threw back his head and laughed with an infectious joy.

"I can show you another reason, too," I said. "Take the helm for a moment; give it a try."

Impressive as was the outward appearance of our compass-pyx, the experienced captain soon discovered that our vessel was no better than a small and barely seaworthy rowboat when it came under his command. The box of ivory and ebony lay inert against his forehead. Only Enkidu besides myself had been entrusted with the power of control, and my nephew, I supposed, was still peacefully at home. Where now I, in truth, fervently wished to be. I had had enough, and more than enough, of adventuring for the time being.

Soon after leaving the land of the Amazons, the pirate king and I separated, still under conditions of mutual respect. I put my pair of passengers ashore on an island of his choosing, on the margin of the Great Sea, from which he seemed supremely confident of being able to make his way to anywhere he wished. And we parted wishing each other success in our respective endeavors.

Antiope gave me a brief wave and then fixed her gaze once more on the man beside her, the one she so adored.

I set my course for home, as well as I was able.

21

Thanatos

IT HAS BEEN my fate, in common with the great majority of human-kind, to meet Death on the surface of the earth. What made my case out of the ordinary was the fact that my first encounter with Thanatos was not my last. As I write these words, I believe that the final con-frontation between the two of us is yet to be. I have heard some say that I am now truly immortal, but in human minds and mouths that word has as many meanings as does human life itself.

But let me tell things in their proper order. The first occasion on which I stood face-to-face with Death (I am here using no mere figure of speech) took place some time before I ever managed to force an entry to the Underworld.

When, in the course of my laborious return alone from the realm of the Amazons, I sailed my *Skyboat* along the coast of the land called Pherae, I found that my reputation had somehow preceded me. It was a fair land, displaying many signs of prosperity, and none at all of recent war.

On most of the islands where I stopped, and in the coastal villages, many people recognized my name and stood back from me in awe. But here and there a few were ready to challenge me to a fight, just for the sake of challenge; and some of these, seeing my youth and unimpressive size, and the fact that my body bore no scars, refused to believe I could be the hero who had slain the Hydra, crushed the ribs of mighty An-taeus, and clubbed to death the sea monster that would otherwise have devoured a Trojan princess. Such would-be rivals I usually managed to put off with soft words and a steady gaze, though one or two required a firmer hand. With a sigh I acknowledged the fact that the days when I could wander the earth in carefree anonymity were gone, and would never return, unless I began to travel in disguise.

———

When the people I spoke to along the way told me that I had reached the realm of King Admetus, my spirits rose. Here I ought to find at least a friendly welcome. Many days ago I had learned, indirectly, by word of mouth from various folk, that I was formally invited to visit King Admetus and his queen, at their court, in a town described as being "below the peak called Chalcodon."

The invitation reached me first when I was in Cadmia, dallying with my new bride, and it had been carried there in a somewhat garbled form. I pondered at the time whether the invitation might be some result of my having saved Hesione from the sea monster, or whether there existed some alliance between these people and the grateful folk at Troy, who might still be trying to find some way to reward me.

The truth, as I discovered later, was somewhat simpler and had little to do with any personal reputation I might have gained: Every member of the original crew of *Argo,* along with their immediate families, was included in the invitation. At least one of Jason's heroes was a native of Pherae.

While I am again on the subject of the Argosy, I should mention that there have been for some years several lists of those names, all differing in detail. Each nation, sometimes it seems each city, puts forward a compilation in which its own representative is prominent. There is inevitably dispute about who joined Jason's crew and when, and who dropped out or died along the way. In some of these rosters, you will find the name of King Admetus himself, which is a mistake.

———

Imagine, then, my dismay at arriving at the court of Admetus only to find that the whole capital city, if not the entire nation, was in mourning and disarray. The grief the people showed was obviously genuine, and disfigured almost every face. The palace, like many other buildings in the city, was draped in swaths of black, and I entered its precincts to the sound of harsh gongs beaten intermittently. Meanwhile the air, indoors and out, was thick with bitter smoke and a fine drift of ashes from the sacrificial fires.

However, the prospect was not one of unrelieved gloom on my part. I had scarcely arrived when I saw a vision which lifted my thoughts momentarily out of the realm of death and sorrow—Deianeira, the sister of Meleager.

Several other guests happened to be present when I arrived in the torchlit courtyard, and my eyes studying the small group immediately picked out green eyes, straight brown hair, and a slender female body, clad in the finest of translucent linen.

I approached Danni at once, and we exchanged friendly greetings— like all other conversation in the palace, less cheerful than they might have been, because of the funereal atmosphere.

"Is it Fate that brings us together, or only chance?" I asked, when we had gone through the customary forms of speech and handclasps.

But Danni had little interest in such questions. Hardly had she greeted me before she was asking if I could tell her any news of Meleager—naturally she had not seen him since the day I pitched him into the harbor at Iolcus, and she had thought that Mel was still with me and the others on the Argosy.

I expressed my regret that I could not give her any news about her brother. In turn she told me that she had come here to the court of King Admetus in response to the general invitation. She was the only representative of Meleager's family who could make the trip.

"My uncle Augeus was unable to leave home, or so he claimed, and we agreed it would be rude for no one of our family to appear. So, here I am."

"And I am glad you came, and that your uncle stayed home."

I learned that the ship that had brought her to Pherae was in the harbor beside my boat. And I was attracted to her at once, though instead of declaring the fact I told her about my marriage.

When Danni heard that, she mentioned, almost casually, that since our last meeting she had been betrothed, to one of her uncle's neighbors, an arrangement for which her uncle had been responsible. But the elderly neighbor had died before the marriage could be solemnized.

"My condolences," I offered.

There was a flash of something bitter in the green eyes. "You may save them for another time. It was a fortunate escape for me."

"In that case, my congratulations."

Our talk turned to the Argosy again, about which many rumors swirled. I now told Danni the story of how I had become separated from her brother and the rest, and she hoped that Meleager had not been involved in what had amounted to my nephew's kidnapping.

"How unfair of them!" she declared. "Are you much saddened, Hercules, to have been left behind, to have missed all their glorious adventures?"

"I have had little time to think about what adventures they might be having. My own life has not been exactly dull."

After some polite conversation with the other guests, I took Danni aside for a more private talk. At the moment I was less interested in telling her my history than in hearing more of hers.

When we were quite alone, she said to me: "My uncle Augeus is insisting that I move in permanently with him. Everyone says it is unseemly for a young unmarried woman to be maintaining her own household."

"I wouldn't want to live with your uncle," I observed.

"Nor do I, and so far I've managed to put him off. My worst fear is that he will get tired of waiting for Mel to come back, and decide to arrange yet another betrothal for me."

That would be tragic, I thought. But the funereal gloom of the real tragedy with which we were surrounded cut short our discussion of other matters. "What has happened here?" I demanded in a lowered voice, waving my hand to include the courtyard and the palace.

Danni was not yet certain, either. But the question was answered by one of the minor court officials when he realized we did not know. "Woe to us all! Our lovely queen is dead!"

Any coherent information on the cause of death was hard to come by, and details were impossible. Contradictory reports were circulating. Yet the main point was inescapable: The beloved young queen was dead. Tragedy had struck the royal family less than a full day ago, and the news was only now being carried by the outlying portions of the realm. Yet tradition, as inflexible here as in many other places, decreed that an appointment made with foreign visitors must be kept.

When the king at last made his appearance, the look on the face of our royal host was so lost, so doomed, that I could not keep from bursting out: "My lord king—my greatest sympathy!"

Admetus turned his gaze in my direction, but he seemed to be looking through me—not out of rudeness, but in pain. He was young. I suppose no older than his wife had been, and seldom have I seen anyone so nearly bereft of his wits by grief. Now I could see that tears were glistening on his bearded cheeks. It was hard for him to choke out even a few words.

"My wife, my queen—is dead."

We all hastened to offer such condolences as we were able. I said to him again: "Majesty, my heartfelt sympathy! Is there anything I can do to ease your pain?"

But the king could say no more at the moment, and abandoned himself once more to quiet weeping.

The traditional feast of welcome, a form required by rigid local custom, was of course no feast at all. Indeed it was a meal in name only, as a succession of elaborate dishes came to the table and were taken away again untouched by any who sat there. Dancers and musicians there were none, but only the harsh sound of the distant gongs at random intervals.

As soon as custom and courtesy allowed, the king arose, murmured a few indistinguishable words, and retreated to his quarters.

At that the gathering broke up. Moments later, I, too, had risen from my chair. We were told that the king would see us again, later in the evening; meanwhile, we were free to move about the palace.

Having located the room where I was to spend the night, I joined the other guests in wandering, and fell in with Danni and a young girl serving as her attendant.

At any other time, the royal art collection would have made a considerable impression, but now our minds were too absorbed in tragedy. As we traversed a hallway, I was able to see, from two or three rooms away, where the dead body of the beloved queen lay in state, gowned in black on a bier of carven ebony. Around her a circle of armed attendants was standing motionless to form a guard of honor. Her comely face looked marvelously pale against the darkness of cloth and wood. Yet her body did not seem shrunken or wasted, or otherwise damaged in any way that I could see.

The official to whom I had spoken earlier, and a court physician to whom I was also introduced, told me in response to my questions that a strange illness had come upon her very suddenly.

Danni was moved again to tears.

I tried to imagine what it would be like to hear that my own beloved Megan had been seized by death; but I soon shuddered inwardly and gave the effort up.

"What was the nature of Her Majesty's illness?" I inquired when next I saw the court physician, no more than an hour later.

"Nothing contagious," he answered shortly. Somewhere in the background, voices quavered in shrill mourning.

"That was not my concern."

He looked at me again and seemed to relax a little. "It was no disease, good Hercules. Nor was it violence, in the ordinary sense."

The physician paused a moment and looked behind him over his shoulder before continuing in a lower voice. "The truth is that she fell victim to a visit from the God of Death himself."

Still I did not quite understand. "I suppose we all do that, Doctor, sooner or later. But—?"

He was shaking his head. "I am not speaking figuratively. I mean that an avatar of Thanatos was here, within these walls—may still be nearby, for all I know—as an active enemy of our king."

"Ah. The king and the god had some dispute?"

"It is a long story, and a tragic one. Suffice it to say that our good king has made an enemy against whom no mere mortal can have any defense." He shuddered slightly. "I don't know if you can understand. Few people have ever actually confronted any god, face-to-face."

"I have," I said. And from the corner of my eye saw Danni turn her face toward me.

"I see." It seemed that my informant believed my claim, and that had made me rise somewhat in his estimation. "Then perhaps you can understand. But *this* god . . ."

Other people were approaching, and our conversation died away.

————————

I might have retired early to my room, except for the king's promise that he would see his guests again, later in the evening. As matters fell out, I never learned precisely what was planned, perhaps some ritual of mourning that would have required the presence of us all at midnight. I was standing in a courtyard of the palace, in the presence of the king himself and several others, guests and members of the household, waiting to be told more, when to the surprise of us all, Thanatos actually appeared.

The God of Death manifested himself, bearing in his arms the queen's dead body. He had emerged from one of the dark doorways leading into the far wing of the palace, looking as if he had every right to be where he was—and I am sure it is the same with any home he enters.

I saw before me a human figure, that of a strong man somewhat taller than myself, draped in a long cloak of black and red. An unkempt dark beard rimmed the lower half of a fierce countenance. And there was just a hint, gone again before I could focus my mortal vision on them, of red and ghostly wings sprouting from broad shoulders. And I understood that once more I was looking at a god. At the same time, the figure before me was thoroughly human. In some way, that made it more frightening, but it was not nearly as overwhelming in its presence as Apollo, or even Hermes.

Danni was outraged, and she clenched her small fists. "Ah, gods, this is unbearable!" Her voice was not loud, but in the silence clearly audible. Death seemed to pay it no attention.

In the next moment she had fastened an appealing gaze on me.

"Oh, if only we could do something! Ah, if my brother was only here! But no, Mel is only human, as mortal as you and I."

I tried to find some words of comfort, but there were none. Meanwhile, Death was carrying the dead queen easily in his arms. So, it is said, Death conveys all whom he harvests to the Underworld; but we all stared, for none of us had ever seen the like before, and I hope I never see it again.

We all, as I say, were standing as if paralyzed, and Thanatos would almost certainly have borne away his prey unchallenged, had he not chosen to delay. But as he walked across the terrace toward the open garden, his eye fell upon me. It was obvious that he recognized me and was not going to let the occasion pass unmarked.

When I saw the way he looked at me, I wondered why such enmity. Was this avatar of Death perhaps a friend of Hera? A question crossed my mind as to whether the God of Death might have defected to the Giants' side, in hopes of being placed in some position of authority when they had finally broken the power of the Olympians on earth. Or was he simply, cravenly, hoping that the Giants would allow him to survive, when all the other Olympians had been wiped out? I had known for some time that Zeus had enemies among the gods, though I doubted that any of them were going to try to strike at him directly.

On the other hand, I supposed it might be possible that Thanatos really cared little, one way or the other, about what Zeus might think. And that this was simply some feud of his with the local king and had nothing to do directly with the great war on which all of my attention had been focused.

He let the black-draped body of the queen slide casually from his grip, as if it had been no more than a slaughtered sheep or deer. Then the God of Death, keeping his smiling gaze fixed on me, assumed a negligent pose with folded arms and empty hands, leaning against one of the columns supporting the roof of a cloister. It was a gesture of leisurely arrogance that seemed to say he wanted to establish himself in a position from which he could give me his full attention.

A tomblike hush had fallen over the entire courtyard; all was so quiet that I could hear the very faint crackling noise of one of the torches in its wall sconce. But more and more people were gathering, and it seemed that with every heartbeat a new face appeared in one of the windows on the upper level, or on the open side of the courtyard, where terrace sloped and blended gradually into a formal garden.

The god allowed the pause to build dramatically before he finally spoke, in a cracked and grating voice.

"You are Hercules." He seemed to make the mere statement of my name a kind of accusation. Somewhere in the distance, one of the gongs of mourning made its random, crashing sound.

"I am," I replied. About then it crossed my mind to wonder whether the Death God was perhaps upset that I had slain Antaeus, with whom Thanatos might have formed some kind of alliance.

Thanatos nodded with the air of a judge confirming a verdict; it was as if I had pleaded guilty, and he now prepared to pronounce the appropriate sentence.

"You are a mortal who has grand ideas about himself," the god went on. "I understand that you are trying to find your way to the Underworld?"

Nothing had ever been further from my thoughts. But I had no intention of meekly submitting for Death's approval any itinerary I might decide on. "And if I am?"

"I can arrange swift passage there for you." And Thanatos smiled an evil smile.

My anger was growing rapidly, driving my own fear before it, and I said: "Before I decide whether to accept your invitation, God of Death, there is a question that I wish you would answer for me."

The dark head bowed. An emanation of cold seemed to proceed from the powerful, twisted figure. "Out of courtesy to your father, I allow you to ask it."

"It is this. What kind of human would deliberately put on that Face that you are wearing? What sort of man are you, who wanted to become Death? What kind of—of creature—would pick up that ghastly *thing*, the Face of Death, and press it against his own eyes and nose and mouth, eager to have *that* sink into his brain?"

Even before I had finished speaking, a very faint hushed gasp went up from the still-growing crowd.

My contempt and defiance were harsh and plain in my voice, and

Death was almost gaping at me, as if he could hardly believe either his eyes or ears.

I had one more good look at Danni, and even from the corner of my eye I could see that her eyes were wide, whether in fright or exhilaration I could not tell.

Presently my antagonist recovered himself sufficiently to speak. "You do indeed have grand ideas. You think that you are strong, young mortal Hercules. It is time you learned something about real strength." Having got over his moment of shock at my defiance, he was as smug, self-satisfied, and certain as any Linus or any lion had ever been.

After a pause he added: "One touch of my hand and you will die."

"I do not think so," my anger answered him.

"I am a god," the slayer said.

"And I, the son of a far greater god than you."

Death's eyes glittered, and I saw the fingers of his right hand working, as if they hungered to grasp and smother. "That may be so, but your father is not here now to save you. I have seen a thousand sons and daughters of Zeus, and gathered them all in. Whether or not he will think you worth trying to ransom, we will discover. Now come along." And he reached out his hand toward me, the gesture of a parent commanding a reluctant child.

22

A Brawl with Death

I STEPPED FORWARD and walked toward Thanatos, not in obedience but with a purpose of my own.

Death abandoned his lounging pose, stood up straight, and fastened his grip upon my left arm. Cold fear struck through me, but I was determined not to yield.

At the moment when Thanatos touched me, I felt a great drain of power and strength, of the very force of life itself. Yet so deep was the reservoir with which Zeus had endowed me that my life stayed in my body, and my body retained its strength. Instead of standing meekly in the grip of Death, I raised my right fist high and struck at him. It was no skilled boxer's blow, but still a solid punch, one that would have killed a mortal man. It grazed his bearded chin and hit him in the chest, and his grip on my arm was broken and he fell back awkwardly, his cloak of red and black swirling about him.

Briefly I had the feeling that I was once more grappling with the Giant Antaeus, but that image did not last. The force arrayed against me now was far greater, though of course Thanatos was not nearly so large as the Giant had been. He was tougher than the Hydra, and I was handicapped by not having my club immediately available.

I had to pummel my opponent with my fists for some time to do him any damage. Meanwhile he struck no real blows, nor did he even attempt any common wrestling holds. Instead he continued to paw and grapple, in the way that only Death can do, trying to draw my life out of my body; but the power of life in me was too great.

Without taking my gaze from my opponent for a moment, I could see from the rim of my vision that the courtyard had become a kind of informal boxing or wrestling ring, surrounded by what must have been half the population of the palace, the other half having precipitately fled.

I bombarded pawing Death with another flurry of punches, and again he went stumbling backward, circling slowly in retreat. From his mouth there came a keening wail of astonishment and rage, along with a trickle of blood, and now I heard the first, soft, unbelieving murmur from the watching crowd, who earlier must have been too shocked to breathe.

Death stepped back, and I advanced.

I was awkward and unskilled in fighting, but so, as I soon realized, was my opponent. Again and again I landed awkward, untaught, swinging blows, any one of which would have pulped the skull or crushed the ribs of any mere human, mangled any natural beast that walked the earth. They did not kill the God of Death, or even break his bones, but again and again they staggered him and knocked him down. Now I saw in his eyes the beginning of understanding that it was truly my father's power that lived in my blood and muscles.

Yet so strong were pride and hatred in my enemy that again and again he leaped to his feet, his cloak flying and the shadowy images of his wings, and hurled himself at me once more.

My own pride, and my anger, were now at full tide. I sent my right fist deep into my charging enemy's midsection, as hard as I could throw it, so that the god gasped and stood for a moment paralyzed, bent almost double. In that moment I drove my left fist down against his head, directly overhand, as if I were pounding a spike through iron. The stone of the patio cracked beneath my victim's feet.

Thus the Death God fell, for the fourth or fifth time. Even under such an impact, Thanatos still did not lose consciousness. But he, and I, and everyone who watched us, knew that he was hopelessly beaten.

I stepped back, like a sportsmanlike boxer, waiting for my opponent to try to rise again.

He raised his face, forehead all smeared with divine blood, and gave me a strange and desperate look, in which terror and disbelief were mingled. Then he began to crawl away. After crawling a few yards Thanatos regained his feet, but kept his back to me and did not pause in his limping, staggering retreat. The circle of watchers, silent again in awe, parted rapidly at his approach. This avatar of Death was not yet dead, but it seemed that his vitality was dangerously low.

At first he hobbled toward the spot where he had set down the pale queen, as if still determined to take her; but I moved quickly to stand in his way, and the God of Death shuddered and reversed himself again.

Thanatos abandoned to me not only the field, but his victim as well, and it seemed he had all that he could do to drag himself away. Before his creeping progress had brought him to the edge of the terrace beside the garden, where anxious onlookers went scurrying ever farther at his approach, his body briefly became transparent and then disappeared. The last I saw of him was the malignant look he turned at me, over his shoulder, just before he vanished.

I turned to look for Danni, but could not immediately locate her in the suddenly milling crowd.

Alcestis the queen, her face as pale as the fate that she had just escaped, still lay where Death had set her down. Her eyes were closed, but we all saw with a shock of joy that she was breathing now. Thanatos had drained her life force away almost to the dregs, but when he was punished, his own existence threatened, what he had drained flowed back to her. Her loving family and her attendants flocked around her with cries of rapture. Soon, in the arms of her rejoicing husband, she had recovered fully from her seeming death.

All the crowd who had watched the fight were awestricken by the power I had demonstrated. Some were already prostrating themselves before me, as if in worship of a god; but I made known my displeasure, and they quickly got to their feet again.

When King Admetus could finally tear himself away from his young wife, he came to me and swore his eternal gratitude, and made extravagant promises of the rewards he was going to give me; and I was very young, and I admit that I believed him for a time.

His cheeks still streamed, but now his tears expressed his joy.

"Half my kingdom, Hercules! I swear by Zeus and by Apollo, that half of everything I own is yours!"

Perhaps I am unjust, and he would really have honored his promise, had I not declined the offer.

"I have no need of kingdoms, Majesty. To give me charge of such immense and complicated matters would only inflict on me an enormous burden."

Then Admetus changed his offer, to endless amounts of jewels and gold and slaves, and swore that he would hear no refusal on my part. But when the promises later turned out to be empty, I was not much upset. The truth was that there was really nothing I needed that was in his power to give.

On that night a certain servant, attendant in the palace, asked so winningly for the honor of sleeping with me that I agreed, and the question never arose as to what otherwise might have happened between me and Meleager's sister.

When full sleep finally claimed me, I was granted only a few hours of peace before Prince Asterion showed his horned head before me in a dream. Even before he spoke, I understood that he had come to give me warning. It seemed to me that the prince and I were standing in a vast, dark room, or hall, swept by a cold wind that blew through open doors and windows. I had the feeling, the inward knowledge, that what he was about to say was so terrible that I awoke, sweating and gasping, before I heard even the first words of what he said. The young attendant who shared my bed was frightened and hurriedly left the room, never to return.

On the next morning I left the king and queen behind, amid a clamor of rejoicing bells. I waved farewell to Danni's haunting green eyes and slender form, and climbed into my little boat and sailed away, my ears almost deafened by a renewed chorus of prayers and good wishes, eager to get home and see my wife and son again.

Now I must pause here in my writing to gather strength to deal with what must next be told.

I have known for some time that for some tasks, even the strength of Hercules may not be enough.

The next leg of my great journey was uneventful. Not many days after departing the kingdom of Admetus, I arrived again in my homeland. Having the speed of the *Skyboat* at my disposal meant that much of the known world was only hours or days away, instead of weeks or months.

On drawing near my homeland, I left the boat at the same place I had moored it on my previous visit, and took to my feet with a light step.

When I was almost within sight of the walls of Cadmia, trudging eagerly up a narrow road, I caught sight of a lone figure standing ahead of me, straight and unmoving in the very middle of the road. It was an ebony figure of shadow, outlined against the mottled clouds of a red sunset. At a distance I could recognize the hair of curly black and the protruding ears. Enkidu had come to welcome me, but he did not advance to meet me, so whatever news he had could not be good. My heart turned over in my breast when I drew near enough to see the look upon my nephew's face, and that he wore the ragged clothes prescribed by tradition for one in mourning.

"Enkidu, you are alone," I said as I approached.

"Everyone else was too much frightened to come with me," he answered softly. His arms hung loose at his sides, and he tried to avoid meeting my eyes.

"Frightened of what?" I asked. Although as I now look back, it seems to me that I already knew.

My nephew had put on weight since I had seen him last, and also gained a little height, but the rags of ritual mourning hung on him loosely. And now his face was so pale that he only looked ill, and not like a young man prosperously married.

His voice, too, seemed unnatural. "Hercules, the prince Asterion appeared to me in a dream and said that you were coming home. He said also that I must be the one to go to meet you."

There followed a long and terrible silence. Then somehow Enkidu managed to speak the necessary words, so that at last I heard the blunt facts, the terrible news of how my wife and child had been horribly murdered. The hands that had done the deed were more than human.

It was as if my spirit had been forced partly out of my body by the shock. The next thing I remember is as if I were observing the scene from outside. I have a kind of vision of myself, sitting helpless in the dust of the road, while Enkidu bent over me, avoiding giving any real answers to the horrible questions that thronged up in my mind. In a kind of madness I kept demanding more details.

What he did tell me was that the bodies of my wife and child had been buried, with honors that made the ceremony almost worthy of a royal funeral. The king had seen to that. Eurystheus had been much saddened by the tragedy, and he sent word that he hoped soon to be able to express his condolences in person.

Enkidu had to help me to my feet. Then he and his young wife took me into their large house, where first servants, and then physicians, were brought to attend me.

There followed a period of time, lasting for days, when fits of senseless violence came over me, and things were broken; fortunately none were human bodies. But eventually such seizures passed, and a time came when others felt safe in approaching me.

From what people told me of the horror of the days just preceding my return home, I realized that Thanatos must have come to wreak destruction on my family as a means of revenge for his humiliating beating.

No other Cadmians had been struck down. None had tried to defend Megan—how could they? I felt no special anger at any of them, from King Eurystheus on down, for their failure. My time for real anger had not come as yet. Never did I see the king, and indeed I had almost forgotten him and his bronze box.

Instead, I was struck by the supreme irony that I had been concerned for what my son would be when he grew up. For that was never going to happen.

Weeks passed. Day after day I sat alone in a room in my nephew's house, or sometimes on a terrace, while all, or almost all, feared to come near me. Once Amphitryon came, and from a little distance murmured his condolences.

It seemed that even before my own arrival, the news had already reached Cadmia of what feat I had achieved at the court of King Admetus. People avoided me and spoke of me in hushed whispers, as they might of any blasphemer who had made an enemy of a powerful deity.

Once—but I am almost sure that this visitation was only in a dream—Apollo himself came to speak to me in soothing words. When I dared to threaten him with my fist, he withdrew himself again—but I was almost sure that it was only in a dream.

And again—and that *this* was a dream I had no doubt—Prince Asterion came to me. He confronted me calmly, even though in the dream I raised my fist against him, as I had in waking life against my other friends. This time he had no words to say in his strange voice, but blessedly he turned aside a nightmare that had begun to ride me, so that I could sink into a kind of rest, oblivion.

And so in time the full madness of grief passed from me, as all things must pass. A day came when I was again aware, however dully, of the songs of birds outside my guest room's window. And somewhere in Enkidu's household a servant's child was crying, and I could find some reassurance in the fact that there were still children in the world.

Pulling myself together, I stood up and tore off the torn and wretched garments of my mourning. I put on a clean tunic and went out of the house in which I had been hiding, to breathe again the outdoor air of the living world.

It seemed that I was doomed to live on for a time, and now I could begin to face the prospect without shrinking. Quietly and reasonably I called for servants to bring me water for a bath, and oil with which to anoint my hair and my youthful beginnings of a beard.

People approached me, cautiously, and now I could speak to them rationally enough. Presently I requested that simple preparations should be made, for I would soon be departing on a journey.

And I called at last for food, for though I had only the beginnings of an appetite, I knew that I would soon need my strength.

———

For the first time in weeks, I took notice of what I ate, and thought the taste of it was pleasant. I was drinking a bowl of soup when Enkidu came to see me.

"What will you do now, Hercules?" my nephew asked, when he had assured himself that I was largely recovered from my madness, but saw that I was determined to leave. His young wife and her attendants stood looking over his shoulders.

"I am going to look for Death," I answered, carefully setting down the bowl.

It took my hearers a moment or two to be sure that I was not talking about suicide.

I was sure now, had finally accepted the fact, that my wife and son were beyond rescue. He who was Death would have made very certain, in this case. I had not seen their bodies buried, but I went to look one final time upon their graves, and this time the sight brought almost the same feeling of finality.

"I will come with you, then," Enkidu said. I think the words cost him a considerable effort, but they were firmly spoken. His body was heavier than it had been, but his cheeks were still quite beardless.

"No, my friend, my comrade," I told him immediately. "I thank you for the offer, but where I am going this time you may not go." And I saw his young wife, still standing behind him, suddenly relax.

Some prominent citizens of Cadmia came to see me. They were worried that Death would return to harry their land again, now that I was gone.

"And so he will," I told them. "Death comes everywhere. But sooner or later he will again find himself in the same place with me."

Now I was determined, as never before, to enter the realm of Death himself and make him pay. Selecting a log of seasoned wild-olive wood, I fashioned myself a new club.

"How and where I do not know," I said, "but somehow I will find his world. He cannot hide from me forever." And I picked up from the dirt of a flower bed a small stone that felt as hard as granite, and between my thumb and fingers absently crushed it into powder.

It seemed to me that no other purpose remained to me in life, except to find my way to the Underworld, and there to have my revenge upon Thanatos.

But when it was actually time to depart, I had to overcome an urge to hesitate. I would take the road back to where the *Skyboat* waited—but then in which direction was I to seek?

━━━━━━

Kneeling in the bottom of the boat, I rested my forehead against the ivory box of the compass-pyx that had once—it seemed so long ago!—been given me by the gods. Then I let my thoughts flow as a dark stream. I would leave it to *Skyboat* to find the way to Hell.

23

Tartarus

THE *SKYBOAT'S* COMPASS-PYX reflected only shadowy images into my mind as I fed it with my hatred—what better fuel for a voyage to Hell?—and the urgency of my need for revenge. Presently my craft jerked into motion, and we were under way. The effort took me a long time—weeks passed, perhaps a month, and whenever I truly relaxed we drifted aimlessly—but in the end I was successful.

The powers of the *Skyboat* were even greater than I had imagined them—or perhaps I give them too much credit. It may be that success was due to my own human, mortal will, stronger than either my friends or enemies had calculated, and to the fuel of hate.

———

My entrance to the Underworld lay in a strange and unfamiliar land, and I reached it near sunset, following a day of oppressive weather, when storms threatened, but no lightning had yet struck to purge the air.

The magic *Skyboat* brought me as far as it could, down one stream and through the Great Sea, then up another watercourse through several branchings, until the stream at last became too shallow, and I was forced to abandon my vessel.

I had left home with a substantial supply of food and still had enough left to maintain my strength for perhaps another week. I carried also a waterskin, which I refilled when I could. These modest supplies, and my club, made up the whole of my equipment. Now I began to climb on foot beside the rivulet, and the sprite, buzzing invisibly as usual, came with me.

Climbing the rough hillside for a hundred yards or so, I came to a growth of cypress and a thicket of cedar on a small shelf of land. In this hidden place the stream I had been following was born, in a pool fed by deep springs. Another and lesser trickle of water fell inconspicuously from the same pond, pouring away out of sight over a narrow lip of stone, vanishing through a hole that opened into a lower darkness between two tilted slabs of granite.

When I put my head into this dark hole, I could hear, rising from far underground, the muted thunder of a small waterfall. Also my nose was attacked by a foul, sulphurous smell, which I took as a hopeful sign. Surely this was the path for the Underworld, to which my boat had done its best to carry me.

I took it as another favorable sign that now the sprite who had come with me on my last climb deserted me abruptly.

I silently waved good-bye to the invisible creature, and to my abandoned *Skyboat*, now also out of sight behind rocks and trees. Shouldering the most recent version of my club, I tried to wedge my body into the dark hole, following the subterranean waterfall.

At the last moment the start of my descent was delayed. The hole in the rock was not quite large enough for me to work my entire body into it; briefly I laid my new club aside, and a moment's work with my two arms wrought a minor dislocation in one of the small bones of the mountain, affording my body now room enough to pass.

Whatever drama might have been inherent in my thus beginning a journey underground was somewhat spoiled by an anticlimax. The way beyond the entrance opening was dark, but never quite too dark for me to find my footing, though I could not determine any source for the faint light.

Minute after minute, and then hour after hour, while the last traces of daylight faded and vanished far behind me, I trod a path that seemed to have been worn into the earth and rock by the passage of innumerable feet. Yet paradoxically I encountered no other travelers. Certainly, I thought, no such army as the silent majority could ever have passed between those granite slabs without leaving many traces. If all the dead of all the world were somehow required to traverse that narrow opening,

I'd have encountered such a crush and press aboveground that I'd still be trying to get through.

No, I thought. The Underworld must receive its recruits, or the great preponderance of them, through some system more complex than that.

When at last I grew weary from my long trek underground, I paused to rest, in a place where dry dust made a pillow softer than plain rock, and fell into a slumber.

As I slept, Apollo appeared to me in a dream, to offer his sympathy on my tragic loss. He also told me he was pleased that I seemed to be recovering from the shock; and he reassured me that his memory, damaged in the Giant's assault that had aborted our journey to Vulcan's workshop, was now largely restored again.

Vaguely I was aware that the prince Asterion was arranging this communication, and from time to time I could see his horned head in the background.

It seemed to me that in my dream I asked, or tried to ask, Apollo whether he could, or would, try to join me in the realm of Hades. And I thought that the Sun God concluded by telling me: "I am not welcome down there, and my appearance would only provoke another terrible fight with Hades, one that our cause can ill afford just now. But I will see you again, Hercules, in waking life, soon after you emerge from the Underworld—provided you are able to do that."

Groaning and sneezing with the dryness of the dust that made my pillow, I awoke from sleep, not knowing for a moment who I was, or where, or why—but then I remembered where I was, and why.

While still only half awake, it seemed to me that I heard a great dog barking in the distance. This made me wonder whether the entrance to the Underworld that I had found might be the one where Cerberus kept watch—or perhaps, I thought, that story was nothing but legend.

When I was fully awake, I heard no barking. Groping around me in the dimness until I found my club, I set it on my shoulder and moved on.

———

That next portion of my descent lasted for what seemed many hours. Where the shadows were thickest I went probing the way ahead with the length of my club, sometimes on a declivity so steep that I had to use it as a staff and grip rock with one hand to keep my balance. Though the darkness was unending, still it never became quite absolute. The tortuous path beside the gurgling rivulet of water at last flattened out into a level space, and the close rocky walls fell back. As I went lower the air grew warmer, but at the same time became thick and foul.

On the way I had had plenty of time to ponder where I was going, and what I was about. I remembered an ancient story that one of my early tutors had required me to memorize: It told of a cave of immeasurable depth, its mouth hidden by the darkness of a forest on the shore of a black lake. No birds flew over those waters or in those woods because of the foul air rising from the lake, whose name, Avernus, meant that it was birdless.

Presently, as I went farther and farther along the level way, the stench that had assailed my nostrils as I reached the depths began to fade—or at least, as is the way with most foul smells, I ceased to notice it.

And then, to my considerable astonishment, I came upon a deserted village—scattered houses, built much in the style of peasants' homes I was familiar with above. It was hard to imagine what fields the villagers might farm, what crops they grew; yet I was unable to shake a feeling that these dwellings ought to be occupied, that very likely there had recently been people in them, and they would be inhabited again as soon as I looked away.

But I knew I must not expect to find things here as they were in the world above. Now I felt that I was truly in the realm of Hades. I had gone beyond worrying over what might happen to me. But it did strike me as odd that so far I had encountered not another soul, neither human, god, nor demon.

Whether there was any longer a solid roof above my head or not, I could not have said. But for a long time now, the stars had ceased to be visible.

———

The whole place was unrelievedly dim and shadowy, with, as far as I could tell, not so much as a mushroom growing anywhere. Still, enough light to let me see where I was going came from somewhere, but I could not identify the source. Such was the effect of those surroundings on my mind and soul that I never doubted that these conditions were doomed to persist eternally. I would have taken an oath that Apollo's blessed sunlight had never touched that gray and lifeless scene, and I could find no reason to believe that it ever would. It seemed I could feel as much as see the clouds that weighed above me, and patches of fog seemed to spring up out of the barren ground.

On I pressed through the forbidding landscape. Looking back now,

I suppose that I must still have nursed a faint hope of being able to save my wife and child, a hope so faint and distant that I dared not acknowledge it to myself—otherwise I might well have been overcome with terror to find myself in such surroundings. No mere curiosity, no thought of material treasure, not even the bitter anger that still held me in its thrall, could have driven me further on.

Somewhere, far behind me now, the stream I had followed from the Upper World had trickled away into the rocks and disappeared. But now again there was water somewhere ahead. I could smell it. It impressed me as the same odor that arises from some deep, natural wells, not quite foul and yet not invitingly clear. One would have to be thirsty indeed to drink willingly from that fount.

———

And now, with every step that I advanced, I felt more certain that my feet were on the true descending path. Here I noted that a groove perhaps a foot wide had been deeply worn into the solid rock, as if by the feet of innumerable numbers of the dead, who had come this way before me. Still, no one beside myself was using the passage now.

There was a murmur of speech from somewhere ahead, voices rising louder now and then, as of two or three people in grim argument. Advancing a little farther, I emerged from the narrow passage into a vast, dim cavern. At a distance of a hundred yards or so, I could perceive dim shapes, as of several people standing on a shore, near a long boat bobbing in the dark and shallow water, almost at their feet.

———

It seemed to me that everyone in the world must remember, from stories heard in childhood, that Charon was the boatman who ferried the newly dead across the river Styx; and I had no doubt of who this boatman was, from the moment I first saw him. My adventures since meeting the Hydra had considerably strengthened my faith in legends.

Pacing steadily closer, I could see the boatman and his clients all more clearly. Charon was a wizened figure, wrapped in dark rags. What little I could see of his face and hands suggested that he was incredibly ancient, yet the way he waved his arms about proved him still briskly active. His boat was as dark as the water it floated on, and some thirty feet long when first I looked at it, though later it seemed shorter. He was alone in the boat now, standing in the rear, from which position he seemed to control his vessel easily with his single pole.

I suppose I might have waded or swum the river, taking my chances with whatever dangers might lie concealed in the dark water. But I preferred to bend Charon to my will, rather than seem to be avoiding him. It was as if I sought out obstacles for the sheer raging joy of forcing my way through them.

By now, I thought, my eyes were as well accustomed to the eternal darkness as they were ever going to be. The Styx was broad and gloomy and slow-moving, with the opposite shore visible only as a suggestion of disturbing shadows. Now and then a few bubbles from some unknown source came rising out of the depths.

Those who stood onshore disputing with the boatman were dim, dark figures, hard to see in any detail, even when I came near them. I took them to be the shades of five or six folk who were new arrivals, like myself. Without thinking about it I at first assumed that, unlike me, they were dead and engaged in the traditional ritual of passage.

But when I came right in among them, I could perceive these others clearly enough to see that two or three were steadily, audibly breathing, and one even seemed to be gasping in terror and exhaustion. Then they were no more dead than I was, at least not finally. I was reminded of the strange condition of Queen Alcestis when Thanatos had her in his grasp.

Most of the legendary tales agreed that at the point where I had now arrived, it was necessary for the newly arrived soul to bargain for its passage. In fact, at the moment of my arrival, one of the men in the group was shrilly demanding to be taken across even though he could not pay.

One of his fellows was nervously trying to calm him, calling him Menippus. I elbowed my way in among the others, stood by the arguer, and would have taken his part in the debate with Charon, except that Menippus glared at me with resentment the first time I opened my mouth on his behalf.

Charon resented my intrusion, too.

"I am Hercules, of Cadmia," I told the boatman when he rounded on me with hand outstretched for payment. And in the next breath I demanded: "I have come to this wretched place looking for Thanatos. Where is he?"

Now Charon looked at me closely for the first time, and his ancient, rheumy eyes went wide. It was doubtless the first time in his miserable life that he had ever heard that question asked; and I saw by his terrified reaction to my name and question that my reputation had preceded me even into Hell. There was no room in his image of the world for any intruder like me. So I waved my club and terrified the boatman into cooperating.

His voice was quavering, though he tried to make it brave. "Lord Hercules, there is the matter of payment—"

I had no patience, either, with one who would ask me to pay for this kind of ride. "Payment? Payment! How do you dare to ask me such a question, you damned unhuman monster? How dare you ask such a thing of anyone?"

"It is . . . it is the custom, sir . . ."

"To the Underworld with your custom!" I roared out, then paused, thinking that the way I had phrased my defiance somehow did not make sense.

Next he protested that his boat was too fragile to take the weight of living flesh and bone, but I disallowed that argument, having already seen that some of the other passengers were breathing. With the exception of Menippus, they all seemed willing to be herded along like sheep.

———

At last we were off, and I had to put up with no more nonsense from our boatman about being charged for the ride. Charon drove his vessel energetically across the broad, dark river, displaying a vigor that the appearance of his crinkled form suggested was quite impossible.

The moment the prow ran ashore on the Hellward bank, I stepped out onto land. As I turned my back on them all, I could hear Menippus resuming his own dispute with the boatman, even after having been ferried across. Now the unhappy passenger was demanding to be returned to the other side, and Charon was responding with abusive threats.

Later, the legends would tell how Charon was punished with a beating by some lieutenant of Hades for allowing me, a live and breathing man, to pass unhindered. It may be so. Still, I suppose it was not the beating he would have absorbed had he tried to stop me.

———

But the fate of the feckless boatman has little to do with the story I have set out to tell. From the shoreline the land sloped up gradually, inland, for thirty or forty paces, and beyond that inclined down again. As I groped and stumbled my way deeper into the Underworld I began to encounter frightening shapes, which I took to be the shades of those who were truly dead.

Here and there across the dark landscape I became aware of slowly moving groups of faintly glowing, marching images, as well as an occasional individual in isolation. Now, in this much later epoch when I write, I realize more clearly that only a few of all the world's dead could have been represented in that place, even by such tenuous forms and shadows. And when I was there I could distinguish, at first glance, between those who moved in solid form, and the others who were only images.

Sometimes both types of figure responded when spoken to, and sometimes the words they spoke seemed to make sense; but no real thought or feeling was behind them. They were images that moved and walked and sometimes uttered words; but when I steeled my nerves to touch one, my hand passed right through, so that my palm and fingers for a moment were brightly lighted.

At first I was truly frightened, for the first time since I began my lonely journey. But when I looked more closely at those that were mere apparitions, I was strongly reminded of the images Atlas had shown me—sometimes these, too, were clear and brilliant, and moved in a way that was almost lifelike. Yet it seemed to me that they were much more like reflections in a fine mirror than they were like spirits who had truly been alive.

Some of these people were trapped here—or at least their images seemed to be—in the same way Prometheus had been trapped, held by the same kind of fetters as those I had once broken. It occurred to me now that his punishment had been a form of Hell on the surface of the earth.

———

Gradually but steadily the impression kept growing on me that whoever or whatever had created Olympus seemed to have manufactured Tartarus as well. There were certain similarities, giving the impression, when I thought about it, of common construction units of some kind. Here again I saw stubby projections from the ground, with a resemblance to tree stumps, but that had an artificial look about them.

Certain others among the frightful shapes only looked at me, and fled in terror when I tried to question them.

Every time I thought some individual among them took notice of me, I demanded of her, or him: "I am Hercules, of Cadmia. Where is my wife, Megan? And where is our child?"

And, when those questions failed, as they did each time, I followed with: "Where is the God of Death?"

But never did I get a useful answer. None of those I sought were anywhere to be found.

────────

It was with mixed feelings of joy and fear that I encountered the shade of my own mother, dressed as I had often seen her in sunlight and in life. Almost I expected to see her sewing basket in her hand.

But though the figure had come walking toward me, as if drawn by some mysterious affinity, it was only an image and, when it came within arm's length, ignored me.

I staggered, and then for a moment I could not move at all. "Mother!" I cried out.

But the eyes of Alcmene's shade were terribly clear and empty, and they looked through me, and then looked on, as if I had not been there at all. There was no awareness in them.

And what wrung my heart almost beyond endurance was that I was granted one last look at the shade of Megan, and that of our babe held in her arms. I believe the only thing that saved my sanity was what I had learned from Atlas, regarding how the machinery of Olympus still made such counterfeit likenesses of many people at the point of death. How such bright shadows were created and preserved, in pursuit of some vast project whose purpose all living minds had long since forgotten. So I knew, even as I saw her, that it was not truly Megan who walked before me, but only an image, like a reflection in a pond.

I realize that this explanation leaves uncertain the fate, the nature, of other individuals I encountered in Tartarus, those who still retained their bodies as solid and breathing as my own. But it seems to me that people in that situation have merely been drained of life force, like Alcestis. As we will see, sufficient life remained to certain dwellers in the Underworld to allow them to move and speak, behaving almost normally. I later had good evidence of the fact that when some of these were able to regain the surface of the earth, they were not much the worse for their dread experience.

────────

Since my visit to the Underworld, I have spoken with wise counselors and have come to understand that human bodies, when imprisoned long enough in that dark realm, change fundamentally, acquire a different nature than the one they were born with. With ordinary mortals, the transformation need not take long—but of course I was protected by my father's power, inherent in each atom of my body.

For one thing, they became immortal, or so long-lived that they are sometimes assumed to be immune to death. Charon was an example.

But it is possible for humans in such a situation to be restored to their original natures, if they return to the more mundane world above, where they were born, and where they naturally die.

Later, when I had more time to ponder these events at leisure, it occurred to me to wonder whether Charon himself might be one of these, no longer truly human. Yet what was he, if not human?

But at the time when I was buried in the Underworld, as when I had confronted Atlas under the great bowl of the sky, my mind simply reeled under these complexities and I made no progress in unraveling them.

The general movement of all the shades and breathing folk around me tended in a certain direction, and I took that heading, too, after pausing to eat the last remaining portion of the food I had brought with me.

I drank from a small cold stream, right at the point where it came trickling from the rock, and hoped that it was not the beginning of Lethe, the source of all forgetfulness.

The scattered population whose movement I had been following gradually thinned out in numbers; where the individual shapes were going, I could not say, but there were ever fewer and fewer of them, and in time I was alone.

After descending a great distance, I was led by a burgeoning red glow to come upon an impressive archway, higher than the walls of Cadmia. This opened into what had to be the throne room of the King of Hell.

Once I had entered this vast chamber I paused, involuntarily, to gape about me. The height of the ceiling seemed impossible, made more so by the clouds of reddish mist that concealed its true distance.

At the far end of the great room, the length of a sports stadium from where I stood, there towered high a great black throne, which seemed of a size to seat a Giant comfortably—but the figure occupying it now was no bigger than a man.

At this depth, the air around me was beginning to turn hot again, and the floor of rock was growing warm beneath my sandaled feet. Drawing a deep breath of the tainted atmosphere, I started the long walk to the throne.

━━━━━━━━

My hopes rose as I advanced and could see that the black throne was indeed occupied. But he who sat on it was not, to my great disappointment, my enemy Thanatos. Instead, the enthroned figure was one I would have no hope of pummeling in the way I had served Death. After all, Hades, called by some Pluto or Dis Pater, was, with Zeus and Poseidon, one of the three who ruled the universe—or so I had been taught.

He slouched on the throne, legs crossed, watching my approach with not enough interest to cause him to sit up straight. A crown of some dull metal, formed into a jagged shape, sat crooked on his great, bearded head, and he was twirling some small object in one hand. I was within a few strides of the foot of the throne before I could feel sure of what it was. And then I knew a shock of disappointment: if the Face of Death was here in the hands of Hades, then the last avatar to wear it was surely dead, and all my hope of revenge was in vain.

This was another god whom I had never seen before, but he knew me, for he nodded and smiled at my approach. I had no doubt that it was Hades himself who sat twirling the Face of Death, which looked like a clear, glassy mask, around his finger, stuck through one of the mask's eyeholes. The thought crossed my mind that he might be pondering which mortal ought to be invested with the powers of Thanatos next. I had no doubt there would be willing applicants.

Hades had a booming, bellowing laugh, which sounded when I drew very near. I had heard such laughter before, on the bright surface of the earth, but only from the hopelessly insane.

"Hail, Hercules," the voice of the Lord of the Underworld boomed out when I stood close before him. "I have been more or less expecting you for some time. But I thought you might come riding on some centaur's back. Have you run out of labors to perform in the world of the living?"

Again it seemed my fame had run ahead of me. "Greetings to you, Lord Hades. I am looking for Thanatos."

"Is that the real reason? Well, this is not the place to find him." In rambling and disjointed words, and with many repetitions, the Lord of the Underworld explained to me that Tartarus was actually a very poor place to look for Thanatos—the Death God spent almost all his time in the world above.

This was not how I would have expected Hades to act. The behavior of the god before me strongly reinforced my suspicions of true madness; I wondered whether being struck by a Giant's weapon might produce that effect. I also wondered whether I should raise the question, but soon decided there was nothing to be gained by doing so.

"Plenty of work up there to keep him busy." He gestured with a great thumb toward the rocky ceiling, and once more he laughed. "Up on the surface is where Thanatos does his work—if you can dignify what he does by that name."

Meanwhile, another handful of ghostly, semitransparent figures trooped by, paying no attention to me, nor even to the ruler of this fantastic domain. As far as I could tell, none of these wraiths had any purpose in their movement, but wandered aimlessly.

"Why do you stare at them, Hercules?" the Lord of the Underworld demanded. "What did you expect to find here, festivals of sunshine?"

"I stare because I still wonder if Thanatos is among them."

"And if he were?" Hades went on in his rambling, disjointed speech. "These are mere witless, lifeless shades, no more than shadows on a wall. What point is there in punishing a shadow?"

I replied to that question with one of my own. "If these are only shadows, tell me this: What is it that casts the shadow? What of their true souls?"

The mad god squinted at me horribly and pointed one great arm in my direction as he nodded for emphasis. "Now *there* is a question. There is a *pro*found mystery. I myself have often wondered about that. But if such things still exist anywhere in the Universe, it is certainly not here."

He paused, then added with a chilling laugh: "If you see *my* true soul anywhere, will you let me know? I fear that someone's stolen it away."

He made a sudden motion with his great right arm, as of scooping up an object I could not see clearly, and putting it on his head. For just an instant, I thought he might be grabbing his true soul. And a moment later I was startled when the figure of Hades abruptly vanished from my sight. Another moment and he was back, still occupying his throne, and laughing his hideous laugh.

It came to me that he must be putting on and taking off his famed Helmet of Invisibility, which had been resting—itself invisible, until he picked it up—beside him, on one broad arm of his throne chair.

Great Hades shifted his weight on his royal seat and looked around, as if seeking someone who ought to be present but was not. Then, in a brief return of mental clarity, he seemed to recall his situation.

"Where is that damned zombie who—? But no, I forget, they've all gone. I am unattended." Leaning a little forward, he fixed me with a terrible gaze. "Would you believe it? *They say I have gone mad.*" The last words came out in a ghastly whisper.

"I suppose I might believe that if I tried."

That, at least, seemed to be logical. If Hades had indeed gone mad, then his consort Persephone and all his usual attendants might well have fled his presence in terror, not knowing what atrocity he might commit on them at any moment. So he sat on the black throne, all alone in the vast throne room, and seemed to pay no attention at all to the ceaseless passage of time.

He did ask me some questions, though. Some of them I do not remember, but some I do.

"Hercules, tell me, have the sun and moon yet fallen from their places? Is the end of the Universe at hand?"

"Not according to Atlas."

"Have you seen *the stars, at bloody wars, in the wounded welkin weeping?*" Again the terrifying whisper.

"I do not understand you," I protested.

"You are no poet, then."

"I never claimed to be."

And then the Lord of the Underworld wondered aloud if I was the first intruder of many who were going to seek shelter in his domain, when that of sun and stars and sea was falling and burning up around them.

Rather than stand tongue-tied, I continued to do my best to answer Hades. I gave him what reassurances I could about the stability of the world above. Also I reminded him about the war.

"Zeus fights the Giants, does he? Well, I could tell him a thing or two about that. I myself went out fighting Giants once . . . yes, I was a true god once, though you might not believe it to look at me."

"Oh, I believe it, Dark One. You are not the only deity who is sometimes called insane."

———

Hades thought no more of receiving the insult than I, in my current state, of giving it. Perhaps he did not even hear it. He went on rambling, and playing with the god-Face in his hands, while I looked around me for any evidence that Thanatos might be going to appear. Alas, I found none.

When the Lord of the Underworld had babbled on a little longer, I suddenly pricked up my ears. He seemed to be claiming that he was now allied with Zeus, Apollo, and other gods of the Upper World. And in later days I was able to verify the fact: he had signed with them a pact of mutual toleration and nonviolence, until their common enemies, the Giants, should be disposed of.

But there was still no sign of the one I had come here seeking. I supposed it might be possible that when Hades learned that I was coming into his domain, he had warned Thanatos, either the old avatar or the new, and sent him to hide somewhere else. But that would require some other explanation of the Face my host was twirling.

At last I said: "I have no quarrel with you just now, Master of the Underworld." Raising an arm, I pointed off to my right. In that direction a different quality in the light, or in the dimness rather, strongly suggested some kind of a broad doorway, at only a moderate distance. "What is there?" I demanded.

"What is anywhere, bold mortal? And why should you care? For a dead man, Hercules, you display an inordinate amount of energy."

"If you think that I am dead, Lord of Hell, watch closely and learn better. Now tell me, is Death hiding in that room?" Once again I jabbed the air with my finger. "Do you fear to give me a plain answer?"

"I fear nothing, dead man!" And he hammered the right arm of his great chair with his clenched fist, so hard that the floor of Hell quivered beneath my feet. "The Thrones of Lethe are in that room. Go see for yourself. Now go away, bother me no longer, I have work to do. Can't you see? A tremendous amount of important work!" And he sank back on this throne and closed his eyes and resumed his twiddling, twirling of the Face of Death.

I turned my back on His Dark Majesty and moved away. But when I had gone only a few paces, he called after me: "What else you find in there may surprise you, Hercules!" And suddenly the laughter of Hades boomed forth again.

Turning my back again on the mad god, I walked steadily away. Ahead of me the outline of a large doorway loomed more clearly through the dimness with every step. And in the same direction I thought I could now hear the sound of men's voices, raised as if in drunken song.

24

The Harrowing

NOW I HEARD the drunken singing, in two voices, from close ahead. The louder and clearer voice was rather deep, and it seemed to me strangely familiar.

On passing through the arched doorway I found myself in another chamber of the Underworld, this one fully as long and wide as the throne room, though not as high. Frozen drops of rock, looking as if they had once been molten, hung from a ceiling that was in places low enough for a tall man to bang his head. I was not tall enough to need to worry. The vast space, mostly empty, was strangely lighted by wall-mounted torches that burned with flames of evil red, flames that shot up to play against the lowering overhead rock without doing very much to relieve the surrounding blackness—and here, as Hades had predicted, I came upon a sight which brought me to a halt in sheer surprise.

Clouds of shadow or dank fog—I suppose there were some of each—filled much of the huge chamber. But when I had walked half its length, I could observe a pair of men occupying two of a long row of low chairs, or perches; knee-high, stumplike projections rising from the ebony floor. It seemed to me at first glance that all the other chairs were empty.

Hades had said something about this room containing the Thrones of Lethe, which sounded to me like seats named for the legendary River of Forgetfulness.

For some reason the two men were arrayed in festive garments, creating a totally incongruous effect in this buried dungeon. They were sitting in slumped positions, the one on the more distant chair looking almost comatose, his bearded jaw moving intermittently as he tried to sing. The other was turning his head from side to side as I approached, but at first he paid me no attention. Their faces remained almost entirely in shadow.

In the gloom, it took me a few moments to determine that the pair were bound in place on their stumps, with shackles around their waists and ankles. They also wore strange-looking caps or helmets, each head-piece connected by a thin cable to the Throne below.

The relatively active man, he who was sitting nearest to the door where I had entered, had somehow managed to get his head almost free of this restraint, so his metal cap had slid far down over his left ear. But his limbs were still firmly bound by chains, much like those Prometheus had endured, and there seemed no possibility that he could ever free himself entirely.

As I drew near, this one stopped turning his head from side to side and focused his gaze on me. "Are you real?" the familiar voice inquired of me as I approached.

"Of course I am," I said.

A well-remembered figure put out a human hand, large and muscular yet trembling, to try to touch my arm. A shaky whisper asked me: "Have you solid human flesh and bone?"

"I have, and I intend to keep them."

After a shocked pause, there came a one-word question: "Hercules?"

My amazement at this encounter was at least as great as his. I had last seen Theseus well aboveground and apparently in good health, in the company of the lovely Antiope, when we parted following our escape from the land of the Amazons. His companion in this grotesque dungeon I could not recognize, but even semiconscious he, too, had a piratic look about him.

Seeing my evident uncertainty, Theseus introduced me to his comrade, naming him Pirithous. It was hard to estimate sizes when both men were sitting down, but I thought Pirithous was nearly as big as Theseus, and more thickly built.

Theseus seemed to think it important to tell me more about his companion. "He was a Lapith chieftain—Hercules, this damned fool once tried to steal some sheep from me, did you know that?"

"No," I said.

When Pirithous would not respond to verbal urgings, Theseus kicked him and swore at him and finally managed to rouse him a little from his stupor.

Meanwhile I was asking: "So how in hell did the two of you ever find your way down into the Underworld? And how long have you been here?"

Theseus frowned and shook his head. His lips moved as if he were making an effort to count something.

"Just got here," said Pirithous, his bass voice full of misplaced confidence, as he added a string of blasphemies against a formidable array of gods. Though he now gave the impression of being more or less aware of his surroundings, it was obvious that neither he nor Theseus had any real idea of how much time had passed.

As I have already mentioned, the row of stumps, or Thrones of Lethe, extended into the distance. A hint of shadowed movement, yards away, suggested that not all the Thrones were empty in that direction.

I was more perturbed, and fascinated, by the prisoners' unique surroundings than they themselves seemed to be.

"Is there no decent *light* down here?" I demanded. "No torches, candles, a simple oil lamp even?" I still could not identify the source of the faint illumination that suggested more than it revealed, and rendered hideous the few details that it did make clear.

Theseus strained against his bonds as if he had suddenly just noticed them, his mighty muscles quivering for a long moment before he slumped back. In an ordinary man, his posture would have suggested something like despair.

"Hercules, can you get us out?"

His voice now sounded muted, and that was the least arrogant thing I had ever heard him say.

"It's possible," I told him. "I have yet to see the bond I couldn't break."

I bent to make a closer examination of the links and clamps that held the pirates to their stumps. The material of the Thrones strongly resembled that of other ancient odylic devices I had encountered recently. Each consisted of a flat seat attached to the top of a short pillar of white stone, smooth as marble, with odd devices connected to it, things that I supposed must have some magical import. The confining chains, like those that had bound Prometheus, were of brass or bronze or iron (it was hard to be sure in the dimness), fastened with clasps of what looked like ebony and ivory to hold the captive's wrists and ankles.

I took some links between my fingers.

"Slain in some sea fight at last, were you?" I demanded of the master pirate. Not that I really thought him or his companion dead—there was too much breath and sweat and profanity about them. At the same time, the shackle holding the right arm of Theseus let go with a ringing snap. Seconds later I heard a metal fragment land on hard rock in the distance.

"No. No, nothing like that." His handsome eyes were clearing now, with activity and the prospect of freedom. "Hercules, it is really you? Damnation, but I think it is. Who else could break these things? So, Thanatos has collected you after all."

"Like hell he has! I'll collect *him* if he comes within my grasp. I'm very much alive."

But there was no use trying to explain my situation to Theseus now, or obtain any useful information from him. Suddenly he was almost comatose again. I pulled his tilted helmet entirely off his head, but that seemed to make little difference. As long as he remained sitting on a Throne of Lethe, it seemed impossible to rouse the Prince of Pirates from his trancelike state for more than a few moments at a stretch. He could only respond feebly when I shook him and called his name.

Exerting my strength against one after another of the material bonds that held him—the chains were tougher than I had expected, but in the end I had my way—I managed to free Theseus entirely, and pulled him to his feet.

He staggered but did not fall. As soon as he had broken contact with the Throne of Lethe, the master pirate gazed at me like a man freshly awakened from some hideous dream, and I saw the sweat break out on his living, breathing face. In the next moment he tore off the festive garments in which he had been dressed, and stood in the noxious darkness naked, his whole body trembling.

Casting another glance down the row of chairs, noting again that there was a third one, in the distance, that also seemed to be occupied, I asked what had happened to the Amazon princess, Antiope, who had been with him when we last met.

Theseus answered shortly that she was not here.

Meanwhile I was methodically working to free Pirithous, who let his festive garments stay on when he got up. He, like his captain, gave every indication of being still actively alive.

I remarked on this, and they emphatically agreed.

"We're no more dead than you are, by the balls of Zeus!" growled Theseus.

"I'd say a lot closer to it, though. Well, if the pair of you were not killed in some sea fight, how *did* you get into this situation?"

"We were hunting Persephone," Pirithous admitted in a mumble.

For a moment I was sure that my ears had betrayed me. "You were hunting *who?*"

"You know, Hades's queen."

"I know who Persephone is; the queen of this place, consort of Hades, or call him Dis or Pluto if you like." Planting my fists on my hips, I shook my head. "What I find hard to believe is that anyone could be stupid enough to try a trick like that."

Theseus shrugged and seemed to revel in the freedom of movement he had now regained. Somehow he was not angered by my harsh words; looking back, I think he was actually pleased to find himself in the company of someone strong enough to assume a kind of authority, for this allowed him to play his favorite role of carefree rebel.

He went on: "My friend Pirithous here had taken a fancy to her. And, well, when that happens, what can a man do? We were going to carry her away. I thought that once we got back to our ship . . ." He shrugged again and let the idea die away.

"You *thought*? That you would simply carry away a goddess? I wouldn't call that thinking. And how did you manage to get in here, anyway? And where's your ship?"

"There's a river, called Acheron, that has it source in the Upper World but drains into a cave. We took that route. But I'm afraid the ship is gone."

I nodded. "It did seem to me that there had to be more than one entrance," I remarked. "Maybe there are many."

Slowly Theseus shook his head. "Not such a good idea, was it?" he admitted. "Well, we were both a little drunk at the time."

"I wouldn't call that an idea at all, kidnapping the consort of Hades! Even a pair of stupid pirates should have known better."

Pirithous groaned something inarticulate. I supposed that Hades, even in his craziness, must have been impressed by their audacity, but certainly not amused by it. When he caught these intruders, the mad Lord of the Underworld had told them they were invited to a banquet, and had dressed them in festive garments. But then Hades had placed them on the Thrones of Lethe, and they were fortunate indeed that he had not yet got around to doing worse.

Theseus had now recovered enough of his wits to feel deeply shaken by the experience. "Were you ever caught up in the hands of a god, Hercules? You may be strong, but . . . just grabbed up, like a child, and then tied down like a laced shoe? There's not much a man can do when that happens to him. Not even a man as powerful as you are."

"No, not much. Let me ask you again, now that you're fully awake: I don't suppose you've seen Thanatos anywhere around here?" Hades had shown me what looked to me like the Face of Death, and told me a story to go with it; but the urge for revenge would not let go of me that easily.

Pirithous shook his head. Theseus said: "No, we've seen no one like that." And now his tone, for once, became suddenly plaintive. "Hercules? Get us out of here?" And Pirithous, with a kind of inarticulate groan, seconded the plea.

"I'll try. But first, I think there's someone else, down that way. Let me see who it is." And I turned away and began to walk along the line of Thrones.

Before I had taken many steps, I heard another strained and strangely familiar voice call my name from that direction.

In another moment I was close enough to get a clear look at the face of Meleager, Danni's brother, who sat chained to another stone tree stump.

I had no surprise left in me.

This third prisoner, dressed in an ordinary tunic that he might have worn while on his Argosy adventure, was more fully conscious than either of the buccaneers had been when on their Thrones.

"Hercules?" he croaked.

"It's me. Hold still, and I'll have you loose in a moment." And I set down my club again.

"I died foolishly, Hercules!" Meleager was plainly in a mood for agonized repentance. "Wickedly abandoning my responsibilities to my family in the Upper World."

"You haven't died at all, not yet," I counseled him. "Not entirely." *Spang* went a chain. Again the spray of fragments, making a fine pattern on distant stone.

"I am dead." Mel contradicted me flatly, speaking in the solemn tone of one who wanted to be finished with all mortal life. "I couldn't be here otherwise. I'm dead and undergoing a just punishment for the evil I have done. For all the good I have failed to do." He paused, wrinkling his brow. "Whereas you're really still alive, aren't you?"

"My body is as solid and hale as ever," I assured him. *Spang*.

Now he was trying to wrench the helmet off his head, but not having any success. "Hercules, if you ever do manage to return to the Upper World alive—"

"I suppose that might happen." I really believe that until that moment I had not thought about it, one way or the other.

"—I entreat you to marry my sister, Deianeira."

———

His words struck me speechless, and my hands ceased their work for a long moment.

"Hercules, she is an innocent young girl. As yet she knows nothing of the ways of Aphrodite, charmer of men."

Remembering our meeting at the court of King Admetus, I was not totally sure about that, but in any case it seemed irrelevant.

"How do you know that you were killed?" I demanded of Meleager, changing the subject. Meanwhile, every time I looked at him or touched him my conviction was reaffirmed that this was indeed a living man. I could watch him breathe, and feel the solidity of his limbs as I peeled away their bonds.

In another moment he was completely free, but seemed unable to give my question a clear answer. "Something hit me in the head. Then there was another fight, and it seemed to me I drowned . . ."

As far as I could tell, there were no other captives in the great prison room; hasty introductions were performed, and the four of us began to look for some way out. I felt reluctant to go back through Hades's throne room; and I got the impression, trying to see through fog and shadow, that the door in that direction was now closed.

Meanwhile, Meleager was not yet fully satisfied that he still breathed. "How could I be here if I wasn't dead?" he insisted, after a few moments of thick-witted attempt at thought.

I shook my head at this. "You're no deader than the rest of us."

Meleager now resumed his attempts to arrange a marriage. Before his plunge into the Underworld, he had been the surviving male head of the family, and as an honorable man had considered his sister his responsibility.

"Hercules, I should never have gone off with Jason on that mad expedition. Not when it meant abandoning my family responsibilities. I have failed in my duty to my sister, because it was entirely up to me to see to it that she makes a good marriage. Now more than ever she needs a decent husband. I'm serious, I entreat you to take her for your wife."

"Why 'more than ever'?"

"Because—I'm dead."

"Oh yes, I had forgotten. Well, finding an acceptable husband for Danni should not be difficult at all—she is a lovely woman."

"That she is." Meleager paused, looked at me closely. Then in a loud, firm voice, he said: "As for 'acceptable,' my standards are quite high. Hercules, if you are able to return to the world above, I charge you with the duty of marrying my sister."

I stared at him, realizing that he was not just dazed, and wondering if he had gone as mad as Hades. But then I remembered that Meleager had not seen me since the day, long months ago, when the Argonauts had left me and my nephew stranded on the shores of Mysia. How long ago that seemed! So it was highly unlikely that Mel could have heard the news of my marriage to Megan, or her recent death.

I find it hard to reconstruct, or understand, my own mental state at this time. Possibly my grief for my lost loved ones had burned so fiercely that already there were only ashes left. Still, it would seem that no thought could be farther from my mind than that of contracting another marriage. But I can only report what truly happened, and the fact is that I heard myself agreeing to Mel's entreaties—perhaps in those circumstances I would have said anything to stop his raving.

Besides, I had to confront the fact that my search for Thanatos in Hell had failed. Before I went elsewhere seeking Death, I might as well take the opportunity to cheat him out of three more victims.

"Stay close behind me, men," I told the trio who now—yes, even Theseus—were looking to me for leadership. "I'm getting out of here, and I don't think anyone will try to stop me as I leave." Privately I told myself that I would welcome any such attempt.

I chose the direction in which the ground beneath our feet seemed to rise a little as we moved, and set out.

Meleager, as we progressed, tearfully confessed that he felt a great responsibility for the kidnapping of Enkidu, which had resulted in the lad's being thrown into the Pool of Pegae, all because most of the Argonauts wanted to delay and get rid of his powerful uncle. Mel said he had not been directly responsible, but he had failed to properly discourage the attempt.

"I am sorry now that I didn't try to stop them, Hercules." His honest face was woebegone.

"It's over now, and no harm done," I told him shortly. "Let it be forgotten."

I gave serious thought to the possibility of summoning my *Skyboat* to come cruising right along the Styx, or the Acheron, and enjoyed a moment of sardonic amusement at the thought of Charon's reaction to such competition. But then I thought of the long, long detour the boat might have to travel to get from the nameless stream where I had left it waiting, and decided it had best stay there.

━━━━━━

The fact was that I had virtually given up trying to find Thanatos in the Underworld. Since entering Hell, I had repeatedly encountered folk whom I could recognize, a state of affairs which seemed unlikely, considering the vast number of people who must have died since the beginning of the world, and of all those who must be dying now, hour by hour and minute by minute, in every nation and in many of the ships at sea, with or without the personal help of Thanatos or any other god. In an Underworld so heavily populated, why, out of all those thousands, nay millions, should I keep encountering so many people I had known?

Surely something more than mere chance must be involved. So, were the Death God here, I thought, I would have found him by now. Since he was not, I would have to seek him elsewhere.

Besides, there had been something convincing in the way that Hades, whether he was insane or not, had twirled what appeared to be the Face of Death around his finger.

As the four of us moved on from room to room, an obstacle to our departure soon presented itself. There came a huge whining and shuffling in the darkness, and then we saw it: what I can only describe as a three-headed dog, shaggy and elephant-sized, though built closer to the ground than any elephant.

When I was on Corycus, several people had told me that at least two versions of Cerberus had been destroyed in recent years—but here was yet another duplication, or perhaps it was a new edition, of the great dog.

Cerberus was stranger than any beast I had encountered on the surface of the earth, perhaps even more bizarre than Antaeus. He, or it, was neither beast, god, nor human, but rather an artifact of the mysterious odylic process.

Each head was equipped with a pair of wide-set yellow eyes and supported by its own set of forelegs, so that the creature walked and ran upon eight legs in all. Each set of jaws was filled with long, sharp teeth.

Pirithous and Meleager retreated hastily, for which I could not blame them. Theseus danced about alertly, keeping out of reach of those six big jaws.

"I think I can grab one leg and hold it, Hercules," he calmly proposed. "Or would you rather I took the tail?"

I thanked him politely but suggested that his best move would be to stay clear. Then I stepped in close to Cerberus, catching all three of its slow brains by surprise, and stunned the one in the middle with a punch. The two remaining heads howled and snarled and snapped. Both tried to get at me at once, with the effect of paralyzing their shared body with contradictory commands.

A bit of scrambling about was necessary before all three heads could be rendered unconscious, and while that was in progress I considered the idea of bringing back to Hephaestus and Daedalus some sample fragment of the great dog's flesh and bone.

Or, for that matter, the whole thing, as I had once brought the Boar. I could picture myself throwing Cerberus down at the feet of Hermes, or of Zeus himself. "Here, you are so obsessed with monsters, take this one!"

But I soon gave up on that plan. Getting the whole beast out alive, with the three heads probably regaining consciousness at random intervals, would certainly have required a terrific struggle.

Pirithous and Meleager soon returned, and the four of us walked on, leaving the monster dog where it had fallen. We had not gone far when it began to whine and whimper in the gloom behind us. But those sounds faded gradually as we moved away.

Finding my way down into Hell had been comparatively easy. But once the decision had been made to get out again, I realized that I faced something of a problem. Simply retracing my steps seemed out of the question; I had the feeling that the scenery here was slowly and continually shifting, so that finding the right way would be hopeless. Theseus and Pirithous had no more idea than I did of which way we ought to go; and Meleager could not even remember how he had been brought into the Underworld.

Doing the best we could, we groped our way through one room and passage after another, praying for providential guidance and trying to climb when we came to anything like a stair or ramp.

Now the stench of sulphur mounted in my nostrils. We had reached the hinterland of Hell, a dark and smoky place enough in its own right, bathed in some kind of volcanic fumes, and frightening in the way that all deeply unsettled things can be.

How long we kept at it I cannot say, but eventually determination was rewarded. What had looked like only more hellish space, only mere fogbank dimness, turned out when I bumped into it to be a solid wall, painted or naturally colored gray, in shadings that gave it the look of fog when seen from only a few feet away.

As soon as I felt it was solid wall, and had made sure there was no door, I hit the blank surface with my fist, putting some energy behind the blow. Something cracked, in the circumstances an encouraging sound. I hit it again, still harder, and then again. Pieces began to fall away, and presently I succeeded in breaking my way through.

Emerging on the other side of the wall, we immediately felt a movement of what smelled and tasted like fresh air. The other aspects of the world were not much changed, but the refreshing draft gave us hope. Finding an ascending slope, we pushed on with fresh energy, drawing in deep breaths.

After a long climb, during which the world around us underwent a gradual alteration, we came to a place where we were undoubtedly aboveground, and the blessed light of Apollo's sun, or Diana's moon, was visible at least dimly, and there were living, growing things about.

I had found my way down into Hell, then fought my way up and out of it again.

But as soon as all immediate challenges had been disposed of, the pointlessness of it all struck me with overwhelming force. The fact that I had survived another adventure was ultimately meaningless. I had really won nothing at all.

Megan was still dead, and so was small Hyllus, whose life I had, without fully realizing it, begun to consider in some ways more important than my own. I saw the world before me as a dark, blank space, devoid of significance.

And when that thought came I collapsed again, sitting on the ground, not knowing what to do or what was to become of me. I felt like most of my self had been consumed in the fires of my own rage and hate.

On my emergence from the Underworld I more than half expected to find Hermes waiting for me, ready to congratulate me on my accomplishments and to tell me that my divine sponsors had a new job for me to undertake. Oh, the Messenger would probably be very glad to see me, having a good reason to fear that a valuable worker had gone to Hell and would not be coming back. And of course he would have good reasons why neither he nor Zeus had gone to Tartarus to look for me.

Not that Zeus was ever going to speak to me directly. But I knew exactly what I was going to tell the Messenger when next I saw him: "If any of you gods have seen my father, I would like to see him, too. No matter if he is not in fact all-powerful. No matter even if there are a hundred Giants stronger than he is, or if he has now gone as mad as

Hades. I won't hold any of those things against him. But I have done all that I swore to do, and more; and I intend to hold him to his promise to meet with me. There are some words I want to say to him."

As soon as we could be sure that we were out, my three companions wept tears of joy and hastened to offer prayers and promise sacrifices of thanksgiving. Meleager, finally convinced that he was still alive, was in ecstasy. Their demonstrations of delight evoked in me nothing but the dregs of my rage at Thanatos, and loathing for the world.

The sky in the east turned light, and presently I could see the sun again, but at first the sight meant nothing to me. The light of sun and moon and stars was only mockery.

When my three companions in escape offered me words of comfort and tried to inspire me to new hope, I raised my fist and roared at them. Two of them prudently retreated. Only one remained, who was still standing near me when I once more raised my head. Again I raised my fist menacingly, but the figure before me did not move.

Theseus, the scoundrel and pirate, was the only one who defied my stupid threats and remained with me. Pirithous had taken to his heels— and so, I observed, had Meleager, who an hour or so ago had pledged himself to me in eternal gratitude and friendship. I groaned out curses at the remaining pirate and warned him to be on his way, too.

But when I looked up again, some minutes later, Theseus was still standing there, exactly where he had been.

He said in a firm voice: "Pull yourself together, shipmate."

I gave him a look that would have driven ten ordinary men away. But Theseus stared right back at me.

He said: "Hell of a thing, what Death did to you. Robbed you all at once of everything you had. I don't know if I could take a punch like that—hell, I know I couldn't. I've never had the guts to live that kind of life. Love people and have them love me, knowing it could all be lost. Which is doubtless why I could never pick one woman and . . ."

An interval of silence passed, while my companion looked away from me, as if he pondered the evils of the world, or perhaps had been surprised by something in himself. Then he came a little closer and squatted down at my side. Presently he sighed, and went on:

"I'm older than you, Hercules, and there's some things I do know. When the whole damned world has fallen on a man's head, he's got to suck in his gut and keep going. Do that, and you can still win. Law of nature. Win, even if the bastards kill you. But if you don't do that, then you've let them win."

"I . . ." It was excruciatingly hard to get out any words at all. "I wanted to find Death. Whether I could beat the hell out of him again, or whether he got me this . . . but instead there sat Hades, gone completely mad. He had the Face of Death in his hands, and he sat there, twirling it around his finger."

My faithful companion nodded, as if he understood. At least he sympathized, and at the moment that was more important. Later I realized that the pirate's understanding went in some ways deeper than my own.

After a while he reassured me: "You'll catch up with him. Sooner or later."

Theseus stayed with me yet for a while longer. Until, I suppose, he saw in me some sign that in my mind I had turned some kind of corner and was going to heed his advice.

"You'll be all right now, Hercules. Yeah, I think you will. Let your friends help you."

And at last he quietly moved on.

25

Wrestling

SKYBOAT HAD NOT yet rejoined me, and I began to travel on my own two legs, looking for a sizable stream where I might hope that it would soon be able to meet me.

After my descent into the Underworld, and after Theseus had given me his necessary pep talk, and I had made my way through the rest of the limbo of the borderlands, I craved a face-to-face meeting with my father even more desperately than before.

Now I was traveling alone again, even though more than ever I needed to talk to someone who could make sense out of what had happened in my own life, and was still happening in the world. I would have given much to have even an hour with Daedalus, but that was not to be.

Danni's green eyes and slender body kept intruding upon my thoughts, and I yearned toward her as if I might find in her a place of refuge from grief and fear and turmoil. Again in memory I saw the face of her brother, deep in Tartarus, and heard him urging me to marry her. The words took on the character of some mystic revelation.

The first time I feel asleep after returning to the world of the living, I had a dream in which I found myself dueling somehow with my father. I thought in my vision that Zeus, huge, gray-bearded, the image of a quintessential patriarch, came at me armed with the sword and shield of the Amazon queen, and my club was awkward, and suddenly it became too heavy for me to lift at all.

It was all unclear in my mind as to whether the duel had anything to do with my promise to marry Danni.

───────

I crossed a small stream or two, but still had not regained the *Skyboat*. I was wandering in an unknown country, far from home, vaguely hoping somehow to regain contact with Apollo.

In my alienated state of mind I kept wondering if all the gods that I had ever met had been deranged or even killed by some effort of our terrible enemies. The dream in which Apollo appeared to me was reassuring, but he might of course have fallen in battle after that.

───────

In the course of my waking wanderings, I came to a town of modest size whose name I did not know; nor was I at all certain what border I had last crossed. But I could understand the speech of those I met, or enough of it to meet my needs, and this satisfied me for the time being.

The townsfolk greeted me with a simple, courteous welcome. It seemed that I now found myself in a land set apart from most of the world's wars and upheavals, where the people seemed simple and for the most part honest. Here and there were simple shrines to the usual gods, the figures considered most likely to be helpful and dependable.

The town's mayor, a gray-bearded elder with massive eyebrows and a pleasant face, came out to offer me official welcome, and did so without indicating that he knew he had a celebrity on his hands. I got the impression that any well-behaved traveler might have been given the same reception.

There was a small speech that I had given often since the beginning of my wanderings, and now I used it yet again.

"My name is Hercules, and I am an honest man. I am also a stranger among you, far from my own home, and I ask for what you can spare me in the way of food and clothing."

"That seems a most reasonable request, and it is granted." The old man, who had shown no reaction when he heard my name, briefly paused to study me before he added: "But will you do us one reasonable favor in return?"

"Very likely. What is it?"

Leaning a little forward, he pronounced the one word carefully: "Wrestle."

"Wrestle?" For a moment I wondered whether I had heard him correctly. "Wrestle who? And where, and why, and when?"

The man looked a little pained, as if the speech he gave me had been enforced upon him. He said: "There is a certain competition pending, in which it is crucial to us that our town should not be utterly disgraced. Understand, stranger, that whether you actually win a single match or not is of small importance. All that really matters is that you make a creditable effort."

"All right." I could feel myself relaxing inwardly. "I can manage that, and it doesn't seem a lot to ask. Far be it from me to bring disgrace upon my hosts."

The mayor smiled. "Good. We will feed you first, of course. We want you to be strong." And he looked at my unimpressive frame with optimistic eyes.

While I attacked the substantial meal that was soon set before me, washing it down with a flagon of good local beer, I heard the explanations of the townsfolk as to why they were in need of another wrestler.

The whole business seemed a little odd, but reasonably straightforward. The wrestling matches were part of a local tradition of competition with a neighboring town. Each town's chosen competitors formed a single line, the two lines approaching each other head-on, from opposite sides of the wrestling ring. The losing contestant in each match, two falls out of three, was eliminated, and the next man in line stood up in his place. When all the members of either one line or the other had been thrown, the opposite team was acclaimed the winner.

Meanwhile, the general populations of the two towns mingled freely; scores of women, children, and elders all gathered outside the ring to watch and to cheer on their respective local heroes in a festive, almost carnival, atmosphere. Similar contests between towns existed in Cadmia, and in my wanderings I had encountered others. As such affairs went, this one seemed notably unbloody. For that reason, I thought, if for no other, it deserved to be encouraged.

I was not surprised to see that most of the other contestants, on both sides, were bigger than me, bulkier with bone and muscle. When we had stripped, put on the traditional loincloths worn in wrestling, and had taken our places for the event, my hosts' line was notably shorter than that of their opponents. As a relatively small man of unproven skill, I was placed at the tail of it, with the stoutest champion at the head.

After a few speeches, mercifully short, the match got under way. Women and children cheered on the sidelines, and the elder men looked on with varying expressions.

My hosts were somewhat downcast, though not especially surprised, when the opposition proved more powerful and our line was soon depleted. When I stepped forward, the opposing line was only a little shorter than it had been at the start, with almost a dozen men remaining. In contrast, I was the last hope for our side.

Still, I would have been willing to lay a small wager that we were not going to lose.

Methodically, I began to work my way through the opposing wrestlers, who, as I had expected, presented no particular problem. For a time I amused myself by throwing them in alternate directions, one this way and the next one that. I allowed each one to struggle and strain for a short time before disposing of him. Of course I grimaced and grunted at appropriate moments, trying to cloak my series of victories in an air of difficulty.

I had gone through six or seven opponents in this fashion, creating something of a sensation in the audience. And now here came the next man in line. His body was muscular but not spectacular, his size was no greater than ordinary, and there was nothing in his face to capture my attention. Some gray was sprinkled in his dark beard, making him seem a little older than his teammates, though still far from ancient.

Reaching out, I seized the rolled cloth belt of his loincloth with one hand, and one of his arms with the other, taking care not to crush the bones and flesh. With gentle force I pulled and pushed—

—and found myself swept helplessly right off my feet, spinning in midair, the world's whirl ending only when my flight ended, with a great thump that left me flat on my back and staring in stupefaction at the sky.

My head was still spinning as I scrambled quickly to all fours, then up into a kind of wrestler's crouch. My opponent was in roughly the same position, looking at me keenly, his expression indicating wariness rather than the triumph or surprise I had expected.

The crowd around us, instead of closing in, had drawn back in apprehension. For a moment there had been shocked silence, and now there was a steady murmuring.

Now at last I took a good look at the man who had actually overpowered me and thrown me to the ground. If he was indeed a god, and I had to assume he was, his appearance still gave no clue to his exact identity.

There was a louder murmuring from the crowd as word spread of the remarkable thing that had just happened. From what I could overhear, I gathered that the onlookers were as amazed as I was, and no one seemed to have any idea of the stranger's identity.

We closed and grappled with each other once again. This time it seemed to me that though my opponent's strength was absolutely fantastic, every bit the equal of my own, he was not as skilled as other men I had encountered, whose skills had of course availed them nothing.

Here and there during my wanderings, including my earlier matches of the day, I had without even trying picked up a trick or two, simply by observing what one wrestler after another tried to do to me.

Attempting one of these tricks now, I put something like my full strength into the effort, and was rewarded by seeing the mystery man swept off his feet, to land awkwardly and with a heavy thud.

To judge by his expression, he was every bit as surprised as I had been—and a moment later, every bit as determined to have revenge.

We grunted a few terse comments at each other.

The noise of the crowd drowned out all else, as we closed and grappled for the third time.

As sometimes happens, more often when neither contestant has much skill, the fall was inconclusive. We staggered and came down together. Before we could regain our feet and try again, eager voices were being raised on all sides. I heard that the mayors of the two towns seemed to be declaring a truce, both of them eager to conclude that the contest had ended in a draw.

───────

By mutual consent my opponent and I let ourselves sink back to the ground. We sat there in the worn dirt, staring at each other, while the sound of my own racing pulse in my ears gradually died away, and the heaving of my chest for air subsided. The man who had managed to throw me to the earth was wearing a little smile now, as if he was quite pleased with the result of our tussle. His face, everything about him looked staggeringly ordinary. And obviously he was waiting for me to speak first.

I tried to speak, failed, and tried again. A third attempt was necessary before I could get out the words, "You are my father."

The smile that great Zeus was wearing broadened, making pleasant creases in his face. I noted that somehow my father's skin was more weathered and lined than mine was, or would ever be.

He said, in a voice that just missed being ordinary: "And you are Hercules. Every bit as strong as I had hoped you would be. Come, we must have a talk."

Jumping to his feet, as if to make a point of the fact that he was fully recovered from our gasping struggle, he offered me a hand and pulled me up. Then he linked his arm with mine and led me away to a place where, for some reason, none of the curious onlookers followed. I could hear them somewhere in the middle distance, marveling loudly over how the pair of champions had suddenly disappeared.

After all my efforts to bring this moment about, I came perilously close to not knowing what to say.

"You are—" But somehow I could not get out the words.

"I am your father. Yes, you were quite right the first time." The Thunderer wiped sweat from his face and chuckled in a very human way.

Despite his show of jumping quickly to his feet, we were both still breathing heavily. At last I managed to find some words: "So, I have outwrestled Zeus himself."

"Only in one fall out of three! I would not brag, upstart, if I were you." Though the words were harsh, the tone in which they were spoken told of pride and even a kind of love.

Then the most powerful god in the Universe cast back over his left shoulder a look that was almost furtive.

"Besides," my father said, "the less closely the world can keep track of my whereabouts, the better. In particular, the Giants are not to know anything at all of where I am, or what I'm doing."

I made an awkward, sweeping gesture. "This whole wrestling contest—"

He nodded. "All designed just so you and I could have this meeting. I have taken considerable pains to arrange it. I wanted to keep it as secret as possible from our enemies, and to make sure that you would be unlikely to refuse to take part."

"I am honored."

"You deserve to be honored. You have done well."

"Thank you," I said. And then: "I have prayed for this meeting."

"That was well done." It seemed a perfectly sincere comment.

"Do gods really hear all their worshipers' prayers?" I asked my father. "There must be thousands and thousands every day."

"More like millions and millions, Hercules. But there is no need for the gods to hear every single one of them, because we know what they are. What they always are, have always been."

I thought that over for a little while. "And do you, great Zeus, know the details of the lives of all your thousands of children?"

"Zeus has thousands of offspring, true. But without his Face in here"—and my father raised a hand to touch his forehead—"I would still be a man; and the man who now wears the Face of Zeus"—he thumped himself on the chest "has only a very few children whom he calls his own."

"And I—"

"And you, Hercules, I am proud to say, are one of them."

We talked for a time of other matters, but inevitably came to the matter of the Giants.

———————

We talked for what seemed a long time, and I do not remember all of what we said. But at one point, I know Zeus told me: "Mortals are always wondering why we have so often withdrawn ourselves from human affairs for extended periods. But few if any have guessed the correct answer."

"Which is simply fear."

"Fear indeed. A god, or goddess, appearing openly among humans will inevitably soon draw a crowd. And crowds are conspicuous and make it easy for our enemies to keep track of where we are."

And I said to him: "Apollo told me that his true name—his first, human name—is Jeremy Redthorn."

"I'm well aware of what the young man told you. But don't expect to hear any similar revelations from me. There are good reasons."

"I don't doubt it, sir."

And then my father began to talk about me. I will not set down here everything that he said, but it turned out that he knew many details of my childhood that I had imagined no one but myself would ever know.

As soon as I had the chance, I began to question him about Hera, the goddess proclaimed by tradition to be his consort, and who, I had some reason to believe, had once sent snakes to kill me in my cradle.

My father frowned. "Sadly, there is some truth in the story. I regret I was not alert enough to prevent it—more proof, if any were needed, of my own distinct lack of omnipotence. But that's all over and done with."

He heaved a sigh, and his face regained cheerfulness. "Hera exists now in a new avatar—have you met her yet?—never mind, you will. No reason to think of her current version as my wife, but she and I are on good terms. No, Hercules, as far as I know, you have nothing to fear from any god or goddess."

"That's good to know, sir." I paused, then added: "But there is one god who has much to fear from me, if I ever get my hands on him again."

"That avatar of Death is himself dead," said Zeus. Then he added: "Of course I would have stopped the horror he committed against your family, had I known in time what he intended. But you must understand that I have my limits, too, especially since I began to encounter Giants. And you must be careful what you do to gods, even the most minor ones. Almost all of them are jealous of our power and status and want no humiliation at the hands of mortals."

"I understand that, sir."

"I remember the day Amphitryon flogged you with a belt," Zeus went on, smiling faintly. "That was one time when there was obviously no need for me to intervene on your behalf."

"I should not have broken his fine dagger."

"No, that was wrong of you. But you were very young; and I, too, have broken many things that I should not, while lacking your excuse."

I wondered, silently, if my father had also been watching on the day when I first made love to Megan. Some part of me wanted to ask him that, but a greater part would not.

And then there was the sad hour in which I had killed Linus. But we did not speak of that time, either.

Now Zeus was looking at me in a way that made me wonder if he could indeed see everything that was in my heart. He said: "Today is a good day, as far as my wits are concerned. I seem to be recovering as rapidly as can be expected from my last duel with a Giant. That is why—that is one reason—I have chosen it for our talk."

We talked, at last, about the final fate of Megan and little Hyllus. "I hope and pray," I said, "their true souls are not wandering lost, somewhere in the Underworld."

"That much I can promise you," my father said.

"Indeed," I said, "I was pretty well convinced that there are no true souls there. I saw strange empty images, and a few bodies that lived and breathed, as lively as my own."

" 'We each of us owe God a death . . . ,' " said the man who was supposed to be the greatest god himself, and I had the impression that he was quoting something. "Someday, Hercules, you and I must have a talk on the subject of life and death."

"In a way, sir," I said impulsively, "you remind me of Daedalus."

"Do I, indeed? I take that as a compliment. I hope the Artisan would feel the same way."

At last, so Zeus told me, he had available the results of the analysis, performed by Vulcan and Daedalus, of the Boar I had brought in alive, and of the other samples of flesh and bone from an assortment of monsters, including Antaeus.

And he got to his feet, with the air of a king about to take his leave.

But before departing, he said to me: "You are my son, and I am proud of you."

"Father!" The word still sounded strange in my own ears. When he paused, I demanded: "When will I see you again? Tell me, what am I to do next?"

Zeus shook his head. "If only I were really as all-powerful as the legends have me! All I can tell you with certainty is that I must go now, and I will see you again when the proper time has come. Meanwhile, here is another you have met, and you must go with him."

My visit with Atlas, and my sojourn underground, had revealed to me too much of the Universe for me to any longer imagine that Zeus or any other individual might be its ruler.

And when my father had said good-bye, I was not much surprised to see Apollo waiting for me in his chariot, ready to convey me to the secret laboratory.

The Far-Worker and I greeted each other joyfully, and I learned with great relief that he had once again regained his mental faculties, and practically all his memory.

He said to me: "We gods are resilient. But how many more times our minds may be so damaged, and still recover . . ." The god shook his head pessimistically.

And yet once more, taking my courage in both hands, I boarded my friend's chariot, not knowing if we could reach our destination before some Giant's weapon, like an invisible arrow, shot us out of the sky.

This time we flew far, and higher than before, so high indeed that my lungs worked hard for breath. My imagination peopled the earth below us thickly with Giants, towering forms who scanned the skies for targets—like hunters with bows and slings, who look for ducks. But if in fact there were any such enemies around, they could not see us, and we were not attacked.

26

Vulcan's Workshop

LIKE EVERYONE ELSE I knew, I had been hearing stories about Vulcan's workshop all my life. It was one of the great establishments of legend, in which, from time immemorial, all manner of marvels had been and were still being produced. And at the end of my second ride in a flying chariot, which concluded much more successfully than my first, I was able to confirm with my own eyes the truth of some of the strangest tales.

By the time we began our second hour of flight, I knew that we were farther north than I had ever been before. As we approached our destination from the air, there appeared before us a rocky island, bound by glaciers, a mile out from the ragged, fog-bound shoreline of a northern ocean, under the slanted light of a western sun. Gray, sullen seas beat on the sharp rocks of the little island, far less than a square mile in area. I would not have wanted to attempt to reach that goal by sea, not even in the *Skyboat*. Even the name of this ocean was unknown to me, and I realized that its waters were connected to those of the Great Sea only by a long, circuitous route.

But thoughts of geography and navigation were secondary at the moment. I scarcely felt the icy wind that tugged at my hair and beard, or the warmth of the low sun in the bright sky. I was no stranger to earthly palaces, but never had I seen, and scarcely had I imagined, anything like this. Looking at the island, and the structure occupying most of its surface, I would never have guessed that it had ever been inhabited by either gods or humans.

The location seemed to have been chosen with the idea of making the fortress on it not only unassailable, but approachable only by gods, or by other beings with a comparable talent for flight.

The whole building—for such my escort assured me it was—seemed little more than a huge slab of dark, slippery rock, perhaps a hundred feet high, tilted only a few degrees out of the vertical, and emerging from a rocky platform only a few feet above the level of the sea. The only sign of artifice was a few reinforcing bands of strong metal, inlaid into the otherwise almost featureless rock.

As the chariot bore us down toward a landing on the platform base, I was puzzled at still being able to see no doors or windows in all the flat expanse of walls. There were indeed huge panels, almost flat and smooth, whose appearance from a quarter of a mile away had suggested that they might be enormous doors. But as we drew nearer still, our flight slowing almost to a stop as it neared its end, I saw that their surfaces were devoid of any lock or hinge or joining, and there appeared to be no way to get a grip to try to open them.

Either Apollo was reading my mind or his powers of observation allowed him to determine just what I was looking at.

"Once I tried my full strength against those portals," he informed me. "And as you see, they are still standing."

I looked at him, and at the rock, and back to him again. "The lord Vulcan must build well, and deserves his reputation," I said.

"Indeed he does. But this time we come with a key and know the secret of the lock."

Apollo's pacing horses seemed to know just where to bring us down, without specific orders from their master. We landed on a small, flat space just in front of the largest flat panel that might have been a door. I believe my escort was just about to put a key into a lock (thought I could not discern the keyhole) when the door was opened for us by the life-sized figure of a slender maiden, completely nude and seeming to be made entirely of shining gold.

As long as we were still airborne, the chariot had glowed with a kind of inner warmth, which had sufficed to keep my mortal flesh from freezing. But when we came to a halt and I jumped out, the full arctic blast of Hyperborean wind struck at me, and I was very glad to follow the gesture of the golden maid, who beckoned me to her through the doorway, into a place of comfortable warmth and cheerful light.

I started to speak to the maid as I hurried past her, but before I had finished a sentence I was completely sure that the figure before me was neither human nor god, but only a device of metal and magic, cunningly formed into the shape of a young girl. Apollo, entering the fortress right behind me, ignored the golden marvel and strode on down a long hallway, halloing ahead in the manner of a man entering a familiar house. The maiden promptly closed the outer door behind us.

Moments later my divine companion and I were standing in a vast room, almost as big as the hall of Hades in the Underworld, furnished with chairs and tables of heroic size, and lit by the orange glow of a distant forge. Another moment after that, and we were being welcomed by a marvelous company, in which Daedalus, the only mortal present besides myself, made the least impressive figure.

Half a dozen tall, formidable figures were gathered in the hall, and most of them turned their heads to look at me as I entered. Their faces wore a variety of expressions, and presently I was being introduced to Hephaestus, also known as Vulcan, or the Smith.

The Smith's hands were big, with gnarled fingers, and he limped on a right leg that was slightly twisted and deformed. His muscular torso was bare and sweating, and he was gripping some tool I did not recognize.

———

Before I could start to worry about any possible awkwardness in my being introduced to Hera, the thing had been accomplished. I bowed low before a majestic woman in formal robes, who responded with a gracious nod. A golden circlet crowned her head, and a peacock was strutting at her feet.

Close beside her was standing Mars, also called Ares, unmistakable with his armor and his spear. I knew a strange sensation down the back of my neck when the God of War nodded to me with respect.

I was sure that my first glance on entering had shown me several other deities in the group, but whoever they might have been, all were gone now, vanished like a rainbow when the sun is suddenly engulfed in clouds.

Daedalus said he had important business to transact with me, now that I was available, and he called me away from the gathering of gods and goddesses as soon as he could without offending any of that company. With one of the golden maidens to assist him, he was prepared to show me the important work that he and Hephaestus were engaged in. Meanwhile I started to tell him about my experience with Atlas.

Gladly I followed the Artisan into another room. I had pictured the inside of this establishment, when I tried to picture it at all, as a gigantic forge or foundry, filled with flame and smoke and the clang of metal, and all of these were present in the central hall; but the first workroom I actually entered was equipped and furnished very differently. Most of the laborers, it seemed to me, were as invisible as so many Dionysian sprites.

Now Daedalus showed me an ongoing laboratory experiment, in which he and the Smith were hand-forging helmets out of a special alloy of bronze, containing a slight mixture of the residue of a fallen Giant's body. Daedalus had hopes that this alloy would effectively shield the wearer's brain from the Giants' destructive rays.

Naturally I rejoiced to hear this news. It was obvious from past experience that the assembled divinities would need some kind of protective devices if they were going to have any chance of making a successful fight of it in the open.

At the time of my arrival, Hephaestus had only one helmet ready. Conferring with Daedalus and his magic helpers, he tried to get a production line going.

Ordinarily, Zeus and his colleagues wore gold or silver, when they encumbered their comely bodies with any metal at all. I got the impression that they all considered helmets, like their other accoutrements, as purely decorative. In the ordinary course of events deities needed no protection, from either violence or weather.

Vulcan put his experimental helmet on his own head. He wanted to demonstrate his own handiwork by getting someone to accompany him in an airborne chariot while he hunted for a Giant and attempted to attack him.

When the Smith's devine peers heard of this planned demonstration, they were upset, and all agreed that he was too important to the cause to risk himself in such a fashion. Naturally no mortal human would be of any use as a subject in this case, and so it was decided to call for volunteers among the lesser deities.

But as soon as word went out from Hephaestus and Daedalus that they were seeking some minor god willing to be experimentally befuddled, Dionysus volunteered at once, saying that such a mental state was nothing out of the ordinary for him.

"I fear my esteemed colleagues do not understand," proclaimed the Twice-Born. "I am no hero. It's just that I expect to experience little difference between the mental state brought on by this experiment and the ecstasy I commonly share with my worshipers."

The Smith shook his head doubtfully. "Then it seems we ought to find some other volunteer for our test. Who else is available?" And this discussion, too, seemed likely to dissolve in hopeless wrangling. I feared there was no way that the important test could be accomplished anytime soon.

After I had been given a preliminary tour of the secret workshop, He- phaestus called me aside, saying he had prepared for me special gifts.

"Hercules, I have heard much of you, and I like what I hear."

This came as a complete surprise to me, but you may believe I followed with alacrity. In another room, where the fire of a smaller forge was burning, he showed me that he had ready a suit of chain mail, forged from a different metal alloy than the gods' helmets, and padded with fine wool. This, he promised me, would be just what I needed. The garment had been forged and trimmed with divine skill into a shape that fit me excellently well.

I put it on at once, found that it allowed me perfect freedom of movement, and once more thanked its creator. It would offer consid- erable protection from any weapon the Giants might strike at me with, and from the arctic blasts of freezing air as well.

I thanked the Smith as politely as I could, while keeping to myself my serious doubts that I would ever need armor of any kind to shield me in a fight—on the other hand, if we were going to fight in a cold climate I would certainly be grateful for something to keep me warm.

Daedalus, who had come to observe the fitting, cautioned me that the suit's materials had not been tested against burns or poisons.

And Hephaestus said: "Since I have been told something of your strength, I have not stinted on the armor's strength by trying to reduce its weight. Few mortal men who wore this would be able to lift their arms, or even move their feet. But you should have no difficulty."

He also told me that his mortal name was Andy Ferrante. "You might as well call me Andy, Hercules. I'm even newer at this game than Apollo is." And he put out his hand for me to shake.

And in the course of our talk, Hephaestus mentioned his dream of someday, somehow, gaining the power of manufacturing Faces. But any such effort would have to wait until the war was over.

When I was dressed in my new suit, and after I had allowed myself a few hours' sleep and had eaten, I resumed my study of the research projects that were currently under way.

There was another golden maiden here, and other inhuman helpers who were less spectacular, if only because they were invisible.

By studying the materials and processes that the Giants had used to create the monsters, the Smith and the Artisan between them thought they had gained some important insight as to the nature of the Giants, and some clues to their special weapon as well. Though the Boar and Hydra, and the sea monster that had almost eaten the Trojan princess, were of course of different species than the Giants, they, too, were designed creatures, incorporating odylic magic.

Part of the work recently accomplished by the Smith and the Artisan had been the building of a kind of greenhouse on a remote high ledge of Vulcan's fortress, and the planting of Apple seeds therein. So far there had not been enough of a crop to allow much in the way of experimentation.

Daedalus told me as he suspected that the Giants, whether moved by some intellectual curiosity or only acting on instinct, had also been experimenting. Not with helmets, unfortunately, but with means of turning all native earthly life into monstrous variations that would cease to reproduce. So far they had had only occasional success.

"And we still don't know with any certainty where the Giants themselves came from—I find it fascinating that Atlas told you they issued from the earth. I wonder if he meant that the first ones grew like plants? Oh, how I wish I had been there when you were talking to him!"

"I wish so, too," I told the Artisan. "Maybe when this war is over we can go back and talk to him again."

———

Almost all the Giants with whom people had reported having encountered were male. But my tutors assured me again that female examples, Giants who seemed to have been modeled in more or less crude imitation of human women, were not unknown.

Though Giants rarely spoke to gods or humans, there had been a few dialogues between the two species over the centuries. Generally these communications consisted of little more than shouted threats, challenges, or warnings. Presumably the Titans communicated more frequently among themselves.

The life span of each Giant seemed to be enormous, though probably not comparable to that of a god.

Neither Daedalus nor Hephaestus had yet been able to learn exactly where on earth the Giants had first sprung to life, or when—except that it must have been in the remote past.

Or whether, somewhere in the dim past, they had actually been human—to me that was the most chilling possibility of all.

———

The more I thought about our race of enemies, the more I realized that I knew almost nothing about them. I spoke my thoughts aloud to Daedalus. "I wonder, are there Giant infants somewhere?"

"I suppose everything that lives must pass through some stage of immaturity. Antaeus, as you describe him, Hercules, must have been quite young, as Giants go."

"That had never occurred to me," I remarked, trying to cast back my thoughts. "True, he had no beard, and I think no hair on chest or belly. It may be he was but half grown." I tried to compare his remembered image with that of the Giant who had shot Apollo's chariot out of the air with me aboard.

As later research demonstrated, those Apples of Hesperides were essential to the Giants' reproduction and important in their nourishment, if not essential to their absolute survival.

"If we can eliminate the Apples entirely from the earth, that ought to make the survival of our enemies much more difficult. It might even finish them off entirely."

It was perfectly true, several deities assured me, that the Giants sometimes sexually assaulted women, and even goddesses. A number of cases had been recorded down through the years. But Daedalus now contended that their assaults on females were only being misinterpreted as sexual.

Hera, who had quietly approached and was listening to the lecture, was not pleased with that point of view and issued a stern decree that the rights of women should be everywhere defended.

The next point to be argued, by some of the other gods, was just what those rights should be. Our discussion was going nowhere when Zeus suddenly joined us, materializing apparently from out of nothing, surprising everyone already inside the laboratory. My father was dressed simply, though much more regally than when I had seen him in the wrestling ring. Especially astonished were those gods, chiefly Vulcan, who thought that all intruders had been effectively excluded. But when they saw who this intruder was, they only shrugged their shoulders.

Diplomatically Zeus sidestepped the debate on women's rights. It seemed that a council of war was about to get under way, and as I was so important to the Olympian cause, I was invited to attend. Zeus now publicly acknowledged me as his son in front of his assembled colleagues, none of whom seemed in the least surprised.

Hephaestus, pleased that I had taken to his customized armor with such enthusiasm, was ready now to show me my new club, which he said he had made from a particular oak tree.

This weapon was no larger than other clubs of similar shape that I had used in the past, but it was certainly heavier, and stronger. This one had been loaded by Vulcan with metal weights, and strengthened with steel bands and rods. I understood that the Artisan had been instrumental in its design.

It was so heavy that Daedalus, after one abortive effort to lift it cleanly, did not try to carry it to me himself, but employed one of the golden maidens for the job. The slender metal figure bore the weapon with an ease that not even an Amazon could have matched.

Daedalus said to me: "An ordinary man would be considered very powerful if he could even lift this weapon, let alone use it. It is designed especially for one of your size and strength."

I swung it a few times in the air, reveling in what seemed perfect balance, and looked about for something to hit.

The inconclusive wrangling of the gods was cut off in midsentence by a Titanic blast, which shook the floor of rock beneath our feet.

My divine allies and I were startled, and some of us were staggered, when rock over our heads shuddered, as if Thor's hammer had struck home, and a fine sprinkling of dust came sifting down.

A moment later, the speeding figure of the Messenger came darting into the vast room from somewhere to warn us all in a stentorian voice that the Giants had taken the offensive and were now bombarding Vulcan's island laboratory with huge rocks, while an actual invasion was about to get under way.

The walls and roof of Vulcan's laboratory, as I have said, looked almost unimaginably strong. But still I had a feeling in my bones that they would give way if that bombardment were continued. Each direct hit sent tremors through the solid rock beneath our feet, shook down a shower of fine debris, and produced an almost deafening gonglike reverberation in the ears of all who occupied the fortress.

The Olympians' immediate response to the attack was to plunge into an argument as to whether the rock and metal walls of the fortress could be depended on to shield their vulnerable brains from memory depletion, as long as they remained inside.

"To the Underworld with memory depletion!" shouted a deity I could not recognize. "We'd better get ourselves out of the way of flying rocks!"

Mars pounded the butt of his spear on the stone floor and roared out his contempt of such a cowardly attitude. Shrinking out of sight of the enemy was no way to win a war.

Meanwhile, I was more than ready to enter combat. Gripping my new club in both hands, I almost cried aloud for joy as I ran toward the place where, as I remembered, a door led to the outside.

Zeus now echoed the War God in a ringing call to arms. And now indeed the numbers in our company were growing. I could not recognize most of the new arrivals, nor tell where they were coming from—perhaps from some other chamber in the fort.

I learned a little later that before the fighting started, Zeus had been sending out messengers, summoning every god and goddess whose support he had any hope of getting, to take part in a climactic battle. He had meant to convene a conference of deities, where he could present to his colleagues a reasoned case for all-out warfare against the Giants; but that argument had now been made for him, and forcefully.

Sprites had done most of the messenger work, maintaining a fairly effective communications network on our side, leaving only a few of the most vitally important missions for Mercury to handle personally.

The invitations, or urgent summonses from Zeus to join the fight, had gone only to his fellow deities—this was not a matter in which mere mortal humans could be expected to be of any help. All the kings and high priests of earthly power would have to remain standing on the sidelines, beside the humbler members of the human race.

Meanwhile, in the main room of the workshop, the molten, carefully blended bronze alloy was being poured into ingots, which were then in turn hammered and welded into the shape of the desired helmets. Something like a production line had been established, operated chiefly by the Smith's two golden metal aides, with help from some Dionysian satyrs, and other creatures I could not immediately identify.

The great building shook under the impact of another enormous boulder as the bombardment continued.

Still, some of the Smith's clients were unhappy with the helmet design. Rarely have I known any group of mortals as prone to argument as were the gods. Some of their number insisted on debating the question of whether Vulcan had got his proportions right in that alloy, and even the relative efficacy of bronze, as compared to iron, or cloth, or simple unalloyed tin or copper.

As I listened to them, there dawned on me suddenly something I ought to have realized before: that deities were no braver than anyone else, when facing what they thought might be a real danger. Some eagerly embraced even the weakest excuses to put off the moment of real testing.

Certain other deities, of course, were at the opposite extreme of readiness. Blustering Ares now demanded that he be given the first helmet. Hephaestus complied, and as soon as Mars had the bronze casque on his head he lived up to his reputation by actually leading the way into combat. The metal was still so hot from the forge that it was almost glowing, but Mars did not appear to notice the heat as he gripped it in both hands.

"If you are looking for some guarantee of perfect safety," he barked at his timorous colleagues, "we will not find it here inside this fort, or anywhere!"

Some of the gods railed at Ares for his bragging, but others shouted their readiness to follow him into battle.

Mars pointed at me and sought to shame them by my example. "Will you stand back and allow a mere mortal to lead the way?"

I was hardly leading the way at the moment, but the War God's point was made. Some responded angrily to this challenge, and others ignored it. It seemed to me that a sizable majority of divinities took to their heels, fleeing through the air invisibly (as they hoped), or tried to hide in an effort to avoid the weapon they could not withstand. At the present rate of production, it seemed that hours or even days must pass before Vulcan's helmets would be available to all the gods who wanted them.

The fact that a great many gods were ready to delegate their fighting to a mere mortal like myself did not disturb me. I understood their necessity for doing what was necessary to protect themselves, at least until the enemy's most effective weapons could be somehow countered. If all my powerful allies should be wiped out, my own chances of success would vanish utterly.

And I thought I had yet to meet the Giant who could do me any deadly harm—I suppose my state of mind at the time could be generously described as the overconfidence of youth.

27

Battle

SEEING THAT I was trying to get out-of-doors and into the fight as quickly as possible, some goddess equipped with flying Sandals—to my embarrassment I could not recognize her—effortlessly picked me up and carried me high into the upper reaches of the laboratory's vast interior.

I had entered Vulcan's laboratory through a door at ground level, but now came out through an opening high in the peaked roof. There my benefactor silently put me down and flew away. On emerging into the open air, I was much comforted to find that my new armor protected me effectively from the arctic blasts of cold wind; I had dreaded being frozen more than I feared anything a Giant was likely to do to me.

As when I entered the fortress, the sun was low in the sky; but now its light fell from a different direction, and I realized that a night had passed while I was inside.

As soon as I got outside I could see that not only was a bombardment in progress, but a strong force of Giants was approaching the island, advancing in a rough semicircle along the fog-shrouded shore a mile away, and out across the water.

Looking down from my high vantage point, it seemed to me that the tallest of the attackers might be closer to fifty feet in height than to a hundred. Even at a distance of half a mile, Alkyoneus was already recognizable, conspicuous among his fellows by his size and bulk. His appearance was also odd, this time, because his body gleamed, as if with metal, from head to foot.

To my further amazement I saw that some of the attackers were actually afloat in the choppy sea, in several kinds of ships and rafts.

Even more astonishing, some, supported by enormous balloons, were airborne over the water.

"Don't tell me they can swim!" barked some minor godlet, hovering just over the sharply peaked roof where I was balancing. "I'd expect them to melt to mud with a good soaking."

I would have expected much the same thing, but that was not the case. Actually the attackers were approaching across and through the water, their weight partially supported by enormous balloons, their stony feet only dragging a little in the waves.

I brandished my new club and announced my readiness to fight.

As soon as I had my feet solidly planted on the peak of the roof, I could see how the outer walls of the fortress had already been damaged, great irregular peelings of stone spalled away by the bombardment, like bark splintered from a tree. Huge rocks were still flying toward us on curved paths out of the gray sky, some of them from clear over the horizon, one arriving at or near the laboratory every few seconds. While still at a distance some of these boulders seemed to float like giant snowflakes, or tufts of thistledown, but as they drew near I could see that they were actually hurtling faster than arrows. Some were so small and approached so swiftly that it taxed my mortal vision to catch sight of them at all.

"So, they are using trebuchets? Or catapults?" I demanded.

The head of the goddess turned in my direction. "I believe they are simply picking up rocks in their hands and throwing them, my lad. Giants can do that."

I was impressed.

Meanwhile, the actual invasion was steadily progressing. Those Giants supported by balloons came floating toward us almost entirely above the water, only dipping in their feet from time to time, taking advantage of an offshore breeze to stay on course to the island. Their massive feet were encased in bundles of hollow reeds that must have given them some buoyancy. It struck me at the time that our monstrous enemies must be very brave to risk the depths of the ocean thus; it seemed to me hardly possible that any of that earthy race could swim, but that rather they must sink like the stones they almost were, once plunged in without support.

Something, it might have been the day's first Arrow from Apollo's Bow, or a slung stone from Mars, punctured the supporting balloons of one advancing figure, and with a great bellowing cry the Giant fell into the ocean. He disappeared completely in a titanic splash, but moments later his head and shoulders surfaced. Plainly he found the water only chest-deep at his point of entry, and he managed to survive, his earthy body more resistant to melting than I had expected.

His fellow Titans were not discouraged by his fate. Anyway, comparatively few were depending on balloons. A majority were paddling enormous boats, approaching our fortress island from several sides at once. The nearest of this latter group were almost ashore now and had abandoned their boats to go wading in the sea, as if indifferent to its icy cold and to the pounding of the surf.

Meanwhile, other attackers continued hurling huge rocks at our fortress island, some from very far away. I was glad to see that the enemy effort was not well coordinated, so that the members of the landing party stood in some danger of being brained by their own side's long-range bombardment. At the same time I wondered how those distant throwers could ever know whether they had the proper range or not.

Even as I watched, the first of the invading Giants actually set his huge feet on the island. And now about a dozen more were just about to follow him. Their seamed and craggy faces loomed not far below me, some bearded and some smooth, all of them hard, all loathsome in my sight.

Now Ares, reining in his black horses so that his chariot hovered in midair, was shouting at his colleagues, trying to convince them that the numbers made this a serious attempt to take the fort, and not just a harassing raid.

Zeus raised his voice and said: "Whatever their intentions may be, here they are, and we'd better start to fight them."

Mars began to roar out orders, but Apollo at the same time seemed to be commanding yet another course of action.

Impatient of watching and waiting, I decided to take the initiative. The way our leaders were contradicting one another, I could hardly fail to find myself acting in obedience to one chief at least, no matter what I did.

Wary about putting myself directly in the path of one of the huge incoming missiles, I impulsively tried catching a small splinter from one of the near misses. A head-sized fragment was arcing toward me slowly enough that I could get my hands in its way. Catching the heavy object spun me around with its velocity, but I was able to keep my grip on it while still retaining my balance on the peaked roof.

In another moment, I had hurled the fragment back, aiming for the spot on the horizon whence most of the big rocks were coming, and putting what I then considered to be nearly all my strength into the throw. Two or three such attempts were necessary for me to get the distance approximately right, as nearly as I could judge from the distant splashes of ice and snow; but it seemed unlikely that I would hit any of my targets, which were invisible to me with distance. I thought I had better direct my energies to matters close at hand.

———

By now, four or five of the Giants' invasion force were already ashore, looking about for enemies to smite, while an equal number of the enormous figures, with more following in the distance, were now wading knee-deep, or thigh-deep, in through the breaking surf.

And now the long-range bombardment ceased abruptly, as if some signal had been given. I wondered if the throwers' sight was keen enough to see the situation from miles away.

Our enemies' willingness to immerse themselves yards deep in water proved to be a mistake when Poseidon, Lord of the Oceans, and some of his lesser associates entered the battle on our side.

I saw Neptune's bearded head above the waves, but only briefly. This first thrust of Poseidon and his forces into combat scored some success for our side. The waves erupted around the ships that were still carrying Giants, capsizing the oversize passengers into the almost frozen sea. Salt water seemed to boil around those wading ashore, and mammoth breakers pounded them against the rocks, bruising and tearing their hard bodies, spilling thick Giant blood into the sea.

Again I saw Neptune riding in his golden chariot, pulled by white horses, with his trident raised high, leading his forces into battle.

Unhappily the Sea God's head was still unprotected, and a Giant mind weapon soon disrupted his attack. He and his escort of lesser gods were driven off with failing memories.

With startling suddenness the huge waves died away, leaving the sea around our island almost calm. The natural sea creatures, killer whales and others who had been following Neptune's orders were left leaderless. Some who persisted in their assaults were scooped out of the sea in Giant hands and hurled against dry rocks.

Finding the surf a perilous place to be themselves, Giants hastened to scramble up onto the shore.

Now a few more of the gods, their noble heads newly ensconced in bronze helmets, came flying out of the fortress, some in chariots and some running like deer with flying Sandals, in a wild sortie.

Immediately several Giants' arms were lifted and pointed at them, blasting the deities with their special weapon. But this time our foes were confounded when the devices for the first time failed to work, or had only marginal effect, even at close range.

Roaring in triumph, our gods, using their own characteristic weapons, struck down a number of Giants, and the rest fell back in a disorderly retreat. The lightning of Zeus struck left and right, the Arrows of Apollo flew, the spear of Mars thrust again and again, with effective violence.

I saw more than one of the Giants' balloons explode into flames, flaring spectacularly when lightning struck, and dropping their weighty burdens on rock or into the sea.

One came down very close to where I stood. The gasbags that gave the huge body buoyancy were pierced by missiles. The Giant's huge frame tottered, and he stumbled on his massive, slow-moving feet. Missiles of his own, that he had not had time to throw, cascaded from his hands to crash hard on the distant ground, and his vast arms, with fingers spread, went groping blindly. More lightning bolts seared down, to right and left, each momentarily painting one side of his body a pure electric white.

His body hit the earth with a crushing impact. The frame of any Giant who fell for any considerable distance broke to pieces on contact with the ground.

———

The losses were not all on one side. I saw some lesser god, whom I could not recognize at that distance, struck down, mashed flat by a huge rock. The victim's god-Face came bursting from his head and went spinning away to fall into the sea. I believe the only human to witness that loss was myself, and I neither needed nor wanted whatever extra powers that Face might have conveyed. If the tales of magic that we all believed were true, then sometime, somewhere, it would be washed ashore where human hands could pick it up.

Meanwhile I still had taken no part in the fight myself and was frantically casting about for some way of actually getting into action. So far, none of our adversaries had come within my reach. (I knew that with a little exertion, I could jump for a great distance; but occasional practice sessions, early in life, had convinced me that I could never be exactly sure just where I was going to come down.)

Months ago, on entering my combat with Antaeus, I had expected a struggle not intrinsically different from an ordinary wrestling match. But now, having survived and profited from that experience, I had some idea of what I was up against. I could only suppose that the truly huge Giants would be vastly stronger even than Antaeus, their bodies tougher and harder to wound or break. I wanted to take full advantage of my new, bigger, heavier club, but I also vowed to tear my opponent apart with my bare hands, if that proved necessary.

I contemplated jumping, or falling, to the ground and attacking one of the advancing Giants at foot level. But Fate provided a more promising opportunity. From the high roof of Vulcan's enormous dwelling I could look right down on the shaggy head of one of the taller Giants as the huge intruder tried to break his way in through what looked like the laboratory's front door.

The business was slightly complicated by the fact that he was actually wearing a kind of helmet, which appeared to be made of several thicknesses of tough leather. But I thought that ought to make little difference to my club.

Boldly I leaped onto my adversary's head, and with my free hand I clutched a handful of his coarse, shaggy hair to keep myself in position. Then with my club I belabored his padded skull.

In such a position I could strike only awkwardly, so it seemed to me that I was only tapping. Still my victim screamed and fell to his knees; his skull was thick, but it was not hard and thick enough.

I had been expecting my gargantuan opponent to collapse as soon as his head was severely damaged, but the collapse was not as quick or as complete as I had hoped.

I pounded him some more, and then leaped free when his body crashed face-first along the stony shore.

———

Several Titans, having identified me as the mortal who was causing them huge problems, surrounded me with the obvious goal of trying to finish me off. They pounded at me with giant clubs, actual tree trunks stripped of branches, whose impact on the island rock I narrowly avoided.

Others came balloon-skipping across the half-frozen sea, carrying oil-soaked tree trunks as great burning brands. Quite a sight in the gray, near arctic twilight, but a poor choice of weapon with which to assault Vulcan's stony stronghold.

But these special weapons were not meant to breach the walls. They were intended to kill me.

Almost the only real pain I had ever felt in my life had come from internal causes—the common bellyaches and toothaches of childhood. The peculiar blister raised on my hand during my fight with the centaurs was a notable exception. I did have good reason to believe that my skin was much more heat-resistant than that of any ordinary human, but whether it could withstand prolonged exposure to fire I did not know, and being reluctant to put it to the ultimate test, I did all I could to avoid the burning tree trunks.

———

Now the voices of several gods were raised in excited cries, sounding a familiar name. I turned to see that the enemy champion was at hand, and I recognized him as the Giant who had shot down Apollo's chariot with me aboard. Alkyoneus had come ashore and was standing on one rocky tip of the laboratory island. The archenemy of the gods was leading the other invaders.

This was my first really good look at Alkyoneus, and I stood stunned, for he was even more impressive when seen at close range. He was clad from head to toe in some kind of metal armor, or at least in a net of chains, the lower links dragging on the earth.

Apollo brought his chariot to a sudden stop beside me, and in a few terse words proposed that we attack this Giant together.

Gripping my club, I stared at the enemy champion. He differed from the others in being not only larger, but more powerfully built. Just as a wrestler is easily distinguished from other men at first glance, so Alkyoneus stood out from his fellow Giants.

"Anytime you're ready, Jeremy Redthorn," I said, over my shoulder.

———

But before Apollo and I could agree on a plan for our attack, the chariot of Mars came hurtling past us at full speed. The War God was charging directly at our common enemy, howling a challenge and raising his mighty spear.

Alkyoneus struck out with one mighty arm, and I gasped in surprise as the rushing chariot of Mars was knocked aside before the god could thrust with his spear.

And in the next moment, the Giant moved in our direction with amazing speed. Before I realized what had happened, Apollo, too, had been somehow beaten to the ground, where his horses lay tangled in their harness; his chariot spun its wheels in the air.

In the next instant my Titanic opponent had somehow spotted my tiny figure and had turned on me with arms outstretched. Perhaps my fame had spread even among Giants, and he knew me by the club I carried. All of his enormous fingers were pointing at me, and he was obviously using the exotic weapon that his kind used against the gods—whether or not the word of my invulnerability had spread among our enemies, he wanted to try for himself whether the special weapon had no effect.

Mighty Alkyoneus was not stupid enough to persist with his useless magic after he saw that it was ineffective.

I ran toward him, but he moved away—not out of fear, I was sure. Rather he was intent on rallying, in a voice of thunder, some of his fellow Giants who were obviously contemplating a retreat.

Another, lesser Giant came at me and repeated another of my earlier opponent's mistakes by trying to step on me, like a man killing a beetle or a mouse. But I was a different sort of mouse than this creature had ever seen before. Bracing the butt end of my club on the ground, like a soldier's pike, I gave him a punctured foot.

The enormous body of my most recent opponent took a long time falling, like a tall tree. The arms were extremely powerful, and by no means clumsy, but still ineffective in breaking the fall. The heavy impact on rock took a lot out of him, and I suspect it cost him a few broken ribs, with likely internal injuries. But he was a fighter, and his fingers kept spasmodically attempting to grab me up. I had to disable most of the fingers before I could get inside the reach of his arms, close to his body, and finish him off.

Just as I did so, gods brought down another Giant only a short distance away. One outflung arm splashed into the ocean. The vast head split open like a melon when it came down hard on a sharp outcropping of rock, and blood and brains spilled out.

Unable to drop upon my opponent's head this time, I started the process of destruction with the big toe. My experience so far indicated that the process of killing a Giant could never be accomplished with a single blow, no matter how powerful.

The first blow of my metal-loaded club shattered the hard skin and splintered the even harder bones of what, even seen at close range, looked superficially like a giant human foot, down to the toenails and the small tufts of hair that grew upon the toes.

It seemed that the bigger the Giant, the tougher his flesh and the stronger his bones. All of these Giants were vastly more powerful than Antaeus had been.

My latest foe hopped and bellowed, as a man might if stung on the big toe by a large wasp.

Another wallop, and a crack appeared in the skin of his feet, running up the ankle, then the calf. Another hard blow on the ankle completed the disabling of the left leg.

One more blow, and he was down on one knee. When the Giant put one hand to the ground for support, I began to destroy that hand even as I had destroyed his foot.

In a way the Giants' size put them at a disadvantage. Daedalus and others have explained to me that it is simply a fact of nature that huge bodies are more vulnerable than small ones to certain common mishaps—such as tripping and falling down.

———

When I had finished destroying my second or third victim in this manner, I leaned on my club, gasping, and looked around. Our surviving foes were now in general retreat. The enemy attack on Vulcan's laboratory had been beaten off, at least for the moment. Apollo was on his feet again, shaking his head to clear it, calming his magic horses and trying to restore his chariot.

———

A distracted Giant was unaware of the radiant presence of Apollo, at a range of only about a mile, until an Arrow smote home like an explosive bullet, blasting and scattering pieces of tough, claylike Giant flesh in all directions, along with shattered fragments of bone.

And with that the fight was on again.

———

The battle that was eventually to decide all of our fates had started almost accidentally. Certainly our side had not chosen that day outside of Vulcan's laboratory as the time and place for a decisive confrontation, and maybe the Giants had not planned it that way, either. But as the fighting went on, both sides kept pouring in reinforcements.

The majority of participants on our side arrived on the scene by air, while most Giants came by water. A few of our enemies seemed to have made a long march overland, then had to find a way to cross approximately a mile of open, relatively shallow water between them and the island.

Daedalus and I were the only mortal humans to witness the entire battle, though the fate of our whole race hung in the balance.

Many more gods, perhaps a majority of all those in the world, chose not to take part, or were simply off on the other side of the world somewhere—I thought that many gods, despite all the educational opportunities that they enjoyed, had probably never realized how truly big the world was. And now it was sadly true that many others were no longer able to remember the size of the earth. And of course most mortals had never suspected the truths of geography, or even thought much on the subject.

The bodies of the Titans, when they employed their huge balloons to assist them in rapid movement, went drifting over sea and land like a flotilla of flying gods . . . still, only one or two, most notably Alkyoneus, could move as fast as most of the gods.

In actual combat, with their huge feet planted firmly on the ground that nourished them, Giants turned and bent and straightened almost gracefully and with amazing speed, their huge arms flailing. Few of our enemies bore weapons, though some had fashioned shields, and some brandished clubs. Most depended on their boulder-sized fists, and the strength and accuracy (which was considerable) of their throwing arms, and with them poured out a hail of devastation, which at one time or another must have knocked to earth a score of gods. On that terrible day, more than one god-Face was forcibly separated from its late wearer's human head. Any human who came within their reach, whether enjoying the powers of a god-Face or not, stood in some danger.

More than once I was hit by a stone or by some Giant's fist or club—my body was sent flying for a considerable distance, or it smashed into a rock wall. Under one such impact the rock cracked, but I still survived without disabling injury. My real test came when the experience was repeated, and I began to realize that there were limits to even my toughness.

Some gods appeared only briefly on the battlefield and then withdrew again. I have already named some who were present, and some I will name, and tell what they did. I will pass over the behavior of certain others in tactful silence.

And there were still other deities who never put in an appearance at all, a few of them for the simple reason that they did not learn of the battle until it was over. A few more were more deliberately circumspect. As far as I knew, Hades himself was still ranting in his madness, while remaining safely and snugly underground. And I thought that perhaps there was some method in his madness after all.

When we had beaten off the Giants' renewed attack, Mars and Zeus assigned a garrison of some less combative deities to hold the laboratory against any possibly renewed assualt. Meanwhile it seemed that we ought to take the offensive with the bulk of our forces—but of course in that company no decision so momentous could be made without a lengthy conference and argument.

While we were resting from our exertions, and while several gods were polishing their arguments, back inside the laboratory, Zeus told me more of my own history. Some years ago, the them-current avatar of Zeus had figured out a way to invest a hujan, or mortal, with divine power, without burdening him with the new vulnerability of a Face.

The idea was that the presumably enormous capabilities of this "designed" human would be immune to the Giants' most effective weapon. But exactly what those capabilities were going to be was very difficult to predict.

Everyone was well aware that such a weapon would take years to develop.

"Perhaps twenty years must pass before it is fully ready," Zeus had argued at the time. "But neither we nor the Giants are going anywhere. And they are not, thank all the Fates, in any hurry about arranging our annihilation. Therefore certainty is more important then speed when we plan our move against them."

Early on, several of those who advised Zeus in his planning devoutly expressed their hopes that this new man, or woman, should not be physically deformed, like Prince Asterion. It could be catastrophic to the plans of Zeus if this planned savior were to find life a burden and be angry at those who had brought him into the world. And what if this human being should be corrupted to turn against the gods who had created him?

"But it is rarley the obviously deformed who find life an unbearable burden," Vulcan reminded his leader now.

"That is true, I had forgotten. It is so very long since I was merely human."

———

I never learned what process of selection had been employed. Whatever it was, it indicated that Alcmene, wife of the Cadmian general Amphitryon, would be the ideal candidate for this breeding. One consideration must have been that the blood of divinity ran in her veins.

"That could be said of a great many people," I observed.

"Not nearly as great a number as would like to claim it for themselves. But Alcmene was indeed a special case." Daedalus, who had evidently been making a study of the matter, went on to explain that Zeus was my mother's great-grandfather on her father's side—and had also been, probably in another avatar, a remote ancestor of her husband.

"An incestuous business," I commented, bleakly considering my own origins. "Or would be, if the same rules applied to gods as to humankind."

"There's no use speaking of gods and rules in the same breath," said Daedalus, and looked around to see who might be listening. "I suppose we will come one day to the point where every human being on earth is descended in some way from Zeus."

———

My father, as I eventually discovered, had planned to wait until I was somewhat older before throwing me into the front line in the struggle against the Giants. But through the years of my childhood, the Giants kept posing a greater and ever greater threat. When my father learned that I had already slain a monstrous lion, and shortly after that the Hydra, he decided I was already old enough, and pushed on with his plan.

(I had the feeling that my father was on the point of telling me something more while we were resting between battles—but that, for good or ill, he could not quite bring himself to do so.)

Some hours passed thus in the laboratory, while we talked and rested (it seemed to me that gods wanted rest, whether they actually needed it or not), and some of us rearmed ourselves before going on with the next phase of the battle. There were some gods ready to fight who still lacked helmets.

Mars ranted and raved, urging us to lose no time in rushing after the fleeing foe. We should strike while the momentum was with us, and before the enemy could find some way of counteracting the protective helmets that had so suddenly provided our side with an advantage. Several times I reminded various deities that whenever we launched our attack, I would need a ride in someone's chariot if I was going to keep up. Zeus assured me that there were fighting gods who lacked the power of flight, so Daedalus and I would not be the only wingless passengers; but there were chariots enough for all to ride.

While some counseled a quick pursuit, other gods were already convinced that the Giants no longer presented an immediate threat to the Olympians' dominance of the world, and that it was time to declare the war won and go home.

Here Zeus did his best to assert his authority, proclaiming that the war was only getting started. In fixture either gods or Giants would rule the earth, and there could be no compromise.

28

We Go A-Hunting

WHEN WE HAD rested for a few hours after beating off the enemy attack Zeus, Hephaestus, and Apollo convened a council of war inside Vulcan's fortress. Daedalus and I, the only mortal humans for many miles around, reentered the vast building and stood by listening, though for some time no one acknowledged our presence.

All the gods recognized the need to follow some unified plan in following up our victory, but there was wide disagreement as to what that plan should be.

Gods and goddesses began to scribble maps on the flat, blank surface of one of Vulcan's interior walls. Someone knew, or claimed to know, where most of the Giants dwelt. Another informed us that Alkyoneus had been seen fleeing in that direction.

Zeus had the place of honor in all ceremonies among the gods, or at least in all of them I ever saw. Hades and Poseidon were next in rank, but even when Hades was not at war with Zeus, or suffering through a bout of madness, he kept almost entirely apart from the others. Poseidon was no enemy of Zeus, but until today he had not been much concerned about the problem posed by Giants.

"Speaking of Poseidon," asked some goddess I did not recognize, "does anyone know if he survived that little skirmish?"

No one could be sure. In any case, Neptune exercised an independent command over his own marine forces. Several witnesses reported seeing him caught without a bronze helmet, and I spoke up to confirm that observation. It was then assumed that he had not joined the council of war because he could not longer remember who he was or what he was supposed to be doing.

Mars, for all his hard fighting and dynamic speeches, failed as an effective leader because he paid too little attention to what his comrades in arms were doing and saying, what they feared and wanted. Though he claimed to be the war chief on land and in the air, a number of his fellow deities were disinclined to listen to him when he began shouting orders.

I was, and still am, no expert on military affairs, but it needed no experience to see that we were not going to present any kind of disciplined, highly organized opposition to the enemy.

Daedalus proclaimed in a firm voice that when at last we set out to carry the fight to the Giants in their own territory, he was coming with us.

Hephaestus announced that he wanted to come, too; and that if we waited a few more hours, his workers would have produced enough bronze helmets to protect everyone. Unfortunately, neither Vulcan nor Daedalus had been able to come up with any weapon that would be especially effective against Giants.

The first phase of the battle had demonstrated that the Smith's defensive helmets were not a total success. Deities fighting with their heads encased in bronze still suffered some loss of memory when the Giants' strange weapon struck at them heavily and repeatedly. However, the helmets did help enormously, and almost every god and goddess who meant to fight was now demanding one. It was still uncertain what would be the long-term fate of those who relied on bronze for protection in battle.

I knew that I could still play an important role in the fighting, but it was now possible to imagine that the gods might win even without my help.

There came a time when the bickering in the great hall died down, and I realized that most of the assembled company were looking at me, and that I was the subject of discussion.

In the background I could hear someone muttering about a prophecy supposedly once made by Hera: that the gods would be victorious in the war only if some mortal human clad in a lion's skin should fight beside them. And there was an old tradition, or superstition, regarding Giants, that their mother, the earth, had made them proof against all weapons of the gods—not, however, against weapons of mortals; and knowing this, Athena was to arrange the birth of a great mortal hero.

Dionysus was saying: "It took the enterprise and the strength of Hercules to make some of the gods realize that the Giants were neither invulnerable nor omnipotent. Humanity invested with the power of gods, but without the need for Faces, could fight and win against them."

Someone else impulsively put forth the proposal that, as soon as an appropriate Face became available, I be granted divine status, as a reward for my success in battle.

I heard this offer with mixed feelings. Of course it was an honor to be so admired, but I was immediately disinclined to accept. There was no Face of Hercules, and I was not at all sure that I wanted to become someone other than who I was.

———

But already the council had moved on to a discussion of our enemies. The Giants had shared the earth with us for a long time. Ancient descriptions spoke of them as towering, terrible creatures, who for the most part sported long beards, and in some cases wore snakes' tails instead of legs.

Humans called some Giants by their own Titanic names, while for others we knew only the names we had devised for them ourselves. Here and there was one who had at some time introduced himself to humanity, on one of those rare occasions when a meeting was peaceful enough to allow for such civility.

Daedalus (who kept reminding everyone that he wanted to accompany our attacking forces) told me he was convinced that the powers giving the special weapon its effectiveness were related to the magic-tech by means of which the race of Giants themselves had somehow been born.

———

Slowly, over centuries, there had come to be more and more Giants on the earth. I suppose we humans, including the earthly gods, could only thank whatever power truly ruled the Universe that our enemies' rate of reproduction was so low—else we would have been overrun, wiped out, many human generations in the past.

Someone said of the Giants: "The damned creatures are just very hard to kill. Sheer physical force still seems like the best bet, but it will have to be applied on a scale that will strain our resources."

And Mercury reported: "They do sometimes have spasms of lust, in which they yearn to force their will upon goddesses. And of course it takes a lot of food to fill their enormous bellies. Hercules and others have seen them eating cattle, chewing up entire bovine bodies like so many little sausages."

After all, I had watched the first Giant I ever saw as he roasted and ate a sheep. I imagined that they might like to eat people even more than sheep or other animals, but like everyone else were forced to take what they could get.

For a time, certain deities who made a practice of studying their opponents thought that Giants might be mutated humans. That idea struck me as extremely strange when I first encountered it, and nothing I learned later made it sound any more reasonable.

What these awkward imitations of ourselves might eventually want to do with the uncountable kinds of other life that grew on earth, once they had established their dominion, was more than any god or mortal in our ranks could say. The Titans were here, and they were hostile to humanity, and that was about all we could be certain of regarding their purposes.

The Smith and the Artisan, basing their arguments largely on evidence I had gathered, tried to convince the assembled Olympians that the Giants were not alien to the earth. They had not come from somewhere out among the stars but were only a part of the earth's own life—a part that in ancient times had been twisted into a strange shape by magic, what some called odylic science.

This suggestion of worlds other than our own sharply called to memory other mysteries that I had recently encountered.

"Atlas was beginning to show me something of the kind," I said, and saw many gods' faces turn toward me in surprise. "But only beginning. We didn't have a chance to get very far with any revelations."

The great contest between Giants and Olympians had gone on for many years. I understood now that it went a long way toward explaining why the gods have been for long periods absent from world affairs.

"But leaving Giants alone does not get rid of them," Zeus reminded his colleagues. "They do not spontaneously disappear. Rather they continue, in their patient, methodical way, to spend their time and energy becoming more and more troublesome to humanity. By means of the strange monsters they create, if for no other reason."

———

For many years the gods had been trying to keep their problem of vulnerability a secret from the bulk of humanity, fearing that if men and women knew their relative weakness, they would take the Titans' side against their own relations.

At one point Zeus said: "I can see now that trying to preserve secrecy was a mistake, and we should have put more trust in our fellow humans." Looking at the only two mortal humans present, he added: "It would be natural for you to side with us rather than the dirt-faces."

Daedalus agreed. "And siding with the Giants would have been a great mistake on our part. In a world ruled by Giants, ordinary people would be reduced to the status of cattle. The centaurs have chosen poorly."

I was sure that some of them, including Pholus, would not be on the Giants' side.

One of the gods philosophized: "After all, we *are* humans, however much we like to call ourselves immortal. Our Faces that we boast about, that other people worship, are only masks that we put on."

Eventually our expeditionary force got under way.

When the time actually came to move out, Apollo reached out an arm and scooped me aboard his chariot. Beside us drove Mars, behind a pair of magnificent black horses, their hoofbeats thundering on air.

Thanks to the speed of movement afforded us by the divine Sandals and chariots, we were able to travel more than a thousand miles to the south in only a few hours. Most of the flight was at high altitude, but the chariot of Apollo provided warmth and somehow even air to keep the Far-Worker's passengers, Daedalus and myself, almost comfortable.

The sprites had provided our leaders with accurate intelligence, and at the expected time we came in sight of a village, built on a gigantic scale, in the midst of a green and sunlit land. Looking over the rail of my host's chariot, I could catch a glimpse in the distance of a broad blue arm of the Great Sea; but it was too far away to let us obtain any help from Neptune and his legions.

A score or more of flying chariots came sweeping in rapidly on a cluster of huge buildings, each tall enough for its builders and owners to stand upright inside. The construction materials used were the trunks of many large trees and huge stone blocks. Roofs had been thatched with giant plants.

The air was much warmer here than it had been around the laboratory's desolate island, and things were green and growing. We had seen only a few humans on our final approach to our objective, but in this climate it seemed likely that Apples could be grown easily and plentifully. As we were on the point of landing, I looked out over long rows of budding trees that would be huge when they had got their growth; another orchard nearby held a smaller number that were already grown and producing fruit.

The inhabitants must have been warned somehow of our approach, for we found not a single Giant in any of the buildings or nearby fields.

Here and there as we came sweeping in, movement swarmed on pairs of tiny legs, no bigger and much weaker than my own—ordinary mortal humans who had been dwelling here with the Giants, or by their sufferance.

"Do they not know that we come to save them from the Giants?" I demanded of the world.

Daedalus shook his head. "They probably realize that we bring war. And a war between gods and Giants is not something that most humans will want to watch at close range."

There were also penned and pastured animals, doubtless being bred for food, that we dispersed by breaking down the fences. I also caught a glimpse of a few centaurs galloping away, but all my thoughts were on other matters at the time.

"I don't suppose this place is the Giants' headquarters," the Artisan observed to me. "But it must be the nearest thing to one that our scouts could find."

"I suppose they must have other orchards elsewhere," I agreed. "There certainly can't be many Giants in the world, if this is their biggest town."

He nodded. "It seems a fair assumption that somewhere they have other settlements and orchards, ten times the size of these."

And then we were on the ground, the silence shattered by a loud rumbling of wheels while our vehicle jolted to a stop. Daedalus prudently stayed with Apollo's chariot, while I jumped out and joined some of the bolder gods in prowling through the buildings, seeking for our foes. They were not to be discovered in that place, but their property was everywhere, in the form of gigantic tools and furnishings.

One of our more bellicose gods was shouting: "Come out, Alkyoneus, come out and play! Where are you hiding?"

But no one, it seemed, was ready just then to join us in another game.

"These are the Apples of the Hesperides," cried Zeus, pulling open a huge bin of fruit, calling everyone's attention to the fact. Everyone could recognize them, from the sample I had earlier obtained. It was impossible to mistake them for any other kind of fruit or vegetable. The yellow, melon-sized fruit were in all the buildings, arrayed on racks or snuggled one or two in a nest, like the eggs of barnyard fowl.

As we broke into the place and battered our way through it, my companions and I stumbled upon an indoor nursery for seedlings, roofed with a kind of oiled paper that let in much sunlight. I pounded the trees and their containers into splinters with my club, and the gods to the right and left of me wrought similar destruction.

"If Hades were here," some minor god suggested, "he might generate a nice earthquake and tumble these walls down."

"It seems we'll have to do as best we can without him," cautioned Zeus.

We also found another huge building, in which the balloons used in the attack on the island had evidently been manufactured.

But we were not going to be allowed to pillage and ruin the enemy stronghold unopposed: In a nearby grove of towering trees forces had been gathering to oppose our invasion, and now they were ready to strike at us. The counterattack was signaled by a new barrage of flying rocks.

The counterattack did not really take us by surprise, but we were too near that situation to feel comfortable about it. Yet another Giant now advanced on me with murderous intent.

Apparently some of our enemies were still ignorant about me. Certainly this advancing Titan, like the others I had faced, must have believed I was a god—or he would not have wasted his special weapon trying to disable me.

Like the others I had so far confronted, this one misplaced his confidence in the magical beams he could project from his fingertips.

As the long day of fighting wore on, I saw some minor goddess struck down, whose name I did not know. Her head was shattered, a sickening display of colors punctuated with pieces of white bone, making a portrait of beauty and power brought low by overwhelming brutal force. If she had been wearing a bronze helmet, it had offered no protection against such a ferocious blow.

I looked at her feet for flying Sandals, thinking that I might gain speed enough to let me catch up with my opponents.

But either she had not been wearing Sandals, or someone else had taken them ahead of me.

Moments later, I saw something I truly had never expected to behold: a momentarily victorious Giant, still feeling desperate enough, or perhaps simply adventurous enough, to try on a Face. He picked it up from the body of his comparatively diminutive slain opponent.

In the hand that raised it, the Face was a tiny, insignificant thing. At a little distance it looked like nothing more or less than a translucent mask designed to fit a mortal human head. It was no match at all for the Giant's great, pale, rocklike sketch of a countenance. And it remained stubbornly unabsorbed when he tried to press it between his eyes with one huge finger.

The Face was still stuck on the end of his fingertip when I got his attention by beginning to cut him down.

Again Alkyoneus, the archenemy of the gods, appeared, clad in rattling strips and chains of metal armor, inspiring the Giant forces to renewed efforts.

Many of the gods recoiled as the Giants' champion strode forward. But again Mars chose to meet him head-on, howling a challenge. Alas, Ares had no more success in this joust than in the previous one.

But our forces rallied, the thunderbolts of Zeus flew thick and fast, the Arrows of Apollo killed and wounded. I could see that Alkyoneus was hurt, but he kept to his feet.

Mars was slower to climb back into his chariot this time, slower to plead with his fellow Olympians that we must pursue the enemy as quickly as we could. Zeus added his own urgings, but it did not matter. Most of the surviving gods insisted on having time to rest.

Not that any who had come this far were ready to quit. We were determined to hunt down and exterminate the fleeing enemy, or at least get rid of Alkyoneus.

Even at the much later date on which I write, the ideal of complete extermination has so far proven impossible to achieve. Some minimize the continued threat. And Poseidon and some of the other gods, who had been deranged and driven early from the field, in later days rejoined divine society having forgotten that there ever was a battle at all. To this day some of them do not remember it; and a few even believe, or pretend to believe, that the whole story is an utter fabrication. My own memory of these events is probably better than that of any god, simply because I never fell victim to the Giants' magic force—and that indeed is one reason why I am writing these memoirs.

———

I was surprised to see how, despite their heavy bodies, the Giants could move quite rapidly over long distances, outpacing racing cameloids when they were forced to make the effort. And I was surprised also at their numbers in their counterattack around their village. Obviously their survivors from the earlier fighting had been reinforced.

In the fierce battles of that day there were perhaps a hundred gods in all, arrayed on one side, and perhaps as many as two hundred Giants on the other—along with certain centaurs and whatever other creatures might have been induced to join them.

At the beginning, and again later, whenever events allowed us a breathing space, the strategic questions were fiercely debated—such as, whether it was possible, or even desirable, to concentrate our forces in one place. But, as I suspect happens in most battles, once the fighting started, fine plans and strategy were all but forgotten by both sides as we concentrated on the mechanics of destruction, and on keeping ourselves alive. On every side the fighting was spreading like wildfire, and the commanders could no more manage it than they could have regulated a conflagration.

———

Many of the gods who did join in the fighting were comparatively minor figures, and some achieved more than their more famous colleagues. I hesitate to name names.

Even Mars was accused of cowardice by some. He could not be everywhere, and others who fought missed seeing him at all.

His appearance whenever he did show up inspired terror in many, including some of our opponents, if one could judge by the speed with which they fled from him.

At one point I saw with horror that the God of War had lost his helmet.

Shortly after that, the Giants scored on him with their special weapon; but in the case of Ares the effect was not what his enemies had hoped. Even when he had almost entirely lost his memory, he charged ahead, caring for nothing but killing.

I saw him send home a spear-thrust that felled a Giant, then whip his chariot horses on in pursuit of his next target.

Running up to one of my huge opponents at the level of his ankles, I prepared to swing my club with force enough to annihilate one of his leg bones, bulging beneath the skin. But the stepping motion of his leg changed at the last moment, and again I lost respect for our enemies' intelligence. This Giant, like several of my earlier opponents, was prepared to stomp on me with a gigantic foot—a moment later he reacted as if he'd stepped on a sharp stone. Partly the result of the fine steel armor with which Hephaestus had provided me—and partly because I held up my club on end to prick his foot.

Some have assured me that Giants have always had a special fear of lightning. But what mortal creature does not fear the thunderbolt? Whether the enemy particularly dreaded them or not, the fulminations of Zeus had a powerful effect. Even when the Thunderer failed to score a direct hit, his blasts still did considerable damage. Daedalus later discovered that the iron component of my club had been magnetized strongly enough to pick up nails.

The Thunderer also gathered thunderbolts into loose magnetic spheres and rolled them at his enemies like bowling balls. On contact they tended to produce truly satisfying explosions.

But Alkyoneus was obviously possessed of some form of immunity. It was as if his whole body served as a kind of lightning rod, conducting the power harmlessly down into the earth.

Later we discovered that his armor, which he had had designed specially for a duel with Zeus, offered an all-metal pathway that kept his body inside it safe.

Neither was I to be outdone when it came to throwing things, small though I was. Zeus and all other gods were able to magically extend the reach of their hands and arms, enabling them to uproot and move whole mountains, or at least small hills, and hurl them as projectiles.

"What's *that?*" I called out in amazement. Around us the whole earth seemed to be shuddering.

"One of them," said Zeus, "is throwing mountains at us."

I choked out something stupid, I am sure, for I could not believe the fact. Later I saw convincing evidence.

"It's true enough," my father told me. "Well, I will show them that I can do the same."

When a god or Giant literally uprooted a mountain, the whole earth quivered for many miles around, and clouds of dust billowed up, darkening the sky. When the Giant or god hurled such a missile, the huge mass cast a cloud-sized shadow in its passage. If it was thrown hard enough, the shock wave in itself was enough to knock down trees and lesser vegetation.

I on the other hand remained limited in my reach, even if my strength was equal to the Thunderer's. I had not my father's power to exert force outside my body, and could never get my arms around such a huge object. But once I had boulders in my grasp, I could propel them with the velocity of pellets shot from a crossbow—or even faster, faster than the eye could follow, if I put all my strength and will into the throw.

Never before in my life, not even, as it seemed to me then, not even in my wrestling match with Zeus, had I ever exerted my full strength.

My aim was not too good at first, and I missed my target by a quarter of a mile—a visible splash, startling white against the wine-dark sea, or a fountain of dust on land, showed where the missile struck—but my skills rapidly improved with practice.

Whenever one of my missiles struck home, it cracked a Giant's skull or ribs. I think I saw one lesser Giant's head carried entirely away, but at that distance it was hard to be sure.

Any lesser being I hit, such as a centaur, was of course obliterated by the impact.

And when a mass of earth or rock, hurled by some Giant, came toward me far too fast for me to dodge, I could only brace myself and try to withstand the impact. A deafening roar was followed by smothering darkness—and then, gasping and choking, I had to dig myself out from under several yards of soil and broken rock.

———

Some have said that when our battle for the Apple orchard had run its course, certain Giants who had been captured alive were locked away in Tartarus by Zeus; that the Thunderer for some reason wanted to spare their lives but doom them to eternal exile. I think this is extremely doubtful. Another legend has it that a remnant of our foes retreated to some portion of the Underworld as to a last defensive redoubt; and the gods decided that the difficulties of digging them out of any fastness so well fortified would have been so great that even Hades had doubts of being able to accomplish it.

Later legends have stated that the gods could do no more than stun the Giants, and depended in every case on the arms of Hercules to provide a finishing blow. In fact, Giants were wounded and killed, often without any help from me, in a number of ways, some particularly gruesome.

Some of our opponents on that day were no bigger than Antaeus had been. But none, I think, were any smaller.

Of course legend has played its role in history, as usual. One hears, for example, that the superhuman giant Tityus, when his body was stretched out at full length, covered nine acres. And Enkelados was so energetic that the whole weight of Mount Aetna was barely enough to keep him from bursting free. These were definitely exaggerations.

To my astonishment, some have lately questioned whether the Giants ever existed, and put forth the foolish argument that if they had, surely some of their bones would still remain as evidence. But the truth, as I have been trying to explain convincingly in these pages, is that when they died, their bones, along with the rest of their vast bodies, soon decayed into a substance indistinguishable from ordinary dirt and gravel.

Diana, traditionally called the twin sister of Apollo, appeared from somewhere to take part in the fighting. She was said to be a virgin huntress, who carried arrows and a spear and was of a vindictive nature.

I saw her kill the Giant called Gration, riddling him with pointed shafts, and I was mightily impressed.

Several of our enemies were especially impressive, too, each in his own way. Briareus in his furious efforts almost proved true the legend that credited him with a hundred arms, while Typhon practically played the part of a volcano, breathing out fire. At various times most of the gods showed some fear of these beings, though not to the degree ascribed by legend, in which the Olympians all fled to Egypt and hid themselves under various forms.

———

The renewed fighting around the devastated Giant village turned fierce indeed.

Porphyrion, while trying to seize Hera, perhaps as a hostage, was overpowered by a team of gods, and Enkelados was slain by Athena. Ephialtes died when one of Apollo's Arrows struck him in the eye.

Apollo in general played a major role in the fighting, his Arrows doing almost as much damage as Zeus accomplished with his mighty bolts of lightning.

Hephaestus also battled fiercely, angered I suppose by the attack upon his laboratory. I saw his figure, looking larger than life-sized, carrying in each hand an enormous gobbet of what must have been molten iron, which he hurled at any of our enemies who came in range.

Alkyoneus was not to be defeated, but soon the landscape was littered with the bodies of dead Giants, and he gave his surviving colleagues the signal to withdraw.

29

The Last Word

OUR PURSUIT OF the fleeing Alkyoneus and his band of surviving Giants carried us closer and ever closer to the part of the world that I associated in my mind with Danni.

The Giants had been airborne when they embarked on this latest leg of their retreat, and yet here we were, following their footprints in the earth. There should be a better word to describe the marks made by their tremendous feet—they were not mere prints, but great crushed craters. Bushes, small trees, and fences were smashed down when in the way. I remember the trail's crossing an abandoned farmyard, where a couple of outbuildings had been flattened, too.

Each segment of visible trail extended for no more than about a hundred yards. Then it would cease abruptly, showing exactly where the massive bodies of our enemies had once more gone airborne. But then after a short flight, usually no more than half a mile, at least one or two Giants returned to earth once more and ran for a short distance on their great legs. Remembering how quickly I had seen them step in battle, I could well believe that their steady running pace would be impressive.

"It's almost as if they wanted to make sure we don't lose their trail," shouted someone flying near me.

I had what I thought was a better idea: that our enemies, depending on the earth for sustenance far more than humans did, could not or dared not remain out of contact with soil and rock for more than a few minutes.

As the miles flew by and the day advanced, and the direction taken by our quarry did not change, I began to feel some immediate concern for Danni, and I promised myself that before I left the area of the estate, I would see to it that she was safe. Several times I told myself that there was no reason to think she stood in any special danger. But my uneasiness persisted.

I had known for some time the approximate location of her home and Meleager's, near the port city of Iolcus—Mel had told me as much, during the brief time when we were Argonauts together. And now I remembered that he had mentioned it again when we were climbing together out of Tartarus. He had been trying to make some preliminary arrangement for my formal betrothal to his sister, while I in my black mood had been paying little attention.

And certainly I remembered where the estate of Augeus was located, whose stables I had once so thoroughly cleansed. And it bothered me that the trail left by the fleeing Giants was now tending in that direction. I thought it was quite possible that Danni happened to be visiting her uncle there again, or that she had been forced by family pressures to relocate in her uncle's house.

As the suspicion grew in me that the Giants were deliberately planning to use her, I wondered: Had word somehow already reached my enemies that Danni and I were now formally engaged, or about to be? Some being had overheard me talking to her brother, down in Tartarus? Plenty of time for the word to spread, while I was wandering around the Upper World again and wrestling with my father.

At nightfall we broke off our pursuit and stopped to rest and eat and make plans for the next day. Whether gods absolutely required physical nourishment or not, a number of them were not going to forgo it for themselves or for their horses, just because we happened to be at war.

By the time we stopped, Daedalus and I were both in serious need of rest. My last sleep, just before that last battle, was a troubled one.

I dreamt that Hades had sent the Face of Death to me by a special messenger, and that I was free to make what disposition of it I wished.

I tried to tear the clear, glassy stuff in two, but the fabric was strong enough to resist even me—which I found a strange sensation indeed, even in a dream. At last I threw the damn thing from me, into a small stream, knowing that it would be washed into a larger river, and then yet a larger one, eventually finding its way to the ocean—let find it who would.

I dreamt that battle was raging again, and that Zeus had been struck down by two mountains hurled at him at once by two Giants, catching him between.

Where my father had been standing, there was now only a huge hole in the earth. I borrowed a chariot and flew desperately toward the center of the crater, which was almost a mile in diameter.

Desperately distressed, I dug frantically into the rubble, sending huge rocks flying this way and that.

At the bottom lay one small human body, somehow still almost intact—or at least recognizable.

I dreamt then that as my father lay dying in my arms, the Face of Zeus came working its way up out of his eyes and forehead, like some long-sunken vessel rising from the deep; and with great reluctance, but a sense of inevitability, I picked it up and put it on.

And then for a time, still dreaming, I reveled in the powers of Zeus. My perception widened, in a way that not even Atlas had been able to accomplish, so that I was granted some idea, some feel, for how great and magnificent the earth was—the deep sky had suddenly become too frightening for me to contemplate.

Great, grumbling, black-bellied cloud masses churned their way across the sky, in obedience to my will. Grand crooked forks of lightning fell from them to devastate my chosen targets. I could see Giants, now shrunken to the scale of small and frightened humans, running for their lives.

Eventually Prince Asterion appeared in my dream and told me he had come to help me out of it and to wish me well in the coming fight.

———

I woke from my troubled sleep to find my living father standing looking at me. Zeus, as God of the Sky, had the governance of lightning, as well as wind and storm in general. And his powers extended beyond the earth, somewhat above the thick blanket of air that Atlas had once shown me. By the commanding power of his will alone, the Thunderer could deflect the rocks that flew unendingly in airless space, when natural causes brought them near Earth, and then guided them like slung missiles against his monstrous enemies.

And the Giants on their side were far from weak and helpless. As whole new hosts and legions of their enormous bodies came tramping or drifting toward us over land and sea, I realized that there were more of them in the world than I had ever imagined. From the talk I heard around me, I understood that at least some of the gods were similarly astonished.

When the fighting resumed, the Arrows of Diana struck home in concert with those of Apollo, and no Giant could stand against that double impact.

When a strong god and I attacked as a team, no Giant whom we challenged could stand for very long before us. Mighty Arrows flew from Apollo's Bow, faster than any human could have aimed and shot them. As the bewildered target tried to fend them off, I moved in close for the attack.

When I had a chance, I looked around for Alkyoneus; but always some other opponent intervened.

In that climactic battle, Athena once more played a considerable role. She fought wearing a helmet, wielding a spear, and guarding herself with the shield called Aegis, which at that time was not yet as famous as it has since become.

As I have already said, there were many other gods engaged on that field of combat, and there are too many stories for me to attempt to tell them all.

It was with a sense of some inevitable fate come due that I saw the Giants' trial lead at last directly to the estate of Danni's uncle Augeus, the same man who had once claimed to offer a great reward for the slaying of the Hydra and had so urgently craved the cleansing of the stables.

The trail led straight to that place, and through it, apparently without pause, as if our enemies' flight had followed this path only by the sheerest accident. Later, of course, I learned that that was not the case. There had been a plan to take Danni hostage and use her somehow against me. But our enemies' plans, like our own, were subject to confusion in the fog of war, and she was never captured.

But I of course demanded that we land, and soon Apollo's chariot came down on the front lawn of Uncle Augeus, and moments later I entered the house, with such an escort as only young men in legends ever have. And Danni was there, of course, free and unharmed, and I will never forget the look in her green eyes when I strode in, with the Lord Apollo half a stride behind me, an Arrow nocked to his Bow.

I think it unlikely that Augeus, in his shocked state, immediately recognized in me a young troublemaker who had once cleaned his stables. But even if he did, he was not about to refuse me permission to marry his young niece—especially not when he had every reason to believe that an army of Giants was about to descend on his estate and trample his accumulated prosperity into dust.

⎯⎯⎯⎯⎯

As soon as Danni saw me, she came to me and took both my hands in hers. I could see she was afraid, but I thought that most of her fear was for me, not for herself.

She said: "Mel has told me of the loss you suffered. It is so terrible, I wonder how you endure it."

"I couldn't endure it. But other things have happened to bring me past it."

"Other things—having to do with me, Hercules?"

"One of them does. Very much so." I suppose my manner, indicated that I would be more specific when the right time came, and sensibly she did not press me at the moment.

We talked of Mel, who had set out to be a hero, and of our current situation regarding the Giants.

"You've cut your hair," I said. It was still straight and brown, but it only just hung past her ears.

"Do you like it?" She shook her head to make her tresses dance.

"I do, whether it is long or short. But then I like everything about you, and it has been that way since the moment we first met." Without pausing, I rushed on:

"I have sworn a solemn oath to marry you."

Danni's face showed no great surprise, and I realized that Mel must have told her of the conversation he and I had shared in Hell.

Suddenly there was a daring glint of humor in her green eyes, and she asked: "Sworn it under what compulsion?" Now I thought that she was testing me, ready either to laugh or to flare in anger.

"Don't you know me better than that? It is impossible to compel Hercules, son of Zeus, to do anything he does not want to do."

"Oh, has that been proven? But I have not tried my hand at such a feat." And I rejoiced to see a spirit of mischief dancing in the green eyes, ready to do battle with anything, especially with fear and sadness. "It would be an interesting challenge."

Now it was my turn to reach out with both hands to her. "Danni, will you be my wife?"

"Hercules, you must know I will. I have been aching to marry you since the day you threw my brother off the dock."

―――――――――

And Zeus himself found time to preside at a brief and simple ceremony, where several other gods and goddesses honored Danni and me by their presence—the business took only a few minutes.

But the wedding feast was going to have to wait, and so was the wedding night. Some people on our side were surprised at that, believing the battle was basically over and that it only remained for us to hunt down Alkyoneus and the other Giants who had fled.

"The battle may well be over," the Thunderer assured them, "but the war certainly is not."

And even those who thought the battle over were seriously mistaken. Now Alkyoneus was in the process of hunting me down, and came raging after me.

For some time now, when traveling long distances, he had been using a pair of flying Sandals, stolen or captured from some unhappy god, which worked as well on his enormous bulk as on a body of merely human size. But when it came time to fight again, he put the Sandals off, so he could better plant his feet and swing his club. He was running at us now, in solid contact with the earth, and it was plain he meant to fight.

―――――――――

And yet again Apollo, bronze helmet and all, had been knocked out of the air by a club in the hands of Alkyoneus, and the Sun God had to take a moment or two to regain his senses.

My case was similar. I never saw the blow that hit me when I came running near, doing my best to get within reach of the Giant's feet. I suppose it was his long club that he swung to swat me off the ground and send me flying—as I had once, long ago, propelled a lion through the air.

It must have been only moments later that a pair of centaurs found me lying stunned, after that terrific blow had bounced me off a rock or two.

Meanwhile the final, desperate battle still raged all around us, but I was only dimly aware of it. At first the centaurs' voices seemed to reach me from a great distance and to be partially muffled. They were debating between themselves as to what to do with me. By now I was beginning to regain my senses.

Kneeling beside me, the two six-limbed beings first tried to pry my club out of my immobile fingers, but I maintained my grip on that glorious weapon even while I continued to feign unconsciousness.

Now I could more clearly hear the centaurs, and recognized one voice as that of Nessus. The words of their debate began to make more sense in my shocked brain.

"Should we kill him immediately?" one asked.

"There's only one way we can do that." The voice of Nessus carried the calm of great insanity. "Are you ready for the sacrifice?"

The nameless centaur sounded considerably more normal than my old enemy. "We have talked that over again and again. No need for any of us to die, if the loss, the donation, is shared among us."

At the time, this made no sense to me. And then, just as I was about to leap up and smite them, Nessus said: "Anyway, we must first take him to Alkyoneus, who wants to see what he is made of."

Struck by a sudden inspiration, I lay still, restricting my impending movement to a few twitches.

"Shall we tie his wrists?" the nameless centaur asked.

"Tie the arms of Hercules?" Nessus was contemptuous. "That would be a useless exercise, wouldn't you say?"

Presently I was lifted and slung over a horselike back. Still I gripped my club, so one end of it went dragging on the ground as I was carried, and I thought surely that would make my would-be captors suspicious. But no, they were certain they had captured me, and I went along with the game as the only means of catching up with Alkyoneus. By now I was convinced that he was too fast on his feet for me to have any chance of overtaking him. Meanwhile, a temporary lull had fallen over the battlefield.

"Put him here," boomed out an enormous voice, and I was dumped from a centaur's back onto a surface as broad and flat and leathery as the floor of an expensive tent. And now the tent floor was moving up, bearing me and the two centaurs with it.

Cracking an eyelid open, I made sure that I had been set down on the palm of a Giant's hand, and that currently I was being held at the level of his chest while he inspected me. The palm of his hand was easily ten feet wide. Taking an iron grip upon my patience, I ordered myself to wait until I could be sure of landing on the great Giant's shoulder if I jumped, and to wait until I had my feet planted on his shoulder before I swung my club.

Presently I heard the Giant's enormous, booming voice again, this time from deafeningly near at hand, conversing with the centaurs in some language I did not understand.

By this time I suppose Alkyoneus was about half convinced that I was finally dead. Now at last he was incautiously holding me close to his head so he could examine me closely. Maybe he was nearsighted. I was prodded, gently, with the tip of a finger that felt like the end of a big log.

Getting my feet under me in a sudden scramble, I suddenly realized there was no need to jump from his hand to his shoulder before I swung—his staring right eye was only a few feet from my face.

But Nessus and his comrade reacted quickly when I moved. Their natural unconsidered instinct was to seize me, and they were quick enough to get some parts of their bodies in the way of my swing when it was launched into the Giant's face.

Thus it was that my club, propelled with all the strength that I could summon up, hit centaur flesh and bone by accident, hit and passed through on its way to its intended target.

What the effect of my unaided swing would have on Alkyoneus I do not know, for just at that moment a timely contribution came from Apollo—one of his Arrows entered the Giant's left eye, detonating a powerful explosion inside his head, even as I knocked the staring right eye of Alkyoneus clear out of his enormous face.

Two slain centaurs and I fell with the great Giant's hand, and fortunately the corpse of Alkyoneus, almost beheaded by the double impact, did not land on top of me; but still a moment later I was writhing and screaming on the ground, in agony from a poisoning by the centaurs' blood. Some of it had splashed me, soaking through the wool with which my suit of Vulcan's chain mail was lined; and I tore desperately at the garment to get it off.

Even in my frenzy, I realized that Danni was there, trying to help me.

Moments later, I fell into a swoon from which I only recovered when the battle was practically over.

The armor made for me by Vulcan, and the quick action of my bride-to-be, had saved me from a worse fate, but I had still been severely burned, as if by acid.

Zeus had failed to warn me, fearful that I would at last turn against him if I knew the secret vulnerability he had designed into my nature.

In planning my existence, Zeus had been as crafty and suspicious as a god could be with the experience of ages to draw upon (at least in those portions of his memory that were not riddled with lacunae). He had feared to create a rival who might someday pose a threat to his own rule. Therefore he had provided his hopeful new monster with a secret weakness, by means of which he would be able to arrange my destruction, if that ever became necessary. The answer, what he thought was an acceptable answer, was found in the chemistry of centaurs' blood.

———

Apollo had survived the fight without any additional damage, and presently he came to do what he could to ease my suffering; and what he could do was quite a lot. Pain subsided to bearable levels, and some of my strength returned.

A small crowd of victorious gods was gathered around the fallen bulk of Alkyoneus; and now it was possible to study the design of his armor, which conducted thunderbolts harmlessly to the ground.

The surviving centaurs had all fled the field; and to this day I have never learned why certain of their race so hated me that they tried to arrange with their Giant allies an elaborate plan for my destruction.

———

My friend Hephaestus still had not abandoned hope of someday discovering the secret of creating Faces. He has told me that he will someday be able in his laboratory to forge the Face of Hercules, who must henceforward be a god. Oh, not great enough to challenge my father, as Vulcan hastens to make clear, or to cause Zeus any uneasy moments. The god Hercules would lack some of the Thunderer's key attributes, while still matching him in general strength and durability.

But if the day ever comes when Vulcan succeeds, I do not think I will accept the gift. Not unless Danni receives her own immortality at the same time.

Certain gods remind me, from time to time, that I am still only mortal—as if the fact gave them cause for worry. It does not much concern me. I have already faced Thanatos once, and in my heart I still believe what I suppose I have always believed, that some inner essence of humanity is naturally immune to death. So, I am no more and no less immortal than Danni at my side, or any of those who envy me my strength—or than any of you who read my words.

Besides, even gods must die, as was thoroughly demonstrated in our war with the Giants. And if Vulcan is ever able to grant me such a gift, and I accept it, then when I die the Face of Hercules must pass to someone else.

———

Here I conclude this story of my life. But my life is not yet over. Danni will bear me sons and daughters, and I do not think any god will be so foolish as to try to serve me as Zeus once served Amphitryon.